OXFORD WORLD'S CLASSICS

WAR AND PEACE

COUNT LEO NIKOLAYEVICH TOLSTOY, the youngest of four brothers, was born in 1828 at Yasnaya Polyana, his father's estate in Tula province, about two hundred miles from Moscow. His mother died when he was 2, and his father when he was 9. He revered their memory, and they were the inspiration for his portraits of Princess Mary and Nicholas Rostov in *War and Peace*. Both his mother and father belonged to the Russian nobility, and Tolstoy always remained highly conscious of his aristocratic status, even when towards the end of his life he embraced and taught doctrines of Christian equality and the brotherhood of man.

He served in the army in the Caucasus and the Crimea, where as an artillery officer at the siege of Sevastopol he wrote his first stories and impressions. After leaving the army he travelled and studied educational theories, which deeply interested him. In 1862 he married Sophie Behrs and for the next fifteen years lived a tranquil and productive life as a country gentleman and author. *War and Peace* was finished in 1869 and *Anna Karenina* in 1877. He had thirteen children. In 1879, after undergoing a severe spiritual crisis, he wrote the autobiographical *A Confession*, and from then on he became a 'Tolstoyan', seeking to propagate his views on religion, morality, non-violence, and renunciation of the flesh. He continued to write, but chiefly in the form of parables, tracts, and morality plays—written 'with the left hand of Tolstoy' as a Russian critic has put it—though he also composed a late novel, *Resurrection*, and one of his finest long tales, *Hadji Murat*. Because of his new beliefs and disciples, and his international fame as pacifist and sage, relations with his wife became strained and family life increasingly difficult. At last in 1910, at the age of 82, he left his home and died of pneumonia at a local railway station.

HENRY GIFFORD, formerly Professor of English and Comparative Literature at the University of Bristol, has written widely on Russian literature. His publications include *The Novel in Russia* (1964) and *Tolstoy* (Past Masters, 1982).

OXFORD WORLD'S CLASSICS

*For over 100 years Oxford World's Classics have brought
readers closer to the world's great literature. Now with over 700
titles—from the 4,000-year-old myths of Mesopotamia to the
twentieth century's greatest novels—the series makes available
lesser-known as well as celebrated writing.*

*The pocket-sized hardbacks of the early years contained
introductions by Virginia Woolf, T. S. Eliot, Graham Greene,
and other literary figures that enriched the experience of reading.
Today the series is recognized for its fine scholarship and
reliability in texts that span world literature, drama and poetry,
religion, philosophy and politics. Each edition includes perceptive
commentary and essential background information to meet the
changing needs of readers.*

OXFORD WORLD'S CLASSICS

LEO TOLSTOY

War and Peace

Translated by
LOUISE AND AYLMER MAUDE

Edited with an Introduction and Notes by
HENRY GIFFORD

OXFORD
UNIVERSITY PRESS

OXFORD
UNIVERSITY PRESS

Great Clarendon Street, Oxford OX2 6DP

Oxford University Press is a department of the University of Oxford.
It furthers the University's objective of excellence in research, scholarship,
and education by publishing worldwide in

Oxford New York

Athens Auckland Bangkok Bogotá Buenos Aires
Cape Town Chennai Dar es Salaam Delhi Florence Hong Kong Istanbul
Karachi Kolkata Kuala Lumpur Madrid Melbourne Mexico City Mumbai
Nairobi Paris São Paulo Shanghai Singapore Taipei Tokyo Toronto Warsaw

with associated companies in Berlin Ibadan

Oxford is a registered trade mark of Oxford University Press
in the UK and in certain other countries

Published in the United States
by Oxford University Press Inc., New York

British Library Cataloguing in Publication Data

Data available

Library of Congress Cataloging in Publication Data

Data available

ISBN–13: 978–0–19–283398–3
ISBN–10: 0–19–283398–7

11

Printed in Great Britain by
Clays Ltd, St Ives plc

CONTENTS

WAR AND PEACE

INTRODUCTION

WAR AND PEACE was not immediately or universally recognized
by its readers as a world's classic. It came out by instalments
between 1865 and 1869, in a time of fierce controversy; and there
were complaints from both left and right about its being tenden-
tious. Tolstoy's contemporaries could few of them stand back and
see the grand design of the book; they were distracted by questions
of genre – was this a novel of family life? an historical chronicle,
not without its distortions? or a panoramic 'poem' like Gogol's
Dead Souls? Tolstoy rejected all these definitions when in 1868 he
published 'Some Words About *War and Peace*' (to be found at the
end of this volume). He claimed that the best things in the fiction
of his countrymen had never conformed to the known genres.
But many of his readers found it difficult to adjust to the changed
perspective in a novel that started with the domestic life of a few
families and moved steadily into the domain of a national epic.
They were even more perplexed when, half-way through it, passages
of theoretical argument about history and free will began to grow
in frequency, until the Second Epilogue left fiction behind altogether,
and hammered out a paradoxical thesis.

Tolstoy tells us in 'Some Words' that he wrote the novel during
'five years of uninterrupted and exceptionally strenuous labour
under the best conditions of life'. It was certainly strenuous labour,
as the many drafts that have survived witness; and the only inter-
ruptions it suffered were those incidental to raising a family –
he had married in 1862 – and farming his estate. He claimed in a
letter of 1863 to be at the height of his powers; and never had
Tolstoy felt so much at harmony with himself. The 'best conditions
of life' meant virtual seclusion on his estate of Yasnaya Polyana.
He wanted explicitly in this novel to celebrate the life of the
Russian nobility (a term including what we should call the gentry)
and the solid agrarian order which found itself under challenge in
a new phase of Russian history following the Emancipation of the
Serfs in 1861. Yasnaya Polyana and all it stood for was very
precious to Tolstoy. The atmosphere of the place is palpable when
he writes of the Rostovs and their country pursuits at Otradnoe.

The challenge, of which Tolstoy was keenly aware, to his own
cherished traditions came from the so-called 'new men' who

began to dominate the intellectual scene after the defeat of Russia in the Crimean War, during which the repressive Tsar Nicholas I had died. The years ensuing were remarkable, even by Russian standards, for their ideological conflict. The leading journal then was *The Contemporary*, edited by the poet Nekrasov, who had been glad to publish Tolstoy's own work from *Childhood* (1852) onwards, and regarded him as a writer of exceptional promise – an opinion shared by Turgenev. But Nekrasov had come increasingly under the influence of two associates, Chernyshevsky and Dobrolyubov, former seminarists whose militant views were odious to Tolstoy. Dogmatically, they put their trust in progress, in the rationality of man once freed from superstition and the constraints of despotism, and in the organization of society on scientific principles. Tolstoy, though himself an unresting inquirer, was no friend to intellectuals: we have only to consider his attitude in *War and Peace* to Speransky. In 1863 Chernyshevsky, although in prison, had been able to publish a novel, *What Is To Be Done?*, which portrayed an emancipated woman who dreams of a radiant future. Tolstoy resented it as an attack on the family, and the many admirers of Chernyshevsky's novel among the intelligentsia could see plainly his polemical intention in *War and Peace*.

At the beginning of the 1860s, after having dropped out of literature for a while, Tolstoy made a start on a novel about the Decembrists. These were the liberal conspirators from the aristocracy who on 14 December 1825 rose against Nicholas I on his accession. In 1856 at the beginning of a new reign those who had survived thirty years of exile in Siberia were allowed to return. Tolstoy was interested in these revolutionaries of an earlier generation. He abandoned his novel about the Decembrists, but Pierre in *War and Peace*, as the First Epilogue reveals, took a leading part in one of the circles leading up to the insurrection, and he admits to Prince Andrew's son that his friend too would have shared their ideas. In these two representatives of the aristocracy, before the modern age which he opposed, Tolstoy could realize the life of thinking men who had liberated themselves from ideology. Prince Andrew tired of Speransky's notions, Freemasonry ceased to enchant Pierre.

The novel about the Decembrists was never written. Now Tolstoy turned to the beginning of the century, when Napoleon filled the western horizon of Russia. He began by narrating the fortunes of a few aristocratic families in those years from 1805. The first instalment to appear bore the title 1805, but it was not until a few months later, in March 1865, that Tolstoy recorded in his diary a new vision of what his novel might be. At one early stage he had thought of calling it *All's Well That Ends Well*, which would seem to tilt the balance towards the domestic, with the war as a temporary disturbance of its peaceful waters. But now he had become absorbed in reading about Napoleon and Alexander, and the idea that came upon him 'like a cloud of joy and of the consciousness of being able to make something great' was that he would write 'the psychological history of the romance between Alexander and Napoleon'. Alexander puzzled him, so intelligent, sensitive, a potentially great man who wavered between liberalism when he supported Speransky, and military harshness when he replaced him by Arakcheev. Tolstoy sees 'confusion outwardly' in Alexander, and yet, within, a spiritual brightness. Reading about the two leaders he had come to see 'all the baseness, all the phrase-making, all the senselessness, all the contradictions of the people surrounding them, and of themselves' – particularly of Napoleon, whom already he condemned as insincere, unfeeling, and self-deluded. Napoleon 'is not interesting, but only the people surrounding him and on whom he acted'. All this gave rise to 'great thoughts' and when Tolstoy conceived his work at this stage as a 'poem' he was aware of its epic possibilities.

He had now become a historical novelist in the most profound sense. His readers might complain that he appeared to forget the original characters of his story, as he came more and more to expatiate upon public events and public figures, and later to challenge the historians and argue with military experts. They had expected a family chronicle, of the kind Tolstoy himself had read in Trollope's work, with admiration for the novelist's mastery, though he soon recognized how much Trollope dealt in the conventional. Tolstoy had a good knowledge of the contemporary English novel, and some respect for it. *War and Peace*, however, developed on lines of its own, and Tolstoy was right when he insisted that it could not be placed in any accepted category.

For the reader in our time, with all the study that has been made of Tolstoy's working methods when he wrote this novel, it no longer perplexes, and the design is fairly simple to see. We know from Russian critics of this century like Shklovsky and Eykhenbaum how he handled his sources, and what transformations the story underwent as it grew in his mind. There is an excellent account of all this in the book by R. F. Christian, *Tolstoy's 'War and Peace': A Study* (Oxford, 1962). For many years the English reader, encouraged in this view by Henry James and his disciple Percy Lubbock, failed to perceive the coherence of Tolstoy's novel. It was indeed open to the winds of his time – Tolstoy allowed no barriers between art and daily living. The world of Alexander's era is not distanced by reminders of its pastness as that of the Regency is in *Vanity Fair*, or Middlemarch in the late 1820s and early 1830s by George Eliot contemplating it fifty years later. Tolstoy writes of the past (though with some deliberate historical colouring) in terms of the present, and *War and Peace* is a novel of the 1860s like any other of that contentious decade, even if the issues are presented in a wider perspective. For this reason it is a developing work, that deepened with Tolstoy's awareness of moral and historical problems. But the flood through all its branches is channelled and controlled. The ideas of the novel – though it adds up to more than its ideas – are linked in a firm structure.

Tolstoy's own experience entered deeply into the novel. His family were quick to recognize many of the people and situations, although no character is to be identified wholly with its prototype. He changed more in a character than a letter or two in the surname (the old Prince Nicholas Bolkonsky from his grandfather Prince Nicholas Volkonsky, or his daughter from Tolstoy's own mother, also Mary, and like her plain and wealthy). Tolstoy's portraits are always subtly enhanced so that, as William James once remarked, 'life indeed seems less real than his tale of it.' Natasha with her extraordinary openness to life is more than an amalgam of Tolstoy's sister-in-law and his wife.

The battle scenes owe much to what he had seen himself in the Crimean War, when at Sevastopol he was present in the dangerous Fourth Bastion. The *Sevastopol Sketches* describing life under siege there have been worked up into the immense and crowded canvas of Napoleon's campaigns in 1805 and 1812. Many years later Tolstoy spoke of his debt to Stendhal who in *La Chartreuse de Parme* depicted the battle of Waterloo as experienced by the bewildered Fabrice, a participant who has utterly lost his bearings. The character of warfare had changed little from Austerlitz to Tolstoy's own time: the weapons had made no striking advance, communications remained slow, intelligence was haphazard; the signals network of a modern army did not exist. The military experts (whom, like experts of every kind, Tolstoy held in contempt) were displeased with his calm dismissal of military science. They could not fail to resent the many gibes at pedantic German theorists (many soldiers of high rank under the imperial regime were German in origin). Prince Andrew, just before Borodino, overhears a brief exchange between the great theorist of war, Clausewitz, and a compatriot. It revolts him by its lack of sensitivity to the suffering in war, which is seen purely in a technical light. However, General Dragomirov, a military critic of War and Peace who dissented strongly from Tolstoy's conclusions about the futility of strategic studies, had to admit that his battle scenes could give 'invaluable practical lessons'. Tolstoy, in a way that very few military historians ever did, showed the experience of war for those taking part in it.

The brush with Clausewitz belongs to a grand strategy pursued throughout the novel. Tolstoy develops his own campaign parallel with Kutuzov's. Each is concerned to repel the foreign invader. Tolstoy's prejudice against Napoleon (and the way he often manipulates his source material exposes the prejudice) is not mere resentment of the national enemy. Napoleon represents the inhumanity that Tolstoy is already beginning to find in modern civilization. Whereas Kutuzov, deliberately set up as the moral opposite to Napoleon, has a natural compassion, it never occurs to Napoleon that war is anything but magnificent theatre with himself in the leading role, that destiny which he has manufactured and wants to serve him. Kutuzov's wisdom is contrasted with Napoleon's delusions of grandeur. And the insincerity, the lack of any real concern for their fellow-men that marks the court circle in Petersburg – so unlike the warm-hearted Rostovs in Moscow – finds its reflection in French manners and its clichés in French speech. Tolstoy knows that for him the genuine is the Russian. The French and the Germans alike are out of touch with actualities. Here, I think, more comes into play than patriotic bias. Tolstoy is pitting the natural against the contrived.

Tolstoy's point of view, consistent and at times heavily stressed, does lead to some tampering with sources. Although he claims in 'Some Words About War and Peace' to have · 'accumulated a whole library of materials', his reading was somewhat narrowly selective and, in the way of genius, desultory. He made use of two standard Russian histories, by Mikhaylovsky-Danilevsky (1844) and Bogdanovich (1859–60); also of Thiers's Histoire du Consulat et de l'Empire (1845–62), which for twenty years held the field against other French accounts of Napoleon. All three works could make available for him vividly recorded scenes. But he explains in 'Some Words' that 'the tasks of artists and historians are quite different'. The historian is dominated by his single idea of a character (though we might argue that Tolstoy is dominated by a single idea of Napoleon); whereas the artist, aware that nothing in life is answerable to tidy schemes, has to approach the historical event from another side (and people show new aspects of themselves under the force of events). 'Either from his own experience, or from letters, memoirs, and accounts, the artist realizes a certain event to himself . . .'. Tolstoy began his preparations for War and

Peace by seeking out the reminiscences of those who had witnessed his chosen period, their letters and diaries – whatever would help him to 'realize to himself' how it had actually looked and felt. This intimate approach was not approved of by all critics.

Turgenev, who made many objections to *War and Peace* that qualified his admiration, thought he could see a deliberate sleight of hand in the method. 'Tolstoy', he wrote, 'astonishes the reader by the pointed toe of Alexander's boot, by Speransky's laugh, making one assume that he must know *everything...*'. The way in which Tolstoy claimed intimacy with his characters and the period as a whole offended the survivors of that age. Old Prince Vyazemsky, long before the friend of Pushkin, himself the son of a leading figure in Catherine's reign, and witness (much like Pierre) of Borodino, was not alone in thinking that Tolstoy had impugned the patriotism of the aristocracy in 1812. There were complaints from others who had known the time that Tolstoy failed to catch the tone and the manners. The son of the egregious Count Rostopchin, Governor-General of Moscow in 1812, was among those who protested at Tolstoy's distortions.

The most memorable episode concerning Rostopchin is that when, shortly before the abandonment of Moscow, he sets the mob on to lynching the unfortunate Vereshchagin, who is to be punished as 'the villain who has caused the ruin of Moscow'. Viktor Shklovsky has carefully examined Tolstoy's narrative in relation to his sources. The actual event is little changed by Tolstoy. He does not put into Rostopchin's mouth words that contradict what eyewitnesses heard, though the scene is made more vivid by repetitions: thus (in the Russian text) Rostopchin four times gives the order 'Cut him down!' In the same way, Tolstoy constantly reminds the reader of Vereshchagin's appearance – 'the young man in the fur-lined coat'; he emphasizes the 'long thin neck', and shows how in Vereshchagin's terror 'A vein in the young man's long thin neck swelled like a cord and went blue behind the ear, and suddenly his face flushed.' Tolstoy brings out magnificently the human pathos of the scene, with the unwilling crowd that 'moaned and heaved forward, but again paused', Vereshchagin's 'timid yet theatrical voice', the worse theatre of Rostopchin's incitations to 'cut him down', and the moment at which 'the barrier of human feeling, strained to the utmost...suddenly broke.' Vereshchagin's 'plaintive moan of reproach' – his cry when struck by the blunt side of the soldier's sabre – is fatal to him, and it is 'drowned by the threatening and angry roar of the crowd'.

The account of Rostopchin's confused feelings in his carriage as he leaves the mob is, of course, wholly of Tolstoy's invention. At the memory of Vereshchagin's words 'Count! One God is above us both!' – Tolstoy tells us 'a disagreeable shiver ran down his back. But this was only a momentary feeling and Count Rostopchin smiled disdainfully at himself. "I had other duties," thought he. "The people had to be appeased..."'. There is no knowing whether Rostopchin entertained such thoughts. Yet the situation would seem to demand them, if he is to live with himself now this outrage has happened. The imaginative truth of this scene is irresistible.

Tolstoy's treatment of Napoleon, as we have noted, is hostile from the beginning, when he had first set down his impressions of the 'romance between Alexander and Napoleon'. Tolstoy felt an antipathy to Napoleon, as he did to the able minister Speransky, because they were plebeians (and no doubt his aversion to Chernyshevsky and Dobrolyubov can be felt here), but even more because they were, in Tolstoy's view, unreal. Napoleon in *War and Peace* appears as a stage emperor, surrounded by burlesque kings of his own creation, and nullified by his own rhetoric. It is hard to believe that Pushkin should have called this mountebank a 'sovereign of our thoughts', or Manzoni have written at Napoleon's death in 1821: 'two centuries/The one armed against the other,/Submissive turned to him/As if they waited on destiny.' Tolstoy denies him all military skill (though it is true that Napoleon lacked his usual flair at Borodino). Since Napoleon has not the root of the matter in him, he is worthless.

Here the philosophy that shaped the novel must be considered. Tolstoy, as we have seen, brought to the interpretation of this history the weight of his own experience. He had become convinced that the outcome of a battle hangs on the plain soldier who does what instinct tells him is right in a moment of crisis. In this way Captain Tushin with a single battery is able to save the army from defeat at Schön Grabern – and is afterwards blamed for abandoning a gun, until Prince Andrew speaks up for him. Later in the book Tolstoy formulates the principle: 'Only unconscious action bears fruit, and he who plays a part in an historic event never understands its significance.' The point of view, as so often in Tolstoy's maxims, is exaggerated; but Tolstoy is able to illustrate this time and again in his account of action – particularly in the experience of Nicholas Rostov. And the submission to events, so unavoidable for the soldier in the thick of an engagement, is something that generals must understand, if they are to fulfil the role that Tolstoy allows to them. Thus Bagration at the same battle does not issue orders, except to confirm what is really happening, but 'owing to the tact Bagration showed, his presence was very valuable'. He is an excellent commander, because he concerns himself with the one thing he can influence, the morale of his troops.

The supreme example of this quality is, of course, Kutuzov, who, worldly and self-indulgent old man that he is, yet remains devoted to the mission he has been chosen to carry out. Kutuzov had been appointed commander-in-chief, after Barclay de Tolly was forced to give up Smolensk, by an unwilling Alexander who bowed to popular pressure. When Pushkin, a strong partisan of Barclay, argued his case in 1836, he did not deny that Kutuzov was the man necessary at the moment.

Only Kutuzov could propose the battle of Borodino; only Kutuzov could yield Moscow to the enemy; only Kutuzov could continue in that wise active inactivity, lulling Napoleon to sleep when Moscow burned and awaiting the fatal moment; because Kutuzov alone was invested with the people's confidence, which so marvellously he justified.

Pushkin's testimony is valuable, because it shows the popular view of Kutuzov, which Tolstoy was right to trust, whatever the quibbles of historians. He probably exaggerates the degree of 'wise passiveness' (to use Wordsworth's term) that Kutuzov displays, but essentially the truth was such. Kutuzov in *War and Peace* dozes through the councils of war, ignores the voices dissenting from him, gives every sign of senility; but all the time he is listening to the groundswell of what the Russian people, soldiers and partisans, have to tell him about the war. He becomes the spokesman of Russian instinct, and it triumphs against all expectation.

Napoleon was no truly great man, because greatness cannot exist 'where simplicity, goodness and truth are absent'. Pierre has long searched for these qualities, which are, of course, manifested in Kutuzov. But Pierre finds them in a common soldier (more accurately, a very uncommon one), Platon Karataev. Whereas Tolstoy's Kutuzov convinces, Platon has not impressed many readers as he did Strakhov, Tolstoy's critic and confidant, for whom this holy fool symbolized 'the strength and beauty of the Russian people'. Tolstoy wanted Platon to be so taken, but whether he achieved the artistic triumph that Strakhov claimed is questionable. Platon represents the very opposite of Prince Andrew, whose pride of intellect and readiness to censure have to be purged in suffering. It is as if Tolstoy sought relief through the conception of Platon from the wearisome struggle with ideas that engaged Prince Andrew and Pierre. This meek peasant is able to give Pierre 'that tranquillity of mind, that inner harmony, which had so impressed him in the soldiers at the battle of Borodino'. Platon lives entirely in the moment, babbling and inconsequential. Yet he is always wise in his unreason. At this time Dostoevsky had just created the image of the 'underground man', set up like Platon (whose name, Plato, could not be more ironically chosen) to counter a life-denying logic. But while the 'underground man' takes obstinate satisfaction in his own meanness, Platon knows nothing of himself; and his love for his neighbour, though unfailing, is involuntary and quite impersonal. Most readers are embarrassed by what they consider to be a rare case of Tolstoy caught faking.

It is only with Platon that he fails to convince in his insistence on the value of 'unconscious' action. The term 'unconsciousness' is disputable, since Kutuzov, for instance, may be called in a deeper sense conscious of what was happening. Tolstoy everywhere places his trust in the primacy of feeling, in the capacity for acting on the spur of the moment when the moment is properly understood. Thus, Nicholas at Voronezh forgets his pledge to Sonya (not spontaneously given) and falls in love with a transformed Princess Mary, when 'a new life-force takes possession of her.' Thus Natasha, who had been so busy organizing the conveyance of the family possessions from Moscow, suddenly insists that the carts should be unloaded to take wounded men. These, and a hundred episodes like them, are persuasive because the decision seems to flow inevitably from the character's awareness.

However, in his quarrel with the historians Tolstoy has not the same authority. We can understand what Turgenev meant when he spoke of 'our genius and crank [taking] the bit between his teeth'. Tolstoy distrusted the historians (who fell under his general ban on specialists) because in the first place they relied upon written reports of warfare which he knew from experience to bear little relation to the facts. Nicholas, called without irony 'a truthful young man', finds that he has to make up a story of what he might have done at Schön Grabern, because his hearers would not have accepted the literal truth. Tolstoy's scepticism spreads also to the explanations that historians give of all human affairs. He is very high-handed, and inaccurate, in his account of historical procedures in the Second Epilogue, because his knowledge of the subject was somewhat hastily gathered. But the underlying question still has to be answered: How are we to account for the upheavals of 1812, that drove millions of men to the east, plundering, burning and slaughtering on their way, and then as suddenly drove them back to the west? Tolstoy was aware of the vast labyrinth of connections that lead up to and flow from every action. Perhaps this is especially a novelist's awareness, since for the novelist the world is made up of countless arresting particulars. There are good reasons, as Isaiah Berlin has shown in *The Hedgehog and the Fox*, for attending seriously to Tolstoy's arguments. Their tone may be brutally dogmatic, yet these are matters of great importance that he discusses, and his attention to them added profundity to his novel, even though the way in which they are presented throws the book to some extent out of balance.

Tolstoy's prejudices, to which his contemporaries were so sensitive, cannot be said to have warped the essential truth of *War and Peace*. Even if, as Konstantin Leontiev complained, his characters think the thoughts of Tolstoy's day rather than their own, there is in the book that permanent truth of feeling which Wordsworth believed to be the concern of poetry. Tolstoy has no rival among the novelists in his capacity to realize life, to reveal human beings in their egotism and their ability at times to fulfil themselves innocently and in harmony with the world. *War and Peace*, though depicting cruelty and disaster on a huge scale, can be fairly described as an essay in harmony. It affirms that man is inescapably a moral creature, and that he achieves his fulfilment in unpretentiously being himself.

HENRY GIFFORD

NOTE ON THE TRANSLATION

AYLMER MAUDE and his wife Louise, the translators responsible
for the *Centenary Edition of Tolstoy's Works* (Oxford, 1928–37), knew
both Tolstoy and Russia intimately. Louise was born in Moscow and
lived there for forty years; Aylmer Maude spent two years at a
Moscow school, and stayed in Russia for twenty-three years. He met
Tolstoy in 1888, and became a friend and a disciple, though with
some reservations. Tolstoy often expressed his gratitude to them both
for their service as translators, because they were fully competent
in both languages, meticulous throughout, and devoted to his work.
Maude's *Life of Tolstoy* (Oxford, 1930) remains a valuable account by
one who understood him well, and had played a useful part in one
of Tolstoy's most cherished projects – the resettlement of the
Dukhobors in Canada.

The Maudes' translation has appeared hitherto in three volumes,
consisting in all of fifteen books and two Epilogues. These have now
been aligned with the standard Russian text in four books and
fifteen parts, after a few minor adjustments.

The translation was accompanied by footnotes, and other more
detailed notes at the end of each volume. Many of these have been
preserved, some augmented, others altogether replaced, and certain
new notes have been written. Of particular interest are the original
notes on Russian manners and customs, from Maude's long familiarity
with the people.

SELECT BIBLIOGRAPHY

The Centenary Edition of Tolstoy in 21 vols. (Oxford, 1928–37) has translations by Louise and Aylmer Maude of his principal works. The World's Classics paperback editions include *Anna Karenina* and *The Raid and Other Stories*.

Tolstoy's *Letters* have been edited in 2 vols. by R. F. Christian (London, 1978).

There are biographies by Aylmer Maude in 2 vols. (Oxford, 1930), E. J. Simmons in 2 vols. (Boston, Mass., 1945–6; Vintage paperback, 1960) and Henri Troyat (London, 1960; Penguin paperback, 1970).

Critical studies include John Bayley, *Tolstoy and the Novel* (London, 1966), R. F. Christian, *Tolstoy: A Critical Introduction* (Cambridge, 1969), Henry Gifford, *Tolstoy* (Oxford: Past Masters, 1982), Malcolm Jones, ed., *New Essays on Tolstoy* (Cambridge, 1978), Ralph E. Matlaw, ed., *Tolstoy: A Collection of Critical Essays* (New Jersey, 1967).

The following have special reference to *War and Peace*: Isaiah Berlin, *The Hedgehog and the Fox* (London, 1953; reprinted in his *Russian Thinkers*, London, 1978); R. F. Christian, *Tolstoy's 'War and Peace': A Study* (Oxford, 1962).

For contemporary criticisms of *War and Peace* see A. V. Knowles, ed., *Tolstoy: The Critical Heritage* (London, 1978).

CHRONOLOGY OF LEO TOLSTOY

1828   28 August (O.S.): born at Yasnaya Polyana, province of Tula, fourth son of Count Nikolay Tolstoy. Mother dies 1830, father 1837.

1844–7   Studies at University of Kazan (Oriental Languages, then Law). Leaves without graduating.

1851   Goes to Caucasus with elder brother. Participates in army raid on local village. Begins to write *Childhood* (publ. 1852).

1854   Commissioned. *Boyhood.** Active service on Danube; gets posting to Sevastopol.

1855   After its fall returns to Petersburg, already famous for his first two *Sevastopol Sketches*. Literary and social life in the capital.

1856   Leaves army. *A Landlord's Morning*.

1857   Visits Western Europe. August: returns to Yasnaya Polyana.

1859   His interest and success in literature wane. Founds on his estate a school for peasant children. *Three Deaths; Family Happiness*.

1860–1   Second visit to Western Europe, in order to study educational methods.

1861   Serves as Arbiter of the Peace, to negotiate land settlements after Emancipation of Serfs.

1862   Death of two brothers. Marries Sophia Behrs, daughter of a Moscow physician. There were to be thirteen children of the marriage, only eight growing up. Publishes educational magazine *Yasnaya Polyana*.

1863   *The Cossacks; Polikushka*. Begins *War and Peace*.

1865–6   *1805* (first part of *War and Peace*).

1866   Unsuccessfully defends at court martial soldier who had struck officer.

1869   *War and Peace* completed; final vols. published.

1870   Studies drama and Greek.

1871–2   Working on *Primer* for children.

1872   *A Prisoner in the Caucasus*.

1873   Goes with family to visit new estate in Samara. Publicizes Samara famine. Begins *Anna Karenina* (completed 1877).

* Tolstoy's works are dated, unless otherwise indicated, according to the year of publication.

1877	His growing religious problems. Dismay over Russo-Turkish War.
1879	Begins *A Confession* (completed 1882).
1881	Letter to new tsar asking for clemency towards assassins of Alexander II.
1882	*What Men Live By*. Begins *Death of Ivan Ilyich* and *What Then Must We Do?* (completed 1886).
1883	Meets Chertkov, afterwards his leading disciple.
1885	Founds with Chertkov's help the *Intermediary*, to publish edifying popular works, including his own stories. Vegetarian, gives up hunting.
1886	*The Death of Ivan Ilyich*. Writes play *The Power of Darkness*.
1889	*The Kreutzer Sonata* completed. Begins *Resurrection*.
1891–2	Organizes famine relief.
1893	*The Kingdom of God is Within You* publ. abroad.
1897	Begins *What is Art?* (publ. 1898) and *Hadji Murat*.
1899	*Resurrection*.
1901	Excommunicated from Orthodox Church. Seriously ill. In Crimea meets Chekhov and Gorky.
1902	*What is Religion?* completed. Working on play *The Light Shineth in Darkness*.
1903	Denounces pogroms against Jews.
1904	*Shakespeare and the Drama* completed. Also *Hadji Murat* (publ. after his death). Pamphlet on Russo–Japanese War, *Bethink Yourselves!*
1906	Death of favourite daughter Masha. Increasing tension with wife.
1908	*I Cannot Be Silent*, opposing capital punishment. 28 August: celebrations for eightieth birthday.
1909	Frequent disputes with wife. Draws up will relinquishing copyrights. His secretary Gusev arrested and exiled.
1910	Flight from home, followed by death at Astapovo railway station, 7 November (O.S.).

PRINCIPAL CHARACTERS
AND GUIDE TO PRONUNCIATION

THE names by which the principal characters are usually known are given in capitals. The stressed syllable is marked with an acute accent; ë is pronounced *yo*, and always stressed. The stress on some of the principal place-names is also given below.

THE BEZÚKHOVS

COUNT Cyril BEZÚKHOV·

PIERRE, his son, legitimized after his father's death, becomes Count Peter BEZÚKHOV.

Princess CATICHE, Pierre's cousin.

THE ROSTÓVS*

COUNT Ilyá ROSTÓV.

COUNTESS Nataly ROSTÓVA, his wife.

Count NICHOLAS Rostóv (Nikólenka), their elder son.

Count Peter Rostóv (PÉTYA), their second son.

Countess VÉRA Rostóva, their elder daughter.

Countess Nataly Rostóva (NATÁSHA), their younger daughter.

SÓNYA, a poor member of the Rostóv family circle.

BERG, Alphonse Kárlich, an officer of German extraction who marries Véra.

THE BOLKÓNSKYS

PRINCE Nicholas BOLKÓNSKY, a retired General-in-Chief.

PRINCE ANDREW Bolkónsky, his son.

PRINCESS MARY (Másha) Bolkónskaya, his daughter.

Princess Elizabeth Bolkónskaya (LISE), Andrew's wife.

TÍKHON, Prince N. Bolkónsky's attendant.

ALPÁTYCH, his steward.

THE KURÁGINS

PRINCE VASÍLI Kurágin.

Prince HIPPOLYTE Kurágin, his elder son.

* So stressed by Maude, probably on the analogy of the place-name; but A. B. Goldenveizer (Vblízi Tolstogo, Moscow 1959, p. 371) reports that Tolstoy himself always stressed it Róstov.

Prince ANATOLE Kurágin, his younger son.

Princess HÉLÈNE Kurágina (Lëlya), his daughter, who marries Pierre.

Princess ANNA MIKHÁYLOVNA Drubetskáya.

Prince BORÍS Drubetskóy (Bóry), her son.

JULIE Karágina, an heiress who marries Borís.

MÁRYA DMÍTRIEVNA Akhrosímova (*le terrible dragon*).

BILÍBIN, a diplomat.

DENÍSOV, Vasíli Dmítrich (Váska), an hussar officer.

Lavrúshka, his batman.

DÓLOKHOV (Fédya), an officer and desperado.

Count Rostopchín, Governor of Moscow.

ANNA PÁVLOVNA Scherer (Annette), Maid of Honour to the ex-Empress Márya Fëdorovna.

Shinshín, a relation of Countess Rostóva's.

Timókhin, an infantry officer.

Túshin, an artillery officer.

Platon KARATÁEV, a peasant.

Boguchárovo	Shevárdino
Borodinó	Smolénsk
Málo–Yaroslávets	Torzhók
Mytíshchi	Vorónezh
Ryazán	Vyázma

DATES OF PRINCIPAL EVENTS

1805

* To adjust nineteenth-century old-style dates to our western calendar twelve days have to be added in each case.

Olmütz

Wischau

Austerlitz

Brünn
Schlappanitz

Guntersdorf

Hollabrünn

Znaim

R. Morava

Vienna

Schön Grabern

Krems

R. Danube

Dürrenstein

Mölk

Ips

Amstetten

R. Ips

R. Enns

Linz

Enns

R. Traun

Lambach

Braunau

R. Danube

R. Inn

Ulm (140 miles)

R. Danube

0   50   100   150 km
0   50   100 miles

1. THE 1805 CAMPAIGN

2. AUSTERLITZ

3. THE 1807 CAMPAIGN

Baltic Sea

St Petersburg

R U S S I A

Riga

R. Dvina
Drissa
Polotsk
Ostrovno
Vitebsk
Rudnia
Orsha
Krasnoe
Smolensk
Dorogobuzh
Vyazma
Tsarevo-Zaymishdie
sad Hills
Gzhatsk
Borodino
Mozhaysk
Moscow
Podolsk
Fominskoe
Krasnaya Pakhra
Tarutino
Malo-Yaroslavets
Kaluga
Serpukhov
R. Oka
Tula
Orel
Kursk

Yaroslav

Vladimir

Ryazan

Voronezh

R. Dnieper
Mogilev
R. Berezina
Borisov
Smorgoni
Vilna
R. Vilya
Grodno
Volkovisk
Kovno
R. Niemen
Tilsit
PRUSSIA
WARSAW
GRAND DUCHY
Ostrolenka
Pultusk

——— Napoleon's advance
·········· Napoleon's retreat

0   100   200 miles
0   100   200   300 km

4. THE WAR OF 1812

5. BORODINO

CHAPTER CONTENTS

BOOK ONE

PART I

PART II

PART III

BOOK TWO

PART I

PART II

PART III

PART V

BOOK THREE

PART I

PART III

BOOK FOUR

PART I

FIRST EPILOGUE

SECOND EPILOGUE

WAR AND PEACE

*

BOOK ONE

PART ONE

1

'WELL, Prince, so Genoa and Lucca are now just family estates of the Buonapartes.* But I warn you, if you don't tell me that this means war, if you still try to defend the infamies and horrors perpetrated by that Antichrist – I really believe he is Antichrist – I will have nothing more to do with you and you are no longer my friend, no longer my "faithful slave", as you call yourself! But how do you do? I see I have frightened you – sit down and tell me all the news.'

It was in July 1805, and the speaker was the well-known Anna Pavlovna Scherer, maid of honour and favourite of the Empress Marya Fëdorovna. With these words she greeted Prince Vasili, a man of high rank and importance, who was the first to arrive at her reception. Anna Pavlovna had had a cough for some days. She was, as she said, suffering from *la grippe*; *grippe* being then a new word in St Petersburg, used only by the *élite*.

All her invitations without exception, written in French, and delivered by a scarlet-liveried footman that morning, ran as follows:

If you have nothing better to do, Count (or Prince), and if the prospect of spending an evening with a poor invalid is not too terrible, I shall be very charmed to see you to-night between 7 and 10.

Annette Scherer.

'Heavens! what a virulent attack!' replied the prince, not in the least disconcerted by this reception. He had just entered, wearing an embroidered court uniform, knee-breeches and shoes, and had stars on his breast and a serene expression on his flat face. He spoke in that refined French in which our grandfathers not only spoke but thought, and with the gentle, patronizing intonation natural to a man of importance who had grown old in society and at court. He went up to Anna Pavlovna, kissed her hand, presenting to her his bald, scented and shining head, and complacently seated himself on the sofa.

'First of all, dear friend, tell me how you are. Set your friend's mind at rest,' said he without altering his tone, beneath the

3

politeness and affected sympathy of which indifference and even irony could be discerned.

'Can one be well while suffering morally? Can one be calm in times like these if one has any feeling?' said Anna Pavlovna. 'You are staying the whole evening, I hope?'

'And the fête at the English Ambassador's? To-day is Wednesday. I must put in an appearance there,' said the prince. 'My daughter is coming for me to take me there.'

'I thought to-day's fête had been cancelled. I confess all these festivities and fireworks are becoming wearisome.'

'If they had known that you wished it, the entertainment would have been put off,' said the prince, who, like a wound-up clock, by force of habit said things he did not even wish to be believed.

'Don't tease! Well, and what has been decided about Novosiltsev's dispatch?* You know everything.'

'What can one say about it?' replied the prince in a cold, listless tone. 'What has been decided? They have decided that Buonaparte has burnt his boats, and I believe that we are ready to burn ours.'

Prince Vasili always spoke languidly, like an actor repeating a stale part. Anna Pavlovna Scherer on the contrary, despite her forty years, overflowed with animation and impulsiveness. To be an enthusiast had become her social vocation and, sometimes even when she did not feel like it, she became enthusiastic in order not to disappoint the expectations of those who knew her. The subdued smile which, though it did not suit her faded features, always played round her lips, expressed, as in a spoilt child, a continual consciousness of her charming defect, which she neither wished, nor could, nor considered it necessary, to correct.

In the midst of a conversation on political matters Anna Pavlovna burst out:

'Oh, don't speak to me of Austria. Perhaps I don't understand things, but Austria never has wished, and does not wish, for war. She is betraying us! Russia alone must save Europe. Our gracious sovereign recognizes his high vocation and will be true to it. That is the one thing I have faith in! Our good and wonderful sovereign has to perform the noblest rôle on earth, and he is so virtuous and noble that God will not forsake him. He will fulfil his vocation and crush the hydra of revolution, which has become more terrible than ever in the person of this murderer and villain! We alone must avenge the blood of the just one ... Whom, I ask you, can we rely on ...? England with her commercial spirit will not and cannot understand the Emperor Alexander's loftiness of soul. She has refused to evacuate Malta. She wanted to find, and still seeks, some secret motive in our actions. What answer did

4

Novosiltsev get? None. The English have not understood and cannot understand the self-abnegation of our Emperor who wants nothing for himself, but only desires the good of mankind. And what have they promised? Nothing! And what little they have promised they will not perform! Prussia has always declared that Buonaparte is invincible and that all Europe is powerless before him ... And I don't believe a word that Hardenberg says, or Haugwitz either. This famous Prussian neutrality is just a trap. I have faith only in God and the lofty destiny of our adored monarch. He will save Europe!'

She suddenly paused, smiling at her own impetuosity.

'I think,' said the prince with a smile, 'that if you had been sent instead of our dear Wintzingerode you would have captured the King of Prussia's consent by assault. You are so eloquent. Will you give me a cup of tea?'

'In a moment. A *propos*,' she added, becoming calm again, 'I am expecting two very interesting men to-night, le Vicomte de Mortemart, who is connected with the Montmorencys through the Rohans, one of the best French families. He is one of the genuine *émigrés*, the good ones. And also the Abbé Morio. Do you know that profound thinker? He has been received by the Emperor. Had you heard?'

'I shall be delighted to meet them,' said the prince. 'But tell me,' he added with studied carelessness as if it had only just occurred to him, though the question he was about to ask was the chief motive of his visit, 'is it true that the Dowager Empress wants Baron Funke to be appointed first secretary at Vienna? The baron by all accounts is a poor creature.'

Prince Vasili wished to obtain this post for his son, but others were trying through the Dowager Empress Marya Fëdorovna to secure it for the baron.

Anna Pavlovna almost closed her eyes to indicate that neither she nor anyone else had a right to criticize what the Empress desired or was pleased with.

'Baron Funke has been recommended to the Dowager Empress by her sister,' was all she said, in a dry and mournful tone.

As she named the Empress, Anna Pavlovna's face suddenly assumed an expression of profound and sincere devotion and respect, mingled with sadness, and this occurred every time she mentioned her illustrious patroness. She added that her Majesty had deigned to show Baron Funke *beaucoup d'estime*, and again her face clouded over with sadness.

The prince was silent and looked indifferent. But, with the womanly and courtier-like quickness and tact habitual to her, Anna

Pavlovna wished both to rebuke him (for daring to speak as he had done of a man recommended to the Empress) and at the same time to console him, so she said—

'Now about your family. Do you know that since your daughter came out everyone has been enraptured by her? They say she is amazingly beautiful.'

The prince bowed to signify his respect and gratitude.

'I often think,' she continued after a short pause, drawing nearer to the prince and smiling amiably at him as if to show that political and social topics were ended and the time had come for intimate conversation – 'I often think how unfairly sometimes the joys of life are distributed. Why has fate given you two such splendid children? I don't speak of Anatole, your youngest. I don't like him,' she added in a tone admitting of no rejoinder and raising her eyebrows. 'Two such charming children. And really you appreciate them less than anyone, and so you don't deserve to have them.'

And she smiled her ecstatic smile.

'I can't help it,' said the prince. 'Lavater would have said I lack the bump of paternity.'

'Don't joke; I mean to have a serious talk with you. Do you know I am dissatisfied with your younger son? Between ourselves' (and her face assumed its melancholy expression) 'he was mentioned at her Majesty's and you were pitied . . .'

The prince answered nothing, but she looked at him significantly, awaiting a reply. He frowned.

'What would you have me do?' he said at last. 'You know I did all a father could for their education, and they have both turned out fools. Hippolyte is at least a quiet fool, but Anatole is an active one. That is the only difference between them.' He said this smiling in a way more natural and animated than usual, so that the wrinkles round his mouth very clearly revealed something unexpectedly coarse and unpleasant.

'And why are children born to such men as you? If you were not a father there would be nothing I could reproach you with,' said Anna Pavlovna, looking up pensively.

'I am your faithful slave, and to you alone I can confess that my children are the bane of my life. It is the cross I have to bear. That is how I explain it to myself. It can't be helped!'

He said no more, but expressed his resignation to cruel fate by a gesture. Anna Pavlovna meditated.

'Have you never thought of marrying your prodigal son Anatole?' she asked. 'They say old maids have a mania for match-making, and though I don't feel that weakness in myself as yet,

I know a little person who is very unhappy with her father. She is a relation of yours, Princess Marya Bolkonskaya.

Prince Vasili did not reply though, with the quickness of memory and perception befitting a man of the world, he indicated by a movement of the head that he was considering this information.

'Do you know,' he said at last, evidently unable to check the sad current of his thoughts, 'that Anatole is costing me forty thousand rubles a year? And', he went on after a pause, 'what will it be in five years, if he goes on like this?' Presently he added: 'That's what we fathers have to put up with ... Is this princess of yours rich?'

'Her father is very rich and stingy. He lives in the country. He is the well-known Prince Bolkonsky who had to retire from the army under the late Emperor, and was nicknamed "the King of Prussia". He is very clever but eccentric, and a bore. The poor girl is very unhappy. She has a brother; I think you know him, he married Lisa Meinen lately. He is an aide-de-camp of Kutuzov's and will be here to-night.'

'Listen, dear Annette,' said the prince, suddenly taking Anna Pavlovna's hand and for some reason drawing it downwards. 'Arrange that affair for me and I shall always be your most devoted slave – *slafe* with an f, as a village elder of mine writes in his reports. She is rich and of good family and that's all I want.'

And with the familiarity and easy grace peculiar to him, he raised the maid of honour's hand to his lips, kissed it, and swung it to and fro as he lay back in his arm-chair, looking in another direction.

'*Attendez*,' said Anna Pavlovna, reflecting, 'I'll speak to Lisa, young Bolkonsky's wife, this very evening, and perhaps the thing can be arranged. It shall be on your family's behalf that I'll start my apprenticeship as old maid.'

2

ANNA PAVLOVNA'S drawing-room was gradually filling. The highest Petersburg society was assembled there: people differing widely in age and character but alike in the social circle to which they belonged. Prince Vasili's daughter, the beautiful Hélène, came to take her father to the ambassador's entertainment; she wore a ball dress and her badge as maid of honour. The youthful little Princess Bolkonskaya, known as *la femme la plus séduisante de Pétersbourg*, was also there. She had been married during the previous winter, and being pregnant did not go to any large gatherings, but only to small receptions. Prince Vasili's son, Hippolyte, had come with Mortemart, whom he introduced. The Abbé Morio and many others had also come.

To each new arrival Anna Pavlovna said, 'You have not yet seen my aunt,' or 'You do not know my aunt?' and very gravely conducted him or her to a little old lady, wearing large bows of ribbons in her cap, who had come sailing in from another room as soon as the guests began to arrive; and slowly turning her eyes from the visitor to her aunt, Anna Pavlovna mentioned each one's name and then left them.

Each visitor performed the ceremony of greeting this old aunt whom not one of them knew, not one of them wanted to know, and not one of them cared about; Anna Pavlovna observed these greetings with mournful and solemn interest and silent approval. The aunt spoke to each of them in the same words, about their health and her own, and the health of her Majesty, 'who, thank God, was better to-day.' And each visitor, though politeness prevented his showing impatience, left the old woman with a sense of relief at having performed a vexatious duty and did not return to her the whole evening.

The young Princess Bolkonskaya had brought some work in a gold-embroidered velvet bag. Her pretty little upper lip, on which a delicate dark down was just perceptible, was too short for her teeth, but it lifted all the more sweetly, and was especially charming when she occasionally drew it down to meet the lower lip. As is always the case with a thoroughly attractive woman, her defect – the shortness of her upper lip and her half open mouth – seemed to be her own special and peculiar form of beauty. Everyone brightened at the sight of this pretty young woman, so soon to become a mother, so full of life and health, and carrying her burden so lightly. Old men and dull dispirited young ones who looked at her, after being in her company and talking to her a little while, felt as if they too were becoming, like her, full of life and health. All who talked to her, and at each word saw her bright smile and the constant gleam of her white teeth, thought that they were in a specially amiable mood that day.

The little princess went round the table with quick short swaying steps, her workbag on her arm, and gaily spreading out her dress sat down on a sofa near the silver samovar, as if all she was doing was a pleasure to herself and to all around her. 'I have brought my work,' said she in French, displaying her bag and addressing all present. 'Mind, Annette, I hope you have not played a wicked trick on me,' she added, turning to her hostess. 'You wrote that it was to be quite a small reception, and just see how badly I am dressed.' And she spread out her arms to show her short-waisted, lace-trimmed, dainty grey dress, girdled with a broad ribbon just below the breast.

'*Soyez tranquille, Lise*, you will always be prettier than anyone else,' replied Anna Pavlovna.

'You know,' said the princess in the same tone of voice and still in French, turning to a general, 'my husband is deserting me? He is going to get himself killed. Tell me what this wretched war is for?' she added, addressing Prince Vasili, and without waiting for an answer she turned to speak to his daughter, the beautiful Hélène.

'What a delightful woman this little princess is!' said Prince Vasili to Anna Pavlovna.

One of the next arrivals was a stout, heavily built young man with close-cropped hair, spectacles, the light-coloured breeches fashionable at that time, a very high ruffle and a brown dress-coat. The stout young man was an illegitimate son of Count Bezukhov, a well-known grandee of Catherine's time who now lay dying in Moscow. The young man had not yet entered either the military or civil service, as he had only just returned from abroad where he had been educated, and this was his first appearance in society. Anna Pavlovna greeted him with the nod she accorded to the lowest hierarchy in her drawing-room. But in spite of this lowest grade greeting, a look of anxiety and fear, as at the sight of something too large and unsuited to the place, came over her face when she saw Pierre enter. Though he was certainly rather bigger than the other men in the room her anxiety could only have reference to the clever though shy, but observant and natural, expression which distinguished him from everyone else in that drawing-room.

'It is very good of you, Monsieur Pierre, to come and visit a poor invalid,' said Anna Pavlovna, exchanging an alarmed glance with her aunt as she conducted him to her.

Pierre murmured something unintelligible, and continued to look round as if in search of something. On his way to the aunt he bowed to the little princess with a pleased smile, as to an intimate acquaintance.

Anna Pavlovna's alarm was justified, for Pierre turned away from the aunt without waiting to hear her speech about her Majesty's health. Anna Pavlovna in dismay detained him with the words:

'Do you know the Abbé Morio? He is a most interesting man.'

'Yes, I have heard of his scheme for perpetual peace, and it is very interesting but hardly feasible.'

'You think so?' rejoined Anna Pavlovna in order to say something and get away to attend to her duties as hostess. But Pierre now committed a reverse act of impoliteness. First he had left a lady before she had finished speaking to him, and now he continued to speak to another who wished to get away. With his head bent, and his big feet spread apart, he began explaining his reasons for thinking the abbé's plan chimerical.

'We will talk of it later,' said Anna Pavlovna with a smile.

And having got rid of this young man who did not know how to behave, she resumed her duties as hostess and continued to listen and watch, ready to help at any point where the conversation might happen to flag. As the foreman of a spinning-mill when he has set the hands to work, goes round and notices, here a spindle that has stopped or there one that creaks or makes more noise than it should, and hastens to check the machine or set it in proper motion, so Anna Pavlovna moved about her drawing-room, approaching now a silent, now a too noisy group, and by a word or slight rearrangement kept the conversational machine in steady, proper and regular motion. But amid these cares her anxiety about Pierre was evident. She kept an anxious watch on him when he approached the group round Mortemart to listen to what was being said there, and again when he passed to another group whose centre was the abbé.

Pierre had been educated abroad, and this reception at Anna Pavlovna's was the first he had attended in Russia. He knew that all the intellectual lights of Petersburg were gathered there and, like a child in a toy shop, did not know which way to look, afraid of missing any clever conversation that was to be heard. Seeing the self-confident and refined expression on the faces of those present he was always expecting to hear something very profound. At last he came up to Morio. Here the conversation seemed interesting and he stood waiting for an opportunity to express his own views, as young people are fond of doing.

3

ANNA PAVLOVNA'S reception was in full swing. The spindles hummed steadily and ceaselessly on all sides. With the exception of the aunt, beside whom sat only one elderly lady, who with her thin careworn face was rather out of place in this brilliant society, the whole company had settled into three groups. One, chiefly masculine, had formed round the abbé. Another, of young people, was grouped round the beautiful Princess Hélène, Prince Vasili's daughter, and the little Princess Bolkonskaya, very pretty and rosy, though rather too plump for her age. The third group was gathered round Mortemart and Anna Pavlovna.

The vicomte was a nice-looking young man with soft features and polished manners, who evidently considered himself a celebrity but out of politeness modestly placed himself at the disposal of the circle in which he found himself. Anna Pavlovna was obviously serving him up as a treat to her guests. As a clever *maître d'hôtel* serves up as a specially choice delicacy a piece of meat that no one who had seen it in the kitchen would have cared to eat, so Anna Pavlovna served up to her guests, first the vicomte and then the abbé, as peculiarly choice morsels. The group about Mortemart immediately began discussing the murder of the Duc d'Enghien.* The vicomte said that the Duc d'Enghien had perished by his own magnanimity, and that there were particular reasons for Buonaparte's hatred of him.

'Ah, yes! Do tell us all about it, vicomte,' said Anna Pavlovna, with a pleasant feeling that there was something *à la Louis* XV in the sound of that sentence: '*Contez nous cela, vicomte.*'

The vicomte bowed and smiled courteously in token of his willingness to comply. Anna Pavlovna arranged a group round him, inviting everyone to listen to his tale.

'The vicomte knew the duc personally,' whispered Anna Pavlovna to one of the guests. 'The vicomte is a wonderful *raconteur*,' said she to another. 'How evidently he belongs to the best society,' said she to a third; and the vicomte was served up to the company in the choicest and most advantageous style, like a well-garnished joint of roast beef on a hot dish.

The vicomte wished to begin his story and gave a subtle smile.

'Come over here, Hélène, dear,' said Anna Pavlovna to the beautiful young princess who was sitting some way off, the centre of another group.

The princess smiled. She rose with the same unchanging smile with which she had first entered the room – the smile of a perfectly beautiful woman. With a slight rustle of her white dress trimmed with moss and ivy, with a gleam of white shoulders, glossy hair and sparkling diamonds, she passed between the men who made way for her, not looking at any of them but smiling on all, as if graciously allowing each the privilege of admiring her beautiful figure and shapely shoulders, back, and bosom – which in the fashion of those days were very much exposed – and she seemed to bring the glamour of a ball-room with her as she moved towards Anna Pavlovna. Hélène was so lovely that not only did she not show any trace of coquetry, but on the contrary she even appeared shy of her unquestionable and all too victorious beauty. She seemed to wish, but to be unable, to diminish its effect.

'How lovely!' said everyone who saw her; and the vicomte lifted his shoulders and dropped his eyes as if startled by something extraordinary when she took her seat opposite and beamed upon him also with her unchanging smile.

'Madame, I doubt my ability before such an audience,' said he, smilingly inclining his head.

The princess rested her bare round arm on a little table and considered a reply unnecessary. She smilingly waited. All the time the story was being told she sat upright, glancing now at her beautiful round arm, altered in shape by its pressure on the table, now at her still more beautiful bosom, on which she readjusted a diamond necklace. From time to time she smoothed the folds of her dress, and whenever the story produced an effect she glanced at Anna Pavlovna, at once adopted just the expression she saw on the maid of honour's face, and again relapsed into her radiant smile.

The little princess had also left the tea-table and followed Hélène.

'Wait a moment, I'll get my work ... Now then, what are you thinking of?' she went on, turning to Prince Hippolyte. 'Fetch me my work-bag.'

There was a general movement as the princess, smiling and talking merrily to everyone at once, sat down and gaily arranged herself in her seat.

'Now I am all right,' she said, and asking the vicomte to begin, she took up her work.

Prince Hippolyte, having brought the work-bag, joined the circle and moving a chair close to hers seated himself beside her.

Le charmant Hippolyte was surprising by his extraordinary resemblance to his beautiful sister, but yet more by the fact that in spite of this resemblance he was exceedingly ugly. His features were like his sister's, but while in her case everything was lit up by a joyous, self-satisfied, youthful, and constant smile of animation, and by the wonderful classic beauty of her figure, his face on the contrary was dulled by imbecility and a constant expression of sullen self-confidence, while his body was thin and weak. His eyes, nose, and mouth all seemed puckered into a vacant, wearied grimace, and his arms and legs always fell into unnatural positions.

'It's not going to be a ghost story?' said he, sitting down beside the princess and hastily adjusting his lorgnette, as if without this instrument he could not begin to speak.

'Why no, my dear fellow,' said the astonished narrator, shrugging his shoulders.

'Because I hate ghost stories,' said Prince Hippolyte in a tone which showed that he only understood the meaning of his words after he had uttered them.

He spoke with such self-confidence that his hearers could not be sure whether what he said was very witty or very stupid. He was dressed in a dark-green dress coat, knee-breeches of the colour of *cuisse de nymphe effrayée*, as he called it, shoes and silk stockings.

The vicomte told his tale very neatly. It was an anecdote, then current, to the effect that the Duc d'Enghien had gone secretly to Paris to visit Mademoiselle George;* that at her house he came upon Bonaparte, who also enjoyed the famous actress's favours, and that in his presence Napoleon happened to fall into one of the fainting fits to which he was subject, and was thus at the duc's mercy. The latter spared him, and this magnanimity Bonaparte subsequently repaid by death.

The story was very pretty and interesting, especially at the point where the rivals suddenly recognized one another; and the ladies looked agitated.

'Charming!' said Anna Pavlovna with an inquiring glance at the little princess.

'Charming!' whispered the little princess, sticking the needle into her work as if to testify that the interest and fascination of the story prevented her from going on with it.

The vicomte appreciated this silent praise and smiling gratefully prepared to continue, but just then Anna Pavlovna, who had kept a watchful eye on the young man who so alarmed her, noticed that he was talking too loudly and vehemently with the abbé, so she hurried to the rescue. Pierre had managed to start a conversation with the abbé about the balance of power, and the latter, evidently interested by the young man's simple-minded eagerness, was explaining his pet theory. Both were talking and listening too eagerly and too naturally, which was why Anna Pavlovna disapproved.

'The means are ... the balance of power in Europe and the rights of the people,' the abbé was saying. 'It is only necessary for one powerful nation like Russia – barbaric as she is said to be – to place herself disinterestedly at the head of an alliance having for its object the maintenance of the balance of power in Europe, and it would save the world!'

'But how are you to get that balance?' Pierre was beginning.

At that moment Anna Pavlovna came up, and looking severely at Pierre, asked the Italian how he stood the Russian climate. The Italian's face instantly changed and assumed an offensively affected, sugary expression, evidently habitual to him when conversing with women.

'I am so enchanted by the brilliancy of the wit and culture of the society, more especially of the feminine society, in which I have had the honour of being received, that I have not yet had time to think of the climate,' said he.

Not letting the abbé and Pierre escape, Anna Pavlovna, the more conveniently to keep them under observation, brought them into the larger circle.

Just then another visitor entered the drawing-room: Prince Andrew Bolkonsky, the little princess's husband. He was a very handsome young man, of medium height, with firm, clear-cut features. Everything about him, from his weary, bored expression to his quiet, measured step, offered a most striking contrast to his lively little wife. It was evident that he not only knew everyone in the drawing-room, but had found them to be so tiresome that it wearied him to look at or listen to them. And among all these faces that he found so tedious, none seemed to bore him so much as that of his pretty wife. He turned away from her with a grimace that distorted his handsome face, kissed Anna Pavlovna's hand, and screwing up his eyes scanned the whole company.

'You are off to the war, Prince?' said Anna Pavlovna.

'General Kutuzov,' said Bolkonsky, speaking French and stressing the last syllable of the general's name like a Frenchman, 'has been pleased to take me as an aide-de-camp. . . .'

'And Lise, your wife?'

'She will go to the country.'

'Are you not ashamed to deprive us of your charming wife?'

'André,' said his wife, addressing her husband in the same coquettish manner in which she spoke to other men, 'the vicomte has been telling us such a · tale about Mademoiselle George and Buonaparte!'

Prince Andrew screwed up his eyes and turned away. Pierre, who from the moment Prince Andrew entered the room had watched him with glad, affectionate eyes, now came up and took his arm. Before he looked round Prince Andrew frowned again, expressing his annoyance with whoever was touching his arm, but when he saw Pierre's beaming face he gave him an unexpectedly kind and pleasant smile.

'There now! . . . So you, too, are in the great world?' said he to Pierre.

'I knew you would be here,' replied Pierre. 'I will come to supper with you. May I?' he added in a low voice so as not to disturb the vicomte who was continuing his story.

'No, impossible!' said Prince Andrew, laughing and pressing Pierre's hand to show that there was no need to ask the question. He wished to say something more, but at that moment Prince Vasili and his daughter got up to go and the two young men rose to let them pass.

'You must excuse me, dear Vicomte,' said Prince Vasili to the Frenchman, holding him down by the sleeve in a friendly way to prevent his rising. 'This unfortunate fête at the ambassador's deprives me of a pleasure, and obliges me to interrupt you. I am very sorry to leave your enchanting party,' said he, turning to Anna Pavlovna.

His daughter, Princess Hélène, passed between the chairs lightly holding up the folds of her dress, and the smile shone still more radiantly on her beautiful face. Pierre gazed at her with rapturous, almost frightened, eyes as she passed him.

'Very lovely,' said Prince Andrew.

'Very,' said Pierre.

In passing, Prince Vasili seized Pierre's hand and said to Anna Pavlovna:

'Educate this bear for me! He has been staying with me a whole month and this is the first time I have seen him in society. Nothing is so necessary for a young man as the society of clever women.'

4

ANNA PAVLOVNA smiled and promised to take Pierre in hand. She knew his father to be a connexion of Prince Vasili's. The elderly lady who had been sitting with the old aunt rose hurriedly and overtook Prince Vasili in the ante-room. All the affectation of interest she had assumed had left her kindly and tear-worn face and it now expressed only anxiety and fear.

'How about my son Boris, Prince?' said she, hurrying after him into the ante-room. 'I can't remain any longer in Petersburg. Tell me what news I may take back to my poor boy.'

Although Prince Vasili listened reluctantly and not very politely to the elderly lady, even betraying some impatience, she gave him an ingratiating and appealing smile, and took his hand that he might not go away.

'What would it cost you to say a word to the Emperor, and then he would be transferred to the Guards at once?' said she.

'Believe me, Princess, I am ready to do all I can,' answered Prince Vasili, 'but it is difficult for me to ask the Emperor. I should advise you to appeal to Rumyantsev through Prince Golitsin. That would be the best way.'

The elderly lady was a Princess Drubetskaya, belonging to one of the best families in Russia, but she was poor, and having long been out of society had lost her former influential connexions. She had now come to Petersburg to procure an appointment in the Guards for her only son. It was, in fact, solely to meet Prince Vasili that she had obtained an invitation to Anna Pavlovna's reception, and had sat listening to the vicomte's story. Prince Vasili's words frightened her, an embittered look clouded her once handsome face, but only for a moment; then she smiled again and clutched Prince Vasili's arm more tightly.

'Listen to me, Prince,' said she. 'I have never yet asked you for anything and I never will again, nor have I ever reminded you of my father's friendship for you; but now I entreat you for God's sake to do this for my son – and I shall always regard you as a benefactor,' she added hurriedly. 'No, don't be angry, but promise! I have asked Golitsin and he has refused. Be the kind-hearted man you always were,' she said, trying to smile though tears were in her eyes.

'Papa, we shall be late,' said Princess Hélène, turning her beautiful head and looking over her classically moulded shoulder as she stood waiting by the door.

Influence in society, however, is capital which has to be economized if it is to last. Prince Vasili knew this, and having once realized that if he asked on behalf of all who begged of him, he would soon be unable to ask for himself, he became chary of using his influence. But in Princess Drubetskaya's case he felt, after her second appeal, something like qualms of conscience. She had reminded him of what was quite true; he had been indebted to her father for the first steps in his career. Moreover, he could see by her manner that she was one of those women – mostly mothers – who having once made up their minds, will not rest until they have gained their end, and are prepared if necessary to go on insisting day after day and hour after hour, and even to make scenes. This last consideration moved him.

'My dear Anna Mikhaylovna,' said he with his usual familiarity and weariness of tone, 'it is almost impossible for me to do what you ask; but to prove my devotion to you and how I respect your father's memory, I will do the impossible – your son shall be transferred to the Guards. Here is my hand on it. Are you satisfied?'

'My dear benefactor! This is what I expected from you – I knew your kindness!' He turned to go.

'Wait – just a word! When he has been transferred to the Guards...' she faltered, 'You are on good terms with Michael Ilarionovich Kutuzov*...recommend Boris to him as adjutant! Then I shall be at rest, and then...'

Prince Vasili smiled.

'No, I won't promise that. You don't know how Kutuzov is pestered since his appointment as Commander-in-Chief. He told me himself that all the Moscow ladies have conspired to give him all their sons as adjutants.'

'No, but do promise! I won't let you go! My dear benefactor...'

'Papa,' said his beautiful daughter in the same tone as before, 'we shall be late.'

'Well, *au revoir!* Good-bye! You hear her?'

'Then to-morrow you will speak to the Emperor?'

'Certainly; but about Kutuzov, I don't promise.'

'Do promise, do promise, Vasili!' cried Anna Mikhaylovna as he went, with the smile of a coquettish girl, which at one time probably came naturally to her, but was now very ill-suited to her care-worn face.

Apparently she had forgotten her age and by force of habit employed all the old feminine arts. But as soon as the prince had gone her face resumed its former cold, artificial expression. She returned to the group where the vicomte was still talking, and again pretended to listen, while waiting till it would be time to leave. Her task was accomplished.

'And what do you think of this latest comedy, the coronation at Milan?' asked Anna Pavlovna, 'and of the comedy of the people of Genoa and Lucca laying their petitions before Monsieur Buonaparte, and Monsieur Buonaparte sitting on a throne and granting the petitions of the nations? Adorable! It is enough to make one's head whirl! It is as if the whole world had gone crazy.'

Prince Andrew looked Anna Pavlovna straight in the face with a sarcastic smile.

' "*Dieu me la donne, gare à qui la touche!*"* (Bonaparte's words at his coronation). They say he was very fine when he said that,' he remarked, repeating the words in Italian: ' "*Dio la dona, gai a qui la tocca!*" '

'I hope this will prove the last drop that will make the glass run over,' Anna Pavlovna continued. 'The sovereigns will not be able to endure this man who is a menace to everything.'

'The sovereigns? I do not speak of Russia,' said the vicomte, polite but hopeless: 'The sovereigns, madame...What have they done for Louis XVII, for the Queen, or for Madame Elizabeth? Nothing!' and he became more animated. 'And believe me, they

17

are reaping the reward of their betrayal of the Bourbon cause. The sovereigns! Why, they are sending ambassadors to compliment the usurper.'

And sighing disdainfully, he again changed his position.

Prince Hippolyte, who had been gazing at the vicomte for some time through his lorgnette, suddenly turned completely round towards the little princess, and having asked for a needle began tracing the Condé coat-of-arms on the table. He explained this to her with as much gravity as if she had asked him to do it.

'*Bâton de gueules, engrêlé de gueules d'azur – maison Condé,*'* said he.

The princess listened, smiling.

'If Buonaparte remains on the throne of France a year longer,' the vicomte continued, with the air of a man who, in a matter with which he is better acquainted than anyone else, does not listen to others but follows the current of his own thoughts, 'things will have gone too far. By intrigues, violence, exile, and executions, French society – I mean good French society – will have been for ever destroyed, and then . . .'

He shrugged his shoulders and spread out his hands. Pierre wished to make a remark for the conversation interested him, but Anna Pavlovna, who had him under observation, interrupted:

'The Emperor Alexander,' said she, with the melancholy which always accompanied any reference of hers to the Imperial family, 'has declared that he will leave it to the French people themselves to choose their own form of government; and I believe that once free from the usurper, the whole nation will certainly throw itself into the arms of its rightful king,' she concluded, trying to be amiable to the royalist emigrant.

'That is doubtful,' said Prince Andrew. 'Monsieur le Vicomte quite rightly supposes that matters have already gone too far. I think it will be difficult to return to the old régime.'

'From what I have heard,' said Pierre, blushing and breaking into the conversation, 'almost all the aristocracy has already gone over to Bonaparte's side.'

'It is the Buonapartists who say that,' replied the vicomte without looking at Pierre. 'At the present time it is difficult to know the real state of French public opinion.'

'Bonaparte has said so,' remarked Prince Andrew with a sarcastic smile.

It was evident that he did not like the vicomte and was aiming his remarks at him, though without looking at him.

'"I showed them the path to glory, but they did not follow it",' Prince Andrew continued after a short silence, again quoting

Napoleon's words. ' "I opened my antechambers and they crowded in." I do not know how far he was justified in saying so.'

'Not in the least,' replied the vicomte. 'After the murder of the duc even the most partial ceased to regard him as a hero. If to some people,' he went on, turning to Anna Pavlovna, 'he ever was a hero, after the murder of the duc there was one martyr more in heaven and one hero less on earth.'

Before Anna Pavlovna and the others had time to smile their appreciation of the vicomte's epigram, Pierre again broke into the conversation, and though Anna Pavlovna felt sure he would say something inappropriate, she was unable to stop him.

'The execution of the Duc d'Enghien,' declared Monsieur Pierre, 'was a political necessity, and it seems to me that Napoleon showed greatness of soul by not fearing to take on himself the whole responsibility of that deed.'

'*Dieu! Mon Dieu!*' muttered Anna Pavlovna in a terrified whisper.

'What, Monsieur Pierre...Do you consider that assassination shows greatness of soul?' said the little princess, smiling and drawing her work nearer to her.

'Oh! Oh!' exclaimed several voices.

'Capital!' said Prince Hippolyte in English, and began slapping his knee with the palm of his hand.

The vicomte merely shrugged his shoulders. Pierre looked solemnly at his audience over his spectacles and continued.

'I say so,' he continued desperately, 'because the Bourbons fled from the Revolution leaving the people to anarchy, and Napoleon alone understood the Revolution and quelled it, and so for the general good, he could not stop short for the sake of one man's life.'

'Won't you come over to the other table?' suggested Anna Pavlovna.

But Pierre continued his speech without heeding her.

'No,' cried he, becoming more and more eager, 'Napoleon is great because he rose superior to the Revolution, suppressed its abuses, preserved all that was good in it – equality of citizenship and freedom of speech and of the press – and only for that reason did he obtain power.'

'Yes, if having obtained power, without availing himself of it to commit murder he had restored it to the rightful king, I should have called him a great man,' remarked the vicomte.

'He could not do that. The people only gave him power that he might rid them of the Bourbons and because they saw that he was a great man. The Revolution was a grand thing!' continued Monsieur Pierre, betraying by this desperate and provocative proposition his extreme youth and his wish to express all that was in his mind.

'What? Revolution and regicide a grand thing? ... Well, after that ... But won't you come to this other table?' repeated Anna Pavlovna.

'Rousseau's *Contrat social*,' said the vicomte with a tolerant smile.

'I am not speaking of regicide, I am speaking about ideas.'

'Yes: ideas of robbery, murder, and regicide,' again interjected an ironical voice.

'Those were extremes, no doubt, but they are not what is most important. What is important are the rights of man, emancipation from prejudices, and equality of citizenship, and all these ideas Napoleon has retained in full force.'

'Liberty and Equality,' said the vicomte contemptuously, as if at last deciding seriously to prove to this youth how foolish his words were, '– high-sounding words which have long been discredited. Who does not love Liberty and Equality? Even our Saviour preached liberty and equality. Have people since the Revolution become happier? On the contrary. We wanted liberty, but Buonaparte has destroyed it.'

Prince Andrew kept looking with an amused smile from Pierre to the vicomte and from the vicomte to their hostess. In the first moment of Pierre's outburst Anna Pavlovna, despite her social experience, was horror-struck. But when she saw that Pierre's sacrilegious words had not exasperated the vicomte, and had convinced herself that it was impossible to stop him, she rallied her forces and joined the vicomte·in a vigorous attack on the orator.

'But, my dear Monsieur Pierre,' said she, 'how do you explain the fact of a great man executing a duke – or even an ordinary man – who is innocent and untried?'

'I should like,' said the vicomte, 'to ask how Monsieur explains the 18th Brumaire; was not that an imposture? It was a swindle, and not at all like the conduct of a great man!'

'And the prisoners he killed in Africa?* That was horrible!' said the little princess, shrugging her shoulders.

'He's a low fellow, say what you will,' remarked Prince Hippolyte.

Pierre, not knowing whom to answer, looked at them all and smiled. His smile was unlike the half-smile of other people. When he smiled his grave, even rather gloomy look was instantaneously replaced by another – a childlike, kindly, even rather silly look, which seemed to ask forgiveness.

The vicomte, who was meeting him for the first time, saw clearly that this young Jacobin was not so terrible as his words suggested. All were silent.

'How do you expect him to answer you all at once?' said Prince Andrew. 'Besides, in the actions of a statesman one has to distinguish between his acts as a private person, as a general, and as an emperor. So it seems to me.'

'Yes, yes, of course!' Pierre chimed in, pleased at the arrival of this reinforcement.

'One must admit,' continued Prince Andrew, 'that Napoleon as a man was great on the bridge of Arcole,* and in the hospital at Jaffa where he gave his hand to the plague-stricken; but . . . but there are other acts which it is difficult to justify.'

Prince Andrew, who had evidently wished to tone down the awkwardness of Pierre's remarks, rose and made a sign to his wife that it was time to go.

Suddenly Prince Hippolyte started up making signs to everyone to attend, and asking them all to be seated began:

'I was told a charming Moscow story to-day, and must treat you to it. Excuse me, Vicomte – I must tell it in Russian or the point will be lost . . .' And Prince Hippolyte began to tell his story in such Russian as a Frenchman would speak after spending about a year in Russia. Everyone waited, so emphatically and eagerly did he demand their attention to his story.

'There is in Moscow a lady, *une dame*, and she is very stingy. She must have two footmen behind her carriage, and very big ones. That was her taste. And she had a lady's maid, also big. She said . . .'

Here Prince Hippolyte paused, evidently collecting his ideas with difficulty.

'She said . . . Oh yes! She said, "girl," to the maid, "put on a livery, get up behind the carriage, and come with me while I make some calls." '

Here Prince Hippolyte spluttered and burst out laughing long before his audience, which produced an effect unfavourable to the narrator. Several persons, among them the elderly lady and Anna Pavlovna, did however smile.

'She went. Suddenly there was a great wind. The girl lost her hat and her long hair came down . . .' Here he could contain himself no longer and went on, between gasps of laughter: 'And the whole world knew . . .'

And so the anecdote ended. Though it was unintelligible why he had told it, or why it had to be told in Russian, still Anna Pavlovna and the others appreciated Prince Hippolyte's social tact in so agreeably ending Pierre's unpleasant and unamiable outburst. After the anecdote the conversation broke up into insignificant small talk about the last and next balls, about theatricals, and who would meet whom, and when and where.

5

HAVING thanked Anna Pavlovna for her charming soirée, the guests began to take their leave.

Pierre was ungainly. Stout, above the average height, broad, with huge red hands, he did not know, as the saying is, how to enter a drawing-room and still less how to leave one; that is, how to say something particularly agreeable before going away. Besides this he was absent-minded. When he rose to go, he took up instead of his own, the general's three-cornered hat, and held it, pulling at the plume, till the general asked him to restore it. All his absent-mindedness and inability to enter a room and converse in it was however redeemed by his kindly, simple, and modest expression. Anna Pavlovna turned towards him and, with a Christian mildness that expressed forgiveness of his indiscretion, nodded and said: 'I hope to see you again, but I also hope you will change your opinions, my dear Monsieur Pierre.'

When she said this, he did not reply and only bowed, but again everybody saw his smile, which said nothing, unless perhaps, 'Opinions are opinions, but you see what a capital, good-natured fellow I am.' And everyone, including Anna Pavlovna, felt this.

Prince Andrew had gone out into the hall, and turning his shoulders to the footman who was helping him on with his cloak, listened indifferently to his wife's chatter with Prince Hippolyte who had also come into the hall. Prince Hippolyte stood close to the pretty, pregnant princess, and stared fixedly at her through his eyeglass.

'Go in, Annette, or you will catch cold,' said the little princess, taking leave of Anna Pavlovna. 'It is settled,' she added in a low voice.

Anna Pavlovna had already managed to speak to Lisa about the match she contemplated between Anatole and the little princess's sister-in-law.

'I rely on you, my dear,' said Anna Pavlovna, also in a low tone. 'Write to her and let me know how her father looks at the matter. Au revoir!' – and she left the hall.

Prince Hippolyte approached the little princess and, bending his face close to her, began to whisper something.

Two footmen, the princess's and his own, stood holding a shawl and a cloak, waiting for the conversation to finish. They listened to the French sentences which to them were meaningless, with an air of understanding but not wishing to appear to do so. The princess as usual spoke smilingly and listened with a laugh.

'I am very glad I did not go to the ambassador's,' said Prince Hippolyte, '– so dull. It has been a delightful evening, has it not? Delightful!'

'They say the ball will be very good,' replied the princess, drawing up her downy little lip. 'All the pretty women in society will be there.'

'Not all, for you will not be there; not all,' said Prince Hippolyte smiling joyfully; and snatching the shawl from the footman, whom he even pushed aside, he began wrapping it round the princess. Either from awkwardness or intentionally (no one could have said which) after the shawl had been adjusted he kept his arm around her for a long time, as though embracing her.

Still smiling, she gracefully moved away, turning and glancing at her husband. Prince Andrew's eyes were closed: he seemed weary and sleepy.

'Are you ready?' he asked his wife, looking past her.

Prince Hippolyte hurriedly put on his cloak, which in the latest fashion reached to his very heels, and stumbling in it, ran out into the porch following the princess, whom a footman was helping into the carriage.

'*Princesse, au revoir*,' cried he, stumbling with his tongue as well as with his feet.

The princess, picking up her dress, was taking her seat in the dark carriage, her husband was adjusting his sabre; Prince Hippolyte, under pretence of helping, was in everyone's way.

'Allow me, sir,' said Prince Andrew in Russian in a cold, disagreeable tone to Prince Hippolyte who was blocking his path.

'I am expecting you, Pierre,' said the same voice, but gently and affectionately.

The postillion started, the carriage wheels rattled. Prince Hippolyte laughed spasmodically as he stood in the porch waiting for the vicomte whom he had promised to take home.

'Well, *mon cher*,' said the vicomte, having seated himself beside Hippolyte in the carriage, 'your little princess is very nice, very nice indeed, quite French,' and he kissed the tips of his fingers. Hippolyte burst out laughing.

'Do you know, you are a terrible chap for all your innocent airs,' continued the vicomte. 'I pity the poor husband, that little officer who gives himself the airs of a monarch.'

Hippolyte spluttered again, and amid his laughter said, 'And you were saying that the Russian ladies are not equal to the French? One has to know how to deal with them.'

Pierre, arriving before the others, went into Prince Andrew's study like one quite at home, and from habit immediately lay down on the sofa, took from the shelf the first book that came to his hand (it was Caesar's *Commentaries*) and resting on his elbow, began reading it in the middle.

'What have you done to Mlle Scherer? She will be quite ill now,' said Prince Andrew, as he entered the study rubbing his small white hands.

Pierre turned his whole body, making the sofa creak. He lifted his eager face to Prince Andrew, smiled, and waved his hand.

'That abbé is very interesting but he does not see the thing in the right light... In my opinion perpetual peace is possible, but – I do not know how to express it... not by a balance of political power....'

It was evident that Prince Andrew was not interested in such abstract conversation.

'One can't everywhere say all one thinks, *mon cher*. Well, have you at last decided on anything? Are you going to be a guardsman or a diplomatist?' asked Prince Andrew after a momentary silence.

Pierre sat up on the sofa, with his legs tucked under him.

'Really, I don't yet know. I don't like either the one or the other.'

'But you must decide on something! Your father expects it.'

Pierre at the age of ten had been sent abroad with an abbé as tutor, and had remained away till he was twenty. When he returned to Moscow his father dismissed the abbé and said to the young man, 'Now go to Petersburg, look round, and choose your profession. I will agree to anything. Here is a letter to Prince Vasili, and here is money. Write to me all about it, and I will help you in everything.' Pierre had already been choosing a career for three months, and had not decided on anything. It was about this choice that Prince Andrew was speaking. Pierre rubbed his forehead.

'But he must be a freemason,' said he, referring to the abbé whom he had met that evening.

'That is all nonsense,' Prince Andrew again interrupted him, 'let us talk business. Have you been to the Horse Guards?'

'No, I have not: but this is what I have been thinking and wanted to tell you. There is a war now against Napoleon. If it were a war for freedom I could understand it and should be the first to enter the army; but to help England and Austria against the greatest man in the world is not right.'

Prince Andrew only shrugged his shoulders at Pierre's childish words. He put on the air of one who finds it impossible to reply to such nonsense, but it would in fact have been difficult to give any other answer than the one Prince Andrew gave to this naïve question.

'If no one fought except on his own conviction, there would be no wars,' he said.

'And that would be splendid,' said Pierre.

Prince Andrew smiled ironically.

'Very likely it would be splendid, but it will never come about. . . .'

'Well, why are *you* going to the war?' asked Pierre.

'What for? I don't know. I must. Besides that I am going . . .'. He paused. 'I am going because the life I am leading here does not suit me!'

6

THE rustle of a woman's dress was heard in the next room. Prince Andrew shook himself as if waking up, and his face assumed the look it had had in Anna Pavlovna's drawing-room. Pierre removed his feet from the sofa. The princess came in. She had changed her gown for a house dress as fresh and elegant as the other. Prince Andrew rose and politely placed a chair for her.

'How is it,' she began, as usual in French, settling down briskly and fussily in the easy chair, 'how is it Annette never got married? How stupid you men all are not to have married her! Excuse me for saying so, but you have no sense about women. What an argumentative fellow you are, Monsieur Pierre!'

'And I am still arguing with your husband. I can't understand why he wants to go to the war,' replied Pierre, addressing the princess with none of the embarrassment so commonly shown by young men in their intercourse with young women.

The princess started. Evidently Pierre's words touched her to the quick.

'Ah, that is just what I tell him!' said she. 'I don't understand it; I don't in the least understand why men can't live without wars. How is it that we women don't want anything of the kind, don't need it? Now you shall judge between us. I always tell him: here he is uncle's aide-de-camp, a most brilliant position. He is so well known, so much appreciated by everyone. The other day at the Apraksins' I heard a lady asking, "Is that the famous Prince

Andrew?" I did indeed.' She laughed. 'He is so well received every-where. He might easily become aide-de-camp to the Emperor. You know the Emperor spoke to him most graciously. Annette and I were speaking of how to arrange it. What do you think?'

Pierre looked at his friend, and noticing that he did not like the conversation, gave no reply.

'When are you starting?' he asked.

'Oh, don't speak of his going, don't! I won't hear it spoken of,' said the princess in the same petulantly playful tone in which she had spoken to Hippolyte in the drawing-room and which was so plainly ill-suited to the family circle of which Pierre was almost a member. 'To-day when I remembered that all these delightful associations must be broken off . . . and then you know, André . . .' (she looked significantly at her husband) 'I'm afraid, I'm afraid!' she whispered, and a shudder ran down her back.

Her husband looked at her as if surprised to notice that some-one besides Pierre and himself was in the room, and addressed her in a tone of frigid politeness.

'What is it you are afraid of, Lise? I don't understand,' said he.

'There, what egotists men all are: all, all egotists! Just for a whim of his own, goodness only knows why, he leaves me and locks me up alone in the country.'

'With my father and sister, remember,' said Prince Andrew gently.

'Alone all the same, without *my* friends. . . . And he expects me not to be afraid.'

Her tone was now querulous and her lip drawn up, giving her not a joyful, but an animal, squirrel-like expression. She paused as if she felt it indecorous to speak of her pregnancy before Pierre, though the gist of the matter lay in that.

'I still can't understand what you are afraid of,' said Prince Andrew slowly, not taking his eyes off his wife.

The princess blushed, and raised her arms with a gesture of despair.

'No, Andrew, I must say you have changed. Oh, how you have . . .'

'Your doctor tells you to go to bed earlier,' said Prince Andrew. 'You had better go.'

The princess said nothing, but suddenly her short downy lip quivered. Prince Andrew rose, shrugged his shoulders, and walked about the room.

Pierre looked over his spectacles with naïve surprise, now at him and now at her, moved as if about to rise too, but changed his mind.

'Why should I mind Monsieur Pierre being here?' exclaimed the little princess suddenly, her pretty face all at once distorted by a tearful grimace. 'I have long wanted to ask you, Andrew, why you have changed so to me? What have I done to you? You are going to the war and have no pity for me. Why is it?'

'Lise!' was all Prince Andrew said. But that one word expressed an entreaty, a threat, and above all conviction that she would herself regret her words. But she went hurriedly:

'You treat me like an invalid or a child. I see it all! Did you behave like that six months ago?'

'Lise, I beg you to desist,' said Prince Andrew still more emphatically.

Pierre who had been growing more and more agitated as he listened to all this, rose and approached the princess. He seemed unable to bear the sight of tears, and was ready to cry himself.

'Calm yourself, Princess! It seems so to you because ... I assure you I myself have experienced ... and so ... because ... No, excuse me! An outsider is out of place here ... No, don't distress yourself ... Good-bye!'

Prince Andrew caught him by the hand.

'No, wait, Pierre! The princess is too kind to wish to deprive me of the pleasure of spending the evening with you.'

'No, he thinks only of himself,' muttered the princess without restraining her angry tears.

'Lise!' said Prince Andrew drily, raising his voice to the pitch which indicates that patience is exhausted.

Suddenly the angry, squirrel-like expression of the princess's pretty face changed into a winning and piteous look of fear. Her beautiful eyes glanced askance at her husband's face, and her own assumed the timid, deprecating expression of a dog when it rapidly but feebly wags its drooping tail.

'Mon Dieu, mon Dieu!' she muttered, and lifting her dress with one hand she went up to her husband and kissed him on the forehead.

'Good-night, Lise,' said he, rising and courteously kissing her hand as he would have done to a stranger.

The friends were silent. Neither cared to begin talking. Pierre continually glanced at Prince Andrew; Prince Andrew rubbed his forehead with his small hand.

'Let us go and have supper,' he said with a sigh, going to the door.

They entered the elegant, newly decorated, and luxurious dining-room. Everything from the table-napkins to the silver, china, and glass, bore that imprint of newness found in the households of the newly married. Half-way through supper Prince Andrew leant his elbows on the table, and with a look of nervous agitation such as Pierre had never before seen on his face, began to talk – as one who has long had something on his mind and suddenly determines to speak out.

'Never, never marry, my dear fellow! That's my advice: never marry till you can say to yourself that you have done all you are capable of, and until you have ceased to love the woman of your choice and have seen her plainly as she is, or else you will make a cruel and irrevocable mistake. Marry when you are old and good for nothing – or all that is good and noble in you will be lost. It will all be wasted on trifles. Yes! Yes! Yes! Don't look at me with such surprise. If you marry expecting anything from yourself in the future you will feel at every step that for you all is ended, all is closed except the drawing-room where you will be ranged side by side with a court lackey and an idiot! . . . But what's the good? . . .' and he waved his arm.*

Pierre took off his spectacles, which made his face seem different and the good-natured expression still more apparent, and gazed at his friend in amazement.

'My wife,' continued Prince Andrew, 'is an excellent woman, one of those rare women with whom a man's honour is safe; but, O God, what would I not give now to be unmarried! You are the first and only one to whom I mention this, because I like you.'

As he said this Prince Andrew was less than ever like that Bolkonsky who had lolled in Anna Pavlovna's easy chairs and with half-closed eyes had uttered French phrases between his teeth. Every muscle of his thin face was now quivering with nervous excitement; his eyes, in which the fire of life had seemed extinguished, now flashed with brilliant light. It was evident that the more lifeless he seemed at ordinary times, the more impassioned he became in these moments of almost morbid irritation.

'You don't understand why I say this,' he continued, 'but it is the whole story of life. You talk of Bonaparte and his career,' said he (though Pierre had not mentioned Bonaparte), 'but Bonaparte when he worked went step by step towards his goal. He was free, he had nothing but his aim to consider, and he reached it. But tie yourself up with a woman, and like a chained convict you lose all freedom! And all you have of hope and strength merely weighs you down and torments you with regret. Drawing-rooms, gossip, balls, vanity, and triviality – these are the enchanted circle I cannot escape from. I am now going to the war, the greatest war there ever was, and I know nothing and am fit for nothing. I am very amiable and have a caustic wit,' continued Prince

Andrew, 'and at Anna Pavlovna's they listen to me. And that stupid set without whom my wife cannot exist, and those women ... If you only knew what those society women are, and women in general! My father is right. Selfish, vain, stupid, trivial in everything – that's what women are when you see them in their true colours! When you meet them in society it seems as if there were something in them, but there's nothing, nothing, nothing! No, don't marry, my dear fellow; don't marry!' concluded Prince Andrew.

'It seems funny to me,' said Pierre, 'that *you, you* should consider yourself incapable and your life a spoilt life. You have everything before you, everything. And you ...'

He did not finish his sentence, but his tone showed how highly he thought of his friend and how much he expected of him in the future.

'How can he talk like that?' thought Pierre. He considered his friend a model of perfection because Prince Andrew possessed in the highest degree just the very qualities Pierre lacked, and which might be best described as strength of will. Pierre was always astonished at Prince Andrew's calm manner of treating everybody, his extraordinary memory, his extensive reading (he had read everything, knew everything, and had an opinion about everything), but above all at his capacity for work and study. And if Pierre was often struck by Andrew's lack of capacity for philosophical meditation (to which he himself was particularly addicted), he regarded even this not as a defect but as a sign of strength.

Even in the best, most friendly and simplest relations of life, praise and commendation are essential, just as grease is necessary to wheels that they may run smoothly.

'My part is played out,' said Prince Andrew. 'What's the use of talking about me? Let us talk about you,' he added after a silence, smiling at his reassuring thoughts.

That smile was immediately reflected on Pierre's face.

'But what is there to say about me?' said Pierre, his face relaxing into a careless, merry smile. 'What am I? An illegitimate son!' He suddenly blushed crimson, and it was plain that he had made a great effort to say this. 'Without a name and without means ... And it really ...' But he did not say what 'it really' was. 'For the present I am free and am all right. Only I haven't the least idea what I am to do; I wanted to consult you seriously.'

Prince Andrew looked kindly at him, yet his glance – friendly and affectionate as it was – expressed a sense of his own superiority.

'I am fond of you, especially as you are the one live man among our whole set. Yes, you're all right! Choose what you will; it's all the same. You'll be all right anywhere. But look here: give up visiting those Kuragins and leading that sort of life. It suits you so badly – all this debauchery, dissipation, and the rest of it!'

'What would you have, my dear fellow?' answered Pierre, shrugging his shoulders. 'Women, my dear fellow; women!'

'I don't understand it,' replied Prince Andrew. 'Women who are *comme il faut*, that's a different matter; but the Kuragins' set of women, "women and wine", I don't understand!'

Pierre was staying at Prince Vasili Kuragin's and sharing the dissipated life of his son Anatole, the son whom they were planning to reform by marrying him to Prince Andrew's sister.

'Do you know?' said Pierre, as if suddenly struck by a happy thought, 'seriously, I have long been thinking of it...Leading such a life I can't decide or think properly about anything. One's head aches, and one spends all one's money. He asked me for to-night, but I won't go.'

'You give me your word of honour not to go?'

'On my honour!'

It was past one o'clock when Pierre left his friend. It was a cloudless, northern, summer night. Pierre took an open cab intending to drive straight home. But the nearer he drew to the house the more he felt the impossibility of going to sleep on such a night. It was light enough to see a long way in the deserted street and it seemed more like morning or evening than night. On the way Pierre remembered that Anatole Kuragin was expecting the usual set for cards that evening, after which there was generally a drinking bout, finishing with visits of a kind Pierre was very fond of.

'I should like to go to Kuragin's,' thought he.

But he immediately recalled his promise to Prince Andrew not to go there. Then, as happens to people of weak character, he desired so passionately once more to enjoy that dissipation he was so accustomed to, that he decided to go. The thought immediately occurred to him that his promise to Prince Andrew was of no account, because before he gave it he had already promised Prince Anatole to come to his gathering; 'besides,' thought he, 'all such "words of honour" are conventional things with no definite meaning, especially if one considers that by to-morrow one may be dead, or something so extraordinary may happen to one that honour and dishonour will be all the same!' Pierre often indulged in reflections of this sort, nullifying all his decisions and intentions. He went to Kuragin's.

Reaching the large house near the Horse Guards' barracks, in which Anatole lived, Pierre entered the lighted porch, ascended the stairs, and went in at the open door. There was no one in the ante-room; empty bottles, cloaks, and over-shoes were lying about; there was a smell of alcohol, and sounds of voices and shouting in the distance.

Cards and supper were over, but the visitors had not yet dispersed. Pierre threw off his cloak and entered the first room, in which were the remains of supper. A footman, thinking no one saw him. was drinking on the sly what was left in the glasses. From the third room came sounds of laughter, the shouting of familiar voices, the growling of a bear, and general commotion. Some eight or nine young men were crowding anxiously round an open window. Three others were romping with a young bear, one pulling him by the chain and trying to set him at the others.

'I bet a hundred on Stevens!' shouted one.

'Mind, no holding on!' cried another.

'I bet on Dolokhov!' cried a third. 'Kuragin, you part our hands.'*

'There, leave Bruin alone; here's a bet on.'

'At one draught, or he loses!' shouted a fourth.

'Jacob, bring a bottle!' shouted the host, a tall handsome fellow who stood in the midst of the group, without a coat, and with his fine linen shirt unfastened in front. 'Wait a bit, you fellows. ... Here is Petya! Good man!' cried he, addressing Pierre.

Another voice, from a man of medium height with clear blue eyes, particularly striking among all these drunken voices by its sober ring, cried from the window: 'Come here; part the bets!' This was Dolokhov, an officer of the Semënov regiment, a notorious gambler and duellist, who was living with Anatole. Pierre smiled, looking about him merrily.

'I don't understand. What 's it all about?'

'Wait a bit, he is not drunk yet! A bottle here,' said Anatole, and taking a glass from the table he went up to Pierre.

'First of all you must drink!'

Pierre drank one glass after another, looking from under his brows at the tipsy guests who were again crowding round the window, and listening to their chatter. Anatole kept on refilling Pierre's glass while explaining that Dolokhov was betting with Stevens, an English naval officer, that he would drink a bottle of rum sitting on the outer ledge of the third-floor window with his legs hanging out.

'Go on, you must drink it all,' said Anatole, giving Pierre the last glass, 'or I won't let you go!'

'No, I won't, said Pierre, pushing Anatole aside, and he went up to the window.

Dolokhov was holding the Englishman's hand and clearly and distinctly repeating the terms of the bet, addressing himself particularly to Anatole and Pierre.

Dolokhov was of medium height, with curly hair and light blue eyes. He was about five-and-twenty. Like all infantry officers he wore no moustache, so that his mouth, the most striking feature of his face, was clearly seen. The lines of that mouth were remarkably finely curved. The middle of the upper lip formed a sharp wedge and closed firmly on the firm lower one, and something like two distinct smiles played continually round the two corners of the mouth; this, together with the resolute, insolent intelligence of his eyes, produced an effect which made it impossible not to notice his face. Dolokhov was a man of small means and no connexions. Yet though Anatole spent tens of thousands of rubles, Dolokhov lived with him and had placed himself on such a footing that all who knew them, including Anatole himself, respected him more than they did Anatole. Dolokhov could play all games and nearly always won. However much he drank he never lost his clear-headedness. Both Kuragin and Dolokhov were at that time notorious among the rakes and scapegraces of Petersburg.

The bottle of rum was brought. The window frame which prevented anyone from sitting on the outer sill, was being forced out by two footmen, who were evidently flurried and intimidated by the directions and shouts of the gentlemen around.

Anatole with his swaggering air strode up to the window. He wanted to smash something. Pushing away the footmen he tugged at the frame, but could not move it. He smashed a pane.

'You have a try, Hercules,' said he, turning to Pierre.

Pierre seized the crossbeam, tugged, and wrenched the oak frame out with a crash.

'Take it right out, or they'll think I'm holding on,' said Dolokhov.

'Is the Englishman bragging.... Eh? Is it all right?' said Anatole.

'First rate,' said Pierre, looking at Dolokhov, who with a bottle of rum in his hand was approaching the window, from which the light of the sky, the dawn merging with the afterglow of sunset, was visible.

Dolokhov, the bottle of rum still in his hand, jumped onto the window-sill. 'Listen!' cried he, standing there and addressing those in the room. All were silent.

'I bet fifty imperials' – he spoke French that the Englishman might understand him, but he did not speak it very well – 'I bet fifty imperials . . . or do you wish to make it a hundred?' added he, addressing the Englishman.

'No, fifty,' replied the latter.

'All right. Fifty imperials . . . that I will drink a whole bottle of rum without taking it from my mouth, sitting outside the window on this spot' (he stooped and pointed to the sloping ledge outside the window), 'and without holding on to anything. Is that right?'

'Quite right,' said the Englishman.

Anatole turned to the Englishman and taking him by one of the buttons of his coat and looking down at him – the Englishman was short – began repeating the terms of the wager to him in English.

'Wait!' cried Dolokhov, hammering with the bottle on the window-sill to attract attention. 'Wait a bit, Kuragin. Listen! If anyone else does the same, I will pay him a hundred imperials. Do you understand?'

The Englishman nodded, but gave no indication whether he intended to accept this challenge or not. Anatole did not release him, and though he kept nodding to show that he understood, Anatole went on translating Dolokhov's words into English. A thin young lad, an hussar of the Life Guards, who had been losing that evening, climbed on the window-sill, leaned over, and looked down.

'Oh! Oh Oh!' he muttered, looking down from the window at the stones of the pavement.

'Shut up!' cried Dolokhov, pushing him away from the window. The lad jumped awkwardly back into the room, tripping over his spurs.

Placing the bottle on the window-sill where he could reach it easily, Dolokhov climbed carefully and slowly through the window and lowered his legs. Pressing against both sides of the window, he adjusted himself on his seat, lowered his hands, moved a little to the right and then to the left and took up the bottle. Anatole brought two candles and placed them on the window-sill, though it was already quite light. Dolokhov's back in his white shirt, and his curly head, were lit up from both sides. Everyone crowded to the window, the Englishman in front. Pierre stood smiling but silent. One man, older than the others present, suddenly pushed forward with a scared and angry look and wanted to seize hold of Dolokhov's shirt.

'I say, this is folly! He'll be killed,' said this more sensible man. Anatole stopped him.

33

'Don't touch him! You'll startle him and then he'll be killed. Eh? . . . What then? . . . Eh?'

Dolokhov turned round, and again holding on with both hands, arranged himself on his seat.

'If anyone comes meddling again,' said he, emitting the words separately through his thin compressed lips, 'I will throw him down there. Now then!'

Saying this he again turned round, dropped his hands, took the bottle and lifted it to his lips, threw back his head, and raised his free hand to balance himself. One of the footmen who had stooped to pick up some broken glass, remained in that position without taking his eyes from the window and from Dolokhov's back. Anatole stood erect with staring eyes. The Englishman looked on sideways pursing up his lips. The man who had wished to stop the affair ran to a corner of the room and threw himself on a sofa with his face to the wall. Pierre hid his face, from which a faint smile forgot to fade though his features now expressed horror and fear. All were still. Pierre took his hand from his eyes, Dolokhov still sat in the same position, only his head was thrown further back till his curly hair touched his shirt collar, and the hand holding the bottle was lifted higher and higher and trembled with the effort. The bottle was emptying perceptibly and rising still higher and his head tilting yet further back. 'Why is it so long?' thought Pierre. It seemed to him that more than half an hour had elapsed. Suddenly Dolokhov made a backward movement with his spine, and his arm trembled nervously; this was sufficient to cause his whole body to slip as he sat on the sloping ledge. As he began slipping down, his head and arm wavered still more with the strain. One hand moved as if to clutch the window-sill, but refrained from touching it. Pierre again covered his eyes and thought he would never open them again. Suddenly he was aware of a stir all around. He looked up: Dolokhov was standing on the window-sill with a pale but radiant face.

'It's empty!'

He threw the bottle to the Englishman, who caught it neatly. Dolokhov jumped down. He smelt strongly of rum.

'Well done! . . . Fine fellow! . . . There's a bet for you! . . . Devil take you!' came from different sides.

The Englishman took out his purse and began counting out the money. Dolokhov stood frowning and did not speak. Pierre jumped upon the window-sill.

'Gentlemen, who wishes to bet with me? I'll do the same thing!' he suddenly cried. 'Even without a bet there! Tell them to bring me a bottle. I'll do it. . . . Bring a bottle!'

'Let him do it, let him do it,' said Dolokhov, smiling.

'What next? Have you gone mad? ... No one would let you ... Why, you go giddy even on a staircase,' exclaimed several voices.

'I'll drink it! Let's have a bottle of rum!' shouted Pierre, banging the table with a determined and drunken gesture and preparing to climb out of the window.

They seized him by his arms; but he was so strong that everyone who touched him was sent flying.

'No, you'll never manage him that way,' said Anatole. 'Wait a bit and I'll get round him ... Listen! I'll take your bet to-morrow, but now we are all going to ——'s.'

'Come on then,' cried Pierre. 'Come on! ... And we'll take Bruin with us.'

And he caught the bear, took it in his arms, lifted it from the ground, and began dancing round the room with it.

7

PRINCE VASILI kept the promise he had given to Princess Drubetskaya who had spoken to him on behalf of her only son Boris on the evening of Anna Pavlovna's soirée. The matter was mentioned to the Emperor, an exception made, and Boris transferred into the regiment of Semënov Guards with the rank of cornet. He received however no appointment to Kutuzov's staff despite all Anna Mikhaylovna's endeavours and entreaties. Soon after Anna Pavlovna's reception Anna Mikhaylovna returned to Moscow and went straight to her rich relations the Rostovs, with whom she stayed when in the town and where her darling Bory, who had only just entered a regiment of the line and was being at once transferred to the Guards as a cornet, had been educated from childhood and lived for years at a time. The Guards had already left Petersburg on the 10th of August, and her son, who had remained in Moscow for his equipment, was to join them on the march to Radzivilov.*

It was St Natalia's day and the name-day of two of the Rostovs – the mother and the youngest daughter – both named Nataly. Ever since the morning carriages with six horses had been coming and going continually, bringing visitors to the Countess Rostova's big house on the Povarskaya, so well known to all Moscow. The countess herself and her handsome eldest daughter were in the drawing-room with the visitors who came to congratulate, and who constantly succeeded one another in relays.

The countess was a woman of about forty-five, with a thin oriental type of face, evidently worn out with child-bearing – she had had twelve. A langour of motion and speech, resulting from weakness, gave her a distinguished air which inspired respect. Princess Anna Mikhaylovna Drubetskaya, who as a member of the household was also seated in the drawing-room, helped to receive and entertain the visitors. The young people were in one of the inner rooms, not considering it necessary to take part in receiving the visitors. The count* met the guests and saw them off, inviting them all to dinner.

'I am very, very grateful to you, *mon cher*' (or '*ma chère*' – he called everyone without exception and without the slightest variation in his tone, 'my dear', whether they were above or below him in rank) – 'I thank you for myself and for our two dear ones whose name-day we are keeping. But mind you come to dinner or I shall be offended, *ma chère*! On behalf of the whole family I beg you to come, *mon cher*!' These words he repeated to everyone without exception or variation, and with the same expression on his full, cheerful, clean-shaven face, the same firm pressure of the hand and the same quick, repeated bows. As soon as he had seen a visitor off he returned to one of those who were still in the drawing-room, drew a chair towards him or her, and jauntily spreading out his legs and putting his hands on his knees with the air of a man who enjoys life and knows how to live, he swayed to and fro with dignity, offered surmises about the weather, or touched on questions of health, sometimes in Russian and sometimes in very bad but self-confident French; then again, like a man weary but unflinching in the fulfilment of duty, he rose to see some visitors off, and stroking his scanty grey hairs over his bald patch, also asked them to dinner. Sometimes on his way back from the ante-room he would pass through the conservatory and pantry into the large marble dining-hall, where tables were being set out for eighty people; and looking at the footmen, who were bringing in silver and china, moving tables, and unfolding damask table-linen, he would call Dmitri Vasilevich, a man of good family and the manager of all his affairs, and while looking with pleasure at the enormous table would say: 'Well, Dmitri, you'll see that things are all as they should be? That's right! The great thing is the serving, that's it.' And with a complacent sigh he would return to the drawing-room.

'Marya Lvovna Karagina and her daughter!' announced the countess's gigantic footman in his bass voice, entering the drawing-room. The countess reflected a moment and took a pinch from a gold snuff-box with her husband's portrait on it.

'I'm quite worn out by these callers. However, I'll see her and no more. She is so affected. Ask her in,' she said to the footman in a sad voice, as if saying: 'Very well, finish me off.'

A tall, stout, proud-looking woman, with a round-faced smiling daughter, entered the drawing-room, their dresses rustling.

'Dear Countess, what an age ... She has been laid up, poor child ... at the Razumovskys' ball ... and Countess Apraksina. ... I was so delighted ...', came the sounds of animated feminine voices, interrupting one another and mingling with the rustling of dresses and the scraping of chairs. Then one of those conversations began which last out until, at the first pause, the guests rise with a rustle of dresses and say, 'I am so delighted ... mamma's health ... and Countess Apraksina ...', and then again rustling, pass into the ante-room, put on cloaks or mantles, and drive away. The conversation was on the chief topic of the day: the illness of the wealthy and celebrated beau of Catherine's day, Count Bezukhov, and about his illegitimate son Pierre, the one who had behaved so improperly at Anna Pavlovna's reception.

'I am so sorry for the poor count,' said the visitor. 'He is in such bad health, and now this vexation about his son is enough to kill him!'

'What is that?' asked the countess as if she did not know what the visitor alluded to, though she had already heard about the cause of Count Bezukhov's distress some fifteen times.

'That's what comes of a modern education,' exclaimed the visitor. 'It seems that while he was abroad this young man was allowed to do as he liked, and now in Petersburg I hear he has been doing such terrible things that he has been expelled by the police.'

'You don't say so!' replied the countess.

'He chose his friends badly,' interposed Anna Mikhaylovna. 'Prince Vasili's son, he and a certain Dolokhov have, it is said, been up to heaven only knows what! And they have had to suffer for it. Dolokhov has been degraded to the ranks and Bezukhov's son sent back to Moscow. Anatole Kuragin's father managed somehow to get his son's affair hushed up, but even he was ordered out of Petersburg.'

'But what have they been up to?' asked the countess.

'They are regular brigands, especially Dolokhov,' replied the visitor. 'He is a son of Marya Ivanovna Dolokhova, such a worthy woman, but there, just fancy! Those three got hold of a bear somewhere, put it in a carriage, and set off with it to visit some actresses! The police tried to interfere, and what did the young men do? They tied a policeman and the bear back to back and put the bear into the Mokya Canal. And there was the bear swimming about with the policeman on his back!'

'What a nice figure the policeman must have cut, my dear!' shouted the count, dying with laughter.

'Oh, how dreadful! How can you laugh at it, Count?'

Yet the ladies themselves could not help laughing.

'It was all they could do to rescue the poor man,' continued the visitor. 'And to think it is Cyril Vladimirovich Bezukhov's son who amuses himself in this sensible manner! And he was said to be so well educated and clever. This is all that his foreign education has done for him! I hope that here in Moscow no one will receive him, in spite of his money. They wanted to introduce him to me, but I quite declined: I have my daughters to consider.'

'Why do you say this young man is so rich?' asked the countess, turning away from the girls, who at once assumed an air of inattention. 'His children are all illegitimate. I think Pierre also is illegitimate.'

The visitor made a gesture with her hand.

'I should think he has a score of them.'

Princess Anna Mikhaylovna intervened in the conversation, evidently wishing to show her connexions and knowledge of what went on in society.

'The fact of the matter is,' said she significantly, and also in a half whisper, 'everyone knows Count Cyril's reputation....He has lost count of his children, but this Pierre was his favourite.'

'How handsome the old man still was only a year ago!' remarked the countess. 'I have never seen a handsomer man.'

'He is very much altered now,' said Anna Mikhaylovna. 'Well, as I was saying, Prince Vasili is the next heir through his wife, but the count is very fond of Pierre, looked after his education, and wrote to the Emperor about him; so that in case of his death – and he is so ill that he may die at any moment, and Dr Lorrain has come from Petersburg – no one knows who will inherit his immense fortune, Pierre or Prince Vasili. Forty thousand serfs and millions of rubles! I know it all very well for Prince Vasili told me himself. Besides, Cyril Vladimirovich is my mother's second cousin. He's also my Bory's godfather,' she added, as if she attached no importance at all to the fact.

'Prince Vasili arrived in Moscow yesterday. I hear he has come on some inspection business,' remarked the visitor.

'Yes, but between ourselves,' said the princess, 'that is a pretext. The fact is he has come to see Count Cyril Vladimirovich, hearing how ill he is.'

'But do you know, my dear, that was a capital joke,' said the count; and seeing that the elder visitor was not listening, he turned to the young ladies. 'I can just imagine what a funny figure that policeman cut!'

And as he waved his arms to impersonate the policeman, his portly form again shook with a deep ringing laugh, the laugh of one who always eats well and, in particular, drinks well. 'So, do come and dine with us!' he said.

8

A SILENCE ensued. The countess looked at her callers, smiling affably, but not concealing the fact that she would not be distressed if they now rose and took their leave. The visitor's daughter was already smoothing down her dress with an inquiring look at her mother, when suddenly from the next room were heard the footsteps of boys and girls running to the door and the noise of a chair falling over, and a girl of thirteen, hiding something in the folds of her short muslin frock, darted in and stopped short in the middle of the room. It was evident that she had not intended her flight to bring her so far. Behind her in the doorway appeared a student with a crimson coat-collar, an officer of the Guards, a girl of fifteen, and a plump rosy-faced boy in a short jacket.

The count jumped up and, swaying from side to side, spread his arms wide and threw them round the little girl who had run in.

'Ah, here she is!' he exclaimed laughing. 'My pet, whose name-day it is. My dear pet!'

'*Ma chère*, there is a time for everything,' said the countess with feigned severity. 'You spoil her, Ilya,' she added, turning to her husband.

'How do you do, my dear? I wish you many happy returns of your name-day,' said the visitor. 'What a charming child,' she added, addressing the mother.

This black-eyed, wide-mouthed girl, not pretty but full of life, with childish bare shoulders which after her run heaved and shook her bodice, with black curls tossed backward, thin bare arms, little legs in lace-frilled drawers, and feet in low slippers – was just at that charming age when a girl is no longer a child, though the child is not yet a young woman. Escaping from her father she ran to hide her flushed face in the lace of her mother's mantilla – not paying the least attention to her severe remark – and began to laugh. She laughed, and in fragmentary sentences tried to explain about a doll which she produced from the folds of her frock.

'Do you see? ... My doll. ... Mimi. ... You see....' was all Natasha managed to utter (to her everything seemed funny). She leaned against her mother and burst into such a loud, ringing fit of laughter that even the prim visitor could not help joining in.

'Now then, go away and take your monstrosity with you,' said the mother, pushing away her daughter with pretended sternness, and turning to the visitor she added: 'She is my youngest girl.'

Natasha, raising her face for a moment from her mother's mantilla, glanced up at her through tears of laughter, and again hid her face.

The visitor, compelled to look on at this family scene, thought it necessary to take some part in it.

'Tell me, my dear,' said she to Natasha, 'is Mimi a relation of yours? A daughter, I suppose?'

Natasha did not like the visitor's tone of condescension to childish things. She did not reply, but looked at her seriously.

Meanwhile the younger generation: Boris, the officer, Anna Mikhaylovna's son; Nicholas, the undergraduate, the count's eldest son; Sonya, the count's fifteen-year-old niece, and little Petya, his youngest boy, had all settled down in the drawing-room and were obviously trying to restrain within the bounds of decorum the excitement and mirth that shone in all their faces. Evidently in the back rooms, from which they had dashed out so impetuously, the conversation had been more amusing than the drawing-room talk of society scandals, the weather, and Countess Apraksina. Now and then they glanced at one another, hardly able to suppress their laughter.

The two young men, the student and the officer, friends from childhood, were of the same age and both handsome fellows, though not alike. Boris was tall and fair, and his calm and handsome face had regular, delicate features. Nicholas was short with curly hair and an open expression. Dark hairs were already showing on his upper lip, and his whole face expressed impetuosity and enthusiasm. Nicholas blushed when he entered the drawing-room. He evidently tried to find something to say, but failed. Boris on the contrary at once found his footing, and related quietly and humorously how he had known that doll Mimi when she was still quite a young lady, before her nose was broken; how she had aged during the five years he had known her, and how her head had cracked right across the skull. Having said this he glanced at Natasha. She turned away from him and glanced at her younger brother, who was screwing up his eyes and shaking with suppressed laughter, and unable to control herself any longer, she jumped up and rushed from the room as fast as her nimble little feet would carry her. Boris did not laugh.

'You were meaning to go out weren't you, mamma? Do you want the carriage?' he asked his mother with a smile.

'Yes, yes, go and tell them to get it ready,' she answered, returning his smile.

Boris quietly left the room and went in search of Natasha. The plump boy ran after them angrily, as if vexed that their programme had been disturbed.

9

THE only young people remaining in the drawing-room, not counting the young lady visitor and the countess's eldest daughter (who was four years older than her sister and behaved already like a grown-up person), were Nicholas and Sonya, the niece. Sonya was a slender little brunette with a tender look in her eyes which were veiled by long lashes, thick black plaits coiling twice round her head, and a tawny tint in her complexion and especially in the colour of her slender but graceful and muscular arms and neck. By the grace of her movements, by the softness and flexibility of her small limbs, and by a certain coyness and reserve of manner, she reminded one of a pretty, half-grown kitten which promises to become a beautiful little cat. She evidently considered it proper to show an interest in the general conversation by smiling, but in spite of herself her eyes under their thick long lashes watched her cousin who was going to join the army, with such passionate girlish adoration that her smile could not for a single instant impose upon anyone, and it was clear that the kitten had settled down only to spring up with more energy and again play with her cousin as soon as they too could, like Natasha and Boris, escape from the drawing-room.

'Ah yes, my dear,' said the count, addressing the visitor and pointing to Nicholas, 'his friend Boris has become an officer, and so for friendship's sake he is leaving the university and me, his old father, and entering the military service, my dear. And there was a place and everything waiting for him in the Archives Department! Isn't that friendship?' remarked the count in an inquiring tone.

'But they say that war has been declared,' replied the visitor.

'They've been saying so a long while,' said the count, 'and they'll say so again and again, and that will be the end of it. My dear, there's friendship for you,' he repeated. 'He's joining the hussars.'

The visitor, not knowing what to say, shook her head.

'It's not at all from friendship,' declared Nicholas, flaring up and turning away as if from a shameful aspersion. 'It is not from friendship at all; I simply feel that the army is my vocation.'

He glanced at his cousin and the young lady visitor; and they were both regarding him with a smile of approbation.

'Schubert, the colonel of the Pavlograd Hussars, is dining with us to-day. He has been here on leave and is taking Nicholas back with him. It can't be helped!' said the count, shrugging his shoulders and speaking playfully of a matter that evidently distressed him.

'I have already told you, papa,' said his son, 'that if you don't wish to let me go, I'll stay. But I know I am no use anywhere except in the army; I am not a diplomat nor a government clerk. – I don't know how to hide what I feel.' As he spoke he kept glancing with the flirtatiousness of a handsome youth at Sonya and the young lady visitor.

The little kitten, feasting her eyes on him, seemed ready at any moment to start her gambols again and display her kittenish nature.

'All right, all right!' said the old count. 'He always flares up! This Buonaparte has turned all their heads; they all think of how he rose from an ensign and became Emperor. Well, well, God grant it,' he added, not noticing his visitor's sarcastic smile.

The elders began talking about Bonaparte. Julie Karagina turned to young Rostov.

'What a pity you weren't at the Arkharovs' on Thursday. I was so dull without you,' said she, giving him a tender smile.

The young man, flattered, sat down nearer to her with a coquettish smile, and engaged the smiling Julie in a confidential conversation without at all noticing that his involuntary smile had stabbed the heart of Sonya, who blushed and smiled unnaturally. In the midst of his talk he glanced round at her. She gave him a passionately angry glance, and hardly able to restrain her tears and maintain the artificial smile on her lips, she got up and left the room. All Nicholas's animation vanished. He waited for the first pause in the conversation, and then with a distressed face left the room to find Sonya.

'How plainly all these young people wear their hearts on their sleeves!' said Anna Mikhaylovna, pointing to Nicholas as he went out. '*Cousinage — dangereux voisinage,*' she added.

'Yes,' said the countess when the brightness these young people had brought into the room had vanished; and as if answering a question no one had put but which was always in her mind, 'and how much suffering, how much anxiety one has had to go through that we might rejoice in them now! And yet really the anxiety is greater now than the joy. One is always, always anxious! Especially just at this age, so dangerous both for girls and boys.'

'It all depends on the bringing up,' remarked the visitor.

'Yes, you're quite right,' continued the countess. 'Till now I have always, thank God, been my children's friend and had their full confidence,' said she, repeating the mistake of so many parents who imagine that their children have no secrets from them. 'I know I shall always be my daughters' first confidante, and that if Nicholas, with his impulsive nature, does get into mischief (a boy can't help it) he will all the same never be like those Petersburg young men.'

'Yes, they are splendid, splendid youngsters,' chimed in the count, who always solved questions that seemed to him perplexing by deciding that everything was splendid. 'Just fancy: wants to be an hussar. What's one, to do, my dear?'

'What a charming creature your younger girl is,' said the visitor; 'a little volcano!'

'Yes, a regular volcano,' said the count. 'Takes after me! And what a voice she has; though she's my daughter, I tell the truth when I say she'll be a singer, a second Salomoni! We have engaged an Italian to give her lessons.'

'Isn't she too young? I have heard that it harms the voice to train it at that age.'

'Oh no, not at all too young! replied the count. 'Why, our mothers used to be married at twelve or thirteen.'

'And she's in love with Boris already. Just fancy!' said the countess with a gentle smile, looking at Boris's mother, and went on, evidently concerned with a thought that always occupied her: 'Now you see if I were to be severe with her and to forbid it . . . goodness knows what they might be up to on the sly' (she meant that they would be kissing), 'but as it is, I know every word she utters. She will come running to me of her own accord in the evening and tell me everything. Perhaps I spoil her, but really that seems the best plan. With her elder sister I was stricter.'

'Yes, I was brought up quite differently,' remarked the handsome elder daughter Countess Vera, with a smile.

But the smile did not enhance Vera's beauty as smiles generally do; on the contrary it gave her an unnatural, and therefore unpleasant, expression. Vera was good-looking, not at all stupid, quick at learning, was well brought up, and had a pleasant voice; what she said was true and appropriate, yet, strange to say, everyone – the visitors and countess alike – turned to look at her as if wondering why she had said it, and they all felt awkward.

'People are always too clever with their eldest children and try to make something exceptional of them,' said the visitor.

'What's the good of denying it, my dear? Our dear countess was too clever with Vera,' said the count. 'Well, what of that? She's turned out splendidly all the same,' he added, winking at Vera.

The guests got up and took their leave, promising to return to dinner.

'What manners! I thought they would never go,' said the countess, when she had seen her guests out.

10

WHEN Natasha ran out of the drawing-room she only went as far as the conservatory. There she paused and stood listening to the conversation in the drawing-room, waiting for Boris to come out. She was already growing impatient, and stamped her foot, ready to cry at his not coming at once, when she heard the young man's discreet steps approaching neither quickly nor slowly. At this Natasha dashed swiftly among the flower-tubs and hid there.

Boris paused in the middle of the room, looked round, brushed a little dust from the sleeve of his uniform, and going to a mirror examined his handsome face. Natasha, very still, peered out from her ambush, waiting to see what he would do. He stood a little while before the glass, smiled, and walked toward the other door. Natasha was about to call him but changed her mind. 'Let him look for me,' thought she. Hardly had Boris gone than Sonya, flushed, in tears, and muttering angrily, came in at the other door. Natasha checked her first impulse to run out to her, and remained in her hiding place, watching – as under an invisible cap – to see what went on in the world. She was experiencing a new and peculiar pleasure. Sonya, muttering to herself, kept looking round towards the drawing-room door. It opened and Nicholas came in.

'Sonya, what is the matter with you? How can you?' said he, running up to her.

'It's nothing, nothing; leave me alone!' sobbed Sonya.

'Ah, I know what it is.'

'Well, if you do, so much the better, and you can go back to her!'

'So-o-onya! Look here! How can you torture me and yourself like that, for a mere fancy?' said Nicholas taking her hand.

Sonya did not pull it away, and left off crying. Natasha, not

44

stirring and scarcely breathing, watched from her ambush with sparkling eyes. 'What will happen now?' thought she.

'Sonya! What is anyone in the world to me? You alone are everything!' said Nicholas. 'And I will prove it to you.'

'I don't like you to talk like that.'

'Well then, I won't; only forgive me, Sonya!' He drew her to him and kissed her.

'Oh, how nice,' thought Natasha; and when Sonya and Nicholas had gone out of the conservatory she followed and called Boris to her.

'Boris, come here,' said she with a sly and significant look. 'I have something to tell you. Here, here!' and she led him into the conservatory to the place among the tubs where she had been hiding.

Boris followed her, smiling.

'What is the *something*?' asked he.

She grew confused, glanced round, and seeing the doll she had thrown down on one of the tubs, picked it up.

'Kiss the doll,' said she.

Boris looked attentively and kindly at her eager face, but did not reply.

'Don't you want to? Well then, come here,' said she, and went further in among the plants and threw down the doll. 'Closer, closer!' she whispered.

She caught the young officer by his cuffs, and a look of solemnity and fear appeared on her flushed face.

'And me? Would you like to kiss me?' she whispered almost inaudibly, glancing up at him from under her brows, smiling, and almost crying from excitement.

Boris blushed.

'How funny you are!' he said, bending down to her and blushing still more, but he waited and did nothing.

Suddenly she jumped up onto a tub to be higher than he, embraced him so that both her slender bare arms clasped him above his neck, and tossing back her hair, kissed him full on the lips.

Then she slipped down among the flower pots on the other side of the tubs and stood, hanging her head.

'Natasha,' he said, 'you know that I love you, but ...'

'You are in love with me?' Natasha broke in.

'Yes, I am, but please don't let us do like that ... In another four years ... then I will ask for your hand.'

Natasha considered.

'Thirteen, fourteen, fifteen, sixteen,' she counted on her slender little fingers. 'All right! Then it's settled?'

A smile of joy and satisfaction lit up her eager face.

'Settled!' replied Boris.

'For ever?' said the little girl. 'Till death itself?'

She took his arm and with a happy face went with him into the adjoining sitting-room.

11

AFTER receiving her visitors the countess was so tired that she gave orders to admit no more, but the porter was told to be sure to invite to dinner all who came 'to congratulate'. The countess wished to have a tête-à-tête talk with the friend of her childhood, Princess Anna Mikhaylovna, whom she had not seen properly since she returned from Petersburg. Anna Mikhaylovna, with her tear-worn but pleasant face, drew her chair nearer to that of the countess.

'With you I will be quite frank,' said Anna Mikhaylovna. 'There are not many left of us old friends! That's why I so value your friendship.'

Anna Mikhaylovna looked at Vera and paused. The countess pressed her friend's hand.

'Vera,' she said to her eldest daughter who was evidently not a favourite, 'how is it you have so little tact? Don't you see you are not wanted here? Go to the other girls, or...'

The handsome Vera smiled contemptuously but did not seem at all hurt.

'If you had told me sooner, mamma, I should have gone,' she replied as she rose to go to her own room.

But as she passed the sitting-room she noticed two couples sitting, one pair at each window. She stopped and smiled scornfully. Sonya was sitting close to Nicholas who was copying out some verses for her, the first he had ever written. Boris and Natasha were at the other window and ceased talking when Vera entered. Sonya and Natasha looked at Vera with guilty, happy faces.

It was pleasant and touching to see these little girls in love; but apparently the sight of them roused no pleasant feeling in Vera.

'How often have I asked you not to take my things?' she said. 'You have a room of your own,' and she took the inkstand from Nicholas.

'In a minute, in a minute,' he said, dipping his pen.

'You always manage to do things at the wrong time,' continued Vera. 'You came rushing into the drawing-room so that everyone felt ashamed of you.'

Though what she said was quite just, perhaps for that very reason no one replied, and the four simply looked at one another. She lingered in the room with the inkstand in her hand.

'And at your age what secrets can there be between Natasha and Boris, or between you two? It's all nonsense!'

'Now? Vera, what does it matter to you?' said Natasha in defence, speaking very gently.

She seemed that day to be more than ever kind and affectionate to everyone.

'Very silly,' said Vera. 'I am ashamed of you. Secrets indeed!'

'All have secrets of their own,' answered Natasha, getting warmer. 'We don't interfere with you and Berg.'

'I should think not,' said Vera, 'because there can never be anything wrong in my behaviour. But I'll just tell mamma how you are behaving with Boris.'

'Natalya Ilyinichna behaves very well to me,' remarked Boris. 'I have nothing to complain of.'

'Don't, Boris! You are such a diplomat that it is really tiresome,' said Natasha in a mortified voice that trembled slightly. (She used the word 'diplomat', which was just then much in vogue among the children, in the special sense they attached to it.) 'Why does she bother me?' And she added, turning to Vera, 'You'll never understand it, because you've never loved anyone. You have no heart! You are a Madame de Genlis and nothing more,' (this nickname, bestowed on Vera by Nicholas, was considered very stinging) 'and your greatest pleasure is to be unpleasant to people! Go and flirt with Berg as much as you please,' she finished quickly.

'I shall at any rate not run after a young man before visitors . . .'

'Well, now you've done what you wanted,' put in Nicholas, '—said unpleasant things to everyone and upset them. Let's go to the nursery.'

All four, like a flock of scared birds, got up and left the room.

'The unpleasant things were said to me,' remarked Vera, 'I said none to anyone.'

'Madame de Genlis! Madame de Genlis!' shouted laughing voices through the door.

The handsome Vera, who produced such an irritating and unpleasant effect on everyone, smiled, and evidently unmoved by what had been said to her, went to the looking-glass and arranged her hair and scarf. Looking at her own handsome face she seemed to become still colder and calmer.

*

In the drawing-room the conversation was still going on.

'Ah, my dear,' said the countess, 'my life is not all roses either. Don't I know that at the rate we are living our means won't last long? It's all the Club and his easy-going nature. Even in the country do we get any rest? Theatricals, hunting, and heaven knows what besides! But don't let's talk about me; tell me how you managed everything. I often wonder at you, Annette, – how at your age you can rush off alone in a carriage to Moscow, to Petersburg, to those ministers and great people, and know how to deal with them all! It's quite astonishing. How did you get things settled? I couldn't possibly do it.'

'Ah, my love,' answered Anna Mikhaylovna, 'God grant you never know what it is to be left a widow without means and with a son you love to distraction! One learns many things then,' she added with a certain pride. 'That lawsuit taught me much. When I want to see one of those big people I write a note: "Princess So-and-So desires an interview with So-and-So," and then I take a cab and go myself two, three, or four times – till I get what I want. I don't mind what they may think of me.'

'Well, and to whom did you apply about Bory?' asked the countess. 'You see yours is already an officer in the Guards, while my Nicholas is going as a cadet. There's no one to interest himself for him. To whom did you apply?

'To Prince Vasili. He was so kind. He at once agreed to everything, and put the matter before the Emperor,' said Princess Anna Mikhaylovna enthusiastically, quite forgetting all the humiliation she had endured to gain her end.

'Has Prince Vasili aged much?' asked the countess. 'I have not seen him since we acted together at the Rumyantsovs' theatricals. I expect he has forgotten me. He paid me attentions in those days,' said the countess, with a smile.

'He is just the same as ever,' replied Anna Mikhaylovna, 'overflowing with amiability. His position has not turned his head at all. He said to me, "I am sorry I can do so little for you, dear Princess. I am at your command." Yes, he is a fine fellow and a very kind relation. But, Nataly, you know my love for my son: I would do anything for his happiness! And my affairs are in such a bad way that my position is now a terrible one,' continued Anna Mikhaylovna, sadly, dropping her voice. 'My wretched lawsuit takes all I have and makes no progress. Would you believe it, I have literally not a penny and don't know how to equip Boris.' She took out her handkerchief and began to cry. 'I need five hundred rubles, and have only one twenty-five ruble note. I am in such a state . . . My only hope now is in Count Cyril Vladimirovich

Bezukhov. If he will not assist his godson – you know he is Bory's godfather – and allow him something for his maintenance, all my trouble will have been thrown away...I shall not be able to equip him.'

The countess's eyes filled with tears and she pondered in silence.

'I often think, though perhaps it's a sin,' said the princess, 'that here lives Count Cyril Vladimirovich Bezukhov so rich, all alone ...that tremendous fortune...and what is his life worth? It's a burden to him, and Bory's life is only just beginning....'

'Surely he will leave something to Boris,' said the countess.

'Heaven only knows, my dear! These rich grandees are so selfish. Still, I will take Boris and go to see him at once, and I shall speak to him straight out. Let people think what they will of me, it's really all the same to me when my son's fate is at stake.' The princess rose. 'It's now two o'clock and you dine at four. There will just be time.'

And like a practical Petersburg lady who knows how to make the most of time, Anna Mikhaylovna sent someone to call her son, and went into the ante-room with him.

'Good-bye, my dear,' said she to the countess who saw her to the door, and added in a whisper so that her son should not hear, 'Wish me good luck.'

'Are you going to Count Cyril Vladimirovich, my dear?' said the count coming out from the dining-hall into the ante-room, and he added: 'If he is better, ask Pierre to dine with us. He has been to the house, you know, and danced with the children. Be sure to invite him, my dear. We will see how Taras distinguishes himself to-day. He says Count Orlov never gave such a dinner as ours will be!'

12

'My dear Boris,' said Princess Anna Mikhaylovna to her son as Countess Rostova's carriage in which they were seated drove over the straw-covered street and turned into the wide courtyard of Count Cyril Vladimirovich Bezukhov's house. 'My dear Boris,' said the mother, drawing her hand from beneath her old mantle and laying it timidly and tenderly on her son's arm, 'be affectionate and attentive to him. Count Cyril Vladimirovich is your godfather after all, and your future depends on him. Remember that, my dear, and be nice to him, as you so well know how to be.'

'If only I knew that anything besides humiliation would come of it...' answered her son coldly. 'But I have promised and will do it for your sake.'

Although the hall-porter saw someone's carriage standing at the entrance, after scrutinizing the mother and son (who without asking to be announced had passed straight through the glass porch between the rows of statues in niches) and looking significantly at the lady's old cloak, he asked whether they wanted the count or the princesses, and hearing that they wished to see the count, said his excellency was worse to-day, and that his excellency was not receiving anyone.

'We may as well go back,' said the son in French.

'My dear!' exclaimed his mother imploringly, again laying her hand on his arm as if that touch might soothe or rouse him.

Boris said no more, but looked inquiringly at his mother without taking off his cloak.

'My friend,' said Anna Mikhaylovna in gentle tones, addressing the hall-porter, 'I know Count Cyril Vladimirovich is very ill ... that's why I have come ... I am a relation. I shall not disturb him, my friend ... I only need see Prince Vasili Sergeevich: he is staying here, is he not? Please announce me.'

The hall-porter sullenly pulled a bell that rang upstairs, and turned away.

'Princess Drubetskaya to see Prince Vasili Sergeevich,' he called to a footman dressed in knee-breeches, shoes, and a swallow-tail coat, who ran downstairs and looked over from the half-way landing.

The mother smoothed the folds of her dyed silk dress before a large Venetian mirror in the wall, and in her trodden-down shoes briskly ascended the carpeted stairs.

'My dear,' she said to her son, once more stimulating him by a touch, 'you promised me!'

The son, lowering his eyes, followed her quietly.

They entered the large hall, from which one of the doors led to the apartments assigned to Prince Vasili.

Just as the mother and son, having reached the middle of the hall, were about to ask their way of an elderly footman who had sprung up as they entered, the bronze handle of one of the doors turned and Prince Vasili came out – wearing a velvet coat with a single star on his breast, as was his custom when at home – taking leave of a good-looking, dark-haired man. This was the celebrated Petersburg doctor, Lorrain.

'Then it is certain?' said the prince.

'Prince, *humanum est errare*, but ...' replied the doctor, swallowing his r's, and pronouncing the Latin words with a French accent.

'Very well, very well ...'

Seeing Anna Mikhaylovna and her son, Prince Vasili dismissed the doctor with a bow and approached them silently and with a look of inquiry. The son noticed that an expression of profound sorrow suddenly clouded his mother's face, and he smiled slightly.

'Ah Prince! In what sad circumstances we meet again! And how is our dear invalid? said she, as though unaware of the cold offensive look fixed on her.

Prince Vasili stared at her and at Boris questioningly and perplexed. Boris bowed politely. Prince Vasili without acknowledging the bow turned to Anna Mikhaylovna, answering her query by a movement of the head and lips indicating very little hope for the patient.

'Is it possible?' exclaimed Anna Mikhaylovna. 'Oh, how awful! It is terrible to think. . . . This is my son,' she added, indicating Boris. 'He wanted to thank you himself.'

Boris again bowed politely.

'Believe me, Prince, a mother's heart will never forget what you have done for us.'

'I am glad I was able to do you a service, my dear Anna Mikhaylovna,' said Prince Vasili, arranging his lace frill, and in tone and manner, here in Moscow to Anna Mikhaylovna whom he had placed under an obligation, assuming an air of much greater importance than he had done in Petersburg at Anna Scherer's reception.

'Try to serve well and show yourself worthy,' added he, addressing Boris with severity. 'I am glad. . . . Are you here on leave?' he went on in his usual tone of indifference.

'I am awaiting orders to join my new regiment, your excellency,' replied Boris, betraying neither annoyance at the prince's brusque manner nor a desire to enter into conversation, but speaking so quietly and respectfully that the prince gave him a searching glance.

'Are you living with your mother?'

'I am living at Countess Rostova's,' replied Boris, again adding, 'your excellency.'

'That is, with Ilya Rostov who married Nataly Shinshina,' said Anna Mikhaylovna.

'I know, I know,' answered Prince Vasili in his monotonous voice. 'I never could understand how Nataly made up her mind to marry that unlicked bear! A perfectly absurd and stupid fellow, and a gambler too, I am told.'

'But a very kind man, Prince,' said Anna Mikhaylovna with a pathetic smile, as though she too knew that Count Rostov deserved this censure, but asked him not to be too hard on the poor old man. 'What do the doctors say?' asked the princess after a pause, her worn face again expressing deep sorrow.

'They give little hope,' replied the prince.

'And I should so like to thank *Uncle* once more for all his kindness to me and to Boris. He is his godson,' she added, her tone suggesting that this fact ought to give Prince Vasili much satisfaction.

Prince Vasili became thoughtful and frowned. Anna Mikhaylovna saw that he was afraid of finding in her a rival for Count Bezukhov's fortune, and hastened to reassure him.

'If it were not for my sincere affection and devotion to *Uncle*,' said she, uttering the word with peculiar assurance and unconcern, 'I know his character: noble, upright ... but you see he has no one with him except the young princesses. ... They are still young. ...' She bent her head and continued in a whisper: 'Has he performed his final duty,* Prince? How priceless are those last moments! It can make things no worse, and it is absolutely necessary to prepare him if he is so ill. We women, Prince,' and she smiled tenderly, 'always know how to say these things. I absolutely must see him, however painful it may be for me. I am used to suffering.'

Evidently the prince understood her, and also understood, as he had done at Anna Pavlovna's, that it would be difficult to get rid of Anna Mikhaylovna.

'Would not such a meeting be too trying for him, dear Anna Mikhaylovna?' said he. 'Let us wait until evening. The doctors are expecting a crisis.'

'But one cannot delay, Prince, at such a moment! Consider that the welfare of his soul is at stake. Ah, it is awful: the duties of a Christian ...'

A door of one of the inner rooms opened and one of the princesses, the count's niece, entered with a cold stern face. The length of her body was strikingly out of proportion to her short legs. Prince Vasili turned to her.

'Well, how is he?'

'Still the same; but what can you expect, this noise ...' said the princess, looking at Anna Mikhaylovna as at a stranger.

'Ah, my dear, I hardly knew you,' said Anna Mikhaylovna with a happy smile, ambling lightly up to the count's niece. 'I have come, and am at your service to help you nurse *my uncle*. I imagine what you have gone through,' and she sympathetically turned up her eyes.

The princess gave no reply and did not even smile, but left the room at once. Anna Mikhaylovna took off her gloves, and occupying the position she had conquered, settled down in an arm-chair, inviting Prince Vasili to take a seat beside her.

'Boris,' she said to her son with a smile, 'I shall go in to see the count, my uncle; but you, my dear, had better go to Pierre meanwhile and don't forget to give him the Rostovs' invitation. They ask him to dinner. I suppose he won't go?' she continued, turning to the prince.

'On the contrary,' replied the prince, who had plainly become depressed, 'I shall be only too glad if you relieve me of that young man ... Here he is, and the count has not once asked for him.'

He shrugged his shoulders. A footman conducted Boris down one flight of stairs and up another, to Pierre's rooms.

13

PIERRE, after all, had not managed to choose a career for himself in Petersburg, and had been expelled from there for riotous conduct and sent to Moscow. The story told about him at Count Rostov's was true. Pierre had taken part in tying a policeman to a bear. He had now been for some days in Moscow and was staying as usual at his father's house. Though he expected that the story of his escapade would be already known in Moscow and that the ladies about his father – who were never favourably disposed towards him – would have used it to turn the count against him, he nevertheless on the day of his arrival went to his father's part of the house. Entering the drawing-room, where the princesses spent most of their time, he greeted the ladies, two of whom were sitting at embroidery frames while a third read aloud. It was the eldest who was reading – the one who had met Anna Mikhaylovna. The two younger ones were embroidering: both were rosy and pretty and they differed only in that one had a little mole on her lip which made her much prettier. Pierre was received as if he were a corpse or a leper. The eldest princess paused in her reading and silently stared at him with frightened eyes; the second assumed precisely the same expression; while the youngest, the one with the mole, who was of a cheerful and lively disposition, bent over her frame to hide a smile probably evoked by the amusing scene she foresaw. She drew her wool down through the canvas and, scarcely able to refrain from laughing, stooped as if trying to make out the pattern.

'How do you do, cousin?' said Pierre. 'You don't recognize me?'

'I recognize you only too well, too well.'

53

'How is the count? Can I see him?' asked Pierre, awkwardly as usual, but unabashed.

'The count is suffering physically and mentally, and apparently you have done your best to increase his mental sufferings.'

'Can I see the count?' Pierre again asked.

'H'm . . . If you wish to kill him, to kill him outright, you can see him . . . Olga, go and see whether uncle's beef-tea is ready – it is almost time,' she added, giving Pierre to understand that they were busy, and busy making his father comfortable, while evidently he, Pierre, was only busy causing him annoyance.

Olga went out. Pierre stood looking at the sisters; then he bowed and said:

'Then I will go to my rooms. You will let me know when I can see him.'

And he left the room, followed by the low but ringing laughter of the sister with the mole.,

Next day Prince Vasili had arrived and settled in the count's house. He sent for Pierre and said to him:

'My dear fellow, if you are going to behave here as you did in Petersburg, you will end very badly; that is all I have to say to you. The count is very, very, ill, and you must not see him at all.'

Since then Pierre had not been disturbed and had spent the whole time in his rooms upstairs.

When Boris appeared at his door Pierre was pacing up and down his room, stopping occasionally at a corner to make menacing gestures at the wall, as if running a sword through an invisible foe, and glaring savagely over his spectacles, and then again resuming his walk, muttering indistinct words, shrugging his shoulders, and gesticulating.

'England is done for,' said he, scowling and pointing his finger at someone unseen. 'Mr Pitt, as a traitor to the nation and to the rights of man, is sentenced to . . .' But before Pierre – who at that moment imagined himself to be Napoleon in person and to have just effected the dangerous crossing of the straits of Dover and captured London – could pronounce Pitt's sentence, he saw a well-built and handsome young officer entering his room. Pierre paused. He had left Moscow when Boris was a boy of fourteen, and had quite forgotten him, but in his usual impulsive and hearty way he took Boris by the hand with a friendly smile.

'Do you remember me?' asked Boris quietly with a pleasant smile. 'I have come with my mother to see the count, but it seems he is not well.'

'Yes, it seems he is ill. People are always disturbing him,' answered Pierre, trying to remember who this young man was.

Boris felt that Pierre did not recognize him but did not consider it necessary to introduce himself, and without experiencing the least embarrassment looked Pierre straight in the face.

'Count Rostov asks you to come to dinner to-day,' said he, after a considerable pause which made Pierre feel uncomfortable.

'Ah, Count Rostov!' exclaimed Pierre joyfully. 'Then you are his son, Ilya? Only fancy, I didn't know you at first. Do you remember how we went to the Sparrow Hills with Madame Jacquot? ... It's such an age ...'

'You are mistaken,' said Boris deliberately, with a bold and slightly sarcastic smile. 'I am Boris, son of Princess Anna Mikhaylovna Drubetskaya. Rostov, the father, is Ilya, and his son is Nicholas. I never knew any Madame Jacquot.'

Pierre shook his head and arms as if attacked by mosquitoes or bees.

'Oh dear, what am I thinking about? I've mixed everything up. One has so many relatives in Moscow! So you are Boris? Of course. Well, now we know where we are. And what do you think of the Boulogne expedition? The English will come off badly, you know, if Napoleon gets across the Channel. I think the expedition is quite feasible. If only Villeneuve doesn't make a mess of things!'

Boris knew nothing about the Boulogne expedition; he did not read the papers and it was the first time he had heard Villeneuve's name.

'We here in Moscow are more occupied with dinner parties and scandal than with politics,' said he in his quiet ironical tone. 'I know nothing about it and have not thought about it. Moscow is chiefly busy with gossip,' he continued. 'Just now they are talking about you and your father.'

Pierre smiled in his good-natured way as if afraid for his companion's sake that the latter might say something he would afterwards regret. But Boris spoke distinctly, clearly and drily, looking straight into Pierre's eyes.

'Moscow has nothing else to do but gossip,' Boris went on. 'Everybody is wondering to whom the count will leave his fortune, though he may perhaps outlive us all, as I sincerely hope he will. . . .'

'Yes, it is all very horrid,' interrupted Pierre, 'very horrid.'

Pierre was still afraid that this officer might inadvertently say something disconcerting to himself.

'And it must seem to you,' said Boris flushing slightly, but not changing his tone or attitude, 'it must seem to you that everyone is trying to get something out of the rich man?'

'So it does,' thought Pierre.

'But I just wish to say, to avoid misunderstandings, that you are quite mistaken if you reckon me or my mother among such people. We are very poor, but for my own part at any rate, for the very reason that your father is rich I don't regard myself as a relation of his, and neither I nor my mother would ever ask or take anything from him.'

For a long time Pierre could not understand, but when he did, he jumped up from the sofa, seized Boris under the elbow in his quick, clumsy way, and blushing far more than Boris, began to speak with a feeling of mingled shame and vexation.

'Well, this is strange! Do you suppose I ... who could think? ... I know very well ...'

But Boris again interrupted him.

'I am glad I have spoken out fully. Perhaps you did not like it? You must excuse me,' said he, putting Pierre at ease instead of being put at ease by him, 'but I hope I have not offended you. I always make it a rule to speak out.... Well, what answer am I to take? Will you come to dinner at the Rostovs?'

And Boris, having apparently relieved himself of an onerous duty and extricated himself from an awkward situation and placed another in it, became quite pleasant again.

'No, but I say,' said Pierre, calming down, 'you are a wonderful fellow! What you have just said is good, very good. Of course you don't know me. We have not met for such a long time ... not since we were children. You might think that I ... I understand, quite understand. I could not have done it myself, I should not have had the courage, but it's splendid. I am very glad to have made your acquaintance. It's queer,' he added after a pause, 'that you should have suspected me!' He began to laugh. 'Well, what of it! I hope we'll get better acquainted,' and he pressed Boris's hand. 'Do you know, I have not once been in to see the count. He has not sent for me ... I am sorry for him as a man, but what can one do?'

'And so you think Napoleon will manage to get an army across?' asked Boris with a smile.

Pierre saw that Boris wished to change the subject, and being of the same mind he began explaining the advantages and disadvantages of the Boulogne expedition.

A footman came in to summon Boris – the princess was going. Pierre, in order to make Boris's better acquaintance, promised to come to dinner, and warmly pressing his hand looked affectionately over his spectacles into Boris's eyes. After he had gone Pierre continued pacing up and down the room for a long time, no longer piercing an imaginary foe with his imaginary sword, but smiling at the remembrance of that pleasant intelligent and resolute young man.

As often happens in early youth, especially to one who leads a lonely life, he felt an unaccountable tenderness for this young man and made up his mind that they would be friends.

Prince Vasili saw the princess off. She held a handkerchief to her eyes and her face was tearful.

'It is dreadful, dreadful!' she was saying, 'but cost me what it may I shall do my duty. I will come and spend the night. He must not be left like this. Every moment is precious. I can't think why his nieces put it off. Perhaps God will help me to find a way to prepare him!... Adieu, Prince! May God support you ...'

'*Adieu, ma bonne,*' answered Prince Vasili turning away from her.

'Oh, he is in a dreadful state,' said the mother to her son when they were in the carriage. 'He hardly recognizes anybody.'

'I don't understand, Mamma – what his attitude is to Pierre?' asked the son.

'The will will show that, my dear; our fate also depends on it ...'

'But why do you expect that he will leave us anything?'

'Ah my dear! He is so rich, and we are so poor!'

'Well, that is hardly a sufficient reason, Mamma ...'

'Oh Heaven! How ill he is!' exclaimed the mother.

14

AFTER Anna Mikhaylovna had driven off with her son to visit Count Cyril Vladimirovich Bezukhov, Countess Rostova sat for a long time all alone applying her handkerchief to her eyes. At last she rang.

'What is the matter with you, my dear?' she said crossly to the maid who kept her waiting some minutes. 'Don't you wish to serve me? Then I'll find you another place.'

The countess was upset by her friend's sorrow and humiliating poverty, and was therefore out of sorts, a state of mind which with her always found expression in calling her maid 'my dear' and speaking to her with exaggerated politeness.

'I am very sorry, ma'am,' answered the maid.

'Ask the count to come to me.'

The count came waddling in to see his wife with a rather guilty look as usual.

'Well, little Countess? What a *sauté* of game *au madère* we are to have, my dear! I tasted it. The thousand rubles I paid for Taras were not ill-spent. He is worth it!'

He sat down by his wife, his elbows on his knees and his hands ruffling his grey hair.

'What are your commands, little Countess?'

'You see, my dear ... What's that mess?' she said, pointing to his waistcoat. 'It's the *sauté*, most likely,' she added with a smile. 'Well, you see, Count, I want some money.'

Her face became sad.

'Oh, little Countess!' ... and the count began bustling to get out his pocket-book.

'I want a great deal, Count! I want five hundred rubles,' and taking out her cambric handkerchief she began wiping her husband's waistcoat.

'Yes, immediately, immediately! Hey, who's there?' he called out in a tone only used by persons who are certain that those they call will rush to obey the summons. 'Send Dmitri to me!'

Dmitri, a man of good family who had been brought up in the count's house and now managed all his affairs, stepped softly into the room.

'This is what I want, my dear fellow,' said the count to the deferential young man who had entered. 'Bring me ...' he reflected a moment, 'yes, bring me seven hundred rubles, yes! But mind, don't bring me such tattered and dirty notes as last time, but nice clean ones for the countess.'

'Yes, Dmitri, clean ones, please,' said the countess, sighing deeply.

'When would you like them, your Excellency?' asked Dmitri. 'Allow me to inform you ... But, don't be uneasy,' he added, noticing that the count was beginning to breathe heavily and quickly which was always a sign of approaching anger. 'I was forgetting ... Do you wish it brought at once?'

'Yes, yes; just so! Bring it. Give it to the countess.'

'What a treasure that Dmitri is,' added the count with a smile when the young man had departed. 'There is never any "impossible" with him. That's a thing I hate! Everything is possible.'

'Ah, money, Count, money! How much sorrow it causes in the world,' said the countess. 'But I am in great need of this sum.'

'You, my little Countess, are a notorious spendthrift,' said the count, and having kissed his wife's hand he went back to his study.

When Anna Mikhaylovna returned from Count Bezukhov's the money, all in clean notes, was lying ready under a handkerchief on the countess's little table, and Anna Mikhaylovna noticed that something was agitating her.

'Well, my dear?' asked the countess.

'Oh, what a terrible state he is in! One would not know him, he is so ill! I was only there a few moments and hardly said a word...'

'Annette, for heaven's sake don't refuse me,' the countess began, with a blush that looked very strange on her thin, dignified, elderly face, and she took the money from under the handkerchief.

Anna Mikhaylovna instantly guessed her intention and stooped to be ready to embrace the countess at the appropriate moment.

'This is for Boris from me for his outfit.'

Anna Mikhaylovna was already embracing her and weeping. The countess wept too. They wept because they were friends, and because they were kind-hearted, and because they – friends from childhood – had to think about such a base thing as money, and because their youth was over.... But those tears were pleasant to them both.

15

COUNTESS ROSTOVA, with her daughters and a large number of guests, was already seated in the drawing-room. The count took the gentlemen into his study, and showed them his choice collection of Turkish pipes. From time to time he went out to ask: 'Hasn't she come yet?' They were expecting Marya Dmitrievna Akhrosimova,* known in society as *le terrible dragon*, a lady distinguished not for wealth or rank, but for common sense and frank plainness of speech. Marya Dmitrievna was known to the Imperial family as well as to all Moscow and Petersburg, and both cities wondered at her, laughed privately at her rudeness, and told good stories about her, while none the less all without exception respected and feared her.

In the count's room, which was full of tobacco-smoke, they talked of the war that had been announced in a manifesto, and about the recruiting. None of them had yet seen the manifesto, but they all knew it had appeared. The count sat on the sofa between two guests who were smoking and talking. He neither smoked nor talked, but bending his head first to one side and then to the other watched the smokers with evident pleasure and listened to the conversation of his two neighbours, whom he egged on against each other.

One of them was a sallow, clean-shaven civilian with a thin and wrinkled face, already growing old, though he was dressed like a most fashionable young man. He sat with his legs up on the sofa as if quite at home, and having stuck an amber mouthpiece far into his mouth, was inhaling the smoke spasmodically and screwing up his eyes. This was an old bachelor, Shinshin, a cousin of the countess's, a man with 'a sharp tongue' as they said in Moscow society. He seemed to be condescending to his companion. The latter, a fresh, rosy officer of the Guards, irreproachably washed, brushed and buttoned, held his pipe in the middle of his mouth and with red lips gently inhaled the smoke, letting it escape from his handsome mouth in rings. This was Lieutenant Berg, an officer in the Semënov regiment with whom Boris was to travel to join the army, and about whom Natasha had teased her elder sister Vera, speaking of Berg as her 'intended'. The count sat between them and listened attentively. His favourite occupation when not playing boston, a card game he was very fond of, was that of listener, especially when he succeeded in setting two loquacious talkers at one another.

'Well then, old chap, *mon très honorable* Alphonse Karlovich,' said Shinshin, laughing ironically and mixing the most ordinary Russian expressions with the choicest French phrases – which was a peculiarity of his speech, 'Vous comptez vous faire des rentes sur l'État; you want to make something out of your company?'

'No, Peter Nikolaevich; I only want to show that in the cavalry the advantages are far less than in the infantry. Just consider my own position now, Peter Nikolaevich . . .'

Berg always spoke quietly, politely, and with great precision. His conversation always related entirely to himself; he would remain calm and silent when the talk related to any topic that had no direct bearing on himself. He could remain silent for hours without being at all put out of countenance himself or making others uncomfortable, but as soon as the conversation concerned himself he would begin to talk circumstantially and with evident satisfaction.

'Consider my position, Peter Nikolaevich. Were I in the cavalry I should get not more than two hundred rubles every four months, even with the rank of lieutenant; but as it is I receive two hundred and thirty,' said he, looking at Shinshin and the count with a joyful, pleasant smile, as if it were obvious to him that his success must always be the chief desire of everyone else.

'Besides that, Peter Nikolaevich, by exchanging into the Guards I shall be in a more prominent position,' continued Berg, 'and vacancies occur much more frequently in the Foot Guards. Then just think what can be done with two hundred and thirty rubles! I even manage to put a little aside and to send something to my father,' he went on, emitting a smoke ring.

'La balance y est. . . . A German knows how to skin a flint, as the proverb says,' remarked Shinshin, moving his pipe to the other side of his mouth and winking at the count.

The count burst out laughing. The other guests seeing that Shinshin was talking came up to listen. Berg, oblivious of irony or indifference continued to explain how by exchanging into the Guards he had already gained a step on his old comrades of the Cadet Corps; how in war-time the company commander might get killed and he, as senior in the company, might easily succeed to the post; how popular he was with everyone in the regiment, and how satisfied his father was with him. Berg evidently enjoyed narrating all this, and did not seem to suspect that others, too, might have their own interests. But all he said was so prettily sedate, and the *naïveté* of his youthful egotism was so obvious, that he disarmed his hearers.

'Well, my boy, you'll get along wherever you go – foot or horse – that I'll warrant,' said Shinshin, patting him on the shoulder and taking his feet off the sofa.

Berg smiled joyously. The count, followed by his guests, went into the drawing-room.

*

It was just the moment before a big dinner when the assembled guests, expecting the summons to *zakúska*,* avoid engaging in any long conversation but think it necessary to move about and talk, in order to show that they are not at all impatient for their food. The host and hostess look towards the door, and now and then glance at one another, and the visitors try to guess from these glances who, or what, they are waiting for – some important relation who has not yet arrived, or a dish that is not yet ready.

Pierre had come just at dinner-time, and was sitting awkwardly in the middle of the drawing-room on the first chair he had come across, blocking the way for everyone. The countess tried to make him talk, but he went on naïvely looking around through his spectacles as if in search of somebody and answered all her questions in monosyllables. He was in the way and was the only one who did not notice the fact. Most of the guests, knowing of the affair with the bear, looked with curiosity at this big, stout, quiet man, wondering how such a clumsy, modest fellow could have played such a prank on a policeman.

'You have only lately arrived?' the countess asked him.

'*Oui, madame,*' replied he, looking around him.

'You have not yet seen my husband?'

'*Non, madame.*' He smiled quite inappropriately.

61

'You have been in Paris recently I believe? I suppose it's very interesting.'

'Very interesting.'

The countess exchanged glances with Anna Mikhaylovna. The latter understood that she was being asked to entertain this young man, and sitting down beside him she began to speak about his father; but he answered her, as he had the countess, only in mono-syllables. The other guests were all conversing with one another. 'The Razumovskys . . . It was charming . . . You are very kind . . . Countess Apraksina . . .' was heard on all sides. The countess rose and went into the ball-room.

'Marya Dmitrievna?' came her voice from there.

'Herself,' came the answer in a rough voice, and Marya Dmitrievna entered the room.

All the unmarried ladies and even the married ones except the very oldest rose. Marya Dmitrievna paused at the door. Tall and stout, holding high her fifty-year-old head with its grey curls, she stood surveying the guests, and leisurely arranged her wide sleeves as if rolling them up. Marya Dmitrievna always spoke in Russian.

'Health and happiness to her whose name-day we are keeping and to her children,' she said, in her loud, full-toned voice which drowned all others. 'Well, you old sinner,' she went on, turning to the count who was kissing her hand, 'you're feeling dull in Moscow, I daresay? Nowhere to hunt with your dogs? But what is to be done, old man? Just see how these nestlings are growing up,' and she pointed to the girls. 'You must look for husbands for them, whether you like it or not.'

'Well,' said she, 'how's my Cossack?' (Marya Dmitrievna always called Natasha a Cossack), and she stroked the child's arm as she came up fearless and gay to kiss her hand. 'I know she's a scamp of a girl, but I like her.'

She took a pair of pear-shaped ruby earrings from her huge reticule, and having given them to the rosy Natasha, who beamed with the pleasure of her saint's-day fête, turned away at once and addressed herself to Pierre.

'Eh, eh, friend! Come here a bit,' said she, assuming a soft high tone of voice. 'Come here, my friend, . . .' and she ominously tucked up her sleeves still higher. Pierre approached, looking at her in a childlike way through his spectacles.

'Come nearer, come nearer, friend! I used to be the only one to tell your father the truth when he was in favour, and in your case it's my evident duty.'

She paused. All were silent, expectant of what was to follow, for this was clearly only a prelude.

'A fine lad! My word! A fine lad!... His father lies on his death-bed and he amuses himself setting a policeman astride a bear! For shame, sir, for shame! It would be better if you went to the war.'

She turned away and gave her hand to the count, who could hardly keep from laughing.

'Well, I suppose it is time we were at table?' said Marya Dmitrievna.

The count went in first with Marya Dmitrievna, the countess followed on the arm of a colonel of hussars, a man of importance to them because Nicholas was to go with him to the regiment; then came Anna Mikhaylovna with Shinshin. Berg gave his arm to Vera. The smiling Julie Karagin went in with Nicholas. After them other couples followed, filling the whole dining-hall, and last of all the children, tutors, and governesses, followed singly. The footmen began moving about, chairs scraped, the band struck up in the gallery, and the guests settled down in their places. Then the strains of the count's household band were replaced by the clatter of knives and forks, the voices of visitors, and the soft steps of the footmen. At one end of the table sat the countess with Marya Dmitrievna on her right and Anna Mikhaylovna on her left, the other lady visitors were farther down. At the other end sat the count, with the hussar colonel on his left and Shinshin and the other male visitors on his right. Midway down the long table on one side sat the grown-up young people: Vera beside Berg, and Pierre beside Boris; and on the other side the children, tutors, and governesses. From behind the crystal decanters and fruit-dishes the count kept glancing at his wife and her tall cap with its light-blue ribbons, and busily filled his neighbours' glasses, not neglecting his own. The countess in turn, without omitting her duties as hostess, threw significant glances from behind the pineapples at her husband whose face and bald head seemed by their redness to contrast more than usual with his grey hair. At the ladies' end an even chatter of voices was heard all the time, at the men's end the voices sounded louder and louder, especially that of the colonel of hussars, who growing more and more flushed, ate and drank so much that the count held him up as a pattern to the other guests. Berg with tender smiles was saying to Vera that love is not an earthly but a heavenly feeling. Boris was telling his new friend Pierre who the guests were and ex- changing glances with Natasha, who was sitting opposite. Pierre spoke little but examined the new faces, and ate a great deal. Of the two soups he chose turtle with savoury patties and went on to the game without omitting a single dish or one of the wines.

These latter the butler thrust mysteriously forward wrapped in a napkin from behind the next man's shoulders and whispered: 'Dry Madeira'...'Hungarian'...or 'Rhine-wine' as the case might be. Of the four crystal glasses engraved with the count's monogram that stood before his plate, Pierre held out one at random and drank with enjoyment, gazing with ever-increasing amiability at the other guests. Natasha, who sat opposite, was looking at Boris as girls of thirteen look at the boy they are in love with and have just kissed for the first time. Sometimes that same look fell on Pierre, and that funny lively little girl's look made him inclined to laugh without knowing why.

Nicholas sat at some distance from Sonya, beside Julie Karagin, to whom he was again talking with the same involuntary smile. Sonya wore a company smile but was evidently tormented by jealousy; now she turned pale, now blushed and strained every nerve to overhear what Nicholas and Julie were saying to one another. The governess kept looking round uneasily as if preparing to resent any slight that might be put upon the children. The German tutor was trying to remember all the dishes, wines, and kinds of dessert, in order to send a full description of the dinner to his people in Germany; and he felt greatly offended when the butler with a bottle wrapped in a napkin passed him by. He frowned, trying to appear as if he did not want any of that wine, but was mortified because no one would understand that it was not to quench his thirst or from greediness that he wanted it, but simply from a conscientious desire for knowledge.

16

AT the men's end of the table the talk grew more and more animated. The colonel told them that the declaration of war had already appeared in Petersburg and that a copy, which he had himself seen, had that day been forwarded by courier to the commander-in-chief.

'And why the deuce are we going to fight Bonaparte?' remarked Shinshin. 'He has stopped Austria's cackle and I fear it will be our turn next.'

The colonel was a stout, tall, plethoric German, evidently devoted to the service and patriotically Russian. He resented Shinshin's remark.

'It is for the reasson, my goot sir,' said he, speaking with a German accent, 'for the reasson zat ze Emperor knows zat. He declares in ze manifessto zat he cannot fiew wiz indifference ze danger vreatening Russia and zat ze safety and dignity of ze Empire as vell as ze sanctity of its *alliances* . . .', he spoke this last word with particular emphasis as if in it lay the gist of the matter.

Then with the unerring official memory that characterized him he repeated from the opening words of the manifesto:

'... *and the wish, which constitutes the Emperor's sole and absolute aim -- to establish peace in Europe on firm foundations -- has now decided him to despatch part of the army abroad and to create a new condition for the attainment of that purpose.*'

'Zat, my dear sir, is vy . . .' he concluded, drinking a tumbler of wine with dignity and looking to the count for approval.

'*Connaissez-vous le proverbe*: "*Jerome, Jerome, do not roam, but turn spindles at home!*"?' said Shinshin, puckering his brows and smiling. '*Cela nous convient à merveille.* Suvorov now -- he knew what he was about; yet they beat him *à plate couture*,* and where are we to find Suvorovs now? *Je vous demande un peu,*' said he, continually changing from French to Russian.

'Ve must vight to the last tr-r-op of our plood!' said the colonel, thumping the table; 'and ve must tie for our Emperor, and zen all vill pe vell. And ve must discuss it as little as po-o-ossible' . . . he dwelt particularly on the word *possible* . . . 'as po-o-ossible,' he ended, again turning to the count. 'Zat is how ve old hussars look at it, and zere's an end of it! And how do you, a young man and a young hussar, how do you judge of it?' he added, addressing Nicholas, who when he heard that the war was being discussed had turned from his partner with eyes and ears intent on the colonel.

'I am quite of your opinion,' replied Nicholas, flaming up, turning his plate round and moving his wine glasses about with as much decision and desperation as though he were at that moment facing some great danger. 'I am convinced that we Russians must die or conquer,' he concluded, conscious -- as were others -- after the words were uttered that his remarks were too enthusiastic and emphatic for the occasion and were therefore awkward.

'What you said just now was splendid!' said his partner Julie.

Sonya trembled all over and blushed to her ears and behind them and down to her neck and shoulders while Nicholas was speaking.

Pierre listened to the colonel's speech and nodded approvingly.

'That's fine,' said he.

'The young man's a real hussar!' shouted the colonel, again thumping the table.

'What are you making such a noise about over there?' Marya Dmitrievna's deep voice suddenly inquired from the other end of the table. 'What are you thumping the table for?' she demanded of the hussar, 'and why are you exciting yourself? Do you think the French are here?'

'I am speaking ze truce,' replied the hussar with a smile.

'It's all about the war,' the count shouted down the table. 'You know my son's going, Marya Dmitrievna? My son is going.'

'I have four sons in the army but still I don't fret. It is all in God's hands. You may die in your bed or God may spare you in a battle,' replied Marya Dmitrievna's deep voice, which easily carried the whole length of the table.

'That's true!'

Once more the conversations concentrated, the ladies' at the one end and the men's at the other.

'You won't ask,' Natasha's little brother was saying; 'I know you won't ask!'

'I will,' replied Natasha.

Her face suddenly flushed with reckless and joyous resolution. She half rose, by a glance inviting Pierre, who sat opposite, to listen to what was coming, and turning to her mother:

'Mamma!' rang out the clear contralto notes of her childish voice, audible the whole length of the table.

'What is it?' asked the countess, startled; but seeing by her daughter's face that it was only mischief, she shook a finger at her sternly with a threatening and forbidding movement of her head.

The conversation was hushed.

'Mamma! What sweets are we going to have?' and Natasha's voice sounded still more firm and resolute.

The countess tried to frown, but could not. Marya Dmitrievna shook her fat finger.

'Cossack!' she said threateningly.

Most of the guests, uncertain how to regard this sally, looked at the elders.

'You had better take care!' said the countess.

'Mamma! What sweets are we going to have?' Natasha again cried boldly, with saucy gaiety, confident that her prank would be taken in good part.

Sonya and fat little Petya doubled up with laughter.

'You see! I *have* asked,' whispered Natasha to her little brother and to Pierre, glancing at him again.

'Ice-pudding, but you won't get any,' said Marya Dmitrievna.

Natasha saw there was nothing to be afraid of and so she braved even Marya Dmitrievna.

'Marya Dmitrievna! What kind of ice-pudding? I don't like ice-cream.'

66

'Carrot-ices.'

'No! What kind, Marya Dmitrievna? What kind?' she almost screamed; 'I want to know!'

Marya Dmitrievna and the countess burst out laughing, and all the guests joined in. Everyone laughed, not at Marya Dmitrievna's answer but at the incredible boldness and smartness of this little girl who had dared to treat Marya Dmitrievna in this fashion.

Natasha only desisted when she had been told that there would be pineapple ice. Before the ices champagne was served round. The band again struck up, the count and countess kissed, and the guests, leaving their seats, went up to 'congratulate' the countess, and reached across the table to clink glasses with the count, with the children, and with one another. Again the footmen rushed about, chairs scraped, and in the same order in which they had entered but with redder faces, the guests returned to the drawing-room and to the count's study.

17

THE card-tables were drawn out, sets made up for boston, and the count's visitors settled themselves, some in the two drawing-rooms, some in the sitting-room, some in the library.

The count, holding his cards fanwise, kept himself with difficulty from dropping into his usual after-dinner nap, and laughed at everything. The young people, at the countess's instigation, gathered round the clavichord and harp. Julie by general request played first. After she had played a little air with variations on the harp, she joined the other young ladies in begging Natasha and Nicholas, who were noted for their musical talent, to sing something. Natasha, who was treated as though she were grown up, was evidently very proud of this but at the same time felt shy.

'What shall we sing?' she asked.

'"The Brook,"' suggested Nicholas.

'Well then let's be quick. Boris, come here,' said Natasha. 'But where is Sonya?'

She looked round and seeing that her friend was not in the room ran to look for her.

Running into Sonya's room and not finding her there, Natasha ran to the nursery, but Sonya was not there either. Natasha concluded that she must be on the chest in the passage. The chest in the passage was the place of mourning for the younger female generation in the Rostov household. And there in fact was Sonya lying face downward on Nurse's dirty feather-bed on the top of the chest, crumpling her gauzy pink dress under her, hiding her face with her slender fingers, and sobbing so convulsively that her bare little shoulders shook. Natasha's face which had been so radiantly happy all that saint's-day, suddenly changed: her eyes became fixed, and then a shiver passed down her broad neck and the corners of her mouth drooped.

'Sonya! What is it?... What is the matter?... Oo... Oo... Oo...!' And Natasha's large mouth widened, making her look quite ugly, and she began to wail like a baby without knowing why, except that Sonya was crying. Sonya tried to lift her head to answer but could not, and hid her face still deeper in the bed. Natasha wept, sitting on the blue-striped feather-bed and hugging her friend. With an effort Sonya sat up and began wiping her eyes and explaining.

'Nicholas is going away in a week's time, his... papers... have come... he told me himself... but still I should not cry,' and she showed a paper she held in her hand – with the verses Nicholas had written, 'still, I should not cry, but you can't... no one can understand... what a soul he has!'

And she began to cry again because he had such a noble soul.

'It's all very well for you... I am not envious... I love you and Boris also,' she went on, gaining a little strength; 'he is nice ... there are no difficulties in your way... But Nicholas is my cousin... one would have to... the Metropolitan himself*... and even then it can't be done. And besides, if she tells Mamma' (Sonya looked upon the countess as her mother and called her so) 'that I am spoiling Nicholas's career and am heartless and ungrateful, while truly... God is my witness,' and she made the sign of the cross, 'I love her so much, and all of you, only Vera... And what for? What have I done to her? I am so grateful to you that I would willingly sacrifice everything, only I have nothing...'

Sonya could not continue, and again hid her face in her hands and in the feather-bed. Natasha began consoling her, but her face showed that she understood all the gravity of her friend's trouble.

'Sonya,' she suddenly exclaimed, as if she had guessed the true reason of her friend's sorrow, 'I'm sure Vera has said something to you since dinner? Hasn't she?'

'Yes, these verses Nicholas wrote himself and I copied some others, and she found them on my table and said she'd show them to Mamma, and that I was ungrateful, and that Mamma would never allow him to marry me, but that he'll marry Julie. You see how he's been with her all day... Natasha, what have I done to deserve it?'

And again she began to sob, more bitterly than before. Natasha lifted her up, hugged her, and smiling through her tears, began comforting her.

'Sonya, don't believe her, darling! Don't believe her! Do you remember how we and Nicholas, all three of us, talked in the sitting-room after supper? Why, we settled how everything was to be. I don't quite remember how, but don't you remember that it could all be arranged and how nice it all was? There's Uncle Shinshin's brother has married his first cousin! And we are only second cousins, you know. And Boris says it is quite possible. You know I have told him all about it. And he is so clever and so good!' said Natasha. 'Don't you cry, Sonya, dear love, darling Sonya;' and she kissed her and laughed. 'Vera's spiteful; never mind her! And all will come right and she won't say anything to Mamma. Nicholas will tell her himself, and he doesn't care at all for Julie.'

Natasha kissed her on the hair.

Sonya sat up. The little kitten brightened, its eyes shone, and it seemed ready to lift its tail, jump down on its soft paws, and begin playing with the ball of worsted as a kitten should.

'Do you think so? ... Really? Truly?' she said, quickly smoothing her frock and hair.

'Really, truly!' answered Natasha, pushing in a crisp lock that had strayed from under her friend's plaits.

Both laughed.

'Well, let's go and sing "The Brook".'

'Come along!'

'Do you know, that fat Pierre who sat opposite me is so funny!' said Natasha, stopping suddenly. 'I feel so happy!'

And she set off at a run along the passage.

Sonya, shaking off some down which clung to her and tucking away the verses in the bosom of her dress close to her bony little chest, ran after Natasha down the passage into the sitting-room with flushed face and light, joyous steps. At the visitors' request the young people sang the quartette 'The Brook', with which every-one was delighted. Then Nicholas sang a song he had just learnt.

> At night time in the moon's fair glow,
>   How sweet, as fancies wander free,
> To feel that *in this world there's one*
> *Who still is thinking but of thee!*
>
> That while her fingers touch the harp
>   Wafting sweet music o'er the lea,
> It is for thee thus swells her heart,
>   Sighing its message out to thee....
>
> A day or two, then bliss unspoilt,
>   But oh! till then I cannot live! ...

He had not finished the last verse before the young people began to get ready to dance in the large hall, and the sound of the feet and the coughing of the musicians were heard from the gallery.

*

Pierre was sitting in the drawing-room where Shinshin had engaged him, as a man recently returned from abroad, in a political conversation in which several others joined but which bored Pierre. When the music began Natasha came in and walking straight up to Pierre said, laughing and blushing:

'Mamma told me to ask you to join the dancers.'

'I am afraid of mixing the figures,' Pierre replied; 'but if you will be my teacher...' And lowering his big arm he offered it to the slender little girl.

While the couples were arranging themselves and the musicians tuning up, Pierre sat down with his little partner. Natasha was perfectly happy; she was dancing with a *grown-up* man, who had been *abroad*. She was sitting in a conspicuous place and talking to him like a grown-up lady. She had a fan in her hand that one of the ladies had given her to hold. Assuming quite the pose of a society woman (heaven knows when and where she had learnt it) she talked with her partner, fanning herself and smiling over the fan.

'Dear, dear! Just look at her!' exclaimed the countess as she crossed the ball-room, pointing to Natasha.

Natasha blushed and laughed.

'Well, really, Mamma! Why should you? What is there to be surprised at?'

In the midst of the third *écossaise* there was a clatter of chairs being pushed back in the sitting-room where the count and Marya Dmitrievna had been playing cards with the majority of the more distinguished and older visitors. They now, stretching themselves after sitting so long, and replacing their purses and pocket-books, entered the ball-room. First came Marya Dmitrievna and the count, both with merry countenances. The count, with playful ceremony somewhat in *ballet* style, offered his bent arm to Marya Dmitrievna. He drew himself up, a smile of debonair gallantry lit up his face, and as soon as the last figure of the *écossaise* was ended, he clapped his hands to the musicians and shouted up to their gallery, addressing the first violin:

'Simën! Do you know the *Daniel Cooper*?'

This was the count's favourite dance, which he had danced in his youth. (Strictly speaking, *Daniel Cooper* was one figure of the *anglaise*.)

'Look at Papa!' shouted Natasha to the whole company, and

quite forgetting that she was dancing with a grown-up partner she bent her curly head to her knees and made the whole room ring with her laughter.

And indeed everybody in the room looked with a smile of pleasure at the jovial old gentleman, who standing beside his tall and stout partner, Marya Dmitrievna, curved his arms, beat time, straightened his shoulders, turned out his toes, tapped gently with his foot, and by a smile that broadened his round face more and more, prepared the onlookers for what was to follow. As soon as the provocatively gay strains of *Daniel Cooper* (somewhat resembling those of a merry peasant dance) began to sound, all the doorways of the ball-room were suddenly filled by the domestic serfs – the men on one side and the women on the other – who with beaming faces had come to see their master making merry.

'Just look at the master! A regular eagle he is!' loudly remarked the nurse, as she stood in one of the doorways.

The count danced well and knew it. But his partner could not and did not want to dance well. Her enormous figure stood erect, her powerful arms hanging down (she had handed her reticule to the countess), and only her stern but handsome face really joined in the dance. What was expressed by the whole of the count's plump figure, in Marya Dmitrievna found expression only in her more and more beaming face and quivering nose. But if the count, getting more and more into the swing of it, charmed the spectators by the unexpectedness of his adroit manœuvres and the agility with which he capered about on his light feet, Marya Dmitrievna produced no less impression by slight exertions – the least effort to move her shoulders or bend her arms when turning, or stamp her foot – which everyone appreciated in view of her size and habitual severity. The dance grew livelier and livelier. The other couples could not attract a moment's attention to their own evolutions and did not even try to do so. All were watching the count and Marya Dmitrievna. Natasha kept pulling everyone by sleeve or dress, urging them to 'look at Papa!' though as it was they never took their eyes off the couple. In the intervals of the dance the count, breathing deeply, waved and shouted to the musicians to play faster. Faster, faster and faster; lightly, more lightly and yet more lightly whirled the count, flying round Marya Dmitrievna, now on his toes, now on his heels; until, turning his partner round to her seat, he executed the final *pas*, raising his light foot backwards, bowing his perspiring head, smiling, and making a wide sweep with his arm, amid a thunder of applause and laughter led by Natasha. Both partners stood still, breathing heavily and wiping their faces with their cambric handkerchiefs.

71

'That's how we used to dance in our time, *ma chère*,' said the count.

'That *was* a *Daniel Cooper!*' exclaimed Marya Dmitrievna, tucking up her sleeves and puffing heavily.

18

WHILE in the Rostovs' ball-room the sixth *anglaise* was being danced, to a tune in which the weary musicians blundered, and while tired footmen and cooks were getting the supper, Count Bezukhov had a sixth stroke. The doctors pronounced recovery impossible. After a mute confession, Communion was administered to the dying man, preparations made for the sacrament of Unction, and in his house there was the bustle and thrill of suspense usual at such moments. Outside the house, beyond the gates, a group of undertakers, who hid whenever a carriage drove up, waited in expectation of an important order for an expensive funeral. The Military Governor of Moscow, who had been assiduous in sending aides-de-camp to inquire after the count's health, came himself that evening to bid a last farewell to the celebrated grandee of Catherine's court, Count Bezukhov.

The magnificent reception-room was crowded. Everyone stood up respectfully when the Military Governor, having stayed about half an hour alone with the dying man, passed out, slightly acknowledging their bows and trying to escape as quickly as possible from the glances fixed on him by the doctors, clergy, and relatives of the family. Prince Vasili, who had grown thinner and paler during the last few days, escorted him to the door, repeating something to him several times in low tones.

When the Military Governor had gone, Prince Vasili sat down all alone on a chair in the ball-room, crossing one leg high over the other, leaning his elbow on his knee and covering his face with his hand. After sitting so for a while he rose, and, looking about him with frightened eyes, went with unusually hurried steps down the long corridor leading to the back of the house, to the room of the eldest princess.

Those who were in the dimly-lit reception-room spoke in nervous whispers, and whenever anyone went into or came from the dying man's room, grew silent and gazed with eyes full of curiosity at his door, which creaked slightly when opened.

'The limits of human life ... are fixed and may not be o'erpassed,' said an old priest to a lady who had taken a seat beside him and was listening naïvely to his words.

'I wonder, is it not too late to administer Unction?' asked the lady, adding the priest's clerical title, as if she had no opinion of her own on the subject.

'Ah madam, it is a great sacrament,' replied the priest, passing his hand over the thin grizzled strands of hair combed back across his bald head.

'Who was that? The Military Governor himself?' was being asked at the other side of the room. 'How young-looking he is!'

'Yes, and he is over sixty. I hear the count no longer recognizes anyone? They wished to administer the sacrament of Unction.'

'I knew someone who received that sacrament seven times.'

The second princess had just come from the sick room with her eyes red from weeping and sat down beside Doctor Lorrain, who was sitting in a graceful pose under a portrait of Catherine, leaning his elbow on a table.

'Beautiful,' said the doctor in answer to a remark about the weather. 'The weather is beautiful, Princess; and besides, in Moscow one feels as if one were in the country.'

'Yes, indeed,' replied the princess with a sigh. 'So he may have something to drink?'

Lorrain considered.

'Has he taken his medicine?'

'Yes.'

The doctor glanced at his watch.

'Take a glass of boiled water and put a pinch of cream of tartar,' and he indicated with his delicate fingers what he meant by a pinch.

'Dere has neffer been a gase,' a German doctor was saying to an aide-de-camp, 'dat one liffs after de sird sdroke.'

'And what a well-preserved man he was!' remarked the aide-de-camp. 'And who will inherit his wealth?' he added in a whisper.

'It von't go begging,' replied the German with a smile.

Everyone again looked towards the door, which creaked as the second princess went in with the drink she had prepared according to Lorrain's instructions. The German doctor went up to Lorrain.

'Do you think he can last till morning?' asked the German, addressing Lorrain in French which he pronounced badly.

Lorrain, pursing up his lips, waved a severely negative finger before his nose.

'To-night, not later,' said he in a low voice, and he moved away with a decorous smile of self-satisfaction at being able clearly to understand and state the patient's condition.

Meanwhile Prince Vasili had opened the door into the princess's room.

In this room it was almost dark; only two tiny lamps were burning before the icons and there was a pleasant scent of flowers and burnt pastilles. The room was crowded with small pieces of furniture, whatnots, cupboards, and little tables. The quilt of a high, white feather-bed was just visible behind a screen. A small dog began to bark.

'Ah, is it you, cousin?'

She rose and smoothed her hair, which was as usual so extremely smooth that it seemed to be made of one piece with her head and covered with varnish.

'Has anything happened?' she asked. 'I am so terrified.'

'No, there is no change. I only came to have a talk about business, Catiche,' muttered the prince, seating himself wearily on the chair she had just vacated. 'You have made the place warm, I must say,' he remarked. 'Well, sit down: let's have a talk.'

'I thought perhaps something had happened,' she said with her unchanging stonily severe expression; and, sitting down opposite the prince, she prepared to listen.

'I wished to get a nap, *mon cousin*, but I can't.'

'Well, my dear?' said Prince Vasili, taking her hand and bending it downwards as was his habit.

It was plain that this 'well?' referred to much that they both understood without naming.

The princess, who had a straight, rigid body, abnormally long for her legs, looked directly at Prince Vasili with no sign of emotion in her prominent grey eyes. Then she shook her head and glanced up at the icons with a sigh. This might have been taken as an expression of sorrow and devotion, or of weariness and hope of resting before long. Prince Vasili understood it as an expression of weariness.

'And I?' he said; 'do you think it is easier for me? I am as worn out as a post-horse, but still I must have a talk with you, Catiche, a very serious talk.'

Prince Vasili said no more and his cheeks began to twitch nervously, now on one side now on the other, giving his face an unpleasant expression which was never to be seen on it in a drawing-room. His eyes too seemed strange: at one moment they looked impudently sly and at the next glanced round in alarm.

The princess, holding her little dog on her lap with her thin bony hands, looked attentively into Prince Vasili's eyes evidently resolved not to be the first to break silence, if she had to wait till morning.

'Well, you see, my dear Princess and cousin, Catherine Semënovna,' continued Prince Vasili, returning to his theme, apparently not without an inner struggle; 'at such a moment as this one must think of everything. One must think of the future, of all of you . . . I love you all, like children of my own, as you know.'

The princess continued to look at him without moving, and with the same dull expression.

'And then of course my family has also to be considered,' Prince Vasili went on, testily pushing away a little table without looking at her. 'You know, Catiche, that we – you three sisters, Mamontov, and my wife – are the count's only direct heirs. I know, I know how hard it is for you to talk or think of such matters. It is no easier for me; but, my dear, I am getting on for sixty and must be prepared for anything. Do you know I have sent for Pierre? The count', pointing to his portrait, 'definitely demanded that he should be called.'

Prince Vasili looked questioningly at the princess, but could not make out whether she was considering what he had just said or whether she was simply looking at him.

'There is one thing I constantly pray God to grant, *mon cousin*,' she replied, 'and it is that He would be merciful to him and would allow his noble soul peacefully to leave this . . .'

'Yes, yes, of course,' interrupted Prince Vasili impatiently, rubbing his bald head and angrily pulling back towards him the little table that he had pushed away. 'But . . . in short the fact is . . . you know yourself that last winter the count made a will by which he left all his property, not to us his direct heirs, but to Pierre.'

'He has made wills enough!' quietly remarked the princess. 'But he cannot leave the estate to Pierre. Pierre is illegitimate.'

'But, my dear,' said Prince Vasili suddenly, clutching the little table and becoming more animated and talking more rapidly: 'what if a letter has been written to the Emperor in which the count asks for Pierre's legitimation? Do you understand that in consideration of the count's services, his request would be granted? . . .'

The princess smiled as people do who think they know more about the subject under discussion than those they are talking with.

'I can tell you more,' continued Prince Vasili, seizing her hand, 'that letter was written, though it was not sent, and the Emperor knew of it. The only question is has it been destroyed or not? If not, then as soon as *all is over*,' and Prince Vasili sighed to intimate what he meant by the words *all is over*, 'and the count's papers are opened, the will and letter will be delivered to the Emperor, and the petition will certainly be granted. Pierre will get everything as the legitimate son.'

'And our share?' asked the princess smiling ironically, as if anything might happen, only not that.

'But, my poor Catiche, it is as clear as daylight! He will then be the legal heir to everything and you won't get anything. You must know, my dear, whether the will and letter were written, and whether they have been destroyed or not. And if they have somehow been overlooked, you ought to know where they are, and must find them, because . . .'

'What next?' the princess interrupted, smiling sardonically and not changing the expression of her eyes. 'I am a woman, and you think we are all stupid; but I know this: an illegitimate son cannot inherit . . . *un bâtard!*' she added, as if supposing that this translation of the word would effectively prove to Prince Vasili the invalidity of his contention.

'Well really, Catiche! Can't you understand! You are so intelligent, how is it you don't see that if the count has written a letter to the Emperor begging him to recognize Pierre as legitimate, it follows that Pierre will not be Pierre but will become Bezukhov, and will then inherit everything under the will? And if the will and letter are not destroyed, then you will have nothing but the consolation of having been dutiful *et tout ce qui s'en suit!* That's certain.'

'I know the will was made, but I also know that it is invalid; and you, *mon cousin,* seem to consider me a perfect fool,' said the princess with the expression women assume when they suppose they are saying something witty and stinging.

'My dear Princess Catherine Semënovna,' began Prince Vasili impatiently, 'I came here not to wrangle with you, but to talk about your interests as with a kinswoman, a good, kind, true relation. And I tell you for the tenth time, that if the letter to the Emperor and the will in Pierre's favour are among the count's papers, then, my dear girl, you and your sisters are not heiresses! If you don't believe me, then believe an expert. I have just been talking to Dmitri Onufrich' (the family solicitor) 'and he says the same.'

At this a sudden change evidently took place in the princess's ideas; her thin lips grew white, though her eyes did not change, and her voice when she began to speak passed through such transitions as she herself evidently did not expect.

'That would be a fine thing!' said she. 'I never wanted anything and I don't now.'

She pushed the little dog off her lap and smoothed her dress.

'And this is gratitude – this is recognition for those who have sacrificed everything for his sake!' she cried. 'It's splendid! Fine! I don't want anything, Prince.'

'Yes, but you are not the only one. There are your sisters . . .' replied Prince Vasili.

But the princess did not listen to him.

'Yes, I knew it long ago but had forgotten. I knew that I could expect nothing but meanness, deceit, envy, intrigue, and ingratitude – the blackest ingratitude – in this house . . .'

'Do you or do you not know where that will is?' insisted Prince Vasili, his cheeks twitching more than ever.

'Yes, I was a fool! I still believed in people, loved them, and sacrificed myself. But only the base, the vile succeed! I know who has been intriguing!'

The princess wished to rise, but the prince held her by the hand. She had the air of one who has suddenly lost faith in the whole human race. She gave her companion an angry glance.

'There is still time, my dear. You must remember, Catiche, that it was all done casually in a moment of anger, of illness, and was afterwards forgotten. Our duty, my dear, is to rectify his mistake, to ease his last moments by not letting him commit this injustice, and not to let him die feeling that he is rendering unhappy those who . . .'

'Who sacrificed everything for him,' chimed in the princess, who would again have risen had not the prince still held her fast, 'though he never could appreciate it. No, *mon cousin*,' she added with a sigh, 'I shall always remember that in this world one must expect no reward, that in this world there is neither honour nor justice. In this world one has to be cunning and cruel.'

'Now come, come! Be reasonable. I know your excellent heart.'

'No, I have a wicked heart.'

'I know your heart,' repeated the prince. 'I value your friendship and wish you to have as good an opinion of me. Don't upset yourself, and let us talk sensibly while there is still time, be it a day or be it but an hour. . . . Tell me all you know about the will, and above all where it is. You must know. We will take it at once and show it to the count. He has no doubt forgotten it and will wish to destroy it. You understand that my sole desire is conscientiously to carry out his wishes; that is my only reason for being here. I came simply to help him and you.'

'Now I see it all! I know who has been intriguing – I know!' cried the princess.

'That's not the point, my dear.'

'It's that protégée of yours, that sweet Princess Drubetskaya, that Anna Mikhaylovna whom I would not take for a housemaid . . . the infamous vile woman!'

'Do not let us lose any time . . .'

'Ah, don't talk to me! Last winter she wheedled herself in here and told the count such vile, disgraceful things about us, especially

77

about Sophie – I can't repeat them – that it made the count quite ill and he would not see us for a whole fortnight. I know it was then he wrote this vile, infamous paper, but I thought the thing was invalid.'

'We've got to it at last – why did you not tell me about it sooner?'

'It's in the inlaid portfolio that he keeps under his pillow,' said the princess, ignoring his question. 'Now I know! Yes; if I have a sin, a great sin, it is hatred of that vile woman!' almost shrieked the princess, now quite changed. 'And what does she come worming herself in here for? But I will give her a piece of my mind. The time will come!'

19

WHILE these conversations were going on in the reception-room and the princess's room, a carriage containing Pierre (who had been sent for) and Anna Mikhaylovna (who found it necessary to accompany him) was driving into the court of Count Bezukhov's house. As the wheels rolled softly over the straw beneath the windows, Anna Mikhaylovna, having turned with words of comfort to her companion realized that he was asleep in his corner and woke him up. Rousing himself, Pierre followed Anna Mikhaylovna out of the carriage, and only then began to think of the interview with his dying father which awaited him. He noticed that they had not come to the front entrance but to the back door. While he was getting down from the carriage steps two men, who looked like tradespeople, ran hurriedly from the entrance and hid in the shadow of the wall. Pausing for a moment, Pierre noticed several other men of the same kind hiding in the shadow of the house on both sides. But neither Anna Mikhaylovna nor the footman nor the coachman, who could not help seeing these people, took any notice of them. 'It seems to be all right,' Pierre concluded, and followed Anna Mikhaylovna. She hurriedly ascended the narrow dimly-lit stone staircase, calling to Pierre, who was lagging behind, to follow. Though he did not see why it was necessary for him to go to the count at all, still less why he had to go by the back stairs, yet judging by Anna Mikhaylovna's air of assurance and haste, Pierre concluded that it was all absolutely necessary. Half-way up the stairs they were almost knocked over by some men who, carrying pails, came running downstairs, their boots clattering. These men pressed close to the wall to let Pierre and Anna Mikhaylovna pass and did not evince the least surprise at seeing them there.

'Is this the way to the princesses' apartments?' asked Anna Mikhaylovna of one of them.

'Yes,' replied a footman in a bold loud voice, as if anything were now permissible; 'the door to the left, ma'am.'

'Perhaps the count did not ask for me,' said Pierre when he reached the landing. 'I'd better go to my own room.'

Anna Mikhaylovna paused and waited for him to come up.

'Ah, my friend!' she said, touching his arm as she had done her son's when speaking to him that afternoon, 'believe me I suffer no less than you do, but be a man!'

'But really, hadn't I better go away?' he asked, looking kindly at her over his spectacles.

'Ah, my dear friend! Forget the wrongs that may have been done you. Think that he is your father ... perhaps in the agony of death.' She sighed. 'I have loved you like a son from the first. Trust yourself to me, Pierre. I shall not forget your interests.'

Pierre did not understand a word, but the conviction that all this had to be grew stronger, and he meekly followed Anna Mikhaylovna who was already opening a door.

This door led into a back ante-room. An old man, a servant of the princesses, sat in a corner knitting a stocking. Pierre had never been in this part of the house and did not even know of the existence of these rooms. Anna Mikhaylovna, addressing a maid who was hurrying past with a decanter on a tray as 'my dear' and 'my sweet', asked about the princesses' health, and then led Pierre along a stone passage. The first door on the left led into the princesses' apartments. The maid with the decanter in her haste had not closed the door (everything in the house was done in haste at that time), and Pierre and Anna Mikhaylovna in passing instinctively glanced into the room, where Prince Vasili and the eldest princess were sitting close together talking. Seeing them pass, Prince Vasili drew back with obvious impatience, while the princess jumped up and with a gesture of desperation slammed the door with all her might.

This action was so unlike her usual composure and the fear depicted on Prince Vasili's face so out of keeping with his dignity, that Pierre stopped and glanced inquiringly over his spectacles at his guide. Anna Mikhaylovna evinced no surprise, she only smiled faintly and sighed, as if to say that this was no more than she had expected.

'Be a man, my friend. I will look after your interests,' said she in reply to his look, and went still faster along the passage.

Pierre could not make out what it was all about, and still less what 'watching over his interests' meant, but he decided that all these things had to be. From the passage they went into a large dimly-lit room adjoining the count's reception-room. It was one of those sumptuous but cold apartments known to Pierre only from the front approach, but even in this room there now stood an empty bath, and water had been spilt on the carpet. They were met by a deacon with a censer and by a servant who passed out on tiptoe without heeding them. They went into the reception-room familiar to Pierre, with two Italian windows opening into the conservatory with its large bust and full-length portrait of Catherine the Great. The same people were still sitting here in almost the same positions as before, whispering to one another. All became silent and turned to look at the pale tear-worn Anna Mikhaylovna as she entered, and at the big stout figure of Pierre who, hanging his head, meekly followed her.

Anna Mikhaylovna's face expressed a consciousness that the decisive moment had arrived. With the air of a practical Petersburg lady she now, keeping Pierre close beside her, entered the room even more boldly than that afternoon. She felt that as she brought with her the person the dying man wished to see her own admission was assured. Casting a rapid glance at all those in the room and noticing the count's confessor there, she glided up to him with a sort of amble, not exactly bowing, yet seeming to grow suddenly smaller, and respectfully received the blessing first of one and then of another priest.

'God be thanked that you are in time,' said she to one of the priests; 'all we relatives have been in such anxiety. This young man is the count's son,' she added more softly. 'What a terrible moment!'

Having said this she went up to the doctor.

'Dear doctor,' said she, 'this young man is the count's son. Is there any hope?'

The doctor cast a rapid glance upwards and silently shrugged his shoulders. Anna Mikhaylovna with just the same movement raised her shoulders and eyes, almost closing the latter, sighed, and moved away from the doctor to Pierre. To him, in a particularly respectful and tenderly sad voice, she said:

'Trust in His mercy!' and pointing out a small sofa for him to sit and wait for her, she went silently towards the door that everyone was watching and it creaked very slightly as she disappeared behind it.

Pierre having made up his mind to obey his monitress implicitly, moved towards the sofa she had indicated. As soon as Anna Mikhaylovna had disappeared he noticed that the eyes of all in the room turned to him with something more than curiosity and sympathy. He noticed that they whispered to one another, casting significant looks at him with a kind of awe and even servility. A deference such as he had never before received was shown him. A strange lady, the one who had been talking to the priests, rose and offered him her seat; an aide-de-camp picked up and returned a glove Pierre had dropped; the doctors became respectfully silent as he passed by, and moved to make way for him. At first Pierre wished to take another seat so as not to trouble the lady, and also to pick up the glove himself and to pass round the doctors who were not even in his way; but all at once he felt that this would not do, and that to-night he was a person obliged to perform some sort of awful rite which everyone expected of him, and that he was therefore bound to accept their services. He took the glove in silence from the aide-de-camp, and sat down in the lady's chair, placing his huge hands symmetrically on his knees in the naïve attitude of an Egyptian statue, and decided in his own mind that all was as it should be, and that in order not to lose his head and do foolish things he must not act on his own ideas to-night, but must yield himself up entirely to the will of those who were guiding him.

Not two minutes had passed before Prince Vasili with head erect majestically entered the room. He was wearing his long coat with three stars on his breast. He seemed to have grown thinner since the morning; his eyes seemed larger than usual when he glanced round and noticed Pierre. He went up to him, took his hand (a thing he never used to do) and drew it downwards as if wishing to ascertain whether it was firmly fixed on.

'Courage, courage, my friend! He has asked to see you. That is well!' and he turned to go.

But Pierre thought it necessary to ask: 'How is . . .' and hesitated, not knowing whether it would be proper to call the dying man 'the count', yet ashamed to call him 'father'.

'He had another stroke about half-an-hour ago. Courage, my friend . . .'

Pierre's mind was in such a confused state that the word 'stroke' suggested to him a blow from something. He looked at Prince Vasili in perplexity, and only later grasped that a stroke was an attack of illness. Prince Vasili said something to Lorrain in passing and went through the door on tiptoe. He could not walk well on tiptoe and his whole body jerked at each step. The eldest princess followed him, and the priests and deacons and some servants also went in at the door. Through that door was heard a noise of things being moved about, and at last Anna Mikhaylovna, still with the same expression, pale but resolute in the discharge of duty, ran out and touching Pierre lightly on the arm said:

'The divine mercy is inexhaustible! Unction is about to be administered. Come.'

Pierre went in at the door, stepping on the soft carpet, and noticed that the strange lady, the aide-de-camp, and some of the servants, all followed him in, as if there were now no further need for permission to enter that room.

20

PIERRE well knew this large room divided by columns and an arch, its walls hung round with Persian carpets. The part of the room behind the columns, with a high silk-curtained mahogany bedstead on one side and on the other an immense case containing icons, was brightly illuminated with red light like a Russian church during evening service. Under the gleaming icons stood a long invalid chair, and in that chair on snowy white smooth pillows, evidently freshly changed, Pierre saw – covered to the waist by a bright green quilt – the familiar, majestic figure of his father, Count Bezukhov, with that grey mane of hair above his broad forehead which reminded one of a lion, and the deep characteristically noble wrinkles of his handsome, ruddy face. He lay just under the icons; his large thick hands outside the quilt. Into the right hand, which was lying palm downwards, a wax taper had been thrust between forefinger and thumb, and an old servant, bending over from behind the chair, held it in position. By the chair stood the priests, their long hair falling over their magnificent glittering vestments, with lighted tapers in their hands, slowly and solemnly conducting the service. A little behind them stood the two younger princesses holding handkerchiefs to their eyes, and just in front of them their eldest sister, Catiche, with a vicious and determined look steadily fixed on the icons, as though declaring to all that she could not answer for herself should she glance round. Anna Mikhaylovna, with a meek, sorrowful, and all-forgiving expression on her face, stood by the door near the strange lady. Prince Vasili in front of the door, near the invalid chair, a wax taper in his left hand, was leaning his left arm on the carved back of a velvet chair he had turned round for the purpose, and was crossing himself with his right hand, turning his eyes upward each time he touched his forehead. His face wore a calm look of piety and resignation to the will of God. 'If you do not understand these sentiments,' he seemed to be saying, 'so much the worse for you!'

Behind him stood the aide-de-camp, the doctors, and the menservants; the men and women had separated as in church. All were silently crossing themselves, and the reading of the church service, the subdued chanting of deep bass voices, and in the intervals sighs and the shuffling of feet, were the only sounds that could be heard. Anna Mikhaylovna, with an air of importance that showed that she felt she quite knew what she was about, went across the room to where Pierre was standing and gave him a taper. He lit it and, distracted by observing those around him, began crossing himself with the hand that held the taper.

Sophie, the rosy, laughter-loving, youngest princess with the mole, watched him. She smiled, hid her face in her handkerchief, and remained with it hidden for a while; then looking up and seeing Pierre she again began to laugh. She evidently felt unable to look at him without laughing, but could not resist looking at him; so to be out of temptation she slipped quietly behind one of the columns. In the midst of the service the voices of the priests suddenly ceased, they whispered to one another, and the old servant who was holding the count's hand got up and said something to the ladies. Anna Mikhaylovna stepped forward and, stooping over the dying man, beckoned to Lorrain from behind her back. The French doctor held no taper; he was leaning against one of the columns in a respectful attitude implying that he, a foreigner, in spite of all differences of faith, understood the full importance of the rite now being performed and even approved of it. He now approached the sick man with the noiseless step of one in full vigour of life, with his delicate white fingers raised from the green quilt the hand that was free, and turning sideways felt the pulse and reflected a moment. The sick man was given something to drink, there was a stir around him, then the people resumed their places and the service continued. During this interval Pierre noticed that Prince Vasili left the chair on which he had been leaning, and – with an air which intimated that he knew what he was about and if others did not understand him it was so much the worse for them – did not go up to the dying man, but passed by him, joined the eldest princess, and moved with her to the side of the room where stood the high bedstead with its silken hangings. On leaving the bed both Prince Vasili and the princess passed out by a back door, but returned to their places one after the other before the service was concluded. Pierre paid no more attention to this occurrence than to the rest of what went on, having made up his mind once for all that what he saw happening around him that evening was in some way essential.

The chanting of the service ceased, and the voice of the priest was heard respectfully congratulating the dying man on having received the sacrament. The dying man lay as lifeless and im-movable as before. Around him everyone began to stir: steps were audible and whispers, among which Anna Mikhaylovna's was the most distinct.

Pierre heard her say:

'Certainly he must be moved onto the bed; here it will be impossible...'

The sick man was so surrounded by doctors, princesses, and servants, that Pierre could no longer see the reddish-yellow face with its grey mane – which, though he saw other faces as well, he had not lost sight of for a single moment during the whole service. He judged by the cautious movements of those who crowded round the invalid chair that they had lifted the dying man and were moving him.

'Catch hold of any arm or you'll drop him!' he heard one of the servants say in a frightened whisper. 'Catch hold from underneath. Here!' exclaimed different voices; and the heavy breathing of the bearers and the shuffling of their feet grew more hurried, as if the weight they were carrying were too much for them.

As the bearers, among whom was Anna Mikhaylovna, passed the young man he caught a momentary glimpse between their heads and backs of the dying man's high, stout, uncovered chest and powerful shoulders, raised by those who were holding him under the armpits, and of his grey, curly, leonine head. This head, with its remarkably broad brow and cheekbones, its handsome, sensual mouth, and its cold, majestic expression, was not disfigured by the approach of death. It was the same as Pierre remembered it three months before, when the count had sent him to Petersburg. But now this head was swaying helplessly with the uneven move-ments of the bearers, and the cold listless gaze fixed itself upon nothing.

After a few minutes' bustle beside the high bedstead, those who had carried the sick man dispersed. Anna Mikhaylovna touched Pierre's hand and said 'Come'. Pierre went with her to the bed on which the sick man had been laid in a stately pose in keeping with the ceremony just completed. He lay with his head propped high on the pillows. His hands were symmetrically placed on the green silk quilt, the palms downwards. When Pierre came up the count was gazing straight at him, but with a look the significance of which could not be understood by mortal man. Either this look meant nothing but that as long as one has eyes they must look somewhere, or it meant too much. Pierre hesitated, not knowing what to do, and glanced inquiringly at his guide. Anna Mikhay-lovna made a hurried sign with her eyes, glancing at the sick man's hand and moving her lips as if to send it a kiss. Pierre, carefully stretching his neck so as not to touch the quilt, followed her suggestion and pressed his lips to the large-boned, fleshy hand. Neither the hand nor a single muscle of the count's face stirred. Once more Pierre looked questioningly at Anna Mikhaylovna to see what he was to do next. Anna Mikhaylovna with her eyes indicated a chair that stood beside the bed. Pierre obediently sat down, his eyes asking if he were doing right. Anna Mikhaylovna nodded approvingly. Again Pierre fell into the naïvely symmetrical pose of an Egyptian statue, evidently distressed that his stout and clumsy body took up so much room and doing his utmost to look as small as possible. He looked at the count, who still gazed at the spot where Pierre's face had been before he sat down. Anna Mikhaylovna indicated by her attitude her consciousness of the pathetic importance of these last moments of meeting between the father and son. This lasted about two minutes, which to Pierre seemed an hour. Suddenly the broad muscles and lines of the count's face began to twitch. The twitching increased, the hand-some mouth was drawn to one side (only now did Pierre realize how near death his father was), and from that distorted mouth issued an indistinct, hoarse sound. Anna Mikhaylovna looked attentively at the sick man's eyes, trying to guess what he wanted; she pointed first to Pierre, then to some drink, then named Prince Vasili in an inquiring whisper, then pointed to the quilt. The eyes and face of the sick man showed impatience. He made an effort to look at the servant who stood constantly at the head of the bed.

'Wants to turn on the other side,' whispered the servant, and got up to turn the count's heavy body towards the wall.

Pierre rose to help him.

While the count was being turned over, one of his arms fell back helplessly and he made a fruitless effort to pull it forward. Whether he noticed the look of terror with which Pierre regarded that life-less arm, or whether some other thought flitted across his dying brain, at any rate he glanced at the refractory arm, at Pierre's terror-stricken face, and again at the arm, and on his face a feeble, piteous smile appeared, quite out of keeping with his features, that seemed to deride his own helplessness. At sight of this smile Pierre felt an unexpected quivering in his breast and a tickling in his nose, and tears dimmed his eyes. The sick man was turned onto his side with his face to the wall. He sighed.

'He is dozing,' said Anna Mikhaylovna, observing that one of the princesses was coming to take her turn at watching. 'Let us go.'

Pierre went out.

THERE was now no one in the reception-room except Prince Vasili and the eldest princess, who were sitting under the portrait of Catherine the Great and talking eagerly. As soon as they saw Pierre and his companion they became silent, and Pierre thought he saw the princess hide something as she whispered:

'I can't bear the sight of that woman.'

'Catiche has had tea served in the small drawing-room,' said Prince Vasili to Anna Mikhaylovna. 'Go and take something, my poor Anna Mikhaylovna, or you will not hold out.'

To Pierre he said nothing, merely giving his arm a sympathetic squeeze below the shoulder. Pierre went with Anna Mikhaylovna into the small drawing-room.

'There is nothing so refreshing after a sleepless night as a cup of this delicious Russian tea,' Lorrain was saying with an air of restrained animation as he stood sipping tea from a delicate Chinese handleless cup before a table on which tea and a cold supper were laid in the small circular room. Around the table all who were at Count Bezukhov's house that night had gathered to fortify themselves. Pierre well remembered this small circular drawing-room with its mirrors and little tables. During balls given at the house, Pierre, who did not know how to dance, had liked sitting in this room to watch the ladies who as they passed through in their ball dresses with diamonds and pearls on their bare shoulders, looked at themselves in the brilliantly lighted mirrors which repeated their reflections several times. Now this same room was dimly lighted by two candles. On one small table tea-things and supper-dishes stood in disorder, and in the middle of the night a motley throng of people sat there, not merry-making, but sombrely whispering, and betraying by every word and movement that they none of them forgot what was happening and what was about to happen in the bedroom. Pierre did not eat anything though he would very much have liked to. He looked inquiringly at his monitress, and saw that she was again going on tiptoe to the reception-room where they had left Prince Vasili and the eldest princess. Pierre concluded that this also was essential, and after a short interval followed her. Anna Mikhaylovna was standing beside the princess, and they were both speaking in excited whispers.

'Permit me, Princess, to know what is necessary and what is not necessary,' said the younger of the two speakers, evidently in the same state of excitement as when she had slammed the door of her room.

'But, my dear Princess,' answered Anna Mikhaylovna blandly but impressively, blocking the way to the bedroom and preventing the other from passing, 'won't this be too much for poor uncle at a moment when he needs repose? Worldly conversation at a moment when his soul is already prepared . . .'

Prince Vasili was seated in an easy chair in his familiar attitude, with one leg crossed high above the other. His cheeks, which were so flabby that they looked heavier below, were twitching violently; but he wore the air of a man little concerned in what the two ladies were saying.

'Come, my dear Anna Mikhaylovna, let Catiche do as she pleases. You know how fond the count is of her.'

'I don't even know what is in this paper,' said the younger of the two ladies, addressing Prince Vasili and pointing to an inlaid portfolio she held in her hand. 'All I know is that his real will is in his writing-table, and this is a paper he has forgotten. . . .'

She tried to pass Anna Mikhaylovna, but the latter sprang so as to bar her path.

'I know, my dear, kind Princess,' said Anna Mikhaylovna, seizing the portfolio so firmly that it was plain she would not let go easily. 'Dear Princess, I beg and implore you, have some pity on him! *Je vous en conjure . . .*'

The princess did not reply. Their efforts in the struggle for the portfolio were the only sounds audible, but it was evident that if the princess did speak, her words would not be flattering to Anna Mikhaylovna. Though the latter held on tenaciously, her voice lost none of its honeyed firmness and softness.

'Pierre, my dear, come here. I think he will not be out of place in a family consultation; is it not so, Prince?'

'Why don't you speak, cousin?' suddenly shrieked the princess, so loud that those in the drawing-room heard her and were startled. 'Why do you remain silent when heaven knows who permits herself to interfere, making a scene on the very threshold of a dying man's room? Intriguer!' she hissed viciously, and tugged with all her might at the portfolio.

But Anna Mikhaylovna went forward a step or two to keep her hold on the portfolio, and changed her grip.

Prince Vasili rose. 'Oh!' said he with reproach and surprise, 'this is absurd! Come, let go I tell you.'

The princess let go.

'And you too!'

But Anna Mikhaylovna did not obey him.

'Let go, I tell you! I will take the responsibility. I myself will go and ask him, I! . . . does that satisfy you?'

'But, Prince,' said Anna Mikhaylovna, 'after such a solemn sacrament, allow him a moment's peace! Here, Pierre, tell them your opinion,' said she, turning to the young man who, having come quite close, was gazing with astonishment at the angry face of the princess which had lost all dignity, and at the twitching cheeks of Prince Vasili.

'Remember that you will answer for the consequences,' said Prince Vasili severely. 'You don't know what you are doing.'

'Vile woman!' shouted the princess, darting unexpectedly at Anna Mikhaylovna and snatching the portfolio from her.

Prince Vasili bent his head and spread out his hands.

At this moment that terrible door, which Pierre had watched so long and which had always opened so quietly, burst noisily open and banged against the wall, and the second of the three sisters rushed out wringing her hands.

'What are you doing!' she cried vehemently. 'He is dying and you leave me alone with him!'

Her sister dropped the portfolio. Anna Mikhaylovna, stooping, quickly caught up the object of contention and ran into the bedroom. The eldest princess and Prince Vasili, recovering themselves, followed her. A few minutes later the eldest sister came out with a pale hard face, again biting her underlip. At sight of Pierre her expression showed an irrepressible hatred.

'Yes, now you may be glad!' said she; 'this is what you have been waiting for.' And bursting into tears she hid her face in her handkerchief and rushed from the room.

Prince Vasili came next. He staggered to the sofa on which Pierre was sitting and dropped onto it, covering his face with his hand. Pierre noticed that he was pale and that his jaw quivered and shook as if in an ague.

'Ah, my friend!' said he, taking Pierre by the elbow; and there was in his voice a sincerity and weakness Pierre had never observed in it before. 'How often we sin, how much we deceive, and all for what? I am near sixty, dear friend . . . I too . . . All will end in death, all! Death is awful . . .' and he burst into tears.

Anna Mikhaylovna came out last. She approached Pierre with slow, quiet steps.

'Pierre!' she said.

Pierre gave her an inquiring look. She kissed the young man on his forehead, wetting him with her tears. Then after a pause she said:

'He is no more . . .'

Pierre looked at her over his spectacles.

'Come, I will go with you. Try to weep, nothing gives such relief as tears.'

She led him into the dark drawing-room and Pierre was glad no one could see his face. Anna Mikháylovna left him, and when she returned he was fast asleep with his head on his arm.

In the morning Anna Mikháylovna said to Pierre:

'Yes, my dear, this is a great loss for us all, not to speak of you. But God will support you: you are young, and are now I hope in command of an immense fortune. The will has not yet been opened. I know you well enough to be sure that this will not turn your head, but it imposes duties on you, and you must be a man.'

Pierre was silent.

'Perhaps later on I may tell you, my dear boy, that if I had not been there, God only knows what would have happened! You know, uncle promised me only the day before yesterday not to forget Boris. But he had no time. I hope, my dear friend, you will carry out your father's wish?'

Pierre understood nothing of all this and colouring shyly looked in silence at Princess Anna Mikháylovna. After her talk with Pierre, Anna Mikháylovna returned to the Rostóvs' and went to bed. On waking in the morning she told the Rostóvs and all her acquaintances the details of Count Bezúkhov's death. She said the count had died as she would herself wish to die, that his end was not only touching but edifying. As to the last meeting between father and son, it was so touching that she could not think of it without tears, and did not know which had behaved better during those awful moments – the father who so remembered everything and everybody at the last and had spoken such pathetic words to the son, or Pierre, whom it had been pitiful to see, so stricken was he with grief, though he tried hard to hide it in order not to sadden his dying father. 'It is painful, but it does one good. It uplifts the soul to see such men as the old count and his worthy son,' said she. Of the behaviour of the eldest princess and Prince Vasíli she spoke disapprovingly, but in whispers and as a great secret.

22

At Bald Hills, Prince Nicholas Andréevich Bolkónsky's* estate, the arrival of young Prince Andrew and his wife was daily expected, but this expectation did not upset the regular routine of life in the old prince's household. General-in-Chief Prince Nicholas Andréevich (nicknamed in society 'the King of Prussia'), ever since the Emperor Paul had exiled him to his country estate had lived there continuously with his daughter, Princess Mary, and her companion Mademoiselle Bourienne. Though in the new reign he was free to return to the capitals he still continued to live in the country, remarking that anyone who wanted to see him could come the hundred miles from Moscow to Bald Hills, while he himself needed no one and nothing. He used to say that there are only two sources of human vice – idleness and superstition, and only two virtues – activity and intelligence. He himself undertook his daughter's education, and to develop these two cardinal virtues in her gave her lessons in algebra and geometry till she was twenty, and arranged her life so that her whole time was occupied. He was himself always occupied: writing his memoirs, solving problems in higher mathematics, turning snuff-boxes on a lathe, working in the garden, or superintending the building that was always going on at his estate. As regularity is a prime condition facilitating activity, regularity in his household was carried to the highest point of exactitude. He always came to table under precisely the same conditions, and not only at the same hour but at the same minute. With those about him, from his daughter to his serfs, the prince was sharp and invariably exacting, so that without being a hard-hearted man he inspired such fear and respect as few hard-hearted men would have aroused. Although he was in retirement and had now no influence in political affairs, every high official appointed to the province in which the prince's estate lay considered it his duty to visit him, and waited in the lofty antechamber just as the architect, gardener, or Princess Mary did, till the prince appeared punctually to the appointed hour. Everyone sitting in this antechamber experienced the same feeling of respect and even fear when the enormously high study door opened and showed the figure of a rather small old man, with powdered wig, small withered hands, and bushy grey eyebrows which, when he frowned, sometimes hid the gleam of his shrewd, youthfully glittering eyes.

On the morning of the day that the young couple were to arrive, Princess Mary entered the antechamber as usual at the time appointed for the morning greeting, crossing herself with trepidation and repeating a silent prayer. Every morning she came in like that, and every morning she prayed that the daily interview might pass off well.

An old powdered man-servant who was sitting in the antechamber rose quietly and said in a whisper: 'Please walk in.'

Through the door came the regular hum of a lathe. The princess timidly opened the door which moved noiselessly and easily. She paused at the entrance. The prince was working at the lathe and after glancing round continued his work.

The enormous study was full of things evidently in constant

use. The large table covered with books and plans, the tall glass-fronted bookcase with keys in the locks, the high desk for writing while standing up, on which lay an open exercise-book, and the lathe with tools laid ready to hand and shavings scattered around – all indicated continuous, varied, and orderly activity. The motion of the small foot shod in a Tartar boot embroidered with silver, and the firm pressure of the lean sinewy hand, showed that the prince still possessed the tenacious endurance and vigour of hardy old age. After a few more turns of the lathe he removed his foot from the pedal, wiped his chisel, dropped it into a leather pouch attached to the lathe, and approaching the table, summoned his daughter. He never gave his children a blessing, so he simply held out his bristly cheek (as yet unshaven) and regarding her tenderly and attentively, said severely:

'Quite well? All right then, sit down.' He took the exercise-book containing lessons in geometry written by himself, and drew up a chair with his foot.

'For to-morrow!' said he, quickly finding the page and making a scratch from one paragraph to another with his hard nail.

The princess bent over the exercise-book on the table.

'Wait a bit, here's a letter for you,' said the old man suddenly, taking a letter addressed in a woman's hand from a bag hanging above the table, onto which he threw it.

At the sight of the letter red patches showed themselves on the princess's face. She took it quickly and bent her head over it.

'From Heloïse?'* asked the prince with a cold smile that showed his still sound, yellowish teeth.

'Yes, it's from Julie,' replied the princess with a timid glance and a timid smile.

'I'll let two more letters pass, but the third I'll read,' said the prince sternly; 'I'm afraid you write much nonsense. I'll read the third!'

'Read this if you like, father,' said the princess, blushing still more and holding out the letter.

'The third, I said the third!' cried the prince abruptly, pushing the letter away, and leaning his elbows on the table he drew towards him the exercise-book containing geometrical figures.

'Well, madam,' he began, stooping over the book close to his daughter and placing an arm on the back of the chair on which she sat, so that she felt herself surrounded on all sides by the acrid scent of old age and tobacco, which she had known so long. 'Now, madam, these triangles are equal; please note that the angle ABC. . . .'

The princess looked in a scared way at her father's eyes glittering close to her; the red patches on her face came and went, and it was plain that she understood nothing and was so frightened that her fear would prevent her understanding any of her father's further explanations, however clear they might be. Whether it was the teacher's fault or the pupil's, this same thing happened every day: the princess's eyes drew dim, she could not see and could not hear anything, but was only conscious of her stern father's withered face close to her, of his breath and the smell of him, and could think only of how to get away quickly to her own room to make out the problem in peace. The old man was beside himself: moved the chair on which he was sitting noisily backwards and forwards, made efforts to control himself and not become vehement, but almost always did become vehement, scolded, and sometimes flung the exercise-book away.

The princess gave a wrong answer.

'Well now, isn't she a fool!' shouted the prince, pushing the book aside and turning sharply away; but rising immediately, he paced up and down, lightly touched his daughter's hair and sat down again.

He drew up his chair and continued to explain.

'This won't do, Princess; it won't do,' said he, when Princess Mary, having taken and closed the exercise-book with the next day's lesson, was about to leave: 'Mathematics are most important, madam! I don't want to have you like our silly ladies. Get used to it and you'll like it,' and he patted her cheek. 'It will drive all the nonsense out of your head.'

She turned to go, but he stopped her with a gesture and took an uncut book from the high desk.

'Here is some sort of *Key to the Mysteries*** that your Heloïse has sent you. Religious! I don't interfere with anyone's belief . . . I have looked at it. Take it. Well, now go. Go.'

He patted her on the shoulder and himself closed the door after her.

Princess Mary went back to her room with the sad, scared expression that rarely left her and which made her plain, sickly face yet plainer. She sat down at her writing-table, on which stood miniature portraits and which was littered with books and papers. The princess was as untidy as her father was tidy. She put down the geometry-book and eagerly broke the seal of her letter. It was from her most intimate friend from childhood; that same Julie Karagin who had been at the Rostovs' name-day party.

Julie wrote in French:

Dear and precious Friend, How terrible and frightful a thing is separation! Though I tell myself that half my life and half my happiness are wrapped up in you, and that in spite of the distance separating us our hearts are united by indissoluble bonds, my heart rebels against fate and in spite of the pleasures and distractions around me I cannot overcome a certain secret sorrow that has been in my heart ever since we parted. Why are we not together as we were last summer, in your big study, on the blue sofa, the confidential sofa? Why cannot I now, as three months ago, draw fresh moral strength from your look, so gentle, calm, and penetrating, a look I loved so well and seem to see before me as I write?

Having read thus far, Princess Mary sighed and glanced into the mirror which stood on her right. It reflected a weak, ungraceful figure and thin face. Her eyes, always sad, now looked with particular hopelessness at her reflection in the glass. 'She flatters me,' thought the princess, turning away and continuing to read. But Julie did not flatter her friend: the princess's eyes – large, deep, and luminous (it seemed as if at times there radiated from them shafts of warm light), were so beautiful that very often in spite of the plainness of her face they gave her an attraction more powerful than that of beauty. But the princess never saw the beautiful expression of her own eyes – the look they had when she was not thinking of herself. As with everyone, her face assumed a forced unnatural expression as soon as she looked in a glass. She went on reading:

All Moscow talks of nothing but war. One of my two brothers is already abroad, the other is with the Guards, who are starting on their march to the frontier. Our dear Emperor has left Petersburg and it is thought intends to expose his precious person to the chances of war. God grant that the Corsican monster who is destroying the peace of Europe may be overthrown by the angel whom it has pleased the Almighty, in His goodness, to give us as sovereign! To say nothing of my brothers, this war has deprived me of one of the associations nearest my heart. I mean young Nicholas Rostov, who with his enthusiasm could not bear to remain inactive and has left the university to join the army. I will confess to you, dear Mary, that in spite of his extreme youth his departure for the army was a great grief to me. This young man, of whom I spoke to you last summer, is so noble-minded and full of that real youthfulness which one seldom finds nowadays among our old men of twenty and, particularly, he is so frank and has so much heart. He is so pure and poetic that my relations with him, transient as they were, have been one of the sweetest comforts to my poor heart, which has already suffered so much. Some day I will tell you about our parting and all that was said then. That is still too fresh. Ah, dear friend, you are happy not to know these poignant joys and sorrows. You are fortunate, for the latter are generally the stronger! I know very well that Count Nicholas is too young ever to be more to me than a friend, but this sweet friendship, this poetic and pure intimacy, were what my heart needed. But enough of this! The chief news, about which all Moscow gossips, is the death of old Count Bezukhov, and his inheritance. Fancy! The three princesses have received very little, Prince Vasili nothing, and it is Monsieur Pierre who has inherited all the property and has besides been recognized as legitimate; so that he is now Count Bezukhov and possessor of the finest fortune in Russia. It is rumoured that Prince Vasili played a very despicable part in this affair and that he returned to Petersburg quite crestfallen.

I confess I understand very little about all these matters of wills and inheritance; but I do know that since this young man, whom we all used to know as plain Monsieur Pierre, has become Count Bezukhov and the owner of one of the largest fortunes in Russia, I am much amused to watch the change in the tone and manners of the mammas burdened by marriageable daughters, and of the young ladies themselves, towards him, though, between you and me, he always seemed to me a poor sort of fellow. As for the past two years people have amused themselves by finding husbands for me (most of whom I don't even know), the matchmaking chronicles of Moscow now speak of me as the future Countess Bezukhova. But you will understand that I have no desire for the post. A *propos* of marriages: do you know that a while ago that *universal auntie* Anna Mikhaylovna told me, under the seal of strict secrecy, of a plan of marriage for you. It is neither more nor less than with Prince Vasili's son Anatole, whom they wish to reform by marrying him to someone rich and *distinguée*, and it is on you that his relations' choice has fallen. I don't know what you will think of it, but I consider it my duty to let you know of it. He is said to be very handsome and a terrible scapegrace. That is all I have been able to find out about him.

But enough of gossip. I am at the end of my second sheet of paper, and mamma has sent for me to go and dine at the Apraksins'. Read the mystical book I am sending you; it has an enormous success here. Though there are things in it difficult for the feeble human mind to grasp, it is an admirable book which calms and elevates the soul. Adieu! Give my respects to monsieur your father and my compliments to Mademoiselle Bourienne. I embrace you as I love you.

JULIE.

P.S. Let me have news of your brother and his charming little wife.

The princess pondered awhile with a thoughtful smile and her luminous eyes lit up so that her face was entirely transformed. Then she suddenly rose and with her heavy tread went up to the table. She took a sheet of paper and her hand moved rapidly over it. This is the reply she wrote, also in French:

Dear and precious Friend, – Your letter of the 13th has given me great delight. So you still love me, my romantic Julie? Separation, of which you say so much that is bad, does not seem to have had its usual effect on you. You complain of our separation. What then should I say, if I *dared* complain, I who am deprived of all who are dear to me? Ah, if we had not religion to console us life would be very sad. Why do you suppose that I should look severely on your affection for that young man? On such matters I am only severe with myself. I understand such feelings in others, and if never having felt them I cannot approve of them, neither do I condemn them. Only it seems to me that Christian love, love of one's neighbour, love of one's enemy, is worthier, sweeter, and better, than the feelings which the beautiful eyes of a young man can inspire in a romantic and loving young girl like yourself.

The news of Count Bezukhov's death reached us before your letter and my father was much affected by it. He says the count was the last representative but one of the great century, and that it is his own turn now, but that he will do all he can to let his turn come as late as possible. God preserve us from that terrible misfortune!

I cannot agree with you about Pierre, whom I knew as a child. He always seemed to me to have an excellent heart, and that is the quality I value most in people. As to his inheritance and the part played by Prince Vasili, it is very sad for both. Ah, my dear friend, our divine Saviour's words, that it is easier for a camel to go through the eye of a needle than for a rich man to enter the Kingdom of God, are terribly true. I pity Prince Vasili but am still more sorry for Pierre. So young, and burdened with such riches – to what temptations he will be exposed! If I were asked what I desire most on earth, it would be to be poorer than the poorest beggar. A thousand thanks, dear friend, for the volume you have sent me and which has such success in Moscow. Yet since you tell me that among some good things it contains others which our weak human understanding cannot grasp, it seems to me rather useless to spend time in reading what is unintelligible and can therefore bear no fruit. I never could understand the fondness some people have for confusing their minds by dwelling on mystical books that merely awaken their doubts and excite their imagination, giving them a bent for exaggeration quite contrary to Christian simplicity. Let us rather read the Epistles and Gospels. Let us not seek to penetrate what mysteries they contain; for how can we, miserable sinners that we are, know the terrible and holy secrets of Providence while we remain in this flesh which forms an impenetrable veil between us and the Eternal? Let us rather confine ourselves to studying those sublime rules which our divine Saviour has left for our guidance here below. Let us try to conform to them and follow them, and let us be persuaded that the less we let our feeble human minds roam, the better we shall please God, who rejects all knowledge that does not come from Him; and the less we seek to fathom what He has been pleased to conceal from us, the sooner will He vouchsafe its revelation to us through His divine Spirit.

My father has not spoken to me of a suitor, but has only told me that he has received a letter and is expecting a visit from Prince Vasili. In regard to this project of marriage for me, I will tell you, dear sweet friend, that I look on marriage as a divine institution to which we must conform. However painful it may be to me, should the Almighty ever lay the duties of wife and mother upon me I shall try to perform them as faithfully as I can, without disquieting myself by examining my feelings towards him whom He may give me for husband.

I have had a letter from my brother, who announces his speedy arrival at Bald Hills with his wife. This pleasure will be but a brief one, however, for he will leave us again to take part in this unhappy war into which we have been drawn God knows how or why. Not only where you are – at the heart of affairs and of the world – is the talk all of war, even here amid field-work and the calm of nature – which townsfolk consider characteristic of the country – rumours of war are heard and painfully felt. My father talks of nothing but marches and counter-marches, things of which I understand nothing; and the day before yesterday during my daily walk through the village I witnessed a heartrending scene ... It was a convoy of conscripts enrolled from our people and starting to join the army. You should have seen the state of the mothers, wives, and children, of the men who were going, and should have heard the sobs. It seems as though mankind has forgotten the laws of its divine Saviour, Who preached love and forgiveness of injuries – and that men attribute the greatest merit to skill in killing one another.

Adieu, dear and kind friend; may our divine Saviour and his most Holy Mother keep you in their holy and all-powerful care!

MARY.

'Ah, you are sending off a letter, Princess? I have already dispatched mine. I have written to my poor mother,' said the smiling Mademoiselle Bourienne rapidly, in her pleasant mellow tones and with guttural r's. She brought into Princess Mary's strenuous mournful and gloomy world a quite different atmosphere, careless, lighthearted, and self-satisfied.

'Princess, I must warn you,' she added, lowering her voice and evidently listening to herself with pleasure, and speaking with exaggerated *grasseyement*,* 'the prince has been scolding Michael Ivanovich. He is in a very bad humour, very morose. Be prepared.'

'Ah, dear friend,' replied Princess Mary, 'I have asked you never to warn me of the humour my father is in. I do not allow myself to judge him and would not have others do so.'

The princess glanced at her watch and seeing that she was five minutes late in starting her practice on the clavichord, went into the sitting-room with a look of alarm. Between twelve and two o'clock, as the day was mapped out, the prince rested and the princess played the clavichord.

THE grey-haired valet was sitting drowsily listening to the snoring of the prince, who was in his large study. From the far side of the house through the closed doors came the sound of difficult passages – twenty times repeated – of a sonata of Dussek's.

Just then a closed carriage and another with a hood drove up to the porch. Prince Andrew got out of the carriage, helped his little wife to alight, and let her pass into the house before him. Old Tikhon, wearing a wig, put his head out of the door of the antechamber, reported in a whisper that the prince was sleeping, and hastily closed the door. Tikhon knew that neither the son's arrival nor any other unusual event must be allowed to disturb the appointed order of the day. Prince Andrew apparently knew this as well as Tikhon; he looked at his watch as if to ascertain whether his father's habits had changed since he was at home last, and, having assured himself that they had not, he turned to his wife.

'He will get up in twenty minutes. Let us go across to Mary's room,' he said.

The little princess had grown stouter during this time, but her eyes and her short, downy, smiling lip lifted when she began to speak just as merrily and prettily as ever.

'Why, this is a palace!' she said to her husband, looking around with the expression with which people compliment their host at a ball. 'Let's come, quick, quick!' And with a glance round, she smiled at Tikhon, at her husband, and at the footman who accompanied them.

'Is that Mary practising? Let's go quietly and take her by surprise.'

Prince Andrew followed her with a courteous but sad expression.

'You've grown older, Tikhon,' he said in passing to the old man, who kissed his hand.

Before they reached the room from which the sounds of the clavichord came, the pretty, fair-haired Frenchwoman, Mademoiselle Bourienne, rushed out apparently beside herself with delight.

'Ah! what joy for the princess!' exclaimed she: 'At last! I must let her know.'

'No, no, please not ... You are Mademoiselle Bourienne,' said the little princess, kissing her. 'I know you already through my sister-in-law's friendship for you. She was not expecting us?'

They went up to the door of the sitting-room from which came the sound of the oft-repeated passage of the sonata. Prince Andrew stopped and made a grimace, as if expecting something unpleasant.

The little princess entered the room. The passage broke off in the middle, a cry was heard, then Princess Mary's heavy tread and the sound of kissing. When Prince Andrew went in the two princesses, who had only met once before for a short time at his wedding, were in each other's arms warmly pressing their lips to whatever place they happened to touch. Mademoiselle Bourienne stood near them pressing her hand to her heart, with a beatific smile and obviously equally ready to cry or to laugh. Prince Andrew shrugged his shoulders and frowned, as lovers of music do when they hear a false note. The two women let go of one another, and then as if afraid of being too late, seized each other's hands, kissing them and pulling them away, and again began kissing each other on the face, and then to Prince Andrew's surprise both began to cry and kissed again. Mademoiselle Bourienne also began to cry. Prince Andrew evidently felt ill at ease, but to the two women it seemed quite natural that they should cry, and apparently it never entered their heads that it could have been otherwise at this meeting.

'Ah! my dear!... Ah! Mary!...' they suddenly exclaimed, and then laughed. 'I dreamt last night...' – 'You were not expecting us?...' – 'Ah! Mary, you have got thinner!...' 'And you have grown stouter!...'

'I knew the princess at once,' put in Mademoiselle Bourienne.

'And I had no idea!...' exclaimed Princess Mary. 'Ah Andrew, I did not see you.'

Prince Andrew and his sister, hand in hand, kissed one another, and he told her she was still the same cry-baby as ever. Princess Mary had turned towards her brother, and through her tears the loving warm gentle look of her large luminous eyes, very beautiful at that moment, rested on Prince Andrew's face.

The little princess talked incessantly, her short downy upper lip continually and rapidly touching her rosy nether lip when necessary and drawing up again next moment when her face broke into a smile of glittering teeth and sparkling eyes. She told of an accident they had had on the Spassky Hill which might have been serious for her in her condition, and immediately after that informed them that she had left all her clothes in Petersburg and that heaven knew what she would have to dress in here; and that Andrew had quite changed, and that Kitty Odyntsova had married an old man, and that there was a suitor for Mary, a real one, but that they would talk of that later. Princess Mary was still looking silently at her brother and her beautiful eyes were full of love and sadness. It was plain that she was following a train of thought independent of her sister-in-law's words. In the midst of a description of the last Petersburg fête she addressed her brother:

'So you are really going to the war, Andrew?' she said sighing. Lise sighed too.

'Yes, and even to-morrow,' replied her brother.

'He is leaving me here; God knows why, when he might have had promotion . . .'

Princess Mary did not listen to the end, but continuing her train of thought turned to her sister-in-law with a tender glance at her figure.

'Is it certain?' she asked.

The face of the little princess changed. She sighed and said :

'Yes, quite certain. Ah! it is very dreadful . . .'

Her lip descended. She brought her face close to her sister-in-law's, and unexpectedly again began to cry.

'She needs rest,' said Prince Andrew with a frown. 'Don't you, Lise? Take her to your room and I'll go to father. How is he? Just the same?'

'Yes, just the same. Though I don't know what your opinion will be,' answered the princess joyfully.

'And are the hours the same? And the walks in the avenues? And the lathe?' asked Prince Andrew, with a scarcely perceptible smile which showed that, in spite of all his love and respect for his father, he was aware of his weaknesses.

'The hours are the same, and the lathe, and also the mathematics and my geometry lessons,' said Princess Mary gleefully, as if her lessons in geometry were among the greatest delights of her life.

When the twenty minutes had elapsed and the time had come for the old prince to get up, Tikhon came to call the young prince to his father. The old man made a departure from his usual routine in honour of his son's arrival: he gave orders to admit him to his apartments while he dressed for dinner. The old prince always dressed in old-fashioned style, wearing an antique coat and powdered hair; and when Prince Andrew entered his father's dressing-room (not with the contemptuous look and manner he wore in drawing-rooms, but with the animated face with which he talked to Pierre) the old man was sitting on a large leather-covered chair, wrapped in a powdering mantle, entrusting his head to Tikhon.

'Ah! here's the warrior! Wants to vanquish Buonaparte?' said the old man, shaking his powdered head as much as the tail, which Tikhon was holding fast to plait, would allow.

'You at least must tackle him properly, or else if he goes on like this he'll soon have us, too, for his subjects! How are you?' And he held out his cheek.

The old man was in a good temper after his nap before dinner. (He used to say, that a nap 'after dinner was silver – before dinner, golden'.) He cast happy, sidelong glances at his son from under his thick bushy eyebrows. Prince Andrew went up and kissed his father on the spot indicated to him. He made no reply on his father's favourite topic – making fun of the military men of the day, and more particularly of Bonaparte.

'Yes, father, I have come to you and brought my wife who is pregnant,' said Prince Andrew, following every movement of his father's face with an eager and respectful look. 'How is your health?'

'Only fools and rakes fall ill, my boy. You know me: I am busy from morning till night and abstemious, so of course I am well.'

'Thank God,' said his son smiling.

'God has nothing to do with it! Well, go on,' he continued, returning to his hobby; 'tell me how the Germans have taught you to fight Buonaparte by this new science you call "strategy"?'

Prince Andrew smiled.

'Give me time to collect my wits, father,' said he, with a smile that showed that his father's foibles did not prevent his son from loving and honouring him. 'Why, I have not yet had time to settle down!'

'Nonsense, nonsense!' cried the old man, shaking his pigtail to see whether it was firmly plaited, and grasping his son by the hand. 'The house for your wife is ready. Princess Mary will take her there and show her over, and they'll talk nineteen to the dozen. That's their woman's way! I am glad to have her. Sit down and talk. About Michelsen's army I understand* – Tolstoy's too . . . a simultaneous expedition. . . . But what's the southern army to do? Prussia is neutral . . . I know that. What about Austria?' said he, rising from his chair and pacing up and down the room followed by Tikhon, who ran after him, handing him different articles of clothing. 'What of Sweden? How will they cross Pomerania?'

Prince Andrew, seeing that his father insisted, began – at first reluctantly, but gradually with more and more animation, and from habit changing unconsciously from Russian to French as he went on – to explain the plan of operation for the coming campaign. He explained how an army, ninety thousand strong, was to threaten Prussia so as to bring her out of her neutrality and draw her into the war; how part of that army was to join some Swedish forces at Stralsund; how two hundred and twenty thousand Austrians, with a hundred thousand Russians, were to operate in Italy and on the Rhine; how fifty thousand Russians and as many English were to land at Naples, and how a total force of five hundred thousand men was to attack the French from different sides. The old prince did not evince the least interest during this explanation, but as if he were not listening to it continued to dress while walking about, and three times unexpectedly interrupted. Once he stopped it by shouting: 'The white one, the white one!'

This meant that Tikhon was not handing him the waistcoat he wanted. Another time he interrupted, saying:

'And will she soon be confined?' and shaking his head reproachfully said: 'That's bad! Go on, go on.'

The third interruption came when Prince Andrew was finishing his description. The old man began to sing, in the cracked voice of old age: '*Malbrook s'en va-t-en guerre. Dieu sait quand reviendra.*'

His son only smiled.

'I don't say it's a plan I approve of,' said the son; 'I am only telling you what it is. Napoleon has also formed his plan by now, not worse than this one.'

'Well you've told me nothing new,' and the old man repeated, meditatively and rapidly:

'*Dieu sait quand reviendra.* Go to the dining-room.'

24

AT the appointed hour the prince, powdered and shaven, entered the dining-room where his daughter-in-law, Princess Mary, and Mademoiselle Bourienne, were already awaiting him together with his architect, who by a strange caprice of his employer's was admitted to table, though the position of that insignificant individual was such as could certainly not have caused him to expect that honour. The prince, who generally kept very strictly to social distinctions and rarely admitted even important government officials to his table, had unexpectedly selected Michael Ivanovich (who always went into a corner to blow his nose on his checked handkerchief) to illustrate the theory that all men are equals, and had more than once impressed on his daughter that Michael Ivanovich was 'not a whit worse than you or I'. At dinner the prince usually spoke to the taciturn Michael Ivanovich more often than to anyone else.

In the dining-room, which like all the rooms in the house was exceedingly lofty, the members of the household, and the footmen – one behind each chair – stood waiting for the prince to enter. The head butler, napkin on arm, was scanning the setting of the table, making signs to the footmen, and anxiously glancing from the clock to the door by which the prince was to enter. Prince Andrew was looking at a large gilt frame, new to him, containing the genealogical tree of the Princes Bolkonsky, opposite which hung another such frame with a badly-painted portrait (evidently by the hand of the artist belonging to the estate) of a ruling prince, in a crown – an alleged descendant of Rurik and ancestor of the Bolkonskys. Prince Andrew, looking again at that genealogical tree, shook his head, laughing as a man laughs who looks at a portrait so characteristic of the original as to be amusing.

'How thoroughly like him that is!' he said to Princess Mary, who had come up to him.

Princess Mary looked at her brother in surprise. She did not understand what he was laughing at. Everything her father did inspired her with reverence and was beyond question.

'Everyone has his Achilles' heel,' continued Prince Andrew. 'Fancy, with *his* powerful mind, indulging in such nonsense!'

Princess Mary could not understand the boldness of her brother's criticism and was about to reply, when the expected footsteps were heard coming from the study. The prince walked in quickly and jauntily as was his wont, as if intentionally contrasting the briskness of his manners with the strict formality of his house. At that moment the great clock struck two, and another with a shrill tone joined in from the drawing-room. The prince stood still; his lively glittering eyes from under their thick bushy eyebrows sternly scanned all present and rested on the little princess. She felt, as courtiers do when the Tsar enters, the sensation of fear and respect which the old man inspired in all around him. He stroked her hair, and then patted her awkwardly on the back of her neck.

'I'm glad, glad, to see you,' he said, looking attentively into her eyes, and then quickly went to his place and sat down. 'Sit down, sit down! Sit down, Michael Ivanovich!'

He indicated a place beside him to his daughter-in-law. A footman moved the chair for her.

'Ho, ho!' said the old man, casting his eyes on her rounded figure. 'You've been in a hurry. That's bad!'

He laughed in his usual dry, cold, unpleasant way, with his lips only and not with his eyes.

'You must walk, as much as possible, as much as possible,' he said.

The little princess did not, or did not wish to, hear his words.

She was silent and seemed confused. The prince asked her about her father, and she began to smile and talk. He asked about mutual acquaintances, and she became still more animated and chattered away giving him greetings from various people and retailing the town gossip.

'Countess Apraksina, poor thing, has lost her husband and she has cried her eyes out,' she said, growing more and more lively.

As she became animated the prince looked at her more and more sternly, and suddenly, as if he had studied her sufficiently and had formed a definite idea of her, he turned away and addressed Michael Ivanovich.

'Well, Michael Ivanovich, our Buonaparte will be having a bad time of it. Prince Andrew' (he always spoke thus of his son) 'has been telling me what forces are being collected against him! While you and I have never thought much of him.'

Michael Ivanovich did not at all know when 'you and I' had said such things about Bonaparte, but understanding that he was wanted as a peg on which to hang the prince's favourite topic, he looked inquiringly at the young prince, wondering what would follow.

'He is a great tactician!' said the prince to his son, pointing to the architect.

And the conversation again turned on the war, on Bonaparte, and the generals and statesmen of the day. The old prince seemed convinced not only that all the men of the day were mere babies who did not know the A B C of war or of politics, and that Bonaparte was an insignificant little Frenchy, successful only because there were no longer any Potëmkins or Suvorovs left to oppose him; but he was also convinced that there were no political difficulties in Europe and no real war, but only a sort of puppet-show at which the men of the day were playing, pretending to do something real. Prince Andrew gaily bore with his father's ridicule of the new men, and drew him on and listened to him with evident pleasure.

'The past always seems good,' said he, 'but did not Suvorov himself fall into a trap Moreau set him, and from which he did not know how to escape?'

'Who told you that? Who?' cried the prince. 'Suvorov!' And he jerked away his plate, which Tikhon briskly caught. 'Suvorov!... Consider, Prince Andrew! Two... Frederick and Suvorov; Moreau! ... Moreau would have been a prisoner if Suvorov had had a free hand; but he had the Hofs-kriegs-wurst-schnapps-Rath* on his hands. It would have puzzled the devil himself! When you get there you'll find out what those Hofs-kriegs-wurst-Raths are! Suvorov couldn't manage them so what chance has Michael Kutuzov? No, my dear boy,' he continued, 'you and your generals won't get on against Buonaparte; you'll have to call in the French, so that birds of a feather may fight together. The German, Pahlen, has been sent to New York in America, to fetch the Frenchman Moreau,* he said, alluding to the invitation made that year to Moreau to enter the Russian service. . . . 'Wonderful! . . . Were the Potëmkins, Suvorovs, and Orlovs Germans? No, lad, either you fellows have all lost your wits, or I have outlived mine. May God help you, but we'll see what will happen. Buonaparte has become a great commander among them! Hm! . . .'

'I don't at all say that all the plans are good,' said Prince Andrew, 'I am only surprised at your opinion of Bonaparte. You may laugh as much as you like, but all the same Bonaparte is a great general!'

'Michael Ivanovich!' cried the old prince to the architect who, busy with his roast meat, hoped he had been forgotten: 'Didn't I tell you Buonaparte was a great tactician? Here, he says the same thing.'

'To be sure, your excellency,' replied the architect.

The prince again laughed his frigid laugh.

'Buonaparte was born with a silver spoon in his mouth. He has got splendid soldiers. Besides he began by attacking Germans. And only idlers have failed to beat the Germans. Since the world began everybody has beaten the Germans. They beat no one – except one another. He made his reputation fighting them.'

And the prince began explaining all the blunders which, according to him, Bonaparte had made in his campaigns and even in politics. His son made no rejoinder, but it was evident that whatever arguments were presented he was as little able as his father to change his opinion. He listened, refraining from a reply, and involuntarily wondered how this old man, living alone in the country for so many years, could know and discuss so minutely and acutely all the recent European military and political events.

'You think I'm an old man and don't understand the present state of affairs?' concluded his father. 'But it troubles me. I don't sleep at night. Come now, where has this great commander of yours shown his skill?' he concluded.

'That would take too long to tell,' answered the son.

'Well, then go off to your Bonaparte! Mademoiselle Bourienne, here's another admirer of that powder-monkey emperor of yours,' he exclaimed in excellent French.

'You know, Prince, I am not a Bonapartist!'

'*Dieu sait quand reviendra*' ... hummed the prince out of tune and, with a laugh still more so, he quitted the table.

The little princess during the whole discussion and the rest of the dinner sat silent, glancing with a frightened look now at her father-in-law and now at Princess Mary. When they left the table she took her sister-in-law's arm and drew her into another room.

'What a clever man your father is,' said she; 'perhaps that is why I am afraid of him.'

'Oh, he is so kind!' answered Princess Mary.

25

PRINCE ANDREW was to leave next evening. The old prince, not altering his routine, retired as usual after dinner. The little princess was in her sister-in-law's room. Prince Andrew in a travelling coat without epaulettes had been packing with his valet in the rooms assigned to him. After inspecting the carriage himself and seeing the trunks put in, he ordered the horses to be harnessed. Only those things he always kept with him remained in his room; a small box, a large canteen fitted with silver plate, two Turkish pistols, and a sabre – a present from his father who had brought it from the siege of Ochakov.* All these travelling effects of Prince Andrew's were in very good order: new, clean, and in cloth covers carefully tied with tapes.

When starting on a journey or changing their mode of life, men capable of reflection are generally in a serious frame of mind. At such moments one reviews the past and plans for the future. Prince Andrew's face looked very thoughtful and tender. With his hands behind him he paced briskly from corner to corner of the room looking straight before him and thoughtfully shaking his head. Did he fear going to the war, or was he sad at leaving his wife? – perhaps both, but evidently he did not wish to be seen in that mood, for hearing footsteps in the passage he hurriedly unclasped his hands, stopped at a table as if tying the cover of the small box, and assumed his usual tranquil and impenetrable expression. It was the heavy tread of Princess Mary that he heard.

'I hear you have given orders to harness,' she cried, panting (she had apparently been running), 'and I did so wish to have another talk with you alone! God knows how long we may again be parted. You are not angry with me for coming? You have changed so, Andrusha,' she added, as if to explain such a question.

She smiled as she uttered his pet name, 'Andrusha'. It was

obviously strange to her to think that this stern handsome man should be Andrusha – the slender mischievous boy who had been her playfellow in childhood.

'And where is Lise?' he asked, answering her question only by a smile.

'She was so tired that she has fallen asleep on the sofa in my room. Oh, Andrew! What a treasure of a wife you have,' said she, sitting down on the sofa, facing her brother. 'She is quite a child: such a dear, merry child. I have grown so fond of her.'

Prince Andrew was silent, but the princess noticed the ironical and contemptuous look that showed itself on his face.

'One must be indulgent to little weaknesses; who is free from them, Andrew? Don't forget that she has grown up and been educated in society, and so her position now is not a rosy one. We should enter into everyone's situation. *Tout comprendre, c'est tout pardonner.* Think what it must be for her, poor thing, after what she has been used to, to be parted from her husband and be left alone in the country, in her condition! It's very hard.'

Prince Andrew smiled as he looked at his sister, as we smile at those we think we thoroughly understand.

'You live in the country and don't think the life terrible,' he replied.

'I . . . that's different. Why speak of me? I don't want any other life, and can't, for I know no other. But think, Andrew: for a young society woman to be buried in the country during the best years of her life, all alone, – for papa is always busy, and I . . . well, you know what poor resources I have for entertaining a woman used to the best society. There is only Mademoiselle Bourienne. . . .'

'I don't like your Mademoiselle Bourienne at all,' said Prince Andrew.

'No? She is very nice and kind, and above all she's much to be pitied. She has no one, no one. To tell the truth, I don't need her, and she's even in my way. You know I always was a savage, and now am even more so. I like being alone. . . . Father likes her very much. She and Michael Ivanovich are the two people to whom he is always gentle and kind, because he has been a benefactor to them both. As Sterne says: "We don't love people so much for the good they have done us, as for the good we have done them." Father took her when she was homeless after losing her own father. She is very good-natured, and my father likes her way of reading. She reads to him in the evenings and reads splendidly.'

'To be quite frank, Mary, I expect father's character sometimes makes things trying for you, doesn't it?' Prince Andrew asked suddenly.

Princess Mary was first surprised and then aghast at this question.

'For me? For me? ... Trying for me! ...' said she.

'He always was rather harsh; and now I should think he's getting very trying,' said Prince Andrew, apparently speaking lightly of their father in order to puzzle or test his sister.

'You are good in every way, Andrew, but you have a kind of intellectual pride,' said the princess, following the train of her own thoughts rather than the trend of the conversation – 'and that's a great sin. How can one judge father? But even if one might, what feeling except veneration could such a man as my father evoke? And I am so contented and happy with him. I only wish you were all as happy as I am.'

Her brother shook his head incredulously.

'The only thing that is hard for me ... I will tell you the truth, Andrew, – is father's way of treating religious subjects. I don't understand how a man of his immense intellect can fail to see what is as clear as day, and can go so far astray. That is the only thing that makes me unhappy. But even in this I can see lately a shade of improvement. His satire has been less bitter of late, and there was a monk he received and had a long talk with.'

'Ah! my dear, I am afraid you and your monk are wasting your powder,' said Prince Andrew banteringly yet tenderly.

'Ah! *mon ami*, I only pray, and hope that God will hear me. Andrew ...' she said timidly after a moment's silence, 'I have a great favour to ask of you.'

'What is it, dear?'

'No – promise that you will not refuse! It will give you no trouble and is nothing unworthy of you, but it will comfort me. Promise, Andrusha! ...' said she, putting her hand in her reticule but not yet taking out what she was holding inside it, as if what she held were the subject of her request and must not be shown before the request was granted.

She looked timidly at her brother.

'Even if it were a great deal of trouble ...' answered Prince Andrew as if guessing what it was about.

'Think what you please! I know you are just like father. Think as you please, but do this for my sake! Please do! Father's father, our grandfather, wore it in all his wars.' (She still did not take out what she was holding in her reticule.) 'So you promise?'

'Of course. What is it?'

'Andrew, I bless you with this icon and you must promise me you will never take it off. Do you promise?'

'If it does not weigh a hundredweight and won't break my

neck ... To please you ...' said Prince Andrew. But immediately, noticing the pained expression his joke had brought to his sister's face, he repented and added: 'I am glad to; really, dear, I am very glad.'

'Against your will He will save and have mercy on you and bring you to Himself, for in Him alone is truth and peace,' said she in a voice trembling with emotion, solemnly holding up in both hands before her brother a small, oval, antique, dark-faced icon of the Saviour in a gold setting, on a finely wrought silver chain.

She crossed herself, kissed the icon, and handed it to Andrew.

'Please, Andrew, for my sake! ...'

Rays of gentle light shone from her large timid eyes. Those eyes lit up the whole of her thin sickly face and made it beautiful. Her brother would have taken the icon, but she stopped him. Andrew understood, crossed himself, and kissed the icon. There was a look of tenderness, for he was touched, but also a gleam of irony on his face.

'Thank you, my dear.' She kissed him on the forehead and sat down again on the sofa. They were silent for a while.

'As I was saying to you, Andrew, be kind and generous as you always used to be. Don't judge Lise harshly,' she began. 'She is so sweet, so good-natured, and her position now is a very hard one.'

'I do not think I have complained of my wife to you, Masha, or blamed her. Why do you say all this to me?'

Red patches appeared on Princess Mary's face and she was silent as if she felt guilty.

'I have said nothing to you, but you have already been talked to. And I am sorry for that,' he went on.

The patches grew deeper on her forehead, neck and cheeks. She tried to say something but could not. Her brother had guessed right: the little princess had been crying after dinner and had spoken of her forebodings about her confinement, and of how she dreaded it, and had complained of her fate, her father-in-law and her husband. After crying she had fallen asleep. Prince Andrew felt sorry for his sister.

'Know this, Masha: I can't reproach, have not reproached, and never shall reproach *my wife* with anything, and I cannot reproach myself with anything in regard to her; and that always will be so in whatever circumstances I may be placed. But if you want to know the truth ... if you want to know whether I am happy? No! Is she happy? No! But why this is so I don't know ...'

As he said this he rose, went to his sister and, stooping, kissed her forehead. His fine eyes lit up with a thoughtful, kindly, and unaccustomed brightness, but he was looking not at his sister but over her head towards the darkness of the open doorway.

'Let us go to her, I must say good-bye. Or – go and wake her, and I'll come in a moment. Petrushka!' he called to his valet: 'Come here, take these away. Put this on the seat and this to the right.'

Princess Mary rose and moved to the door, then stopped and said:

'Andrew, if you had faith you would have turned to God and asked him to give you the love you do not feel, and your prayer would have been answered.'

'Well, maybe!' said Prince Andrew. 'Go, Masha; I'll come immediately.'

On the way to his sister's room, in the passage which connected one wing with the other, Prince Andrew met Mademoiselle Bourienne smiling sweetly. It was the third time that day that, with an ecstatic and artless smile, she had met him in secluded passages.

'Oh! I thought you were in your room,' she said, for some reason blushing and dropping her eyes.

Prince Andrew looked sternly at her and an expression of anger suddenly came over his face. He said nothing to her but looked at her forehead and hair without looking at her eyes, with such contempt that the Frenchwoman blushed and went away without a word. When he reached his sister's room his wife was already awake and her merry voice, hurrying one word after another, came through the open door. She was speaking as usual in French, and as if after long self-restraint she wished to make up for lost time.

'No, but imagine the old Countess Zubova,* with false curls and her mouth full of false teeth, as if she were trying to cheat old age. . . . Ha, ha, ha! Mary!'

This very sentence about Countess Zubova and this same laugh Prince Andrew had already heard from his wife in the presence of others some five times. He entered the room softly. The little princess, plump and rosy, was sitting in an easy chair with her work in her hands, talking incessantly, repeating Petersburg reminiscences and even phrases. Prince Andrew came up, stroked her hair, and asked if she felt rested after their journey. She answered him, and continued her chatter.

The coach with six horses was waiting at the porch. It was an autumn night, so dark that the coachman could not see the carriage-pole. Servants with lanterns were bustling about in the porch. The immense house was brilliant with lights shining through its lofty windows. The domestic serfs were crowding in the hall, waiting to bid good-bye to the young prince. The members of the household were all gathered in the reception hall: Michael Ivanovich, Mademoiselle Bourienne, Princess Mary, and the little princess. Prince Andrew had been called to his father's study, as the latter wished to say good-bye to him alone. All were waiting for them to come out.

When Prince Andrew entered the study the old man in his old-age spectacles and white dressing-gown, in which he received no one but his son, sat at the table writing. He glanced round.

'Going?' And he went on writing.

'I've come to say good-bye.'

'Kiss me here,' and he touched his cheek: 'Thanks, thanks!'

'What do you thank me for?'

'For not dilly-dallying and not hanging to a woman's apron-strings. The Service before everything. Thanks, thanks!' And he went on writing, so that his quill spluttered and squeaked. 'If you have anything to say, say it. These two things can be done together,' he added.

'About my wife.... I am ashamed as it is to leave her on your hands....'

'Why talk nonsense? Say what you want.'

'When her confinement is due, send to Moscow for an *accoucheur* ... Let him be here....'

The old prince stopped writing and, as if not understanding, fixed his stern eyes on his son.

'I know that no one can help if nature does not do her work,' said Prince Andrew, evidently confused. 'I know that out of a million cases only one goes wrong, but it is her fancy and mine. They have been telling her things. She has had a dream and is frightened.'

'Hm... Hm...' muttered the old prince to himself, finishing what he was writing. 'I'll do it.'

He signed with a flourish and suddenly turning to his son began to laugh.

'It's a bad business, eh?'

'What is bad, father?'

'The wife!' said the old prince, briefly and significantly.

'I don't understand!' said Prince Andrew.

'Yes, it can't be helped, lad,' said the prince. 'They're all like that; one can't unmarry. Don't be afraid; I won't tell anyone, but you know it yourself.'

He seized his son by the hand with small bony fingers, shook it, looked straight into his son's face with keen eyes which seemed to see through him, and again laughed his frigid laugh.

The son sighed, thus admitting that his father had understood him. The old man continued to fold and seal his letter, snatching up and throwing down the wax, the seal, and the paper, with his accustomed rapidity.

'What's to be done? She's pretty! I will do everything. Make your mind easy,' said he in abrupt sentences while sealing his letter.

Andrew did not speak; he was both pleased and displeased that his father understood him. The old man got up and gave the letter to his son.

'Listen!' said he; 'don't worry about your wife: what can be done shall be. Now listen! Give this letter to Michael Ilarionovich.* I have written that he should make use of you in proper places and not keep you long as an adjutant: a bad position! Tell him I remember and like him. Write and tell me how he receives you. If he is all right – serve him. Nicholas Bolkonsky's son need not serve under anyone if he is in disfavour. Now come here.'

He spoke so rapidly that he did not finish half his words, but his son was accustomed to understand him. He led him to the desk, raised the lid, drew out a drawer, and took out an exercise-book filled with his bold, tall, close handwriting.

'I shall probably die before you. So remember, these are my memoirs; hand them to the Emperor after my death. Now here is a Lombard-bond* and a letter; it is a premium for the man who writes a history of Suvorov's wars. Send it to the Academy. Here are some jottings for you to read when I am gone. You will find them useful.'

Andrew did not tell his father that he would no doubt live a long time yet. He felt that he must not say it.

'I will do it all, father,' he said.

'Well, now, good-bye!' He gave his son his hand to kiss, and embraced him. 'Remember this, Prince Andrew, if they kill you it will hurt me, your old father. . . .' He paused unexpectedly, and then in a querulous voice suddenly shrieked: 'but if I hear that you have not behaved like a son of Nicholas Bolkonsky, I shall be ashamed!'

'You need not have said that to me, father,' said the son with a smile.

The old man was silent.

'I also wanted to ask you,' continued Prince Andrew, 'if I'm killed and if I have a son, do not let him be taken away from you – as I said yesterday . . . let him grow up with you . . . Please.'

'Not let the wife have him?' said the old man, and laughed.

They stood silent, facing one another. The old man's sharp eyes were fixed straight on his son's. Something twitched in the lower part of the old prince's face.

'We've said good-bye. Go!' he suddenly shouted in a loud, angry voice, opening his door.

'What is it? What?' asked both princesses when they saw for a moment at the door Prince Andrew and the figure of the old man in a white dressing-gown, spectacled and wigless, shouting in an angry voice.

Prince Andrew sighed and made no reply.

'Well!' he said, turning to his wife.

And this 'Well!' sounded coldly ironic, as if he were saying: 'Now go through your performance.'

'Andrew, already!' said the little princess, turning pale and looking with dismay at her husband.

He embraced her. She screamed and fell unconscious on his shoulder.

He cautiously released the shoulder she leant on, looked into her face, and carefully placed her in an easy chair.

'Adieu, Mary,' said he gently to his sister, taking her by the hand and kissing her, and then he left the room with rapid steps.

The little princess lay in the arm-chair, Mademoiselle Bourienne chafing her temples. Princess Mary, supporting her sister-in-law, still looked with her beautiful eyes full of tears at the door through which Prince Andrew had gone, and made the sign of the cross in his direction. From the study, like pistol shots, came the frequent sound of the old man angrily blowing his nose. Hardly had Prince Andrew gone when the study door opened quickly, and the stern figure of the old man in the white dressing-gown looked out.

'Gone? That's all right!' said he; and looking angrily at the unconscious little princess, he shook his head reprovingly and slammed the door.

END OF PART ONE

PART TWO

1

In October 1805 a Russian army was occupying the villages and towns of the Archduchy of Austria, and yet other regiments freshly arriving from Russia were settling near the fortress of Braunau and burdening the inhabitants on whom they were quartered. Braunau was the head-quarters of the commander-in-chief, Kutuzov.

On October 11th, 1805, one of the infantry regiments that had just reached Braunau had halted half a mile from the town, waiting to be inspected by the commander-in-chief. Despite the un-Russian appearance of the locality and surroundings – fruit gardens, stone fences, tiled roofs, and hills in the distance – and despite the fact that the inhabitants (who gazed with curiosity at the soldiers) were not Russians, the regiment had just the appearance of any Russian regiment preparing for an inspection anywhere in the heart of Russia.

On the evening of the last day's march an order had been received that the commander-in-chief would inspect the regiment on the march. Though the words of the order were not clear to the regimental commander, and the question arose whether the troops were to be in marching order or not, it was decided at a consultation between the battalion commanders, to present the regiment in parade order, on the principle that it is always better to 'bow too low than not bow low enough'. So the soldiers, after a twenty-mile march, were kept mending and cleaning all night long without closing their eyes, while the adjutants and company commanders calculated and reckoned, and by morning the regiment – instead of the straggling, disorderly crowd it had been on its last march the day before – presented a well-ordered array of two thousand men each of whom knew his place and his duty, had every button and every strap in place, and shone with cleanliness. And not only externally was all in order, but had it pleased the commander-in-chief to look under the uniforms he would have found on every man a clean shirt, and in every knapsack, the appointed number of articles, 'awl, soap, and all', as the soldiers say. There was only one circumstance concerning which no one could be at ease. It was the state of the soldiers' boots. More than half the men's boots were in holes. But this defect was not due to any fault of the regimental commander, for in spite of repeated demands boots had not been issued by the Austrian commissariat, and the regiment had marched some seven hundred miles.

The commander of the regiment was an elderly, choleric, stout and thick-set general with grizzled eyebrows and whiskers, and wider from chest to back than across the shoulders. He had on a brand new uniform showing the creases where it had been folded, and thick gold epaulettes which seemed to stand rather than lie down on his massive shoulders. He had the air of a man happily performing one of the most solemn duties of his life. He walked about in front of the line and at every step pulled himself up, slightly arching his back. It was plain that the commander admired his regiment, rejoiced in it, and that his whole mind was engrossed by it, yet his strut seemed to indicate that besides military matters social interests and the fair sex occupied no small part of his thoughts.

'Well, Michael Mitrich, sir?' he said, addressing one of the battalion commanders who smilingly pressed forward (it was plain that they both felt happy). 'We had our hands full last night. However, I think the regiment is not a bad one, eh?'

The battalion commander perceived the jovial irony and laughed.

'It would not be turned off the field even on the Tsaritsin Meadow.'*

'What?' asked the commander.

At that moment, on the road from the town on which signallers had been posted, two men appeared on horseback. They were an aide-de-camp followed by a Cossack.

The aide-de-camp was sent to confirm the order which had not been clearly worded the day before, namely, that the commander-in-chief wished to see the regiment just in the state in which it had been on the march: in their greatcoats, and packs, and without any preparation whatever.

A member of the Hofkriegsrath from Vienna had come to Kutuzov the day before with proposals and demands for him to join up with the army of the Archduke Ferdinand and Mack, and Kutuzov, not considering this junction advisable, meant among other arguments in support of his view, to show the Austrian general the wretched state in which the troops arrived from Russia. With this object he intended to meet the regiment; so the worse the condition it was in, the better pleased the commander-in-chief would be. Though the aide-de-camp did not know these circumstances, he nevertheless delivered the definite order that the men should be in their greatcoats and in marching-order, and that the commander-in-chief would otherwise be dissatisfied. On hearing this the regimental commander hung his head, silently shrugged his shoulders, and spread out his arms with a choleric gesture.

'A fine mess we've made of it!' he remarked.

'There now! Didn't I tell you, Michael Mitrich, that if it was said "on the march" it meant in greatcoats?' said he reproachfully to the battalion commander. Oh, my God!' he added stepping resolutely forward. 'Company commanders!' he shouted in a voice accustomed to command. 'Sergeant-majors! . . . How soon will he be here?' he asked the aide-de-camp with a respectful politeness evidently relating to the personage he was referring to.

'In an hour's time, I should say.'

'Shall we have time to change clothes?'

'I don't know, general. . . .'

The regimental commander, going up to the line himself, ordered the soldiers to change into their greatcoats. The company commanders ran off to their companies, the sergeant-majors began bustling (the greatcoats were not in very good condition), and instantly the squares that had up to then been in regular order and silent, began to sway and stretch and hum with voices. On all sides soldiers were running to and fro, throwing up their knapsacks with a jerk of their shoulders and pulling the straps over their heads, unstrapping their overcoats and drawing the sleeves on with upraised arms.

In half an hour all was again in order, only the squares had become grey instead of black. The regimental commander walked with his jerky steps to the front of the regiment and examined it from a distance.

'Whatever is this? This!' he shouted and stood still. 'Commander of the third company!'

'Commander of the third company wanted by the general! . . . commander to the general . . . third company to the commander.' The words passed along the lines and an adjutant ran to look for the missing officer.

When the eager but misrepeated words had reached their destination in a cry of: 'The general to the third company,' the missing officer appeared from behind his company, and though he was a middle-aged man and not in the habit of running, trotted awkwardly stumbling on his toes towards the general. The captain's face showed the uneasiness of a schoolboy who is told to repeat a lesson he has not learnt. Spots appeared on his nose, the redness of which was evidently due to intemperance, and his mouth twitched nervously. The general looked the captain up and down as he came up panting, slackening his pace as he approached.

'You will soon be dressing your men in petticoats! What is this?' shouted the regimental commander, thrusting forward his jaw and pointing at a soldier in the ranks of the third company in a great-coat of bluish cloth, which contrasted with the others. 'What have you been after? The commander-in-chief is expected and you leave your place? Eh? I'll teach you to dress the men in fancy coats for a parade.... Eh ... ?'

The commander of the company, with his eyes fixed on his superior pressed two fingers more and more rigidly to his cap, as if in this pressure lay his only hope of salvation.

'Well, why don't you speak? Whom have you got there dressed up as a Hungarian?' said the commander with an austere gibe.

'Your Excellency ...'

'Well, your Excellency what? Your Excellency! But what about your Excellency? ... nobody knows.'

'Your Excellency, it's the officer Dolokhov, who has been reduced to the ranks,' said the captain softly.

'Well? Has he been degraded into a field-marshal, or into a soldier? If a soldier, he should be dressed in regulation uniform like the others.'

'Your Excellency, you gave him leave yourself, on the march.'

'Gave him leave? Leave? That's just like you young men,' said the regimental commander, cooling down a little. 'Leave indeed. ... One says a word to you and you ... What?' he added with renewed irritation, 'I beg you to dress your men decently.'

And the commander, turning to look at the adjutant, directed his jerky steps down the line. He was evidently pleased at his own display of anger and walking up to the regiment wished to find a further excuse for wrath. Having snapped at an officer for an unpolished badge, at another because his line was not straight, he reached the third company.

'H-o-o-w are you standing? Where's your leg? Your leg?' shouted the commander with a tone of suffering in his voice, while there were still five men between him and Dolokhov with his bluish-grey uniform.

Dolokhov slowly straightened his bent knee, looking straight with his clear, insolent eyes in the general's face.

'Why a blue coat? Off with it ... Sergeant-major! Change his coat ... the ras ...'. He did not finish.

'General, I must obey orders, but I am not bound to endure ...' Dolokhov hurriedly interrupted.

'No talking in the ranks! . . . No talking, no talking!'

'Not bound to endure insults,' Dolokhov concluded in loud, ringing tones.

The eyes of the general and the soldier met. The general became silent, angrily pulling down his tight scarf.

'I request you to have the goodness to change your coat,' he said as he turned away.

2

'HE'S coming!' shouted the signaller at that moment.

The regimental commander, flushing, ran to his horse, seized the stirrup with trembling hands, threw his body across the saddle, righted himself, drew his sabre, and with a happy and resolute countenance, opening his mouth awry, prepared to shout. The regiment fluttered like a bird preening its plumage, and became motionless.

'Att-ention!' shouted the regimental commander in a soul-shaking voice which expressed joy for himself, severity for the regiment, and welcome for the approaching chief.

Along the broad country road, edged on both sides by trees, came a high, light-blue Viennese calèche, slightly creaking on its springs and drawn by six horses at a smart trot. Behind the calèche galloped the suite and a convoy of Croats. Beside Kutuzov sat an Austrian general, in a white uniform that looked strange among the Russian black ones. The calèche stopped in front of the regiment. Kutuzov and the Austrian general were talking in low voices, and Kutuzov smiled slightly as treading heavily he stepped down from the carriage just as if those two thousand men breathlessly gazing at him and the regimental commander did not exist.

The word of command rang out, and again the regiment quivered, as with a jingling sound it presented arms. Then amidst a dead silence the feeble voice of the commander-in-chief was heard. The regiment roared, 'Health to your Ex . . . len . . . len . . . lency!' and again all became silent. At first Kutuzov stood still while the regiment moved; then he and the general in white, accompanied by the suite, walked between the ranks.

From the way the regimental commander saluted the commander-in-chief and devoured him with his eyes, drawing himself up obsequiously, and from the way he walked through the ranks behind the generals, bending forward and hardly able to restrain his jerky movements, and from the way he darted forward at every word or gesture of the commander-in-chief, it was evident that he performed his duty as a subordinate with even greater zeal than his duty as a commander. Thanks to the strictness and assiduity of its commander the regiment, in comparison with others that had reached Braunau at the same time, was in splendid condition. There were only 217 sick and stragglers. Everything was in good order except the boots.

Kutuzov walked through the ranks, sometimes stopping to say a few friendly words to officers he had known in the Turkish war, sometimes also to the soldiers. Looking at their boots he several times shook his head sadly, pointing them out to the Austrian general with an expression which seemed to say that he was not blaming anyone, but could not help noticing what a bad state of things it was. The regimental commander ran forward on each such occasion fearing to miss a single word of the commander-in-chief's regarding the regiment. Behind Kutuzov, at a distance that allowed every softly spoken word to be heard, followed some twenty men of his suite. These gentlemen talked among themselves and sometimes laughed. Nearest of all to the commander-in-chief walked a handsome adjutant. This was Prince Bolkonsky. Beside him was his comrade Nesvitsky, a tall staff-officer, extremely stout, with a kindly, smiling, handsome face and moist eyes. Nesvitsky could hardly keep from laughter provoked by a swarthy hussar officer who walked beside him. This hussar, with a grave face and without a smile or a change in the expression of his fixed eyes, watched the regimental commander's back and mimicked his every movement. Each time the commander started and bent forward, the hussar started and bent forward in exactly the same manner, Nesvitsky laughed and nudged the others to make them look at the wag.

Kutuzov walked slowly and languidly past thousands of eyes which were starting from their sockets to watch their chief. On reaching the third company he suddenly stopped. His suite not having expected this, involuntarily came closer to him.

'Ah, Timokhin!' said he, recognizing the red-nosed captain who had been reprimanded on account of the blue greatcoat.

One would have thought it impossible for a man to stretch himself more than Timokhin had done when he was reprimanded by the regimental commander, but now that the commander-in-chief addressed him he drew himself up to such an extent that it seemed he could not have sustained it had the commander-in-chief continued to look at him, and so Kutuzov, who evidently understood his case and wished him nothing but good, quickly turned away, a scarcely perceptible smile flitting over his scarred and puffy face.

'Another Ismail comrade,' said he. 'A brave officer! Are you satisfied with him?' he asked the regimental commander.

And the latter – unconscious that he was being reflected in the hussar officer as in a looking-glass – started, moved forward, and answered: 'Highly satisfied, your Excellency!'

'We all have our weaknesses,' said Kutuzov smiling and walking away from him. 'He used to have a predilection for Bacchus.'

The regimental commander was afraid he might be blamed for this, and did not answer. The hussar at that moment noticed the face of the red-nosed captain and his drawn-in stomach, and mimicked his expression and pose with such exactitude that Nesvitsky could not help laughing. Kutuzov turned round. The officer evidently had complete control of his face, and while Kutuzov was turning managed to make a grimace and then assume a most serious, deferential, and innocent expression.

The third company was the last, and Kutuzov pondered, apparently trying to recollect something. Prince Andrew stepped forward from among the suite and said softly in French:

'You told me to remind you of the officer Dolokhov, reduced to the ranks in this regiment.'

Dolokhov, who had already changed into a soldier's grey greatcoat, did not wait to be called. The shapely figure of the fair-haired soldier, with his clear blue eyes, stepped forward from the ranks, went up to the commander-in-chief, and presented arms.

'Have you a complaint to make?' Kutuzov asked with a slight frown.

'This is Dolokhov,' said Prince Andrew.

'Ah!' said Kutuzov. 'I hope this will be a lesson to you. Do your duty. The Emperor is gracious, and I shan't forget you if you deserve well.'

The clear blue eyes looked at the commander-in-chief just as boldly as they had looked at the regimental commander, seeming by their expression to tear open the veil of convention that separates a commander-in-chief so widely from a private.

'One thing I ask of your Excellency,' Dolokhov said in his firm, ringing, deliberate voice. 'I ask an opportunity to atone for my fault and prove my devotion to his Majesty the Emperor and to Russia!'

Kutuzov turned away. The same smile of the eyes with which he had turned from Captain Timokhin again flitted over his face. He turned away with a grimace as if to say that everything Dolokhov had said to him and everything he could say had long been known to him, that he was weary of it and it was not at all what he wanted. He turned away and went to the carriage.

The regiment broke up into companies, which went to their appointed quarters near Braunau, where they hoped to receive boots and clothes and to rest after their hard marches.

'You won't bear me a grudge, Prokhor Ignatych?' said the regimental commander, overtaking the third company on its way to its quarters and riding up to Captain Timokhin who was walking in front. (The regimental commander's face now that the inspection was happily over beamed with irrepressible delight.) 'It's in the Emperor's service . . . it can't be helped . . . one is sometimes a bit hasty on parade . . . I am the first to apologize, you know me! . . . He was very pleased!' And he held out his hand to the captain.

'Don't mention it, General, as if I'd be so bold!' replied the captain, his nose growing redder as he gave a smile which showed where two front teeth were missing that had been knocked out by the butt end of a gun at Ismail.

'And tell Mr Dolokhov that I won't forget him – he may be quite easy. And tell me, please – I've been meaning to ask – how is he behaving himself, and in general . . .'

'As far as the service goes he is quite punctilious, your Excellency; but his character . . .' said Timokhin.

'And what about his character?' asked the regimental commander.

'It's different on different days,' answered the captain. 'One day he is sensible, well educated and good-natured, and the next he's a wild beast. . . . In Poland, if you please, he nearly killed a Jew.'

'Oh, well, well!' remarked the regimental commander. 'Still, one must have pity on a young man in misfortune. You know he has important connexions . . . Well then, you just . . .'

'I will, your Excellency,' said Timokhin, showing by his smile that he understood his commander's wish.

'Well, of course, of course!'

The regimental commander sought out Dolokhov in the ranks, and reining in his horse, said to him:

'After the next affair . . . epaulettes.'

Dolokhov looked round but did not say anything, nor did the mocking smile on his lips change.

'Well, that's all right,' continued the regimental commander. 'A cup of vodka for the men from me,' he added so that the soldiers could hear. 'I thank you all! God be praised!' and he rode past that company and overtook the next one.

'Well, he's really a good fellow, one can serve under him,' said Timokhin to the subaltern beside him.

'In a word, a hearty one...' said the subaltern, laughing (the regimental commander was nicknamed *King of Hearts*).

The cheerful mood of their officers after the inspection infected the soldiers. The company marched on gaily. The soldiers' voices could be heard on every side.

'And they said Kutuzov was blind of one eye?'

'And so he is! Quite blind!'

'No, friend, he is sharper eyed than you are. Boots and leg-bands* ... he noticed everything...'

'When he looked at my feet, friend... well, thinks I...'

'And that other one with him, the Austrian, looked as if he were smeared with chalk – as white as flour! I suppose they polish him up as they do the guns.'

'I say, Fedeshon!... Did he say when the battles are to begin? You were near him. Everybody said that Buonaparte himself was at Braunau.'

'Buonaparte himself... Just listen to the fool, what he doesn't know! The Prussians are up in arms now. The Austrians, you see, are putting them down. When they've been put down, the war with Buonaparte will begin. And he says Buonaparte is in Braunau! Shows you're a fool. You'd better listen more carefully!'

'What devils these quartermasters are! See, the fifth company is turned into the village already... they will have their buck-wheat cooked before we reach our quarters.'

'Give me a biscuit, you devil!'

'And did you give me tobacco yesterday? That's just it, friend! Ah well, never mind, here you are.'

'They might call a halt here or we'll have to do another four miles without eating.'

'Wasn't it fine when those Germans gave us lifts!* You just sit still and are drawn along.'

'And here, friend, the people are quite beggarly. There they all seemed to be Poles – all under the Russian crown – but here they're all regular Germans.'

'Singers to the front!' came the captain's order.

And from the different ranks some twenty men ran to the front. A drummer, their leader, turned round facing the singers, and flourishing his arm began a long-drawn-out soldiers' song, commencing with the words: '*Morning dawned, the sun was rising*' and concluding: '*On then, brothers, on to glory, led by Father Kamensky.*' This song had been composed in the Turkish campaign and was now being sung in Austria, the only change being that the words 'Father Kamensky' were replaced by 'Father Kutuzov'.

Having jerked out these last words as soldiers do and waved his arms as if flinging something to the ground, the drummer – a lean, handsome soldier of forty – looked sternly at the singers and screwed up his eyes. Then having satisfied himself that all eyes were fixed on him, he raised both arms as if carefully lifting some invisible but precious object above his head and, holding it there for some seconds, suddenly flung it down and began:

'*Oh, my bower, oh, my bower . . .!*'

'*Oh, my bower new . . .!*' chimed in twenty voices, and the castanet-player in spite of the burden of his equipment rushed out to the front and walking backwards before the company jerked his shoulders and flourished his castanets as if threatening someone. The soldiers, swinging their arms and keeping time spontaneously, marched with long steps. Behind the company the sound of wheels, the creaking of springs, and the tramp of horses' hoofs were heard. Kutuzov and his suite were returning to the town. The commander-in-chief made a sign that the men should continue to march at ease, and he and all his suite showed pleasure at the sound of the singing and the sight of the dancing soldier and the gay and smartly marching men. In the second file from the right flank, beside which the carriage passed the company, a blue-eyed soldier involuntarily attracted notice. It was Dolokhov marching with particular grace and boldness in time to the song and looking at those driving past as if he pitied all who were not at that moment marching with the company. The hussar cornet of Kutuzov's suite who had mimicked the regimental commander, fell back from the carriage and rode up to Dolokhov.

Hussar cornet Zherkov had at one time, in Petersburg, belonged to the wild set led by Dolokhov. Zherkov had met Dolokhov abroad as a private and had not seen fit to recognize him. But now that Kutuzov had spoken to the gentleman-ranker, he addressed him with the cordiality of an old friend.

'My dear fellow how are you?' said he through the singing, making his horse keep pace with the company.

'How am I?' Dolokhov answered coldly. 'I am as you see.'

The lively song gave a special flavour to the tone of free and easy gaiety with which Zherkov spoke, and to the intentional coldness of Dolokhov's reply.

'And how do you get on with the officers?' inquired Zherkov.

'All right. They are good fellows. And how have you wriggled onto the staff?'

'I was attached; I'm on duty.'

Both were silent.

'*She let the hawk fly upward from her wide right sleeve,*' went the song, arousing an involuntary sensation of courage and cheerfulness. Their conversation would probably have been different but for the effect of that song.

'Is it true the Austrians have been beaten?' asked Dolokhov.

'The devil only knows! They say so.'

'I'm glad,' answered Dolokhov briefly and clearly, as the song demanded.

'I say, come round some evening and we'll have a game of faro!' said Zherkov.

'Why, have you too much money?'

'Do come.'

'I can't. I've sworn not to. I won't drink and won't play till I get reinstated.'

'Well that's only till the first engagement.'

'We shall see.'

They were again silent.

'Come if you need anything. One can at least be of use on the staff . . .'

Dolokhov smiled. 'Don't trouble. If I want anything, I won't beg – I'll take it!'

'Well, never mind; I only . . .'

'And I only . . .'

'Good-bye.'

'Good health . . .'

> *'It's a long, long way*
> *To my native land . . .'*

Zherkov touched his horse with the spurs; it pranced excitedly from foot to foot uncertain with which to start, then settled down, galloped past the company, and overtook the carriage, still keeping time to the song.

3

ON returning from the review Kutuzov took the Austrian general into his private room, and calling his adjutant, asked for some papers relating to the condition of the troops on their arrival, and the letters that had come from the Archduke Ferdinand, who was in command of the advanced army. Prince Andrew Bolkonsky came into the room with the required papers. Kutuzov and the Austrian member of the Hofkriegsrath were sitting at the table on which a plan was spread out.

'Ah! . . .' said Kutuzov glancing at Bolkonsky as if by this exclamation he was asking the adjutant to wait, and he went on with the conversation in French.

'All I can say, General,' said he with a pleasant elegance of expression and intonation that obliged one to listen to each deliberately spoken word. It was evident that Kutuzov himself listened with pleasure to his own voice. 'All I can say, General, is that if the matter depended on my personal wishes, the will of his Majesty the Emperor Francis would have been fulfilled long ago. I should long ago have joined the archduke. And believe me on my honour that to me personally it would be a pleasure to hand over the supreme command of the army into the hands of a better informed and more skilful general – of whom Austria has so many – and to lay down all this heavy responsibility. But circumstances are sometimes too strong for us, General.'

And Kutuzov smiled in a way that seemed to say, 'You are quite at liberty not to believe me and I don't even care whether you do or not, but you have no grounds for telling me so. And that is the whole point.'

The Austrian general looked dissatisfied, but had no option but to reply in the same tone.

'On the contrary,' he said, in a querulous and angry tone that contrasted with his flattering words, 'on the contrary, your Excellency's participation in the common action is highly valued by his Majesty; but we think the present delay is depriving the splendid Russian troops and their commander of the laurels they have been accustomed to win in their battles,' he concluded his evidently pre-arranged sentence.

Kutuzov bowed with the same smile.

'But that is my conviction, and judging by the last letter with which his Highness the Archduke Ferdinand has honoured me, I imagine that the Austrian troops, under the direction of so skilful a leader as General Mack have by now already gained a decisive victory and no longer need our aid,' said Kutuzov.

The general frowned. Though there was no definite news of an Austrian defeat, there were many circumstances confirming the unfavourable rumours that were afloat, and so Kutuzov's suggestion of an Austrian victory sounded much like irony. But Kutuzov went on blandly smiling with the same expression, which seemed to say that he had a right to suppose so. And in fact the last letter he had received from Mack's army informed him of a victory and stated that strategically the position of the army was very favourable.

'Give me that letter,' said Kutuzov turning to Prince Andrew. 'Please have a look at it' – and Kutuzov with an ironical smile about the corners of his mouth read to the Austrian general the following passage, in German, from the Archduke Ferdinand's letter.

'We have fully concentrated forces of nearly seventy thousand men with which to attack and defeat the enemy should he cross the Lech. Also, as we are masters of Ulm, we cannot be deprived of the advantage of commanding both sides of the Danube, so that should the enemy not cross the Lech, we can cross the Danube, throw ourselves on his line of communication, recross the river lower down, and frustrate his intention should he try to direct his whole force against our faithful ally. We shall therefore confidently await the moment when the Imperial Russian army will be fully equipped, and shall then, in conjunction with it, easily find a way to prepare for the enemy the fate he deserves.'

Kutuzov sighed deeply on finishing this paragraph and looked at the member of the Hofkriegsrath mildly and attentively.

'But you know the wise maxim, your Excellency, advising one to expect the worst,' said the Austrian general, evidently wishing to have done with jests and to come to business. He involuntarily looked round at the aide-de-camp.

'Excuse me, General,' interrupted Kutuzov, also turning to Prince Andrew. 'Look here, my dear fellow, get from Kozlovsky all the reports from our scouts. Here are two letters from Count Nostitz and here is one from his Highness the Archduke Ferdinand and here are these,' he said, handing him several papers, 'make a neat memorandum in French out of all this, showing all the news we have had of the movements of the Austrian army, and then give it to his Excellency.'

Prince Andrew bowed his head in token of having understood from the first not only what had been said but also what Kutuzov would have liked to tell him. He gathered up the papers and, with a bow to both, stepped softly over the carpet and went out into the waiting-room.

Though not much time had passed since Prince Andrew had left Russia, he had changed greatly during that period. In the expression of his face, in his movements, in his walk, scarcely a trace was left of his former affected languor and indolence. He now looked like a man who has no time to think of the impression he makes on others, but is occupied with agreeable and interesting work. His face expressed more satisfaction with himself and those around him, his smile and glance were brighter and more attractive.

Kutuzov, whom he had overtaken in Poland, had received him very kindly, promised not to forget him, distinguished him above the other adjutants, and had taken him to Vienna and given him the more serious commissions. From Vienna Kutuzov wrote to his old comrade, Prince Andrew's father:

'Your son bids fair to become an officer distinguished by his industry, firmness, and expedition. I consider myself fortunate to have such a subordinate by me.'

On Kutuzov's staff, among his fellow-officers and in the army generally, Prince Andrew had, as he had had in Petersburg society, two quite opposite reputations. Some, a minority, acknowledged him to be different from themselves and from everyone else, expected great things of him, listened to him, admired, and imitated him, and with them Prince Andrew was natural and pleasant. Others, the majority, disliked him and considered him conceited, cold, and disagreeable. But among these people Prince Andrew knew how to take his stand so that they respected and even feared him.

Coming out of Kutuzov's room into the waiting-room with the papers in his hand Prince Andrew came up to his comrade, the aide-de-camp on duty, Kozlovsky, who was sitting at the window with a book.

'Well, Prince?' asked Kozlovsky.

'I am ordered to write a memorandum explaining why we are not advancing.'

'And why is it?'

Prince Andrew shrugged his shoulders.

'Any news from Mack?'

'No.'

'If it were true that he has been beaten news would have come.'

'Probably,' said Prince Andrew moving towards the outer door.

But at that instant a tall Austrian general in a greatcoat, with the order of Maria Theresa on his neck and a black bandage round his head, who had evidently just arrived, entered quickly, slamming the door. Prince Andrew stopped short.

'Commander-in-chief Kutuzov?' said the newly-arrived general, speaking quickly with a harsh German accent, looking to both sides and advancing straight towards the inner door.

'The commander-in-chief is engaged,' said Kozlovsky, going hurriedly up to the unknown general and blocking his way to the door. 'Whom shall I announce?'

The unknown general looked disdainfully down at Kozlovsky, who was rather short, as if surprised that anyone should not know him.

'The commander-in-chief is engaged,' repeated Kozlovsky calmly.

The general's face clouded, his lips quivered and trembled. He took out a notebook, hurriedly scribbled something in pencil, tore out the leaf, gave it to Kozlovsky, stepped quickly to the window and threw himself into a chair, gazing at those in the room as if asking, 'Why do they look at me?' Then he lifted his head, stretched his neck as if he intended to say something, but immediately, with affected indifference, began to hum to himself, producing a queer sound which immediately broke off. The door of the private room opened and Kutuzov appeared in the doorway. The general with the bandaged head bent forward as though running away from some danger, and making long quick strides with his thin legs, went up to Kutuzov.

'*Vous voyez le malheureux Mack,*' he uttered in a broken voice.

Kutuzov's face as he stood in the open door-way remained perfectly immobile for a few moments. Then wrinkles ran over his face like a wave and his forehead became smooth again, he bowed his head respectfully, closed his eyes, silently let Mack enter his room before him, and closed the door himself behind him.

The report which had been circulated that the Austrians had been beaten and that the whole army had surrendered at Ulm proved to be correct. Within half an hour adjutants had been sent in various directions with orders which showed that the Russian troops, who had hitherto been inactive, would also have to meet the enemy.

Prince Andrew was one of those rare staff-officers whose chief interest lay in the general progress of the war. When he saw Mack and heard the details of his disaster he understood that half the campaign was lost, understood all the difficulties of the Russian army's position, and vividly imagined what awaited it and the part he would have to play. Involuntarily he felt a joyful agitation at the thought of the humiliation of arrogant Austria and that in a week's time he might, perhaps, see and take part in the first Russian encounter with the French since Suvorov met them. He feared that Bonaparte's genius might outweigh all the courage of the Russian troops, and at the same time could not admit the idea of his hero being disgraced.

Excited and irritated by these thoughts Prince Andrew went towards his room to write to his father, to whom he wrote every day. In the corridor he met Nesvitsky with whom he shared a room, and the wag Zherkov; they were as usual laughing.

'Why are you so glum?' asked Nesvitsky noticing Prince Andrew's pale face and glittering eyes.

'There's nothing to be gay about,' answered Bolkonsky.

Just as Prince Andrew met Nesvitsky and Zherkov, there came towards them from the other end of the corridor, Strauch, an Austrian general who was on Kutuzov's staff in charge of the provisioning of the Russian army, and the member of the Hofkriegsrath who had arrived the previous evening. There was room enough in the wide corridor for the generals to pass the three officers quite easily, but Zherkov, pushing Nesvitsky aside with his arm, said in a breathless voice,

'They're coming! . . . they're coming . . . Stand aside, make way, please make way!'

The generals were passing by, looking as if they wished to avoid embarrassing attentions. On the face of the wag Zherkov there suddenly appeared a stupid smile of glee which he seemed unable to suppress.

'Your Excellency,' said he in German, stepping forward and addressing the Austrian general, 'I have the honour to congratulate you.'

He bowed his head and scraped first with one foot and then with the other, awkwardly, like a child at a dancing-lesson.

The member of the Hofkriegsrath looked at him severely, but seeing the seriousness of his stupid smile, could not but give him a moment's attention. He screwed up his eyes showing that he was listening.

'I have the honour to congratulate you. General Mack has arrived, quite well, only a little bruised just here,' he added, pointing with a beaming smile to his head.

The general frowned, turned away, and went on.

'*Gott, wie naiv!*' said he angrily, after he had gone a few steps.

Nesvitsky with a laugh threw his arms round Prince Andrew, but Bolkonsky, turning still paler, pushed him away with an angry look and turned to Zherkov. The nervous irritation aroused by the appearance of Mack, the news of his defeat, and the thought of what lay before the Russian army, found vent in anger at Zherkov's untimely jest.

'If you, sir, choose to make a *buffoon* of yourself,' he said sharply, with a slight trembling of the lower jaw, 'I can't prevent your doing so; but I warn you that if you *dare* to play the fool in my presence, I will teach you to behave yourself.'

Nesvitsky and Zherkov were so surprised by this outburst that they gazed at Bolkonsky silently with wide-open eyes.

'What's the matter? I only congratulated them,' said Zherkov.

'I am not jesting with you; please be silent!' cried Bolkonsky, and taking Nesvitsky's arm he left Zherkov, who did not know what to say.

'Come, what's the matter, old fellow?' said Nesvitsky trying to soothe him.

'What's the matter?' exclaimed Prince Andrew standing still in his excitement. 'Don't you understand that either we are officers serving our Tsar and our country, rejoicing in the successes and grieving at the misfortunes of our common cause, or we are merely lackeys who care nothing for their master's business. *Quarante mille hommes massacrés et l'armée de nos alliés détruite, et vous trouvez là le mot pour rire,*' he said, as if strengthening his views by this French sentence. '*C'est bien pour un garçon de rien comme cet individu dont vous avez fait un ami, mais pas pour vous, pas pour vous.* Only a *hobbledehoy* could amuse himself in this way,' he added in Russian – but pronouncing the word with a French accent – having noticed that Zherkov could still hear him.

He waited a moment to see whether the cornet would answer, but he turned and went out of the corridor.

4

THE Pavlograd hussars were stationed two miles from Braunau. The squadron in which Nicholas Rostov served as a cadet was quartered in the German village of Salzeneck. The best quarters in the village were assigned to cavalry-captain Denisov, the squadron commander, known throughout the whole cavalry division as Vaska Denisov. Cadet Rostov ever since he had overtaken the regiment in Poland had lived with the squadron commander.

On October 11th, the day when all was astir at head-quarters over the news of Mack's defeat, the camp life of the officers of this squadron was proceeding as usual. Denisov, who had been losing at cards all night, had not yet come home when Rostov rode back early in the morning from a foraging expedition. Rostov in his cadet uniform, with a jerk to his horse rode up to the porch, swung his leg over the saddle with a supple youthful movement, stood for a moment in the stirrup as if loth to part from his horse, and at last sprang down and called to his orderly.

'Ah, Bondarenko, dear friend!' said he to the hussar who rushed up headlong to the horse. 'Walk him up and down, my dear fellow,' he continued, with that gay brotherly cordiality which good-hearted young people show to everyone when they are happy.

'Yes, your Excellency,' answered the Ukrainian gaily, tossing his head.

'Mind, walk him up and down well!'

Another hussar also rushed towards the horse, but Bondarenko had already thrown the reins of the snaffle-bridle over the horse's head. It was evident that the cadet was liberal with his tips and that it paid to serve him. Rostov patted the horse's neck and then his flank, and lingered for a moment.

'Splendid! What a horse he will be!' he thought with a smile, and holding up his sabre, his spurs jingling, he ran up the steps of the porch. His landlord, who in a waistcoat and a pointed cap, pitchfork in hand, was clearing manure from the cow-house, looked out, and his face immediately brightened on seeing Rostov. '*Schön gut Morgen! Schön gut Morgen!*' he said winking with a merry smile, evidently pleased to greet the young man.

'*Schon fleissig?*'* said Rostov with the same gay brotherly smile which did not leave his eager face. '*Hoch Oestreicher! Hoch Russen! Kaiser Alexander hoch!*'* said he, quoting words often repeated by the German landlord.

The German laughed, came out of the cowshed, pulled off his cap, and waving it above his head cried:

'*Und die ganze Welt hoch!*'

Rostov waved his cap above his head like the German and cried laughing, '*Und vivat die ganze Welt!*' Though neither the German cleaning his cowshed, nor Rostov back with his platoon from foraging for hay, had any reason for rejoicing, they looked at each other with joyful delight and brotherly love, wagged their heads in token of their mutual affection, and parted smiling, the German returning to his cowshed and Rostov going to the cottage he occupied with Denisov.

'What about your master?' he asked Lavrushka, Denisov's orderly, whom all the regiment knew for a rogue.

'Hasn't been in since the evening. Must have been losing,' answered Lavrushka. 'I know by now, if he wins he comes back to brag about it, but if he stays out till morning it means he's lost and will come back in a rage. Will you have coffee?'

'Yes, bring some.'

Ten minutes later Lavrushka brought the coffee. 'He's coming!' said he. 'Now for trouble!' Rostov looked out of the window and saw Denisov coming home. Denisov was a small man with a red face, sparkling black eyes, and black tousled moustache and hair. He wore an unfastened cloak, wide breeches hanging down in creases, and a crumpled shako on the back of his head. He came up to the porch gloomily, hanging his head.

'Lavwuska!' he shouted loudly and angrily, 'take it off, block-head!'

'Well, I am taking it off,' replied Lavrushka's voice.

'Ah, you're up already,' said Denisov, entering the room.

'Long ago,' answered Rostov, 'I have already been for the hay, and have seen Fräulein Mathilde.'

'Weally! And I've been losing, bwother. I lost yesterday like a damned fool!' cried Denisov, not pronouncing his r's. 'Such ill

130

luck! Such ill luck. As soon as you left, it began and went on. Hullo there! Tea!'

Puckering up his face as though smiling, and showing his short strong teeth, he began with the stubby fingers of both hands to ruffle up his thick tangled black hair.

'And what devil made me go to that wat?' (an officer nicknamed 'the rat') he said, rubbing his forehead and whole face with both hands. 'Just fancy, he didn't let me win a single cahd, not one cahd.'

He took the lighted pipe that was offered to him, gripped it in his fist, and tapped it on the floor, making the sparks fly, while he continued to shout.

'He lets one win the singles and collahs it as soon as one doubles it; gives the singles and snatches the doubles!'

He scattered the burning tobacco, smashed the pipe, and threw it away. Then he remained silent for a while, and all at once looked cheerfully with his glittering, black eyes at Rostov.

'If at least we had some women here; but there's nothing foh one to do but dwink. If we could only get to fighting soon. Hullo, who's there?' he said, turning to the door as he heard a tread of heavy boots and the clinking of spurs that came to a stop, and a respectful cough.

'The squadron quartermaster!' said Lavrushka.

Denisov's face puckered still more.

'Wetched!' he muttered, throwing down a purse with some gold in it. 'Wostov, deah fellow, just see how much there is left and shove the purse undah the pillow,' he said, and went out to the quartermaster.

Rostov took the money and, mechanically arranging the old and new coins in separate piles, began counting them.

'Ah! Telyanin! How d'ye do? They plucked me last night,' came Denisov's voice from the next room.

'Where? At Bykov's, at the rat's ... I knew it,' replied a piping voice, and Lieutenant Telyanin, a small officer of the same squadron, entered the room.

Rostov thrust the purse under the pillow and shook the damp little hand which was offered him. Telyanin for some reason had been transferred from the Guards just before this campaign. He behaved very well in the regiment but was not liked; Rostov especially detested him and was unable to overcome or conceal his groundless antipathy to the man.

'Well, young cavalryman, how is my Rook behaving?' he asked. (Rook was a young horse Telyanin had sold to Rostov.)

The lieutenant never looked the man he was speaking to

straight in the face; his eyes continually wandered from one object to another.

'I saw you riding this morning . . .' he added.

'Oh, he's all right, a good horse,' answered Rostov, though the horse for which he had paid seven hundred rubles was not worth half that sum. 'He's begun to go a little lame on the left foreleg,' he added.

'The hoof's cracked! That's nothing. I'll teach you what to do and show you what kind of rivet to use.'

'Yes, please do,' said Rostov.

'I'll show you, I'll show you! It's not a secret. And it's a horse you'll thank me for.'

'Then I'll have it brought round,' said Rostov wishing to avoid Telyanin, and he went out to give the order.

In the passage Denisov, with a pipe, was squatting on the threshold facing the quartermaster who was reporting to him. On seeing Rostov Denisov screwed up his face and pointing over his shoulder with his thumb to the room where Telyanin was sitting, he frowned and gave a shudder of disgust.

'Ugh! I don't like that fellow,' he said, regardless of the quartermaster's presence.

Rostov shrugged his shoulders as much as to say: 'Nor do I, but what's one to do?' and having given his order, he returned to Telyanin.

Telyanin was sitting in the same indolent pose in which Rostov had left him, rubbing his small white hands.

'Well there certainly are disgusting people,' thought Rostov as he entered.

'Have you told them to bring the horse?' asked Telyanin, getting up and looking carelessly about him.

'I have.'

'Let us go ourselves. I only came round to ask Denisov about yesterday's order. Have you got it, Denisov?'

'Not yet. But where are you off to?'

'I want to teach this young man how to shoe a horse,' said Telyanin.

They went through the porch and into the stable. The lieutenant explained how to rivet the hoof and went away to his own quarters.

When Rostov went back there was a bottle of vodka and a sausage on the table. Denisov was sitting there scratching with his pen on a sheet of paper. He looked gloomily in Rostov's face and said:

'I am witing to her.'

He leant his elbows on the table with his pen in his hand, and evidently glad of a chance to say quicker in words what he wanted to write, told Rostov the contents of his letter.

'You see, my fwiend,' he said, 'we sleep when we don't love. We are childwen of the dust . . . but one falls in love and one is a God, one is pua' as on the fihst day of cweation . . . Who's that now? Send him to the devil, I'm busy!' he shouted to Lavrushka, who went up to him not in the least abashed.

'Who should it be? You yourself told him to come. It's the quartermaster for the money.'

Denisov frowned and was about to shout some reply but stopped.

'Wetched business,' he muttered to himself. 'How much is left in the puhse?' he asked, turning to Rostov.

'Seven new and three old imperials.'

'Oh, it's wetched! Well, what are you standing there for, you sca'cwow? Call the quahtehmasteh,' he shouted to Lavrushka.

'Please, Denisov, let me lend you some: I have some, you know,' said Rostov, blushing.

'Don't like borrowing from my own fellows, I don't,' growled Denisov.

'But if you won't accept money from me like a comrade, you will offend me. Really I have some,' Rostov repeated.

'No, I tell you.'

And Denisov went to the bed to get the purse from under the pillow.

'Where have you put it, Wostov?'

'Under the lower pillow.'

'It's not there.'

Denisov threw both pillows on the floor. The purse was not there.

'That's odd.'

'Wait, haven't you dropped it?' said Rostov, picking up the pillows one at a time and shaking them.

He pulled off the quilt and shook it. The purse was not there.

'Dear me, can I have forgotten? No, I remember thinking that you kept it under your head like treasure,' said Rostov. 'I put it just here. Where is it?' he asked, turning to Lavrushka.

'I haven't been in the room. It must be where you put it.'

'But it isn't! . . .'

'You're always like that; you thwow a thing down anywhere and forget it. Feel in your pockets.'

'No, if I hadn't had the thought of treasure,' said Rostov, 'but that's why I remember putting it there.'

Lavrushka turned all the bedding over, looked under the bed and under the table, searched everywhere, and stood still in the middle of the room. Denisov silently watched Lavrushka's movements, and when the latter threw up his arms in surprise saying it was nowhere to be found, Denisov glanced at Rostov.

'Wostov, you've not been playing schoolboy twicks....'

Rostov felt Denisov's gaze fixed on him, raised his eyes, and instantly dropped them again. All the blood which had seemed congested somewhere below his throat rushed to his face and eyes. He could not draw breath.

'And there hasn't been anyone in the room except the lieutenant and yourselves. It must be here somewhere,' said Lavrushka.

'Now then, you devil's puppet, look alive and hunt for it!' shouted Denisov suddenly, turning purple and rushing at the man with a threatening gesture. 'If the purse isn't found I'll flog you, I'll flog you all.'

Rostov, his eyes avoiding Denisov, began buttoning his coat, buckled on his sabre, and put on his cap.

'I must have that purse, I tell you,' shouted Denisov, shaking his orderly by the shoulders and knocking him against the wall.

'Denisov, let him alone, I know who has taken it,' said Rostov going towards the door without raising his eyes.

Denisov paused, thought a moment, and evidently understanding what Rostov hinted at, seized his arm.

'Nonsense!' he cried, and the veins on his forehead and neck stood out like cords. 'You are mad, I tell you. I won't allow it. The purse is here! I'll flay this scoundwel alive, and it will be found.'

'I know who has taken it,' repeated Rostov in an unsteady voice, and went to the door.

'And I tell you, don't you dahe to do it!' shouted Denisov, rushing at the cadet to restrain him.

But Rostov pulled away his arm and with as much anger as though Denisov were his worst enemy firmly fixed his eyes directly on his face.

'Do you understand what you're saying?' he said in a trembling voice. 'There was no one else in the room except myself. So that if it is not so, then ...'

He could not finish and ran out of the room.

'Ah, may the devil take you and everybody,' were the last words Rostov heard.

Rostov went to Telyanin's quarters.

'The master is not in, he's gone to head-quarters,' said Telyanin's orderly. 'Has something happened?' he added, surprised at the cadet's troubled face.

'No, nothing.'

'You've only just missed him,' said the orderly.

The head-quarters were situated two miles away from Salzeneck, and Rostov, without returning home, took a horse and rode there. There was an inn in the village which the officers frequented. Rostov rode up to it and saw Telyanin's horse at the porch.

In the second room of the inn the lieutenant was sitting over a dish of sausages and a bottle of wine.

'Ah, you've come here too, young man!' he said, smiling and raising his eyebrows.

'Yes,' said Rostov as if it cost him a great effort to utter the word; and he sat down at the nearest table.

Both were silent. There were two Germans and a Russian officer in the room. No one spoke and the only sounds heard were the clatter of knives and the munching of the lieutenant.

When Telyanin had finished his lunch he took out of his pocket a double purse, and drawing its rings aside with his small, white, turned-up fingers, drew out a gold imperial, and lifting his eyebrows gave it to the waiter.

'Please be quick,' he said.

The coin was a new one. Rostov rose and went up to Telyanin.

'Allow me to look at your purse,' he said in a low, almost inaudible, voice.

With shifting eyes but eyebrows still raised, Telyanin handed him the purse.

'Yes, it's a nice purse. Yes, yes,' he said growing suddenly pale, and added, 'Look at it, young man.'

Rostov took the purse in his hand, examined it and the money in it, and looked at Telyanin. The lieutenant was looking about in his usual way and suddenly seemed to grow very merry.

'If we get to Vienna I'll get rid of it there, but in these wretched little towns there's nowhere to spend it,' said he. 'Well, let me have it, young man, I'm going.'

Rostov did not speak.

'And you? Are you going to have lunch too? They feed you quite decently here,' continued Telyanin. 'Now then, let me have it.'

He stretched out his hand to take hold of the purse. Rostov let go of it. Telyanin took the purse and began carelessly slipping it into the pocket of his riding-breeches with his eyebrows lifted and his mouth slightly open, as if to say, 'Yes, yes, I am putting my purse in my pocket and that's quite simple and is no one else's business.'

'Well, young man?' he said with a sigh, and from under his lifted brows he glanced into Rostov's eyes.

Some flash as of an electric spark shot from Telyanin's eyes to Rostov's and back, and back again and again in an instant.

'Come here,' said Rostov, catching hold of Telyanin's arm and almost dragging him to the window. 'That money is Denisov's; you took it . . .' he whispered just above Telyanin's ear.

'What? What? How dare you? What?' said Telyanin.

But these words came like a piteous, despairing cry and an entreaty for pardon. As soon as Rostov heard them, an enormous load of doubt fell from him. He was glad, and at the same instant began to pity the miserable man who stood before him, but the task he had begun had to be completed.

'Heaven only knows what the people here may imagine,' muttered Telyanin, taking up his cap and moving towards a small empty room. 'We must have an explanation . . .'

'I know it and shall prove it,' said Rostov.

'I . . .'

Every muscle of Telyanin's pale terrified face began to quiver, his eyes still shifted from side to side but with a downward look not rising to Rostov's face, and his sobs were audible.

'Count! . . . Don't ruin a young fellow . . . here is this wretched money, take it . . .' He threw it on the table. 'I have an old father and mother! . . .'

Rostov took the money, avoiding Telyanin's eyes, and went out of the room without a word. But at the door he stopped and then retraced his steps. 'O God,' he said with tears in his eyes, 'how could you do it?'

'Count, . . .' said Telyanin drawing nearer to him.

'Don't touch me,' said Rostov, drawing back. 'If you need it, take the money,' and he threw the purse to him and ran out of the inn.

5

THAT same evening there was an animated discussion among the squadron's officers in Denisov's quarters.

'And I tell you, Rostov, that you must apologize to the colonel!' said a tall, grizzly-haired staff-captain with enormous moustaches and many wrinkles on his large features, to Rostov who was crimson with excitement.

The staff-captain, Kirsten, had twice been reduced to the ranks for affairs of honour and had twice regained his commission.

'I will allow no one to call me a liar!' cried Rostov. 'He told me I lied, and I told him he lied. And there it rests. He may keep me on duty every day, or may place me under arrest, but no one can make me apologize, because if he, as commander of this regiment, thinks it beneath his dignity to give me satisfaction, then . . .'

'You just wait a moment, my dear fellow, and listen,' interrupted the staff-captain in his deep bass, calmly stroking his long moustache. 'You tell the colonel in the presence of other officers that an officer has stolen . . .'

'I'm not to blame that the conversation began in the presence of other officers. Perhaps I ought not to have spoken before them, but I am not a diplomatist. That's why I joined the hussars, thinking that here one would not need finesse; and he tells me that I am lying – so let him give me satisfaction . . .'

'That's all right. No one thinks you a coward, but that's not the point. Ask Denisov whether it is not out of the question for a cadet to demand satisfaction of his regimental commander?'

Denisov sat gloomily biting his moustache and listening to the conversation, evidently with no wish to take part in it. He answered the staff-captain's question by a disapproving shake of his head.

'You speak to the colonel about this nasty business before other officers,' continued the staff-captain, 'and Bogdanich' (the colonel was called Bogdanich) 'shuts you up.'

'He did not shut me up, he said I was telling an untruth.'

'Well, have it so, and you talked a lot of nonsense to him and must apologize.'

'Not on any account!' exclaimed Rostov.

'I did not expect this of you,' said the staff-captain seriously and severely. 'You don't wish to apologize, but, man, it's not only to him but to the whole regiment – all of us – you're to blame all round. The case is this: you ought to have thought the matter over and taken advice; but no, you go and blurt it all straight out before the officers. Now what was the colonel to do? Have the officer tried and disgrace the whole regiment? Is that how you look at it? We don't see it like that. And Bogdanich was a brick: he told you you were saying what was not true. It's not pleasant, but what's to be done, my dear fellow? You landed yourself in it. And now, when one wants to smooth the thing over, some conceit prevents your apologizing, and you wish to make the whole affair public. You are offended at being put on duty a bit, but why not apologize to an old and honourable officer? Whatever Bogdanich may be, anyway he is an honourable and brave old colonel! You're quick at taking offence, but you don't mind disgracing the whole regiment!' The staff-captain's voice began to tremble. 'You have been in the regiment next to no time, my lad, you're here to-day and to-morrow you'll be appointed adjutant somewhere and can snap your fingers when it is said, "There are thieves among the Pavlograd officers!" But it's not all the same to us! Am I not right, Denisov? It's not the same!'

Denisov remained silent and did not move, but occasionally looked with his glittering black eyes at Rostov.

'You value your own pride and don't wish to apologize,' continued the staff-captain, 'but we old fellows, who have grown up in and God willing are going to die in the regiment, we prize the honour of the regiment, and Bogdanich knows it. Oh we do prize it, old fellow! And all this is not right, it's not right! You may take offence or not but I always stick to mother truth. It's not right!'

And the staff-captain rose and turned away from Rostov.

'That's twue, devil take it!' shouted Denisov, jumping up. 'Now then, Wostov, now then!'

Rostov, growing red and pale alternately, looked first at one officer and then at the other.

'No, gentlemen, no . . . you mustn't think . . . I quite understand. You're wrong to think that of me . . . I . . . for me . . . for the honour of the regiment I'd . . . Ah well, I'll show that in action, and for me the honour of the flag . . . Well, never mind, it's true I'm to blame, to blame all round. Well, what else do you want? . . .'

'Come, that's right, Count!' cried the staff-captain, turning round the clapping Rostov on the shoulder with his big hand.

'I tell you,' shouted Denisov, 'he's a fine fellow.'

'That's better, Count,' said the staff-captain, beginning to address Rostov by his title, as if in recognition of his confession. 'Go and apologize, your Excellency. Yes, go!'

'Gentlemen, I'll do anything. No one shall hear a word from me,' said Rostov in an imploring voice, 'but I can't apologize, by God I can't, do what you will! How can I go and apologize like a little boy asking forgiveness?'

Denisov began to laugh.

'It'll be worse for you. Bogdanich is vindictive and you'll pay for your obstinacy,' said Kirsten.

'No, on my word it's not obstinacy! I can't describe the feeling. I can't . . .'

'Well it's as you like,' said the staff-captain. 'And what has become of that scoundrel?' he asked Denisov.

'He has weported himself sick, he's to be stwuck off the list to-mowow,' muttered Denisov.

'It is an illness, there's no other way of explaining it,' said the staff-captain.

'Illness or not, he'd better not cwoss my path. I'd kill him!' shouted Denisov in a bloodthirsty tone.

Just then Zherkov entered the room.

'What brings you here?' cried the officers turning to the new-comer.

'We're to go into action, gentlemen! Mack has surrendered with his whole army.'

'It's not true!'

'I've seen him myself!'

'What? Saw the real Mack? With hands and feet?'

'Into action! Into action! Bring him a bottle for such news! But how did you come here?'

'I've been sent back to the regiment all on account of that devil, Mack. An Austrian general complained of me. I congratulated him on Mack's arrival ... What's the matter, Rostov? You look as if you'd just come out of a hot bath.'

'Oh, my dear fellow, we're in such a stew here these last two days.'

The regimental adjutant came in and confirmed the news brought by Zherkov. They were under orders to advance next day.

'We're going into action, gentlemen!'

'Well, thank God! We've been sitting here too long!'

6

KUTUZOV fell back towards Vienna,* destroying behind him the bridges over the rivers Inn (at Braunau) and Traun (near Linz). On October 23rd the Russian troops were crossing the river Enns. At mid-day the Russian baggage-train, the artillery, and columns of troops, were defiling through the town of Enns on both sides of the bridge.

It was a warm, rainy, autumnal day. The wide expanse that opened out before the heights on which the Russian batteries stood guarding the bridge, was at times veiled by a diaphanous curtain of slanting rain, and then, suddenly spread out in the sunlight, far-distant objects could be clearly seen glittering as though freshly varnished. Down below, the little town could be seen with its white, red-roofed houses, its cathedral, and its bridge, on both sides of which streamed jostling masses of Russian troops. At the bend of the Danube, vessels, an island, and a castle with a park surrounded by the waters of the confluence of the Enns and the Danube, became visible, and the rocky left bank of the Danube covered with pine forests, with a mystic background of green tree-tops and bluish gorges. The turrets of a convent stood out beyond a wild virgin pine-forest, and far away on the other side of the Enns the enemy's horse patrols could be discerned.

Among the field-guns on the brow of the hill the general in command of the rearguard stood with a staff-officer, scanning the country through his field-glass. A little behind them Nesvitsky, who had been sent to the rearguard by the commander-in-chief, was sitting on the trail of a gun-carriage. A Cossack who accompanied him had handed him a knapsack and a flask, and Nesvitsky was treating some officers to pies and real *doppel-kümmel*. The officers gladly gathered round him, some on their knees, some squatting Turkish fashion on the wet grass.

'Yes, the Austrian prince who built that castle was no fool. It's a fine place! Why are you not eating anything, gentlemen?' Nesvitsky was saying.

'Thank you very much, Prince,' answered one of the officers, pleased to be talking to a staff-officer of such importance. 'It's a lovely place! We passed close to the park and saw two deer ... and what a splendid house!'

'Look, Prince,' said another, who would have dearly liked to take another pie but felt shy, and therefore pretended to be examining the countryside – 'See, our infantrymen have already got there. Look there in the meadow behind the village, three of them are dragging something. They'll ransack that castle,' he remarked with evident approval.

'So they will,' said Nesvitsky. 'No, but what I should like,' added he, munching a pie in his moist-lipped handsome mouth, 'would be to slip in over there.'

He pointed with a smile to a turreted nunnery, and his eyes narrowed and gleamed.

'That would be fine, gentlemen!'

The officers laughed.

'Just to flutter the nuns a bit. They say there are Italian girls among them. On my word I'd give five years of my life for it!'

'They must be feeling dull, too,' said one of the bolder officers, laughing.

Meanwhile the staff-officer standing in front pointed out something to the general, who looked through his field-glass.

'Yes, so it is, so it is,' said the general angrily, lowering the field-glass and shrugging his shoulders, 'so it is! They'll be fired on at the crossing. And why are they dawdling there?'

On the opposite side the enemy could be seen by the naked eye, and from their battery a milk-white cloud arose. Then came the distant report of a shot, and our troops could be seen hurrying to the crossing.

Nesvitsky rose puffing, and went up to the general smiling.

'Would not your Excellency like a little refreshment?' he said.

'It's a bad business,' said the general without answering him, 'our men have been wasting time.'

'Hadn't I better ride over, your Excellency?' asked Nesvitsky.

'Yes, please do,' answered the general, and he repeated the order that had already once been given in detail: 'and tell the hussars that they are to cross last and to fire the bridge as I ordered; and the inflammable material on the bridge must be re-inspected.'

'Very good,' answered Nesvitsky.

He called the Cossack with his horse, told him to put away the knapsack and flask, and swung his heavy person easily into the saddle.

'I'll really call in on the nuns,' he said to the officers who watched him smilingly, and he rode off by the winding path down the hill.

'Now then let's see how far it will carry, Captain. Just try!' said the general, turning to an artillery officer. 'Have a little fun to pass the time.'

'Crew, to your guns!' commanded the officer.

In a moment the men came running gaily from their camp fires and began loading.

'One!' came the command.

Number one jumped briskly aside. The gun rang out with a deafening metallic roar, and a whistling grenade flew above the heads of our troops below the hill and fell far short of the enemy, a little smoke showing the spot where it burst.

The faces of officers and men brightened up at the sound. Everyone got up and began watching the movements of our troops below, as plainly visible as if but a stone's throw away, and the movements of the approaching enemy farther off. At the same instant the sun came fully out from behind the clouds, and the clear sound of the solitary shot and the brilliance of the bright sunshine merged in a single joyous and spirited impression.

7

TWO of the enemy's shots had already flown across the bridge, where there was a crush. Half-way across stood Prince Nesvitsky, who had alighted from his horse and whose big body was jammed against the railings. He looked back laughing to the Cossack who stood a few steps behind him holding two horses by their bridles. Each time Prince Nesvitsky tried to move on, soldiers and carts pushed him back again and pressed him against the railings, and all he could do was to smile.

'What a fellow you are, friend!' said the Cossack to a convoy-soldier with a wagon, who was pressing onto the infantrymen who were crowded together close to his wheels and his horses. 'What a fellow! You can't wait a moment! Don't you see the General wants to pass?'

But the convoyman took no notice of the word 'General', and shouted at the soldiers who were blocking his way. 'Hi there boys! Keep to the left! Wait a bit.' But the soldiers, crowded together shoulder to shoulder, their bayonets interlocking, moved over the bridge in a dense mass. Looking down over the rails Prince Nesvitsky saw the rapid, noisy little waves of the Enns, which rippling and eddying round the piles of the bridge chased each other along. Looking on the bridge he saw equally uniform living waves of soldiers, shoulder-straps, covered shakos, knapsacks, bayonets, long muskets, and under the shakos faces with broad cheekbones, sunken cheeks, and listless tired expressions, and feet that moved through the sticky mud that covered the planks of the bridge. Sometimes through the monotonous waves of men, like a fleck of white foam on the waves of the Enns, an officer in a cloak, and with a type of face different from that of the men, squeezed his way along; sometimes like a chip of wood whirling in the river, an hussar on foot, an orderly, or a townsman, was carried through the waves of infantry; and sometimes like a log floating down the river, an officers' or company's baggage wagon, piled high, leather-covered, and hemmed in on all sides, moved across the bridge.

'It's as if a dam had burst,' said the Cossack hopelessly. 'Are there many more of you to come?'

'A million all but one!' replied a waggish soldier in a torn coat with a wink, and passed on followed by another, an old man.

'If *he*' (*he* meant the enemy) 'begins popping at the bridge now,' said the old soldier dismally to a comrade, 'you'll forget to scratch yourself.'

That soldier passed on, and after him came another sitting on a cart.

'Where the devil have the leg-bands been shoved to?' said an orderly, running behind the cart and fumbling in the back of it.

And he also passed on with the wagon. Then came some merry soldiers who had evidently been drinking.

'And then, old fellow, he gives him one in the teeth with the butt end of his gun . . .' a soldier whose greatcoat was well tucked up said gaily, with a wide swing of his arm.

'Yes, the ham was just delicious . . .' answered another, with a loud laugh. And they, too, passed on, so that Nesvitsky did not learn who had been struck on the teeth, or what the ham had to do with it.

'Bah! How they scurry. He just sends a ball and they think they'll all be killed,' a sergeant was saying angrily and reproachfully.

'As it flies past me, Daddy, the ball I mean,' said a young soldier with an enormous mouth, hardly refraining from laughing, 'I felt like dying of fright. I did, 'pon my word, I got that frightened!' said he, as if bragging of having been frightened.

That one also passed. Then followed a cart unlike any that had gone before. It was a German cart with a pair of horses led by a German, and seemed loaded with a whole houseful of effects. A fine brindled cow with a large udder was attached to the cart behind. A woman with an unweaned baby, an old woman, and a healthy German girl with bright red cheeks, were sitting on some feather-beds. Evidently these fugitives were allowed to pass by special permission. The eyes of all the soldiers turned towards the women, and while the vehicle was passing at foot pace all the soldiers' remarks related to the two young ones. Every face bore almost the same smile, expressing unseemly thoughts about the women.

'Just see, the German sausage is making tracks, too!'

'Sell me the missis,' said another soldier, addressing the German, who angry and frightened, strode energetically along with downcast eyes.

'See how smart she's made herself! Oh, the devils!'

'There, Fedotov, you should be quartered on them!'

'I have seen as much before now, mate!'

'Where are you going?' asked an infantry officer who was eating an apple, also half smiling as he looked at the handsome girl.

The German closed his eyes, signifying that he did not understand.

'Take it if you like,' said the officer, giving the girl an apple.

The girl smiled and took it. Nesvitsky like the rest of the men on the bridge did not take his eyes off the women till they had passed. When they had gone by the same stream of soldiers followed, with the same kind of talk, and at last all stopped. As often happens, the horses of a convoy-wagon became restive at the end of the bridge, and the whole crowd had to wait.

143

'And why are they stopping? There's no proper order!' said the soldiers. 'Where are you shoving to? Devil take you! Can't you wait? It'll be worse if he fires the bridge. See, here's an officer jammed in too,' – different voices were saying in the crowd, as the men looked at one another, and all pressed towards the exit from the bridge.

Looking down at the waters of the Enns under the bridge, Nesvitsky suddenly heard a sound new to him, of something swiftly approaching ... something big, that splashed into the water.

'Just see where it carries to!' a soldier near by said sternly, looking round at the sound.

'Encouraging us to get along quicker,' said another uneasily.

The crowd moved on again. Nesvitsky realized that it was a cannon-ball.

'Hey, Cossack, my horse!' he said. 'Now then, you there! get out of the way! Make way!'

With great difficulty he managed to get to his horse, and shouting continually he moved on. The soldiers squeezed themselves to make way for him, but again pressed on him so that they jammed his leg, and those nearest him were not to blame, for they were themselves pressed still harder from behind.

'Nesvitsky, Nesvitsky! you numskull!' came a hoarse voice from behind him.

Nesvitsky looked round, and saw, some fifteen paces away but separated by the living mass of moving infantry, Vaska Denisov, red and shaggy, with his cap on the back of his black head and a cloak hanging jauntily over his shoulder.

'Tell these devils, these fiends, to let me pass!' shouted Denisov evidently in a fit of rage, his coal-black eyes with their bloodshot whites glittering and rolling as he waved his sheathed sabre in a small bare hand as red as his face.

'Ah, Vaska!' joyfully replied Nesvitsky. 'What's up with you?'

'The squadwon can't pass,' shouted Vaska Denisov, showing his white teeth fiercely and spurring his black thoroughbred Arab, which twitched its ears as the bayonets touched it, and snorted, spurting white foam from its bit, tramping the planks of the bridge with his hoofs, and apparently ready to jump over the railings had his rider let him. 'What is this? They're like sheep! Just like sheep! Out of the way! ... Let us pass! ... Stop there, you devil with the cart! I'll hack you with my sabre!' he shouted, actually drawing his sabre from its scabbard and flourishing it.

The soldiers crowded against one another with terrified faces, and Denisov joined Nesvitsky.

'How's it you're not drunk to-day?' said Nesvitsky when the other had ridden up to him.

'They don't even give one time to dwink!' answered Vaska Denisov. They keep dwagging the wegiment to and fwo all day. If they mean to fight, let's fight. But the devil knows what this is.'

'What a dandy you are to-day!' said Nesvitsky, looking at Denisov's new cloak and saddle-cloth.

Denisov smiled, took out of his sabretache a handkerchief that diffused a smell of perfume, and put it to Nesvitsky's nose.

'Of course. I'm going into action! I've shaved, bwushed my teeth, and scented myself.'

The imposing figure of Nesvitsky followed by his Cossack, and the determination of Denisov who flourished his sword and shouted frantically, had such an effect that they managed to squeeze through to the farther side of the bridge and stopped the infantry. Beside the bridge Nesvitsky found the colonel to whom he had to deliver the order, and having done this he rode back.

Having cleared the way Denisov stopped at the end of the bridge. Carelessly holding in his stallion that was neighing and pawing the ground eager to rejoin its fellows, he watched his squadron draw nearer. Then the clang of hoofs, as of several horses galloping, resounded on the planks of the bridge, and the squadron, officers in front and men four abreast, spread across the bridge and began to emerge on his side of it.

The infantry who had been stopped crowded near the bridge in the trampled mud, and gazed, with that particular feeling of ill-will, estrangement, and ridicule with which troops of different arms usually encounter one another, at the clean smart hussars who moved past them in regular order.

'Smart lads! Only fit for a fair!' said one.

'What good are they? They're led about just for show!' remarked another.

'Don't kick up the dust, you infantry!' jested an hussar whose prancing horse had splashed mud over some foot-soldiers.

'I'd like to put you on a two-days' march with a knapsack! Your fine cords would soon get a bit rubbed,' said an infantryman, wiping the mud off his face with his sleeve. 'Perched up there, you're more like a bird than a man.'

'There now, Zikin, they ought to put you on a horse. You'd look fine,' said a corporal, chaffing a thin little soldier who bent under the weight of his knapsack.

'Take a stick between your legs, that'll suit you for a horse!' the hussar shouted back.

THE last of the infantry hurriedly crossed the bridge, squeezing together as they approached it as if passing through a funnel. At last the baggage-wagons had all crossed, the crush was less, and the last battalion came onto the bridge. Only Denisov's squadron of hussars remained on the farther side of the bridge facing the enemy, who could be seen from the hill on the opposite bank but was not yet visible from the bridge, for the horizon as seen from the valley through which the river flowed was formed by the rising ground only half a mile away. At the foot of the hill lay waste land over which a few groups of our Cossack scouts were moving. Suddenly on the road at the top of the high ground, artillery and troops in blue uniform were seen. These were the French. A group of Cossack scouts retired down the hill at a trot. All the officers and men of Denisov's squadron, though they tried to talk of other things and to look in other directions, thought only of what was there on the hilltop, and kept constantly looking at the patches appearing on the sky-line, which they knew to be the enemy's troops. The weather had cleared again since noon and the sun was descending brightly upon the Danube and the dark hills around it. It was calm, and at intervals the bugle-calls and the shouts of the enemy could be heard from the hill. There was no one now between the squadron and the enemy except a few scattered skirmishers. An empty space of some seven hundred yards was all that separated them. The enemy ceased firing, and that stern, threatening, inaccessible and intangible line which separates two hostile armies was all the more clearly felt.

'One step beyond that boundary line which resembles the line dividing the living from the dead, lies uncertainty, suffering, and death. And what is there? Who is there? – there beyond that field, that tree, that roof lit up by the sun? No one knows, but one wants to know. You fear and yet long to cross that line, and know that sooner or later it must be crossed and you will have to find out what is there, just as you will inevitably have to learn what lies the other side of death. But you are strong, healthy, cheerful, and excited, and are surrounded by other such excitedly-animated and healthy men.' So thinks, or at any rate feels, anyone who comes in sight of the enemy, and that feeling gives a particular glamour and glad keenness of impression to everything that takes place at such moments.

On the high ground where the enemy was, the smoke of a

cannon rose, and a ball flew whistling over the heads of the hussar squadron. The officers who had been standing together rode off to their places. The hussars began carefully aligning their horses. Silence fell on the whole squadron. All were looking at the enemy in front and at the squadron commander, awaiting the word of command. A second and a third cannon-ball flew past. Evidently they were firing at the hussars, but the balls with rapid rhythmic whistle flew over the heads of the horsemen and fell somewhere beyond them. The hussars did not look round, but at the sound of each shot, as at the word of command, the whole squadron with its rows of faces so alike yet so different, holding its breath while the ball flew past, rose in the stirrups and sank back again. The soldiers without turning their heads glanced at one another, curious to see their comrades' impression. Every face, from Denisov's to that of the bugler, showed one common expression of conflict, irritation, and excitement, around chin and mouth. The quartermaster frowned, looking at the soldiers as if threatening to punish them. Cadet Mironov ducked every time a ball flew past. Rostov on the left flank, mounted on his Rook – a handsome horse despite its game leg – had the happy air of a schoolboy called up before a large audience for an examination in which he feels sure he will distinguish himself. He was glancing at everyone with a clear bright expression, as if asking them to notice how calmly he sat under fire. But despite himself, on his face too that same indication of something new and stern showed round the mouth.

'Who's that curtseying there? Cadet Miwonov! That's not wight! Look at me,' cried Denisov who, unable to keep still on one spot, kept turning his horse in front of the squadron.

The black, hairy, snub-nosed face of Vaska Denisov, and his whole short sturdy figure with the sinewy hairy hand and stumpy fingers in which he held the hilt of his naked sabre, looked just as it usually did, especially towards evening when he had emptied his second bottle; he was only redder than usual. With his shaggy head thrown back like birds when they drink, pressing his spurs mercilessly into the sides of his good horse Bedouin and sitting as though falling backwards in the saddle, he galloped to the other flank of the squadron and shouted in a hoarse voice to the men to look to their pistols. He rode up to Kirsten. The staff-captain on his broad-backed steady mare came at a walk to meet him. His face with its long moustache was serious as always, only his eyes were brighter than usual.

'Well, what about it?' said he to Denisov. 'It won't come to a fight. You'll see – we shall retire.'

'The devil only knows what they're about!' muttered Denisov.

'Ah, Wostov,' he cried noticing the cadet's bright face, 'you've got it at last.'

And he smiled approvingly, evidently pleased with the cadet. Rostov felt perfectly happy. Just then the commander appeared on the bridge. Denisov galloped up to him.

'Your Excellency! Let us attack them! I'll dwive them off.'

'Attack indeed!' said the colonel in a bored voice, puckering up his face as if driving off a troublesome fly. 'And why are you stopping here? Don't you see the skirmishers are retreating? Lead the squadron back.'

The squadron crossed the bridge and drew out of range of fire without having lost a single man. The second squadron that had been in the front line followed them across and the last Cossacks quitted the farther side of the river.

The two Pavlograd squadrons, having crossed the bridge, retired up the hill one after the other. Their colonel, Karl Bogdanich Schubert,* came up to Denisov's squadron and rode at a foot-pace not far from Rostov, without taking any notice of him although they were now meeting for the first time since their encounter concerning Telyanin. Rostov feeling that he was at the front and in the power of a man towards whom he now admitted that he had been to blame, did not lift his eyes from the colonel's athletic back, his nape covered with light hair, and his red neck. It seemed to Rostov that Bogdanich was only pretending not to notice him, and that his whole aim now was to test the cadet's courage, so he drew himself up and looked around him merrily; then it seemed to him that Bogdanich rode so near in order to show him his courage. Next he thought that his enemy would send the squadron on a desperate attack just to punish him – Rostov. Then he imagined how, after the attack, Bogdanich would come up to him as he lay wounded and would magnanimously extend the hand of reconciliation.

The high-shouldered figure of Zherkov, familiar to the Pavlograds as he had but recently left their regiment, rode up to the colonel. After his dismissal from head-quarters Zherkov had not remained in the regiment, saying he was not such a fool as to slave at the front when he could get more rewards by doing nothing on the staff, and had succeeded in attaching himself as an orderly officer to Prince Bagration. He now came to his former chief with an order from the commander of the rearguard.

'Colonel,' he said, addressing Rostov's enemy with an air of gloomy gravity and glancing round at his comrades, 'there is an order to stop and fire the bridge.'

'An order to who?' asked the colonel morosely.

'I don't myself know "to who",' replied the cornet in a serious tone, 'but the prince told me to "go and tell the colonel that the hussars must return quickly and fire the bridge".'

Zherkov was followed by an officer of the suite who rode up to the colonel of hussars with the same order. After him the stout Nesvitsky came galloping up on a Cossack horse that could scarcely carry his weight.

'How's this, Colonel?' he shouted as he approached. 'I told you to fire the bridge, and now someone has gone and blundered; they are all beside themselves over there and one can't make anything out.'

The colonel deliberately stopped the regiment and turned to Nesvitsky.

'You spoke to me of inflammable material,' said he, 'but you said nothing about firing it.'

'But, my dear sir,' said Nesvitsky as he drew up, taking off his cap and smoothing his hair wet with perspiration with his plump hand, 'wasn't I telling you to fire the bridge, when inflammable material had been put in position?'

'I am not your "dear sir," Mr Staff-officer, and you did not tell me to burn the bridge! I know the service, and it is my habit orders strictly to obey. You said the bridge would be burnt, but who would it burn, I could not know by the holy spirit!'

'Ah, that's always the way!' said Nesvitsky with a wave of the hand. 'How did you get here?' said he, turning to Zherkov.

'On the same business. But you *are* damp! Let me wring you out!'

'You were saying, Mr Staff-officer ...' continued the colonel in an offended tone.

'Colonel,' interrupted the officer of the suite, 'you must be quick or the enemy will bring up his guns to use grape-shot.'

The colonel looked silently at the officer of the suite, at the stout staff-officer, and at Zherkov, and he frowned.

'I will the bridge fire,' he said in a solemn tone, as if to announce that in spite of all the unpleasantness he had to endure he would still do the right thing.

Striking his horse with his long muscular legs as if it were to blame for everything, the colonel moved forward and ordered the second squadron, that in which Rostov was serving under Denisov, to return to the bridge.

'There, it's just as I thought,' said Rostov to himself. 'He wishes to test me!' His heart contracted and the blood rushed to his face. 'Let him see whether I am a coward!' he thought.

Again on all the bright faces of the squadron the serious

expression appeared that they had worn when under fire. Rostov watched his enemy, the colonel, closely – to find in his face confirmation of his own conjecture, but the colonel did not once glance at Rostov, and looked as he always did when at the front, solemn and stern. Then came the word of command.

'Look sharp! Look sharp!' several voices repeated around him.

Their sabres catching in the bridles and their spurs jingling, the hussars hastily dismounted, not knowing what they were to do. The men were crossing themselves. Rostov no longer looked at the colonel, he had no time. He was afraid of falling behind the hussars, so much afraid that his heart stood still. His hand trembled as he gave his horse into an orderly's charge, and he felt the blood rush to his heart with a thud. Denisov rode past him, leaning back and shouting something. Rostov saw nothing but the hussars running all around him, their spurs catching and their sabres clattering.

'Stretchers!' shouted someone behind him.

Rostov did not think what this call for stretchers meant; he ran on, trying only to be ahead of the others; but just at the bridge, not looking at the ground, he came on some sticky, trodden mud, stumbled, and fell on his hands. The others outstripped him.

'At boss zides, Captain,' he heard the voice of the colonel, who, having ridden ahead, had pulled up his horse near the bridge, with a triumphant, cheerful face.

Rostov wiping his muddy hands on his breeches looked at his enemy, and was about to run on, thinking that the farther he went to the front the better. But Bogdanich, without looking at or recognizing Rostov, shouted to him:

'Who's that running on the middle of the bridge? To the right! Come back, Cadet!' he cried angrily; and turning to Denisov, who, showing off his courage, had ridden on to the planks of the bridge:

'Why run risks, Captain? You should dismount,' he said.

'Oh, every bullet has its billet,' answered Vaska Denisov, turning in his saddle.

Meanwhile Nesvitsky, Zherkov, and the officer of the suite were standing together out of range of the shots, watching, now the small group of men with yellow shakos, dark-green jackets braided with cord, and blue riding-breeches, who were swarming near the bridge, and then what was approaching in the distance from the opposite side – the blue uniforms and groups with horses, easily recognizable as artillery.

'Will they burn the bridge or not? Who'll get there first? Will they get there and fire the bridge or will the French get within grape-shot range and wipe them out?' These were the questions each man of the troops on the high ground above the bridge involuntarily asked himself with a sinking heart – watching the bridge and the hussars in the bright evening light and the blue tunics advancing from the other side with their bayonets and guns.

'Ugh! The hussars will get it hot!' said Nesvitsky; 'they are within grape-shot range now.'

'He shouldn't have taken so many men,' said the officer of the suite.

'True enough,' answered Nesvitsky; 'two smart fellows could have done the job just as well.'

'Ah, your Excellency,' put in Zherkov, his eyes fixed on the hussars, but still with that naïve air that made it impossible to know whether he was speaking in jest or in earnest. 'Ah, your Excellency! How you look at things! Send two men? And who then would give us the Vladimir medal and ribbon? But now, even if they do get peppered, the squadron may be recommended for honours and he may get a ribbon. Our Bogdanich knows how things are done.'

'There now!' said the officer of the suite, 'that's grapeshot.'

He pointed to the French guns, the limbers of which were being detached and hurriedly removed.

On the French side, amid the groups with cannon, a cloud of smoke appeared, then a second and a third almost simultaneously, and at the moment when the first report was heard a fourth was seen. Then two reports one after another, and a third.

'Oh! Oh!' groaned Nesvitsky, as if in fierce pain, seizing the officer of the suite by the arm. 'Look! A man has fallen! Fallen, fallen!'

'Two, I think.'

'If I were Tsar I would never go to war,' said Nesvitsky, turning away.

The French guns were hastily reloaded. The infantry in their blue uniforms advanced towards the bridge at a run. Smoke appeared again but at irregular intervals, and grape-shot cracked and rattled onto the bridge. But this time Nesvitsky could not see what was happening there, as a dense cloud of smoke arose from it. The hussars had succeeded in setting it on fire and the French batteries were now firing at them, no longer to hinder them but because the guns were trained and there was someone to fire at.

The French had time to fire three rounds of grape-shot before the hussars got back to their horses. Two were misdirected and the shot went too high, but the last round fell in the midst of a group of hussars and knocked three of them over.

Rostov, absorbed by his relations with Bogdanich, had paused on the bridge, not knowing what to do. There was no one to hew down (as he had always imagined battles to himself), nor could he help to fire the bridge because he had not brought any burning straw with him like the other soldiers. He stood looking about him, when suddenly he heard a rattle on the bridge as if nuts were being spilt, and the hussar nearest to him fell against the rails with a groan. Rostov ran up to him with the others. Again someone shouted, 'Stretchers!' Four men seized the hussar and began lifting him.

'Oooh! For Christ's sake let me alone!' cried the wounded man, but still he was lifted and laid on the stretcher.

Nicholas Rostov turned away and, as if searching for something, gazed into the distance, at the waters of the Danube, at the sky, and at the sun. How beautiful the sky looked; how blue, how calm, and how deep! How bright and glorious was the setting sun! With what soft glitter the waters of the distant Danube shone. And fairer still were the far away blue mountains beyond the river, the nunnery, the mysterious gorges, and the pine forests veiled in mist to their summits ... There was peace and happiness ... 'I should wish for nothing else, nothing, if only I were there,' thought Rostov. 'In myself alone and in that sunshine there is so much happiness; but here ... groans, suffering, fear, and this uncertainty and hurry ... There – they are shouting again, and again are all running back somewhere, and I shall run with them, and it, death, is here above me and around ... Another instant and I shall never again see the sun, this water, that gorge! ...'

At that instant the sun began to hide behind the clouds, and other stretchers came in view before Rostov. And the fear of death and of the stretchers, and love of the sun and of life, all merged into one feeling of sickening agitation.

'O Lord God! Thou who art in that heaven, save, forgive, and protect me!' Rostov whispered.

The hussars ran back to the men who held their horses; their voices sounded louder and calmer, the stretchers disappeared from sight.

'Well, fwiend? So you've smelt powdah!' shouted Vaska Denisov just above his ear.

'It's all over; but I am a coward – yes, a coward!' thought Rostov, and sighing deeply he took Rook, his horse, which stood resting one foot, from the orderly, and began to mount.

'Was that grape-shot?' he asked Denisov.

'Yes and no mistake!' cried Denisov. 'You worked like wegular bwicks and it's nasty work! An attack's pleasant work! Hacking away at the dogs! But this sort of thing is the very devil, with them shooting at you like a target.'

And Denisov rode up to a group that had stopped near Rostov, composed of the colonel, Nesvitsky, Zherkov, and the officer from the suite.

'Well it seems that no one has noticed,' thought Rostov. And this was true. No one had taken any notice, for everyone knew the sensation which the cadet under fire for the first time had experienced.

'Here's something for you to report,' said Zherkov. 'See if I don't get promoted to a sub-lieutenancy.'

'Inform the prince that I the bridge fired!' said the colonel triumphantly and gaily.

'And if he asks about the losses?'

'A trifle,' said the colonel in his bass voice: 'two hussars wounded, and one knocked out,' he added, unable to restrain a happy smile, and pronouncing the phrase 'knocked out' with ringing distinctness.

9

PURSUED by the French army of a hundred thousand men under the command of Bonaparte, encountering a population that was unfriendly to it, losing confidence in its allies, suffering from shortness of supplies, and compelled to act under conditions of war unlike anything that had been foreseen, the Russian army of thirty-five thousand men commanded by Kutuzov was hurriedly retreating along the Danube, stopping where overtaken by the enemy and fighting rearguard actions only as far as necessary to enable it to retreat without losing its heavy equipment. There had been actions at Lambach, Amstetten, and Mölk;* but despite the courage and endurance – acknowledged even by the enemy – with which the Russians fought, the only consequence of these actions was a yet more rapid retreat. Austrian troops that had escaped capture at Ulm and had joined Kutuzov at Braunau, now separated from the Russian army, and Kutuzov was left with only his own weak and exhausted forces. The defence of Vienna was no longer to be thought of. Instead of an offensive, the plan of which, carefully prepared in accord with the modern science of strategics, had been handed to Kutuzov when he was in Vienna by the Austrian Hofkriegsrath, the sole and almost unattainable aim remaining for him was to effect a junction with the forces that were advancing from Russia, without losing his army as Mack had done at Ulm.

On the 28th of October Kutuzov with his army crossed to the left bank of the Danube and took up a position for the first time with the river between himself and the main body of the French. On the 30th he attacked Mortier's division which was on the left bank, and broke it up. In this action for the first time trophies were taken: banners, cannon, and two enemy generals. For the first time, after a fortnight's retreat, the Russian troops had halted and after a fight had not only held the field but had repulsed the French. Though the troops were ill-clad, exhausted, and had lost a third of their number in killed, wounded, sick, and stragglers; though a number of sick and wounded had been abandoned on the other side of the Danube with a letter in which Kutuzov entrusted them to the humanity of the enemy; and though the big hospitals and the houses in Krems converted into military hospitals could no longer accommodate all the sick and wounded, yet the stand made at Krems and the victory over Mortier raised the spirits of the army considerably. Throughout the whole army and at head-quarters most joyful though erroneous rumours were rife of the imaginary approach of columns from Russia, of some victory gained by the Austrians, and of the retreat of the frightened Bonaparte.

Prince Andrew during the battle had been in attendance on the Austrian General Schmidt, who was killed in the action. His horse had been wounded under him and his own arm slightly grazed by a bullet. As a mark of the commander-in-chief's special favour he was sent with the news of this victory to the Austrian Court, now no longer at Vienna (which was threatened by the French) but at Brünn. Despite his apparently delicate build Prince Andrew could endure physical fatigue far better than many very muscular men, and on the night of the battle, having arrived at Krems, excited but not weary, with despatches from Dokhturov to Kutuzov, he was sent immediately with a special despatch to Brünn. To be so sent meant not only a reward but an important step towards promotion.

The night was dark but starry, the road showed black in the snow that had fallen the previous day – the day of the battle. Reviewing his impressions of the recent battle, picturing pleasantly to himself the impression his news of a victory would create, or recalling the send-off given him by the commander-in-chief and his fellow-officers, Prince Andrew was galloping along in a post-chaise enjoying the feelings of a man who has at length begun to attain a long-desired happiness. As soon as he closed his eyes his ears seemed filled with the rattle of the wheels and the sensation of victory. Then he began to imagine that the Russians were running away and that he himself was killed, but he quickly roused himself with a feeling of joy, as if learning afresh that this was not so but that on the contrary the French had run away. He again recalled all the details of the victory and his own calm courage during the battle, and feeling reassured he dozed off . . . The dark starry night was followed by a bright cheerful morning. The snow was thawing in the sunshine, the horses galloped quickly, and on both sides of the road were forests of different kinds, fields, and villages.

At one of the post-stations he overtook a convoy of Russian wounded. The Russian officer in charge of the transport lolled back in the front cart, shouting and scolding a soldier with coarse abuse. In each of the long German carts six or more pale, dirty, bandaged men were being jolted over the stony road. Some of them were talking (he heard Russian words), others were eating bread; the more severely wounded looked silently, with the languid interest of sick children, at the envoy hurrying past them.

Prince Andrew told his driver to stop, and asked a soldier in what action they had been wounded. 'Day before yesterday, on the Danube,' answered the soldier. Prince Andrew took out his purse and gave the soldier three gold pieces.

'That's for them all,' he said to the officer who came up.

'Get well soon, lads!' he continued, turning to the soldiers. 'There's plenty to do still.'

'What news, sir?' asked the officer, evidently anxious to start a conversation.

'Good news! . . . Go on!' he shouted to the driver, and they galloped on.

It was already quite dark when Prince Andrew rattled over the paved streets of Brünn and found himself surrounded by high buildings, the lights of shops, houses, and street-lamps, fine carriages, and all that atmosphere of a large and active town which is always so attractive to a soldier after camp life. Despite his rapid journey and sleepless night, Prince Andrew when he drove up to the palace felt even more vigorous and alert than he had done the day before. Only his eyes gleamed feverishly and his thoughts followed one another with extraordinary clearness and rapidity. He again vividly recalled the details of the battle, no longer dim, but definite and in the concise form in which he imagined himself stating them to the Emperor Francis. He vividly imagined the casual questions that might be put to him and the answers he would give. He expected to be at once presented to the Emperor.

At the chief entrance to the palace, however, an official came running out to meet him, and learning that he was a special messenger led him to another entrance.

'To the right from the corridor, *Euer Hochgeboren!* There you will find the adjutant on duty,' said the official. 'He will conduct you to the Minister of War.'

The adjutant on duty, meeting Prince Andrew, asked him to wait, and went in to the Minister of War. Five minutes later he returned and bowing with particular courtesy ushered Prince Andrew before him along a corridor to the cabinet where the Minister of War was at work. The adjutant by his elaborate courtesy appeared to wish to ward off any attempt at familiarity on the part of the Russian messenger.

Prince Andrew's joyous feeling was considerably weakened as he approached the door of the minister's room. He felt offended, and without his noticing it the feeling of offence immediately turned into one of disdain which was quite uncalled for. His fertile mind instantly suggested to him a point of view which gave him a right to despise the adjutant and the minister. 'Away from the smell of powder, they probably think it easy to gain victories!' he thought. His eyes narrowed disdainfully, he entered the room of the Minister of War with peculiarly deliberate steps. This feeling of disdain was heightened when he saw the minister seated at a large table reading some papers and making pencil notes on them, and for the first two or three minutes taking no notice of his arrival. A wax candle stood at each side of the minister's bent bald head with its grey temples. He went on reading to the end, without raising his eyes at the opening of the door and the sound of footsteps.

'Take this and deliver it,' said he to his adjutant, handing him the papers and still taking no notice of the special messenger.

Prince Andrew felt that either the actions of Kutuzov's army interested the Minister of War less than any of the other matters he was concerned with, or he wanted to give the Russian special messenger that impression. 'But that is a matter of perfect in-difference to me,' he thought. The minister drew the remaining papers together, arranged them evenly, and then raised his head. He had an intellectual and distinctive head, but the instant he turned to Prince Andrew the firm, intelligent expression on his face changed in a way evidently deliberate and habitual to him. His face took on the stupid artificial smile (which does not even attempt to hide its artificiality) of a man who is continually receiving many petitioners one after another.

'From General Field-Marshal Kutuzov?' he asked. 'I hope it is good news? There has been an encounter with Mortier? A victory? It was high time!'

He took the despatch which was addressed to him and began to read it with a mournful expression.

'Oh, my God! Schmidt!' he exclaimed in German. 'What a calamity! What a calamity!'

Having glanced through the despatch he laid it on the table and looked at Prince Andrew, evidently considering something.

'Ah, what a calamity! You say the affair was decisive? But Mortier is not captured.' Again he pondered. 'I'm very glad you have brought good news, though Schmidt's death is a heavy price to pay for the victory. His Majesty will no doubt wish to see you, but not to-day. I thank you! You must have a rest. Be at the levee to-morrow after the parade. However I will let you know.'

The stupid smile, which had left his face while he was speaking, reappeared.

'Au revoir! Thank you very much. His Majesty will probably desire to see you,' he added, bowing his head.

When Prince Andrew left the palace he felt that all the interest and happiness the victory had afforded him had been now left in the indifferent hands of the Minister of War and the polite adjutant. The whole tenor of his thoughts instantaneously changed; the battle seemed the memory of a remote event long past.

10

PRINCE ANDREW stayed at Brünn with Bilibin, a Russian acquaintance of his in the diplomatic service.

'Ah, my dear Prince! I could not have a more welcome visitor,' said Bilibin as he came out to meet Prince Andrew. 'Franz, put the prince's things in my bedroom,' said he to the servant who was ushering Bolkonsky in. 'So you're a messenger of victory, eh? Splendid! And I am sitting here ill, as you see.'

After washing and dressing, Prince Andrew came into the diplomat's luxurious study and sat down to the dinner prepared for him. Bilibin settled down comfortably beside the fire.

After his journey and the campaign during which he had been deprived of all the comforts of cleanliness and all the refinements of life, Prince Andrew felt a pleasant sense of repose among luxurious surroundings such as he had been accustomed to from childhood. Besides it was pleasant, after his reception by the Austrians, to speak if not in Russian (for they were speaking French) at least with a Russian who would, he supposed, share the general

Russian antipathy to the Austrians which was then particularly strong.

Bilibin was a man of thirty-five, a bachelor and of the same circle as Prince Andrew. They had known each other previously in Petersburg, but had become more intimate when Prince Andrew was in Vienna with Kutuzov. Just as Prince Andrew was a young man who gave promise of rising high in the military profession, so to an even greater extent, Bilibin gave promise of rising in his diplomatic career. He was still a young man but no longer a young diplomat, as he had entered the service at the age of sixteen, had been in Paris and Copenhagen, and now held a rather important post in Vienna. Both the foreign minister and our ambassador in Vienna knew him and valued him. He was not one of those many diplomats who are esteemed because they have certain negative qualities, avoid doing certain things, and speak French. He was one of those who, liking work, knew how to do it, and despite his indolence would sometimes spend a whole night at his writing-table. He worked equally well whatever the import of his work. It was not the question 'What for?' but the question 'How?' that interested him. What the diplomatic matter might be he did not care, but it gave him great pleasure to prepare a circular, memorandum, or report, skilfully, pointedly and elegantly. Bilibin's services were valued not only for what he wrote, but also for his skill in dealing and conversing with those in the highest spheres.

Bilibin liked conversation as he liked work, only when it could be made elegantly witty. In society he always awaited an opportunity to say something striking, and took part in a conversation only when that was possible. His conversation was always sprinkled with wittily original, finished phrases of general interest. These sayings were prepared in the inner laboratory of his mind in a portable form as if intentionally, so that insignificant society people might carry them from drawing-room to drawing-room. And in fact Bilibin's witticisms were hawked about in the Viennese drawing-rooms and often had an influence on matters considered important.

His thin, worn, sallow face was covered with deep wrinkles, which always looked as clean and well washed as the tips of one's fingers after a Russian bath. The movement of these wrinkles formed the principal play of expression on his face. Now his forehead would pucker into deep folds and his eyebrows were lifted, then his eyebrows would descend and deep wrinkles would crease his cheeks. His small, deep-set eyes always twinkled and looked out straight.

'Well, now tell me about your exploits,' said he.

Bolkonsky, very modestly without once mentioning himself, described the engagement and his reception by the Minister of War.

'They received me and my news as one receives a dog in a game of skittles,' said he in conclusion.

Bilibin smiled and the wrinkles on his face disappeared.

'*Cependant, mon cher,*' he remarked, examining his nails from a distance and puckering the skin above his left eye, '*malgré la haute estime que je professe pour* the Orthodox Russian army, *j'avoue que votre victoire n'est pas des plus victorieuses.*'

He went on talking in this way in French, uttering only those words in Russian on which he wished to put a contemptuous emphasis.

'Come now! You with all your forces fall on the unfortunate Mortier and his one division, and even then Mortier slips through your fingers! Where's the victory?'

'But seriously,' said Prince Andrew, 'we can at any rate say without boasting that it was a little better than at Ulm...'

'Why didn't you capture one, just one, marshal for us?'

'Because not everything happens as one expects with the smoothness of a parade. We had expected, as I told you, to get at their rear by seven in the morning but had not reached it by five in the afternoon.'

'And why didn't you do it at seven in the morning? You ought to have been there at seven in the morning,' returned Bilibin with a smile. 'You ought to have been there at seven in the morning.'

'Why did you not succeed in impressing on Bonaparte by diplomatic methods that he had better leave Genoa alone?' retorted Prince Andrew in the same tone.

'I know,' interrupted Bilibin, 'you're thinking it's very easy to take marshals, sitting on a sofa by the fire! That is true, but still why didn't you capture him? So don't be surprised if not only the Minister of War but also his Most August Majesty the Emperor and King Francis is not much delighted by your victory. Even I, a poor secretary of the Russian Embassy, do not feel any need, in token of my joy, to give my Franz a *thaler*, or let him go with his *Liebchen* to the Prater... True, we have no Prater here...'

He looked straight at Prince Andrew and suddenly unwrinkled his forehead.

'It is now my turn to ask you "why?" *mon cher*,' said Bolkonsky. 'I confess I do not understand: perhaps there are diplomatic subtleties here beyond my feeble intelligence, but I can't make it out. Mack loses a whole army, the Archduke Ferdinand and the

Archduke Karl give no signs of life and make blunder after blunder. Kutuzov alone at last gains a real victory, destroying the spell of the invincibility of the French, and the Minister of War does not even care to hear the details.'

'That's just it, my dear fellow! You see it's *hurrah* for the Tsar, for Russia, for the Orthodox Greek faith! All that is beautiful, but what do we, I mean the Austrian Court, care for your victories? Bring us nice news of a victory by the Archduke Karl or Ferdinand (one archduke's as good as another, as you know) and even if it is only over a fire-brigade of Bonaparte's, that will be another story and we'll fire off some cannon! But this sort of thing seems done on purpose to vex us. The Archduke Karl does nothing, the Archduke Ferdinand disgraces himself. You abandon Vienna, give up its defence – as much as to say: "Heaven is with us, but heaven help you and your capital!" The one general whom we all loved, Schmidt, you expose to a bullet, and then you congratulate us on the victory! Admit that more irritating news than yours could not have been conceived. It's as if it had been done on purpose, on purpose. Besides, suppose you did gain a brilliant victory, if even the Archduke Karl gained a victory, what effect would that have on the general course of events? It's too late now when Vienna is occupied by the French army!'

'What? Occupied? Vienna occupied?'

'Not only occupied, but Bonaparte is at Schönbrunn, and the count, our dear Count Vrbna, goes to him for orders.'

After the fatigues and impressions of the journey, his reception, and especially after having dined, Bolkonsky felt that he could not take in the full significance of the words he heard.

'Count Lichtenfels was here this morning,' Bilibin continued, 'and showed me a letter in which the parade of the French in Vienna was fully described: Prince Murat *et tout le tremblement* ... * You see that your victory is not a matter of great rejoicing and that you can't be received as a saviour.'

'Really I don't care about that, I don't care at all,' said Prince Andrew, beginning to understand that his news of the battle before Krems was really of small importance in view of such events as the fall of Austria's capital. 'How is it Vienna was taken? What of the bridge and its celebrated bridge-head and Prince Auersperg? We heard reports that Prince Auersperg was defending Vienna,' said he.

'Prince Auersperg is on this, on our side of the river, and is defending us – doing it very badly I think, but still he is defending us. But Vienna is on the other side. No, the bridge has not yet been taken and I hope it will not be, for it is mined and orders have been given to blow it up. Otherwise we should long ago have been in the mountains of Bohemia, and you and your army would have spent a bad quarter of an hour between two fires.'

'But still this does not mean that the campaign is over,' said Prince Andrew.

'Well, I think it is. The bigwigs here think so too, but they daren't say so. It will be as I said at the beginning of the campaign, it won't be your skirmishing at Dürrenstein, or gunpowder at all that will decide the matter, but those who devised it,' said Bilibin, quoting one of his own *mots*, releasing the wrinkles on his forehead, and pausing. 'The only question is what will come of the meeting between the Emperor Alexander and the King of Prussia in Berlin?* If Prussia joins the allies, Austria's hand will be forced and there will be war. If not it is merely a question of settling where the preliminaries of the new Campo Formio are to be drawn up.'

'What an extraordinary genius!' Prince Andrew suddenly exclaimed, clenching his small hand and striking the table with it, 'and what luck the man has!'

'Buonaparte?' said Bilibin inquiringly, puckering up his forehead to indicate that he was about to say something witty. 'Buonaparte?' he repeated, accentuating the *u*: 'I think, however, now that he lays down laws for Austria at Schönbrunn, *il faut lui faire grâce de l'u!** I shall certainly adopt an innovation and call him simply Bonaparte!'

'But joking apart,' said Prince Andrew, 'do you really think the campaign is over?'

'This is what I think. Austria has been made a fool of, and she is not used to it. She will retaliate. And she has been fooled in the first place because her provinces have been pillaged – they say the Holy Russian army loots terribly – her army is destroyed, her capital taken, and all this for the *beaux yeux* of His Sardinian Majesty.* And therefore – this is between ourselves – I instinctively feel that we are being deceived, my instinct tells me of negotiations with France and projects for peace, a secret peace concluded separately.'

'Impossible!' cried Prince Andrew. 'That would be too base.'

'If we live we shall see,' replied Bilibin, his face again becoming smooth as a sign that the conversation was at an end.

When Prince Andrew reached the room prepared for him and lay down in a clean shirt on the feather-bed with its warmed and fragrant pillows, he felt that the battle of which he had brought tidings was far far away from him. The alliance with Prussia, Austria's treachery, Bonaparte's new triumph, to-morrow's levee and parade, and the audience with the Emperor Francis, occupied his thoughts.

He closed his eyes, and immediately a sound of cannonading, of musketry, and the rattling of carriage wheels seemed to fill his ears, and now again drawn out in a thin line the musketeers were descending the hill, the French were firing, and he felt his heart palpitating as he rode forward beside Schmidt with the bullets merrily whistling all around, and he experienced tenfold the joy of living, as he had not done since childhood.

He woke up . . .

'Yes, that all happened!' he said, and smiling happily to himself like a child, he fell into a deep youthful slumber.

11

NEXT day he woke late. Recalling his recent impressions the first thought that came into his mind was that to-day he had to be presented to the Emperor Francis; he remembered the Minister of War, the polite Austrian adjutant, Bilibin, and last night's conversation. Having dressed for his attendance at court in full parade uniform, which he had not worn for a long time, he went into Bilibin's study fresh, animated and handsome, with his hand bandaged. In the study were four gentlemen of the diplomatic corps. With Prince Hippolyte Kuragin, who was a secretary to the embassy, Bolkonsky was already acquainted. Bilibin introduced him to the others.

The gentlemen assembled at Bilibin's were young, wealthy, gay, society men, who here, as in Vienna, formed a special set which Bilibin, their leader, called *les nôtres*. This set, consisting almost exclusively of diplomats, evidently had its own interests which had nothing to do with war or politics but related to high society, to certain women, and to the official side of the service. These gentlemen received Prince Andrew as one of themselves, an honour they did not extend to many. From politeness and to start conversation, they asked him a few questions about the army and the battle, and then the talk went off into merry jests and gossip.

'But the best of it was,' said one, telling of the misfortune of a fellow diplomat, 'that the Chancellor told him flatly that his appointment to London was a promotion and that he was so to regard it. Can you fancy the figure he cut . . .?'

'But the worst of it, gentlemen – I am giving Kuragin away to you – is that that man suffers, and this Don Juan, wicked fellow, is taking advantage of it!'

Prince Hippolyte was lolling in a lounge chair with his legs over its arm. He began to laugh.

'Tell me about that!' he said.

'Oh, you Don Juan! You serpent!' cried several voices.

'You, Bolkonsky, don't know,' said Bilibin turning to Prince Andrew, 'that all the atrocities of the French army (I nearly said of the Russian army) are nothing compared to what this man has been doing among the women!'

'*La femme est la campagne de l'homme,*' announced Prince Hippolyte, and began looking through a lorgnette at his elevated legs.

Bilibin and the rest of 'ours' burst out laughing in Hippolyte's face, and Prince Andrew saw that Hippolyte, of whom – he had to admit – he had almost been jealous on his wife's account, was the butt of this set.

'Oh, I must give you a treat,' Bilibin whispered to Bolkonsky. 'Kuragin is exquisite when he discusses politics – you should see his gravity!'

He sat down beside Hippolyte and wrinkling his forehead began talking to him about politics. Prince Andrew and the others gathered round these two.

'The Berlin cabinet cannot express a feeling of alliance,' began Hippolyte gazing round with importance at the others, 'without expressing . . . as in its last note . . . you understand . . . Besides, unless his Majesty the Emperor derogates from the principle of our alliance . . .

'Wait, I have not finished . . .' he said to Prince Andrew, seizing him by the arm, 'I believe that intervention will be stronger than non-intervention. And . . .' he paused. 'Finally one cannot impute the non-receipt of our despatch of November 18. That is how it will end.' And he released Bolkonsky's arm to indicate that he had now quite finished.

'Demosthenes, I know thee by the pebble thou secretest in thy golden mouth!' said Bilibin, and the mop of hair on his head moved with satisfaction.

Everybody laughed, and Hippolyte louder than anyone. He was evidently distressed, and breathed painfully, but could not restrain the wild laughter that convulsed his usually impassive features.

'Well now, gentlemen,' said Bilibin, 'Bolkonsky is my guest in this house and in Brünn itself. I want to entertain him, as far as I can, with all the pleasures of life here. If we were in Vienna it would be easy, but here, in this wretched Moravian hole, it is more difficult, and I beg you all to help me. Brünn's attractions must be shown him. You can undertake the theatre, I society, and you, Hippolyte, of course the women.'

'We must let him see Amelie, she's exquisite!' said one of 'ours', kissing his finger-tips.

'In general we must turn this bloodthirsty soldier to more humane interests,' said Bilibin.

'I shall scarcely be able to avail myself of your hospitality, gentlemen, it is already time for me to go,' replied Prince Andrew looking at his watch.

'Where to?'

'To the Emperor.'

'Oh! Oh! Oh!'

'Well, *au revoir*, Bolkonsky! *Au revoir*, Prince! Come back early to dinner,' cried several voices. 'We'll take you in hand.'

'When speaking to the Emperor, try as far as you can to praise the way that provisions are supplied and the routes indicated,' said Bilibin, accompanying him to the hall.

'I should like to speak well of them, but as far as I know the facts, I can't,' replied Bolkonsky, smiling.

'Well, talk as much as you can, anyway. He has a passion for giving audiences, but he does not like talking himself and can't do it, as you will see.'

12

AT the levee Prince Andrew stood among the Austrian officers as he had been told to, and the Emperor Francis merely looked fixedly into his face and just nodded to him with his long head. But after it was over the adjutant he had seen the previous day ceremoniously informed Bolkonsky that the Emperor desired to give him an audience. The Emperor Francis received him standing in the middle of the room. Before the conversation began Prince Andrew was struck by the fact that the Emperor seemed confused and blushed as if not knowing what to say.

'Tell me, when did the battle begin?' he asked hurriedly.

Prince Andrew replied. Then followed other questions just as simple: 'Was Kutuzov well? When had he left Krems?' and so on. The Emperor spoke as if his sole aim were to put a given number of questions – the answers to these questions, as was only too evident, did not interest him.

'At what o'clock did the battle begin?' asked the Emperor.

'I cannot inform your Majesty at what o'clock the battle began at the front, but at Dürrenstein, where I was, our attack began after five in the afternoon,' replied Bolkonsky growing more animated and expecting that he would have a chance to give a reliable account, which he had ready in his mind, of all he knew and had seen. But the Emperor smiled and interrupted him.

'How many miles?'

'From where to where, your Majesty?'

'From Dürrenstein to Krems.'

'Three and a half miles, your Majesty.'

'The French have abandoned the left bank?'

'According to the scouts the last of them crossed on rafts during the night.'

'Is there sufficient forage in Krems?'

'Forage had not been supplied to the extent . . .'

The Emperor interrupted him.

'At what o'clock was General Schmidt killed?'

'At seven o'clock, I believe.'

'At seven o'clock? It's very sad, very sad!'

The Emperor thanked Prince Andrew and bowed. Prince Andrew withdrew and was immediately surrounded by courtiers on all sides. Everywhere he saw friendly looks and heard friendly words. Yesterday's adjutant reproached him for not having stayed at the palace, and offered him his own house. The Minister of War came up and congratulated him on the Maria Theresa Order of the third grade, which the Emperor was conferring on him. The Empress's chamberlain invited him to see her Majesty. The archduchess also wished to see him. He did not know whom to answer, and for a few seconds collected his thoughts. Then the Russian ambassador took him by the shoulder, led him to the window, and began to talk to him.

Contrary to Bilibin's forecast the news he had brought was joyfully received. A thanksgiving service was arranged, Kutuzov was awarded the Grand Cross of Maria Theresa, and the whole army received rewards. Bolkonsky was invited everywhere, and had to spend the whole morning calling on the principal Austrian dignitaries. Between four and five in the afternoon, having made all his calls, he was returning to Bilibin's house thinking out a letter to his father about the battle and his visit to Brünn. At the door he found a vehicle half full of luggage. Franz, Bilibin's man, was dragging a portmanteau with some difficulty out of the front door.

Before returning to Bilibin's Prince Andrew had gone to a bookshop to provide himself with some books for the campaign, and had spent some time in the shop.

'What is it?' he asked.

'Oh, your Excellency!' said Franz, with difficulty rolling the portmanteau into the vehicle, 'we are to move on still farther. The scoundrel is again at our heels!'

'Eh? What?' asked Prince Andrew.

Bilibin came out to meet him. His usually calm face showed excitement.

'There now! Confess that this is delightful,' said he. 'This affair of the Thabor Bridge, at Vienna ... They have crossed without striking a blow!'

Prince Andrew could not understand.

'But where do you come from not to know what every coachman in the town knows?'

'I come from the archduchess's. I heard nothing there.'

'And you didn't see that everybody is packing up?'

'I did not ... What is it all about?' inquired Prince Andrew impatiently.

'What's it all about? Why, the French have crossed the bridge that Auersperg was defending, and the bridge was not blown up: so Murat is now rushing along the road to Brünn and will be here in a day or two.'

'What? Here? But why did they not blow up the bridge, if it was mined?'

'That is what I ask you. No one, not even Bonaparte, knows why.'

Bolkonsky shrugged his shoulders.

'But if the bridge is crossed it means that the army too is lost! It will be cut off,' said he.

'That's just it,' answered Bilibin. 'Listen! The French entered Vienna as I told you. Very well. Next day, which was yesterday, those gentlemen, *messieurs les maréchaux*, Murat, Lannes, and Belliard, mount and ride to the bridge. (Observe that all three are Gascons.) "Gentlemen," says one of them, "you know the Thabor Bridge is mined and doubly mined and that there are menacing fortifications at its head and an army of fifteen thousand men has been ordered to blow up the bridge and not let us cross? But it will please our sovereign the Emperor Napoleon if we take this bridge, so let us three go and take it!" "Yes, let's!" say the others. And off they go and take the bridge, cross it, and now with their whole army are on this side of the Danube, marching on us, you, and your lines of communication.'

'Stop jesting,' said Prince Andrew sadly and seriously. This news grieved him and yet he was pleased.

As soon as he learned that the Russian army was in such a hopeless situation it occurred to him that it was he who was destined to lead it out of this position; that here was the Toulon that would lift him from the ranks* of obscure officers and offer him the first step to fame! Listening to Bilibin he was already imagining how on reaching the army he would give an opinion at the war council which would be the only one that could save the army, and how he alone would be entrusted with the execution of the plan.

'Stop this jesting,' he said.

'I am not jesting,' Bilibin went on. 'Nothing is truer or sadder. These gentlemen ride onto the bridge alone and wave white handkerchiefs; they assure the officer on duty that they, the marshals, are on their way to negotiate with Prince Auersperg. He lets them enter the *tête-de-pont*. They spin him a thousand gasconades, saying that the war is over, that the Emperor Francis is arranging a meeting with Bonaparte, that they desire to see Prince Auersperg, and so on. The officer sends for Auersperg; these gentlemen embrace the officers, crack jokes, sit on the cannon, and meanwhile a French battalion gets to the bridge unobserved, flings the bags of incendiary material into the water, and approaches the *tête-de-pont*. At length appears the lieutenant-general, our dear Prince Auersperg von Mautern himself. 'Dearest foe! Flower of the Austrian army, hero of the Turkish wars! Hostilities are ended, we can shake one another's hand ... The Emperor Napoleon burns with impatience to make Prince Auersperg's acquaintance.' In a word those gentlemen, Gascons indeed, so bewildered him with fine words, and he is so flattered by his rapidly established intimacy with the French marshals, and so dazzled by the sight of Murat's mantle and ostrich plumes, *qu'il n'y voit que du feu, et oublie celui qu'il devait faire, faire sur l'ennemi!'* In spite of the animation of his speech Bilibin did not forget to pause after this *mot* to give time for its due appreciation. 'The French battalion rushes to the bridge-head, spikes the guns, and the bridge is taken! But what is best of all,' he went on, his excitement subsiding under the delightful interest of his own story, 'is that the sergeant in charge of the cannon which was to give the signal to fire the mines and blow up the bridge, this sergeant seeing that the French troops were running onto the bridge, was about to fire, but Lannes stayed his hand. The sergeant, who was evidently wiser than his general, goes up to Auersperg and says: "Prince, you are being deceived, here are the French!" Murat, seeing that all is lost if the sergeant is allowed to speak, turns to Auersperg with feigned astonishment (he is a true Gascon) and says: "I don't recognize the world-famous Austrian discipline, if you allow a subordinate to address you like that!" It was a stroke of genius. Prince Auersperg feels his dignity at stake and orders the sergeant to be arrested. Come, you must own that this affair of the Thabor Bridge is delightful! It is not exactly stupidity, nor rascality . . .'

'It may be treachery,' said Prince Andrew, vividly imagining the grey overcoats, wounds, the smoke of gunpowder, the sounds of firing, and the glory that awaited him.

'Not that either. That puts the court in too bad a light,' replied Bilibin. 'It's not treachery nor rascality not stupidity: it is just as at Ulm . . . it is . . .' – he seemed to be trying to find the right expression. 'C'est . . . c'est du Mack. Nous sommes mackés,' he concluded, feeling that he had produced a good epigram, a fresh one that would be repeated. His hitherto puckered brow became smooth as a sign of pleasure, and with a slight smile he began to examine his nails.

'Where are you off to?' he said suddenly to Prince Andrew who had risen and was going towards his room.

'I am going away.'

'Where to?'

'To the army.'

'But you meant to stay another two days?'

'But now I am off at once.'

And Prince Andrew after giving directions about his departure went to his room.

'Do you know, mon cher,' said Bilibin following him, 'I have been thinking about you. Why are you going?'

And in proof of the conclusiveness of his opinion all the wrinkles vanished from his face.

Prince Andrew looked inquiringly at him and gave no reply.

'Why are you going? I know you think it your duty to gallop back to the army now that it is in danger. I understand that. Mon cher, it is heroism!'

'Not at all,' said Prince Andrew.

'But as you are a philosopher, be a consistent one, look at the other side of the question and you will see that your duty, on the contrary, is to take care of yourself. Leave it to those who are no longer fit for anything else. . . . You have not been ordered to return and have not been dismissed from here; therefore you can stay and go with us wherever our ill-luck takes us. They say we are going to Olmütz, and Olmütz is a very decent town. You and I will travel comfortably in my calèche.'

'Do stop joking, Bilibin,' cried Bolkonsky.

'I am speaking sincerely as a friend! Consider! Where and why are you going, when you might remain here? You are faced by one of two things,' and the skin over his left temple puckered, 'either you will not reach your regiment before peace is concluded, or you will share defeat and disgrace with Kutuzov's whole army.'

And Bilibin unwrinkled his temple, feeling that the dilemma was insoluble.

'I cannot argue about it,' replied Prince Andrew coldly, but he thought: 'I am going to save the army.'

'My dear fellow, you are a hero!' said Bilibin.

13

THAT same night, having taken leave of the Minister of War, Bolkonsky set off to rejoin the army, not knowing where he would find it and fearing to be captured by the French on the way to Krems.

In Brünn everybody attached to the court was packing up, and the heavy baggage was already being dispatched to Olmütz. Near Hetzelsdorf Prince Andrew struck the high road along which the Russian army was moving with great haste and in the greatest disorder. The road was so obstructed with carts that it was impossible to get by in a carriage. Prince Andrew took a horse and a Cossack from a Cossack commander, and hungry and weary, making his way past the baggage-wagons, rode in search of the commander-in-chief and of his own luggage. Very sinister reports of the position of the army reached him as he went along, and the appearance of the troops in their disorderly flight confirmed these rumours.

'Cette armée russe que l'or de l'Angleterre a transportée des extrémités de l'univers, nous allons lui faire éprouver le même sort – (le sort de l'armée d'Ulm).' He remembered these words in Bonaparte's address to his army at the beginning of the campaign, and they awoke in him astonishment at the genius of his hero, a feeling of wounded pride, and a hope of glory. 'And should there be nothing left but to die?' he thought. 'Well, if need be, I shall do it no worse than others.'

He looked with disdain at the endless confused mass of detachments, carts, guns, artillery, and again baggage-wagons and vehicles of all kinds, overtaking one another and blocking the muddy road, three and sometimes four abreast. From all sides, behind and before, as far as ear could reach, there was the rattle of wheels, the creaking of carts and gun-carriages, the tramp of horses, the crack of whips, shouts, the urging of horses, and the swearing of soldiers, orderlies and officers. All along the sides of the road fallen horses were to be seen, some flayed, some not, and broken-down carts beside which solitary soldiers sat waiting for something, and again soldiers straggling from their companies, crowds of whom set off to the neighbouring villages, or returned from them dragging sheep, fowls, hay, and bulging sacks. At each ascent or descent of the road the crowds were yet denser and the din of shouting more incessant. Soldiers floundering knee-deep in mud pushed the guns and wagons themselves. Whips cracked, hoofs slipped, traces broke, and lungs were strained with shouting. The officers directing the march rode backward and forward between the carts. Their voices were but feebly heard amid the uproar and one saw by their faces that they despaired of the possibility of checking this disorder.

'Here is our dear Orthodox Russian army,' thought Bolkonsky, recalling Bilibin's words.

Wishing to find out where the commander-in-chief was, he rode up to a convoy. Directly opposite to him came a strange one-horse vehicle, evidently rigged up by soldiers out of any available materials and looking like something between a cart, a cabriolet, and a calèche. A soldier was driving, and a woman enveloped in shawls sat behind the apron under the leather hood of the vehicle. Prince Andrew rode up and was just putting his question to a soldier when his attention was diverted by the desperate shrieks of the woman in the vehicle. An officer in charge of transport was beating the soldier who was driving the woman's vehicle for trying to get ahead of others, and the strokes of his whip fell on the apron of the equipage. The woman screamed piercingly. Seeing Prince Andrew she leaned out from behind the apron, and waving her thin arms from under the woollen shawl, cried:

'Mr Aide-de-camp! Mr Aide-de-camp!... For heaven's sake... Protect me! What will become of us? I am the wife of the doctor of the Seventh Chasseurs... They won't let us pass, we are left behind and have lost our people...'

'I'll flatten you into a pancake!' shouted the angry officer to the soldier. 'Turn back with your slut!'

'Mr Aide-de-camp! Help me!... What does it all mean?' screamed the doctor's wife.

'Kindly let this cart pass. Don't you see it's a woman?' said Prince Andrew riding up to the officer.

The officer glanced at him, and without replying turned again to the soldier. 'I'll teach you to push on!... Back!'

'Let them pass, I tell you!' repeated Prince Andrew, compressing his lips.

'And who are you?' cried the officer, turning on him with tipsy rage, 'who are *you*? Are you in command here? Eh? I am commander here, not you! Go back or I'll flatten you into a pancake,' repeated he. This expression evidently pleased him.

'That was a nice snub for the little aide-de-camp,' came a voice from behind.

Prince Andrew saw that the officer was in that state of senseless tipsy rage when a man does not know what he is saying. He saw that his championship of the doctor's wife in her queer trap might expose him to what he dreaded more than anything in the world – to ridicule; but his instinct urged him on. Before the officer finished his sentence Prince Andrew, his face distorted with fury, rode up to him and raised his riding-whip.

'Kind . . . ly let – them – pass!'

The officer flourished his arm and hastily rode away.

'It's all the fault of these fellows on the staff that there's this disorder,' he muttered. 'Do as you like.'

Prince Andrew without lifting his eyes rode hastily away from the doctor's wife, who was calling him her deliverer, and recalling with a sense of disgust the minutest details of this humiliating scene he galloped on to the village where he was told that the commander-in-chief was.

On reaching the village he dismounted and went to the nearest house, intending to rest if but for a moment, eat something, and try to sort out the stinging and tormenting thoughts that confused his mind. 'This is a mob of scoundrels and not an army,' he was thinking as he went up to the window of the first house, when a familiar voice called him by name.

He turned round. Nesvitsky's handsome face looked out of the little window. Nesvitsky, moving his moist lips as he chewed something, and flourishing his arm, called him to enter.

'Bolkonsky! Bolkonsky! . . . Don't you hear? Eh? Come quick . . .' he shouted.

Entering the house, Prince Andrew saw Nesvitsky and another adjutant having something to eat. They hastily turned round to him asking if he had any news. On their familiar faces he read agitation and alarm. This was particularly noticeable on Nesvitsky's usually laughing countenance.

'Where is the commander-in-chief?' asked Bolkonsky.

'Here, in that house,' answered the adjutant.

'Well, is it true that it's peace and capitulation?' asked Nesvitsky.

'I was going to ask you. I know nothing except that it was all I could do to get here.'

'And we, my dear boy! It's terrible! I was wrong to laugh at

Mack, we're getting it still worse,' said Nesvitsky. 'But sit down and have something to eat.'

'You won't be able to find either your baggage or anything else now, Prince. And God only knows where your man Peter is,' said the other adjutant.

'Where are head-quarters?'

'We are to spend the night in Znaim.'

'Well, I have got all I need into packs for two horses,' said Nesvitsky. 'They've made up splendid packs for me – fit to cross the Bohemian mountains with. It's a bad look-out, old fellow! But what's the matter with you? You must be ill to shiver like that,' he added, noticing that Prince Andrew winced as at an electric shock.

'It's nothing,' replied Prince Andrew.

He had just remembered his recent encounter with the doctor's wife and the convoy officer.

'What is the commander-in-chief doing here?' he asked.

'I can't make out at all,' said Nesvitsky.

'Well, all I can make out is that everything is abominable, abominable, quite abominable!' said Prince Andrew, and he went off to the house where the commander-in-chief was.

Passing by Kutuzov's carriage and the exhausted saddle-horses of his suite, with their Cossacks who were talking loudly together, Prince Andrew entered the passage. Kutuzov himself, he was told, was in the house with Prince Bagration and Weyrother. Weyrother was the Austrian general who had succeeded Schmidt. In the passage little Kozlovsky was squatting on his heels in front of a clerk. The clerk, with cuffs turned up, was hastily writing at a tub turned bottom upwards. Kozlovsky's face looked worn – he too had evidently not slept all night. He glanced at Prince Andrew and did not even nod to him.

'Second line . . . have you written it?' he continued dictating to the clerk. 'The Kiev Grenadiers, Podolian . . .'

'One can't write so fast, your honour,' said the clerk, glancing angrily and disrespectfully at Kozlovsky.

Through the door came the sounds of Kutuzov's voice, excited and dissatisfied, interrupted by another, an unfamiliar voice. From the sound of these voices, the inattentive way Kozlovsky looked at him, the disrespectful manner of the exhausted clerk, the fact that the clerk and Kozlovsky were squatting on the floor by a tub so near to the commander-in-chief, and from the noisy laughter of the Cossacks holding the horses near the window, Prince Andrew felt that something important and disastrous was about to happen.

He turned to Kozlovsky with urgent questions.

'Immediately, Prince,' said Kozlovsky. 'Dispositions for Bagration.'

'What about capitulation?'

'Nothing of the sort. Orders are issued for a battle.'

Prince Andrew moved towards the door from whence voices were heard. Just as he was going to open it the sounds ceased, the door opened, and Kutuzov with his eagle nose and puffy face appeared in the doorway. Prince Andrew stood right in front of Kutuzov but the expression of the commander-in-chief's one sound eye showed him to be so preoccupied with thoughts and anxieties as to be oblivious of his presence. He looked straight at his adjutant's face without recognizing him.

'Well, have you finished?' said he to Kozlovsky.

'One moment, your Excellency.'

Bagration, a gaunt middle-aged man of medium height with a firm, impassive face of oriental type, came out after the commander-in-chief.

'I have the honour to present myself,' repeated Prince Andrew rather loudly, handing Kutuzov an envelope.

'Ah, from Vienna? Very good. Later, later!'

Kutuzov went out into the porch with Bagration.

'Well, good-bye, Prince,' said he to Bagration. 'My blessing, and may Christ be with you in your great endeavour!'

His face suddenly softened and tears came into his eyes. With his left hand he drew Bagration towards him, and with his right, on which he wore a ring, he made the sign of the cross over him with a gesture evidently habitual, offering his puffy cheek, but Bagration kissed him on the neck instead.

'Christ be with you!' Kutuzov repeated and went towards his carriage. 'Get in with me,' said he to Bolkonsky.

'Your Excellency, I should like to be of use here. Allow me to remain with Prince Bagration's detachment.'

'Get in,' said Kutuzov, and noticing that Bolkonsky still delayed, he added: 'I need good officers myself, need them myself!'

They got into the carriage and drove for a few minutes in silence.

'There is still much, much before us,' he said, as if with an old man's penetration he understood all that was passing in Bolkonsky's mind. 'If a tenth part of his detachment returns I shall thank God,' he added as if speaking to himself.

Prince Andrew glanced at Kutuzov's face only a foot distant from him and involuntarily noticed the carefully washed seams of the scar near his temple, where an Ismail bullet had pierced his skull, and the empty eye-socket. 'Yes, he has a right to speak so calmly of those men's death,' thought Bolkonsky.

'That is why I beg to be sent to that detachment,' he said.

Kutuzov did not reply. He seemed to have forgotten what he had been saying, and sat plunged in thought. Five minutes later, gently swaying on the soft springs of the carriage, he turned to Prince Andrew. There was not a trace of agitation on his face. With delicate irony he questioned Prince Andrew about the details of his interview with the Emperor, about the remarks he had heard at court concerning the Krems affair, and about some ladies they both knew.

14

On November 1st Kutuzov had received through a spy news that the army he commanded was in an almost hopeless position. The spy reported that the French, after crossing the bridge at Vienna, were advancing in immense force upon Kutuzov's line of communication with the troops that were arriving from Russia. If Kutuzov decided to remain at Krems, Napoleon's army of one hundred and fifty thousand men would cut him off completely and surround his exhausted army of forty thousand, and he would find himself in the position of Mack at Ulm. If Kutuzov decided to abandon the road connecting him with the troops arriving from Russia, he would have to march with no road into unknown parts of the Bohemian mountains, defending himself against superior forces of the enemy and abandoning all hopes of a junction with Buxhöwden. If Kutuzov decided to retreat along the road from Krems to Olmütz, to unite with the troops arriving from Russia, he risked being forestalled on that road by the French who had crossed the Vienna bridge, and encumbered by his baggage and transport, having to accept battle on the march against an enemy three times as strong, who would hem him in from two sides.

Kutuzov chose this latter course.

The French, the spy reported, having crossed the Vienna bridge were advancing by forced marches towards Znaim, which lay a hundred versts off on the line of Kutuzov's retreat. If he reached Znaim before the French, there would be great hope of saving the army; to let the French forestall him at Znaim meant the exposure of his whole army to a disgrace such as that of Ulm, or to utter destruction. But to forestall the French with his whole army was impossible. The road for the French from Vienna to Znaim was shorter and better than the road for the Russians from Krems to Znaim.

The night he received the news, Kutuzov sent Bagration's vanguard, four thousand strong, to the right across the hills from the Krems–Znaim to the Vienna–Znaim road. Bagration was to make this march without resting and to halt facing Vienna with Znaim to his rear, and if he succeeded in forestalling the French he was to delay them as long as possible. Kutuzov himself with all his transport took the road to Znaim.

Marching thirty miles that stormy night across roadless hills, with his hungry, ill-shod soldiers, and losing a third of his men as stragglers by the way, Bagration came out on the Vienna–Znaim road at Hollabrünn a few hours ahead of the French who were approaching Hollabrünn from Vienna. Kutuzov with his transport had still to march for some days before he could reach Znaim. Hence Bagration with his four thousand hungry exhausted men, would have to detain for days the whole enemy army that came upon him at Hollabrünn, which was clearly impossible. But a freak of fate made the impossible possible. The success of the trick that had placed the Vienna bridge in the hands of the French without a fight, led Murat to try to deceive Kutuzov in a similar way. Meeting Bagration's weak detachment on the Znaim road he supposed it to be Kutuzov's whole army. To be able to crush it absolutely he awaited the arrival of the rest of the troops who were on their way from Vienna, and with this object offered a three days' truce on condition that both armies should remain in position without moving. Murat declared that negotiations for peace were already proceeding, and that he therefore offered this truce to avoid unnecessary bloodshed. Count Nostitz, the Austrian general occupying the advanced posts, believed Murat's emissary and retired, leaving Bagration's division exposed. Another emissary rode to the Russian line to announce the peace negotiations and to offer the Russian army the three days' truce. Bagration replied that he was not authorized either to accept or refuse a truce, and sent his adjutant to Kutuzov to report the offer he had received.

A truce was Kutuzov's sole chance of gaining time, giving Bagration's exhausted troops some rest, and letting the transport and heavy convoys (whose movements were concealed from the French) advance if but one stage nearer Znaim. The offer of a truce gave the only, and a quite unexpected, chance of saving the army. On receiving the news he immediately dispatched Adjutant-General Wintzingerode, who was in attendance on him, to the enemy camp. Wintzingerode was not merely to agree to the truce but also to offer terms of capitulation, and meanwhile Kutuzov sent his adjutants back to hasten to the utmost the movements of the baggage-trains of the entire army along the Krems–Znaim road. Bagration's exhausted and hungry detachment which alone covered this movement of the transport and of the whole army, had to remain stationary in face of an enemy eight times as strong as itself.

Kutuzov's expectations that the proposals of capitulation (which were in no way binding) might give time for part of the transport to pass, and also that Murat's mistake would very soon be discovered proved correct. As soon as Bonaparte (who was at Schönbrunn, sixteen miles from Hollabrünn) received Murat's despatch with the proposal of a truce and a capitulation, he detected a ruse and wrote the following letter to Murat:

Schönbrunn, 25th Brumaire, 1805,
at eight o'clock in the morning.

To Prince Murat,

I cannot find words to express to you my displeasure. You command only my advance-guard, and have no right to arrange an armistice without my order. You are causing me to lose the fruits of a campaign. Break the armistice immediately and march on the enemy. Inform him that the general who signed that capitulation had no right to do so, and that no one but the Emperor of Russia has that right.

If however the Emperor of Russia ratifies that convention, I will ratify it; but it is only a trick. March on, destroy the Russian army ... You are in a position to seize its baggage and artillery.

The Russian Emperor's aide-de-camp is an impostor. Officers are nothing when they have no powers; this one had none ... The Austrians let themselves be tricked at the crossing of the Vienna bridge, you are letting yourself be tricked by an aide-de-camp of the Emperor.

Napoleon.*

Bonaparte's adjutant rode full gallop with this menacing letter to Murat. Bonaparte himself, not trusting to his generals, moved with all the Guards to the field of battle, afraid of letting a ready victim escape, and Bagration's four thousand men merrily lighted camp fires, dried and warmed themselves, cooked their porridge for the first time for three days, and not one of them knew or imagined what was in store for him.

15

BETWEEN three and four o'clock in the afternoon Prince Andrew, who had persisted in his request to Kutuzov, arrived at Grunth and reported himself to Bagration. Bonaparte's adjutant had not yet reached Murat's detachment and the battle had not yet begun. In Bagration's detachment no one knew anything of the general position of affairs. They talked of peace but did not believe in its possibility; others talked of a battle but also disbelieved in the nearness of an engagement. Bagration, knowing Bolkonsky to be a favourite and trusted adjutant, received him with distinction and special marks of favour, explaining to him that there would probably be an engagement that day or the next, and giving him full liberty to remain with him during the battle or to join the rearguard and have an eye on the order of retreat, 'which is also very important'.

'However there will hardly be an engagement to-day,' said Bagration as if to reassure Prince Andrew.

'If he is one of the ordinary little staff-dandies sent to earn a medal, he can get his reward just as well in the rearguard, but if he wishes to stay with me, let him...he'll be of use here if he's a brave officer,' thought Bagration. Prince Andrew, without replying, asked the prince's permission to ride round the position to see the disposition of the forces, so as to know his bearings should he be sent to execute an order. The officer on duty, a handsome, elegantly dressed man with a diamond ring on his forefinger, who was fond of speaking French though he spoke it badly, offered to conduct Prince Andrew.

On all sides they saw rain-soaked officers with dejected faces who seemed to be seeking something, and soldiers dragging doors, benches, and fencing, from the village.

'There now, Prince! We can't stop those fellows,' said the staff-officer pointing to the soldiers. 'The officers don't keep them in hand. And there,' he pointed to a sutler's tent, 'they crowd in and sit. This morning I turned them all out and now look, it's full again. I must go there, Prince, and scare them a bit. It won't take a moment.'

'Yes, let's go in and I will get myself a roll and some cheese,' said Prince Andrew who had not yet had time to eat anything.

'Why didn't you mention it, Prince? I would have offered you something.'

They dismounted and entered the tent. Several officers, with flushed and weary faces, were sitting at the table eating and drinking.

'Now what does this mean, gentlemen?' said the staff-officer, in the reproachful tone of a man who has repeated the same thing more than once. 'You know it won't do to leave your posts like this. The prince gave orders that no one should leave his post. Now you, Captain,' and he turned to a thin, dirty little artillery officer who without his boots (he had given them to the canteen keeper to dry) in only his stockings, rose when they entered, smiling not altogether comfortably.

'Well, aren't you ashamed of yourself, Captain Tushin?' he

continued. 'One would think that as an artillery officer you would set a good example, yet here you are without your boots! The alarm will be sounded and you'll be in a pretty position without your boots!' (The staff-officer smiled.) 'Kindly return to your posts, gentlemen, all of you, all!' he added in a tone of command.

Prince Andrew smiled involuntarily as he looked at the artillery officer Tushin, who silent and smiling, shifting from one stockinged foot to the other, glanced inquiringly with his large, intelligent, kindly eyes from Prince Andrew to the staff-officer.

'The soldiers say it feels easier without boots,' said Captain Tushin smiling shyly in his uncomfortable position, evidently wishing to adopt a jocular tone. But before he had finished he felt that his jest was unacceptable and had not come off. He grew confused.

'Kindly return to your posts,' said the staff-officer trying to preserve his gravity.

Prince Andrew glanced again at the artillery officer's small figure. There was something peculiar about it, quite unsoldierly, rather comic, but extremely attractive.

The staff-officer and Prince Andrew mounted their horses and rode on.

Having ridden beyond the village, continually meeting and over-taking soldiers and officers of various regiments, they saw on their left some entrenchments being thrown up, the freshly-dug clay of which showed up red. Several battalions of soldiers, in their shirt-sleeves despite the cold wind, swarmed in these earthworks like a ghost of white ants; spadesful of red clay were continually being thrown up from behind the bank by unseen hands. Prince Andrew and the officer rode up, looked at the entrenchment, and went on again. Just behind it they came upon some dozens of soldiers, continually replaced by others, who ran from the entrenchment. They had to hold their noses and put their horses to a trot to escape from the poisoned atmosphere of these latrines.

'Voilà l'agrément des camps, monsieur le prince,' said the staff-officer.

They rode up the opposite hill. From there the French could already be seen. Prince Andrew stopped and began examining the position.

'That's our battery,' said the staff-officer indicating the highest point. 'It's in charge of the queer fellow we saw without his boots. You can see everything from there; let's go there, Prince.'

'Thank you very much, I will go on alone,' said Prince Andrew, wishing to rid himself of this staff-officer's company, 'please don't trouble yourself further.'

The staff-officer remained behind and Prince Andrew rode on alone. The farther forward and nearer the enemy he went, the more orderly and cheerful were the troops. The greatest disorder and depression had been in the baggage-train he had passed that morning on the Znaim road seven miles away from the French. At Grunth also some apprehension and alarm could be felt, but the nearer Prince Andrew came to the French lines the more confident was the appearance of our troops. The soldiers in their greatcoats were ranged in lines, the sergeant-majors and company officers were counting the men, poking the last man in each section in the ribs and telling him to hold his hand up. Soldiers scattered over the whole place were dragging logs and brushwood and were building shelters with merry chatter and laughter; around the fires sat others, dressed and undressed, drying their shirts and leg-bands or mending boots or overcoats and crowding round the boilers and porridge-cookers. In one company dinner was ready and the soldiers were gazing eagerly at the steaming boiler, waiting till the sample, which a quartermaster-sergeant was carrying in a wooden bowl to an officer who sat on a log before his shelter, had been tasted.

Another company, a lucky one for not all the companies had vodka, crowded round a pock-marked, broad-shouldered sergeant-major who, tilting a keg, filled one after another the canteen-lids held out to him. The soldiers lifted the canteen-lids to their lips with reverential faces, emptied them rolling the vodka in their mouths, and walked away from the sergeant-major with brightened expressions, licking their lips and wiping them on the sleeves of their greatcoats. All their faces were as serene as if all this were happening at home awaiting peaceful encampment, and not within sight of the enemy before an action in which at least half of them would be left on the field. After passing a chasseur regiment and in the lines of the Kiev grenadiers – fine fellows busy with similar peaceful affairs – near the shelter of the regimental commander, higher than and different from the others, Prince Andrew came out in front of a platoon of grenadiers before whom lay a naked man. Two soldiers held him while two others were flourishing their switches and striking him regularly on his bare back. The man shrieked unnaturally. A stout major was pacing up and down the line, and regardless of the screams kept repeating:

'It's a shame for a soldier to steal; a soldier must be honest, honourable, and brave, but if he robs his fellows there is no honour in him, he's a scoundrel. Go on! Go on!'

So the swishing sounds of the strokes, and the desperate but unnatural screams, continued.

'Go on, go on!' said the major.

A young officer with a bewildered and pained expression on his face stepped away from the man and looked round inquiringly at the adjutant as he rode by.

Prince Andrew, having reached the front line, rode along it. Our front line and that of the enemy were far apart on the right and left flanks, but in the centre where the men with a flag of truce had passed that morning, the lines were so near together that the men could see one another's faces and speak to one another. Besides the soldiers who formed the picket line on either side, there were many curious onlookers who, jesting and laughing, stared at their strange foreign enemies.

Since early morning – despite an injunction not to approach the picket line – the officers had been unable to keep sightseers away. The soldiers forming the picket line, like showmen exhibiting a curiosity, no longer looked at the French but paid attention to the sightseers and grew weary waiting to be relieved. Prince Andrew halted to have a look at the French.

'Look! Look there!' one soldier was saying to another, pointing to a Russian musketeer who had gone up to the picket line with an officer and was rapidly and excitedly talking to a French grenadier. 'Hark to him jabbering! Fine, isn't it? It's all the Frenchy can do to keep up with him. There now, Sidorov!'

'Wait a bit and listen. It's fine!' answered Sidorov, who was considered an adept at French.

The soldier to whom the laughers referred was Dolokhov. Prince Andrew recognized him and stopped to listen to what he was saying. Dolokhov had come from the left flank where their regiment was stationed, with his captain.

'Now then, go on, go on!' incited the officer, bending forward and trying not to lose a word of the speech which was incomprehensible to him. 'More, please: more! What's he saying?'

Dolokhov did not answer the captain; he had been drawn into a hot dispute with the French grenadier. They were naturally talking about the campaign. The Frenchman, confusing the Austrians with the Russians, was trying to prove that the Russians had surrendered and had fled all the way from Ulm, while Dolokhov maintained that the Russians had not surrendered but had beaten the French.

'We have orders to drive you off here, and we shall drive you off,' said Dolokhov.

'Only take care you and your Cossacks are not all captured!' said the French grenadier.

The French onlookers and listeners laughed.

'We'll make you dance as we did under Suvorov...(*on vous fera danser*),' said Dolokhov.

'*Qu'est-ce qu'il chante?* (What's he singing about?)' asked a Frenchman.

'It's ancient history,' said another, guessing that it referred to a former war. 'The Emperor will teach your Suvara as he has taught the others...'

'Bonaparte...' began Dolokhov, but the Frenchman interrupted him.

'Not Bonaparte. He is the Emperor! *Sacré nom...*!' cried he angrily.

'The devil skin your Emperor.'

And Dolokhov swore at him in coarse soldier's Russian and shouldering his musket walked away.

'Let us go, Ivan Lukich,' he said to the captain.

'Ah, that's the way to talk French,' said the picket soldiers. 'Now, Sidorov, you have a try!'

Sidorov, turning to the French, winked, and began to jabber meaningless sounds very fast: '*Kari, mala, tafa, safi, muter, Kaská,*' he said, trying to give an expressive intonation to his voice.

'Ho! ho! ho! Ha! ha! ha! ha! Ouh! ouh!' came peals of such healthy and good-humoured laughter from the soldiers that it infected the French involuntarily, so much so that the only thing left to do seemed to be to unload the muskets, explode the ammunition, and all return home as quickly as possible.

But the guns remained loaded, the loop-holes in block-houses and entrenchments looked out just as menacingly, and the unlimbered cannon confronted one another as before.

16

HAVING ridden round the whole line from right flank to left, Prince Andrew made his way up to the battery from which the staff-officer had told him the whole field could be seen. Here he dismounted, and stopped beside the farthest of the four unlimbered cannon. Before the guns an artillery sentry was pacing up and down; he stood at attention when the officer arrived, but at a sign resumed his measured, monotonous pacing. Behind the guns were their limbers, and still farther back picket-ropes and artillerymen's bonfires. To the left, not far from the farthest cannon, was a small newly-constructed wattle-shed from which came the sound of officers' voices in eager conversation.

It was true that a view over nearly the whole Russian position and the greater part of the enemy's opened out from this battery. Just facing it, on the crest of the opposite hill, the village of Schön Grabern could be seen, and in three places to left and right the French troops amid the smoke of their camp fires, the greater part of whom were evidently in the village itself and behind the hill. To the left from that village, amid the smoke, was something resembling a battery, but it was impossible to see it clearly with the naked eye. Our right flank was posted on a rather steep incline which dominated the French position. Our infantry were stationed there, and at the farthest point the dragoons. In the centre, where Tushin's battery stood and from which Prince Andrew was surveying the position, was the easiest and most direct descent and ascent to the brook separating us from Schön Grabern. On the left our troops were close to a copse, in which smoked the bonfires of our infantry who were felling wood. The French line was wider than ours, and it was plain that they could easily outflank us on both sides. Behind our position was a steep and deep dip, making it difficult for artillery and cavalry to retire. Prince Andrew took out his notebook, and leaning on the cannon, sketched a plan of the position. He made some notes on two points, intending to mention them to Bagration. His idea was, first to concentrate all the artillery in the centre, and secondly, to withdraw the cavalry to the other side of the dip. Prince Andrew, being always near the commander-in-chief, closely following the mass movements and general orders, and constantly studying historical accounts of battles, involuntarily pictured to himself the course of events in the forthcoming action in broad outline. He imagined only important possibilities: 'If the enemy attacks the right flank,' he said to himself, 'the Kiev grenadiers and the Podolsk chasseurs must hold their position till reserves from the centre come up. In that case the dragoons could successfully make a flank counter-attack. If they attack our centre we, having the centre battery on this high ground, shall withdraw the left flank under its cover, and retreat to the dip by echelons.' So he reasoned ... All the time he had been beside the gun he had heard the voices of the officers distinctly, but as often happens had not understood a word of what they were saying. Suddenly however he was struck by a voice coming from the shed, and its tone was so sincere that he could not but listen.

'No, friend,' said a pleasant and as it seemed to Prince Andrew a familiar voice, 'what I say is that if it were possible to know what is beyond death, none of us would be afraid of it. That's so, friend.'

Another, a younger voice, interrupted him:

'Afraid or not, you can't escape it anyhow.'

'All the same, one is afraid! Oh, you clever people,' said a third manly voice interrupting them both. 'Of course you artillerymen are very wise, because you can take everything along with you – vodka and snacks.'

And the owner of the manly voice, evidently an infantry officer, laughed.

'Yes, one is afraid,' continued the first speaker, he of the familiar voice. 'One is afraid of the unknown, that's what it is. Whatever we may say about the soul going to the sky ... we know there is no sky but only an atmosphere.'

The manly voice again interrupted the artillery officer.

'Well, stand us some of your herb-vodka, Tushin,' it said.

'Why,' thought Prince Andrew, 'that's the captain who stood up in the sutler's hut without his boots.' He recognized the agreeable philosophizing voice with pleasure.

'Some herb-vodka? Certainly!' said Tushin, '– but still, to conceive a future life ...'

He did not finish. Just then there was a whistle in the air; nearer and nearer, faster and louder, louder and faster, a cannon-ball, as if it had not finished saying what was necessary, thudded into the ground near the shed with superhuman force, throwing up a mass of earth. The ground seemed to groan at the terrible impact.

And immediately Tushin, with a short pipe in the corner of his mouth and his kind intelligent face rather pale, rushed out of the shed followed by the owner of the manly voice, a dashing infantry officer who hurried off to his company, buttoning up his coat as he ran.

17

MOUNTING his horse again Prince Andrew lingered with the battery, looking at the puff from the gun that had sent the ball. His eyes ran rapidly over the wide space, but he only saw that the hitherto motionless masses of the French now swayed, and that there really was a battery to their left. The smoke above it had not yet dispersed. Two mounted Frenchmen, probably adjutants, were galloping up the hill. A small but distinctly visible enemy column was moving down the hill, probably to strengthen the front line. The smoke of the first shot had not yet dispersed before another puff appeared, followed by a report. The battle had begun! Prince Andrew turned his horse and galloped back to Grunth to find Prince Bagration. He heard the cannonade behind him growing louder and more frequent. Evidently our guns had begun to reply.

From the bottom of the slope, where the parleys had taken place, came the report of musketry.

Lemarrois had just arrived at a gallop with Bonaparte's stern letter, and Murat, humiliated and anxious to expiate his fault, had at once moved his forces to attack the centre and outflank both the Russian wings, hoping before evening and before the arrival of the Emperor to crush the contemptible detachment that stood before him.

'It has begun. Here it is!' thought Prince Andrew, feeling the blood rush to his heart. 'But where and how will my Toulon* present itself?'

Passing between the companies that had been eating porridge and drinking vodka a quarter of an hour before he saw everywhere the same rapid movement of soldiers forming ranks and getting their muskets ready, and on all their faces he recognized the same eagerness that filled his heart. 'It has begun! Here it is, dreadful but enjoyable!' was what the face of each soldier and each officer seemed to say.

Before he had reached the embankments that were being thrown up, he saw, in the light of the dull autumn evening, mounted men coming towards him. The foremost, wearing a Cossack cloak and lambskin cap and riding a white horse, was Prince Bagration. Prince Andrew stopped, waiting for him to come up; Prince Bagration reined in his horse and recognizing Prince Andrew nodded to him. He still looked ahead while Prince Andrew told him what he had seen.

The feeling, 'It has begun! Here it is!' was seen even on Prince Bagration's hard brown face with its half-closed dull sleepy eyes. Prince Andrew gazed with anxious curiosity at that impassive face and wished he could tell what, if anything, this man was thinking and feeling at that moment. 'Is there anything at all behind that impassive face?' Prince Andrew asked himself as he looked. Prince Bagration bent his head in sign of agreement with what Prince Andrew told him, and said, 'Very good!' in a tone that seemed to imply that everything that took place and was reported to him was exactly what he had foreseen. Prince Andrew, out of breath with his rapid ride, spoke quickly. Prince Bagration, uttering his words with an oriental accent,* spoke particularly slowly, as if to impress the fact that there was no need to hurry. However he put his horse to a trot in the direction of Tushin's battery. Prince Andrew followed with the suite. Behind Prince Bagration rode an officer of the suite, the prince's personal adjutant, Zherkov, an orderly officer, the staff-officer on duty, riding a fine bob-tailed horse, and a civilian – an accountant who had asked permission to be present at the battle out of curiosity. The accountant, a stout full-faced man, looked around him with a naïve smile of satisfaction and presented a strange appearance among the hussars, Cossacks and adjutants, in his camlet coat as he jolted on his horse with a convoy-officer's saddle.

'He wants to see a battle,' said Zherkov to Bolkonsky, pointing to the accountant, 'but he feels a pain in the pit of his stomach already.'

'Oh, leave off!' said the accountant with a beaming but rather cunning smile, as if flattered at being made the subject of Zherkov's joke, and purposely trying to appear stupider than he really was.

'It is very strange, *mon Monsieur Prince*,' said the staff-officer. (He remembered that in French there is some peculiar way of addressing a prince, but could not get it quite right.)

By this time they were all approaching Tushin's battery, and a ball struck the ground in front of them.

'What's that that has fallen?' asked the accountant with a naïve smile.

'A French pancake,' answered Zherkov.

'So that's what they hit with?' asked the accountant. 'How awful!'

He seemed to swell with satisfaction. He had hardly finished when they again heard an unexpectedly violent whistling which suddenly ended with a thud into something soft . . . f-f-flop! and a Cossack, riding a little to their right and behind the accountant, crashed to earth with his horse. Zherkov and the staff-officer bent over their saddles and turned their horses away. The accountant stopped facing the Cossack and examined him with attentive curiosity. The Cossack was dead, but the horse still struggled.

Prince Bagration screwed up his eyes, looked round, and seeing the cause of the confusion, turned away with indifference, as if to say, 'Is it worth while noticing trifles?' He reined in his horse with the ease of a skilful rider, and slightly bending over, disengaged his sabre which had caught in his cloak. It was an old-fashioned sabre of a kind no longer in general use. Prince Andrew remembered the story of Suvorov giving his sabre to Bagration in Italy, and the recollection was particularly pleasant at that moment. They had reached the battery at which Prince Andrew had been when he examined the battlefield.

'Whose company?' asked Prince Bagration of an artilleryman standing by the ammunition-wagon.

He asked, 'Whose company?' but he really meant, 'Are you frightened here?' and the artilleryman understood him.

'Captain Tushin's, your Excellency!' shouted the red-haired, freckled gunner in a merry voice, standing to attention.

'Yes, yes,' muttered Bagration as if considering something, and he rode past the limbers to the farthest cannon.

As he approached, a ringing shot issued from it deafening him and his suite, and in the smoke that suddenly surrounded the gun they could see the gunners who had seized it straining to roll it quickly back to its former position. A huge broad-shouldered gunner, Number One, holding a mop, his legs far apart, sprang to the wheel; while Number Two with a trembling hand placed a charge in the cannon's mouth. The short round-shouldered Captain Tushin, stumbling over the trail of the gun-carriage, moved forward, and not noticing the general, looked out shading his eyes with his small hand.

'Lift it two lines more and it will be just right,' cried he in a feeble voice to which he tried to impart a dashing note, ill suited to his weak figure. 'Number Two!' he squeaked. 'Fire Medvedev!'

Bagration called to him, and Tushin, raising three fingers to his cap, with a bashful and awkward gesture not at all like a military salute but like a priest's benediction, approached the general. Though Tushin's guns had been intended to cannonade the valley, he was firing incendiary balls at the village of Schön Grabern visible just opposite, in front of which large masses of French were advancing.

No one had given Tushin orders where and at what to fire, but after consulting his sergeant-major Zakharchenko for whom he had great respect, he had decided that it would be a good thing to set fire to the village. 'Very good!' said Bagration in reply to the officer's report, and began deliberately to examine the whole battle-field extended before him. The French had advanced nearest on our right. Below the height on which the Kiev regiment was stationed, in the hollow where the rivulet flowed, the soul-stirring rolling and crackling of musketry was heard, and much farther to the right, beyond the dragoons, the officer of the suite pointed out to Bagration a French column that was outflanking us. To the left the horizon was bounded by the adjacent wood. Prince Bagration ordered two battalions from the centre to be sent to reinforce the right flank. The officers of the suite ventured to remark to the prince that if these battalions went away, the guns would remain without support. Prince Bagration turned to the officer and with his dull eyes looked at him in silence. It seemed to Prince Andrew that the officer's remark was just and that really no answer could be made to it. But at that moment an adjutant galloped up with a message from the commander of the regiment in the hollow and news that immense masses of the French were coming down upon them, and that his regiment was in disorder and was retreating upon the Kiev grenadiers. Prince Bagration bowed his head in sign of assent and approval. He rode off at a walk to the right and sent an adjutant to the dragoons with orders to attack the French. But this adjutant returned half-an-hour later with the news that the commander of the dragoons had already retreated beyond the dip in the ground, as a heavy fire had been opened on him and he was losing men uselessly, and so had hastened to throw some sharpshooters into the wood.

'Very good!' said Bagration.

As he was leaving the battery, firing was heard on the left also, and as it was too far to the left flank for him to have time to go there himself, Prince Bagration sent Zherkov to tell the general in command (the one who had paraded his regiment before Kutuzov at Braunau) that he must retreat as quickly as possible behind the hollow in the rear, as the right flank would probably not be able to withstand the enemy's attack very long. About Tushin and the battalion that had been in support of his battery, all was forgotten. Prince Andrew listened attentively to Bagration's colloquies with the commanding officers and the orders he gave them, and to his surprise found that no orders were really given but that Prince Bagration tried to make it appear that everything done by necessity, by accident, or by the will of subordinate commanders, was done, if not by his direct command at least in accord with his intentions. Prince Andrew noticed however that though what happened was due to chance and was independent of the commander's will, owing to the tact Bagration showed, his presence was very valuable. Officers who approached him with disturbed countenances became calm; soldiers and officers greeted him gaily, grew more cheerful in his presence, and were evidently anxious to display their courage before him.

18

PRINCE BAGRATION, having reached the highest point of our right flank, began riding downhill to where the roll of musketry was heard but where on account of the smoke nothing could be seen. The nearer they got to the hollow the less they could see but the more they felt the nearness of the actual battlefield. They began to meet wounded men. One with a bleeding head and no cap was being dragged along by two soldiers who supported him under the arms. There was a gurgle in his throat and he was spitting blood. A bullet had evidently hit him in the throat or mouth. Another was walking sturdily by himself but without his musket, groaning aloud and swinging his arm which had just been hurt, while blood from it was streaming over his greatcoat as from a bottle. He had that moment been wounded and his face showed fear rather than suffering. Crossing a road they descended a steep incline and saw several men lying on the ground, they also met a crowd of soldiers some of whom were unwounded. The soldiers were ascending the hill breathing heavily, and despite the general's presence were talking loudly and gesticulating. In front of them rows of grey cloaks were already visible through the smoke, and an officer catching sight of Bagration rushed shouting after the crowd of retreating soldiers, ordering them back. Bagration rode up to the ranks along which shots crackled now here and now there, drowning the sound of voices and the shouts of command. The whole air reeked with smoke. The excited faces of the soldiers were blackened with it. Some were using their ramrods, others putting powder on the touch-pans or taking charges from their pouches, while others were firing, though who they were firing at could not be seen for the smoke which there was no wind to carry away. A pleasant humming and whistling of bullets was often heard. 'What is this?' thought Prince Andrew approaching the crowd of soldiers. 'It can't be an attack for they are not moving; it can't be a square – for they are not drawn up for that.'

The commander of the regiment, a thin, feeble-looking old man with a pleasant smile – his eyelids drooping more than half over his old eyes giving him a mild expression, rode up to Bagration and welcomed him as a host welcomes an honoured guest. He reported that his regiment had been attacked by French cavalry and that, though the attack had been repulsed, he had lost more than half his men. He said the attack had been repulsed, employing this military term to describe what had occurred to his regiment, but in reality he did not himself know what had happened during that half-hour to the troops entrusted to him, and could not say with certainty whether the attack had been repulsed or his regiment had been broken up. All he knew was that at the commencement of the action balls and shells began flying all over his regiment and hitting men, and that afterwards someone had shouted 'Cavalry!' and our men had begun firing. They were still firing, not at the cavalry which had disappeared, but at French infantry who had come into the hollow and were firing at our men. Prince Bagration bowed his head as a sign that this was exactly what he had desired and expected. Turning to his adjutant he ordered him to bring down the two battalions of the Sixth Chasseurs whom they had just passed. Prince Andrew was struck by the changed expression on Prince Bagration's face at this moment. It expressed the concentrated and happy resolution you see on the face of a man who on a hot day takes a final run before plunging into the water. The dull sleepy expression was no longer there, nor the affectation of profound thought. The round, steady, hawk's eyes looked before him eagerly and rather disdainfully, not resting on anything although his movements were still slow and measured.

The commander of the regiment turned to Prince Bagration entreating him to go back as it was too dangerous to remain where they were. 'Please, your Excellency, for God's sake!' he kept saying, glancing for support at an officer of the suite who turned away from him. 'There, you see!' and he drew attention to the bullets whistling, singing and hissing continually around them. He spoke in the tone of entreaty and reproach that a carpenter uses to a gentleman who has picked up an axe: 'We are used to it, but you, sir, will blister your hands.' He spoke as if those bullets could not kill him, and his half-closed eyes gave still more persuasiveness to his words. The staff-officer joined in the colonel's appeals, but Bagration did not reply; he only gave an order to cease firing and re-form, so as to give room for the two approaching battalions. While he was speaking the curtain of smoke that had concealed the hollow, driven by a rising wind, began to move from right to left, as if drawn by an invisible hand, and the hill opposite with the French moving about on it opened out before them. All eyes fastened involuntarily on this French column advancing against them and winding down over the uneven ground. One could already see the soldiers' shaggy caps, distinguish the officers from the men, and see the standard flapping against its staff.

'They march splendidly,' remarked someone in Bagration's suite.

The head of the column had already descended into the hollow. The clash would take place on this side of it . . .

The remains of our regiment which had been in action rapidly formed up and moved to the right; from behind it, dispersing the laggards, came two battalions of the Sixth Chasseurs in fine order. Before they had reached Bagration the weighty tread of the mass of men marching in step could be heard. On their left flank, nearest to Bagration, marched a company commander, a fine round-faced man with a stupid and happy expression – the same man who had rushed out of the wattle-shed. At that moment he was clearly thinking of nothing but how dashing a fellow he would appear as he passed the commander.

With the self-satisfaction of a man on parade, he stepped lightly with his muscular legs as if sailing along, stretching himself to his full height without the smallest effort, his ease contrasting with the heavy tread of the soldiers who were keeping step with him. He carried close to his leg a narrow unsheathed sword (small, curved, and not like a real weapon) and looked now at the superior officers and now back at his men without losing step, his whole powerful body turning flexibly. It was as if all the powers of his soul were concentrated on passing the commander in the best possible manner, and feeling that he was doing it well, he was happy. 'Left ... left ... left ...' he seemed to repeat to himself at each alternate step; and in time to this with stern but varied faces, the wall of soldiers burdened with knapsacks and muskets, marched in step, and each one of these hundreds of soldiers seemed to be repeating to himself at each alternate step, 'Left ... left ... left ...' A fat major skirted a bush, puffing and falling out of step; a soldier who had fallen behind, his face showing alarm at his defection, ran at a trot, panting, to catch up with his company. A cannon-ball cleaving the air flew over the heads of Bagration and his suite and fell into the column to the measure of 'Left ... left!' 'Close up!' came the company commander's voice in jaunty tones. The soldiers passed in a semi-circle round something where the ball had fallen, and an old trooper on the flank, a non-commissioned officer, who had stopped beside the dead men, ran to catch up his line and falling into step with a hop, looked back angrily, and through the ominous silence and the regular tramp of feet beating the ground in unison, one seemed to hear left ... left ... left.

'Well done, lads!' said Prince Bagration.

'Glad to do our best, your Ex'len-lency!' came a confused shout from the ranks. A morose soldier marching on the left turned his eyes on Bagration as he shouted, with an expression that seemed to say: 'We know that ourselves!' Another, without looking round, as though fearing to relax, shouted with his mouth wide open and passed on.

The order was given to halt and down knapsacks.

Bagration rode round the ranks that had marched past him and dismounted. He gave the reins to a Cossack, took off and handed over his felt coat, stretched his legs, and set his cap straight. The head of the French column, with its officers leading, appeared from below the hill.

'Forward, with God!' said Bagration in a resolute sonorous voice, turning for a moment to the front line, and, slightly swinging his arms, he went forward uneasily over the rough field with the awkward gait of a cavalryman. Prince Andrew felt that an invisible power was leading him forward, and experienced great happiness.

The French were already near. Prince Andrew walking beside

Bagration, could clearly distinguish their bandoliers, red epaulettes, and even their faces. (He distinctly saw an old French officer, who with gaitered legs and turned-out toes climbed the hill with difficulty.) Prince Bagration gave no further orders and silently continued to walk on in front of the ranks. Suddenly one shot after another rang out from among the French, smoke appeared all along their uneven ranks, and musket shots sounded. Several of our men fell, among them the round-faced officer who had marched so gaily and complacently. But at the moment the first report was heard, Bagration looked round and shouted 'Hurrah!'

'Hurrah – ah! – ah!' rang a long-drawn shout from our ranks, and passing Bagration and racing one another, they rushed in an irregular but joyous and eager crowd down the hill at their disordered foe.*

19

THE attack of the Sixth Chasseurs secured the retreat of our right flank. In the centre Tushin's forgotten battery, which had managed to set fire to the Schön Grabern village, delayed the French advance. The French were putting out the fire which the wind was spreading, and thus gave us time to retreat. The retirement of the centre to the other side of the dip in the ground at the rear was hurried and noisy, but the different companies did not get mixed. But our left – which consisted of the Azov and Podolsk infantry and the Pavlograd hussars – was simultaneously attacked and outflanked by superior French forces under Lannes, and was thrown into confusion. Bagration had sent Zherkov to the general commanding that left flank with orders to retreat immediately.

Zherkov, not removing his hand from his cap, turned his horse about and galloped off. But no sooner had he left Bagration than his courage failed him. He was seized by panic and could not go where it was dangerous.

Having reached the left bank, instead of going to the front where the firing was, he began to look for the general and his staff where they could not possibly be, and so did not deliver the order.

The command of the left flank belonged by seniority to the commander of the regiment Kutuzov had reviewed at Braunau and in which Dolokhov was serving as a private. But the command of the extreme left flank had been assigned to the commander of the Pavlograd regiment in which Rostov was serving, and a misunderstanding arose. The two commanders were much exasperated with one another and long after the action had begun on the right flank and the French were already advancing, were engaged in discussion, with the sole object of offending one another. But the regiments, both cavalry and infantry, were by no means ready for the impending action. From privates to general they were not expecting a battle and were engaged in peaceful occupations, the cavalry feeding their horses and the infantry collecting wood.

'He higher iss dan I in rank,' said the German colonel of the hussars, flushing and addressing an adjutant who had ridden up, 'so let him do vhat he vill, but I cannot sacrifice my hussars ... Bugler, sount ze retreat!'

But haste was becoming imperative. Cannon and musketry mingling together, thundered on the right and in the centre, while the capotes of Lannes's sharpshooters were already seen crossing the mill-dam and forming up within twice the range of a musket-shot. The general in command of the infantry went towards his horse with jerky steps, and having mounted drew himself up very straight and tall and rode to the Pavlograd commander. The commanders met with polite bows but with secret malevolence in their hearts.

'Once again, Colonel,' said the general, 'I can't leave half my men in the wood. I *beg* of you, I *beg* of you,' he repeated, 'to occupy the *position* and prepare for an attack.'

'I peg of you yourself not to mix in vot is not your pusiness!' suddenly replied the irate colonel. 'If you vere in the cavalry ...'

'I am not in the cavalry, Colonel, but I am a Russian general and if you are not aware of the fact ...'

'Quite avare, your Excellency,' suddenly shouted the colonel, touching his horse and turning purple in the face. 'Vill you be so goot to come to ze front and see dat zis position iss no goot? I don't vish to desstroy my men for your pleasure!'

'You forget yourself, Colonel. I am not considering my own pleasure and I won't allow it to be said!'

Taking the colonel's outburst as a challenge to his courage, the general expanded his chest and rode, frowning, beside him to the front line, as if their differences would be settled there amongst the bullets. They reached the front, several bullets sped over them, and they halted in silence. There was nothing fresh to be seen from the line, for from where they had been before it had been evident that it was impossible for cavalry to act among the bushes and broken ground, as well as that the French were outflanking our left. The general and colonel looked sternly and significantly at one another like two fighting-cocks preparing for battle, each vainly trying to detect signs of cowardice in the other. Both passed the examination successfully. As there was nothing to be said, and neither wished to give occasion for it to be alleged that he had been the first to leave the range of fire, they would have remained there for a long time testing each other's courage, had it not been that just then they heard the rattle of musketry and a muffled shout almost behind them in the wood. The French had attacked the men collecting wood in the copse. It was no longer possible for the hussars to retreat with the infantry. They were cut off from the line of retreat on the left by the French. However inconvenient the position, it was now necessary to attack in order to cut a way through for themselves.

The squadron in which Rostov was serving had scarcely time to mount before it was halted facing the enemy. Again, as at the Enns bridge, there was nothing between the squadron and the enemy, and again that terrible dividing line of uncertainty and fear – resembling the line separating the living from the dead – lay between them. All were conscious of this unseen line, and the question whether they would cross it or not, and how they would cross it, agitated them all.

The colonel rode to the front, angrily gave some reply to questions put to him by the officers, and like a man desperately insisting on having his own way, gave an order. No one said anything definite, but the rumour of an attack spread through the squadron. The command to form up rang out and the sabres whizzed as they were drawn from their scabbards. Still no one moved. The troops of the left flank, infantry and hussars alike, felt that the commander did not himself know what to do, and this irresolution communicated itself to the men.

'If only they would be quick!' thought Rostov, feeling that at last the time had come to experience the joy of an attack of which he had so often heard from his fellow hussars.

'Fo'ward, with God, lads!' rang out Denisov's voice. 'At a twot, fo'ward!'

The horses' croups began to sway in the front line. Rook pulled at the reins and started of his own accord.

Before him on the right Rostov saw the front lines of his hussars, and still farther ahead a dark line, which he could not see distinctly but took to be the enemy. Shots could be heard, but some way off.

'Faster!' came the word of command, and Rostov felt Rook's flanks drooping as he broke into a gallop.

Rostov anticipated his horse's movements and became more and more elated. He had noticed a solitary tree ahead of him. This tree had been in the middle of the line that had seemed so terrible – and now he had crossed that line, and not only was there nothing terrible, but everything was becoming more and more happy and animated. 'Oh, how I will slash at him!' thought Rostov, gripping the hilt of his sabre.

'Hurr-a-a-a-ah!' came a roar of voices. 'Let anyone come my way now,' thought Rostov driving his spurs into Rook and letting him go at full gallop so that he outstripped the others. Ahead the enemy was already visible. Suddenly something like a birch-broom seemed to sweep over the squadron. Rostov raised his sabre ready to strike, but at that instant the trooper Nikitenko who was galloping ahead, shot away from him, and Rostov felt as in a dream that he continued to be carried forward with unnatural speed but yet stayed on the same spot. From behind him Bondarchuk, an hussar he knew, jolted against him and looked at him angrily. Bondarchuk's horse swerved and galloped past.

'How is it I am not moving? I have fallen, I am killed!' Rostov asked and answered at the same instant. He was alone in the middle of a field. Instead of the moving horses and hussars' backs, he saw nothing before him but the motionless earth and the stubble around him. There was warm blood under his arm. 'No, I am wounded and the horse is killed.' Rook tried to rise on his forelegs but fell back, pinning his rider's leg. Blood was flowing from his head, he struggled but could not rise. Rostov also tried to rise but fell back, his sabretache having become entangled in the saddle. Where our men were, and where the French, he did not know. There was no one near.

Having disentangled his leg, he rose. 'Where, on which side, was now the line that had so sharply divided the two armies?' he asked himself and could not answer. 'Can something bad have happened to me?' he wondered as he got up; and at that moment he felt that something superfluous was hanging on his benumbed left arm. The wrist felt as if it were not his. He examined his hand carefully, vainly trying to find blood on it. 'Ah, here are people coming,' he thought joyfully, seeing some men running towards him. 'They will help me!' In front came a man wearing a strange shako and a blue cloak, swarthy, sunburnt, and with a hooked nose. Then came two more, and many more running behind. One of them said something strange, not in Russian. In among the hindmost of these men wearing similar shakos was a Russian hussar. He was being held by the arms, and his horse was being led behind him.

'It must be one of ours, a prisoner. Yes. Can it be that they will take me too? Who are these men?' thought Rostov scarcely believing his eyes. 'Can they be French?' He looked at the approaching Frenchmen, and though but a moment before he had been galloping to get at them and hack them to pieces, their proximity now seemed so awful that he could not believe his eyes. 'Who are they? Why are they running? Can they be coming at me? And why? To kill me? *Me* whom everyone is so fond of?' He remembered his mother's love for him, and his family's, and his friends', and the enemy's intention to kill him seemed impossible. 'But perhaps they may do it!' For more than ten seconds he stood not moving from the spot or realizing the situation. The foremost Frenchman, the one with the hooked nose, was already so close that the expression of his face could be seen. And the excited, alien face of that man, his bayonet hanging down, holding his breath, and running so lightly, frightened Rostov. He seized his pistol, and instead of firing it flung it at the Frenchman and ran with all his might towards the bushes. He did not now run with the feeling of doubt and conflict with which he had trodden the Enns bridge, but with the feeling of a hare fleeing from the hounds. One single sentiment, that of fear for his young and happy life, possessed his whole being. Rapidly leaping the furrows he fled across the field with the impetuosity he used to show at catchplay, now and then turning his good-natured, pale, young face to look back. A shudder of terror went through him: 'No, better not look,' he thought, but having reached the bushes he glanced round once more. The French had fallen behind, and just as he looked round the first man changed his run to a walk, and turning, shouted something loudly to a comrade farther back. Rostov paused. 'No, there's some mistake,' thought he. 'They can't have wanted to kill me.' But at the same time his left arm felt as heavy as if a five-stone weight were tied to it. He could run no more. The Frenchman also stopped and took aim. Rostov closed his eyes and stooped down. One bullet and then another whistled past him. He mustered his last remaining strength, took hold of his left hand with his right and reached the bushes. Behind these were some Russian sharpshooters.

20

THE infantry regiments that had been caught unawares in the outskirts of the wood ran out of it, the different companies getting mixed, and retreated as a disorderly crowd. One soldier in his fear uttered the senseless cry, 'Cut off!' that is so terrible in battle, and that word infected the whole crowd with a feeling of panic.

'Surrounded! Cut off! We're lost!' shouted the fugitives.

The moment he heard the firing and the cry from behind, the general realized that something dreadful had happened to his regiment, and the thought that he, an exemplary officer of many years' service who had never been to blame, might be held responsible at head-quarters for negligence or inefficiency, so staggered him that forgetting the recalcitrant cavalry colonel, his own dignity as a general, and above all quite forgetting the danger and all regard for self-preservation, he clutched the pommel of his saddle and spurring his horse galloped to the regiment under a hail of bullets which fell around, but fortunately missed him. His one desire was to know what was happening and at any cost correct, or remedy, the mistake if he had made one, so that he, an exemplary officer of twenty-two years' service who had never been censured, should not be held to blame.

Having galloped safely through the French, he reached a field behind the copse across which our men, regardless of orders, were running, and descending the valley. That moment of moral hesitation which decides the fate of battles had arrived. Would this disorderly crowd of soldiers attend to the voice of their commander, or would they, disregarding him, continue their flight? Despite his desperate shouts that used to seem so terrible to the soldiers, despite his furious purple countenance distorted out of all likeness to his former self, and the flourishing of his sabre, the soldiers all continued to run, talking, firing into the air and disobeying orders. The moral hesitation which decides the fate of battles was evidently culminating in a panic.

The general had a fit of coughing as a result of shouting and of the powder-smoke, and stopped in despair. Everything seemed lost. But at that moment the French who were attacking, suddenly and without any apparent reason, ran back and disappeared from the outskirts, and Russian sharpshooters showed themselves in the copse. It was Timokhin's company, which alone had maintained its order in the wood, and having lain in ambush in a ditch now attacked the French unexpectedly. Timokhin armed only with a sword, had rushed at the enemy with such a desperate cry and such mad drunken determination, that taken by surprise the French had thrown down their muskets and run. Dolokhov, running beside Timokhin, killed a Frenchman at close quarters and was the first to seize the surrendering French officer by his collar. Our fugitives returned, the battalions re-formed, and the French who had nearly cut our left flank in half, were for the moment repulsed. Our reserve units were able to join up, and the fight was at an end. The regimental commander and Major Ekonomov had stopped beside a bridge letting the retreating companies pass by them, when a soldier came up and took hold of the commander's stirrup almost leaning against him. The man was wearing a bluish coat of broadcloth, he had no knapsack or cap, his head was bandaged, and over his shoulder a French munition pouch was slung. He had an officer's sword in his hand. The soldier was pale, his blue eyes looked impudently into the commander's face, and his lips were smiling. Though the commander was occupied in giving instructions to Major Ekonomov, he could not help taking notice of the soldier.

'Your Excellency, here are two trophies,' said Dolokhov, pointing to the French sword and pouch. 'I have taken an officer prisoner. I stopped the company.' Dolokhov breathed heavily from weariness and spoke in abrupt sentences. 'The whole company can bear witness. I beg you will remember this, your Excellency!'

'All right, all right,' replied the commander, and turned to Major Ekonomov.

But Dolokhov did not go away; he untied the handkerchief around his head, pulled it off, and showed the blood congealed on his hair.

'A bayonet wound. I remained at the front. Remember, your Excellency!'

*

Tushin's battery had been forgotten and only at the very end of the action did Prince Bagration, still hearing the cannonade in the centre, send his orderly staff-officer and later Prince Andrew also, to order the battery to retire as quickly as possible. When the supports attached to Tushin's battery had been moved away in the middle of the action by someone's order, the battery had continued firing and was only not captured by the French because the enemy could not surmise that anyone could have the effrontery to continue firing from four quite undefended guns. On the contrary, the energetic action of that battery led the French to suppose that here – in the centre – the main Russian forces were concentrated. Twice they had attempted to attack this point, but on each occasion had been driven back by grapeshot from the four isolated guns on the hillock.

Soon after Prince Bagration had left him, Tushin had succeeded in setting fire to Schön Grabern.

'Look at them scurrying! It's burning! Just see the smoke! Fine! Grand! Look at the smoke, the smoke!' exclaimed the artillerymen, brightening up.

All the guns without waiting for orders, were being fired in the direction of the conflagration. As if urging each other on the soldiers cried at each shot: 'Fine! That's good! Look at it . . . Grand!' The fire, fanned by the breeze, was rapidly spreading. The French columns that had advanced beyond the village went back, but as though in revenge for this failure, the enemy placed ten guns to the right of the village and began firing them at Tushin's battery.

In their childlike glee, aroused by the fire and their luck in successfully cannonading the French, our artillerymen only noticed this battery when two balls, and then four more, fell among our guns, one knocking over two horses and another tearing off a munition-wagon driver's leg. Their spirits once roused were however not diminished, but only changed character. The horses were replaced by others from a reserve gun-carriage, the wounded were carried away, and the four guns were turned against the ten-gun battery. Tushin's companion officer had been killed at the beginning of the engagement and within an hour seventeen of the forty men of the guns' crews had been disabled, but the artillerymen were still as merry and lively as ever. Twice they noticed the French appearing below them, and then they fired grape-shot at them.

Little Tushin, moving feebly and awkwardly, kept telling his orderly to 'refill my pipe for that one!' and then, scattering sparks from it, ran forward shading his eyes with his small hand to look at the French.

'Smack at 'em, lads!' he kept saying, seizing the guns by the wheels and working the screws himself.

Amid the smoke, deafened by the incessant reports which always made him jump. Tushin, not taking his pipe from his mouth, ran from gun to gun, now aiming, now counting the charges, now giving orders about replacing dead or wounded horses and harnessing fresh ones, and shouting in his feeble voice, so high-pitched and irresolute. His face grew more and more animated. Only when a man was killed or wounded did he frown and turn away from the sight, shouting angrily at the men who, as is always the case, hesitated about lifting the injured or dead. The soldiers, for the most part handsome fellows and, as is always the case in an artillery company, a head and shoulders taller and twice as broad as their officer – all looked at their commander like children in an embarrassing situation, and the expression on his face was invariably reflected on theirs.

Owing to the terrible uproar and the necessity for concentration and activity, Tushin did not experience the slightest unpleasant sense of fear, and the thought that he might be killed or badly wounded never occurred to him. On the contrary he became more and more elated. It seemed to him that it was a very long time ago, almost a day, since he had first seen the enemy and fired the first shot, and that the corner of the field he stood on was well known and familiar ground. Though he thought of everything, considered everything, and did everything the best of officers could do in his position, he was in a state akin to feverish delirium or drunkenness.

From the deafening sounds of his own guns around him, the whistle and thud of the enemy's cannon-balls, from the flushed and perspiring faces of the crews bustling round the guns, from the sight of the blood of men and horses, from the little puffs of smoke on the enemy's side (always followed by a ball flying past and striking the earth, a man, a gun, or a horse), from the sight of all these things a fantastic world of his own had taken possession of his brain and at that moment afforded him pleasure. The enemy's guns were in his fancy not guns but pipes from which occasional puffs were blown by an invisible smoker.

'There ... he's puffing again,' muttered Tushin to himself as a small cloud rose from the hill and was borne in a streak to the left by the wind. 'Now look out for the ball ... we'll throw it back.'

'What do you want, your honour?' asked an artilleryman standing close by, who heard him muttering.

'Nothing ... only a shell ...' he answered.

'Come along, our Matvevna!' he said to himself. 'Matvevna' (daughter of Matthew) was the name his fancy gave to the farthest gun of the battery, which was large and of an old pattern. The French swarming round their guns seemed to him like ants. In that world the handsome drunkard, Number One of the second gun's crew, was 'uncle'; Tushin looked at him more often than at anyone else, and took delight in his every movement. The sound of musketry at the foot of the hill, now diminishing now increasing, seemed like someone's breathing. He listened intently to the ebb and flow of these sounds.

'Ah! Breathing again, breathing!' he muttered to himself.

He imagined himself as an enormously tall, powerful man who was throwing cannon-balls at the French with both hands.

'Now then, Matvevna, dear old lady, don't let me down!' he was saying as he moved from the gun, when a strange, unfamiliar voice called above his head: 'Captain Tushin! Captain!'

Tushin turned round in dismay. It was the staff-officer who had turned him out of the booth at Grunth. He was shouting in a gasping voice:

'Are you mad? You have twice been ordered to retreat, and you ...'

'Why are they down on me?' thought Tushin, looking in alarm at his superior.

'I...don't...' he muttered, holding up two fingers to his cap. 'I...'

But the staff-officer did not finish what he wanted to say. A cannon-ball flying close to him caused him to duck and bend over his horse. He paused, and just as he was about to say something more another ball stopped him. He turned his horse and galloped off.

'Retire! All to retire!' he shouted from a distance.

The soldiers laughed. A moment later an adjutant arrived with the same order.

It was Prince Andrew. The first thing he saw on riding up to the space where Tushin's guns were stationed was an unharnessed horse with a broken leg, that lay screaming piteously beside the harnessed horses. Blood was gushing from its leg as from a spring. Among the limbers lay several dead men. One ball after another passed over as he approached and he felt a nervous shudder run down his spine. But the mere thought of being afraid roused him again. 'I cannot be afraid,' thought he, and dismounted slowly among the guns. He delivered the order and did not leave the battery. He decided to have the guns removed from their positions and withdrawn in his presence. Together with Tushin, stepping across the bodies and under a terrible fire from the French, he attended to the removal of the guns.

'A staff-officer was here a minute ago but skipped off,' said an artilleryman to Prince Andrew. 'Not like your honour!'

Prince Andrew said nothing to Tushin. They were both so busy as to seem not to notice one another. When, having limbered up the only two cannon that remained uninjured out of the four, they began moving down the hill (one shattered gun and one unicorn* were left behind), Prince Andrew rode up to Tushin.

'Well, till we meet again...' he said, holding out his hand to Tushin.

'Good-bye, my dear fellow,' said Tushin. 'Dear soul! Good-bye, my dear fellow!' and for some unknown reason tears suddenly filled his eyes.

21

THE wind had fallen and black clouds, merging with the powder-smoke, hung low over the field of battle on the horizon. It was growing dark and the glow of two conflagrations was the more conspicuous. The cannonade was dying down, but the rattle of musketry behind and on the right sounded oftener and nearer. As soon as Tushin with his guns, continually driving round or coming upon wounded men, was out of range of fire and had descended into the dip, he was met by some of the staff, among them the staff-officer and Zherkov, who had been twice sent to Tushin's battery but had never reached it. Interrupting one another they all gave, and transmitted, orders as to how to proceed, reprimanding and reproaching him. Tushin gave no orders, and silently – fearing to speak because at every word he felt ready to weep without knowing why – rode behind on his artillery nag. Though the orders were to abandon the wounded, many of them dragged themselves after the troops and begged for seats on the gun-carriages. The jaunty infantry officer who just before the battle had rushed out of Tushin's wattle-shed, was laid, with a bullet in his stomach, on Matvevna's carriage. At the foot of the hill a pale hussar cadet supporting one hand with the other, came up to Tushin and asked for a seat.

'Captain, for God's sake! I've hurt my arm,' he said timidly. 'For God's sake . . . I can't walk. For God's sake!'

It was plain that this cadet had already repeatedly asked for a lift and been refused. He asked in a hesitating, piteous voice.

'Tell them to give me a seat, for God's sake!'

'Give him a seat,' said Tushin. 'Lay a cloak for him to sit on, lad,' he said, addressing his favourite soldier. 'And where is the wounded officer?'

'He has been set down. He died,' replied someone.

'Help him up. Sit down, dear fellow, sit down! Spread out the cloak, Antonov.'

The cadet was Rostov. With one hand he supported the other; he was pale and his jaw trembled, shivering feverishly. He was placed on 'Matvevna', the gun from which they had removed the dead officer. The cloak they spread under him was wet with blood which stained his breeches and arm.

'What, are you wounded, my lad?' said Tushin, approaching the gun on which Rostov sat.

'No, it's a sprain.'

'Then what is this blood on the gun-carriage?' inquired Tushin.

'It was the officer, your honour, stained it,' answered the artillery-man, wiping away the blood with his coat-sleeve as if apologizing for the state of his gun.

It was all that they could do to get the guns up the rise, aided by the infantry, and having reached the village of Guntersdorf they halted. It had grown so dark that one could not distinguish the uniforms ten paces off, and the firing had begun to subside. Suddenly, nearby on the right, shouting and firing were again heard. Flashes of shots gleamed in the darkness. This was the last

French attack, and was met by soldiers who had sheltered in the village houses. They all rushed out of the village again, but Tushin's guns could not move, and the artillerymen, Tushin, and the cadet, exchanged silent glances as they awaited their fate. The firing died down, and soldiers talking eagerly streamed out of a side-street.

'Not hurt, Petrov?' asked one.

'We've given it 'em hot, mate! They won't make another push now,' said another.

'You couldn't see a thing. How they shot at their own fellows! Nothing could be seen. Pitch dark, brother! Isn't there something to drink?'

The French had been repulsed for the last time. And again and again in the complete darkness Tushin's guns moved forward, surrounded by the humming infantry as by a frame.

In the darkness it seemed as though a gloomy unseen river was flowing always in one direction, humming with whispers and talk and the sound of hoofs and wheels. Amid the general rumble the groans and voices of the wounded were more distinctly heard than any other sound in the darkness of the night. The gloom that enveloped the army was filled with their groans, which seemed to melt into one with the darkness of the night. After a while the moving mass became agitated, someone rode past on a white horse followed by his suite, and said something in passing: 'What did he say? Where to, now? Halt, is it? Did he thank us?' came eager questions from all sides. The whole moving mass began pressing closer together and a report spread that they were ordered to halt: evidently those in front had halted. All remained where they were in the middle of the muddy road.

Fires were lighted and the talk became more audible. Captain Tushin, having given orders to his company, sent a soldier to find a dressing station or a doctor for the cadet, and sat down by a bonfire the soldiers had kindled on the road. Rostov, too, dragged himself to the fire. From pain, cold and damp, a feverish shivering shook his whole body. Drowsiness was irresistibly mastering him, but he was kept awake by an excruciating pain in his arm for which he could find no satisfactory position. He kept closing his eyes and then again looking at the fire, which seemed to him dazzling red, and at the feeble round-shouldered figure of Tushin who was sitting cross-legged like a Turk beside him. Tushin's large kind intelligent eyes were fixed with sympathy and commiseration on Rostov, who saw that Tushin with his whole heart wished to help him but could not.

From all sides were heard the footsteps and talk of the infantry, who were walking, driving past, and settling down all around. The sound of voices, the tramping feet, the horses' hoofs moving in the mud, the crackling of wood fires near and afar, merged into one tremulous rumble.

It was no longer as before, a dark unseen river flowing through the gloom, but a dark sea swelling and gradually subsiding after a storm. Rostov looked at and listened listlessly to what passed before and around him. An infantryman came to the fire, squatted on his heels, held his hands to the blaze, and turned away his face.

'You don't mind, your honour?' he asked Tushin. 'I've lost my company, your honour. I don't know where ... such bad luck!'

With the soldier an infantry officer with a bandaged cheek came up to the bonfire, and addressing Tushin asked him to have the guns moved a trifle to let a wagon go past. After he had gone two soldiers rushed to the camp fire. They were quarrelling and fighting desperately, each trying to snatch from the other a boot they were both holding on to.

'You picked it up? ... I dare say! You're very smart!' one of them shouted hoarsely.

Then a thin pale soldier, his neck bandaged with a blood-stained leg-band, came up and in angry tones asked the artillerymen for water.

'Must one die like a dog?' said he.

Tushin told them to give the man some water. Then a cheerful soldier ran up begging a little fire for the infantry.

'A nice little hot torch for the infantry! Good luck to you, fellow countrymen. Thanks for the fire – we'll return it with interest,' said he carrying away into the darkness a glowing stick.

Next came four soldiers carrying something heavy on a cloak, and passed by the fire. One of them stumbled.

'Who the devil has put logs on the road?' snarled he.

'He's dead – why carry him?' said another.

'Shut up!'

And they disappeared into the darkness with their load.

'Still aching?' Tushin asked Rostov in a whisper.

'Yes.'

'Your honour, you're wanted by the general. He is in the hut here,' said a gunner, coming up to Tushin.

'Coming, friend.'

Tushin rose and buttoning his greatcoat and pulling it straight, walked away from the fire.

Not far from the artillery camp-fire, in a hut that had been prepared for him, Prince Bagration sat at dinner, talking with some commanding officers who had gathered at his quarters. The little old man with the half-closed eyes was there, greedily gnawing a mutton-bone, and the general who had served blamelessly for twenty-two years, flushed by a glass of vodka and the dinner; and the staff-officer with the signet-ring, and Zherkov uneasily glancing at them all, and Prince Andrew, pale, with compressed lips and feverishly glittering eyes.

In a corner of the hut stood a standard captured from the French, and the accountant with the naïve face was feeling its texture, shaking his head in perplexity – perhaps because the banner really interested him, perhaps because it was hard for him, hungry as he was, to look on at a dinner where there was no place for him. In the next hut there was a French colonel who had been taken prisoner by our dragoons. Our officers were flocking in to look at him. Prince Bagration was thanking the individual commanders and inquiring into details of the action and our losses. The general whose regiment had been inspected at Braunau was informing the prince that as soon as the action began he had withdrawn from the wood, mustered the men who were wood-cutting, and allowing the French to pass him had made a bayonet charge with two battalions and had broken up the French troops.

'When I saw, your Excellency, that their first battalion was disorganized, I stopped in the road and thought: "I'll let them come on and will meet them with the fire of the whole battalion" – and that's what I did.'

The general had so wished to do this, and was so sorry he had not managed to do it, that it seemed to him as if it had really happened. Perhaps it might really have been so? Could one possibly make out amid all that confusion, what did or did not happen?

'By the way, your Excellency, I should inform you,' he continued – remembering Dolokhov's conversation with Kutuzov, and his last interview with the gentleman-ranker – 'that Private Dolokhov, who was reduced to the ranks, took a French officer prisoner in my presence and particularly distinguished himself.'

'I saw the Pavlograd hussars attack there, your Excellency,' chimed in Zherkov, looking uneasily around. He had not seen the hussars all that day, but had heard about them from an infantry officer. 'They broke up two squares, your Excellency.'

Several of those present smiled at Zherkov's words expecting one of his usual jokes, but noticing that what he was saying redounded to the glory of our arms and of the day's work, they assumed a serious expression, though many of them knew that what he was saying was a lie devoid of any foundation. Prince Bagration turned to the old colonel:

'Gentlemen, I thank you all; all arms have behaved heroically: infantry, cavalry, and artillery. How was it that two guns were abandoned in the centre?' he inquired, searching with his eyes for someone. (Prince Bagration did not ask about the guns on the left flank; he knew that all the guns there had been abandoned at the very beginning of the action.) 'I think I sent you?' he added turning to the staff-officer on duty.

'One was damaged,' answered the staff-officer, 'and the other I can't understand. I was there all the time giving orders, and had only just left . . . It is true it was hot there,' he added modestly.

Someone mentioned that Captain Tushin was bivouacking close to the village and had already been sent for.

'Oh, but you were there?' said Prince Bagration, addressing Prince Andrew.

'Of course, we only just missed one another,' said the staff-officer, with a smile to Bolkonsky.

'I had not the pleasure of seeing you,' said Prince Andrew coldly and abruptly.

All were silent. Tushin appeared at the threshold and made his way timidly from behind the backs of the generals. As he stepped past the generals in the crowded hut, feeling embarrassed as he always was by the sight of his superiors, he did not notice the staff of the banner and stumbled over it. Several of those present laughed.

'How is it a gun was abandoned?' asked Bagration, frowning, not so much at the captain as at those who were laughing, among whom Zherkov laughed loudest.

Only now, when he was confronted by the stern authorities, did his guilt and the disgrace of having lost two guns and yet remaining alive, present themselves to Tushin in all their horror. He had been so excited that he had not thought about it until that moment. The officers' laughter confused him still more. He stood before Bagration with his lower jaw trembling, and was hardly able to mutter:

'I don't know . . . your Excellency . . . I had no men . . . your Excellency.'

'You might have taken some from the covering troops.'

Tushin did not say that there were no covering troops though that was perfectly true. He was afraid of getting some other officer into trouble, and silently fixed his eyes on Bagration as a schoolboy who has blundered looks at an examiner.

The silence lasted some time. Prince Bagration, apparently not wishing to be severe, found nothing to say, the others did not venture to intervene. Prince Andrew looked at Tushin from under his brows and his fingers twitched nervously.

'Your Excellency!' Prince Andrew broke the silence with his abrupt voice, 'you were pleased to send me to Captain Tushin's battery. I went there and found two-thirds of the men and horses knocked out, two guns smashed, and no supports at all.'

Prince Bagration and Tushin looked with equal intentness at Bolkonsky who spoke with suppressed agitation.

'And if your Excellency will allow me to express my opinion,' he continued, 'we owe to-day's success chiefly to the action of that battery and the heroic endurance of Captain Tushin and his company,' and without awaiting a reply, Prince Andrew rose and left the table.

Prince Bagration looked at Tushin, evidently reluctant to show distrust in Bolkonsky's emphatic opinion yet not feeling able fully to credit it, bent his head, and told Tushin that he could go. Prince Andrew went out with him.

'Thank you; you saved me, my dear fellow!' said Tushin.

Prince Andrew gave him a look, but said nothing and went away. He felt sad and depressed. It was all so strange, so unlike what he had hoped.

*

'Who are they? Why are they here? What do they want? And when will this all end?' thought Rostov looking at the changing shadows before him. The pain in his arm became more and more intense. Irresistible drowsiness overpowered him, red rings danced before his eyes, and the impression of those voices and faces and a sense of loneliness merged with the physical pain. It was they, these soldiers – wounded and unwounded – it was they who were crushing, weighing down and twisting the sinews and scorching the flesh of his sprained arm and shoulder. To rid himself of them he closed his eyes.

For a moment he dozed, but in that short interval innumerable things appeared to him in a dream: his mother and her large white hand, Sonya's thin little shoulders, Natasha's eyes and laughter, Denisov with his voice and moustache, and Telyanin, and all that affair with Telyanin and Bogdanich. That affair was the same thing as this soldier with the harsh voice, and it was that affair and this soldier that were so agonizingly, incessantly, pulling and pressing his arm and always dragging it in one direction. He tried to get away from them, but they would not for an instant let his shoulder move a hair's breadth. It would not ache – it would be well – if only they did not pull it, but it was impossible to get rid of them.

He opened his eyes and looked up. The black canopy of night

hung less than a yard above the glow of the charcoal. Flakes of falling snow were fluttering in that light. Tushin had not returned, the doctor had not come. He was alone now except for a soldier who was sitting naked at the other side of the fire warming his thin yellow body.

'Nobody wants me!' thought Rostov. 'There is no one to help me or pity me. Yet I was once at home, strong, happy, and loved.' He sighed, and doing so groaned involuntarily.

'Eh, is anything hurting you?' asked the soldier, shaking his shirt out over the fire, and not waiting for an answer he gave a grunt and added: 'What a lot of men have been crippled to-day – frightful!'

Rostov did not listen to the soldier. He looked at the snowflakes fluttering above the fire, and remembered a Russian winter at his warm bright home, his fluffy fur coat, his quickly-gliding sledge, his healthy body, and all the affection and care of his family. 'And why did I come here?' he wondered.

Next day the French did not renew their attack, and the remnant of Bagration's detachment was reunited to Kutuzov's army.

END OF PART TWO

PART THREE

1

PRINCE VASILI was not a man who deliberately thought out his plans. Still less did he think of injuring anyone for his own advantage. He was merely a man of the world who had got on and to whom getting on had become a habit. Schemes and devices for which he never rightly accounted to himself, but which formed the whole interest of his life, were constantly shaping themselves in his mind, arising from the circumstances and persons he met. Of these plans he had not merely one or two in his head but dozens, some only beginning to form themselves, some approaching achievement, and some in course of disintegration. He did not, for instance, say to himself: 'This man now has influence, I must gain his confidence and friendship and through him obtain a special grant.' Nor did he say to himself: 'Pierre is a rich man, I must entice him to marry my daughter and lend me the forty thousand rubles I need.' But when he came across a man of position his instinct immediately told him that this man could be useful, and without any premeditation Prince Vasili took the first opportunity to gain his confidence, flatter him, become intimate with him, and finally make his request.

He had Pierre at hand in Moscow and procured for him an appointment as Gentleman of the Bed-chamber, which at that time conferred the status of Councillor of State,* and insisted on the young man accompanying him to Petersburg and staying at his house. With apparent absent-mindedness, yet with unhesitating assurance that he was doing the right thing, Prince Vasili did everything to get Pierre to marry his daughter. Had he thought out his plans beforehand he could not have been so natural and shown such unaffected familiarity in intercourse with everybody, both above and below him in social standing. Something always drew him towards those richer and more powerful than himself and he had rare skill in seizing the most opportune moment for making use of people.

Pierre on unexpectedly becoming Count Bezukhov and a rich man, felt himself after his recent loneliness and freedom from cares, so beset and preoccupied that only in bed was he able to be by himself. He had to sign papers, to present himself at government offices the function of which was not clear to him, to question his chief steward, to visit his estate near Moscow, and to receive many people who formerly did not even wish to know of his existence but would now have been offended and grieved had he chosen not to see them. These different people – business men, relations, and acquaintances alike – were all disposed to treat the young heir in the most friendly and flattering manner: they were all evidently firmly convinced of Pierre's noble qualities. He was always hearing such words as: 'With your remarkable kindness,' or, 'With your excellent heart,' 'You are yourself so honourable, Count,' or, 'Were he as clever as you,' and so on, till he began sincerely to believe in his own exceptional kindness and extraordinary intelligence, the more so as in the depth of his heart it had always seemed to him that he really was very kind and intelligent. Even people who had formerly been spiteful towards him and evidently unfriendly now became gentle and affectionate. The angry eldest princess with the long waist and hair plastered down like a doll's, had come into Pierre's room after the funeral. With drooping eyes and frequent blushes she told him she was very sorry about their past misunderstandings and did not now feel she had a right to ask him for anything, except only for permission, after the blow she had received, to remain for a few weeks longer in the house she so loved and where she had sacrificed so much. She could not refrain from weeping at these words. Touched that this statuesque princess could so change, Pierre took her hand and begged her forgiveness, without knowing what for. From that day the eldest princess quite changed towards Pierre and began knitting a striped scarf for him.

'Do this for my sake, *mon cher*; after all, she had to put up with a great deal from the deceased,' said Prince Vasili to him, handing him a deed to sign for the princess's benefit.

Prince Vasili had come to the conclusion that it was necessary to throw this bone – a bill for thirty thousand rubles – to the poor princess, that it might not occur to her to speak of his share in the affair of the inlaid portfolio. Pierre signed the deed, and after that the princess grew still kinder. The younger sisters also became affectionate to him, especially the youngest, the pretty one with the mole, who often made him feel confused by her smiles and her own confusion when meeting him.

It seemed so natural to Pierre that everyone should like him, and it would have seemed so unnatural had anyone disliked him, that he could not but believe in the sincerity of those around him.

Besides he had no time to ask himself whether these people were sincere or not. He was always busy and always felt in a state of mild and cheerful intoxication. He felt as though he were the centre of some important and general movement; that something was constantly expected of him, that if he did not do it he would grieve and disappoint many people, but if he did this and that, all would be well; and he did what was demanded of him, but still that happy result always remained in the future.

More than anyone else Prince Vasili took possession of Pierre's affairs and of Pierre himself in those early days. From the death of Count Bezukhov he did not let go his hold of the lad. He had the air of a man oppressed by business, weary and suffering, who yet would not, for pity's sake, leave this helpless youth who after all was the son of his old friend and the possessor of such enormous wealth, to the caprice of fate and the designs of rogues. During the few days he spent in Moscow after the death of Count Bezukhov, he would call Pierre, or go to him himself, and tell him what ought to be done in a tone of weariness and assurance, as if he were adding every time: 'You know I am overwhelmed with business and it is purely out of charity that I trouble myself about you, and you also know quite well that what I propose is the only thing possible.'

'Well, my dear fellow, to-morrow we are off at last,' said Prince Vasili one day, closing his eyes and fingering Pierre's elbow, speaking as if he were saying something which had long since been agreed upon and could not now be altered. 'We start to-morrow and I'm giving you a place in my carriage. I am very glad. All our important business here is now settled, and I ought to have been off long ago. Here is something I have received from the chancellor. I asked him for you, and you have been entered in the diplomatic corps and made a Gentleman of the Bed-chamber. The diplomatic career now lies open before you.'

Notwithstanding the tone of wearied assurance with which these words were pronounced, Pierre, who had so long been considering his career, wished to make some suggestion. But Prince Vasili interrupted him in the special deep cooing tone, precluding the possibility of interrupting his speech, which he used in extreme cases when special persuasion was needed.

'Mais, mon cher, I did this for my own sake, to satisfy my conscience, and there is nothing to thank me for. No one has ever complained yet of being too much loved; and besides, you are free, you could throw it up to-morrow. But you will see everything for yourself when you get to Petersburg. It is high time for you to get away from these terrible recollections.' Prince Vasili sighed.

'Yes, yes, my boy. And my valet can go in your carriage. Ah! I was nearly forgetting,' he added. 'You know, *mon cher*, your father and I had some accounts to settle, so I have received what was due from the Ryazan estate and will keep it; you won't require it. We'll go into the accounts later.'

By 'what was due from the Ryazan estate' Prince Vasili meant several thousand rubles quit-rent received from Pierre's peasants, which the prince had retained for himself.

In Petersburg as in Moscow, Pierre found the same atmosphere of gentleness and affection. He could not refuse the post, or rather the rank (for he did nothing), that Prince Vasili had procured for him, and acquaintances, invitations, and social occupations were so numerous that even more than in Moscow he felt a sense of bewilderment, bustle, and continual expectation of some good, always in front of him but never attained.

Of his former bachelor acquaintances many were no longer in Petersburg. The Guards had gone to the front; Dolokhov had been reduced to the ranks; Anatole was in the army somewhere in the provinces; Prince Andrew was abroad; so Pierre had not the opportunity to spend his nights as he used to like to spend them, or to open his mind by intimate talks with a friend older than himself and whom he respected. His whole time was taken up with dinners and balls, and was spent chiefly at Prince Vasili's house in the company of the stout princess, his wife, and his beautiful daughter Hélène.

Like the others, Anna Pavlovna Scherer showed Pierre the change of attitude towards him that had taken place in society.

Formerly in Anna Pavlovna's presence Pierre had always felt that what he was saying was out of place, tactless and unsuitable, that remarks which seemed to him clever while they formed in his mind became foolish as soon as he uttered them, while on the contrary Hippolyte's stupidest remarks came out clever and apt. Now everything Pierre said was *charmant*. Even if Anna Pavlovna did not say so he could see that she wished to, and only refrained out of regard for his modesty.

In the beginning of the winter of 1805–6 Pierre received one of Anna Pavlovna's usual notes with an invitation to which was added: 'You will find the beautiful Hélène here, whom it is always delightful to see.'

When he read that sentence Pierre felt for the first time that some link which other people recognized, had grown up between himself and Hélène, and that thought both alarmed him, as if some obligation were being imposed on him which he could not fulfil, and pleased him as an entertaining supposition.

Anna Pavlovna's 'At home' was like the former one, only the novelty she offered her guests this time was not Mortemart, but a diplomatist fresh from Berlin with the very latest details of the Emperor Alexander's visit to Potsdam, and of how the two august friends had pledged themselves in an indissoluble alliance to uphold the cause of justice against the enemy of the human race. Anna Pavlovna received Pierre with a shade of melancholy, evidently relating to the young man's recent loss by the death of Count Bezukhov (everyone constantly considered it a duty to assure Pierre that he was greatly afflicted by the death of the father he had hardly known), and her melancholy was just like the august melancholy she showed at the mention of her most august Majesty the Empress Marya Fëdorovna. Pierre felt flattered by this. Anna Pavlovna arranged the different groups in her drawing-room with her habitual skill. The large group, in which were Prince Vasili and the generals, had the benefit of the diplomat. Another group was at the tea table. Pierre wished to join the former, but Anna Pavlovna – who was in the excited condition of a commander on a battlefield to whom thousands of new and brilliant ideas occur which there is hardly time to put in action – seeing Pierre touched his sleeve with her finger, saying:

'Wait a bit, I have something in view for you this evening.' (She glanced at Hélène and smiled at her.) 'My dear Hélène, be charitable to my poor aunt who adores you. Go and keep her company for ten minutes. And that it may not be too dull, here is the dear Count who will not refuse to accompany you.'

The beauty went to the aunt, but Anna Pavlovna detained Pierre, looking as if she had to give some final necessary instructions.

'Isn't she exquisite?' she said to Pierre, pointing to the stately beauty as she glided away. 'And how she carries herself! For so young a girl, such tact, such masterly perfection of manner! It comes from her heart. Happy the man who wins her! With her the least worldly of men would occupy a most brilliant position in society. Don't you think so? I only wanted to know your opinion,' and Anna Pavlovna let Pierre go.

Pierre in reply sincerely agreed with her as to Hélène's perfection of manner. If he ever thought of Hélène it was just of her beauty and her remarkable skill in appearing silently dignified in society.

The old aunt received the two young people in her corner, but seemed desirous of hiding her adoration for Hélène and inclined rather to show her fear of Anna Pavlovna. She looked at her niece as if inquiring what she was to do with these people. On leaving them Anna Pavlovna again touched Pierre's sleeve, saying: 'I hope you won't say that it is dull in my house again,' and she glanced at Hélène.

Hélène smiled, with a look implying that she did not admit the possibility of anyone seeing her without being enchanted. The aunt coughed, swallowed, and said in French that she was very pleased to see Hélène, then she turned to Pierre with the same words of welcome and the same look. In the middle of a dull and halting conversation Hélène turned to Pierre with the beautiful bright smile she gave everyone. Pierre was so used to that smile, and it had so little meaning for him, that he paid no attention to it. The aunt was just speaking of a collection of snuff-boxes that had belonged to Pierre's father, Count Bezukhov, and showed them her own box. Princess Hélène asked to see the portrait of the aunt's husband on the box-lid.

'That is probably the work of Vinesse,' said Pierre, mentioning a celebrated miniaturist, and he leant over the table to take the snuff-box while trying to hear what was being said at the other table.

He half rose, meaning to go round, but the aunt handed him the snuff-box, passing it across Hélène's back. Hélène stooped forward to make room, and looked round with a smile. She was, as always at evening parties, wearing a dress such as was then fashionable, cut very low at front and back. Her bust, which had always seemed like marble to Pierre, was so close to him that his short-sighted eyes could not but perceive the living charm of her neck and shoulders, so near to his lips that he need only have bent his head a little to have touched them. He was conscious of the warmth of her body, the scent of perfume, and the creaking of her corset as she moved. He did not see her marble beauty forming a complete whole with her dress, but all the charm of her body only covered by her garments. And having once seen this he could not help being aware of it, just as we cannot renew an illusion we have once seen through.

'So you have never before noticed how beautiful I am?' Hélène seemed to say. 'You had not noticed that I am a woman? Yes, I am a woman who may belong to anyone – to you too,' said her glance. And at that moment Pierre felt that Hélène not only could, but must, be his wife, and that it could not be otherwise.

He knew this at that moment as surely as if he had been standing at the altar with her. How and when this would be he did not know, he did not even know if it would be a good thing (he even felt, he knew not why, that it would be a bad thing) but he knew it would happen.

Pierre dropped his eyes, lifted them again, and wished once more to see her as a distant beauty far removed from him, as he had seen her every day until then, but he could no longer do it. He could not, any more than a man who has been looking at a tuft of steppe grass through the mist and taking it for a tree, can again take it for a tree after he has once recognized it to be a tuft of grass. She was terribly close to him. She already had power over him, and between them there was no longer any barrier except the barrier of his own will.

'Well, I will leave you in your little corner,' came Anna Pavlovna's voice, 'I see you are all right there.'

And Pierre, anxiously trying to remember whether he had done anything reprehensible, looked round with a blush. It seemed to him that everyone knew what had happened to him as he knew it himself.

A little later when he went up to the large circle, Anna Pavlovna said to him: 'I hear you are refitting your Petersburg house?'

This was true. The architect had told him it was necessary, and Pierre, without knowing why, was having his enormous Petersburg house done up.

'That's a good thing, but don't move from Prince Vasili's. It is good to have a friend like the prince,' she said smiling at Prince Vasili. 'I know something about that. Don't I? And you are still so young. You need advice. Don't be angry with me for exercising an old woman's privilege.'

She paused as women always do, expecting something after they have mentioned their age. 'If you marry it will be a different thing,' she continued, uniting them both in one glance. Pierre did not look at Hélène nor she at him. But she was just as terribly close to him. He muttered something, and coloured.

When he got home he could not sleep for a long time for thinking of what had happened. What had happened? Nothing. He had merely understood that the woman he had known as a child, of whom when her beauty was mentioned he had said absent-mindedly: 'Yes, she's good-looking,' he had understood that this woman might belong to him.

'But she's stupid. I have myself said she is stupid,' he thought. 'There is something nasty, something wrong, in the feeling she excites in me. I have been told that her brother Anatole was in love with her and she with him, that there was quite a scandal and that that's why he was sent away. Hippolyte is her brother... Prince Vasili is her father... It's bad...' he reflected, but while he was thinking this (the reflection was still incomplete) he caught himself smiling and was conscious that another line of thought had sprung up, and while thinking of her worthlessness he was also dreaming of how she would be his wife, how she would love him and become quite different, and how all he had thought and heard of her might be false. And he again saw her not as the daughter of Prince Vasili, but visualized her whole body only veiled by its grey dress. 'But no! Why did this thought never occur to me before?' and again he told himself that it was impossible, that there would be something unnatural, and as it seemed to him dishonourable, in this marriage. He recalled her former words and looks and the words and looks of those who had seen them together. He recalled Anna Pavlovna's words and looks when she spoke to him about his house, recalled thousands of such hints from Prince Vasili and others, and was seized by terror lest he had already in some way bound himself to do something that was evidently wrong, and that he ought not to do. But at the very time he was expressing this conviction to himself, in another part of his mind her image rose in all its womanly beauty.

2

In November 1805 Prince Vasili had to go on a tour of inspection in four different provinces. He had arranged this for himself so as to visit his neglected estates at the same time, and pick up his son Anatole where his regiment was stationed, and take him to visit Prince Nicholas Bolkonsky in order to arrange a match for him with the daughter of that rich old man. But before leaving home and undertaking these new affairs, Prince Vasili had to settle matters with Pierre, who it is true had latterly spent whole days at home, that is in Prince Vasili's house where he was staying, and had been absurd, excited, and foolish in Hélène's presence (as a lover should be) but had not yet proposed to her.

'This is all very fine, but things must be settled,' said Prince Vasili to himself with a sorrowful sigh one morning, feeling that Pierre who was under such obligations to him ('But never mind that') was not behaving very well in this matter. 'Youth, frivolity ... well, God be with him,' thought he, relishing his own goodness of heart, 'but it must be brought to a head. The day after to-morrow will be Lëlya's* nameday. I will invite two or three people, and if he does not understand what he ought to do, then it will be my affair – yes, my affair. I am her father.'

Six weeks after Anna Pavlovna's 'At home' and after the sleepless night when he had decided that to marry Hélène would be a calamity and that he ought to avoid her and go away, Pierre, despite that decision, had not left Prince Vasili's and felt with terror that in people's eyes he was every day more and more connected with her, that it was impossible for him to return to his former conception of her, that he could not break away from her, and that though it would be a terrible thing he would have to unite his fate with hers. He might perhaps have been able to free himself but that Prince Vasili (who had rarely before given receptions) now hardly let a day go by without having an evening party at which Pierre had to be present unless he wished to spoil the general pleasure and disappoint everyone's expectation. Prince Vasili in the rare moments when he was at home, would take Pierre's hand in passing and draw it downwards, or absent-mindedly hold out his wrinkled, clean-shaven cheek for Pierre to kiss, and would say: 'Till to-morrow,' or, 'Be in to dinner or I shall not see you,' or, 'I am staying in for your sake,' and so on. And though Prince Vasili when he stayed in (as he said) for Pierre's sake, hardly exchanged a couple of words with him, Pierre felt unable to disappoint him. Every day he said to himself one and the same thing: 'It is time I understood her and made up my mind what she really is. Was I mistaken before, or am I mistaken now? No, she is not stupid, she is an excellent girl,' he sometimes said to himself, 'she never makes a mistake, never says anything stupid. She says little, but what she does say is always clear and simple, so she is not stupid. She never was abashed and is not abashed now, so she cannot be a bad woman!' He had often begun to make reflections or think aloud in her company, and she had always answered him either by a brief but appropriate remark – showing that it did not interest her – or by a silent look and smile which more palpably than anything else showed Pierre her superiority. She was right in regarding all arguments as nonsense in comparison with that smile.

She always addressed him with a radiantly confiding smile meant for him alone, in which there was something more significant than in the general smile that usually brightened her face. Pierre knew that everyone was waiting for him to say a word and cross a certain line, and he knew that sooner or later he would step across it, but an incomprehensible terror seized him at the thought of that dreadful step. A thousand times during that month and a half while he felt himself drawn nearer and nearer to that dreadful abyss, Pierre said to himself: 'What am I doing? I need resolution. Can it be that I have none?'

He wished to take a decision, but felt with dismay that in this matter he lacked that strength of will which he had known in himself and really possessed. Pierre was one of those who are only strong when they feel themselves quite innocent, and since that day when he was overpowered by a feeling of desire while stooping over the snuff-box at Anna Pavlovna's, an unacknowledged sense of the guilt of that desire paralysed his will.

On Hélène's nameday a small party of just their own people – as his wife said – met for supper at Prince Vasili's. All these friends and relations had been given to understand that the fate of the young girl would be decided that evening. The visitors were seated at supper. Princess Kuragina, a portly imposing woman who had once been handsome, was sitting at the head of the table. On either side of her sat the more important guests – an old general and his wife, and Anna Pavlovna Scherer. At the other end sat the younger and less important guests, and there too sat the members of the family, and Pierre and Hélène side by side. Prince Vasili was not having any supper: he went round the table in a merry mood sitting down now by one now by another of the guests. To each of them he made some careless and agreeable remark except to Pierre and Hélène, whose presence he seemed not to notice. He enlivened the whole party. The wax candles burned brightly, the silver and crystal gleamed, so did the ladies, *toilettes* and the gold and silver of the men's epaulettes; servants in scarlet liveries moved round the table, and the clatter of plates, knives, and glasses, mingled with the animated hum of several conversations. At one end of the table an old chamberlain was heard assuring an old baroness that he loved her passionately at which she laughed; at the other could be heard the story of the misfortunes of some Mary Viktorovna or other. At the centre of the table Prince Vasili attracted everybody's attention. With a facetious smile on his face he was telling the ladies about last Wednesday's meeting of the Imperial Council, at which Sergey Kuzmich Vyazmitinov, the new military governor-general of Petersburg, had received and read the then famous rescript of the Emperor Alexander from the army to Sergey Kuzmich, in which the Emperor said that he was receiving from all sides declarations of the people's loyalty, that the declaration from Petersburg gave him particular pleasure, and that he was proud to be at the head of such a nation and would endeavour to be worthy of it. This rescript began with the words: 'Sergey Kuzmich, From all sides reports reach me,' etc.

'Well, and so he never got farther than: "Sergey Kuzmich"?' asked one of the ladies.

'Exactly, not a hair's breadth farther,' answered Prince Vasili laughing, '"Sergey Kuzmich... From all sides... From all sides ... Sergey Kuzmich..." Poor Vyazmitinov could not get any farther. He began the rescript again and again but as soon as he uttered *"Sergey"* he sobbed, *"Kuz-mi-ch"* tears, and *"From all sides"* was smothered in sobs, and he could get no farther. And again his handkerchief, and again: *"Sergey Kuzmich, From all sides,"* . . . and tears, till at last somebody else was asked to read it.'

'Kuzmich . . . From all sides . . . and then tears,' someone repeated laughing.

'Don't be unkind,' cried Anna Pavlovna from her end of the table, holding up a threatening finger. 'He is such a worthy and excellent man, our dear Vyazmitinov . . .'

Everybody laughed a great deal. At the head of the table, where the honoured guests sat, everyone seemed to be in high spirits and under the influence of a variety of exciting sensations. Only Pierre and Hélène sat silently side by side almost at the bottom of the table, a suppressed smile brightening both their faces, a smile that had nothing to do with Sergey Kuzmich – a smile of bashfulness at their own feelings. But much as all the rest laughed, talked, and joked, much as they enjoyed their Rhine wine, *sauté*, and ices, and however they avoided looking at the young couple, and heedless and unobservant as they seemed of them, one could feel by the occasional glances they gave that the story about Sergey Kuzmich, the laughter and the food, were all a pretence, and that the whole attention of that company was directed to – Pierre and Hélène. Prince Vasili mimicked the sobbing of Sergey Kuzmich and at the same time his eyes glanced towards his daughter, and while he laughed the expression on his face clearly said: 'Yes . . . it's getting on, it will all be settled to-day.' Anna Pavlovna threatened him on behalf of 'our dear Vyazmitinov', and in her eyes, which for an instant glanced at Pierre, Prince Vasili read a congratulation on his future son-in-law and on his daughter's happiness. The old princess sighed sadly as she offered some wine to the old lady next to her and glanced angrily at her daughter, and her sigh seemed to say: 'Yes, there's nothing left for you and me but to sip sweet wine, my dear, now that the time has come for these young ones to be thus boldly, provocatively happy.' 'And what nonsense all this is that I am saying!' thought a diplomatist, glancing at the happy faces of the lovers. 'That's happiness!'

Into the insignificant, trifling, and artificial interests uniting that society, had entered the simple feeling of the attraction of a healthy and handsome young man and woman for one another. And this human feeling dominated everything else and soared above all their affected chatter. Jests fell flat, news was not interesting, and the animation was evidently forced. Not only the guests but even the footmen waiting at table seemed to feel this, and they forgot their duties as they looked at the beautiful Hélène with her radiant face and at the red, broad, and happy though uneasy face of Pierre. It seemed as if the very light of the candles was focused on those two happy faces alone.

Pierre felt that he was the centre of it all, and this both pleased and embarrassed him. He was like a man entirely absorbed in some occupation. He did not see, hear, or understand anything clearly. Only now and then detached ideas and impressions from the world of reality shot unexpectedly through his mind.

'So it is all finished!' he thought, 'And how has it all happened? How quickly! Now I know that not because of her alone, nor of myself alone, but because of everyone, *it* must inevitably come about. They are all expecting *it*, they are so sure that it will happen that I cannot, I cannot, disappoint them. But how will it be? I do not know, but it will certainly happen!' thought Pierre, glancing at those dazzling shoulders close to his eyes.

Or he would suddenly feel ashamed of he knew not what. He felt it awkward to attract everyone's attention and to be considered a lucky man and, with his plain face, to be looked on as a sort of Paris possessed of a Helen. 'But no doubt it always is and must be so!' he consoled himself. 'And besides, what have I done to bring it about? How did it begin? I travelled from Moscow with Prince Vasili. Then there was nothing. So why should I not stay at his house? Then I played cards with her and picked up her reticule and drove out with her. How did it begin, when did it all come about?' And here he was sitting by her side as her betrothed, seeing, hearing, feeling her nearness, her breathing, her movements, her beauty. Then it would suddenly seem to him that it was not she but he who was so unusually beautiful, and that that was why they all looked so at him, and flattered by this general admiration he would expand his chest, raise his head, and rejoice at his good fortune. Suddenly he heard a familiar voice repeating something to him a second time. But Pierre was so absorbed that he did not understand what was said.

'I am asking you when you last heard from Bolkonsky,' repeated Prince Vasili a third time. 'How absent-minded you are, my dear fellow.'

Prince Vasili smiled, and Pierre noticed that everyone was smiling at him and Hélène. 'Well what of it, if you all know it?' thought Pierre. 'What of it? It's the truth!' and he himself smiled his gentle childlike smile, and Hélène smiled too.

'When did you get the letter? Was it from Olmütz?' repeated Prince Vasili, who pretended to want to know this in order to settle a dispute.

'How can one talk or think of such trifles?' thought Pierre.

'Yes, from Olmütz,' he answered with a sigh.

After supper Pierre with his partner followed the others into the drawing-room. The guests began to disperse, some without taking leave of Hélène. Some as if unwilling to distract her from an important occupation, came up to her for a moment and made haste to go away, refusing to let her see them off. The diplomatist preserved a mournful silence as he left the drawing-room. He pictured the vanity of his diplomatic career in comparison with Pierre's happiness. The old general grumbled at his wife when she asked how his leg was. 'Oh, the old fool,' he thought. 'That Princess Hélène will be beautiful still when she's fifty.'

'I think I may congratulate you,' whispered Anna Pavlovna to the old princess, kissing her soundly. 'If I hadn't this headache I'd have stayed longer.'

The old princess did not reply, she was tormented by jealousy of her daughter's happiness.

While the guests were taking their leave Pierre remained for a long time alone with Hélène in the little drawing-room where they were sitting. He had often before, during the last six weeks, remained alone with her, but had never spoken to her of love. Now he felt that it was inevitable, but he could not make up his mind to take the final step. He felt ashamed; he felt that he was occupying someone else's place here beside Hélène. 'This happiness is not for you,' some inner voice whispered to him. 'This happiness is for those who have not in them what there is in you.'

But as he had to say something, he began by asking her whether she was satisfied with the party. She replied in her usual simple manner that this name-day of hers had been one of the pleasantest she had ever had.

Some of the nearest relatives had not yet left. They were sitting in the large drawing-room. Prince Vasili came up to Pierre with languid footsteps. Pierre rose, and said it was getting late. Prince Vasili gave him a look of stern inquiry, as though what Pierre had just said was so strange that one could not take it in. But then the expression of severity changed and he drew Pierre's hand downwards, made him sit down, and smiled affectionately.

'Well, Lëlya?' he asked, turning instantly to his daughter and addressing her with the careless tone of habitual tenderness natural to parents who have petted their children from babyhood, but which Prince Vasili had only acquired by imitating other parents.

And he again turned to Pierre.

'Sergey Kuzmich – from all sides—,' he said unbuttoning the top button of his waistcoat.

Pierre smiled, but his smile showed that he knew it was not the story about Sergey Kuzmich that interested Prince Vasili just then, and Prince Vasili saw that Pierre knew this. He suddenly muttered something and went away. It seemed to Pierre that even the prince was disconcerted. The sight of the discomposure of that old man of the world touched Pierre: he looked at Hélène and she too seemed disconcerted, and her look seemed to say: 'Well, it is your own fault.'

'The step must be taken but I cannot, I cannot!' thought Pierre, and he again began speaking about indifferent matters, about Sergey Kuzmich, asking what the point of the story was as he had not heard it properly. Hélène answered with a smile that she too had missed it.

When Prince Vasili returned to the drawing-room the princess, his wife, was talking in low tones to the elderly lady about Pierre.

'Of course it is a very brilliant match, but happiness, my dear . . .'

'Marriages are made in heaven,' replied the elderly lady.

Prince Vasili passed by, seeming not to hear the ladies, and sat down on a sofa in a far corner of the room. He closed his eyes and seemed to be dozing. His head sank forward and then he roused himself.

'Aline,' he said to his wife, 'go and see what they are about.'

The princess went up to the door, passed by it with a dignified and indifferent air and glanced into the little drawing-room. Pierre and Hélène still sat talking just as before.

'Still the same,' she said to her husband.

Prince Vasili frowned, twisting his mouth, his cheeks quivered and his face assumed the coarse unpleasant expression peculiar to him. Shaking himself, he rose, threw back his head and with resolute steps went past the ladies into the little drawing-room. With quick steps he went joyfully up to Pierre. His face was so unusually triumphant that Pierre rose in alarm on seeing it.

'Thank God!' said Prince Vasili. 'My wife has told me everything!' – (He put one arm around Pierre and the other around his daughter.) – 'My dear boy . . . Lëlya . . . I am very pleased.' (His voice trembled.) 'I loved your father . . . and she will make you a good wife . . . God bless you! . . .'

He embraced his daughter, and then again Pierre, and kissed him with his malodorous mouth. Tears actually moistened his cheeks.

'Princess, come here!' he shouted.

The old princess came in, and also wept. The elderly lady was using her handkerchief too. Pierre was kissed, and he kissed the beautiful Hélène's hand several times. After a while they were left alone again.

'All this had to be and could not be otherwise,' thought Pierre, 'so it is useless to ask whether it is good or bad. It is good because it's definite and one is rid of the old tormenting doubt.' Pierre held the hand of his betrothed in silence, looking at her beautiful bosom as it rose and fell.

'Hélène!' he said aloud and paused.

'Something special is always said in such cases,' he thought, but could not remember what it was that people say. He looked at her face. She drew nearer to him. Her face flushed.

'Oh, take those off ... those ...' she said pointing to his spectacles.

Pierre took them off, and his eyes besides the strange look eyes have from which spectacles have just been removed, had also a frightened and inquiring look. He was about to stoop over her hand and kiss it, but with a rapid, almost brutal movement of her head she intercepted his lips and met them with her own. Her face struck Pierre by its altered, unpleasantly excited expression.

'It is too late now, it's done; besides I love her,' thought Pierre.

'*Je vous aime!*' he said, remembering what has to be said at such moments: but his words sounded so weak that he felt ashamed of himself.

Six weeks later he was married, and settled in Count Bezukhov's large newly-furnished, Petersburg house, the happy possessor, as people said, of a wife who was a celebrated beauty, and of millions of money.

3

OLD Prince Nicholas Bolkonsky received a letter from Prince Vasili in November 1805 announcing that he and his son would be paying him a visit. 'I am starting on a journey of inspection, and of course I shall think nothing of an extra seventy miles to come and see you at the same time, my honoured benefactor,' wrote Prince Vasili. 'My son Anatole is accompanying me on his way to the army, so I hope you will allow him personally to express the deep respect that, emulating his father, he feels for you.'

'It seems there will be no need to bring Mary out, suitors are coming to us of their own accord,' incautiously remarked the little princess on hearing the news.

Prince Nicholas frowned, but said nothing.

A fortnight after the letter Prince Vasili's servants came one evening in advance of him, and he and his son arrived next day.

Old Bolkonsky had always had a poor opinion of Prince Vasili's character, but more so recently, since in the new reigns of Paul and Alexander Prince Vasili had risen to high position and honours. And now from the hints contained in his letter and given by the little princess, he saw which way the wind was blowing, and his low opinion changed into a feeling of contemptuous ill will. He snorted whenever he mentioned him. On the day of Prince Vasili's arrival Prince Bolkonsky was particularly discontented and out of temper. Whether he was in a bad temper because Prince Vasili was coming, or whether his being in a bad temper made him specially annoyed at Prince Vasili's visit, he was in a bad temper, and in the morning Tikhon had already advised the architect not to go to the prince with his report.

'Do you hear how he's walking?' said Tikhon, drawing the architect's attention to the sound of the prince's footsteps. 'Stepping flat on his heels – we know what that means . . .'

However, at nine o'clock the prince, in his velvet coat with a sable collar and cap, went out for his usual walk. It had snowed the day before and the path to the hot-house, along which the prince was in the habit of walking, had been swept: the marks of the broom were still visible in the snow and a shovel had been left sticking in one of the soft snow banks that bordered both sides of the path. The prince went through the conservatories, the serfs' quarters, and the out-buildings, frowning and silent.

'Can a sledge pass?' he asked his overseer, a venerable man resembling his master in manners and looks, who was accompanying him back to the house.

'The snow is deep. I am having the avenue swept, your honour.'

The prince bowed his head and went up to the porch. 'God be thanked,' thought the overseer, 'the storm has blown over!'

'It would have been hard to drive up, your honour,' he added. 'I heard, your honour, that a minister is coming to visit your honour.'

The prince turned round to the overseer and fixed his eyes on him frowning.

'What? A minister? What minister? Who gave orders?' he said in his shrill harsh voice. 'The road is not swept for the princess, my daughter, but for a minister! For me there are no ministers!'

'Your honour, I thought . . .'

'You thought!' shouted the prince, his words coming more and more rapidly and indistinctly. 'You thought! . . . Rascals! Blackguards! . . . I'll teach you to think!' and lifting his stick he swung it and would have hit Alpatych, the overseer, had not the latter instinctively avoided the blow. 'Thought ... Blackguards ...' shouted the prince rapidly.

But although Alpatych, frightened at his own temerity in avoiding the stroke, came up to the prince bowing his bald head resignedly before him, or perhaps for that very reason, the prince, though he continued to shout: 'Blackguards! ... Throw the snow back on the road!' did not lift his stick again but hurried into the house.

Before dinner Princess Mary and Mademoiselle Bourienne, who knew that the prince was in a bad humour, stood awaiting him; Mademoiselle Bourienne with a radiant face that said: 'I know nothing, I am the same as usual,' and Princess Mary, pale, frightened and with downcast eyes. What she found hardest to bear was to know that on such occasions she ought to behave like Mademoiselle Bourienne, but could not. She thought: 'If I seem not to notice he will think that I do not sympathize with him; if I seem sad and out of spirits myself, he will say (as he has done before) that I'm in the dumps.'

The prince looked at his daughter's frightened face and snorted.

'Fool ... or dummy!' he muttered.

'And the other one is not here. They've been telling tales,' he thought – referring to the little princess who was not in the dining-room.

'Where is the princess?' he asked. 'Hiding?'

'She is not very well,' answered Mademoiselle Bourienne with a bright smile, 'she won't come down. It is natural in her state.'

'Hm! Hm!' muttered the prince sitting down.

His plate seemed to him not quite clean, and pointing to a spot he flung it away. Tikhon caught it and handed it to a footman. The little princess was not unwell, but had such an overpowering fear of the prince that, hearing he was in a bad humour, she had decided not to appear.

'I am afraid for the baby,' she said to Mademoiselle Bourienne: 'Heaven knows what a fright might do.'

In general at Bald Hills the little princess lived in constant fear, and with a sense of antipathy to the old prince which she did not realize because the fear was so much the stronger feeling. The prince reciprocated this antipathy, but it was overpowered by his contempt for her. When the little princess had grown accustomed to life at Bald Hills, she took a special fancy to Mademoiselle Bourienne, spent whole days with her, asked her to sleep in her room, and often talked with her about the old prince and criticized him.

'So we are to have visitors, *mon prince?*' remarked Mademoiselle Bourienne, unfolding her white napkin with her rosy fingers. 'His Excellency Prince Vasili Kuragin and his son, I understand?' she said inquiringly.

'Hm! – his Excellency is a puppy ... I got him his appointment in the service,' said the prince disdainfully. 'Why his son is coming I don't understand. Perhaps Princess Elizabeth and Princess Mary know. I don't know why he brings his son here. I don't want him.' (He looked at his blushing daughter.) 'Are you unwell to-day? Eh? Afraid of the "minister" as that idiot Alpatych called him this morning?'

'No, *mon père.*'

Though Mademoiselle Bourienne had been so unsuccessful in her choice of a subject she did not stop talking, but chattered about the conservatories, and the beauty of a flower that had just opened, and after the soup the prince became more genial.

After dinner he went to see his daughter-in-law. The little princess was sitting at a small table chattering with Masha, her maid. She grew pale on seeing her father-in-law.

She was much altered. She was now plain rather than pretty. Her cheeks had sunk, her lip was drawn up, and her eyes drawn down.

'Yes, I feel a kind of oppression,' she said in reply to the prince's question as to how she felt.

'Do you want anything?'

'No, *merci, mon père.*'

'Well, all right, all right.'

He left the room and went to the waiting-room, where Alpatych stood with bowed head.

'Has the snow been shovelled back?'

'Yes, your Excellency. Forgive me for heaven's sake ... It was only my stupidity.'

'All right, all right,' interrupted the prince, and laughing in his unnatural way he stretched out his hand for Alpatych to kiss and then proceeded to his study.

Prince Vasili arrived that evening. He was met in the avenue by coachmen and footmen, who with loud shouts dragged his sledges up to one of the lodges over the road purposely laden with snow.

Prince Vasili and Anatole had separate rooms assigned to them.

Anatole having taken off his overcoat, sat with arms akimbo before a table on a corner of which he smilingly and absent-mindedly fixed his large and handsome eyes. He regarded his whole life as a continual round of amusement which someone for some reason had to provide for him. And he looked on this visit to a churlish old man and a rich and ugly heiress in the same way. All this might, he thought, turn out very well and amusingly. 'And why not marry her if she really has so much money? That never does any harm,' thought Anatole.

He shaved and scented himself with the care and elegance which had become habitual to him, and his handsome head held high, entered his father's room with the good-humoured and victorious air natural to him. Prince Vasili's two valets were busy dressing him, and he looked round with much animation and cheerfully nodded to his son as the latter entered, as if to say: 'Yes, that's how I want you to look.'

'I say, father, joking apart, is she very hideous?' Anatole asked, as if continuing a conversation the subject of which had often been mentioned during the journey.

'Enough! What nonsense! Above all, try to be respectful and cautious with the old prince.'

'If he starts a row I'll go away,' said Prince Anatole. 'I can't bear those old men! Eh?'

'Remember, for you everything depends on this.'

In the meantime not only was it known in the maidservants' rooms that the minister and his son had arrived, but the appearance of both had been minutely described. Princess Mary was sitting alone in her room vainly trying to master her agitation.

'Why did they write, why did Lise tell me about it? It can never happen!' she said looking at herself in the glass. 'How shall I enter the drawing-room? Even if I like him I can't now be myself with him.' The mere thought of her father's look filled her with terror. The little princess and Mademoiselle Bourienne had already received from Masha, the lady's maid, the necessary report of how handsome the minister's son was, with his rosy cheeks and dark eyebrows, and with what difficulty the father had dragged his legs upstairs while the son had followed him like an eagle, three steps at a time. Having received this information the little princess and Mademoiselle Bourienne, whose chattering voices had reached her from the corridor, went into Princess Mary's room.

'You know they've come, Marie?' said the little princess, waddling in, and sinking heavily into an arm-chair.

She was no longer in the loose gown she generally wore in the morning, but had on one of her best dresses. Her hair was carefully done and her face was animated, which, however, did not conceal its sunken and faded outlines. Dressed as she used to be in Petersburg society, it was still more noticeable how much plainer she had become. Some unobtrusive touch had been added to Mademoiselle

Bourienne's toilette which rendered her fresh and pretty face yet more attractive.

'What! Are you going to remain as you are, dear princess?' she began. 'They'll be announcing that the gentlemen are in the drawing-room and we shall have to go down, and you have not smartened yourself up at all!'

The little princess got up, rang for the maid, and hurriedly and merrily began to devise and carry out a plan of how Princess Mary should be dressed. Princess Mary's self-esteem was wounded by the fact that the arrival of a suitor agitated her, and still more so by both her companions not having the least conception that it could be otherwise. To tell them that she felt ashamed for herself and for them would be to betray her agitation, while to decline their offers to dress her would prolong their banter and insistence. She flushed, her beautiful eyes grew dim, red blotches came on her face and it took on the unattractive martyr-like expression it so often wore, as she submitted herself to Mademoiselle Bourienne and Lise. Both these women *quite sincerely* tried to make her look pretty. She was so plain that neither of them could think of her as a rival, so they began dressing her with perfect sincerity, and with the naïve and firm conviction women have that dress can make a face pretty.

'No really, my dear, this dress is not pretty,' said Lise, looking sideways at Princess Mary from a little distance. 'You have a maroon dress, have it fetched. Really! You know the fate of your whole life may be at stake. But this one is too light, it's not becoming!'

It was not the dress, but the face and whole figure of Princess Mary that was not pretty, but neither Mademoiselle Bourienne nor the little princess felt this, they still thought that if a blue ribbon were placed in the hair, the hair combed up, and the blue scarf arranged lower on the best maroon dress, and so on, all would be well. They forgot that the frightened face and the figure could not be altered, and that however they might change the setting and adornment of that face it would still remain piteous and plain. After two or three changes to which Princess Mary meekly submitted, just as her hair had been arranged on the top of her head (a style that quite altered and spoilt her looks) and she had put on a maroon dress with a pale-blue scarf, the little princess walked twice round her, now adjusting a fold of the dress with her little hand, now arranging the scarf and looking at her with her head bent first on one side and then on the other.

'No, it will not do,' she said decidedly, clasping her hands. 'No, Mary, really this dress does not suit you. I prefer you in your little grey everyday dress. Now please, do it for my sake. Katie,' she said to the maid, 'bring the princess her grey dress, and you'll see, Mademoiselle Bourienne, how I shall arrange it,' she added, smiling with a foretaste of artistic pleasure.

But when Katie brought the required dress Princess Mary remained sitting motionless before the glass looking at her face, and saw in the mirror her eyes full of tears and her mouth quivering, ready to burst into sobs.

'Come, dear princess,' said Mademoiselle Bourienne, 'just one more little effort.'

The little princess, taking the dress from the maid, came up to Princess Mary.

'Well, now we'll arrange something quite simple and becoming,' she said.

The three voices, hers, Mademoiselle Bourienne's, and Katie's who was laughing at something, mingled in a merry sound like the chirping of birds.

'No, leave me alone,' said Princess Mary.

Her voice sounded so serious and so sad that the chirping of the birds was silenced at once. They looked at the beautiful, large, thoughtful eyes full of tears and of thoughts, gazing shiningly and imploringly at them, and understood that it was useless and even cruel to insist.

'At least, change your coiffure,' said the little princess. 'Didn't I tell you,' she went on, turning reproachfully to Mademoiselle Bourienne, 'Mary's is a face which such a coiffure does not suit in the least. Not in the least! Please change it.'

'Leave me alone, please leave me alone! It is all quite the same to me,' answered a voice struggling with tears.

Mademoiselle Bourienne and the little princess had to own to themselves that Princess Mary in this guise looked very plain, worse than usual, but it was too late. She was looking at them with an expression they both knew, an expression thoughtful and sad. This expression in Princess Mary did not frighten them (she never inspired fear in anyone) but they knew that when it appeared on her face she became mute and was not to be shaken in her determination.

'You will change it, won't you?' said Lise. And as Princess Mary gave no answer she left the room.

Princess Mary was left alone. She did not comply with Lise's request, she not only left her hair as it was but did not even look in her glass. Letting her arms fall helplessly she sat with downcast eyes and pondered. A husband, a man, a strong dominant and strangely attractive being rose in her imagination, and carried her into a totally different happy world of his own. She fancied a child, *her own* – such as she had seen the day before in the arms of her nurse's daughter – at her own breast, the husband standing by and gazing tenderly at her and the child. 'But no, it is impossible, I am too ugly,' she thought.

'Please come to tea. The prince will be out in a moment,' came the maid's voice at the door.

She roused herself, and felt appalled at what she had been thinking, and before going down she went into the room where the icons hung and, her eyes fixed on the dark face of a large icon of the Saviour lit up by a lamp, she stood before it with folded hands for a few moments. A painful doubt filled her soul. Could the joy of love, of earthly love for a man, be for her? In her thoughts of marriage Princess Mary dreamed of happiness and of children, but her strongest most deeply-hidden longing was for earthly love. The more she tried to hide this feeling from others and even from herself, the stronger it grew. 'O God,' she said, 'how am I to stifle in my heart these temptations of the devil? How am I to renounce for ever these vile fancies, so as peacefully to fulfil Thy will?' And scarcely had she put that question than God gave her the answer in her own heart. 'Desire nothing for thyself, seek nothing, be not anxious or envious. Man's future and thy own fate must remain hidden from thee, but live so that thou mayest be ready for anything. If it be God's will to prove thee in the duties of marriage, be ready to fulfil His will.' With this consoling thought (but yet with a hope for the fulfilment of her forbidden earthly longing) Princess Mary sighed, and having crossed herself went down, thinking neither of her gown and coiffure nor of how she would go in nor of what she would say. What could all that matter in comparison with the will of God, without Whose care not a hair of man's head can fall?

4

WHEN Princess Mary came down, Prince Vasili and his son were already in the drawing-room talking to the little princess and Mademoiselle Bourienne. When she entered with her heavy step, treading on her heels, the gentlemen and Mademoiselle Bourienne rose and the little princess, indicating her to the gentlemen, said: '*Voilà Marie!*' Princess Mary saw them all and saw them in detail. She saw Prince Vasili's face, serious for an instant at the sight of her, but immediately smiling again, and the little princess curiously noting the impression 'Marie' produced on the visitors.

And she saw Mademoiselle Bourienne with her ribbon and pretty face and her unusually animated look which was fixed on *him*, but *him* she could not see, she only saw something large, brilliant and handsome moving towards her as she entered the room. Prince Vasili approached first, and she kissed the bald forehead that bent over her hand and answered his question by saying that, on the contrary, she remembered him quite well. Then Anatole came up to her. She still could not see him. She only felt a soft hand taking hers firmly, and she touched with her lips a white forehead over which was beautiful light-brown hair smelling of pomade. When she looked up at him she was struck by his beauty. Anatole stood with his right thumb under a button of his uniform, his chest expanded and his back drawn in, slightly swinging one foot and, with his head a little bent, looked with beaming face at the princess without speaking and evidently not thinking about her at all. Anatole was not quick-witted, not ready or eloquent in conversation, but he had the faculty, so invaluable in society, of composure and imperturbable self-possession. If a man lacking in self-confidence remains dumb on a first introduction and betrays a consciousness of the impropriety of such silence and an anxiety to find something to say, the effect is bad. But Anatole was dumb, swung his foot, and smilingly examined the princess's hair. It was evident that he could be silent in this way for a very long time. 'If anyone finds this silence inconvenient, let him talk, but I don't want to,' he seemed to say. Besides this, in his behaviour to women Anatole had a manner which particularly inspired in them curiosity, awe, and even love – a supercilious consciousness of his own superiority. It was as if he said to them: 'I know you, I know you, but why should I bother about you? You'd be only too glad, of course.' Perhaps he did not really think this when he met women – even probably he did not, for in general he thought very little – but his looks and manner gave that impression. The princess felt this, and as if wishing to show him that she did not even dare expect to interest him, she turned to his father. The conversation was general and animated, thanks to Princess Lise's voice and little downy lip that lifted over her white teeth. She met Prince Vasili with that playful manner often employed by lively chatty people, and consisting in the assumption that between the person they so address and themselves there are some semi-private long-established jokes and amusing reminiscences, though no such reminiscences really exist – just as none existed in this case. Prince Vasili readily adopted her tone and the little princess also drew Anatole, whom she hardly knew, into these amusing recollections of things that had never occurred. Mademoiselle Bourienne also shared them and even Princess Mary felt herself pleasantly made to share in these merry reminiscences.

'Here at least we shall have the benefit of your company all to ourselves, dear Prince,' said the little princess (of course in French) to Prince Vasili. 'It's not as at Annette's receptions where you always ran away; you remember *cette chère Annette!*'

'Ah, but you won't talk politics to me like Annette!'

'And our little tea-table?'

'Oh, yes!'

'Why is it you were never at Annette's?' the little princess asked Anatole. 'Ah, I know, I know,' she said with a sly glance, 'your brother Hippolyte told me about your goings on. Oh!' and she shook her finger at him, 'I have even heard of your doings in Paris!'

'And didn't Hippolyte tell you?' asked Prince Vasili, turning to his son and seizing the little princess's arm as if she would have run away and he had just managed to catch her, 'didn't he tell you how he himself was pining for the dear princess, and how she showed him the door? Oh, she is a pearl among women, Princess,' he added, turning to Princess Mary.

When Paris was mentioned, Mademoiselle Bourienne for her part seized the opportunity of joining in the general current of recollections.

She took the liberty of inquiring whether it was long since Anatole had left Paris and how he had liked that city. Anatole answered the Frenchwoman very readily, and looking at her with a smile talked to her about her native land. When he saw the pretty little Bourienne, Anatole came to the conclusion that he would not find Bald Hills dull either. 'Not at all bad!' he thought, examining her, 'not at all bad, that little companion! I hope she will bring her along with her when we're married, *la petite est gentille.*'

The old prince dressed leisurely in his study, frowning and considering what he was to do. The coming of these visitors annoyed him. 'What are Prince Vasili and that son of his to me? Prince Vasili is a shallow braggart and his son, no doubt, is a fine specimen,' he grumbled to himself. What angered him was that the coming of these visitors revived in his mind an unsettled question he always tried to stifle, one about which he always deceived himself. The question was whether he could ever bring himself to part from his daughter and give her to a husband. The prince never directly asked himself that question, knowing beforehand that he would have to answer it justly, and justice clashed not only with his feelings but with the very possibility of life. Life without Princess Mary, little as he seemed to value her, was unthinkable to him. 'And why should she marry?' he thought. 'To be unhappy for certain. There's Lise, married to Andrew – a better husband one would think could hardly be found nowadays – but is she contented with her lot? And who would marry Marie for love? Plain and awkward! They'll take her for her connexions and wealth. Are there no women living unmarried, and even the happier for it?' So thought Prince Bolkonsky while dressing, and yet the question he was always putting off demanded an immediate answer. Prince Vasili had brought his son with the evident intention of proposing, and to-day or to-morrow he would probably ask for an answer. His birth and position in society were not bad. 'Well, I've nothing against it,' the prince said to himself, 'but he must be worthy of her. And that is what we shall see.'

'That is what we shall see! That is what we shall see!' he added aloud.

He entered the drawing-room with his usual alert step, glancing rapidly round the company. He noticed the change in the little princess's dress, Mademoiselle Bourienne's ribbon, Princess Mary's unbecoming coiffure, Mademoiselle Bourienne's and Anatole's smiles, and the loneliness of his daughter amid the general conversation. 'Got herself up like a fool!' he thought, looking irritably at her. 'She is shameless, and he ignores her!'

He went straight up to Prince Vasili.

'Well! How d'ye do? How d'ye do? Glad to see you!'

'Friendship laughs at distance,' began Prince Vasili in his usual rapid, self-confident, familiar tone. 'Here is my second son; please love and befriend him.'

Prince Bolkonsky surveyed Anatole.

'Fine young fellow! Fine young fellow!' he said. 'Well, come and kiss me,' and he offered his cheek.

Anatole kissed the old man, and looked at him with curiosity and perfect composure, waiting for a display of the eccentricities his father had told him to expect.

Prince Bolkonsky sat down in his usual place in the corner of the sofa, and drawing up an arm-chair for Prince Vasili pointed to it and began questioning him about political affairs and news. He seemed to listen attentively to what Prince Vasili said, but kept glancing at Princess Mary.

'And so they are writing from Potsdam already?' he said, repeating Prince Vasili's last words. Then rising he suddenly went up to his daughter.

'Is it for visitors you've got yourself up like that, eh?' said he. 'Fine, very fine! You have done up your hair in this new way

233

for the visitors, and before the visitors I tell you that in future you are never to dare to change your way of dress without my consent.'

'It was my fault, *mon père*,' interceded the little princess with a blush.

'You must do as you please,' said Prince Bolkonsky, bowing to his daughter-in-law, 'but she need not make a guy of herself, she's plain enough as it is.'

And he sat down again, paying no more attention to his daughter who was reduced to tears.

'On the contrary that coiffure suits the princess very well,' said Prince Vasili.

'Now you, young Prince, what's your name?' said Prince Bolkonsky turning to Anatole, 'come here, let us talk and get acquainted.'

'Now the fun begins,' thought Anatole, sitting down with a smile beside the old prince.

'Well, my dear boy, I hear you've been educated abroad, not taught to read and write by the deacon like your father and me. Now tell me, my dear boy, are you serving in the Horse Guards?' asked the old man, scrutinizing Anatole closely and intently.

'No, I have been transferred to the line,' said Anatole hardly able to restrain his laughter.

'Ah! That's a good thing. So, my dear boy, you wish to serve the Tsar and the country? It is war time. Such a fine fellow must serve. Well, are you off to the front?'

'No, Prince, our regiment has gone to the front, but I am attached ... what is it I am attached to, papa?' said Anatole, turning to his father with a laugh.

'A splendid soldier, splendid! "What am I attached to!" Ha, ha, ha!' laughed Prince Bolkonsky, and Anatole laughed still louder. Suddenly Prince Bolkonsky frowned.

'You may go,' he said to Anatole.

Anatole returned smiling to the ladies.

'And so you've had him educated abroad, Prince Vasili, haven't you?' said the old prince to Prince Vasili.

'I have done my best for him, and I can assure you the education there is much better than ours.'

'Yes, everything is different nowadays, everything is changed. The lad's a fine fellow, a fine fellow! Well, come with me now.' He took Prince Vasili's arm and led him to his study. As soon as they were alone together Prince Vasili announced his hopes and wishes to the old prince.

'Well, do you think I shall prevent her, that I can't part from her?' said the old prince angrily. 'What an idea! I'm ready for it to-morrow! Only let me tell you, I want to know my son-in-law better. You know my principles – everything above-board! I will ask her to-morrow in your presence; if she is willing, then he can stay on. He can stay and I'll see.' The old prince snorted. 'Let her marry, it's all the same to me!' he screamed in the same piercing tone as when parting from his son.

'I will tell you frankly,' said Prince Vasili in the tone of a crafty man convinced of the futility of being cunning with so keen-sighted a companion. 'You know, you see right through people. Anatole is no genius, but he is an honest, good-hearted lad; an excellent son or kinsman.'

'All right, all right, we'll see!'

As always happens when women lead lonely lives for any length of time without male society, on Anatole's appearance all the three women of Prince Bolkonsky's household felt that their life had not been real till then. Their powers of reasoning, feeling, and observing, immediately increased tenfold, and their life, which seemed to have been passed in darkness, was suddenly lit up by a new brightness full of significance.

Princess Mary grew quite unconscious of her face and coiffure. The handsome open face of the man who might perhaps be her husband absorbed all her attention. He seemed to her kind, brave, determined, manly, and magnanimous. She felt convinced of that. Thousands of dreams of a future family life continually rose in her imagination. She drove them away and tried to conceal them.

'But am I not too cold with him?' thought the princess. 'I try to be reserved because in the depth of my soul I feel too near to him already, but then he cannot know what I think of him and may imagine that I do not like him.'

And Princess Mary tried, but could not manage, to be cordial to her new guest. 'Poor girl, she's devilish ugly!' thought Anatole.

Mademoiselle Bourienne, also roused to great excitement by Anatole's arrival, thought in another way. Of course she, a handsome young woman without any definite position, without relations or even a country, did not intend to devote her life to serving Prince Bolkonsky, to reading aloud to him and being friends with Princess Mary. Mademoiselle Bourienne had long been waiting for a Russian prince who, able to appreciate at a glance her superiority to the plain, badly dressed, ungainly Russian princesses, would fall in love with her and carry her off; and here at last was the Russian prince. Mademoiselle Bourienne knew a story, heard from her aunt but finished in her own way, which she liked to repeat to herself. It was the story of a girl who had been seduced, and to whom her poor mother (*sa pauvre mère*) appeared, and reproached her for yielding to a man without being married. Mademoiselle Bourienne was often touched to tears as in imagination she told this story to *him*, her seducer. And now *he*, a real Russian prince, had appeared. He would carry her away and then *sa pauvre mère* would appear and he would marry her. So her future shaped itself in Mademoiselle Bourienne's head at the very time she was talking to Anatole about Paris. It was not calculation that guided her (she did not even for a moment consider what she should do) but all this had long been familiar to her, and now that Anatole had appeared it just grouped itself around him and she wished and tried to please him as much as possible.

The little princess, like an old war-horse that hears the trumpet, unconsciously and quite forgetting her condition prepared for the familiar gallop of coquetry, without any ulterior motive or any struggle but with naïve and light-hearted gaiety.

Although in female society Anatole usually assumed the role of a man tired of being run after by women, his vanity was flattered by the spectacle of his power over these three women. Besides that he was beginning to feel for the pretty and provocative Mademoiselle Bourienne that passionate animal feeling which was apt to master him with great suddenness and prompt him to the coarsest and most reckless actions.

After tea the company went into the sitting-room and Princess Mary was asked to play on the clavichord. Anatole laughing and in high spirits, came and leaned on his elbow, facing her and beside Mademoiselle Bourienne. Princess Mary felt his look with a painfully joyous emotion. Her favourite sonata bore her into a most intimately poetic world, and the look she felt upon her made that world still more poetic. But Anatole's expression, though his eyes were fixed on her, referred not to her but to the movements of Mademoiselle Bourienne's little foot, which he was then touching with his own under the clavichord. Mademoiselle Bourienne was also looking at Princess Mary, and in her lovely eyes there was a look of fearful joy and hope that was also new to the princess.

'How she loves me!' thought Princess Mary. 'How happy I am now, and how happy I may be with such a friend and such a husband! Husband? Can it be possible?' she thought, not daring to look at his face, but still feeling his eyes gazing at her.

In the evening after supper when all were about to retire, Anatole kissed Princess Mary's hand. She did not know how she found the courage, but she looked straight into his handsome face as it came near to her short-sighted eyes. Turning from Princess

Mary he went up and kissed Mademoiselle Bourienne's hand. (This was not etiquette, but then he did everything so simply and with such assurance!) Mademoiselle Bourienne flushed, and gave the princess a frightened look.

'What delicacy!' thought the princess. 'Is it possible that Amélie' (Mademoiselle Bourienne) 'thinks I could be jealous of her, and not value her pure affection and devotion to me?' She went up to her and kissed her warmly. Anatole went up to kiss the little princess's hand.

'No! No! No! When your father writes to tell me that you are behaving well I will give you my hand to kiss. Not till then!' she said. And smilingly raising a finger at him she left the room.

5

THEY all separated, but except Anatole who fell asleep as soon as he got into bed, all kept awake a long time that night.

'Is he really to be my husband, this stranger who is so kind – yes, kind, that is the chief thing,' thought Princess Mary, and fear, which she had seldom experienced, came upon her. She feared to look round, it seemed to her that someone was there standing behind the screen in the dark corner. And this someone was *he* – the devil – and *he* was also this man with the white forehead, black eyebrows, and red lips.

She rang for her maid, and asked her to sleep in her room.

Mademoiselle Bourienne walked up and down the conservatory for a long time that evening vainly expecting someone, now smiling at someone, now working herself up to tears with the imaginary words of her *pauvre mère* rebuking her for her fall.

The little princess grumbled to her maid that her bed was badly made. She could not lie either on her face or on her side. Every position was awkward and uncomfortable, and her burden oppressed her now more than ever because Anatole's presence had vividly recalled to her the time when she was not like that, and when everything was light and gay. She sat in an arm-chair in her dressing jacket and night-cap, and Katie, sleepy and dishevelled, beat and turned the heavy feather-bed for the third time, muttering to herself.

'I told you it was all lumps and holes!' the little princess repeated. 'I should be glad enough to fall asleep, so it's not my fault!' and her voice quivered like that of a child about to cry.

The old prince did not sleep either. Tikhon, half asleep, heard him pacing angrily about and snorting. The old prince felt as though he had been insulted through his daughter. The insult was the more pointed because it concerned not himself but another, his daughter, whom he loved more than himself. He kept telling himself that he would consider the whole matter and decide what was right and how he should act, but instead of that he only excited himself more and more.

'The first man that turns up – she forgets her father and everything else, runs upstairs and does up her hair and wags her tail and is unlike herself! Glad to throw her father over! And she knew I should notice it. Frr...frr...frr...! And don't I see that that idiot had eyes only for Bourienne – I shall have to get rid of her. And how is it she has not pride enough to see it? If she has no pride for herself she might at least have some for my sake! She must be shown that the blockhead thinks nothing of her and looks only at Bourienne. No, she has no pride...but I'll let her see...'

The old prince knew that if he told his daughter she was making a mistake, and that Anatole meant to flirt with Mademoiselle Bourienne, Princess Mary's self-esteem would be wounded and his point (not to be parted from her) would be gained, so pacifying himself with this thought he called Tikhon and began to undress.

'What devil brought them here?' thought he while Tikhon was putting the night-shirt over his dried-up old body and grey-haired chest. 'I never invited them. They came to disturb my life – and there is not much of it left.'

'Devil take 'em!' he muttered, while his head was still covered by the shirt.

Tikhon knew his master's habit of sometimes thinking aloud, and therefore met with unaltered looks the angrily inquisitive expression of the face that emerged from the shirt.

'Gone to bed?' asked the prince.

Tikhon, like all good valets, instinctively knew the direction of his master's thoughts. He guessed that the question referred to Prince Vasili and his son.

'They have gone to bed and put out their lights, your Excellency.'

'No good...no good...' said the prince rapidly, and thrusting his feet into his slippers and his arms into the sleeves of his dressing-gown, he went to the couch on which he slept.

Though no words had passed between Anatole and Mademoiselle Bourienne they quite understood one another as to the first part of their romance, up to the appearance of the *pauvre mère*; they understood that they had much to say to one another in private and so they had been seeking an opportunity since morning to meet one another alone. When Princess Mary went to her father's room at the usual hour, Mademoiselle Bourienne and Anatole met in the conservatory.

Princess Mary went to the door of the study with special trepidation. It seemed to her that not only did everybody know that her fate would be decided that day, but that they also knew what she thought about it. She read this in Tikhon's face and in that of Prince Vasili's valet who made her a low bow when she met him in the corridor carrying hot water.

The old prince was very affectionate and careful in his treatment of his daughter that morning. Princess Mary well knew this painstaking expression of her father's. His face wore that expression when his dry hands clenched with vexation at her not understanding a sum in arithmetic, when rising from his chair he would walk away from her repeating in a low voice the same words several times over.

He came to the point at once, treating her ceremoniously.

'I have had a proposition made me concerning you,' he said with an unnatural smile. 'I expect you have guessed that Prince Vasili has not come and brought his pupil with him' (for some reason Prince Bolkonsky referred to Anatole as a 'pupil') 'for the sake of my beautiful eyes. Last night a proposition was made me on your account and, as you know my principles, I refer it to you.'

'How am I to understand you, *mon père?*' said the princess, growing pale and then blushing.

'How understand me!' cried her father angrily. 'Prince Vasili finds you to his taste as a daughter-in-law and makes a proposal to you on his pupil's behalf. That's how it's to be understood! "How understand it"!... And I ask you!'

'I do not know what you think, father,' whispered the princess.

'I? I? What of me? Leave me out of the question. I'm not going to get married. What about *you?* That's what I want to know.'

The princess saw that her father regarded the matter with disapproval, but at that moment the thought occurred to her that her fate would be decided now or never. She lowered her eyes so as not to see the gaze under which she felt that she could not think but would be only able to submit from habit, and she said:

'I wish only to do your will, but if I had to express my own desire...' She had no time to finish. The old prince interrupted her.

'That's admirable!' he shouted. 'He will take you with your

dowry and take Mademoisella Bourienne into the bargain. She'll be the wife, while you . . .'

The prince stopped. He saw the effect these words had produced on his daughter. She lowered her head and was ready to burst into tears.

'Now then, now then, I'm only joking!' he said. 'Remember this, Princess, I hold to the principle that a maiden has a full right to choose. I give you freedom. Only remember that your life's happiness depends on your decision. Never mind me!'

'But I do not know, father!'

'There's no need to talk! He receives his orders and will marry you or anybody; but you are free to choose . . . Go to your room, think it over, and come back in an hour and tell me in his presence: yes, or no, I know you will pray over it. Well, pray if you like, but you had better *think* it over. Go! Yes or no, yes or no, yes or no!' he still shouted, when the princess, as if lost in a fog, had already staggered out of the study.

Her fate was decided and happily decided. But what her father had said about Mademoiselle Bourienne was dreadful. It was untrue to be sure, but still it was terrible, and she could not help thinking of it. She was going straight on through the conservatory, neither seeing nor hearing anything, when suddenly the well-known whispering of Mademoiselle Bourienne aroused her. She raised her eyes, and two steps away saw Anatole embracing the Frenchwoman and whispering something to her. With a horrified expression on his handsome face Anatole looked at Princess Mary, but did not at once take his arm from the waist of Mademoiselle Bourienne who had not yet seen her.

'Who's that? Why? Wait a moment!' Anatole's face seemed to say. Princess Mary looked at them in silence. She could not understand it. At last Mademoiselle Bourienne gave a scream and ran away. Anatole bowed to Princess Mary with a gay smile, as if inviting her to join in a laugh at this strange incident, and then shrugging his shoulders went to the door that led to his own apartments.

An hour later Tikhon came to call Princess Mary to the old prince; he added that Prince Vasili was also there. When Tikhon came over to her, Princess Mary was sitting on the sofa in her room holding the weeping Mademoiselle Bourienne in her arms and gently stroking her hair. The princess's beautiful eyes with all their former calm radiance were looking with tender affection and pity at Mademoiselle Bourienne's pretty face.

'No, Princess, I have lost your affection for ever!' said Mademoiselle Bourienne.

'Why? I love you more than ever,' said Princess Mary, 'and I will try to do all I can for your happiness.'

'But you despise me. You who are so pure can never understand being so carried away by passion. Oh, only my poor mother . . .'

'I quite understand,' answered Princess Mary with a sad smile. 'Calm yourself, my dear. I will go to my father,' she said, and went out.

Prince Vasili, with one leg thrown high over the other and a snuff-box in his hand, was sitting there with a smile of deep emotion on his face, as if stirred to his heart's core and himself regretting and laughing at his own sensibility, when Princess Mary entered. He hurriedly took a pinch of snuff.

'Ah, my dear, my dear!' he began, rising and taking her by both hands. Then, sighing, he added: 'My son's fate is in your hands. Decide, my dear, good, gentle Marie, whom I have always loved as a daughter!'

He drew back, and a real tear appeared in his eye.

'Fr . . . fr . . .' snorted Prince Bolkonsky. 'The prince is making a proposition to you in his pupil's — I mean his son's — name. Do you wish, or not, to be Prince Anatole Kuragin's wife? Reply: yes or no,' he shouted, 'and then I shall reserve the right to state my opinion also. Yes, my opinion, and only my opinion,' added Prince Bolkonsky, turning to Prince Vasili and answering his imploring look. 'Yes, or no?'

'My desire is never to leave you, father, never to separate my life from yours. I don't wish to marry,' she answered positively, glancing at Prince Vasili and at her father with her beautiful eyes.

'Humbug! Nonsense! Humbug, humbug, humbug!' cried Prince Bolkonsky, frowning, and taking his daughter's hand he did not kiss her, but only, bending his forehead to hers, just touched it, and pressed her hand so that she winced and uttered a cry.

Prince Vasili rose.

'My dear, I must tell you that this is a moment I shall never, never forget. But, my dear, will you not give us a little hope of touching this heart, so kind and generous? Say "perhaps" . . . The future is so long. Say "perhaps".'

'Prince, what I have said is all there is in my heart. I thank you for the honour, but I shall never be your son's wife.'

'Well, so that's finished, my dear fellow! I am very glad to have seen you. Very glad! Go back to your rooms, Princess. Go!' said the old prince. 'Very, very glad to have seen you,' repeated he, embracing Prince Vasili.

'My vocation is a different one,' thought Princess Mary. 'My vocation is to be happy with another kind of happiness, the happiness of love and self-sacrifice. And cost what it may, I will arrange poor Amélie's happiness, she loves him so passionately, and so passionately repents. I will do all I can to arrange the match between them. If he is not rich I will give her the means; I will ask my father and Andrew. I shall be so happy when she is his wife. She is so unfortunate, a stranger, alone, helpless! And, oh God, how passionately she must love him if she could so far forget herself! Perhaps I might have done the same!...' thought Princess Mary.

6

IT was long since the Rostovs had news of Nicholas. Not till mid-winter was the count at last handed a letter addressed in his son's handwriting. On receiving it he ran on tiptoe to his study in alarm and haste trying to escape notice, closed the door and began to read the letter.

Anna Mikhaylovna, who always knew everything that passed in the house, on hearing of the arrival of the letter went softly into the room and found the count with it in his hand sobbing and laughing at the same time.

Anna Mikhaylovna though her circumstances had improved was still living with the Rostovs.

'My dear friend?' said she in a tone of pathetic inquiry, prepared to sympathize in any way.

The count sobbed yet more.

'Nikolenka...a letter...wa...a...s...wounded...my darling boy...the countess...promoted to be an officer...thank God...How tell the little countess!'

Anna Mikhaylovna sat down beside him, with her own handkerchief wiped the tears from his eyes and from the letter, then having dried her own eyes she comforted the count, and decided that at dinner and till tea-time she would prepare the countess, and after tea with God's help would inform her.

At dinner Anna Mikhaylovna talked the whole time about the war news and about Nikolenka, twice asked when the last letter had been received from him, though she knew that already, and remarked that they might very likely be getting a letter from him that day. Each time that these hints began to make the countess anxious and she glanced uneasily at the count and at Anna Mikhaylovna, the latter very adroitly turned the conversation to insignificant matters. Natasha, who of the whole family was the most gifted with a capacity to feel any shades of intonation, look, and expression, pricked up her ears from the beginning of the meal, and was certain that there was some secret between her father and Anna Mikhaylovna, that it had something to do with her brother, and that Anna Mikhaylovna was preparing them for it. Bold as she was, Natasha, who knew how sensitive her mother was to anything relating to Nikolenka, did not venture to ask any questions at dinner, but she was too excited to eat anything and kept wriggling about on her chair regardless of her governess's remarks. After dinner she rushed headlong after Anna Mikhaylovna, and dashing at her, flung herself on her neck as soon as she overtook her in the sitting-room.

'Auntie darling, do tell me what it is!'

'Nothing, my dear.'

'No, dearest, sweet one, honey, I won't give up – I know you know something.'

Anna Mikhaylovna shook her head.

'You are a little sly-boots,' she said.

'A letter from Nikolenka! I'm sure of it!' exclaimed Natasha, reading confirmation in Anna Mikhaylovna's face.

'But for God's sake be careful, you know how it may affect your mamma.'

'I will, I will, only tell me! You won't? Then I will go and tell at once.'

Anna Mikhaylovna in a few words told her the contents of the letter, on condition that she should tell no one.

'No, on my true word of honour,' said Natasha crossing herself, 'I won't tell anyone!' and she ran off at once to Sonya.

'Nikolenka ... wounded ... a letter,' she announced in gleeful triumph.

'Nicholas!' was all Sonya said, instantly turning white.

Natasha seeing the impression the news of her brother's wound produced on Sonya, felt for the first time the sorrowful side of the news.

She rushed to Sonya, hugged her, and began to cry.

'A little wound, but he has been made an officer; he is well now, he wrote himself,' said she through her tears.

'There now! It's true that all you women are cry-babies,' remarked Petya, pacing the room with large, resolute strides. 'Now I'm very glad, very glad indeed, that my brother has distinguished himself so. You are all blubberers and understand nothing.'

Natasha smiled through her tears.

'You haven't read the letter?' asked Sonya.

'No, but she said that it was all over and that he's now an officer.'

'Thank God!' said Sonya, crossing herself. 'But perhaps she deceived you. Let us go to Mamma.'

Petya paced the room in silence for a time.

'If I'd been in Nikolenka's place I would have killed even more of those Frenchmen,' he said. 'What nasty brutes they are! I'd have killed so many that there'd have been a heap of them.'

'Hold your tongue, Petya, what a goose you are!'

'I'm not a goose, but they are who cry about trifles,' said Petya.

'Do you remember him?' Natasha suddenly asked, after a moment's silence.

Sonya smiled.

'Do I remember Nicholas?'

'No, Sonya, but do you remember so that you remember him perfectly, remember everything?' said Natasha with an expressive gesture, evidently wishing to give her words a very definite meaning. 'I remember Nikolenka too, I remember him well,' she said. 'But I don't remember Boris. I don't remember him a bit.'

'What! You don't remember Boris?' asked Sonya in surprise.

'It's not that I don't remember – I know what he is like, but not as I remember Nikolenka. Him – I just shut my eyes and remember, but Boris . . . No!' (She shut her eyes.) 'No! there's nothing at all.'

'Oh, Natasha!' said Sonya, looking ecstatically and earnestly at her friend as if she did not consider her worthy to hear what she meant to say, and as if she were saying it to someone else with whom joking was out of the question, 'I am in love with your brother once for all, and whatever may happen to him or to me I shall never cease to love him as long as I live.'

Natasha looked at Sonya with wondering and inquisitive eyes, and said nothing. She felt that Sonya was speaking the truth, that there was love such as Sonya was speaking of. But Natasha had not yet felt anything like it. She believed it could be, but did not understand it.

'Shall you write to him?' she asked.

Sonya became thoughtful. The question of how to write to Nicholas, and whether she ought to write, tormented her. Now that he was already an officer and a wounded hero would it be right to remind him of herself and, as it might seem, of the obligations to her he had taken on himself?

'I don't know. I think if he writes, I will write too,' she said blushing.

'And you won't feel ashamed to write to him?'

Sonya smiled.

'No.'

'And I should be ashamed to write to Boris. I'm not going to.'

'Why should you be ashamed?'

'Well, I don't know. It's awkward, and would make me ashamed.'

'And I know why she'd be ashamed,' said Petya, offended by Natasha's previous remark. 'It's because she was in love with that fat one in spectacles' (that was how Petya described his namesake, the new Count Bezukhov), 'and now she's in love with that singer' (he meant Natasha's Italian singing-master), 'that's why she's ashamed!'

'Petya, you're a stupid!' said Natasha.

'Not more stupid than you, madam,' said the nine-year-old Petya, with the air of an old brigadier.

The countess had been prepared by Anna Mikhaylovna's hints at dinner. On retiring to her own room, she sat in an arm-chair, her eyes fixed on a miniature portrait of her son on the lid of a snuff-box, while the tears kept coming into her eyes. Anna Mikhaylovna, with the letter, came on tiptoe to the countess's door and paused.

'Don't come in,' she said to the old count who was following her. 'Come later.' And she went in, closing the door behind her.

The count put his ear to the keyhole and listened.

At first he heard the sound of indifferent voices, then Anna Mikhaylovna's voice alone in a long speech, then a cry, then silence, then both voices together with glad intonations, and then footsteps. Anna Mikhaylovna opened the door. Her face wore the proud expression of a surgeon who has just performed a difficult operation, and admits the public to appreciate his skill.

'It is done!' she said to the count, pointing triumphantly to the countess, who sat holding in one hand the snuff-box with its portrait and in the other the letter, and pressing them alternately to her lips.

When she saw the count she stretched out her arms to him, embraced his bald head, over which she again looked at the letter and the portrait, and in order to press them again to her lips she lightly pushed away the bald head. Vera, Natasha, Sonya, and Petya now entered the room, and the reading of the letter began. After a brief description of the campaign and the two battles in which he had taken part, and his promotion, Nicholas said that he kissed his father's and mother's hands asking for their blessing, and that he kissed Vera, Natasha, and Petya. Besides that he sent greetings to Monsieur Schelling, Madame Schoss, and his old nurse, and asked them to kiss for him 'dear Sonya, whom he loved and thought of just the same as ever'. When she heard this, Sonya blushed so that tears came into her eyes, and unable to bear the looks turned upon her, ran away into the dancing hall, whirled round it at full speed with her dress puffed out like a balloon, and flushed and smiling, plumped down on the floor. The countess was crying.

'Why are you crying, Mamma?' asked Vera. 'From all he says one should be glad and not cry.'

This was quite true, but the count, the countess, and Natasha, looked at her reproachfully. 'And who is it she takes after?' thought the countess.

Nicholas's letter was read over hundreds of times, and those who were considered worthy to hear it had to come to the countess, for she did not let it out of her hands. The tutors came, and the nurses, and Dmitri, and several acquaintances, and the countess re-read the letter each time with fresh pleasure and each time discovered in it fresh proofs of Nikolenka's virtues. How strange, how extraordinary, how joyful it seemed, that her son, the scarcely perceptible motion of whose tiny limbs she had felt twenty years ago within her, that son about whom she used to have quarrels with the too-indulgent count, that son who had first learnt to say 'pear' and then 'granny', that this son should now be away in a foreign land amid strange surroundings, a manly warrior doing some kind of man's work of his own without help or guidance. The universal experience of ages, showing that children do grow imperceptibly from the cradle to manhood, did not exist for the countess. Her son's growth towards manhood at each of its stages had seemed as extraordinary to her as if there had never existed the millions of human beings who grew up in the same way. As twenty years before it seemed impossible that the little creature who lived somewhere under her heart would ever cry, suck her breast, and begin to speak, so now she could not believe that that little creature could be this strong, brave man, this model son and officer, that judging by this letter, he now was.

'What a *style*! How charmingly he describes!' said she, reading the descriptive part of the letter. 'And what a soul! Not a word about himself ... Not a word! About some Denisov or other, though he himself I dare say is braver than any of them! He says nothing about his sufferings. What a heart! How like him it is! And how he has remembered everybody! Not forgetting anyone. I always said when he was only so high – I always said ...'

For more than a week preparations were being made, rough drafts of letters to Nicholas from all the household were written and copied out, while under the supervision of the countess and the solicitude of the count, money and all things necessary for the uniform and equipment of the newly commissioned officer were collected. Anna Mikhaylovna, practical woman that she was, had even managed by favour with the army authorities to secure advantageous means of communication for herself and her son. She had opportunities of sending her letters to the Grand Duke Constantine Pavlovich who commanded the Guards. The Rostovs supposed that *The Russian Guards, Abroad,* was a quite definite address, and that if a letter reached the Grand Duke in command of the Guards there was no reason why it should not reach the Pavlograd regiment, which was presumably somewhere in the same neighbourhood. And so it was decided to send the letters and money by the Grand Duke's courier to Boris, and Boris was to forward them to Nicholas. The letters were from the old count, the countess, Petya, Vera, Natasha and Sonya, and finally there were six thousand rubles for his outfit and various other things the old count sent to his son.

7

ON the 12th of November Kutuzov's active army, in camp before Olmütz, was preparing to be reviewed next day by the two Emperors – the Russian and the Austrian. The Guards, just arrived from Russia, spent the night ten miles from Olmütz, and next morning were to come straight to the review, reaching the field at Olmütz by ten o'clock.

That day Nicholas Rostov received a letter from Boris telling him that the Ismaylov* regiment was quartered for the night ten miles from Olmütz, and that he wanted to see him as he had a letter and money for him. Rostov was particularly in need of money now that the troops, after their active service, were stationed near Olmütz and the camp swarmed with well-provisioned sutlers and Austrian Jews offering all sorts of tempting wares. The Pavlograds held feast after feast celebrating awards they had received for the campaign, and made expeditions to Olmütz to visit a certain Caroline the Hungarian, who had recently opened a restaurant there with girls as waitresses. Rostov who had just celebrated his promotion to a cornetcy and bought Denisov's horse, Bedouin, was in debt all round, to his comrades and the sutlers. On receiving Boris's letter he rode with a fellow-officer to Olmütz, dined there, drank a bottle of wine, and then set off alone to the Guards' camp to find his old playmate. Rostov had not yet had time to get his uniform. He had on a shabby cadet jacket decorated with a soldier's cross, equally shabby cadet's riding breeches lined with worn leather, and an officer's sabre with a sword-knot. The Don horse he was riding was one he had bought from a Cossack during the campaign, and he wore a crumpled hussar cap stuck jauntily back on one side of his head. As he rode up to the camp he thought how he would impress Boris and all his comrades of the Guards by his appearance – that of a fighting hussar who had been under fire.

The Guards had made their whole march as if on a pleasure trip, parading their cleanliness and discipline. They had come by easy stages, their knapsacks conveyed on carts, and the Austrian authorities had provided excellent dinners for the officers at every halting-place. The regiments had entered and left the towns with their bands playing, and by the Grand Duke's orders the men had marched all the way in step (a practice on which the Guards prided themselves), the officers on foot and at their proper posts. Boris had been quartered, and had marched all the way, with Berg who was already in command of a company. Berg, who had obtained his captaincy during the campaign, had gained the confidence of his superiors by his promptitude and accuracy and had arranged his money matters very satisfactorily. Boris during the campaign had made the acquaintance of many persons who might prove useful to him, and by a letter of recommendation he had brought from Pierre, had become acquainted with Prince Andrew Bolkonsky through whom he hoped to obtain a post on the commander-in-chief's staff. Berg and Boris having rested after yesterday's march, were sitting, clean and neatly dressed at a round table in the clean quarters allotted to them, playing chess. Berg held a smoking pipe between his knees. Boris in the accurate way characteristic of him was building a little pyramid of chessmen with his delicate white fingers while awaiting Berg's move, and watched his opponent's face, evidently thinking about the game, as he always thought only of whatever he was engaged on.

'Well, how are you going to get out of that?' he remarked.

'We'll try to,' replied Berg, touching a pawn and then removing his hand.

At that moment the door opened.

'Here he is at last!' shouted Rostov. 'And Berg too! Oh, you *petisenfans, allay cushay dormir!*' he exclaimed, imitating his Russian nurse's French, at which he and Boris used to laugh long ago.

'Dear me, how you have changed!'

Boris rose to meet Rostov, but in doing so did not omit to steady and replace some chessmen that were falling. He was about to embrace his friend but Nicholas avoided him. With that peculiar feeling of youth, that dread of beaten tracks, and wish to express itself in a manner different from that of its elders which is often insincere, Nicholas wished to do something special on meeting his friend. He wanted to pinch him, push him, do anything but kiss him – a thing everybody did. But notwithstanding this, Boris embraced him in a quiet friendly way and kissed him three times.

They had not met for nearly half a year and, being at the age when young men take their first steps on life's road, each saw immense changes in the other, quite a new reflection of the society in which they had taken those first steps. Both had changed greatly since they last met and both were in a hurry to show the changes that had taken place in them.

'Oh, you damned dandies! Clean and fresh as if you'd been to a fête, not like us sinners of the line,' cried Rostov, with martial swagger and with baritone notes in his voice new to Boris, pointing to his own mud-bespattered breeches. The German landlady, hearing Rostov's loud voice, popped her head in at the door.

'Eh, is she pretty?' he asked with a wink.

'Why do you shout so? You'll frighten them!' said Boris. 'I did not expect you to-day,' he added. 'I only sent you the note yesterday by Bolkonsky – an adjutant of Kutuzov's, who's a friend of mine. I did not think he would get it to you so quickly ... Well, how are you? Been under fire already?' asked Boris.

Without answering, Rostov shook the soldier's Cross of St George fastened to the cording of his uniform, and indicating his bandaged arm, glanced at Berg with a smile.

'As you see,' he said.

'Indeed? Yes, yes!' said Boris with a smile. 'And we too have had a splendid march. You know of course that his Imperial Highness rode with our regiment all the time, so that we had every comfort and every advantage. What receptions we had in Poland! What dinners and balls! I can't tell you. And the Tsarevich was very gracious to all our officers.'

And the two friends told each other of their doings, the one of his hussar revels, and life in the fighting line, the other of the pleasures and advantages of service under members of the Imperial family.

'Oh, you Guards!' said Rostov. 'I say, send for some wine.'

Boris made a grimace.

'If you really want it,' said he.

He went to his bed, drew a purse from under the clean pillow, and sent for wine.

'Yes, and I have some money and a letter to give you,' he added.

Rostov took the letter, and throwing the money on the sofa put both arms on the table and began to read. After reading a few lines he glanced angrily at Berg, then, meeting his eyes, hid his face behind the letter.

'Well, they've sent you a tidy sum,' said Berg, eyeing the heavy purse that sank into the sofa. 'As for us, Count, we get along on our pay. I can tell you for myself . . .'

'I say Berg, my dear fellow,' said Rostov, 'when you get a letter from home and meet one of your own people whom you want to talk everything over with, and I happen to be there, I'll go at once, to be out of your way! Do go somewhere, anywhere . . . to the devil!' he exclaimed, and immediately seizing him by the shoulder and looking amiably into his face, evidently wishing to soften the rudeness of his words, he added, 'Don't be hurt, my dear fellow; you know I speak from my heart as to an old acquaintance.'

'Oh, don't mention it, Count! I quite understand,' said Berg, getting up and speaking in a muffled and guttural voice.

'Go across to our hosts: they invited you,' added Boris.

Berg put on the cleanest of coats, without a spot or speck of dust, stood before a looking-glass and brushed the hair on his temples upwards, in the way affected by the Emperor Alexander, and having assured himself from the way Rostov looked at it that his coat had been noticed, left the room with a pleasant smile.

'Oh dear, what a beast I am!' muttered Rostov, as he read the letter.

'Why?'

'Oh, what a pig I am, not once to have written, and to have given them such a fright! Oh, what a pig I am!' he repeated, flushing suddenly. 'Well, have you sent Gabriel for some wine? All right, let's have some!'

In the letter from his parents was enclosed a letter of recommendation to Bagration which the old countess at Anna Mikhaylovna's advice had obtained through an acquaintance and sent to her son, asking him to take it to its destination and make use of it.

'What nonsense! Much I need it!' said Rostov, throwing the letter under the table.

'Why have you thrown that away?' asked Boris.

'It is some letter of recommendation . . . what the devil do I want it for!'

'Why "What the devil"?' said Boris, picking it up and reading the address. 'This letter would be of great use to you.'

'I want nothing, and I won't be anyone's adjutant.'

'Why not?' inquired Boris.

'It's a lackey's job!'

'You are still the same dreamer, I see,' remarked Boris, shaking his head.

'And you're still the same diplomatist! But that's not the point. ... Come, how are you?' asked Rostov.

'Well, as you see. So far everything's all right, but I confess I should much like to be an adjutant and not remain at the front.'

'Why?'

'Because when once a man starts on military service he should try to make as successful a career of it as possible.'

'Oh, that's it!' said Rostov, evidently thinking of something else.

He looked intently and inquiringly into his friend's eyes, evidently trying in vain to find the answer to some question.

Old Gabriel brought in the wine.

'Shouldn't we now send for Berg?' asked Boris. 'He would drink with you. I can't.'

'Well, send for him ... and how do you get on with that German?' said Rostov with a contemptuous smile.

'He is a very, very nice, honest, and pleasant fellow,' answered Boris.

Again Rostov looked intently into Boris's eyes and sighed. Berg returned, and over the bottle of wine conversation between the three officers grew animated. The Guardsmen told Rostov of their march and how they had been made much of in Russia, Poland, and abroad. They spoke of the sayings and doings of their commander, the Grand Duke, and told stories of his kindness and irascibility. Berg as usual kept silent when the subject did not relate to himself, but in connexion with the stories of the Grand Duke's quick temper he related with gusto how in Galicia he had managed to deal with the Grand Duke when the latter made a tour of the regiments and was annoyed at the irregularity of a movement. With a pleasant smile Berg related how the Grand Duke had ridden up to him in a violent passion shouting: 'Arnauts!* (Arnauts was the Tsarevich's favourite expression when he was in a rage) and called for the company commander.

'Would you believe it, Count, I was not at all alarmed, because I knew I was right. Without boasting, you know, I may say that I know the Army Orders by heart and know the Regulations as well as I do the Lord's Prayer. So, Count, there never is any negligence in my company, and so my conscience was at ease. I came forward ...' (Berg stood up and showed how he presented himself, with his hand to his cap, and really it would have been difficult for a face to express greater respect and self-complacency than his did.) 'Well he stormed at me, as the saying is, stormed and stormed and stormed! It was not a matter of life but rather of death, as the saying is. "Albanians!" and "devils!" and "To Siberia!"' said Berg with a sagacious smile. 'I knew I was in the right so I kept silent; was not that best, Count? . . . "Hey, are you dumb?" he shouted. Still I remained silent. And what do you think, Count? The next day it was not even mentioned in the Orders of the Day! That's what keeping one's head means. That's the way, Count,' said Berg, lighting his pipe and emitting rings of smoke.

'Yes, that was fine,' said Rostov smiling.

But Boris noticed that he was preparing to make fun of Berg, and skilfully changed the subject. He asked him to tell them how and where he got his wound. This pleased Rostov and he began talking about it, and as he went on became more and more animated. He told them of his Schön Grabern affair just as those who have taken part in a battle generally do describe it, that is, as they would like it to have been, as they have heard it described by others, and as sounds well, but not at all as it really was. Rostov was a truthful young man and would on no account have told a deliberate lie. He began his story meaning to tell everything just as it happened, but imperceptibly, involuntarily, and inevitably he lapsed into falsehood. If he had told the truth to his hearers – who like himself had often heard stories of attacks and had formed a definite idea of what an attack was and were expecting to hear just such a story – they would either not have believed him or, still worse, would have thought that Rostov was himself to blame since what generally happens to the narrators of cavalry attacks had not happened to him. He could not tell them simply that everyone went at a trot, and that he fell off his horse and sprained his arm and then ran as hard as he could from a Frenchman into the wood. Besides, to tell everything as it really happened it would have been necessary to make an effort of will to tell only what happened. It is very difficult to tell the truth, and young people are rarely capable of it. His hearers expected a story of how beside himself and all aflame with excitement, he had flown like a storm at the square, cut his way in, slashed right and left, how his sabre had tasted flesh, and he had fallen exhausted, and so on. And so he told them all that.

In the middle of his story, just as he was saying: 'You cannot imagine what a strange frenzy one experiences during an attack,' Prince Andrew, whom Boris was expecting, entered the room. Prince Andrew, who liked to help young men, was flattered by being asked for his assistance, and being well-disposed towards

Boris who had managed to please him the day before, he wished to do what the young man wanted. Having been sent with papers from Kutuzov to the Tsarevich he looked in on Boris hoping to find him alone. When he came in and saw an hussar of the line recounting his military exploits (Prince Andrew could not endure that sort of man) he gave Boris a pleasant smile, frowned as with half-closed eyes he looked at Rostov, bowed slightly and wearily, and sat down languidly on the sofa: he felt it unpleasant to have dropped in on bad company. Rostov flushed up on noticing this, but he did not care, this was a mere stranger. Glancing however at Boris he saw that he too seemed ashamed of the hussar of the line.

In spite of Prince Andrew's disagreeable, ironical tone, in spite of the contempt with which Rostov from his *fighting* army point of view regarded all these little adjutants on the staff, of whom the newcomer was evidently one, Rostov felt confused, blushed, and became silent. Boris inquired what news there might be on the staff, and what, without indiscretion, one might ask about our plans.

'We shall probably advance,' replied Bolkonsky, evidently reluctant to say more in the presence of a stranger.

Berg took the opportunity to ask, with great politeness, whether, as was rumoured, the allowance of forage-money to captains of companies would be doubled. To this Prince Andrew answered with a smile that he could give no opinion on such an important government order, and Berg laughed gaily.

'As to your business,' Prince Andrew continued, addressing Boris, 'we will talk of it later' (and he looked round at Rostov). 'Come to me after the review and we will do what is possible.'

And having glanced round the room Prince Andrew turned to Rostov, whose state of unconquerable childish embarrassment now changing to anger he did not condescend to notice, and said:

'I think you were talking of the Schön Grabern affair? Were you there?'

'I was there,' said Rostov angrily as if intending to insult the aide-de-camp.

Bolkonsky noticed the hussar's state of mind, and it amused him. With a slightly contemptuous smile he said:

'Yes, there are many stories now told about that affair!'

'Yes, stories!' repeated Rostov loudly, looking with eyes suddenly grown furious, now at Boris, now at Bolkonsky. 'Yes, many stories! But our stories are the stories of men who have been under the enemy's fire! *Our* stories have some weight, not like the stories of those fellows on the staff who get rewards without doing anything!'

'Of whom you imagine me to be one?' said Prince Andrew with a quiet and particularly amiable smile.

A strange feeling of exasperation and yet of respect for this man's self-possession mingled at that moment in Rostov's soul.

'I am not talking about you,' he said, 'I don't know you and frankly I don't want to. I am speaking of the staff in general.'

'And I will tell you this,' Prince Andrew interrupted in a tone of quiet authority, 'you wish to insult me, and I am ready to agree with you that it would be very easy to do so if you haven't sufficient self-respect, but admit that the time and place are very badly chosen. In a day or two we shall all have to take part in a greater and more serious duel, and besides, Drubetskoy, who says he is an old friend of yours, is not at all to blame that my face has the misfortune to displease you. However,' he added rising, 'you know my name and where to find me, but don't forget that I do not regard either myself or you as having been at all insulted, and as a man older than you, my advice is to let the matter drop. Well then, on Friday after the review I shall expect you, Drubetskoy. Au revoir!' exclaimed Prince Andrew and with a bow to them both he went out.

Only when Prince Andrew was gone did Rostov think of what he ought to have said. And he was still more angry at having omitted to say it. He ordered his horse at once, and coldly taking leave of Boris, rode home. Should he go to head-quarters next day and challenge that affected adjutant, or really let the matter drop, was the question that worried him all the way. He thought angrily of the pleasure he would have at seeing the fright of that small and frail but proud man when covered by his pistol, and then he felt with surprise that of all the men he knew there was none he would so much like to have for a friend as that very adjutant whom he so hated.

8

THE day after Rostov had been to see Boris, a review was held of the Austrian and Russian troops, both those freshly arrived from Russia and those who had been campaigning under Kutuzov. The two Emperors, the Russian with his heir the Tsarevich, and the Austrian with the Archduke, inspected the Allied army of eighty thousand men.

From early morning the smart clean troops were on the move, forming up on the field before the fortress. Now thousands of feet and bayonets moved and halted at the officer's command, turned with banners flying, formed up at intervals, and wheeled round other similar masses of infantry in different uniforms; now was heard the rhythmic beat of hoofs and the jingling of showy cavalry in blue, red, and green braided uniforms, with smartly dressed bandsmen in front mounted on black, roan, or grey horses; then again, spreading out with the brazen clatter of the polished shining cannon that quivered on the gun-carriages and with the smell of linstocks, came the artillery which crawled between the infantry and cavalry and took up its appointed position. Not only the generals in full parade uniforms, with their thin or thick waists drawn in to the utmost, their red necks squeezed into their stiff collars, and wearing scarves and all their decorations, not only the elegant, pomaded officers, but every soldier with his freshly washed and shaven face and his weapons clean and polished to the utmost, and every horse groomed till its coat shone like satin and every hair of its wetted mane lay smooth – felt that no small matter was happening, but an important and solemn affair. Every general and every soldier was conscious of his own insignificance, aware of being but a drop in that ocean of men, and yet at the same time was conscious of his strength as a part of that enormous whole.

From early morning strenuous activities and efforts had begun and by ten o'clock all had been brought into due order. The ranks were drawn up on the vast field. The whole army was extended in three lines: the cavalry in front, behind it the artillery, and behind that again the infantry.

A space like a street was left between each two lines of troops. The three parts of that army were sharply distinguished: Kutuzov's fighting army (with the Pavlograds on the right flank of the front); those recently arrived from Russia, both Guards and regiments of the line; and the Austrian troops. But they all stood in the same lines, under one command, and in a like order.

Like wind over leaves ran an excited whisper: 'They're coming! They're coming!' Alarmed voices were heard, and a stir of final preparation swept over all the troops.

From the direction of Olmütz in front of them, a group was seen approaching. And at that moment, though the day was still, a light gust of wind blowing over the army slightly stirred the streamers on the lances and the unfolded standards fluttered against their staffs. It looked as if by that slight motion the army itself was expressing its joy at the approach of the Emperors. One voice was heard shouting: 'Eyes front!' Then, like the crowing of cocks at sunrise, this was repeated by others from various sides and all became silent.

In the deathlike stillness only the tramp of horses was heard.

This was the Emperors' suites. The Emperors rode up to the flank, and the trumpets of the first cavalry regiment played the general march. It seemed as though not the trumpeters were playing, but as if the army itself, rejoicing at the Emperor's approach, had naturally burst into music. Amid these sounds, only the youthful kindly voice of the Emperor Alexander was clearly heard. He gave the words of greeting, and the first regiment roared 'hurrah!' so deafeningly, continuously, and joyfully, that the men themselves were awed by their multitude and the immensity of the power they constituted.

Rostov standing in the front lines of Kutuzov's army which the Tsar approached first, experienced the same feeling as every other man in that army: a feeling of self-forgetfulness, a proud consciousness of might, and a passionate attraction to him who was the cause of this triumph.

He felt that at a single word from that man all this vast mass (and he himself an insignificant atom in it) would go through fire and water, commit crime, die, or perform deeds of highest heroism, and so he could not but tremble and his heart stand still at the imminence of that word.

'Hurrah! Hurrah! Hurrah!' thundered from all sides, one regiment after another greeting the Tsar with the strains of the march, and then 'hurrah!' . . . Then the general march, and again 'hurrah! hurrah!' growing ever stronger, and fuller, and merging into a deafening roar.

Till the Tsar reached it, each regiment in its silence and immobility seemed like a lifeless body, but as soon as he came up it became alive, its thunder joining the roar of the whole line along which he had already passed. Through the terrible and deafening roar of those voices, amid the square masses of troops standing motionless as if turned to stone, hundreds of riders composing the suites moved carelessly but symmetrically and above all freely, and in front of them two men – the Emperors. Upon them the undivided, tensely passionate attention of that whole mass of men was concentrated.

The handsome young Emperor Alexander, in the uniform of the Horse Guards, wearing a cocked hat with its peaks front and back, with his pleasant face and resonant though not loud voice, attracted everyone's attention.

Rostov was not far from the trumpeters, and with his keen sight had recognized the Tsar and watched his approach. When he was within twenty paces, and Nicholas could clearly distinguish every detail of his handsome, happy young face, he experienced a feeling of tenderness and ecstasy such as he had never before known. Every trait and every movement of the Tsar's seemed to him enchanting.

Stopping in front of the Pavlograds, the Tsar said something in French to the Austrian Emperor and smiled.

Seeing that smile Rostov involuntarily smiled himself and felt a still stronger flow of love for his sovereign. He longed to show that love in some way, and knowing that this was impossible was ready to cry. The Tsar called the colonel of the regiment and said a few words to him.

'Oh God, what would happen to me if the Emperor spoke to me?' thought Rostov. 'I should die of happiness!'

The Tsar addressed the officers also: 'I thank you all, gentlemen, I thank you with my whole heart.' To Rostov every word sounded like a voice from heaven. How gladly would he have died at once for his Tsar!

'You have earned the St George's standards and will be worthy of them.'

'Oh, to die, to die for him!' thought Rostov.

The Tsar said something more which Rostov did not hear, and the soldiers, straining their lungs, shouted 'hurrah!'

Rostov too, bending over his saddle, shouted 'hurrah!' with all his might, feeling that he would like to injure himself by that shout, if only to express his rapture fully.

The Tsar stopped a few minutes in front of the hussars as if undecided.

'How can the Emperor be undecided?' thought Rostov, but then even this indecision appeared to him majestic and enchanting, like everything else the Tsar did.

That hesitation lasted only an instant. The Tsar's foot, in the narrow pointed boot then fashionable, touched the groin of the bob-tailed bay mare he rode, his hand in a white glove gathered up the reins, and he moved off accompanied by an irregularly swaying sea of aides-de-camp. Farther and farther he rode away, stopping at the other regiments, till at last only his white plumes were visible to Rostov from amid the suites that surrounded the Emperors.

Among the gentlemen of the suite Rostov noticed Bolkonsky, sitting his horse indolently and carelessly. Rostov recalled their quarrel of yesterday and the question presented itself whether he ought or ought not to challenge Bolkonsky. 'Of course not!' he now thought. 'Is it worth thinking or speaking of it at such a moment? At a time of such love, such rapture, and such self-sacrifice, what do any of our quarrels and affronts matter? I love and forgive everybody now.'

When the Emperor had passed nearly all the regiments, the troops began a ceremonial march past him, and Rostov on Bedouin, recently purchased from Denisov, rode past too, at the rear of his squadron – that is, alone and in full view of the Emperor.

Before he reached him, Rostov, who was a splendid horseman, spurred Bedouin twice and successfully put him to the showy trot in which the animal went when excited. Bending his foaming muzzle to his chest, his tail extended, Bedouin, as if also conscious of the Emperor's eye upon him, passed splendidly, lifting his feet with a high and graceful action as if flying through the air without touching the ground.

Rostov himself, his legs well back and his stomach drawn in and feeling himself one with his horse, rode past the Emperor with a frowning but blissful face 'like a vewy devil', as Denisov expressed it.

'Fine fellows, the Pavlograds!' remarked the Emperor.

'My God, how happy I should be if he ordered me to leap into the fire this instant!' thought Rostov.

When the review was over the newly arrived officers, and also Kutuzov's, collected in groups and began to talk about the awards, about the Austrians and their uniforms, about their lines, about Bonaparte, and how badly the latter would fare now, especially if the Essen corps arrived and Prussia took our side.

But the talk in every group was chiefly about the Emperor Alexander. His every word and movement was described with ecstasy.

They all had but one wish: to advance as soon as possible against the enemy under the Emperor's command. Commanded by the Emperor himself they could not fail to vanquish anyone, be it whom it might: so thought Rostov and most of the officers after the review.

All were then more confident of victory than the winning of two battles would have made them.

9

THE day after the review, Boris in his best uniform and with his comrade Berg's best wishes for success, rode to Olmütz to see Bolkonsky, wishing to profit by his friendliness and obtain for himself the best post he could – preferably that of adjutant to some important personage, a position in the army which seemed to him most attractive. 'It is all very well for Rostov whose father sends him ten thousand rubles at a time, to talk about not wishing to cringe to anybody and not be anyone's lackey, but I who have nothing but my brains, have to make a career, and must not miss opportunities but must avail myself of them!' he reflected.

He did not find Prince Andrew in Olmütz that day, but the appearance of the town where the head-quarters and the diplomatic corps were stationed, and the two Emperors were living with their suites, households, and courts, only strengthened his desire to belong to that higher world.

He knew no one, and despite his smart Guardsman's uniform, all these exalted personages passing in the streets in their elegant carriages with their plumes, ribbons, and medals, both courtiers and military men, seemed so immeasurably above him, an insignificant officer of the Guards, that they not only did not wish to, but simply could not be aware of his existence. At the quarters of the commander-in-chief, Kutuzov, where he inquired for Bolkonsky, all the adjutants and even the orderlies looked at him as if they wished to impress on him that a great many officers like him were always coming there and that everybody was heartily sick of them. In spite of this, or rather because of it, next day, November the 15th, after dinner he again went to Olmütz, and entering the house occupied by Kutuzov, asked for Bolkonsky. Prince Andrew was in and Boris was shown into a large hall probably formerly used for dancing, but in which five beds now stood, and furniture of various kinds: a table, chairs, and a clavichord. One adjutant, nearest the door, was sitting at the table in a Persian dressing-gown, writing. Another, the red stout Nesvitsky, lay on a bed with his arms under his head, laughing with an officer who had sat down beside him. A third was playing a Viennese waltz on the clavichord, while a fourth, lying on the clavichord, sang the tune. Bolkonsky was not there. None of these gentlemen changed his position on seeing Boris. The one who was writing, and whom Boris addressed, turned round crossly and told him Bolkonsky was on duty, and that he should go through the door on the left into the reception-room if he wished to see him. Boris thanked him and went to the reception-room, where he found some ten officers and generals.

When he entered, Prince Andrew, his eyes drooping contemptuously (with that peculiar expression of polite weariness which plainly says, 'if it were not my duty I would not talk to you for a moment'), was listening to an old Russian general with decorations, who stood very erect, almost on tiptoe, with a soldier's obsequious expression on his purple face, reporting something.

'Very well, then, be so good as to wait,' said Prince Andrew to the general in Russian, speaking with the French intonation he affected when he wished to speak contemptuously, and noticing Boris, Prince Andrew, paying no more heed to the general who ran after him imploring him to hear something more, nodded and turned to him with a cheerful smile.

At that moment Boris clearly realized what he had before surmised, that in the army, besides the subordination and discipline prescribed in the military code, which he and the others knew in the regiment, there was another, more important, subordination, which made this tight-laced, purple-faced general wait respectfully while Captain Prince Andrew for his own pleasure chose to chat with Lieutenant Drubetskoy. More than ever was Boris resolved to serve in future not according to the written code, but under this unwritten law. He felt now that merely by having been recommended to Prince Andrew he had already risen above the general who at the front had the power to annihilate him, a lieutenant of the Guards. Prince Andrew came up to him and took his hand.

'I am very sorry you did not find me in yesterday. I was fussing about with Germans all day. We went with Weyrother to survey the dispositions. When Germans start being accurate there's no end to it!'

Boris smiled, as if he understood what Prince Andrew was alluding to as something generally known. But it was the first time he had heard Weyrother's name, or even the term 'dispositions'.

'Well, my dear fellow, so you still want to be an adjutant? I have been thinking about you.'

'Yes, I was thinking' – for some reason Boris could not help blushing – 'of asking the commander-in-chief. He has had a letter from Prince Kuragin about me. I only wanted to ask because I fear the Guards won't be in action,' he added as if in apology.

'All right, all right. We'll talk it over,' replied Prince Andrew. 'Only let me report this gentleman's business, and I shall be at your disposal.'

While Prince Andrew went to report about the purple-faced general, that gentleman – evidently not sharing Boris's conception of the advantages of the unwritten code of subordination – looked so fixedly at the presumptuous lieutenant who had prevented his finishing what he had to say to the adjutant, that Boris felt uncomfortable. He turned away and waited impatiently for Prince Andrew's return from the commander-in-chief's room.

'You see, my dear fellow, I have been thinking about you,' said Prince Andrew when they had gone into the large room where the clavichord was. 'It's no use your going to the commander-in-chief. He would say a lot of pleasant things, ask you to dinner' ('that would not be bad as regards the unwritten code,' thought Boris), 'but nothing more would come of it. There will soon be a battalion of us aides-de-camp and adjutants! But this is what we'll do: I have a good friend, an adjutant-general and an excellent fellow, Prince Dolgorukov; and though you may not know it, the fact is that now Kutuzov with his staff and all of us count for nothing. Everything is now centred round the Emperor. So we will go to Dolgorukov; I have to go there anyhow, and I have already spoken to him about you. We shall see whether he cannot attach you to himself or find a place for you somewhere nearer the sun.'

Prince Andrew always became specially keen when he had to guide a young man and help him to worldly success. Under cover of obtaining help of this kind for another, which from pride he would never accept for himself, he kept in touch with the circle which confers success and which attracted him. He very readily took up Boris's cause and went with him to Dolgorukov.

It was late in the evening when they entered the palace at Olmütz occupied by the Emperors and their retinues.

That same day a council of war had been held in which all the members of the Hofkriegsrath and both Emperors took part. At that council, contrary to the views of the old generals Kutuzov and Prince Schwartzenberg, it had been decided to advance immediately and give battle to Bonaparte. The council of war was just over when Prince Andrew accompanied by Boris arrived at the palace to find Dolgorukov. Everyone at head-quarters was still under the spell of the day's council, at which the party of the young had triumphed. The voices of those who counselled delay and advised waiting for something else before advancing, had been so completely silenced and their arguments confuted by such conclusive evidence of the advantages of attacking, that what had been discussed at the council – the coming battle and the victory that would certainly result from it – no longer seemed to be in the future but in the past. All the advantages were on our side. Our enormous forces, undoubtedly superior to Napoleon's, were concentrated in one place, the troops inspired by the Emperor's presence were eager for action. The strategic position where the operations would take place was familiar in all its details to the Austrian General Weyrother: a lucky accident had ordained that the Austrian army should manœuvre the previous year on the very fields where the French had now to be fought; the adjacent locality was known and shown in every detail on the maps, and Bonaparte, evidently weakened, was undertaking nothing.

Dolgorukov, one of the warmest advocates of an attack, had just returned from the council, tired and exhausted but eager and proud of the victory that had been gained. Prince Andrew introduced his protégé, but Prince Dolgorukov politely and firmly pressing his hand said nothing to Boris, and evidently unable to suppress the thoughts which were uppermost in his mind at that moment, addressed Prince Andrew in French.

'Ah, my dear fellow, what a battle we have gained! God grant that the one that will result from it will be as victorious! However, my dear fellow,' he said abruptly and eagerly, 'I must confess to having been unjust to the Austrians and especially to Weyrother. What exactitude, what minuteness, what knowledge of the locality, what foresight for every eventuality, every possibility, even to the smallest detail! No, my dear fellow, no conditions better than our present ones could have been devised. This combination of Austrian precision with Russian valour – what more could be wished for?'

'So the attack is definitely resolved on?' asked Bolkonsky.

'And do you know, my dear fellow, it seems to me that Bonaparte has decidedly lost his bearings, you know that a letter was received from him to-day for the Emperor.' Dolgorukov smiled significantly.

'Is that so? And what does he say?' inquired Bolkonsky.

'What can he say? Tra-di-ri-di-ra and so on ... merely to gain time. I tell you he is in our hands, that's certain! But what was most amusing,' he continued, with a sudden, good-natured laugh, 'was that we could not think how to address the reply! If not as "Consul" and of course not as "Emperor", it seemed to me it should be to "General Bonaparte".'

'But between not recognizing him as Emperor and calling him General Bonaparte there is a difference,' remarked Bolkonsky.

'That's just it,' interrupted Dolgorukov quickly, laughing. 'You know Bilibin – he's a very clever fellow. He suggested addressing him as "Usurper and Enemy of Mankind".'

Dolgorukov laughed merrily.

'Only that?' said Bolkonsky.

'All the same it was Bilibin who found a suitable form for the address. He is a wise and clever fellow.'

'What was it?'

'To the Head of the French Government ... *Au chef du gouvernement français*,' said Dolgorukov with grave satisfaction. 'Good, wasn't it?'

'Yes, but he will dislike it extremely,' said Bolkonsky.

'Oh yes, very much! My brother knows him, he's dined with him – the present Emperor – more than once in Paris, and tells me he never met a more cunning or subtle diplomatist – you know, a combination of French adroitness and Italian play-acting! Do you know the tale about him and Count Markov? Count Markov was the only man who knew how to handle him. You know the story of the handkerchief? It is delightful!'

And the talkative Dolgorukov, turning now to Boris now to Prince Andrew, told how Bonaparte wishing to test Markov, our ambassador, purposely dropped a handkerchief in front of him and stood looking at Markov, probably expecting Markov to pick it up for him, and how Markov immediately dropped his own beside it and picked it up without touching Bonaparte's.

'Delightful!' said Bolkonsky. 'But I have come to you, Prince, as a petitioner on behalf of this young man. You see . . .' but before Prince Andrew could finish, an aide-de-camp came in to summon Dolgorukov to the Emperor.

'Oh, what a nuisance,' said Dolgorukov, getting up hurriedly and pressing the hands of Prince Andrew and Boris. 'You know I should be very glad to do all in my power both for you and for this dear young man.' Again he pressed the hand of the latter with an expression of good-natured, sincere, and animated levity. 'But you see . . . another time!'

Boris was excited by the thought of being so close to the higher powers as he felt himself to be at that moment. He was conscious that here he was in contact with the springs that set in motion the enormous movements of the mass of which in his regiment he felt himself a tiny, obedient, and insignificant atom. They followed Prince Dolgorukov out into the corridor, and met – coming out of the door of the Emperor's room by which Dolgorukov had entered – a short man in civilian clothes with a clever face and sharply projecting jaw which, without spoiling his face, gave him a peculiar vivacity and shiftiness of expression. This short man nodded to Dolgorukov as to an intimate friend, and stared at Prince Andrew with cool intensity, walking straight towards him and evidently expecting him to bow or to step out of his way. Prince Andrew did neither: a look of animosity appeared on his face and the other turned away and went down the side of the corridor.

'Who was that?' asked Boris.

'He is one of the most remarkable, but to me most unpleasant of men – the Minister of Foreign Affairs, Prince Adam Czartoryski . . . It is such men as he who decide the fate of nations,' added Bolkonsky with a sigh he could not suppress, as they passed out of the palace.

Next day the army began its campaign, and up to the very battle of Austerlitz Boris was unable to see either Prince Andrew or Dolgorukov again, and remained for a while with the Ismaylov regiment.

At dawn on the 16th of November Denisov's squadron, in which Nicholas Rostov served and which was in Prince Bagration's detachment, moved from the place where it had spent the night, advancing into action as arranged, and after going behind other columns for about a verst, was stopped on the high road. Rostov saw the Cossacks and then the first and second squadrons of hussars, and infantry battalions and artillery pass by and go forward, and then Generals Bagration and Dolgorukov ride past with their adjutants. All the fear before action which he had experienced as previously, all the inner struggle to conquer that fear, all his dreams of distinguishing himself as a true hussar in this battle, had been wasted. Their squadron remained in reserve and Nicholas Rostov spent that day in a dull and wretched mood. At nine in the morning he heard firing in front and shouts of *hurrah*, and saw wounded being brought back (there were not many of them), and at last he saw how a whole detachment of French cavalry was brought in, convoyed by a sótnya* of Cossacks. Evidently the affair was over, and though not big, had been a successful engagement. The men and officers returning spoke of a brilliant victory, of the occupation of the town of Wischau and the capture of a whole French squadron. The day was bright and sunny after a sharp night frost, and the cheerful glitter of that autumn day was in keeping with the news of victory which was conveyed not only by the tales of those who had taken part in it, but also by the joyful expression on the faces of soldiers, officers, generals, and adjutants, as they passed Rostov going or coming. And Nicholas, who had vainly suffered all the dread that precedes a battle and had spent that happy day in inactivity, was all the more depressed.

'Come here, Wostov. Let's dwink to dwown our gwief!' shouted Denisov, who had settled down by the roadside with a flask and some food.

The officers gathered round Denisov's canteen, eating and talking.

'There! They are bringing another!' cried one of the officers, indicating a captive French dragoon who was being brought in on foot by two Cossacks.

One of them was leading by the bridle a fine large French horse he had taken from the prisoner.

'Sell us that horse!' Denisov called out to the Cossacks.

'If you like, your honour!'

The officers got up and stood round the Cossacks and their prisoner. The French dragoon was a young Alsatian who spoke French with a German accent. He was breathless with agitation, his face was red, and when he heard some French spoken he at once began speaking to the officers, addressing first one, then another. He said he would not have been taken, it was not his fault but the corporal's who had sent him to seize some horse-cloths, though he had told him the Russians were there. And at every word he added: 'But don't hurry my little horse!' and stroked the animal. It was plain that he did not quite grasp where he was. Now he excused himself for having been taken prisoner, and now imagining himself before his own officers, insisted on his soldierly discipline and zeal in the service. He brought with him into our rearguard all the freshness of atmosphere of the French army, which was so alien to us.

The Cossacks sold the horse for two gold pieces, and Rostov, being the richest of the officers now that he had received his money, bought it.

'But don't hurt my little horse!' said the Alsatian good-naturedly to Rostov when the animal was handed over to the hussar.

Rostov smilingly reassured the dragoon and gave him money.

'Alley! Alley!' said the Cossack, touching the prisoner's arm to make him go on.

'The Emperor! The Emperor!' was suddenly heard among the hussars.

All began to run and bustle, and Rostov saw coming up the road behind him several riders with white plumes in their hats. In a moment everyone was in his place, waiting.

Rostov did not know or remember how he ran to his place and mounted. Instantly his regret at not having been in action and his dejected mood amid people of whom he was weary, had gone, instantly every thought of himself had vanished. He was filled with happiness at his nearness to the Emperor. He felt that this nearness by itself made up to him for the day he had lost. He was happy as a lover when the longed-for moment of meeting arrives. Not daring to look round and without looking round, he was ecstatically conscious of *his* approach. He felt it not only from the sound of the hoofs of the approaching cavalcade, but because as *he* drew near everything grew brighter, more joyful, more significant, and more festive around him. Nearer and nearer to Rostov came that sun shedding beams of mild and majestic light around, and already he felt himself enveloped in those beams, he heard *his* voice, that kindly, calm, and majestic voice, that was yet so simple! And as if in accord with Rostov's feeling, there was a deathly stillness amid which was heard the Emperor's voice.

'The Pavlograd hussars?' he inquired.

'The reserves, sire!' replied a voice, a very human one compared to that which had said: 'The Pavlograd hussars?'

The Emperor drew level with Rostov and halted. Alexander's face was even more beautiful than it had been three days before at the review. It shone with such gaiety and youth, such innocent youth, that it suggested the liveliness of a fourteen-year-old boy, and yet it was the face of the majestic Emperor. Casually, while surveying the squadron, the Emperor's eyes met Rostov's and rested on them for not more than two seconds. Whether or no the Emperor understood what was going on in Rostov's soul (it seemed to Rostov that he understood everything), at any rate his blue eyes gazed for about two seconds into Rostov's face. A gentle, mild light poured from them. Then all at once he raised his eyebrows, abruptly touched his horse with his left foot, and galloped on.

The young Emperor could not restrain his wish to be present at the battle and, in spite of the remonstrances of his courtiers, at twelve o'clock left the third column with which he had been, and galloped towards the vanguard. Before he came up with the hussars several adjutants met him with news of the successful result of the action.

This battle which consisted in the capture of a French squadron, was represented as a brilliant victory over the French, and so the Emperor and the whole army, especially while the smoke hung over the battlefield, believed that the French had been defeated and were retreating against their will. A few minutes after the Emperor had passed, the Pavlograd division was ordered to advance. In Wischau itself, a pretty German town, Rostov saw the Emperor again. In the market-place where there had been some rather heavy firing before the Emperor's arrival, lay several killed and wounded soldiers whom there had not been time to move. The Emperor, surrounded by his suite of officers and courtiers, was riding a bob-tailed chestnut mare, a different one from that which he had ridden at the review, and bending to one side he gracefully held a gold lorgnette to his eyes and looked at a soldier who lay prone, with blood on his uncovered head. The wounded soldier was so dirty, coarse, and revolting, that his proximity to the Emperor shocked Rostov. Rostov saw how the Emperor's rather round shoulders shuddered as if a cold shiver had run down them, how his left foot began convulsively tapping the horse's side with the spur, and how the well-trained horse looked round unconcerned and did not stir. An adjutant, dismounting, lifted the soldier under the arms to place him on a stretcher that had been brought. The soldier groaned.

'Gently, gently! Can't you do it more gently?' said the Emperor, apparently suffering more than the dying soldier, and he rode away.

Rostov saw tears filling the Emperor's eyes and heard him, as he was riding away, say to Czartoryski:

'What a terrible thing war is: what a terrible thing! *Quelle terrible chose que la guerre!*'

The troops of the vanguard were stationed before Wischau within sight of the enemy's lines, which all day long had yielded ground to us at the least firing. The Emperor's gratitude was announced to the vanguard, rewards were promised and the men received a double ration of vodka. The camp-fires crackled and the soldiers' songs resounded even more merrily than on the previous night. Denisov celebrated his promotion to the rank of major, and Rostov, who had already drunk enough, at the end of the feast proposed the Emperor's health. 'Not "our Sovereign, the Emperor", as they say at official dinners,' said he, 'but the health of our Sovereign, that good, enchanting, and great man! Let us drink to his health and to the certain defeat of the French!'

'If we fought before,' he said, 'not letting the French pass, as at Schön Grabern, what shall we not do now when *he* is at the front? We will all die for him gladly! Is it not so, gentlemen? Perhaps I am not saying it right, I have drunk a good deal – but that is how I feel, and so do you too! To the health of Alexander the First! Hurrah!'

'Hurrah!' rang the enthusiastic voices of the officers.

And the old cavalry captain Kirsten shouted enthusiastically and no less sincerely than the twenty-year-old Rostov.

When the officers had emptied and smashed their glasses, Kirsten filled others, and in shirt-sleeves and breeches went glass in hand to the soldiers' bonfires and with his long grey moustache, his white chest showing from under his open shirt, he stood in a majestic pose in the light of the camp-fire, waving his uplifted arm.

'Lads! here's to our Sovereign, the Emperor, and victory over our enemies! Hurrah!' he exclaimed in his dashing, old, hussar's baritone.

The hussars crowded round and responded heartily with loud shouts.

Late that night when all had separated, Denisov with his short hand patted his favourite, Rostov, on the shoulder.

'As there's no one to fall in love with on campaign, he's fallen in love with the Tsar,' he said.

'Denisov, don't make fun of it!' cried Rostov. 'It is such a lofty, beautiful feeling, such a ...'

'I believe it, I believe it, fwiend, and I share and appwove ...'

'No, you don't understand!'

And Rostov got up and went wandering among the camp-fires dreaming of what happiness it would be to die – not in saving the Emperor's life (he did not even dare to dream of that) but simply to die before his eyes. He really was in love with the Tsar and the glory of the Russian arms and the hope of future triumph. And he was not the only man to experience that feeling during those memorable days preceding the battle of Austerlitz; nine-tenths of the men in the Russian army were then in love, though less ecstatically, with their Tsar and the glory of the Russian arms.

11

THE next day the Emperor stopped at Wischau, and Villier, his physician, was repeatedly summoned to see him. At head-quarters and among the troops near by the news spread that the Emperor was unwell. He ate nothing and had slept badly that night, those around him reported. The cause of this indisposition was the strong impression made on his sensitive mind by the sight of the killed and wounded.

At daybreak on the 17th a French officer, who had come with a flag of truce demanding an audience with the Russian Emperòr, was brought into Wischau from our outposts. This officer was Savary. The Emperor had only just fallen asleep and so Savary had to wait. At midday he was admitted to the Emperor, and an hour later he rode off with Prince Dolgorukov to the advanced post of the French army.

It was rumoured that Savary had been sent to propose to Alexander a meeting with Napoleon. To the joy and pride of the whole army a personal interview was refused, and instead of the Sovereign, Prince Dolgorukov, the victor at Wischau, was sent with Savary to negotiate with Napoleon, if contrary to expectation these negotiations were actuated by a real desire for peace.

Towards evening Dolgorukov came back, went straight to the Tsar, and remained alone with him for a long time.

On the 18th and 19th of November the army advanced two days' march, and the enemy's outposts after a brief interchange of shots retreated. In the highest army circles from midday on the 19th a great, excitedly bustling activity began which lasted till the morning of the 20th, when the memorable battle of Austerlitz was fought.

Till midday on the 19th the activity, the eager talk, running to and fro, and dispatching of adjutants, was confined to the Emperor's head-quarters. But on the afternoon of that day this activity reached Kutuzov's head-quarters and the staffs of the commanders of columns. By evening the adjutants had spread it to all ends and parts of the army, and in the night from the 19th to the 20th the whole eighty thousand allied troops rose from their bivouacs to the hum of voices, and the army swayed and started in one enormous mass six miles long.

The concentrated activity which had begun at the Emperor's head-quarters in the morning and had started the whole movement that followed, was like the first movement of the main wheel of a large tower-clock. One wheel slowly moved, another was set in motion, and a third, and wheels began to revolve faster and faster, levers and cogwheels to work, chimes to play, figures to pop out, and the hands to advance with regular motion as a result of all that activity.

Just as in the mechanism of a clock, so in the mechanism of the military machine, an impulse once given leads to the final result; and just as indifferently quiescent till the moment when motion is transmitted to them are the parts of the mechanism which the impulse has not yet reached. Wheels creak on their axles as the cogs engage one another and the revolving pulleys whirr with the rapidity of their movement, but a neighbouring wheel is as quiet and motionless as though it were prepared to remain so for a hundred years; but the moment comes when the lever catches it, and obeying the impulse that wheel begins to creak, and joins in the common motion the result and aim of which are beyond its ken.

Just as in a clock the result of the complicated motion of innumerable wheels and pulleys is merely a slow and regular movement of the hands which show the time, so the result of all the complicated human activities of 160,000 Russians and French – all their passions, desires, remorse, humiliations, sufferings, outbursts of pride, fear, and enthusiasm – was only the loss of the battle of Austerlitz, the so-called battle of the three Emperors – that is to say, a slow movement of the hand on the dial of human history.

Prince Andrew was on duty that day and in constant attendance on the commander-in-chief.

At six in the evening Kutuzov went to the Emperor's head-quarters and after staying but a short time with the Tsar went to see the grand marshal of the court, Count Tolstoy.

Bolkonsky took the opportunity to go in to get some details of the coming action from Dolgorukov. He felt that Kutuzov was upset and dissatisfied about something and that at head-quarters they were dissatisfied with him, and also that at the Emperor's head-quarters everyone adopted towards him the tone of men who knew something others did not know: he therefore wished to speak to Dolgorukov.

'Well, how d'you do, my dear fellow?' said Dolgorukov who was sitting at tea with Bilibin. 'The fête is for to-morrow. How is your old fellow? Out of sorts?'

'I won't say he is out of sorts, but I fancy he would like to be heard.'

'But they heard him at the council of war and will hear him when he talks sense, but to temporize and wait for something now when Bonaparte fears nothing so much as a general battle is impossible.'

'Yes, you have seen him?' said Prince Andrew. 'Well, what is Bonaparte like? How did he impress you?'

'Yes, I saw him, and am convinced that he fears nothing so much as a general engagement,' repeated Dolgorukov, evidently prizing this general conclusion which he had arrived at from his interview with Napoleon. 'If he weren't afraid of a battle why did he ask for that interview? Why negotiate, and above all why retreat, when to retreat is so contrary to his method of conducting war? Believe me he is afraid, afraid of a general battle. His hour has come! Mark my words!'

'But tell me, what is he like, eh?' said Prince Andrew again.

'He is a man in a grey overcoat, very anxious that I should call him "Your Majesty", but who to his chagrin got no title from me! That's the sort of man he is, and nothing more,' replied Dolgorukov, looking round at Bilibin with a smile.

'Despite my great respect for old Kutuzov,' he continued, 'we should be a nice set of fellows if we were to wait about and so give him a chance to escape, or to trick us, now that we certainly have him in our hands! No, we mustn't forget Suvorov and his rule – not to put yourself in a position to be attacked, but yourself to attack. Believe me in war the energy of young men often shows the way better than all the experience of old Cunctators.'

'But in what position are we going to attack him? I have been at the outposts to-day and it is impossible to say where his chief forces are situated,' said Prince Andrew.

He wished to explain to Dolgorukov a plan of attack he had himself formed.

'Oh, that is all the same,' Dolgorukov said quickly, and getting up he spread a map on the table. 'All eventualities have been foreseen. If he is standing before Brunn . . .'

And Prince Dolgorukov rapidly but indistinctly explained Weyrother's plan of a flanking movement.

Prince Andrew began to reply and to state his own plan, which might have been as good as Weyrother's but for the disadvantage that Weyrother's had already been approved. As soon as Prince Andrew began to demonstrate the defects of the latter and the merits of his own plan, Prince Dolgorukov ceased to listen to him and gazed absent-mindedly not at the map but at Prince Andrew's face.

'There will be a council of war at Kutuzov's to-night though; you can say all this there,' remarked Dolgorukov.

'I will do so,' said Prince Andrew, moving away from the map.

'Whatever are you bothering about, gentlemen?' said Bilibin, who till then had listened with an amused smile to their conversation and now was evidently ready with a joke. 'Whether to-morrow brings victory or defeat the glory of our Russian arms is secure. Except your Kutuzov there is not a single Russian in command of a column! The commanders are: Herr General Wimpfen, le Comte de Langeron, le Prince de Lichtenstein, le Prince de Hohenlohe, and finally Prishprish,* and so on like all those Polish names.'

'Be quiet, backbiter!' said Dolgorukov. 'It is not true; there are now two Russians, Miloradovich and Dokhturov, and there would be a third, Count Arakcheev, if his nerves were not too weak.'

'However, I think General Kutuzov has come out,' said Prince Andrew. 'I wish you good luck and success, gentlemen!' he added, and went out after shaking hands with Dolgorukov and Bilibin.

On the way home Prince Andrew could not refrain from asking Kutuzov, who was sitting silently beside him, what he thought of to-morrow's battle.

Kutuzov looked sternly at his adjutant and after a pause replied: 'I think the battle will be lost, and so I told Count Tolstoy and asked him to tell the Emperor. What do you think he replied? "My dear General, I am engaged with rice and cutlets, look after military matters yourself!" Yes . . . That was the answer I got!'

SHORTLY after nine o'clock that evening Weyrother drove with his plans to Kutuzov's quarters where the council of war was to be held. All the commanders of columns were summoned to the commander-in-chief's and with the exception of Prince Bagration, who declined to come, were all there at the appointed time.

Weyrother who was in full control of the proposed battle, by his eagerness and briskness presented a marked contrast to the dissatisfied and drowsy Kutuzov who reluctantly played the part of chairman and president of the council of war. Weyrother evidently felt himself to be at the head of a movement that had already become unrestrainable. He was like a horse running downhill harnessed to a heavy cart. Whether he was pulling it or being pushed by it he did not know, but rushed along at headlong speed with no time to consider what this movement might lead to. Weyrother had been twice that evening to the enemy's picket line to reconnoitre personally, and twice to the Emperors, Russian and Austrian, to report and explain, and to his head-quarters where he had dictated the disposition in German, and now much exhausted he arrived at Kutuzov's.

He was evidently so busy that he even forgot to be polite to the commander-in-chief. He interrupted him, talked rapidly and indistinctly without looking at the man he was addressing, and did not reply to questions put to him. He was bespattered with mud and had a pitiful, weary, and distracted air, though at the same time he was haughty and self-confident.

Kutuzov was occupying a nobleman's castle of modest dimensions near Ostralitz. In the large drawing-room which had become the commander-in-chief's office, were gathered Kutuzov himself, Weyrother, and the members of the council of war. They were drinking tea, and only awaited Prince Bagration to begin the council. At last Bagration's orderly came with the news that the prince could not attend. Prince Andrew came in to inform the commander-in-chief of this, and availing himself of permission previously given him by Kutuzov to be present at the council, he remained in the room.

'Since Prince Bagration is not coming we may begin,' said Weyrother, hurriedly rising from his seat and going up to the table on which an enormous map of the environs of Brunn was spread out.

Kutuzov, with his uniform unbuttoned so that his fat neck bulged over his collar as if escaping, was sitting almost asleep in a low chair with his podgy old hands resting symmetrically on its arms. At the sound of Weyrother's voice he opened his one eye with an effort.

'Yes, yes, if you please! It is already late,' said he, and nodding his head he let it droop and again closed his eye.

If at first the members of the council thought that Kutuzov was pretending to be asleep, the sounds his nose emitted during the reading that followed proved that the commander-in-chief at that moment was absorbed by a far more serious matter than a desire to show his contempt for the dispositions or anything else – he was engaged in satisfying the irresistible human need for sleep. He really was asleep. Weyrother, with the gesture of a man too busy to lose a moment, glanced at Kutuzov and having convinced himself that he was asleep, took up a paper and in a loud monotonous voice began to read out the dispositions for the impending battle, under a heading which he also read out:

'Dispositions for an attack on the enemy position behind Kobelnitz and Sokolnitz, 30th November* 1805.'

The dispositions were very complicated and difficult. They began as follows:

'As the enemy's left wing rests on wooded hills and his right extends along Kobelnitz and Sokolnitz behind the ponds that are there, while we on the other hand with our left wing by far outflank his right, it is advantageous to attack the enemy's latter wing especially if we occupy the villages of Sokolnitz and Kobelnitz, whereby we can both fall on his flank and pursue him over the plain between Schlappanitz and the Thuerassa forest, avoiding the defiles of Schlappanitz and Bellowitz which cover the enemy's front. For this object it is necessary that ... The first column marches ... The second column marches ... The third column marches ...' and so on, read Weyrother.

The generals seemed to listen reluctantly to the difficult dispositions. The tall fair-haired General Buxhöwden stood leaning his back against the wall, his eyes fixed on a burning candle, and seemed not to listen nor even to wish to be thought to listen. Exactly opposite Weyrother, with his glistening wide-open eyes fixed upon him and his moustache twisted upwards, sat the ruddy Miloradovich in a military pose, his elbows turned outwards, his hands on his knees, and his shoulders raised. He remained stubbornly silent, gazing at Weyrother's face, and only turned away his eyes when the Austrian chief-of-staff finished reading. Then Miloradovich looked round significantly at the other generals. But one could not tell from that significant look whether he agreed or disagreed and was satisfied or not with the arrangements. Next to Weyrother sat Count Langeron who, with a subtle smile that never left his typically southern French face during the whole time of the reading, gazed at his delicate fingers which rapidly twirled by its corners a gold snuff-box on which was a portrait. In the middle of one of the longest sentences he stopped the rotary motion of the snuff-box, raised his head, and with inimical politeness lurking in the corners of his thin lips, interrupted Weyrother wishing to say something. But the Austrian general continuing to read, frowned angrily and jerked his elbows, as if to say: 'You can tell me your views later, but now be so good as to look at the map and listen.' Langeron lifted his eyes with an expression of perplexity, turned round to Miloradovich as if seeking an explanation, but meeting the latter's impressive but meaningless gaze, drooped his eyes sadly and again took to twirling his snuff-box.

'A geography lesson!' he muttered as if to himself, but loud enough to be heard.

Przebyszewski, with respectful but dignified politeness, held his hand to his ear towards Weyrother with the air of a man absorbed in attention. Dokhturov, a little man, sat opposite Weyrother with an assiduous and modest mien, and stooping over the outspread map conscientiously studied the dispositions and the unfamiliar locality. He asked Weyrother several times to repeat words he had not clearly heard and the difficult names of villages. Weyrother complied and Dokhturov noted them down.

When the reading which lasted more than an hour was over, Langeron again brought his snuff-box to rest and, without looking at Weyrother or at anyone in particular, began to say how difficult it was to carry out such a plan in which the enemy's position was assumed to be known, whereas it was perhaps not known, since the enemy was in movement. Langeron's objections were valid but it was obvious that their chief aim was to show General Weyrother – who had read his dispositions with as much self-confidence as if he were addressing school-children – that he had to do not with fools but with men who could teach him something in military matters.

When the monotonous sound of Weyrother's voice ceased, Kutuzov opened his eye as a miller wakes up when the soporific drone of the mill-wheel is interrupted. He listened to what Langeron said, as if remarking, 'So you are still at that silly business!' quickly closed his eye again and let his head sink still lower.

Langeron, trying as virulently as possible to sting Weyrother's vanity as author of the military plan, argued that Bonaparte might easily attack instead of being attacked, and so render the whole of this plan perfectly worthless. Weyrother met all objections with a firm and contemptuous smile, evidently prepared beforehand to meet all objections be they what they might.

'If he could attack us he would have done so to-day,' said he.

'So you think he is powerless?' said Langeron.

'He has forty thousand men at most,' replied Weyrother with the smile of a doctor to whom an old wife wishes to explain the treatment of a case.

'In that case he is inviting his doom by awaiting our attack,' said Langeron with a subtly ironical smile, again glancing round for support to Miloradovich who was near him.

But Miloradovich was at that moment evidently thinking of anything rather than of what the generals were disputing about.

'*Ma foi!*' said he, 'to-morrow we shall see all that on the battlefield.'

Weyrother again gave that smile which seemed to say that to him it was strange and ridiculous to meet objections from Russian generals, and to have to prove to them what he had not merely convinced himself of, but had also convinced the sovereign Emperors of.

'The enemy has quenched his fires and a continual noise is heard from his camp,' said he. 'What does that mean? Either he is retreating, which is the only thing we need fear, or he is changing his position.' (He smiled ironically.) 'But even if he also took up a position in the Thuerassa, he merely saves us a great deal of trouble and all our arrangements to the minutest detail remain the same.'

'How is that? . . .' began Prince Andrew, who had for long been awaiting an opportunity to express his doubts.

Kutuzov here woke up, coughed heavily, and looked round at the generals.

'Gentlemen, the dispositions for to-morrow – or rather for to-day, for it is past midnight – cannot now be altered,' said he. 'You have heard them, and we shall all do our duty. But before a battle there is nothing more important . . .' he paused, 'than to have a good sleep.'

He moved as if to rise. The generals bowed and retired. It was past midnight. Prince Andrew went out.

The council of war, at which Prince Andrew had not been able to express his opinion as he had hoped to, left on him a vague and uneasy impression. Whether Dolgorukov and Weyrother, or Kutuzov, Langeron, and the others who did not approve of the plan of attack, were right – he did not know. 'But was it really not possible for Kutuzov to state his views plainly to the Emperor?

Is it possible that on account of court and personal considerations tens of thousands of lives, and my life, *my* life,' he thought, 'must be risked?'

'Yes, it is very likely that I shall be killed to-morrow,' he thought. And suddenly at this thought of death a whole series of most distant, most intimate, memories rose in his imagination: he remembered his last parting from his father and his wife; he remembered the days when he first loved her. He thought of her pregnancy and felt sorry for her and for himself, and in a nervously emotional and softened mood he went out of the hut in which he was billeted with Nesvitsky and began to walk up and down before it.

The night was foggy and through the fog the moonlight gleamed mysteriously. 'Yes, to-morrow, to-morrow!' he thought. 'To-morrow everything may be over for me! All these memories will be no more, none of them will have any meaning for me. To-morrow perhaps, even certainly, I have a presentiment that for the first time I shall have to show all I can do.' And his fancy pictured the battle, its loss, the concentration of fighting at one point, and the hesitation of all the commanders. And then that happy moment, that Toulon for which he had so long waited, presents itself to him at last. He firmly and clearly expresses his opinion to Kutuzov, to Weyrother, and to the Emperors. All are struck by the justness of his views but no one undertakes to carry them out, so he takes a regiment, a division – stipulates that no one is to interfere with his arrangements – leads his division to the decisive point, and gains the victory alone. 'But death and suffering?' suggested another voice. Prince Andrew however did not answer that voice and went on dreaming of his triumphs. The dispositions for the next battle are planned by him alone. Nominally he is only an adjutant on Kutuzov's staff, but he does everything alone. Kutuzov is removed and he is appointed . . . 'Well and then?' asked the other voice. 'If before that you are not ten times wounded, killed, or betrayed, well . . . what then? . . .'* 'Well then,' Prince Andrew answered himself, 'I don't know what will happen and don't want to know, and can't, but if I want this – want glory, want to be known to men, want to be loved by them, it is not my fault that I want it and want nothing but that and live only for that. Yes, for that alone! I shall never tell anyone, but, oh God! what am I to do if I love nothing but fame and men's love? Death, wounds, the loss of family – I fear nothing. And precious and dear as many persons are to me – father, sister, wife – those dearest to me – yet dreadful and unnatural as it seems, I would give them all at once for a moment of glory, of triumph over men, of love from men I don't know and never shall know, for the love of these men here,' he thought, as he listened to voices in Kutuzov's courtyard. The voices were those of the orderlies who were packing up; one voice, probably a coachman's, was teasing Kutuzov's old cook whom Prince Andrew knew, and who was called Tit. He was saying, 'Tit, I say, Tit!'

'Well?' returned the old man.

'Go, Tit, thresh a bit!' said the wag.

'Oh, go to the devil!' called out a voice, drowned by the laughter of the orderlies and servants.

'All the same, I love and value nothing but triumph over them all, I value this mystic power and glory that is floating here above me in this mist!'

13

THAT same night Rostov was with a platoon on skirmishing duty in front of Bagration's detachment. His hussars were placed along the line in couples and he himself rode along the line trying to master the sleepiness that kept coming over him. An enormous space, with our army's camp fires dimly glowing in the fog, could be seen behind him, in front of him was misty darkness. Rostov could see nothing, peer as he would into that foggy distance: now something gleamed grey, now there was something black, now little lights seemed to glimmer where the enemy ought to be, now he fancied it was only something in his own eyes. His eyes kept closing, and in his fancy appeared – now the Emperor, now Denisov, and now Moscow memories – and he again hurriedly opened his eyes and saw close before him the head and ears of the horse he was riding, and sometimes when he came within six paces of them, the black figures of hussars, but in the distance was still the same misty darkness. 'Why not? ... it might easily happen,' thought Rostov, 'that the Emperor will meet me and give me an order as he would to any other officer; he'll say: "Go and find out what's there." There are many stories of his getting to know an officer in just such a chance way and attaching him to himself! What if he gave me a place near him? Oh, how I would guard him, how I would tell him the truth, how I would unmask his deceivers!' And in order to realize vividly his love and devotion to the sovereign, Rostov pictured to himself an enemy or a deceitful German, whom he would not only kill with pleasure but whom he would slap in the face before the Emperor. Suddenly a distant shout aroused him. He started and opened his eyes.

'Where am I? Oh yes, in the skirmishing line ... pass and

watchword – *shaft, Olmütz*. What a nuisance that our squadron will be in reserve to-morrow,' he thought. 'I'll ask leave to go to the front, this may be my only chance of seeing the Emperor. It won't be long now before I am off duty. I'll take another turn and when I get back I'll go to the general and ask him.' He readjusted himself in the saddle and touched up his horse to ride once more round his hussars. It seemed to him that it was getting lighter. To the left he saw a sloping descent lit up, and facing it a black knoll that seemed as steep as a wall. On this knoll there was a white patch that Rostov could not at all make out: was it a glade in the wood lit up by the moon, or some unmelted snow, or some white houses? He even thought something moved on that white spot. 'I expect it's snow . . . that spot . . . a spot – *une tache*,' he thought. 'There now . . . it's not a *tache* . . . Natasha . . . sister, black eyes . . . Na . . . tasha . . . (won't she be surprised when I tell her how I've seen the Emperor?) Natasha . . . take my *sabretache* . . .' – 'Keep to the right, your honour, there are bushes here,' came the voice of an hussar past whom Rostov was riding in the act of falling asleep. Rostov lifted his head that had sunk almost to his horse's mane and pulled up beside the hussar. He was succumbing to irresistible, youthful, childish drowsiness. 'But what was I thinking? I mustn't forget. How I shall speak to the Emperor? No, that's not it – that's to-morrow. Oh yes! Na-tasha . . . *sabretache* . . . sabre them . . . Whom? The hussars . . . Ah, the hussars with moustaches. Along the Tverskaya Street rode that hussar with moustaches . . . I thought about him too just opposite Guryev's house . . . Old Guryev . . . Oh, but Denisov's a fine fellow. But that's all nonsense. The chief thing is that the Emperor is here. How he looked at me and wished to say something, but dared not . . . No, it was I who dared not. But that's nonsense, the chief thing is not to forget the important thing I was thinking of. Yes, Na-tasha, *sabretache*, oh, yes, yes! That's right!' And his head once more sank to his horse's neck. All at once it seemed to him that he was being fired at. 'What? What? What? . . . Cut them down! What? . . .' said Rostov, waking up. At the moment he opened his eyes he heard in front of him, where the enemy was, the long-drawn shouts of thousands of voices. His horse and the horse of the hussar near him pricked their ears at these shouts. Over there, where the shouting came from, a fire flared up and went out again, then another, and all along the French line on the hill fires flared up and the shouting grew louder and louder. Rostov could hear the sound of French words but could not distinguish them. The din of many voices was too great; all he could hear was: 'ahahah!' and 'rrrr!'

'What's that? What do you make of it?' said Rostov to the hussar beside him. 'That must be the enemy's camp!'

The hussar did not reply.

'Why, don't you hear it?' Rostov asked again, after waiting for a reply.

'Who can tell, your honour?' replied the hussar reluctantly.

'From the direction it must be the enemy,' repeated Rostov.

'It may be him or it may be nothing,' muttered the hussar. 'It's dark . . . Steady!' he cried to his fidgeting horse.

Rostov's horse was also getting restive: it pawed the frozen ground, pricking its ears at the noise and looking at the lights. The shouting grew still louder and merged into a general roar that only an army of several thousand men could produce. The lights spread farther and farther, probably along the line of the French camp. Rostov no longer wanted to sleep. The gay triumphant shouting of the enemy army had a stimulating effect on him. '*Vive l'Empereur! l'Empereur!*' he now heard distinctly.

'They can't be far off, probably just beyond the stream,' he said to the hussar beside him.

The hussar only sighed without replying, and coughed angrily. The sound of horse's hoofs approaching at a trot along the line of hussars was heard, and out of the foggy darkness the figure of a sergeant of hussars suddenly appeared, looming huge as an elephant.

'Your honour, the generals!' said the sergeant, riding up to Rostov.

Rostov, still looking round towards the fires and the shouts, rode with the sergeant to meet some mounted men who were riding along the line. One was on a white horse. Prince Bagration and Prince Dolgorukov with their adjutants had come to witness the curious phenomenon of the lights and shouts in the enemy's camp. Rostov rode up to Bagration, reported to him, and then joined the adjutants listening to what the generals were saying.

'Believe me,' said Prince Dolgorukov, addressing Bagration, 'it is nothing but a trick! He has retreated and ordered the rearguards to kindle fires and make a noise to deceive us.'

'Hardly,' said Bagration. 'I saw them this evening on that knoll; if they had retreated they would have withdrawn from that too . . . Officer!' said Bagration to Rostov, 'are the enemy's skirmishers still there?'

'They were there this evening, but now I don't know, your Excellency. Shall I go with some of my hussars to see?' replied Rostov.

Bagration stopped, and before replying tried to see Rostov's face in the mist.

'Well, go and see,' he said, after a pause.

'Yes, sir.'

Rostov spurred his horse, called to Sergeant Fedchenko and two other hussars, told them to follow him, and trotted downhill in the direction from which the shouting came. He felt both frightened and pleased to be riding alone with three hussars into that mysterious and dangerous misty distance where no one had been before him. Bagration called to him from the hill not to go beyond the stream, but Rostov pretended not to hear him and did not stop but rode on and on, continually mistaking bushes for trees and gullies for men, and continually discovering his mistakes. Having descended the hill at a trot he no longer saw either our own or the enemy's fires, but heard the shouting of the French more loudly and distinctly. In the valley he saw before him something like a river, but when he reached it he found it was a road. Having come out onto the road he reined in his horse, hesitating whether to ride along it or cross it and ride over the black field up the hill-side. To keep to the road which gleamed white in the mist would have been safer because it would be easier to see people coming along it. 'Follow me!' said he, crossed the road, and began riding up the hill at a gallop towards the point where the French pickets had been standing that evening.

'Your honour, there he is!' cried one of the hussars behind him. And before Rostov had time to make out what the black thing was that had suddenly appeared in the fog, there was a flash followed by a report, and a bullet whizzing high up in the mist with a plaintive sound passed out of hearing. Another musket missed fire but flashed in the pan. Rostov turned his horse and galloped back. Four more reports followed at intervals, and the bullets passed somewhere in the fog singing in different tones. Rostov reined in his horse, whose spirits had risen like his own at the firing, and went back at a foot-pace. 'Well, some more! Some more!' a merry voice was saying in his soul. But no more shots came.

Only when approaching Bagration did Rostov let his horse gallop again, and with his hand at the salute rode up to the general.

Dolgorukov was still insisting that the French had retreated and had only lit fires to deceive us.

'What does that prove?' he was saying as Rostov rode up. 'They might retreat and leave the pickets.'

'It's plain they have not all gone yet, Prince,' said Bagration. 'Wait till to-morrow morning, we'll find out everything to-morrow.'

'The picket is still on the hill, your Excellency, just where it was in the evening,' reported Rostov, stooping forward with his hand at the salute and unable to repress the smile of delight induced by his ride and especially by the sound of the bullets.

'Very good, very good,' said Bagration. 'Thank you, officer.'

'Your Excellency,' said Rostov, 'may I ask a favour?'

'What is it?'

'To-morrow our squadron is to be in reserve. May I ask to be attached to the first squadron?'

'What's your name?'

'Count Rostov.'

'Oh, very well, you may stay in attendance on me.'

'Count Ilya Rostov's son?' asked Dolgorukov.

But Rostov did not reply.

'Then I may reckon on it, your Excellency?'

'I will give the order.'

'To-morrow very likely I may be sent with some message to the Emperor,' thought Rostov. 'Thank God!'

The fires and shouting in the enemy's army were occasioned by the fact that while Napoleon's proclamation was being read to the troops the Emperor himself rode round his bivouacs. The soldiers on seeing him lit wisps of straw and ran after him shouting, 'Vive l'Empereur!' Napoleon's proclamation was as follows:

Soldiers! The Russian army is advancing against you to avenge the Austrian army of Ulm. They are the same battalions you broke at Hollabrünn* and have pursued ever since to this place. The position we occupy is a strong one, and while they are marching to go round me on the right they will expose a flank to me. Soldiers! I will myself direct your battalions. I will keep out of fire if you with your habitual valour carry disorder and confusion into the enemy's ranks, but should victory be in doubt even for a moment, you will see your Emperor exposing himself to the first blows of the enemy, for there must be no doubt of victory, especially on this day when what is at stake is the honour of the French infantry, so necessary to the honour of our nation.

Do not break your ranks on the plea of removing the wounded! Let every man be fully imbued with the thought that we must defeat these hirelings of England, inspired by such hatred of our nation! This victory will conclude our campaign and we can return to winter quarters, where fresh French troops who are being raised in France will join us, and the peace I shall conclude will be worthy of my people, of you, and of myself.

Napoleon.

At five in the morning it was still quite dark. The troops of the centre, the reserves, and Bagration's right flank, had not yet moved, but on the left flank the columns of infantry, cavalry, and artillery which were to be the first to descend the heights to attack the French right flank and drive it into the Bohemian mountains according to plan, were already up and astir. The smoke of the camp-fires, into which they were throwing everything superfluous, made the eyes smart! It was cold and dark. The officers were hurriedly drinking tea and breakfasting, the soldiers, munching biscuit and beating a tattoo with their feet to warm themselves, gathering round the fires throwing into the flames the remains of sheds, chairs, tables, wheels, tubs, and everything that they did not want or could not carry away with them. Austrian column-guides were moving in and out among the Russian troops and served as heralds of the advance. As soon as an Austrian officer showed himself near a commanding officer's quarters the regiment began to move: the soldiers ran from the fires, thrust their pipes into their boots, their bags into the carts, got their muskets ready, and formed rank. The officers buttoned up their coats, buckled on their swords and pouches, and moved along the ranks shouting. The train-drivers and orderlies harnessed and packed the wagons and tied on the loads. The adjutants and battalion and regimental commanders mounted, crossed themselves, gave final instructions, orders, and commissions to the baggage men who remained behind, and the monotonous tramp of thousands of feet resounded. The columns moved forward without knowing where, and unable from the masses around them, the smoke, and the increasing fog, to see either the place they were leaving or that to which they were going.

A soldier on the march is hemmed in and borne along by his regiment as much as a sailor is by his ship. However far he has walked, whatever strange, unknown, and dangerous places he reaches, just as a sailor is always surrounded by the same decks, masts, and rigging of his ship, so the soldier always has around him the same comrades, the same ranks, the same sergeant-major Ivan Mitrich, the same company dog Jack, and the same commanders. The sailor rarely cares to know the latitude in which his ship is sailing, but on the day of battle – heaven knows how and whence – a stern note of which all are conscious sounds in the moral atmosphere of an army, announcing the approach of something decisive and solemn, and awakening in the men an unusual curiosity. On the day of battle the soldiers excitedly try to get beyond the interests of their regiment, they listen intently, look about, and eagerly ask concerning what is going on around them.

The fog had grown so dense that though it was growing light they could not see ten paces ahead. Bushes looked like gigantic trees and level ground like cliffs and slopes. Anywhere, on any side, one might encounter an enemy invisible ten paces off. But the columns advanced for a long time, always in the same fog, descending and ascending hills, avoiding gardens and enclosures, going over new and unknown ground, and nowhere encountering the enemy. On the contrary, the soldiers became aware that in front, behind, and on all sides, other Russian columns were moving in the same direction. Every soldier felt glad to know that to the unknown place where he was going, many many more of our men were going too.

'There now, the Kurskies have also gone past,' was being said in the ranks.

'It's wonderful what a lot of our troops have gathered, lads! Last night I looked at the camp-fires and there was no end of them. A regular Moscow!'

Though none of the column commanders rode up to the ranks or talked to the men (the commanders, as we saw at the council of war, were out of humour and dissatisfied with the affair, and so did not extend themselves to cheer the men but merely carried out the orders), yet the troops marched gaily, as they always do when going into action, especially to an attack. But when they had marched for about an hour in the dense fog, the greater part of the men had to halt, and an unpleasant consciousness of some dislocation and blunder spread through the ranks. How such a consciousness is communicated is very difficult to define, but it certainly is communicated very surely, and flows rapidly, imperceptibly, and irresponsibly, as water does in a creek. Had the Russian army been alone without any allies, it might perhaps have been a long time before this consciousness of mismanagement became a general conviction, but as it was, the disorder was readily and naturally attributed to the stupid Germans, and everyone was convinced that a dangerous muddle had been occasioned by the sausage-eaters.

'Why have we stopped? Is the way blocked? Or have we already come up against the French?'

'No, one can't hear them. They'd be firing if we had.'

'They were in hurry enough to start us, and now here we stand in the middle of a field without rhyme or reason. It's all those damned Germans' muddling! What stupid devils!'

'Yes, I'd send them on in front, but no fear, they're crowding up behind. And now here we stand hungry.'

'I say, shall we soon be clear? They say the cavalry are blocking the way,' said an officer.

'Ah, those damned Germans! They don't know their own country!' said another.

'What division are you?' shouted an adjutant, riding up.

'The Eighteenth.'

'Then why are you here? You should have gone on long ago, now you won't get there till evening.'

'What stupid orders! They don't themselves know what they are doing!' said the officer and rode off.

Then a general rode past shouting something angrily, not in Russian.

'Tafa-lafa! But what he's jabbering no one can make out,' said a soldier, mimicking the general who had ridden away. 'I'd shoot them, the scoundrels!'

'We were ordered to be at the place before nine, but we haven't got halfway. Fine orders!' was being repeated on different sides.

And the feeling of energy with which the troops had started began to turn into vexation and anger at the stupid arrangements, and at the Germans.

The cause of the confusion was that while the Austrian cavalry was moving towards our left flank, the higher command found that our centre was too far separated from our right flank and the cavalry were all ordered to turn back to the right. Several thousand cavalry crossed in front of the infantry, who had to wait.

At the front an altercation occurred between an Austrian guide and a Russian general. The general shouted a demand that the cavalry should be halted, the Austrian argued that not he, but the higher command, was to blame. The troops meanwhile stood growing listless and dispirited. After an hour's delay they at last moved on, descending the hill. The fog that was dispersing on the hill lay still more densely below, where they were descending. In front in the fog a shot was heard and then another, at first irregularly at varying intervals – trata . . . tat – and then more and more regularly and rapidly, and the action at the Goldbach stream began.

Not expecting to come on the enemy down by the stream, and having stumbled on him in the fog, hearing no encouraging word from their commanders, and with a consciousness of being too late spreading through the ranks, and above all being unable to see anything in front or around them in the thick fog, the Russians exchanged shots with the enemy lazily, and advanced and again halted, receiving no timely orders from the officers or adjutants who wandered about in the fog in those unknown surroundings unable to find their own regiments. In this way the action began for the first, second, and third columns, which had gone down into the valley. The fourth column, with which Kutuzov was, stood on the Pratzen heights.

Below, where the fight was beginning, there was still thick fog; on the higher ground it was clearing, but nothing could be seen of what was going on in front. Whether all the enemy forces were, as we supposed, six miles away, or whether they were near by in that sea of mist, no one knew till after eight o'clock.

It was nine o'clock in the morning. The fog lay unbroken like a sea down below, but higher up at the village of Schlappanitz where Napoleon stood with his marshals around him, it was quite light. Above him was a clear blue sky, and the sun's vast orb quivered like a huge, hollow, crimson float on the surface of that milky sea of mist. The whole French army, and even Napoleon himself with his staff, were not on the far side of the streams and hollows of Sokolnitz and Schlappanitz beyond which we intended to take up our position and begin the action, but were on this side, so close to our own forces that Napoleon with the naked eye could distinguish a mounted man from one on foot. Napoleon, in the blue cloak which he had worn on his Italian campaign, sat on his small grey Arab horse a little in front of his marshals. He gazed silently at the hills which seemed to rise out of the sea of mist and on which the Russian troops were moving in the distance, and he listened to the sounds of firing in the valley. Not a single muscle of his face – which in those days was still thin – moved. His gleaming eyes were fixed intently on one spot. His predictions were being justified. Part of the Russian force had already descended into the valley towards the ponds and lakes, and part were leaving these Pratzen heights which he intended to attack and regarded as the key to the position. He saw over the mist that in a hollow between two hills near the village of Pratzen, the Russian columns, their bayonets glittering, were moving continuously in one direction towards the valley and disappearing one after another into the mist. From information he had received the evening before, from the sound of wheels and footsteps heard by the outposts during the night, by the disorderly movement of the Russian columns, and from all indications, he saw clearly that the allies believed him to be far away in front of them, and that the columns moving near Pratzen constituted the centre of the Russian army, and that centre was already sufficiently weakened to be successfully attacked. But still he did not begin the engagement.

To-day was a great day for him – the anniversary of his coronation. Before dawn he had slept for a few hours, and refreshed, vigorous, and in good spirits, he mounted his horse and rode out into the field in that happy mood in which everything seems possible and everything succeeds. He sat motionless, looking at the heights visible above the mist, and his cold face wore that special look of confident, self-complacent happiness that one sees on the face of a boy happily in love. The marshals stood behind him not venturing to distract his attention. He looked now at the Pratzen heights, now at the sun floating up out of the mist.

When the sun had entirely emerged from the fog, and fields and mist were aglow with dazzling light – as if he had only awaited this to begin the action – he drew the glove from his shapely white hand, made a sign with it to the marshals, and ordered the action to begin. The marshals, accompanied by adjutants, galloped off in different directions, and a few minutes later the chief forces of the French army moved rapidly towards those Pratzen heights which were being more and more denuded by Russian troops moving down the valley to their left.

15

AT eight o'clock Kutuzov rode to Pratzen at the head of the fourth column, Miloradovich's, the one that was to take the place of Przebyszewski's and Langeron's columns which had already gone down into the valley. He greeted the men of the foremost regiment and gave them the order to march, thereby indicating that he intended to lead that column himself. When he had reached the village of Pratzen he halted. Prince Andrew was behind, among the immense number forming the commander-in-chief's suite. He was in a state of suppressed excitement and irritation, though controlledly calm as a man is at the approach of a long-awaited moment. He was firmly convinced that this was the day of his Toulon, or his bridge of Arcole. How it would come about he did not know, but he felt sure it would do so. The locality and the position of our troops were known to him as far as they could be known to anyone in our army. His own strategic plan, which obviously could not now be carried out, was forgotten. Now, entering into Weyrother's plan, Prince Andrew considered possible contingencies and formed new projects such as might call for his rapidity of perception and decision.

To the left down below in the mist, the musketry fire of unseen forces could be heard. It was there Prince Andrew thought the fight would concentrate. 'There we shall encounter difficulties, and there,' thought he, 'I shall be sent with a brigade or division, and there, standard in hand, I shall go forward and break whatever is in front of me.'

He could not look calmly at the standards of the passing battalions. Seeing them he kept thinking, 'That may be the very standard with which I shall lead the army.'

In the morning all that was left of the night-mist on the heights was a hoar frost now turning to dew, but in the valleys it still lay like a milk-white sea. Nothing was visible in the valley to the left into which our troops had descended and from whence came the sounds of firing. Above the heights was the dark clear sky, and to the right the vast orb of the sun. In front, far off on the farther shore of that sea of mist some wooded hills were discernible, and it was there the enemy probably was, for something could be descried. On the right the Guards were entering the misty region with a sound of hoofs and wheels and now and then a gleam of bayonets; to the left beyond the village similar masses of cavalry came up and disappeared in the sea of mist. In front and behind moved infantry. The commander-in-chief was standing at the end of the village letting the troops pass by him. That morning Kutuzov seemed worn and irritable. The infantry passing before him came to a halt without any command being given, apparently obstructed by something in front.

'Do order them to form into battalion columns and go round the village!' he said angrily to a general who had ridden up. 'Don't you understand, your Excellency, my dear sir, that you must not defile through narrow village streets when we are marching against the enemy?'

'I intended to re-form them beyond the village, your Excellency,' answered the general.

Kutuzov laughed bitterly.

'You'll make a fine thing of it, deploying in sight of the enemy! Very fine!'

'The enemy is still far away, your Excellency. According to the dispositions . . .'

'The dispositions!' exclaimed Kutuzov bitterly. 'Who told you that? . . . Kindly do as you are ordered.'

'Yes, sir.'

'My dear fellow,' Nesvitsky whispered to Prince Andrew, 'the old man is as surly as a dog.'

An Austrian officer in a white uniform with green plumes in

his hat galloped up to Kutuzov and asked in the Emperor's name, Had the fourth column advanced into action?

Kutuzov turned round without answering and his eye happened to fall upon Prince Andrew, who was beside him. Seeing him, Kutuzov's malevolent and caustic expression softened, as if admitting that what was being done was not his adjutant's fault, and still not answering the Austrian adjutant, he addressed Bolkonsky.

'Go, my dear fellow, and see whether the third division has passed the village. Tell it to stop and await my orders.'

Hardly had Prince Andrew started than he stopped him.

'And ask whether sharpshooters have been posted,' he added. 'What are they doing? What are they doing?' he murmured to himself, still not replying to the Austrian.

Prince Andrew galloped off to execute the order.

Overtaking the battalions that continued to advance, he stopped the third division and convinced himself that there really were no sharpshooters in front of our columns. The colonel at the head of the regiment was much surprised at the commander-in-chief's order to throw out skirmishers. He had felt perfectly sure that there were other troops in front of him and that the enemy must be at least six miles away. There was really nothing to be seen in front except a barren descent hidden by dense mist. Having given orders in the commander-in-chief's name to rectify this omission, Prince Andrew galloped back. Kutuzov, still in the same place, his stout body resting heavily in the saddle with the lassitude of age, sat yawning wearily with closed eyes. The troops were no longer moving, but stood with the butts of their muskets on the ground.

'All right, all right!' he said to Prince Andrew, and turned to a general who watch in hand was saying it was time they started as all the left flank columns had already descended.

'Plenty of time, your Excellency,' muttered Kutuzov in the midst of a yawn. 'Plenty of time,' he repeated.

Just then at a distance behind Kutuzov was heard the sound of regiments saluting, and this sound rapidly came nearer along the whole extended line of the advancing Russian columns. Evidently the person they were greeting was riding quickly. When the soldiers of the regiment in front of which Kutuzov was standing began to shout, he rode a little to one side and looked round with a frown. Along the road from Pratzen galloped what looked like a squadron of horsemen in various uniforms. Two of them rode side by side in front, at full gallop. One in a black uniform with white plumes in his hat rode a bob-tailed chestnut horse, the other who was in a white uniform, rode a black one. These were the two Emperors followed by their suites. Kutuzov, affecting the manners of an old soldier at the front, gave the command 'Attention!' and rode up to the Emperors with a salute. His whole appearance and manner was suddenly transformed. He put on the air of a subordinate who obeys without reasoning. With an affectation of respect which evidently struck Alexander unpleasantly, he rode up and saluted.

This unpleasant impression merely flitted over the young and happy face of the Emperor like a cloud of haze across a clear sky, and vanished. After his illness he looked rather thinner that day than on the field of Olmütz where Bolkonsky had seen him for the first time abroad, but there was still the same bewitching combination of majesty and mildness in his fine grey eyes, and on his delicate lips the same capacity for varying expression and the same prevalent appearance of good-hearted innocent youth.

At the Olmütz review he had seemed more majestic, here he seemed brighter and more energetic. He was slightly flushed after galloping two miles, and reining in his horse he sighed restfully and looked round at the faces of his suite, young and animated as his own. Czartoryski, Novosiltsev, Prince Volkonsky, Strogonov and the others, all richly dressed gay young men on splendid, well-groomed, fresh, only slightly heated horses, exchanging remarks and smiling, had stopped behind the Emperor. The Emperor Francis, a rosy long-faced young man, sat very erect on his handsome black horse looking about him in a leisurely and preoccupied manner. He beckoned to one of his white adjutants and asked some question – 'Most likely he is asking at what o'clock they started,' thought Prince Andrew, watching his old acquaintance with a smile he could not repress as he recalled his reception at Brünn. In the Emperors' suite were the picked young orderly officers of the Guard and line regiments, Russian and Austrian. Among them were grooms leading the Tsar's beautiful relay horses covered with embroidered cloths.

As when a window is opened a whiff of fresh air from the fields enters a stuffy room, so a whiff of youthfulness, energy, and confidence of success reached Kutuzov's cheerless staff with the galloping advent of all these brilliant young men.

'Why aren't you beginning, Michael Ilarinovich?'* said the Emperor Alexander hurriedly to Kutuzov, glancing courteously at the same time at the Emperor Francis.

'I am waiting, your Majesty,' answered Kutuzov, bending forward respectfully.

The Emperor, frowning slightly, bent his ear forward as if he had not quite heard.

'Waiting, your Majesty,' repeated Kutuzov. (Prince Andrew noted that Kutuzov's upper lip twitched unnaturally as he said the word 'waiting'). 'Not all the columns have formed up yet, your Majesty.'

The Tsar heard but obviously did not like the reply; he shrugged his rather round shoulders and glanced at Novosiltsev who was near him, as if complaining of Kutuzov.

'You know, Michael Ilarionovich, we are not on the Empress's Field where a parade does not begin till all the troops are assembled,' said the Tsar with another glance at the Emperor Francis, as if inviting him if not to join in at least to listen to what he was saying. But the Emperor Francis continued to look about him and did not listen.

'That is just why I do not begin, sire,' said Kutuzov in a resounding voice, apparently to preclude the possibility of not being heard, and again something in his face twitched – 'That is just why I do not begin, sire, because we are not on parade and not on the Empress's Field,' said he clearly and distinctly.

In the Emperor's suite all exchanged rapid looks that expressed dissatisfaction and reproach. 'Old though he may be, he should not, he certainly should not, speak like that,' their glances seemed to say.

The Tsar looked intently and observantly into Kutuzov's eye waiting to hear whether he would say anything more. But Kutuzov, with respectfully bowed head, seemed also to be waiting. The silence lasted for about a minute.

'However, if you command it, your Majesty,' said Kutuzov, lifting his head and again assuming his former tone of a dull, unreasoning, but submissive general.

He touched his horse and having called Miloradovich, the commander of the column, gave him the order to advance.

The troops again began to move, and two battalions of the Novgorod and one of the Apsheron regiment went forward past the Emperor.

As this Apsheron battalion marched by, the red-faced Miloradovich, without his greatcoat, with his Orders on his breast and an enormous tuft of plumes in his cocked hat worn on one side with its corners front and back, galloped strenuously forward, and with a dashing salute reined in his horse before the Emperor.

'God be with you, general!' said the Emperor.

'*Ma foi, sire, nous ferons ce qui sera dans notre possibilité, sire,*' he answered gaily, raising nevertheless ironic smiles among the gentlemen of the Tsar's suite by his poor French.

Miloradovich wheeled his horse sharply and stationed himself a little behind the Emperor. The Apsheron men, excited by the

Tsar's presence, passed in step before the Emperors and their suites at a bold brisk pace.

'Lads!' shouted Miloradovich in a loud self-confident and cheery voice, obviously so elated by the sound of firing, by the prospect of battle, and by the sight of the gallant Apsherons, his comrades in Suvorov's time, now passing so gallantly before the Emperors, that he forgot the sovereigns' presence. 'Lads, it's not the first village you've had to take,' cried he.

'Glad to do our best!' shouted the soldiers.

The Emperor's horse started at the sudden cry. This horse that had carried the sovereign at reviews in Russia bore him also here on the field of Austerlitz, enduring the heedless blows of his left foot and pricking its ears at the sound of shots just as it had done on the Empress's Field, not understanding the significance of the firing, nor of the nearness of the Emperor Francis's black cob, nor of all that was being said, thought, and felt that day by its rider.

The Emperor turned with a smile to one of his followers and made a remark to him, pointing to the gallant Apsherons.

16

KUTUZOV accompanied by his adjutants rode at a walking pace behind the carabineers.

When he had gone less than half a mile in the rear of the column he stopped at a solitary, deserted house that had probably once been an inn, where two roads parted. Both of them led down-hill and troops were marching along both.

The fog had begun to clear and enemy troops were already dimly visible about a mile and a half off on the opposite heights. Down below, on the left, the firing became more distinct. Kutuzov had stopped and was speaking to an Austrian general. Prince Andrew, who was a little behind and looking at them, turned to an adjutant to ask him for a field-glass.

'Look, look!' said this adjutant, looking not at the troops in the distance, but down the hill before him. 'It's the French!'

The two generals and the adjutant took hold of the field-glass, trying to snatch it from one another. The expression on all their faces suddenly changed to one of horror. The French were supposed to be a mile and a half away, but had suddenly and unexpectedly appeared just in front of us.

'It's the enemy?...No!...Yes, see it is!...for certain...But how is that?' said different voices.

With the naked eye Prince Andrew saw below them to the right, not more than five hundred paces from where Kutuzov was standing, a dense French column coming up to meet the Apsherons.

'Here it is! The decisive moment has arrived. My turn has come,' thought Prince Andrew, and striking his horse he rode up to Kutuzov.

'The Apsherons must be stopped, your Excellency,' cried he. But at that very instant a cloud of smoke spread all round, firing was heard quite close at hand and a voice of naïve terror barely two steps from Prince Andrew, shouted, 'Brothers! All's lost!' And at this voice, as if at a command, everyone began to run.

Confused and ever-increasing crowds were running back to where five minutes before the troops had passed the Emperors. Not only would it have been difficult to stop that crowd, it was even impossible not to be carried back with it oneself. Bolkonsky only tried not to lose touch with it, and looked around bewildered and unable to grasp what was happening in front of him. Nesvitsky with an angry face, red and unlike himself, was shouting to Kutuzov that if he did not ride away at once he would certainly be taken prisoner. Kutuzov remained in the same place, and without answering drew out a handkerchief. Blood was flowing from his cheek. Prince Andrew forced his way to him.

'You are wounded?' he asked, hardly able to master the trembling of his lower jaw.

'The wound is not here, it is there!' said Kutuzov, pressing the handkerchief to his wounded cheek and pointing to the fleeing soldiers. 'Stop them!' he shouted, and at the same moment, probably realizing that it was impossible to stop them, spurred his horse and rode to the right.

A fresh wave of the flying mob caught him and bore him back with it.

The troops were running in such a dense mass that once surrounded by them it was difficult to get out again. One was shouting 'Get on! Why are you hindering us?' Another in the same place turned round and fired in the air; a third was striking the horse Kutuzov himself rode. Having by a great effort got away to the left from that flood of men, Kutuzov, with his suite diminished by more than half, rode towards a sound of artillery fire near by. Having forced his way out of the crowd of fugitives, Prince Andrew, trying to keep near Kutuzov, saw on the slope of the hill amid the smoke a Russian battery that was still firing and Frenchmen running towards it. Higher up stood some Russian infantry, neither moving forward to protect the battery nor backward with the fleeing crowd. A mounted general separated himself from the infantry and approached Kutuzov. Of Kutuzov's suite only four remained. They were all pale and exchanged looks in silence.

'Stop those wretches!' gasped Kutuzov to the regimental commander, pointing to the flying soldiers; but at that instant, as if to punish him for those words, bullets flew hissing across the regiment and across Kutuzov's suite like a flock of little birds.

The French had attacked the battery, and seeing Kutuzov, were firing at him. After this volley the regimental commander clutched at his leg; several soldiers fell, and a second lieutenant who was holding the flag let it fall from his hands. It swayed and fell, but caught on the muskets of the nearest soldiers. The soldiers started firing without orders.

'Oh! Oh! Oh!' groaned Kutuzov despairingly and looked around ... 'Bolkonsky!' he whispered, his voice trembling from a consciousness of the feebleness of age, 'Bolkonsky!' he whispered pointing to the disordered battalion and at the enemy, 'What's that?'

But before he had finished speaking, Prince Andrew, feeling tears of shame and anger choking him, had already leapt from his horse and run to the standard.

'Forward, lads!' he shouted in a voice piercing as a child's.

'Here it is!' thought he, seizing the staff of the standard and hearing with pleasure the whistle of bullets evidently aimed at him. Several soldiers fell.

'Hurrah!' shouted Prince Andrew, and scarcely able to hold up the heavy standard, he ran forward with full confidence that the whole battalion would follow him.

And really he only ran a few steps alone. One soldier moved and then another and soon the whole battalion ran forward shouting 'hurrah!' and overtook him. A sergeant of the battalion ran up and took the flag that was swaying from its weight in Prince Andrew's hands, but he was immediately killed. Prince Andrew again seized the standard, and dragging it by the staff ran on with the battalion. In front he saw our artillerymen, some of whom were fighting, while others having abandoned their guns were running towards him. He also saw French infantry soldiers who were seizing the artillery horses and turning the guns round. Prince Andrew and the battalion were already within twenty paces of the cannon. He heard the whistle of bullets above him unceasingly and to right and left of him soldiers continually groaned and dropped. But he did not look at them: he looked only at what was going on in front of him – at the battery. He now saw clearly the figure of a red-haired gunner with his shako knocked awry, pulling one end of a mop while a French soldier tugged at the other. He could distinctly see the distraught yet angry expression on the faces of these two men, who evidently did not realize what they were doing.

'What are they about?' thought Prince Andrew as he gazed at them. 'Why doesn't the red-haired gunner run away as he is unarmed? Why doesn't the Frenchman stab him? He will not get away before the Frenchman remembers his bayonet and stabs him . . .'

And really another French soldier, trailing his musket, ran up to the struggling men and the fate of the red-haired gunner who had triumphantly secured the mop and still did not realize what awaited him, was about to be decided. But Prince Andrew did not see how it ended. It seemed to him as though one of the soldiers near him hit him on the head with the full swing of a bludgeon. It hurt a little, but the worst of it was that the pain distracted him and prevented his seeing what he had been looking at.

'What's this? Am I falling? My legs are giving way,' thought he, and fell on his back. He opened his eyes, hoping to see how the struggle of the Frenchmen with the gunners ended, whether the red-haired gunner had been killed or not, and whether the cannon had been captured or saved. But he saw nothing. Above him there was now nothing but the sky – the lofty sky, not clear yet still immeasurably lofty, with grey clouds gliding slowly across it. 'How quiet, peaceful, and solemn, not at all as I ran,' thought Prince Andrew '– not as we ran, shouting and fighting, not at all as the gunner and the Frenchman with frightened and angry faces struggled for the mop: how differently do those clouds glide across that lofty infinite sky! How was it I did not see that lofty sky before? And how happy I am to have found it at last! Yes! All is vanity, all falsehood, except that infinite sky. There is nothing, nothing, but that. But even it does not exist, there is nothing but quiet and peace. Thank God! . . .'

17

ON our right flank commanded by Bagration, at nine o'clock the battle had not yet begun. Not wishing to agree to Dolgorukov's demand to commence the action, and wishing to avert responsibility from himself, Prince Bagration proposed to Dolgorukov to send to inquire of the commander-in-chief. Bagration knew that as the distance between the two flanks was more than six miles, even if the messenger were not killed (which he very likely would be), and found the commander-in-chief (which would be very difficult), he would not be able to get back before evening.

Bagration cast his large, expressionless, sleepy eyes round his suite, and the boyish face of Rostov, breathless with excitement and hope, was the first to catch his eye. He sent him.

'And if I should meet his Majesty before I meet the commander-in-chief, your Excellency?' said Rostov, with his hand to his cap.

'You can give the message to his Majesty,' said Dolgorukov, hurriedly interrupting Bagration.

On being relieved from picket duty Rostov had managed to get a few hours' sleep before morning, and felt cheerful, bold, and resolute, with elasticity of movement, faith in his good fortune, and generally in that state of mind which makes everything seem possible, pleasant and easy.

All his wishes were being fulfilled that morning: there was to be a general engagement in which he was taking part, more than that, he was orderly to the bravest general, and still more, he was going with a message to Kutuzov, perhaps even to the sovereign himself. The morning was bright, he had a good horse under him, and his heart was full of joy and happiness. On receiving the order he gave his horse the rein and galloped along the line. At first he rode along the line of Bagration's troops, which had not yet advanced into action but were standing motionless; then he came to the region occupied by Uvarov's cavalry and here he noticed a stir and signs of preparation for battle; having passed Uvarov's cavalry he clearly heard the sound of cannon and musketry ahead of him. The firing grew louder and louder.

In the fresh morning air were now heard, not two or three musket shots at irregular intervals as before, followed by one or two cannon shots, but a roll of volleys of musketry from the slopes of the hill before Pratzen, interrupted by such frequent reports of cannon that sometimes several of them were not separated from one another but merged into a general roar.

He could see puffs of musketry smoke that seemed to chase one another down the hillsides, and clouds of cannon smoke rolling, spreading, and mingling with one another. He could also, by the gleam of bayonets visible through the smoke, make out moving masses of infantry and narrow lines of artillery with green caissons.

Rostov stopped his horse for a moment on a hillock to see what was going on, but strain his attention as he would he could not understand or make out anything of what was happening: there in the smoke men of some sort were moving about, and in front and behind moved lines of troops; but why, whither, and who they were, it was impossible to make out. These sights and sounds had no depressing or intimidating effect on him, on the contrary they stimulated his energy and determination.

'Go on! Go on! Give it them!' he mentally exclaimed at these sounds, and again proceeded to gallop along the line, penetrating farther and farther into the region where the army was already in action.

'How it will be there I don't know, but all will be well!' thought Rostov.

After passing some Austrian troops he noticed that the next part of the line (the Guards) was already in action.

'So much the better! I shall see it close,' he thought.

He was riding almost along the front line. A handful of men came galloping towards him. They were our Uhlans who with disordered ranks were returning from the attack. Rostov got out of their way, involuntarily noticed that one of them was bleeding, and galloped on.

'That is no business of mine,' he thought. He had not ridden many hundred yards after that before he saw to his left, across the whole width of the field, an enormous mass of cavalry in brilliant white uniforms, mounted on black horses, trotting straight towards him and across his path. Rostov put his horse to full gallop to get out of the way of these men, and he would have got clear had they continued at the same speed, but they kept increasing their pace, so that some of the horses were already galloping. Rostov heard the thud of their hoofs and the jingle of their weapons and saw their horses, their figures, and even their faces, more and more distinctly. They were our Horse Guards, advancing to attack the French cavalry that was coming to meet them.

The Horse Guards were galloping, but still holding in their horses. Rostov could already see their faces and heard the command: 'Charge!' shouted by an officer who was urging his thoroughbred to full speed. Rostov fearing to be crushed or swept into the attack on the French, galloped along the front as hard as his horse could go, but still was not in time to avoid them.

The last of the Horse Guards, a huge pock-marked fellow, frowned angrily on seeing Rostov before him, with whom he would inevitably collide. This Guardsman would certainly have bowled Rostov and his Bedouin over (Rostov felt himself quite tiny and weak compared to these gigantic men and horses) had it not occurred to Rostov to flourish his whip before the eyes of the Guardsman's horse. The heavy black horse, sixteen hands high, shied, throwing back its ears; but the pock-marked Guardsman drove his huge spurs in violently, and the horse flourishing its tail and extending its neck, galloped on yet faster. Hardly had the Horse Guards passed Rostov before he heard them shout, 'Hurrah!' and looking back saw that their foremost ranks were mixed up with some foreign cavalry with red epaulettes, probably French. He could see nothing more, for immediately afterwards cannon began firing from somewhere and smoke enveloped everything.

At that moment, as the Horse Guards having passed him disappeared in the smoke, Rostov hesitated whether to gallop after them or to go where he was sent. This was the brilliant charge of the Horse Guards that amazed the French themselves. Rostov was horrified to hear later that of all that mass of huge and handsome men, of all those brilliant, rich youths, officers and cadets, who had galloped past him on their thousand-ruble horses, only eighteen were left after the charge.

'Why should I envy them? My chance is not lost, and maybe I shall see the Emperor immediately!' thought Rostov and galloped on.

When he came level with the Foot Guards he noticed that about them and around them cannon-balls were flying, of which he was aware not so much because he heard their sound as because he saw uneasiness on the soldiers' faces, and unnatural warlike solemnity on those of the officers.

Passing behind one of the lines of a regiment of Foot Guards he heard a voice calling him by name.

'Rostov!'

'What?' he answered, not recognizing Boris.

'I say, we've been in the front line! Our regiment attacked!' said Boris with the happy smile seen on the faces of young men who have been under fire for the first time.

Rostov stopped.

'Have you?' he said. 'Well, how did it go?'

'We drove them back!' said Boris with animation, growing talkative. 'Can you imagine it?' and he began describing how the Guards having taken up their position and seeing troops before them, thought they were Austrians, and all at once discovered from the cannon-balls discharged by those troops, that they were themselves in the front line and had unexpectedly to go into action. Rostov without hearing Boris to the end spurred his horse.

'Where are you off to?' asked Boris.

'With a message to his Majesty.'

'There he is!' said Boris, thinking Rostov had said 'his Highness' and pointing to the Grand Duke who with his high shoulders and frowning brows stood a hundred paces away from them in his helmet and horse guards' jacket, shouting something to a pale, white-uniformed Austrian officer.

'But that's the Grand Duke, and I want the commander-in-chief or the Emperor,' said Rostov, and was about to spur his horse.

'Count! Count!' shouted Berg who ran up from the other side as eager as Boris. 'Count! I am wounded in my right hand' (and he showed his bleeding hand with a handkerchief tied round it) 'and I remained at the front. I held my sword in my left hand, Count. All our family – the von Bergs – have been knights!'

He said something more, but Rostov did not wait to hear it and rode away.

Having passed the Guards and traversed an empty space, Rostov to avoid again getting in front of the first line as he had done when the Horse Guards charged, followed the line of reserves, going far round the place where the hottest musket-fire and cannonade was heard. Suddenly he heard musket-fire quite close in front of him and behind our troops, where he could never have expected the enemy to be.

'What can it be?' he thought. 'The enemy in the rear of our army? Impossible!' And suddenly he was seized by a panic of fear for himself and for the issue of the whole battle. 'But be that what it may,' he reflected, 'there is no riding round it now. I must look for the commander-in-chief here, and if all is lost it is for me to perish with the rest.'

The foreboding of evil that had suddenly come over Rostov was more and more confirmed the farther he rode into the region behind the village of Pratzen, which was full of troops of all kinds.

'What does it mean? What is it? Whom are they firing at? Who is firing?' Rostov kept asking as he came up to Russian and Austrian soldiers running in confused crowds across his path.

'The devil knows! They've killed everybody! It's all up now!' he was told in Russian, German, and Czech, by the crowd of fugitives who understood what was happening as little as he did.

'Kill the Germans!' shouted one.

'May the devil take them – the traitors!'

'*Zum Henker diese Russen!*' muttered a German.

Several wounded men passed along the road, and words of abuse, screams, and groans mingled in a general hubbub, then the firing died down. Rostov learnt later that Russian and Austrian soldiers had been firing at one another.

'My God! What does it all mean?' thought he. 'And here, where at any moment the Emperor may see them ... But no, these must be only a handful of scoundrels. It will soon be over, it can't be *that*, it can't be! Only to get past them quicker, quicker!'

The idea of defeat and flight could not enter Rostov's head. Though he saw French cannon and French troops on the Pratzen heights just where he had been ordered to look for the commander-in-chief, he could not, did not wish, to believe *that*.

18

ROSTOV had been ordered to look for Kutuzov and the Emperor near the village of Pratzen. But neither they nor a single commanding officer was there, only disorganized crowds of troops of various kinds. He urged on his already weary horse to get quickly past these crowds, but the farther he went the more disorganized they were. The high road on which he had come out was thronged with calèches, carriages of all sorts, and Russian and Austrian soldiers of all arms, some wounded and some not. This whole mass droned and jostled in confusion under the dismal influence of cannon-balls flying from the French batteries stationed on the Pratzen heights.

'Where is the Emperor? Where is Kutuzov?' Rostov kept asking everyone he could stop, but got no answer from anyone.

At last seizing a soldier by his collar he forced him to answer.

'Eh, brother! They've all bolted long ago!' said the soldier, laughing for some reason and shaking himself free.

Having left that soldier who was evidently drunk, Rostov stopped the horse of a batman or groom of some important personage and began to question him. The man announced that the Tsar had been driven in a carriage at full speed about an hour before along that very road and that he was dangerously wounded.

'It can't be!' said Rostov. 'It must have been someone else.'

'I saw him myself,' replied the man with a self-confident smile of derision. 'I ought to know the Emperor by now, after the times I've seen him in Petersburg. I saw him just as I see you ... There he sat in the carriage as pale as anything. How they made the four black horses fly! Gracious me, they did rattle past! It's time I knew the imperial horses and Ilya Ivanych. I don't think Ilya drives anyone except the Tsar!'

Rostov let go of the horse and was about to ride on, when a wounded officer passing by addressed him:

'Who is it you want?' he asked. 'The commander-in-chief? He was killed by a cannon-ball – struck in the breast before our regiment.'

'Not killed – wounded!' another officer corrected him.

'Who? Kutuzov?' asked Rostov.

'Not Kutuzov, but what's his name – well, never mind ... there are not many left alive. Go that way, to that village, all the commanders are there,' said the officer, pointing to the village of Hosjeradek, and he walked on.

Rostov rode on at a foot pace not knowing why nor to whom he was now going. The Emperor was wounded, the battle lost. It was impossible to doubt it now. Rostov rode in the direction pointed out to him, in which he saw turrets and a church. What need to hurry? What was he now to say to the Tsar or to Kutuzov, even if they were alive and unwounded?

'Take this road, your honour, that way you will be killed at once!' a soldier shouted to him. 'They'd kill you there!'

'Oh, what are you talking about?' said another. 'Where is he to go? That way is nearer.'

Rostov considered, and then went in the direction where they said he would be killed.

'It's all the same now. If the Emperor is wounded, am I to try to save myself?' he thought. He rode on to the region where the greatest number of men had perished in fleeing from Pratzen. The French had not yet occupied that region, and the Russians – the uninjured and slightly wounded – had left it long ago. All about the field, like heaps of manure on well-kept plough-land, lay from ten to fifteen dead and wounded to each couple of acres. The wounded crept together in twos and threes and one could hear their distressing screams and groans, sometimes feigned – or so it seemed to Rostov. He put his horse to a trot to avoid seeing all these suffering men, and he felt afraid – not for his life, but for the courage he needed and which he knew would not stand the sight of these unfortunates.

The French, who had ceased firing at this field strewn with dead and wounded where there was no one left to fire at, on seeing an adjutant riding over it trained a gun on him and fired several shots. The sensation of those terrible whistling sounds and of the corpses around him merged in Rostov's mind into a single feeling of terror and pity for himself. He remembered his mother's last letter. 'What would she feel,' thought he, 'if she saw me here now on this field with the cannon aimed at me?'

In the village of Hosjeradek there were Russian troops retiring from the field of battle, who though still in some confusion were less disordered. The French cannon did not reach there and the musketry fire sounded far away. Here everyone clearly saw and said that the battle was lost. No one whom Rostov asked could tell him where the Emperor or Kutuzov was. Some said the report that the Emperor was wounded was correct, others that it was not, and explained the false rumour that had spread by the fact that the Emperor's carriage had really galloped from the field of battle with the pale and terrified Ober-Hofmarschal Count Tolstoy, who had ridden out to the battlefield with others in the Emperor's suite. One officer told Rostov that he had seen someone from headquarters behind the village to the left, and thither Rostov rode, not hoping to find anyone but merely to ease his conscience. When he had ridden about two miles and had passed the last of the Russian troops, he saw, near a kitchen-garden with a ditch round it, two men on horseback facing the ditch. One with a white plume in his hat seemed familiar to Rostov; the other on a beautiful chestnut horse (which Rostov fancied he had seen before) rode up to the ditch, struck his horse with his spurs, and giving it the rein leaped lightly over. Only a little earth crumbled from the bank under the horse's hind hoofs. Turning the horse sharply, he again jumped the ditch, and deferentially addressed the horseman with the white plumes, evidently suggesting that he should do the same. The rider, whose figure seemed familiar to Rostov and involuntarily riveted his attention, made a gesture of refusal with his head and hand and by that gesture Rostov instantly recognized his lamented and adored monarch.

'But it can't be he, alone in the midst of this empty field!' thought Rostov. At that moment Alexander turned his head and Rostov saw the beloved features that were so deeply engraved on his memory. The Emperor was pale, his cheeks sunken and his eyes hollow, but the charm, the mildness of his features, was all the greater. Rostov was happy in the assurance that the rumours about the Emperor being wounded were false. He was happy to be seeing him. He knew that he might, and even ought, to go straight to him and give the message Dolgorukov had ordered him to deliver.

But as a youth in love trembles, is unnerved, and dares not utter the thoughts he has dreamt of for nights, but looks around for help or a chance of delay and flight when the longed-for moment comes and he is alone with *her*, so Rostov, now that he had attained what he had longed for more than anything else in the world, did not know how to approach the Emperor, and a thousand reasons occurred to him why it would be inconvenient, unseemly, and impossible to do so.

'What! It is as if I were glad of a chance to take advantage of his being alone and despondent! A strange face may seem unpleasant or painful to him at this moment of sorrow; besides, what can I say to him now, when my heart fails me and my mouth feels dry at the mere sight of him?' Not one of the innumerable speeches addressed to the Emperor that he had composed in his imagination could he now recall. Those speeches were intended for quite other conditions, they were for the most part to be spoken at a moment of victory and triumph, generally when he was dying of wounds and the sovereign had thanked him for heroic deeds, and while dying he expressed the love his actions had proved.

'Besides how can I ask the Emperor for his instructions for the right flank now that it is nearly four o'clock and the battle is lost? No, certainly I must not approach him, I must not intrude on his reflections. Better die a thousand times than risk receiving an unkind look or bad opinion from him,' Rostov decided, and sorrowfully and with a heart full of despair he rode away, continually looking back at the Tsar, who still remained in the same attitude of indecision.

While Rostov was thus arguing with himself and riding sadly away, Captain von Toll chanced to ride to the same spot, and seeing the Emperor at once rode up to him, offered his services, and assisted him to cross the ditch on foot. The Emperor, wishing to rest and feeling unwell, sat down under an apple-tree and von Toll remained beside him. Rostov from a distance saw with envy and remorse how von Toll spoke long and warmly to the Emperor and how the Emperor, evidently weeping, covered his eyes with his hand and pressed von Toll's hand.

'And I might have been in his place!' thought Rostov, and hardly restraining his tears of pity for the Emperor, he rode on in utter despair, not knowing where to or why he was now riding.

His despair was all the greater from feeling that his own weakness was the cause of his grief.

He might . . . not only might but should, have gone up to the sovereign. It was a unique chance to show his devotion to the Emperor and he had not made use of it . . . 'What have I done?' thought he. And he turned round and galloped back to the place where he had seen the Emperor, but there was no one beyond the ditch now. Only some carts and carriages were passing by. From one of the drivers he learnt that Kutuzov's staff were not far off, in the village the vehicles were going to. Rostov followed them. In front of him walked Kutuzov's groom leading horses in horsecloths. Then came a cart, and behind that walked an old, bandy-legged domestic serf in a peaked cap and sheepskin coat.

'Tit! I say, Tit!' said the groom.

'What?' answered the old man absent-mindedly.

'Go Tit! Thresh a bit!'

'Oh, you fool!' said the old man, spitting angrily. Some time passed in silence, and then the same joke was repeated.

Before five in the evening the battle had been lost at all points. More than a hundred cannon were already in the hands of the French.

Przebyszewski and his corps had laid down their arms. Other columns after losing half their men were retreating in disorderly confused masses.

The remains of Langeron's and Dokhturov's mingled forces were crowding around the dams and banks of the ponds near the village of Augesd.

After five o'clock it was only at the Augesd dam that a hot cannonade (delivered by the French alone) was still to be heard from numerous batteries ranged on the slopes of the Pratzen heights, directed at our retreating forces.

In the rearguard Dokhturov and others, rallying some battalions, kept up a musketry fire at the French cavalry that was pursuing our troops. It was growing dusk. On the narrow Augesd dam where for so many years the old miller had been accustomed to sit in his tasselled cap peacefully angling, while his grandson, with shirtsleeves rolled up, handled the floundering silvery fish in the watering-can, on that dam over which for so many years Moravians in shaggy caps and blue jackets had peacefully driven their two-horse carts loaded with wheat and had returned dusty with flour whitening their carts – on that narrow dam amid the wagons and the cannon, under the horse's hoofs and between the wagon wheels, men disfigured by fear of death now crowded together, crushing one another, dying, stepping over the dying and killing one another, only to move on a few steps and be killed themselves in the same way.

Every ten seconds a cannon-ball flew compressing the air around, or a shell burst in the midst of that dense throng, killing some and splashing with blood those near them.

Dolokhov – now an officer – wounded in the arm, and on foot, with the regimental commander on horseback and some ten men of his company, represented all that was left of that whole regiment. Impelled by the crowd they had got wedged in at the approach to the dam and, jammed in on all sides, had stopped because a horse in front had fallen under a cannon and the crowd were dragging it out. A cannon-ball killed someone behind them, another fell in front and splashed Dolokhov with blood. The crowd, pushing forward desperately, squeezed together, moved a few steps, and again stopped.

'Move on a hundred yards and we are certainly saved, remain here another two minutes and it is certain death,' thought each one.

Dolokhov who was in the midst of the crowd forced his way to the edge of the dam, throwing two soldiers off their feet, and ran onto the slippery ice that covered the mill-pool.

'Turn this way!' he shouted, jumping over the ice which creaked under him; 'turn this way!' he shouted to those with the gun. 'It bears! . . .'

The ice bore him but it swayed and creaked, and it was plain that it would give way not only under a cannon or a crowd, but very soon even under his weight alone. The men looked at him and pressed to the bank, hesitating to step onto the ice. The general on horseback at the entrance to the dam, raised his hand and opened his mouth to address Dolokhov. Suddenly a cannon-ball hissed so low above the crowd that everyone ducked. It flopped into something moist, and the general fell from his horse in a pool of blood. Nobody gave him a look or thought of raising him.

'Get onto the ice, over the ice! Go on! Turn! Don't you hear? Go on!' innumerable voices suddenly shouted after the ball had struck the general, the men themselves not knowing what, or why, they were shouting.

One of the hindmost guns that was going onto the dam turned off onto the ice. Crowds of soldiers from the dam began running onto the frozen pond. The ice gave way under one of the foremost soldiers, and one leg slipped into the water. He tried to right himself but fell in up to his waist. The nearest soldiers shrank back, the gun-driver stopped his horse, but from behind still came the shouts: 'Onto the ice, why do you stop? Go on! Go on!' And cries of horror were heard in the crowd. The soldiers near the gun waved their arms and beat the horses to make them turn and move on. The horses moved off the bank. The ice, that had held under those on foot, collapsed in a great mass, and some forty men who were on it dashed, some forwards and some back, drowning one another.

Still the cannon-balls continued regularly to whistle and flop onto the ice and into the water, and oftenest of all among the crowd that covered the dam, the pond, and the bank.

19

ON the Pratzen heights, where he had fallen with the flagstaff in his hand, lay Prince Andrew Bolkonsky bleeding profusely and unconsciously uttering a gentle, piteous, and childlike moan.

Towards evening he ceased moaning and became quite still. He did not know how long his unconsciousness lasted. Suddenly he again felt that he was alive and suffering from a burning, lacerating pain in his head.

'Where is it, that lofty sky that I did not know till now, but saw to-day?' was his first thought. 'And I did not know this suffering either,' he thought. 'Yes, I did not know anything, anything at all till now. But where am I?'

He listened, and heard the sound of approaching horses, and voices speaking French. He opened his eyes. Above him again was the same lofty sky with clouds that had risen and were floating still higher, and between them gleamed blue infinity. He did not turn his head and did not see those who, judging by the sound of hoofs and voices, had ridden up and stopped near him.

It was Napoleon accompanied by two aides-de-camp. Bonaparte riding over the battlefield had given final orders to strengthen the batteries firing at the Augesd dam, and was looking at the killed and wounded left on the field.

'Fine men!' remarked Napoleon, looking at a dead Russian grenadier who with his face buried in the ground and a blackened nape, lay on his stomach with an already stiffened arm flung wide.

'The ammunition for the guns in position is exhausted, your Majesty,' said an adjutant who had come from the batteries that were firing at Augesd.

'Have some brought from the reserve,' said Napoleon, and having gone on a few steps he stopped before Prince Andrew, who lay on his back with the flagstaff that had been dropped beside him. (The flag had already been taken by the French as a trophy.)

'That's a fine death!' said Napoleon as he gazed at Bolkonsky.

Prince Andrew understood that this was said of him, and that it was Napoleon who said it. He heard the speaker addressed as *Sire*. But he heard the words as he might have heard the buzzing of a fly. Not only did they not interest him, but he took no notice of them and at once forgot them. His head was burning, he felt himself bleeding to death, and he saw above him the remote, lofty, and everlasting sky. He knew it was Napoleon – his hero – but at that moment Napoleon seemed to him such a small insignificant creature compared with what was passing now between himself and that lofty infinite sky with the clouds flying over it. At that moment it meant nothing to him who might be standing over him, or what was said of him; he was only glad that people were standing near him, and only wished that they would help him and bring him back to life, which seemed to him so beautiful now that he had to-day learned to understand it so differently. He collected all his strength, to stir and utter a sound. He feebly moved his leg, and uttered a weak sickly groan which aroused his own pity.

'Ah! He is alive,' said Napoleon. 'Lift this young man up and carry him to the dressing-station.'

Having said this, Napoleon rode on to meet Marshal Lannes, who, hat in hand, rode up smiling to the Emperor to congratulate him on the victory.

Prince Andrew remembered nothing more: he lost consciousness from the terrible pain of being lifted onto the stretcher, the jolting while being moved, and the probing of his wound at the dressing-station. He did not regain consciousness till late in the day, when with other wounded and captured Russian officers he was carried to the hospital. During this transfer he felt a little stronger and was to look about him and even speak.

The first words he heard on coming to his senses were those of a French convoy officer, who said rapidly:

'We must halt here: the Emperor will pass here immediately; it will please him to see these gentlemen prisoners.'

'There are so many prisoners to-day, nearly the whole Russian army, that he is probably tired of them,' said another officer.

'All the same! They say this one is the commander of all the Emperor Alexander's Guards,' said the first one, indicating a Russian officer in the white uniform of the Horse Guards.

Bolkonsky recognized Prince Repnin whom he had met in Petersburg society. Beside him stood a lad of nineteen, also a wounded officer of the Horse Guards.

Bonaparte, having come up at a gallop, stopped his horse.

'Which is the senior?' he asked, on seeing the prisoners.

They named the colonel, Prince Repnin.

'You are the commander of the Emperor Alexander's regiment of Horse Guards?' asked Napoleon.

'I commanded a squadron,' replied Repnin.

'Your regiment fulfilled its duty honourably,' said Napoleon.

'The praise of a great commander is a soldier's highest reward,' said Repnin.

'I bestow it with pleasure,' said Napoleon. 'And who is that young man beside you?'

Prince Repnin named Lieutenant Sukhtelen.

After looking at him Napoleon smiled.

'He's very young to come to meddle with us.'

'Youth is no hindrance to courage,' muttered Sukhtelen in a failing voice.

'A splendid reply!' said Napoleon. 'Young man, you will go far!'

Prince Andrew, who had also been brought forward before the

Emperor's eyes to complete the show of prisoners, could not fail to attract his attention. Napoleon apparently remembered seeing him on the battlefield, and addressing him, again used the epithet 'young man' that was connected in his memory with Prince Andrew.

'Well, and you, young man,' said he. 'How do you feel, *mon brave*?'

Though five minutes before Prince Andrew had been able to say a few words to the soldiers who were carrying him, now with his eyes fixed straight on Napoleon, he was silent ... So insignificant at that moment seemed to him all the interests that engrossed Napoleon, so mean did his hero himself with his paltry vanity and joy in victory appear, compared to the lofty, equitable, and kindly sky which he had seen and understood, that he could not answer him.

Everything seemed so futile and insignificant in comparison with the stern and solemn train of thought that weakness from loss of blood, suffering, and the nearness of death, aroused in him. Looking into Napoleon's eyes Prince Andrew thought of the insignificance of greatness, the unimportance of life which no one could understand, and the still greater unimportance of death, the meaning of which no one alive could understand or explain.

The Emperor without waiting for an answer turned away, and said to one of the officers as he went:

'Have these gentlemen attended to and taken to my bivouac; let my doctor Larrey examine their wounds. Au *revoir*, Prince Repnin!' and he spurred his horse and galloped away.

His face shone with self-satisfaction and pleasure.

The soldiers who had carried Prince Andrew had noticed and taken the little gold icon Princess Mary had hung round her brother's neck, but seeing the favour the Emperor showed the prisoners, they now hastened to return the holy image.

Prince Andrew did not see how and by whom it was replaced, but the little icon with its thin gold chain suddenly appeared upon his chest outside his uniform.

'It would be good,' thought Prince Andrew, glancing at the icon his sister had hung round his neck with such emotion and reverence, 'it would be good if everything were as clear and simple as it seems to Mary. How good it would be to know where to seek for help in this life, and what to expect after it beyond the grave! How happy and calm I should be if I could now say: "Lord, have mercy on me!" ... but to whom should I say that? Either to a Power indefinable, incomprehensible, which I not only cannot address but which I cannot even express in words – the Great All or Nothing –' said he to himself, 'or to that God who has been sewn into this amulet by Mary! There is nothing certain, nothing at all except the unimportance of everything I understand, and the greatness of something incomprehensible but all-important.'

The stretchers moved on. At every jolt he again felt unendurable pain; his feverishness increased and he grew delirious. Visions of his father, wife, sister, and future son, and the tenderness he had felt the night before the battle, the figure of the insignificant little Napoleon, and above all this the lofty sky, formed the chief subjects of his delirious fancies.

The quiet home life and peaceful happiness of Bald Hills presented itself to him. He was already enjoying that happiness when that little Napoleon had suddenly appeared with his unsympathizing look of short-sighted delight at the misery of others, and doubts and torments had followed, and only the heavens promised peace. Towards morning all these dreams melted and merged into the chaos and darkness of unconsciousness and oblivion, which in the opinion of Napoleon's doctor, Larrey, was much more likely to end in death than in convalescence.

'He is a nervous, bilious subject,' said Larrey, 'and will not recover.'

And Prince Andrew, with others fatally wounded, was left to the care of the inhabitants of the district.

END OF BOOK ONE

WAR AND PEACE

*

BOOK TWO

PART ONE

1

Early in the year 1806 Nicholas Rostov returned home on leave. Denisov was going home to Voronezh and Rostov persuaded him to travel with him as far as Moscow and to stay with him there. Meeting a comrade at the last post-station but one before Moscow, Denisov had drunk three bottles of wine with him, and despite the jolting ruts across the snow-covered road, did not once wake up, on the way to Moscow, but lay at the bottom of the sledge beside Rostov, who grew more and more impatient the nearer they got to Moscow.

'How much longer? How much longer? Oh, these insufferable streets, shops, bakers' signboards, street lamps and sledges!' thought Rostov when their leave-permits had been passed at the town gate, and they had entered Moscow.

'Denisov! We're here! He's asleep,' he added, leaning forward with his whole body as if in that position he hoped to hasten the speed of the sledge.

Denisov gave no answer.

'There's the corner at the cross-roads, where the cabman Zakhar has his stand, and there's Zakhar himself and still the same horse! And here's the little shop where we used to buy gingerbread! Can't you hurry up? Now then!'

'Which house is it?' asked the driver.

'Why that one, right at the end, the big one. Don't you see? That's our house,' said Rostov. 'Of course it's our house! Denisov, Denisov! We're almost there!'

Denisov raised his head, coughed, and made no answer.

'Dmitri,' said Rostov to his valet on the box, 'those lights are in our house, aren't they?'

'Yes, sir, and there's a light in your father's study.'

'Then they've not gone to bed yet? What do you think? Mind now, don't forget to put out my new coat,' added Rostov, fingering his new moustache. 'Now then, get on,' he shouted to the driver. 'Do wake up, Vaska,' he went on, turning to Denisov, whose head was again nodding. 'Come, get on! You shall have three rubles for vodka – get on!' Rostov shouted, when the sledge was only three houses from his door. It seemed to him the horses were not moving at all. At last the sledge bore to the right, drew up at an entrance, and Rostov saw overhead the old familiar cornice with a bit of plaster broken off, the porch, and the post by the side of the pavement. He sprang out before the sledge stopped, and ran into the hall. The house stood cold and silent, as if quite regardless of who had come to it. There was no one in the hall. 'Oh God! Is everyone all right?' he thought, stopping for a moment with a sinking heart and then immediately starting to run along the hall and up the warped steps of the familiar staircase. The well-known old door-handle, which always angered the countess when it was not properly cleaned, turned as loosely as ever. A solitary tallow candle burnt in the ante-room.

Old Michael was asleep on the chest. Prokofy, the footman, who was so strong that he could lift the back of the carriage from behind, sat plaiting slippers out of cloth selvedges. He looked up at the opening door and his expression of sleepy indifference suddenly changed to one of delighted amazement.

'Gracious heavens! The young Count!' he cried, recognizing his young master. 'Can it be? My treasure!' and Prokofy, trembling with excitement rushed towards the drawing-room door, probably in order to announce him, but changing his mind came back and stooped to kiss the young man's shoulder.

'All well?' asked Rostov, drawing away his arm.

'Yes, God be thanked! Yes! They've just finished supper. Let me have a look at you, your Excellency.'

'Is everything quite all right?'

'The Lord be thanked, yes!'

Rostov, who had completely forgotten Denisov, not wishing any one to forestall him, threw off his fur coat and ran on tiptoe through the large dark ball-room. All was the same: there were the same old card-tables and the same chandelier with a cover over it; but someone had already seen the young master, and before he had reached the drawing-room something flew out from a side door like a tornado and began hugging and kissing him. Another and yet another creature of the same kind sprang from a second door and a third; more hugging, more kissing, more outcries, and tears of joy. He could not distinguish which was papa, which Natasha, and which Petya. Everyone shouted, talked, and kissed him at the same time. Only his mother was not there, he noticed that.

'And I did not know ... Nicholas ... My darling ... !'

'Here he is ... our own ... Kolya, dear fellow ... How he has changed! ... Where are the candles? ... Tea! ...'

'And me, kiss me!'

'Dearest . . . and me!'

Sonya, Natasha, Petya, Anna Mikhaylovna, Vera, and the old count were all hugging him, and the serfs, men and maids, flocked into the room, exclaiming and oh-ing and ah-ing.

Petya, clinging to his legs, kept shouting, 'And me too!'

Natasha, after she had pulled him down towards her and covered his face with kisses, holding him tight by the skirt of his coat, sprang away and pranced up and down in one place like a goat, and shrieked piercingly.

All around were loving eyes glistening with tears of joy, and all around were lips seeking a kiss.

Sonya too, all rosy red, clung to his arm and, radiant with bliss, looked eagerly towards his eyes, waiting for the look for which she longed. Sonya now was sixteen and she was very pretty, especially at this moment of happy rapturous excitement. She gazed at him, not taking her eyes off him, and smiling and holding her breath. He gave her a grateful look, but was still expectant and looking for someone. The old countess had not yet come. But now steps were heard at the door, steps so rapid that they could hardly be his mother's.

Yet it was she, dressed in a new gown which he did not know, made since he had left. All the others let him go, and he ran to her. When they met she fell on his breast, sobbing. She could not lift her face, but only pressed it to the cold braiding of his hussar's jacket. Denisov, who had come into the room unnoticed by anyone, stood there and wiped his eyes at the sight.

'Vasili Denisov, your son's friend,' he said, introducing himself to the count who was looking inquiringly at him.

'You are most welcome! I know, I know,' said the count, kissing and embracing Denisov. 'Nicholas wrote us . . . Natasha, Vera, look! Here is Denisov!'

The same happy rapturous faces turned to the shaggy figure of Denisov.

'Darling Denisov!' screamed Natasha beside herself with rapture, springing to him, putting her arms round him, and kissing him. This escapade made everybody feel confused. Denisov blushed too, but smiled, and taking Natasha's hand kissed it.

Denisov was shown to the room prepared for him, and the Rostovs all gathered round Nicholas in the sitting-room.

The old countess, not letting go of his hand and kissing it every moment, sat beside him: the rest, crowding round him, watched every movement, word, or look of his, never taking their blissfully adoring eyes off him. His brother and sisters struggled for the

313

places nearest to him, and disputed with one another who should bring him his tea, handkerchief, and pipe.

Rostov was very happy in the love they showed him; but the first moment of meeting had been so beatific that his present joy seemed insufficient, and he kept expecting something more, more, and yet more.

Next morning, after the fatigues of their journey, the travellers slept till ten o'clock.

In the room next their bedroom there was a confusion of sabres, satchels, sabretaches, open portmanteaus, and dirty boots. Two freshly cleaned pairs with spurs had just been placed by the wall. The servants were bringing in jugs and basins, hot water for shaving, and their well-brushed clothes. There was a masculine odour and a smell of tobacco.

'Hallo, Gwishka – my pipe!' came Vasili Denisov's husky voice. 'Wostov, get up!'

Rostov, rubbing his eyes that seemed glued together, raised his dishevelled head from the hot pillow.

'Why, is it late?'

'Late! It's nearly ten o'clock,' answered Natasha's voice. A rustle of starched petticoats and the whispering and laughter of girls' voices came from the adjoining room. The door was opened a crack, and there was a glimpse of something blue, of ribbons, black hair and merry faces. It was Natasha, Sonya, and Petya, who had come to see whether they were getting up.

'Nicholas! Get up!' Natasha's voice was again heard at the door. 'Directly!'

Meanwhile Petya having found and seized the sabres in the outer room, with the delight boys feel at the sight of a military elder brother, and forgetting that it was unbecoming for the girls to see men undressed, opened the bedroom door.

'Is this your sabre?' he shouted.

The girls sprang aside. Denisov hid his hairy legs under the blanket, looking with a scared face at his comrade for help. The door having let Petya in, closed again. A sound of laughter came from behind it.

'Nicholas! Come out in your dressing-gown!' said Natasha's voice.

'Is this your sabre?' asked Petya, 'Or is it yours?' he said, addressing the black-moustached Denisov with servile deference.

Rostov hurriedly put something on his feet, drew on his dressing-gown, and went out. Natasha had put on one spurred boot and was just getting her foot into the other. Sonya when he came in was twirling round and was about to expand her dress into a balloon and sit down. They were dressed alike in new pale-blue frocks, and were both fresh, rosy, and bright. Sonya ran away, but Natasha, taking her brother's arm, led him into the sitting-room, where they began talking. They hardly gave one another time to ask questions and give replies concerning a thousand little matters which could not interest anyone but themselves. Natasha laughed at every word he said or that she said herself, not because what they were saying was amusing, but because she felt happy and was unable to control her joy which expressed itself by laughter.

'Oh, how nice, how splendid!' she said to everything.

Rostov felt that under the influence of the warm rays of love, that childlike smile which had not once appeared on his face since he left home, now for the first time after eighteen months again brightened his soul and his face.

'No, but listen,' she said, 'now you are quite a man, aren't you? I'm awfully glad you're my brother.' She touched his moustache. 'I want to know what you men are like. Are you the same as we? No?'

'Why did Sonya run away?' asked Rostov.

'Ah, yes! That's a whole long story! How are you going to speak to her – *Thou* or *you*?'

'As may happen,' said Rostov.

'No, call her *you*, please! I'll tell you all about it some other time. No, I'll tell you now. You know Sonya's my dearest friend. Such a friend that I burnt my arm for her sake. Look here!'

She pulled up her muslin sleeve and showed him a red scar on her long, slender, delicate arm, high above the elbow on the part that is covered even by a ball-dress.

'I burnt this to prove my love for her. I just heated a ruler in the fire and pressed it there!'

Sitting on the sofa with the little cushions on its arms, in what used to be his old schoolroom, and looking into Natasha's wildly bright eyes, Rostov re-entered that world of home and childhood which had no meaning for anyone else, but gave him some of the best joys of his life; and the burning of an arm with a ruler as a proof of love did not seem to him senseless, he understood and was not surprised at it.

'Well, and is that all?' he asked.

'We are such friends, such friends! All that ruler business was just nonsense, but we are friends for ever. She if she loves anyone, does it for life, but I don't understand that, I forget quickly.'

'Well, what then?'

'Well, she loves me and you like that.'

Natasha suddenly flushed.

'Why, you remember before you went away? . . . Well, she says you are to forget all that . . . She says: "I shall love him always, but let him be free." Isn't that lovely and noble! Yes, very noble? Isn't it?' asked Natasha so seriously and excitedly that it was evident that what she was now saying she had talked of before with tears.

Rostov became thoughtful.

'I never go back on my word,' he said. 'Besides, Sonya is so charming that only a fool would renounce such happiness.'

'No, no!' cried Natasha, 'she and I have already talked it over. We knew you'd say so. But it won't do, because you see, if you say that – if you consider yourself bound by your promise – it will seem as if she had not meant it seriously. It makes it as if you were marrying her because you must, and that wouldn't do at all.'

Rostov saw that it had been well considered by them. Sonya had already struck him by her beauty on the preceding day. To-day, when he had caught a glimpse of her, she seemed still more lovely. She was a charming girl of sixteen, evidently passionately in love with him (he did not doubt that for an instant). Why should he not love her now, and even marry her, Rostov thought, but just now there were so many other pleasures and interests before him! 'Yes, they have taken a wise decision,' he thought. 'I must remain free.'

'Well then, that's excellent,' said he. 'We'll talk it over later on. Oh, how glad I am to have you!'

'Well, and are you still true to Boris?' he continued.

'Oh, what nonsense!' cried Natasha laughing. 'I don't think about him or anyone else, and I don't want anything of the kind.'

'Dear me! Then what are you up to now?'

'Now?' repeated Natasha, and a happy smile lit up her face. 'Have you seen Duport?'

'No.'

'Not seen Duport – the famous dancer? Well then, you won't understand. That's what I'm up to.'

Curving her arms, Natasha held out her skirt as dancers do, ran back a few steps, turned, cut a caper, brought her little feet sharply together, and made some steps on the very tips of her toes.

'See, I'm standing! See!' she said, but could not maintain herself on her toes any longer. 'So that's what I'm up to! I'll never marry anyone, but will be a dancer. Only don't tell anyone.'

Rostov laughed so loud and merrily that Denisov in the bedroom felt envious and Natasha could not help joining in.

'No, but don't you think it's nice?' she kept repeating.

'Nice! And so you no longer wish to marry Boris?'

Natasha flared up. 'I don't want to marry anyone. And I'll tell him so when I see him!'

'Dear me!' said Rostov.

'But that's all rubbish,' Natasha chattered on. 'And is Denisov nice?' she asked.

'Yes, indeed!'

'Oh, well then, good-bye: go and dress. Is he very terrible, Denisov?'

'Why terrible?' asked Nicholas. 'No, Vaska is a splendid fellow.'

'You call him Vaska? That's funny! And is he very nice?'

'Very.'

'Well then, be quick. We'll all have breakfast together.'

And Natasha rose and went out of the room on tiptoe like a ballet dancer, but smiling as only happy girls of fifteen can smile. When Rostov met Sonya in the drawing-room he reddened. He did not know how to behave with her. The evening before, in the first happy moment of meeting, they had kissed each other, but to-day they felt it could not be done; he felt that everybody, including his mother and sisters, was looking inquiringly at him and watching to see how he would behave with her. He kissed her hand and addressed her not as *thou* but as *you* – Sonya. But their eyes met and said *thou*, and exchanged tender kisses. Her looks asked him to forgive her for having dared, by Natasha's intermediacy, to remind him of his promise, and then thanked him for his love. His looks thanked her for offering him his freedom, and told her that one way or other he would never cease to love her, for that would be impossible.

'How strange it is,' said Vera, selecting a moment when all were silent, 'that Sonya and Nicholas now say *you* to one another and meet like strangers.'

Vera's remark was correct as her remarks always were, but like most of her observations it made everyone feel uncomfortable, not only Sonya, Nicholas, and Natasha, but even the old countess, who – dreading this love affair which might hinder Nicholas from making a brilliant match – blushed like a girl.

Denisov to Rostov's surprise appeared in the drawing-room with pomaded hair, perfumed, and in a new uniform, looking just as smart as he made himself when going into battle, and he was more amiable to the ladies and gentlemen than Rostov had ever expected to see him.

2

ON his return to Moscow from the army Nicholas Rostov was welcomed by his home circle as the best of sons, a hero, and their darling Nikolenka, by his relations as a charming, attractive, and polite young man, by his acquaintances as a handsome lieutenant of hussars, a good dancer, and one of the best matches in the city.

The Rostovs knew everybody in Moscow. The old count had money enough that year, as all his estates had been re-mortgaged, and so Nicholas, acquiring a trotter of his own, very stylish riding-breeches of the latest cut, such as no one else yet had in Moscow, and boots of the latest fashion with extremely pointed toes and small silver spurs, passed his time very gaily. After a short period of adapting himself to the old conditions of life, Nicholas found it very pleasant to be at home again. He felt that he had grown up and matured very much. His despair at failing in a Scripture examination, his borrowing money from Gavril to pay a sledge-driver, his kissing Sonya on the sly – he now recalled all this as childishness he had left immeasurably behind. Now he was a lieutenant of hussars, in a jacket laced with silver, and wearing the cross of St George awarded to soldiers for bravery in action, and in the company of well-known, elderly and respected racing-men was training a trotter of his own for a race. He knew a lady on one of the boulevards whom he visited of an evening. He led the mazurka at the Arkharovs' ball, talked about the war with Field-Marshal Kamensky, visited the English Club,* and was on intimate terms with a colonel of forty to whom Denisov had introduced him.

His passion for the Emperor had cooled somewhat in Moscow. But still, as he did not see him and had no opportunity of seeing him, he often spoke about him and about his love for him, letting it be understood that he had not told all and that there was some-thing in his feelings for the Emperor not everyone could under-stand, and with his whole soul he shared the adoration then com-mon in Moscow for the Emperor, who was spoken of as the 'angel incarnate'.

During Rostov's short stay in Moscow before rejoining the army he did not draw closer to Sonya, but rather drifted away from her. She was very pretty and sweet, and evidently deeply in love with him, but he was at the period of youth when there seems so much to do that there is *no time* for that sort of thing and a young man fears to bind himself, and prizes his freedom which he needs for so many other things. When he thought of Sonya during this stay in

Moscow he said to himself, 'Ah, there will be, and there are, many more such girls somewhere whom I do not yet know. There will be time enough to think about love when I want to, but now I have no time.' Besides it seemed to him that the society of women was rather derogatory to his manhood. He went to balls and into ladies' society with an affectation of doing so against his will. The races, the English Club, sprees with Denisov and visits to a certain house – that was another matter and quite the thing for a dashing young hussar!

At the beginning of March old Count Ilya Rostov was very busy arranging a dinner in honour of Prince Bagration at the English Club.

The count walked up and down the hall in his dressing-gown, giving orders to the club steward and to the famous Feoktist, the club's head cook, about asparagus, fresh cucumbers, strawberries, veal, and fish for this dinner. The count had been a member and on the committee of the club from the day it was founded. To him the club entrusted the arrangement of the festival in honour of Bagration, for few men knew so well how to arrange a feast on an open-handed, hospitable scale, and still fewer men would be so well able and willing to make up out of their own resources what might be needed for the success of the fête. The club cook and the steward listened to the count's orders with pleased faces, for they knew that under no other management could they so easily extract a good profit for themselves from a dinner costing several thousand rubles.

'Well then, mind and have cocks' combs in the turtle soup, you know!'

'Shall we have three cold dishes then?' asked the cook.

The count considered.

'We can't have less – yes, three . . . the mayonnaise, that's one,' said he, bending down a finger.

'Then am I to order those large sterlets?' asked the steward.

'Yes, it can't be helped if they won't take less. Ah, dear me! I was forgetting. We must have another entrée. Ah, goodness gracious!' he clutched at his head. 'Who is going to get me the flowers? Dmitri! Eh, Dmitri! Gallop off to our Moscow estate,' he said to the factotum who appeared at his call. 'Hurry off and tell Maksim, the gardener, to set the serfs to work. Say that everything out of the hothouses must be brought here well wrapped up in felt: I must have two hundred pots here on Friday.'

Having given several more orders he was about to go to his 'little Countess' to have a rest, but remembering something else of importance, he returned again, called back the cook and the club steward, and again began giving orders. A light footstep and the clinking of spurs were heard at the door, and the young count, handsome, rosy, with a dark little moustache, evidently rested and made sleeker by his easy life in Moscow, entered the room.

'Ah, my boy, my head's in a whirl!' said the old man with a smile as if he felt a little confused before his son. 'Now if you would only help a bit! I must have singers too. I shall have my own orchestra, but shouldn't we get the gipsy singers as well? You military men like that sort of thing.'

'Really, papa, I believe Prince Bagration worried himself less before the battle of Schön Grabern than you do now,' said his son with a smile.

The old count pretended to be angry.

'Yes, you talk, but try it yourself!'

And the count turned to the cook, who with a shrewd and respectful expression, looked observantly and sympathetically at the father and son.

'What have the young people come to nowadays, eh, Feoktist?' said he ' – laughing at us old fellows!'

'That's so, your Excellency, all they have to do is to eat a good dinner, but providing it and serving it all up, that's not their business!'

'That's it, that's it!' exclaimed the count, and gaily seizing his son by both hands he cried, 'Now I've got you, so take the sledge and pair at once, and go to Bezukhov's, and tell him "Count Ilya has sent you to ask for strawberries and fresh pineapples." We can't get them from anyone else. He's not there himself, so you'll have to go in and ask the princesses; and from there go on to the Rasgulyay – the coachman Ipatka knows – and look up the gipsy Ilyushka, the one who danced at Count Orlov's, you remember, in a white Cossack coat, and bring him along to me.'

'And am I to bring the gipsy girls along with him?' asked Nicholas laughing. 'Dear, dear!' . . .

At that moment, with noiseless footsteps and with the business-like, preoccupied, yet meekly Christian look which never left her face, Anna Mikhaylovna entered the hall. Though she came upon the count in his dressing-gown every day, he invariably became confused and begged her to excuse his costume.

'No matter at all, my dear Count,' she said, meekly closing her eyes. 'But I'll go to Bezukhov's myself. Pierre has arrived, and now we shall get anything we want from his hothouses. I have to see him in any case. He has forwarded me a letter from Boris. Thank God, Boris is now on the staff.'

The count was delighted at Anna Mikhaylovna's taking upon

herself one of his commissions, and ordered the small closed carriage for her.

'Tell Bezukhov to come. I'll put his name down. Is his wife with him?' he asked.

Anna Mikhaylovna turned up her eyes, and profound sadness was depicted on her face.

'Ah, dear friend, he is very unfortunate,' she said. 'If what we hear is true, it is dreadful. How little we dreamed of such a thing when we were rejoicing at his happiness! And such a lofty angelic soul as young Bezukhov! Yes, I pity him from my heart, and shall try to give him what consolation I can.'

'Wh-what is the matter?' asked both the young and old Rostov.

Anna Mikhaylovna sighed deeply.

'Dolokhov, Mary Ivanovna's son,' she said in a mysterious whisper, 'has compromised her completely, they say. Pierre took him up, invited him to his house in Petersburg, and now . . . she has come here and that dare-devil after her!' said Anna Mikhaylovna, wishing to show her sympathy for Pierre, but by involuntary intonations and a half-smile betraying her sympathy for the 'dare-devil', as she called Dolokhov. 'They say Pierre is quite broken by his misfortune.'

'Dear, dear! But still tell him to come to the Club – it will all blow over. It will be a tremendous banquet.'

Next day, the 3rd of March, soon after one o'clock, two hundred and fifty members of the English Club and fifty guests were awaiting the guest of honour and hero of the Austrian campaign, Prince Bagration, to dinner.

On the first arrival of the news of the battle of Austerlitz, Moscow had been bewildered. At that time the Russians were so used to victories that on receiving news of a defeat some would simply not believe it, while others sought some extraordinary explanation of so strange an event. In the English Club where all who were distinguished, important, and well-informed, foregathered, when the news began to arrive in December nothing was said about the war and the last battle, as though all were in a conspiracy of silence. The men who set the tone in conversation* – Count Rostopchin, Prince Yuri Dolgorukov, Valuev, Count Markov and Prince Vyazemsky – did not show themselves at the Club but met in private houses in intimate circles, and the Moscovites who took their opinions from others – Ilya Rostov among them – remained for a while without any definite opinion on the subject of the war, and without leaders. The Moscovites felt that something was wrong, and that to discuss the bad news was difficult, and so it was best to be silent. But after a while, just as a jury comes out of its room, the bigwigs who guided the Club's opinion reappeared, and everybody began speaking clearly and definitely. Reasons were found for the incredible, unheard-of, and impossible event of a Russian defeat, everything became clear, and in all corners of Moscow the same things began to be said. These reasons were the treachery of the Austrians, a defective commissariat, the treachery of the Pole Przebyszewski and of the Frenchman Langeron, Kutuzov's incapacity, and (it was whispered) the youth and inexperience of the sovereign, who had trusted worthless and insignificant people. But the army, the Russian army, everyone declared was extraordinary, and had achieved miracles of valour. The soldiers, officers, and generals were heroes. But the hero of heroes was Prince Bagration, distinguished by his Schön Grabern affair and by the retreat from Austerlitz, where he alone had withdrawn his column unbroken, and had all day beaten back an enemy force twice as numerous as his own. What also conduced to Bagration being selected as Moscow's hero was the fact that he had no connexions in the city and was a stranger there. In his person honour was shown to a simple fighting Russian soldier without connexions and intrigues, and to one who was associated by memories of the Italian campaign with the name of Suvorov. Moreover paying such honour to Bagration was the best way of expressing disapproval and dislike of Kutuzov.

'Had there been no Bagration it would have been necessary to invent him,' said the wit Shinshin, parodying the words of Voltaire. Kutuzov no one spoke of, except some who abused him in whispers, calling him a court-weathercock and an old satyr.

All Moscow repeated Prince Dolgorukov's saying: 'If you go on modelling and modelling you must get smeared with clay,' suggesting consolation for our defeat by the memory of former victories; and the words of Rostopchin, that French soldiers have to be incited to battle by high-falutin' words, and Germans by logical arguments to show them that it is more dangerous to run away than to advance, but that Russian soldiers only need to be restrained and held back! On all sides new and fresh anecdotes were heard of individual examples of heroism shown by our officers and men at Austerlitz. One had saved a standard, another had killed five Frenchmen, a third had loaded five cannon single-handed. Berg was mentioned by those who did not know him, as having when wounded in the right hand, taken his sword in the left, and gone forward. Of Bolkonsky nothing was said, and only those who knew him intimately regretted that he had died so young, leaving a pregnant wife with his eccentric father.

ON that 3rd of March all the rooms in the English Club were filled with a hum of conversation, like the hum of bees swarming in spring-time. The members and guests of the club wandered hither and thither, sat, stood, met, and separated, some in uniform and some in evening dress and a few here and there with powdered hair and in Russian *kaftáns*. Powdered footmen in livery with buckled shoes and smart stockings stood at every door anxiously noting visitors' every movement in order to offer their services. Most of those present were elderly respected men with broad self-confident faces, fat fingers, and resolute gestures and voices. This class of guests and members sat in certain habitual places and met in certain habitual groups. A minority of those present were casual guests – chiefly young men, among whom were Denisov, Rostov and Dolokhov – who was now again an officer in the Semënov regiment. The faces of these young people, especially those who were military men, bore that expression of condescending respect for their elders which seems to say to the older generation, 'We are prepared to respect and honour you, but all the same remember that the future belongs to us.'

Nesvitsky was there as an old member of the club. Pierre, who at his wife's command had let his hair grow and abandoned his spectacles, went about the rooms fashionably dressed but looking sad and dull. Here as elsewhere he was surrounded by an atmosphere of subservience to his wealth, and being in the habit of lording it over these people he treated them with absent-minded contempt.

By his age he should have belonged to the younger men, but by his wealth and connexions he belonged to the groups of old and honoured guests, and so he went from one group to another. Some of the most important old men were the centre of groups which even strangers approached respectfully to hear the voices of well-known men. The largest circles formed round Count Rostopchin, Valuev, and Naryshkin. Rostopchin was describing how the Russians had been overwhelmed by flying Austrians and had had to force their way through them with bayonets.

Valuev was confidentially telling that Uvarov had been sent from Petersburg to ascertain what Moscow was thinking about Austerlitz.

In a third circle Naryshkin was speaking of the meeting of the Austrian Council of War at which Suvorov crowed like a cock in reply to the nonsense talked by the Austrian generals. Shinshin, standing close by, tried to make a joke, saying that Kutuzov had evidently failed to learn from Suvorov even so simple a thing as the art of crowing like a cock, but the elder members glanced severely at the wit, making him feel that in that place and on that day it was improper to speak so of Kutuzov.

Count Ilya Rostov, hurried and preoccupied, went about in his soft boots between the dining and drawing-rooms hastily greeting the important and unimportant, all of whom he knew, as if they were all equals, while his eyes occasionally sought out his fine well-set-up young son, resting on him and winking joyfully at him. Young Rostov stood at a window with Dolokhov, whose acquaintance he had lately made and highly valued. The old count came up to them and pressed Dolokhov's hand.

'Please come and visit us ... you know my brave boy ... been together out there ... both playing the hero ... Ah, Vasíli Ignato-vich ... How d'ye do, old fellow?' he said, turning to an old man who was passing, but before he had finished his greeting there was a general stir, and a footman who had run in announced with a frightened face: 'He's arrived!'

Bells rang, the stewards rushed forward, and – like rye shaken together in a shovel – the guests who had been scattered about in different rooms came together and crowded in the large drawing-room by the door of the ball-room.

Bagration appeared in the doorway of the ante-room without hat or sword, which in accord with the Club custom he had given up to the hall-porter. He had no lambskin cap on his head, nor had he a loaded whip over his shoulder, as when Rostov had seen him on the eve of the battle of Austerlitz, but wore a tight new uniform with Russian and foreign Orders, and the Star of St George on his left breast. Evidently just before coming to the dinner he had had his hair and whiskers trimmed, which changed his appearance for the worse. There was something naïvely festive in his air, which in conjunction with his firm and virile features gave him a rather comical expression. Bekleshëv and Theodore Uvarov who had arrived with him, paused at the doorway to allow him, as the guest of honour, to enter first. Bagration was embarrassed, not wishing to avail himself of their courtesy, and this caused some delay at the doors, but after all he did at last enter first. He walked shyly and awkwardly over the parquet floor of the reception-room not knowing what to do with his hands; he was more accustomed to walk over a ploughed field under fire, as he had done at the head of the Kursk regiment at Schön Grabern – and he would have found that easier. The committee-men met him at the first door and expressing their delight at seeing such a highly honoured guest, took possession of him as it were, without waiting for his reply, surrounded him, and led him to the drawing-room. It was at first impossible to enter the drawing-room door for the crowd of members and guests jostling one another and trying to get a good look at Bagration over each other's shoulders, as if he were some rare animal. Count Ilya Rostov, laughing and repeating the words, 'Make way, dear boy! Make way, make way!' pushed through the crowd more energetically than anyone, led the guests into the drawing-room, and seated them on the centre sofa. The bigwigs, the most respected members of the Club, beset the new arrivals. Count Ilya again thrusting his way through the crowd, went out of the drawing-room, and reappeared a minute later with another committee-man, carrying a large silver salver which he presented to Prince Bagration. On the salver lay some verses composed and printed in the hero's honour. Bagration on seeing the salver glanced around in dismay, as though seeking help. But all eyes demanded that he should submit. Feeling himself in their power, he resolutely took the salver with both hands and looked sternly and reproachfully at the count who had presented it to him. Someone obligingly took the dish from Bagration (or he would, it seemed, have held it till evening and have gone in to dinner with it) and drew his attention to the verses. 'Well, I will read them, then!' Bagration seemed to say, and fixing his weary eyes on the paper, began to read them with a fixed and serious expression. But the author himself took the verses and began reading them aloud. Bagration bowed his head and listened:*

> Bring glory then to Alexander's reign
> And on the throne our Titus shield.
> A dreaded foe be thou, kind-hearted as a man,
> A Rhipheus at home, a Caesar in the field!
>
> E'en fortunate Napoleon
> Knows by experience, now, Bagration,
> And dare not Herculean Russians trouble....

But before he had finished reading, a stentorian major-domo announced that dinner was ready. The door opened, and from the dining-room came the resounding strains of the Polonaise:

> Conquest's joyful thunder waken,
> Triumph, valiant Russians, now!...

and Count Rostov, glancing angrily at the author who went on reading his verses, bowed to Bagration. Everyone rose, feeling that dinner was more important than verses, and Bagration, again preceding all the rest, went in to dinner. He was seated in the place of honour between two Alexanders – Bekleshëv and Naryshkin – which was a significant allusion to the name of the sovereign. Three hundred persons took their seats in the dining-room, according to their rank and importance: the more important nearer to the honoured guest, as naturally as water flows deepest where the land lies lowest.

Just before dinner Count Ilya Rostov presented his son to Bagration, who recognized him and said a few words to him, disjointed and awkward, as were all the words he spoke that day, and Count Ilya looked joyfully and proudly around while Bagration spoke to his son.

Nicholas Rostov, with Denisov and his new acquaintance Dolokhov, sat almost at the middle of the table. Facing them sat Pierre beside Prince Nesvitsky. Count Ilya Rostov with the other members of the committee sat facing Bagration, and as the very personification of Moscow hospitality did the honours to the Prince.

His efforts had not been in vain. The dinner, both the lenten and the other fare, was splendid, yet he could not feel quite at ease till the end of the meal. He winked at the butler, whispered directions to the footmen, and awaited each expected dish with some anxiety. Everything was excellent. With the second course, a gigantic sterlet (at sight of which Ilya Rostov blushed with self-conscious pleasure), the footmen began popping corks and filling the champagne glasses. After the fish, which made a certain sensation, the count exchanged glances with the other committee-men. 'There will be many toasts, it's time to begin,' he whispered, and taking up his glass he rose. All were silent, waiting for what he would say.

'To the health of our Sovereign, the Emperor!' he cried, and at the same moment his kindly eyes grew moist with tears of joy and enthusiasm. The band immediately struck up 'Conquest's joyful thunder waken ...' All rose and cried 'hurrah!' Bagration also rose, and shouted 'hurrah!' in exactly the same voice in which he had shouted it on the field at Schön Grabern. Young Rostov's ecstatic voice could be heard above the three hundred others. He nearly wept. 'To the health of our Sovereign, the Emperor!' he roared, 'hurrah!' and emptying his glass at one gulp he dashed it to the floor. Many followed his example, and the loud shouting continued for a long time. When the voices subsided, the footmen cleared away the broken glass and everybody sat down again, smiling at the noise they had made and exchanging remarks. The old count rose once more, glanced at a note lying beside his plate, and proposed a toast, 'To the health of the hero of our last campaign, Prince Peter Ivanovich Bagration!', and again his blue eyes grew moist. 'Hurrah!' cried the three hundred voices again, but instead

of the band a choir began singing a cantata composed by Paul
Ivanovich Kutuzov:*

> Russians! O'er all barriers on!
> Courage conquest guarantees;
> Have we not Bagration?
> He brings foemen to their knees, . . . &c.

As soon as the singing was over, another and another toast was
proposed and Count Ilya Rostov became more and more moved,
more glass was smashed and the shouting grew louder. They drank
to Bekleshëv, Naryshkin, Uvarov, Dolgorukov, Apraksin, Valuev,
to the committee, to all the Club members and to all the Club
guests, and finally to Count Ilya Rostov separately, as the organizer
of the banquet. At that toast the count took out his handkerchief
and, covering his face, wept outright.

4

PIERRE sat opposite Dolokhov and Nicholas Rostov. As usual he
ate and drank much and eagerly. But those who knew him intimately noticed that some great change had come over him that
day. He was silent all through dinner and looked about, blinking
and scowling, or with fixed eyes and a look of complete absent-
mindedness kept rubbing the bridge of his nose. His face was
depressed and gloomy. He seemed to see and hear nothing of what
was going on around him and to be absorbed by some depressing
and unsolved problem.

The unsolved problem that tormented him was caused by hints
given by the princess, his cousin, at Moscow, concerning Dolokhov's
intimacy with his wife, and by an anonymous letter he had received
that morning, which in the mean jocular way common to anonymous letters said that he saw badly through his spectacles, but that
his wife's connexion with Dolokhov was a secret to no one but
himself. Pierre absolutely disbelieved both the princess's hints and
the letter, but he feared now to look at Dolokhov, who was sitting
opposite him. Every time he chanced to meet Dolokhov's handsome
insolent eyes, Pierre felt something terrible and monstrous rising
in his soul and turned quickly away. Involuntarily recalling his
wife's past and her relations with Dolokhov, Pierre saw clearly
that what was said in the letter might be true, or might at least
seem to be true had it not referred to *his wife*. He involuntarily
remembered how Dolokhov who had fully recovered his former
position after the campaign, had returned to Petersburg and come

to him. Availing himself of his friendly relations with Pierre as a boon companion, Dolokhov had come straight to his house, and Pierre had put him up and lent him money. Pierre recalled how Hélène had smilingly expressed disapproval of Dolokhov's living at their house, and how cynically Dolokhov had praised his wife's beauty to him and from that time till they came to Moscow had not left them for a day.

'Yes, he is very handsome,' thought Pierre, 'and I know him. It would be particularly pleasant to him to dishonour my name and ridicule me, just because I have exerted myself on his behalf, befriended him and helped him. I know and understand what a spice that would add to the pleasure of deceiving me, if it really were true. Yes, if it were true, but I do not believe it. I have no right to, and can't believe it.' He remembered the expression Dolokhov's face assumed in his moments of cruelty, as when tying the policeman to the bear and dropping them into the water, or when he challenged a man to a duel without any reason, or shot a postboy's horse with a pistol. That expression was often on Dolokhov's face when looking at him. 'Yes, he is a bully,' thought Pierre, 'to kill a man means nothing to him. It must seem to him that everyone is afraid of him, and that must please him. He must think that I, too, am afraid of him – and in fact I am afraid of him,' he thought, and again he felt something terrible and monstrous rising in his soul. Dolokhov, Denisov, and Rostov, were now sitting opposite Pierre and seemed very gay. Rostov was talking merrily to his two friends, one of whom was a dashing hussar and the other a notorious duellist and rake, and every now and then he glanced ironically at Pierre whose preoccupied, absent-minded, and massive figure was a very noticeable one at the dinner. Rostov looked inimically at Pierre, first because Pierre appeared to his hussar eyes as a rich civilian, the husband of a beauty, and in a word – an old woman, and secondly because Pierre in his preoccupation and absent-mindedness had not recognized Rostov and had not responded to his greeting. When the Emperor's health was drunk Pierre, lost in thought, did not rise or lift his glass.

'What are you about?' shouted Rostov looking at him in an ecstasy of exasperation. 'Don't you hear it's his Majesty the Emperor's health?'

Pierre sighed, rose submissively, emptied his glass, and waiting till all were seated again turned with his kindly smile to Rostov.

'Why, I didn't recognize you!' he said. But Rostov was otherwise engaged; he was shouting 'hurrah!'

'Why don't you renew the acquaintance?' said Dolokhov to Rostov.

'Confound him, he's a fool!' said Rostov.

'One should make up to the husbands of pretty women,' said Denisov.

Pierre did not catch what they were saying, but knew they were talking about him. He reddened and turned away.

'Well, now to the health of handsome women!' said Dolokhov, and with a serious expression, but with a smile lurking at the corners of his mouth, he turned with his glass to Pierre.

'Here's to the health of lovely women, Peterkin – and their lovers!' he added.

Pierre with downcast eyes drank out of his glass without looking at Dolokhov or answering him. The footman, who was distributing leaflets with Kutuzov's cantata, laid one before Pierre as one of the principal guests. He was just going to take it when Dolokhov, leaning across, snatched it from his hand and began reading it. Pierre looked at Dolokhov and his eyes dropped, the something terrible and monstrous that had tormented him all dinner-time rose and took possession of him. He leaned his whole massive body across the table.

'How dare you take it?' he shouted.

Hearing that cry and seeing to whom it was addressed, Nesvitsky and the neighbour on his right quickly turned in alarm to Bezukhov.

'Don't! Don't! What are you about?' whispered their frightened voices.

Dolokhov looked at Pierre with clear mirthful cruel eyes, and that smile of his which seemed to say, 'Ah! This is what I like!'

'You shan't have it!' he said distinctly.

Pale, with quivering lips, Pierre snatched the copy.

'You . . . ! you . . . scoundrel! I challenge you!' he ejaculated, and pushing back his chair he rose from the table.

At the very instant he did this and uttered those words Pierre felt that the question of his wife's guilt which had been tormenting him the whole day, was finally and indubitably answered in the affirmative. He hated her and was for ever sundered from her. Despite Denisov's request that he would take no part in the matter, Rostov agreed to be Dolokhov's second, and after dinner he discussed the arrangements for the duel with Nesvitsky, Bezukhov's second. Pierre went home, but Rostov with Dolokhov and Denisov stayed on at the club till late, listening to the gipsies and other singers.

'Well, then, till to-morrow at Sokolniki,' said Dolokhov as he took leave of Rostov in the club porch.

'And do you feel quite calm?' Rostov asked.

Dolokhov paused.

'Well, you see, I'll tell you the whole secret of duelling in two words. If you are going to fight a duel, and you make a will and write affectionate letters to your parents, and if you think you may be killed, you are a fool and are lost for certain. But go with the firm intention of killing your man as quickly and surely as possible, and then all will be right, as our bear-huntsman at Kostroma used to tell me. "Everyone fears a bear," he says, "but when you see one your fear's all gone, and your only thought is not to let him get away!" And that's how it is with me. *A demain, mon cher.*'

Next day at eight in the morning Pierre and Nesvitsky drove to the Sokolniki forest and found Dolokhov, Denisov and Rostov already there. Pierre had the air of a man preoccupied with considerations which had no connexion with the matter in hand. His haggard face was yellow. He had evidently not slept that night. He looked about distractedly and screwed up his eyes as if dazzled by the sun. He was entirely absorbed by two considerations: his wife's guilt, of which after his sleepless night he had not the slightest doubt, and the guiltlessness of Dolokhov, who had no reason to preserve the honour of a man who was nothing to him ... 'I should perhaps have done the same in his place,' thought Pierre. 'It's even certain that I should have done the same, then why this duel, this murder? Either I shall kill him, or he will hit me in the head, or elbow, or knee. Can't I go away from here, run away, bury myself somewhere?' passed through his mind. But just at moments when such thoughts occurred to him, he would ask in a particularly calm and absent-minded way, which inspired the respect of the onlookers, 'Will it be long? Are things ready?'

When all was ready, the sabres struck in the snow to mark the barriers, and the pistols loaded, Nesvitsky went up to Pierre.

'I should not be doing my duty, Count,' he said in timid tones, 'and should not justify your confidence and the honour you have done me in choosing me for your second, if at this grave, this very grave, moment I did not tell you the whole truth. I think there is no sufficient ground for this affair, or for blood to be shed over it. ... You were not right, not quite in the right, you were impetuous ...'

'Oh yes, it is horribly stupid,' said Pierre.

'Then allow me to express your regrets, and I am sure your opponent will accept them,' said Nesvitsky (who like the others concerned in the affair, and like everyone in similar cases, did not yet believe that the affair had come to an actual duel). 'You know, Count, it is much more honourable to admit one's mistake than to let matters become irreparable. There was no insult on either side. Allow me to convey . . .'

'No! What is there to talk about?' said Pierre. 'It's all the same . . . Is everything ready?' he added. 'Only tell me where to go and where to shoot,' he said with an unnaturally gentle smile.

He took the pistol in his hand and began asking about the working of the trigger, as he had not before held a pistol in his hand – a fact he did not wish to confess.

'Oh yes, like that, I know, I only forgot,' said he.

'No apologies, none whatever,' said Dolokhov to Denisov (who on his side had been attempting a reconciliation) and he also went up to the appointed place.

The spot chosen for the duel was some eighty paces from the road where the sledges had been left, in a small clearing in the pine forest covered with melting snow, the frost having begun to break up during the last few days. The antagonists stood forty paces apart at the farther edge of the clearing. The seconds, measuring the paces, left tracks in the deep wet snow between the place where they had been standing and Nesvitsky's and Dolokhov's sabres, which were stuck into the ground ten paces apart to mark the barrier. It was thawing and misty, at forty paces' distance nothing could be seen. For three minutes all had been ready, but they still delayed and all were silent.

5

'WELL, begin!' said Dolokhov.

'All right,' said Pierre still smiling in the same way.

A feeling of dread was in the air. It was evident that the affair so lightly begun could no longer be averted but was taking its course independently of men's will. Denisov first went to the barrier and announced:

'As the adve'sawies have wefused a weconciliation, please pwoceed. Take your pistols, and at the word *thwee* begin to advance.'

'O-ne! T-wo! Thwee!' he shouted angrily and stepped aside.

The combatants advanced along the trodden tracks, nearer and nearer to one another, beginning to see one another through the mist. They had the right to fire when they liked as they approached the barrier. Dolokhov walked slowly without raising his pistol, looking intently with his bright sparkling blue eyes into his antagonist's face. His mouth wore its usual semblance of a smile.

'So I can fire when I like!' said Pierre, and at the word 'three' he went quickly forward missing the trodden path and stepping into the deep snow. He held the pistol in his right hand at arm's length, apparently afraid of shooting himself with it. His left hand he held carefully back, because he wished to support his right hand with it and knew he must not do so. Having advanced six paces and strayed off the track into the snow, Pierre looked down at his feet, then quickly glanced at Dolokhov and bending his finger as he had been shown, fired. Not at all expecting so loud a report, Pierre shuddered at the sound, and then smiling at his own sensations, stood still. The smoke, rendered denser by the mist, prevented him from seeing anything for an instant, but there was no second report as he had expected. He only heard Dolokhov's hurried steps, and his figure came in view through the smoke. He was pressing one hand to his left side, while the other clutched his drooping pistol. His face was pale. Rostov ran towards him and said something.

'No-o-o!' muttered Dolokhov through his teeth, 'no, it's not over.' And after stumbling a few staggering steps right up to the sabre, he sank on the snow beside it. His left hand was bloody; he wiped it on his coat and supported himself with it. His frowning face was pallid and quivered.

'Plea ...' began Dolokhov, but could not at first pronounce the word.

'Please,' he uttered with an effort.

Pierre hardly restraining his sobs, began running towards Dolokhov and was about to cross the space between the barriers, when Dolokhov cried:

'To your barrier!' and Pierre, grasping what was meant, stopped by his sabre. Only ten paces divided them. Dolokhov lowered his head to the snow, greedily bit at it, again raised his head, adjusted himself, drew in his legs and sat up, seeking a firm centre of gravity. He sucked and swallowed the cold snow, his lips quivered, but his eyes, still smiling, glittered with effort and exasperation as he mustered his remaining strength. He raised his pistol and aimed.

'Sideways! Cover yourself with your pistol!' ejaculated Nesvitsky.

'Cover yourself!' even Denisov cried to his adversary.

Pierre with a gentle smile of pity and remorse, his arms and legs helplessly spread out, stood with his broad chest directly facing Dolokhov and looked sorrowfully at him. Denisov, Rostov, and Nesvitsky closed their eyes. At the same instant they heard a report and Dolokhov's angry cry.

'Missed!' shouted Dolokhov, and he lay helplessly face downwards on the snow.

Pierre clutched his temples, and turning round went into the forest, trampling through the deep snow, and muttering incoherent words:

'Folly . . . folly! Death . . . lies . . .' he repeated, puckering his face. Nesvitsky stopped him and took him home.

Rostov and Denisov drove away with the wounded Dolokhov.

The latter lay silent in the sledge with closed eyes, and did not answer a word to the questions addressed to him. But on entering Moscow he suddenly came to, and lifting his head with an effort, took Rostov, who was sitting beside him, by the hand. Rostov was struck by the totally altered and unexpectedly rapturous and tender expression on Dolokhov's face.

'Well? How do you feel?' he asked.

'Bad! But it's not that, my friend –' said Dolokhov with a gasping voice. 'Where are we? In Moscow, I know. I don't matter, but I have killed her, killed . . . She won't get over it! She won't survive . . .'

'Who?' asked Rostov.

'My mother! My mother, my angel, my adored angel-mother,' and Dolokhov pressed Rostov's hand and burst into tears.

When he had become a little quieter he explained to Rostov that he was living with his mother, who if she saw him dying would not survive it. He implored Rostov to go on and prepare her.

Rostov went on ahead to do what was asked, and to his great surprise learned that Dolokhov the brawler, Dolokhov the bully, lived in Moscow with an old mother and a hunchback sister, and was the most affectionate of sons and brothers.

6

PIERRE had of late rarely seen his wife alone. Both in Petersburg and in Moscow their house was always full of visitors. The night after the duel he did not go to his bedroom, but as he often did, remained in his father's room, that huge room in which Count Bezukhov had died.

He lay down on the sofa meaning to fall asleep and forget all that had happened to him, but could not do so. Such a storm of feelings, thoughts, and memories suddenly arose within him, that he could not fall asleep, nor even remain in one place, but had to jump up and pace the room with rapid steps. Now he seemed to see her in the early days of their marriage, with bare shoulders and a languid, passionate look on her face, and then immediately he saw beside her Dolokhov's handsome, insolent, hard and mocking face as he had seen it at the banquet, and then that same face pale, quivering, and suffering as it had been when he reeled and sank on the snow.

'What has happened?' he asked himself. 'I have killed her *lover*, yes, killed my wife's lover. Yes, that was it! And why? How did I come to do it?' – 'Because you married her,' answered an inner voice.

'But in what was I to blame?' he asked. 'In marrying her without loving her; in deceiving yourself and her.' And he vividly recalled that moment after supper at Prince Vasili's, when he spoke those words he had found so difficult to utter. 'I love you.' 'It all comes from that! Even then I felt it,' he thought. 'I felt then that it was not so, that I had no right to do it. And so it turns out.'

He remembered his honeymoon, and blushed at the recollection. Particularly vivid, humiliating, and shameful was the recollection of how one day soon after his marriage he came out of the bedroom into his study a little before noon in his silk dressing-gown, and found his head-steward there, who, bowing respectfully, looked into his face and at his dressing-gown, and smiled slightly, as if expressing respectful understanding of his employer's happiness.

'But how often I have felt proud of her, proud of her majestic beauty and social tact,' thought he; 'been proud of my house, in which she received all Petersburg, proud of her unapproachability and beauty. So this is what I was proud of! I then thought that I did not understand her. How often when considering her character I have told myself that I was to blame for not understanding her, for not understanding that constant composure and complacency and lack of all interests or desires, and the whole secret lies in the terrible truth that she is a depraved woman. Now I have spoken that terrible word to myself all has become clear.

'Anatole used to come to borrow money from her* and used to kiss her naked shoulders. She did not give him the money but let herself be kissed. Her father in jest tried to rouse her jealousy, and she replied with a calm smile that she was not so stupid as to be jealous: "Let him do what he pleases," she used to say of me. One day I asked her if she felt any symptoms of pregnancy. She laughed contemptuously and said she was not a fool to want to have children, and that she was not going to have any children by *me*.'

Then he recalled the coarseness and bluntness of her thoughts and the vulgarity of the expressions that were natural to her, though she had been brought up in the most aristocratic circles.

'I'm not such a fool ... Just you try it on ... *Allez-vous promener*,' she used to say. Often seeing the success she had with

334

young and old men and women Pierre could not understand why he did not love her.

'Yes, I never loved her,' said he to himself; 'I knew she was a depraved woman,' he repeated, 'but dared not admit it to myself. And now there's Dolokhov sitting in the snow with a forced smile and perhaps dying, while meeting my remorse with some forced bravado!'

Pierre was one of those people who, in spite of an appearance of what is called weak character, do not seek a confidant in their troubles. He digested his sufferings alone.

'It is all, all her fault,' he said to himself; 'but what of that? Why did I bind myself to her? Why did I say "*Je vous aime*" to her, which was a lie, and worse than a lie? I am guilty and must endure... what? A slur on my name? A misfortune for life? Oh, that's nonsense,' he thought. 'The slur on my name and honour – that's all apart from myself.'

'Louis XVI was executed because they said he was dishonourable and a criminal,' came into Pierre's head, 'and from their point of view they were right, as were those too who canonised him and died a martyr's death for his sake. Then Robespierre was beheaded for being a despot. Who is right and who is wrong? No one! But if you are alive – live: to-morrow you'll die as I might have died an hour ago. And is it worth tormenting oneself, when one has only a moment of life in comparison with eternity?'

But at the moment when he imagined himself calmed by such reflections, *she* suddenly came into his mind as she was at the moments when he had most strongly expressed his insincere love for her, and he felt the blood rush to his heart and had again to get up and move about and break and tear whatever came to his hand. 'Why did I tell her that "*Je vous aime*"?' he kept repeating to himself. And when he had said it for the tenth time, Moliere's words: *Mais que diable alloit-il faire dans cette galère** occurred to him, and he began to laugh at himself.

In the night he called his valet and told him to pack up to go to Petersburg. He could not imagine how he could speak to her now. He resolved to go away next day and leave a letter informing her of his intention to part from her for ever.

Next morning when the valet came into the room with his coffee, Pierre was lying asleep on the ottoman with an open book in his hand.

He woke up and looked round for awhile with a startled expression, unable to realize where he was.

'The countess told me to inquire whether your Excellency was at home,' said the valet.

But before Pierre could decide what answer he would send, the countess herself in a white satin dressing-gown embroidered with silver and with simply dressed hair (two immense plaits twice round her lovely head like a coronet) entered the room, calm and majestic, except that there was a wrathful wrinkle on her rather prominent marble brow. With her imperturbable calm she did not begin to speak in front of the valet. She knew of the duel and had come to speak about it. She waited till the valet had set down the coffee things and left the room. Pierre looked at her timidly over his spectacles, and like a hare surrounded by hounds who lays back her ears and continues to crouch motionless before her enemies he tried to continue reading. But feeling this to be senseless and impossible, he again glanced timidly at her. She did not sit down but looked at him with a contemptuous smile, waiting for the valet to go.

'Well, what's this now? What have you been up to now, I should like to know?' she asked sternly.

'I? What have I...?' stammered Pierre.

'So it seems you're a hero, eh? Come now, what was this duel about? What is it meant to prove? What? I ask you.'

Pierre turned over heavily on the ottoman and opened his mouth, but could not reply.

'If you won't answer, I'll tell you...' Hélène went on. 'You believe everything you're told. You were told...' Hélène laughed, 'that Dolokhov was my lover,' she said in French with her coarse plainness of speech, uttering the word *amant* as casually as any other word, 'and you believed it! Well, what have you proved? What does this duel prove? That you're a fool, *que vous êtes un sot*, but everybody knew that. What will be the result? That I shall be the laughing-stock of all Moscow, that everyone will say that you, drunk and not knowing what you were about, challenged a man you are jealous of without cause.' Hélène raised her voice and became more and more excited, 'a man who's a better man than you in every way...'

'Hm...Hm...!' growled Pierre, frowning without looking at her, and not moving a muscle.

'And how could you believe he was my lover? Why? Because I like his company? If you were cleverer and more agreeable, I should prefer yours.'

'Don't speak to me...I beg you,' muttered Pierre hoarsely.

'Why shouldn't I speak? I can speak as I like, and I tell you plainly that there are not many wives with husbands such as you who would not have taken lovers (*des amants*), but I have not done so,' said she.

Pierre wished to say something, looked at her with eyes whose strange expression she did not understand, and lay down again. He was suffering physically at that moment, there was a weight on his chest and he could not breathe. He knew that he must do something to put an end to this suffering, but what he wanted to do was too terrible.

'We had better separate,' he muttered in a broken voice.

'Separate? Very well, but only if you give me a fortune,' said Hélène. 'Separate! That's a thing to frighten me with!'

Pierre leaped up from the sofa and rushed staggering towards her.

'I'll kill you!' he shouted, and seizing the marble top of a table with a strength he had never before felt, he made a step towards her brandishing the slab.

Hélène's face became terrible, she shrieked and sprang aside. His father's nature showed itself in Pierre. He felt the fascination and delight of frenzy. He flung down the slab, broke it, and swooping down on her with outstretched hands shouted, 'Get out!' in such a terrible voice that the whole house heard it with horror. God knows what he would have done at that moment had Hélène not fled from the room.

*

A week later Pierre gave his wife full power to control all his estates in Great Russia, which formed the larger part of his property, and left for Petersburg alone.

7

Two months had elapsed since the news of the battle of Austerlitz and the loss of Prince Andrew had reached Bald Hills, and in spite of the letters sent through the embassy and all the searches made, his body had not been found nor was he on the list of prisoners. What was worst of all for his relations was the fact that there was still a possibility of his having been picked up on the battlefield by the people of the place and that he might now be lying, recovering or dying, alone among strangers and unable to send news of himself. The gazettes from which the old prince first heard of the defeat at Austerlitz stated, as usual very briefly and vaguely, that after brilliant engagements the Russians had had to retreat and had made their withdrawal in perfect order. The old prince understood from this official report that our army had been defeated. A week after the gazette report of the battle of Austerlitz came a letter from Kutuzov informing the prince of the fate that had befallen his son.

'Your son,' wrote Kutuzov, 'fell before my eyes, a standard in his hand and at the head of a regiment – he fell as a hero, worthy of his father and his fatherland. To the great regret of myself and of the whole army it is still uncertain whether he is alive or not. I comfort myself and you with the hope that your son is alive, for otherwise he would have been mentioned among the officers found on the field of battle, a list of whom has been sent me under flag of truce.'

After receiving this news late in the evening, when he was alone in his study, the old prince went for his walk as usual next morning, but he was silent with his steward, the gardener, and the architect, and though he looked very grim he said nothing to anyone.

When Princess Mary went to him at the usual hour he was working at his lathe and, as usual, did not look round at her.

'Ah, Princess Mary!' he said suddenly in an unnatural voice, throwing down his chisel. (The wheel continued to revolve by its own impetus, and Princess Mary long remembered the dying creak of that wheel which merged in her memory with what followed.)

She approached him, saw his face, and something gave way within her. Her eyes grew dim. By the expression of her father's face, not sad, not crushed, but angry and working unnaturally, she saw that hanging over her and about to crush her was some terrible misfortune, the worst in life, one she had not yet experienced, irreparable and incomprehensible – the death of one she loved.

'Father! Andrew!' – said the ungraceful, awkward princess with such an indescribable charm of sorrow and self-forgetfulness that her father could not bear her look but turned away with a sob.

'Bad news! He's not among the prisoners nor among the killed! Kutuzov writes . . .' and he screamed as piercingly as if he wished to drive the princess away by that scream . . . 'Killed!'

The princess did not fall down or faint. She was already pale, but on hearing these words her face changed and something brightened in her beautiful radiant eyes. It was as if joy – a supreme joy apart from the joys and sorrows of this world – overflowed the great grief within her. She forgot all fear of her father, went up to him, took his hand, and drawing him down put her arm round his thin scraggy neck.

'Father,' she said, 'do not turn away from me, let us weep together.'

'Scoundrels! Blackguards!' shrieked the old man, turning his face away from her. 'Destroying the army, destroying the men! And why? Go, go and tell Lise.'

The princess sank helplessly into an arm-chair beside her father and wept. She saw her brother now as he had been at the moment when he took leave of her and of Lise, his look tender yet proud. She saw him tender and amused as he was when he put on the little icon. 'Did he believe? Had he repented of his unbelief? Was he now there? There in the realms of eternal peace and blessedness?' she thought.

'Father, tell me how it happened,' she asked through her tears.

'Go! Go! Killed in battle, where the best of Russian men and Russia's glory were led to destruction. Go, Princess Mary. Go and tell Lise. I will follow.'

When Princess Mary returned from her father, the little princess sat working, and looked up with that curious expression of inner, happy calm peculiar to pregnant women. It was evident that her eyes did not see Princess Mary but were looking within . . . into herself . . . at something joyful and mysterious taking place within her.

'Mary,' she said, moving away from the embroidery-frame and lying back, 'give me your hand.' She took her sister-in-law's hand and held it below her waist.

Her eyes were smiling expectantly, her downy lip rose, and remained lifted in child-like happiness.

Princess Mary knelt down before her and hid her face in the folds of her sister-in-law's dress.

'There, there! Do you feel it? I feel so strange. And do you know, Mary, I am going to love him very much,' said Lise, looking with bright and happy eyes at her sister-in-law.

Princess Mary could not lift her head, she was weeping.

'What is the matter, Mary?'

'Nothing . . . only I feel sad . . . sad about Andrew,' she said, wiping away her tears on her sister-in-law's knee.

Several times in the course of the morning Princess Mary began trying to prepare her sister-in-law, and every time began to cry. Unobservant as was the little princess, these tears, the cause of which she did not understand, agitated her. She said nothing but looked about uneasily as if in search of something. Before dinner the old prince, of whom she was always afraid, came into her room with a peculiarly restless and malign expression, and went out again without saying a word. She looked at Princess Mary, then sat thinking for awhile with that expression of attention to something within her that is only seen in pregnant women, and suddenly began to cry.

'Has anything come from Andrew?' she asked.

'No, you know it's too soon for news. But my father is anxious and I feel afraid.'

'So there's nothing?'

'Nothing,' answered Princess Mary, looking firmly with her radiant eyes at her sister-in-law.

She had determined not to tell her, and persuaded her father to hide the terrible news from her till after her confinement, which was expected within a few days. Princess Mary and the old prince each bore and hid their grief in their own way. The old prince would not cherish any hope; he made up his mind that Prince Andrew had been killed, and though he sent an official to Austria to seek for traces of his son, he ordered a monument from Moscow which he intended to erect in his own garden to his memory, and he told everybody that his son had been killed. He tried not to change his former way of life, but his strength failed him. He walked less, ate less, slept less, and became weaker every day. Princess Mary hoped. She prayed for her brother as living, and was always awaiting news of his return.

8

'DEAREST,' said the little princess after breakfast on the morning of the 19th of March, and her downy little lip rose from old habit, but as sorrow was manifest in every smile, the sound of every word, and even every footstep in that house since the terrible news had come, so now the smile of the little princess – influenced by the general mood though without knowing its cause – was such as to remind one still more of the general sorrow.

'Dearest, I'm afraid this morning's fruschtique* – as Foka the cook calls it – has disagreed with me.'

'What is the matter with you, my darling? You look pale. Oh, you are very pale!' said Princess Mary in alarm, running with her soft, ponderous steps up to her sister-in-law.

'Your Excellency, should not Mary Bogdanovna be sent for?' said one of the maids who was present. (Mary Bogdanovna was a midwife from the neighbouring town who had been at Bald Hills for the last fortnight.)

'Oh yes,' assented Princess Mary, 'perhaps that's it. I'll go. Courage, my angel.' She kissed Lise and was about to leave the room.

'Oh, no, no!' And besides the pallor and the physical suffering on the little princess's face, an expression of childish fear of inevitable pain showed itself.

'No, it's only indigestion . . . ! Say it's only indigestion, say so, Mary! Say . . .' And the little princess began to cry capriciously like a suffering child, and to wring her little hands even with some affectation. Princess Mary ran out of the room to fetch Mary Bogdanovna.

'Mon Dieu! Mon Dieu! Oh!' she heard as she left the room.

The midwife was already on her way to meet her, rubbing her small plump white hands with an air of calm importance.

'Mary Bogdanovna, I think it's beginning!' said Princess Mary looking at the midwife with wide-open eyes of alarm.

'Well, the Lord be thanked, Princess,' said Mary Bogdanovna, not hastening her steps. 'You young ladies should not know anything about it.'

'But how is it the doctor from Moscow is not here yet?' said the princess. (In accordance with Lise's and Prince Andrew's wishes they had sent in good time to Moscow for a doctor and were expecting him at any moment.)

'No matter, Princess, don't be alarmed,' said Mary Bogdanovna. 'We'll manage very well without a doctor.'

Five minutes later Princess Mary from her room heard something heavy being carried by. She looked out. The menservants were carrying the large leather sofa from Prince Andrew's study into the bedroom. On their faces was a quiet and solemn look.

Princess Mary sat alone in her room listening to the sounds in the house, now and then opening her door when someone passed and watching what was going on in the passage. Some women passing with quiet steps in and out of the bedroom glanced at the princess and turned away. She did not venture to ask any questions, and shut the door again, now sitting down in her easy chair, now taking her prayer book, now kneeling before the icon-stand. To her surprise and distress she found that her prayers did not calm her excitement. Suddenly her door opened softly and her old nurse, Praskovya Savishna, who hardly ever came to that room, as the old prince had forbidden it, appeared on the threshold with a shawl round her head.

'I've come to sit with you a bit, Masha,' said the nurse, 'and here I've brought the prince's wedding candles to light before his saint, my angel,' she said with a sigh.

'Oh, nurse, I'm so glad!'

'God is merciful, birdie.'

The nurse lit the gilt candles before the icons and sat down by the door with her knitting. Princess Mary took a book and began reading. Only when footsteps or voices were heard did they look at one another, the princess anxious and inquiring, the nurse encouraging. Everyone in the house was dominated by the same feeling that Princess Mary experienced as she sat in her room. But owing to the superstition that the fewer the people who know of it the less a woman in travail suffers, everyone tried to pretend not to know; no one spoke of it, but apart from the ordinary staid and respectful good manners habitual in the prince's household, a common anxiety, a softening of the heart, and a consciousness that something great and mysterious was being accomplished at that moment, made itself felt.

There was no laughter in the maids' large hall. In the men-servants' hall all sat waiting, silently and alert. In the outlying serfs' quarters torches and candles were burning and no one slept. The old prince, stepping on his heels, paced up and down his study and sent Tikhon to ask Mary Bogdanovna what news? – 'Say only that "the prince told me to ask", and come and tell me her answer.'

'Inform the prince that labour has begun,' said Mary Bogdanovna, giving the messenger a significant look.

Tikhon went and told the prince.

'Very good!' said the prince closing the door behind him, and Tikhon did not hear the slightest sound from the study after that.

After a while he re-entered it as if to snuff the candles, and seeing that the prince was lying on the sofa, looked at him, noticed his perturbed face, shook his head, and going up to him, silently kissed him on the shoulder and left the room without snuffing the candles or saying why he had entered. The most solemn mystery in the world continued its course. Evening passed, night came, and the feeling of suspense and softening of heart in the presence of the unfathomable did not lessen but increased. No one slept.

*

It was one of those March nights when winter seems to wish to resume its sway, and scatters its last snows and storms with desperate fury. A relay of horses had been sent up the high road to meet the German doctor from Moscow who was expected every moment, and men on horseback with lanterns were sent to the cross-roads to guide him over the country road with its hollows and snow-covered pools of water.

Princess Mary had long since put aside her book: she sat silent, her luminous eyes fixed on her nurse's wrinkled face (every line of which she knew so well), on the lock of grey hair that escaped from under the kerchief, and the loose skin that hung under her chin.

Nurse Savishna, knitting in hand, was telling in low tones, scarcely hearing or understanding her own words, what she had told hundreds of times before: how the late princess had given birth to Princess Mary in Kishenëv with only a Moldavian peasant woman to help instead of a midwife.

'God is merciful, doctors are never needed,' she said.

Suddenly a gust of wind beat violently against the casement of the window, from which the double frame had been removed (by order of the prince, one window frame was removed in each room as soon as the larks returned), and forcing open a loosely closed latch, set the damask curtain flapping and blew out the candle with its chill, snowy draught. Princess Mary shuddered; her nurse, putting down the stockings she was knitting, went to the window and leaning out tried to catch the open casement. The cold wind flapped the ends of her kerchief and her loose locks of grey hair.

'Princess, my dear, there's someone driving up the avenue!' she said, holding the casement and not closing it. 'With lanterns. Most likely the doctor.'

'Oh, my God! thank God!' said Princess Mary. 'I must go and meet him, he does not know Russian.'

Princess Mary threw a shawl over her head and ran to meet the newcomer. As she was crossing the ante-room she saw through the window a carriage with lanterns standing at the entrance. She went out on the stairs. On a banister-post stood a tallow candle which guttered in the draught. On the landing below, Philip, the footman, stood looking scared and holding another candle. Still lower, beyond the turn of the staircase, one could hear the footstep of someone in thick felt boots, and a voice that seemed familiar to Princess Mary was saying something.

'Thank God!' said the voice. 'And father?'

'Gone to bed,' replied the voice of Demyan the house-steward, who was downstairs.

Then the voice said something more, Demyan replied, and the steps in the felt boots approached the unseen bend of the staircase more rapidly.

'It's Andrew!' thought Princess Mary. 'No it can't be, that would be too extraordinary,' and at the very moment she thought this, the face and figure of Prince Andrew, in a fur cloak the deep collar of which was covered with snow, appeared on the landing where the footman stood with the candle. Yes, it was he, pale, thin, with a changed and strangely softened but agitated expression on his face. He came up the stairs and embraced his sister.

'You did not get my letter?' he asked, and not waiting for a reply – which he would not have received, for the princess was unable to speak – he turned back, rapidly mounted the stairs again with the doctor who had entered the hall after him (they had met at the last post-station) and again embraced his sister.

'What a strange fate, Masha darling!' And having taken off his cloak and felt boots, he went to the little princess's apartment.

THE little princess lay supported by pillows, with a white cap on her head (the pains had just left her). Strands of her black hair lay round her inflamed and perspiring cheeks, her charming rosy mouth with its downy lip was open and she was smiling joyfully. Prince Andrew entered, and paused facing her at the foot of the sofa on which she was lying. Her glittering eyes, filled with child-like fear and excitement, rested on him without changing their expression. 'I love you all and have done no harm to anyone; why must I suffer so? help me!' her look seemed to say. She saw her husband, but did not realize the significance of his appearance before her now. Prince Andrew went round the sofa and kissed her forehead.

'My darling!' he said – a word he had never used to her before. 'God is merciful . . .'

She looked at him inquiringly and with childlike reproach.

'I expected help from you and I get none, none from you either!' said her eyes. She was not surprised at his having come; she did not realize that he had come. His coming had nothing to do with her sufferings or with their relief. The pangs began again and Mary Bogdanovna advised Prince Andrew to leave the room.

The doctor entered. Prince Andrew went out and meeting Princess Mary, again joined her. They began talking in whispers, but their talk broke off at every moment. They waited and listened.

'Go, dear,' said Princess Mary.

Prince Andrew went again to his wife and sat waiting in the room next to hers. A woman came from the bedroom with a frightened face and became confused when she saw Prince Andrew. He covered his face with his hands and remained so for some minutes. Piteous, helpless, animal moans came through the door. Prince Andrew got up, went to the door, and tried to open it. Someone was holding it shut.

'You can't come in! You can't!' said a terrified voice from within.

He began pacing the room. The screaming ceased, and a few more seconds went by. Then suddenly a terrible shriek – it could not be hers, she could not scream like that – came from the bed-room. Prince Andrew ran to the door; the scream ceased and he heard the wail of an infant.

'What have they taken a baby in there for?' thought Prince Andrew in the first second. 'A baby? What baby . . . ? Why is there a baby there? Or is the baby born?'

Then suddenly he realized the joyful significance of that wail; tears choked him, and leaning his elbows on the window-sill he began to cry, sobbing like a child. The door opened. The doctor with his shirt-sleeves tucked up, without a coat, pale and with a trembling jaw, came out of the room. Prince Andrew turned to him, but the doctor gave him a bewildered look and passed by without a word. A woman rushed out and seeing Prince Andrew stopped, hesitating on the threshold. He went into his wife's room. She was lying dead, in the same position he had seen her in five minutes before, and despite the fixed eyes and the pallor of the cheeks, the same expression was on her charming childlike face with its upper lip covered with tiny black hair.

'I love you all, and have done no harm to anyone; and what have you done to me?' – said her charming, pathetic, dead face.

In a corner of the room something red and tiny gave a grunt and squealed in Mary Bogdanovna's trembling white hands.

Two hours later Prince Andrew stepping softly went into his father's room. The old man already knew everything. He was standing close to the door and as soon as it opened his rough old arms closed like a vice round his son's neck, and without a word he began to sob like a child.

*

Three days later the little princess was buried, and Prince Andrew went up the steps to where the coffin stood, to give her the fare-well kiss. And there in the coffin was the same face, though with closed eyes. 'Ah, what have you done to me?' it still seemed to say, and Prince Andrew felt that something gave way in his soul, and that he was guilty of a sin he could neither remedy nor forget. He could not weep. The old man too came up and kissed the waxen little hands that lay quietly crossed one on the other on her breast, and to him, too, her face seemed to say: 'Ah, what have you done to me, and why?' And at the sight the old man turned angrily away.

*

Another five days passed, and then the young Prince Nicholas Andreevich was baptized. The wet-nurse supported the coverlet with her chin, while the priest with a goose feather anointed the boy's little red and wrinkled soles and palms.

His grandfather, who was his godfather, trembling and afraid of dropping him, carried the infant round the battered tin font, and handed him over to the godmother, Princess Mary. Prince Andrew sat in another room, faint with fear lest the baby should be drowned in the font, and awaited the termination of the ceremony. He looked up joyfully at the baby when the nurse brought it to him, and nodded approval when she told him that the wax with the baby's hair had not sunk in the font but had floated.*

10

ROSTOV'S share in Dolokhov's duel with Bezukhov was hushed up by the efforts of the old count, and instead of being degraded to the ranks as he expected he was appointed an adjutant to the governor-general of Moscow. As a result he could not go to the country with the rest of the family, but was kept all summer in Moscow by his new duties. Dolokhov recovered, and Rostov became very friendly with him during his convalescence. Dolokhov lay ill at his mother's who loved him passionately and tenderly, and old Mary Ivanovna, who had grown fond of Rostov for his friendship to her Fedya, often talked to him about her son.

'Yes, Count,' she would say, 'he is too noble and pure-souled for our present, depraved world. No one now loves virtue, it seems like a reproach to everyone. Now tell me, Count, was it right, was it honourable, of Bezukhov? And Fedya, with his noble spirit, loved him and even now never says a word against him. Those pranks in Petersburg when they played some tricks on a policeman, didn't they do it together? And there! Bezukhov got off scot free, while Fedya had to bear the whole burden on his shoulders. Fancy what he had to go through! It's true he has been reinstated, but how could they fail to do that? I think there were not many such gallant sons of the fatherland out there as he. And now – this duel! Have these people no feeling, or honour? Knowing him to be an only son, to challenge him and shoot so straight! It's well God had mercy on us. And what was it for? Who doesn't have intrigues nowadays? Why, if he was so jealous, as I see things he should have shown it sooner, but he lets it go on for months. And then to call him out, reckoning on Fedya not fighting because he owed him money! What baseness! What meanness! I know you understand Fedya, my dear Count, that, believe me, is why I am so fond of you. Few people do understand him. His is such a lofty, heavenly soul!'

Dolokhov himself during his convalescence spoke to Rostov in a way no one would have expected of him.

'I know people consider me a bad man!' he said. 'Let them! I don't care a straw about anyone but those I love; but those I love, I love so that I would give my life for them, and the others I'd throttle if they stood in my way. I have an adored, a priceless mother, and two or three friends – you among them, and as for the rest I only care about them in so far as they are harmful or useful. And most of them are harmful, especially the women. Yes, dear boy,' he continued, 'I have met loving, noble, high-minded men, but I have not yet met any women – countesses or cooks – who were not venal. I have not yet met that divine purity and devotion I look for in woman. If I found such a one I'd give my life for her! But those!...' and he made a gesture of contempt. 'And believe me, if I still value my life it is only because I still hope to meet such a divine creature, who will regenerate, purify, and elevate me. But you don't understand it.'

'Oh, yes, I quite understand,' answered Rostov, who was under his new friend's influence.

*

In the autumn the Rostovs returned to Moscow. Early in the winter Denisov also came back and stayed with them. The first half of the winter of 1806 which Nicholas Rostov spent in Moscow, was one of the happiest, merriest times for him and the whole family. Nicholas brought many young men to his parents' house. Vera was a handsome girl of twenty; Sonya a girl of sixteen with all the charm of an opening flower; Natasha, half grown up and half child, was now childishly amusing, now girlishly enchanting.

At that time in the Rostovs' house there prevailed an amorous atmosphere characteristic of homes where there are very young and very charming girls. Every young man who came to the house, seeing those impressionable, smiling, young faces (smiling probably at their own happiness), feeling the eager bustle around him, and hearing the fitful bursts of song and music and the inconsequent but friendly prattle of young girls ready for anything and full of hope – experienced the same feeling; sharing with the young folk of the Rostovs' household a readiness to fall in love and an expectation of happiness.

Among the young men introduced by Rostov one of the first was Dolokhov, whom everyone in the house liked except Natasha. She almost quarrelled with her brother about him. She insisted that he was a bad man, and that in the duel with Bezukhov, Pierre was right and Dolokhov wrong, and further that he was disagreeable and unnatural.

'There's nothing for me to understand,' she cried out with resolute self-will, 'he is wicked and heartless. There now, I like your Denisov though he is a rake and all that, still I like him; so you see I do understand. I don't know how to put it ... with this one everything is calculated, and I don't like that. But Denisov ...'

'Oh, Denisov is quite different,' replied Nicholas, implying that even Denisov was nothing compared to Dolokhov – 'you must understand what a soul there is in Dolokhov, you should see him with his mother. What a heart!'

'Well, I don't know about that, but I am uncomfortable with him. And do you know he has fallen in love with Sonya?'

'What nonsense ...'

'I'm certain of it, you'll see.'

Natasha's prediction proved true. Dolokhov, who did not usually care for the society of ladies, began to come often to the house, and the question for whose sake he came (though no one spoke of it) was soon settled. He came because of Sonya. And Sonya, though she would never have dared to say so, knew it and blushed scarlet every time Dolokhov appeared.

Dolokhov often dined at the Rostovs', never missed a performance at which they were present, and went to Iogel's balls for young people which the Rostovs always attended. He was pointedly attentive to Sonya, and looked at her in such a way that not only could she not bear his glances without colouring, but even the old countess and Natasha blushed when they saw his looks.

It was evident that this strange, strong man was under the irresistible influence of the dark graceful girl who loved another.

Rostov noticed something new in Dolokhov's relations with Sonya, but he did not explain to himself what these new relations were. 'They're always in love with someone,' he thought of Sonya and Natasha. But he was not as much at ease with Sonya and Dolokhov as before, and was less frequently at home.

In the autumn of 1806 everybody had again begun talking of the war with Napoleon* with even greater warmth than the year before. Orders were given to raise recruits, ten men in every thousand for the regular army, and besides this, nine men in every thousand for the militia. Everywhere Bonaparte was anathematized and in Moscow nothing but the coming war was talked of. For the Rostov family the whole interest of these preparations for war lay in the fact that Nicholas would not hear of remaining in Moscow, and only awaited the termination of Denisov's furlough after Christmas, to return with him to their regiment. His approaching departure did not prevent his amusing himself, but rather gave zest to his pleasures. He spent the greater part of his time away from home, at dinners, parties, and balls.

11

On the third day after Christmas Nicholas dined at home, a thing he had rarely done of late. It was a grand farewell dinner, as he and Denisov were leaving to join their regiment after Epiphany. About twenty people were present, including Dolokhov and Denisov.

Never had love been so much in the air, and never had the amorous atmosphere made itself so strongly felt in the Rostovs' house as at this holiday time. 'Seize the moments of happiness, love and be loved! That is the only reality in the world, all else is folly. It is the one thing we are interested in here,' said the spirit of the place.

Nicholas, having as usual exhausted two pairs of horses, without visiting all the places he meant to go to and where he had been invited, returned home just before dinner. As soon as he entered he noticed and felt the tension of the amorous air in the house, and also noticed a curious embarrassment among some of those present. Sonya, Dolokhov, and the old countess were especially disturbed, and to a lesser degree Natasha. Nicholas understood that something must have happened between Sonya and Dolokhov before dinner, and with the kindly sensitiveness natural to him was very gentle and wary with them both at dinner. On that same evening there was to be one of the balls that Iogel (the dancing master) gave for his pupils during the holidays.

'Nicholas, will you come to Iogel's? Please do!' said Natasha. 'He asked you, and Vasili Dmitrich (Denisov) is also going.'

'Where would I not go at the countess's command!' said Denisov, who at the Rostovs' had jocularly assumed the role of Natasha's knight. 'I'm even weady to dance the *pas de châle*.'

'If I have time,' answered Nicholas. 'But I promised the Arkharovs; they have a party.'

'And you?' he asked Dolokhov, but as soon as he had asked the question he noticed that it should not have been put.

'Perhaps,' coldly and angrily replied Dolokhov, glancing at Sonya, and, scowling, he gave Nicholas just such a look as he had given Pierre at the Club dinner.

'There is something up,' thought Nicholas, and he was further confirmed in this conclusion by the fact that Dolokhov left immediately after dinner. He called Natasha and asked her what was the matter.

'And I was looking for you,' said Natasha running out to him. 'I told you, but you would not believe it,' she said triumphantly. 'He has proposed to Sonya!'

Little as Nicholas had occupied himself with Sonya of late, something seemed to give way within him at this news. Dolokhov was a suitable and in some respects a brilliant match for the dowerless, orphan girl. From the point of view of the old countess and of society it was out of the question for her to refuse him. And therefore Nicholas's first feeling on hearing the news was one of anger with Sonya . . . He tried to say, 'That's capital; of course she'll forget her childish promises and accept the offer,' but before he had time to say it Natasha began again.

'And fancy! She refused him quite definitely!' adding, after a pause, 'She told him she loved another.'

'Yes, my Sonya could not have done otherwise!' thought Nicholas.

'Much as Mamma pressed her, she refused, and I know she won't change once she has said . . .'

'And Mamma pressed her!' said Nicholas reproachfully.

'Yes,' said Natasha. 'Do you know, Nicholas – don't be angry – but I know you will not marry her. I know, Heaven knows how, but I know for certain that you won't marry her.'

'Now you don't know that at all!' said Nicholas. 'But I must talk to her. What a darling Sonya is!' he added with a smile.

'Ah, she is indeed a darling! I'll send her to you.'

And Natasha kissed her brother and ran away.

A minute later Sonya came in with a frightened, guilty, and scared look. Nicholas went up to her and kissed her hand. This was the first time since his return that they had talked alone and about their love.

'Sophie,' he began, timidly at first and then more and more boldly, 'if you wish to refuse one who is not only a brilliant and advantageous match but a splendid, noble fellow . . . he is my friend . . .'

Sonya interrupted him.

'I have already refused,' she said hurriedly.

'If you are refusing for my sake, I am afraid that I . . .'

Sonya again interrupted. She gave him an imploring, frightened look.

'Nicholas, don't tell me that!' she said.

'No, but I must. It may be arrogant of me, but still it is best to say it. If you refuse him on my account, I must tell you the whole truth. I love you, and I think I love you more than anyone else . . .'

'That is enough for me,' said Sonya, blushing.

'No, but I have been in love a thousand times and shall fall in love again, though for no one have I such a feeling of friendship, confidence, and love as I have for you. Then I am young. Mamma does not wish it. In a word, I make no promise. And I beg you to consider Dolokhov's offer,' he said, articulating his friend's name with difficulty.

'Don't say that to me! I want nothing. I love you as a brother and always shall, and I want nothing more.'

'You are an angel: I am not worthy of you, but I am afraid of misleading you.'

And Nicholas again kissed her hand.

12

IOGEL'S were the most enjoyable balls in Moscow. So said the mothers as they watched their young people executing their newly-learned steps, and so said the youths and maidens themselves as they danced till they were ready to drop, and so said the grown-up young men and women who came to these balls with an air of condescension, and found them most enjoyable. That year two marriages had come of these balls. The two pretty young Princesses Gorchakov met suitors there and were married, and so further increased the fame of these dances. What distinguished them from others was the absence of host or hostess and the presence of the good-natured Iogel, flying about like a feather and bowing according to the rules of his art, as he collected the tickets from all his visitors. There was the fact that only those came who wished to dance and amuse themselves as girls of thirteen and fourteen do who are wearing long dresses for the first time. With scarcely any exceptions they all were, or seemed to be, pretty – so rapturous were their smiles and so sparkling their eyes. Sometimes the best of the pupils, of whom Natasha, who was exceptionally graceful, was first, even danced the *pas de châle*, but at this last ball only the écossaise, the anglaise, and the mazurka which was just coming into fashion, were danced. Iogel had taken a ballroom in Bezukhov's house, and the ball, as everyone said, was a great success. There were many pretty girls and the Rostov girls were among the prettiest. They were both particularly happy and gay. That evening, proud of Dolokhov's proposal, her refusal, and her explanation with Nicholas, Sonya twirled about before she left home so that the maid could hardly get her hair plaited, and was transparently radiant with impulsive joy.

Natasha no less proud of her first long dress and of being at a real ball was even happier. They were both dresed in white muslin with pink ribbons.

Natasha fell in love the very moment she entered the ballroom. She was not in love with anyone in particular, but with everyone. Whatever person she happened to look at she was in love with for that moment.

'Oh, how delightful it is!' she kept saying, running up to Sonya.

Nicholas and Denisov were walking up and down, looking with kindly patronage at the dancers.

'How sweet she is, – she will be a weal beauty!' said Denisov.

'Who?'

'Countess Natasha,' answered Denisov.

'And how she dances! What gwace!' he said again after a pause.

'Who are you talking about?'

'About your sister,' ejaculated Denisov testily.

Rostov smiled.

'My dear Count, you were one of my best pupils, – you must dance,' said little Iogel coming up to Nicholas. 'Look how many charming young ladies—' He turned with the same request to Denisov who was also a former pupil of his.

'No, my dear fellow, I'll be a wallflower,' said Denisov. 'Don't you wecollect what bad use I made of your lessons?'

'Oh no!' said Iogel, hastening to reassure him. 'You were only inattentive, but you had talent, – oh yes, you had talent!'

The band struck up the newly introduced mazurka. Nicholas could not refuse Iogel, and asked Sonya to dance. Denisov sat down by the old ladies and leaning on his sabre and beating time with his foot, told them something funny and kept them amused, while he watched the young people dancing. Iogel with Natasha, his pride and his best pupil, were the first couple. Noiselessly, skilfully stepping with his little feet in low shoes, Iogel flew first across the hall with Natasha, who though shy, went on carefully executing her steps. Denisov did not take his eyes off her and beat time with his sabre in a way that clearly indicated that if he was not dancing it was because he would not and not because he could not. In the middle of a figure he beckoned to Rostov who was passing:

'This is not at all the thing,' he said. 'What sort of a Polish mazuwka is this? But she does dance splendidly.'

Knowing that Denisov had a reputation even in Poland for the masterly way in which he danced the mazurka, Nicholas ran up to Natasha:

'Go and choose Denisov. He is a real dancer, a wonder!' he said.

When it came to Natasha's turn to choose a partner, she rose and, tripping rapidly across in her little shoes trimmed with bows, ran timidly to the corner where Denisov sat. She saw that everybody was looking at her and waiting. Nicholas saw that Denisov and she were smilingly disputing, and that Denisov was refusing though he smiled delightedly. He ran up to them.

'Please, Vasili Dmitrich,' Natasha was saying, 'do come!'

'Oh no, let me off, Countess,' Denisov replied.

'Now then, Vaska,' said Nicholas.

'They coax me as if I were Vaska the cat!' said Denisov jokingly.

'I'll sing for you a whole evening,' said Natasha.

'Oh, the faiwy! She can do anything with me!' said Denisov, and he unhooked his sabre. He came out from behind the chairs, clasped his partner's hand firmly, threw back his head and advanced his foot, waiting for the beat. Only on horseback and in the mazurka was Denisov's short stature not noticeable and he looked the fine fellow he felt himself to be. At the right beat of the music he looked sideways at his partner with a merry and triumphant air, suddenly stamped with one foot, bounded from the floor like a ball, and flew round the room taking his partner with him. He glided silently on one foot half across the room, and seeming not to notice the chairs was dashing straight at them, when suddenly, clinking his spurs and spreading out his legs, he stopped short on his heels, stood so a second, stamped on the spot clanking his spurs, whirled rapidly round, and striking his left heel against his right, flew round again in a circle. Natasha guessed what he meant to do, and abandoning herself to him followed his lead hardly knowing how. First he spun her round, holding her now with his left now with his right hand, then falling on one knee he twirled her round him, and again jumping up, dashed so impetuously forward that it seemed as if he would rush through the whole suite of rooms without drawing breath, and then he suddenly stopped and performed some new and unexpected steps. When at last, smartly whirling his partner round in front of her chair, he drew up with a click of his spurs and bowed to her, Natasha did not even make him a curtsey. She fixed her eyes on him in amazement, smiling as if she did not recognize him.

'What does this mean?' she brought out.

Although Iogel did not acknowledge this to be the real mazurka, everyone was delighted with Denisov's skill, he was asked again and again as a partner, and the old men began smilingly to talk about Poland and the good old days. Denisov, flushed after the mazurka and mopping himself with his handkerchief, sat down by Natasha and did not leave her for the rest of the evening.

13

For two days after that Rostov did not see Dolokhov at his own or at Dolokhov's home: on the third day he received a note from him:

'As I do not intend to be at your house again for reasons you know of, and am going to rejoin my regiment, I am giving a farewell supper to-night to my friends – come to the English Hotel.'

About ten o'clock Rostov went to the English Hotel straight from the theatre, where he had been with his family and Denisov. He was at once shown to the best room, which Dolokhov had taken for that evening. Some twenty men were gathered round a table at which Dolokhov sat between two candles. On the table was a pile of gold and paper money, and he was keeping the bank. Rostov had not seen him since his proposal and Sonya's refusal, and felt uncomfortable at the thought of how they would meet.

Dolokhov's clear cold glance met Rostov as soon as he entered the door, as though he had long expected him.

'It's a long time since we met,' he said. 'Thanks for coming. I'll just finish dealing, and then Ilyushka will come with his chorus.'

'I called once or twice at your house,' said Rostov, reddening.

Dolokhov made no reply.

'You may punt,' he said.

Rostov recalled at that moment a strange conversation he had once had with Dolokhov. 'None but fools trust to luck in play,' Dolokhov had then said.

'Or are you afraid to play with me?' Dolokhov now asked as if guessing Rostov's thought.

Beneath his smile Rostov saw in him the mood he had shown at the Club dinner and at other times, when as if tired of everyday life he had felt a need to escape from it by some strange, and usually cruel, action.

Rostov felt ill at ease. He tried, but failed, to find some joke with which to reply to Dolokhov's words. But before he had thought of anything, Dolokhov, looking straight in his face, said slowly and deliberately so that everyone could hear:

'Do you remember we had a talk about cards..."He's a fool who trusts to luck, one should make certain," and I want to try.'

'To try his luck or the certainty?' Rostov asked himself.

'Well you'd better not play,' Dolokhov added, and springing a new pack of cards said: 'Bank, gentlemen!'

Moving the money forward he prepared to deal. Rostov sat down by his side and at first did not play. Dolokhov kept glancing at him.

'Why don't you play?' he asked.

And strange to say Nicholas felt that he could not help taking up a card, putting a small stake on it, and beginning to play.

'I have no money with me,' he said.

'I'll trust you.'

Rostov staked five rubles on a card and lost, staked again, and again lost. Dolokhov 'killed', that is, beat, ten cards of Rostov's running.

'Gentlemen,' said Dolokhov after he had dealt for some time. 'Please place your money on the cards or I may get muddled in the reckoning.'

One of the players said he hoped he might be trusted.

'Yes, you might, but I am afraid of getting the accounts mixed. So I ask you to put the money on your cards,' replied Dolokhov. 'Don't stint yourself, we'll settle afterwards,' he added, turning to Rostov.

The game continued; a waiter kept handing round champagne.

All Rostov's cards were beaten and he had eight hundred rubles scored up against him. He wrote '800 rubles' on a card, but while the waiter filled his glass he changed his mind, and altered it to his usual stake of twenty rubles.

'Leave it,' said Dolokhov, though he did not seem to be even looking at Rostov, 'you'll win it back all the sooner. I lose to the others but win from you. Or are you afraid of me?' he asked again.

Rostov submitted. He let the eight hundred remain and laid down a seven of hearts with a torn corner, which he had picked up from the floor. He well remembered that seven afterwards. He laid down the seven of hearts, on which with a broken bit of chalk he had written '800 rubles' in clear upright figures; he emptied the glass of warm champagne that was handed him, smiled at Dolokhov's words, and with a sinking heart, waiting for a seven to turn up, gazed at Dolokhov's hands which held the pack. Much depended on Rostov's winning or losing on that seven of hearts. On the previous Sunday the old count had given his son two thousand rubles, and though he always disliked speaking of money difficulties had told Nicholas that this was all he could let him have till May, and asked him to be more economical this time. Nicholas had replied that it would be more than enough for him, and that he gave his word of honour not to take anything more till the spring. Now only twelve hundred rubles was left of that money, so that this seven of hearts meant for him not only the loss of sixteen hundred rubles, but the necessity of going back on his word. With a sinking heart he watched Dolokhov's hands and thought, 'Now then, make haste and let me have this card and I'll take my cap and drive home to supper with Denisov, Natasha, and Sonya, and will certainly never touch a card again.' At that moment his home life, jokes with Petya, talks with Sonya, duets with Natasha, picquet with his father, and even his comfortable bed in the house on the Povarskaya, rose before him with such vividness, clearness, and charm that it seemed as if it were all a lost and unappreciated bliss, long past. He could not conceive that a stupid chance, letting the seven be dealt to the right rather than to the left, might deprive him of all this happiness, newly appreciated and newly illumined, and plunge him into the depths of unknown and undefined misery. That could not be, yet he awaited with a sinking heart the movement of Dolokhov's hands. Those broad, reddish hands, with hairy wrists visible from under the shirt-cuffs, laid down the pack and took up a glass and a pipe that were handed him.

'So you are not afraid to play with me?' repeated Dolokhov, and as if about to tell a good story he put down the cards, leant back in his chair, and began deliberately with a smile:

'Yes, gentlemen, I've been told there's a rumour going about Moscow that I'm a sharper, so I advise you to be careful.'

'Come now, deal!' exclaimed Rostov.

'Oh, those Moscow gossips!' said Dolokhov, and he took up the cards with a smile.

'Aah!' Rostov almost screamed lifting both hands to his head. The seven he needed was lying uppermost, the first card in the pack. He had lost more than he could pay.

'Still, don't ruin yourself!' said Dolokhov with a side glance at Rostov as he continued to deal.

14

An hour and a half later most of the players were but little interested in their own play.

The whole interest was concentrated on Rostov. Instead of sixteen hundred rubles he had a long column of figures scored against him, which he had reckoned up to ten thousand, but that now, as he vaguely supposed, must have risen to fifteen thousand. In reality it already exceeded twenty thousand rubles. Dolokhov was no longer listening to stories or telling them, but followed every movement of Rostov's hands and occasionally ran his eyes over the score against him. He had decided to play until that score reached forty-three thousand. He had fixed on that number because forty-three was the sum of his and Sonya's joint ages. Rostov, leaning his head on both hands, sat at the table which was scrawled over with figures, wet with spilt wine, and littered with cards. One tormenting impression did not leave him: that those broad-boned reddish hands with hairy wrists visible from under the shirt-sleeves, those hands which he loved and hated, held him in their power.

'Six hundred rubles, ace, a corner, a nine... winning it back's impossible... Oh, how pleasant it was at home!... The knave, double or quits... it can't be!... And why is he doing this to me?' Rostov pondered. Sometimes he staked a large sum, but Dolokhov refused to accept it and fixed the stake himself. Nicholas submitted to him, and at one moment prayed to God as he had done on the battlefield at the bridge over the Enns, and then guessed that the card that came first to hand from the crumpled heap under the table would save him, now counted the cords on his coat and took a card with that number and tried staking the total of his losses on it, then he looked round for aid from the other players, or peered at the now cold face of Dolokhov and tried to read what was passing in his mind.

'He knows of course what this loss means to me. He can't want my ruin. Wasn't he my friend? Wasn't I fond of him? But it's not his fault. What's he to do if he has such luck?... And it's not my fault either,' he thought to himself. 'I have done nothing wrong. Have I killed anyone, or insulted or wished harm to anyone? Why such a terrible misfortune? And when did it begin? Such a little while ago I came to this table with the thought of winning a hundred rubles to buy that casket for mamma's name-day and then going home. I was so happy, so free, so light-hearted! And I did not realize how happy I was! When did that end and when did this new, terrible state of things begin? What marked the change? I sat all the time in this same place at this table, chose and placed cards, and watched those broad-boned agile hands in the same way. When did it happen and what has happened? I am well and strong, and still the same and in the same place. No, it can't be! Surely it will all end in nothing!'

He was flushed and bathed in perspiration, though the room was not hot. His face was terrible and piteous to see, especially from its helpless efforts to seem calm.

The score against him reached the fateful sum of forty-three thousand. Rostov had just prepared a card, by bending the corner of which he meant to double the three thousand just put down to his score, when Dolokhov, slamming down the pack of cards, put it aside and began rapidly adding up the total of Rostov's debt, breaking the chalk as he marked the figures in his clear, bold hand.

'Supper, it's time for supper! And here are the gipsies!'

Some swarthy men and women were really entering from the cold outside, and saying something in their gipsy accents. Nicholas understood that it was all over; but he said in an indifferent tone:

'Well, won't you go on? I had a splendid card all ready,' as if it were the fun of the game which interested him most.

'It's all up! I'm lost!' thought he. 'Now a bullet through my brain – that's all that's left me!' And at the same time he said in a cheerful voice:

'Come now, just this one more little card!'

'All right!' said Dolokhov, having finished the addition. 'All right! Twenty-one rubles,' he said, pointing to the figure twenty-one by which the total exceeded the round sum of forty-three thousand; and taking up a pack he prepared to deal. Rostov submissively unbent the corner of his card and, instead of the six thousand he had intended, carefully wrote twenty-one.

'It's all the same to me,' he said. 'I only want to see whether you will let me win this ten, or beat it.'

Dolokhov began to deal seriously. Oh, how Rostov detested at that moment those hands with their short reddish fingers and hairy wrists, which held him in their power . . . The ten fell to him.

'You owe forty-three thousand, Count,' said Dolokhov, and stretching himself he rose from the table. 'One does get tired sitting so long,' he added.

'Yes, I'm tired too,' said Rostov.

Dolokhov cut him short, as if to remind him that it was not for him to jest.

'When am I to receive the money, Count?'

Rostov, flushing, drew Dolokhov into the next room.

'I cannot pay it all immediately. Will you take an I.O.U.?' he said.

'I say, Rostov,' said Dolokhov clearly, smiling, and looking Nicholas straight in the eyes, 'You know the saying, "Lucky in love unlucky at cards." Your cousin is in love with you, I know.'

'Oh, it's terrible to feel oneself so in this man's power,' thought Rostov. He knew what a shock he would inflict on his father and mother by the news of this loss, he knew what a relief it would be to escape it all, and felt that Dolokhov knew that he could save him from all this shame and sorrow, but wanted now to play with him as a cat does with a mouse.

'Your cousin . . .' Dolokhov started to say, but Nicholas interrupted him.

'My cousin has nothing to do with this and it's not necessary to mention her!' he exclaimed fiercely.

'Then when am I to have it?'

'To-morrow,' replied Rostov and left the room.

15

To say 'to-morrow' and keep up a dignified tone was not difficult, but to go home alone, see his sisters, brother, mother, and father, confess and ask for money he had no right to after giving his word of honour, was terrible.

At home they had not yet gone to bed. The young people after returning from the theatre had had supper, and were grouped round the clavichord. As soon as Nicholas entered he was enfolded in that poetic atmosphere of love which pervaded the Rostov household that winter, and now after Dolokhov's proposal and Iogel's ball seemed to have grown thicker round Sonya and Natasha as the air does before a thunderstorm. Sonya and Natasha in the light blue dresses they had worn at the theatre, looking pretty and conscious of it, were standing by the clavichord happy and smiling. Vera was playing chess with Shinshin in the drawing-room. The old countess, waiting for the return of her husband and son, sat playing patience with the old gentlewoman who lived in their house. Denisov, with sparkling eyes and ruffled hair, sat at the clavichord striking chords with his short fingers, his legs thrown back and his eyes rolling as he sang, with his small, husky, but true voice, some verses called 'Enchantress'* which he had composed, and to which he was trying to fit music.

> Enchantress say, to my forsaken lyre
> What magic power is this recalls me still?
> What spark has set my inmost soul on fire,
> What is this bliss that makes my fingers thrill?

– He was singing in passionate tones, gazing with his sparkling black agate eyes at the frightened and happy Natasha.

'Splendid! Excellent!' exclaimed Natasha. 'Another verse,' she said without noticing Nicholas.

'Everything's still the same with them,' thought Nicholas, glancing into the drawing-room, where he saw Vera and his mother with the old lady.

'Ah, and here's Nicholas!' cried Natasha running up to him.

'Is papa at home?' he asked.

'I am so glad you've come!' said Natasha without answering him. 'We *are* enjoying ourselves! Vasili Dmitrich is staying a day longer for my sake! Did you know?'

'No, papa is not back yet,' said Sonya.

'Nicholas, have you come? Come here, dear!' called the old countess from the drawing-room.

Nicholas went to her, kissed her hand, and sitting down silently at her table began to watch her hands arranging the cards. From the dancing-room they still heard the laughter, and merry voices trying to persuade Natasha to sing.

"All wight! All wight!' shouted Denisov, 'It's no good making excuses now! It's your turn to sing the ba'cawolle – I entweat you!'

The countess glanced at her silent son.

'What is the matter?' she asked.

'Oh, nothing,' said he as if weary of being continually asked the same question. 'Will Papa be back soon?'

'I expect so.'

'Everything's the same with them. They know nothing about it! Where am I to go?' thought Nicholas, and went again into the dancing-room where the clavichord stood.

Sonya was sitting at the clavichord playing the prelude to Denisov's favourite barcarolle. Natasha was preparing to sing. Denisov was looking at her with enraptured eyes.

Nicholas began pacing up and down the room.

'Why do they want to make her sing? How can she sing? There's nothing to be happy about!' thought he.

Sonya struck the first chord of the prelude.

'My God, I'm a ruined and dishonoured man! A bullet through my brain is the only thing left me – not singing!' his thoughts ran on. 'Go away? But where to? It's all one – let them sing!'

He continued to pace the room looking gloomily at Denisov and the girls and avoiding their eyes.

'Nikolenka, what is the matter?' Sonya's eyes fixed on him seemed to ask. She noticed at once that something had happened to him.

Nicholas turned away from her. Natasha too, with her quick instinct, had instantly noticed her brother's condition. But though she noticed it, she was herself in such high spirits at that moment, so far from sorrow, sadness or self-reproach, that she purposely deceived herself as young people often do. 'No, I am too happy now to spoil my enjoyment by sympathy with anyone's sorrow,' she felt, and she said to herself: 'No, I must be mistaken, he must be feeling happy just as I am.'

'Now Sonya!' she said, going to the very middle of the room where she considered the resonance was best.

Having lifted her head and let her arms droop lifelessly as ballet-dancers do, Natasha, rising energetically from her heels to her toes, stepped to the middle of the room and stood still.

'Yes, that's me!' she seemed to say, answering the rapt gaze with which Denisov followed her.

'And what is she so pleased about?' thought Nicholas, looking at his sister. 'Why isn't she dull and ashamed?'

Natasha took the first note, her throat swelled, her chest rose, her eyes became serious. At that moment she was oblivious of her surroundings, and from her smiling lips flowed sounds which any one may produce at the same intervals and hold for the same time, but which leave you cold a thousand times and the thousand and first time thrill you and make you weep.

Natasha that winter had for the first time begun to sing seriously, mainly because Denisov so delighted in her singing. She no longer sang as a child, there was no longer in her singing that comical, childish, painstaking effect that had been in it before; but she did not yet sing well, as all the connoisseurs who heard her said: 'It is not trained, but it is a beautiful voice that must be trained.' Only they generally said this some time after she had finished singing. While that untrained voice with its incorrect breathing and laboured transitions was sounding, even the connoisseurs said nothing, but only delighted in it and wished to hear it again. In her voice there was a virginal freshness, an unconsciousness of her own powers, and an as yet untrained velvety softness, which so mingled with her lack of art in singing that it seemed as if nothing in that voice could be altered without spoiling it.

'What is this?' thought Nicholas, listening to her with widely opened eyes. 'What has happened to her? How she is singing to-day!' And suddenly the whole world centred for him on anticipation of the next note, the next phrase, and everything in the world was divided into three beats: *Oh mio crudele affetto* ... One, two, three ... one, two, three ... One ... *Oh mio crudele affetto* ... One, two, three ... One. 'Oh, this senseless life of ours!' thought Nicholas. 'All this misery, and money, and Dolokhov, and anger, and honour – it's all nonsense ... but this is real ... Now then, Natasha, now then, dearest! Now then, darling! How will she take that *si*? She's taken it! Thank God!' And without noticing that he was singing, to strengthen the *si* he sung a second, a third below the high note. 'Ah, God! How fine! Did I really take it? How fortunate!' he thought.

Oh, how that chord vibrated, and how moved was something

that was finest in Rostov's soul! And this something was apart from everything else in the world and above everything in the world. 'What were losses, and Dolokhov, and words of honour? . . . All nonsense! One might kill and rob and yet be happy . . .'

16

IT was long since Rostov had felt such enjoyment from music as he did that day. But no sooner had Natasha finished her barcarolle than reality again presented itself. He got up without saying a word and went downstairs to his own room. A quarter of an hour later the old count came in from his Club cheerful and contented. Nicholas, hearing him drive up, went to meet him.

'Well – had a good time?' said the old count, smiling gaily and proudly at his son.

Nicholas tried to say 'Yes,' but could not: and he nearly burst into sobs. The count was lighting his pipe and did not notice his son's condition.

'Ah, it can't be avoided!' thought Nicholas for the first and last time. And suddenly, in the most casual tone, which made him feel ashamed of himself, he said, as if merely asking his father to let him have the carriage to drive into town:

'Papa, I have come on a matter of business. I was nearly forgetting. I need some money.'

'Dear me!' said his father who was in a specially good humour. 'I told you it would not be enough. How much?'

'Very much,' said Nicholas flushing, and with a stupid careless smile for which he was long unable to forgive himself, 'I have lost a little, I mean a good deal, a great deal – forty-three thousand.'

'What! To whom? . . . Nonsense!' cried the count, suddenly reddening with an apoplectic flush over neck and nape as old people do.

'I promised to pay to-morrow,' said Nicholas.

'Well! . . .' said the old count, spreading out his arms and sinking helplessly on the sofa.

'It can't be helped! It happens to everyone!' said the son with a bold, free and easy tone, while in his soul he regarded himself as a worthless scoundrel whose whole life could not atone for his crime. He longed to kiss his father's hands and kneel to beg his forgiveness, but said, in a careless and even rude voice, that it happens to everyone!

The old count cast down his eyes on hearing his son's words, and began bustlingly searching for something.

'Yes, yes,' he muttered, 'it will be difficult, I fear, difficult to raise.... happens to everybody! Yes, who has not done it?'

And with a furtive glance at his son's face the count went out of the room ... Nicholas had been prepared for resistance, but had not at all expected this.

'Papa! Pa-pa!' he called after him sobbing, 'forgive me!' And seizing his father's hand, he pressed it to his lips and burst into tears.

*

While father and son were having their explanation, the mother and daughter were having one not less important. Natasha came running to her mother quite excited.

'Mamma! ... Mamma! ... He has made me ...'

'Made what?'

'Made, made me an offer, mamma! Mamma!' she exclaimed.

The countess did not believe her ears. Denisov had proposed. To whom? To this chit of a girl, Natasha, who not so long ago was playing with dolls and who was still having lessons.

'Don't, Natasha! What nonsense!' she said, hoping it was a joke.

'Nonsense indeed! I am telling you the fact,' said Natasha indignantly. 'I come to ask you what to do, and you call it "nonsense!"'

The countess shrugged her shoulders.

'If it is true that Monsieur Denisov has made you a proposal, tell him he is a fool, that's all!'

'No, he's not a fool!' replied Natasha indignantly and seriously.

'Well then, what do you want? You're all in love nowadays. Well, if you are in love, marry him!' said the countess with a laugh of annoyance. 'Good luck to you!'

'No, mamma, I'm not in love with him, I suppose I'm not in love with him.'

'Well then, tell him so.'

'Mamma, are you cross? Don't be cross, dear! Is it my fault?'

'No, but what is it, my dear? Do you want me to go and tell him?' said the countess smiling.

'No, I will do it myself, only tell me what to say. It's all very well for you,' said Natasha, with a responsive smile. 'You should have seen how he said it! I know he did not mean to say it, but it came out accidentally.'

'Well, all the same, you must refuse him.'

'No, I mustn't. I am so sorry for him! He's so nice.'

'Well then, accept his offer. It's high time for you to be married,' answered the countess sharply and sarcastically.

'No, mamma, but I'm so sorry for him. I don't know how I'm to say it.'

'And there's nothing for you to say. I shall speak to him myself,' said the countess, indignant that they should have dared to treat this little Natasha as grown up.

'No, not on any account! I will tell him myself, and you'll listen at the door,' and Natasha ran across the drawing-room to the dancing-hall, where Denisov was sitting on the same chair by the clavichord with his face in his hands.

He jumped up at the sound of her light step.

'Natalie,' he said, moving with rapid steps towards her, 'decide my fate. It is in your hands.'

'Vasili Dmitrich, I'm so sorry for you!...No, but you are so nice...but it won't do...not that...but as a friend I shall always love you.'

Denisov bent over her hand and she heard strange sounds she did not understand. She kissed his rough curly black head. At this instant they heard the quick rustle of the countess's dress. She came up to them.

'Vasili Dmitrich, I thank you for the honour,' she said, with an embarrassed voice, though it sounded severe to Denisov '– but my daughter is so young, and I thought that, as my son's friend, you would have addressed yourself first to me. In that case you would not have obliged me to give this refusal.'

'Countess...' said Denisov with downcast eyes and a guilty face. He tried to say more, but faltered.

Natasha could not remain calm seeing him in such a plight. She began to sob aloud.

'Countess, I have done w'ong,' Denisov went on in an unsteady voice, 'but believe me, I so adore your daughter and all your family that I would give my life twice over...' He looked at the countess, and seeing her severe face said: 'Well, good-bye, Countess,' and kissing her hand, he left the room with quick resolute strides, without looking at Natasha.

*

Next day Rostov saw Denisov off. He did not wish to stay another day in Moscow. All Denisov's Moscow friends gave him a farewell entertainment at the gipsies', with the result that he had no recollection of how he was put in the sledge or of the first three stages of his journey.

After Denisov's departure Rostov spent another fortnight in Moscow, without going out of the house, waiting for the money his father could not at once raise, and he spent most of his time in the girls' room.

Sonya was more tender and devoted to him than ever. It was as if she wanted to show him that his losses were an achievement that made her love him all the more, but Nicholas now considered himself unworthy of her.

He filled the girls' albums with verses and music, and having at last sent Dolokhov the whole forty-three thousand rubles and received his receipt, he left at the end of November without taking leave of any of his acquaintances, to overtake his regiment which was already in Poland.

END OF PART ONE

PART TWO

1

AFTER his interview with his wife Pierre left for Petersburg. At the Torzhok post-station either there were no horses or the post-master would not supply them. Pierre was obliged to wait. Without undressing, he lay down on the leather sofa in front of a round table, put his big feet in their over-boots on the table and began to reflect.

'Will you have the portmanteaux brought in? And a bed got ready, and tea?' asked his valet.

Pierre gave no answer, for he neither heard nor saw anything. He had begun to think at the last station and was still pondering on the same question – one so important that he took no notice of what went on around him. Not only was he indifferent as to whether he got to Petersburg earlier or later, or whether he secured accommodation at this station, but compared to the thoughts that now occupied him it was a matter of indifference whether he remained there for a few hours or for the rest of his life.

The post-master, his wife, the valet, and a peasant woman selling Torzhok embroidery, came into the room offering their services. Without changing his careless attitude Pierre looked at them over his spectacles unable to understand what they wanted or how they could go on living without having solved the problems that so absorbed him. He had been engrossed by the same thoughts ever since the day he returned from Sokolniki after the duel and had spent that first agonizing, sleepless night. But now in the solitude of the journey they seized him with special force. No matter what he thought about, he always returned to these same questions which he could not solve and yet could not cease to ask himself. It was as if the thread of the chief screw which held his life together were stripped, so that the screw could not get in or out, but went on turning uselessly in the same place.

The post-master came in and began obsequiously to beg his Excellency to wait only two hours, when, come what might, he would let his Excellency have the courier-horses. It was plain that

367

he was lying and only wanted to get more money from the traveller.

'Is this good or bad?' Pierre asked himself. 'It is good for me, bad for another traveller, and for himself it's unavoidable because he needs money for food; the man said an officer had once given him a thrashing for letting a private traveller have the courier-horses. But the officer thrashed him because he had to get on as quickly as possible. And I,' continued Pierre, 'shot Dolokhov because I considered myself injured, and Louis XVI was executed because they considered him a criminal, and a year later they executed those who had executed him – also for some reason. What is bad? What is good? What should one love and what hate? What does one live for? And what am I? What is life, and what is death? What Power governs it all?'

There was no answer to any of these questions, except one, and that not a logical answer and not at all a reply to them. The answer was: 'You'll die and all will end. You'll die and know all, or cease asking.' But dying was also dreadful.

The Torzhok pedlar woman in a whining voice went on offering her wares, especially a pair of goat-skin slippers. 'I have hundreds of rubles I don't know what to do with, and she stands in her tattered cloak looking timidly at me,' he thought. 'And what does she want the money for? As if that money could add a hair's breadth to her happiness or peace of mind. Can anything in the world make her or me less a prey to evil and death? – death which ends all and must come to-day or to-morrow – at any rate in an instant as compared with eternity.' And again he twisted the screw with the stripped thread, and again it turned uselessly in the same place.

His servant handed him a half-cut novel, in the form of letters, by Madame de Souza.* He began reading about the sufferings and virtuous struggles of a certain Émilie de Mansfeld. 'And why did she resist her seducer when she loved him?' he thought. 'God could not have put into her heart an impulse that was against His will. My wife – as she once was – did not struggle, and perhaps she was right. Nothing has been found out, nothing discovered,' Pierre again said to himself. 'All we can know is that we know nothing. And that's the height of human wisdom.'

Everything within and around him seemed confused, senseless, and repellent. Yet in this very repugnance to all his circumstances Pierre found a kind of tantalizing satisfaction.

'I make bold to ask your Excellency to move a little for this gentleman,' said the post-master, entering the room followed by another traveller also detained for lack of horses.

The newcomer was a short, large-boned, yellow-faced, wrinkled old man, with grey bushy eyebrows overhanging bright eyes of an indefinite greyish colour.

Pierre took his feet off the table, stood up, and lay down on a bed that had been got ready for him, glancing now and then at the newcomer, who with a gloomy and tired face was wearily taking off his wraps with the aid of his servant, and not looking at Pierre. With a pair of felt boots on his thin bony legs, and keeping on a worn, nankeen-covered sheep-skin coat, the traveller sat down on the sofa, leant back his big head with its broad temples and close-cropped hair, and looked at Bezukhov. The stern, shrewd, and penetrating expression of that look struck Pierre. He felt a wish to speak to the stranger, but by the time he had made up his mind to ask him a question about the roads, the traveller had closed his eyes. His shrivelled old hands were folded and on the finger of one of them Pierre noticed a large cast-iron ring with a seal representing a death's head. The stranger sat without stirring, either resting or, as it seemed to Pierre, sunk in profound and calm meditation. His servant was also a yellow, wrinkled old man, without beard or moustache, evidently not because he was shaven but because they had never grown. The active old servant was unpacking the traveller's canteen and preparing tea. He brought in a boiling samovar. When everything was ready, the stranger opened his eyes, moved to the table, filled a tumbler with tea for himself and one for the beardless old man to whom he passed it. Pierre began to feel a sense of uneasiness, and the need, even the inevitability, of entering into conversation with this stranger.

The servant brought back his tumbler turned upside down with an unfinished bit of nibbled sugar, and asked if anything more would be wanted.*

'No. Give me the book,' said the stranger.

The servant handed him a book which Pierre took to be a devotional work, and the traveller became absorbed in it. Pierre looked at him. All at once the stranger closed the book, putting in a marker, and again, leaning with his arms on the back of the sofa, sat in his former position with his eyes shut. Pierre looked at him and had not time to turn away when the old man, opening his eyes, fixed his steady and severe gaze straight on Pierre's face.

Pierre felt confused, and wished to avoid that look, but the bright old eyes attracted him irresistibly.

'I HAVE the pleasure of addressing Count Bezukhov if I am not mistaken,' said the stranger in a deliberate and loud voice.

Pierre looked silently and inquiringly at him over his spectacles.

'I have heard of you, my dear sir,' continued the stranger, 'and of your misfortune.' He seemed to emphasize the last word, as if to say – 'Yes, misfortune! Call it what you please, I know that what happened to you in Moscow was a misfortune.' – 'I regret it very much, my dear sir.'

Pierre flushed, and hurriedly putting his legs down from the bed, bent forward towards the old man with a forced and timid smile.

'I have not referred to this out of curiosity, my dear sir, but for graver reasons.'

He paused, his gaze still on Pierre, and moved aside on the sofa by way of inviting the other to take a seat beside him. Pierre felt reluctant to enter into conversation with this old man, but submitting to him involuntarily, came up and sat down beside him.

'You are unhappy, my dear sir,' the stranger continued. 'You are young and I am old. I should like to help you as far as lies in my power.'

'Oh, yes!' said Pierre, with a forced smile. 'I am very grateful to you. Where are you travelling from?'

The stranger's face was not genial, it was even cold and severe, but in spite of this, both the face and words of his new acquaintance were irresistibly attractive to Pierre.

'But if for any reason you don't feel inclined to talk to me,' said the old man, 'say so, my dear sir.' And he suddenly smiled in an unexpected and tenderly paternal way.

'Oh no, not at all! On the contrary I am very glad to make your acquaintance,' said Pierre. And again glancing at the stranger's hands he looked more closely at the ring with its skull – a masonic sign.

'Allow me to ask,' he said, 'are you a mason?'

'Yes, I belong to the Brotherhood of the Freemasons,'* said the stranger, looking deeper and deeper into Pierre's eyes. 'And in their name and my own I hold out a brotherly hand to you.'

'I am afraid,' said Pierre, smiling, and wavering between the confidence the personality of the freemason inspired in him and his own habit of ridiculing the masonic beliefs '– I am afraid I am very far from understanding – how am I to put it? – I am afraid my way of looking at the world is so opposed to yours that we shall not understand one another.'

'I know your outlook,' said the mason, 'and the view of life you mention, and which you think is the result of your own mental efforts, is the one held by the majority of people, and is the invariable fruit of pride, indolence, and ignorance. Forgive me, my dear sir, but if I had not known it I should not have addressed you. Your view of life is a regrettable delusion.'

'Just as I may suppose you to be deluded,' said Pierre with a faint smile.

'I should never dare to say that I know the truth,' said the mason, whose words struck Pierre more and more by their precision and firmness. 'No one can attain to truth by himself. Only by laying stone on stone with the co-operation of all, by the millions of generations from our forefather Adam to our own times, is that temple reared which is to be a worthy dwelling-place of the Great God,' he added, and closed his eyes.

'I ought to tell you that I do not believe ... do not believe in God,' said Pierre regretfully and with an effort, feeling it essential to speak the whole truth.

The mason looked intently at Pierre and smiled as a rich man with millions in hand might smile at a poor fellow who told him that he, poor man, had not the five rubles that would make him happy.

'Yes, you do not know Him, my dear sir,' said the mason. 'You cannot know Him. You do not know Him and that is why you are unhappy.'

'Yes, yes, I am unhappy,' assented Pierre. 'But what am I to do?'

'You know Him not, my dear sir, and so you are very unhappy. You do not know Him, but He is here. He is in me, He is in my words, He is in thee, and even in those blasphemous words thou hast just uttered!' pronounced the mason in a stern and tremulous voice.

He paused and sighed, evidently trying to calm himself.

'If He were not,' he said quietly, 'you and I would not be speaking of Him, my dear sir. Of what, of whom, are we speaking? Whom hast thou denied?' he suddenly asked with exulting austerity and authority in his voice. 'Who invented Him, if He does not exist? Whence came thy conception of the existence of such an incomprehensible Being? Why didst thou, and why did the whole world, conceive the idea of the existence of such an incomprehensible Being, a Being all-powerful, eternal, and infinite in all His attributes? ...'

He stopped and remained silent for a long time.

Pierre could not and did not wish to break this silence.

'He exists, but to understand Him is hard,' the mason began again, looking not at Pierre but straight before him, and turning the leaves of his book with his old hands which from excitement he could not keep still. 'If it were a man whose existence thou didst doubt I could bring him to thee, could take him by the hand and show him to thee. But how can I, an insignificant mortal, show His omnipotence, His infinity, and all His mercy to one who is blind, or who shuts his eyes that he may not see or understand Him and may not see or understand his own vileness and sinfulness?' He paused again. 'Who art thou? Thou dreamest that thou art wise because thou couldst utter those blasphemous words,' he went on with a sombre and scornful smile. 'And thou art more foolish and unreasonable than a little child, who playing with the parts of a skilfully made watch dares to say that, as he does not understand its use, he does not believe in the master who made it. To know Him is hard ... For ages, from our forefather Adam to our own day, we labour to attain that knowledge and are still infinitely far from our aim; but in our lack of understanding we see only our weakness and His greatness ...'

Pierre listened with swelling heart, gazing into the mason's face with shining eyes, not interrupting or questioning him but believing with his whole soul what the stranger said. Whether he accepted the wise reasoning contained in the mason's words, or believed as a child believes, in the speaker's tone of conviction and earnestness or the tremor of the speaker's voice – which sometimes almost broke – or those brilliant aged eyes grown old in this conviction, or the calm firmness and certainty of his vocation, which radiated from his whole being (and which struck Pierre especially by contrast with his own dejection and hopelessness) – at any rate Pierre longed with his whole soul to believe and he did believe, and felt a joyful sense of comfort, regeneration, and return to life.

'He is not to be apprehended by reason, but by life,' said the mason.

'I do not understand,' said Pierre, feeling with dismay doubts reawakening. He was afraid of any want of clearness, any weakness, in the mason's arguments, he dreaded not to be able to believe in him. 'I don't understand,' he said, 'how it is that the mind of man cannot attain the knowledge of which you speak?'

The mason smiled with his gentle fatherly smile.

'The highest wisdom and truth are like the purest liquid we may wish to imbibe,' he said. 'Can I receive that pure liquid into an impure vessel and judge of its purity? Only by the inner purification of myself can I retain in some degree of purity the liquid I receive.'

'Yes, yes, that is so,' said Pierre joyfully.

'The highest wisdom is not founded on reason alone, not on those worldly sciences of physics, history, chemistry, and the like, into which intellectual knowledge is divided. The highest wisdom is one. The highest wisdom has but one science – the science of the whole – the science explaining the whole creation and man's place in it. To receive that science it is necessary to purify and renew one's inner self, and so before one can know, it is necessary to believe and to perfect one's self. And to attain this end we have the light called conscience, that God has implanted in our souls.'

'Yes, yes,' assented Pierre.

'Look then at thy inner self with the eyes of the spirit, and ask thyself whether thou art content with thyself. What hast thou attained relying on reason only? What art thou? You are young, you are rich, you are clever, you are well educated. And what have you done with all these good gifts? Are you content with yourself and with your life?'

'No, I hate my life,' Pierre muttered, wincing.

'Thou hatest it. Then change it, purify thyself; and as thou art purified thou wilt gain wisdom. Look at your life, my dear sir. How have you spent it? In riotous orgies and debauchery, receiving everything from society and giving nothing in return. You have become the possessor of wealth. How have you used it? What have you done for your neighbour? Have you ever thought of your tens of thousands of slaves? Have you helped them physically and morally? No! You have profited by their toil to lead a profligate life. That is what you have done. Have you chosen a post in which you might be of service to your neighbour? No! You have spent your life in idleness. Then you married, my dear sir – took on yourself responsibility for the guidance of a young woman, and what have you done? You have not helped her to find the way of truth, my dear sir, but have thrust her into an abyss of deceit and misery. A man offended you and you shot him, and you say you do not know God and hate your life. There is nothing strange in that, my dear sir!'

After these words the mason, as if tired by his long discourse, again leant his arms on the back of the sofa and closed his eyes. Pierre looked at that aged, stern, motionless, almost lifeless face, and moved his lips without uttering a sound. He wished to say, 'Yes, a vile, idle, vicious life!' but dared not break the silence.

The mason cleared his throat huskily as old men do, and called his servant.

'How about the horses?' he asked, without looking at Pierre.

'The exchange horses have just come,' answered the servant. 'Will you not rest here?'

'No, tell them to harness.'

'Can he really be going away and leaving me alone without having told me all, and without promising to help me?' thought Pierre rising with downcast head; and he began to pace the room, glancing occasionally at the mason. 'Yes, I never thought of it, but I have led a contemptible and profligate life though I did not like it and did not want to,' thought Pierre. 'But this man knows the truth, and if he wished to, could disclose it to me.'

Pierre wished to say this to the mason, but did not dare to. The traveller, having packed his things with his practised hands, began fastening his coat. When he had finished he turned to Bezukhov, and said in a tone of indifferent politeness:

'Where are you going now, my dear sir?'

'I? ... I'm going to Petersburg,' answered Pierre in a childlike hesitating voice. 'I thank you. I agree with all you have said. But do not suppose me to be so bad. With my whole soul I wish to be what you would have me be, but I have never had help from anyone ... But it is I, above all, who am to blame for everything. Help me, teach me, and perhaps I may ...'

Pierre could not go on. He gulped and turned away.

The mason remained silent for a long time, evidently considering.

'Help comes from God alone,' he said, 'but such measure of help as our Order can bestow it will render you, my dear sir. You are going to Petersburg. Hand this to Count Willarski' (he took out his notebook and wrote a few words on a large sheet of paper folded in four). 'Allow me to give you a piece of advice. When you reach the capital, first of all devote some time to solitude and self-examination and do not resume your former way of life. And now I wish you a good journey, my dear sir,' he added, seeing that his servant had entered ... 'and success.'

The traveller was Joseph Alexeevich Bazdeev, as Pierre saw from the post-master's book. Bazdeev had been one of the best-known freemasons and Martinists even in Novikov's time.* For a long while after he had gone Pierre did not go to bed or order horses but paced up and down the room pondering over his vicious past, and with a rapturous sense of beginning anew pictured to himself the blissful irreproachable virtuous future that seemed to him so easy. It seemed to him that he had been vicious only because he had somehow forgotten how good it is to be virtuous. Not a trace of his former doubts remained in his soul. He firmly believed in the

possibility of the brotherhood of men united in the aim of supporting one another in the path of virtue, and that is how freemasonry
presented itself to him.

3

ON reaching Petersburg Pierre did not let anyone know of his
arrival, he went nowhere and spent whole days in reading Thomas
à Kempis,* whose book had been sent him by someone unkown.
One thing he continually realized as he read that book: the joy,
hitherto unknown to him, of believing in the possibility of attaining perfection and in the possibility of active brotherly love among
men, which Joseph Alexeevich had revealed to him. A week after
his arrival the young Polish count Willarski, whom Pierre had
known slightly in Petersburg society, came into his room one
evening in the official and ceremonious manner with which Dolokhov's second had called on him, and having closed the door
behind him and satisfied himself that there was nobody else in
the room, addressed Pierre.

'I have come to you with a message and an offer, Count,' he
said without sitting down. 'A person of very high standing in our
Brotherhood has made application for 'you to be received into our
Order before the usual term, and has proposed to me to be your
sponsor. I consider it a sacred duty to fulfil that person's wishes.
Do you wish to enter the Brotherhood of Freemasons under my
sponsorship?'

The cold austere tone of this man, whom he had almost always
before met at balls amiably smiling in the society of the most
brilliant women, surprised Pierre.

'Yes, I do wish it,' said he.

Willarski bowed his head.

'One more question, Count,' he said, 'which I beg you to
answer in all sincerity – not as a future mason but as an honest
man: have you renounced your former convictions – do you believe
in God?'

Pierre considered.

'Yes . . . yes, I believe in God,' he said.

'In that case . . .' began Willarski, but Pierre interrupted him.

'Yes, I do believe in God,' he repeated.

'In that case we can go,' said Willarski. 'My carriage is at your
service.'

Willarski was silent throughout the drive. To Pierre's inquiries
as to what he must do and how he should answer, Willarski only

replied that brothers more worthy than he would test him, and that Pierre had only to tell the truth.*

Having entered the courtyard of a large house where the Lodge had its quarters, and having ascended a dark staircase, they entered a small well-lit ante-room where they took off their cloaks without the aid of a servant. From there they passed into another room. A man in strange attire appeared at the door. Willarski, stepping towards him, said something to him in French in an undertone and then went up to a small wardrobe in which Pierre noticed garments such as he had never seen before. Having taken a kerchief from the cupboard, Willarski bound Pierre's eyes with it and tied it in a knot behind, catching some hairs painfully in the knot. Then he drew his face down, kissed him, and taking him by the hand led him forward. The hairs tied in the knot hurt Pierre and there were lines of pain on his face and a shamefaced smile. His huge figure, with arms hanging down and with a puckered though smiling face, moved after Willarski with uncertain timid steps.

Having led him about ten paces, Willarski stopped.

'Whatever happens to you,' he said, 'you must bear it all manfully if you have firmly resolved to join our Brotherhood.' (Pierre nodded affirmatively.) 'When you hear a knock at the door you will uncover your eyes,' added Willarski. 'I wish you courage and success,' and pressing Pierre's hand, he went out.

Left alone, Pierre went on smiling in the same way. Once or twice he shrugged his shoulders and raised his hand to the kerchief as if wishing to take it off, but let it drop again. The five minutes spent with his eyes bandaged seemed to him an hour. His arm felt numb, his legs almost gave way, it seemed to him that he was tired out. He experienced a variety of most complex sensations. He felt afraid of what would happen to him, and still more afraid of showing his fear. He felt curious to know what was going to happen and what would be revealed to him; but most of all he felt joyful that the moment had come when he would at last start on that path of regeneration and on the actively virtuous life of which he had been dreaming since he met Joseph Alexeevich. Loud knocks were heard at the door. Pierre took the bandage off his eyes and glanced around him. The room was in black darkness, only a small lamp was burning inside something white. Pierre went nearer and saw that the lamp stood on a black table on which lay an open book. The book was the Gospel, and the white thing with the lamp inside was a human skull with its cavities and teeth. After reading the first words of the Gospel: 'In the beginning was the Word, and the Word was with God', Pierre went round the table and saw a large open box filled with something. It was a coffin with bones inside. He was not at all surprised by what he saw. Hoping to enter on an entirely new life quite unlike the old one, he expected everything to be unusual, even more unusual than what he was seeing. A skull, a coffin, the Gospel – it seemed to him that he had expected all this and even more. Trying to stimulate his emotions he looked around. 'God, death, love, the brotherhood of man,' he kept saying to himself, associating these words with vague yet joyful ideas. The door opened and someone came in.

By the dim light to which Pierre had already become accustomed, he saw a rather short man. Having evidently come from the light into the darkness, the man paused, then moved with cautious steps towards the table and placed on it his small leather-gloved hands.

This short man had on a white leather apron which covered his chest and part of his legs, and a kind of necklace above which rose a high white ruffle, outlining his rather long face which was lit up from below.

'For what have you come hither?' asked the newcomer turning in Pierre's direction at a slight rustle made by the latter. 'Why have you, who do not believe in the truth of the light and who have not seen the light, come here? What do you seek from us? Wisdom, virtue, enlightenment?'

At the moment the door opened and the stranger came in Pierre felt a sense of awe and veneration such as he had experienced in his boyhood at confession; he felt himself in the presence of one socially a complete stranger, yet near to him through the brotherhood of man. With bated breath and beating heart he moved towards the Rhetor (by which name the brother who prepared a seeker for entrance into the Brotherhood was known). Drawing nearer, he recognized in the Rhetor a man he knew, Smolyaninov, and it mortified him to think that the newcomer was an acquaintance – he wished him simply a brother and a virtuous instructor. For a long time he could not utter a word, so that the Rhetor had to repeat his question.

'Yes ... I ... I ... desire regeneration,' Pierre uttered with difficulty.

'Very well,' said Smolyaninov, and went on at once: 'Have you any idea of the means by which our holy Order will help you to reach your aim?' said he quietly and quickly.

'I ... hope ... for guidance ... help ... in regeneration,' said Pierre with a trembling voice and some difficulty in utterance, due to his excitement and to being unaccustomed to speak of abstract matters in Russian.

'What is your conception of Freemasonry?'

'I imagine that Freemasonry is the fraternity and equality of men who have virtuous aims,' said Pierre, feeling ashamed of the inadequacy of his words for the solemnity of the moment, as he spoke. 'I imagine . . .'

'Good!' said the Rhetor quickly, apparently quite satisfied with this answer. 'Have you sought for means of attaining your aim in religion?'

'No, I considered it erroneous and did not follow it,' said Pierre, so softly that the Rhetor did not hear him and asked him what he was saying. 'I have been an atheist,' answered Pierre.

'You are seeking for truth in order to follow its laws in your life, therefore you seek wisdom and virtue. Is that not so?' said the Rhetor after a moment's pause.

'Yes, yes,' assented Pierre.

The Rhetor cleared his throat, crossed his gloved hands on his breast and began to speak.

'Now I must disclose to you the chief aim of our Order,' he said, 'and if this aim coincides with yours, you may enter our Brotherhood with profit. The first and chief object of our Order, the foundation on which it rests and which no human power can destroy, is the preservation and handing on to posterity of a certain important mystery . . . which has come down to us from the remotest ages, even from the first man – a mystery on which perhaps the fate of mankind depends. But since this mystery is of such a nature that nobody can know or use it unless he be prepared by long and diligent self-purification, not everyone can hope to attain it quickly. Hence we have a secondary aim, that of preparing our members as much as possible to reform their hearts, to purify and enlighten their minds, by means handed on to us by tradition from those who have striven to attain this mystery, and thereby to render them capable of receiving it.

'By purifying and regenerating our members we try, thirdly, to improve the whole human race, offering it in our members an example of piety and virtue, and thereby try with all our might to combat the evil which sways the world. Think this over and I will come to you again.'

'To combat the evil which sways the world . . .' Pierre repeated, and a mental image of his future activity in this direction rose in his mind. He imagined men such as he had himself been a fortnight ago, and he addressed an edifying exhortation to them. He imagined to himself vicious and unfortunate people whom he would assist by word and deed, imagined oppressors whose victims he would rescue. Of the three objects mentioned by the Rhetor this last, that of improving mankind, specially appealed to Pierre.

The important mystery mentioned by the Rhetor, though it aroused his curiosity, did not seem to him essential, and the second aim, that of purifying and regenerating himself, did not much interest him because at that moment he felt with delight that he was already perfectly cured of his former faults and was ready for all that was good.

Half an hour later the Rhetor returned to inform the seeker of the seven virtues, corresponding to the seven steps of Solomon's temple, which every freemason should cultivate in himself. These virtues were: 1. *Discretion*, the keeping of the secrets of the Order. 2. *Obedience* to those of higher ranks in the Order. 3. *Morality*. 4. *Love of mankind*. 5. *Courage*. 6. *Generosity*. 7. *The love of death*.

'In the *seventh* place, try by the frequent thought of death,' the Rhetor said, 'to bring yourself to regard it not as a dreaded foe, but as a friend that frees the soul grown weary in the labours of virtue from this distressful life, and leads it to its place of recompense and peace.'

'Yes, that must be so,' thought Pierre when after these words the Rhetor went away leaving him to solitary meditation. 'It must be so, but I am still so weak that I love my life, the meaning of which is only now gradually opening before me.' But five of the other virtues, which Pierre recalled, counting them on his fingers, he felt already in his soul: *Courage, generosity, morality, love of mankind*, and especially *obedience* – which did not even seem to him a virtue, but a joy. (He now felt so glad to be free from his own lawlessness and to submit his will to those who knew the indubitable truth.) He forgot what the seventh virtue was, and could not recall it.

The third time the Rhetor came back more quickly, and asked Pierre whether he was still firm in his intention and determined to submit to all that would be required of him.

'I am ready for everything,' said Pierre.

'I must also inform you,' said the Rhetor, 'that our Order delivers its teaching not in words only but also by other means, which may perhaps have a stronger effect on the sincere seeker after wisdom and virtue than mere words. This chamber with what you see therein, should already have suggested to your heart, if it is sincere, more than words could do. You will perhaps also see in your further initiation a like method of enlightenment. Our Order imitates the ancient societies that explained their teaching by hieroglyphics. A hieroglyph,' said the Rhetor, 'is an emblem of something not cognizable by the senses but which possesses qualities resembling those of the symbol.'

Pierre knew very well what a hieroglyph was, but dared not

speak. He listened to the Rhetor in silence, feeling from all he said that his ordeal was about to begin.

'If you are resolved, I must begin your initiation,' said the Rhetor coming closer to Pierre. 'In token of generosity I ask you to give me all your valuables.'

'But I have nothing here,' replied Pierre, supposing that he was asked to give up all he possessed.

'What you have with you: watch, money, rings...'

Pierre quickly took out his purse and watch, but could not manage for some time to get the wedding ring off his fat finger. When that had been done the Rhetor said:

'In token of obedience I ask you to undress.'

Pierre took off his coat, waistcoat, and left boot according to the Rhetor's instructions. The mason drew the shirt back from Pierre's left breast, and stooping down pulled up the left leg of his trousers to above the knee. Pierre hurriedly began taking off his right boot also and was going to tuck up the other trouser-leg to save this stranger the trouble, but the mason told him that was not necessary and gave him a slipper for his left foot. With a childlike smile of embarrassment, doubt, and self-derision, which appeared on his face against his will, Pierre stood with his arms hanging down and legs apart before his brother Rhetor, and awaited his further commands.

'And now in token of candour, I ask you to reveal to me your chief passion,' said the latter.

'My passion! I have had so many,' replied Pierre.

'That passion which more than all others caused you to waver on the path of virtue,' said the mason.

Pierre paused, seeking a reply.

'Wine? Gluttony? Idleness? Laziness? Irritability? Anger? Women?' He went over his vices in his mind not knowing to which of them to give the pre-eminence.

'Women,' he said in a low, scarcely audible voice.

The mason did not move and for a long time said nothing after this answer. At last he moved up to Pierre and, taking the kerchief that lay on the table, again bound his eyes.

'For the last time I say to you – turn all your attention upon yourself, put a bridle on your senses, and seek blessedness not in passion but in your own heart. The source of blessedness is not without us but within...'

Pierre had already long been feeling in himself that refreshing source of blessedness which now flooded his heart with glad emotion.

4

SOON after this there came into the dark chamber to fetch Pierre, not the Rhetor but Pierre's sponsor Willarski, whom he recognized by his voice. To fresh questions as to the firmness of his resolution Pierre replied: 'Yes, yes, I agree,' and with a beaming, childlike smile, his fat chest uncovered, stepping unevenly and timidly in one slippered and one booted foot, he advanced, while Willarski held a sword to his bare chest. He was conducted from that room along passages that turned backwards and forwards, and was at last brought to the doors of the Lodge. Willarski coughed, he was answered by the masonic knock with mallets, the doors opened before them. A bass voice (Pierre was still blindfold) questioned him as to who he was, when and where he was born, and so on. Then he was again led somewhere still blindfold, and as they went along he was told allegories of the toils of his pilgrimage, of holy friendship, of the Eternal Architect of the universe, and of the courage with which he should endure toils and dangers. During these wanderings Pierre noticed that he was spoken of now as the 'Seeker', now as the 'Sufferer', and now as the 'Postulant', to the accompaniment of various knockings with mallets and swords. As he was being led up to some object he noticed a hesitation and uncertainty among his conductors. He heard those around him disputing in whispers and one of them insisting that he should be led along a certain carpet. After that they took his right hand, placed it on something, and told him to hold a pair of compasses to his left breast with the other hand and to repeat, after someone who read aloud, an oath of fidelity to the laws of the Order. The candles were then extinguished and some spirit lighted, as Pierre knew by the smell, and he was told that he would now see the lesser light. The bandage was taken off his eyes and by the faint light of the burning spirit Pierre, as in a dream, saw several men standing before him, wearing aprons like the Rhetor's and holding swords in their hands pointed at his breast. Among them stood a man whose white shirt was stained with blood. On seeing this Pierre moved forward with his breast towards the swords, meaning them to pierce it. But the swords were drawn back from him and he was at once blindfolded again.

'Now thou hast seen the lesser light,' uttered a voice. Then the candles were relit and he was told that he would see the full light; the bandage was again removed and more than ten voices said together: 'Sic transit gloria mundi.'

Pierre gradually began to recover himself, and looked about at the room and at the people in it. Round a long table covered with black sat some twelve men in garments like those he had already seen. Some of them Pierre had met in Petersburg society. In the President's chair sat a young man he did not know, with a peculiar cross hanging from his neck. On his right sat the Italian abbé whom Pierre had met at Anna Pavlovna's two years before. There were also present a very distinguished dignitary, and a Swiss who had formerly been tutor at the Kuragins. All maintained a solemn silence, listening to the words of the President, who held a mallet in his hand. Let into the wall was a star-shaped light. At one side of the table was a small carpet with various figures worked upon it, at the other was something resembling an altar on which lay a Testament and a skull. Round it stood seven large candlesticks like those used in churches. Two of the brothers led Pierre up to the altar, placed his feet at right angles, and bade him lie down, saying that he must prostrate himself at the Gates of the Temple.

'He must first receive the trowel,' whispered one of the brothers.

'Oh, hush, please!' said another.

Pierre, perplexed, looked round with his short-sighted eyes without obeying, and suddenly doubts rose in his mind. 'Where am I? What am I doing? Aren't they laughing at me? Shan't I be ashamed to remember this?' But these doubts only lasted a moment. Pierre glanced at the serious faces of those around, remembered all he had already gone through, and realized that he could not stop half-way. He was aghast at his hesitation, and trying to arouse his former devotional feeling, prostrated himself before the Gates of the Temple. And really the feeling of devotion returned to him even more strongly than before. When he had lain there some time he was told to get up, and a white leather apron such as the others wore was put on him; he was given a trowel and three pairs of gloves, and then the Grand Master addressed him. He told him that he should try to do nothing to stain the whiteness of that apron, which symbolized strength and purity; then of the unexplained trowel, he told him to toil with it to cleanse his own heart from vice, and indulgently to smooth with it the heart of his neighbour. As to the first pair of gloves, a man's, he said that Pierre could not know their meaning but must keep them. The second pair of man's gloves he was to wear at the meetings, and finally of the third, a pair of women's gloves, he said: 'Dear brother, these woman's gloves are intended for you too. Give them to the woman whom you shall honour most of all. This gift will be a pledge of your purity of heart to her whom you select to be your worthy helpmeet in masonry.' And after a pause he added:

'But beware, dear brother, that these gloves do not deck hands that are unclean.' While the Grand Master said these last words it seemed to Pierre that he grew embarrassed. Pierre himself grew still more confused, blushed like a child till tears came into his eyes, began looking about him uneasily, and an awkward pause followed.

This silence was broken by one of the Brethren who led Pierre up to the rug and began reading to him from a manuscript book an explanation of all the figures on it: the sun, the moon, a hammer, a plumb-line, a trowel, a rough stone and a squared stone, a pillar, three windows, and so on. Then a place was assigned to Pierre, he was shown the signs of the Lodge, told the password, and at last was permitted to sit down. The Grand Master began reading the statutes. They were very long, and Pierre, from joy, agitation, and embarrassment, was not in a state to understand what was being read. He managed to follow only the last words of the statutes and these remained in his mind.

'In our temples we recognize no other distinctions,' read the Grand Master, 'but those between virtue and vice. Beware of making any distinctions which may infringe equality. Fly to a brother's aid whoever he may be, exhort him who goeth astray, raise him that falleth, and never bear malice or enmity towards thy brother. Be kindly and courteous. Kindle in all hearts the flame of virtue. Share thy happiness with thy neighbour, and may envy never dim the purity of that bliss. Forgive thy enemy, do not avenge thyself except by doing him good. Thus fulfilling the highest law thou shalt regain traces of the ancient dignity which thou hast lost.'

He finished, and getting up embraced and kissed Pierre, who with tears of joy in his eyes looked round him, not knowing how to answer the congratulations and greetings from acquaintances that met him on all sides. He acknowledged no acquaintances but saw in all these men only brothers, and burnt with impatience to set to work with them.

The Grand Master rapped with his mallet. All the masons sat down in their places, and one of them read an exhortation on the necessity of humility.

The Grand Master proposed that the last duty should be performed, and the distinguished dignitary who bore the title of 'Collector of Alms', went round to all the brothers. Pierre would have liked to subscribe all he had, but fearing that it might look like pride, subscribed the same amount as the others.

The meeting was at an end, and on reaching home Pierre felt as if he had returned from a long journey on which he had spent dozens of years, had become completely changed, and had quite left behind his former habits and way of life.

5

THE day after he had been received into the Lodge Pierre was sitting at home reading a book and trying to fathom the significance of the Square, one side of which symbolized God, another moral things, a third physical things, and the fourth a combination of these. Now and then his attention wandered from the book and the Square and he formed in imagination a new plan of life. On the previous evening at the Lodge he had heard that a rumour of his duel had reached the Emperor, and that it would be wiser for him to leave Petersburg. Pierre proposed going to his estates in the south and there attending to the welfare of his serfs. He was joyfully planning this new life, when Prince Vasili suddenly entered the room.

'My dear fellow, what have you been up to in Moscow? Why have you quarrelled with Hélène, *mon cher*? You are under a delusion,' said Prince Vasili as he entered. 'I know all about it, and I can tell you positively that Hélène is as innocent before you as Christ was before the Jews.'

Pierre was about to reply but Prince Vasili interrupted him.

'And why didn't you simply come straight to me as to a friend? I know all about it and understand it all,' he said. 'You behaved as becomes a man who values his honour, perhaps too hastily, but we won't go into that. But consider the position in which you are placing her and me in the eyes of society, and even of the Court,' he added, lowering his voice. 'She is living in Moscow and you are here. Remember, dear boy,' and he drew Pierre's arm downwards, 'it is simply a misunderstanding. I expect you feel it so yourself. Let us write her a letter at once, and she'll come here and all will be explained, or else, my dear boy, let me tell you it's quite likely you'll have to suffer for it.'

Prince Vasili gave Pierre a significant look.

'I know from reliable sources that the Dowager Empress is taking a keen interest in the whole affair. You know she is very gracious to Hélène.'

Pierre tried several times to speak, but on one hand Prince Vasili did not let him and on the other Pierre himself feared to begin to speak in the tone of decided refusal and disagreement in which he had firmly resolved to answer his father-in-law. Moreover the words of the masonic statutes, 'be kindly and courteous', recurred to him. He blinked, went red, got up and sat down again, struggling with himself to do what was for him the most difficult thing in life – to say an unpleasant thing to a man's face, to say what the other, whoever he might be, did not expect. He was so used to submitting to Prince Vasili's tone of careless self-assurance that he felt he would be unable to withstand it now, but he also felt that on what he said now his future depended – whether he would follow the same old road, or that new path so attractively shown him by the masons, on which he firmly believed he would be reborn to a new life.

'Now, dear boy,' said Prince Vasili playfully, 'say "yes", and I'll write to her myself, and we will kill the fatted calf.'

But before Prince Vasili had finished his playful speech, Pierre without looking at him, and with a kind of fury that made him like his father, muttered in a whisper:

'Prince, I did not ask you here. Go, please go!' And he jumped up and opened the door for him.

'Go!' he repeated, amazed at himself and glad to see the look of confusion and fear that showed itself on Prince Vasili's face.

'What's the matter with you? Are you ill?'

'Go!' the quivering voice repeated. And Prince Vasili had to go without receiving any explanation.

A week later Pierre, having taken leave of his new friends, the masons, and leaving large sums of money with them for alms, went away to his estates. His new brethren gave him letters to the Kiev and Odessa masons and promised to write to him and guide him in his new activity.

6

THE duel between Pierre and Dolokhov was hushed up and, in spite of the Emperor's severity regarding duels at that time, neither the principals nor their seconds suffered for it. But the story of the duel, confirmed by Pierre's rupture with his wife, was the talk of society. Pierre, who had been regarded with patronizing condescension when he was an illegitimate son, and petted and extolled when he was the best match in Russia, had sunk greatly in the esteem of society after his marriage – when the marriageable daughters and their mothers had nothing to hope from him – especially as he did not know how, and did not wish, to court society's favour. Now he alone was blamed for what had happened, he was said to be insanely jealous, and subject like his father to fits of bloodthirsty rage. And when after Pierre's departure Hélène returned to Petersburg, she was received by all her acquaintances not only cordially, but even with a shade of deference due to her misfortune. When conversation turned on her husband Hélène assumed a dignified expression, which with characteristic tact she had acquired though she did not understand its significance. This expression suggested that she had resolved to endure her troubles uncomplainingly, and that her husband was a cross laid upon her by God. Prince Vasili expressed his opinion more openly. He shrugged his shoulders when Pierre was mentioned and pointing to his forehead, remarked:

'A bit touched – I always said so.'

'I said from the first,' declared Anna Pavlovna referring to Pierre, 'I said at the time and before anyone else' (she insisted on her priority), 'that that senseless young man was spoilt by the depraved ideas of these days. I said so even at the time when everybody was in raptures about him, when he had just returned from abroad and when, if you remember, he posed as a sort of Marat at one of my soirées. And how has it ended? I was against this marriage even then, and foretold all that has happened.'

Anna Pavlovna continued to give on free evenings the same kind of soirées as before – such as she alone had the gift of arranging – at which was to be found 'the cream of really good society, the bloom of the intellectual essence of Petersburg', as she herself put it. Besides this refined selection of society Anna Pavlovna's receptions were also distinguished by the fact that she always presented some new and interesting persons to the visitors, and that nowhere else was the state of the political thermometer of legitimate Petersburg Court society so clearly and distinctly indicated.

Towards the end of 1806, when all the sad details of Napoleon's destruction of the Prussian Army at Jena and Auerstadt and the surrender of most of the Prussian fortresses had been received, when our troops had already entered Prussia and our second war with Napoleon was beginning, Anna Pavlovna gave one of her soirées. The 'cream of really good society' consisted of the fascinating Hélène, forsaken by her husband, Mortemart, the delightful Prince Hippolyte who had just returned from Vienna, two diplomatists, the old aunt, a young man referred to in that drawing-room as 'a man of great merit' (un homme de beaucoup de mérite), a newly-appointed maid of honour and her mother, and several other less noteworthy persons.

The novelty Anna Pavlovna was setting before her guests that evening was Boris Drubetskoy, who had just arrived as a special messenger from the Prussian army and was aide-de-camp to a very important personage.

The temperature shown by the political thermometer to the company that evening was this:

'Whatever the European sovereigns and commanders may do to countenance Bonaparte, and to cause *me*, and *us* in general, annoyance and mortification, our opinion of Bonaparte cannot alter. We shall not cease to express our sincere views on that subject, and can only say to the King of Prussia and others: "So much the worse for you. *Tu l'as voulu, George Dandin*",* that's all we have to say about it!'

When Boris who was to be served up to the guests entered the drawing-room, almost all the company had assembled, and the conversation, guided by Anna Pavlovna, was about our diplomatic relations with Austria and the hope of an alliance with her.

Boris, grown more manly and looking fresh, rosy, and self-possessed, entered the drawing-room elegantly dressed in the uniform of an aide-de-camp, and was duly conducted to pay his respects to the aunt and then brought back to the general circle.

Anna Pavlovna gave him her shrivelled hand to kiss, and introduced him to several persons whom he did not know, giving him a whispered description of each.

'Prince Hippolyte Kuragin – charming young fellow; M. Krug – *chargé d'affaires* from Copenhagen – a profound intellect,' and simply, 'Mr Shitov – a man of great merit,' – this of the man usually so described.

Thanks to Anna Mikhaylovna's efforts, his own tastes, and the peculiarities of his reserved nature, Boris had managed during his service to place himself very advantageously. He was aide-de-camp to a very important personage, had been sent on a very important mission to Prussia, and had just returned from there as a special messenger. He had become thoroughly conversant with that unwritten code with which he had been so pleased at Olmütz and according to which an ensign might rank incomparably higher than a general, and according to which what was needed for success in the service was not effort or work, or courage, or perseverance, but only the knowledge of how to get on with those who can grant rewards, and he was himself often surprised at the rapidity of his success, and at the inability of others to understand these things. In consequence of this discovery his whole manner of life, all his relations with old friends, all his plans for his future, were completely altered. He was not rich, but would spend his last groat to be better dressed than others, and would rather deprive himself of many pleasures than allow himself to be seen in a shabby equipage or appear in the streets of Petersburg in an old uniform. He made friends with and sought the acquaintance of only those above him in position and who could therefore be of use to him. He liked Petersburg and despised Moscow. The remembrance of the Rostovs' house and of his childish love for Natasha was unpleasant to him and he had not once been to see the Rostovs since the day of his departure for the army. To be in Anna Pavlovna's drawing-room he considered an important step up in the service, and he at once understood his rôle, letting his hostess make use of whatever interest he had to offer. He himself carefully scanned each face, appraising the possibilities of establishing intimacy with each of those present, and the advantages that might accrue. He took the seat indicated to him beside the fair Hélène, and listened to the general conversation.

'Vienna considers the bases of the proposed treaty so unattainable* that not even a continuity of most brilliant successes would secure them, and she doubts the means we have of gaining them. That is the actual phrase used by the Vienna cabinet,' said the Danish *chargé d'affaires*.

'The doubt is flattering,' said 'the man of profound intellect',* with a subtle smile.

'We must distinguish between the Vienna cabinet and the Emperor of Austria,' said Mortemart. 'The Emperor of Austria can never have thought of such a thing, it is only the cabinet that says it.'

'Ah, my dear Vicomte,' put in Anna Pavlovna, '*L'Urope*' (for some reason she called it *Urope* as if that were a specially refined French pronunciation which she could allow herself when conversing with a Frenchman), '*L'Urope ne sera jamais notre alliée sincère.*'

After that Anna Pavlovna led up to the courage and firmness of the King of Prussia, in order to draw Boris into the conversation.

Boris listened attentively to each of the speakers, awaiting his turn, but managed meanwhile to look round repeatedly at his neighbour, the beautiful Hélène, whose eyes several times met those of the handsome young aide-de-camp with a smile.

Speaking of the position of Prussia, Anna Pavlovna very naturally asked Boris to tell them about his journey to Glogau and in what state he found the Prussian army. Boris, speaking with deliberation, told them in pure correct French many interesting details about the armies and the Court, carefully abstaining from expressing an opinion of his own about the facts he was recounting. For some time he engrossed the general attention, and Anna Pavlovna felt that the novelty she had served up was received with pleasure by all her visitors. The greatest attention of all to Boris's narrative was shown by Hélène. She asked him several questions about his journey and seemed greatly interested in the state of the Prussian army. As soon as he had finished she turned to him with her usual smile.

'You absolutely must come and see me,' she said in a tone that implied that for certain considerations he could not know of this was absolutely necessary. 'On Tuesday, between eight and nine. It will give me great pleasure.'

Boris promised to fulfil her wish and was about to begin a conversation with her, when Anna Pavlovna called him away on the pretext that her aunt wished to hear him.

'You know her husband, of course?' said Anna Pavlovna, closing her eyes and indicating Hélène with a sorrowful gesture. 'Ah, she is such an unfortunate and charming woman! Don't mention him before her – please don't! It is too painful for her!'

7

WHEN Boris and Anna Pavlovna returned to the others Prince Hippolyte had the ear of the company. Bending forward in his arm-chair he said: '*Le Roi de Prusse!*' and having said this laughed. Everyone turned towards him.

'*Le Roi de Prusse?*' Hippolyte said interrogatively, again laughing, and then calmly and seriously sat back in his chair. Anna Pavlovna waited for him to go on, but as he seemed quite decided to say no more she began to tell of how at Potsdam the impious Bonaparte had stolen the sword of Frederick the Great.

'It is the sword of Frederick the Great which I . . .' she began, but Hippolyte interrupted her with the words: '*Le Roi de Prusse . . .*' and again as soon as all turned towards him, excused himself and said no more.

Anna Pavlovna frowned. Mortemart, Hippolyte's friend, addressed him firmly.

'Come now, what about your *Roi de Prusse?*'

Hippolyte laughed as if ashamed of laughing.

'Oh, it's nothing. I only wished to say . . .' (He wanted to repeat a joke he had heard in Vienna and which he had been trying all that evening to get in) 'I only wished to say that we are wrong to fight, *pour le Roi de Prusse!*'*

Boris smiled circumspectly, so that it might be taken as ironical or appreciative according to the way the joke was received. Everybody laughed.

'Your joke is too bad, it's witty but unjust,' said Anna Pavlovna, shaking her little shrivelled finger at him.

'We are not fighting *pour le Roi de Prusse*, but for right principles. Oh, that wicked Prince Hippolyte!' she said.

The conversation did not flag all evening and turned chiefly on the political news. It became particularly animated towards the end of the evening when the rewards bestowed by the Emperor were mentioned.

'You know N— N— received a snuff-box with the portrait last year?' said 'the man of profound intellect'. 'Why shouldn't S— S— get the same distinction?'

'Pardon me! A snuff-box with the Emperor's portrait is a reward but not a distinction,' said the diplomatist – 'A gift, rather.'

'There are precedents, I may mention Schwarzenberg.'

'It's impossible,' replied another.

'Will you bet? The ribbon of the order is a different matter...'

When everybody rose to go, Hélène who had spoken very little all the evening again turned to Boris, asking him in a tone of caressing significant command, to come to her on Tuesday.

'It is of great importance to me,' she said, turning with a smile towards Anna Pavlovna, and Anna Pavlovna with the same sad smile with which she spoke of her exalted patroness, supported Hélène's wish.

It seemed as if from some words Boris had spoken that evening about the Prussian army, Hélène had suddenly found it necessary to see him. She seemed to promise to explain that necessity to him when he came on Tuesday.

But on Tuesday evening, having come to Hélène's splendid salon, Boris received no clear explanation of why it had been necessary for him to come. There were other guests and the countess talked little to him, and only as he kissed her hand on taking leave, said unexpectedly and in a whisper, with a strangely unsmiling face: 'Come to dinner to-morrow... in the evening. You must come... Come!'

During that stay in Petersburg, Boris became an intimate in the countess's house.

8

THE war was flaming up and nearing the Russian frontier. Everywhere one heard curses on Bonaparte, 'the enemy of mankind'. Militiamen and recruits were being enrolled in the villages, and from the seat of war came contradictory news, false as usual and therefore variously interpreted.

The life of old Prince Bolkonsky, Prince Andrew, and Princess Mary, had greatly changed since 1805.

In 1806 the old prince was made one of the eight commanders-in-chief then appointed to supervise the enrolment decreed throughout Russia. Despite the weakness of age, which had become particularly noticeable since the time when he thought his son had been killed, he did not think it right to refuse a duty to which he had been appointed by the Emperor himself, and this fresh opportunity for action gave him new energy and strength. He was continually travelling through the three provinces entrusted to him, was pedantic in the fulfilment of his duties, severe to cruelty with his subordinates, and went into everything down to the minutest details himself. Princess Mary had ceased taking lessons in mathematics from her father, and when the old prince was at home went to his study with the wet-nurse and little Prince Nicholas (as his grandfather called him). The baby Prince Nicholas lived with his wet-nurse and nurse Savishna in the late princess's rooms and Princess Mary spent most of the day in the nursery, taking a mother's place to her little nephew as best she could. Mademoiselle Bourienne, too, seemed passionately fond of the boy, and Princess Mary often deprived herself to give her friend the pleasure of dandling the little *angel* – as she called her nephew – and playing with him.

Near the altar of the church at Bald Hills there was a chapel over the tomb of the little princess, and in this chapel was a marble monument brought from Italy, representing an angel with outspread wings ready to fly upwards. The angel's upper lip was slightly raised as though about to smile, and once on coming out of the chapel Prince Andrew and Princess Mary admitted to one another that the angel's face reminded them strangely of the little princess. But what was still stranger, though of this Prince Andrew said nothing to his sister, was that in the expression the sculptor had happened to give the angel's face, Prince Andrew read the same mild reproach he had read on the face of his dead wife: 'Ah, why have you done this to me?'

Soon after Prince Andrew's return the old prince made over to him a large estate, Bogucharovo, about twenty-five miles from Bald Hills. Partly because of the depressing memories associated with Bald Hills, partly because Prince Andrew did not always feel equal to bearing with his father's peculiarities, and partly because he needed solitude, Prince Andrew made use of Bogucharovo, began building, and spent most of his time there.

After the Austerlitz campaign Prince Andrew had firmly resolved not to continue his military service, and when the war recommenced and everybody had to serve, he took a post under his father in the recruitment so as to avoid active service. The old prince and his son seemed to have changed rôles since the campaign of 1805. The old man, roused by activity, expected the best results from the new campaign, while Prince Andrew on the contrary, taking no part in the war and secretly regretting this, saw only the dark side.

On 26th February 1807 the old prince set off on one of his circuits. Prince Andrew remained at Bald Hills as usual during his father's absence. Little Nicholas had been unwell for four days. The coachman who had driven the old prince to town returned bringing papers and letters for Prince Andrew.

Not finding the young prince in his study the valet went with the letters to Princess Mary's apartments, but did not find him there. He was told that the prince had gone to the nursery.

'If you please, your Excellency, Petrusha has brought some papers,' said one of the nursemaids to Prince Andrew who was sitting on a child's little chair while, frowning and with trembling hands, he poured drops from a medicine bottle into a wineglass half full of water.

'What is it?' he said crossly, and his hand shaking unintentionally, he poured too many drops into the glass. He threw the mixture onto the floor and asked for some more water. The maid brought it.

There were in the room a child's cot, two boxes, two arm-chairs, a table, a child's table, and the little chair on which Prince Andrew was sitting. The curtains were drawn, and a single candle was burning on the table, screened by a bound music-book so that the light did not fall on the cot.

'My dear,' said Princess Mary, addressing her brother from beside the cot where she was standing, 'better wait a bit... later...'

'Oh, leave off, you always talk nonsense and keep putting things off – and this is what comes of it!' said Prince Andrew in an exasperated whisper, evidently meaning to wound his sister.

'My dear, really... it's better not to wake him... he's asleep,' said the princess in a tone of entreaty.

Prince Andrew got up, and went on tiptoe up to the little bed, wineglass in hand.

'Perhaps we'd really better not wake him,' he said hesitating.

'As you please... really... I think so... but as you please,' said Princess Mary, evidently intimidated and confused that her opinion had prevailed. She drew her brother's attention to the maid who was calling him in a whisper.

It was the second night that neither of them had slept, watching the boy who was in a high fever. These last days, mistrusting their household doctor and expecting another for whom they had sent to town, they had been trying first one remedy and then another. Worn out by sleeplessness and anxiety they threw their burden of sorrow on one another, and reproached and disputed with each other.

'Petrusha has come with papers from your father,' whispered the maid.

Prince Andrew went out.

'Devil take them!' he muttered, and after listening to the verbal instructions his father had sent and taking the correspondence and his father's letter, he returned to the nursery.

'Well?' he asked.

'Still the same. Wait, for heaven's sake. Karl Ivanich always says that sleep is more important than anything,' whispered Princess Mary with a sigh.

Prince Andrew went up to the child and felt him. He was burning hot.

'Confound you and your Karl Ivanich!' He took the glass with the drops and again went up to the cot.

'Andrew, don't!' said Princess Mary.

But he scowled at her angrily though also with suffering in his eyes, and stooped glass in hand over the infant.

'But I wish it,' he said. 'I beg you – give it him!'

Princess Mary shrugged her shoulders but took the glass submissively, and calling the nurse began giving the medicine. The child screamed hoarsely. Prince Andrew winced, and clutching his head went out and sat down on a sofa in the next room.

He still had all the letters in his hand. Opening them mechanically he began reading. The old prince, now and then using abbreviations, wrote in his large elongated hand on blue paper as follows:

'Have just this moment received by special messenger very joyful news – if it's not false. Bennigsen seems to have obtained a complete victory over Buonaparte at Eylau.* In Petersburg everyone is rejoicing, and the rewards sent to the army are innumerable. Though he is a German – I congratulate him! I can't make out what the commander at Korchevo – a certain Khandrikov – is up to; till now the additional men and provisions have not arrived. Gallop off to him at once and say I'll have his head off if everything is not here in a week. Have received another letter about the Preussisch-Eylau battle from Petenka – he took part in it – and it's all true. When mischief-makers don't meddle even a German beats Buonaparte. He is said to be fleeing in great disorder. Mind you

393

gallop off to Korchevo without delay and carry out instructions!'

Prince Andrew sighed and broke the seal of another envelope. It was a closely written letter of two sheets from Bilibin. He folded it up without reading it and re-read his father's letter, ending with the words: 'Gallop off to Korchevo and carry out instructions!'

'No, pardon me, I won't go now till the child is better,' thought he, going to the door and looking into the nursery.

Princess Mary was still standing by the cot, gently rocking the baby.

'Ah yes, and what else did he say that's unpleasant?' thought Prince Andrew, recalling his father's letter. 'Yes, we have gained a victory over Bonaparte, just when I'm not serving. Yes, yes, he's always poking fun at me ... Ah, well! Let him!' And he began reading Bilibin's letter which was written in French. He read without understanding half of it, read only to forget, if but for a moment, what he had too long been thinking of so painfully to the exclusion of all else.

9

BILIBIN was now at army head-quarters in a diplomatic capacity, and though he wrote in French and used French jests and French idioms, he described the whole campaign with a fearless self-censure and self-derision genuinely Russian. Bilibin wrote that the obligation of diplomatic discretion tormented him, and he was happy to have in Prince Andrew a reliable correspondent to whom he could pour out the bile he had accumulated at the sight of all that was being done in the army. The letter was old, having been written before the battle at Preussisch-Eylau.

Since the day of our brilliant success at Austerlitz, [wrote Bilibin] as you know, my dear Prince, I never leave head-quarters. I have certainly acquired a taste for war, and it is just as well for me; what I have seen during these last three months is incredible.

I begin *ab ovo*. 'The enemy of the human race', as you know, attacks the Prussians. The Prussians are our faithful allies who have only betrayed us three times in three years. We take up their cause, but it turns out that 'the enemy of the human race' pays no heed to our fine speeches and in his rude and savage way throws himself on the Prussians without giving them time to finish the parade they had begun, and in two twists of the hand he breaks them to smithereens and installs himself in the palace at Potsdam.

'I most ardently desire,' writes the King of Prussia to Bonaparte, 'that your Majesty should be received and treated in my palace in a manner agreeable to yourself, and in so far as circumstances allowed,

I have hastened to take all steps to that end. May I have succeeded!'
The Prussian generals pride themselves on being polite to the French and lay down their arms at the first demand.

The head of the garrison at Glogau, with ten thousand men, asks the King of Prussia what he is to do if he is summoned to surrender ... All this is absolutely true.

In short, hoping to settle matters by taking up a war-like attitude, it turns out that we have landed ourselves in war, and what is more, in war on our own frontiers, *with* and *for* the King of Prussia. We have everything in perfect order, only one little thing is lacking, namely, a commander-in-chief. As it was considered that the Austerlitz success might have been more decisive had the commander-in-chief not been so young, all our octogenarians were reviewed, and of Prozorovsky and Kamensky the latter was preferred. The general comes to us, Suvorov-like, in a *kibitka,** and is received with acclamations of joy and triumph.

On the 4th, the first courier arrives from Petersburg. The mails are taken to the field-marshal's room, for he likes to do everything himself. I am called in to help sort the letters and take those meant for us. The field-marshal looks on and waits for letters addressed to him. We search, but none are to be found. The field-marshal grows impatient and sets to work himself, and finds letters from the Emperor to Count T., Prince V., and others. Then he bursts into one of his wild furies and rages at everyone and everything, seizes the letters, opens them, and reads those from the Emperor addressed to others. 'Ah! So that's the way they treat me! No confidence in me! Ah, ordered to keep an eye on me! Very well then! Get along with you!' So he writes the famous order of the day to General Bennigsen:

'I am wounded and cannot ride, and consequently cannot command the army. You have brought your army corps to Pultusk, routed: here it is exposed, and without fuel or forage, so something must be done, and, as you yourself reported to Count Buxhöwden yesterday, you must think of retreating to our frontier – which do to-day.'

'From all my riding,' he writes to the Emperor, 'I have got a saddle-sore, which coming after all my previous journeys quite prevents my riding and commanding so vast an army, so I have passed on the command to the general next in seniority, Count Buxhöwden, having sent him my whole staff and all that belongs to it, advising him if there is a lack of bread, to move farther into the interior of Prussia, for only one day's ration of bread remains, and in some regiments none at all, as reported by the division commanders, Ostermann and Sedmoretzky, and all that the peasants had has been eaten up. I myself will remain in hospital at Ostrolenka till I recover. In regard to which I humbly submit my report, with the information that if the army remains in its present bivouac another fortnight there will not be a healthy man left in it by spring.

'Grant leave to retire to his country seat to an old man who is already in any case dishonoured by being unable to fulfil the great and glorious task for which he was chosen. I shall await your most gracious permission here in hospital, that I may not have to play the part of a *secretary* rather than *commander* in the army. My removal from the army does not produce the slightest stir – a blind man has left it. There are thousands such as I in Russia.'

The field-marshal is angry with the Emperor and he punishes us all, isn't it logical?

This is the first act. Those that follow are naturally increasingly interesting and entertaining. After the field-marshal's departure it appears that we are within sight of the enemy and must give battle. Buxhöwden is commander-in-chief by seniority, but General Bennigsen does not quite see it; more particularly as it is he and his corps who are within sight of the enemy and he wishes to profit by the opportunity to fight a battle 'on his own hand' as the Germans say. He does so. This is the battle of Pultusk, which is considered a great victory but in my opinion was nothing of the kind. We civilians, as you know, have a very bad way of deciding whether a battle was won or lost. Those who retreat after a battle have lost it, is what we say; and according to that it is we who lost the battle of Pultusk. In short, we retreat after the battle but send a courier to Petersburg with news of a victory, and General Bennigsen hoping to receive from Petersburg the post of commander-in-chief as a reward for his victory, does not give up the command of the army to General Buxhöwden. During this interregnum we begin a very original and interesting series of manœuvres. Our aim is no longer, as it should be, to avoid or attack the enemy, but solely to avoid General Buxhöwden who by right of seniority should be our chief. So energetically do we pursue this aim that after crossing an unfordable river we burn the bridges to separate ourselves from our enemy, who at the moment is not Bonaparte but Buxhöwden. General Buxhöwden was all but attacked and captured by a superior enemy force as a result of one of these manœuvres that enabled us to escape him. Buxhöwden pursues us – we scuttle. He hardly crosses the river to our side before we recross to the other. At last our enemy, Buxhöwden, catches us and attacks. Both generals are angry, and the result is a challenge on Buxhöwden's part and an epileptic fit on Bennigsen's. But at the critical moment the courier, who carried the news of our victory at Pultusk to Petersburg, returns bringing our appointment as commander-in-chief, and our first foe, Buxhöwden, is vanquished; we can now turn our thoughts to the second, Bonaparte. But as it turns out, just at that moment a third enemy rises before us – namely the *Orthodox Russian soldiers*, loudly demanding bread, meat, biscuits, fodder, and what not! The stores are empty, the roads impassable. The Orthodox begin looting, and in a way of which our last campaign can give you no idea. Half the regiments form bands and scour the countryside and put everything to fire and sword. The inhabitants are totally ruined, the hospitals overflow with sick, and famine is everywhere. Twice the marauders even attack our head-quarters and the commander-in-chief has to ask for a battalion to disperse them. During one of these attacks they carried off my empty portmanteau and my dressing-gown. The

Emperor proposes to give all commanders of divisions the right to shoot marauders, but I much fear this will oblige one-half the army to shoot the other.

At first Prince Andrew read with his eyes only, but after a while in spite of himself (although he knew how far it was safe to trust Bilibin) what he read began to interest him more and more. When he had read thus far, he crumpled the letter up and threw it away. It was not what he had read that vexed him, but the fact that the life out there in which he had now no part could perturb him. He shut his eyes, rubbed his forehead as if to rid himself of all interest in what he had read, and listened to what was passing in the nursery. Suddenly he thought he heard a strange noise through the door. He was seized with alarm lest something should have happened to the child while he was reading the letter. He went on tiptoe to the nursery door and opened it.

Just as he went in he saw that the nurse was hiding something from him with a scared look, and that Princess Mary was no longer by the cot.

'My dear,' he heard what seemed to him her despairing whisper behind him.

As often happens after long sleeplessness and long anxiety, he was seized by an unreasoning panic – it occurred to him that the child was dead. All that he saw and heard seemed to confirm this terror.

'All is over,' he thought, and a cold sweat broke out on his forehead. He went to the cot in confusion, sure that he would find it empty and that the nurse had been hiding the dead baby. He drew the curtain aside and for some time his frightened, restless eyes could not find the baby. At last he saw him: the rosy boy had tossed about till he lay across the bed with his head lower than the pillow, and was smacking his lips in his sleep and breathing evenly.

Prince Andrew was as glad to find the boy like that as if he had already lost him. He bent over him and, as his sister had taught him, tried with his lips whether the child was still feverish. The soft forehead was moist. Prince Andrew touched the head with his hand; even the hair was wet, so profusely had the child perspired. He was not dead: evidently the crisis was over and he was convalescent. Prince Andrew longed to snatch up, to squeeze, to hold to his heart, this helpless little creature, but dared not do so. He stood over him, gazing at his head and at the little arms and legs which showed under the blanket. He heard a rustle behind him and a shadow appeared under the curtain of the cot. He did not look round, but still gazing at the infant's face listened to his regular breathing. The dark shadow was Princess Mary, who had come up to the cot with noiseless steps, lifted the curtain, and dropped it again behind her. Prince Andrew recognized her without looking and held out his hand to her. She pressed it.

'He has perspired,' said Prince Andrew.

'I was coming to tell you so.'

The child moved slightly in his sleep, smiled, and rubbed his forehead against the pillow.

Prince Andrew looked at his sister. In the dim shadow of the curtain her luminous eyes shone more brightly than usual from the tears of joy that were in them. She leaned over to her brother and kissed him, slightly catching the curtain of the cot. Each made the other a warning gesture, and stood still in the dim light beneath the curtain as if not wishing to leave that seclusion where they three were shut off from all the world. Prince Andrew was the first to move away, ruffling his hair against the muslin of the curtain.

'Yes, this is the one thing left me now,' he said with a sigh.

10

SOON after his admission to the Masonic Brotherhood Pierre went to the Kiev province, where he had the greatest number of serfs, taking with him full directions which he had written down for his own guidance as to what he should do on his estates.

When he reached Kiev he sent for all his stewards to the head office and explained to them his intentions and wishes. He told them that steps would be taken immediately to free his serfs – and that till then they were not to be overburdened with labour, women while nursing their babies were not to be sent to work, assistance was to be given to the serfs, punishments were to be admonitory and not corporal, and hospitals, asylums, and schools were to be established on all the estates. Some of the stewards (there were semi-literate foremen among them) listened with alarm, supposing these words to mean that the young count was displeased with their management and embezzlement of money, some after their first fright were amused by Pierre's lisp and the new words they had not heard before, others simply enjoyed hearing how the master talked, while the cleverest among them, including the chief steward, understood from this speech how they could best handle the master for their own ends.

The chief steward expressed great sympathy with Pierre's intentions, but remarked that besides these changes it would be necessary to go into the general state of affairs which was far from satisfactory.

Despite Count Bezukhov's enormous wealth, since he had come into an income which was said to amount to five hundred thousand rubles a year, Pierre felt himself far poorer than when his father had made him an allowance of ten thousand rubles. He had a dim perception of the following budget:

About 80,000 went in payments on all the estates to the Land Bank; about 30,000 went for the upkeep of the estate near Moscow, the town house, and the allowance to the three princesses; about 15,000 was given in pensions and the same amount for asylums; 150,000 alimony was sent to the countess; about 70,000 went for interest on debts. The building of a new church previously begun, had cost about 10,000 in each of the last two years, and he did not know how the rest, about 100,000 rubles, was spent, and almost every year he was obliged to borrow. Besides this the chief steward wrote every year telling him of fires and bad harvests, or of the necessity of rebuilding factories and workshops. So the first task Pierre had to face was one for which he had very little aptitude or inclination – practical business.

He discussed estate affairs every day with his chief steward. But he felt that this did not forward matters at all. He felt that these consultations were detached from real affairs and did not link up with them or make them move. On the one hand the chief steward put the state of things to him in the very worst light, pointing out the necessity of paying off the debts and undertaking new activities with serf-labour, to which Pierre did not agree. On the other hand Pierre demanded that steps should be taken to liberate the serfs, which the steward met by showing the necessity of first paying off the loans from the Land Bank, and the consequent impossibility of a speedy emancipation.

The steward did not say it was quite impossible, but suggested selling the forests in the province of Kostroma, the land lower down the river, and the Crimean estate, in order to make it possible: all of which operations according to him were connected with such complicated measures – the removal of injunctions, petitions, permits, and so on – that Pierre became quite bewildered and only replied:

'Yes, yes, do so.'

Pierre had none of the practical persistence that would have enabled him to attend to the business himself, and so he disliked it and only tried to pretend to the steward that he was attending to it. The steward for his part tried to pretend to the count that he considered these consultations very valuable for the proprietor and troublesome to himself.

In Kiev Pierre found some people he knew, and strangers hastened to make his acquaintance and joyfully welcomed the rich newcomer, the largest landowner of the province. Temptations to Pierre's greatest weakness – the one to which he had confessed when admitted to the Lodge – were so strong that he could not resist them. Again whole days, weeks, and months of his life passed in as great a rush, and were as much occupied with evening parties, dinners, lunches and balls, giving him no time for reflection, as in Petersburg. Instead of the new life he had hoped to lead he still lived the old life, only in new surroundings.

Of the three precepts of freemasonry Pierre realized that he did not fulfil the one which enjoined every mason to set an example of moral life, and that of the seven virtues he lacked two – morality and the love of death. He consoled himself with the thought that he fulfilled another of the precepts – that of reforming the human race – and had other virtues – love of his neighbour and especially generosity.

In the spring of 1807 he decided to return to Petersburg. On the way he intended to visit all his estates and see for himself how far his orders had been carried out and in what state were the serfs whom God had entrusted to his care and whom he intended to benefit.

The chief steward, who considered the young count's attempts almost insane – unprofitable to himself, to the count, and to the serfs – made some concessions. Continuing to represent the liberation of the serfs as impracticable, he arranged for the erection of large buildings – schools, hospitals, and asylums – on all the estates before the master arrived. Everywhere preparations were made not for ceremonious welcomes (which he knew Pierre would not like), but for just such gratefully religious ones, with offerings of icons and the bread and salt of hospitality, as according to his understanding of his master would touch and delude him.

The southern spring, the comfortable rapid travelling in a Vienna carriage and the solitude of the road, all had a gladdening effect on Pierre. The estates he had not before visited were each more picturesque than the other; the serfs everywhere seemed thriving and touchingly grateful for the benefits conferred on them. Everywhere were receptions, which though they embarrassed Pierre awakened a joyful feeling in the depth of his heart. In one place the peasants presented him with bread and salt and an icon of St Peter and St Paul, asking permission, as a mark of their gratitude for the benefits he had conferred on them, to build a new chantry to the church at their own expense in honour of Peter and Paul, his patron saints. In another place the women with infants in arms met him to thank him for releasing them from hard work. On a third estate the priest, bearing a cross, came to meet him surrounded by children whom, by the count's generosity, he was instructing in reading, writing, and religion. On all his estates Pierre saw with his own eyes brick buildings erected or in course of erection, all on one plan, for hospitals, schools, and almshouses, which were soon to be opened. Everywhere he saw the stewards' accounts, according to which the serfs' manorial labour had been diminished, and heard the touching thanks of deputations of serfs in their full-skirted blue coats.

What Pierre did not know was that the place where they presented him with bread and salt and wished to build a chantry in honour of Peter and Paul was a market-village where a fair was held on St Peter's day,* and that the richest peasants (who formed the deputations) had begun the chantry long before, and that nine-tenths of the peasants in that village were in a state of the greatest poverty. He did not know that since the nursing mothers were no longer sent to work on his land, they did still harder work on their own land. He did not know that the priest who met him with the cross oppressed the peasants by his exactions, and that the pupils' parents wept at having to let him take their children and secured their release by heavy payments. He did not know that the brick buildings, built to plan, were being built by serfs whose manorial labour was thus increased, though lessened on paper. He did not know that where the steward had shown him in the accounts that the serfs' payments had been diminished by a third, their obligatory manorial work had been increased by a half. And so Pierre was delighted with his visit to his estates and quite recovered the philanthropic mood in which he had left Petersburg, and wrote enthusiastic letters to his 'brother-instructor' as he called the Grand Master.

'How easy it is, how little effort it needs, to do so much good,' thought Pierre, 'and how little attention we pay to it!'

He was pleased at the gratitude he received, but felt abashed at receiving it. This gratitude reminded him of how much more he might do for these simple kindly people.

The chief steward, a very stupid but cunning man who saw perfectly through the naïve and intelligent count and played with him as with a toy, seeing the effect these prearranged receptions had on Pierre, pressed him still harder with proofs of the impossibility and above all the uselessness of freeing the serfs, who were quite happy as it was.

Pierre in his secret soul agreed with the steward that it would be difficult to imagine happier people, and that God only knew what would happen to them when they were free, but he insisted, though reluctantly, on what he thought right. The steward promised to do all in his power to carry out the count's wishes, seeing clearly that not only would the count never be able to find out whether all measures had been taken for the sale of the land and forests and to release them from the Land Bank, but would probably never even inquire, and would never know that the newly-erected buildings were standing empty, and that the serfs continued to give in money and work all that other people's serfs gave – that is to say, all that could be got out of them.

11

RETURNING from his journey through South Russia in the happiest state of mind, Pierre carried out an intention he had long had of visiting his friend Bolkonsky whom he had not seen for two years.

Bogucharovo lay in a flat uninteresting part of the country among fields and forests of fir and birch, which were partly cut down. The house lay behind a newly-dug pond filled with water to the brink and with banks still bare of grass. It was at the end of a village that stretched along the high road in the midst of a young copse in which were a few fir trees.

The homestead consisted of a threshing floor, outhouses, stables, a bath-house, a lodge, and a large brick house with semicircular façade still in course of construction. Round the house was a garden newly laid out. The fences and gates were new and solid; two fire pumps and a water-cart, painted green, stood in a shed; the paths were straight, the bridges were strong and had hand-rails. Everything bore an impress of tidiness and good management. Some domestic serfs Pierre met, in reply to inquiries as to where the prince lived, pointed out a small newly-built lodge close to the pond. Anton, a man who had looked after Prince Andrew in his boyhood, helped Pierre out of his carriage, said that the prince was at home, and showed him into a clean little ante-room.

Pierre was struck by the modesty of the small though clean house after the brilliant surroundings in which he had last met his friend in Petersburg.

He quickly entered the small reception-room with its still un-plastered wooden walls redolent of pine, and would have gone farther, but Anton ran ahead on tiptoe and knocked at a door.

'Well, what is it?' came a sharp, unpleasant voice.

'A visitor,' answered Anton.

'Ask him to wait,' and the sound was heard of a chair being pushed back.

Pierre went with rapid steps to the door and suddenly came face to face with Prince Andrew, who came out frowning and looking old. Pierre embraced him, and lifting his spectacles kissed his friend on the cheek and looked at him closely.

'Well, I did not expect you, I am very glad,' said Prince Andrew.

Pierre said nothing; he looked fixedly at his friend with surprise. He was struck by the change in him. His words were kindly and there was a smile on his lips and face, but his eyes were dull and lifeless and in spite of his evident wish to do so he could not give them a joyous and glad sparkle. Prince Andrew had grown thinner, paler, and more manly looking, but what amazed and estranged Pierre till he got used to it was his inertia and a wrinkle on his brow indicating prolonged concentration on some one thought.

As is usually the case with people meeting after a prolonged separation, it was long before their conversation could settle on anything. They put questions and gave brief replies about things they knew ought to be talked over at length. At last the conversation gradually settled on some of the topics at first lightly touched on: their past life, plans for the future, Pierre's journeys and occupations, the war, and so on. The preoccupation and despondency which Pierre had noticed in his friend's look was now still more clearly expressed in the smile with which he listened to Pierre, especially when he spoke with joyful animation of the past or the future. It was as if Prince Andrew would have liked to sympathize with what Pierre was saying, but could not. The latter began to feel that it was in bad taste to speak of his enthusiasms, dreams, and hopes of happiness or goodness, in Prince Andrew's presence. He was ashamed to express his new masonic views, which had been particularly revived and strengthened by his late tour. He checked himself, fearing to seem naïve, yet he felt an irresistible desire to show his friend as soon as possible that he was now a quite different, and better, Pierre than he had been in Petersburg.

'I can't tell you how much I have lived through since then. I hardly know myself again.'

'Yes, we have altered much, very much, since then,' said Prince Andrew.

'Well, and you? What are your plans?'

'Plans!' repeated Prince Andrew ironically. 'My plans?' he said, as if astonished at the word. 'Well, you see, I'm building. I mean to settle here altogether next year . . .'

Pierre looked silently and searchingly into Prince Andrew's face, which had grown much older.

'No, I meant to ask . . .' Pierre began, but Prince Andrew interrupted him.

'But why talk of me? . . . Talk *to* me, yes, tell me about your travels and all you have been doing on your estates.'

Pierre began describing what he had done on his estates, trying as far as possible to conceal his own part in the improvements that had been made. Prince Andrew several times prompted Pierre's story of what he had been doing, as though it were all an old-time story, and he listened not only without interest but even as if ashamed of what Pierre was telling him.

Pierre felt uncomfortable and even depressed in his friend's company and at last became silent.

'I'll tell you what, my dear fellow,' said Prince Andrew, who evidently also felt depressed and constrained with his visitor. 'I am only bivouacking here, and have just come to look round. I am going back to my sister to-day. I will introduce you to her. But of course you know her already,' he said, evidently trying to entertain a visitor with whom he now found nothing in common. 'We will go after dinner. And would you now like to look round my place?'

They went out and walked about till dinner-time, talking of the political news and common acquaintances, like people who do not know each other intimately. Prince Andrew spoke with some animation and interest only of the new homestead he was constructing and its buildings, but even here, while on the scaffolding, in the midst of a talk explaining the future arrangements of the house, he interrupted himself:

'However, this is not at all interesting. Let us have dinner, and then we'll set off.'

At dinner conversation turned on Pierre's marriage.

'I was very much surprised when I heard of it,' said Prince Andrew.

Pierre blushed, as he always did when it was mentioned, and said hurriedly:

'I will tell you some time how it all happened. But you know it is all over, and for ever.'

'For ever?' said Prince Andrew. 'Nothing's for ever.'

'But you know how it all ended, don't you? You heard of the duel?'

'And so you had to go through that too!'

'One thing I thank God for, is that I did not kill that man,' said Pierre.

'Why so?' asked Prince Andrew. 'To kill a vicious dog is a very good thing really.'

'No, to kill a man is bad – wrong.'

'Why is it wrong?' urged Prince Andrew. 'It is not given to man to know what is right and what is wrong. Men always did and always will err and in nothing more than in what they consider right and wrong.'

'What does harm to another is wrong,' said Pierre, feeling with pleasure that for the first time since his arrival Prince Andrew was roused, had begun to talk, and wanted to express what had brought him to his present state.

'And who has told you what is bad for another man?' he asked.

'Bad! Bad!' exclaimed Pierre. 'We all know what is bad for ourselves.'

'Yes we know that, but the harm I am conscious of in myself is something I cannot inflict on others,' said Prince Andrew, growing more and more animated and evidently wishing to express his new outlook to Pierre. He spoke in French. 'I only know two very real evils in life: remorse and illness. The only good is the absence of those evils. To live for myself avoiding those two evils is my whole philosophy now.'

'And love of one's neighbour, and self-sacrifice?' began Pierre. 'No, I can't agree with you! To live only so as not to do evil and not to have to repent, is not enough. I lived like that, I lived for myself and ruined my life. And only now when I am living, or at least trying' (Pierre's modesty made him correct himself) 'to live for others, only now have I understood all the happiness of life. No, I shall not agree with you, and you do not really believe what you are saying.'

Prince Andrew looked silently at Pierre with an ironic smile.

'When you see my sister, Princess Mary, you'll get on with her,' he said. 'Perhaps you are right for yourself,' he added after a short pause, 'but everyone lives in his own way. You lived for yourself and say you nearly ruined your life and only found happiness when you began living for others. I experienced just the reverse. I lived for glory. – And after all what is glory? The same love of others, a desire to do something for them, a desire for their approval. – So I lived for others, and not almost, but quite, ruined my life. And I have become calmer since I began to live only for myself.'

'But what do you mean by living only for yourself?' asked

Pierre growing excited. 'What about your son, your sister, and your father?'

'But that's just the same as myself – they are not *others*,' explained Prince Andrew. 'The others, one's neighbours, *le prochain*, as you and Princess Mary call it, are the chief source of all error and evil. *Le prochain* – your Kiev peasants to whom you want to do good.'

And he looked at Pierre with a mocking, challenging expression. He evidently wished to draw him on.

'You are joking,' replied Pierre, growing more and more excited. 'What error or evil can there be in my wishing to do good, and even doing a little – though I did very little and did it very badly? – What evil can there be in it if unfortunate people, our serfs, people like ourselves, were growing up and dying with no idea of God and truth beyond ceremonies and meaningless prayers, and are now instructed in a comforting belief in future life, retribution, recompense, and consolation? What evil and error is there in it, if people were dying of disease without help while material assistance could so easily be rendered, and I supplied them with a doctor, a hospital, and an asylum for the aged? And is it not a palpable, unquestionable good if a peasant, or a woman with a baby has no rest day or night, and I give them rest and leisure?' said Pierre, hurrying and lisping. 'And I have done that though badly and to a small extent, but I have done something towards it, and you cannot persuade me that it was not a good action, and more than that, you can't make me believe that you do not think so yourself. And the main thing is,' he continued, 'that I know, and know for certain, that the enjoyment of doing this good is the only sure happiness in life.'

'Yes, if you put it like that it's quite a different matter,' said Prince Andrew. 'I build a house and lay out a garden, and you build hospitals. The one and the other may serve as a pastime. But what's right and what's good must be judged by one who knows all, but not by us. Well, you want an argument,' he added, 'come on then.'

They rose from the table and sat down in the entrance porch which served as a verandah.

'Come, let's argue then,' said Prince Andrew. 'You talk of schools,' he went on, crooking a finger, 'education and so forth; that is, you want to raise him' (pointing to a peasant who passed by them taking off his cap) 'from his animal condition and awaken in him spiritual needs, while it seems to me that animal happiness is the only happiness possible, and that is just what you want to deprive him of. I envy him, but you want to make him what I am, without giving him my means. Then you say, "lighten his toil". But as I see it, physical labour is as essential to him, as much a condition of his existence, as mental activity is to you or me. You can't help thinking. I go to bed after two in the morning, thoughts come and I can't sleep but toss about till dawn, because I think and can't help thinking, just as he can't help ploughing and mowing; if he didn't he would go to the drink shop or fall ill. Just as I could not stand his terrible physical labour but should die of it in a week, so he could not stand my physical idleness, but would grow fat and die. The third thing – what else was it you talked about?' and Prince Andrew crooked a third finger, 'Ah, yes, hospitals, medicine. He has a fit, he is dying, and you come and bleed him and patch him up. He will drag about as a cripple, a burden to everybody, for another ten years. It would be far easier and simpler for him to die. Others are being born and there are plenty of them as it is. It would be different if you grudged losing a labourer – that's how I regard him – but you want to cure him from love of him. And he does not want that. And besides, what a notion that medicine ever cured anyone! Killed them, yes!' said he, frowning angrily and turning away from Pierre.

Prince Andrew expressed his ideas so clearly and distinctly that it was evident he had reflected on this subject more than once, and he spoke readily and rapidly like a man who has not talked for a long time. His glance became more animated as his conclusions became more hopeless.

'Oh, that is dreadful, dreadful!' said Pierre. 'I don't understand how one can live with such ideas. I had such moments myself not long ago, in Moscow and when travelling, but at such times I collapse so that I don't live at all – everything seems hateful to me . . . myself most of all. Then I don't eat, don't wash . . . and how is it with you? . . .'

'Why not wash? That is not cleanly,' said Prince Andrew; 'on the contrary one must try to make one's life as pleasant as possible. I'm alive; that is not my fault, so I must live out my life as best I can, without hurting others.'

'But with such ideas what motive have you for living? One would sit without moving, undertaking nothing . . .'

'Life as it is leaves one no peace. I should be thankful to do nothing, but here on the one hand the local nobility have done me the honour to choose me to be their marshal;* it was all I could do to get out of it. They could not understand that I have not the necessary qualifications for it – the kind of good-natured, fussy shallowness necessary for the position. Then there's this house,

407

which must be built in order to have a nook of one's own in which to be quiet. And now there's this recruiting.'

'Why aren't you serving in the army?'

'After Austerlitz!' said Prince Andrew gloomily. 'No, thank you very much! I have promised myself not to serve again in the active Russian army. And I won't – not even if Bonaparte were here at Smolensk threatening Bald Hills – even then I wouldn't serve in the Russian army! Well, as I was saying,' he continued, recovering his composure, 'now there's this recruiting. My father is chief in command of the 3rd District, and my only way of avoiding active service is to serve under him.'

'Then you are serving?'

'I am.'

He paused a little while.

'And why do you serve?'

'Why, for this reason! My father is one of the most remarkable men of his time. But he is growing old, and though not exactly cruel, he has too energetic a character. He is so accustomed to unlimited power that he is terrible, and now he has this authority of a commander-in-chief of the recruiting, granted by the Emperor. If I had been two hours late a fortnight ago he would have had a paymaster's clerk at Yukhnova hanged,' said Prince Andrew with a smile. 'So I am serving because I alone have any influence with my father, and now and then can save him from actions which would torment him afterwards.'

'Well, there you see!'

'Yes, but it is not as you imagine,' Prince Andrew continued, 'I did not, and do not, in the least care about that scoundrel of a clerk who had stolen some boots from the recruits, I should even have been very glad to see him hanged, but I was sorry for my father – that again is for myself.'

Prince Andrew grew more and more animated. His eyes glittered feverishly while he tried to prove to Pierre that in his actions there was no desire to do good to his neighbour.

'There now, you wish to liberate your serfs,' he continued, 'that is a very good thing, but not for you – I don't suppose you ever had anyone flogged or sent to Siberia – and still less for your serfs. If they are beaten, flogged, or sent to Siberia, I don't suppose they are any the worse off. In Siberia they lead the same animal life, and the stripes on their bodies heal, and they are happy as before. But it is a good thing for proprietors who perish morally, bring remorse upon themselves, stifle this remorse and grow callous, as a result of being able to inflict punishments justly and unjustly. It is those people I pity, and for their sake I should like to liberate the serfs. You may not have seen, but I have seen, how good men brought up in those traditions of unlimited power, in time when they grow more irritable, become cruel and harsh, are conscious of it, but cannot restrain themselves and grow more and more miserable.'

Prince Andrew spoke so earnestly that Pierre could not help thinking that these thoughts had been suggested to Prince Andrew by his father's case.

He did not reply.

'So that's what I am sorry for – human dignity, peace of mind, purity, and not the serfs' backs and foreheads, which, beat and shave as you may,* always remain the same backs and foreheads.'

'No, no! A thousand times no! I shall never agree with you,' said Pierre.

12

IN the evening Andrew and Pierre got into an open carriage and drove to Bald Hills. Prince Andrew, glancing at Pierre, broke the silence now and then with remarks which showed that he was in a good temper.

Pointing to the fields, he spoke of the improvements he was making in his husbandry.

Pierre remained gloomily silent, answering in monosyllables and apparently immersed in his own thoughts.

He was thinking that Prince Andrew was unhappy, had gone astray, did not see the true light, and that he, Pierre, ought to aid, enlighten, and raise him. But as soon as he thought of what he should say, he felt that Prince Andrew with one word, one argument, would upset all his teaching, and he shrank from beginning, afraid of exposing to possible ridicule what to him was precious and sacred.

'No, but why do you think so?' Pierre suddenly began, lowering his head and looking like a bull about to charge, 'why do you think so? You should not think so.'

'Think? What about?' asked Prince Andrew with surprise.

'About life, about man's destiny. It can't be so. I myself thought like that, and do you know what saved me? Freemasonry! No, don't smile. Freemasonry is not a religious ceremonial sect, as I thought it was: freemasonry is the best expression of the best, the eternal, aspects of humanity.'

And he began to explain freemasonry as he understood it to Prince Andrew. He said that freemasonry is the teaching of

Christianity freed from the bonds of State and Church, a teaching of equality, brotherhood, and love.

'Only our holy Brotherhood has the real meaning of life, all the rest is a dream,' said Pierre. 'Understand, my dear fellow, that outside this union all is filled with deceit and falsehood and I agree with you that nothing is left for an intelligent and good man but to live out his life, like you, merely trying not to harm others. But make our fundamental convictions your own, join our Brotherhood, give yourself up to us, let yourself be guided, and you will at once feel yourself, as I have felt myself, a part of that vast invisible chain the beginning of which is hidden in Heaven,' said Pierre.

Prince Andrew looking straight in front of him listened in silence to Pierre's words. More than once when the noise of the wheels prevented his catching what Pierre said, he asked him to repeat it, and by the peculiar glow that came into Prince Andrew's eyes and by his silence, Pierre saw that his words were not in vain and that Prince Andrew would not interrupt him nor laugh at what he said.

They reached a river that had overflowed its banks and which they had to cross by ferry. While the carriage and horses were being placed on it, they also stepped on the raft.

Prince Andrew leaning his arms on the raft railing, gazed silently at the flooding waters glittering in the setting sun.

'Well, what do you think about it?' Pierre asked. 'Why are you silent?'

'What do I think about it? I am listening to you. It's all very well . . . You say: join our Brotherhood and we will show you the aim of life, the destiny of man, and the laws which govern the world. But who are *we*? Men. How is it you know everything? Why do I alone not see what you see? You see a reign of goodness and truth on earth, but I don't see it.'

Pierre interrupted him.

'Do you believe in a future life?' he asked.

'A future life?' Prince Andrew repeated, but Pierre, giving him no time to reply, took the repetition for a denial, the more readily as he knew Prince Andrew's former atheistic convictions.

'You say you can't see a reign of goodness and truth on earth. Nor could I, and it cannot be seen if one looks on our life here as the end of everything. On *earth*, here on this earth' (Pierre pointed to the fields), 'there is no truth, all is false and evil; but in the universe, in the whole universe, there is a kingdom of truth, and we who are now the children of earth are – eternally – children of the whole universe. Don't I feel in my soul that I am part of

410

this vast harmonious whole? Don't I feel that I form one link, one step, between the lower and higher beings, in this vast harmonious multitude of beings in whom the Deity – the Supreme Power if you prefer the term – is manifest? If I see, clearly see, that ladder leading from plant to man, why should I suppose it breaks off at me and does not go farther and farther? I feel that I cannot vanish, since nothing vanishes in this world, but that I shall always exist and always have existed. I feel that beyond me and above me there are spirits, and that in this world there is truth.'

'Yes, that is Herder's theory,' said Prince Andrew, 'but it is not that which can convince me, dear friend – life and death are what convince. What convinces is when one sees a being dear to one, bound up with one's own life, before whom one was to blame and had hoped to make it right' (Prince Andrew's voice trembled and he turned away), 'and suddenly that being is seized with pain, suffers, and ceases to exist ... Why? It cannot be that there is no answer. And I believe there is ... That's what convinces, that is what has convinced me,' said Prince Andrew.

'Yes, yes, of course,' said Pierre, 'isn't that what I'm saying?'

'No. All I say is that it is not argument that convinces me of the necessity of a future life, but this: when you go hand in hand with someone and all at once that person vanishes *there, into nowhere*, and you yourself are left facing that abyss, and look in. And I have looked in ...'

'Well, that's it then! You know that there is a *there* and there is a *Someone? There* is the future life. The *Someone* is – God.'

Prince Andrew did not reply. The carriage and horses had long since been taken off, onto the farther bank, and reharnessed. The sun had sunk half below the horizon and an evening frost was starring the puddles near the ferry, but Pierre and Andrew, to the astonishment of the footmen, coachmen, and ferrymen, still stood on the raft and talked.

'If there is a God and future life there is truth and good, and man's highest happiness consists in striving to attain them. We must live, we must love, and we must believe that we live not only to-day on this scrap of earth but have lived and shall live for ever, there, in the Whole,' said Pierre, and he pointed to the sky.

Prince Andrew stood leaning on the railing of the raft listening to Pierre, and he gazed with his eyes fixed on the red reflection of the sun gleaming on the blue waters. There was perfect stillness. Pierre became silent. The raft had long since stopped, and only the waves of the current beat softly against it below. Prince

Andrew felt as if the sound of the waves kept up a refrain to Pierre's words, whispering:

'It is true, believe it.'

He sighed, and glanced with a radiant, childlike, tender look at Pierre's face, flushed and rapturous, but yet shy before his superior friend.

'Yes, if only it were so!' said Prince Andrew. 'However, it is time to get on,' he added, and stepping off the raft he looked up at the sky to which Pierre had pointed, and for the first time since Austerlitz saw that high everlasting sky he had seen while lying on that battlefield; and something that had long been slumbering, something that was best within him, suddenly awoke, joyful and youthful, in his soul. It vanished as soon as he returned to the customary conditions of his life, but he knew that this feeling which he did not know how to develop, existed within him. His meeting with Pierre formed an epoch in Prince Andrew's life. Though outwardly he continued to live in the same old way, inwardly he began a new life.

13

IT was getting dusk when Prince Andrew and Pierre drove up to the front entrance of the house at Bald Hills. As they approached the house Prince Andrew with a smile drew Pierre's attention to a commotion going on at the back porch. A woman bent with age, with a wallet on her back, and a short, long-haired young man in a black garment, had rushed back to the gate on seeing the carriage driving up. Two women ran out after them, and all four, looking round at the carriage, ran in dismay up the steps of the back porch.

'Those are Mary's "God's folk",'* said Prince Andrew. 'They have mistaken us for my father. This is the one matter in which she disobeys him. He orders these pilgrims to be driven away, but she receives them.'

'But what are "God's folk"?' asked Pierre.

Prince Andrew had no time to answer. The servants came out to meet them, and he asked where the old prince was and whether he was expected back soon.

The old prince had gone to the town and was expected back any minute.

Prince Andrew led Pierre to his own apartments, which were always kept in perfect order and readiness for him in his father's house; he himself went to the nursery.

'Let us go and see my sister,' he said to Pierre when he returned. 'I have not found her yet, she is hiding now, sitting with her "God's folk". It will serve her right, she will be confused, but you will see her "God's folk". It's really very curious.'

'What are "God's folk"?' asked Pierre.

'Come, and you'll see for yourself.'

Princess Mary really was disconcerted and red patches came on her face when they went in. In her snug rooms, with lamps burning before the icon-stand, a young lad with a long nose and long hair, wearing a monk's cassock, sat on the sofa beside her, behind a samovar. Near them in an arm-chair sat a thin, shrivelled old woman, with a meek expression on her childlike face.

'Andrew, why didn't you warn me?' said the princess with mild reproach, as she stood before her pilgrims like a hen before her chickens.

'*Charmée de vous voir. Je suis très contente de vous voir*,' she said to Pierre as he kissed her hand. She had known him as a child, and now his friendship with Andrew, his misfortune with his wife, and above all, his kindly simple face, disposed her favourably towards him. She looked at him with her beautiful radiant eyes and seemed to say, 'I like you very much, but please don't laugh at my people.' After exchanging the first greetings they sat down.

'Ah, and Ivanushka is here too!' said Prince Andrew, glancing with a smile at the young pilgrim.

'Andrew!' said Princess Mary imploringly.

'*Il faut que vous sachiez que c'est une femme*,' said Prince Andrew to Pierre.

'Andrew, *au nom de Dieu!*' Princess Mary repeated.

It was evident that Prince Andrew's ironical tone towards the pilgrims, and Princess Mary's helpless attempts to protect them, were their customary long-established relations on the matter.

'*Mais, ma bonne amie*,' said Prince Andrew, '*vous devriez au contraire m'être reconnaissante de ce que j'explique à Pierre votre intimité avec ce jeune homme.*'*

'Really?' said Pierre, gazing over his spectacles with curiosity and seriousness (for which Princess Mary was specially grateful to him) into Ivanushka's face, who seeing that she was being spoken about, looked round at them all with crafty eyes.

Princess Mary's embarrassment on *her people's* account was quite unnecessary. They were not in the least abashed. The old woman, lowering her eyes but casting side-glances at the new-comers, had turned her cup upside down and placed a nibbled bit of sugar beside it, and sat quietly in her arm-chair, though hoping to be offered another cup of tea. Ivanushka, sipping out of her saucer, looked with sly womanish eyes from under her brows at the young men.

'Where have you been? To Kiev?' Prince Andrew asked the old woman.

'I have, good sir,' she answered garrulously. 'Just at Christmas time I was deemed worthy to partake of the holy and heavenly sacrament at the shrine of the saint. And now I'm from Kolyazin, master, where a great and wonderful blessing has been revealed.'

'And was Ivanushka with you?'

'I go by myself, benefactor,' said Ivanushka, trying to speak in a bass voice. 'I only came across Pelageya in Yukhnovo . . .'

Pelageya interrupted her companion; she evidently wished to tell of what she had seen.

'In Kolyazin, master, a wonderful blessing has been revealed.'

'What is it? Some new relics?' asked Prince Andrew.

'Andrew, do leave off,' said Princess Mary. 'Don't tell him, Pelageya.'

'No . . . why not, my dear, why shouldn't I? I like him. He is kind, he is one of God's chosen, he's a benefactor, he once gave me ten rubles, I remember. When I was in Kiev, Crazy Cyril says to me (he's one of God's own and goes barefoot summer and winter), he says, "Why are you not going to the right place? Go to Kolyazin where a wonder-working icon of the holy Mother of God has been revealed." On hearing these words I said good-bye to the holy folk and went.'

All were silent, only the pilgrim woman went on in measured tones, drawing in her breath.

'So I come, master, and the people say to me: "A great blessing has been revealed, holy oil trickles from the cheeks of our blessed Mother, the holy Virgin Mother of God." . . .'

'All right, all right, you can tell us afterwards,' said Princess Mary flushing.

'Let me ask her,' said Pierre. 'Did you see it yourselves?' he inquired.

'Oh, yes, master, I was found worthy. Such a brightness on the face like the light of heaven, and from the blessed Mother's cheek it drops and drops . . .'

'But, dear me, that must be a fraud!' said Pierre naïvely, who had listened attentively to the pilgrim.

'Oh, master, what are you saying?' exclaimed the horrified Pelageya, turning to Princess Mary for support.

'They impose on the people,' he repeated.

'Lord Jesus Christ!' exclaimed the pilgrim woman crossing herself. 'Oh, don't speak so, master! There was a general who did not

414

believe, and said, "The monks cheat," and as soon as he'd said it he went blind. And he dreamt that the Holy Virgin Mother of the Kiev catacombs came to him and said, "Believe in me and I will make you whole." So he begged: "Take me to her, take me to her." It's the real truth I'm telling you, I saw it myself. So he was brought, quite blind, straight to her, and he goes up to her and falls down and says, "Make me whole," says he, "and I'll give thee what the Tsar bestowed on me." I saw it myself, master; the star is fixed into the icon. Well, and what do you think? He received his sight! It's a sin to speak so. God will punish you,' she said admonishingly, turning to Pierre.

'How did the star get into the icon?' Pierre asked.

'And was the Holy Mother promoted to the rank of general?' said Prince Andrew with a smile.

Pelageya suddenly grew quite pale and clasped her hands.

'Oh, master, master, what a sin! And you who have a son!' she began, her pallor suddenly turning to a vivid red. 'Master, what have you said? God forgive you!' And she crossed herself. 'Lord forgive him! My dear, what does it mean? . . .' she asked, turning to Princess Mary. She got up and, almost crying, began to arrange her wallet. She evidently felt frightened and ashamed to have accepted charity in a house where such things could be said, and was at the same time sorry to have now to forgo the charity of this house.

'Now, why need you do it?' said Princess Mary. 'Why did you come to me? . . .'

'Come, Pelageya, I was joking,' said Pierre. '*Princesse, ma parole, je n'ai pas voulu l'offenser.* I did not mean anything, I was only joking,' he said, smiling shyly and trying to efface his offence. 'It was all my fault, and Andrew was only joking.'

Pelageya stopped doubtfully, but in Pierre's face there was such a look of sincere penitence, and Prince Andrew glanced so meekly now at her and now at Pierre, that she was gradually reassured.

14

THE pilgrim woman was appeased, and being encouraged to talk gave a long account of Father Amphilochus, who led so holy a life that his hands smelt of incense, and how on her last visit to Kiev some monks she knew let her have the keys of the catacombs, and how she, taking some dried bread with her, had spent two days in the catacombs with the saints. 'I'd pray awhile to one, ponder awhile, then go on to another. I'd sleep a bit and then again go and kiss the relics, and there was such peace all around, such blessedness, that you don't want to come out even into the light of heaven again.'

Pierre listened to her attentively and seriously. Prince Andrew went out of the room, and then, leaving 'God's folk' to finish their tea, Princess Mary took Pierre into the drawing-room.

'You are very kind,' she said to him.

'Oh, I really did not mean to hurt her feelings. I understand them so well and have the greatest respect for them.'

Princess Mary looked at him silently and smiled affectionately.

'I have known you a long time, you see, and am as fond of you as of a brother,' she said. 'How do you find Andrew?' she added hurriedly, not giving him time to reply to her affectionate words. 'I am very anxious about him. His health was better in the winter, but last spring his wound reopened and the doctor said he ought to go away for a cure. And I am also very much afraid for him spiritually. He has not a character like us women who when we suffer can weep away our sorrows. He keeps it all within him. To-day he is cheerful and in good spirits, but that is the effect of your visit – he is not often like that. If you could persuade him to go abroad! He needs activity, and this quiet regular life is very bad for him. Others don't notice it, but I see it.'

Towards ten o'clock the menservants rushed to the front door hearing the bells of the old prince's carriage approaching. Prince Andrew and Pierre also went out into the porch.

'Who's that?' asked the old prince, noticing Pierre as he got out of the carriage.

'Ah! Very glad! Kiss me,' he said, having learnt who the young stranger was.

The old prince was in a good temper and very gracious to Pierre.

Before supper Prince Andrew, coming back to his father's study, found him disputing hotly with his visitor. Pierre was maintaining that a time would come when there would be no more wars. The old prince disputed it chaffingly, but without getting angry.

'Drain the blood from men's veins and put in water instead, then there will be no more war! Old women's nonsense – old women's nonsense!' he repeated, but still he patted Pierre affectionately on the shoulder, and then went up to the table where Prince Andrew, evidently not wishing to join in the conversation, was looking over the papers his father had brought from town. The old prince went up to him and began to talk business.

'The marshal, a Count Rostov, hasn't sent half his contingent. He came to town and wanted to invite me to dinner – I gave him a pretty dinner! ... And there, look at this ... Well, my boy,' the old prince went on, addressing his son and patting Pierre on the shoulder. 'A fine fellow – your friend – I like him! He stirs me up. Another says clever things and one doesn't care to listen, but this one talks rubbish yet stirs an old fellow up. Well, go! Get along! Perhaps I'll come and sit with you at supper. We'll have another dispute. Make friends with my little fool, Princess Mary,' he shouted after Pierre through the door.

Only now on his visit to Bald Hills did Pierre fully realize the strength and charm of his friendship with Prince Andrew. That charm was not expressed so much in his relations with him, as with all his family and with the household. With the stern old prince and the gentle timid Princess Mary, though he had scarcely known them, Pierre at once felt like an old friend. They were all fond of him already. Not only Princess Mary, who had been won by his gentleness with the pilgrims, gave him her most radiant looks, but even the one-year-old 'Prince Nicholas' (as his grandfather called him) smiled at Pierre and let himself be taken in his arms, and Michael Ivanovich and Mademoiselle Bourienne looked at him with pleasant smiles when he talked to the old prince.

The old prince came in to supper; this was evidently on Pierre's account. And during the two days of the young man's visit he was extremely kind to him, and told him to visit them again.

When Pierre had gone and the members of the household met together, they began to express their opinions of him as people always do after a new acquaintance has left, but as seldom happens, no one said anything but good of him.

15

When returning from his leave Rostov felt for the first time how close was the bond that united him to Denisov and the whole regiment.

On approaching it Rostov felt as he had done when approaching his home in Moscow. When he saw the first hussar with the unbuttoned uniform of his regiment, when he recognized red-haired Dementyev and saw the picket ropes of the roan horses, when Lavrushka gleefully shouted to his master, 'The Count has come!' and Denisov, who had been asleep on his bed, ran all dishevelled out of the mud hut to embrace him, and the officers collected round to greet the new arrival, Rostov experienced the same feeling as when his mother, his father, and his sister had embraced him, and tears of joy choked him so that he could not speak. The regiment was also a home, and as unalterably dear and precious as his parents' house.

When he had reported himself to the commander of the regiment and been re-assigned to his former squadron, had been on duty and gone out foraging, when he had again entered into all the little interests of the regiment and felt himself deprived of liberty and bound in one narrow unchanging frame, he experienced the same sense of peace, of moral support, and the same sense of being at home here in his own place, as he had felt under the parental roof. But here was none of all that turmoil of the world at large where he did not know his right place and took mistaken decisions, here was no Sonya with whom he ought, or ought not, to have an explanation; here was no possibility of going there or not going there; here there were not twenty-four hours in the day which could be spent in such a variety of ways; there was not that innumerable crowd of people of whom not one was nearer to him or farther from him than another; there were none of those uncertain and undefined money relations with his father, and nothing to recall that terrible loss to Dolokhov. Here in the regiment all was clear and simple. The whole world was divided into two unequal parts: one, our Pavlograd regiment; the other, all the rest. And the rest was no concern of his. In the regiment everything was definite: who was lieutenant, who captain, who was a good fellow, who a bad one, and most of all, who was a comrade. The canteen-keeper gave one credit, one's pay came every four months, there was nothing to think out or decide, you had only to do nothing that was considered bad in the Pavlograd regiment and, when given an order, to do what was clearly, distinctly, and definitely ordered – and all would be well.

Having once more entered into the definite conditions of this regimental life, Rostov felt the joy and relief a tired man feels on lying down to rest. Life in the regiment during this campaign was all the pleasanter for him because after his loss to Dolokhov (for which, in spite of all his family's efforts to console him, he could not forgive himself) he had made up his mind to atone for his fault by serving not as he had done before, but really well, and by being a perfectly first-rate comrade and officer – in a word, a splendid man altogether, a thing which seemed so difficult out *in the world*, but so possible in the regiment.

After his losses he had determined to pay back his debt to his parents in five years. He received ten thousand rubles a year, but now resolved to take only two thousand and leave the rest to repay the debt to his parents.

Our army, after repeated retreats and advances and battles at Pultusk and Preussisch-Eylau, was concentrated near Bartenstein. It was awaiting the Emperor's arrival and the beginning of a new campaign.

The Pavlograd regiment, belonging to that part of the army which had served in the 1805 campaign, had been recruiting up to strength in Russia, and arrived too late to take part in the first actions of the campaign. It had been neither at Pultusk nor at Preussisch-Eylau, and, when it joined the army in the field in the second half of the campaign, was attached to Platov's division.*

Platov's division was acting independently of the main army. Several times parts of the Pavlograd regiment had exchanged shots with the enemy, had taken prisoners, and once had even captured Marshal Oudinot's carriages. In April the Pavlograds were stationed immovably for some weeks near a totally ruined and deserted German village.

A thaw had set in, it was muddy and cold, the ice on the river broke, and the roads became impassable. For days neither provisions for the men nor fodder for the horses had been issued.* As no transports could arrive the men dispersed about the abandoned and deserted villages searching for potatoes, but found few even of these.

Everything had been eaten up and the inhabitants had all fled – if any remained they were worse than beggars and nothing more could be taken from them; even the soldiers, usually pitiless enough, instead of taking anything from them often gave them the last of their rations.

The Pavlograd regiment had had only two men wounded in action but had lost nearly half its men from hunger and sickness. In the hospitals death was so certain that soldiers suffering from fever, or the swelling that came from bad food, preferred to remain on duty, and hardly able to drag their legs went to the front rather than to the hospitals. When spring came on the soldiers found a plant just showing out of the ground that looked like asparagus, which for some reason they called 'Mashka's sweet root'. It was very bitter, but they wandered about the fields seeking it and dug it out with their sabres and ate it, though they were ordered not to do so as it was a noxious plant. That spring a new disease broke out among the soldiers, a swelling of the arms, legs, and face, which the doctors attributed to eating this root. But in spite of all this, the soldiers of Denisov's squadron fed chiefly on 'Mashka's sweet root', because it was the second week that the last of the biscuits were being doled out at the rate of half a pound a man, and the last potatoes received had sprouted and frozen.

The horses also had been fed for a fortnight on straw from the thatched roofs, and had become terribly thin, though still covered with tufts of felty winter hair.

Despite this destitution the soldiers and officers went on living just as usual. Despite their pale swollen faces and tattered uniforms, the hussars formed line for roll-call, kept things in order, groomed their horses, polished their arms, brought in straw from the thatched roofs in place of fodder, and sat down to dine round the cauldrons from which they rose up hungry, joking about their nasty food and their hunger. As usual in their spare time they lit bonfires, steamed themselves before them naked, smoked, picked out and baked sprouting rotten potatoes, told and listened to stories of Potëmkin's and Suvorov's campaigns, or to legends of Alësha the Sly, or the priest's labourer Mikolka.

The officers as usual lived in twos and threes in the roofless half-ruined houses. The seniors tried to collect straw and potatoes, and in general food for the men. The younger ones occupied themselves as before, some playing cards (there was plenty of money though there was no food), some with more innocent games such as quoits and skittles.* The general trend of the campaign was rarely spoken of partly because nothing certain was known about it, partly because there was a vague feeling that in the main it was going badly.

Rostov lived as before with Denisov, and since their furlough they had become more friendly than ever. Denisov never spoke of Rostov's family, but by the tender friendship his commander showed him, Rostov felt that the elder hussar's luckless love for Natasha played a part in strengthening their friendship. Denisov evidently tried to expose Rostov to danger as seldom as possible, and after an action greeted his safe return with evident joy. On one of his foraging expeditions, in a deserted and ruined village to which he had come in search of provisions, Rostov found a family consisting of an old Pole and his daughter with an infant in arms. They were half-clad, hungry, too weak to get away on foot, and had no means of obtaining a conveyance. Rostov brought them to his quarters, placed them in his own lodging, and kept them for some weeks while the old man was recovering. One of his comrades, talking of women, began chaffing Rostov, saying that he was more wily than any of them and that it would not be a bad thing if he introduced to them the pretty Polish girl he had saved. Rostov took the joke as an insult, flared up, and said such unpleasant things to the officer that it was all Denisov could do to prevent a duel. When the officer had gone away, Denisov, who did not himself know what Rostov's relations with the Polish girl might be, began to upbraid him for his quickness of temper, and Rostov replied:

'Say what you like ... She is like a sister to me, and I can't tell you how it offended me ... because ... well, for that reason ...'

Denisov patted him on the shoulder, and began rapidly pacing the room without looking at Rostov, as was his way at moments of deep feeling.

'Ah, what a mad bweed you Wostovs are!' he muttered, and Rostov noticed tears in his eyes.

16

In April the troops were enlivened by news of the Emperor's arrival, but Rostov had no chance of being present at the review he held at Bartenstein, as the Pavlograds were at the outposts far beyond that place.

They were bivouacking. Denisov and Rostov were living in an earth hut, dug out for them by the soldiers and roofed with branches and turf. The hut was made in the following manner, which had then come into vogue. A trench was dug three and a half feet wide, four feet eight inches deep, and eight feet long. At one end of the trench steps were cut out and these formed the entrance and vestibule. The trench itself was the room, in which the lucky ones, such as the squadron-commander, had a board lying on piles at the end opposite the entrance, to serve as a table. On each side of the trench the earth was cut out to a breadth of about two and a half feet, and this did duty for bedsteads and couches. The roof was so constructed that one could stand up in the middle of the trench, and could even sit up on the beds if one drew close to the table. Denisov, who was living luxuriously because the soldiers of his squadron liked him, had also a board in the roof at the farther end, with a piece of (broken but mended) glass in it for a window. When it was very cold, embers from the soldiers' camp fire were placed on a bent sheet of iron on the steps in the 'reception room' – as Denisov called that part of the hut – and it was then so warm that the officers, of whom there were always some with Denisov and Rostov, sat in their shirt-sleeves.

In April Rostov was on orderly duty. One morning between seven and eight, returning after a sleepless night, he sent for embers, changed his rain-soaked underclothes, said his prayers, drank tea, got warm, then tidied up the things on the table and in his own corner and, his face glowing from exposure to the wind and with nothing on but his shirt, lay down on his back putting his arms under his head. He was pleasantly considering the probability of being promoted in a few days for his last reconnoitring expedition, and was awaiting Denisov, who had gone out somewhere and with whom he wanted a talk.

Suddenly he heard Denisov shouting in a vibrating voice behind the hut, evidently much excited. Rostov moved to the window to see whom he was speaking to, and saw the quartermaster Topcheenko.

'I ordered you not to let them eat that Mashka woot stuff!' Denisov was shouting. 'And I saw with my own eyes how Lazarchuk bwought some fwom the fields.'

'I have given the order again and again, your honour, but they don't obey,' answered the quartermaster.

Rostov lay down again on his bed, and thought complacently: 'Let him fuss and bustle now, my job's done and I'm lying down – capitally!' He could hear that Lavrushka – that sly, bold orderly of Denisov's – was talking, as well as the quartermaster. Lavrushka was saying something about loaded wagons, biscuits and oxen, he had seen when he had gone out for provisions.

Then Denisov's voice was heard shouting farther and farther away. 'Saddle! Second platoon!'

'Where are they off to now?' thought Rostov.

Five minutes later Denisov came into the hut, climbed with muddy boots on the bed, lit his pipe, furiously scattered his things about, took his leaded whip, buckled on his sabre, and went out again. In answer to Rostov's inquiry where he was going, he answered vaguely and crossly that he had some business.

'Let God and our great monarch judge me afterwards!' said Denisov going out, and Rostov heard the hoofs of several horses splashing through the mud. He did not even trouble to find out where Denisov had gone. Having got warm in his corner he fell asleep and did not leave the hut till towards evening. Denisov had not yet returned. The weather had cleared up, and near the next hut two officers and a cadet were playing svayka, laughing as they threw their missiles which buried themselves in the soft mud. Rostov joined them. In the middle of the game the officers saw some wagons approaching with fifteen hussars on their skinny horses behind them. The wagons escorted by the hussars drew up to the picket ropes and a crowd of hussars surrounded them.

'There now, Denisov has been worrying,' said Rostov, 'and here are the provisions.'

'So they are!' said the officers. 'Won't the soldiers be glad!'

A little behind the hussars came Denisov, accompanied by two infantry officers with whom he was talking.

Rostov went to meet them.

'I warn you, Captain,' one of the officers, a short thin man, evidently very angry, was saying.

'Haven't I told you I won't give them up?' replied Denisov.

'You will answer for it, Captain. It is mutiny – seizing the transport of one's own army. Our men have had nothing to eat for two days.'

'And mine have had nothing for two weeks,' said Denisov.

'It is robbery! You'll answer for it, sir!' said the infantry officer raising his voice.

'Now what are you pestewing me for?' cried Denisov, suddenly losing his temper. 'I shall answer for it and not you, and you'd better not buzz about here till you get hurt. Be off! Go!' he shouted at the officers.

'Very well, then!' shouted the little officer, undaunted and not riding away. 'If you are determined to rob, I'll . . .'

'Go to the devil! Quick ma'ch, while you're safe and sound!' and Denisov turned his horse on the officer.

'Very well, very well!' muttered the officer threateningly, and turning his horse he trotted away, jolting in his saddle.

'A dog astwide a fence! A weal dog astwide a fence!' shouted Denisov after him (the most insulting expression a cavalryman can address to a mounted infantryman) and riding up to Rostov he burst out laughing.

'I've taken twansports from the infantwy by force!' he said. 'After all, can't let our men starve.'

The wagons that had reached the hussars had been consigned to an infantry regiment, but learning from Lavrushka that the transport was unescorted, Denisov with his hussars had seized it by force. The soldiers had biscuits dealt out to them freely, and they even shared them with the other squadrons.

The next day the regimental commander sent for Denisov, and holding his fingers spread out before his eyes said:

'This is how I look at this affair: I know nothing about it and won't begin proceedings, but I advise you to ride over to the staff, and settle the business there in the commissariat department, and if possible sign a receipt for such and such stores received. If not, as the demand was booked against an infantry regiment, there will be a row and the affair may end badly.'

From the regimental commander's Denisov rode straight to the staff with a sincere desire to act on this advice. In the evening he came back to his dug-out in a state such as Rostov had never yet seen him in. Denisov could not speak, and gasped for breath. When Rostov asked what was the matter, he only uttered some incoherent oaths and threats in a hoarse feeble voice.

Alarmed at Denisov's condition, Rostov suggested that he should undress, drink some water and send for the doctor.

'Twy me for wobbewy . . . oh! Some more water . . . Let them twy me, but I'll always thwash scoundwels . . . and I'll tell the Empewo' . . . Ice . . .' he muttered.

The regimental doctor when he came said it was absolutely necessary to bleed Denisov. A deep saucer of black blood was taken from his hairy arm, and only then was he able to relate what had happened to him.

'I get there,' began Denisov. '"Now then, where's your chief's quarters?" They were pointed out. "Please to wait." "I've widden twenty miles and have duties to attend to and no time to wait. Announce me." Vewy well, so out comes their head thief – also took it into his head to lecture me: "It's wobbewy!" – "Wobbewy," I say, "is not done by a man who seizes pwovisions to feed his soldiers, but by him who takes them to fill his own pockets!" "Will you please be silent?" "Vewy good!" Then he says: "Go and give a weceipt to the commissioner, but your affair will be passed on to head-quarters." I go to the commissioner. I enter, and at the table . . . who do you think? No, but wait a bit! . . . Who is it that's starving us?' shouted Denisov, hitting the table with the fist of his newly-bled arm so violently that the table nearly broke down and the tumblers on it jumped about. 'Telyanin! "What? So it's you who's starving us to death! Is it? Take this and this!" and I hit him so pat, stwaight on his snout . . . "Ah, what a . . . what a . . . !" and I sta'ted fwashing him . . . Well I've had a bit of fun I can tell you!' cried Denisov, gleeful and yet angry, his white teeth showing under his black moustache. 'I'd have killed him if they hadn't taken him away!'

'But what are you shouting for? Calm yourself,' said Rostov. 'You've set your arm bleeding afresh. Wait, we must tie it up again.'

Denisov was bandaged up again and put to bed. Next day he woke calm and cheerful.

But at noon the adjutant of the regiment came into Rostov's and Denisov's dug-out with a grave and serious face, and regretfully showed them a paper addressed to Major Denisov from the regimental commander, in which inquiries were made about yesterday's occurrence. The adjutant told them that the affair was likely to take a very bad turn: that a court-martial had been appointed, and that in view of the severity with which marauding and insubordination were now regarded, degradation to the ranks would be the best that could be hoped for.

The case as presented by the offended parties was that after seizing the transports, Major Denisov, being drunk, went to the chief quartermaster and without any provocation called him a thief, threatened to strike him, and on being led out had rushed into the office and given two officials a thrashing, and dislocated the arm of one of them.

In answer to Rostov's renewed questions, Denisov said, laughing, that he thought he remembered that some other fellow had got mixed up in it, but that it was all nonsense and rubbish, and he did not in the least fear any kind of trial, and that if those scoundrels dared attack him he would give them an answer they would not easily forget.

Denisov spoke contemptuously of the whole matter, but Rostov knew him too well not to detect that (while hiding it from others) at heart he feared a court-martial and was worried over the affair, which was evidently taking a bad turn. Every day letters of inquiry and notices from the Court arrived, and on the first of May Denisov was ordered to hand the squadron over to the next in seniority and appear before the staff of his division to explain his violence at the commissariat office. On the previous day Platov reconnoitred with two Cossack regiments and two squadrons of hussars. Denisov, as was his wont, rode out in front of the outposts parading his courage. A bullet fired by a French sharpshooter hit him in the fleshy part of his leg. Perhaps at another time Denisov would not have left the regiment for so slight a wound, but now he took advantage of it to excuse himself from appearing at the staff, and went into hospital.

17

IN June the battle of Friedland was fought, in which the Pavlograds did not take part, and after that an armistice was proclaimed. Rostov, who felt his friend's absence very much, having no news of him since he left and feeling anxious about his wound and the progress of his affairs, took advantage of the armistice to get leave to visit Denisov in hospital.

The hospital was in a small Prussian town that had been twice devastated by Russian and French troops. Because it was summer, when it is so beautiful out in the fields, the little town presented a particularly dismal appearance with its broken roofs and fences, its foul streets, tattered inhabitants, and the sick and drunken soldiers wandering about.

The hospital was in a brick building with some of the window frames and panes broken, and a courtyard surrounded by the remains of a wooden fence that had been pulled to pieces. Several bandaged soldiers, with pale swollen faces, were sitting or walking about in the sunshine in the yard.

Directly Rostov entered the door he was enveloped by a smell of putrefaction and hospital air. On the stairs he met a Russian army doctor smoking a cigar. The doctor was followed by a Russian assistant.

'I can't tear myself in pieces,' the doctor was saying. 'Come to Makar Alexeevich in the evening. I shall be there.'

The assistant asked some further questions.

'Oh, do the best you can! Isn't it all the same?' The doctor noticed Rostov coming upstairs.

'What do you want, sir?' said the doctor. 'What do you want? The bullets having spared you, do you want to try typhus? This is a pest-house, sir.'

'How so?' asked Rostov.

'Typhus, sir. It's death to go in. Only we two, Makeev and I' (he pointed to the assistant) 'keep on here. Some five of us doctors have died in this place . . . When a new one comes he is done for in a week,' said the doctor with evident satisfaction. 'Prussian doctors have been invited here but our allies don't like it at all.'

Rostov explained that he wanted to see Major Denisov of the hussars, who was wounded.

'I don't know. I can't tell you, sir. Only think! I am alone in charge of three hospitals with more than four hundred patients! It's well that the charitable Prussian ladies send us two pounds of coffee and some lint each month or we should be lost!' he laughed. 'Four hundred, sir, and they're always sending me fresh ones. There *are* four hundred? Eh?' he asked, turning to his assistant.

The assistant looked fagged out. He was evidently vexed, and impatient for the talkative doctor to go.

'Major Denisov,' Rostov said again. 'He was wounded at Molliten.'

'Dead, I fancy. Eh, Makeev?' queried the doctor in a tone of indifference.

The assistant however did not confirm the doctor's words.

'Is he tall and with reddish hair?' asked the doctor.

Rostov described Denisov's appearance.

'There was one like that,' said the doctor, as if pleased. 'That one is dead, I fancy. However, I'll look up our list. We had a list. Have you got it, Makeev?'

'Makar Alexeevich has the list,' answered the assistant. 'But if you'll step into the officers' wards you'll see for yourself,' he added, turning to Rostov.

'Ah, you'd better not go, sir,' said the doctor, 'or you may have to stay here yourself.'

But Rostov bowed himself away from the doctor and asked the assistant to show him the way.

'Only don't blame me!' the doctor shouted up after him.

Rostov and the assistant went into the dark corridor. The smell was so strong there that Rostov held his nose, and had to pause and collect his strength before he could go on. A door opened to the right, and an emaciated sallow man on crutches, barefoot and in underclothing, limped out, and leaning against the doorpost looked with glittering envious eyes at those who were passing. Glancing in at the door, Rostov saw that the sick and wounded were lying on the floor on straw and overcoats.

'May I go in and look?'

'What is there to see?' said the assistant.

But just because the assistant evidently did not want him to go in, Rostov entered the soldiers' ward. The foul air to which he had already begun to get used in the corridor was still stronger here. It was a little different, more pungent, and one felt that this was where it originated.

In the long room, brightly lit up by the sun through the large windows, the sick and wounded lay in two rows with their heads to the walls, and leaving a passage in the middle. Most of them were unconscious and paid no attention to the newcomers. Those who were conscious raised themselves or lifted their thin yellow faces, and all looked intently at Rostov with the same expression of hope, of relief, reproach, and envy of another's health. Rostov went to the middle of the room, and looking through the open doors into the two adjoining rooms saw the same thing there. He stood still looking silently around. He had not at all expected such a sight. Just before him, almost across the middle of the passage on the bare floor, lay a sick man, probably a Cossack to judge by the cut of his hair. The man lay on his back, his huge arms and legs outstretched. His face was purple, his eyes were rolled back so that only the whites were seen, and on his bare legs and arms which were still red, the veins stood out like cords. He was knocking the back of his head against the floor, hoarsely uttering some word which he kept repeating. Rostov listened and made out the word. It was 'drink, drink, a drink!' Rostov glanced round, looking for someone who would put this man back in his place and bring him water.

'Who looks after the sick here?' he asked the assistant.

Just then a commissariat soldier, a hospital orderly, came in from the next room, marching stiffly, and drew up in front of Rostov.

'Good day, your honour!' he shouted, rolling his eyes at Rostov and evidently mistaking him for one of the hospital authorities.

'Get him to his place and give him some water,' said Rostov, pointing to the Cossack.

'Yes, your honour,' the soldier replied complacently, and rolling his eyes more than ever he drew himself up still straighter, but did not move.

'No, it's impossible to do anything here,' thought Rostov, lowering his eyes, and he was going out, but became aware of an intense look fixed on him on his right, and he turned. Close to the corner, on an overcoat, sat an old unshaven grey-bearded soldier as thin as a skeleton, with a stern sallow face and eyes intently fixed on Rostov. The man's neighbour on one side whispered something to him, pointing at Rostov, who noticed that the old man wanted to speak to him. He drew nearer and saw that the old man had only one leg bent under him, the other had been amputated above the knee. His neighbour on the other side, who lay motionless some distance from him with his head thrown back, was a young soldier with a snub nose. His pale waxen face was still freckled, and his eyes were rolled back. Rostov looked at the young soldier and a cold chill ran down his back.

'Why, this one seems . . .' he began, turning to the assistant.

'And how we've been begging, your honour,' said the old soldier, his jaw quivering. 'He's been dead since morning. After all we're men, not dogs.'

'I'll send someone at once. He shall be taken away – taken away at once,' said the assistant hurriedly. 'Let us go, your honour.'

'Yes, yes, let us go,' said Rostov hastily, and lowering his eyes and shrinking, he tried to pass unnoticed between the rows of reproachful envious eyes that were fixed upon him, and went out of the room.

18

GOING along the corridor the assistant led Rostov to the officers' wards, consisting of three rooms, the doors of which stood open. There were beds in these rooms and the sick and wounded officers were lying or sitting on them. Some were walking about the rooms in hospital dressing-gowns. The first person Rostov met in the officers' ward was a thin little man with one arm, who was walking about the first room in a nightcap and a hospital dressing-gown with a pipe between his teeth. Rostov looked at him trying to remember where he had seen him before.

'See where we've met again!' said the little man. 'Tushin, Tushin, don't you remember, who gave you a lift at Schön Grabern? And I've had a bit cut off, you see...' he went on with a smile, pointing to the empty sleeve of his dressing-gown. 'Looking for Vasili Dmitrich Denisov? My neighbour,' he added when he heard who Rostov wanted. 'Here, here', and Tushin led him into the next room, from whence came sounds of several laughing voices.

'How can they laugh, or even live at all here?' thought Rostov, still aware of that smell of decomposing flesh that had been so strong in the soldiers' ward, and still seeming to see fixed on him those envious looks which had followed him out from both sides, and the face of that young soldier with eyes rolled back.

Denisov lay asleep on his bed with his head under the blanket, though it was nearly noon.

'Ah, Wostov? How are you, how are you?' he called out, still in the same voice as in the regiment, but Rostov noticed sadly that under this habitual ease and animation some new, sinister, hidden feeling showed itself in the expression of Denisov's face and the intonations of his voice.

His wound, though such a slight one, had not yet healed even now six weeks after he had been hit. His face had the same swollen pallor as the faces of the other hospital patients, but it was not this that struck Rostov. What struck him was that Denisov did not seem glad to see him, and smiled at him unnaturally. He did not ask about the regiment, nor about the general state of affairs, and when Rostov spoke of these matters did not listen.

Rostov even noticed that Denisov did not like to be reminded of the regiment, or in general of that other, free life which was going on outside the hospital. He seemed to try to forget that old life and was only interested in the affair with the commissariat officers. On Rostov's inquiry as to how that matter stood, he at once produced from under his pillow a paper he had received from the commission and the rough draft of his answer to it. He became animated when he began reading his paper, and specially drew Rostov's attention to the stinging rejoinders he made to his enemies. His hospital companions, who had gathered round Rostov – a fresh arrival from the world outside – gradually began to disperse as soon as Denisov began reading his answer. Rostov noticed by their faces that all those gentlemen had already heard that story more than once and were tired of it. Only the man who had the next bed, a stout Uhlan, continued to sit on his bed gloomily frowning and smoking a pipe, and little one-armed Tushin still listened, shaking his head disapprovingly. In the middle of the reading the Uhlan interrupted Denisov.

'But what I say is,' he said, turning to Rostov, 'it would be best simply to petition the Emperor for pardon. They say great rewards will now be distributed, and surely a pardon would be granted...'

'Me petition the Empewo'!' exclaimed Denisov in a voice to which he tried hard to give the old energy and fire, but which sounded like an expression of irritable impotence. 'What for? If I were a wobber I would ask mercy, but I'm being court-martialled for bwinging wobbers to book. Let them twy me, I'm not afwaid of anyone. I've served the Tsar and my countwy honouwably and have not stolen! And am I to be degwaded? ... Listen, I'm w'iting to them stwaight. This is what I say: "If I had wobbed the Tweasury..."'

'It's well written certainly,' said Tushin, 'but that's not the point, Vasili Dmitrich,' and he also turned to Rostov. 'One has to submit, and Vasili Dmitrich doesn't want to. You know the auditor told you it was a bad business.'

'Well, let it be bad,' said Denisov.

'The auditor wrote out a petition for you,' continued Tushin, 'and you ought to sign it and ask this gentleman to take it. No doubt he' (indicating Rostov) 'has connexions on the staff. You won't find a better opportunity.'

'Haven't I said I'm not going to gwovel?' Denisov interrupted him, and went on reading his paper.

Rostov had not the courage to persuade Denisov, though he instinctively felt that the way advised by Tushin and the other officers was the safest, and though he would have been glad to be of service to Denisov. He knew his stubborn will and straight-forward hasty temper.

When the reading of Denisov's virulent reply, which took more than an hour, was over, Rostov said nothing, and he spent the rest of the day in a most dejected state of mind amid Denisov's hospital comrades who had gathered around him, telling them what he knew and listening to their stories. Denisov was moodily silent all the evening.

Late in the evening when Rostov was about to leave, he asked Denisov whether he had no commission for him.

'Yes, wait a bit,' said Denisov glancing round at the officers, and taking his papers from under his pillow he went to the window where he had an inkpot, and sat down to write.

'It seems it's no use knocking one's head against a wall!' he said, coming from the window and giving Rostov a large envelope.

In it was the petition to the Emperor drawn up by the auditor, in which Denisov without alluding to the offences of the commissariat officials, simply asked for pardon.

'Hand it in. It seems . . .'

He did not finish but gave a painfully unnatural smile.

19

HAVING returned to the regiment and told the commander the state of Denisov's affairs, Rostov rode to Tilsit with the letter to the Emperor.

On the 13th of June the French and Russian Emperors arrived in Tilsit.* Boris Drubetskoy had asked the important personage on whom he was in attendance to include him in the suite appointed for the stay at Tilsit.

'I should like to see the great man,' he said alluding to Napoleon, whom hitherto he like everyone else had always called Buonaparte.

'You are speaking of Buonaparte?' asked the general, smiling.

Boris looked at his general inquiringly and immediately saw that he was being tested.

'I am speaking, Prince, of the Emperor Napoleon,' he replied. The general patted him on the shoulder with a smile.

'You will go far,' he said, and took him to Tilsit with him.

Boris was among the few present at the Niemen on the day the two Emperors met. He saw the raft, decorated with monograms, saw Napoleon pass before the French Guards on the farther bank of the river, saw the pensive face of the Emperor Alexander as he sat in silence in a tavern on the bank of the Niemen awaiting Napoleon's arrival, saw both Emperors get into boats, and saw how Napoleon – reaching the raft first – stepped quickly forward to meet Alexander and held out his hand to him, and how they both retired into the pavilion. Since he had begun to move in the highest circles Boris had made it his habit to watch attentively all that went on around him and to note it down. At the time of the meeting at Tilsit he asked the names of those who had come with Napoleon and about the uniforms they wore, and listened attentively to words spoken by important personages. At the moment the Emperors went into the pavilion he looked at his watch, and did not forget to look at it again when Alexander came out. The interview had lasted an hour and fifty-three minutes. He noted this down that same evening among other facts he felt to be of historic importance. As the Emperor's suite was a very small one it was

431

a matter of great importance, for a man who valued his success in the service, to be at Tilsit on the occasion of this interview between the two Emperors, and having succeeded in this, Boris felt that henceforth his position was fully assured. He had not only become known, but people had grown accustomed to him and accepted him. Twice he had executed commissions to the Emperor himself, so that the latter knew his face, and all those at Court, far from cold-shouldering him as at first when they considered him a newcomer, would now have been surprised had he been absent.

Boris lodged with another adjutant, the Polish Count Zhilinski. Zhilinski, a Pole brought up in Paris, was rich, and passionately fond of the French, and almost every day of the stay at Tilsit, French officers of the Guard and from French head-quarters were dining and lunching with him and Boris.

On the evening of the 24th of June, Count Zhilinski was giving a supper to his French friends. The guest of honour was an aide-de-camp of Napoleon's, there were also several French officers of the Guard, and a page of Napoleon's, a young lad of an old aristocratic French family. That very·day Rostov, profiting by the darkness to avoid being recognized in civilian dress, came to Tilsit and went to the lodging occupied by Boris and Zhilinski.

Rostov, in common with the whole army from which he came, was far from having experienced the change of feeling towards Napoleon and the French – who from being foes had suddenly become friends – that had taken place at head-quarters and in Boris. In the army, Bonaparte and the French were still regarded with mingled feelings of anger, contempt, and fear. Only recently, talking with one of Platov's Cossack officers, Rostov had argued that if Napoleon were taken prisoner he would be treated not as a sovereign, but as a criminal. Quite lately happening to meet a wounded French colonel on the road, Rostov had maintained with heat that peace was impossible between a legitimate sovereign and the criminal Bonaparte. Rostov was therefore unpleasantly struck by the presence of French officers in Boris's lodgings, dressed in uniforms he had been accustomed to see from quite a different point of view from the outposts of the flank. As soon as he noticed a French officer who thrust his head out of the door, that warlike feeling of hostility which he always experienced at the sight of the enemy, suddenly seized him. He stopped at the threshold and asked in Russian whether Drubetskoy lived there. Boris, hearing a strange voice in the ante-room, came out to meet him. An expression of annoyance showed itself for a moment on his face on first recognizing Rostov.

'Ah, it's you? Very glad, very glad to see you,' he said however, coming towards him with a smile. But Rostov had noticed his first impulse.

'I've come at a bad time I think. I should not have come, but I have business,' he said coldly.

'No, I only wonder how you managed to get away from your regiment. *Dans un moment je suis à vous*,' he said, answering someone who called him.

'I see I'm intruding,' Rostov repeated.

The look of annoyance had already disappeared from Boris's face: having evidently reflected and decided how to act he very quietly took both Rostov's hands and led him into the next room. His eyes, looking serenely and steadily at Rostov, seemed to be veiled by something, as if screened by blue spectacles of conventionality. So it seemed to Rostov.

'Oh come now! As if you could come at a wrong time!' said Boris, and he led him into the room where the supper table was laid and introduced him to his guests, explaining that he was not a civilian, but an hussar officer, and an old friend of his.

'Count Zhilinski – *le Comte* N. N. – *le Capitaine* S. S.' said he, naming his guests. Rostov looked frowningly at the Frenchmen, bowed reluctantly, and remained silent.

Zhilinski evidently did not receive this new Russian person very willingly into his circle, and did not speak to Rostov. Boris did not appear to notice the constraint the newcomer produced, and with the same pleasant composure and the same veiled look in his eyes with which he had met Rostov, tried to enliven the conversation. One of the Frenchmen, with the politeness characteristic of his countrymen, addressed the obstinately taciturn Rostov, saying that the latter had probably come to Tilsit to see the Emperor.

'No, I came on business,' replied Rostov briefly.

Rostov had been out of humour from the moment he noticed the look of dissatisfaction on Boris's face, and as always happens to those in a bad humour, it seemed to him that everyone regarded him with aversion and that he was in everybody's way. He really was in their way, for he alone took no part in the conversation which again became general. The looks the visitors cast on him seemed to say: 'And what is he sitting here for?' He rose and went up to Boris.

'Anyhow I'm in your way,' he said in a low tone. 'Come and talk over my business and I'll go away.'

'Oh, no, not at all,' said Boris. 'But if you are tired, come and lie down in my room and have a rest.'

'Yes, really . . .'

They went into the little room where Boris slept. Rostov without

433

sitting down, began at once, irritably (as if Boris were to blame in some way) telling him about Denisov's affair, asking him whether, through his general, he could and would intercede with the Emperor on Denisov's behalf and get Denisov's petition handed in. When he and Boris were alone, Rostov felt for the first time that he could not look Boris in the face without a sense of awkwardness. Boris, with one leg crossed over the other and stroking his left hand with the slender fingers of his right, listened to Rostov as a general listens to the report of a subordinate, now looking aside and now gazing straight into Rostov's eyes with the same veiled look. Each time this happened Rostov felt uncomfortable and cast down his eyes.

'I have heard of such cases and know that his Majesty is very severe in such affairs. I think it would be best not to bring it before the Emperor, but to apply to the commander of the corps ... But in general, I think ...'

'So you don't want to do anything? Well then, say so!' Rostov almost shouted, not looking Boris in the face.

Boris smiled.

'On the contrary I will do what I can. Only I thought ...'

At that moment Zhilinski's voice was heard calling Boris.

'Well then, go, go, go ...' said Rostov, and refusing supper and remaining alone in the little room, he walked up and down for a long time hearing the light-hearted French conversation from the next room.

20

ROSTOV had come to Tilsit on the day least suitable for a petition on Denisov's behalf. He could not himself go to the general in attendance as he was in mufti and had come to Tilsit without permission to do so, and Boris, even had he wished to, could not have done so on the following day. On that day, June 27th, the preliminaries of peace were signed. The Emperors exchanged decorations: Alexander received the Cross of the Legion of Honour, and Napoleon the Order of St Andrew of the First Degree, and a dinner had been arranged for the evening, given by a battalion of the French Guards to the Preobrazhensk battalion. The Emperors were to be present at that banquet.

Rostov felt so ill at ease and uncomfortable with Boris, that when the latter looked in after supper he pretended to be asleep, and early next morning went away, avoiding Boris. In his civilian clothes and a round hat he wandered about the town, staring at the

French and their uniforms and at the streets and houses where the Russian and French Emperors were staying. In a square he saw tables being set up and preparations made for the dinner, he saw the Russian and French colours draped from side to side of the streets with huge monograms A. and N. In the windows of the houses also, flags and bunting were displayed.

'Boris doesn't want to help me and I don't want to ask him. That's settled,' thought Nicholas. 'All is over between us, but I won't leave here without having done all I can for Denisov and certainly not without getting his letter to the Emperor. The Emperor! . . . He is here!' thought Rostov who had unconsciously returned to the house where Alexander lodged.

Saddled horses were standing before the house and the suite were assembling, evidently preparing for the Emperor to come out.

'I may see him at any moment,' thought Rostov. 'If only I were to hand the letter direct to him and tell him all . . . could they really arrest me for my civilian clothes? Surely not! He would understand on whose side justice lies. He understands everything, knows everything. Who can be more just, more magnanimous than he? And even if they did arrest me for being here, what would it matter?' thought he, looking at an officer who was entering the house the Emperor occupied. 'After all, people do go in . . . It's all nonsense! I'll go in and hand the letter to the Emperor myself, so much the worse for Drubetskoy who drives me to it!' And suddenly with a determination he himself did not expect, Rostov felt for the letter in his pocket and went straight to the house.

'No, I won't miss my opportunity now as I did after Austerlitz,' he thought, expecting every moment to meet the monarch, and conscious of the blood that rushed to his heart at the thought. 'I will fall at his feet and beseech him. He will lift me up, will listen, and will even thank me. "I am happy when I can do good, but to remedy injustice is the greatest happiness,"' Rostov fancied the sovereign saying. And passing people who looked after him with curiosity, he entered the porch of the Emperor's house.

A broad staircase led straight up from the entry, and to the right he saw a closed door. Below, under the staircase, was a door leading to the lower floor.

'Whom do you want?' someone inquired.

'To hand in a letter, a petition, to his Majesty,' said Nicholas, with a tremor in his voice.

'A petition? This way, to the officer on duty' (he was shown the door leading downstairs) 'only it won't be accepted.'

On hearing this indifferent voice Rostov grew frightened at what he was doing; the thought of meeting the Emperor at any moment was so fascinating and consequently so alarming, that he was ready to run away, but the official who had questioned him opened the door, and Rostov entered.

A short stout man of about thirty, in white breeches and high boots and a batiste shirt that he had evidently only just put on, was standing in that room, and his valet was buttoning onto the back of his breeches a new pair of handsome silk-embroidered braces that for some reason attracted Rostov's attention. This man was speaking to someone in the adjoining room.

'A good figure and in her first bloom,' he was saying, but on seeing Rostov he stopped short and frowned.

'What is it? A petition?'

'What is it?' asked the person in the other room.

'Another petitioner,' answered the man with the braces.

'Tell him to come later. He'll be coming out directly, we must go.'

'Later ... later! To-morrow. It's too late ...'

Rostov turned and was about to go, but the man in the braces stopped him.

'Whom have you come from? Who are you?'

'I come from Major Denisov,' answered Rostov.

'Are you an officer?'

'Lieutenant Count Rostov.'

'What audacity! Hand it in through your commander. And go along with you ... go'; and he continued to put on the uniform the valet handed him.

Rostov went back into the hall and noticed that in the porch there were many officers and generals in full parade uniform whom he had to pass.

Cursing his temerity, his heart sinking at the thought of finding himself at any moment face to face with the Emperor and being put to shame and arrested in his presence, fully alive now to the impropriety of his conduct and repenting of it, Rostov with downcast eyes was making his way out of the house through the brilliant suite, when a familiar voice called him and a hand detained him.

'What are you doing here, sir, in civilian dress?' asked a deep voice.

It was a cavalry general who had obtained the Emperor's special favour during this campaign, and who had formerly commanded the division in which Rostov was serving.

Rostov in dismay began justifying himself, but seeing the kindly, jocular face of the general, he took him aside and in an excited voice told him the whole affair, asking him to intercede for Denisov, whom the general knew. Having heard Rostov to the end the general shook his head gravely.

'I'm sorry, sorry for that fine fellow. Give me the letter.'

Hardly had Rostov handed him the letter and finished explaining Denisov's case, when hasty steps and the jingling of spurs was heard on the stairs, and the general, leaving him, went to the porch. The gentlemen of the Emperor's suite ran down the stairs and went to their horses. Hayne, the same groom who had been at Austerlitz, led up the Emperor's horse, and the faint creak of a footstep Rostov knew at once, was heard on the stairs. Forgetting the danger of being recognized, Rostov went close to the porch together with some inquisitive civilians, and again after two years saw those features he adored: that same face and same look and step, and the same union of majesty and mildness ... And the feeling of enthusiasm and love for his sovereign rose again in Rostov's soul in all its old force. In the uniform of the Preobrazhensk regiment – white chamois-leather breeches and high boots – and wearing a star Rostov did not know (it was that of the *Légion d'honneur*), the monarch came out into the porch, putting on his gloves and carrying his hat under his arm. He stopped and looked about him, brightening everything around by his glance. He spoke a few words to some of the generals, and recognizing the former commander of Rostov's division smiled and beckoned to him.

All the suite drew back, and Rostov saw the general talking for some time to the Emperor.

The Emperor said a few words to him and took a step towards his horse. Again the crowd of members of the suite and street-gazers (among whom was Rostov) moved nearer to the Emperor. Stopping beside his horse with his hand on the saddle, the Emperor turned to the cavalry general and said in a loud voice, evidently wishing to be heard by all:

'I cannot do it, General. I cannot, because the law is stronger than I,' and he raised his foot to the stirrup.

The general bowed his head respectfully, and the monarch mounted and rode down the street at a gallop. Beside himself with enthusiasm Rostov ran after him with the crowd.

21

THE Emperor rode to the square where, facing one another, a battalion of the Preobrazhensk regiment stood on the right and a battalion of the French Guards in their bearskin caps on the left.

As the Tsar rode up to one flank of the battalions, which presented arms, another group of horsemen galloped up to the opposite flank, and at the head of them Rostov recognized Napoleon. It could be no one else. He came at a gallop, wearing a small hat, a blue uniform open over a white vest, and the St Andrew ribbon over his shoulder. He was riding a very fine thoroughbred grey Arab horse with a crimson gold-embroidered saddle-cloth. On approaching Alexander he raised his hat, and as he did so Rostov, with his cavalryman's eye, could not help noticing that Napoleon did not sit well or firmly in the saddle. The battalions shouted 'Hurrah!' and '*Vive l'Empereur!*' Napoleon said something to Alexander, and both Emperors dismounted and took each other's hands. Napoleon's face wore an unpleasant and artificial smile. Alexander was saying something affable to him.

In spite of the trampling of the French gendarmes' horses which were pushing back the crowd, Rostov kept his eyes on every movement of Alexander and Bonaparte. It struck him as a surprise that Alexander treated Bonaparte as an equal and that the latter was quite at ease with the Tsar, as if such relations with an Emperor were an everyday matter to him.

Alexander and Napoleon, with the long train of their suites, approached the right flank of the Preobrazhensk battalion and came straight up to the crowd standing there. The crowd unexpectedly found itself so close to the Emperors that Rostov, standing in the front row, was afraid he might be recognized.

'Sire, I ask your permission to present the Legion of Honour to the bravest of your soldiers,' said a sharp, precise voice articulating every letter.

This was said by the undersized Napoleon, looking up straight into Alexander's eyes. Alexander listened attentively to what was said to him, and bending his head smiled pleasantly.

'To him who has borne himself most bravely in this last war,' added Napoleon, accentuating each syllable, as with a composure and assurance exasperating to Rostov he ran his eye over the Russian ranks drawn up before him, who all presented arms with their eyes fixed on their Emperor.

'Will your Majesty allow me to consult the colonel?' said Alexander and took a few hasty steps towards Prince Kozlovsky, the commander of the battalion.

Bonaparte meanwhile began taking the glove off his small white hand, tore it in so doing and threw it away. An aide-de-camp behind him rushed forward and picked it up.

'To whom shall it be given?' the Emperor Alexander asked Kozlovsky in Russian in a low voice.

'To whomever your Majesty commands.'

438

The Emperor knit his brows with dissatisfaction, and glancing back remarked:

'But we must give him an answer.'

Kozlovsky scanned the ranks resolutely, and included Rostov in his scrutiny.

'Can it be me?' thought Rostov.

'Lazarev!' the colonel called with a frown, and Lazarev, the first soldier in the rank, stepped briskly forward.

'Where are you off to? Stop here!' voices whispered to Lazarev who did not know where to go. Lazarev stopped, casting a sidelong look at his colonel in alarm. His face twitched, as often happens to soldiers called before the ranks.

Napoleon slightly turned his head, and put his plump little hand out behind him as if to take something. The members of his suite, guessing at once what he wanted, moved about and whispered as they passed something from one to another, and a page – the same one Rostov had seen the previous evening at Boris's – ran forward, and bowing respectfully over the outstretched hand and not keeping it waiting a moment, laid in it an Order on a red ribbon. Napoleon without looking pressed two fingers together and the badge was between them. Then he approached Lazarev (who rolled his eyes and persistently gazed at his own monarch), looked round at the Emperor Alexander to imply that what he was now doing was done for the sake of his ally, and the small white hand holding the Order touched one of Lazarev's buttons. It was as if Napoleon knew that it was only necessary for his hand to deign to touch that soldier's breast for the soldier to be for ever happy, rewarded, and distinguished from everyone else in the world. Napoleon merely laid the cross on Lazarev's breast and, dropping his hand, turned towards Alexander as though sure that the cross would adhere there. And it really did.

Officious hands, Russian and French, immediately seized the cross and fastened it to the uniform. Lazarev glanced morosely at the little man with white hands who was doing something to him, and still standing motionless presenting arms, looked again straight into Alexander's eyes as if asking whether he should stand there, or go away, or do something else. But receiving no orders he remained for some time in that rigid position.

The Emperors remounted and rode away. The Preobrazhensk battalion, breaking rank, mingled with the French Guards and sat down at the tables prepared for them.

Lazarev sat in the place of honour. Russian and French officers embraced him, congratulated him, and pressed his hands. Crowds of officers and civilians drew near merely to see him. A rumble of

Russian and French voices and laughter filled the air round the tables in the square. Two officers with flushed faces, looking cheerful and happy, passed by Rostov.

'What d'you think of the treat? All on silver plate,' one of them was saying. 'Have you seen Lazarev?'

'I have.'

'To-morrow, I hear, the Preobrazhenskys will give them a dinner.'

'Yes, but what luck for Lazarev! Twelve hundred francs pension for life.'

'Here's a cap, lads!' shouted a Preobrazhensk soldier, donning a shaggy French cap.

'It's a fine thing! First rate!'

'Have you heard the password?' asked one Guards' officer of another. 'The day before yesterday it was, "*Napoléon, France, bravoure*"; yesterday, "*Alexandre, Russie, grandeur*". One day our Emperor gives it and next day Napoleon. To-morrow our Emperor will send a St George's Cross to the bravest of the French Guards. It has to be done. He must respond in kind.'

Boris too with his friend Zhilinski, came to see the Preobrazhensk banquet. On his way back he noticed Rostov standing by the corner of a house.

'Rostov! How d'you do? We missed one another,' he said, and could not refrain from asking what was the matter, so strangely dismal and troubled was Rostov's face.

'Nothing, nothing,' replied Rostov.

'You'll call round?'

'Yes, I will.'

Rostov stood at that corner for a long time, watching the feast from a distance. In his mind a painful process was going on which he could not bring to a conclusion. Terrible doubts rose in his soul. Now he remembered Denisov with his changed expression, his submission, and the whole hospital, with arms and legs torn off and its dirt and disease. So vividly did he recall that hospital stench of dead flesh that he looked round to see where the smell came from. Next he thought of that self-satisfied Bonaparte with his small white hand, who was now an Emperor, liked and respected by Alexander. Then why those severed arms and legs and those dead men? . . . Then again he thought of Lazarev rewarded and Denisov punished and unpardoned. He caught himself harbouring such strange thoughts that he was frightened.

The smell of food the Preobrazhenskys were eating, and a sense of hunger, recalled him from these reflections; he had to get something to eat before going away. He went to an hotel he had noticed that morning. There he found so many people, among them officers who like himself had come in civilian clothes, that he had difficulty in getting a dinner. Two officers of his own division joined him. The conversation naturally turned on the peace. The officers, his comrades, like most of the army, were dissatisfied with the peace concluded after the battle of Friedland. They said that had we held out a little longer Napoleon would have been done for, as his troops had neither provisions nor ammunition. Nicholas ate and drank (chiefly the latter) in silence. He finished a couple of bottles of wine by himself. The process in his mind went on tormenting him without reaching a conclusion. He feared to give way to his thoughts yet he could not get rid of them. Suddenly, on one of the officers saying that it was humiliating to look at the French, Rostov began shouting with uncalled-for warmth, and therefore much to the surprise of the officers:

'How can you judge what's best?' he cried, the blood suddenly rushing to his face. 'How can you judge the Emperor's actions? What right have we to argue? We cannot comprehend either the Emperor's aims or his actions!'

'But I never said a word about the Emperor!' said the officer, justifying himself, and unable to understand Rostov's outburst except on the supposition that he was drunk.

But Rostov did not listen to him.

'We are not diplomatic officials, we are soldiers and nothing more,' he went on. 'If we are ordered to die, we must die. If we're punished, it means that we have deserved it, it's not for us to judge. If the Emperor pleases to recognize Bonaparte as Emperor and to conclude an alliance with him, it means that that is the right thing to do. If once we begin judging and arguing about everything, nothing sacred will be left! That way we shall be saying there is no God – nothing!' shouted Nicholas banging the table – very little to the point as it seemed to his listeners, but quite relevantly to the course of his own thoughts.

'Our business is to do our duty, to fight and not to think! That's all . . .' said he.

'And to drink,' said one of the officers, not wishing to quarrel.

'Yes, and to drink,' assented Nicholas. 'Hullo there! Another bottle!' he shouted.

END OF PART TWO

PART THREE

1

In 1808 the Emperor Alexander went to Erfurt for a fresh interview with the Emperor Napoleon, and in the upper circles of Petersburg there was much talk of the grandeur of this important meeting.

In 1809 the intimacy between 'the world's two arbiters', as Napoleon and Alexander were called, was such that when Napoleon declared war on Austria a Russian corps crossed the frontier to co-operate with our old enemy Bonaparte against our old ally the Emperor of Austria, and in court circles the possibility of marriage between Napoleon and one of Alexander's sisters was spoken of. But besides considerations of foreign policy the attention of Russian society was at that time keenly directed on the internal changes that were being undertaken in all the departments of government.

Life meanwhile – real life, with its essential interests of health and sickness, toil and rest, and its intellectual interests in thought, science, poetry, music, love, friendship, hatred, and passions – went on as usual, independently of and apart from political friendship or enmity with Napoleon Bonaparte and from all the schemes of reconstruction.

*

Prince Andrew had spent two years continuously in the country.

All the plans Pierre had attempted on his estates – and constantly changing from one thing to another had never accomplished – were carried out by Prince Andrew without display and without perceptible difficulty.

He had in the highest degree a practical tenacity which Pierre lacked, and without fuss or strain on his part this set things going.

On one of his estates the three hundred serfs were liberated and became free agricultural labourers – this being one of the first examples of the kind in Russia. On other estates the serfs' compulsory labour was commuted for a quit-rent. A trained midwife was engaged for Bogucharovo at his expense, and a priest was paid to teach reading and writing to the children of the peasants and household serfs.

Prince Andrew spent half his time at Bald Hills with his father and his son, who was still in the care of nurses. The other half he spent in 'Bogucharovo Cloister', as his father called Prince Andrew's estate. Despite the indifference to the affairs of the world he had expressed to Pierre, he diligently followed all that went on, received many books, and to his surprise noticed that when he or his father had visitors from Petersburg, the very vortex of life, these people lagged behind himself – who never left the country – in knowledge of what was happening in home and foreign affairs.

Besides being occupied with his estates, and reading a great variety of books, Prince Andrew was at this time busy with a critical survey of our last two unfortunate campaigns, and with drawing up a proposal for a reform of the army rules and regulations.

In the spring of 1809 he went to visit the Ryazan estates which his son, whose guardian he was, had inherited.

Warmed by the spring sunshine he sat in the calèche looking at the new grass, the first leaves on the birches and the first puffs of white spring clouds floating across the clear blue sky. He was not thinking of anything, but looked absent-mindedly and cheerfully from side to side.

They crossed the ferry where he had talked with Pierre the year before. They went through the muddy village, past threshing-floors and green fields of winter rye, downhill where snow still lodged near the bridge, uphill where the clay had been liquefied by the rain, past strips of stubble land and bushes touched with green here and there, and into a birch forest growing on both sides of the road. In the forest it was almost hot, no wind could be felt. The birches with their sticky green leaves were motionless, and lilac-coloured flowers and the first blades of green grass were pushing up and lifting last year's leaves. The coarse evergreen colour of the small fir-trees scattered here and there among the birches was an unpleasant reminder of winter. On entering the forest the horses began to snort, and sweated visibly.

Peter the footman made some remark to the coachman; the latter assented. But apparently the coachman's sympathy was not enough for Peter, and he turned on the box towards his master.

'How pleasant it is, your Excellency!' he said with a respectful smile.

'What?'

'It's pleasant, your Excellency!'

'What is he talking about?' thought Prince Andrew. 'Oh, the spring, I suppose,' he thought as he turned round. 'Yes, really everything is green already ... How early! The birches and cherry and alders too are coming out ... But the oaks show no sign yet. Ah, here is one oak!'

At the edge of the road stood an oak. Probably ten times the age of the birches that formed the forest, it was ten times as thick and twice as tall as they. It was an enormous tree, its girth twice as great as a man could embrace, and evidently long ago some of its branches had been broken off and its bark scarred. With its huge ungainly limbs sprawling unsymmetrically, and its gnarled hands and fingers, it stood an aged, stern, and scornful monster among the smiling birch-trees. Only the dead-looking evergreen firs dotted about in the forest, and this oak, refused to yield to the charm of spring, or notice either the spring or the sunshine.

'Spring, love, happiness!' this oak seemed to say. 'Are you not weary of that stupid, meaningless, constantly repeated fraud? Always the same and always a fraud! There is no spring, no sun, no happiness! Look at those cramped dead firs, ever the same, and at me too, sticking out my broken and barked fingers just where they have grown, whether from my back or my sides: as they have grown so I stand, and I do not believe in your hopes and your lies.'

As he passed through the forest Prince Andrew turned several times to look at that oak, as if expecting something from it. Under the oak, too, were flowers and grass, but it stood among them scowling, rigid, misshapen, and grim as ever.

'Yes, the oak is right, a thousand times right,' thought Prince Andrew. 'Let others – the young – yield afresh to that fraud, but we know life, our life is finished!'

A whole sequence of new thoughts, hopeless but mournfully pleasant, rose in his soul in connexion with that tree. During this journey he, as it were, considered his life afresh and arrived at his old conclusion, restful in its hopelessness: that it was not for him to begin anything anew – but that he must live out his life, content to do no harm, and not disturbing himself or desiring anything.

2

PRINCE ANDREW had to see the Marshal of the Nobility for the district in connexion with the affairs of the Ryazan estate of which he was trustee. This Marshal was Count Ilya Rostov, and in the middle of May Prince Andrew went to visit him.

It was now hot spring weather. The whole forest was already

clothed in green. It was dusty, and so hot that on passing near water one longed to bathe.

Prince Andrew, depressed, and preoccupied with the business about which he had to speak to the Marshal, was driving up the avenue in the grounds of the Rostovs' house at Otradnoe. He heard merry girlish cries behind some trees on the right, and saw a group of girls running to cross the path of his calèche. Ahead of the rest and nearer to him ran a dark-haired, remarkably slim, pretty girl in a yellow chintz dress, with a white handkerchief on her head from under which loose locks of hair escaped. The girl was shouting something, but seeing that he was a stranger, ran back laughing without looking at him.

Suddenly, he did not know why, he felt a pang. The day was so beautiful, the sun so bright, everything around so gay, but that slim pretty girl did not know, or wish to know, of his existence and was contented and cheerful in her own separate – probably foolish – but bright and happy life. 'What is she so glad about? What is she thinking of? Not of the military regulations or of the arrangement of the Ryazan serfs' quit-rents. Of what is she thinking? Why is she so happy?' Prince Andrew asked himself with instinctive curiosity.

In 1809 Count Ilya Rostov was living at Otradnoe just as he had done in former years, that is, entertaining almost the whole province with hunts, theatricals, dinners, and music. He was glad to see Prince Andrew, as he was to see any new visitor, and insisted on his staying the night.

During the dull day, in the course of which he was entertained by his elderly hosts and by the more important of the visitors (the old count's house was crowded on account of an approaching name-day), Prince Andrew repeatedly glanced at Natasha, gay and laughing among the younger members of the company, and asked himself each time, 'What is she thinking about? Why is she so glad?'

That night, alone in new surroundings, he was long unable to sleep. He read awhile and then put out his candle, but relit it. It was hot in the room, the inside shutters of which were closed. He was cross with the stupid old man (as he called Rostov), who had made him stay by assuring him that some necessary documents had not yet arrived from town, and he was vexed with himself for having stayed.

He got up and went to the window to open it. As soon as he opened the shutters the moonlight, as if it had long been watching for this, burst into the room. He opened the casement. The night was fresh, bright, and very still. Just before the window was a row of pollard-trees, looking black on one side and with a silvery light on the other. Beneath the trees grew some kind of lush, wet, bushy vegetation with silver-lit leaves and stems here and there. Farther back beyond the dark trees a roof glittered with dew, to the right was a leafy tree with brilliantly white trunk and branches, and above it shone the moon, nearly at its full, in a pale, almost starless, spring sky. Prince Andrew leaned his elbows on the window-ledge and his eyes rested on that sky.

His room was on the first floor. Those in the rooms above were also awake. He heard female voices overhead.

'Just once more,' said a girlish voice above him which Prince Andrew recognized at once.

'But when are you coming to bed?' replied another voice.

'I won't, I can't sleep, what's the use? Come now, for the last time.'

Two girlish voices sang a musical passage – the end of some song.

'Oh, how lovely! Now go to sleep, and there's an end of it.'

'You go to sleep, but I can't,' said the first voice, coming nearer to the window. She was evidently leaning right out, for the rustle of her dress and even her breathing could be heard. Everything was stone-still, like the moon and its light and the shadows. Prince Andrew, too, dared not stir, for fear of betraying his unintentional presence.

'Sonya! Sonya!' he again heard the first speaker. 'Oh, how can you sleep? Only look how glorious it is! Ah, how glorious! Do wake up, Sonya!' she said almost with tears in her voice. 'There never, never was such a lovely night before!'

Sonya made some reluctant reply.

'Do just come and see what a moon!... Oh, how lovely! Come here... Darling, sweetheart, come here! There, you see? I feel like sitting down on my heels, putting my arms round my knees like this, straining tight, as tight as possible, and flying away! Like this...'*

'Take care, you'll fall out.'

He heard the sound of a scuffle and Sonya's disapproving voice: 'It's past one o'clock.'

'Oh, you only spoil things for me. All right, go, go!'

Again all was silent, but Prince Andrew knew she was still sitting there. From time to time he heard a soft rustle, and at times a sigh.

'O God, O God! What does it mean?' she suddenly exclaimed. 'To bed then, if it must be!' and she slammed the casement.

'For her I might as well not exist!' thought Prince Andrew while he listened to her voice, for some reason expecting yet fearing that she might say something about him. 'There she is again! As if it were on purpose,' thought he.

In his soul there suddenly arose such an unexpected turmoil of youthful thoughts and hopes, contrary to the whole tenor of his life, that unable to explain his condition to himself he lay down and fell asleep at once.

3

NEXT morning, having taken leave of no one but the count, and not waiting for the ladies to appear, Prince Andrew set off for home.

It was already the beginning of June when on his return journey he drove into the birch forest where the gnarled old oak had made so strange and memorable an impression on him. In the forest the harness-bells sounded yet more muffled than they had done six weeks before, for now all was thick, shady and dense, and the young firs dotted about in the forest did not jar on the general beauty but, lending themselves to the mood around, were delicately green with fluffy young shoots.

The whole day had been hot. Somewhere a storm was gathering, but only a small cloud had scattered some rain-drops lightly, sprinkling the road and the sappy leaves. The left side of the forest was dark in the shade, the right side glittered in the sunlight, wet and shiny and scarcely swayed by the breeze. Everything was in blossom, the nightingales trilled, and their voices reverberated now near now far away.

'Yes, here in this forest was that oak with which I agreed,' thought Prince Andrew. 'But where is it?' he again wondered, gazing at the left side of the road, and without recognizing it he looked with admiration at the very oak he sought. The old oak, quite transfigured, spreading out a canopy of sappy dark-green foliage, stood rapt and slightly trembling in the rays of the evening sun. Neither gnarled fingers nor old scars nor old doubts and sorrows were any of them in evidence now. Through the hard century-old bark, even where there were no twigs, leaves had sprouted such as one could hardly believe the old veteran could have produced.

'Yes, it is the same oak,' thought Prince Andrew, and all at once he was seized by an unreasoning spring-time feeling of joy and renewal. All the best moments of his life suddenly rose to his memory. Austerlitz with the lofty heavens, his wife's dead reproachful face, Pierre at the ferry, that girl thrilled by the beauty of the night, and that night itself and the moon, and . . . all this rushed suddenly to his mind.

'No, life is not over at thirty-one!' Prince Andrew suddenly decided finally and decisively. 'It is not enough for me to know what I have in me – everyone must know it: Pierre, and that young girl who wanted to fly away into the sky, everyone must know me, so that my life may not be lived for myself alone while others live so apart from it, but so that it may be reflected in them all, and they and I may live in harmony.'

On reaching home Prince Andrew decided to go to Petersburg that autumn and found all sorts of reasons for this decision. A whole series of sensible and logical considerations showing it to be essential for him to go to Petersburg, and even to re-enter the service, kept springing up in his mind. He could not now understand how he could ever even have doubted the necessity of taking an active share in life, just as a month before he had not understood how the idea of leaving the quiet country could ever enter his head. It now seemed clear to him that all his experience of life must be sense-lessly wasted unless he applied it to some kind of work and again played an active part in life. He did not even remember how formerly, on the strength of similar wretched logical arguments, it had seemed obvious that he would be degrading himself if he now, after the lessons he had had in life, allowed himself to believe in the possibility of being useful and in the possibility of happiness or love. Now reason suggested quite the opposite. After that journey to Ryazan he found the country dull; his former pursuits no longer interested him, and often when sitting alone in his study he got up, went to the mirror and gazed a long time at his own face. Then he would turn away to the portrait of his dead Lise, who with hair curled *à la grecque* looked tenderly and gaily at him out of the gilt frame. She did not now say those former terrible words to him, but looked simply, merrily, and inquisitively at him. And Prince Andrew, crossing his arms behind him, long paced the room, now frowning now smiling, as he reflected on those irrational, inexpressible thoughts, secret as a crime, which altered his whole life and were connected with Pierre, with fame, with the girl at the window, the oak, and woman's beauty and love. And if anyone came into his room at such moments he was particularly cold, stern, and above all, unpleasantly logical.

'My dear,' Princess Mary entering at such a moment would say, 'little Nicholas can't go out to-day, it's very cold.'

'If it were hot,' Prince Andrew would reply at such times very drily to his sister, 'he could go out in his smock, but as it is cold he

449

must wear warm clothes, which were designed for that purpose. That is what follows from the fact that it is cold; and not that a child who needs fresh air should remain at home,' he would add with extreme logic, as if punishing someone for those secret illogical emotions that stirred within him.

At such moments Princess Mary would think how intellectual work dries men up.

4

PRINCE ANDREW arrived in Petersburg in August 1809. It was the time when the youthful Speransky was at the zenith of his fame* and his reforms were being pushed forward with the greatest energy. That same August the Emperor was thrown from his calèche, injured his leg, and remained three weeks at Peterhof, receiving Speransky every day and no one else. At that time the two famous decrees were being prepared that so agitated society – abolishing court ranks and introducing examinations to qualify for the grades of Collegiate Assessor and State Councillor* – and not merely these but a whole State constitution, intended to change the existing order of government in Russia: legal, administrative, and financial, from the Council of State down to the district tribunals. Now those vague liberal dreams with which the Emperor Alexander had ascended the throne, and which he had tried to put into effect with the aid of his associates, Czartoryski, Novosiltsev, Kochubey, and Stroganov – whom he himself in jest had called his *Comité de salut public* – were taking shape and being realized.

Now all these men were replaced by Speransky on the civil side and Arakcheev* on the military. Soon after his arrival Prince Andrew, as a gentleman of the chamber, presented himself at court and at a levée. The Emperor, though he met him twice, did not favour him with a single word. It had always seemed to Prince Andrew before that he was antipathetic to the Emperor and that the latter disliked his face and personality generally, and in the cold, repellent glance the Emperor gave him, he now found further confirmation of this surmise. The courtiers explained the Emperor's neglect of him by his Majesty's displeasure at Bolkonsky's not having served since 1805.

'I know myself that one cannot help one's sympathies and antipathies,' thought Prince Andrew, 'so it will not do to present my proposal for the reform of the army regulations to the Emperor personally, but the project will speak for itself.'

He mentioned what he had written to an old field-marshal, a

friend of his father's. The field-marshal made an appointment to see him, received him graciously, and promised to inform the Emperor. A few days later Prince Andrew received notice that he was to go to see the Minister of War, Count Arakcheev.

On the appointed day Prince Andrew entered Count Arakcheev's waiting-room at nine in the morning.

He did not know Arakcheev personally, had never seen him, and all he had heard of him inspired him with but little respect for the man.

'He is Minister of War, a man trusted by the Emperor, and I need not concern myself about his personal qualities: he has been commissioned to consider my project, so he alone can get it adopted,' thought Prince Andrew as he waited among a number of important and unimportant people in Count Arakcheev's waiting-room.

During his service, chiefly as an adjutant, Prince Andrew had seen the ante-rooms of many important men, and the different types of such rooms were well known to him. Count Arakcheev's ante-room had quite a special character. The faces of the unimportant people awaiting their turn for an audience showed embarrassment and servility; the faces of those of higher rank expressed a common feeling of awkwardness, covered by a mask of unconcern and ridicule of themselves, their situation, and the person for whom they were waiting. Some walked thoughtfully up and down, others whispered and laughed. Prince Andrew heard the nickname 'Sila Andreevich'* and the words, '*Uncle* will give it us hot,' in reference to Count Arakcheev. One general (an important personage) evidently feeling offended at having to wait so long, sat crossing and uncrossing his legs and smiling contemptuously to himself.

But the moment the door opened one feeling alone appeared on all faces – that of fear. Prince Andrew for the second time asked the adjutant on duty to take in his name, but received an ironical look and was told that his turn would come in due course. After some others had been shown in and out of the minister's room by the adjutant on duty, an officer who struck Prince Andrew by his humiliated and frightened air was admitted at that terrible door. This officer's audience lasted a long time. Then suddenly the grating sound of a harsh voice was heard from the other side of the door, and the officer – with pale face and trembling lips – came out and passed through the waiting-room clutching his head.

After this Prince Andrew was conducted to the door and the officer on duty said in a whisper. 'To the right, at the window.'

Prince Andrew entered a plain tidy room, and saw at the table a man of forty with a long waist, a long closely cropped head, deep wrinkles, scowling brows above dull greenish-hazel eyes, and an overhanging red nose. Arakcheev turned his head towards him without looking at him.

'What is your petition?' asked Arakcheev.

'I am not petitioning, your Excellency,' returned Prince Andrew quietly.

Arakcheev's eyes turned towards him.

'Sit down,' said he. 'Prince Bolkonsky?'

'I am not petitioning about anything. His Majesty the Emperor has deigned to send your Excellency a project submitted by me . . .'

'You see, my dear sir, I have read your project,' interrupted Arakcheev, uttering only the first words amiably and then – again without looking at Prince Andrew – relapsing gradually into a tone of grumbling contempt. 'You are proposing new military laws? There are many laws but no one to carry out the old ones. Nowadays everybody designs laws, it is easier writing than doing.'

'I came at his Majesty the Emperor's wish to learn from your Excellency how you propose to deal with the memorandum I have presented,' said Prince Andrew politely.

'I have endorsed a resolution on your memorandum and sent it to the Committee. I do *not* approve of it,' said Arakcheev rising and taking a paper from his writing-table. 'Here!' and he handed it to Prince Andrew.

Across the paper was scrawled in pencil, without capital letters, misspelt, and without punctuation: 'Unsoundly constructed because resembles an imitation of the French military code and from the Articles of War needlessly deviating.'

'To what Committee has the memorandum been referred?' inquired Prince Andrew.

'To the Committee on Army Regulations, and I have recommended that your honour should be appointed a member, but without a salary.'

Prince Andrew smiled.

'I don't want one.'

'A member without salary,' repeated Arakcheev. 'I have the honour . . . Eh! Call the next one! Who else is there?' he shouted, bowing to Prince Andrew.

5

WHILE waiting for the announcement of his appointment to the Committee, Prince Andrew looked up his former acquaintances, particularly those he knew to be in power and whose aid he might need. In Petersburg he now experienced the same feeling he had had on the eve of a battle, when troubled by anxious curiosity and irresistibly attracted to the ruling circles where the future, on which the fate of millions depended, was being shaped. From the irritation of the older men, the curiosity of the uninitiated, the reserve of the initiated, the hurry and preoccupation of everyone, and the innumerable committees and commissions of whose existence he learnt every day, he felt that now, in 1809, here in Petersburg a vast civil conflict was in preparation, the commander-in-chief of which was a mysterious person he did not know, but who was supposed to be a man of genius – Speransky. And this movement of reconstruction of which Prince Andrew had a vague idea, and Speransky its chief promoter, began to interest him so keenly that the question of the army regulations quickly receded to a secondary place in his consciousness.

Prince Andrew was most favourably placed to secure a good reception in the highest and most diverse Petersburg circles of the day. The reforming party cordially welcomed and courted him, in the first place because he was reputed to be clever and very well-read, and secondly because by liberating his serfs he had obtained the reputation of being a liberal. The party of the old and dissatisfied, who censured the innovations, turned to him expecting his sympathy in their disapproval of the reforms, simply because he was the son of his father. The feminine society world welcomed him gladly, because he was rich, distinguished, a good match, and almost a newcomer, with a halo of romance on account of his supposed death and the tragic loss of his wife. Besides this the general opinion of all who had known him previously was that he had greatly improved during these last five years, having softened and grown more manly, lost his former affectation, pride and contemptuous irony, and acquired the serenity that comes with years. People talked about him, were interested in him, and wanted to meet him.

The day after his interview with Count Arakcheev, Prince Andrew spent the evening at Count Kochubey's.* He told the count of his interview with *Sila Andreevich* (Kochubey spoke of Arakcheev by that nickname with the same vague irony Prince Andrew had noticed in the Minister of War's ante-room).

'*Mon cher*, even in this case you can't do without Michael Mikhaylovich Speransky. He manages everything. I'll speak to him. He has promised to come this evening.'

'What has Speransky to do with the army regulations?' asked Prince Andrew.

Kochubey shook his head smilingly, as if surprised at Bolkonsky's simplicity.

'We were talking to him about you a few days ago,' Kochubey continued, 'and about your free ploughmen.'

'Oh, is it you, Prince, who have freed your serfs?' said an old man of Catherine's day, turning contemptuously towards Bolkonsky.

'It was a small estate that brought in no profit,' replied Prince Andrew, trying to extenuate his action so as not to irritate the old man uselessly.

'Afraid of being late...' said the old man, looking at Kochubey.

'There's one thing I don't understand,' he continued. 'Who will plough the land if they are set free? It is easy to write laws, but difficult to rule... Just the same as now – I ask you, Count – who will be heads of the departments when everybody has to pass examinations?'

'Those who pass the examinations, I suppose,' replied Kochubey crossing his legs and glancing round.

'Well, I have Pryanichnikov serving under me, a splendid man, a priceless man, but he's sixty. Is he to go up for examination?'

'Yes, that's a difficulty, as education is not at all general, but...'

Count Kochubey did not finish. He rose, took Prince Andrew by the arm, and went to meet a tall, bald, fair man of about forty with a large open forehead and a long face of unusual and peculiar whiteness, who was just entering. The newcomer wore a blue swallow-tail coat with a cross suspended from his neck and a star on his left breast. It was Speransky. Prince Andrew recognized him at once, and felt a throb within him, as happens at critical moments of life. Whether it was from respect, envy, or anticipation, he did not know. Speransky's whole figure was of a peculiar type that made him easily recognizable. In the society in which Prince Andrew lived he had never seen anyone who together with awkward and clumsy gestures possessed such calmness and self-assurance; he had never seen so resolute yet gentle an expression as that in those half-closed, rather humid eyes, or so firm a smile that expressed nothing; nor had he heard such a refined, smooth, soft voice; above all he had never seen such delicate whiteness of face or hands – hands which were broad, but very plump, soft, and white. Such whiteness and softness Prince Andrew had only seen on the faces of soldiers who had been long in hospital. This was

Speransky, Secretary of State, reporter to the Emperor and his companion at Erfurt, where he had more than once met and talked with Napoleon.

Speransky did not shift his eyes from one face to another as people involuntarily do on entering a large company, and was in no hurry to speak. He spoke slowly, with assurance that he would be listened to, and he looked only at the person with whom he was conversing.

Prince Andrew followed Speransky's every word and movement with particular attention. As happens to some people, especially to men who judge those near to them severely, he always on meeting anyone new – especially anyone whom, like Speransky, he knew by reputation – expected to discover in him the perfection of human qualities.

Speransky told Kochubey he was sorry he had been unable to come sooner, as he had been detained at the palace. He did not say that the Emperor had kept him, and Prince Andrew noticed this affectation of modesty. When Kochubey introduced Prince Andrew, Speransky slowly turned his eyes to Bolkonsky with his customary smile, and looked at him in silence.

'I am very glad to make your acquaintance. I had heard of you, as everyone has,' he said after a pause.

Kochubey said a few words about the reception Arakcheev had given Bolkonsky. Speransky smiled more markedly.

'The chairman of the Committee on Army Regulations is my good friend Monsieur Magnitsky,' he said, fully articulating every word and syllable, 'and if you like I can put you in touch with him.' He paused at the full stop. 'I hope you will find him sympathetic, and ready to co-operate in promoting all that is reasonable.'

A circle soon formed round Speransky, and the old man who had talked about his subordinate Pryanichnikov addressed a question to him.

Prince Andrew without joining in the conversation watched every movement of Speransky's: this man, not long since an insignificant divinity student, who now, Bolkonsky thought, held in his hands – those plump white hands – the fate of Russia. Prince Andrew was struck by the extraordinarily disdainful composure with which Speransky answered the old man. He appeared to address condescending words to him from an immeasurable height. When the old man began to speak too loud, Speransky smiled and said he could not judge of the advantage or disadvantage of what pleased the sovereign.

Having talked for a little while in the general circle, Speransky rose and coming up to Prince Andrew took him along to the other end of the room. It was clear that he thought it necessary to interest himself in Bolkonsky.

'I had no chance to talk with you, Prince, during the animated conversation in which that venerable gentleman involved me,' he said with a mildly contemptuous smile, as if intimating by that smile that he and Prince Andrew understood the insignificance of the people with whom he had just been talking. This flattered Prince Andrew. 'I have known of you for a long time: first from your action with regard to your serfs, a first example, of which it is very desirable that there should be more imitators; and secondly because you are one of those gentlemen of the chamber who have not considered themselves offended by the new decree concerning the ranks allotted to courtiers, which is causing so much gossip and tittle-tattle.'

'No,' said Prince Andrew, 'my father did not wish me to take advantage of the privilege. I began the service from the lower grade.'

'Your father, a man of the last century, evidently stands above our contemporaries who so condemn this measure which merely re-establishes natural justice.'

'I think, however, that these condemnations have some ground,' returned Prince Andrew, trying to resist Speransky's influence, of which he began to be conscious. He did not like to agree with him in everything and felt a wish to contradict. Though he usually spoke easily and well, he felt a difficulty in expressing himself now while talking with Speransky. He was too much absorbed in observing the famous man's personality.

'Grounds of personal ambition maybe,' Speransky put in quietly.

'And of state-interest to some extent,' said Prince Andrew.

'What do you mean?' asked Speransky quietly, lowering his eyes.

'I am an admirer of Montesquieu,'* replied Prince Andrew, 'and his idea that *le principe des monarchies est l'honneur, me paraît incontestable. Certains droits et privilèges de la noblesse me paraissent être des moyens de soutenir ce sentiment.*'

The smile vanished from Speransky's white face, which was much improved by the change. Probably Prince Andrew's thought interested him.

'*Si vous envisagez la question sous ce point de vue,*' he began, pronouncing French with evident difficulty, and speaking even slower than in Russian but quite calmly.

Speransky went on to say that honour, *l'honneur*, cannot be upheld by privileges harmful to the service; that honour, *l'honneur*, is either a negative concept of not doing what is blameworthy, or it is a source of emulation in pursuit of commendation and rewards, which recognize it. His arguments were concise, simple, and clear.

'An institution upholding honour, the source of emulation, is one similar to the *Légion d'honneur* of the great Emperor Napoleon, not harmful but helpful to the success of the service, but not a class or court privilege.'

'I do not dispute that, but it cannot be denied that court privileges have attained the same end,' returned Prince Andrew. 'Every courtier considers himself bound to maintain his position worthily.'

'Yet you do not care to avail yourself of the privilege, Prince,' said Speransky, indicating by a smile that he wished to finish amiably an argument which was embarrassing for his companion. 'If you will do me the honour of calling on me on Wednesday,' he added, 'I will, after talking with Magnitsky, let you know what may interest you, and shall also have the pleasure of a more detailed chat with you.'

Closing his eyes, he bowed *à la française*, without taking leave, and trying to attract as little attention as possible, he left the room.

6

DURING the first weeks of his stay in Petersburg Prince Andrew felt the whole trend of thought he had formed during his life of seclusion quite overshadowed by the trifling cares that engrossed him in that city.

On returning home in the evening he would jot down in his notebook four or five necessary calls or appointments for certain hours. The mechanism of life, the arrangement of the day so as to be in time everywhere, absorbed the greater part of his vital energy. He did nothing, did not even think or find time to think, but only talked, and talked successfully, of what he had thought while in the country.

He sometimes noticed with dissatisfaction that he repeated the same remark on the same day in different circles. But he was so busy for whole days together that he had no time to notice that he was thinking of nothing.

As he had done on their first meeting at Kochubey's, Speransky produced a strong impression on Prince Andrew on the Wednesday, when he received him *tête-à-tête* at his own house and talked to him long and confidentially.

To Bolkonsky so many people appeared contemptible and insignificant creatures, and he so longed to find in someone the living ideal of that perfection towards which he strove, that he readily believed that in Speransky he had found this ideal of a perfectly rational and virtuous man. Had Speransky sprung from the same class as himself and possessed the same breeding and traditions, Bolkonsky would soon have discovered his weak, human, unheroic sides; but as it was, Speransky's strange and logical turn of mind inspired him with respect all the more because he did not quite understand him. Moreover Speransky, either because he appreciated the other's capacity or because he considered it necessary to win him to his side, showed off his dispassionate calm reasonableness before Prince Andrew and flattered him with that subtle flattery which goes hand in hand with self-assurance, and consists in a tacit assumption that one's companion is the only man besides oneself capable of understanding the folly of the rest of mankind, and the reasonableness and profundity of one's own ideas.

During their long conversation on Wednesday evening, Speransky more than once remarked: 'We regard everything that is above the common level of rooted custom'...; or, with a smile: 'But we want the wolves to be fed and the sheep to be safe...' or: 'They cannot understand this...' and all in a way that seemed to say: 'We, you and I, understand what they are and who we are.'

This first long conversation with Speransky only strengthened in Prince Andrew the feeling he had experienced towards him at their first meeting. He saw in him a remarkable, clear-thinking man of vast intellect who by his energy and persistence had attained power, which he was using solely for the welfare of Russia. In Prince Andrew's eyes Speransky was the man he would himself have wished to be – one who explained all the facts of life reasonably, considered important only what was rational, and was capable of applying the standard of reason to everything. Everything seemed so simple and clear in Speransky's exposition that Prince Andrew involuntarily agreed with him about everything. If he replied and argued, it was only because he wished to maintain his independence and not submit to Speransky's opinions entirely. Everything was right and everything was as it should be: only one thing disconcerted Prince Andrew. This was Speransky's cold, mirror-like look, which did not allow one to penetrate to his soul, and his delicate white hands, which Prince Andrew involuntarily watched as one does watch the hands of those who possess power. This mirror-like gaze and those delicate hands irritated Prince Andrew, he knew not why. He was unpleasantly struck, too, by the excessive contempt for others that he observed in Speransky, and by the diversity of lines of argument he used to support his opinions. He made use of every kind of mental device, except analogy, and passed too boldly, it seemed to Prince Andrew, from one to another. Now he would take up the position of a practical man and condemn dreamers; now that of a satirist, and laugh ironically at his opponents; now grow severely logical, or suddenly rise to the realm of metaphysics. (This last resource was one he very frequently employed.) He would transfer a question to metaphysical heights, pass on to definitions of space, time, and thought, and having deduced the refutation he needed, would again descend to the level of the original discussion.

In general the trait of Speransky's mentality which struck Prince Andrew most was his absolute and unshakable belief in the power and authority of reason. It was evident that the thought could never occur to him which to Prince Andrew seemed so natural, namely, that it is after all impossible to express all one thinks; and that he had never felt the doubt, 'Is not all I think and believe nonsense?' And it was just this peculiarity of Speransky's mind that particularly attracted Prince Andrew.

During the first period of their acquaintance Bolkonsky felt a passionate admiration for him similar to that which he had once felt for Bonaparte. The fact that Speransky was the son of a village priest, and that stupid people might meanly despise him on account of his humble origin (as in fact many did), caused Prince Andrew to cherish his sentiment for him the more, and unconsciously to strengthen it.

On that first evening Bolkonsky spent with him, having mentioned the Commission for the Revision of the Code of Laws, Speransky told him sarcastically that the Commission had existed for a hundred and fifty years, had cost millions, and had done nothing except that Rosenkampf had stuck labels on the corresponding paragraphs of the different codes.

'And that is all the State has for the millions it has spent,' said he. 'We want to give the Senate new juridical powers, but we have no laws. That is why it is a sin for men like you, Prince, not to serve in these times!'

Prince Andrew said that for that work an education in jurisprudence was needed which he did not possess.

'But nobody possesses it, so what would you have? It is a vicious circle from which we must break a way out.'

A week later Prince Andrew was a member of the Committee on Army Regulations, and – what he had not at all expected – was chairman of a section of the Committee for the revision of the laws. At Speransky's request he took the first part of the Civil Code that was being drawn up, and with the aid of the *Code Napoléon* and the Institutes of Justinian he worked at formulating the section on Personal Rights.

NEARLY two years before this, in 1808, Pierre on returning to Petersburg after visiting his estates had involuntarily found himself in a leading position among the Petersburg Freemasons. He arranged dining and funeral Lodge meetings, enrolled new members, and busied himself uniting various Lodges and acquiring authentic charters. He gave money for the erection of temples, and supplemented as far as he could the collection of alms, in regard to which the majority of members were stingy and irregular. He supported almost single-handed a poorhouse the Order had founded in Petersburg.

His life meanwhile continued as before, with the same infatuations and dissipations. He liked to dine and drink well, and though he considered it immoral and humiliating could not resist the temptations of the bachelor circles in which he moved.

Amid the turmoil of his activities and distractions, however, Pierre at the end of a year began to feel that the more firmly he tried to rest upon it, the more the masonic ground on which he stood gave way under him. At the same time he felt that the deeper the ground sank under him the closer bound he involuntarily became to the Order. When he had joined the Freemasons he had experienced the feeling of one who confidently steps onto the smooth surface of a bog. When he put his foot down it sank in. To make quite sure of the firmness of the ground, he put his other foot down and sank deeper still, became stuck in it, and involuntarily waded knee-deep in the bog.

Joseph Alexeevich was not in Petersburg – he had of late stood aside from the affairs of the Petersburg Lodges and lived almost entirely in Moscow. All the members of the Lodges were men Pierre knew in ordinary life, and it was difficult for him to regard them merely as Brothers in Freemasonry and not as Prince B. or Ivan Vasilevich D., whom he knew in society mostly as weak and insignificant men. Under the masonic aprons and insignia he saw the uniforms and decorations at which they aimed in ordinary life. Often after collecting alms, and reckoning up twenty to thirty rubles received for the most part in promises from a dozen members, of whom half were as well able to pay as himself, Pierre remembered the masonic vow in which each Brother promised to devote all his belongings to his neighbour, and doubts, on which he tried not to dwell, arose in his soul.

He divided the Brothers he knew into four categories. In the first he put those who did not take an active part in the affairs of the Lodges or in human affairs, but were exclusively occupied with the mystical science of the Order: with questions of the threefold designation of God, the three primordial elements – sulphur, mercury, and salt* – or the meaning of the square and all the various figures of the temple of Solomon. Pierre respected this class of Brothers, to which the elder ones chiefly belonged, including, Pierre thought, Joseph Alexeevich himself, but he did not share their interests. His heart was not in the mystical aspect of Freemasonry.

In the second category Pierre reckoned himself and others like him, seeking and vacillating, who had not yet found in Freemasonry a straight and comprehensible path, but hoped to do so.

In the third category he included those Brothers (the majority) who saw nothing in Freemasonry but the external forms and ceremonies, and prized the strict performance of these forms without troubling about their purport or significance. Such were Willarski and even the Grand Master of the principal Lodge.

Finally, to the fourth category also a great many Brothers belonged, particularly those who had lately joined. These according to Pierre's observation were men who had no belief in anything, nor desire for anything, but joined the Freemasons merely to associate with the wealthy young Brothers who were influential through their connexions or rank, and of whom there were very many in the Lodge.

Pierre began to feel dissatisfied with what he was doing. Freemasonry, at any rate as he saw it here, sometimes seemed to him based merely on externals. He did not think of doubting Freemasonry itself, but suspected that Russian Masonry had taken a wrong path and deviated from its original principles. And so towards the end of the year he went abroad to be initiated into the higher secrets of the Order.

In the summer of 1809 Pierre returned to Petersburg. Our Freemasons knew from correspondence with those abroad that Bezukhov had obtained the confidence of many highly placed persons, had been initiated into many mysteries, had been raised to a higher grade, and was bringing back with him much that might conduce to the advantage of the masonic cause in Russia. The Petersburg Freemasons all came to see him, tried to ingratiate themselves with him, and it seemed to them all that he was preparing something for them and concealing it.

A solemn meeting of the Lodge of the second degree was convened, at which Pierre promised to communicate to the Petersburg Brothers what he had to deliver to them from the highest leaders of their Order. The meeting was a full one. After the usual ceremonies Pierre rose and began his address.

'Dear Brothers,' he began, blushing and stammering, with a written speech in his hand, 'it is not sufficient to observe our mysteries in the seclusion of our Lodge – we must act – act! We are drowsing, but we must act.' Pierre raised his notebook and began to read.

'For the dissemination of pure truth and to secure the triumph of virtue,' he read, 'we must cleanse men from prejudice, diffuse principles in harmony with the spirit of the times, undertake the education of the young, unite ourselves in indissoluble bonds with the wisest men, boldly yet prudently overcome superstitions, infidelity, and folly, and form of those devoted to us a body linked together by unity of purpose and possessed of authority and power.

'To attain this end we must ensure a preponderance of virtue over vice, and must endeavour to secure that the honest man may, even in this world, receive a lasting reward for his virtue. But in these great endeavours we are gravely hampered by the political institutions of to-day. What is to be done in these circumstances? To favour revolutions, overthrow everything, repel force by force? ...No! We are very far from that. Every violent reform deserves censure, for it quite fails to remedy evil while men remain what they are, and also because wisdom needs no violence.

'The whole plan of our Order should be based on the idea of preparing men of firmness and virtue bound together by unity of conviction – aiming at the punishment of vice and folly, and patronizing talent and virtue: raising worthy men from the dust and attaching them to our Brotherhood. Only then will our Order have the power unobtrusively to bind the hands of the protectors of disorder and to control them without their being aware of it. In a word, we must found a form of government holding universal sway, which should be diffused over the whole world without destroying the bonds of citizenship, and beside which all other governments can continue in their customary course and do every-thing except what impedes the great aim of our Order, which is to obtain for virtue the victory over vice. This aim was that of Christianity itself. It taught men to be wise and good, and for their own benefit to follow the example and instruction of the best and wisest men.

'At that time, when everything was plunged in darkness, preaching alone was of course sufficient. The novelty of Truth endowed her with special strength, but now we need much more powerful methods. It is now necessary that man governed by his senses should find in virtue a charm palpable to those senses. It is impossible to eradicate the passions; but we must strive to direct them to a noble aim, and it is therefore necessary that everyone should be able to satisfy his passions within the limits of virtue. Our Order should provide means to that end.

'As soon as we have a certain number of worthy men in every State, each of them again training two others and all being closely united, everything will be possible for our Order, which has already in secret accomplished much for the welfare of mankind.'

This speech not only made a strong impression, but created excitement in the Lodge. The majority of the Brothers, seeing in it dangerous designs of Illuminism,* met it with a coldness that surprised Pierre. The Grand Master began answering him, and Pierre began developing his views with more and more warmth. It was long since there had been so stormy a meeting. Parties were formed, some accusing Pierre of Illuminism, others supporting him. At that meeting he was struck for the first time by the endless variety of men's minds, which prevents a truth from ever presenting itself identically to two persons. Even those members who seemed to be on his side understood him in their own way, with limitations and alterations he could not agree to, as what he always wanted most was to convey his thought to others just as he himself understood it.

At the end of the meeting the Grand Master reproved Bezukhov with irony and ill will for his vehemence, and said it was not love of virtue alone, but also a love of strife that had moved him in the dispute. Pierre did not answer him, and asked briefly whether his proposal would be accepted. He was told that it would not, and without waiting for the usual formalities he left the Lodge and went home.

8

AGAIN Pierre was overtaken by the depression he so dreaded. For three days after the delivery of his speech at the Lodge* he lay on a sofa at home receiving no one and going nowhere.

It was just then that he received a letter from his wife, who implored him to see her, telling him how grieved she was about him and how she wished to devote her whole life to him.

At the end of the letter she informed him that in a few days she would return to Petersburg from abroad.

Following this letter one of the masonic Brothers whom Pierre respected less than the others forced his way in to see him and turning the conversation upon Pierre's matrimonial affairs, by way of fraternal advice expressed the opinion that his severity to his wife was wrong, and that he was neglecting one of the first rules of Freemasonry by not forgiving the penitent.

At the same time his mother-in-law, Prince Vasili's wife, sent to him imploring him to come if only for a few minutes to discuss a most important matter. Pierre saw that there was a conspiracy against him and that they wanted to reunite him with his wife, and in the mood he then was in, this was not even unpleasant to him. Nothing mattered to him. Nothing in life seemed to him of much importance, and under the influence of the depression that possessed him he valued neither his liberty nor his resolution to punish his wife.

'No one is right and no one is to blame; so she too is not to blame,' he thought.

If he did not at once give his consent to a reunion with his wife, it was only because in his state of depression he did not feel able to take any step. Had his wife come to him, he would not have turned her away. Compared to what preoccupied him, was it not a matter of indifference whether he lived with his wife or not?

Without replying either to his wife or his mother-in-law, Pierre late one night prepared for a journey and started for Moscow to see Joseph Alexeevich. This is what he noted in his diary:

Moscow, 17th November.
I have just returned from my benefactor, and hasten to write down what I have experienced. Joseph Alexeevich is living poorly and has for three years been suffering from a painful disease of the bladder. No one has ever heard him utter a groan or a word of complaint. From morning till late at night, except when he eats his very plain food, he is working at science. He received me graciously and made me sit down on the bed on which he lay. I made the sign of the Knights of the East and of Jerusalem, and he responded in the same manner, asking me with a mild smile what I had learned and gained in the Prussian and Scottish Lodges. I told him everything as best I could, and told him what I had proposed to our Petersburg Lodge, of the bad reception I had encountered, and of my rupture with the Brothers. Joseph Alexeevich, having remained silent and thoughtful for a good while, told me his view of the matter, which at once lit up for me my whole past, and the future path I should follow. He surprised me by asking whether I remembered the threefold aim of the Order: (1) The preservation and study of the mystery. (2) The purification and reformation of oneself for its reception, and (3) The improvement of the human race by striving for such purification. Which is the principal *aim* of these three? Certainly self-reformation and self-purification. Only to this aim can we always strive independently of circumstances. But at the same time, just this aim demands

the greatest efforts of us; and so, led astray by pride, losing sight of this aim, we occupy ourselves either with the mystery which in our impurity we are unworthy to receive, or seek the reformation of the human race while ourselves setting an example of baseness and profligacy. Illuminism is not a pure doctrine just because it is attracted by social activity and puffed up by pride. On this ground Joseph Alexeevich condemned my speech and my whole activity, and in the depth of my soul I agreed with him. Talking of my family affairs he said to me, 'the chief duty of a true Mason, as I have told you, lies in perfecting himself. We often think that by removing all the diffi-culties of our life we shall more quickly reach our aim, but on the con-trary, my dear sir, it is only in the midst of worldly cares that we can attain our three chief aims: (1) Self-knowledge – for man can only know himself by comparison. (2) Self-perfecting, which can only be attained by conflict, and (3) The attainment of the chief virtue – love of death. Only the vicissitudes of life can show us its vanity, and develop our innate love of death or of rebirth to a new life.' These words are all the more remarkable because, in spite of his great physical sufferings, Joseph Alexeevich is never weary of life though he loves death, for which – in spite of the purity and loftiness of his inner man – he does not yet feel himself sufficiently prepared. My benefactor then explained to me fully the meaning of the Great Square of creation, and pointed out to me that the numbers three and seven are the basis of everything. He advised me not to avoid inter-course with the Petersburg Brothers, but to take up only second-grade posts in the Lodge, to try, while diverting the Brothers from pride, to turn them towards the true path of self-knowledge and self-perfecting. Besides this he advised me for myself personally above all to keep a watch over myself, and to that end he gave me a note-book, the one I am now writing in, and in which I will in future note down all my actions.

Petersburg, 23rd November.

I am again living with my wife. My mother-in-law came to me in tears and said that Hélène was here and that she implored me to hear her; that she was innocent and unhappy at my desertion, and much more. I knew that if I once let myself see her I should not have strength to go on refusing what she wanted. In my perplexity I did not know whose aid and advice to seek. Had my benefactor been here he would have told me what to do. I went to my room and re-read Joseph Alexeevich's letters and recalled my conversations with him, and deduced from it all that I ought not to refuse a suppliant, and ought to reach out a helping hand to everyone – especially to one so closely bound to me – and that I must bear my cross. But if I forgive her for the sake of doing right, then let union with her have only a spiritual aim. That is what I decided, and what I wrote to Joseph Alexeevich. I told my wife that I begged her to forget the past, to forgive me whatever wrong I may have done her, and that I had nothing to forgive. It gave me joy to tell her this. She need not know how hard it was for me to see her again. I have settled on the upper floor of this big house, and am experiencing a happy feeling of regeneration.

9

AT that time, as always happens, the highest society that met at Court and at the grand balls was divided into several circles, each with its own particular tone. The largest of these was the French circle of the Napoleonic alliance, the circle of Count Rumyantsev and Caulaincourt.* In this group Hélène, as soon as she had settled in Petersburg with her husband, took a very prominent place. She was visited by the members of the French embassy and by many belonging to that circle and noted for their intellect and polished manners.

Hélène had been at Erfurt* during the famous meeting of the Emperors, and had brought from there these connexions with the Napoleonic notabilities. At Erfurt her success had been brilliant. Napoleon himself had noticed her in the theatre, and said of her: '*C'est un superbe animal.*' Her success as a beautiful and elegant woman did not surprise Pierre, for she had become even handsomer than before. What did surprise him was that during these last two years his wife had succeeded in gaining the reputation '*d'une femme charmante, aussi spirituelle que belle*'. The distinguished Prince de Ligne* wrote her eight-page letters. Bilibin saved up his epigrams to produce them in Countess Bezukhova's presence. To be received in the Countess Bezukhova's salon was regarded as a diploma of intellect. Young men read books before attending Hélène's evenings, to have something to say in her salon, and secretaries of the embassy, and even ambassadors, confided diplomatic secrets to her, so that in a way Hélène was a power. Pierre, who knew she was very stupid, sometimes attended, with a strange feeling of perplexity and fear, her evenings and dinner parties, where politics, poetry, and philosophy were discussed. At these parties his feelings were like those of a conjuror who always expects his trick to be found out at any moment. But whether because stupidity was just what was needed to run such a salon, or because those who were deceived found pleasure in the deception, at any rate it remained unexposed and Hélène Bezukhova's reputation as a lovely and clever woman became so firmly established that she could say the emptiest and stupidest things and yet everybody would go into raptures over every word of hers, and look for a profound meaning in it of which she herself had no conception.

Pierre was just the husband needed for a brilliant society woman. He was that absent-minded crank, a *grand seigneur* husband who was in no one's way, and far from spoiling the high tone and general impression of the drawing-room, he served, by the contrast he presented to her, as an advantageous background to his elegant and tactful wife. Pierre during the last two years, as a result of his continual absorption in abstract interests and his sincere contempt for all else, had acquired in his wife's circle, which did not interest him, that air of unconcern, indifference, and benevolence towards all, which cannot be acquired artificially, and therefore inspires involuntary respect. He entered his wife's drawing-room as one enters a theatre, was acquainted with everybody, equally pleased to see everyone and equally indifferent to them all. Sometimes he joined in a conversation which interested him and, regardless of whether any 'gentlemen of the embassy' were present or not, lispingly expressed his views, which were sometimes not at all in accord with the accepted tone of the moment. But the general opinion concerning the queer husband of 'the most distinguished woman in Petersburg' was so well established that no one took his freaks seriously.

Among the many young men who frequented her house every day, Boris Drubetskoy, who had already achieved great success in the service, was the most intimate friend of the Bezukhov household since Hélène's return from Erfurt. Hélène spoke of him as '*mon page*', and treated him like a child. Her smile for him was the same as for everybody, but sometimes that smile made Pierre uncomfortable. Towards him, Boris behaved with a particularly dignified and sad deference. This shade of deference also disturbed Pierre. He had suffered so painfully three years before from the mortification to which his wife had subjected him, that he now protected himself from the danger of its repetition, first by not being a husband to his wife, and secondly by not allowing himself to suspect.

'No, now that she has become a blue-stocking she has finally renounced her former infatuations,' he told himself. 'There has never been an instance of a blue-stocking being carried away by affairs of the heart' – a statement which, though gathered from an unknown source, he believed implicitly. Yet strange to say Boris's presence in his wife's drawing-room (and he was almost always there) had a physical effect upon Pierre; it constricted his limbs and destroyed the unconsciousness and freedom of his movements.

'What a strange antipathy,' thought Pierre, 'yet I used to like him very much.'

In the eyes of the world Pierre was a great gentleman, the rather blind and absurd husband of a distinguished wife, a clever crank who did nothing, but harmed nobody, and was a first-rate, good-natured fellow. But a complex and difficult process of internal development was taking place all this time in Pierre's soul, revealing much to him and causing him many spiritual doubts and joys.

10

PIERRE went on with his diary, and this is what he wrote in it during that time:

24th November.
Got up at eight, read the Scriptures, then went to my duties.

(By Joseph Alexeevich's advice Pierre had entered the service of the State and served on one of the committees.)

Returned home for dinner and dined alone – the countess had many visitors I do not like. I ate and drank moderately, and after dinner copied out some passages for the Brothers. In the evening I went down to the countess and told a funny story about B., and only remembered that I ought not to have done so when everybody laughed loudly at it.

I am going to bed with a happy and tranquil mind. Great God, help me to walk in Thy paths, (1) to conquer anger by calmness and deliberation, (2) to vanquish lust by self-restraint and repulsion, (3) to withdraw from worldliness, but not avoid (*a*) the service of the State, (*b*) family duties, (*c*) relations with my friends, and (*d*) the management of my affairs.

27th November.
I got up late. On waking I lay long in bed yielding to sloth. O God, help and strengthen me that I may walk in Thy ways! Read the Scriptures, but without proper feeling. Brother Urusov came and we talked about worldly vanities. He told me of the Emperor's new projects. I began to criticize them, but remembered my rules and my benefactor's words – that a true Freemason should be a zealous worker for the State when his aid is required and a quiet onlooker when not called on to assist. My tongue is my enemy. Brothers G. V. and O. visited me and we had a preliminary talk about the reception of a new Brother. They laid on me the duty of Rhetor. I feel myself weak and unworthy. Then our talk turned to the interpretation of the seven pillars and steps of the Temple, the seven sciences, the seven virtues, the seven vices, and the seven gifts of the Holy Spirit. Brother O. was very eloquent. In the evening the admission took place. The new decoration of the premises contributed much to the magnificence of the spectacle. It was Boris Drubetskoy who was admitted. I nominated him and was the Rhetor. A strange feeling agitated me all the time I was alone with him in the dark chamber. I caught myself harbour-

ing a feeling of hatred towards him which I vainly tried to overcome. That is why I should really like to save him from evil and lead him into the path of truth, but evil thoughts of him did not leave me. It seemed to me that his object in entering the Brotherhood was merely to be intimate and in favour with members of our Lodge. Apart from the fact that he had asked me several times whether N. and S. were members of our Lodge (a question to which I could not reply) and that according to my observation he is incapable of feeling respect for our holy Order and is too preoccupied and satisfied with the outer man to desire spiritual improvement, I had no cause to doubt him, but he seemed to me insincere, and all the time I stood alone with him in the dark temple it seemed to me that he was smiling contemptuously at my words, and I wished really to stab his bare breast with the sword I held to it. I could not be eloquent, nor could I frankly mention my doubts to the Brothers and to the Grand Master. Great Architect of Nature, help me to find the true path out of the labyrinth of lies!

After this three pages were left blank in the diary, and then the following was written:

I have had a long and instructive talk alone with Brother V., who advised me to hold fast by Brother A. Though I am unworthy, much was revealed to me. Adonai is the name of the creator of the world. Elohim is the name of the ruler of all. The third name is the name unutterable which means the All. Talks with Brother V. strengthen, refresh, and support me in the path of virtue. In his presence doubt has no place. The distinction between the poor teachings of mundane science and our sacred all-embracing teaching is clear to me. Human sciences dissect everything to comprehend it, and kill everything to examine it. In the holy science of our Order all is one, all is known in its entirety and life. The Trinity – the three elements of matter – are sulphur, mercury, and salt. Sulphur is of an oily and fiery nature; in combination with salt by its fiery nature it arouses a desire in the latter by means of which it attracts mercury, seizes it, holds it, and in combination produces other bodies. Mercury is a fluid, volatile, spiritual essence. Christ, the Holy Spirit, Him! ...

3rd December.
Awoke late, read the Scriptures but was apathetic. Afterwards went and paced up and down the large hall. I wished to meditate, but instead my imagination pictured an occurrence of four years ago, when Dolokhov, meeting me in Moscow after our duel, said he hoped I was enjoying perfect peace of mind in spite of my wife's absence. At the time I gave him no answer. Now I recalled every detail of that meeting and in my mind gave him the most malevolent and bitter replies. I recollected myself and drove away that thought only when I found myself glowing with anger, but I did not sufficiently repent. Afterwards Boris Drubetskoy came and began relating various adventures. His coming vexed me from the first, and I said

something disagreeable to him. He replied. I flared up and said much that was unpleasant and even rude to him. He became silent, and I recollected myself only when it was too late. My God, I cannot get on with him at all. The cause of this is my egotism. I set myself above him and so become much worse than he, for he is lenient to my rudeness while I on the contrary nourish contempt for him. O God, grant that in his presence I may rather see my own vileness, and behave so that he too may benefit. After dinner I fell asleep and as I was drowsing off I clearly heard a voice saying in my left ear, 'Thy day!'

I dreamt that I was walking in the dark and was suddenly surrounded by dogs, but I went on undismayed. Suddenly a smallish dog seized my left thigh with its teeth and would not let go. I began to throttle it with my hands. Scarcely had I torn it off before another, a bigger one, began biting me. I lifted it up but the higher I lifted it the bigger and heavier it grew. And suddenly Brother A. came and, taking my arm, led me to a building, to enter which we had to pass along a narrow plank. I stepped on it, but it bent and gave way and I began to clamber up a fence which I could scarcely reach with my hands. After much effort I dragged myself up, so that my legs hung down on one side and my body on the other. I looked round and saw Brother A. standing on the fence and pointing me to a broad avenue and garden, and in the garden was a large and beautiful building. I woke up. O Lord, great Architect of Nature, help me to tear from myself these dogs – my passions – especially the last, which unites in itself the strength of all the former ones, and aid me to enter that temple of virtue to a vision of which I attained in my dream.

7th December.

I dreamt that Joseph Alexeevich was sitting in my house, and that I was very glad, and wished to entertain him. It seemed as if I chattered incessantly with other people and suddenly remembered that this could not please him, and I wished to come close to him and embrace him. But as soon as I drew near, I saw that his face had changed and grown young, and he was quietly telling me something about the teaching of our Order, but so softly that I could not hear it. Then it seemed that we all left the room and something strange happened. We were sitting or lying on the floor. He was telling me something, and I wished to show him my sensibility, and not listening to what he was saying, I began picturing to myself the condition of my inner man and the grace of God sanctifying me. And tears came into my eyes, and I was glad he noticed this. But he looked at me with vexation and jumped up, breaking off his remarks. I felt abashed and asked whether what he had been saying did not concern me; but he did not reply, gave me a kind look, and then we suddenly found ourselves in my bedroom where there is a double bed. He lay down on the edge of it and I burned with longing to caress him and lie down too. And he said, 'Tell me frankly what is your chief temptation? Do you know it? I think you know it already.' Abashed by this question, I replied that sloth was my chief temptation. He shook his head incredulously; and even more abashed, I said that though I was living with my wife as he advised, I was not living with her as her husband. To this he replied that one should not deprive a wife of one's embraces, and gave me to understand that that was my duty. But I replied that I should be ashamed to do it, and suddenly everything vanished. And I awoke and found in my mind the text from the Gospel: 'The life was the light of men. And the light shineth in darkness; and the darkness comprehended it not.' Joseph Alexeevich's face had looked young and bright. That day I received a letter from my benefactor in which he wrote about 'conjugal duties'.

9th December.

I had a dream from which I awoke with a throbbing heart. I saw that I was in Moscow in my house, in the big sitting-room, and Joseph Alexeevich came in from the drawing-room. I seemed to know at once that the process of regeneration had already taken place in him, and I rushed to meet him. I embraced him and kissed his hands, and he said, 'Hast thou noticed that my face is different?' I looked at him, still holding him in my arms, and saw that his face was young, but that he had no hair on his head and his features were quite changed. And I said, 'I should have known you had I met you by chance,' and I thought to myself, 'Am I telling the truth?' And suddenly I saw him lying like a dead body; then he gradually recovered and went with me into my study carrying a large book of sheets of drawing paper; I said, 'I drew that,' and he answered by bowing his head. I opened the book, and on all the pages there were excellent drawings. And in my dream I knew that these drawings represented the love adventures of the soul with its beloved. And on its pages I saw a beautiful representation of a maiden in transparent garments and with a transparent body, flying up to the clouds. And I seemed to know that this maiden was nothing else than a representation of the Song of Songs. And looking at those drawings I dreamed I felt that I was doing wrong, but could not tear myself away from them. Lord, help me! My God, if Thy forsaking me is Thy doing, Thy will be done; but if I am myself the cause, teach me what I should do! I shall perish of my debauchery if Thou utterly desertest me!

11

THE Rostovs' monetary affairs had not improved during the two years they had spent in the country.

Though Nicholas Rostov had kept firmly to his resolution and was still serving modestly in an obscure regiment spending comparatively little, the way of life at Otradnoe – Mitinka's management of affairs, in particular – was such that the debts inevitably increased every year. The only resource obviously presenting itself to the old count was to apply for an official post, so he had come to Petersburg to look for one and also, as he said, to let the lassies enjoy themselves for the last time.

Soon after their arrival in Petersburg, Berg proposed to Vera and was accepted.

Though in Moscow the Rostovs belonged to the best society without themselves giving it a thought, yet in Petersburg their circle of acquaintances was a mixed and indefinite one. In Petersburg they were provincials, and the very people they had entertained in Moscow without inquiring to what set they belonged, here looked down on them.

The Rostovs lived in the same hospitable way in Petersburg as in Moscow, and the most diverse people met at their suppers. Country neighbours from Otradnoe, impoverished old squires and their daughters, Peronskaya a maid of honour, Pierre Bezukhov, and the son of their district postmaster, who had obtained a post in Petersburg. Among the men who very soon became frequent visitors at the Rostovs' house in Petersburg were Boris, Pierre whom the count had met in the street and dragged home with him, and Berg who spent whole days at the Rostovs' and paid the eldest daughter, Countess Vera, the attentions a young man pays when he intends to propose.

Not in vain had Berg shown everybody his right hand wounded at Austerlitz and held a perfectly unnecessary sword in his left. He narrated that episode so persistently and with so important an air that everyone believed in the merit and usefulness of his deed, and he had obtained two decorations for Austerlitz.

In the Finnish war he also managed to distinguish himself. He had picked up the scrap of a grenade that had killed an aide-de-camp standing near the commander-in-chief, and had taken it to his commander. Just as he had done after Austerlitz, he related this occurrence at such length and so insistently that everyone again believed it had been necessary to do this, and he received two decorations for the Finnish war also. In 1809 he was a captain in the Guards, wore medals, and held some special lucrative posts in Petersburg.

Though some sceptics smiled when told of Berg's merits, it could not be denied that he was a painstaking and brave officer, on excellent terms with his superiors, and a moral young man with a brilliant career before him and an assured position in society.

Four years before, meeting a German comrade in the stalls of a Moscow theatre, Berg had pointed out Vera Rostova to him and had said in German, '*das soll mein Weib werden*', and from that moment had made up his mind to marry her. Now in Petersburg, having considered the Rostovs' position and his own, he decided that the time had come to propose.

Berg's proposal was at first received with a perplexity that was not flattering to him. At first it seemed strange that the son of an obscure Livonian gentleman should propose marriage to a Countess Rostova; but Berg's chief characteristic was such a naïve and good-natured egotism that the Rostovs involuntarily came to think it would be a' good thing, since he himself was so firmly convinced that it was good, indeed excellent. Moreover, the Rostovs' affairs were seriously embarrassed, as the suitor could not but know; and above all, Vera was twenty-four, had been taken out everywhere, and though she was certainly good-looking and sensible, no one up to now had proposed to her. So they gave their consent.

'You see,' said Berg to his comrade, whom he called 'friend' only because he knew that everyone has friends, 'You see, I have considered it all, and should not marry if I had not thought it all out or if it were in any way unsuitable. But on the contrary, my papa and mamma are now provided for – I have arranged that rent for them in the Baltic Provinces* – and I can live in Petersburg on my pay, and with her fortune and my good management we can get along nicely. I am not marrying for money – I consider that dishonourable – but a wife should bring her share and a husband his. I have my position in the service, she has connexions and some means. In our times that is worth something, isn't it? But above all, she is a handsome, estimable girl, and she loves me . . .'

Berg blushed and smiled.

'And I love her, because her character is sensible and very good. Now the other sister, though they are the same family, is quite different – an unpleasant character and has not the same intelligence. She is so . . . you know? . . . Unpleasant . . . But my fiancée . . .! Well, you will be coming' – he was going to say 'to dine', but changed his mind and said 'to take tea with us', and quickly doubling up his tongue he blew a small round ring of tobacco smoke, perfectly embodying his dream of happiness.

After the first feeling of perplexity aroused in the parents by Berg's proposal, the holiday tone of joyousness usual at such times took possession of the family, but the rejoicing was external and insincere. In the family's feeling towards this wedding a certain awkwardness and constraint was evident: as if they were ashamed of not having loved Vera sufficiently and of being so ready to get her off their hands. The old count felt this most. He would probably have been unable to state the cause of his embarrassment, but it resulted from the state of his affairs. He did not know at all how much he had, what his debts amounted to, or what dowry he could give Vera. When his daughters were born he had assigned to each of them, for her dowry, an estate with three hundred serfs; but one of those estates had already been sold, and the other was mortgaged, and the interest so much in arrears that it would have to be sold, so that it was impossible to give it to Vera. Nor had he any money.

Berg had already been engaged a month, and only a week remained before the wedding, but the count had not yet decided in his own mind the question of the dowry, nor spoken to his wife about it. At one time the count thought of giving her the Ryazan estate, or of selling a forest, at another time of borrowing money on a note of hand. A few days before the wedding Berg entered the count's study early one morning, and with a pleasant smile respectfully asked his future father-in-law to let him know what Vera's dowry would be. The count was so disconcerted by this long-foreseen inquiry that without consideration he gave the first reply that came into his head. 'I like your being business-like about it . . . I like it. You shall be satisfied . . .'

And patting Berg on the shoulder he got up, wishing to end the conversation. But Berg, smiling pleasantly, explained that if he did not know for certain how much Vera would have and did not receive at least part of the dowry in advance, he would have to break matters off.

'Because, consider, Count – if I allowed myself to marry now without having definite means to maintain my wife, I should be acting badly . . .'

The conversation ended by the count, who wished to be generous and to avoid further importunity, saying that he would give a note of hand for eighty thousand rubles. Berg smiled meekly, kissed the count on the shoulder, and said that he was very grateful, but that it was impossible for him to arrange his new life without receiving thirty thousand in ready money. 'Or at least twenty thousand, Count,' he added, 'and then a note of hand for only sixty thousand.'

'Yes, yes, all right!' said the count hurriedly. 'Only excuse me, my dear fellow, I'll give you twenty thousand and a note of hand for eighty thousand as well. Yes, yes! Kiss me.'

12

NATASHA was sixteen and it was the year 1809, the very year to which she had counted on her fingers with Boris after they had kissed four years ago. Since then she had not once seen him. Before Sonya and her mother, if Boris happened to be mentioned, she spoke quite freely of that episode as of some childish, long-forgotten matter that was not worth mentioning. But in the secret depths of her soul the question whether her engagement to Boris was a jest or an important, binding promise tormented her.

Since Boris left Moscow in 1805 to join the army he had not seen the Rostovs. He had been in Moscow several times, and had passed near Otradnoe, but had never been to see them.

Sometimes it occurred to Natasha that he did not wish to see her, and this conjecture was confirmed by the sad tone in which her elders spoke of him.

'Nowadays old friends are not remembered,' the countess would say when Boris was mentioned.

Anna Mikhaylovna also had of late visited them less frequently, seemed to hold herself with particular dignity, and always spoke rapturously and gratefully of the merits of her son and the brilliant career on which he had entered. When the Rostovs came to Petersburg, Boris called on them.

He drove to their house in some agitation. The memory of Natasha was his most poetic recollection. But he went with the firm intention of letting her and her parents feel that the childish relations between himself and Natasha could not be binding either on her or on him. He had a brilliant position in society thanks to his intimacy with Countess Bezukhova, a brilliant position in the service thanks to the patronage of an important personage whose complete confidence he enjoyed, and he was beginning to make plans for marrying one of the richest heiresses in Petersburg, plans which might very easily be realized. When he entered the Rostovs' drawing-room Natasha was in her own room. When she heard of his arrival she almost ran into the drawing-room, flushed, and beaming with a more than cordial smile.

Boris remembered Natasha in a short dress, with dark eyes shining from under her curls and boisterous, childish laughter, as he had known her four years before; and so he was taken aback when quite a different Natasha entered, and his face expressed rapturous astonishment. This expression on his face pleased Natasha.

'Well, do you recognize your little madcap playmate?' asked the countess.

Boris kissed Natasha's hand and said that he was astonished at the change in her.

'How handsome you have grown!'

'I should think so!' replied Natasha's laughing eyes.

'And is papa older?' she asked.

Natasha sat down and, without joining in Boris's conversation with the countess, silently and minutely studied her childhood's suitor. He felt the weight of that resolute and affectionate scrutiny, and glanced at her occasionally.

Boris's uniform, spurs, tie, and the way his hair was brushed, were all *comme il faut* and in the latest fashion. This Natasha noticed at once. He sat rather sideways in the arm-chair next to the countess, arranging with his right hand the cleanest of gloves that fitted his left hand like a skin, and he spoke with a particularly refined compression of his lips about the amusements of the highest Petersburg society, recalling with mild irony old times in Moscow and Moscow acquaintances. It was not accidentally, Natasha felt, that he alluded, when speaking of the highest aristocracy, to an ambassador's ball he had attended, and to invitations he had received from N. N. and S. S.

All this time Natasha sat silent, glancing up at him from under her brows. This gaze disturbed and confused Boris more and more. He looked round more frequently towards her, and broke off in what he was saying. He did not stay more than ten minutes, then rose and took his leave. The same inquisitive, challenging, and rather mocking eyes still looked at him. After his first visit Boris said to himself that Natasha attracted him just as much as ever, but that he must not yield to that feeling, because to marry her, a girl almost without fortune, would mean ruin to his career, while to renew their former relations without intending to marry her would be dishonourable. Boris made up his mind to avoid meeting Natasha, but despite that resolution he called again a few days later, and began calling often and spending whole days at the Rostovs'. It seemed to him that he ought to have an explanation with Natasha and tell her that the old times must be forgotten, that in spite of everything . . . she could not be his wife, that he had no means, and they would never let her marry him. But he failed to do so, and felt awkward about entering on such an explanation. From day to day he became more and more entangled. It seemed to her mother and Sonya that Natasha was in love with Boris as of old. She sang him his favourite songs, showed him her album, making him write in it, did not allow him to allude to the past, letting it be understood how delightful was the present; and every day he went away in a fog, without having said what he meant to, and not knowing what he was doing or why he came, or how it would all end. He left off visiting Hélène and received reproachful notes from her every day, and yet he continued to spend whole days with the Rostovs.

ONE night when the old countess, in night-cap and dressing-jacket, without her false curls, and with her poor little knob of hair showing under her white cotton cap, knelt sighing and groaning on a rug and bowing to the ground in prayer, her door creaked and Natasha, also in a dressing-jacket with slippers on her bare feet and her hair in curl-papers, ran in. The countess – her prayerful mood dispelled – looked round and frowned. She was finishing her last prayer: 'Can it be that this couch will be my grave?' Natasha, flushed and eager, seeing her mother in prayer suddenly checked her rush, half sat down, and unconsciously put out her tongue as if chiding herself. Seeing that her mother was still praying she ran on tiptoe to the bed and, rapidly slipping one little foot against the other, pushed off her slippers and jumped onto the bed the countess had feared might become her grave. This couch was high, with a feather-bed and five pillows each smaller than the one below. Natasha jumped on it, sank into the feather-bed, rolled over to the wall, and began snuggling up the bedclothes as she settled down, raising her knees to her chin, kicking out and laughing almost inaudibly, now covering herself up head and all, and now peeping at her mother. The countess finished her prayers and came to the bed with a stern face, but seeing that Natasha's head was covered, she smiled in her kind, weak way.

'Now then, now then!' said she.

'Mamma, can we have a talk? Yes?' said Natasha. 'Now, just one on your throat and another . . . that'll do!' And seizing her mother round the neck, she kissed her on the throat. In her behaviour to her mother Natasha seemed rough, but she was so sensitive and tactful that however she clasped her mother, she always managed to do it without hurting her, or making her feel uncomfortable or displeased.

'Well, what is it to-night?' said the mother, having arranged her pillows and waited until Natasha, after turning over a couple of times, had settled down beside her under the quilt, spread out her arms, and assumed a serious expression.

These visits of Natasha's at night, before the count returned from his club, were one of the greatest pleasures of both mother and daughter.

'What is it to-night? – But I have to tell you . . .'

Natasha put her hand on her mother's mouth.

'About Boris . . . I know,' she said seriously; 'that's what I have come about. Don't say it – I know. No, do tell me!' and she removed her hand. 'Tell me, mamma! He's nice?'

'Natasha, you are sixteen. At your age I was married. You say Boris is nice. He is very nice, and I love him like a son. But what then...? What are you thinking about? You have quite turned his head, I can see that...'

As she said this the countess looked round at her daughter. Natasha was lying looking steadily straight before her at one of the mahogany sphinxes carved on the corners of the bedstead, so that the countess only saw her daughter's face in profile. That face struck her by its peculiarly serious and concentrated expression.

Natasha was listening and considering.

'Well, what then?' said she.

'You have quite turned his head, and why? What do you want of him? You know you can't marry him.'

'Why not?' said Natasha, without changing her position.

'Because he is young, because he is poor, because he is a relation... and because you yourself don't love him.'

'How do you know?'

'I know. It is not right, darling!'

'But if I want to...' said Natasha.

'Leave off talking nonsense,' said the countess.

'But if I want to...'

'Natasha, I am in earnest...'

Natasha did not let her finish. She drew the countess's large hand to her, kissed it on the back and then on the palm, then again turned it over and began kissing first one knuckle,* then the space between the knuckles, then the next knuckle, whispering, 'January, February, March, April, May. Speak, mamma, why don't you say anything? Speak!' said she, turning to her mother, who was tenderly gazing at her daughter and in that contemplation seemed to have forgotten all she had wished to say.

'It won't do, my love! Not everyone will understand this friendship dating from your childish days, and to see him so intimate with you may injure you in the eyes of other young men who visit us, and above all, it torments him for nothing. He may already have found a suitable and wealthy match, and now he's half crazy.'

'Crazy?' repeated Natasha.

'I'll tell you some things about myself. I had a cousin...'

'I know! Cyril Matveich... but he is old.'

'He was not always old. But this is what I'll do, Natasha, I'll have a talk with Boris. He need not come so often...'

'Why not, if he likes to?'

'Because I know it will end in nothing...'

'How can you know? No, mamma, don't speak to him! What nonsense!' said Natasha in the tone of one being deprived of her property. 'Well, I won't marry, but let him come if he enjoys it and I enjoy it.' Natasha smiled and looked at her mother. 'Not to marry, but just *so*,' she added.

'How *so*, my pet?'

'Just *so*. There's no need for me to marry him. But . . . just *so*.'

'Just so, just so,' repeated the countess, and shaking all over, she went off into a good-humoured, unexpected, elderly laugh.

'Don't laugh, stop!' cried Natasha. 'You're shaking the whole bed! You're awfully like me, just such another giggler . . . Wait . . .' and she seized the countess's hands and kissed a knuckle of the little finger, saying, 'June,' and continued, kissing, 'July, August' on the other hand. 'But, mamma, is he very much in love? What do you think? Was anybody ever so much in love with you? And he's very nice, very, very nice. Only not quite my taste – he is so narrow, like the dining-room clock . . . Don't you understand? Narrow, you know – grey, light grey . . .'

'What rubbish you're talking!' said the countess.

Natasha continued:

'Don't you really understand? Nicholas would understand . . . Bezukhov, now, is blue, dark blue and red, and he is square.'

'You flirt with him too,' said the countess, laughing.

'No, he is a Freemason, I have found out. He is fine, dark blue and red . . . How can I explain it to you?'

'Little Countess!' the count's voice called from behind the door. 'You're not asleep?' Natasha jumped up, snatched up her slippers, and ran barefoot to her own room.

It was a long time before she could sleep. She kept thinking that no one could understand all that she understood and all there was in her.

'Sonya?' she thought, glancing at that curled-up, sleeping little kitten with her enormous plait of hair. 'No, how could she? She's virtuous. She fell in love with Nicholas and does not wish to know anything more. Even mamma does not understand. It is wonderful how clever I am and how . . . charming she is,' she went on, speaking of herself in the third person, and imagining it was some very wise man – the wisest and best of men – who was saying it of her. 'There is everything, everything in her,' continued this man. 'She is unusually intelligent, charming . . . and then she is pretty, uncommonly pretty, and agile – she swims and rides splendidly . . . and her voice! One can really say it's a wonderful voice!'

She hummed a scrap from her favourite opera by Cherubini, threw herself on her bed, laughed at the pleasant thought that she would immediately fall asleep, called Dunyasha, the maid, to put out the candle, and before Dunyasha had left the room had already passed into another yet happier world of dreams, where everything was as light and beautiful as in reality, and even more so because it was different.

Next day the countess called Boris aside and had a talk with him, after which he ceased coming to the Rostovs.

14

ON the 31st of December, New Year's Eve 1810, an old grandee of Catherine's day was giving a ball and midnight supper. The diplomatic corps and the Emperor himself were to be present.

The grandee's well-known mansion on the English Quay glittered with innumerable lights. Police were stationed at the brightly lit entrance which was carpeted with red baize, and not only gendarmes but dozens of police officers and even the police-master himself stood at the porch. Carriages kept driving away and fresh ones arriving, with red-liveried footmen and footmen in plumed hats. From the carriages emerged men wearing uniforms, stars, and ribbons, while ladies in satin and ermine cautiously descended the carriage steps which were let down for them with a clatter, and then walked hurriedly and noiselessly over the baize at the entrance.

Almost every time a new carriage drove up a whisper ran through the crowd and caps were doffed.

'The Emperor? . . . No, a minister . . . prince . . . ambassador. Don't you see the plumes? . . .' was whispered among the crowd.

One person, better dressed than the rest, seemed to know everyone and mentioned by name the greatest dignitaries of the day.

A third of the visitors had already arrived, but the Rostovs, who were to be present, were still hurrying to get dressed.

There had been many discussions and preparations for this ball in the Rostov family, many fears that the invitation would not arrive, that the dresses would not be ready, or that something would not be arranged as it should be.

Marya Ignatevna Peronskaya, a thin and sallow maid of honour at the court of the Dowager Empress, who was a friend and relation of the countess and piloted the provincial Rostovs in Petersburg high society, was to accompany them to the ball.

They were to call for her at her house in the Taurida Gardens at ten o'clock, but it was already five minutes to ten and the girls were not yet dressed.

Natasha was going to her first grand ball. She had got up at eight that morning and had been in a fever of excitement and activity all day. All her powers since morning had been concentrated on ensuring that they all – she herself, mamma, and Sonya – should be as well dressed as possible. Sonya and her mother put themselves entirely in her hands. The countess was to wear a claret-coloured velvet dress, and the two girls white gauze over pink silk slips, with roses on their bodices and their hair dressed à la grecque.

Everything essential had already been done; feet, hands, necks, and ears washed, perfumed, and powdered, as befits a ball; the open-work silk stockings and white satin shoes with ribbons were already on; the hairdressing was almost done. Sonya was finishing dressing and so was the countess, but Natasha, who had bustled about helping them all, was behindhand. She was still sitting before a looking-glass with a dressing-jacket thrown over her slender shoulders. Sonya stood ready dressed in the middle of the room, and pressing the head of a pin till it hurt her dainty finger, was fixing on a last ribbon that squeaked as the pin went through it.

'That's not the way, that's not the way, Sonya!' cried Natasha turning her head and clutching with both hands at her hair which the maid, who was dressing it, had not time to release. 'That bow is not right. Come here!'

Sonya sat down and Natasha pinned the ribbon on differently.

'Allow me, Miss! I can't do it like that,' said the maid who was holding Natasha's hair.

'Oh dear! Well then, wait. That's right, Sonya.'

'Aren't you ready? It is nearly ten,' came the countess's voice.

'Directly! Directly! And you, mamma?'

'I have only my cap to pin on.'

'Don't do it without me!' called Natasha. 'You won't do it right.'

'But it's already ten.'

They had decided to be at the ball by half-past ten, and Natasha had still to get dressed and they had to call at the Taurida Gardens.

When her hair was done, Natasha, in her short petticoat from under which her dancing shoes showed, and in her mother's dressing-jacket, ran up to Sonya, scrutinized her, and then ran to her mother. Turning her mother's head this way and that, she fastened on the cap and hurriedly kissing her grey hair ran back to the maids who were turning up the hem of her skirt.

The cause of the delay was Natasha's skirt, which was too long. Two maids were turning up the hem and hurriedly biting off the ends of thread. A third with pins in her mouth was running about between the countess and Sonya, and a fourth held the whole of the gossamer garment up high on one uplifted hand.

'Mavra, quicker, darling!'

'Give me my thimble, Miss, from there . . .'

'Whenever will you be ready?' asked the count coming to the door. 'Here is some scent. Peronskaya must be tired of waiting.'

'It's ready, Miss,' said the maid, holding up the shortened gauze dress with two fingers, and blowing and shaking something off it, as if by this to express a consciousness of the airiness and purity of what she held.

Natasha began putting on the dress.

'In a minute! In a minute! Don't come in, papa!' she cried to her father as he opened the door – speaking from under the filmy skirt which still covered her whole face.

Sonya slammed the door to. A minute later they let the count in. He was wearing a blue swallow-tail coat, shoes and stockings, and was perfumed and his hair pomaded.

'Oh, papa! how nice you look! Charming!' cried Natasha, as she stood in the middle of the room smoothing out the folds of the gauze.

'If you please, Miss! allow me,' said the maid, who on her knees was pulling the skirt straight and shifting the pins from one side of her mouth to the other with her tongue.

'Say what you like,' exclaimed Sonya, in a despairing voice as she looked at Natasha, 'say what you like, it is still too long.'

Natasha stepped back to look at herself in the pier-glass. The dress *was* too long.

'Really, madam, it is not at all too long,' said Mavra, crawling on her knees after her young lady.

'Well, if it's too long we'll tack it up . . . we'll tack it up in one minute,' said the resolute Dunyasha taking a needle that was stuck on the front of her little shawl and, still kneeling on the floor, set to work once more.

At that moment, with soft steps, the countess came in shyly, in her cap and velvet gown.

'Oo-oo, my beauty!' exclaimed the count, 'she looks better than any of you!'

He would have embraced her but, blushing, she stepped aside fearing to be rumpled.

'Mamma, your cap, more to this side,' said Natasha. 'I'll arrange it,' and she rushed forward so that the maids who were tacking up her skirt could not move fast enough and a piece of gauze was torn off.

'Oh, goodness! What has happened? Really it was not my fault!'

'Never mind, I'll run it up, it won't show,' said Dunyasha.

'What a beauty – a very queen!' said the nurse as she came to the door. 'And Sonya! They are lovely!'

At a quarter past ten they at last got into their carriages and started. But they had still to call at the Taurida Gardens.

Peronskaya was quite ready. In spite of her age and plainness she had gone through the same process as the Rostovs, but with less flurry – for to her it was a matter of routine. Her ugly old body was washed, perfumed, and powdered, in just the same way. She had washed behind her ears just as carefully, and when she entered her drawing-room in her yellow dress, wearing her badge as maid of honour, her old lady's maid was as full of rapturous admiration as the Rostovs' servants had been.

She praised the Rostovs' toilettes. They praised her taste and toilette, and at eleven o'clock, careful of their *coiffures* and dresses, they settled themselves in their carriages and drove off.

15

NATASHA had not had a moment free since early morning and had not once had time to think of what lay before her.

In the damp chill air and crowded closeness of the swaying carriage, she for the first time vividly imagined what was in store for her there at the ball, in those brightly lighted rooms – with music, flowers, dances, the Emperor, and all the brilliant young people of Petersburg. The prospect was so splendid that she hardly believed it would come true, so out of keeping was it with the chill darkness and closeness of the carriage. She understood all that awaited her only when, after stepping over the red baize at the entrance, she entered the hall, took off her fur cloak and, beside Sonya and in front of her mother, mounted the brightly illuminated stairs between the flowers. Only then did she remember how she must behave at a ball, and tried to assume the majestic air she considered indispensable for a girl on such an occasion. But, fortunately for her, she felt her eyes growing misty, she saw nothing clearly, her pulse beat a hundred to the minute and the blood throbbed at her heart. She could not assume that pose, which would have made her ridiculous, and she moved on almost fainting from excitement and trying with all her might to conceal it. And this was the very attitude that became her best. Before and behind them other visitors were entering, also talking in low tones and wearing ball-dresses. The mirrors on the landing reflected ladies in white, pale-blue, and pink dresses, with diamonds and pearls on their bare necks and arms.

Natasha looked in the mirrors and could not distinguish her reflection from the others. All was blent into one brilliant procession. On entering the ball-room the regular hum of voices, footsteps, and greetings deafened Natasha, and the light and glitter dazzled her still more. The host and hostess, who had already been standing at the door for half an hour repeating the same words to the various arrivals, '*Charmé de vous voir,*' greeted the Rostovs and Peronskaya in the same manner.

The two girls in their white dresses, each with a rose in her black hair, both curtsied in the same way, but the hostess's eye involuntarily rested longer on the slim Natasha. She looked at her and gave her alone a special smile, in addition to her usual smile as hostess. Looking at her she may have recalled the golden, irrevocable days of her own girlhood and her own first ball. The host also followed Natasha with his eyes and asked the count which was his daughter.

'Charming!' said he, kissing the tips of his fingers.

In the ball-room guests stood crowding at the entrance doors awaiting the Emperor. The countess took up a position in one of the front rows of that crowd. Natasha heard and felt that several people were asking about her and looking at her. She realized that those noticing her liked her, and this observation helped to calm her.

'There are some like ourselves and some worse,' she thought.

Peronskaya was pointing out to the countess the most important people at the ball.

'That is the Dutch ambassador, do you see? That grey-haired man,' she said, indicating an old man with a profusion of silver-grey curly hair, who was surrounded by ladies laughing at something he said.

'Ah, here she is, the Queen of Petersburg, Countess Bezukhova,' said Peronskaya, indicating Hélène who had just entered. 'How lovely! She is quite equal to Marya Antonovna.* See how the men, young and old, pay court to her. Beautiful and clever . . . they say Prince —— is quite mad about her. But see, those two, though not good-looking, are even more run after.'

She pointed to a lady who was crossing the room followed by a very plain daughter.

'She is a splendid match, a millionairess,' said Peronskaya. 'And look, here come her suitors.'

'That is Bezukhova's brother, Anatole Kuragin,' she said, indicating a handsome officer of the Horse Guards who passed by them with head erect, looking at something over the heads of the ladies. 'He's handsome, isn't he? I hear they will marry him to that rich girl. But your cousin, Drubetskoy, is also very attentive to her. They say she has millions. Oh yes, that's the French ambassador himself!' she replied to the countess's inquiry about Caulaincourt. 'Looks as if he were a king! All the same, the French are charming, very charming. No one more charming in society. Ah, here she is! Yes, she is still the most beautiful of them all, our Marya Antonovna! And how simply she is dressed! Lovely! And that stout one in spectacles is the universal Freemason,' she went on, indicating Pierre. 'Put him beside his wife and he looks a regular buffoon!'

Pierre, swaying his stout body, advanced making way through the crowd and nodding to right and left as casually and good-naturedly as if he were passing through a crowd at a fair. He pushed through, evidently looking for someone.

Natasha looked joyfully at the familiar face of Pierre, 'the buffoon', as Peronskaya had called him, and knew he was looking for them, and for her in particular. He had promised to be at the ball and introduce partners to her.

But before he reached them Pierre stopped beside a very handsome, dark man of middle height, and in a white uniform, who stood by a window talking to a tall man wearing stars and a ribbon. Natasha at once recognized the shorter and younger man in the white uniform: it was Bolkonsky, who seemed to her to have grown much younger, happier, and better-looking.

'There's someone else we know – Bolkonsky, do you see, mamma?' said Natasha, pointing out Prince Andrew. 'You remember, he stayed a night with us at Otradnoe.'

'Oh, you know him?' said Peronskaya. 'I can't bear him. *Il fait à présent la pluie et le beau temps.* He's too proud for anything. Takes after his father. And he's hand in glove with Speransky, writing some projects or other. Just look how he treats the ladies! There's one talking to him, and he has turned away,' she said, pointing at him. 'I'd give it him if he treated me as he does those ladies.'

16

SUDDENLY everybody stirred, began talking, and pressed forward and then back, and between the two rows, which separated, the Emperor entered to the sounds of music that had immediately struck up. Behind him walked his host and hostess. He walked in rapidly, bowing to right and left as if anxious to get the first moments of the reception over. The band played the polonaise in vogue at that time on account of the words that had been set to it, beginning: 'Alexander, Elisaveta, all our hearts you ravish quite...' The Emperor passed on to the drawing-room, the crowd made a rush for the doors, and several persons with excited faces hurried there and back again. Then the crowd hastily retired from the drawing-room door, at which the Emperor reappeared talking to the hostess. A young man, looking distraught, pounced down on the ladies, asking them to move aside. Some ladies, with faces betraying complete forgetfulness of all the rules of decorum, pushed forward to the detriment of their toilettes. The men began to choose partners and take their places for the polonaise.

Everyone moved back, and the Emperor came smiling out of the drawing-room leading his hostess by the hand but not keeping time to the music. The host followed with Marya Antonovna Naryshkina; then came ambassadors, ministers, and various generals, whom Peronskaya diligently named. More than half the ladies already had partners and were taking up, or preparing to take up, their positions for the polonaise. Natasha felt that she would be left with her mother and Sonya among a minority of women who crowded near the wall, not having been invited to dance. She stood with her slender arms hanging down, her scarcely defined bosom rising and falling regularly, and with bated breath and glittering, frightened eyes gazed straight before her, evidently prepared for the height of joy or misery. She was not concerned about the Emperor, or any of those great people whom Peronskaya was pointing out – she had but one thought: 'Is it possible no one will ask me, that I shall not be among the first to dance? Is it possible that not one of all these men will notice me? They do not even seem to see me, or if they do, they look as if they were saying, "Ah, she's not the one I'm after, so it's not worth looking at her!" No, it's impossible,' she thought. 'They must know how I long to dance, how splendidly I dance, and how they would enjoy dancing with me.'

The strains of the polonaise, which had continued for a considerable time, had begun to sound like a sad reminiscence in Natasha's ears. She wanted to cry. Peronskaya had left them. The count was at the other end of the room. She and the countess and Sonya were standing by themselves as in the depths of a forest, amid that crowd of strangers, with no one interested in them and not wanted by anyone. Prince Andrew with a lady passed by, evidently not recognizing them. The handsome Anatole was smilingly talking to a partner on his arm, and looked at Natasha as one looks at a wall. Boris passed them twice and each time turned away. Berg and his wife, who were not dancing, came up to them.

This family gathering seemed humiliating to Natasha – as if there were nowhere else for the family to talk but here at the ball. She did not listen to or look at Vera, who was telling her something about her own green dress.

At last the Emperor stopped beside his last partner (he had danced with three) and the music ceased. A worried aide-de-camp ran up to the Rostovs requesting them to stand farther back, though as it was they were already close to the wall, and from the gallery resounded the distinct, precise, enticingly rhythmical strains of a valse. The Emperor looked smilingly down the room. A minute passed but no one had yet begun dancing. An aide-de-camp, the Master of Ceremonies, went up to Countess Bezukhova and asked her to dance. She smilingly raised her hand and laid it on his shoulder without looking at him. The aide-de-camp, an adept in his art, grasping his partner firmly round her waist, with confident deliberation started smoothly, gliding first round the edge of the circle, then at the corner of the room he caught Hélène's left hand and turned her, the only sound audible, apart from the ever-quickening music, being the rhythmic click of the spurs on his rapid, agile feet, while at every third beat his partner's velvet dress spread out and seemed to flash as she whirled round. Natasha gazed at them and was ready to cry because it was not she who was dancing that first turn of the valse.

Prince Andrew, in the white uniform of a cavalry colonel, wearing stockings and dancing-shoes, stood looking animated and bright in the front row of the circle not far from the Rostovs. Baron Firhoff was talking to him about the first sitting of the Council of State to be held next day. Prince Andrew, as one closely connected with Speransky and participating in the work of the legislative commission, could give reliable information about that sitting, concerning which various rumours were current. But not listening to what Firhoff was saying, he was gazing now at the sovereign, and now at the men intending to dance who had not yet gathered courage to enter the circle.

Prince Andrew was watching these men abashed by the Emperor's presence, and the women who were breathlessly longing to be asked to dance.

Pierre came up to him and caught him by the arm.

'You always dance. I have a protégée, the young Rostova, here. Ask her,' he said.

'Where is she?' asked Bolkonsky. 'Excuse me!' he added, turning to the baron, 'we will finish this conversation elsewhere – at a ball one must dance.' He stepped forward in the direction Pierre indicated. The despairing, dejected expression of Natasha's face caught his eye. He recognized her, guessed her feelings, saw that it was her début, remembered her conversation at the window, and with an expression of pleasure on his face approached Countess Rostova.

'Allow me to introduce you to my daughter,' said the countess, with heightened colour.

'I have the pleasure of being already acquainted, if the Countess remembers me,' said Prince Andrew with a low and courteous bow quite belying Peronskaya's remarks about his rudeness, and approaching Natasha he held out his arm to grasp her waist before he had completed his invitation. He asked her to valse. That tremulous expression on Natasha's face, prepared either for despair or rapture, suddenly brightened into a happy, grateful, childlike smile. 'I have long been waiting for you,' that frightened happy little girl seemed to say by the smile that replaced the threatened tears, as she raised her hand to Prince Andrew's shoulder. They were the second couple to enter the circle. Prince Andrew was one of the best dancers of his day and Natasha danced exquisitely. Her little feet in their white satin dancing-shoes did their work swiftly, lightly, and independently of herself, while her face beamed with ecstatic happiness. Her slender bare arms and neck were not beautiful – compared to Hélène's her shoulders looked thin and her bosom undeveloped. But Hélène seemed, as it were, hardened by a varnish left by the thousands of looks that had scanned her person, while Natasha was like a girl exposed for the first time, who would have felt very much ashamed had she not been assured that this was absolutely necessary.

Prince Andrew liked dancing, and wishing to escape as quickly as possible from the political and clever talk which everyone addressed to him, wishing to break up the circle of restraint he disliked, caused by the Emperor's presence, he danced, and had chosen Natasha because Pierre pointed her out to him and because she was the first pretty girl who caught his eye; but scarcely had he embraced that slender supple figure, and felt her stirring so close to him and smiling so near him, than the wine of her charm rose to his head, and he felt himself revived and rejuvenated when after leaving her he stood breathing deeply and watching the other dancers.

17

AFTER Prince Andrew, Boris came up to ask Natasha for a dance, and then the aide-de-camp who had opened the ball, and several other young men, so that, flushed and happy, and passing on her superfluous partners to Sonya, she did not cease dancing all the evening. She noticed and saw nothing of what occupied everyone else. Not only did she fail to notice that the Emperor talked a long time with the French ambassador, and how particularly gracious he was to a certain lady, or that Prince So-and-so and So-and-so did and said this and that, and that Hélène had great success and was honoured by the special attention of So-and-so, but she did not even see the Emperor, and only noticed that he had gone because the ball became livelier after his departure. For one of the merry cotillions before supper Prince Andrew was again her partner. He reminded her of their first encounter in the Otradnoe avenue, and how she had been unable to sleep that moonlight night, and told her how he had involuntarily overheard her. Natasha blushed at that recollection and tried to excuse herself, as if there had been something to be ashamed of in what Prince Andrew had overheard.

Like all men who have grown up in society, Prince Andrew liked meeting someone there not of the conventional society stamp. And such was Natasha, with her surprise, her delight, her shyness, and even her mistakes in speaking French. With her he behaved with special care and tenderness, sitting beside her and talking of the simplest and most unimportant matters; he admired the joyous brightness of her eyes and smile, which related not to what was said but to her own happiness. When she was chosen by a dancer, and rose with a smile and danced round the room, Prince Andrew particularly admired her shy grace. In the middle of the cotillion, having completed one of the figures, Natasha, still out of breath, was returning to her seat when another dancer chose her. She was tired and panting and evidently thought of declining, but immediately put her hand gaily on the man's shoulder, smiling at Prince Andrew.

'I'd be glad to sit beside you and rest: I'm tired; but you see how they keep asking me, and I'm glad of it, I'm happy and I love everybody, and you and I understand it all,' and much, much more was said in her smile. When her partner left her, Natasha ran across the room to choose two ladies for the figure.

'If she goes to her cousin first and then to another lady, she will be my wife,' said Prince Andrew to himself, quite to his own surprise, as he watched her. She did go first to her cousin.

'What rubbish sometimes enters one's head!' thought Prince Andrew, 'but what is certain is that that girl is so charming, so original, that she won't be dancing here a month before she will be married . . . Such as she are rare here,' he thought, as Natasha, readjusting a rose that was slipping on her bodice, settled herself beside him.

When the cotillion was over the old count in his blue coat came up to the dancers. He invited Prince Andrew to come and see them, and asked his daughter whether she was enjoying herself. Natasha did not answer at once, but only looked up with a smile that said reproachfully: 'How can you ask such a question?'

'I have never enjoyed myself so much before!' she said, and Prince Andrew noticed how her thin arms rose quickly as if to embrace her father, and instantly dropped again. Natasha was happier than she had ever been in her life. She was at that height of bliss when one becomes completely kind and good, and does not believe in the possibility of evil, unhappiness, or sorrow.

At that ball Pierre for the first time felt humiliated by the position his wife occupied in court circles. He was gloomy and absent-minded. A deep furrow ran across his forehead, and standing by a window he stared over his spectacles seeing no one.

On her way to supper Natasha passed him.

Pierre's gloomy, unhappy look struck her. She stopped in front of him. She wished to help him, to bestow on him the superabundance of her own happiness.

'How delightful it is, Count!' said she. 'Isn't it?'

Pierre smiled absent-mindedly, evidently not grasping what she said.

'Yes, I am very glad,' he said.

'How can people be dissatisfied with anything?' thought Natasha. 'Especially such a capital fellow as Bezukhov!' In Natasha's eyes all the people at the ball alike were good, kind, and splendid people, loving one another; none of them capable of injuring another – and so they ought all to be happy.

18

NEXT day Prince Andrew thought of the ball, but his mind did not dwell on it long. 'Yes, it was a very brilliant ball,' and then ... 'Yes, that little Rostova is very charming. There's something fresh, original, unPetersburg-like about her that distinguishes her.' That was all he thought about yesterday's ball, and after his morning tea he set to work.

But either from fatigue or want of sleep he was ill-disposed for work and could get nothing done. He kept criticizing his own work as he often did, and was glad when he heard someone coming.

The visitor was Bitsky, who served on various committees, frequented all the societies in Petersburg, and was a passionate devotee of the new ideas and of Speransky, and a diligent Petersburg newsmonger – one of those men who choose their opinions like their clothes, according to the fashion, but who for that very reason appear to be the warmest partisans. Hardly had he got rid of his hat before he ran into Prince Andrew's room with a preoccupied air and at once began talking. He had just heard particulars of that morning's sitting of the Council of State opened by the Emperor, and he spoke of it enthusiastically. The Emperor's speech had been extraordinary. It had been a speech such as only consti-tutional monarchs deliver. 'The sovereign plainly said that the Council and Senate are *estates* of the realm, he said that the govern-ment must rest not on authority but on secure bases. The Emperor said that the fiscal system must be reorganized and the accounts published,' recounted Bitsky, emphasizing certain words and open-ing his eyes significantly.

'Ah, yes. To-day's events mark an epoch, the greatest epoch in our history,' he concluded.

Prince Andrew listened to the account of the opening of the Council of State, which he had so impatiently awaited and to which he had attached such importance, and was surprised that this event, now that it had taken place, did not affect him, and even seemed quite insignificant. He listened with quiet irony to Bitsky's enthusiastic account of it. A very simple thought occurred to him: 'What does it matter to me or to Bitsky what the Emperor was pleased to say at the Council? Can all that make me any happier or better?'

And this simple reflection suddenly destroyed all the interest Prince Andrew had felt in the impending reforms. He was going to dine that evening at Speransky's, 'with only a few friends', as the host had said when inviting him. The prospect of that dinner in the intimate home circle of the man he so admired had greatly interested Prince Andrew, especially as he had not yet seen Speransky in his domestic surroundings, but now he felt disinclined to go to it.

At the appointed hour, however, he entered the modest house Speransky owned in the Taurida Gardens. In the parqueted dining-room of this small house, remarkable for its extreme cleanliness (suggesting that of a monastery), Prince Andrew, who was rather late, found the friendly gathering of Speransky's intimate acquaint-ances already assembled at five o'clock. There were no ladies present except Speransky's little daughter (long-faced like her father) and her governess. The other guests were Gervais, Magnitsky, and Stolypin.* While still in the ante-room, Prince Andrew heard loud voices and a ringing staccato laugh – a laugh such as one hears on the stage. Someone – it sounded like Speransky – was distinctly ejaculating *ha-ha-ha*. Prince Andrew had never before heard Speransky's famous laugh, and this ringing, high-pitched laughter from a statesman made a strange impression on him.

He entered the dining-room. The whole company were standing

between two windows, at a small table laid with hors-d'œuvres. Speransky, wearing a grey swallow-tail coat with a star on the breast, and evidently still the same waistcoat and high white stock he had worn at the meeting of the Council of State, stood at the table with a beaming countenance. His guests surrounded him. Magnitsky, addressing himself to Speransky, was relating an anecdote, and Speransky was laughing in advance at what Magnitsky was going to say. When Prince Andrew entered the room Magnitsky's words were again drowned by laughter. Stolypin gave a deep bass guffaw as he munched a piece of bread and cheese. Gervais laughed softly with a hissing chuckle, and Speransky in a high-pitched staccato manner.

Still laughing, Speransky held out his soft white hand to Prince Andrew.

'Very pleased to see you, Prince,' he said. 'One moment...' he went on, turning to Magnitsky and interrupting his story. 'We have agreed that this is a dinner for recreation, with not a word about business!' and turning again to the narrator he began to laugh afresh.

Prince Andrew looked at the laughing Speransky with astonishment, regret, and disillusionment. It seemed to him that this was not Speransky but someone else. Everything that had formerly appeared mysterious and fascinating in Speransky suddenly became plain and unattractive.

At dinner the conversation did not cease for a moment, and seemed to consist of the contents of a book of funny anecdotes. Before Magnitsky had finished his story, someone else was anxious to relate something still funnier. Most of the anecdotes, if not relating to the State service, related to people in the service. It seemed that in this company the insignificance of those people was so definitely accepted that the only possible attitude towards them was one of good-humoured ridicule. Speransky related how at the Council that morning, a deaf dignitary, when asked his opinion, replied that he thought so too. Gervais gave a long account of an official revision, remarkable for the stupidity of everybody concerned. Stolypin, stuttering, broke into the conversation and began excitedly talking of the abuses that existed under the former order of things – threatening to give a serious turn to the conversation. Magnitsky starting quizzing Stolypin about his vehemence. Gervais intervened with a joke, and the talk reverted to its former lively tone.

Evidently Speransky liked to rest after his labours and find amusement in a circle of friends, and his guests, understanding his wish, tried to enliven him and amuse themselves. But their gaiety seemed to Prince Andrew mirthless and tiresome. Speransky's high-pitched voice struck him unpleasantly, and the incessant laughter grated on him like a false note. Prince Andrew did not laugh and feared that he would be a damper on the spirits of the company, but no one took any notice of his being out of harmony with the general mood. They all seemed very gay.

He tried several times to join in the conversation, but his remarks were tossed aside each time like a cork thrown out of the water, and he could not jest with them.

There was nothing wrong or unseemly in what they said, it was witty, and might have been funny, but it lacked just that something which is the salt of mirth, and they were not even aware that such a thing existed.

After dinner Speransky's daughter and her governess rose. He patted the little girl with his white hand and kissed her. And that gesture, too, seemed unnatural to Prince Andrew.

The men remained at table over their port – English fashion. In the midst of a conversation that was started about Napoleon's Spanish affairs,* which they all agreed in approving, Prince Andrew began to express a contrary opinion. Speransky smiled and, with an evident wish to prevent the conversation from taking an unpleasant course, told a story that had no connexion with the previous conversation. For a few moments all were silent.

Having sat some time at table, Speransky corked a bottle of wine, and remarking, 'Nowadays good wine rides in a carriage and pair,' passed it to the servant and got up. All rose, and continuing to talk loudly went into the drawing-room. Two letters brought by a courier were handed to Speransky, and he took them to his study. As soon as he had left the room the general merriment stopped and the guests began to converse sensibly and quietly with one another.

'Now for the recitation!' said Speransky on returning from his study. 'A wonderful talent!' he said to Prince Andrew and Magnitsky immediately assumed a pose and began reciting some humorous verses in French which he had composed about various well-known Petersburg people. He was interrupted several times by applause. When the verses were finished, Prince Andrew went up to Speransky and took his leave.

'Where are you off to so early?' asked Speransky.

'I promised to go to a reception.'

They said no more. Prince Andrew looked closely into those mirror-like, impenetrable eyes, and felt that it had been ridiculous of him to have expected anything from Speransky and from any of his own activities connected with him, or ever to have attributed

493

importance to what Speransky was doing. That precise, mirthless laughter rang in Prince Andrew's ears long after he had left the house.

When he reached home Prince Andrew began thinking of his life in Petersburg during those last four months, as if it were something new. He recalled his exertions and solicitations, and the history of his project of army reform, which had been accepted for consideration and which they were trying to pass over in silence simply because another, a very poor one, had already been prepared and submitted to the Emperor. He thought of the meetings of a committee of which Berg was a member. He remembered how carefully and at what length everything relating to form and procedure was discussed at those meetings, and how sedulously and promptly all that related to the gist of the business was evaded. He recalled his labours on the Legal Code, and how painstakingly he had translated the articles of the Roman and French codes into Russian, and he felt ashamed of himself. Then he vividly pictured to himself Bogucharovo, his occupations in the country, his journey to Ryazan, he remembered the peasants, and Dron the village elder, and mentally applying to them the Personal Rights he had divided into paragraphs, he felt astonished that he could have spent so much time on such useless work.

19

NEXT day Prince Andrew called at a few houses he had not visited before, and among them at the Rostovs' with whom he had renewed acquaintance at the ball. Apart from considerations of politeness which demanded the call, he wanted to see that original, eager girl who had left such a pleasant impression on his mind, in her own home.

Natasha was one of the first to meet him. She was wearing a dark-blue house-dress, in which Prince Andrew thought her even prettier than in her ball-dress. She and all the Rostov family welcomed him as an old friend, simply and cordially. The whole family, whom he had formerly judged severely, now seemed to him to consist of excellent, simple, and kindly people. The old count's hospitality and good nature, which struck one especially in Petersburg as a pleasant surprise, were such that Prince Andrew could not refuse to stay to dinner. 'Yes,' he thought, 'they are capital people, who of course have not the slightest idea what a treasure they possess in Natasha; but they are kindly folk and form the best possible setting for this strikingly poetic, charming girl, overflowing with life!'

In Natasha Prince Andrew was conscious of a strange world completely alien to him and brimful of joys unknown to him, a different world that in the Otradnoe avenue and at the window that moonlight night had already begun to disconcert him. Now this world disconcerted him no longer and was no longer alien to him, but he himself, having entered it, found in it a new enjoyment.

After dinner Natasha, at Prince Andrew's request, went to the clavichord and began singing. Prince Andrew stood by a window talking to the ladies and listened to her. In the midst of a phrase he ceased speaking and suddenly felt tears choking him, a thing he had thought impossible for him. He looked at Natasha as she sang, and something new and joyful stirred in his soul. He felt happy and at the same time sad. He had absolutely nothing to weep about yet he was ready to weep. What about? His former love? The little princess? His disillusionments? ... His hopes for the future? ... Yes and no. The chief reason was a sudden, vivid sense of the terrible contrast between something infinitely great and illimitable within him, and that limited and material something that he, and even she, was. This contrast weighed on and yet cheered him while she sang.

As soon as Natasha had finished she went up to him and asked how he liked her voice. She asked this and then became confused, feeling that she ought not to have asked it. He smiled, looking at her, and said he liked her singing as he liked everything she did.

Prince Andrew left the Rostovs' late in the evening. He went to bed from habit, but soon realized that he could not sleep. Having lit his candle he sat up in bed, then got up, then lay down again not at all troubled by his sleeplessness: his soul was as fresh and joyful as if he had stepped out of a stuffy room into God's own fresh air. It did not enter his head that he was in love with Natasha, he was not thinking about her, but only picturing her to himself, and in consequence all life appeared in a new light. 'Why do I strive, why do I toil in this narrow, confined frame, when life, all life with all its joys, is open to me?' said he to himself. And for the first time for a very long while he began making happy plans for the future. He decided that he must attend to his son's education by finding a tutor and putting the boy in his charge, then he ought to retire from the service and go abroad, and see England, Switzerland, and Italy. 'I must use my freedom while I feel so much strength and youth in me,' he said to himself. 'Pierre was right when he said one must believe in the possibility of happiness in order to be happy, and now I do believe in it. Let the dead bury their dead, but while one has life one must live and be happy!' thought he.

20

ONE morning Colonel Adolf Berg, whom Pierre knew as he knew everybody in Moscow and Petersburg, came to see him. Berg arrived in an immaculate brand-new uniform, with his hair pomaded and brushed forward over his temples as the Emperor Alexander wore his hair.

'I have just been to see the countess, your wife. Unfortunately she could not grant my request, but I hope, Count, I shall be more fortunate with you,' he said with a smile.

'What is it you wish, Colonel? I am at your service.'

'I have now quite settled in my new rooms, Count, (Berg said this with perfect conviction that this information could not but be agreeable) 'and so I wish to arrange just a small party for my own and my wife's friends.' (He smiled still more pleasantly.) 'I wished to ask the countess and you to do me the honour of coming to tea and to supper.'

Only Countess Hélène, considering the society of such people as the Bergs beneath her, could be cruel enough to refuse such an invitation. Berg explained so clearly why he wanted to collect at his house a small but select company, and why this would give him pleasure, and why though he grudged spending money on cards or anything harmful, he was prepared to run into some expense for the sake of good society – that Pierre could not refuse, and promised to come.

'But don't be late, Count, if I may venture to ask; about ten minutes to eight, please. We shall make up a rubber. Our general is coming. He is very good to me. We shall have supper, Count. So you will do me the favour.'

Contrary to his habit of being late, Pierre on that day arrived at the Bergs' house, not at ten but at fifteen minutes to eight.

Having prepared everything necessary for the party, the Bergs were ready for their guests' arrival.

In their new, clean, and light study, with its small busts and pictures and new furniture, sat Berg and his wife. Berg, closely buttoned up in his new uniform, sat beside his wife, explaining to her that one always could and should be acquainted with people above one, because only then does one get satisfaction from acquaintances.

'You can get to know something, you can ask for something. See how I managed from my first promotion.' (Berg measured his life not by years but by promotions.) 'My comrades are still nobodies, while I am only waiting for a vacancy to command a regiment, and have the happiness to be your husband.' (He rose and kissed Vera's hand, and on the way to her straightened out a turned-up corner of the carpet.) 'And how have I obtained all this? Chiefly by knowing how to choose my acquaintances. It goes without saying that one must be conscientious and methodical.'

Berg smiled with a sense of his superiority over a weak woman, and paused, reflecting that this dear wife of his was after all but a weak woman who could not understand all that constitutes a man's dignity, what it was *ein Mann zu sein*. Vera at the same time was smiling with a sense of superiority over her good, conscientious husband, who all the same understood life wrongly as, according to Vera, all men did. Berg, judging by his wife, thought all women weak and foolish. Vera, judging only by her husband and generalizing from that observation, supposed that all men, though they understand nothing and are conceited and selfish, ascribe common sense to themselves alone.

Berg rose and embraced his wife carefully, so as not to crush her lace fichu for which he had paid a good price, kissing her straight on the lips.

'The only thing is, we mustn't have children too soon,' he continued, following an unconscious sequence of ideas.

'Yes,' answered Vera, 'I don't at all want that. We must live for society.'

'Princess Yusupova wore one exactly like this,' said Berg, pointing to the fichu with a happy and kindly smile.

Just then Count Bezukhov was announced. Husband and wife glanced at one another, both smiling with self-satisfaction, and each mentally claiming the honour of this visit.

'This is what comes of knowing how to make acquaintances,' thought Berg. 'This is what comes of knowing how to conduct oneself.'

'But please don't interrupt me when I am entertaining the guests,' said Vera, 'because I know what interests each of them and what to say to different people.'

Berg smiled again.

'It can't be helped: men must sometimes have masculine conversation,' said he.

They received Pierre in their small, new drawing-room, where it was impossible to sit down anywhere without disturbing its symmetry, neatness, and order; so it was quite comprehensible and not strange that Berg, having generously offered to disturb the symmetry of an arm-chair or of the sofa for his dear guest, but being apparently painfully undecided on the matter himself, eventually left the visitor to settle the question of selection. Pierre disturbed the symmetry by moving a chair for himself, and Berg and Vera immediately began their evening party, interrupting each other in their efforts to entertain their guest.

Vera, having decided in her own mind that Pierre ought to be entertained with conversation about the French embassy, at once began accordingly. Berg, having decided that masculine conversation was required, interrupted his wife's remarks and touched on the question of the war with Austria, and unconsciously jumped from the general subject to personal considerations as to the proposals made him to take part in the Austrian campaign, and the reasons why he had declined them. Though the conversation was very incoherent and Vera was angry at the intrusion of the masculine element, both husband and wife felt with satisfaction that, even if only one guest was present, their evening had begun very well and was as like as two peas to every other evening party with its talk, tea, and lighted candles.

Before long Boris, Berg's old comrade, arrived. There was a shade of condescension and patronage in his treatment of Berg and Vera. After Boris came a lady with the colonel, then the general himself, then the Rostovs, and the party became unquestionably exactly like all other evening parties. Berg and Vera could not repress their smiles of satisfaction at the sight of all this movement in their drawing-room, at the sound of the disconnected talk, the rustling of dresses, and the bowing and scraping. Everything was just as everybody always has it, especially so the general, who admired the apartment, patted Berg on the shoulder, and with parental authority superintended the setting-out of the table for boston.* The general sat down by Count Ilya Rostov, who was next to himself the most important guest. The old people sat with the old, the young with the young, and the hostess at the tea-table, on which stood exactly the same kind of cakes in a silver cake-basket as the Panins had at their party. Everything was just as it was everywhere else.

21

PIERRE, as one of the principal guests, had to sit down to boston with Count Rostov, the general, and the colonel. At the card-table he happened to be directly facing Natasha, and was struck by a curious change that had come over her since the ball. She was silent, and not only less pretty than at the ball, but only redeemed from plainness by her look of gentle indifference to everything around.

'What's the matter with her?' thought Pierre, glancing at her. She was sitting by her sister at the tea-table, and reluctantly, without looking at him, made some reply to Boris who sat down beside her. After playing out a whole suit and to his partner's delight taking five tricks, Pierre, hearing greetings and the steps of someone who had entered the room while he was picking up his tricks, glanced again at Natasha.

'What has happened to her?' he asked himself with still greater surprise.

Prince Andrew was standing before her, saying something to her with a look of tender solicitude. She having raised her head, was looking up at him, flushed and evidently trying to master her rapid breathing. And the bright glow of some inner fire that had been suppressed was again alight in her. She was completely transformed, and from a plain girl had again become what she had been at the ball.

Prince Andrew went up to Pierre, and the latter noticed a new and youthful expression in his friend's face.

Pierre changed places several times during the game, sitting now with his back to Natasha and now facing her, but during the whole of the six rubbers he watched her and his friend.

'Something very important is happening between them,' thought Pierre, and a feeling that was both joyful and painful agitated him and made him neglect the game.

After six rubbers the general got up, saying that it was no use playing like that, and Pierre was released. Natasha on one side was talking with Sonya and Boris, and Vera with a subtle smile was saying something to Prince Andrew. Pierre went up to his friend, and asking whether they were talking secrets, sat down beside them. Vera having noticed Prince Andrew's attentions to Natasha, decided that at a party, a real evening party, subtle allusions to the tender passion were absolutely necessary, and seizing a moment when Prince Andrew was alone, began a conversation with him about feelings in general and about her sister. With so intellectual a guest as she considered Prince Andrew to be, she felt that she had to employ her diplomatic tact.

When Pierre went up to them he noticed that Vera was being carried away by her self-satisfied talk, but that Prince Andrew seemed embarrassed, a thing that rarely happened with him.

'What do you think?' Vera was saying with an arch smile. 'You are so discerning, Prince, and understand people's characters so well at a glance. What do you think of Natalie? Could she be constant in her attachments? Could she, like other women' (Vera meant herself) 'love a man once for all and remain true to him for ever? That is what I consider true love. What do you think, Prince?'

'I know your sister too little,' replied Prince Andrew, with a sarcastic smile under which he wished to hide his embarrassment, 'to be able to solve so delicate a question, and then I have noticed that the less attractive a woman is the more constant she is likely to be,' he added, and looked up at Pierre who was just approaching them.

'Yes, that is true, Prince. In our days,' continued Vera – mentioning 'our days' as people of limited intelligence are fond of doing, imagining that they have discovered and appraised the peculiarities of 'our days' and that human characteristics change with the times – 'In our days a girl has so much freedom that the pleasure of being courted often stifles real feeling in her. And it must be confessed that Natalie is very susceptible.' This return to the subject of Natalie caused Prince Andrew to knit his brows with discomfort: he was about to rise, but Vera continued with a still more subtle smile:

'I think no one has been more courted than she,' she went on, 'but till quite lately she never cared seriously for anyone. Now you know, Count,' she said to Pierre, 'even our dear cousin Boris, who, between ourselves, was very far gone in the land of tenderness ...' (alluding to a map of love much in vogue at that time).

Prince Andrew frowned and remained silent.

'You are friendly with Boris, aren't you?' asked Vera.

'Yes, I know him ...'

'I expect he has told you of his childish love for Natasha?'

'Oh, there was a childish love?' suddenly asked Prince Andrew, blushing unexpectedly.

'Yes, you know between cousins intimacy often leads to love. *Le cousinage est un dangereux voisinage.* Don't you think so?'

'Oh, undoubtedly!' said Prince Andrew, and with sudden and unnatural liveliness he began chaffing Pierre about the need to be very careful with his fifty-year-old Moscow cousins, and in the midst of these jesting remarks he rose, taking Pierre by the arm, and drew him aside.

'Well?' asked Pierre, seeing his friend's strange animation with surprise, and noticing the glance he turned on Nastasha as he rose.

'I must ... I must have a talk with you,' said Prince Andrew. 'You know that pair of women's gloves?' (He referred to the masonic gloves given to a newly initiated Brother to present to the woman he loved.) 'I ... but no, I will talk to you later on,' and with a strange light in his eyes and restlessness in his movements, Prince Andrew approached Natasha and sat down beside her. Pierre saw how Prince Andrew asked her something and how she flushed as she replied.

But at that moment Berg came to Pierre and began insisting that he should take part in an argument between the general and the colonel on the affairs in Spain.

Berg was satisfied and happy. The smile of pleasure never left his face. The party was very successful and quite like other parties he had seen. Everything was similar: the ladies' subtle talk, the cards, the general raising his voice at the card-table, and the samovar and the tea-cakes; only one thing was lacking that he had always seen at the evening parties he wished to imitate. They had not yet had a loud conversation among the men and a dispute about something important and clever. Now the general had begun such a discussion and so Berg drew Pierre to it.

22

NEXT day, having been invited by the count, Prince Andrew dined with the Rostovs and spent the rest of the day there.

Everyone in the house realized for whose sake Prince Andrew came, and without concealing it he tried to be with Natasha all day. Not only in the soul of the frightened yet happy and enraptured Natasha, but in the whole house, there was a feeling of awe at something important that was bound to happen. The countess looked with sad and sternly serious eyes at Prince Andrew when he talked to Natasha, and timidly started some artificial conversation about trifles as soon as he looked her way. Sonya was afraid to leave Natasha and afraid of being in the way when she was with them. Natasha grew pale, in a panic of expectation, when she remained alone with him for a moment. Prince Andrew surprised her by his timidity. She felt that he wanted to say something to her but could not bring himself to do so.

In the evening, when Prince Andrew had left, the countess went up to Natasha and whispered:

'Well, what?'

'Mamma! For heaven's sake don't ask me anything now! One can't talk about that,' said Natasha.

But all the same that night Natasha, now agitated and now frightened, lay a long time in her mother's bed gazing straight before her. She told her how he had complimented her, how he told her he was going abroad, asked her where they were going to spend the summer, and then how he had asked her about Boris.

'But such a . . . such a . . . never happened to me before!' she said. 'Only I feel afraid in his presence. I am always afraid when I'm with him. What does that mean? Does it mean that it's the real thing? Yes? Mamma, are you asleep?'

'No, my love; I am frightened myself,' answered her mother. 'Now go!'

'All the same I shan't sleep. What silliness, to sleep! Mummy! Mummy! such a thing never happened to me before,' she said, surprised and alarmed at the feeling she was aware of in herself. 'And could we ever have thought! . . .'

It seemed to Natasha that even at the time she first saw Prince Andrew at Otradnoe, she had fallen in love with him. It was as if she feared this strange, unexpected happiness of meeting again the very man she had then chosen (she was firmly convinced she had done so), and of finding him, as it seemed, not indifferent to her.

'And it had to happen that he should come specially to Petersburg while we are here. And it had to happen that we should meet at that ball. It is fate. Clearly it is fate, that everything led up to this! Already *then*, directly I saw him I felt something peculiar.'

'What else did he say to you? What are those verses? Read them, . . .' said her mother, thoughtfully, referring to some verses Prince Andrew had written in Natasha's album.

'Mamma, one need not be ashamed of his being a widower?'

' 'Don't, Natasha! Pray to God. "Marriages are made in heaven",' said her mother.

At that very time Prince Andrew was sitting with Pierre and telling him of his love for Natasha and his firm resolve to make her his wife.

That day Countess Hélène had a reception at her house. The French ambassador was there, and a foreign Prince of the Blood who had of late become a frequent visitor of hers, and many brilliant ladies and gentlemen. Pierre, who had come downstairs, walked through the rooms and struck everyone by his preoccupied, absent-minded and morose air.

Since the ball he had felt the approach of a fit of nervous depression and had made desperate efforts to combat it. Since the intimacy of his wife with the royal prince, Pierre had unexpectedly been made a gentleman of the bedchamber, and from that time he had begun to feel oppressed and ashamed in court society, and dark thoughts of the vanity of all things human came to him oftener than before. At the same time the feeling he had noticed between his protégée Natasha and Prince Andrew accentuated his gloom by the contrast between his own position and his friend's. He tried equally to avoid thinking about his wife, and about Natasha and Prince Andrew; and again everything seemed to him insignificant in comparison with eternity; again the question: For what? presented itself; and he forced himself to work day and night at masonic labours, hoping to drive away the evil spirit that threatened him. Towards midnight, after he had left the countess's apartments, he was sitting upstairs in a shabby dressing-gown, copying out the original transactions of the Scottish Lodge of Freemasons, at a table in his low room cloudy with tobacco smoke, when someone came in. It was Prince Andrew.

'Ah, it's you!' said Pierre with a preoccupied, dissatisfied air. 'And I, you see, am hard at it,' he pointed to his manuscript-book with that air of escaping from the ills of life with which unhappy people look at their work.

Prince Andrew, with a beaming, ecstatic expression of renewed life on his face, paused in front of Pierre and, not noticing his sad look, smiled at him with the egotism of joy.

'Well, dear heart,' said he, 'I wanted to tell you about it yesterday, and I have come to do so to-day. I never experienced anything like it before. I am in love, my friend!'

Suddenly Pierre heaved a deep sigh and dumped his heavy person down on the sofa beside Prince Andrew.

'With Natasha Rostova, yes?' said he.

'Yes, yes! Who else should it be? I should never have believed it, but the feeling is stronger than I. Yesterday I tormented myself and suffered, but I would not exchange even that torment for anything in the world, I have not lived till now. At last I live, but I can't live without her! But can she love me? . . . I am too old for her . . . Why don't you speak?'

'I? I? What did I tell you?' said Pierre suddenly, rising and beginning to pace up and down the room. 'I always thought it . . . That girl is such a treasure . . . she is a rare girl . . . My dear friend, I entreat you, don't philosophize, don't doubt, marry, marry, marry . . . And I am sure there will not be a happier man than you.'

'But what of her?'

'She loves you.'

'Don't talk rubbish, . . .' said Prince Andrew, smiling and looking into Pierre's eyes.

'She does, I know,' Pierre cried fiercely.

'But do listen,' returned Prince Andrew, holding him by the arm. 'Do you know the condition I am in? I must talk about it to someone.'

'Well, go on, go on. I am very glad,' said Pierre, and his face really changed, his brow became smooth, and he listened gladly to Prince Andrew. Prince Andrew seemed, and really was, quite a different, quite a new man. Where was his spleen, his contempt for life, his disillusionment? Pierre was the only person to whom he made up his mind to speak openly; and to him he told all that was in his soul. Now he boldly and lightly made plans for an extended future, said he could not sacrifice his own happiness to his father's caprice, and spoke of how he would either make his father consent to this marriage and love her, or would do without his consent; then he marvelled at the feeling that had mastered him, as at something strange, apart from and independent of himself.

'I should not have believed anyone who told me that I was capable of such love,' said Prince Andrew. 'It is not at all the same feeling that I knew in the past. The whole world is now for me divided into two halves: one half is she, and there all is joy, hope, light; the other half is everything where she is not, and there all is gloom and darkness...'

'Darkness and gloom,' reiterated Pierre; 'yes, yes, I understand that.'

'I cannot help loving the light, it is not my fault. And I am very happy! You understand me? I know you are glad for my sake.'

'Yes, yes,' Pierre assented, looking at his friend with a touched and sad expression in his eyes. The brighter Prince Andrew's lot appeared to him, the gloomier seemed his own.

23

PRINCE ANDREW needed his father's consent to his marriage, and to obtain this he started for the country next day.

His father received his son's communication with external composure, but inward wrath. He could not comprehend how anyone could wish to alter his life or introduce anything new into it, when his own life was already ending. 'If only they would let me end my days as I want to,' thought the old man, 'then they might do as they please.' With his son, however, he employed the diplomacy he reserved for important occasions and, adopting a quiet tone, discussed the whole matter.

In the first place the marriage was not a brilliant one as regards birth, wealth, or rank. Secondly, Prince Andrew was no longer as young as he had been and his health was poor (the old man laid special stress on this), while she was very young. Thirdly, he had a son whom it would be a pity to entrust to a chit of a girl. 'Fourthly and finally,' the father said, looking ironically at his son, 'I beg you to put it off for a year: go abroad, take a cure, look out, as you wanted to, for a German tutor for Prince Nicholas. Then if your love or passion or obstinacy – as you please – is still as great, marry! And that's my last word on it. Mind, the last! . . .' concluded the prince, in a tone which showed that nothing would make him alter his decision.

Prince Andrew saw clearly that the old man hoped that his feelings, or his fiancée's, would not stand a year's test, or that he (the old prince himself) would die before then, and he decided to conform to his father's wish – to propose, and postpone the wedding for a year.

Three weeks after the last evening he had spent with the Rostovs, Prince Andrew returned to Petersburg.

Next day after her talk with her mother Natasha expected Bolkonsky all day, but he did not come. On the second and third day it was the same. Pierre did not come either and Natasha, not knowing that Prince Andrew had gone to see his father, could not explain his absence to herself.

Three weeks passed in this way. Natasha had no desire to go out anywhere, and wandered from room to room like a shadow, idle and listless; she wept secretly at night and did not go to her mother in the evenings. She blushed continually and was irritable. It seemed to her that everybody knew about her disappointment, and was laughing at her and pitying her. Strong as was her inward grief, this wound to her vanity intensified her misery.

Once she came to her mother, tried to say something, and suddenly began to cry. Her tears were those of an offended child who does not know why it is being punished.

The countess began to soothe Natasha, who after first listening to her mother's words, suddenly interrupted her:

'Leave off, mamma! I don't think, and don't want to think about it! He just came and then left off, left off . . .'

Her voice trembled, and she again nearly cried, but recovered and went on quietly:

'And I don't at all want to get married. And I am afraid of him; I have now become quite, quite calm.'

The day after this conversation Natasha put on the old dress which she knew had the peculiar property of conducing to cheerfulness in the mornings, and that day she returned to the old way of life which she had abandoned since the ball. Having finished her morning tea she went to the ball-room, which she particularly liked for its loud resonance, and began singing her solfeggio. When she had finished her first exercise she stood still in the middle of the room and sang a musical phrase that particularly pleased her. She listened joyfully (as though she had not expected it) to the charm of the notes reverberating, filling the whole empty ball-room, and slowly dying away; and all at once she felt cheerful. 'What's the good of making so much of it? Things are nice as it is,' she said to herself, and she began walking up and down the room, not stepping simply on the resounding parquet but treading with each step from the heel to the toe (she had on a new and favourite pair of shoes) and listening to the regular tap of the heel and creak of the toe as gladly as she had to the sounds of her own voice. Passing a mirror she glanced into it. 'There, that's me!' the expression of her face seemed to say as she caught sight of herself. 'Well, and very nice too! I need nobody.'

A footman wanted to come in to clear away something in the room, but she would not let him, and having closed the door behind him continued her walk. That morning she had returned to her favourite mood – love of, and delight in, herself. 'How charming that Natasha is!' she said again, speaking as some third, collective, male person. 'Pretty, a good voice, young, and in nobody's way if only they leave her in peace.' But however much they left her in peace, she could not now be at peace, and immediately felt this.

In the hall the porch-door opened, and someone asked, 'At home?' and then footsteps were heard. Natasha was looking at the mirror, but did not see herself. She listened to the sounds in the hall. When she saw herself, her face was pale. It was *he*. She knew this for certain, though she hardly heard his voice through the closed doors.

Pale and agitated, Natasha ran into the drawing-room.

'Mamma! Bolkonsky has come!' she said. 'Mamma, it is awful, it is unbearable! I don't want ... to be tormented! What am I to do? ...'

Before the countess could answer, Prince Andrew entered the room with an agitated and serious face. As soon as he saw Natasha his face brightened. He kissed the countess's hand and Natasha's, and sat down beside the sofa.

'It is long since we had the pleasure ...' began the countess, but Prince Andrew interrupted her by answering her intended question, obviously in haste to say what he had to.

'I have not been to see you all this time because I have been at my father's. I had to talk over a very important matter with him. I only got back last night,' he said, glancing at Natasha; 'I want to have a talk with you, Countess,' he added after a moment's pause.

The countess lowered her eyes, sighing deeply.

'I am at your disposal,' she murmured.

Natasha knew that she ought to go away, but was unable to do so: something gripped her throat, and regardless of manners she stared straight at Prince Andrew with wide-open eyes.

'At once? This instant!...No, it can't be!' she thought.

Again he glanced at her, and that glance convinced her that she was not mistaken. Yes, at once, that very instant, her fate would be decided.

'Go, Natasha! I will call you,' said the countess in a whisper.

Natasha glanced with frightened imploring eyes at Prince Andrew and at her mother, and went out.

'I have come, Countess, to ask for your daughter's hand,' said Prince Andrew.

The countess's face flushed hotly, but she said nothing.

'Your offer...' she began at last sedately. He remained silent, looking into her eyes. 'Your offer...' (she grew confused) 'is agreeable to us, and...I accept your offer. I am glad. And my husband...I hope...but it will depend on her...'

'I will speak to her when I have your consent...Do you give it to me?' said Prince Andrew.

'Yes,' replied the countess. She held out her hand to him, and with a mixed feeling of estrangement and tenderness pressed her lips to his forehead as he stooped to kiss her hand. She wished to love him as a son, but felt that to her he was a stranger and a terrifying man. 'I am sure my husband will consent,' said the countess, 'but your father...'

'My father, to whom I have told my plans, has made it an express condition of his consent that the wedding is not to take place for a year. And I wished to tell you of that,' said Prince Andrew.

'It is true that Natasha is still young, but – so long as that?...'

'It is unavoidable,' said Prince Andrew with a sigh.

'I will send her to you,' said the countess, and left the room.

'Lord have mercy upon us!' she repeated while seeking her daughter.

Sonya said that Natasha was in her bedroom. Natasha was sitting on the bed, pale and dry-eyed, and was gazing at the icons and whispering something as she rapidly crossed herself. Seeing her mother, she jumped up and flew to her.

'Well, mamma?...Well?...'

'Go, go to him. He is asking for your hand,' said the countess, coldly it seemed to Natasha. 'Go...go,' said the mother, sadly and reproachfully, with a deep sigh, as her daughter ran away.

Natasha never remembered how she entered the drawing-room. When she came in and saw him she paused. 'Is it possible that this stranger has now become *everything* to me?' she asked herself, and immediately answered, 'Yes, everything! He alone is now dearer to me than everything in the world.' Prince Andrew came up to her with downcast eyes.

'I have loved you from the very first moment I saw you. May I hope?'

He looked at her and was struck by the serious impassioned expression of her face. Her face said: 'Why ask? Why doubt what you cannot but know? Why speak, when words cannot express what one feels?'

She drew near to him and stopped. He took her hand and kissed it.

'Do you love me?'

'Yes, yes!' Natasha murmured as if in vexation. Then she sighed loudly and, catching her breath more and more quickly, began to sob.

'What is it? What's the matter?'

'Oh, I am so happy!' she replied, smiled through her tears, bent over closer to him, paused for an instant as if asking herself whether she might, and then kissed him.

Prince Andrew held her hands, looked into her eyes, and did not find in his heart his former love for her. Something in him had suddenly changed; there was no longer the former poetic and mystic charm of desire, but there was pity for her feminine and childish weakness, fear at her devotion and trustfulness, and an oppressive yet joyful sense of the duty that now bound him to her for ever. The present feeling, though not so bright and poetic as the former, was stronger and more serious.

'Did your mother tell you that it cannot be for a year?' asked Prince Andrew, still looking into her eyes.

'Is it possible that I – the "chit of a girl", as everybody called me,' thought Natasha, 'is it possible that I am now to be the *wife* and the equal of this strange, dear, clever man, whom even my father looks up to? Can it be true? Can it be true that there can be no more playing with life, that now I am grown up, that on me now lies a responsibility for my every word and deed? Yes, but what did he ask me?'

'No,' she replied, but she had not understood his question.

'Forgive me!' he said. 'But you are so young, and I have already been through so much in life. I am afraid for you, you do not yet know yourself.'

Natasha listened with concentrated attention, trying but failing to take in the meaning of his words.

'Hard as this year which delays my happiness will be,' continued

508

Prince Andrew, 'it will give you time to be sure of yourself. I ask you to make me happy in a year, but you are free: our engagement shall remain a secret, and should you find that you do not love me, or should you come to love...' said Prince Andrew with an unnatural smile.

'Why do you say that?' Natasha interrupted him. 'You know that from the very day you first came to Otradnoe I have loved you,' she cried, quite convinced that she spoke the truth.

'In a year you will learn to know yourself...'

'A whole year!' Natasha repeated suddenly, only now realizing that the marriage was to be postponed for a year. 'But why a year? Why a year?...'

Prince Andrew began to explain to her the reasons for this delay. Natasha did not hear him.

'And can't it be helped?' she asked. Prince Andrew did not reply, but his face expressed the impossibility of altering that decision.

'It's awful! Oh, it's awful! awful!' Natasha suddenly cried, and again burst into sobs. 'I shall die, waiting a year: it's impossible, it's awful!' She looked into her lover's face and saw in it a look of commiseration and perplexity.

'No, no! I'll do anything!' she said, suddenly checking her tears. 'I am so happy.'

The father and mother came into the room and gave the betrothed couple their blessing.

From that day Prince Andrew began to frequent the Rostovs' as Natasha's affianced lover.

24

No betrothal ceremony took place and Natasha's engagement to Bolkonsky was not announced; Prince Andrew insisted on that. He said that as he was responsible for the delay, he ought to bear the whole burden of it; that he had given his word and bound himself for ever, but that he did not wish to bind Natasha and gave her perfect freedom. If after six months she felt that she did not love him, she would have full right to reject him. Naturally neither Natasha nor her parents wished to hear of this, but Prince Andrew was firm. He came every day to the Rostovs', but did not behave to Natasha as an affianced lover: he did not use the familiar *thou*, but said *you* to her, and kissed only her hand. After their engagement, quite different, intimate, and natural relations sprang up between them. It was as if they had not known each other till now. Both liked to recall how they had regarded each other when as yet they were *nothing* to one another; they felt themselves now quite different beings: then they were artificial, now natural and sincere. At first the family felt some constraint in intercourse with Prince Andrew; he seemed a man from another world, and for a long time Natasha trained the family to get used to him, proudly assuring them all that he only appeared to be different, but was really just like all of them, and that she was not afraid of him and no one else ought to be. After a few days they grew accustomed to him, and without restraint in his presence pursued their usual way of life, in which he took his part. He could talk about rural economy with the count, fashions with the countess and Natasha, and about albums and fancy-work with Sonya. Sometimes the household both among themselves and in his presence expressed their wonder at how it had all happened, and at the evident omens there had been of it: Prince Andrew's coming to Otradnoe and their coming to Petersburg, and the likeness between Natasha and Prince Andrew which her nurse had noticed on his first visit, and Andrew's encounter with Nicholas in 1805, and many other incidents betokening that it had to be.

In the house that poetic dullness and quiet reigned which always accompanies the presence of a betrothed couple. Often when all sitting together everyone kept silent. Sometimes the others would get up and go away and the couple, left alone, still remained silent. They rarely spoke of their future life. Prince Andrew was afraid and ashamed to speak of it. Natasha shared this as she did all his feelings, which she constantly divined. Once she began questioning him about his son. Prince Andrew blushed, as he often did now – Natasha particularly liked it in him – and said that his son would not live with them.

'Why not?' asked Natasha in a frightened tone.

'I cannot take him away from his grandfather, and besides . . .'

'How I should have loved him!' said Natasha, immediately guessing his thought; 'but I know you wish to avoid any pretext for finding fault with us.'

Sometimes the old count would come up, kiss Prince Andrew, and ask his advice about Petya's education or Nicholas's service. The old countess sighed as she looked at them; Sonya was always getting frightened lest she should be in the way, and tried to find excuses for leaving them alone, even when they did not wish it. When Prince Andrew spoke (he could tell a story very well) Natasha listened to him with pride; when she spoke, she noticed with fear and joy that he gazed attentively and scrutinizingly at her. She asked herself in perplexity: 'What does he look for in me? He is trying to discover something by looking at me! What if what he seeks in me is not there?' Sometimes she fell into one of the mad, merry moods characteristic of her, and then she particularly loved to hear and see how Prince Andrew laughed. He seldom laughed, but when he did he abandoned himself entirely to his laughter, and after such a laugh she always felt nearer to him. Natasha would have been completely happy if the thought of the separation awaiting her and drawing near had not terrified her, just as the mere thought of it made him turn pale and cold.

On the eve of his departure from Petersburg Prince Andrew brought with him Pierre, who had not been to the Rostovs' once since the ball. Pierre seemed disconcerted and embarrassed. He was talking to the countess, and Natasha sat down beside a little chess-table with Sonya, thereby inviting Prince Andrew to come too. He did so.

'You have known Bezukhov a long time?' he asked. 'Do you like him?'

'Yes, he's a dear, but very absurd.'

And, as usual when speaking of Pierre, she began to tell anecdotes of his absent-mindedness, some of which had even been invented about him.

'Do you know I have entrusted him with our secret? I have known him from childhood. He has a heart of gold. I beg you, Natalie,' Prince Andrew said with sudden seriousness – 'I am going away, and heaven knows what may happen. You may cease to . . . all right, I know I am not to say that. Only this, then: whatever may happen to you when I am not there . . .'

'What can happen?'

'Whatever trouble may come,' Prince Andrew continued, 'I beg you, Mademoiselle Sophie, whatever may happen, to turn to him alone for advice and help! He is a most absent-minded and absurd fellow, but he has a heart of gold.'

Neither her father, nor her mother, nor Sonya, nor Prince Andrew himself, could have foreseen how the separation from her lover would act on Natasha. Flushed and agitated she went about the house all that day, dry-eyed, occupied with most trivial matters as if not understanding what awaited her. She did not even cry when, on taking leave, he kissed her hand for the last time. 'Don't go!' she said in a tone that made him wonder whether he really ought not to stay and which he remembered long afterwards. Nor did she cry when he was gone; but for several days she sat in her room dry-eyed, taking no interest in anything and only saying now and then, 'Oh, why did he go away?'

But a fortnight after his departure, to the surprise of those around her, she recovered from her mental sickness just as suddenly and

511

became her old self again, but with a change in her moral physiognomy, as a child gets up after a long illness with a changed expression of face.

DURING that year after his son's departure, Prince Nicholas Bolkonsky's health and temper became much worse. He grew still more irritable, and it was Princess Mary who generally bore the brunt of his frequent fits of unprovoked anger. He seemed carefully to seek out her tender spots so as to torture her mentally as harshly as possible. Princess Mary had two passions and consequently two joys – her nephew, little Nicholas, and religion – and these were the favourite subjects of the prince's attacks and ridicule. Whatever was spoken of he would bring round to the superstitiousness of old maids, or the petting and spoiling of children. 'You want to make him' – little Nicholas – 'into an old maid like yourself! A pity! Prince Andrew wants a son and not an old maid,' he would say. Or, turning to Mademoiselle Bourienne, he would ask her in Princess Mary's presence how she liked our village priests and icons, and would joke about them.

He continually hurt Princess Mary's feelings and tormented her, but it cost her no effort to forgive him. Could he be to blame towards her, or could her father, who she knew loved her in spite of it all, be unjust? And what is justice? The princess never thought of that proud word 'justice'. All the complex laws of man centred for her in one clear and simple law – the law of love and self-sacrifice taught us by Him who lovingly suffered for mankind though He Himself was God. What had she to do with the justice or injustice of other people? She had to endure and love, and that she did.

During the winter Prince Andrew had come to Bald Hills, and had been gay, gentle, and more affectionate than Princess Mary had known him for a long time past. She felt that something had happened to him, but he said nothing to her about his love. Before he left he had a long talk with his father about something, and Princess Mary noticed that before his departure they were dissatisfied with one another.

Soon after Prince Andrew had gone, Princess Mary wrote to her friend Julie Karagina in Petersburg, whom she had dreamed (as all girls dream) of marrying to her brother, and who was at that time in mourning for her own brother, killed in Turkey.*

Sorrow, it seems, is our common lot, my dear, tender friend Julie.

Your loss is so terrible that I can only explain it to myself as a special providence of God who, loving you, wishes to try you and your excellent mother. Oh, my friend! Religion, and religion alone, can – I will not say comfort us – but save us from despair. Religion alone can explain to us what without its help man cannot comprehend: why, for what cause, kind and noble beings, able to find happiness in life – not merely harming no one, but necessary to the happiness of others – are called away to God, while cruel, useless, harmful persons, or such as are a burden to themselves and to others, are left living. The first death I saw, and one I shall never forget – that of my dear sister-in-law – left that impression on me. Just as you ask destiny why your splendid brother had to die, so I asked why that angel Lise, who not only never wronged anyone, but in whose soul there were never any unkind thoughts, had to die. And what do you think, dear friend? Five years have passed since then, and already I, with my petty understanding, begin to see clearly why she had to die, and in what way that death was but an expression of the infinite goodness of the Creator, whose every action, though generally incomprehensible to us, is but a manifestation of His infinite love for His creatures. Perhaps, I often think, she was too angelically innocent to have the strength to perform all a mother's duties. As a young wife she was irreproachable; perhaps she could not have been so as a mother. As it is, not only has she left us, and particularly Prince Andrew, with the purest regrets and memories, but probably she will *there* receive a place I dare not hope for myself. But not to speak of her alone, that early and terrible death has had the most beneficent influence on me and on my brother in spite of all our grief. Then, at the moment of our loss, these thoughts could not occur to me; I should then have dismissed them with horror, but now they are very clear and certain. I write all this to you, dear friend, only to convince you of the Gospel truth which has become for me a principle of life: not a single hair of our heads will fall without His will. And His will is governed only by infinite love for us, and so whatever befalls us is for our good.

You ask whether we shall spend next winter in Moscow. In spite of my wish to see you, I do not think so and do not want to do so. You will be surprised to hear that the reason for this is Buonaparte! The case is this: my father's health is growing noticeably worse, he cannot stand any contradiction and is becoming irritable. This irritability is, as you know, chiefly directed to political questions. He cannot endure the notion that Buonaparte is negotiating on equal terms with all the sovereigns of Europe, and particularly with our own, the grandson of the Great Catherine! As you know, I am quite indifferent to politics, but from my father's remarks and his talks with Michael Ivanovich I know all that goes on in the world, and especially about the honours conferred on Buonaparte, who only at Bald Hills in the whole world, it seems, is not accepted as a great man, still less as Emperor of France. And my father cannot stand this. It seems to me that it is chiefly because of his political views that my father is reluctant to speak of going to Moscow; for he foresees the encounters that would result from his way of expressing his views regardless of anybody. All the benefit he might derive from a course of treatment, he would lose as a result of the disputes about Buonaparte which would be inevitable. In any case it will be decided very shortly.

Our family life goes on in the old way except for my brother Andrew's absence. He, as I wrote you before, has changed very much of late. After his sorrow he only this year quite recovered his spirits. He has again become as I used to know him when a child: kind, affectionate, with that heart of gold to which I know no equal. He has realized, it seems to me, that life is not over for him. But together with this mental change he has grown physically much weaker. He has become thinner and more nervous. I am anxious about him and glad he is taking this trip abroad which the doctors recommended long ago. I hope it will cure him. You write that in Petersburg he is spoken of as one of the most active, cultivated, and capable of the young men. Forgive my vanity as a relation, but I never doubted it. The good he has done to everybody here, from his peasants up to the gentry, is incalculable. On his arrival in Petersburg he received only his due. I always wonder at the way rumours fly from Petersburg to Moscow, especially such false ones as that you write about – I mean the report of my brother's betrothal to the little Rostova. I do not think my brother will ever marry again, and certainly not her; and this is why: first, I know that though he rarely speaks about the wife he has lost, the grief of that loss has gone too deep in his heart for him ever to decide to give her a successor and our little angel a step-mother. Secondly because, as far as I know, that girl is not the kind of girl who could please Prince Andrew. I do not think he would choose her for a wife, and frankly I do not wish it. But I am running on too long and am at the end of my second sheet. Good-bye, my dear friend. May God keep you in His holy and mighty care. My dear friend, Mademoiselle Bourienne, sends you kisses.

Mary.

26

IN the middle of the summer Princess Mary received an unexpected letter from Prince Andrew in Switzerland in which he gave her strange and surprising news. He informed her of his engagement to Natasha Rostova. The whole letter breathed loving rapture for his betrothed and tender and confiding affection for his sister. He wrote that he had never loved as he did now, and that only now did he understand and know what life was. He asked his sister to forgive him for not having told her of his resolve when he had last visited Bald Hills, though he had spoken of it to his father. He had not done so for fear Princess Mary should ask her father to give his consent, irritating him and having to bear the brunt of his displeasure without attaining her object.

Besides [he wrote] the matter was not then so definitely settled as it is now. My father then insisted on a delay of a year and now already *six months*, half of that period, has passed, and my resolution is firmer than ever. If the doctors did not keep me here at the spas I should be back in Russia, but as it is I have to postpone my return for three months. You know me and my relations with father. I want nothing from him. I have been and always shall be independent; but to go against his will and arouse his anger, now that he may perhaps remain with us such a short time, would destroy half my happiness. I am now writing to him about the same question, and beg you to choose a good moment to hand him the letter, and to let me know how he looks at the whole matter and whether there is hope that he may consent to reduce the term by four months.

After long hesitations, doubts and prayers, Princess Mary gave the letter to her father. The next day the old prince said to her quietly:

'Write and tell your brother to wait till I am dead ... It won't be long – I shall soon set him free.'

The princess was about to reply, but her father would not let her speak and raising his voice more and more, cried:

'Marry, marry, my boy! ... A good family! ... Clever people, eh? Rich, eh? Yes, a nice step-mother little Nicholas will have! Write and tell him that he may marry to-morrow if he likes. She will be little Nicholas's step-mother and I'll marry Bourienne! ... Ha, ha, ha! He mustn't be without a step-mother either! Only one thing, no more women are wanted in my house – let him marry and live by himself. Perhaps you will go and live with him too?' he added, turning to Princess Mary. 'Go in heaven's name! Go out into the frost ... the frost ... the frost!'

After this outburst the prince did not speak any more about the matter. But repressed vexation at his son's poor-spirited behaviour found expression in his treatment of his daughter. To his former pretexts for irony a fresh one was now added – allusions to stepmothers, and amiabilities to Mademoiselle Bourienne.

'Why shouldn't I marry her?' he asked his daughter. 'She'll make a splendid princess!'

And latterly, to her surprise and bewilderment, Princess Mary noticed that her father was really associating more and more with the Frenchwoman. She wrote to Prince Andrew about the reception of his letter, but comforted him with hopes of reconciling their father to the idea.

Little Nicholas and his education, her brother Andrew, and

religion, were Princess Mary's joys and consolations; but besides that, since everyone must have personal hopes, Princess Mary in the profoundest depths of her heart had a hidden dream and hope that supplied the chief consolation of her life. This comforting dream and hope were given her by *God's folk* – the half-witted and other pilgrims who visited her without the prince's knowledge. The longer she lived, the more experience and observation she had of life, the greater was her wonder at the short-sightedness of men who seek enjoyment and happiness here on earth: toiling, suffering, struggling, and harming one another, to obtain that impossible, visionary, sinful happiness. Prince Andrew had loved his wife, she died, but that was not enough, he wanted to bind his happiness to another woman. Her father objected to this because he wanted a more distinguished and wealthier match for Andrew. And they all struggled and suffered and tormented one another and injured their souls, their eternal souls, for the attainment of benefits which endure but for an instant. Not only do we know this ourselves, but Christ, the Son of God, came down to earth and told us that this life is but for a moment and is a probation; yet we cling to it and think to find happiness in it. 'How is it that no one realizes this?' thought Princess Mary. 'No one except these despised *God's folk* who, wallet on back, come to me by the back door, afraid of being seen by the prince, not for fear of ill-usage by him but for fear of causing him to sin. To leave family, home, and all the cares of worldly welfare, in order without clinging to anything to wander in hempen rags from place to place under an assumed name, doing no one any harm but praying for all – for those who drive one away as well as for those who protect one: higher than that life and truth there is no life or truth!'

There was one pilgrim, a quiet pock-marked little woman of fifty called Theodosia, who for over thirty years had gone about barefoot and worn heavy chains. Princess Mary was particularly fond of her. Once when in a room with a lamp dimly lit before the icon Theodosia was talking of her life, the thought that Theodosia alone had found the true path of life suddenly came to Princess Mary with such force that she resolved to become a pilgrim herself. When Theodosia had gone to sleep Princess Mary thought about this for a long time, and at last made up her mind that, strange as it might seem, she must go on pilgrimage. She disclosed this thought to no one but to her confessor, Father Akinfi, the monk, and he approved of her intention. Under guise of a present for the pilgrims, Princess Mary prepared a pilgrim's complete costume for herself: a coarse smock, bast shoes, a rough coat and a black kerchief. Often, approaching the chest of drawers containing this secret treasure,

Princess Mary paused, uncertain whether the time had not already come to put her project into execution.

Often listening to the pilgrims' tales she was so stimulated by their simple speech, mechanical to them but to her so full of deep meaning, that several times she was on the point of abandoning everything and running away from home. In imagination she already pictured herself by Theodosia's side, dressed in coarse rags, walking with a staff, a wallet on her back, along the dusty road, directing her wanderings from one saint's shrine to another, free from envy, earthly love, or desire, and reaching at last the place where there is no more sorrow or sighing, but eternal joy and bliss.

'I shall come to a place and pray there, and before having time to get used to it or getting to love it, I shall go farther. I will go on till my legs fail, and I'll lie down and die somewhere, and shall at last reach that eternal, quiet haven, where there is neither sorrow nor sighing . . .' thought Princess Mary.

But afterwards, when she saw her father and especially little Koko (Nicholas) her resolve weakened. She wept quietly, and felt that she was a sinner who loved her father and little nephew more than God.

END OF PART THREE

PART FOUR

1

THE Bible legend tells us that the absence of labour – idleness –
was a condition of the first man's blessedness before the Fall. Fallen
man has retained a love of idleness, but the curse weighs on the race
not only because we have to seek our bread in the sweat of our
brows, but because our moral nature is such that we cannot be both
idle and at ease. An inner voice tells us we are in the wrong if we
are idle. If man could find a state in which he felt that though idle
he was fulfilling his duty, he would have found one of the conditions of man's primitive blessedness. And such a state of obligatory and irreproachable idleness is the lot of a whole class – the
military. The chief attraction of military service has consisted and
will consist in this compulsory and irreproachable idleness.

Nicholas Rostov experienced this blissful condition to the full
when after 1807 he continued to serve in the Pavlograd regiment,
in which he already commanded the squadron he had taken over
from Denisov.

Rostov had become a bluff, good-natured fellow, whom his
Moscow acquaintances would have considered rather bad form, but
who was liked and respected by his comrades, subordinates, and
superiors, and was well contented with his life. Of late, in 1809, he
found in letters from home more frequent complaints from his
mother that their affairs were falling into greater and greater disorder, and that it was time for him to come back to gladden and
comfort his old parents.

Reading these letters Nicholas felt a dread of their wanting to
take him away from surroundings in which, protected from all the
entanglements of life, he was living so calmly and quietly. He felt
that sooner or later he would have to re-enter that whirlpool of life,
with its embarrassments and affairs to be straightened out, its
accounts with stewards, quarrels, and intrigues, its ties, society, and
with Sonya's love and his promise to her. It was all dreadfully
difficult and complicated; and he replied to his mother in cold,
formal letters in French, beginning: 'My dear mamma' and ending:
'Your obedient son', which said nothing of when he would return.

In 1810 he received letters from his parents in which they told him of Natasha's engagement to Bolkonsky, and that the wedding would be in a year's time because the old prince made difficulties. This letter grieved and mortified Nicholas. In the first place he was sorry that Natasha, for whom he cared more than for anyone else in the family, should be lost to the home; and secondly, from his hussar point of view, he regretted not to have been there to show that fellow Bolkonsky that connexion with him was no such great honour after all, and that if he loved Natasha he might dispense with permission from his dotard father. For a moment he hesitated whether he should not apply for leave in order to see Natasha before she was married, but then came the manœuvres, and considerations about Sonya and about the confusion of their affairs, and Nicholas again put it off. But in the spring of that year he received a letter from his mother, written without his father's knowledge, and that letter persuaded him to return. She wrote that if he did not come and take matters in hand, their whole property would be sold by auction and they would all have to go begging. The count was so weak, and trusted Mitenka so much, and was so good-natured, that everybody took advantage of him and things were going from bad to worse. 'For God's sake, I implore you, come at once, if you do not wish to make me and the whole family wretched,' wrote the countess.

This letter touched Nicholas. He had that common sense of a matter-of-fact man which showed him what he ought to do.

The right thing now was, if not to retire from the service, at any rate to go home on leave. Why he had to go he did not know; but after his after-dinner nap he gave orders to saddle Mars, an extremely vicious grey stallion that had not been ridden for a long time, and when he returned with the horse all in a lather, he informed Lavrushka (Denisov's servant who had remained with him) and his comrades who turned up in the evening, that he was applying for leave and was going home. Difficult and strange as it was for him to reflect that he would go away without having heard from the staff – and this interested him extremely – whether he was promoted to a captaincy or would receive the Order of St Anne for the last manœuvres; strange as it was to think that he would go away without having sold his three roans to the Polish Count Goluchowski, who was bargaining for the horses Rostov had betted he would sell for two thousand rubles; incomprehensible as it seemed that the ball the hussars were giving in honour of the Polish Mademoiselle Przazdziecka (out of rivalry to the uhlans, who had given one in honour of their Polish Mademoiselle Borzozowska) would take place without him – he knew he must go away from this good, bright world, to somewhere where everything was stupid and confused. A week later he obtained his leave. His hussar comrades – not only those of his own regiment, but the whole brigade – gave Rostov a dinner to which the subscription was fifteen rubles a head, and at which there were two bands and two choirs of singers. Rostov danced the Trepak with Major Basov; the tipsy officers tossed, embraced, and dropped Rostov; the soldiers of the third squadron tossed him too, and shouted 'hurrah!', and then they put him in his sledge and escorted him as far as the first post-station.

During the first half of the journey – from Kremenchug to Kiev – all Rostov's thoughts, as is usual in such cases, were behind him, with the squadron; but when he had gone more than half-way he began to forget his three roans and Dozhoyveyko, his quartermaster, and to wonder anxiously how things would be at Otradnoe and what he would find there. Thoughts of home grew stronger the nearer he approached it – far stronger, as though this feeling of his was subject to the law by which the force of attraction is in inverse proportion to the square of the distance. At the last post-station before Otradnoe he gave the driver a three-ruble tip, and on arriving he ran breathlessly, like a boy, up the steps of his home.

After the rapture of meeting, and after that odd feeling of un-satisfied expectation – the feeling that 'everything is just the same, so why did I hurry?' – Nicholas began to settle down in his old home world. His father and mother were much the same, only a little older. What was new in them was a certain uneasiness and occasional discord, which there used not to be, and which, as Nicholas soon found out, was due to the bad state of their affairs. Sonya was nearly twenty, she had stopped growing prettier and promised nothing more than she was already, but that was enough. She exhaled happiness and love from the time Nicholas returned, and the faithful, unalterable love of this girl had a gladdening effect on him. Petya and Natasha surprised Nicholas most. Petya was a big, handsome boy of thirteen, merry, witty, and mischievous, with a voice that was already breaking. As for Natasha, for a long while Nicholas wondered and laughed whenever he looked at her.

'You're not the same at all,' he said.

'How? Am I uglier?'

'On the contrary, but what dignity! A princess!' he whispered to her.

'Yes, yes, yes!' cried Natasha joyfully.

She told him all about her romance with Prince Andrew and of his visit to Otradnoe, and showed him his last letter.

'Well, are you glad?' Natasha asked. 'I am so tranquil and happy now.'

'Very glad,' answered Nicholas. 'He is an excellent fellow ... And are you very much in love?'

'How shall I put it?' replied Natasha. 'I was in love with Boris, with my teacher, and with Denisov, but this is quite different. I feel at peace and settled. I know that no better man than he exists, and I am calm and contented now. Not at all as before.'

Nicholas expressed his disapproval of the postponement of the marriage for a year; but Natasha attacked her brother with exasperation, proving to him that it could not be otherwise, and that it would be a bad thing to enter a family against the father's will, and that she herself wished it so.

'You don't at all understand,' she said.

Nicholas was silent and agreed with her.

Her brother often wondered as he looked at her. She did not seem at all like a girl in love and parted from her affianced husband. She was even-tempered and calm, and quite as cheerful as of old. This amazed Nicholas and even made him regard Bolkonsky's courtship sceptically. He could not believe that her fate was sealed, especially as he had not seen her with Prince Andrew. It always seemed to him that there was something not quite right about this intended marriage.

'Why this delay? Why no betrothal?' he thought. Once, when he had touched on this topic with his mother, he discovered, to his surprise and somewhat to his satisfaction, that in the depth of her soul she too had doubts about this marriage.

'You see he writes,' said she, showing her son a letter of Prince Andrew's with that latent grudge a mother always has in regard to a daughter's future married happiness, 'he writes that he won't come before December. What can be keeping him? Illness, probably! His health is very delicate. Don't tell Natasha. And don't attach importance to her being so bright: that's because she's living through the last days of her girlhood, but I know what she is like every time we receive a letter from him! However, God grant that everything turns out well!' (she always ended with these words). 'He is an excellent man!'

2

AFTER reaching home Nicholas was at first serious and even dull. He was worried by the impending necessity of interfering in the stupid business matters for which his mother had called him home. To throw off this burden as quickly as possible, on the third day after his arrival he went, angry and scowling and without answering questions as to where he was going, to Mitenka's lodge, and demanded an *account of everything*. But what an *account of everything* might be Nicholas knew even less than the frightened and bewildered Mitenka. The conversation and the examination of the accounts with Mitenka did not last long. The village elder, a peasant delegate, and the village clerk, who were waiting in the passage, heard with fear and delight first the young count's voice roaring and snapping and rising louder and louder, and then words of abuse, dreadful words, ejaculated one after the other.

'Robber! . . . Ungrateful wretch! . . . I'll hack the dog to pieces! I'm not my father! . . . Robbing us! . . .' and so on.

Then with no less fear and delight they saw how the young count, red in the face and with bloodshot eyes, dragged Mitenka out by the scruff of the neck and applied his foot and knee to him behind with great agility at convenient moments between his words, shouting, 'Be off! Never let me see your face here again, you villain!'

Mitenka flew headlong down the six steps and ran away into the shrubbery. (This shrubbery was a well-known haven of refuge for culprits at Otradnoe. Mitenka himself, returning tipsy from the town, used to hide there, and many of the residents at Otradnoe, hiding from Mitenka, knew of its protective qualities.)

Mitenka's wife and sister-in-law thrust their heads and frightened faces out of the door of a room where a bright samovar was boiling and where the steward's high bedstead stood with its patchwork quilt.

The young count paid no heed to them, but breathing hard passed by with resolute strides and went into the house.

The countess, who heard at once from the maids what had happened at the lodge, was calmed by the thought that now their affairs would certainly improve, but on the other hand felt anxious as to the effect this excitement might have on her son. She went several times to his door on tiptoe and listened, as he lighted one pipe after another.

Next day the old count called his son aside and with an embarrassed smile said to him:

'But you know, my dear boy, it's a pity you got excited! Mitenka has told me all about it.'

'I knew,' thought Nicholas, 'that I should never understand anything in this crazy world.'

'You were angry that he had not entered those 700 rubles. But they were carried forward – and you did not look at the other page.'

'Papa, he is a blackguard and a thief! I know he is! And what I have done, I have done; but if you like I won't speak to him again.'

'No, my dear boy' (the count, too, felt embarrassed. He knew he had mismanaged his wife's property and was to blame towards his children, but he did not know how to remedy it). 'No, I beg you to attend to the business. I am old. I . . .'

'No, papa. Forgive me if I have caused you unpleasantness. I understand it all less than you do.'

'Devil take all these peasants, and money matters, and carryings forward from page to page,' he thought. 'I used to understand what a "corner" and the stakes at cards meant, but carrying forward to another page I don't understand at all,' said he to himself, and after that he did not meddle in business affairs. But once the countess called her son and informed him that she had a promissory note from Anna Mikháylovna for two thousand rubles, and asked him what he thought of doing with it.

'This,' answered Nicholas. 'You say it rests with me. Well, I don't like Anna Mikháylovna, and I don't like Borís, but they were our friends and poor. Well then, this!' and he tore up the note, and by so doing caused the old countess to weep tears of joy. After that, young Rostóv took no further part in any business affairs, but devoted himself with passionate enthusiasm to what was to him a new pursuit – the chase – for which his father kept a large establishment.

3

THE weather was already growing wintry, and morning frosts congealed an earth saturated by autumn rains. The verdure had thickened, and its bright green stood out sharply against the brownish strips of winter rye trodden down by the cattle, and against the pale yellow stubble of the spring sowing and the reddish strips of buckwheat. The wooded ravines and the copses, which at the end of August had still been green islands amid black fields and stubble, had become golden and bright-red islands amid the green winter rye. The hares had already half changed their summer coats, the fox-cubs were beginning to scatter, and the young wolves were bigger than dogs. It was the best time of year for the chase. The hounds of that ardent young sportsman Rostóv had not merely reached hard winter condition, but were so jaded that at a meeting of the huntsmen it was decided to give them a three days' rest and then, on the 16th of September, to go on a distant expedition, starting from the oak grove where there was an undisturbed litter of wolf-cubs.

All that day the hounds remained at home. It was frosty and the air was sharp, but towards evening the sky became overcast and it began to thaw. On the 15th, when young Rostov in his dressing-gown looked out of the window, he saw it was an unsurpassable morning for hunting:* it was as if the sky were melting and sinking to the earth without any wind. The only motion in the air was that of the dripping, microscopic particles of drizzling mist. The bare twigs in the garden were hung with transparent drops which fell on the freshly fallen leaves. The earth in the kitchen-garden looked wet and black and glistened like poppy-seed and at a short distance merged into the dull moist veil of mist. Nicholas went out into the wet and muddy porch. There was a smell of decaying leaves and of dog. Milka, a black-spotted broad-haunched bitch with prominent black eyes, got up on seeing her master, stretched her hind legs, lay down like a hare and then suddenly jumped up and licked him right on his nose and moustache. Another borzoi, a dog, catching sight of his master from the garden path, arched his back and rushing headlong towards the porch with lifted tail began rubbing himself against his legs.

'O-hoy!' came at that moment that inimitable huntsman's call which unites the deepest bass with the shrillest tenor, and round the corner came Daniel the head huntsman and head kennel-man, a grey, wrinkled old man with hair cut straight over his forehead, Ukrainian fashion, a long bent whip in his hand, and that look of independence and scorn of everything that is only seen in huntsmen. He doffed his Circassian cap to his master and looked at him scornfully. This scorn was not offensive to his master. Nicholas knew that this Daniel, disdainful of everybody and who considered himself above them, was all the same his serf and huntsman.

'Daniel!' Nicholas said timidly, conscious at the sight of the weather, the hounds, and the huntsman, that he was being carried away by that irresistible passion for sport which makes a man forget all his previous resolutions, as a lover forgets in the presence of his mistress.

'What orders, your Excellency?' said the huntsman in his deep bass, deep as a proto-deacon's and hoarse with hallooing – and two flashing black eyes gazed from under his brows at his master, who was silent. 'Can you resist it?' those eyes seemed to be asking.

'It's a good day, eh? For a hunt and a gallop, eh?' asked Nicholas, scratching Milka behind the ears.

Daniel did not answer, but winked instead.

'I sent Uvarka at dawn to listen,' his bass boomed out after a minute's pause. 'He says *she's moved them* into the Otradnoe enclosure. They were howling there.' (This meant that the she-wolf, about whom they both knew, had moved with her cubs to the Otradnoe copse, a small place two versts from the house.)

'We ought to go, don't you think so?' said Nicholas. 'Come to me with Uvarka.'

'As you please.'

'Then put off feeding them.'

'Yes, sir.'

Five minutes later Daniel and Uvarka were standing in Nicholas's big study. Though Daniel was not a big man, to see him in a room was like seeing a horse or a bear on the floor among the furniture and surroundings of human life. Daniel himself felt this, and as usual stood just inside the door, trying to speak softly and not move, for fear of breaking something in the master's apartment, and he hastened to say all that was necessary so as to get from under that ceiling, out into the open under the sky once more.

Having finished his inquiries and extorted from Daniel an opinion that the hounds were fit (Daniel himself wished to go hunting), Nicholas ordered the horses to be saddled. But just as Daniel was about to go, Natasha came in with rapid steps, not having done up her hair or finished dressing, and with her old nurse's big shawl wrapped round her. Petya ran in at the same time.

'You are going?' asked Natasha. 'I knew you would! Sonya said you wouldn't go, but I knew that to-day is the sort of day when you couldn't help going.'

'Yes, we are going,' replied Nicholas reluctantly, for to-day as he intended to hunt seriously he did not want to take Natasha and Petya. 'We are going, but only wolf-hunting: it would be dull for you.'

'You know it is my greatest pleasure,' said Natasha. 'It's not fair; you are going by yourself, are having the horses saddled, and said nothing to us about it.'

'"No barrier bars a Russian's path" – we'll go!' shouted Petya.

'But you can't. Mamma said you mustn't,' said Nicholas to Natasha.

'Yes, I'll go. I shall certainly go,' said Natasha decisively. 'Daniel, tell them to saddle for us, and Michael must come with my dogs,' she added to the huntsman.

It seemed to Daniel irksome and improper to be in a room at all, but to have anything to do with a young lady seemed to him impossible. He cast down his eyes and hurried out as if it were none of his business, careful as he went not to inflict any accidental injury on the young lady.

4

THE old count, who had always kept up an enormous hunting establishment but had now handed it all completely over to his son's care, being in very good spirits on this 15th of September, prepared to go out with the others.

In an hour's time the whole hunting party was at the porch. Nicholas, with a stern and serious air which showed that now was no time for attending to trifles, went past Natasha and Petya who were trying to tell him something. He had a look at all the details of the hunt, sent a pack of hounds and huntsmen on ahead to find the quarry, mounted his chestnut Donets, and whistling to his own leash of borzois, set off across the threshing-ground to a field leading to the Otradnoe wood. The old count's horse, a sorrel gelding called Viflyanka, was led by the groom in attendance on him, while the count himself was to drive in a small trap straight to a spot reserved for him.

They were taking fifty-four hounds with six hunt-attendants and whippers-in. Besides the family there were eight borzoi kennel-men and more than forty borzois, so that, with the borzois on leash belonging to members of the family, there were about a hundred and thirty dogs and twenty horsemen.

Each dog knew its master and its call. Each man in the hunt knew his business, his place, and what he had to do. As soon as they had passed the fence they all spread out evenly and quietly without noise or talk, along the road and field leading to the Otradnoe covert.

The horses stepped over the field as over a thick carpet, now and then splashing into puddles as they crossed a road. The misty sky still seemed to descend evenly and imperceptibly towards the earth, the air was still, warm, and silent. Occasionally the whistle of a huntsman, the snort of a horse, the crack of a whip, or the whine of a straggling hound, could be heard.

When they had gone about a verst, five more riders with dogs appeared out of the mist, approaching the Rostovs. In front rode a fresh-looking handsome old man with a large grey moustache.

'Good morning, Uncle!' said Nicholas when the old man drew near.

'That's it. Come on!...I was sure of it,' began 'Uncle'. (He was a distant relative of the Rostovs', a man of small means, and their neighbour.) 'I knew you wouldn't be able to resist it and it's a good thing you're going. That's it! Come on!' (This was 'Uncle's'

527

favourite expression.) 'Take the covert at once, for my Girchik says the Ilagins are at Korniki with their hounds. That's it. Come on! . . . They'll take the cubs from under your very nose.'

'That's where I'm going. Shall we join up our packs?' asked Nicholas.

The hounds were joined into one pack, and 'Uncle' and Nicholas rode on side by side. Natasha, muffled up in shawls which did not hide her eager face and shining eyes, galloped up to them. She was followed by Petya who always kept close to her, by Michael a huntsman, and by a groom appointed to look after her. Petya, who was laughing, whipped and pulled at his horse. Natasha sat easily and confidently on her black Arabchick and reined him in without effort with a firm hand.

'Uncle' looked round disapprovingly at Petya and Natasha. He did not like to combine frivolity with the serious business of hunting.

'Good morning, Uncle! We are going too!' shouted Petya.

'Good morning, good morning! But don't go overriding the hounds,' said 'Uncle' sternly.

'Nicholas, what a fine dog Trunila is! He knew me,' said Natasha, referring to her favourite hound.

'In the first place Trunila is not a "dog" but a harrier,' thought Nicholas, and looked sternly at his sister, trying to make her feel the distance that ought to separate them at that moment. Natasha understood it.

'You mustn't think we'll be in anyone's way, Uncle,' she said. 'We'll go to our places and won't budge.'

'A good thing too, little Countess,' said 'Uncle', 'only mind you don't fall off your horse,' he added, 'because – that's it, come on! – you've nothing to hold on to.'

The oasis of the Otradnoe covert came in sight a couple of hundred yards off, the huntsmen were already nearing it. Rostov, having finally settled with 'Uncle' where they should set on the hounds, and having shown Natasha where she was to stand – a spot where nothing could possibly run out – went round above the ravine.

'Well, nephew, you're going for a big wolf,' said 'Uncle'. 'Mind and don't let her slip!'

'That's as may happen,' answered Rostov. 'Karay, here!' he shouted, answering 'Uncle's' remark by this call to his borzoi. Karay was a shaggy old dog with a hanging jowl, famous for having tackled a big wolf unaided. They all took up their places.

The old count, knowing his son's ardour in the hunt, hurried so as not to be late, and the huntsmen had not yet reached their places when Count Ilya Rostov, cheerful, flushed, and with quivering cheeks, drove up with his black horses over the winter rye to the place reserved for him where a wolf might come out. Having straightened his coat and fastened on his hunting-knives and horn, he mounted his good, sleek, well-fed and comfortable horse, Viflyanka, which was turning grey like himself. His horses and trap were sent home. Count Ilya Rostov, though not at heart a keen sportsman, knew the rules of the hunt well, and rode to the bushy edge of the wood where he was to stand, arranged his reins, settled himself in the saddle and, feeling that he was ready, looked about with a smile.

Beside him was Simon Chekmar, his personal attendant, an old horseman now somewhat stiff in the saddle. Chekmar held in leash three formidable wolf-hounds, who had, however, grown fat like their master and his horse. Two wise old dogs lay down unleashed. Some hundred paces farther along the edge of the wood stood Mitka, the count's other groom, a daring horseman and keen rider to hounds. Before the hunt, by old custom, the count had drunk a silver cupful of mulled brandy, taken a snack, and washed it down with half a bottle of his favourite Bordeaux.

He was somewhat flushed with the wine and the drive. His eyes were rather moist and glittered more than usual, and as he sat in his saddle wrapped up in his fur coat he looked like a child taken for an outing.

The thin, hollow-cheeked Chekmar, having got everything ready, kept glancing at his master with whom he had lived on the best of terms for thirty years, and understanding the mood he was in, expected a pleasant chat. A third person rode up circumspectly through the wood (it was plain that he had had a lesson) and stopped behind the count. This person was a grey-bearded old man in a woman's cloak with a tall peaked cap on his head. He was the buffoon, who went by a woman's name, Nastasya Ivanovna.*

'Well, Nastasya Ivanovna!' whispered the count, winking at him. 'If you scare away the beast, Daniel'll give it you!'

'I know a thing or two myself!' said Nastasya Ivanovna.

'Hush!' whispered the count and turned to Simon. 'Have you seen the young countess?' he asked. 'Where is she?'

'With young Count Peter, by the Zharov rank grass,' answered Simon, smiling. 'Though she's a lady she's very fond of hunting.'

'And you're surprised at the way she rides, Simon, eh?' said the count. 'She's as good as many a man!'

'Of course! It's marvellous. So bold, so easy!'

'And Nicholas? Where is he? By the Lyadov upland, isn't he?'

'Yes sir. He knows where to stand. He understands the matter so well that Daniel and I are often quite astounded,' said Simon, well knowing what would please his master.

'Rides well, eh? And how well he looks on his horse, eh?'

'A perfect picture! How he chased a fox out of the rank grass by the Zavarzinsk thicket the other day! Leapt a fearful place; what a sight when they rushed from the covert . . . the horse worth a thousand rubles and the rider beyond all price! Yes, one would have to search far to find another as smart.'

'To search far . . .' repeated the count, evidently sorry Simon had not said more. 'To search far,' he said, turning back the skirt of his coat to get at his snuff-box.

'The other day when he came out from Mass in full uniform, Michael Sidorych . . .' Simon did not finish, for on the still air he had distinctly caught the music of the hunt with only two or three hounds giving tongue. He bent down his head and listened, shaking a warning finger at his master. 'They are on the scent of the cubs . . .' he whispered, 'straight to the Lyadov uplands.'

The count, forgetting to smooth out the smile on his face, looked into the distance straight before him, down the narrow open space, holding the snuff-box in his hand but not taking any. After the cry of the hounds came the deep tones of the wolf-call from Daniel's hunting-horn; the pack joined the first three hounds and they could be heard in full cry, with that peculiar lift in the note that indicates that they are after a wolf. The whippers-in no longer set on the hounds, but changed to the cry of *ulyulyu*, and above the others rose Daniel's voice, now a deep bass, now piercingly shrill. His voice seemed to fill the whole wood and carried far beyond out into the open field.

After listening a few moments in silence the count and his attendant convinced themselves that the hounds had separated into two packs: the sound of the larger pack, eagerly giving tongue, began to die away in the distance, the other pack rushed by the wood past the count, and it was with this that Daniel's voice was heard calling *ulyulyu*. The sounds of both packs mingled and broke apart again, but both were becoming more distant.

Simon sighed and stooped to straighten the leash a young borzoi had entangled, the count too sighed, and noticing the snuff-box in his hand opened it and took a pinch. 'Back!' cried Simon to a borzoi that was pushing forward out of the wood. The count started and dropped the snuff-box. Nastasya Ivanovna dismounted to pick it up. The count and Simon were looking at him.

Then unexpectedly, as often happens, the sounds of the hunt suddenly approached, as if the hounds in full cry and Daniel *ulyulyuing* were just in front of them.

The count turned and saw on his right Mitka, staring at him with eyes starting out of his head, raising his cap and pointing before him to the other side.

'Look out!' he shouted in a voice plainly showing that he had long fretted to utter that word, and letting the borzois slip he galloped towards the count.

The count and Simon galloped out of the wood, and saw on their left a wolf which, softly swaying from side to side was coming at a quiet lope farther to the left to the very place where they were standing. The angry borzois whined, and getting free of the leash rushed past the horses' feet at the wolf.

The wolf paused, turned its heavy forehead towards the dogs awkwardly, like a man suffering from the quinsy, and still slightly swaying from side to side, gave a couple of leaps and with a swish of its tail disappeared into the skirt of the wood. At the same instant, with a cry like a wail, first one hound, then another, and then another, sprang out helter-skelter from the wood opposite and the whole pack rushed across the field towards the very spot where the wolf had disappeared. The hazel bushes parted behind the hounds, and Daniel's chestnut horse appeared, dark with sweat. On its long back sat Daniel, hunched forward, capless, his dishevelled grey hair hanging over his flushed, perspiring face.

'Ulyulyulyu! ulyulyu! . . .' he cried. When he caught sight of the count his eyes flashed lightning.

'Blast you!' he shouted, holding up his whip threateningly at the count.

'You've let the wolf go! . . . What sportsmen!' and as if scorning to say more to the frightened and shamefaced count, he lashed the heaving flanks of his sweating chestnut gelding with all the anger the count had aroused, and flew off after the hounds. The count, like a punished schoolboy, looked round trying by a smile to win Simon's sympathy for his plight. But Simon was no longer there. He was galloping round by the bushes while the field was coming up on both sides, all trying to head the wolf, but it vanished into the wood before they could do so.

5

NICHOLAS ROSTOV meanwhile remained at his post waiting for the wolf. By the way the hunt approached and receded, by the cries of the dogs whose notes were familiar to him, by the way the voices of the huntsmen approached, receded, and rose, he realized what was happening at the copse. He knew that young and old wolves were there, that the hounds had separated into two packs, that somewhere a wolf was being chased, and that something had gone wrong. He expected the wolf to come his way any moment. He made thousands of different conjectures as to where and from what side the beast would come and how he would set upon it. Hope alternated with despair. Several times he addressed a prayer to God that the wolf should come his way. He prayed with that passionate and shamefaced feeling with which men pray at moments of great excitement arising from trivial causes. 'What would it be to Thee to do this for me?' he said to God. 'I know Thou art great, and that it is a sin to ask this of Thee, but for God's sake do let the old wolf come my way and let Karay spring at it – in sight of "Uncle" who is watching from over there – and seize it by the throat in a death-grip!' A thousand times during that half-hour Rostov cast eager and restless glances over the edge of the wood, with the two scraggy oaks rising above the aspen undergrowth and the gully with its water-worn side and 'Uncle's' cap just visible above the bush on his right.

'No, I shan't have such luck,' thought Rostov, 'yet what wouldn't it be worth! It is not to be! Everywhere, at cards and in war, I am always unlucky.' Memories of Austerlitz and of Dolokhov flashed rapidly and clearly through his mind. 'Only once in my life to get an old wolf, I want only that!' thought he, straining eyes and ears and looking to the left and then to the right, and listening to the slightest variation of note in the cries of the dogs.

Again he looked to the right, and saw something running towards him across the deserted field. 'No, it can't be!' thought Rostov taking a deep breath, as a man does at the coming of something long hoped for. The height of happiness was reached – and so simply, without warning, or noise, or display, that Rostov could not believe his eyes and remained in doubt for over a second. The wolf ran forward and jumped heavily over a gully that lay in her path. She was an old animal, with a grey back and big reddish belly. She ran without hurry, evidently feeling sure that no one saw her. Rostov, holding his breath, looked round at the borzois. They stood or lay not seeing the wolf or understanding the situation. Old Karay had turned his head and was angrily searching for fleas, baring his yellow teeth and snapping at his hind legs.

'Ulyulyulyu!' whispered Rostov pouting his lips. The borzois jumped up, jerking the rings of the leashes and pricking their ears. Karay finished scratching his hind quarters, and cocking his ears, got up with quivering tail from which tufts of matted hair hung down.

'Shall I loose them or not?' Nicholas asked himself as the wolf approached him coming from the copse. Suddenly the wolf's whole physiognomy changed; she shuddered, seeing what she had probably never seen before – human eyes fixed upon her, and turning her head a little towards Rostov she paused.

'Back or forward? Eh, no matter, forward...' the wolf seemed to say to herself, and she moved forward without again looking round, and with a quiet, long, easy yet resolute lope.

'*Ulyulyu!*' cried Nicholas in a voice not his own, and of its own accord his good horse darted headlong downhill leaping over gullies to head off the wolf, and the borzois passed it running faster still. Nicholas did not hear his own cry nor feel that he was galloping, nor see the borzois, nor the ground over which he went: he saw only the wolf, who increasing her speed bounded on in the same direction along the hollow. The first to come into view was Milka, with her black markings and powerful quarters, gaining upon the wolf. Nearer and nearer... now she was ahead of it; but the wolf turned its head to face her, and instead of putting on speed as she usually did Milka suddenly raised her tail and stiffened her forelegs.

'*Ulyulyulyulyu!*' shouted Nicholas.

The reddish Lyubim rushed forward from behind Milka, sprang impetuously at the wolf and seized it by its hind quarters, but immediately jumped aside in terror. The wolf crouched, gnashed her teeth, and again rose and bounded forward, followed at the distance of a couple of feet by all the borzois, who did not get any closer to her.

'She'll get away! No, it's impossible!' thought Nicholas, still shouting with a hoarse voice.

'Karay, *ulyulyu!*...' he shouted, looking round for the old borzoi who was now his only hope. Karay, with all the strength age had left him, stretched himself to the utmost, and watching the wolf galloped heavily aside to intercept it. But the quickness of the wolf's lope and the borzoi's slower pace made it plain that Karay had miscalculated. Nicholas could already see not far in front of him the wood, where the wolf would certainly escape should she reach it. But coming towards him he saw hounds and a huntsman galloping almost straight at the wolf. There was still hope. A long yellowish young borzoi, one Nicholas did not know, from another leash, rushed impetuously at the wolf from in front and almost knocked her over. But the wolf jumped up more quickly than anyone could have expected and, gnashing her teeth, flew at the yellowish borzoi, which with a piercing yelp fell with its head on the ground, bleeding from a gash in its side.

'Karay! Old fellow!...' wailed Nicholas.

Thanks to the delay caused by this crossing of the wolf's path, the old dog with its felted hair hanging from its thigh was within five paces of it. As if aware of her danger the wolf turned her eyes on Karay, tucked her tail yet further between her legs, and increased her speed. But here Nicholas only saw that something happened to Karay – the borzoi was suddenly on the wolf, and they rolled together down into a gully just in front of them.

That instant when Nicholas saw the wolf struggling in the gully with the dogs, while from under them could be seen her grey hair and outstretched hind leg and her frightened choking head with ears laid back (Karay was pinning her by the throat), was the happiest moment of his life. With his hand on his saddle-bow he was ready to dismount and stab the wolf, when she suddenly thrust her head up from among that mass of dogs, and then her fore-paws were on the edge of the gully. She clicked her teeth (Karay no longer had her by the throat), leapt with a movement of her hind legs out of the gully, and having disengaged herself from the dogs, with tail tucked in again went forward. Karay, his hair bristling, and probably bruised or wounded, climbed with difficulty out of the gully.

'Oh my God! Why?' Nicholas cried in despair.

'Uncle's' huntsman was galloping from the other side across the wolf's path and his borzois once more stopped the animal's advance. She was again hemmed in.

Nicholas and his attendant, with 'Uncle' and his huntsman, were all riding round the wolf, crying '*ulyulyu!*', shouting and preparing to dismount each moment that the wolf crouched back, and starting forward again every time she shook herself and moved towards the wood where she would be safe.

Already at the beginning of this chase Daniel, hearing the *ulyulyuing*, had rushed out from the wood. He saw Karay seize the wolf, and checked his horse supposing the affair to be over. But when he saw that the horsemen did not dismount and that the wolf shook herself and ran for safety, Daniel set his chestnut galloping not at the wolf but straight towards the wood, just as Karay had run to cut the animal off. As a result of this he galloped up to the wolf just when she had been stopped a second time by 'Uncle's' borzois.

Daniel galloped up silently, holding a naked dagger in his left hand and thrashing the labouring sides of his chestnut horse with his whip as if it were a flail.

Nicholas neither saw nor heard Daniel until the chestnut, breathing heavily, panted past him, and he heard the fall of a body and saw Daniel lying on the wolf's back among the dogs trying to seize her by the ears. It was evident to the dogs, the hunters, and to the wolf herself, that all was now over. The terrified wolf pressed back her ears and tried to rise, but the borzois stuck to her. Daniel rose a little, took a step, and with his whole weight, as if lying down to rest, fell on the wolf, seizing her by the ears. Nicholas was about to stab her, but Daniel whispered, 'Don't, we'll gag her!' and changing his position set his foot on the wolf's neck. A stick was thrust between her jaws and she was fastened with a leash, as if bridled, her legs were bound together, and Daniel rolled her over once or twice from side to side.

With happy, exhausted faces they laid the old wolf, alive, on a shying and snorting horse, and accompanied by the dogs yelping at her, took her to the place where they were all to meet. The hounds had killed two of the cubs and the borzois three. The huntsmen assembled with their booty and their stories, and all came to look at the wolf, which with her broad-browed head hanging down and the bitten stick between her jaws, gazed with great glassy eyes at this crowd of dogs and men surrounding her. When she was touched, she jerked her bound legs and looked wildly yet simply at everybody. Old Count Rostov also rode up and touched the wolf.

'Oh, what a formidable one!' said he. 'A formidable one, eh?' he asked Daniel, who was standing near.

'Yes, your Excellency,' answered Daniel quickly doffing his cap.

The count remembered the wolf he had let slip and his encounter with Daniel.

'Ah, but you are a crusty fellow, friend!' said the count.

For sole reply Daniel gave him a shy, childlike, meek and amiable smile.

6

THE old count went home and Natasha and Petya promised to return very soon, but as it was still early the hunt went farther. At midday they put the hounds into a ravine thickly overgrown with young trees. Nicholas standing in a fallow field could see all his whips.

Facing him lay a field of winter rye, and there his own huntsman stood alone in a hollow behind a hazel bush. The hounds had scarcely been loosed before Nicholas heard one he knew, Voltorn, giving tongue at intervals, other hounds joined in, now pausing and now again giving tongue. A moment later he heard a cry from the wooded ravine that a fox had been found, and the whole pack, joining together, rushed along the ravine towards the rye-field and away from Nicholas.

He saw the whips in their red caps galloping along the edge of the ravine, he even saw the hounds, and was expecting a fox to show itself at any moment on the rye-field opposite.

The huntsman standing in the hollow moved and loosed his borzois, and Nicholas saw a queer, short-legged red fox with a fine brush going hard across the field. The borzois bore down on it . . . Now they drew close to the fox which began to dodge between the field in sharper and sharper curves, trailing its brush, when suddenly a strange white borzoi dashed in followed by a black one, and everything was in confusion; the borzois formed a star-shaped figure, scarcely swaying their bodies and with tails turned away from the centre of the group. Two huntsmen galloped up to the dogs, one in a red cap, the other, a stranger, in a green coat.

'What's this?' thought Nicholas. 'Where's that huntsman from? He is not "Uncle's" man.'

The huntsman got the fox, but stayed there a long time without strapping it to the saddle. Their horses, bridled and with high saddles, stood near them and there too the dogs were lying. The huntsmen waved their arms and did something to the fox. Then from that spot came the sound of a horn, with the signal agreed on in case of a fight.

'That's Ilagin's huntsman having a row with our Ivan,' said Nicholas's groom.

Nicholas sent the man to call Natasha and Petya to him, and rode at a foot-pace to the place where the whips were getting the hounds together. Several of the field galloped to the spot where the fight was going on.

Nicholas dismounted, and with Natasha and Petya who had ridden up, stopped near the hounds, waiting to see how the matter would end. Out of the bushes came the huntsman who had been fighting, and rode towards his young master with the fox tied to his crupper. While still at a distance he took off his cap and tried to speak respectfully, but he was pale and breathless and his face was angry. One of his eyes was black, but he probably was not even aware of it.

'What has happened?' asked Nicholas.

'A likely thing, killing a fox our dogs had hunted! And it was my grey bitch that caught it! Go to law, indeed! . . . He snatches at the fox! I gave him one with the fox. Here it is on my saddle! Do you want a taste of this? . . .' said the huntsman, pointing to his dagger and probably imagining himself still speaking to his foe.

Nicholas, not stopping to talk to the man, asked his sister and Petya to wait for him and rode to the spot where the enemy's, Ilagin's, hunting-party was.

The victorious huntsman rode off to join the field, and there, surrounded by inquiring sympathizers, recounted his exploits.

The facts were that Ilagin, with whom the Rostovs had a quarrel and were at law, hunted over places that belonged by custom to the Rostovs, and had now, as if purposely, sent his men to the very woods the Rostovs were hunting, and let his man snatch a fox their dogs had chased.

Nicholas, though he had never seen Ilagin, with his usual absence of moderation in judgement, hated him cordially from reports of his arbitrariness and violence, and regarded him as his bitterest foe. He rode in angry agitation towards him, firmly grasping his whip and fully prepared to take the most resolute and desperate steps to punish his enemy.

Hardly had he passed an angle of the wood before a stout gentleman in a beaver cap came riding towards him on a handsome raven-black horse, accompanied by two hunt-servants.

Instead of an enemy, Nicholas found in Ilagin a stately and courteous gentleman who was particularly anxious to make the young count's acquaintance. Having ridden up to Nicholas, Ilagin raised his beaver cap and said he much regretted what had occurred and would have the man punished who had allowed himself to seize a fox hunted by someone else's borzois. He hoped to become better acquainted with the count and invited him to draw his covert.

Natasha, afraid that her brother would do something dreadful, had followed him in some excitement. Seeing the enemies exchanging friendly greetings she rode up to them. Ilagin lifted his beaver cap still higher to Natasha, and said with a pleasant smile that the young countess resembled Diana in her passion for the chase as well as in her beauty, of which he had heard much.

To expiate his huntsman's offence Ilagin pressed the Rostovs to come to an upland of his about a verst away which he usually kept for himself and which, he said, swarmed with hares. Nicholas agreed, and the hunt, now doubled, moved on.

The way to Ilagin's upland was across the fields. The hunt-servants fell into line. The masters rode together, 'Uncle', Rostov, and Ilagin, kept stealthily glancing at one another's dogs, trying not to be observed by their companions and searching uneasily for rivals to their own borzois.

Rostov was particularly struck by the beauty of a small, pure bred, red-spotted bitch on Ilagin's leash, slender but with muscles like steel, a delicate muzzle and prominent black eyes. He had heard of the swiftness of Ilagin's borzois, and in that beautiful bitch saw a rival to his own Milka.

In the middle of a sober conversation begun by Ilagin about the year's harvest, Nicholas pointed to the red-spotted bitch.

'A fine little bitch, that!' said he in a careless tone. 'Is she swift?'

'That one? Yes, she's a good dog, gets what she's after,' answered Ilagin indifferently of the red-spotted bitch Erza, for which a year before he had given a neighbour three families of house-serfs. 'So in your parts, too, the harvest is nothing to boast of, Count?' he went on, continuing the conversation they had begun. And considering it polite to return the young count's compliment, Ilagin looked at his borzois and picked out Milka, who attracted his attention by her breadth. 'That black-spotted one of yours is fine – well-shaped!' said he.

'Yes, she's fast enough,' replied Nicholas, and thought: 'If only a full-grown hare would cross the field now, I'd show you what sort of a borzoi she is,' and turning to his groom he said he would give a ruble to anyone who found a hare.

'I don't understand,' continued Ilagin, 'how some sportsmen can be so jealous about game and dogs. For myself, I can tell you, Count, I enjoy riding in company such as this ... what could be better?' (he again raised his cap to Natasha), 'but as for counting skins and what one takes, I don't care about that.'

'Of course not!'

'Or being upset because someone else's borzoi and not mine catches something. All I care about is to enjoy seeing the chase, is it not so, Count? For I consider that ...'

'A-tu!' came the long-drawn cry of one of the borzoi-whippers-in who had halted. He stood on a knoll in the stubble holding his whip aloft, and again repeated his long-drawn cry, 'a-tu!' (This call and the uplifted whip meant that he saw a sitting hare.)

'Ah, he has found one, I think,' said Ilagin carelessly. 'Well, let us course it, Count.'

'Yes, we must ride up ... Shall we both course it?' answered Nicholas, seeing in Erza and 'Uncle's' red Rugay two rivals he had never yet had a chance of pitting against his own borzois. 'And suppose they outdo my Milka at once!' he thought, as he rode with 'Uncle' and Ilagin towards the hare.

'A full-grown one?' asked Ilagin as he approached the whip who had sighted the hare – and not without agitation he looked round and whistled to Erza.

'And you, Michael Nikanorovich?' he said, addressing 'Uncle'.

The latter was riding with a sullen expression on his face.

'How can I join in? Why you've given a village for each of your borzois! That's it, come on! Yours are worth thousands. Try yours against one another, you two, and I'll look on!'

'Rugay, hey, hey!' he shouted. 'Rugayushka!' he added, involuntarily by this diminutive expressing his affection and the hopes he placed on this red borzoi. Natasha saw and felt the agitation the two elderly men and her brother were trying to conceal, and was herself excited by it.

The huntsman stood half-way up the knoll holding up his whip and the gentlefolk rode up to him at a foot-pace; the hounds that were far off on the horizon turned away from the hare, and the whips, but not the gentlefolk, also moved away. All were moving slowly and sedately.

'How is it pointing?' asked Nicholas, riding a hundred paces towards the whip who had sighted the hare.

But before the whip could reply, the hare, scenting the frost coming next morning, was unable to rest and leapt up. The pack on leash rushed downhill in full cry after the hare, and from all sides the borzois that were not on leash darted after the hounds and the hare. All the hunt, who had been moving slowly, shouted 'Stop!', calling in the hounds, while the borzoi-whips, with a cry of 'a-tu!', galloped across the field setting the borzois on the hare. The tranquil Ilagin, Nicholas, Natasha, and 'Uncle', flew, reckless of where or how they went, seeing only the borzois and the hare and fearing only to lose sight even for an instant of the chase. The hare they had started was a strong and swift one. When he jumped up he did not run at once, but pricked his ears listening to the shouting and trampling that resounded from all sides at once. He took a dozen bounds not very quickly, letting the borzois gain on him, and finally, having chosen his direction and realized his danger, laid back his ears and rushed off headlong. He had been lying in the stubble, but in front of him was the autumn-sowing where the ground was soft. The two borzois of the huntsman who had sighted him, having been the nearest, were the first to see and pursue him, but they had not gone far before Ilagin's red-spotted Erza passed them, got within a length, flew at the hare with terrible swiftness aiming at his scut, and thinking she had seized him rolled over like a ball. The hare arched his back and bounded off yet more swiftly. From behind Erza rushed the broad-haunched black-spotted Milka and began rapidly gaining on the hare.

'Milashka, dear!' rose Nicholas's triumphant cry. It looked as if Milka would immediately pounce on the hare, but she overtook him and flew past. The hare had squatted. Again the beautiful Erza reached him, but when close to the hare's scut paused as if measuring the distance so as not to make a mistake this time but seize his hind leg.

'Erza, darling!' Ilagin wailed in a voice unlike his own. Erza did not hearken to his appeal. At the very moment when she would have seized her prey, the hare moved and darted along the balk between the winter rye and the stubble. Again Erza and Milka were abreast, running like a pair of carriage horses, and began to overtake the hare, but it was easier for the hare to run on the balk and the borzois did not overtake him so quickly.

'Rugay, Rugayushka! That's it, come on!' came a third voice just then, and 'Uncle's' red borzoi, straining and curving its back, caught up with the two foremost borzois, pushed ahead of them, regardless of the terrible strain put on speed close to the hare, knocked it off the balk onto the rye-field, again put on speed still more viciously, sinking to his knees in the muddy field, and all one could see was how, muddying his back, he rolled over with the hare. A ring of borzois surrounded him. A moment later everyone had drawn up around the crowd of dogs. Only the delighted 'Uncle' dismounted, and cut off a pad, shaking the hare for the blood to drip off, and anxiously glancing round with restless eyes while his arms and legs twitched. He spoke without himself knowing whom to or what about. 'That's it, come on! That's a dog!... There, it has beaten them all, the thousand-ruble as well as the one-ruble borzois. That's it, come on!' said he, panting and looking wrathfully around as if he were abusing someone, and as if they were all his enemies, had insulted him, and only now had he at last succeeded in justifying himself. 'There are your thousand-ruble ones... That's it, come on!...'

'Rugay, here's a pad for you!' he said, throwing down the hare's muddy pad. 'You've deserved it, that's it, come on!'

'She'd tired herself out, she'd run it down three times by herself,' said Nicholas, also not listening to anyone and regardless of whether he were heard or not.

'But what is there in running across it like that?' said Ilagin's groom.

'Once she had missed it and turned it away, any mongrel could take it,' Ilagin was saying at the same time, breathless from his gallop and his excitement. At the same moment Natasha, without drawing breath, screamed joyously, ecstatically, and so piercingly that it set everyone's ears tingling. By that shriek she expressed what the others expressed by all talking at once, and it was so strange that she must herself have been ashamed of so wild a cry, and everyone else would have been amazed at it, at any other time. 'Uncle' himself twisted up the hare, threw it neatly and smartly across his horse's back as if by that gesture he meant to rebuke everybody, and with an air of not wishing to speak to anyone mounted his bay and rode off. The others all followed dispirited and shamefaced, and only much later were they able to regain their former affectation of indifference. For a long time they continued to look at red Rugay who, his arched back spattered with mud and clanking the ring of his leash, walked along just behind 'Uncle's' horse with the serene air of a conqueror.

'Well, I am like any other dog as long as it's not a question of coursing. But when it is, then look out!' his appearance seemed to Nicholas to be saying.

When, much later, 'Uncle' rode up to Nicholas and began talking to him, he felt flattered that, after what had happened, 'Uncle' deigned to speak to him.

7

TOWARDS evening Ilagin took leave of Nicholas, who found that they were so far from home that he accepted 'Uncle's' offer that the hunting-party should spend the night in his little village of Mikhaylovna.

'And if you put up at my house that will be better still. That's it, come on!' said 'Uncle'. 'You see it's damp weather, and you could rest, and the little countess could be driven home in a trap.'

'Uncle's' offer was accepted. A huntsman was sent to Otradnoe for a trap, while Nicholas rode with Natasha and Petya to 'Uncle's' house.

Some five male domestic serfs, big and little, rushed out to the front porch to meet their master. A score of women serfs old and young, as well as children, popped out from the back entrance to have a look at the hunters who were arriving. The presence of Natasha – a woman, a lady, and on horseback – raised the curiosity of the serfs to such a degree that many of them came up to her, stared her in the face, and unabashed by her presence made remarks about her as though she were some prodigy on show, and not a human being able to hear or understand what was said about her.

'Arinka! Look, she sits sideways! There she sits and her skirt dangles . . . See, she's got a little hunting-horn!'

'Goodness gracious! See her knife? . . .'

'Isn't she a Tartar!'

'How is it you didn't go head over heels?' asked the boldest of all, addressing Natasha directly.

'Uncle' dismounted at the porch of his little wooden house, which stood in the midst of an overgrown garden, and after a glance at his retainers shouted authoritatively that the superfluous ones should take themselves off and that all necessary preparations should be made to receive the guests and the visitors.

The serfs all dispersed. 'Uncle' lifted Natasha off her horse, and taking her hand led her up the rickety wooden steps of the porch. The house with its bare unplastered log-walls was not over-clean – it did not seem that those living in it aimed at keeping it spotless – but neither was it noticeably neglected. In the entry there was a smell of fresh apples, and wolf and fox skins hung about.

'Uncle' led his visitors through the ante-room into a small hall with a folding table and red chairs, then into the drawing-room with a round birch-wood table and a sofa, and finally into his private room, where there was a tattered sofa, a worn carpet, and portraits of Suvorov, of the host's father and mother, and of himself in military uniform. The study smelt strongly of tobacco and dogs. 'Uncle' asked his visitors to sit down and make themselves at home, and then went out of the room. Rugay, his back still muddy, came into the room and lay down on the sofa, cleaning himself with his tongue and teeth. Leading from the study was a passage in which a partition with ragged curtains could be seen. From behind this came women's laughter and whispers. Natasha, Nicholas, and Petya took off their wraps and sat down on the sofa. Petya, leaning on his elbow, fell asleep at once. Natasha and Nicholas were silent. Their faces glowed, they were hungry and very cheerful. They looked at one another (now that the hunt was over and they were in the house, Nicholas no longer considered it necessary to show his manly superiority over his sister), Natasha gave him a wink, and neither refrained long from bursting into a peal of ringing laughter even before they had a pretext ready to account for it.

After a while 'Uncle' came in, in a Cossack coat, blue trousers, and small top-boots. And Natasha felt that this costume, the very one she had regarded with surprise and amusement at Otradnoe, was just the right thing and not at all worse than a swallow-tail or frock coat. 'Uncle' too was in high spirits, and far from being offended by the brother's and sister's laughter (it could never enter his head that they might be laughing at his way of life), he himself joined in their spontaneous merriment.

'That's right, young Countess, that's it, come on! I never saw anyone like her!' said he, offering Nicholas a pipe with a long stem and with a practised motion of three fingers taking down another that had been cut short. 'She's ridden all day like a man, and is as fresh as ever!'

Soon after 'Uncle's' reappearance the door was opened, evidently from the sound by a bare-footed girl, and a stout, rosy, good-looking woman of about forty, with a double chin and full red lips, entered carrying a large loaded tray. With hospitable dignity and cordiality in her glance and in every motion, she looked at the visitors and, with a pleasant smile, bowed respectfully. In spite of her exceptional stoutness, which caused her to protrude her chest and stomach and throw back her head, this woman (who was 'Uncle's' housekeeper) trod very lightly. She went to the table, set down the tray, and with her plump white hands deftly took from it the bottles and various hors-d'œuvre and dishes, and arranged them on the table. When she had finished, she stepped aside and stopped at the door with a smile on her face. 'Here I am. I am she! Now do you understand "Uncle"?' her expression said to Rostov. How could one help understanding? Not only Nicholas but even Natasha understood the meaning of his puckered brow and the happy complacent smile that slightly puckered his lips when Anisya Fëdorovna entered. On the tray was a bottle of herb-wine, different kinds of vodka, pickled mushrooms, rye-cakes made with buttermilk, honey in the comb, still mead and sparkling mead, apples, nuts (raw and roasted), and nut-and-honey sweets. Afterwards she brought a freshly roasted chicken, ham, preserves made with honey, and preserves made with sugar.

All this was the fruit of Anisya Fëdorovna's housekeeping, gathered and prepared by her. The smell and taste of it all had a smack of Anisya Fëdorovna herself; a savour of juiciness, cleanliness, whiteness, and pleasant smiles.

'Take this, little Lady-Countess!' she kept saying, as she offered Natasha first one thing and then another.

Natasha ate of everything and thought she had never seen or eaten such buttermilk-cakes, such aromatic jam, such honey-and-nut sweets, or such a chicken anywhere. Anisya Fëdorovna left the room.

After supper over their cherry brandy Rostov and 'Uncle' talked of past and future hunts, of Rugay and Ilagin's dogs, while Natasha sat upright on the sofa and listened with sparkling eyes. She tried several times to wake Petya that he might eat something, but he only muttered incoherent words without waking up. Natasha felt so light-hearted and happy in these novel surroundings that she only feared the trap would come for her too soon. After a casual pause such as often occurs when receiving friends for the first time in one's own house, 'Uncle', answering a thought that was in his visitors' minds, said:

'This, you see, is how I am finishing my days ... Death will come. That's it, come on! Nothing will remain. Then why harm anyone?'

'Uncle's' face was very significant and even handsome as he said this. Involuntarily Rostov recalled all the good he had heard about him from his father and the neighbours. Throughout the whole province 'Uncle' had the reputation of being the most honourable and disinterested of cranks. They called him in to decide family disputes, chose him as executor, confided secrets to him, elected him to be a justice and to other posts; but he always persistently refused public appointments, passing the autumn and spring in the fields on his bay gelding, sitting at home in winter, and lying in his overgrown garden in summer.

'Why don't you enter the service, Uncle?'

'I did once, but gave it up. I am not fit for it. That's it, come on! I can't make head or tail of it. That's for you – I haven't brains enough. Now hunting is another matter – that's it, come on! Open the door, there!' he shouted. 'Why have you shut it?'

The door at the end of the passage led to the huntsmen's room, as they called the room for the hunt-servants.

There was a rapid patter of bare feet, and an unseen hand opened the door into the huntsmen's room, from which came the clear sounds of a balalayka, on which someone who was evidently a master of the art was playing. Natasha had been listening to those strains for some time and now went out into the passage to hear better.

'That's Mitka, my coachman ... I have got him a good balalayka. I'm fond of it,' said 'Uncle'.

It was the custom for Mitka to play the balalayka in the huntsmen's room when 'Uncle' returned from the chase. 'Uncle' was fond of such music.

'How good! Really very good!' said Nicholas with some unintentional superciliousness, as if ashamed to confess that the sounds pleased him very much.

'Very good?' said Natasha reproachfully, noticing her brother's tone. 'Not "very good" – it's simply delicious!'

Just as 'Uncle's' pickled mushrooms, honey, and cherry brandy had seemed to her the best in the world, so also that song, at that moment, seemed to her the acme of musical delight.

'More, please, more!' cried Natasha at the door as soon as the balalayka ceased. Mitka tuned up afresh, and recommenced thrumming the balalayka to the air of *My Lady*, with trills and variations. 'Uncle' sat listening, slightly smiling with his head on one side. The air was repeated a hundred times. The balalayka was retuned several times and the same notes were thrummed again, but the listeners did not grow weary of it and wished to hear it again and again. Anisya Fëdorovna came in and leaned her portly person against the door-post.

'You like listening?' she said to Natasha, with a smile extremely like 'Uncle's'. 'That's a good player of ours,' she added.

'He doesn't play that part right!' said 'Uncle' suddenly, with an energetic gesture. 'Here he ought to burst out – that's it, come on! – ought to burst out.'

'Do you play then?' asked Natasha.

'Uncle' did not answer, but smiled.

'Anisya, go and see if the strings of my guitar are all right. I haven't touched it for a long time. That's it – come on! I've given it up.'

Anisya Fëdorovna with her light step willingly went to fulfil her errand, and brought back the guitar.

Without looking at anyone, 'Uncle' blew the dust off it, and tapping the case with his bony fingers tuned the guitar and settled himself in his arm-chair. He took the guitar a little above the finger-board, arching his left elbow with a somewhat theatrical gesture, and with a wink at Anisya Fëdorovna struck a single chord, pure and sonorous, and then quietly, smoothly, and confidently began playing in very slow time not *My Lady*, but the well-known song *Came a maiden down the street*. The tune played with precision and in exact time began to thrill in the hearts of Nicholas and Natasha, arousing in them the same kind of sober mirth as radiated from Anisya Fëdorovna's whole being. Anisya Fëdorovna flushed, and drawing her kerchief over her face went laughing out of the room. 'Uncle' continued to play correctly, carefully, with energetic firmness, looking with a changed and inspired expression at the spot where Anisya Fëdorovna had just stood. Something seemed to be laughing a little on one side of his face under his grey moustaches, especially as the song grew brisker and the time quicker, and when, here and there, as he ran his fingers over the strings, something seemed to snap.

'Lovely, lovely! Go on, Uncle, go on!' shouted Natasha as soon as he had finished. She jumped up and hugged and kissed him. 'Nicholas, Nicholas!' she said, turning to her brother, as if asking him: 'What is it moves me so?'

Nicholas too was greatly pleased by 'Uncle's' playing, and 'Uncle' played the piece over again. Anisya Fëdorovna's smiling face re-appeared in the doorway and behind hers other faces . . .

> *Fetching water clear and sweet,*
> *Stop, dear maiden, I entreat –*

played 'Uncle' once more, running his fingers skilfully over the strings, and then he stopped short and jerked his shoulders.

'Go on, Uncle dear,' Natasha wailed in an imploring tone as if her life depended on it.

'Uncle' rose, and it was as if there were two men in him: one of them smiled seriously at the merry fellow, while the merry fellow struck a naïve and precise attitude preparatory to a folk-dance.

'Now then, niece!' he exclaimed, waving to Natasha the hand that had just struck a chord.

Natasha threw off the shawl from her shoulders, ran forward to face 'Uncle', and setting her arms akimbo, also made a motion with her shoulders and struck an attitude.

Where, how, and when had this young countess, educated by an *émigrée* French governess, imbibed from the Russian air she breathed that spirit, and obtained that manner which the *pas de châle** would, one would have supposed, long ago have effaced? But the spirit and the movements were those inimitable and unteachable Russian ones that 'Uncle' had expected of her. As soon as she had struck her pose and smiled triumphantly, proudly, and with sly merriment, the fear that had at first seized Nicholas and the others that she might not do the right thing was at an end, and they were already admiring her.

She did the right thing with such precision, such complete precision, that Anisya Fëdorovna, who had at once handed her the handkerchief she needed for the dance, had tears in her eyes, though she laughed as she watched this slim, graceful countess, reared in silks and velvets and so different from herself, who yet was able to understand all that was in Anisya and in Anisya's father and mother and aunt, and in every Russian man and woman.

'Well, little Countess; that's it - come on!' cried 'Uncle' with a joyous laugh, having finished the dance. 'Well done, niece! Now a fine young fellow must be found as husband for you. That's it - come on!'

'He's chosen already,' said Nicholas smiling.

'Oh?' said 'Uncle' in surprise, looking inquiringly at Natasha, who nodded her head with a happy smile.

'And such a one!' she said. But as soon as she had said it a new train of thoughts and feelings arose in her. 'What did Nicholas's smile mean when he said "chosen already"? Is he glad of it or not? It is as if he thought my Bolkonsky would not approve of or understand our gaiety. But he would understand it all. Where is he now?' she thought, and her face suddenly became serious. But this lasted only a second. 'Don't dare to think about it,' she said to herself, and sat down again smilingly beside 'Uncle', begging him to play something more.

'Uncle' played another song and a valse; then after a pause he cleared his throat, and sang his favourite hunting song:

> As 'twas growing dark last night
> Fell the snow so soft and light...

'Uncle' sang as peasants sing, with full and naïve conviction that the whole meaning of a song lies in the words, and that the tune comes of itself, and that apart from the words there is no tune, which exists only to give measure to the words. As a result of this the unconsidered tune, like the song of a bird, was extraordinarily good. Natasha was in ecstasies over 'Uncle's' singing. She resolved to give up learning the harp, and to play only the guitar. She asked 'Uncle' for his guitar and at once found the chords of the song.

After nine o'clock two traps and three mounted men, who had been sent to look for them, arrived to fetch Natasha and Petya. The count and countess did not know where they were and were very anxious, said one of the men.

Petya was carried out like a log and laid in the larger of the two traps. Natasha and Nicholas got into the other. 'Uncle' wrapped Natasha up warmly, and took leave of her with quite a new tenderness. He accompanied them on foot as far as a bridge that could not be crossed, so that they had to go round by the ford, and he sent huntsmen to ride in front with lanterns.

'Good-bye, dear niece,' his voice called out of the darkness – not the voice Natasha had known previously, but the one that had sung *As 'twas growing dark last night.*

In the village through which they passed there were red lights and a cheerful smell of smoke.

'What a darling "Uncle" is!' said Natasha, when they had come out onto the high road.

'Yes,' returned Nicholas. 'You're not cold?'

'No. I'm quite, quite all right. I feel so comfortable!' answered Natasha, almost perplexed by her feelings. They remained silent a long while. The night was dark and damp. They could not see the horses, but only heard them splashing through the unseen mud.

What was passing in that receptive childlike soul that so eagerly caught and assimilated all the diverse impressions of life? How did they all find place in her? But she was very happy. As they were nearing home she suddenly struck up the air of *As 't was growing dark last night* – the tune of which she had all the way been trying to get, and had at last caught.

'Got it?' said Nicholas.

'What were you thinking about just now, Nicholas?' inquired Natasha.

They were fond of asking one another that question.

'I?' said Nicholas, trying to remember. 'Well, you see, first I thought that Rugay, the red hound, was like "Uncle", and that if he were a man he would always keep "Uncle" near him, if not for his riding then for his manner. What a good fellow "Uncle" is! Don't you think so? Well, and you?'

'I?' Wait a bit, wait. Yes, first I thought that we are driving along and imagining that we are going home, but that heaven knows where we are really going in the darkness, and that we shall arrive and suddenly find that we are not in Otradnoe but in Fairyland. And then I thought . . . No, nothing else.'

'I know, I expect you thought of him,' said Nicholas, smiling as Natasha knew by the sound of his voice.

'No,' said Natasha, though she had in reality been thinking about Prince Andrew at the same time as of the rest, and of how he would have liked 'Uncle'. 'And then I was saying to myself all the way, "How well Anisya carried herself, how well!"' And Nicholas heard her spontaneous, happy, ringing laughter. 'And do you know,' she suddenly said, 'I know that I shall never again be as happy and tranquil as I am now.'

'Rubbish, nonsense, humbug!' exclaimed Nicholas, and he thought: 'How charming this Natasha of mine is! I have no other friend like her, and never shall have. Why should she marry? We might always drive about together!'

'What a darling this Nicholas of mine is!' thought Natasha.

'Ah, there are still lights in the drawing-room!' she said, pointing to the windows of the house that gleamed invitingly in the moist velvety darkness of the night.

8

Count Ilya Rostov had resigned the position of Marshal of the Nobility because it involved him in too much expense, but still his affairs did not improve. Natasha and Nicholas often noticed their parents conferring together anxiously and privately, and heard suggestions of selling the fine ancestral house and estate near Moscow. It was not necessary to entertain so freely as when the count had been Marshal, and life at Otradnoe was quieter than in former years, but still the enormous house and its lodges were full of people, and more than twenty sat down to table every day. These were all their own people who had settled down in the house almost as members of the family, or persons who were, it seemed, obliged to live in the count's house. Such were Dimmler the musician* and his wife, Vogel the dancing-master and his family, Belova, an old maiden lady, an inmate of the house, and many others such as Petya's tutors, the girls' former governess, and other people who simply found it preferable and more advantageous to live in the count's house than at home. They had not as many visitors as before, but the old habits of life, without which the count and countess could not conceive of existence, remained unchanged. There was still the hunting establishment which Nicholas had even enlarged, the same fifty horses and fifteen grooms in the stables, the same expensive presents and dinner-parties to the whole district on name-days; there were still the count's games of whist and boston, at which – spreading out his cards so that everyone could see them – he let himself be plundered of hundreds of rubles every day by neighbours, who looked upon an opportunity to play a rubber with Count Rostov as a most profitable source of income.

The count moved in his affairs as in a huge net, trying not to believe that he was entangled but becoming more and more so at every step, and feeling too feeble to break the meshes or to set to work carefully and patiently to disentangle them. The countess with her loving heart felt that her children were being ruined, that it was not the count's fault, for he could not help being what he was – that (though he tried to hide it) he himself suffered from the consciousness of his own and his children's ruin, and she tried to find means of remedying the position. From her feminine point of view she could see only one solution, namely, for Nicholas to marry a rich heiress. She felt this to be their last hope, and that if Nicholas refused the match she had found for him, she would have to abandon the hope of ever getting matters right. This match was with Julie Karagina, the daughter of excellent and virtuous parents, a girl the Rostovs had known from childhood, and who had now become a wealthy heiress through the death of the last of her brothers.

The countess had written direct to Julie's mother in Moscow, suggesting a marriage between their children, and had received a favourable answer from her. Karagina had replied that for her part she was agreeable, and everything would depend on her daughter's inclination. She invited Nicholas to come to Moscow.

Several times the countess, with tears in her eyes, told her son that now that both her daughters were settled her only wish was to see him married. She said she could lie down in her grave peacefully if that were accomplished. Then she told him that she knew of a splendid girl, and tried to discover what he thought about marriage.

At other times she praised Julie to him, and advised him to go to Moscow during the holidays to amuse himself. Nicholas guessed what his mother's remarks were leading to, and during one of these conversations induced her to speak quite frankly. She told him that her only hope of getting their affairs disentangled, now lay in his marrying Julie Karagina.

'But, mamma, suppose I loved a girl who has no fortune, would you expect me to sacrifice my feelings and my honour for the sake of money?' he asked his mother, not realizing the cruelty of his question and only wishing to show his noble-mindedness.

'No, you have not understood me,' said his mother, not knowing how to justify herself. 'You have not understood me, Nikolenka. It is your happiness I wish for,' she added, feeling that she was telling an untruth and was becoming entangled. She began to cry.

'Mamma, don't cry. Only tell me that you wish it, and you know I will give my life, anything, to put you at ease,' said Nicholas. 'I would sacrifice anything for you – even my feelings.'

But the countess did not want the question put like that: she did not want a sacrifice from her son, she herself wished to make a sacrifice for him.

'No, you have not understood me, don't let us talk about it,' she replied, wiping away her tears.

'Maybe I do love a poor girl,' said Nicholas to himself. 'Am I to sacrifice my feelings and my honour for money? I wonder how mamma could speak so to me. Because Sonya is poor I must not love her,' he thought, 'must not respond to her faithful, devoted love? Yet I should certainly be happier with her than with some doll-like Julie. I can always sacrifice my feelings for my family's welfare,' he said to himself, 'but I can't coerce my feelings. If I love Sonya, that feeling is for me stronger and higher than all else.'

Nicholas did not go to Moscow, and the countess did not renew the conversation with him about marriage. She saw with sorrow, and sometimes with exasperation, symptoms of a growing attachment between her son and the portionless Sonya. Though she blamed herself for it, she could not refrain from grumbling at and worrying Sonya, often pulling her up without reason, addressing her stiffly as 'my dear', and using the formal 'you' instead of the intimate 'thou' in speaking to her. The kind-hearted countess was the more vexed with Sonya because that poor, dark-eyed niece of hers was so meek, so kind, so devotedly grateful to her benefactors, and so faithfully, unchangingly and unselfishly in love with Nicholas, that there were no grounds for finding fault with her.

Nicholas was spending the last of his leave at home. A fourth letter had come from Prince Andrew, from Rome, in which he wrote that he would have been on his way back to Russia long ago had not his wound unexpectedly reopened in the warm climate, which obliged him to defer his return till the beginning of the new year. Natasha was still as much in love with her betrothed, found the same comfort in that love, and was still as ready to throw herself into all the pleasures of life as before; but at the end of the fourth month of their separation she began to have fits of depression which she could not master. She felt sorry for herself; sorry that she was being wasted all this time, and of no use to anyone – while she felt herself so capable of loving and being loved.

Things were not cheerful in the Rostovs' home.

9

CHRISTMAS came, and except for the ceremonial Mass, the solemn and wearisome Christmas congratulations from neighbours and servants, and the new dresses everyone put on, there were no special festivities, though the calm frost of twenty degrees Réaumur,* the dazzling sunshine by day, and the starlight of the winter nights, seemed to call for some special celebration of the season.

On the third day of Christmas week, after the midday dinner all the inmates of the house dispersed to various rooms. It was the dullest time of the day. Nicholas, who had been visiting some neighbours that morning, was asleep on the sitting-room sofa. The old count was resting in his study. Sonya sat in the drawing-room at the round table, copying a design for embroidery. The countess was playing patience. Nastasya Ivanovna, the buffoon, sat with a sad face at the window with two old ladies. Natasha came into the room, went up to Sonya, glanced at what she was doing, and then went up to her mother and stood without speaking.

'Why are you wandering about like an outcast?' asked her mother. 'What do you want?'

'Him . . . I want him . . . now, this minute! I want him!' said Natasha, with glittering eyes and no sign of a smile.

The countess lifted her head and looked attentively at her daughter.

'Don't look at me, mamma! Don't look; I shall cry directly.'

'Sit down with me a little,' said the countess.

'Mamma, I want him. Why should I be wasted like this, mamma?'

Her voice broke, tears gushed from her eyes, and she turned quickly to hide them and left the room.

She passed into the sitting-room, stood there thinking awhile, and then went into the maids' room. There an old maid-servant was grumbling at a young girl who stood panting, having just run in through the cold from the serfs' quarters.

'Stop playing – there's a time for everything,' said the old woman.

'Let her alone, Kondratevna,' said Natasha. 'Go, Mavrusha, go.'

Having released Mavrusha, Natasha crossed the dancing-hall and went to the vestibule. There an old footman and two young ones were playing cards. They broke off and rose as she entered.

'What can I do with them?' thought Natasha.

'Oh, Nikita, please go ... where can I send him? ... Yes, go to the yard and fetch a fowl, please, a cock, and you, Misha, bring me some oats.'*

'Just a few oats?' said Misha cheerfully and readily.

'Go, go quickly,' the old man urged him.

'And you, Theodore, get me a piece of chalk.'

On her way past the butler's pantry she told them to set a samovar, though it was not at all the time for tea.

Foka, the butler, was the most ill-tempered person in the house. Natasha liked to test her power over him. He distrusted the order and asked whether the samovar was really wanted.

'Oh dear, what a young lady!' said Foka, pretending to frown at Natasha.

No one in the house sent people about or gave them as much trouble as Natasha did. She could not see people unconcernedly, but had to send them on some errand. She seemed to be trying whether any of them would get angry or sulky with her; but the serfs fulfilled no one's orders so readily as they did hers. 'What can I do, where can I go?' thought she, as she went slowly along the passage.

'Nastasya Ivanovna, what sort of children shall I have?' she asked the buffoon, who was coming towards her in a woman's jacket.

'Why, fleas, crickets, grasshoppers,' answered the buffoon.

'O Lord, O Lord, it's always the same! Oh, where am I to go? What am I to do with myself?' And tapping with her heels she ran quickly upstairs to see Vogel and his wife who lived on the upper storey.

Two governesses were sitting with the Vogels at a table on which were plates of raisins, walnuts, and almonds. The governesses were discussing whether it was cheaper to live in Moscow or Odessa. Natasha sat down, listened to their talk with a serious and thoughtful air, and then got up again.

'The island of Madagascar,' she said, 'Ma-da-gas-car,' she repeated, articulating each syllable distinctly, and, not replying to Madame Schoss who asked what she was saying, she went out of the room.

Her brother Petya was upstairs too; with the man in attendance on him he was preparing fireworks to let off that night.

'Petya! Petya!' she called to him. 'Carry me downstairs.'

Petya ran up and offered her his back. She jumped on it putting her arms round his neck, and he pranced along with her.

'No don't ... the island of Madagascar!' she said, and jumping off his back she went downstairs.

Having as it were reviewed her kingdom, tested her power, and made sure that everyone was submissive, but that all the same it was dull, Natasha betook herself to the ball-room, picked up her guitar, sat down in a dark corner behind a bookcase and began to run her fingers over the strings in the bass, picking out a passage she recalled from an opera she had heard in Petersburg with Prince Andrew. What she drew from the guitar would have had no meaning for other listeners, but in her imagination a whole series of reminiscences arose from those sounds. She sat behind the bookcase with her eyes fixed on a streak of light escaping from the pantry door, and listened to herself and pondered. She was in a mood for brooding on the past.

Sonya passed to the pantry with a glass in her hand. Natasha glanced at her and at the crack in the pantry door, and it seemed to her that she remembered the light falling through that crack once before and Sonya passing with a glass in her hand. 'Yes, it was exactly the same,' thought Natasha.

'Sonya, what is this?' she cried, twanging a thick string.

'Oh, you are there!' said Sonya with a start, and came near and listened. 'I don't know. A storm?' she ventured timidly, afraid of being wrong.

'There! That's just how she started and just how she came up smiling timidly when all this happened before,' thought Natasha, 'and in just the same way I thought there was something lacking in her.'

'No, it's the chorus from the *Water-Carrier*, listen!' and Natasha sang the air of the chorus so that Sonya should catch it. 'Where were you going?' she asked.

'To change the water in this glass. I am just finishing the design.'

'You always find something to do, but I can't,' said Natasha. 'And where's Nicholas?'

'Asleep, I think.'

'Sonya, go and wake him,' said Natasha. 'Tell him I want him to come and sing.'

She sat awhile, wondering what the meaning of it all having happened before could be, and without solving this problem, or at all regretting not having done so, she again passed in fancy to the time when she was with *him* and he was looking at her with a lover's eyes.

'Oh, if only he would come quicker! I am so afraid it will never be! And worst of all, I am growing old – that's the thing! There won't then be in me what there is now. But perhaps he'll come to-day, will come immediately. Perhaps he has come and is sitting in the drawing-room. Perhaps he came yesterday and I have forgotten it.' She rose, put down the guitar, and went to the drawing-room.

All the domestic circle, tutors, governesses, and guests, were already at the tea-table. The servants stood round the table – but Prince Andrew was not there and life was going on as before.

'Ah, here she is!' said the old count when he saw Natasha enter. 'Well, sit down by me.' But Natasha stayed by her mother and glanced round as if looking for something.

'Mamma!' she muttered, 'give him to me, give him, mamma, quickly, quickly!' and she again had difficulty in repressing her sobs.

She sat down at the table and listened to the conversation between the elders and Nicholas, who had also come to the table. 'My God, my God! The same faces, the same talk, papa holding his cup and blowing in the same way!' thought Natasha, feeling with horror a sense of repulsion rising up in her for the whole household because they were always the same.

After tea Nicholas, Sonya, and Natasha went to the sitting-room, to their favourite corner where their most intimate talks always began.

10

'DOES it ever happen to you,' said Natasha to her brother when they had settled down in the sitting-room, 'does it ever happen to you to feel as if there were nothing more to come – nothing; that everything good is past? And to feel not exactly dull, but sad?'

'I should think so!' he replied. 'I have felt like that when everything was all right and everyone was cheerful. The thought has come into my mind that I was already tired of it all, and that we must all die. Once in the regiment I had not gone to some merry-making where there was music ... and suddenly I felt so depressed ...'

'Oh yes, I know, I know!' Natasha interrupted him. 'When I was quite little that used to be so with me. Do you remember when I was punished once about some plums? You were all dancing, and I sat sobbing in the school-room? I shall never forget it: I felt sad and sorry for everyone, for myself, and for everyone.

And I was innocent – that was the chief thing,' said Natasha. 'Do you remember?'

'I remember,' answered Nicholas. 'I remember that I came to you afterwards and wanted to comfort you but, do you know, I felt ashamed to. We were terribly absurd. I had a funny doll then and wanted to give it you. Do you remember?'

'And do you remember,' Natasha asked with a pensive smile, 'how once, long long ago, when we were quite little, uncle called us into the study – that was in the old house – and it was dark – we went in and suddenly there stood . . .'

'A negro,' chimed in Nicholas with a smile of delight. 'Of course I remember. Even now I don't know whether there really was a negro, or if we only dreamt it or were told about him.'

'He was grey, you remember, and had white teeth, and stood and looked at us . . .'

'Sonya, do you remember?' asked Nicholas.

'Yes, yes, I do remember something too,' Sonya answered timidly.

'You know I have asked papa and mamma about that negro,' said Natasha, 'and they say there was no negro at all. But you see, you remember!'

'Of course I do, I remember his teeth as if I had just seen them.'

'How strange it is! It's as if it were a dream! I like that.'

'And do you remember how we rolled hard-boiled eggs in the ball-room, and suddenly two old women began spinning round on the carpet? Was that real or not? Do you remember what fun it was?'

'Yes, and you remember how papa in his blue overcoat fired a gun in the porch?'

So they went through their memories, smiling with pleasure: not the sad memories of old age, but poetic, youthful ones – those impressions of one's most distant past in which dreams and realities blend – and they laughed with quiet enjoyment.

Sonya, as always, did not quite keep pace with them, though they shared the same reminiscences.

Much that they remembered had slipped from her mind, and what she recalled did not arouse the same poetic feeling as they experienced. She simply enjoyed their pleasure and tried to fit in with it.

She only really took part when they recalled Sonya's first arrival. She told them how afraid she had been of Nicholas because he had on a corded jacket, and her nurse had told her that she, too, would be sewn up with cords.

'And I remember their telling me that you had been born under a cabbage,' said Natasha, 'and I remember that I dared not disbelieve it then, but knew it was not true, and I felt so uncomfortable.'

While they were talking a maid thrust her head in at the other door of the sitting-room.

'They have brought the cock, Miss,' she said in a whisper.

'It isn't wanted, Polya. Tell them to take it away,' replied Natasha.

In the middle of their talk in the sitting-room, Dimmler came in and went up to the harp that stood there in a corner. He took off its cloth covering, and the harp gave out a jarring sound.

'Mr Dimmler, please play my favourite nocturne by Field,'* came the old countess's voice from the drawing-room.

Dimmler struck a chord, and turning to Natasha, Nicholas and Sonya, remarked: 'How quiet you young people are!'

'Yes, we're philosophizing,' said Natasha, glancing round for a moment and then continuing the conversation. They were now discussing dreams.

Dimmler began to play, Natasha went on tiptoe noiselessly to the table, took up a candle, carried it out and returned, seating herself quietly in her former place. It was dark in the room, especially where they were sitting on the sofa, but through the big windows the silvery light of the full moon fell on the floor. Dimmler had finished the piece but still sat softly running his fingers over the strings, evidently uncertain whether to stop or to play something else.

'Do you know,' said Natasha in a whisper, moving closer to Nicholas and Sonya, 'that when one goes on and on recalling memories, one at last begins to remember what happened before one was in the world . . .'

'That is metempsychosis,' said Sonya, who had always learned well, and remembered everything. 'The Egyptians believed that our souls have lived in animals, and will go back into animals again.'

'No, I don't believe we ever were in animals,' said Natasha, still in a whisper though the music had ceased. 'But I am certain that we were angels somewhere *there*, and have been here, and that is why we remember . . .'

'May I join you?' said Dimmler who had come up quietly, and he sat down by them.

'If we have been angels, why have we fallen lower?' said Nicholas. 'No, that can't be!'

'Not lower, who said we were lower? . . . How do I know what I was before?' Natasha rejoined with conviction. 'The soul is immortal – well then, if I shall always live I must have lived before, lived for a whole eternity.'

'Yes, but it is hard for us to imagine eternity,' remarked Dimmler, who had joined the young folk with a mildly condescending smile but now spoke as quietly and seriously as they.

'Why is it hard to imagine eternity?' said Natasha. 'It is now to-day, and it will be to-morrow, and always; and there was yesterday, and the day before ...'

'Natasha! Now it's your turn. Sing me something,' they heard the countess say. 'Why are you sitting there like conspirators?'

'Mamma, I don't at all want to,' replied Natasha, but all the same she rose.

None of them, not even the middle-aged Dimmler, wanted to break off their conversation and quit that corner in the sitting-room, but Natasha got up and Nicholas sat down at the clavichord. Standing as usual in the middle of the hall, and choosing the place where the resonance was best, Natasha began to sing her mother's favourite song.

She had said she did not want to sing, but it was long since she had sung, and long before she again sang as she did that evening. The count, from his study where he was talking to Mitenka, heard her, and like a schoolboy in a hurry to run out to play, blundered in his talk while giving orders to the steward, and at last stopped, while Mitenka stood in front of him, also listening and smiling. Nicholas did not take his eyes off his sister and drew breath in time with her. Sonya, as she listened, thought of the immense difference there was between herself and her friend, and how impossible it was for her to be anything like as bewitching as her cousin. The old countess sat with a blissful yet sad smile and with tears in her eyes, occasionally shaking her head. She thought of Natasha and of her own youth, and of how there was something unnatural and dreadful in this impending marriage of Natasha and Prince Andrew.

Dimmler, who had seated himself beside the countess, listened with closed eyes.

'Ah, Countess,' he said at last, 'that's a European talent, she has nothing to learn – what softness, tenderness, and strength ...'

'Ah, how afraid I am for her, how afraid I am!' said the countess, not realizing to whom she was speaking. Her maternal instinct told her that Natasha had too much of something, and that because of this she would not be happy. Before Natasha had finished singing, fourteen-year-old Petya rushed in delightedly to say that some mummers had arrived.

Natasha stopped abruptly.

'Idiot!' she screamed at her brother and running to a chair threw herself on it sobbing so violently that she could not stop for a long time.

557

'It's nothing, mamma, really it's nothing; only Petya startled me,' she said trying to smile, but her tears still flowed and sobs still choked her.

The mummers (some of the house-serfs), dressed up as bears, Turks, inn-keepers, and ladies – frightening and funny – bringing in with them the cold from outside and a feeling of gaiety, crowded, at first timidly, in the ante-room, then hiding behind one another they pushed into the ball-room where, shyly at first and then more and more merrily and heartily, they started singing, dancing, and playing Christmas games. The countess, when she had identified them and laughed at their costumes, went into the drawing-room. The count sat in the ball-room smiling radiantly and applauding the players. The young people had disappeared.

Half an hour later there appeared among the other mummers in the ball-room an old lady in a hooped skirt – this was Nicholas. A Turkish girl was Petya. A clown was Dimmler. An hussar was Natasha, and a Circassian was Sonya with burnt-cork moustache and eyebrows.

After the condescending surprise, non-recognition, and praise, of those who were not themselves dressed up, the young people decided that their costumes were so good that they ought to be shown elsewhere.

Nicholas, who as the roads were in splendid condition wanted to take them all for a drive in his troyka, proposed to take with them about a dozen of the serf-mummers and drive to 'Uncle's'.

'No, why disturb the old fellow?' said the countess, 'besides, you wouldn't have room to turn round there. If you must go, go to the Melyukovs'.'

Melyukova was a widow, who with her family and their tutors and governesses lived three miles from the Rostovs.

'That's right, my dear,' chimed in the old count, thoroughly aroused. I'll dress up at once and go with them. I'll make Pashette open her eyes.'

But the countess would not agree to his going; he had had a bad leg all these days. It was decided that the count must not go, but that if Louisa Ivanovna (Madame Schoss) would go with them, the young ladies might go to the Melyukovs', Sonya, generally so timid and shy, begging Louisa Ivanovna not to refuse more urgently than anyone.

Sonya's costume was the best of all. Her moustache and eyebrows were extraordinarily becoming. Everyone told her she looked very handsome, and she was in a spirited and energetic mood unusual with her. Some inner voice told her that now or never her fate would be decided, and in her male attire she seemed quite a different person. Louisa Ivanovna consented to go, and in half an hour four troyka-sledges with large and small bells, their runners squeaking and whistling over the frozen snow, drove up to the porch.

Natasha was foremost in setting a merry holiday tone, which passing from one to another grew stronger and stronger and reached its climax when they all came out into the frost and got into the sledges, talking, calling to one another, laughing and shouting.

Two of the troykas were the usual household sledges, the third was the old count's with a trotter from the Orlov stud as shaft-horse, the fourth was Nicholas's own with a short shaggy black shaft-horse. Nicholas, in his old lady's dress, over which he had belted his hussar overcoat, stood in the middle of the sledge reins in hand.

It was so light that he could see the moonlight reflected from the metal harness disks and from the eyes of the horses, who looked round in alarm at the noisy party under the shadow of the porch-roof.

Natasha, Sonya, Madame Schoss and two maids got into Nicholas's sledge, Dimmler, his wife, and Petya into the old count's, and the rest of the mummers seated themselves in the other two sledges.

'You go ahead, Zakhar!' shouted Nicholas to his father's coach-man, wishing for a chance to race past him.

The old count's troyka, with Dimmler and his party, started forward squeaking on its runners as though freezing to the snow, its deep-toned bell clanging. The side-horses, pressing against the shafts of the middle horse, sank in the snow which was dry and glittered like sugar, and threw it up.

Nicholas set off following the first sledge: behind him the others moved noisily, their runners squeaking. At first they drove at a steady trot along the narrow road. While they drove past the garden, the shadows of the bare trees fell across the road and hid the brilliant moonlight, but as soon as they were past the fence, the snowy plain, bathed in moonlight and motionless, spread out before them glittering like diamonds and dappled with bluish shadows. *Bang, bang!* went the first sledge over a cradle-hole in the snow of the road, and each of the other sledges jolted in the same way, and rudely breaking the frost-bound stillness the troykas began to speed along the road one after the other.

'A hare's track, a lot of tracks!' rang out Natasha's voice through the frost-bound air.

'How light it is, Nicholas!' came Sonya's voice.

Nicholas glanced round at Sonya, and bent down to see her

face closer. Quite a new, sweet face with black eyebrows and moustaches peeped up at him from her sable furs – so close and yet so distant – in the moonlight.

'That used to be Sonya,' thought he, and looked at her closer and smiled.

'What is it, Nicholas?'

'Nothing,' said he and turned again to the horses.

When they came out onto the beaten high road – polished by sledge-runners and cut up by rough-shod hoofs, the marks of which were visible in the moonlight – the horses began to tug at the reins of their own accord and increased their pace. The near side-horse, arching his head and breaking into a short canter, tugged at his traces. The shaft-horse swayed from side to side moving his ears as if asking: 'Isn't it time to begin now?' In front, already far ahead, the deep bell of the sledge ringing farther and farther off, the black horses driven by Zakhar could be clearly seen against the white snow. From that sledge one could hear the shouts, laughter, and voices of the mummers.

'Gee up, my darlings!' shouted Nicholas pulling the reins to one side and flourishing the whip.

It was only by the keener wind that met them and the jerks given by the side-horses who pulled harder – ever increasing their gallop – that one noticed how fast the troyka was flying. Nicholas looked back. With screams, squeals, and waving of whips, that caused even the shaft-horses to gallop – the other sledges followed. The shaft-horse swung steadily beneath the bow over its head, with no thought of slackening pace and ready to put on speed when required.

Nicholas overtook the first sledge. They were driving down hill and coming out upon a broad trodden track across a meadow near a river.

'Where are we?' thought he. 'It's the Kosoy meadow, I suppose. But no – this is something new I've never seen before. This isn't the Kosoy meadow, nor the Dëmkin hill, and heaven only knows what it is! It is something new and enchanted. Well, whatever it may be . . .' And shouting to his horses he began to pass the first troyka.

Zakhar held back his horses and turned his face, which was already covered with hoar-frost to his eyebrows.

Nicholas gave the horses the rein, and Zakhar, stretching out his arms, clucked his tongue and let his horses go.

'Now, look out, Master!' he cried.

Faster still the two troykas flew, side by side, and faster moved the feet of the galloping side-horses. Nicholas began to draw ahead. Zakhar, while still keeping his arms extended, raised one hand with the reins.

'No you won't, Master!' he shouted.

Nicholas put all his horses to a gallop and passed Zakhar. The horses showered the fine dry snow on the faces of those in the sledge – beside them sounded quick ringing bells and they caught confused glimpses of swiftly moving legs and the shadows of the troyka they were passing. The whistling sound of the runners on the snow and the voices of girls shrieking, were heard from different sides.

Again checking his horses, Nicholas looked around him. They were still surrounded by the magic plain bathed in moonlight and spangled with stars.

'Zakhar is shouting that I should turn to the left, but why to the left?' thought Nicholas. 'Are we getting to the Melyukovs'? Is this Melyukovka? Heaven only knows where we are going, and heaven knows what is happening to us – but it is very strange and pleasant whatever it is.' And he looked round in the sledge.

'Look, his moustache and eyelashes are all white!' said one of the strange, pretty, unfamiliar people – the one with fine eyebrows and moustache.

'I think this used to be Natasha,' thought Nicholas, 'and that was Madame Schoss, but perhaps it's not, and this Circassian with the moustache I don't know, but I love her.'

'Aren't you cold?' he asked.

They did not answer but began to laugh. Dimmler from the sledge behind shouted something – probably something funny – but they could not make out what he said.

'Yes, yes!' some voices answered, laughing.

'But here was a fairy forest with black moving shadows, and a glitter of diamonds and a flight of marble steps and the silver roofs of fairy buildings and the shrill yells of some animals. And if this is really Melyukovka it is still stranger that we drove heaven knows where and have come to Melyukovka,' thought Nicholas.

It really was Melyukovka, and maids and footmen with merry faces came running out to the porch, carrying candles.

'Who is it?' asked someone in the porch.

'The mummers from the count's. I know by the horses,' replied some voices.

11

PELAGEYA Danilovna Melyukova, a broadly built, energetic woman wearing spectacles, sat in the drawing-room in a loose dress surrounded by her daughters whom she was trying to keep from feeling dull. They were quietly dropping melted wax into snow and looking at the shadows the wax figures would throw on the wall, when they heard the steps and voices of new arrivals in the vestibule.

Hussars, ladies, witches, clowns and bears, after clearing their throats and wiping the hoar-frost from their faces in the vestibule, came into the ball-room where candles were hurriedly lighted. The clown – Dimmler – and the lady – Nicholas – started a dance. Surrounded by the screaming children the mummers, covering their faces and disguising their voices, bowed to their hostess and arranged themselves about the room.

'Dear me! there's no recognizing them! And Natasha! See whom she looks like! She really reminds me of somebody. But Herr Dimmler – isn't he good! I didn't know him! And how he dances. Dear me, there's a Circassian. Really how becoming it is to dear Sonya. And who is that? Well you have cheered us up! Nikita and Vanya – clear away the tables! And we were sitting so quietly. Ha, ha, ha!... The hussar, the hussar! Just like a boy! And the legs!... I can't look at him...' different voices were saying.

Natasha, the young Melyukovs' favourite, disappeared with them into the back rooms where a cork, and various dressing-gowns and male garments were called for, and received from the footman by bare girlish arms from behind the door. Ten minutes later all the young Melyukovs joined the mummers.

Pelageya Danilovna, having given orders to clear the rooms for the visitors, and arranged about refreshments for the gentry and the serfs, went about among the mummers without removing her spectacles, peering into their faces with a suppressed smile and failing to recognize any of them. It was not merely Dimmler and the Rostovs she failed to recognize, she did not even recognize her own daughters, or her late husband's dressing-gowns and uniforms, which they had put on.

'And who is this?' she asked her governess, peering into the face of her own daughter dressed up as a Kazan-Tartar. 'I suppose it is one of the Rostovs! Well, Mr Hussar, and what regiment do you serve in?' she asked Natasha. 'Here, hand some fruit-jelly to the Turk!' she ordered the butler who was handing things round. 'That's not forbidden by his law.'

Sometimes, as she looked at the strange but amusing capers cut by the dancers, who – having decided once for all that being disguised no one would recognize them – were not at all shy, Pelageya Danilovna hid her face in her handkerchief, and her whole stout body shook with irrepressible, kindly, elderly laughter.

'My little Sasha! Look at Sasha!' she said.

After Russian country-dances and chorus-dances, Pelageya Danilovna made the serfs and gentry join in one large circle: a ring, a string, and a silver ruble were fetched, and they all played games together.

In an hour all the costumes were crumpled and disordered. The corked eyebrows and moustaches were smeared over the perspiring, flushed, and merry faces. Pelageya Danilovna began to recognize the mummers, admired their cleverly contrived costumes, and particularly how they suited the young ladies, and she thanked them all for having entertained her so well. The visitors were invited to supper in the drawing-room, and the serfs had something served to them in the ball-room.

'Now to tell one's fortune in the empty bath-house is frightening!' said an old maid who lived with the Melyukovs, during supper.

'Why?' asked the eldest Melyukov girl.

'You wouldn't go, it takes courage . . .'

'I'll go,' said Sonya.

'Tell what happened to the young lady!' said the second Melyukov girl.

'Well,' began the old maid, 'a young lady once went out, took a cock, laid the table for two, all properly, and sat down. After sitting a while, she suddenly hears someone coming . . . a sledge drives up with harness bells; she hears him coming! He comes in, just in the shape of a man, like an officer – comes in and sits down to table with her.'

'Ah! ah!' screamed Natasha, rolling her eyes with horror.

'Yes? And how . . . did he speak?'

'Yes, like a man. Everything quite all right, and he began persuading her; and she should have kept him talking till cock-crow, but she got frightened, just got frightened and hid her face in her hands. Then he caught her up. It was lucky the maids ran in just then . . .'

'Now, why frighten them?' said Pelageya Danilovna.

'Mamma, you used to try your fate yourself . . .' said her daughter.

'And how does one do it in a barn?' inquired Sonya.

'Well, say you went to the barn now, and listened. It depends on what you hear; hammering and knocking – that's bad; but a sound of shifting grain is good, and one sometimes hears that, too.'

'Mamma, tells us what happened to you in the barn.'

Pelageya Danilovna smiled.

'Oh, I've forgotten . . .' she replied. 'But none of you would go?'

'Yes, I will, Pelageya Danilovna, let me! I'll go,' said Sonya.

'Well why not, if you're not afraid?'

'Louisa Ivanovna, may I?' asked Sonya.

Whether they were playing the ring and string game, or the ruble game, or talking as now, Nicholas did not leave Sonya's side, and gazed at her with quite new eyes. It seemed to him that it was only to-day, thanks to that burnt-cork moustache, that he had fully learnt to know her. And really that evening Sonya was brighter, more animated, and prettier, than Nicholas had ever seen her before.

'So that's what she is like; what a fool I have been!' he thought, gazing at her sparkling eyes, and under the moustache a happy, rapturous smile dimpled her cheeks, a smile he had never seen before.

'I'm not afraid of anything,' said Sonya. 'May I go at once?' She got up.

They told her where the barn was and how she should stand silent and listen, and they handed her a fur cloak. She threw this over her head and shoulders and glanced at Nicholas.

'What a darling that girl is!' thought he. 'And what have I been thinking of till now?'

Sonya went out into the passage to go to the barn. Nicholas went hastily to the front porch, saying he felt too hot. The crowd of people really had made the house stuffy.

Outside there was the same cold stillness, and the same moon, but even brighter than before. The light was so strong and the snow sparkled with so many stars, that one did not wish to look up at the sky and the real stars were unnoticed. The sky was black and dreary, while the earth was gay.

'I am a fool, a fool! what have I been waiting for?' thought Nicholas, and running out from the porch he went round the corner of the house and along the path that led to the back porch. He knew Sonya would pass that way. Half-way lay some snow-covered piles of firewood, and across and along them a network of shadows from the bare old lime trees fell on the snow and on the path. This path led to the barn. The log walls of the barn and its snow-covered roof, that looked as if hewn out of some precious stone, sparkled in the moonlight. A tree in the garden snapped with the frost, and then all was again perfectly silent. His bosom seemed to inhale not air, but the strength of eternal youth and gladness.

From the back porch came the sound of feet descending the steps, the bottom step, upon which snow had fallen, gave a ringing creak and he heard the voice of an old maidservant saying, 'Straight, straight along the path, Miss. Only don't look back.'

'I am not afraid,' answered Sonya's voice, and along the path towards Nicholas came the crunching, whistling sound of Sonya's feet in her thin shoes.

Sonya came along wrapped in her cloak. She was only a couple of paces away when she saw him, and to her too he was not the Nicholas she had known and always slightly feared. He was in a woman's dress, with tousled hair and a happy smile new to Sonya. She ran rapidly towards him.

'Quite different and yet the same,' thought Nicholas looking at her face all lit up by the moonlight. He slipped his arms under the cloak that covered her head, embraced her, pressed her to him, and kissed her on the lips that wore a moustache and had a smell of burnt cork. Sonya kissed him full on the lips, and disengaging her little hands, pressed them to his cheeks.

'Sonya!' ... 'Nicholas!' ... was all they said. They ran to the barn and then back again, re-entering, he by the front and she by the back porch.

12

WHEN they all drove back from Pelageya Danilovna's, Natasha, who always saw and noticed everything, arranged that she and Madame Schoss should go back in the sledge with Dimmler, and Sonya with Nicholas and the maids.

On the way back Nicholas drove at a steady pace instead of racing, and kept peering by that fantastic all-transforming light into Sonya's face and searching beneath the eyebrows and moustache for his former and his present Sonya from whom he had resolved never to be parted again. He looked, and recognizing in her both the old and the new Sonya, and being reminded by the smell of burnt cork of the sensation of her kiss, inhaled the frosty air with a full breast and, looking at the ground flying beneath him and at the sparkling sky, felt himself again in fairyland.

'Sonya, is it well with *thee*?' he asked from time to time.

'Yes!' she replied. 'And with *thee*?'

When half-way home, Nicholas handed the reins to the coachman and ran for a moment to Natasha's sledge and stood on its wing.

'Natasha!' he whispered in French, 'do you know I have made up my mind about Sonya?'

'Have you told her?' asked Natasha, suddenly beaming all over with joy.

'Oh, how strange you are with that moustache and those eyebrows! ... Natasha – are you glad?'

'I am so glad, so glad! I was beginning to be vexed with you.

I did not tell you, but you have been treating her badly. What a heart she has, Nicholas! I am horrid sometimes but I was ashamed to be happy while Sonya was not,' continued Natasha. 'Now I am so glad! Well, run back to her.'

'No, wait a bit . . . Oh, how funny you look!' cried Nicholas peering into her face and finding in his sister too something new, unusual, and bewitchingly tender, that he had not seen in her before. 'Natasha, it's magical, isn't it?'

'Yes,' she replied. 'You have done splendidly.'

'Had I seen her before as she is now,' thought Nicholas, 'I should long ago have asked her what to do, and have done whatever she told me, and all would have been well.'

'So you are glad, and I have done right?'

'Oh, quite right! I had a quarrel with mamma some time ago about it. Mamma said she was angling for you. How could she say such a thing! I nearly stormed at mamma. I will never let anyone say anything bad of Sonya, for there is nothing but good in her.'

'Then it's all right?' said Nicholas again scrutinizing the expression of his sister's face to see if she was in earnest. Then he jumped down and, his boots scrunching the snow, ran back to his sledge. The same happy smiling Circassian with moustache and beaming eyes looking up from under a sable hood, was still sitting there, and that Circassian was Sonya, and that Sonya was certainly his future happy and loving wife.

When they reached home and had told their mother how they had spent the evening at the Melyukovs', the girls went to their bed-room. When they had undressed, but without washing off the cork moustaches, they sat a long time talking of their happiness. They talked of how they would live when they were married, how their husbands would be friends, and how happy they would be. On Natasha's table stood two looking-glasses which Dunyasha had prepared beforehand.

'Only when will all that be? I am afraid never . . . It would be too good!' said Natasha, rising and going to the looking-glasses.

'Sit down, Natasha; perhaps you'll see him,' said Sonya.

Natasha lit the candles, one on each side of one of the looking-glasses, and sat down.

'I see someone with a moustache,' said Natasha, seeing her own face.

'You mustn't laugh, Miss,' said Dunyasha.

With Sonya's help and the maid's, Natasha got the glass she held into the right position opposite the other; her face assumed a serious expression, and she sat silent. She sat a long time looking at the receding line of candles reflected in the glasses and expecting (from tales she had heard) to see a coffin, or *him*, Prince Andrew, in that last dim, indistinctly outlined, square. But ready as she was to take the smallest speck for the image of a man or of a coffin, she saw nothing. She began blinking rapidly and moved away from the looking-glasses.

'Why is it others see things and I don't?' she said. 'You sit down now, Sonya. You absolutely must, to-night! Do it for me ... To-day I feel so frightened!'

Sonya sat down before the glasses, got the right position, and began looking.

'Now, Miss Sonya is sure to see something,' whispered Dunyasha; 'while you do nothing but laugh.'

Sonya heard this and Natasha's whisper:

'I know she will. She saw something last year.'

For about three minutes all were silent.

'Of course she will!' whispered Natasha, but did not finish ... suddenly Sonya pushed away the glass she was holding and covered her eyes with her hand.

'Oh, Natasha!' she cried.

'Did you see? Did you? What was it?' exclaimed Natasha, holding up the looking-glass.

Sonya had not seen anything, she was just wanting to blink and to get up when she heard Natasha say, 'Of course she will!' She did not wish to disappoint either Dunyasha or Natasha, but it was hard to sit still. She did not herself know how or why the exclamation escaped her when she covered her eyes.

'You saw him?' urged Natasha, seizing her hand.

'Yes. Wait a bit ... I ... saw him,' Sonya could not help saying, not yet knowing whom Natasha meant by *him*, Nicholas or Prince Andrew.

'But why shouldn't I say I saw something? Others do see! Besides, who can tell whether I saw anything or not?' flashed through Sonya's mind.

'Yes, I saw him,' she said.

'How? Standing or lying?'

'No, I saw ... At first there was nothing, then I saw him lying down.'

'Andrew lying? Is he ill?' asked Natasha, her frightened eyes fixed on her friend.

'No, on the contrary, on the contrary! His face was cheerful, and he turned to me.' And when saying this she herself fancied she had really seen what she described.

'Well and then, Sonya? ...'

'After that, I could not make out what there was; something blue and red . . .'

'Sonya! When will he come back? When shall I see him! O, God, how afraid I am for him and for myself and about everything! . . .' Natasha began, and without replying to Sonya's words of comfort she got into bed, and long after her candle was out lay open-eyed and motionless, gazing at the moonlight through the frosty window-panes.

13

Soon after the Christmas holidays Nicholas told his mother of his love for Sonya and of his firm resolve to marry her. The countess who had long noticed what was going on between them and was expecting this declaration, listened to him in silence, and then told her son that he might marry whom he pleased, but that neither she nor his father would give their blessing to such a marriage. Nicholas, for the first time, felt that his mother was displeased with him and that, despite her love for him, she would not give way. Coldly, without looking at her son, she sent for her husband, and when he came tried briefly and coldly to inform him of the facts, in her son's presence, but unable to restrain herself she burst into tears of vexation and left the room. The old count began irresolutely to admonish Nicholas and beg him to abandon his purpose. Nicholas replied that he could not go back on his word, and his father, sighing and evidently disconcerted, very soon became silent and went in to the countess. In all his encounters with his son the count was always conscious of his own guilt towards him for having wasted the family fortune, and so he could not be angry with him for refusing to marry an heiress and choosing the dower-less Sonya. On this occasion he was only more vividly conscious of the fact that if his affairs had not been in disorder, no better wife for Nicholas than Sonya could have been wished for, and that no one but himself, with his Mitenka and his unconquerable habits, was to blame for the condition of the family finances.

The father and mother did not speak of the matter to their son again, but a few days later the countess sent for Sonya and, with a cruelty neither of them expected, reproached her niece for trying to catch Nicholas and for ingratitude. Sonya listened silently with downcast eyes to the countess's cruel words, without understanding what was required of her. She was ready to sacrifice everything for her benefactors. Self-sacrifice was her most cherished idea; but in this case she could not see what she ought to sacrifice, or for whom.

She could not help loving the countess and the whole Rostov family, but neither could she help loving Nicholas and knowing that his happiness depended on that love. She was silent and sad, and did not reply. Nicholas felt the situation to be intolerable and went to have an explanation with his mother. He first implored her to forgive him and Sonya and consent to their marriage, then he threatened that if she molested Sonya he would at once marry her secretly.

The countess, with a coldness her son had never seen in her before, replied that he was of age, that Prince Andrew was marrying without his father's consent, and he could do the same, but that she would never receive that *intriguer* as her daughter.

Exploding at the word *intriguer*, Nicholas, raising his voice, told his mother he had never expected her to try to force him to sell his feelings, but if that were so, he would say for the last time ... But he had no time to utter the decisive word which the expression of his face caused his mother to await with terror, and which would perhaps have for ever remained a cruel memory to them both. He had not time to say it, for Natasha, with a pale and set face, entered the room from the door at which she had been listening.

'Nicholas, you are talking nonsense! Be quiet, be quiet, be quiet, I tell you! ...' she almost screamed, so as to drown his voice.

'Mamma darling, it's not at all so ... my poor, sweet darling,' she said to her mother, who conscious that they had been on the brink of a rupture, gazed at her son with terror, but in the obstinacy and excitement of the conflict could not and would not give way.

'Nicholas, I'll explain to you. Go away! Listen, mamma darling,' said Natasha.

Her words were incoherent, but they attained the purpose at which she was aiming.

The countess, sobbing heavily, hid her face on her daughter's breast, while Nicholas rose, clutching his head, and left the room.

Natasha set to work to effect a reconciliation, and so far succeeded that Nicholas received a promise from his mother that Sonya should not be troubled, while he on his side promised not to undertake anything without his parents' knowledge.

Firmly resolved, after putting his affairs in order in the regiment, to retire from the army and return and marry Sonya, Nicholas, serious, sorrowful, and at variance with his parents, but as it seemed to him passionately in love, left at the beginning of January to rejoin his regiment.

After Nicholas had gone things in the Rostov household were

more depressing than ever, and the countess fell ill from mental agitation.

Sonya was unhappy at the separation from Nicholas, and still more so on account of the hostile tone the countess could not help adopting towards her. The count was more perturbed than ever by the condition of his affairs, which called for some decisive action. Their town house and estate near Moscow had inevitably to be sold, and for this they had to go to Moscow. But the countess's health obliged them to delay their departure from day to day.

Natasha, who had borne the first period of separation from her betrothed lightly and even cheerfully, now grew more agitated and impatient every day. The thought that her best days, which she would have employed in loving him, were being vainly wasted with no advantage to anyone, tormented her incessantly. His letters for the most part irritated her. It hurt her to think that while she lived only in the thought of him, he was living a real life, seeing new places and new people that interested him. The more interesting his letters were the more vexed she felt. Her letters to him, far from giving her any comfort, seemed to her a wearisome and artificial obligation. She could not write, because she could not conceive the possibility of expressing sincerely in a letter even a thousandth part of what she expressed by voice, smile, and glance. She wrote to him formal, monotonous, and dry letters, to which she attached no importance herself, and in the rough copies of which the countess corrected her mistakes in spelling.

There was still no improvement in the countess's health, but it was impossible to defer the journey to Moscow any longer. Natasha's trousseau had to be ordered and the house sold. Moreover Prince Andrew was expected in Moscow, where old Prince Bolkonsky was spending the winter, and Natasha felt sure he had already arrived.

So the countess remained in the country, and the count, taking Sonya and Natasha with him, went to Moscow at the end of January.

END OF PART FOUR

PART FIVE

1

AFTER Prince Andrew's engagement to Natasha, Pierre without any apparent cause suddenly felt it impossible to go on living as before. Firmly convinced as he was of the truths revealed to him by his benefactor, and happy as he had been in perfecting his inner man, to which he had devoted himself with such ardour – all the zest of such a life vanished after the engagement of Andrew and Natasha, and the death of Joseph Alexeevich, the news of which reached him almost at the same time. Only the skeleton of life remained: his house, a brilliant wife who now enjoyed the favours of a very important personage, acquaintance with all Petersburg, and his Court service with its dull formalities. And this life suddenly seemed to Pierre unexpectedly loathsome. He ceased keeping a diary, avoided the company of the Brothers, began going to the club again, drank a great deal, and came once more in touch with the bachelor sets, leading such a life that the Countess Hélène thought it necessary to speak severely to him about it. Pierre felt that she was right, and to avoid compromising her went away to Moscow.

In Moscow as soon as he entered his huge house in which the faded and fading princesses still lived, with its enormous retinue: as soon as, driving through the town, he saw the Iberian shrine with innumerable tapers burning before the golden settings of the icons, the Kremlin Square with its snow undisturbed by vehicles, the sledge-drivers and hovels of the Sivtsev Vrazhok,* those old Muscovites who desired nothing, hurried nowhere, and were ending their days leisurely; when he saw those old Moscow ladies, the Moscow balls and the English Club, he felt himself at home in a quiet haven. In Moscow he felt at peace, at home, warm and dirty as in an old dressing-gown.

Moscow society, from the old women down to the children, received Pierre like a long-expected guest whose place was always ready, awaiting him. For Moscow society Pierre was the nicest, kindest, most intellectual, merriest, and most magnanimous of cranks, a heedless, genial nobleman of the old Russian type. His purse was always empty because it was open to everyone.

Benefit performances, poor pictures, statues, benevolent societies, gipsy choirs, schools, subscription dinners, sprees, Freemasons, churches, and books – no one and nothing met with a refusal from him, and had it not been for two friends who had borrowed large sums from him and taken him under their protection, he would have given everything away. There was never a dinner or soirée at the club without him. As soon as he sank into his place on the sofa after two bottles of Margaux he was surrounded, and talking, disputing, and joking began. When there were quarrels, his kindly smile and well-timed jests reconciled the antagonists. The masonic dinners were dull and dreary when he was not there.

When after a bachelor supper he rose with his amiable and kindly smile, yielding to the entreaties of the festive company to drive off somewhere with them, shouts of delight and triumph arose among the young men. At balls he danced if a partner was needed. Young ladies, married and unmarried, liked him because, without making love to any one of them, he was equally amiable to all, especially after supper. '*Il est charmant; il n'a pas de sexe,*' they said of him.

Pierre was one of those retired gentlemen-in-waiting of whom there were hundreds, good-humouredly ending their days in Moscow.

How horrified he would have been seven years before, when he first arrived from abroad, had he been told that there was no need for him to seek or plan anything, that his rut had long been shaped, eternally predetermined, and that wriggle as he might, he would be what all in his position were. He could not have believed it! Had he not at one time longed with all his heart to establish a republic in Russia; then himself to be a Napoleon; then to be a philosopher; and then a strategist and the conqueror of Napoleon? Had he not seen the possibility of, and passionately desired, the regeneration of the sinful human race, and his own progress to the highest degree of perfection? Had he not established schools and hospitals and liberated his serfs?

But instead of all that – here he was, the wealthy husband of an unfaithful wife, a retired gentleman-in-waiting, fond of eating and drinking and, as he unbuttoned his waistcoat, of abusing the government a bit, a member of the Moscow English Club and a universal favourite in Moscow society. For a long time he could not reconcile himself to the idea that he was one of those same retired Moscow gentlemen-in-waiting he had so despised seven years before.

Sometimes he consoled himself with the thought that he was only living this life temporarily; but then he was shocked by the thought of how many, like himself, had entered that life and that club temporarily, with all their teeth and hair, and had only left it when not a single tooth or hair remained.

In moments of pride, when he thought of his position it seemed to him that he was quite different and distinct from those other retired gentlemen-in-waiting he had formerly despised: they were empty, stupid, contented fellows, satisfied with their position, 'while I am still discontented and want to do something for mankind. But perhaps all these comrades of mine struggled just like me and sought something new, a path in life of their own, and like me were brought by force of circumstances, society, and race – by that elemental force against which man is powerless – to the condition I am in,' said he to himself in moments of humility; and after living some time in Moscow he no longer despised, but began to grow fond of, to respect, and to pity, his comrades in destiny, as he pitied himself.

Pierre no longer suffered moments of despair, hypochondria, and disgust with life, but the malady that had formerly found expression in such acute attacks was driven inwards and never left him for a moment. 'What for? Why? What is going on in the world?' he would ask himself in perplexity several times a day, involuntarily beginning to reflect anew on the meaning of the phenomena of life; but knowing by experience that there were no answers to these questions he made haste to turn away from them, and took up a book, or hurried off to the club or to Apollon Nikolaevich's, to exchange the gossip of the town.

'Hélène, who has never cared for anything but her own body and is one of the stupidest women in the world,' thought Pierre, 'is regarded by people as the acme of intelligence and refinement, and they pay homage to her. Napoleon Bonaparte was despised by all as long as he was great, but now that he has become a wretched comedian the Emperor Francis wants to offer him his daughter in an illegal marriage.* The Spaniards, through the Catholic clergy, offer praise to God for their victory over the French on the 14th of June,* and the French, also through the Catholic clergy, offer praise because on that same 14th of June they defeated the Spaniards. My brother Masons swear by the blood that they are ready to sacrifice everything for their neighbour, but they do not give a ruble each to the collections for the poor, and they intrigue, the Astræa Lodge against the Manna Seekers,* and fuss about an authentic Scotch carpet* and a charter that nobody needs, and the meaning of which the very man who wrote it does not understand. We all profess the Christian law of forgiveness of injuries and love of our neighbours, the law in honour of which we have built in Moscow forty times forty churches – but yesterday a deserter was knouted to death and a minister of that same law of love and forgiveness, a priest, gave the soldier a cross to kiss before his execution.' So thought Pierre, and the whole of this general deception which everyone accepts, accustomed as he was to it, astonished him each time as if it were something new. 'I understand the deception and confusion,' he thought, 'but how am I to tell them all that I see? I have tried, and have always found that they too in the depths of their souls understand it as I do, and only try not to see it. So it appears that it must be so! But I – what is to become of me?' thought he. He had the unfortunate capacity many men, especially Russians, have of seeing and believing in the possibility of goodness and truth, but of seeing the evil and falsehood of life too clearly to be able to take a serious part in it. Every sphere of work was connected, in his eyes, with evil and deception. Whatever he tried to be, whatever he engaged in, the evil and falsehood of it repulsed him and blocked every path of activity. Yet he had to live and to find occupation. It was too dreadful to be under the burden of these insoluble problems, so he abandoned himself to any distraction in order to forget them. He frequented every kind of society, drank much, bought pictures, engaged in building, and above all – read.

He read, and read everything that came to hand. On coming home, while his valets were still taking off his things, he picked up a book and began to read. From reading he passed to sleeping, from sleeping to gossip in drawing-rooms of the club, from gossip to carousals and women; from carousals back to gossip, reading, and wine. Drinking became more and more a physical and also a moral necessity. Though the doctors warned him that with his corpulence wine was dangerous for him, he drank a great deal. He was only quite at ease when, having poured several glasses of wine mechanically into his large mouth, he felt a pleasant warmth in his body, an amiability towards all his fellows, and a readiness to respond superficially to every ideal without probing it deeply. Only after emptying a bottle or two did he feel dimly that the terribly tangled skein of life which previously had terrified him was not as dreadful as he had thought. He was always conscious of some aspect of that skein, as with a buzzing in his head after dinner or supper he chatted or listened to conversation, or read. But under the influence of wine he said to himself: 'It doesn't matter. I'll get it unravelled. I have a solution ready, but have no time now – I'll think it all out later on!' But the *later on* never came.

In the morning, on an empty stomach, all the old questions

appeared as insoluble and terrible as ever, and Pierre hastily picked up a book, and if anyone came to see him he was glad.

Sometimes he remembered how he had heard that soldiers in war when entrenched under the enemy's fire, if they have nothing to do, try hard to find some occupation the more easily to bear the danger. To Pierre all men seemed like those soldiers, seeking refuge from life: some in ambition, some in cards, some in framing laws, some in women, some in toys, some in horses, some in politics, some in sport, some in wine, and some in governmental affairs. 'Nothing is trivial, and nothing is important, it's all the same – only to save oneself from it as best one can,' thought Pierre. 'Only not to see *it*, that dreadful *it*!'

2

AT the beginning of winter Prince Nicholas Bolkonsky and his daughter moved to Moscow. At that time enthusiasm for the Emperor Alexander's regime had weakened, and a patriotic and anti-French tendency prevailed there, and this together with his past and his intellect and his originality, at once made Prince Nicholas Bolkonsky an object of particular respect to the Moscovites, and the centre of the Moscow opposition to the government.

The prince had aged very much that year. He showed marked signs of senility by a tendency to fall asleep, forgetfulness of quite recent events, remembrance of remote ones, and the childish vanity with which he accepted the role of head of the Moscow opposition. In spite of this the old man inspired in all his visitors alike a feeling of respectful veneration – especially of an evening when he came in to tea in his old-fashioned coat and powdered wig and, aroused by anyone, told his abrupt stories of the past, or uttered yet more abrupt and scathing criticisms of the present. For them all, that old-fashioned house with its gigantic mirrors, pre-Revolution furniture, powdered footmen, and the stern shrewd old man (himself a relic of the past century) with his gentle daughter and the pretty Frenchwoman who were reverently devoted to him, presented a majestic and agreeable spectacle. But the visitors did not reflect that besides the couple of hours during which they saw their host, there were also twenty-two hours in the day during which the private and intimate life of the house continued.

Latterly that private life had become very trying for Princess Mary. There in Moscow she was deprived of her greatest pleasures – talks with the pilgrims and the solitude which refreshed her at Bald Hills – and she had none of the advantages and pleasures of city life. She did not go out into society; everyone knew that her father would not let her go anywhere without him, and his failing health prevented his going out himself, so that she was not invited to dinners and evening parties. She had quite abandoned the hope of getting married. She saw the coldness and malevolence with which the old prince received and dismissed the young men, possible suitors, who sometimes appeared at their house. She had no friends: during this visit to Moscow she had been disappointed in the two who had been nearest to her. Mademoiselle Bourienne, with whom she had never been able to be quite frank, had now become unpleasant to her, and for various reasons Princess Mary avoided her. Julie, with whom she had corresponded for the last five years, was in Moscow, but proved to be quite alien to her when they met. Just then Julie, who by the death of her brothers had become one of the richest heiresses in Moscow, was in the full whirl of society pleasures. She was surrounded by young men who, she fancied, had suddenly learnt to appreciate her worth. Julie was at that stage in the life of a society woman when she feels that her last chance of marrying has come, and that her fate must be decided now or never. On Thursdays Princess Mary remembered with a mournful smile that she now had no one to write to, since Julie – whose presence gave her no pleasure – was here and they met every week. Like the old *émigré* who declined to marry the lady with whom he had spent his evenings for years, she regretted Julie's presence and having no one to write to. In Moscow Princess Mary had no one to talk to, no one to whom to confide her sorrow, and much sorrow fell to her lot just then. The time for Prince Andrew's return and marriage was approaching, but his request to her to prepare his father for it had not been carried out; in fact it seemed as if matters were quite hopeless, for at every mention of the young Countess Rostova the old Prince (who apart from that was usually in a bad temper) lost control of himself. Another lately added sorrow arose from the lessons she gave her six-year-old nephew. To her consternation she detected in herself in relation to little Nicholas some symptoms of her father's irritability. However often she told herself that she must not get irritable when teaching her nephew, almost every time that, pointer in hand, she sat down to show him the French alphabet, she so longed to pour her own knowledge quickly and easily into the child – who was already afraid that Auntie might at any moment get angry – that at his slightest inattention she trembled, became flustered and heated, raised her voice, and sometimes pulled him by the arm and put him in the corner. Having put him in the corner she would herself begin to cry over her cruel, evil nature, and little Nicholas, follow-ing her example, would sob, and without permission would leave his corner, come to her, pull her wet hands from her face, and comfort her. But what distressed the princess most of all was her father's irritability, which was always directed against her and had of late amounted to cruelty. Had he forced her to prostrate herself to the ground all night, had he beaten her, or made her fetch wood or water, it would never have entered her mind to think her position hard; but this loving despot – the more cruel because he loved her and for that reason tormented himself and her – knew how not merely to hurt and humiliate her deliberately, but to show her that she was always to blame for everything. Of late he had exhibited a new trait that tormented Princess Mary more than anything else; this was his ever-increasing intimacy with Mademoiselle Bourienne. The idea that at the first moment of receiving the news of his son's intentions had occurred to him in jest – that if Andrew got married, he himself would marry Bourienne – had evidently pleased him, and latterly he had persistently, and as it seemed to Princess Mary merely to offend her, shown special endearments to the companion, and expressed his dissatisfaction with his daughter by demonstrations of love for Bourienne.

One day in Moscow in Princess Mary's presence (she thought her father did it purposely when she was there) the old prince kissed Mademoiselle Bourienne's hand and, drawing her to him, embraced her affectionately. Princess Mary flushed and ran out of the room. A few minutes later Mademoiselle Bourienne came into Princess Mary's room smiling and making cheerful remarks in her agreeable voice. Princess Mary hastily wiped away her tears, went resolutely up to Mademoiselle Bourienne, and evidently unconscious of what she was doing began shouting in angry haste at the Frenchwoman, her voice breaking: 'It's horrible, vile, inhuman, to take advantage of the weakness ...' She did not finish. 'Leave my room,' she exclaimed, and burst into sobs.

Next day the prince did not say a word to his daughter, but she noticed that at dinner he gave orders that Mademoiselle Bourienne should be served first. After dinner, when the footman handed coffee, and from habit began with the princess, the prince suddenly grew furious, threw his stick at Philip, and instantly gave instructions to have him conscripted for the army.

'He doesn't obey ... I said it twice ... and he doesn't obey! She is the first person in this house; she's my best friend,' cried the prince. 'And if you allow yourself,' he screamed in a fury, addressing Princess Mary for the first time, 'to forget yourself again before her as you dared to do yesterday, I will show you who is master in this house. Go! Don't let me set eyes on you; beg her pardon!'

Princess Mary asked Mademoiselle Bourienne's pardon, and also her father's pardon for herself and for Philip the footman, who had begged for her intervention.

At such moments something like a pride of sacrifice gathered in her soul. And suddenly that father, whom she had judged, would look for his spectacles in her presence, fumbling near them and not seeing them, or would forget something that had just occurred, or take a false step with his failing legs and turn to see if anyone had noticed his feebleness, or, worst of all, at dinner when there were no visitors to excite him, would suddenly fall asleep, letting his napkin drop and his shaking head sink over his plate. 'He is old and feeble, and I dare to condemn him!' she thought at such moments, with a feeling of revulsion against herself.

3

IN 1811 there was living in Moscow a French doctor – Métivier – who had rapidly become the fashion. He was enormously tall, handsome, amiable as Frenchmen are, and was, as all Moscow said, an extraordinarily clever doctor. He was received in the best houses not merely as a doctor, but as an equal.

Prince Nicholas had always ridiculed medicine, but latterly on Mademoiselle Bourienne's advice had allowed this doctor to visit him and had grown accustomed to him. Métivier came to see the prince about twice a week.

On December 6th – St Nicholas's day and the prince's name-day – all Moscow came to the prince's front door, but he gave orders to admit no one, and to invite to dinner only a small number, a list of whom he gave to Princess Mary.

Métivier, who came in the morning with his felicitations, considered it proper in his quality of doctor *de forcer la consigne*, as he told Princess Mary, and went in to see the prince. It happened that on that morning of his name-day the prince was in one of his worst moods. He had been going about the house all the morning finding fault with everyone and pretending not to understand what was said to him and not to be understood himself. Princess Mary well knew this mood of quiet absorbed querulousness, which generally culminated in a burst of rage, and she went about all that morning as though facing a cocked and loaded gun and awaited the inevitable explosion. Until the doctor's arrival the morning had passed off safely. After admitting the doctor, Princess Mary sat down with a book in the drawing-room near the door through which she could hear all that passed in the study.

At first she only heard Métivier's voice, then her father's, then both voices began speaking at the same time, the door was flung open, and on the threshold appeared the handsome figure of the terrified Métivier with his shock of black hair, and the prince in his dressing-gown and fez, his face distorted with fury and the pupils of his eyes rolled downwards.

'You don't understand?' shouted the prince, 'but I do! French spy, slave of Buonaparte, spy, get out of my house! Be off, I tell you . . .' and he slammed the door.

Métivier, shrugging his shoulders, went up to Mademoiselle Bourienne, who at the sound of shouting had run in from an adjoining room.

'The prince is not very well: bile and rush of blood to the head. Keep calm, I will call again to-morrow,' said Métivier, and putting his fingers to his lips he hastened away.

Through the study-door came the sound of slippered feet and the cry: 'Spies, traitors, traitors everywhere! Not a moment's peace in my own house!'

After Métivier's departure the old prince called his daughter in, and the whole weight of his wrath fell on her. She was to blame that a spy had been admitted. Had he not told her, yes, told her to make a list, and not to admit anyone who was not on that list? Then why was that scoundrel admitted? She was the cause of it all. With her, he said, he could not have a moment's peace, and could not die quietly.

'No, ma'am! We must part, we must part! Understand that, understand it! I cannot endure any more,' he said, and left the room. Then, as if afraid she might find some means of consolation, he returned and trying to appear calm added: 'And don't imagine I have said this in a moment of anger. I am calm, I have thought it over, and it will be carried out – we must part; so find some place for yourself! . . .' But he could not restrain himself and, with the virulence of which only one who loves is capable, evidently suffering himself, he shook his fists at her and screamed:

'If only some fool would marry her!' Then he slammed the door, sent for Mademoiselle Bourienne and subsided in his study.

At two o'clock the six chosen guests assembled for dinner.

These guests – the famous Count Rostopchin, Prince Lopukhin and his nephew, General Chatrov, an old war comrade of the prince's, and of the younger generation Pierre and Boris Drubetskoy – awaited the prince in the drawing-room.

Boris, who had come to Moscow on leave a few days before, had been anxious to be presented to Prince Nicholas Bolkonsky, and had contrived to ingratiate himself so well that the old prince in his case made an exception to the rule of not receiving bachelors in his house.

The prince's house did not belong to what is known as *fashionable society*, but his little circle – though not much talked about in town – was one it was more flattering to be received in than any other. Boris had realized this the week before, when the commander-in-chief in his presence invited Rostopchin to dinner on St Nicholas's day, and Rostopchin had replied that he could not come:

'On that day I always go to pay my devotions to the relics of Prince Nicholas Bolkonsky.'

'Oh, yes, yes!' replied the commander-in-chief. 'How is he? . . .'

The small group that assembled before dinner in the lofty old-fashioned drawing-room, with its old furniture, resembled the solemn gathering of a Court of Justice. All were silent or talked in low tones. Prince Nicholas came in serious and taciturn. Princess Mary seemed even quieter and more diffident than usual. The guests were reluctant to address her, feeling that she was in no mood for their conversation. Count Rostopchin alone kept the conversation going, now relating the latest town news, and now the latest political gossip.

Lopukhin and the old general occasionally took part in the conversation. Prince Bolkonsky listened as a presiding judge receives a report, only now and then, silently or by a brief word, showing that he took heed of what was being reported to him. The tone of the conversation was such as indicated that no one approved of what was being done in the political world. Incidents were related evidently confirming the opinion that everything was going from bad to worse, but whether telling a story or giving an opinion the speaker always stopped, or was stopped, at the point beyond which his criticism might touch the sovereign himself.

At dinner the talk turned on the latest political news: Napoleon's seizure of the Duke of Oldenburg's territory,* and the Russian Note, hostile to Napoleon, which had been sent to all the European courts.

'Bonaparte treats Europe as a pirate does a captured vessel,' said Count Rostopchin, repeating a phrase he had uttered several times before. 'One only wonders at the long-suffering or blindness of the crowned heads. Now the Pope's turn has come, and Bonaparte doesn't scruple to depose the head of the Catholic Church – yet all keep silent! Our sovereign alone has protested against the seizure of the Duke of Oldenburg's territory, and even . . .' Count Rostopchin paused, feeling that he had reached the limit beyond which censure was impossible.

'Other territories have been offered in exchange for the Duchy of Oldenburg,' said Prince Bolkonsky. 'He shifts the Dukes about as I might move my serfs from Bald Hills to Bogucharovo or my Ryazan estates.'

'The Duke of Oldenburg bears his misfortunes with admirable strength of character and resignation,' remarked Boris, joining in respectfully.

He said this because on his journey from Petersburg he had had the honour of being presented to the Duke. Prince Bolkonsky glanced at the young man as if about to say something in reply, but changed his mind, evidently considering him too young.

'I have read our protest about the Oldenburg affair and was surprised how badly the Note was worded,' remarked Count Rostopchin in the casual tone of a man dealing with a subject quite familiar to him.

Pierre looked at Rostopchin with naïve astonishment, not understanding why he should be disturbed by the bad composition of the Note.

'Does it matter, Count, how the Note is worded,' he asked, 'so long as its substance is forceful?'

'My dear fellow, with our five hundred thousand troops it should be easy to have a good style,' returned Count Rostopchin.

Pierre now understood the count's dissatisfaction with the wording of the Note.

'One would have thought quill-drivers enough had sprung up,' remarked the old prince. 'There in Petersburg they are always writing – not Notes only but even new laws. My Andrew there has written a whole volume of laws for Russia. Nowadays they are always writing!' and he laughed unnaturally.

There was a momentary pause in the conversation; the old general cleared his throat to draw attention.

'Did you hear of the last event at the review in Petersburg? The figure cut by the new French ambassador.'

'Eh? Yes, I heard something: he said something awkward in his Majesty's presence.'

'His Majesty drew his attention to the Grenadier division and to the march past,' continued the general, 'and it seems the ambassador took no notice and allowed himself to reply that: "We in France pay no attention to such trifles!" The Emperor did not condescend to reply. At the next review, they say, the Emperor did not once deign to address him.'

All were silent. On this fact relating to the Emperor personally, it was impossible to pass any judgment.

'Impudent fellows!' said the prince. 'You know Métivier? I turned him out of my house this morning. He was here; they admitted him in spite of my request that they should let no one in,' he went on, glancing angrily at his daughter.

And he narrated his whole conversation with the French doctor and the reasons that convinced him that Métivier was a spy. Though these reasons were very insufficient and obscure, no one made any rejoinder.

After the roast, champagne was served. The guests rose to congratulate the old prince. Princess Mary, too, went round to him.

He gave her a cold, angry look, and offered her his wrinkled, clean-shaven cheek to kiss. The whole expression of his face told her that he had not forgotten the morning's talk, that his decision remained in force, and only the presence of visitors hindered his speaking of it to her now.

When they went into the drawing-room where coffee was served, the old men sat together.

Prince Nicholas grew more animated and expressed his views on the impending war.

He said that our wars with Bonaparte would be disastrous so long as we sought alliances with the Germans and thrust ourselves into European affairs, into which we had been drawn by the Peace of Tilsit. 'We ought not to fight either for or against Austria. Our political interests are all in the East, and in regard to Bonaparte the only thing is to have an armed frontier and a firm policy, and he will never dare to cross the Russian frontier, as was the case in 1807!'

'How can we fight the French, Prince?' said Count Rostopchin. 'Can we arm ourselves against our teachers and divinities? Look at our youths, look at our ladies! The French are our Gods: Paris is our Kingdom of Heaven.'

He began speaking louder, evidently to be heard by everyone.

'French dresses, French ideas, French feelings! There now, you turned Métivier out by the scruff of his neck because he is a Frenchman and a scoundrel, but our ladies crawl after him on their knees. I went to a party last night, and there out of five ladies three were Roman Catholics and had the Pope's indulgence for doing wool-work on Sundays. And they themselves sit there nearly naked, like the sign-boards at our Public Baths, if I may say so. Ah, when one looks at our young people, Prince, one would like to take Peter the Great's old cudgel out of the museum and belabour them in the Russian way till all the nonsense jumps out of them.'

All were silent. The old prince looked at Rostopchin with a smile and wagged his head approvingly.

'Well, good-bye, your Excellency, keep well!' said Rostopchin, getting up with characteristic briskness and holding out his hand to the prince.

'Good-bye, my dear fellow . . . His words are music, I never tire of hearing him!' said the old prince, keeping hold of the hand and offering his cheek to be kissed.

Following Rostopchin's example the others also rose.

4

PRINCESS MARY, as she sat listening to the old men's talk and fault-finding, understood nothing of what she heard; she only wondered whether the guests had all observed her father's hostile attitude towards her. She did not even notice the special attentions and amiabilities shown her during dinner by Boris Drubetskoy, who was visiting them for the third time already.

Princess Mary turned with an absent-minded questioning look to Pierre, who hat in hand and with a smile on his face was the last of the guests to approach her after the old prince had gone out and they were left alone in the drawing-room.

'May I stay a little longer?' he said, letting his stout body sink into an arm-chair beside her.

'Oh yes,' she answered. 'You noticed nothing?' her look asked.

Pierre was in an agreeable after-dinner mood. He looked straight before him and smiled quietly.

'Have you known that young man long, Princess?' he asked.

'Who?'

'Drubetskoy.'

'No, not long . . .'

'Do you like him?'

'Yes, he is an agreeable young man . . . Why do you ask me that?' said Princess Mary, still thinking of that morning's conversation with her father.

'Because I have noticed that when a young man comes on leave from Petersburg to Moscow it is usually with the object of marrying an heiress.'

'You have observed that?' said Princess Mary.

'Yes,' returned Pierre with a smile, 'and this young man now manages matters so that where there is a wealthy heiress, there he is too. I can read him like a book. At present he is hesitating whom to lay siege to – you or Mademoiselle Julie Karagina. He is very attentive to her.'

'He visits them?'

'Yes, very often. And do you know the new way of courting?'

583

said Pierre with an amused smile, evidently in that cheerful mood of good-humoured raillery for which he so often reproved himself in his diary.

'No,' replied Princess Mary.

'To please Moscow girls nowadays one has to be melancholy. He is very melancholy with Mademoiselle Karagina,' said Pierre.

'Really?' asked Princess Mary, looking into Pierre's kindly face and still thinking of her own sorrow. 'It would be a relief,' thought she, 'if I ventured to confide what I am feeling to someone. I should like to tell everything to Pierre. He is kind and generous. It would be a relief. He would give me advice.'

'Would you marry him?'

'Oh, my God, Count, there are moments when I would marry anybody!' she cried suddenly to her own surprise and with tears in her voice. 'Ah, how bitter it is to love someone near to you and to feel that...' she went on in a trembling voice, 'that you can do nothing for him but grieve him, and to know that you cannot alter this. Then there is only one thing left – to go away, but where could I go?'

'What is wrong? What is it, Princess?'

But without finishing what she was saying, Princess Mary burst into tears.

'I don't know what is the matter with me to-day. Don't take any notice – forget what I have said!'

Pierre's gaiety vanished completely. He anxiously questioned the princess, asked her to speak out fully and confide her grief to him; but she only repeated that she begged him to forget what she had said, that she did not remember what she had said, and that she had no trouble except the one he knew of – that Prince Andrew's marriage threatened to cause a rupture between father and son.

'Have you any news of the Rostovs?' she asked, to change the subject. 'I was told they are coming soon. I am also expecting Andrew any day. I should like them to meet here.'

'And how does he now regard the matter?' asked Pierre, referring to the old prince.

Princess Mary shook her head.

'What is to be done? In a few months the year will be up. The thing is impossible. I only wish I could spare my brother the first moments. I wish they would come sooner. I hope to be friends with her. You have known them a long time,' said Princess Mary. 'Tell me honestly the whole truth: what sort of a girl is she, and what do you think of her? – The real truth, because you know Andrew is risking so much doing this against his father's will, that I should like to know . . .'

An undefined instinct told Pierre that these explanations, and repeated requests to be told the *whole truth*, expressed ill will on the princess's part towards her future sister-in-law, and a wish that he should disapprove of Andrew's choice; but in reply he said what he felt rather than what he thought.

'I don't know how to answer your question,' he said, blushing without knowing why. 'I really don't know what sort of girl she is; I can't analyse her at all. She is enchanting, but what makes her so I don't know. That is all one can say about her.'

Princess Mary sighed, and the expression on her face said: 'Yes, that's what I expected and feared.'

'Is she clever?' she asked.

Pierre considered.

'I think not,' he said, 'and yet – yes. She does not deign to be clever . . . Oh no, she is simply enchanting, and that is all.'

Princess Mary again shook her head disapprovingly.

'Ah, I so long to like her! Tell her so, if you see her before I do.'

'I hear they are expected very soon,' said Pierre.

Princess Mary told Pierre of her plan to become intimate with her future sister-in-law as soon as the Rostovs arrived and to try to accustom the old prince to her.

5

BORIS had not succeeded in making a wealthy match in Petersburg, so with the same object in view he came to Moscow. There he wavered between the two richest heiresses, Julie and Princess Mary. Though Princess Mary despite her plainness seemed to him more attractive than Julie, he, without knowing why, felt awkward about paying court to her. When they had last met, on the old prince's name-day, she had answered at random all his attempts to talk sentimentally, evidently not listening to what he was saying.

Julie on the contrary accepted his attentions readily, though in a manner peculiar to herself.

She was twenty-seven. After the death of her brothers she had become very wealthy. She was by now decidedly plain, but thought herself not merely as good-looking as before but even far more attractive. She was confirmed in this delusion by the fact that she had become a very wealthy heiress and also by the fact that the older she grew the less dangerous she became to men, and the more freely they could associate with her and avail themselves of her suppers, soirées, and the animated company that assembled at her house, without incurring any obligation. A man who would have been afraid ten years before of going every day to the house when there was a girl of seventeen there, for fear of compromising her and committing himself, would now go boldly every day and treat her not as a marriageable girl but as a sexless acquaintance.

That winter the Karagins' house was the most agreeable and hospitable in Moscow. In addition to the formal evening and dinner parties, a large company, chiefly of men, gathered there every day, supping at midnight and staying till three in the morning. Julie never missed a ball, a promenade, or a play. Her dresses were always of the latest fashion. But in spite of that she seemed to be disillusioned about everything, and told everyone that she did not believe either in friendship or in love, or any of the joys of life, and expected peace only 'yonder'. She adopted the tone of one who has suffered a great disappointment, like a girl who has either lost the man she loved or been cruelly deceived by him. Though nothing of the kind had happened to her, she was regarded in that light and had even herself come to believe that she had suffered much in life. This melancholy, which did not prevent her amusing herself, did not hinder the young people who came to her house from passing the time pleasantly. Every visitor who came to the house paid his tribute to the melancholy mood of the hostess, and then amused himself with society gossip, dancing, intellectual games, and *bouts rimés*, which were in vogue at the Karagins'. Only a few of these young men, among them Boris, entered more deeply into Julie's melancholy, and with these she had prolonged conversations in private on the vanity of all worldly things, and to them she showed her albums, filled with mournful sketches, maxims, and verses.

To Boris Julie was particularly gracious: she regretted his early disillusionment with life, offered him such consolation of friendship as she, who had herself suffered so much, could render, and showed him her album. Boris sketched two trees in the album, and wrote: 'Rustic trees, your dark branches shed gloom and melancholy upon me.'

On another page he drew a tomb, and wrote:

> La mort est secourable et la mort est tranquille.
> Ah! contre les douleurs il n'y a pas d'autre asile.

Julie said this was charming.

'There is something so enchanting in the smile of melancholy,' she said to Boris, repeating word for word a passage she had copied from a book. 'It is a ray of light in the darkness, a shade between sadness and despair, showing the possibility of consolation.'

In reply Boris wrote these lines:

> *Aliment de poison d'une âme trop sensible,*
> *Toi, sans qui le bonheur me serait impossible,*
> *Tendre mélancolie, ah, viens me consoler,*
> *Viens calmer les tourments de ma sombre retraite*
> *Et mêle une douceur secrète*
> *A ces pleurs, que je sens couler.*

For Boris Julie played most doleful nocturnes on her harp. Boris read *Poor Liza* aloud to her, and more than once interrupted the reading because of the emotions that choked him. Meeting at large gatherings Julie and Boris looked on one another as the only souls who understood one another in a world of indifferent people.

Anna Mikhaylovna, who often visited the Karagins, while playing cards with the mother made careful inquiries as to Julie's dowry (she was to have two estates in Penza and the Nizhegorod forests). Anna Mikhaylovna regarded the refined sadness that united her son to the wealthy Julie with emotion and resignation to the Divine will.

'You are always charming and melancholy, my dear Julie,' she said to the daughter. 'Boris says his soul finds repose at your house. He has suffered so many disappointments and is so sensitive,' said she to the mother. 'Ah, my dear, I can't tell you how fond I have grown of Julie latterly,' she said to her son. 'But who could help loving her? She is an angelic being! Ah, Boris, Boris!' – she paused. 'And how I pity her mother,' she went on; 'to-day she showed me her accounts and letters from Penza (they have enormous estates there) and she, poor thing, has no one to help her, and they do cheat her so!'

Boris smiled almost imperceptibly while listening to his mother. He laughed blandly at her naïve diplomacy but listened to what she had to say, and sometimes questioned her carefully about the Penza and Nizhegorod estates.

Julie had long been expecting a proposal from her melancholy adorer and was ready to accept it; but some secret feeling of repulsion for her, for her passionate desire to get married, for her artificiality, and a feeling of horror at renouncing the possibility of real love, still restrained Boris. His leave was expiring. He spent every day and whole days at the Karagins', and every day on thinking the matter over told himself that he would propose to-morrow. But in Julie's presence, looking at her red face and chin (nearly always powdered), her moist eyes, and her expression of continual readiness to pass at once from melancholy to an unnatural rapture of married bliss, Boris could not utter the decisive words, though in imagination he had long regarded himself as the possessor of those Penza and Nizhegorod estates and had apportioned the use of the income from them. Julie saw Boris's indecision and sometimes the thought occurred to her that she was repulsive to him, but her feminine self-deception immediately supplied her with consolation, and she told herself that he was only shy from love. Her melancholy however began to turn to irritability, and not long before Boris's departure she formed a definite plan of action. Just as Boris's leave of absence was expiring, Anatole Kuragin made his appearance in Moscow, and of course in the Karagins' drawing-room, and Julie, suddenly abandoning her melancholy, became cheerful and very attentive to Kuragin.

'My dear,' said Anna Mikhaylovna to her son, 'I know from a reliable source that Prince Vasili has sent his son to Moscow to get him married to Julie. I am so fond of Julie that I should be sorry for her. What do you think of it, my dear?'

The idea of being made a fool of, and of having thrown away that whole month of arduous melancholy service to Julie, and of seeing all the revenue from the Penza estates, which he had already mentally apportioned and put to proper use, fall into the hands of another, and especially into the hands of that idiot Anatole, pained Boris. He drove to the Karagins' with the firm intention of proposing. Julie met him in a gay, careless manner, spoke casually of how she had enjoyed yesterday's ball, and asked when he was leaving. Though Boris had come intentionally to speak of his love and therefore meant to be tender, he began speaking irritably of feminine inconstancy, of how easily women can turn from sadness to joy, and how their moods depend solely on who happens to be paying court to them. Julie was offended, and replied that it was true that a woman needs variety, and the same thing over and over again would weary anyone.

'Then I should advise you . . .' Boris began, wishing to sting her; but at that instant the galling thought occurred to him that he might have to leave Moscow without having accomplished his aim, and have vainly wasted his efforts – which was a thing he never allowed to happen.

He checked himself in the middle of the sentence, lowered his eyes to avoid seeing her unpleasantly irritated and irresolute face, and said:

'I did not come here at all to quarrel with you. On the contrary . . .'

He glanced at her to make sure that he might go on. Her irritability had suddenly quite vanished, and her anxious, imploring eyes were fixed on him with greedy expectation. 'I can always arrange so as not to see her often,' thought Boris. 'The affair has been begun and must be finished!' He blushed hotly, raised his eyes to hers, and said:

'You know my feelings for you!'

There was no need to say more: Julie's face shone with triumph and self-satisfaction; but she forced Boris to say all that is said on such occasions – that he loved her and had never loved any other woman more than her. She knew that for the Penza estates and Nizhegorod forests she could demand this, and she received what she demanded.

The affianced couple, no longer alluding to trees that shed gloom and melancholy upon them, planned the arrangements of a splendid house in Petersburg, paid calls, and prepared everything for a brilliant wedding.

6

At the end of January old Count Rostov went to Moscow with Natasha and Sonya. The countess was still unwell and unable to travel but it was impossible to wait for her recovery. Prince Andrew was expected in Moscow any day, the trousseau had to be ordered and the estate near Moscow had to be sold, besides which the opportunity of presenting his future daughter-in-law to old Prince Bolkonsky while he was in Moscow could not be missed. The Rostovs' Moscow house had not been heated that winter and, as they had come only for a short time and the countess was not with them, the count decided to stay with Marya Dmitrievna Akhrosimova, who had long been pressing her hospitality on them.

Late one evening the Rostovs' four sledges drove into Marya Dmitrievna's courtyard in the old Konyusheny Street. Marya Dmitrievna lived alone. She had already married off her daughter, and her sons were all in the service.

She held herself as erect, told everyone her opinion as candidly, loudly, and bluntly, as ever, and her whole bearing seemed a reproach to others for any weakness, passion, or temptation – the possibility of which she did not admit. From early in the morning, wearing a dressing-jacket, she attended to her household affairs, and then she drove out: on holy days to church, and after the service to jails and prisons on affairs of which she never spoke to anyone.* On ordinary days, after dressing, she received petitioners of various classes, of whom there were always some. Then she had dinner, a substantial and appetizing meal at which there were always three or four guests; after dinner she played a game of boston, and at night she had the newspapers or a new book read to her while she knitted. She rarely made an exception and went out to pay visits, and then only to the most important persons in the town.

She had not yet gone to bed when the Rostovs arrived and the pulley of the hall-door squeaked as it let in the Rostovs and their servants from the cold. Marya Dmitrievna, with her spectacles hanging down on her nose and her head flung back, stood in the hall doorway looking with a stern, grim face at the new arrivals. One might have thought she was angry with the travellers and would immediately turn them out, had she not at the same time been giving careful instructions to the servants for the accommodation of the visitors and their belongings.

'The Count's things? Bring them here,' she said, pointing to the portmanteaux and not greeting anyone. 'The young ladies'? There to the left. Now what are you dawdling for?' she cried to the maids. 'Get the samovar ready!... You've grown plumper and prettier,' she remarked, drawing Natasha (whose cheeks were glowing from the cold) to her by the hood. 'Foo! You *are* cold! Now take off your things, quick!' she shouted to the count who was going to kiss her hand. 'You're half frozen, I'm sure! Bring some rum for tea!... *Bonjour*, Sonya dear!' she added, turning to Sonya and indicating by this French greeting her slightly contemptuous though affectionate attitude towards her.

When they came in to tea, having taken off their outdoor things and tidied themselves up after their journey, Marya Dmitrievna kissed them all in due order.

'I'm heartily glad you have come and are staying with me. It was high time,' she said, giving Natasha a significant look. 'The old man is here and his son's expected any day. You'll have to make his acquaintance. But we'll speak of that later on,' she added, glancing at Sonya with a look that showed she did not want to speak of it in her presence. 'Now listen,' she said to the count. 'What do you want to-morrow? Whom will you send for? Shinshin?' She crooked one of her fingers. 'The snivelling Anna Mikhaylovna? That's two. She's here with her son. The son is getting married! Then Bezukhov, eh? He is here too, with his wife. He ran away from her and she came galloping after him. He dined with me on Wednesday. As for them' – and she pointed to the girls – 'to-morrow I'll take then first to the Iberian shrine of the Mother of God, and then we'll drive to the Super-Rogue's.* I suppose you'll have everything new. Don't judge by me: sleeves nowadays are this size! The other day young Princess Irina Vasilevna came to see me; she was an awful sight – looked as if she had put two barrels on her arms. You know not a day passes now without some new fashion. And what have you to do yourself?' she asked the count sternly.

'One thing has come on top of another: her rags to buy, and now a purchaser has turned up for the Moscow estate and for the house. If you will be so kind, I'll fix a time and go down to the estate just for a day, and leave my lassies with you.'

'All right. All right. They'll be safe with me, as safe as in Chancery! I'll take them where they must go, scold them a bit, and pet them a bit,' said Marya Dmitrievna, touching her god-daughter and favourite, Natasha, on the cheek with her large hand.

Next morning Marya Dmitrievna took the young ladies to the Iberian shrine of the Mother of God and to Madame Suppert-Roguet, who was so afraid of Marya Dmitrievna that she always let her have costumes at a loss merely to get rid of her. Marya Dmitrievna ordered almost the whole trousseau. When they got home she turned everybody out of the room except Natasha, and then called her pet to her arm-chair.

'Well, now we'll talk. I congratulate you on your betrothed. You've hooked a fine fellow! I am glad for your sake, and I've known him since he was so high.' She held her hand a couple of feet from the ground. Natasha blushed happily. 'I like him and all his family. Now listen! You know that old Prince Nicholas much dislikes his son's marrying. The old fellow's crotchety! Of course Prince Andrew is not a child and can shift without him, but it's not nice to enter a family against a father's will. One wants to do it peacefully and lovingly. You're a clever girl and you'll know how to manage. Be kind, and use yours wits. Then all will be well.'

Natasha remained silent, from shyness Marya Dmitrievna supposed, but really because she disliked anyone interfering in what touched her love of Prince Andrew, which seemed to her so apart from all human affairs that no one could understand it. She loved and knew Prince Andrew, he loved her only, and was to come one of these days and take her. She wanted nothing more.

'You see, I have known him a long time and am also fond of Mary, your future sister-in-law. "Husbands' sisters bring up blisters", but this one wouldn't hurt a fly. She has asked me to bring you two together. To-morrow you'll go with your father to see her. Be very nice and affectionate to her: you're younger than she. When *he* comes, he'll find you already know his sister and father and are liked by them. Am I right or not? Won't that be best?'

'Yes, it will,' Natasha answered reluctantly.

NEXT day, on Marya Dmitrievna's advice, Count Rostov took Natasha to call on Prince Nicholas Bolkonsky. The count did not set out cheerfully on this visit, at heart he felt afraid. He well remembered the last interview he had had with the old prince, at the time of the enrolment, when in reply to an invitation to dinner he had had to listen to an angry reprimand for not having provided his full quota of men. Natasha, on the other hand, having put on her best gown was in the highest spirits. 'They can't help liking me,' she thought. 'Everybody always has liked me, and I am so willing to do anything they wish, so ready to be fond of him – for being *his* father – and of her – for being *his* sister – that there is no reason for them not to like me . . .'

They drove up to the gloomy old house on the Vozdvizhenka and entered the vestibule.

'Well, the Lord have mercy on us!' said the count, half in jest, half in earnest; but Natasha noticed that her father was flurried on entering the ante-room, and inquired timidly and softly whether the prince and princess were at home.

When they had been announced a perturbation was noticeable among the servants. The footman who had gone to announce them was stopped by another in the large hall and they whispered to one another. Then a maidservant ran into the hall and hurriedly said something, mentioning the princess. At last an old, cross-looking footman came and announced to the Rostovs that the prince was not receiving, but that the princess begged them to walk up. The first person who came to meet the visitors was Mademoiselle Bourienne. She greeted the father and daughter with special politeness, and showed them to the princess's room. The princess, looking excited and nervous, her face flushed in patches, ran in to meet the visitors, treading heavily, and vainly trying to appear cordial and at ease. From the first glance Princess Mary did not like Natasha. She thought her too fashionably dressed, frivolously gay, and vain. She did not at all realize that before having seen her future sister-in-law she was prejudiced against her by involuntary envy of her beauty, youth, and happiness, as well as by jealousy of her brother's love for her. Apart from this insuperable antipathy to her, Princess Mary was agitated just then because on the Rostovs being announced, the old prince had shouted that he did not wish to see them, that Princess Mary might do so if she chose, but they were not to be admitted to him. She had decided to receive them, but feared lest the prince might at any moment indulge in some freak, as he seemed much upset by the Rostovs' visit.

'There, my dear Princess, I've brought you my songstress,' said the count, bowing, and looking round uneasily as if afraid the old prince might appear. 'I am so glad you should get to know one another . . . very sorry the prince is still ailing,' and after a few more commonplace remarks he rose. 'If you'll allow me to leave my Natasha in your hands for a quarter of an hour, Princess, I'll drive round to see Anna Semënovna, it's quite near, in the Dogs' Square, and then I'll come back for her.'

The count had devised this diplomatic ruse (as he afterwards told his daughter) to give the future sisters-in-law an opportunity to talk to one another freely, but another motive was to avoid the danger of encountering the old prince, of whom he was afraid. He did not mention this to his daughter, but Natasha noticed her father's nervousness and anxiety and felt mortified by it. She blushed for him, grew still angrier at having blushed, and looked at the princess with a bold and defiant expression which said that she was not afraid of anybody. The princess told the count that she would be delighted, and only begged him to stay longer at Anna Semënovna's, and he departed.

Despite the uneasy glances thrown at her by Princess Mary – who wished to have a tête-à-tête with Natasha – Mademoiselle Bourienne remained in the room and persistently talked about Moscow amusements and theatres. Natasha felt offended by the hesitation she had noticed in the ante-room, by her father's nervousness, and by the unnatural manner of the princess who – she thought – was making a favour of receiving her, and so everything displeased her. She did not like Princess Mary, whom she thought very plain, affected, and dry. Natasha suddenly shrank into herself, and involuntarily assumed an off-hand air which alienated Princess Mary still more. After five minutes of irksome, constrained conversation, they heard the sound of slippered feet rapidly approaching. Princess Mary looked frightened. The door opened, and the old prince, in a dressing-gown and a white night-cap, came in.

'Ah, madam!' he began. 'Madam, Countess . . . Countess Rostova, if I am not mistaken . . . I beg you to excuse me, to excuse me . . . I did not know, madam. God is my witness, I did not know you had honoured us with a visit, and I came in such a costume only to see my daughter. I beg you to excuse me . . . God is my witness, I didn't know –' he repeated, stressing the word 'God' so unnaturally and so unpleasantly that Princess Mary stood with downcast eyes, not daring to look either at her father or at Natasha.

Nor did the latter, having risen and curtsied, know what to do. Mademoiselle Bourienne alone smiled agreeably.

'I beg you to excuse me, excuse me! God is my witness, I did not know,' muttered the old man, and after looking Natasha over from head to foot he went out.

Mademoiselle Bourienne was the first to recover herself after this apparition, and began speaking about the prince's indisposition. Natasha and Princess Mary looked at one another in silence, and the longer they did so, without saying what they wanted to say, the greater grew their antipathy to one another.

When the count returned, Natasha was impolitely pleased, and hastened to get away: at that moment she hated the stiff, elderly princess, who could place her in such an embarrassing position and had spent half an hour with her without once mentioning Prince Andrew. 'I couldn't begin talking about him in the presence of that Frenchwoman,' thought Natasha. The same thought was meanwhile tormenting Princess Mary. She knew what she ought to have said to Natasha, but she had been unable to say it because Mademoiselle Bourienne was in the way, and because, without knowing why, she felt it very difficult to speak of the marriage. When the count was already leaving the room, Princess Mary went up hurriedly to Natasha, took her by the hand, and said with a deep sigh:

'Wait, I must . . .'

Natasha glanced at her ironically, without knowing why.

'Dear Natalie,' said Princess Mary, 'I want you to know that I am glad my brother has found happiness . . .'

She paused, feeling that she was not telling the truth. Natasha noticed this and guessed its reason.

'I think, Princess, it is not convenient to speak of that now,' she said with external dignity and coldness, though she felt the tears choking her.

'What have I said and what have I done?' thought she, as soon as she was out of the room.

They waited a long time for Natasha to come to dinner that day. She sat in her room crying like a child, blowing her nose and sobbing. Sonya stood beside her, kissing her hair.

'Natasha, what is it about?' she asked. 'What do they matter to you? It will all pass, Natasha.'

'But if you only knew how offensive it was . . . as if I . . .'

'Don't talk about it, Natasha. It wasn't your fault, so why should you mind? Kiss me,' said Sonya.

Natasha raised her head and, kissing her friend on the lips, pressed her wet face against her.

'I can't tell you, I don't know. No one's to blame,' said Natasha – 'It's my fault. But it all hurts terribly, Oh, why doesn't he come? . . .'

She came in to dinner with red eyes. Marya Dmitrievna, who

knew how the prince had received the Rostovs, pretended not to notice how upset Natasha was, and jested resolutely and loudly at table with the count and the other guests.

8

THAT evening the Rostovs went to the Opera, for which Marya Dmitrievna had taken a box.

Natasha did not want to go, but could not refuse Marya Dmitrievna's kind offer which was intended expressly for her. When she came ready dressed into the ball-room to await her father and looking in the large mirror there saw that she was pretty, very pretty, she felt even more sad, but it was a sweet, tender sadness.

'O, God, if he were here now I would not behave as I did then, but differently. I would not be silly and afraid of things, I would simply embrace him, cling to him, and make him look at me with those searching inquiring eyes with which he has so often looked at me, and then I would make him laugh as he used to laugh. And his eyes – how I see those eyes!' thought Natasha. 'And what do his father and sister matter to me? I love him alone, him, him, with that face and those eyes, with his smile, manly and yet child-like ... No, I had better not think of him; not think of him but forget him, quite forget him for the present. I can't bear this waiting and I shall cry in a minute!' and she turned away from the glass, making an effort not to cry. 'And how can Sonya love Nicholas so calmly and quietly and wait so long and so patiently?' thought she, looking at Sonya, who also came in quite ready, with a fan in her hand. 'No, she's altogether different. I can't!'

Natasha at that moment felt so softened and tender that it was not enough for her to love and know she was beloved, she wanted now, at once, to embrace the man she loved, to speak and hear from him words of love such as filled her heart. While she sat in the carriage beside her father, pensively watching the lights of the street-lamps flickering on the frozen window, she felt still sadder and more in love, and forgot where she was going and with whom. Having fallen into the line of carriages, the Rostovs' carriage drove up to the theatre, its wheels squeaking over the snow. Natasha and Sonya, holding up their dresses, jumped out quickly. The count got out helped by the footmen, and, passing among men and women who were entering, and the programme sellers, they all three went along the corridor to the first row of boxes. Through the closed doors the music was already audible.

595

'Natasha, your hair!' ... whispered Sonya.

An attendant deferentially and quickly slipped before the ladies and opened the door of their box. The music sounded louder, and through the door rows of brightly lit boxes in which ladies sat with bare arms and shoulders, and noisy stalls brilliant with uniforms, glittered before their eyes. A lady entering the next box shot a glance of feminine envy at Natasha. The curtain had not yet risen and the overture was being played. Natasha, smoothing her gown, went in with Sonya and sat down, scanning the brilliant tiers of boxes opposite. A sensation she had not experienced for a long time – that of hundreds of eyes looking at her bare arms and neck – suddenly affected her both agreeably and disagreeably and called up a whole crowd of memories, desires, and emotions associated with that feeling.

The two remarkably pretty girls, Natasha and Sonya, with Count Rostov who had not been seen in Moscow for a long time, attracted general attention. Moreover, everybody knew vaguely of Natasha's engagement to Prince Andrew, and knew that the Rostovs had lived in the country ever since, and all looked with curiosity at a fiancée who was making one of the best matches in Russia.

Natasha's looks, as everyone told her, had improved in the country, and that evening thanks to her agitation she was particularly pretty. She struck those who saw her by her fullness of life and beauty, combined with her indifference to everything about her. Her black eyes looked at the crowd without seeking anyone, and her delicate arm, bare to above the elbow, lay on the velvet edge of the box, while, evidently unconsciously, she opened and closed her hand in time to the music, crumpling her programme.

'Look, there's Alenina,' said Sonya, 'with her mother, isn't it?'

'Dear me, Michael Kirilovich has grown still stouter!' remarked the count.

'Look at our Anna Mikhaylovna – what a head-dress she has on!'

'The Karagins, Julie – and Boris with them. One can see at once that they're engaged ...'

'Drubetskoy has proposed?'

'Oh, yes, I heard it to-day,' said Shinshin, coming into the Rostovs' box.

Natasha looked in the direction in which her father's eyes were turned, and saw Julie sitting beside her mother with a happy look on her face and a string of pearls round her thick red neck – which Natasha knew was covered with powder. Behind them, wearing a smile and leaning over with an ear to Julie's mouth, was Boris's handsome smoothly brushed head. He looked at the Rostovs from under his brows and said something, smiling, to his betrothed.

'They are talking about us, about me and him!' thought Natasha. 'And he no doubt is calming her jealousy of me. They needn't trouble themselves! If only they knew how little I am concerned about any of them.'

Behind them sat Anna Mikhaylovna wearing a green head-dress, and with a happy look of resignation to the will of God on her face. Their box was pervaded by that atmosphere of an affianced couple which Natasha knew so well and liked so much. She turned away and suddenly remembered all that had been so humiliating in her morning's visit.

'What right has he not to wish to receive me into his family? Oh, better not think of it – not till he comes back!' she told herself, and began looking at the faces, some strange and some familiar, in the stalls. In the front, in the very centre, leaning back against the orchestra-rail, stood Dolokhov in a Persian dress, his curly hair brushed up into a huge shock. He stood in full view of the audience, well aware that he was attracting everyone's attention, yet as much at ease as though he were in his own room. Around him thronged Moscow's most brilliant young men, whom he evidently dominated.

The count, laughing, nudged the blushing Sonya and pointed to her former adorer.

'Do you recognize him?' said he. 'And where has he sprung from?' he asked, turning to Shinshin. 'Didn't he vanish somewhere?'

'He did,' replied Shinshin. 'He was in the Caucasus and ran away from there. They say he has been acting as minister to some ruling prince in Persia, where he killed the Shah's brother. Now all the Moscow ladies are mad about him! It's "Dolokhov the Persian" that does it! We never hear a word but Dolokhov is mentioned. They swear by him, they offer him to you as they would a dish of choice sterlet. Dolokhov and Anatole Kuragin have turned all our ladies' heads.'

A tall, beautiful woman with a mass of plaited hair and much exposed plump white shoulders and neck, round which she wore a double string of large pearls, entered the adjoining box rustling her heavy silk dress, and took a long time settling into her place.

Natasha involuntarily gazed at that neck, those shoulders and pearls and *coiffure*, and admired the beauty of the shoulders and the pearls. While Natasha was fixing her gaze on her for the second time the lady looked round, and meeting the count's eyes nodded to him and smiled. She was the Countess Bezukhova, Pierre's wife, and the count, who knew everyone in society, leaned over and spoke to her.

'Have you been here long, Countess?' he inquired. 'I'll call, I'll call to kiss your hand. I'm here on business and have brought my girls with me. They say Semënova acts marvellously. Count Pierre never used to forget us. Is he here?'

'Yes, he meant to look in,' answered Hélène, and glanced attentively at Natasha.

Count Rostov resumed his seat.

'Handsome, isn't she?' he whispered to Natasha.

'Wonderful!' answered Natasha. 'She's a woman one could easily fall in love with.'

Just then the last chords of the overture were heard and the conductor tapped with his stick. Some latecomers took their seats in the stalls and the curtain rose.

As soon as it rose everyone in the boxes and stalls became silent, and all the men, old and young, in uniform and evening dress, and all the women with gems on their bare flesh, turned their whole attention with eager curiosity to the stage. Natasha too began to look at it.

9

THE floor of the stage consisted of smooth boards, at the sides was some painted cardboard representing trees, and at the back was a cloth stretched over boards. In the centre of the stage sat some girls in red bodices and white skirts. One very fat girl in a white silk dress sat apart on a low bench, to the back of which a piece of green cardboard was glued. They all sang something. When they had finished their song the girl in white went up to the prompter's box, and a man with tight silk trousers over his stout legs, and holding a plume and a dagger, went up to her and began singing, waving his arms about.

First the man in the tight trousers sang alone, then she sang, then they both paused while the orchestra played and the man fingered the hand of the girl in white, obviously awaiting the beat to start singing with her. They sang together and everyone in the theatre began clapping and shouting, while the man and woman on the stage – who represented lovers – began smiling, spreading out their arms, and bowing.

After her life in the country, and in her present serious mood, all this seemed grotesque and amazing to Natasha. She could not follow the opera nor even listen to the music, she saw only the painted cardboard and the queerly dressed men and women who moved, spoke, and sang so strangely in that brilliant light. She knew what it was all meant to represent, but it was so pretentiously false and unnatural that she first felt ashamed for the actors and then amused at them. She looked at the faces of the audience, seeking in them the same sense of ridicule and perplexity she herself experienced, but they all seemed attentive to what was happening on the stage, and expressed delight which to Natasha seemed feigned. 'I suppose it has to be like this!' she thought. She kept looking round in turn at the rows of pomaded heads in the stalls and then at the semi-nude women in the boxes, especially at Hélène in the next box, who – apparently quite unclothed – sat with a quiet tranquil smile, not taking her eyes off the stage. And feeling the bright light that flooded the whole place and the warm air heated by the crowd, Natasha little by little began to pass into a state of intoxication she had not experienced for a long while. She did not realize who and where she was, nor what was going on before her. As she looked and thought, the strangest fancies unexpectedly and disconnectedly passed through her mind: the idea occurred to her of jumping onto the edge of the box and singing the air the actress was singing, then she wished to touch with her fan an old gentleman sitting not far from her, then to lean over to Hélène and tickle her.

At a moment when all was quiet before the commencement of a song, a door leading to the stalls on the side nearest the Rostovs' box creaked, and the steps of a belated arrival were heard. 'There's Kuragin!' whispered Shinshin. Countess Bezukhova turned smiling to the newcomer, and Natasha, following the direction of that look, saw an exceptionally handsome adjutant approaching their box with a self-assured yet courteous bearing. This was Anatole Kuragin whom she had seen and noticed long ago at the ball in Petersburg. He was now in an adjutant's uniform with one epaulette and a shoulder-knot. He moved with a restrained swagger which would have been ridiculous had he not been so good-looking and had his handsome face not worn such an expression of good-humoured complacency and gaiety. Though the performance was proceeding, he walked deliberately down the carpeted gangway, his sword and spurs slightly jingling and his handsome perfumed head held high. Having looked at Natasha he approached his sister, laid his well-gloved hand on the edge of her box, nodded to her, and leaning forward asked a question, with a motion towards Natasha.

'Mais charmante!' said he, evidently referring to Natasha, who did not exactly hear his words but understood them from the movement of his lips. Then he took his place in the first row of the stalls and sat down beside Dolokhov, nudging with his elbow in a friendly and off-hand way that Dolokhov whom others treated so fawningly. He winked at him gaily, smiled, and rested his foot against the orchestra-screen.

'How like the brother is to the sister,' remarked the count. 'And how handsome they both are!'

Shinshin, lowering his voice, began to tell the count of some intrigue of Kuragin's in Moscow, and Natasha tried to overhear it just because he had said she was *'charmante'*.

The first act was over. In the stalls everyone began moving about, going out and coming in.

Boris came to the Rostovs' box, received their congratulations very simply, and raising his eyebrows with an absent-minded smile conveyed to Natasha and Sonya his fiancée's invitation to her wedding, and went away. Natasha with a gay coquettish smile talked to him, and congratulated on his approaching wedding that same Boris with whom she had formerly been in love. In the state of intoxication she was in everything seemed simple and natural.

The scantily clad Hélène was sitting near her, smiling at everyone with the same smile and Natasha gave Boris just such a smile.

Hélène's box was filled, and surrounded from the stalls, by the most distinguished and intellectual men, who seemed to vie with one another in their wish to let everyone see that they knew her.

During the whole of that *entr'acte* Kuragin stood with Dolokhov in front of the orchestra partition looking at the Rostovs' box. Natasha knew he was talking about her and this afforded her pleasure. She even turned so that he should see her profile in what she thought was its most becoming aspect. Before the beginning of the second act Pierre appeared in the stalls. The Rostovs had not seen him since their arrival. His face looked sad, and he had grown still stouter since Natasha last saw him. He passed up to the front rows not noticing anyone. Anatole went up to him and began speaking to him, looking at and indicating the Rostovs' box. On seeing Natasha Pierre grew animated and, hastily passing between the rows, came towards their box. When he got there he leaned on his elbows and, smiling, talked to her for a long time. While conversing with Pierre Natasha heard a man's voice in Countess Bezukhova's box and something told her it was Kuragin. She turned and their eyes met. Almost smiling, he gazed straight into her eyes with such an enraptured caressing look that it seemed strange to be so near him, to look at him like that, to be so sure he admired her, and not to be acquainted with him.

In the second act there was scenery representing tombstones, and there was a round hole in the canvas to represent the moon, shades were raised over the footlights, and from horns and contra-bass came deep notes while many people appeared from right and left wearing black cloaks and holding things like daggers in their hands. They began waving their arms. Then some other people ran in and began dragging away the maiden who had been in white and was now in light blue. They did not drag her away at once, but sang with her for a long time, and then at last dragged her off, and behind the scenes something metallic was struck three times and everyone knelt down and sang a prayer. All these things were repeatedly interrupted by the enthusiastic shouts of the audience.

During this act every time Natasha looked towards the stalls she saw Anatole Kuragin, with an arm thrown across the back of his chair, staring at her. She was pleased to see that he was captivated by her and it did not occur to her that there was anything wrong in it.

When the second act was over Countess Bezukhova rose, turned to the Rostovs' box – her whole bosom completely exposed – beckoned the old count with a gloved finger, and paying no attention to those who had entered her box, began talking to him with an amiable smile.

'Do make me acquainted with your charming daughters,' said she. 'The whole town is singing their praises and I don't even know them.'

Natasha rose and curtsied to the splendid countess. She was so pleased by praise from this brilliant beauty that she blushed with pleasure.

'I want to become a Moscovite too, now,' said Hélène. 'How is it you're not ashamed to bury such pearls in the country?'

Countess Bezukhova quite deserved her reputation of being a fascinating woman. She could say what she did not think – especially what was flattering – quite simply and naturally.

'Dear Count, you must let me look after your daughters! Though I am not staying here long this time – nor are you – I will try to amuse them. I have already heard much of you in Petersburg and wanted to get to know you,' said she to Natasha with her stereotyped and lovely smile. 'I had heard about you from my page, Drubetskoy. Have you heard he is getting married? And also from my husband's friend, Bolkonsky, Prince Andrew Bolkonsky,' she went on with special emphasis, implying that she knew of his relation to Natasha. To get better acquainted she asked that one of the young ladies should come into her box for the rest of the performance, and Natasha moved over to it.

The scene of the third act represented a palace in which many candles were burning and pictures of knights with short beards hung on the walls. In the middle stood what were probably a king and a queen. The king waved his right arm and, evidently nervous, sang something badly and sat down on a crimson throne. The maiden who had been first in white and then in light blue, now wore only a smock, and stood beside the throne with her hair down. She sang something mournfully, addressing the queen, but the king waved his arm severely, and men and women with bare legs came in from both sides and began dancing all together. Then the violins played very shrilly and merrily and one of the women with thick bare legs and thin arms, separating from the others, went behind the wings, adjusted her bodice, returned to the middle of the stage, and began jumping and striking one foot rapidly against the other. In the stalls everyone clapped and shouted 'bravo!' Then one of the men went into a corner of the stage. The cymbals and horns in the orchestra struck up more loudly, and this man with bare legs jumped very high and waved his feet about very rapidly. (He was Duport, who received sixty thousand rubles a year for this art.) Everybody in the stalls, boxes, and galleries began clapping and shouting with all their might, and the man stopped and began smiling and bowing to all sides. Then other men and women danced with bare legs. Then the king again shouted to the sound of music and they all began singing. But suddenly a storm came on, chromatic scales and diminished sevenths were heard in the orchestra, everyone ran off, again dragging one of their number away, and the curtain dropped. Once more there was a terrible noise and clatter among the audience, and with rapturous faces everyone began shouting: 'Duport! Duport! Duport!' Natasha no longer thought this strange. She looked about with pleasure, smiling joyfully.

'Isn't Duport delightful?' Hélène asked her.

'Oh yes,' replied Natasha.

10

DURING the *entr'acte* a whiff of cold air came into Hélène's box, the door opened and Anatole entered, stooping and trying not to brush against anyone.

'Let me introduce my brother to you,' said Hélène, her eyes shifting uneasily from Natasha to Anatole.

Natasha turned her pretty little head towards the elegant young officer, and smiled at him over her bare shoulder. Anatole, who was as handsome at close quarters as at a distance, sat down beside her and told her he had long wished to have this happiness – ever since the Naryshkins' ball, in fact, at which he had had the well-remembered pleasure of seeing her. Kuragin was much more sensible and simple with women than among men. He talked boldly and naturally, and Natasha was strangely and agreeably struck by the fact that there was nothing formidable in this man about whom there was so much talk, but that on the contrary his smile was most naïve, cheerful, and good-natured.

Kuragin asked her opinion of the performance, and told her how at a previous performance Seménova had fallen down on the stage, 'And do you know, Countess,' he said, suddenly addressing her as an old, familiar acquaintance, 'we are getting up a costume-tournament; you ought to take part in it! It will be great fun. We shall all meet at the Karagins! Please come! No! Really, eh?' said he.

While saying this he never removed his smiling eyes from her face, her neck, and her bare arms. Natasha knew for certain that he was enraptured by her. This pleased her, yet his presence made her feel constrained and oppressed. When she was not looking at him she felt that he was looking at her shoulders, and she involuntarily caught his eye so that he should look into hers rather than this. But looking into his eyes she was frightened, realizing that there was not that barrier of modesty she had always felt between herself and other men. She did not know how it was that within five minutes she had come to feel herself terribly near to this man. When she turned away she feared he might seize her from behind by her bare arm and kiss her on the neck. They spoke of most ordinary things, yet she felt that they were closer to one another than she had ever been to any man. Natasha kept turning to Hélène and to her father, as if asking what it all meant, but Hélène was engaged in conversation with a general, and did not answer her look, and her father's eyes said nothing but what they always said: 'Having a good time? Well, I'm glad of it!'

During one of these moments of awkward silence when Anatole's prominent eyes were gazing calmly and fixedly at her, Natasha, to break the silence, asked him how he liked Moscow. She asked the question and blushed. She felt all the time that by talking to him she was doing something improper. Anatole smiled as though to encourage her.

'At first I did not like it much, because what makes a town pleasant *ce sont les jolies femmes*, isn't that so? But now I like it very much indeed,' he said, looking at her significantly. 'You'll come to the costume-tournament, Countess? Do come!' and putting out his hand to her bouquet and dropping his voice, he added, 'You will be the prettiest there. Do come, dear Countess, and give me this flower as a pledge!'

Natasha did not understand what he was saying any more than he did himself, but she felt that his incomprehensible words had an improper intention. She did not know what to say, and turned away as if she had not heard his remark. But as soon as she had turned away she felt that he was there, behind, so close behind her.

'How is he now? Confused? Angry? Ought I to put it right?' she asked herself, and she could not refrain from turning round. She looked straight into his eyes, and his nearness, self-assurance, and the good-natured tenderness of his smile, vanquished her. She smiled just as he was doing, gazing straight into his eyes. And again she felt with horror that no barrier lay between him and her.

The curtain rose again. Anatole left the box, serene and gay. Natasha went back to her father in the other box, now quite submissive to the world she found herself in. All that was going on before her now seemed quite natural, but on the other hand all her previous thoughts of her betrothed, of Princess Mary, or of life in the country, did not once recur to her mind and were as if belonging to a remote past.

In the fourth act there was some sort of a devil who sang, waving his arm about, till the boards were withdrawn from under him and he disappeared down below. That was the only part of the fourth act that Natasha saw. She felt agitated and tormented, and the cause of this was Kuragin, whom she could not help watching. As they were leaving the theatre Anatole came up to them, called their carriage and helped them in. As he was putting Natasha in he pressed her arm above the elbow. Agitated and flushed she turned round. He was looking at her with glittering eyes, smiling tenderly.

Only after she had reached home was Natasha able clearly to think over what had happened to her, and suddenly remembering Prince Andrew she was horrified, and at tea to which all had sat down after the opera, she gave a loud exclamation, flushed, and ran out of the room.

'O God! I am lost!' she said to herself. 'How could I let him?' She sat for a long time hiding her flushed face in her hands trying to realize what had happened to her, but was unable either to understand what had happened or what she felt. Everything seemed dark, obscure, and terrible. There in that enormous, illuminated theatre where the bare-legged Duport, in a tinsel-decorated jacket, jumped about to the music on wet boards, and young girls and old men, and the nearly naked Hélène with her proud, calm smile, rapturously cried 'bravo!' – there in the presence of that Hélène it had all seemed clear and simple; but now, alone, by herself, it was incomprehensible. 'What is it? What was that terror I felt of him? What is this gnawing of conscience I am feeling now?' she thought.

Only to the old countess at night in bed could Natasha have told all she was feeling. She knew that Sonya with her severe and simple views would either not understand it at all or would be horrified at such a confession. So Natasha tried to solve what was torturing her by herself.

'Am I spoilt for Andrew's love or not?' she asked herself, and with soothing irony replied: 'What a fool I am to ask that! What did happen to me? Nothing! I have done nothing, I didn't lead him on at all. Nobody will know and I shall never see him again,' she told herself. 'So it is plain that nothing has happened and there is nothing to repent of, and Andrew can love me still. But why "still"? O God, O God, why isn't he here?' Natasha quieted herself for a moment but again some instinct told her that though all this was true, and though nothing had happened, yet the former purity of her love for Prince Andrew had perished. And again in imagination she went over her whole conversation with Kuragin, and again saw the face, gestures, and tender smile of that bold handsome man when he pressed her arm.

11

ANATOLE KURAGIN was staying in Moscow because his father had sent him away from Petersburg, where he had been spending twenty thousand rubles a year in cash, besides running up debts for as much more which his creditors demanded from his father.

His father announced to him that he would now pay half his debts for the last time, but only on condition that he went to Moscow as adjutant to the commander-in-chief – a post his father had procured for him – and would at last try to make a good match there. He indicated to him Princess Mary and Julie Karagina.

Anatole consented and went to Moscow, where he put up at Pierre's house. Pierre received him unwillingly at first, but got used to him after a while, sometimes even accompanied him on his carousals, and gave him money under the guise of loans.

As Shinshin had remarked, from the time of his arrival Anatole had turned the heads of the Moscow ladies, especially by the fact that he slighted them and plainly preferred the gipsy-girls and French actresses – with the chief of whom, Mademoiselle George, he was said to be in intimate relations. He never missed a carousal at Danilov's or other Moscow revellers, drank whole nights through, outvying everyone else, and was at all the balls and parties of the best society. There was talk of his intrigues with some of the ladies, and he flirted with a few of them at the balls. But he did not run after the unmarried girls, especially the rich heiresses who were most of them plain. There was a special reason for this, as he had got married two years before – a fact known only to his most intimate friends. At that time, while with his regiment in Poland, a Polish landowner of small means had forced him to marry his daughter. Anatole had very soon abandoned his wife, and for a payment which he agreed to send to his father-in-law had arranged to be free to pass himself off as a bachelor.

Anatole was always content with his position, with himself, and with others. He was instinctively and thoroughly convinced that it was impossible for him to live otherwise than as he did, and that he had never in his life done anything base. He was incapable of considering how his actions might affect others, or what the consequences of this or that action of his might be. He was convinced that, as a duck is so made that it must live in water, so God had made him such that he must spend thirty thousand rubles a year and always occupy a prominent position in society. He believed this so firmly that others, looking at him, were persuaded of it too, and did not refuse him either a leading place in society, or money, which he borrowed from anyone and everyone and evidently would not repay.

He was not a gambler, at any rate he did not care about winning. He was not vain. He did not mind what people thought of him. Still less could he be accused of ambition. More than once he had vexed his father by spoiling his own career, and he laughed at distinctions of all kinds. He was not mean, and did not refuse anyone who asked of him. All he cared about was gaiety and women, and as according to his ideas there was nothing dishonourable in these tastes, and he was incapable of considering what the gratification of his tastes entailed for others, he honestly considered himself irreproachable, sincerely despised rogues and bad people, and with a tranquil conscience carried his head high.

Rakes, those male Magdalenes, have a secret feeling of innocence similar to that which female Magdalenes have, based on the same hope of forgiveness. 'All will be forgiven her, for she loved much; and all will be forgiven him, for he enjoyed much.'

Dolokhov, who had reappeared that year in Moscow after his exile and his Persian adventures, and was leading a life of luxury, gambling and dissipation, associated with his old Petersburg comrade Kuragin and made use of him for his own ends.

Anatole was sincerely fond of Dolokhov for his cleverness and audacity. Dolokhov, who needed Anatole Kuragin's name, position, and connexions as a bait to draw rich young men into his gambling set, made use of him and amused himself at his expense without letting the other feel it. Apart from the advantage he derived from Anatole, the very process of dominating another's will was in itself a pleasure, a habit, and a necessity to Dolokhov.

Natasha had made a strong impression on Kuragin. At supper after the opera he described to Dolokhov, with the air of a connoisseur, the attractions of her arms, shoulders, feet and hair, and expressed his intention of making love to her. Anatole had no notion, and was incapable of considering, what might come of such love-making, as he never had any notion of the outcome of any of his actions.

'She's first-rate, my dear fellow, but not for us,' replied Dolokhov.

'I will tell my sister to ask her to dinner,' said Anatole, 'Eh?'

'You'd better wait till she's married . . .'

'You know, I adore little girls, they lose their heads at once,' pursued Anatole.

'You have been caught once already by a "little girl",' said Dolokhov, who knew of Kuragin's marriage. 'Take care!'

'Well, that can't happen twice! Eh?' said Anatole, with a good-humoured laugh.

12

THE day after the opera the Rostovs went nowhere and nobody came to see them. Marya Dmitrievna talked to the count about something which they concealed from Natasha. Natasha guessed they were talking about the old prince and planning something, and this disquieted and offended her. She was expecting Prince Andrew any moment, and twice that day sent a manservant to the Vozdvizhenka to ascertain whether he had come. He had not arrived. She suffered more now than during her first days in Moscow. To her impatience and pining for him were now added the unpleasant recollection of her interview with Princess Mary and the old prince, and a fear and anxiety of which she did not understand the cause. She continually fancied that either he would never come, or that something would happen to her before he came. She could no longer think of him by herself calmly and continuously as she had done before. As soon as she began to think of him, the recollection of the old prince, of Princess Mary, of the theatre, and of Kuragin, mingled with her thoughts. The question again presented itself whether she was not guilty, whether she had not already broken faith with Prince Andrew, and again she found herself recalling to the minutest detail, every word, every gesture, and every shade in the play of expression on the face of the man who had been able to arouse in her such an incomprehensible and terrifying feeling. To the family Natasha seemed livelier than usual, but she was far less tranquil and happy than before.

On Sunday morning Marya Dmitrievna invited her visitors to Mass at her parish church – the Church of the Assumption built over the graves of victims of the plague.

'I don't like those fashionable churches,' she said, evidently priding herself on her independence of thought. 'God is the same everywhere. We have an excellent priest, he conducts the service decently and with dignity, and the deacon is the same. What holiness is there in giving concerts in the choir? I don't like it, it's just self-indulgence!'

Marya Dmitrievna liked Sundays and knew how to keep them. Her whole house was scrubbed and cleaned on Saturdays; neither she nor the servants worked, and they all wore holiday dress and went to church. At her table there were extra dishes at dinner, and the servants had vodka and roast goose or sucking-pig. But in nothing in the house was the holiday so noticeable as in Marya Dmitrievna's broad, stern face, which on that day wore an invariable look of solemn festivity.

After Mass, when they had finished their coffee, in the dining-room where the loose covers had been removed from the furniture, a servant announced that the carriage was ready, and Marya Dmitrievna rose with a stern air. She wore her holiday shawl, in which she paid calls, and announced that she was going to see Prince Nicholas Bolkonsky to have an explanation with him about Natasha.

After she had gone, a dressmaker from Madame Suppert-Roguet waited on the Rostovs, and Natasha, very glad of this diversion, having shut herself into a room adjoining the drawing-room, occupied herself trying on the new dresses. Just as she had put on a bodice without sleeves and only tacked together, and was turning her head to see in the glass how the back fitted, she heard in the drawing-room the animated sounds of her father's voice and another's – a woman's – that made her flush. It was Hélène. Natasha had not time to take off the bodice before the door opened and Countess Bezukhova, dressed in a purple velvet gown with a high collar, came into the room beaming with good-humoured amiable smiles.

'Oh, my enchantress!' she cried to the blushing Natasha. 'Charming! No, this is really beyond anything, my dear Count,' said she to Count Rostov who had followed her in. 'How can you live in Moscow and go nowhere? No, I won't let you off! Mademoiselle George will recite at my house to-night, and there'll be some people, and if you don't bring your lovely girls – who are prettier than Mademoiselle George – I won't know you! My husband is away in Tver or I would send him to fetch you. You must come. You positively must! Between eight and nine.'

She nodded to the dressmaker, whom she knew and who had curtsied respectfully to her, and seated herself in an arm-chair beside the looking-glass draping the folds of her velvet dress picturesquely. She did not cease chattering good-naturedly and gaily, continually praising Natasha's beauty. She looked at Natasha's dresses and praised them, as well as a new dress of her own, made of 'metallic gauze', which she had received from Paris, and advised Natasha to have one like it.

'But anything suits you, my charmer!' she remarked.

A smile of pleasure never left Natasha's face. She felt happy and as if she were blossoming, under the praise of this dear Countess Bezukhova who had formerly seemed to her so un-approachable and important and was now so kind to her. Natasha brightened up and felt almost in love with this woman, who was so beautiful and so kind. Hélène for her part was sincerely delighted with Natasha and wished to give her a good time. Anatole had asked her to bring him and Natasha together, and she was calling on the Rostovs for that purpose. The idea of throwing her brother and Natasha together amused her.

Though at one time, in Petersburg, she had been annoyed with Natasha for drawing Boris away, she did not think of that now, and in her own way heartily wished Natasha well. As she was leaving the Rostovs she called her protégée aside.

'My brother dined with me yesterday – we nearly died of laughter – he ate nothing and kept sighing for you, my charmer! He is madly, quite madly, in love with you, my dear.'

Natasha blushed scarlet when she heard this.

'How she blushes, how she blushes, my pretty!' said Hélène. 'You must certainly come. If you love somebody, my charmer, that is not a reason to shut yourself up. Even if you are engaged, I am sure your fiancé would wish you to go into society rather than be bored to death.'

'So she knows I am engaged, and she and her husband Pierre – that good Pierre – have talked and laughed about this. So it's all right.' And again, under Hélène's influence, what had seemed terrible now seemed simple and natural. 'And she is such a *grande dame*, so kind, and evidently likes me so much. And why not enjoy myself?' thought Natasha gazing at Hélène with wide-open, wondering eyes.

Marya Dmitrievna came back to dinner taciturn and serious.

having evidently suffered a defeat at the old prince's. She was still too agitated by the encounter to be able to talk of the affair calmly. In answer to the count's inquiries she replied that things were all right and that she would tell about it next day. On hearing of Countess Bezukhova's visit and the invitation for that evening, Marya Dmitrievna remarked:

'I don't care to have anything to do with Bezukhova and don't advise you to; however, if you've promised – go. It will divert your thoughts,' she added, addressing Natasha.

13

COUNT ROSTOV took the girls to Countess Bezukhova's. There were a good many people there, but nearly all strangers to Natasha. Count Rostov was displeased to see that the company consisted almost entirely of men and women known for the freedom of their conduct. Mademoiselle George was standing in a corner of the drawing-room surrounded by young men. There were several Frenchmen present, among them Métivier, who from the time Hélène reached Moscow had been an intimate in her house. The count decided not to sit down to cards or let his girls out of his sight, and to get away as soon as Mademoiselle George's performance was over.

Anatole was at the door, evidently on the look-out for the Rostovs. Immediately after greeting the count he went up to Natasha and followed her. As soon as she saw him she was seized by the same feeling she had had at the opera – gratified vanity at his admiration of her, and fear at the absence of a moral barrier between them.

Hélène welcomed Natasha delightedly and was loud in admiration of her beauty and her dress. Soon after their arrival Mademoiselle George went out of the room to change her costume. In the drawing-room people began arranging the chairs and taking their seats. Anatole moved a chair for Natasha and was about to sit down beside her, but the count, who never lost sight of her, took the seat himself. Anatole sat down behind her.

Mademoiselle George, with her bare, fat, dimpled arms, and a red shawl draped over one shoulder, came into the space left vacant for her, and assumed an unnatural pose. Enthusiastic whispering was audible.

Mademoiselle George looked sternly and gloomily at the audience, and began reciting some French verses describing her guilty love for her son. In some places she raised her voice, in others she whispered, lifting her head triumphantly, sometimes she paused and uttered hoarse sounds, rolling her eyes.

'Adorable! divine! delicious!' was heard from every side.

Natasha looked at the fat actress, but neither saw nor heard nor understood anything of what went on before her. She only felt herself again completely borne away into this strange senseless world – so remote from her old world – a world in which it was impossible to know what was good or bad, reasonable or senseless. Behind her sat Anatole, and conscious of his proximity she experienced a frightened sense of expectancy.

After the first monologue the whole company rose and surrounded Mademoiselle George, expressing their enthusiasm.

'How beautiful she is!' Natasha remarked to her father, who had also risen and was moving through the crowd towards the actress.

'I don't think so when I look at you!' said Anatole, following Natasha. He said this at a moment when she alone could hear him. 'You are enchanting . . . from the moment I saw you I have never ceased . . .'

'Come, come, Natasha!' said the count, as he turned back for his daughter. 'How beautiful she is!'

Natasha without saying anything stepped up to her father and looked at him with surprised inquiring eyes.

After giving several recitations, Mademoiselle George left, and Countess Bezukhova asked her visitors into the ball-room.

The count wished to go home, but Hélène entreated him not to spoil her improvised ball, and the Rostovs stayed on. Anatole asked Natasha for a valse and as they danced he pressed her waist and hand and told her she was bewitching and that he loved her. During the Écossaise, which she also danced with him, Anatole said nothing when they happened to be by themselves, but merely gazed at her. Natasha lifted her frightened eyes to him, but there was such confident tenderness in his affectionate look and smile that she could not, whilst looking at him, say what she had to say. She lowered her eyes.

'Don't say such things to me. I am betrothed and love another,' she said rapidly . . . She glanced at him.

Anatole was not upset or pained by what she had said.

'Don't speak to me of that! What can I do?' said he. 'I tell you I am madly, madly, in love with you! Is it my fault that you are enchanting? . . . It's our turn to begin.'

Natasha, animated and excited, looked about her with wide-open frightened eyes and seemed merrier than usual. She understood hardly anything that went on that evening. They danced the

Écossaise and the *Grossvater*. Her father asked her to come home, but she begged to remain. Wherever she went and whomever she was speaking to, she felt *his* eyes upon her. Later on she recalled how she had asked her father to let her go to the dressing-room to rearrange her dress, that Hélène had followed her and spoken laughingly of her brother's love, and that she again met Anatole in the little sitting-room. Hélène had disappeared leaving them alone, and Anatole had taken her hand and said in a tender voice:

'I cannot come to visit you but is it possible that I shall never see you? I love you madly. Can I never . . . ?' and, blocking her path, he brought his face close to hers.

His large, glittering, masculine eyes were so close to hers that she saw nothing but them.

'Natalie?' he whispered inquiringly while she felt her hands being painfully pressed. 'Natalie?'

'I don't understand. I have nothing to say,' her eyes replied.

Burning lips were pressed to hers, and at the same instant she felt herself released, and Hélène's footsteps and the rustle of her dress were heard in the room. Natasha looked round at her, and then, red and trembling, threw a frightened look of inquiry at Anatole and moved towards the door.

'One word, just one, for God's sake!' cried Anatole.

She paused. She so wanted a word from him that would explain to her what had happened, and to which she could find an answer.

'Natalie, just a word, only one!' he kept repeating, evidently not knowing what to say – and he repeated it till Hélène came up to them.

Hélène returned with Natasha to the drawing-room. The Rostovs went away without staying for supper.

After reaching home Natasha did not sleep all night. She was tormented by the insoluble question whether she loved Anatole or Prince Andrew. She loved Prince Andrew – she remembered distinctly how deeply she loved him. But she also loved Anatole, of that there was no doubt. 'Else how could all this have happened?' thought she. 'If, after that, I could return his smile when saying good-bye, if I was able to let it come to that, it means that I loved him from the first. It means that he is kind, noble, and splendid, and I could not help loving him. What am I to do if I love him and the other one too?' she asked herself, unable to find an answer to these terrible questions.

MORNING came with its cares and bustle. Everyone got up and began to move about and talk, dressmakers came again, Marya Dmitrievna appeared, and they were called to breakfast. Natasha kept looking uneasily at everybody with wide-open eyes, as if wishing to intercept every glance directed towards her, and tried to appear the same as usual.

After breakfast, which was her best time, Marya Dmitrievna sat down in her arm-chair and called Natasha and the count to her.

'Well, friends, I have now thought the whole matter over and this is my advice,' she began. 'Yesterday, as you know, I went to see Prince Bolkonsky. Well, I had a talk with him ... He took it into his head to begin shouting, but I am not one to be shouted down. I said what I had to say!'

'Well, and he?' asked the count.

'He? He's crazy ... he did not want to listen. But what's the use of talking? As it is we have worn the poor girl out,' said Marya Dmitrievna. 'My advice to you is, finish your business and go back home to Otradnoe ... and wait there.'

'Oh, no!' exclaimed Natasha.

'Yes, go back,' said Marya Dmitrievna, 'and wait there. If your betrothed comes here now – there will be no avoiding a quarrel; but alone with the old man he will talk things over and then come on to you.'

Count Rostov approved of this suggestion, appreciating its reasonableness. If the old man came round it would be all the better to visit him in Moscow or at Bald Hills later on; and if not, the wedding, against his wishes, could only be arranged at Otradnoe.

'That is perfectly true. And I am sorry I went to see him and took her,' said the old count.

'No, why be sorry! Being here you had to pay your respects. But if he won't – that's his affair,' said Marya Dmitrievna, looking for something in her reticule. 'Besides, the trousseau is ready, so there is nothing to wait for; and what is not ready I'll send after you. Though I don't like letting you go, it is the best way. So go, with God's blessing!'

Having found what she was looking for in the reticule she handed it to Natasha. It was a letter from Princess Mary.

'She has written to you. How she torments herself, poor thing! She's afraid you might think that she does not like you.'

'But she doesn't like me,' said Natasha.

'Don't talk nonsense!' cried Marya Dmitrievna.

'I shan't believe anyone, I know she doesn't like me,' replied

Natasha boldly as she took the letter, and her face expressed a cold and angry resolution that caused Marya Dmitrievna to look at her more intently and to frown.

'Don't answer like that, my good girl!' she said. 'What I say is true! Write an answer!'

Natasha did not reply, and went to her own room to read Princess Mary's letter.

Princess Mary wrote that she was in despair at the misunderstanding that had occurred between them. Whatever her father's feelings might be, she begged Natasha to believe that she could not help loving her as the one chosen by her brother, for whose happiness she was ready to sacrifice everything.

'Do not think, however,' she wrote, 'that my father is ill-disposed towards you. He is an invalid and an old man who must be forgiven; but he is good and magnanimous, and will love her who makes his son happy.' Princess Mary went on to ask Natasha to fix a time when she could see her again.

After reading the letter Natasha sat down at the writing-table to answer it. 'Dear Princess,' she wrote in French quickly and mechanically, and then paused. What more could she write after all that had happened the evening before? 'Yes, yes! All that has happened, and now all is changed,' she thought as she sat with the letter she had begun before her. 'Must I break off with him? Must I really? That's awful!...' and to escape from these dreadful thoughts she went to Sonya and began sorting patterns with her.

After dinner Natasha went to her room and again took up Princess Mary's letter. 'Can it be that it is all over?' she thought. 'Can it be that all this has happened so quickly and has destroyed all that went before?' She recalled her love for Prince Andrew in all its former strength, and at the same time felt that she loved Kuragin. She vividly pictured herself as Prince Andrew's wife, and the scenes of happiness with him she had so often repeated in her imagination, and at the same time, aglow with excitement, recalled every detail of yesterday's interview with Anatole.

'Why could that not be as well?' she sometimes asked herself in complete bewilderment. 'Only so could I be completely happy; but now I have to choose, and I can't be happy without either of them. Only,' she thought, 'to tell Prince Andrew what has happened or to hide it from him are both equally impossible. But with *that one* nothing is spoilt. But am I really to abandon for ever the joy of Prince Andrew's love, in which I have lived so long?'

'Please, Miss!' whispered a maid entering the room with a mysterious air. 'A man told me to give you this –' and she handed Natasha a letter.

'Only, for Christ's sake . . .' the girl went on, as Natasha, without thinking, mechanically broke the seal and read a love-letter from Anatole, of which, without taking in a word, she understood only that it was a letter from him – from the man she loved. Yes, she loved him, or else how could that have happened which had happened? And how could she have a love-letter from him in her hand?

With trembling hands Natasha held that passionate love-letter which Dolokhov had composed for Anatole, and as she read it, she found in it an echo of all that she herself imagined she was feeling.

'Since yesterday evening my fate has been sealed; to be loved by you or to die. There is no other way for me,' the letter began. Then he went on to say that he knew her parents would not give her to him – for this there were secret reasons he could reveal only to her – but that if she loved him, she need only say the word Yes, and no human power could hinder their bliss. Love would conquer all. He would steal her away and carry her off to the ends of the earth.

'Yes, yes! I love him!' thought Natasha, reading the letter for the twentieth time and finding some peculiarly deep meaning in each word of it.

That evening Marya Dmitrievna was going to the Akharovs' and proposed to take the girls with her. Natasha, pleading a headache, remained at home.

15

On returning late in the evening Sonya went to Natasha's room, and to her surprise found her still dressed, and asleep on the sofa. Open on the table beside her lay Anatole's letter. Sonya picked it up and read it.

As she read she glanced at the sleeping Natasha, trying to find in her face an explanation of what she was reading, but did not find it. Her face was calm, gentle, and happy. Clutching her breast to keep herself from choking, Sonya, pale and trembling with fear and agitation, sat down in an arm-chair and burst into tears.

'How was it I noticed nothing? How could it go so far? Can she have left off loving Prince Andrew? And how could she let Kuragin go to such lengths? He is a deceiver and a villain, that's plain! What will Nicholas, dear noble Nicholas, do when he hears of it? So this is the meaning of her excited, resolute, unnatural look the the day before yesterday, yesterday, and to-day,' thought Sonya. 'But it can't be that she loves him! She probably opened the letter without knowing whom it was from. Probably she is offended by it. She could not do such a thing!'

Sonya wiped away her tears and went up to Natasha, again scanning her face.

'Natasha!' she said, just audibly.

Natasha awoke and saw Sonya.

'Ah, you're back?'

And with the decision and tenderness that often come at the moment of awakening, she embraced her friend, but noticing Sonya's look of embarrassment, her own face expressed confusion and suspicion.

'Sonya, you've read that letter?' she demanded.

'Yes,' answered Sonya softly.

Natasha smiled rapturously.

'No, Sonya, I can't any longer!' she said. 'I can't hide it from you any longer. You know we love one another! Sonya, darling, he writes . . . Sonya . . .'

Sonya stared open-eyed at Natasha, unable to believe her ears.

'And Bolkonsky?' she asked.

'Ah, Sonya, if you only knew how happy I am!' cried Natasha. 'You don't know what love is . . .'

'But, Natasha, can *that* be all over?'

Natasha looked at Sonya with wide-open eyes as if she could not grasp the question.

'Well then, are you refusing Prince Andrew?' said Sonya.

'Oh, you don't understand anything! Don't talk nonsense, just listen!' said Natasha, with momentary vexation.

'But I can't believe it,' insisted Sonya. 'I don't understand. How is it you have loved a man for a whole year and suddenly . . . Why, you have only seen him three times! Natasha, I don't believe you, you're joking! In three days to forget everything and so . . .'

'Three days?' said Natasha. 'It seems to me I've loved him a hundred years. It seems to me that I have never loved anyone before. You can't understand it. Sonya, wait a bit, sit here,' and Natasha embraced and kissed her.

'I had heard that it happens like this, and you must have heard it too, but it's only now that I feel such love. It's not the same as before. As soon as I saw him I felt he was my master and I his slave, and that I could not help loving him. Yes, his slave! Whatever he orders I shall do. You don't understand that. What can I do? What can I do, Sonya?' cried Natasha with a happy yet frightened expression.

'But think what you are doing,' cried Sonya. 'I can't leave it like this. This secret correspondence . . . How could you let him go so

616

far?' she went on, with a horror and disgust she could hardly conceal.

'I told you that I have no will,' Natasha replied. 'Why can't you understand? I love him!'

'Then I won't let it come to that . . . I shall tell!' cried Sonya, bursting into tears.

'What do you mean? For God's sake . . . If you tell, you are my enemy!' declared Natasha. 'You want me to be miserable, you want us to be separated . . .'

When she saw Natasha's fright, Sonya shed tears of shame and pity for her friend.

'But what has happened between you?' she asked. 'What has he said to you? Why doesn't he come to the house?'

Natasha did not answer her questions.

'For God's sake, Sonya, don't tell anyone, don't torture me,' Natasha entreated. 'Remember no one ought to interfere in such matters! I have confided in you . . .'

'But why this secrecy? Why doesn't he come to the house?' asked Sonya. 'Why doesn't he openly ask for your hand? You know Prince Andrew gave you complete freedom – if it is really so; but I don't believe it! Natasha, have you considered what these *secret reasons* can be?'

Natasha looked at Sonya with astonishment. Evidently this question presented itself to her mind for the first time and she did not know how to answer it.

'I don't know what the reasons are. But there must be reasons!'

Sonya sighed and shook her head incredulously.

'If there were reasons . . .' she began.

But Natasha, guessing her doubts, interrupted her in alarm.

'Sonya, one can't doubt him! One can't, one can't! Don't you understand?' she cried.

'Does he love you?'

'Does he love me?' Natasha repeated with a smile of pity at her friend's lack of comprehension. 'Why, you have read his letter and you have seen him.'

'But if he is dishonourable?'

'*He!* dishonourable? If you only knew!' exclaimed Natasha.

'If he is an honourable man he should either declare his intentions, or cease seeing you; and if you won't do this, I will. I will write to him, and I will tell papa!' said Sonya resolutely.

'But I can't live without him!' cried Natasha.

'Natasha, I don't understand you. And what are you saying! Think of your father and of Nicholas.'

'I don't want anyone, I don't love anyone but him. How dare

you say he is dishonourable? Don't you know that I love him?' screamed Natasha. 'Go away, Sonya! I don't want to quarrel with you, but go, for God's sake go! You see how I am suffering!' Natasha cried angrily, in a voice of despair and repressed irritation. Sonya burst into sobs and ran from the room.

Natasha went to the table and without a moment's reflection wrote that answer to Princess Mary which she had been unable to write all the morning. In this letter she said briefly that all their misunderstandings were at an end; that availing herself of the magnanimity of Prince Andrew, who when he went abroad had given her her freedom, she begged Princess Mary to forget everything and forgive her if she had been to blame towards her, but that she could not be his wife. At that moment this all seemed quite easy, simple, and clear to Natasha.

On Friday the Rostovs were to return to the country, but on Wednesday the count went with the prospective purchaser to his estate near Moscow.

On the day the count left, Sonya and Natasha were invited to a big dinner-party at the Karagins', and Marya Dmitrievna took them there. At that party Natasha again met Anatole, and Sonya noticed that she spoke to him, trying not to be overheard, and that all through dinner she was more agitated than ever. When they got home Natasha was the first to begin the explanation Sonya expected.

'There, Sonya, you were talking all sorts of nonsense about him,' Natasha began in a mild voice such as children use when they wish to be praised. 'We have had an explanation to-day.'

'Well, what happened? What did he say? Natasha, how glad I am you're not angry with me! Tell me everything – the whole truth. What did he say?'

Natasha became thoughtful.

'Oh, Sonya, if you knew him as I do! He said . . . He asked me what I had promised Bolkonsky. He was glad I was free to refuse him.'

Sonya sighed sorrowfully.

'But you haven't refused Bolkonsky?' said she.

'Perhaps I have. Perhaps all is over between me and Bolkonsky. Why do you think so badly of me?'

'I don't think anything, only I don't understand this . . .'

'Wait a bit, Sonya, you'll understand everything. You'll see what a man he is! Don't think badly of me or of him. I don't think badly of anyone: I love and pity everybody. But what am I to do?'

Sonya did not succumb to the tender tone Natasha used towards her. The more emotional and ingratiating the expression of Natasha's face became, the more serious and stern grew Sonya's.

'Natasha,' said she, 'you asked me not to speak to you, and I haven't spoken, but now you yourself have begun. I don't trust him, Natasha. Why this secrecy?'

'Again, again!' interrupted Natasha.

'Natasha, I am afraid for you!'

'Afraid of what?'

'I am afraid you're going to your ruin,' said Sonya resolutely, and was herself horrified at what she had said.

Anger again showed in Natasha's face.

'And I'll go to my ruin, I will, as soon as possible! It's not your business! It won't be you, but I, who'll suffer. Leave me alone, leave me alone! I hate you!'

'Natasha!' moaned Sonya, aghast.

'I hate you, I hate you! You're my enemy for ever!' And Natasha ran out of the room.

Natasha did not speak to Sonya again, and avoided her. With the same expression of agitated surprise and guilt she went about the house, taking up now one occupation, now another, and at once abandoning them.

Hard as it was for Sonya, she watched her friend and did not let her out of her sight.

The day before the count was to return, Sonya noticed that Natasha sat by the drawing-room window all the morning, as if expecting something, and that she made a sign to an officer who drove past, whom Sonya took to be Anatole.

Sonya began watching her friend still more attentively, and noticed that at dinner and all that evening Natasha was in a strange and unnatural state. She answered questions at random, began sentences she did not finish, and laughed at everything.

After tea Sonya noticed a housemaid at Natasha's door timidly waiting to let her pass. She let the girl go in, and then listening at the door, learnt that another letter had been delivered.

Then suddenly it became clear to Sonya that Natasha had some dreadful plan for that evening. Sonya knocked at her door. Natasha did not let her in.

'She will run away with him!' thought Sonya. 'She is capable of anything. There was something particularly pathetic and resolute in her face to-day. She cried as she said good-bye to uncle,' Sonya remembered. 'Yes, that's it, she means to elope with him, but what am I to do?' thought she, recalling all the signs that clearly indicated that Natasha had some terrible intention. 'The count is away.

What am I to do? Write to Kuragin demanding an explanation? But what is there to oblige him to reply? Write to Pierre, as Prince Andrew asked me to in case of some misfortune? ... But perhaps she really has already refused Bolkonsky – she sent a letter to Princess Mary yesterday. And uncle is away ...' To tell Marya Dmitrievna who had such faith in Natasha, seemed to Sonya terrible. 'Well anyway,' thought Sonya as she stood in the dark passage, 'now or never I must prove that I remember the family's goodness to me and that I love Nicholas. Yes! If I don't sleep for three nights I'll not leave this passage, and will hold her back by force and not let the family be disgraced,' she thought.

16

ANATOLE had lately moved to Dolokhov's. The plan for Natalie Rostova's abduction had been arranged and the preparations made by Dolokhov a few days before, and on the day that Sonya, after listening at Natasha's door, resolved to safeguard her, it was to have been put into execution. Natasha had promised to come out to Kuragin at the back porch at ten that evening. Kuragin was to put her into a troyka he would have ready, and to drive her forty miles to the village of Kamenka, where an unfrocked priest was in readiness to perform a marriage ceremony over them. At Kamenka a relay of horses was to wait which would take them to the Warsaw high road, and from there they would hasten abroad with post-horses.

Anatole had a passport, an order for post-horses, ten thousand rubles he had taken from his sister and another ten thousand borrowed with Dolokhov's help.

Two witnesses for the mock marriage – Khvostikov, a retired petty official whom Dolokhov made use of in his gambling transactions, and Makarin, a retired hussar, a kindly, weak fellow who had an unbounded affection for Kuragin – were sitting at tea in Dolokhov's front room.

In his large study, the walls of which were hung to the ceiling with Persian rugs, bearskins, and weapons, sat Dolokhov in a travelling cloak and high boots, at an open desk on which lay an abacus and some bundles of paper money. Anatole, with uniform unbuttoned, walked to and fro between the room where the witnesses were sitting, the study, and the room behind, where his French valet and others were packing the last of his things. Dolokhov was counting the money and noting something down.

'Well,' he said, 'Khvostikov must have two thousand.'

'Give it him, then,' said Anatole.

'Makarka' (their name for Makarin) 'will go through fire and water for you for nothing. So here are our accounts all settled,' said Dolokhov, showing him the memorandum. 'Is that right?'

'Yes, of course,' returned Anatole, evidently not listening to Dolokhov and looking straight before him with a smile that did not leave his face.

Dolokhov banged down the lid of his desk, and turned to Anatole with an ironic smile:

'Do you know? You'd really better drop it all. There's still time!'

'Fool,' retorted Anatole. 'Don't talk nonsense! If you only knew ... it's the devil knows what!'

'No, really, give it up!' said Dolokhov. 'I am speaking seriously. It's no joke, this plot you've hatched.'

'What, teasing again? Go to the devil! Eh?' said Anatole, making a grimace. 'Really it's no time for your stupid jokes,' and he left the room.

Dolokhov smiled contemptuously and condescendingly when Anatole had gone out.

'You wait a bit,' he called after him. 'I'm not joking, I'm talking sense. Come here, come here!'

Anatole returned and looked at Dolokhov, trying to give him his attention and evidently submitting to him involuntarily.

'Now listen to me. I'm telling you this for the last time. Why should I joke about it? Did I hinder you? Who arranged everything for you? Who found the priest and got the passport? Who raised the money? I did it all.'

'Well, thank you for it. Do you think I am not grateful?' And Anatole sighed and embraced Dolokhov.

'I helped you, but all the same I must tell you the truth; it is a dangerous business, and if you think about it – a stupid business. Well, you'll carry her off – all right! Will they let it stop at that? It will come out that you're already married. Why, they'll have you in the criminal court ...'

'Oh, nonsense, nonsense!' Anatole ejaculated and again made a grimace. 'Didn't I explain to you? What?' And Anatole, with the partiality dull-witted people have for any conclusion they have reached by their own reasoning, repeated the argument he had already put to Dolokhov a hundred times. 'Didn't I explain to you that I have come to this conclusion: if this marriage is invalid,' he went on, crooking one finger, 'then I have nothing to answer for; but if it is valid, no matter! Abroad no one will know anything about it. Isn't that so? And don't talk to me, don't don't!'

'Seriously, you'd better drop it! You'll only get yourself into a mess!'

'Go to the devil!' cried Anatole and clutching his hair left the room, but returned at once and dropped into an arm-chair in front of Dolokhov with his feet tucked under him. 'It's the very devil! What? Feel how it beats!' He took Dolokhov's hand and put it on his heart. 'What a foot, my dear fellow! What a glance! A goddess!' he added in French. 'What?'

Dolokhov with a cold smile and a gleam in his handsome insolent eyes looked at him – evidently wishing to get some more amusement out of him.

'Well, and when the money's gone, what then?'

'What then? Eh?' repeated Anatole, sincerely perplexed by a thought of the future. 'What then? ... Then, I don't know ... But why talk nonsense!' He glanced at his watch. 'It's time!'

Anatole went into the back room.

'Now then! Nearly ready? You're dawdling!' he shouted to the servants.

Dolokhov put away the money, called a footman whom he ordered to bring something for them to eat and drink before the journey, and went into the room where Khvostikov and Makarin were sitting.

Anatole lay on the sofa in the study leaning on his elbow and smiling pensively, while his handsome lips muttered tenderly to himself.

'Come and eat something. Have a drink!' Dolokhov shouted to him from the other room.

'I don't want to,' answered Anatole continuing to smile.

'Come! Balaga is here.'

Anatole rose and went into the dining-room. Balaga was a famous troyka driver who had known Dolokhov and Anatole some six years and had given them good service with his troykas. More than once when Anatole's regiment was stationed at Tver he had taken him from Tver in the evening, brought him to Moscow by daybreak, and driven him back again the next night. More than once he had enabled Dolokhov to escape when pursued. More than once he had driven them through the town with gipsies and 'ladykins' as he called the *cocottes*. More than once in their service he had run over pedestrians and upset vehicles in the streets of Moscow, and had always been protected from the consequences by 'my gentlemen' as he called them. He had ruined more than one horse in their service. More than once they had beaten him, and more than once they had made him drunk on champagne and madeira, which he loved; and he knew more than one thing about each of them which would long ago have sent an ordinary man to Siberia. They often called Balaga into their orgies and made him drink and dance at the gipsies', and more than one thousand rubles of their money had passed through his hands. In their service he risked his skin and his life twenty times a year, and in their service had lost more horses than the money he had from them would buy. But he liked them; liked that mad driving at twelve miles an hour, liked upsetting a driver, or running down a pedestrian, and flying at full gallop through the Moscow streets. He liked to hear those wild, tipsy shouts behind him: 'Get on! Get on!' when it was impossible to go any faster. He liked giving a painful lash on the neck to some peasant who, more dead than alive, was already hurrying out of his way. 'Real gentlemen!' he considered them.

Anatole and Dolokhov liked Balaga too, for his masterly driving and because he liked the things they liked. With others Balaga bargained, charging twenty-five rubles for a two-hours' drive, and rarely drove himself, generally letting his young men do so. But with 'his gentlemen' he always drove himself, and never demanded anything for his work. Only a couple of times a year – when he knew from their valets that they had money in hand – he would turn up of a morning quite sober, and with a deep bow would ask them to help him. The gentlemen always made him sit down.

'Do help me out, Theodore Ivanych, sir,' or 'your Excellency,' he would say. 'I am quite out of horses. Let me have what you can to go to the fair.'

And Anatole and Dolokhov, when they had money, would give him a thousand or a couple of thousand rubles.

Balaga was a fair-haired, short, and snub-nosed peasant of about twenty-seven, red-faced, with a particularly red thick neck, glittering little eyes, and a small beard. He wore a fine, dark-blue, silk-lined cloth coat over a sheepskin.

On entering the room now, he crossed himself, turning towards the front corner of the room, and went up to Dolokhov holding out a small, black hand.

'Theodore Ivanych!' he said, bowing.

'How d'you do, friend? Well, here he is!'

'Good day, your Excellency!' he said, again holding out his hand to Anatole who had just come in.

'I say, Balaga,' said Anatole, putting his hands on the man's shoulders, 'do you care for me or not? Eh? Now, do me a service ... What horses have you come with? Eh?'

'As your messenger ordered, your special beasts,' replied Balaga.

'Well, listen, Balaga! Drive all three to death, but get me there in three hours. Eh?'

'When they are dead, what shall I drive?' said Balaga with a wink.

'Mind, I'll smash your face in! Don't make jokes!' cried Anatole, suddenly rolling his eyes.

'Why joke?' said the driver, laughing. 'As if I'd grudge my gentlemen anything! As fast as ever the horses can gallop, so fast we'll go!'

'Ah!' said Anatole. 'Well, sit down.'

'Yes, sit down!' said Dolokhov.

'I'll stand, Theodore Ivanych.'

'Sit down; nonsense! Have a drink!' said Anatole, and filled a large glass of madeira for him.

The driver's eyes sparkled at the sight of the wine. After refusing it for manners' sake, he drank it and wiped his mouth with a red silk handkerchief he took out of his cap.

'And when are we to start, your Excellency?'

'Well...' Anatole looked at his watch. 'We'll start at once. Mind, Balaga! You'll get there in time? Eh?'

'That depends on our luck in starting, else why shouldn't we be there in time?' replied Balaga. 'Didn't we get you to Tver in seven hours? I think you remember that, your Excellency?'

'Do you know, one Christmas I drove from Tver,' said Anatole, smiling at the recollection and turning to Makarin who gazed rapturously at him with wide-open eyes. 'Will you believe it, Makarka, it took one's breath away, the rate we flew. We came across a train of loaded sledges, and drove right over two of them. Eh?'

'Those were horses!' Balaga continued the tale. 'That time I'd harnessed two young side-horses with the bay in the shafts,' he went on, turning to Dolokhov. 'Will you believe it, Theodore Ivanych, those animals flew forty miles? I couldn't hold them in, my hands grew numb in the sharp frost so that I threw down the reins – "Catch hold yourself, your Excellency!" says I, and I just tumbled on the bottom of the sledge and sprawled there. It wasn't a case of urging them on, there was no holding them in till we reached the place. The devils took us there in three hours! Only the near one died of it.'

ANATOLE went out of the room and returned a few minutes later wearing a fur coat girt with a silver belt and a sable cap jauntily set on one side and very becoming to his handsome face. Having looked in a mirror, and standing before Dolokhov in the same pose he had assumed before it, he lifted a glass of wine.

'Well, good-bye, Theodore. Thank you for everything and farewell!' said Anatole. 'Well, comrades and friends...' he considered for a moment, '...of my youth, farewell!' he said, turning to Makarin and the others.

Though they were all going with him, Anatole evidently wished to make something touching and solemn out of this address to his comrades. He spoke slowly in a loud voice, and throwing out his chest slightly swayed one leg.

'All take glasses; you too, Balaga. Well, comrades and friends of my youth, we've had our fling and lived and revelled. Eh? And now, when shall we meet again? I am going abroad. We have had a good time – now farewell, lads! To our health! Hurrah!...' he cried, and emptying his glass flung it on the floor.

'To your health!' said Balaga who also emptied his glass, and wiped his mouth with his handkerchief.

Makarin embraced Anatole with tears in his eyes.

'Ah, Prince, how sorry I am to part from you?'

'Let's go. Let's go!' cried Anatole.

Balaga was about to leave the room.

'No, stop!' said Anatole. 'Shut the door; we have first to sit down.* That's the way.'

They shut the door and all sat down.

'Now, quick march, lads!' said Anatole, rising.

Joseph, his valet, handed him his sabretache and sabre, and they all went out into the vestibule.

'And where's the fur cloak?' asked Dolokhov. 'Hey, Ignatka! Go to Matrëna Matrevna and ask her for the sable cloak. I have heard what elopements are like,' continued Dolokhov with a wink. 'Why, she'll rush out more dead than alive just in the things she is wearing; if you delay at all, there'll be tears and "papa" and "mamma", and she's frozen in a minute and must go back – but you wrap the fur cloak round her first thing and carry her to the sledge.'

The valet brought a woman's fox-lined cloak.

'Fool, I told you the sable one! Hey, Matrëna, the sable!' he shouted, so that his voice rang far through the rooms.

A handsome, slim, and pale-faced gipsy-girl with glittering black eyes and curly blue-black hair, wearing a red shawl, ran out with a sable mantle on her arm.

'Here, I don't grudge it – take it!' she said, evidently afraid of her master and yet regretful of her cloak.

Dolokhov, without answering, took the cloak, threw it over Matrëna and wrapped her up in it.

'That's the way,' said Dolokhov, 'and then so!' and he turned the collar up round her head, leaving only a little of the face uncovered. 'And then so, do you see?' and he pushed Anatole's head forward to meet the gap left by the collar, through which Matrëna's brilliant smile was seen.

'Well, good-bye, Matrëna,' said Anatole, kissing her. 'Ah, my revels here are over. Remember me to Stëshka.* There, good-bye! Good-bye, Matrëna, wish me luck!'

'Well, Prince, may God give you great luck!' said Matrëna in her gipsy accent.

Two troykas were standing before the porch and two young drivers were holding the horses. Balaga took his seat in the front one, and holding his elbows high arranged the reins deliberately. Anatole and Dolokhov got in with him. Makarin, Khvostikov, and a valet seated themselves in the other sledge.

'Well, are you ready?' asked Balaga.

'Go!' he cried, twisting the reins round his hands, and the troyka tore down the Nikitsky Boulevard.

'Tproo! Get out of the way! Hi!... Tproo!...' The shouting of Balaga and of the sturdy young fellow seated on the box was all that could be heard. On the Arbat Square the troyka caught against a carriage; something cracked, shouts were heard, and the troyka flew along the Arbat Street.

After taking a turn along the Podnovinsky Boulevard, Balaga began to rein in, and turning back drew up at the crossing of the old Konyusheny Street.

The young fellow on the box jumped down to hold the horses, and Anatole and Dolokhov went along the pavement. When they reached the gate Dolokhov whistled. The whistle was answered, and a maidservant ran out.

'Come into the courtyard or you'll be seen; she'll come out directly,' said she.

Dolokhov stayed by the gate. Anatole followed the maid into the courtyard, turned the corner, and ran up into the porch.

He was met by Gabriel, Marya Dmitrievna's gigantic footman.

'Come to the mistress, please,' said the footman in his deep bass, intercepting any retreat.

626

'To what mistress? Who are you?' asked Anatole in a breathless whisper.

'Kindly step in, my orders are to bring you in.'

'Kuragin! Come back!' shouted Dolokhov. 'Betrayed! Back!'

Dolokhov, after Anatole entered, had remained at the wicket-gate, and was struggling with the yard-porter who was trying to lock it. With a last desperate effort Dolokhov pushed the porter aside, and when Anatole ran back seized him by the arm, pulled him through the wicket, and ran back with him to the troyka.

18

MARY DMITRIEVNA having found Sonya weeping in the corridor, made her confess everything, and intercepting the note to Natasha she read it and went into Natasha's room with it in her hand.

'You shameless good-for-nothing!' said she. 'I won't hear a word.'

Pushing back Natasha, who looked at her with astonished but tearless eyes, she locked her in, and having given orders to the yard-porter to admit the persons who would be coming that evening, but not to let them out again, and having told the footman to bring them up to her, she seated herself in the drawing-room to await the abductors.

When Gabriel came to inform her that the men who had come had run away again, she rose frowning, and clasping her hands behind her paced through the rooms a long time considering what she should do. Towards midnight she went to Natasha's room finger-ing the key in her pocket. Sonya was sitting sobbing in the corridor. 'Marya Dmitrievna, for God's sake let me in to her!' she pleaded, but Marya Dmitrievna unlocked the door and went in without giving her an answer ... 'Disgusting, abominable ... In my house ... horrid girl, hussy! I'm only sorry for her father!' thought she, trying to restrain her wrath. 'Hard as it may be, I'll tell them all to hold their tongues, and will hide it from the count.' She entered the room with resolute steps. Natasha was lying on the sofa, her head hidden in her hands, and she did not stir. She was in just the same position in which Marya Dmitrievna had left her.

'A nice girl! Very nice!' said Marya Dmitrievna. 'Arranging meetings with lovers in my house! It's no use pretending: you listen when I speak to you!' And Marya Dmitrievna touched her arm. 'Listen when I speak! You've disgraced yourself like the lowest of hussies. I'd treat you differently, but I'm sorry for your father, so I will conceal it.'

Natasha did not change her position, but her whole body heaved with noiseless, convulsive sobs which choked her. Marya Dmitrievna glanced round at Sonya and seated herself on the sofa beside Natasha.

'It's lucky for him that he escaped me; but I'll find him!' she said in her rough voice. 'Do you hear what I am saying or not?' she added.

She put her large hand under Natasha's face and turned it towards her. Both Marya Dmitrievna and Sonya were amazed when they saw how Natasha looked. Her eyes were dry and glistening, her lips compressed, her cheeks sunken.

'Let me be!... What is it to me?... I shall die!' she muttered, wrenching herself from Marya Dmitrievna's hands with a vicious effort and sinking down again into her former position.

'Natalie!' said Marya Dmitrievna. 'I wish for your good. Lie still, stay like that then, I won't touch you. But listen. I won't tell you how guilty you are. You know that yourself. But when your father comes back to-morrow – what am I to tell him? Eh?'

Again Natasha's body shook with sobs.

'Suppose he finds out, and your brother, and your betrothed?'

'I have no betrothed: I have refused him!' cried Natasha.

'That's all the same,' continued Marya Dmitrievna. 'If they hear of this will they let it pass? He, your father, I know him ... if he challenges him to a duel will that be all right? Eh?'

'Oh, let me be! Why have you interfered at all? Why? Why? Who asked you to?' shouted Natasha, raising herself on the sofa and looking malignantly at Marya Dmitrievna.

'But what did you want?' cried Marya Dmitrievna, growing angry again. 'Were you kept under lock and key? Who hindered his coming to the house? Why carry you off as if you were some gipsy singing-girl?... Well, if he had carried you off ... 'do you think they wouldn't have found him? Your father, or brother, or your betrothed? And he's a scoundrel, a wretch – that's a fact!'

'He is better than any of you!' exclaimed Natasha getting up. 'If you hadn't interfered ... Oh, my God! What is it all? What is it? Sonya, why ...? Go away!'

And she burst into sobs with the despairing vehemence with which people bewail disasters they feel they have themselves caused. Marya Dmitrievna was about to speak again, but Natasha cried out:

'Go away! Go away! You all hate and despise me!' and she threw herself back on the sofa.

Marya Dmitrievna went on admonishing her for some time, enjoining on her that it must all be kept from her father and assuring her that nobody would know anything about it if only Natasha herself would undertake to forget it all and not let anyone see that something had happened. Natasha did not reply, nor did she sob any longer, but she grew cold and had a shivering fit. Marya Dmitrievna put a pillow under her head, covered her with two quilts, and herself brought her some lime-flower water, but Natasha did not respond to her.

'Well, let her sleep,' said Marya Dmitrievna as she went out of the room supposing Natasha to be asleep.

But Natasha was not asleep; with pale face and fixed wide-open eyes she looked straight before her. All that night she did not sleep or weep, and did not speak to Sonya who got up and went to her several times.

Next day Count Rostov returned from his estate near Moscow in time for lunch as he had promised. He was in very good spirits; the affair with the purchaser was going on satisfactorily, and there was nothing to keep him any longer in Moscow, away from the countess whom he missed. Marya Dmitrievna met him and told him that Natasha had been very unwell the day before and that they had sent for the doctor, but that she was better now. Natasha had not left her room that morning. With compressed and parched lips, and dry fixed eyes, she sat at the window, uneasily watching the people who drove past, and hurriedly glancing round at anyone who entered the room. She was evidently expecting news of him and that he would come or would write to her.

When the count came to see her she turned anxiously round at the sound of a man's footstep, and then her face resumed its cold and malevolent expression. She did not even get up to greet him.

'What is the matter with you, my angel? Are you ill?' asked the count.

After a moment's silence Natasha answered: 'Yes, ill.'

In reply to the count's anxious inquiries as to why she was so dejected and whether anything had happened to her betrothed, she assured him that nothing had happened and asked him not to worry. Marya Dmitrievna confirmed Natasha's assurances that nothing had happened. From the pretence of illness, from his daughter's distress, and by the embarrassed faces of Sonya and Marya Dmitrievna, the count saw clearly that something had gone wrong during his absence, but it was so terrible for him to think that anything disgraceful had happened to his beloved daughter, and he so prized his own cheerful tranquillity, that he avoided inquiries and tried to assure himself that nothing particular had happened, and he was only dissatisfied that her indisposition delayed their return to the country.

FROM the day his wife arrived in Moscow Pierre had been intending to go away somewhere, so as not to be near her. Soon after the Rostovs came to Moscow the effect Natasha had on him made him hasten to carry out his intention. He went to Tver to see Joseph Alexeevich's widow, who had long since promised to hand over to him some papers of her deceased husband's.

When he returned to Moscow Pierre was handed a letter from Marya Dmitrievna asking him to come and see her on a matter of great importance relating to Andrew Bolkonsky and his betrothed. Pierre had been avoiding Natasha because it seemed to him that his feeling for her was stronger than a married man's should be for his friend's fiancée. Yet some fate constantly threw them together.

'What can have happened? And what can they want with me?' thought he as he dressed to go to Marya Dmitrievna's. 'If only Prince Andrew would hurry up and come and marry her!' thought he on his way to the house.

On the Tverskoy Boulevard a familiar voice called to him.

'Pierre! Been back long?' someone shouted. Pierre raised his head. In a sledge drawn by two grey trotting-horses that were bespattering the dashboard with snow, Anatole and his constant companion Makarin dashed past. Anatole was sitting upright in the classic pose of military dandies, the lower part of his face hidden by his beaver collar and his head slightly bent. His face was fresh and rosy, his white-plumed hat, tilted to one side, disclosed his curled and pomaded hair besprinkled with powdery snow.

'Yes, indeed, that's a true sage,' thought Pierre. 'He sees nothing beyond the pleasure of the moment, nothing troubles him and so he is always cheerful, satisfied, and serene. What wouldn't I give to be like him!' he thought enviously.

In Marya Dmitrievna's ante-room the footman who helped him off with his fur coat said that the mistress asked him to come to her bedroom.

When he opened the ball-room door Pierre saw Natasha sitting at the window, with a thin, pale, and spiteful face. She glanced round at him, frowned, and left the room with an expression of cold dignity.

'What has happened?' asked Pierre, entering Marya Dmitrievna's room.

'Fine doings!' answered Marya Dmitrievna. 'For fifty-eight years have I lived in this world and never known anything so disgraceful.'

And having put him on his honour not to repeat anything she

told him, Marya Dmitrievna informed him that Natasha had refused Prince Andrew without her parents' knowledge, and that the cause of this was Anatole Kuragin into whose society Pierre's wife had thrown her, and with whom Natasha had tried to elope during her father's absence, in order to be married secretly.

Pierre raised his shoulders and listened open-mouthed to what was told him, scarcely able to believe his own ears. That Prince Andrew's deeply loved affianced wife – the same Natasha Rostova who used to be so charming – should give up Bolkonsky for that fool Anatole who was already secretly married (as Pierre knew), and should be so in love with him as to agree to run away with him, was something Pierre could not conceive and could not imagine.

He could not reconcile the charming impression he had of Natasha, whom he had known from a child, with this new conception of her baseness, folly, and cruelty. He thought of his wife. 'They are all alike!' he said to himself, reflecting that he was not the only man unfortunate enough to be tied to a bad woman. But still he pitied Prince Andrew to the point of tears and sympathized with his wounded pride, and the more he pitied his friend the more did he think with contempt and even with disgust of that Natasha who had just passed him in the ball-room with such a look of cold dignity. He did not know that Natasha's soul was overflowing with despair, shame, and humiliation, and that it was not her fault that her face happened to assume an expression of calm dignity and severity.

'But how get married?' said Pierre, in answer to Marya Dmitrievna. 'He could not marry – he is married!'

'Things get worse from hour to hour!' ejaculated Marya Dmitrievna. 'A nice youth! What a scoundrel! And she's expecting him – expecting him since yesterday. She must be told! Then at least she won't go on expecting him.'

After hearing the details of Anatole's marriage from Pierre, and giving vent to her anger against Anatole in words of abuse, Marya Dmitrievna told Pierre why she had sent for him. She was afraid that the count or Bolkonsky, who might arrive at any moment, if they knew of this affair (which she hoped to hide from them) might challenge Anatole to a duel, and she therefore asked Pierre to tell his brother-in-law in her name to leave Moscow and not dare to let her set eyes on him again. Pierre – only now realizing the danger to the old count, Nicholas, and Prince Andrew – promised to do as she wished. Having briefly and exactly explained her wishes to him, she let him go to the drawing-room.

'Mind, the count knows nothing. Behave as if you know nothing either,' she said. 'And I will go and tell her it is no use expecting him! And stay to dinner if you care to!' she called after Pierre.

Pierre met the old count, who seemed nervous and upset. That morning Natasha had told him that she had rejected Bolkonsky.

'Troubles, troubles, my dear fellow!' he said to Pierre. 'What troubles one has with these girls without their mother! I do so regret having come here. I will be frank with you. Have you heard she has broken off her engagement without consulting anybody? It's true this engagement never was much to my liking. Of course he is an excellent man, but still, with his father's disapproval they wouldn't have been happy, and Natasha won't lack suitors. Still, it has been going on so long, and to take such a step without father's or mother's consent! And now she's ill, and God knows what! It's hard, Count, hard to manage daughters in their mother's absence . . .'

Pierre saw that the count was much upset, and tried to change the subject, but the count returned to his troubles.

Sonya entered the room with an agitated face.

'Natasha is not quite well; she's in her room and would like to see you. Marya Dmitrievna is with her and she too asks you to come.'

'Yes, you are a great friend of Bolkonsky's, no doubt she wants to send him a message,' said the count. 'Oh dear! Oh dear! How happy it all was!'

And clutching the spare grey locks on his temples the count left the room.

When Marya Dmitrievna told Natasha that Anatole was married, Natasha did not wish to believe it, and insisted on having it confirmed by Pierre himself. Sonya told Pierre this as she led him along the corridor to Natasha's room.

Natasha, pale and stern, was sitting beside Marya Dmitrievna, and her eyes, glittering feverishly, met Pierre with a questioning look the moment he entered. She did not smile or nod, but only gazed fixedly at him, and her look asked only one thing: was he a friend, or like the others an enemy in regard to Anatole? As for himself, Pierre evidently did not exist for her.

'He knows all about it,' said Marya Dmitrievna pointing to Pierre and addressing Natasha. 'Let him tell you whether I have told you the truth.'

Natasha looked from one to the other as a hunted and wounded animal looks at the approaching dogs and sportsmen.

'Natalya Ilynichna,' Pierre began, dropping his eyes with a feeling of pity for her and loathing for the thing he had to do, 'whether it is true or not should make no difference to you, because . . .'

'Then it is not true that he's married!'

'Yes, it is true.'

'Has he been married long?' she asked. 'On your honour? . . .'

Pierre gave his word of honour.

'Is he still here?' she asked, quickly.

'Yes, I have just seen him.'

She was evidently unable to speak, and made a sign with her hands that they should leave her alone.

20

PIERRE did not stay for dinner, but left the room and went away at once. He drove through the town seeking Anatole Kuragin, at the thought of whom now the blood rushed to his heart and he felt a difficulty in breathing. He was not at the ice-hills, nor at the gipsies', nor at Komoneno's. Pierre drove to the club. In the club all was going on as usual. The members who were assembling for dinner were sitting about in groups; they greeted Pierre and spoke of the town news. The footman having greeted him, knowing his habits and his acquaintances, told him there was a place left for him in the small dining-room, and that Prince Michael Zakharych was in the library, but Paul Timofeevich had not yet arrived. One of Pierre's acquaintances, while they were talking about the weather, asked if he had heard of Kuragin's abduction of Rostova which was talked of in the town, and was it true? Pierre laughed and said it was nonsense for he had just come from the Rostovs'. He asked everyone about Anatole. One man told him he had not come yet, and another that he was coming to dinner. Pierre felt it strange to see this calm, indifferent crowd of people unaware of what was going on in his soul. He paced through the ball-room, waited till everyone had come, and as Anatole had not turned up, did not stay for dinner but drove home.

Anatole, for whom Pierre was looking, dined that day with Dolokhov, consulting him as to how to remedy this unfortunate affair. It seemed to him essential to see Natasha. In the evening he drove to his sister's to discuss with her how to arrange a meeting. When Pierre returned home after vainly hunting all over Moscow, his valet informed him that Prince Anatole was with the countess. The countess's drawing-room was full of guests.

Pierre without greeting his wife whom he had not seen since his return – at that moment she was more repulsive to him than ever – entered the drawing-room and seeing Anatole went up to him.

'Ah, Pierre,' said the countess going up to her husband. 'You don't know what a plight our Anatole . . .'

She stopped, seeing in the forward thrust of her husband's head,

633

in his glowing eyes and his resolute gait, the terrible indications of that rage and strength which she knew, and had herself experienced after his duel with Dolokhov.

'Where you are, there is vice and evil!' said Pierre to his wife. 'Anatole, come with me! I must speak to you,' he added in French.

Anatole glanced round at his sister and rose submissively, ready to follow Pierre. Pierre, taking him by the arm, pulled him towards himself and was leading him from the room.

'If you allow yourself in my drawing-room . . .' whispered Hélène, but Pierre did not reply and went out of the room.

Anatole followed him with his usual jaunty step but his face betrayed anxiety.

Having entered his study Pierre closed the door, and addressed Anatole without looking at him.

'You promised Countess Rostova to marry her and were about to elope with her, is that so?'

'*Mon cher*,' answered Anatole (their whole conversation was in French), 'I don't consider myself bound to answer questions put to me in that tone.'

Pierre's face, already pale, became distorted by fury. He seized Anatole by the collar of his uniform with his big hand, and shook him from side to side till Anatole's face showed a sufficient degree of terror.

'When I tell you that I must talk to you! . . .' repeated Pierre.

'Come now, this is stupid. What?' said Anatole, fingering a button of his collar that had been wrenched loose with a bit of the cloth.

'You're a scoundrel and a blackguard, and I don't know what restrains me from the pleasure of smashing your head with this,' said Pierre, expressing himself so artificially because he was talking French.

He took a heavy paper-weight and lifted it threateningly, but at once put it back in its place.

'Did you promise to marry her?'

'I . . . I . . . I didn't think of it. I never promised, because . . .'

Pierre interrupted him.

'Have you any letters of hers? Any letters?' he said, moving towards Anatole.

Anatole glanced at him and immediately thrust his hand into his pocket and drew out his pocket-book.

Pierre took the letter Anatole handed him, and pushing aside a table that stood in his way, threw himself on the sofa.

'I shan't be violent, don't be afraid,' said Pierre in answer to a frightened gesture of Anatole's. 'First, the letters,' said he, as if repeating a lesson to himself. 'Secondly,' he continued after a short pause, again rising and again pacing the room, 'to-morrow you must get out of Moscow.'

'But how can I . . . ?'

'Thirdly,' Pierre continued without listening to him, 'you must never breathe a word of what has passed between you and Countess Rostova. I know I can't prevent your doing so, but if you have a spark of conscience . . .' Pierre paced the room several times in silence.

Anatole sat at the table frowning and biting his lips.

'After all, you must understand that besides your pleasure there is such a thing as other people's happiness and peace, and that you are ruining a whole life for the sake of amusing yourself! Amuse yourself with women like my wife – with them you are within your rights, for they know what you want of them. They are armed against you by the same experience of debauchery; but to promise *a maid* to marry her . . . to deceive, to kidnap . . . Don't you understand that it is as mean as beating an old man or a child? . . .'

Pierre paused and looked at Anatole no longer with an angry, but with a questioning look.

'I don't know about that, eh?' said Anatole, growing more confident as Pierre mastered his wrath. 'I don't know that and don't want to,' he said, not looking at Pierre, and with a slight tremor of his lower jaw, 'but you have used such words to me – "mean" and so on, which as a man of honour I can't allow anyone to use.'

Pierre glanced at him with amazement, unable to understand what he wanted.

'Though it was tête-à-tête,' Anatole continued, 'still I can't . . .'

'Is it satisfaction you want?' said Pierre ironically.

'You could at least take back your words. What? If you want me to do as you wish, eh?'

'I take them back, I take them back!' said Pierre, 'and I ask you to forgive me.' Pierre involuntarily glanced at the loose button. 'And if you require money for your journey . . .'

Anatole smiled. The expression of that base and cringing smile, which Pierre knew so well in his wife, revolted him.

'Oh, vile and heartless brood!' he exclaimed, and left the room.

Next day Anatole left for Petersburg.

21

PIERRE drove to Marya Dmitrievna's to tell her of the fulfilment of her wish that Kuragin should be banished from Moscow. The whole house was in a state of alarm and commotion. Natasha was very ill, having, as Marya Dmitrievna told him in secret, poisoned herself the night after she had been told that Anatole was married, with some arsenic she had stealthily procured. After swallowing a little she had been so frightened that she woke Sonya and told her what she had done. The necessary antidotes had been administered in time and she was now out of danger, though still so weak that it was out of the question to move her to the country, and so the countess had been sent for. Pierre saw the distracted count and Sonya, who had a tear-stained face, but he could not see Natasha.

Pierre dined at the club that day and heard on all sides gossip about the attempted abduction of Rostova. He resolutely denied these rumours, assuring everyone that nothing had happened except that his brother-in-law had proposed to her and been refused. It seemed to Pierre that it was his duty to conceal the whole affair and re-establish Natasha's reputation.

He was awaiting Prince Andrew's return with dread, and went every day to the old prince's for news of him.

Old Prince Bolkonsky heard all the rumours current in the town from Mademoiselle Bourienne, and had read the note to Princess Mary in which Natasha had broken off her engagement. He seemed in better spirits than usual and awaited his son with great impatience.

Some days after Anatole's departure Pierre received a note from Prince Andrew, informing him of his arrival and asking him to come to see him.

Directly he reached Moscow Prince Andrew had received from his father Natasha's note to Princess Mary breaking off her engagement (Mademoiselle Bourienne had purloined it from Princess Mary and given it to the old prince) and he heard from him the story of Natasha's elopement, with additions.

Prince Andrew had arrived in the evening and Pierre came to see him next morning. Pierre expected to find Prince Andrew in almost the same state as Natasha, and was therefore surprised on entering the drawing-room to hear him in the study talking in a loud animated voice about some intrigue going on in Petersburg. The old prince's voice and another now and then interrupted him. Princess Mary came out to meet Pierre. She sighed, looking towards the door of the room where Prince Andrew was, evidently intending to express her sympathy with his sorrow, but Pierre saw by her face that she was glad both at what had happened and at the way her brother had taken the news of Natasha's faithlessness.

'He says he expected it,' she remarked. 'I know his pride will not let him express his feelings, but still he has taken it better, far better, than I expected. Evidently it had to be . . .'

'But is it possible that all is really ended?' asked Pierre.

Princess Mary looked at him with astonishment. She did not understand how he could ask such a question. Pierre went into the study. Prince Andrew, greatly changed and plainly in better health, but with a fresh horizontal wrinkle between his brows, stood in civilian dress facing his father and Prince Meshchersky, warmly disputing and vigorously gesticulating. The conversation was about Speransky – the news of whose sudden exile and alleged treachery had just reached Moscow.*

'Now he is censured and accused by all who were enthusiastic about him a month ago,' Prince Andrew was saying, 'and by those who were unable to understand his aims. To judge a man who is in disfavour and to throw on him all the blame of other men's mistakes is very easy, but I maintain that if anything good has been accomplished in this reign it was done by him, by him alone.'

He paused at the sight of Pierre. His face quivered and immediately assumed a vindictive expression.

'Posterity will do him justice,' he concluded, and at once turned to Pierre.

'Well, how are you? Still getting stouter?' he said with animation, but the new wrinkle on his forehead deepened. 'Yes, I am well,' he said in answer to Pierre's question, and smiled.

To Pierre that smile said plainly: 'I am well, but my health is now of no use to anyone.'

After a few words to Pierre about the awful roads from the Polish frontier, about people he had met in Switzerland who knew Pierre, and about M. Dessalles, whom he had brought from abroad to be his son's tutor, Prince Andrew again joined warmly in the conversation about Speransky which was still going on between the two old men.

'If there were treason, or proofs of secret relations with Napoleon, they would have been made public,' he said with warmth and haste. 'I do not, and never did, like Speransky personally, but I like justice!'

Pierre now recognized in his friend a need with which he was only too familiar, to get excited and to have arguments about extraneous matters in order to stifle thoughts that were too oppressive and too intimate.

When Prince Meshchersky had left, Prince Andrew took Pierre's arm and asked him into the room that had been assigned him. A bed had been made up there, and some open portmanteaux and trunks stood about. Prince Andrew went to one and took out a small casket, from which he drew a packet wrapped in paper. He did it all silently and very quickly. He stood up and coughed. His face was gloomy and his lips compressed.

'Forgive me for troubling you . . .'

Pierre saw that Prince Andrew was going to speak of Natasha, and his broad face expressed pity and sympathy. This expression irritated Prince Andrew, and in a determined, ringing, and unpleasant tone he continued:

'I have received a refusal from Countess Rostova, and have heard reports of your brother-in-law having sought her hand, or something of that kind. Is that true?'

'Both true and untrue,' Pierre began; but Prince Andrew interrupted him.

'Here are her letters and her portrait,' said he.

He took the packet from the table and handed it to Pierre.

'Give this to the countess . . . if you see her.'

'She is very ill,' said Pierre.

'Then she is here still?' said Prince Andrew. 'And Prince Kuragin?' he added quickly.

'He left long ago. She has been at death's door.'

'I much regret her illness,' said Prince Andrew; and he smiled like his father, coldly, maliciously, and unpleasantly.

'So Monsieur Kuragin has not honoured Countess Rostova with his hand?' said Prince Andrew, and he snorted several times.

'He could not marry, for he was married already,' said Pierre.

Prince Andrew laughed disagreeably, again reminding one of his father.

'And where is your brother-in-law now, if I may ask?' he said.

'He has gone to Peters. . . . But I don't know,' said Pierre.

'Well, it doesn't matter,' said Prince Andrew. 'Tell Countess Rostova that she was and is perfectly free, and that I wish her all that is good.'

Pierre took the packet. Prince Andrew, as if trying to remember whether he had something more to say, or waiting to see if Pierre would say anything, looked fixedly at him.

'I say, do you remember our discussion in Petersburg?' asked Pierre, 'about . . .'

'Yes,' returned Prince Andrew hastily. 'I said that a fallen woman should be forgiven, but I didn't say I could forgive her. I can't.'

'But can this be compared . . . ?' said Pierre.

Prince Andrew interrupted him, and cried sharply:

'Yes, ask her hand again, be magnanimous, and so on? . . . Yes, that would be very noble, but I am unable to follow in that gentleman's footsteps. If you wish to be my friend never speak to me of that . . . of all that! Well, good-bye. So you'll give her the packet?'

Pierre left the room and went to the old prince and Princess Mary. The old man seemed livelier than usual. Princess Mary was the same as always, but beneath her sympathy for her brother Pierre noticed her satisfaction that the engagement had been broken off. Looking at them Pierre realized what contempt and animosity they all felt for the Rostovs, and that it was impossible in their presence even to mention the name of her who could give up Prince Andrew for anyone else.

At dinner the talk turned on the war, the approach of which was becoming evident. Prince Andrew talked incessantly, arguing now with his father, now with the Swiss tutor Dessalles, and showing an unnatural animation, the cause of which Pierre so well understood.

22

THAT same evening Pierre went to the Rostovs' to fulfil the commission entrusted to him. Natasha was in bed, the count at the club, and Pierre, after giving the letters to Sonya, went to Marya Dmitrievna who was interested to know how Prince Andrew had taken the news. Ten minutes later Sonya came to Marya Dmitrievna.

'Natasha insists on seeing Count Peter Kirilovich,' said she.

'But how? Are we to take him up to her? The room there has not been tidied up.'

'No, she has dressed and gone into the drawing-room,' said Sonya.

Marya Dmitrievna only shrugged her shoulders.

'When will her mother come? She has worried me to death! Now mind, don't tell her everything!' said she to Pierre. 'One hasn't the heart to scold her, she is so much to be pitied, so much to be pitied.'

Natasha was standing in the middle of the drawing-room, emaciated, with a pale set face, but not at all shamefaced as Pierre expected to find her. When he appeared at the door she grew flurried, evidently undecided whether to go to meet him or to wait till he came up.

Pierre hastened to her. He thought she would give him her hand as usual; but she, stepping up to him, stopped, breathing heavily, her arms hanging lifelessly just in the pose she used to stand in when she went to the middle of the ball-room to sing, but with quite a different expression of face.

'Peter Kirilovich,' she began rapidly, 'Prince Bolkonsky was your friend – is your friend,' she corrected herself. (It seemed to her that everything that had once been, must now be different.) 'He told me once to apply to you . . .'

Pierre sniffed as he looked at her, but did not speak. Till then he had reproached her in his heart and tried to despise her, but he now felt so sorry for her that there was no room in his soul for reproach.

'He is here now: tell him . . . to for . . . forgive me!'

She stopped and breathed still more quickly, but did not shed tears.

'Yes . . . I will tell him,' answered Pierre; 'but . . .'

He did not know what to say.

Natasha was evidently dismayed at the thought of what he might think she had meant.

'No, I know all is over,' she said hurriedly. 'No, that can never be. I'm only tormented by the wrong I have done him. Tell him only that I beg him to forgive, forgive, forgive me for everything . . .'

She trembled all over and sat down on a chair.

A sense of pity he had never before known overflowed Pierre's heart.

'I will tell him, I will tell him everything once more,' said Pierre. 'But . . . I should like to know one thing . . .'

'Know what?' Natasha's eyes asked.

'I should like to know, did you love . . .' Pierre did not know how to refer to Anatole and flushed at the thought of him – 'did you love that bad man?'

'Don't call him bad!' said Natasha. 'But I don't know, don't know at all . . .'

She began to cry, and a still greater sense of pity, tenderness, and love, welled up in Pierre. He felt the tears trickle under his spectacles and hoped they would not be noticed.

'We won't speak of it any more, my dear,' said Pierre, and his gentle, cordial tone suddenly seemed very strange to Natasha.

'We won't speak of it, my dear – I'll tell him everything; but one thing I beg of you, consider me your friend and if you want help, advice, or simply to open your heart to someone – not now but when your mind is clearer – think of me!' He took her hand and kissed it. 'I shall be happy if it's in my power . . .'

Pierre grew confused.

'Don't speak to me like that. I am not worth it!' exclaimed Natasha and turned to leave the room, but Pierre held her hand.

He knew he had something more to say to her. But when he said it he was amazed at his own words.

'Stop, stop! You have your whole life before you,' said he to her.

'Before me? No! All is over for me,' she replied with shame and self-abasement.

'All over?' he repeated. 'If I were not myself, but the handsomest, cleverest, and best man in the world, and were free, I would this moment ask on my knees for your hand and your love!'

For the first time for many days Natasha wept tears of gratitude and tenderness, and glancing at Pierre she went out of the room.

Pierre, too, when she had gone almost ran into the ante-room, restraining tears of tenderness and joy that choked him, and without finding the sleeves of his fur cloak threw it on and got into his sledge.

'Where to now, your Excellency?' asked the coachman.

'Where to?' Pierre asked himself. 'Where can I go now? Surely not to the club or to pay calls?' All men seemed so pitiful, so poor, in comparison with this feeling of tenderness and love he experienced: in comparison with that softened, grateful, last look she had given him through her tears.

'Home!' said Pierre, and despite ten degrees of frost he threw open the bearskin cloak from his broad chest and inhaled the air with joy.

It was clear and frosty. Above the dirty ill-lit streets, above the black roofs, stretched the dark starry sky. Only looking up at the sky did Pierre cease to feel how sordid and humiliating were all mundane things compared with the heights to which his soul had just been raised. At the entrance to the Arbat Square an immense expanse of dark starry sky presented itself to his eyes. Almost in the centre of it, above the Prechistenka Boulevard, surrounded and sprinkled on all sides by stars but distinguished from them all by its nearness to the earth, its white light, and its long uplifted tail, shone the enormous and brilliant comet of the year 1812 – the comet which was said to portend all kinds of woes and the end of the world. In Pierre, however, that comet with its long luminous tail aroused no feeling of fear. On the contrary he gazed joyfully, his eyes moist with tears, at this bright comet which, having travelled in its orbit with inconceivable velocity through immeasurable space, seemed suddenly – like an arrow piercing the earth – to remain fixed in a chosen spot, vigorously holding its tail erect, shining, and displaying its white light amid countless other scintillating stars. It seemed to Pierre that this comet fully responded to what was passing in his own softened and uplifted soul, now blossoming into a new life.

END OF BOOK TWO

WAR AND PEACE

*

BOOK THREE

PART ONE

1

FROM the close of the year 1811 an intensified arming and concentrating of the forces of Western Europe began, and in 1812 these forces – millions of men reckoning those transporting and feeding the army – moved from the west eastwards to the Russian frontier, towards which since 1811 Russian forces had been similarly drawn. On the 12th of June 1812 the forces of Western Europe crossed the Russian frontier and war began, that is, an event took place opposed to human reason and to human nature. Millions of men perpetrated against one another such innumerable crimes, frauds, treacheries, thefts, forgeries, issues of false money, burglaries, incendiarisms, and murders, as in whole centuries are not recorded in the annals of all the law courts of the world, but which those who committed them did not at the time regard as being crimes.*

What produced this extraordinary occurrence? What were its causes? The historians tell us with naïve assurance that its causes were the wrongs inflicted on the Duke of Oldenburg, the non-observance of the Continental System, the ambition of Napoleon, the firmness of Alexander, the mistakes of the diplomatists, and so on.

Consequently it would only have been necessary for Metternich, Rumyantsev, or Talleyrand, between a levée and an evening party, to have taken proper pains and written a more adroit note, or for Napoleon to have written to Alexander: 'My respected Brother, I consent to restore the duchy to the Duke of Oldenburg' – and there would have been no war.

We can understand that the matter seemed like that to contemporaries. It naturally seemed to Napoleon that the war was caused by England's intrigues (as in fact he said on the island of St Helena). It naturally seemed to members of the English Parliament that the cause of the war was Napoleon's ambition; to the Duke of Oldenburg that the cause of the war was the violence done to him; to businessmen that the cause of the war was the Continental System which was ruining Europe; to the generals and old soldiers that the chief reason for the war was the necessity of giving them employment; to the legitimists of that day that it was the need of re-establishing *les bons principes*, and to the diplomatists of that time that it all resulted from the fact that the alliance between Russia and Austria in 1809 had not been sufficiently well concealed from Napoleon, and from the awkward wording of Memorandum No. 178. It is natural that these and a countless and infinite quantity of other reasons, the number depending on the endless diversity of points of view, presented themselves to the men of that day; but to us, to posterity who view the thing that happened in all its magnitude and perceive its plain and terrible meaning, these causes seem insufficient. To us it is incomprehensible that millions of Christian men killed and tortured each other either because Napoleon was ambitious or Alexander was firm, or because England's policy was astute or the Duke of Oldenburg wronged. We cannot grasp what connexion such circumstances have with the actual fact of slaughter and violence: why because the Duke was wronged, thousands of men from the other side of Europe killed and ruined the people of Smolensk and Moscow and were killed by them.

To us their descendants, who are not historians and are not carried away by the process of research, and can therefore regard the event with unclouded common sense, an incalculable number of causes present themselves. The deeper we delve in search of these causes the more of them we find; and each separate cause or whole series of causes appears to us equally valid in itself and equally false by its insignificance compared to the magnitude of the events, and by its impotence – apart from the co-operation of all the other coincident causes – to occasion the event. To us the wish or objection of this or that French corporal to serve a second term appears as much a cause as Napoleon's refusal to withdraw his troops beyond the Vistula and to restore the duchy of Oldenburg; for had he not wished to serve, and had a second, a third, and a thousandth corporal and private also refused, there would have been so many less men in Napoleon's army and the war could not have occurred.

Had Napoleon not taken offence at the demand that he should withdraw beyond the Vistula, and not ordered his troops to advance, there would have been no war; but had all his sergeants objected to serving a second term then also there could have been no war. Nor could there have been a war had there been no English intrigues and no Duke of Oldenburg, and had Alexander not felt insulted, and had there not been an autocratic government in Russia, or a Revolution in France and a subsequent dictatorship and Empire, or all the things that produced the French Revolution, and so on. Without each of these causes nothing could have happened. So all these causes – myriads of causes – coincided to bring it about. And so there was no one cause for that occurrence, but it had to occur because it had to. Millions of men, renouncing their human feelings and reason, had to go from west to east to slay their fellows, just as some centuries previously hordes of men had come from the east to the west slaying their fellows.

The actions of Napoleon and Alexander, on whose words the event seemed to hang, were as little voluntary as the actions of any soldier who was drawn into the campaign by lot or by conscription. This could not be otherwise, for in order that the will of Napoleon and Alexander (on whom the event seemed to depend) should be carried out, the concurrence of innumerable circumstances was needed without any one of which the event could not have taken place. It was necessary that millions of men in whose hands lay the real power – the soldiers who fired, or transported provisions and guns – should consent to carry out the will of these weak individuals, and should have been induced to do so by an infinite number of diverse and complex causes.

We are forced to fall back on fatalism as an explanation of irrational events (that is to say, events the reasonableness of which we do not understand). The more we try to explain such events in history reasonably, the more unreasonable and incomprehensible do they become to us.

Each man lives for himself, using his freedom to attain his personal aims, and feels with his whole being that he can now do or abstain from doing this or that action; but as soon as he has done it, that action performed at a certain moment in time becomes irrevocable and belongs to history, in which it has not a free but a predestined significance.

There are two sides to the life of every man, his individual life which is the more free the more abstract its interests, and his elemental swarm-life in which he inevitably obeys laws laid down for him.

Man lives consciously for himself, but is an unconscious instrument in the attainment of the historic, universal, aims of humanity. A deed done is irrevocable, and its result coinciding in time with the actions of millions of other men assumes an historic significance. The higher a man stands on the social ladder, the more people he is connected with and the more power he has over others, the more evident is the predestination and inevitability of his every action.

'The king's heart is in the hands of the Lord.'

A king is history's slave.

History, that is, the unconscious, general, swarm-life of mankind, uses every moment of the life of kings as a tool for its own purposes.

Though Napoleon at that time, in 1812, was more convinced than ever that it depended on him, *verser (ou ne pas verser) le sang de ses peuples* – as Alexander expressed it in the last letter he wrote him – he had never been so much in the grip of inevitable laws, which compelled him, while thinking that he was acting on his own volition, to perform for the swarm-life – that is to say for history – whatever had to be performed.

The people of the west moved eastwards to slay their fellow men, and by the law of coincidence thousands of minutes causes fitted in and co-ordinated to produce that movement and war: reproaches for the non-observance of the Continental System, the Duke of Oldenburg's wrongs, the movement of troops into Prussia – undertaken (as it seemed to Napoleon) only for the purpose of securing an armed peace, the French Emperor's love and habit of war coinciding with his people's inclinations, allurement by the grandeur of the preparations, and the expenditure on those preparations, and the need of obtaining advantages to compensate for that expenditure, the intoxicating honours he received in Dresden,* the diplomatic negotiations which in the opinion of contemporaries were carried on with a sincere desire to attain peace but which only wounded the self-love of both sides, and millions and millions of other causes that adapted themselves to the event that was happening or coincided with it.

When an apple has ripened and falls, why does it fall? Because of its attraction to the earth, because its stalk withers, because it is dried by the sun, because it grows heavier, because the wind shakes it, or because the boy standing below wants to eat it?

Nothing is the cause. All this is only the coincidence of conditions in which all vital organic and elemental events occur. And the botanist who finds that the apple falls because the cellular tissue decays and so forth, is equally right with the child who stands under the tree and says the apple fell because he wanted to eat it and prayed for it. Equally right or wrong is he who says that Napoleon went to Moscow because he wanted to, and perished because Alexander desired his destruction, and he who says that an undermined hill weighing a million tons fell because the last navvy struck it for the last time with his mattock. In historic events the so-called great men are labels giving names to events, and like labels they have but the smallest connexion with the event itself.

Every act of theirs, which appears to them an act of their own will, is in an historical sense involuntary, and is related to the whole course of history and predestined from eternity.

2

On the 29th of May Napoleon left Dresden, where he had spent three weeks surrounded by a court that included princes, dukes, kings, and even an emperor. Before leaving, Napoleon showed favour to the emperor, kings and princes who had deserved it, reprimanded the kings and princes with whom he was dissatisfied, presented pearls and diamonds of his own – that is which he had taken from other kings – to the Empress of Austria, and having, as his historian tells us, tenderly embraced the Empress Marie Louise – who regarded him as her husband though he had left another wife in Paris – left her grieved by the parting which she seemed hardly able to bear. Though the diplomatists still firmly believed in the possibility of peace, and worked zealously to that end, and though the Emperor Napoleon himself wrote a letter to Alexander calling him *Monsieur mon frère*, and sincerely assured him that he did not want war and would always love and honour him – yet he set off to join his army, and at every station gave fresh orders to accelerate the movement of his troops from west to east. He went in a travelling coach with six horses, surrounded by pages, aides-de-camp, and an escort, along the road to Posen, Thorn, Danzig, and Königsberg. At each of these towns thousands of people met him with excitement and enthusiasm.

The army was moving from west to east and relays of six horses carried him in the same direction. On the 10th of June, coming up with the army, he spent the night in apartments prepared for him on the estate of a Polish count in the Vilkavisski forest.

Next day, overtaking the army, he went in a carriage to the Niemen, and changing into a Polish uniform in order to select a place for the crossing, he drove to the river bank.

Seeing on the other side some Cossacks (*les Cosaques*) and the wide-spreading steppes in the midst of which lay the holy city of Moscow (*Moscou, la ville sainte*), the capital of a realm such as the Scythia into which Alexander the Great had marched – Napoleon unexpectedly, and contrary alike to strategic and diplomatic considerations, ordered an advance, and the next day his army began to cross the Niemen.

Early in the morning of the 12th of June he came out of his tent which was pitched that day on the steep left bank of the Niemen, and looked through a spy-glass at the streams of his troops pouring out of the Vilkavisski forest and flowing over the three bridges thrown across the river. The troops, knowing of the Emperor's presence, were on the look-out for him, and when they caught sight of a figure in an overcoat and a cocked hat standing apart from his suite in front of his tent on the hill, they threw up their caps and shouted: '*Vive l'Empereur!*' and one after another poured in a ceaseless stream out of the vast forest that had concealed them and, separating, flowed on and on by the three bridges to the other side.

'Now we'll go into action. Oh, when he takes it in hand himself things get hot ... by heaven! ... There he is! ... *Vive l'Empereur!* So these are the steppes of Asia! It's a nasty country all the same. *Au revoir*, Beauché; I'll keep the best place in Moscow for you! *Au revoir*. Good luck! ... Did you see the Emperor? *Vive l'Empereur!* ... *preur!* – If they make me Governor of India, Gérard, I'll make you Minister of Kashmir – that's settled. *Vive l'Empereur!* Hurrah, hurrah! hurrah! The Cossacks – those rascals – see how they run! *Vive l'Empereur!* There he is, do you see him? I've seen him twice, as I see you now. The little corporal ... I saw him give the cross to one of the veterans ... *Vive l'Empereur!*' came the voices of men, old and young, of most diverse characters and social positions. On the faces of all was one common expression of joy at the commencement of the long-expected campaign and of rapture and devotion to the man in the grey coat who was standing on the hill.

On the 13th of June a rather small, thoroughbred Arab horse was brought to Napoleon. He mounted it and rode at a gallop to one of the bridges over the Niemen, deafened continually by incessant and rapturous acclamations which he evidently endured only because it was impossible to forbid the soldiers to express their love of him by such shouting, but the shouting which accompanied him everywhere disturbed him and distracted his mind from the military cares that had occupied him from the time he joined the army. He rode across one of the swaying pontoon bridges to the farther side, turned sharply to the left and galloped in the direction of Kovno, preceded by enraptured, mounted chasseurs of the Guard who, breathless with delight, galloped ahead to clear a path for him through the troops. On reaching the broad river Viliya he stopped near a regiment of Polish Uhlans stationed by the river.

'*Vivat!*' shouted the Poles ecstatically, breaking their ranks and pressing against one another to see him.

Napoleon looked up and down the river, dismounted, and sat down on a log that lay on the bank. At a mute sign from him a telescope was handed him which he rested on the back of a happy page who had run up to him, and he gazed at the opposite bank. Then he became absorbed in a map laid out on the logs. Without lifting his head he said something and two of his aides-de-camp galloped off to the Polish Uhlans.

'What? What did he say?' was heard in the ranks of the Polish Uhlans when one of the aides-de-camp rode up to them.

The order was to find a ford and to cross the river. The colonel of Polish Uhlans, a handsome old man, flushed, and fumbling in his speech from excitement asked the aide-de-camp whether he would be permitted to swim the river with his Uhlans instead of seeking a ford. In evident fear of refusal, like a boy asking for permission to get on a horse, he begged to be allowed to swim across the river before the Emperor's eyes. The aide-de-camp replied that probably the Emperor would not be displeased at this excess of zeal.

As soon as the aide-de-camp had said this, the old moustached officer with a happy face and sparkling eyes raised his sabre, shouted 'Vivat!' and, commanding the Uhlans to follow him, spurred his horse and galloped into the river. He gave an angry thrust to his horse which had grown restive under him, and plunged into the water, heading for the deepest part where the current was swift. Hundreds of Uhlans galloped in after him. It was cold and uncanny in the rapid current in the middle of the stream, and the Uhlans caught hold of one another as they fell off their horses. Some of the horses were drowned and some of the men, the others tried to swim on, some in the saddle and some clinging to their horses' manes. They tried to make their way forward to the opposite bank, and though there was a ford half a verst away, were proud that they were swimming and drowning in this river under the eyes of the man who sat on the log and was not even looking at what they were doing. When the aide-de-camp having returned and choosing an opportune moment ventured to draw the Emperor's attention to the devotion of the Poles to his person, the little man in the grey overcoat got up and having summoned Berthier* began pacing up and down the bank with him, giving him instructions and occasionally glancing disapprovingly at the drowning Uhlans who distracted his attention.

For him it was no new conviction that his presence in any part of the world, from Africa to the steppes of Muscovy alike, was enough to dumbfound people and impel them to insane self-oblivion. He called for his horse and rode to his quarters.

Some forty Uhlans were drowned in the river though boats were sent to their assistance. The majority struggled back to the bank from which they had started. The colonel and some of his men got across, and with difficulty clambered out on the further bank. And as soon as they had got out, in their soaked and streaming clothes, they shouted 'Vivat!' and looked ecstatically at the spot where Napoleon had been but where he no longer was, and at that moment considered themselves happy.

That evening, between issuing one order that the forged Russian paper money prepared for use in Russia should be delivered as quickly as possible, and another that a Saxon on whom a letter containing information about the orders to the French army had been found should be shot, Napoleon also gave instructions that the Polish colonel who had needlessly plunged into the river should be enrolled in the *Légion d'honneur* of which Napoleon was himself the head.

*Quos vult perdere dementat.**

3

THE Emperor of Russia had meanwhile been in Vilna for more than a month, reviewing troops and holding manœuvres. Nothing was ready for the war that everyone expected and to prepare for which the Emperor had come from Petersburg. There was no general plan of action. The vacillation between the various plans that were proposed had even increased after the Emperor had been at head-quarters for a month. Each of the three armies had its own commander-in-chief,* but there was no supreme commander of all the forces, and the Emperor did not assume that responsibility himself.

The longer the Emperor remained in Vilna the less did everybody – tired of waiting – prepare for the war. All the efforts of those who surrounded the sovereign seemed directed merely to making him spend his time pleasantly and forget that war was impending.

In June, after many balls and fêtes given by the Polish magnates, by the courtiers, and by the Emperor himself, it occurred to one of the Polish aides-de-camp in attendance that a dinner and ball should be given for the Emperor by his aides-de-camp. This idea was eagerly received. The Emperor gave his consent. The aides-de-camp collected money by subscription. The lady who was thought to be most pleasing to the Emperor was invited to act as hostess. Count Bennigsen, being a landowner in the Vilna province, offered his country house for the fête, and the 13th of June was fixed for a ball, dinner, regatta, and fireworks at Zakret, Count Bennigsen's country seat.

The very day that Napoleon issued the order to cross the Niemen, and his vanguard, driving off the Cossacks, crossed the Russian frontier, Alexander spent the evening at the entertainment given by his aides-de-camp at Bennigsen's country house.

It was a gay and brilliant fête. Connoisseurs of such matters declared that rarely had so many beautiful women been assembled in one place. Countess Bezukhova was present among other Russian ladies who had followed the sovereign from Petersburg to Vilna, and eclipsed the refined Polish ladies by her massive, so-called Russian, type of beauty. The Emperor noticed her, and honoured her with a dance.

Boris Drubetskoy, having left his wife in Moscow and being for the present *en garçon* (as he phrased it), was also there and, though not an aide-de-camp, had subscribed a large sum towards the expenses. Boris was now a rich man who had risen to high honours, and no longer sought patronage but stood on an equal footing with the highest of those of his own age. He was meeting Hélène in Vilna after not having seen her for a long time, and did not recall the past, but as Hélène was enjoying the favours of a very important personage and Boris had only recently married, they met as good friends of long standing.

At midnight dancing was still going on. Hélène, not having a suitable partner, herself offered to dance the mazurka with Boris. They were the third couple. Boris, coolly looking at Hélène's dazzling bare shoulders which emerged from a dark, gold-embroidered, gauze gown, talked to her of old acquaintances, and at the same time, unaware of it himself and unnoticed by others, never for an instant ceased to observe the Emperor who was in the same room. The Emperor was not dancing, he stood in the doorway, stopping now one pair and now another with gracious words that he alone knew how to utter.

As the mazurka began, Boris saw that Adjutant-General Balashev, one of those in closest attendance on the Emperor, went up to him, and contrary to court etiquette stood near him while he was talking to a Polish lady. Having finished speaking to her, the Emperor looked inquiringly at Balashev and, evidently understanding that he only acted thus because there were important reasons for so doing, nodded slightly to the lady and turned to him. Hardly had Balashev begun to speak before a look of amazement appeared on the Emperor's face. He took Balashev by the arm and crossed the room with him, unconsciously clearing a path seven yards wide as the people on both sides made way for him. Boris noticed Arakcheev's excited face when the sovereign went out with Balashev. Arakcheev looked at the Emperor from under his brow, and sniffing with his red nose stepped forward from the crowd as if expecting the Emperor to address him. (Boris understood that Arakcheev envied Balashev and was displeased that evidently important news had reached the Emperor otherwise than through himself.)

But the Emperor and Balashev passed out into the illuminated garden without noticing Arakcheev who, holding his sword and glancing wrathfully around, followed some twenty paces behind them.

All the time Boris was going through the figures of the mazurka he was worried by the question of what news Balashev had brought, and how he could find it out before others.

In the figure in which he had to choose two ladies, he whispered to Hélène that he meant to choose Countess Potocka who he thought had gone out on to the veranda, and glided over the parquet to the door opening into the garden, where, seeing Balashev and the Emperor returning to the veranda, he stood still. They were moving towards the door. Boris, fluttering as if he had not had time to withdraw, respectfully pressed close to the doorpost with bowed head.

The Emperor, with the agitation of one who has been personally affronted, was finishing with these words:

'To enter Russia without declaring war! I will not make peace as long as a single armed enemy remains in my country!'

It seemed to Boris that it gave the Emperor pleasure to utter these words. He was satisfied with the form in which he had expressed his thought, but displeased that Boris had overheard it.

'Let no one know of it!' the Emperor added with a frown.

Boris understood that this was meant for him, and closing his eyes slightly bowed his head. The Emperor re-entered the ball-room and remained there about another half-hour.

Boris was thus the first to learn the news that the French army had crossed the Niemen, and thanks to this was able to show certain important personages that much that was concealed from others was usually known to him, and by this means he rose higher in their estimation.

The unexpected news of the French having crossed the Niemen was particularly startling after a month of unfulfilled expectations, and at a ball. On first receiving the news, under the influence of indignation and resentment the Emperor had found a phrase that pleased him, fully expressed his feelings, and has since become famous. On returning home at two o'clock that night he sent for his secretary, Shishkov, and told him to write an order to the troops and a rescript to Field-Marshal Prince Saltykov, in which he insisted on the words being inserted that he would not make peace so long as a single armed Frenchman remained on Russian soil.

Next day the following letter was sent to Napoleon:

Monsieur mon frère,
Yesterday I learnt that, despite the loyalty with which I have kept my engagements with your Majesty, your troops have crossed the Russian frontier, and I have this moment received from Petersburg a note in which Count Lauriston* informs me, as a reason for this aggression, that your Majesty has considered yourself to be in a state of war with me from the time Prince Kurakin* asked for his passports. The reason on which the Duc de Bassano based his refusal to deliver them to him would never have led me to suppose that that incident could serve as a pretext for aggression. In fact the ambassador, as he himself has declared, was never authorized to make that demand, and as soon as I was informed of it I let him know how much I disapproved of it, and ordered him to remain at his post. If your Majesty does not intend to shed the blood of our peoples for such a misunderstanding, and consents to withdraw your troops from Russian territory, I will regard what has passed as not having occurred and an understanding between us will be possible. In the contrary case, your Majesty, I shall see myself forced to repel an attack that nothing on my part has provoked. It still depends on your Majesty to preserve humanity from the calamity of another war.

I am, &c.,
(Signed) Alexander.

4

AT two in the morning of the 14th of June the Emperor, having sent for Balashev and read him his letter to Napoleon, ordered him to take it and hand it personally to the French Emperor. When dispatching Balashev the Emperor repeated to him the words that he would not make peace so long as a single armed enemy remained on Russian soil, and told him to transmit those words to Napoleon. Alexander did not insert them in his letter to Napoleon because, with his characteristic tact, he felt it would be injudicious to use them at a moment when a last attempt at reconciliation was being made, but he definitely instructed Balashev to repeat them personally to Napoleon.

Having set off in the small hours of the 14th, accompanied by a bugler and two Cossacks, Balashev reached the French outposts at the village of Rykonty, on the Russian side of the Niemen, by dawn. There he was stopped by French cavalry sentinels.

A French non-commissioned officer of hussars, in crimson uniform and a shaggy cap, shouted to the approaching Balashev to halt. Balashev did not do so at once, but continued to advance along the road at a walking pace.

The non-commissioned officer frowned, and muttering words of abuse advanced his horse's chest against Balashev, put his hand to his sabre, and shouted rudely at the Russian general, asking: was he deaf that he did not do as he was told? Balashev mentioned who he was. The non-commissioned officer began talking with his comrades about regimental matters without looking at the Russian general.

After living at the seat of the highest authority and power, after conversing with the Emperor less than three hours before, and in general being accustomed to the respect due to his rank in the service, Balashev found it very strange here on Russian soil to encounter this hostile, and still more this disrespectful, application of brute force to himself.

The sun was only just appearing from behind the clouds, the air was fresh and dewy. A herd of cattle was being driven along the road from the village, and over the fields the larks rose trilling, one after another, like bubbles rising in water.

Balashev looked around him awaiting the arrival of an officer from the village. The Russian Cossacks and bugler and the French hussars looked silently at one another from time to time.

A French colonel of hussars, who had evidently just left his bed, came riding from the village on a handsome sleek grey horse, accompanied by two hussars. The officer, the soldiers, and their horses, all looked smart and well-kept.

It was that first period of a campaign when troops are still in full trim almost like that of peace-time manœuvres, but with a shade of martial swagger in their clothes, and a touch of the gaiety and spirit of enterprise which always accompany the opening of a campaign.

The French colonel with difficulty repressed a yawn, but was polite and evidently understood Balashev's importance. He led him past his soldiers and behind the outposts, and told him that his wish to be presented to the Emperor would most likely be satisfied immediately, as the Emperor's quarters were, he believed, not far off.

They rode through the village of Rykonty, past tethered French hussar horses, past sentinels and men who saluted their colonel and stared with curiosity at a Russian uniform, and came out at the other end of the village. The colonel said that the commander of the division was a mile and a quarter away and would receive Balashev and conduct him to his destination.

The sun had by now risen and shone gaily on the bright verdure.

They had hardly ridden up a hill, past a tavern, before they saw a group of horsemen coming towards them. In front of the group, on a black horse with trappings that glittered in the sun, rode a tall man with plumes in his hat and black hair curling down to his shoulders. He wore a red mantle, and stretched his long legs forward in French fashion. The man rode towards Balashev at a gallop, his plumes flowing and his gems and gold lace glittering in the bright June sunshine.

Balashev was only two horses' length from the equestrian with the bracelets, plumes, necklaces, and gold embroidery, who was galloping towards him with a theatrically solemn countenance, when Julner, the French colonel, whispered respectfully: 'The King of Naples!' It was in fact Murat, now called 'King of Naples'. Though it was quite incomprehensible why he should be King of Naples he was called so, and was himself convinced that he was so, and therefore assumed a more solemn and important air than formerly. He was so sure that he really was the King of Naples that when on the eve of his departure from that city, while walking through the streets with his wife, some Italians called out to him: 'Viva il re!' he turned to his wife with a pensive smile and said: 'Poor fellows, they don't know that I am leaving them to-morrow!'

But though he firmly believed himself to be King of Naples, and pitied the grief felt by the subjects he was abandoning, latterly, after he had been ordered to return to military service, and especially since his last interview with Napoleon in Danzig, when his august brother-in-law had told him: 'I made you King that you should reign in my way, but not in yours!' – he had cheerfully taken up his familiar business, and – like a well-fed but not over-fat horse that feels himself in harness and grows skittish between the shafts – he dressed up in clothes as variegated and expensive as possible, and gaily and contentedly galloped along the roads of Poland, without himself knowing why or where.

On seeing the Russian general he threw back his head, with its long hair curling to his shoulders, in a majestically royal manner, and looked inquiringly at the French colonel. The colonel respectfully informed his Majesty of Balashev's mission, whose name he could not pronounce.

'De Bal-machève!' said the King (overcoming by his assurance the difficulty that had presented itself to the colonel). 'Charmed to make your acquaintance, General!' he added with a gesture of kingly condescension.

As soon as the King began to speak loud and fast his royal dignity instantly forsook him, and without noticing it he passed into his natural tone of good-natured familiarity. He laid his hand on the withers of Balashev's horse and said:

'Well, General, it all looks like war,' as if regretting a circumstance of which he was unable to judge.

'Your Majesty,' replied Balashev, 'my master, the Emperor, does not desire war and as your Majesty sees . . .' said Balashev, using the words *your* Majesty at every opportunity, with the affectation unavoidable in frequently addressing one to whom the title was still a novelty.

Murat's face beamed with stupid satisfaction as he listened to 'Monsieur de Balachoff'. But *royauté oblige!* and he felt it incumbent on him, as a king and an ally to confer on state affairs with Alexander's envoy. He dismounted, took Balashev's arm, and moving a few steps away from his suite which waited respectfully, began to pace up and down with him trying to speak significantly. He referred to the fact that the Emperor Napoleon had resented the demand that he should withdraw his troops from Prussia, especially when that demand became generally known and the dignity of France was thereby offended.

Balashev replied that there was nothing offensive in the demand, because . . . but Murat interrupted him.

'Then you don't consider the Emperor Alexander the aggressor?' he asked unexpectedly, with a kindly and foolish smile.

Balashev told him why he considered Napoleon to be the originator of the war.

'Oh, my dear General!' Murat again interrupted him, 'with all my heart I wish the Emperors may arrange the affair between them, and that the war begun by no wish of mine may finish as quickly as possible!' said he, in the tone of a servant who wants to remain good friends with another despite a quarrel between their masters.

And he went on to inquiries about the Grand Duke and the state of his health, and to reminiscences of the gay and amusing times he had spent with him in Naples. Then suddenly, as if remembering his royal dignity, Murat solemnly drew himself up, assumed the pose in which he had stood at his coronation, and waving his right arm, said:

'I won't detain you longer, General. I wish success to your mission,' and with his embroidered red mantle, his flowing feathers, and his glittering ornaments, he rejoined his suite who were respectfully awaiting him.

Balashev rode on, supposing from Murat's words that he would very soon be brought before Napoleon himself. But instead of that, at the next village the sentinels of Davout's infantry corps detained him, as the pickets of the vanguard had done, and an adjutant of the corps-commander, who was fetched, conducted him into the village to Marshal Davout.

5

DAVOUT was to Napoleon what Arakcheev was to Alexander – though not a coward like Arakcheev, he was as precise, as cruel, and as unable to express his devotion to his monarch except by cruelty.

In the organism of States such men are necessary, as wolves are necessary in the organism of Nature, and they always exist, always appear and hold their own, however incongruous their presence and their proximity to the head of the government may be. This inevitability alone can explain how the cruel Arakcheev, who tore out a grenadier's moustache with his own hands, whose weak nerves rendered him unable to face danger, and who was neither an educated man nor a courtier, was able to maintain his powerful position with Alexander, whose own character was chivalrous, noble, and gentle.

Balashev found Davout seated on a barrel in the shed of a peasant's hut writing – he was auditing accounts. Better quarters could have been found him, but Marshal Davout was one of those men who purposely put themselves in most depressing conditions to have a justification for being gloomy. For the same reason they are always hard at work and in a hurry. 'How can I think of the bright side of life when, as you see, I am sitting on a barrel and working in a dirty shed?' the expression of his face seemed to say. The chief pleasure and necessity of such men, when they encounter anyone who shows animation, is to flaunt their own dreary, persistent activity. Davout allowed himself that pleasure when Balashev was brought in. He became still more absorbed in his task when the Russian general entered, and after glancing over his spectacles at Balashev's face, which was animated by the beauty of the morning and by his talk with Murat, he did not rise or even stir, but scowled still more and sneered malevolently.

When he noticed in Balashev's face the disagreeable impression this reception produced, Davout raised his head and coldly asked what he wanted.

Thinking he could have been received in such a manner only because Davout did not know that he was adjutant-general to the Emperor Alexander and even his envoy to Napoleon, Balashev hastened to inform him of his rank and mission. Contrary to his expectation, Davout after hearing him became still surlier and ruder.

'Where is your dispatch?' he inquired. 'Give it to me. I will send it to the Emperor.'

Balashev replied that he had been ordered to hand it personally to the Emperor.

'Your Emperor's orders are obeyed in your army, but here,' said Davout, 'you must do as you're told.'

And as if to make the Russian general still more conscious of his dependence on brute force, Davout sent an adjutant to call the officer on duty.

Balashev took out the packet containing the Emperor's letter and laid it on the table (made of a door with its hinges still hanging on it, laid across two barrels). Davout took the packet and read the inscription.

'You are perfectly at liberty to treat me with respect or not,' protested Balashev, 'but permit me to observe that I have the honour to be adjutant-general to his Majesty . . .'

Davout glanced at him silently and plainly derived pleasure from the signs of agitation and confusion which appeared on Balashev's face.

'You will be treated as is fitting,' said he, and putting the packet in his pocket left the shed.

A minute later the marshal's adjutant, de Castrés, came in and conducted Balashev to the quarters assigned him.

That day he dined with the marshal, at the same board on the barrels.

Next day Davout rode out early, and after asking Balashev to come to him peremptorily requested him to remain there; to move on with the baggage-train should orders come for it to move, and to talk to no one except Monsieur de Castrés.

After four days of solitude, ennui, and consciousness of his impotence and insignificance – particularly acute by contrast with the sphere of power in which he had so lately moved – and after several marches with the marshal's baggage and the French army, which occupied the whole district, Balashev was brought to Vilna – now occupied by the French – through the very gate by which he had left it four days previously.

Next day the imperial gentleman-in-waiting, Comte de Turenne, came to Balashev and informed him of the Emperor Napoleon's wish to honour him with an audience.

Four days before, sentinels of the Preobrazhensk regiment had stood in front of the house to which Balashev was conducted, and now two French grenadiers stood there, in blue uniforms unfastened in front and with shaggy caps on their heads, and an escort of hussars and uhlans and a brilliant suite of aides-de-camp, pages, and generals, who were waiting for Napoleon to come out, were standing at the porch round his saddle-horse and his Mameluke, Rustan.*

Napoleon received Balashev in the very house in Vilna from which Alexander had dispatched him on his mission.

6

THOUGH Balashev was used to imperial pomp he was amazed at the luxury and magnificence of Napoleon's court.

Comte de Turenne showed him into a large reception room, where many generals, gentlemen-in-waiting, and Polish magnates – several of whom Balashev had seen at the court of the Emperor of Russia – were waiting. Duroc said that Napoleon would receive the Russian general before going for his ride.

After some minutes the gentleman-in-waiting who was on duty came into the great reception room and bowing politely, asked Balashev to follow him.

Balashev went into a small reception room one door of which led into a study, the very one from which the Russian Emperor had dispatched him on his mission. He stood a minute or two waiting. He heard hurried footsteps beyond the door, both halves of it were opened rapidly; all was silent and then from the study the sound was heard of other steps, firm and resolute – they were those of Napoleon. He had just finished dressing for his ride, and wore a blue uniform opening in front over a white waistcoat, so long that it covered his rotund stomach, white leather breeches tightly fitting the fat thighs of his short legs, and Hessian boots. His short hair had evidently just been brushed, but one lock hung down in the middle of his broad forehead. His plump white neck stood out sharply above the black collar of his uniform, and he smelt of eau-de-cologne. His full face, rather young-looking, with its prominent chin, wore a gracious and majestic expression of imperial welcome.

He entered briskly, with a jerk at every step and his head slightly thrown back. His whole short corpulent figure with broad thick shoulders, and chest and stomach involuntarily protruding, had that imposing and stately appearance one sees in men of forty who live in comfort. It was evident, too, that he was in the best of spirits that day.

He nodded in answer to Balashev's low and respectful bow, and coming up to him at once began speaking like a man who values every moment of his time and does not condescend to prepare what he has to say, but is sure he will always say the right thing and say it well.*

'Good day, General!' said he. 'I have received the letter you brought from the Emperor Alexander and am very glad to see you.'

He glanced with his large eyes into Balashev's face and immediately looked past him.

It was plain that Balashev's personality did not interest him at all. Evidently only what took place within *his own* mind interested him. Nothing outside himself had any significance for him because everything in the world, it seemed to him, depended entirely on his will.

'I do not, and did not, desire war,' he continued, 'but it has been forced on me. Even *now*' (he emphasized the word), 'I am ready to receive any explanations you can give me.'

And he began clearly and concisely to explain his reasons for dissatisfaction with the Russian government. Judging by the calmly moderate and amicable tone in which the French Emperor spoke, Balashev was firmly persuaded that he wished for peace and intended to enter into negotiations.

When Napoleon having finished speaking looked inquiringly at the Russian envoy, Balashev began a speech he had prepared long before: 'Sire! The Emperor, my master...' but the sight of the Emperor's eyes bent on him confused him. 'You are flurried – compose yourself!' Napoleon seemed to say, as with a scarcely perceptible smile he looked at Balashev's uniform and sword.

Balashev recovered himself and began to speak. He said that the Emperor Alexander did not consider Kurakin's demand for his passports a sufficient cause for war; that Kurakin had acted on his own initiative and without his sovereign's assent, that the Emperor Alexander did not desire war, and had no relations with England.

'Not *yet*!' interposed Napoleon, and, as if fearing to give vent to his feelings, he frowned and nodded slightly as a sign that Balashev might proceed.

After saying all he had been instructed to say, Balashev added that the Emperor Alexander wished for peace, but would not enter into negotiations except on condition that... Here Balashev hesitated: he remembered the words the Emperor Alexander had not written in his letter, but had specially inserted in the rescript to Saltykov and had told Balashev to repeat to Napoleon. Balashev remembered these words, 'So long as a single armed foe remains on Russian soil', but some complex feeling restrained him. He could not utter them, though he wished to do so. He grew confused, and said: 'On condition that the French army retires beyond the Niemen.'

Napoleon noticed Balashev's embarrassment when uttering these last words: his face twitched and the calf of his left leg began to quiver rhythmically. Without moving from where he stood he began speaking in a louder tone and more hurriedly than before.

During the speech that followed Balashev, who more than once lowered his eyes, involuntarily noticed the quivering of Napoleon's left leg which increased the more, the more Napoleon raised his voice.

'I desire peace no less than the Emperor Alexander,' he began. 'Have I not for eighteen months been doing everything to obtain it? I have waited eighteen months for explanations. But in order to begin negotiations what is demanded of me?' he said frowning and making an energetic gesture of inquiry with his small, white, plump hand.

'The withdrawal of your army beyond the Niemen, Sire,' replied Balashev.

'The Niemen?' repeated Napoleon. 'So now you want me to retire beyond the Niemen – only the Niemen?' repeated Napoleon, looking straight at Balashev.

The latter bowed his head respectfully.

Instead of the demand of four months earlier to withdraw from Pomerania, only a withdrawal beyond the Niemen was now demanded. Napoleon turned quickly and began to pace the room.

'You say the demand now is that I am to withdraw beyond the Niemen before commencing negotiations, but in just the same way two months ago the demand was that I should withdraw beyond the Vistula and the Oder, and yet you are willing to negotiate.'

He went in silence from one corner of the room to the other and again stopped in front of Balashev. Balashev noticed that his left leg was quivering faster than before and his face seemed petrified in its stern expression. This quivering of his left leg was a thing Napoleon was conscious of. 'The vibration of my left calf is a great sign with me,' he remarked at a later date.

'Such demands as to retreat beyond the Vistula and Oder may be made to a Prince of Baden, but not to me!' Napoleon almost screamed, quite to his own surprise. 'If you gave me Petersburg and Moscow I could not accept such conditions. You say I have begun this war! But who first joined his army? The Emperor Alexander, not I! And you offer me negotiations when I have expended millions, when you are in alliance with England, and when your position is a bad one. You offer me negotiations! But what is the aim of your alliance with England? What has she given you?' he continued hurriedly, evidently no longer trying to show the advantages of peace and discuss its possibility, but only to prove his own rectitude and power and Alexander's errors and duplicity.

The commencement of his speech had obviously been made with the intention of demonstrating the advantages of his position and showing that he was nevertheless willing to negotiate. But he had begun talking, and the more he talked the less could he control his words.

The whole purport of his remarks now was evidently to exalt himself and insult Alexander – just what he had least desired at the commencement of the interview.

'I hear you have made peace with Turkey?'*

Balashev bowed his head affirmatively.

'Peace has been concluded . . .' he began.

But Napoleon did not let him speak. He evidently wanted to do all the talking himself and continued to talk with the sort of eloquence and unrestrained irritability to which spoilt people are so prone.

'Yes, I know you have made peace with the Turks without obtaining Moldavia and Wallachia; I would have given your sovereign those provinces as I gave him Finland. Yes,' he went on, 'I promised and would have given the Emperor Alexander Moldavia and Wallachia, and now he won't have those splendid provinces. Yet he might have united them to his empire and in a single reign would have extended Russia from the Gulf of Bothnia to the mouths of the Danube. Catherine the Great could not have done more,' said Napoleon, growing more and more excited as he paced up and down the room repeating to Balashev almost the very words he had used to Alexander himself at Tilsit. 'All that, he would have owed to my friendship. Oh, what a splendid reign!' he repeated several times, then paused, drew from his pocket a gold snuff-box, lifted it to his nose, and greedily sniffed at it.

'What a splendid reign the Emperor Alexander's *might have been!*'

He looked compassionately at Balashev, and as soon as the latter tried to make some rejoinder hastily interrupted him.

'What could he wish or look for that he would not have obtained through my friendship?' demanded Napoleon, shrugging his shoulders in perplexity. 'But no, he has preferred to surround himself with my enemies, and with whom? With Steins, Armfelts, Bennigsens, and Wintzingerodes!* Stein, a traitor expelled from his own country; Armfelt, a rake and an intriguer; Wintzingerode, a fugitive French subject; Bennigsen, rather more of a soldier than the others, but all the same an incompetent, who was unable to do anything in 1807 and who should awaken terrible memories in the Emperor Alexander's mind . . . Granted that were they competent they might be made use of,' continued Napoleon – hardly able to keep pace in words with the rush of thoughts that incessantly sprang up proving how right and strong he was (in his perception the two were one and the same) – 'but they are not even that!

They are neither fit for war nor peace! Barclay is said to be the most capable of them all, but I cannot say so judging by his first movements. And what are they doing, all these courtiers? Pfuel proposes, Armfelt disputes, Bennigsen considers, and Barclay, called on to act, does not know what to decide on, and time passes bringing no result. Bagration alone is a military man. He's stupid, but he has experience, a quick eye, and resolution ... And what role is your young monarch playing in that monstrous crowd? They compromise him and throw on him the responsibility for all that happens. A sovereign should not be with the army unless he is a general!' said Napoleon, evidently uttering these words as a direct challenge to the Emperor. He knew how Alexander desired to be a military commander.

'The campaign only began a week ago, and you haven't even been able to defend Vilna. You are cut in two and have been driven out of the Polish provinces. Your army is grumbling.'

'On the contrary, your Majesty,' said Balashev, hardly able to remember what had been said to him, and following these verbal fireworks with difficulty, 'the troops are burning with eagerness ...'

'I know everything!' Napoleon interrupted him. 'I know everything. I know the number of your battalions as exactly as I know my own. You have not two hundred thousand men, and I have three times that number. I give you my word of honour,' said Napoleon, forgetting that this word of honour could carry no weight – 'I give you my word of honour that I have five hundred and thirty thousand men this side of the Vistula. The Turks will be of no use to you; they are worth nothing and have shown it by making peace with you. As for the Swedes – it is their fate to be governed by mad kings. Their king was insane and they changed him for another – Bernadotte,* who promptly went mad – for no Swede would ally himself with Russia unless he were mad.'

Napoleon grinned maliciously and again raised his snuff-box to his nose.

Balashev knew how to reply to each of Napoleon's remarks, and would have done so; he continually made the gesture of a man wishing to say something, but Napoleon always interrupted him. To the alleged insanity of the Swedes, Balashev wished to reply that when Russia is on her side Sweden is practically an island; but Napoleon gave an angry exclamation to drown his voice. Napoleon was in that state of irritability in which a man has to talk, talk, and talk, merely to convince himself that he is in the right. Balashev began to feel uncomfortable: as envoy he feared to demean his dignity and felt the necessity of replying; but as a man he shrank before the transport of groundless wrath that had evidently seized Napoleon. He knew that none of the words now uttered by Napoleon had any significance, and that Napoleon himself would be ashamed of them when he came to his senses. Balashev stood with downcast eyes, looking at the movements of Napoleon's stout legs and trying to avoid meeting his eyes.

'But what do I care about your allies?' said Napoleon. 'I have allies – the Poles. There are eighty thousand of them and they fight like lions! And there will be two hundred thousand of them.'

And probably still more perturbed by the fact that he had uttered this obvious falsehood, and that Balashev still stood silently before him in the same attitude of submission to fate, Napoleon abruptly turned round, drew close to Balashev's face, and gesticulating rapidly and energetically with his white hands almost shouted:

'Know that if you stir up Prussia against me, I'll wipe it off the map of Europe!' he declared, his face pale and distorted by anger, and he struck one of his small hands energetically with the other. 'Yes, I will throw you back beyond the Dvina and beyond the Dnieper, and will re-erect against you that barrier* which it was criminal and blind of Europe to allow to be destroyed. Yes, that is what will happen to you. That is what you have gained by alienating me!' And he walked silently several times up and down the room, his fat shoulders twitching.

He put his snuff-box into his waistcoat pocket, took it out again, lifted it several times to his nose, and stopped in front of Balashev. He paused, looked ironically straight into Balashev's eyes, and said in a quiet voice:

'And yet what a splendid reign your master *might have had!*'

Balashev, feeling it incumbent on him to reply, said that from the Russian side things did not appear in so gloomy a light. Napoleon was silent, still looking derisively at him, and evidently not listening to him. Balashev said that in Russia the best results were expected from the war. Napoleon nodded condescendingly, as if to say, 'I know it's your duty to say that, but you don't believe it yourself. I have convinced you.'

When Balashev had ended, Napoleon again took out his snuff-box, sniffed at it, and stamped his foot twice on the floor as a signal. The door opened, a gentleman-in-waiting, bending respectfully, handed the Emperor his hat and gloves, another brought him a pocket-handkerchief. Napoleon, without giving them a glance, turned to Balashev:

'Assure the Emperor Alexander from me,' said he, taking his hat, ' that I am as devoted to him as before: I know him thoroughly and very highly esteem his lofty qualities. I will detain you no longer, General; you shall receive my letter to the Emperor.'

And Napoleon went quickly to the door. Everyone in the reception-room rushed forward and descended the staircase.

7

AFTER all that Napoleon had said to him – those bursts of anger and the last dryly spoken words: 'I will detain you no longer, General; you shall receive my letter,' Balashev felt convinced that Napoleon would not wish to see him, and would even avoid another meeting with him – an insulted envoy – especially as he had witnessed his unseemly anger. But to his surprise Balashev received, through Duroc, an invitation to dine with the Emperor that day.

Bessières,* Caulaincourt, and Berthier were present at that dinner.

Napoleon met Balashev cheerfully and amiably. He not only showed no sign of constraint or self-reproach on account of his outburst that morning, but on the contrary tried to reassure Balashev. It was evident that he had long been convinced that it was impossible for him to make a mistake, and that in his perception whatever he did was right, not because it harmonized with any idea of right and wrong, but because he did it.

The Emperor was in very good spirits after his ride through Vilna, where crowds of people had rapturously greeted and followed him. From all the windows of the streets through which he rode rugs, flags, and his monogram were displayed, and the Polish ladies welcoming him waved their handkerchiefs to him.

At dinner, having placed Balashev beside him, Napoleon not only treated him amiably but behaved as if Balashev were one of his own courtiers, one of those who sympathized with his plans and ought to rejoice at his success. In the course of conversation he mentioned Moscow, and questioned Balashev about the Russian capital, not merely as an interested traveller asks about a new city he intends to visit, but as if convinced that Balashev, as a Russian, must be flattered by his curiosity.

'How many inhabitants are there in Moscow? How many houses? Is it true that Moscow is called "Holy Moscow"? How many churches are there in Moscow?' he asked.

And receiving the reply that there were more than two hundred churches, he remarked:

'Why such a quantity of churches?'

'The Russians are very devout,' replied Balashev.

667

'But a large number of monasteries and churches is always a sign of the backwardness of a people,' said Napoleon, turning to Caulaincourt for appreciation of this remark.

Balashev respectfully ventured to disagree with the French Emperor.

'Every country has its own character,' said he.

'But nowhere in Europe is there anything like that,' said Napoleon.

'I beg your Majesty's pardon,' returned Balashev, 'besides Russia there is Spain, where there are also many churches and monasteries.'

This reply of Balashev's, which hinted at the recent defeats of the French in Spain,* was much appreciated when he related it at Alexander's court, but it was not much appreciated at Napoleon's dinner, where it passed unnoticed.

The uninterested and perplexed faces of the marshals showed that they were puzzled as to what Balashev's tone suggested. 'If there is a point we don't see it, or it is not at all witty,' their expressions seemed to say. So little was his rejoinder appreciated that Napoleon did not notice it at all, and naïvely asked Balashev through what towns the direct road from there to Moscow passed. Balashev, who was on the alert all through the dinner, replied that just as 'all roads lead to Rome,' so all roads lead to Moscow: there were many roads, and 'among them the road through *Poltava*,* which Charles XII chose'. Balashev involuntarily flushed with pleasure at the aptness of this reply, but hardly had he uttered the word *Poltava* before Caulaincourt began speaking of the badness of the road from Petersburg to Moscow and of his Petersburg reminiscences.

After dinner they went to drink coffee in Napoleon's study, which four days previously had been that of the Emperor Alexander. Napoleon sat down, toying with his Sèvres coffee cup, and motioned Balashev to a chair beside him.

Napoleon was in that well-known after-dinner mood which, more than any reasoned cause, makes a man contented with himself and disposed to consider everyone his friend. It seemed that he was surrounded by men who adored him; and he felt convinced that, after his dinner, Balashev too was his friend and worshipper. Napoleon turned to him with a pleasant though slightly ironic smile.

'They tell me this is the room the Emperor Alexander occupied? Strange, isn't it, General?' he said, evidently not doubting that this remark would be agreeable to his hearer since it went to prove his, Napoleon's, superiority to Alexander.

Balashev could make no reply and bowed his head in silence.

'Yes. Four days ago in this room, Wintzingerode and Stein were deliberating,' continued Napoleon with the same derisive and self-confident smile. 'What I can't understand,' he went on, 'is that the Emperor Alexander has surrounded himself with my personal enemies. That I do not ... understand. Has he not thought that I may do the same?' and he turned inquiringly to Balashev, and evidently this thought turned him back on to the track of his morning's anger, which was still fresh in him.

'And let him know that I will do so!' said Napoleon, rising and pushing his cup away with his hand. 'I'll drive all his Würtemberg, Baden, and Weimar relations out of Germany ... Yes. I'll drive them out. Let him prepare an asylum for them in Russia!'

Balashev bowed his head with an air indicating that he would like to make his bow and leave, and only listened because he could not help hearing what was said to him. Napoleon did not notice this expression; he treated Balashev not as an envoy from his enemy, but as a man now fully devoted to him and who must rejoice at his former master's humiliation.

'And why has the Emperor Alexander taken command of the armies? What is the good of that? War is my profession, but his business is to reign and not to command armies! Why has he taken on himself such a responsibility?'

Again Napoleon brought out his snuff-box, paced several times up and down the room in silence, and then suddenly and unexpectedly went up to Balashev, and with a slight smile as confidently, quickly, and simply as if he were doing something not merely important but pleasing to Balashev, he raised his hand to the forty-year-old Russian general's face, and taking him by the ear pulled it gently, smiling with his lips only.

To have one's ear pulled by the Emperor was considered the greatest honour and mark of favour at the French court.

'Well, adorer and courtier of the Emperor Alexander, why don't you say anything?' said he, as if it was ridiculous, in his presence, to be the adorer and courtier of any one but himself, Napoleon. 'Are the horses ready for the General?' he added, with a slight inclination of his head in reply to Balashev's bow. 'Let him have mine, he has *a long way to go!*'

The letter taken by Balashev was the last Napoleon sent to Alexander. Every detail of the interview was communicated to the Russian monarch, and the war began ...

8

AFTER his interview with Pierre in Moscow, Prince Andrew went to Petersburg, on business as he told his family, but really to meet Anatole Kuragin whom he felt it necessary to encounter. On reaching Petersburg he inquired for Kuragin but the latter had already left the city. Pierre had warned his brother-in-law that Prince Andrew was on his track. Anatole Kuragin promptly obtained an appointment from the Minister of War and went to join the army in Moldavia.* While in Petersburg Prince Andrew met Kutuzov, his former commander who was always well disposed towards him, and Kutuzov suggested that he should accompany him to the army in Moldavia to which the old general had been appointed commander-in-chief. So Prince Andrew, having received an appointment on the head-quarters staff, left for Turkey.

Prince Andrew did not think it proper to write and challenge Kuragin. He thought that if he challenged him without some fresh cause it might compromise the young Countess Rostova, and so he wanted to meet Kuragin personally in order to find a fresh pretext for a duel. But he again failed to meet Kuragin in Turkey, for soon after Prince Andrew arrived the latter returned to Russia. In a new country, amid new conditions, Prince Andrew found life easier to bear. After his betrothed had broken faith with him – which he felt the more acutely the more he tried to conceal its effects – the surroundings in which he had been happy became trying to him, and the freedom and independence he had once prized so highly were still more so. Not only could be no longer think the thoughts that had first come to him as he lay gazing at the sky on the field of Austerlitz and had later enlarged upon with Pierre, and which had filled his solitude at Bogucharovo and then in Switzerland and Rome, but he even dreaded to recall them and the bright and boundless horizons they had revealed. He was now concerned only with the nearest practical matters unrelated to his past interests, and he seized on these the more eagerly the more those past interests were closed to him. It was as if that lofty infinite canopy of heaven that had once towered above him had suddenly turned into a low solid vault that weighed him down, in which all was clear, but nothing eternal or mysterious.

Of the activities that presented themselves to him, army service was the simplest and most familiar. As a general on duty on Kutuzov's staff he applied himself to business with zeal and perseverance, and surprised Kutuzov by his willingness and accuracy in work. Not having found Kuragin in Turkey, Prince Andrew did not think it necessary to rush back to Russia after him, but all the same he knew that however long it might be before he met Kuragin, despite his contempt for him and despite all the proofs he deduced to convince himself that it was not worth stooping to a conflict with him – he knew that when he did meet him he would not be able to resist calling him out, any more than a ravenous man can help snatching at food. And the consciousness that the insult was not yet avenged, that his rancour was still unspent, weighed on his heart and poisoned the artificial tranquillity which he managed to obtain in Turkey by means of restless, plodding, and rather vainglorious and ambitious activity.

In the year 1812, when news of the war with Napoleon reached Bucharest – where Kutuzov had been living for two months passing his days and nights with a Wallachian woman – Prince Andrew asked Kutuzov to transfer him to the Western Army. Kutuzov, who was already weary of Bolkonsky's activity which seemed to reproach his own idleness, very readily let him go, and gave him a mission to Barclay de Tolly.

Before joining the Western Army which was then, in May, encamped at Drissa,* Prince Andrew visited Bald Hills which was directly on his way, being only three versts off the Smolensk high road. During the last three years there had been so many changes in his life, he had thought, felt, and seen so much (having travelled both in the east and the west) that on reaching Bald Hills it struck him as strange and unexpected to find the way of life there unchanged and still the same in every detail. He entered through the gates with their stone pillars, and drove up the avenue leading to the house as if he were entering an enchanted, sleeping castle. The same old stateliness, the same cleanliness, the same stillness reigned there, and inside there was the same furniture, the same walls, sounds, and smell, and the same timid faces, only somewhat older. Princess Mary was still the same timid, plain, maiden getting on in years, uselessly and joylessly passing the best years of her life in fear and constant suffering. Mademoiselle Bourienne was the same coquettish, self-satisfied girl, enjoying every moment of her existence and full of joyous hopes for the future. She had merely become more self-confident, Prince Andrew thought. Dessalles, the tutor he had brought from Switzerland, was wearing a coat of Russian cut and talking broken Russian to the servants, but was still the same narrowly intelligent, conscientious, and pedantic preceptor. The old prince had changed in appearance only by the loss of a tooth, which left a noticeable gap on one side of his mouth: in character he was the same as ever, only showing still more irritability and scepticism as to what was happening in the world.

Little Nicholas alone had changed. He had grown, become rosier, had curly dark hair, and when merry and laughing quite unconsciously lifted the upper lip of his pretty little mouth just as the little princess used to do. He alone did not obey the law of immutability in the enchanted sleeping castle. But though externally all remained as of old, the inner relations of all these people had changed since Prince Andrew had seen them last. The household was divided into two alien and hostile camps, who changed their habits for his sake and only met because he was there. To the one camp belonged the old prince, Mademoiselle Bourienne, and the architect; to the other Princess Mary, Dessalles, little Nicholas, and all the old nurses and maids.

During his stay at Bald Hills all the family dined together, but they were ill at ease and Prince Andrew felt that he was a visitor for whose sake an exception was being made, and that his presence made them all feel awkward. Involuntarily feeling this, at dinner on the first day he was taciturn, and the old prince noticing this also became morosely dumb, and retired to his apartments directly after dinner. In the evening when Prince Andrew went to him, and, trying to rouse him, began to tell him of the young Count Kamensky's campaign, the old prince began unexpectedly to talk about Princess Mary, blaming her for her superstitions and her dislike of Mademoiselle Bourienne, who he said was the only person truly attached to him.

The old prince said that if he was ill it was only because of Princess Mary: that she purposely worried and irritated him, and that by indulgence and silly talk she was spoiling little Prince Nicholas. The old prince knew very well that he tormented his daughter and that her life was very hard, but he also knew that he could not help tormenting her and that she deserved it. 'Why does Prince Andrew, who sees this, say nothing to me about his sister? Does he think me a scoundrel, or an old fool who without any reason keeps his own daughter at a distance and attaches this Frenchwoman to himself? He doesn't understand, so I must explain it, and he must hear me out,' thought the old prince. And he began explaining why he could not put up with his daughter's unreasonable character.

'If you ask me,' said Prince Andrew without looking up (he was censuring his father for the first time in his life), 'I did not wish to speak about it, but as you ask me I will give you my frank opinion. If there is any misunderstanding and discord between you and Mary, I can't blame her for it at all. I know how she loves and respects you. Since you ask me,' continued Prince Andrew, becoming irritable – as he was always liable to do of late – 'I can only say that if there are any misunderstandings they are caused by that worthless woman, who is not fit to be my sister's companion.'

The old man at first stared fixedly at his son, and an unnatural smile disclosed the fresh gap between his teeth to which Prince Andrew could not get accustomed.

'What companion, my dear boy? Eh? You've already been talking it over! Eh?'

'Father, I did not want to judge,' said Prince Andrew in a hard and bitter tone, 'but you challenged me, and I have said, and always shall say, that Mary is not to blame, but those to blame – the one to blame – is that Frenchwoman.'

'Ah, he has passed judgement ... passed judgement!' said the old man in a low voice and, as it seemed to Prince Andrew, with some embarrassment, but then he suddenly jumped up and cried: 'Be off, be off! Let not a trace of you remain here! ...'

Prince Andrew wished to leave at once, but Princess Mary persuaded him to stay another day. That day he did not see his father, who did not leave his room and admitted no one but Mademoiselle Bourienne and Tikhon, but asked several times whether his son had gone. Next day before leaving Prince Andrew went to his son's rooms. The boy, curly-headed like his mother and glowing with health, sat on his knee, and Prince Andrew began telling him the story of Bluebeard, but fell into a reverie without finishing the story. He thought not of this pretty child, his son whom he held on his knee, but of himself. He sought in himself either remorse for having angered his father, or regret at leaving home for the first time in his life on bad terms with him, and was horrified to find neither. What meant still more to him was, that he sought and did not find in himself the former tenderness for his son which he had hoped to reawaken by caressing the boy and taking him on his knee.

'Well, go on!' said his son.

Prince Andrew without replying put him down from his knee and went out of the room.

As soon as Prince Andrew had given up his daily occupations, and especially on returning to the old conditions of life amid which he had been happy, weariness of life overcame him with its former intensity, and he hastened to escape from these memories and to find some work as soon as possible.

'So you've decided to go, Andrew?' asked his sister.

'Thank God that I can,' replied Prince Andrew. 'I am very sorry you can't.'

'Why do you say that?' replied Princess Mary. 'Why do you

say that, when you are going to this terrible war, and he is so old? Mademoiselle Bourienne says he has been asking about you . . .'

As soon as she began to speak of that, her lips trembled and her tears began to fall. Prince Andrew turned away and began pacing the room.

'Ah, my God! my God! When one thinks who and what – what trash – can cause people misery!' he said with a malignity that alarmed Princess Mary.

She understood that when speaking of 'trash' he referred not only to Mademoiselle Bourienne, the cause of her misery, but also to the man who had ruined his own happiness.

'Andrew! One thing I beg, I entreat of you!' she said, touching his elbow and looking at him with eyes that shone through her tears. 'I understand you' (she looked down). 'Don't imagine that sorrow is the work of men. Men are His tools.' She looked a little above Prince Andrew's head with the confident, accustomed look with which one looks at the place where a familiar portrait hangs. 'Sorrow is sent by *Him*, not by men. Men are His instruments, they are not to blame. If you think someone has wronged you, forget it and forgive! We have no right to punish. And then you will know the happiness of forgiving.'

'If I were a woman I would do so, Mary. That is a woman's virtue. But a man should not and cannot forgive and forget,' he replied; and though till that moment he had not been thinking of Kuragin all his unexpended anger suddenly swelled up in his heart.

'If Mary is already persuading me to forgive, it means that I ought long ago to have punished him,' he thought. And giving her no further reply, he began thinking of the glad vindictive moment when he would meet Kuragin who he knew was now in the army.

Princess Mary begged him to stay one day more, saying that she knew how unhappy her father would be if Andrew left without being reconciled to him, but Prince Andrew replied that he would probably soon be back again from the army, and would certainly write to his father, but that the longer he stayed now the more embittered their difference would become.

'Good-bye, Andrew! Remember that misfortunes come from God, and men are never to blame,' were the last words he heard from his sister when he took leave of her.

'Then it must be so!' thought Prince Andrew as he drove out of the avenue from the house at Bald Hills. 'She, poor innocent creature, is left to be victimized by an old man who has outlived his wits. The old man feels he is guilty, but cannot change himself. My boy is growing up and rejoices in life, in which like everybody else he will deceive or be deceived. And I am off to the army.

Why? I myself don't know. I want to meet that man whom I despise, so as to give him a chance to kill and laugh at me!'

These conditions of life had been the same before, but then they were all connected, while now they had all tumbled to pieces. Only senseless things, lacking coherence, presented themselves one after another to Prince Andrew's mind.

9

PRINCE ANDREW reached the general head-quarters of the army at the end of June. The first army with which was the Emperor, occupied the fortified camp at Drissa, the second army* was retreating, trying to effect a junction with the first one from which it was said to be cut off by large French forces. Everyone was dissatisfied with the general course of affairs in the Russian army, but no one anticipated any danger of an invasion of the Russian provinces, and no one thought the war would extend farther than the western, the Polish, provinces.*

Prince Andrew found Barclay de Tolly, to whom he had been assigned, on the bank of the Drissa. As there was not a single town or large village in the vicinity of the camp, the immense number of generals and courtiers accompanying the army were living in the best houses of the villages on both sides of the river, over a radius of six miles. Barclay de Tolly was quartered nearly three miles from the Emperor. He received Bolkonsky stiffly and coldly, and told him in his foreign accent that he would mention him to the Emperor for a decision as to his employment, but asked him meanwhile to remain on his staff. Anatole Kuragin, whom Prince Andrew had hoped to find with the army, was not there. He had gone to Petersburg, but Prince Andrew was glad to hear this. His mind was occupied by the interests of the centre that was conducting a gigantic war, and he was glad to be free for a while from the distraction caused by the thought of Kuragin. During the first four days, while no duties were required of him, Prince Andrew rode round the whole fortified camp and, by the aid of his own knowledge and by talks with experts, tried to form a definite opinion about it. But the question whether the camp was advantageous or disadvantageous remained for him undecided. Already from his military experience and what he had seen in the Austrian campaign, he had come to the conclusion that in war the most deeply considered plans have no significance, and that all depends on the way unexpected movements of the enemy – that cannot be foreseen – are met, and on how and by whom the whole matter is handled. To clear up this last point for himself Prince Andrew, utilizing his position and acquaintances, tried to fathom the character of the control of the army and of the men and parties engaged in it, and he deduced for himself the following idea of the state of affairs.

While the Emperor had still been at Vilna the forces had been divided into three armies. First, the army under Barclay de Tolly, secondly, the army under Bagration, and thirdly the one commanded by Tormasov. The Emperor was with the first army but not as commander-in-chief. In the orders issued it was stated, not that the Emperor would take command, but only that he would be with the army. The Emperor moreover had with him not a commander-in-chief's staff but the imperial head-quarters staff. In attendance on him was the head of the imperial staff, Quartermaster-General Prince Volkonsky, as well as generals, imperial aides-de-camp, diplomatic officials, and a large number of foreigners, but not the army staff. Besides these there were in attendance on the Emperor without any definite appointments: Arakcheev, the ex-Minister of War; Count Bennigsen, the senior general in rank; the Grand Duke Tsarevich Constantine Pavlovich; Count Rumyantsev, the Chancellor; Stein, a former Prussian minister; Armfelt, a Swedish general; Pfuel, the chief author of the plan of campaign; Paulucci,* an adjutant-general and Sardinian *émigré;* Wolzogen* – and many others. Though these men had no military appointment in the army their position gave them influence, and often a corps commander, or even the commander-in-chief, did not know in what capacity he was questioned by Bennigsen, the Grand Duke, Arakcheev, or Prince Volkonsky, or was given this or that advice, and did not know whether a certain order received in the form of advice emanated from the man who gave it or from the Emperor, and whether it had to be executed or not. But this was only the external condition; the essential significance of the presence of the Emperor and of all these people, from a courtier's point of view (and in an Emperor's vicinity all become courtiers), was clear to everyone. It was this: the Emperor did not assume the title of commander-in-chief but disposed of all the armies; the men around him were his assistants. Arakcheev was a faithful custodian to enforce order, and acted as the sovereign's bodyguard. Bennigsen was a landlord in the Vilna province who appeared to be doing the honours of the district, but was in reality a good general, useful as an adviser and ready at hand to replace Barclay. The Grand Duke was there because it suited him to be. The ex-Minister Stein was there because his advice was useful and the Emperor Alexander held him in high esteem personally. Armfelt virulently hated Napoleon and was a general full of self-confidence, a quality that always influenced Alexander. Paulucci was there because he was bold and decided in speech. The adjutants-general were there because they always accompanied the Emperor, and lastly and chiefly Pfuel was there because he had drawn up the plan of campaign against Napoleon, and, having induced Alexander to believe in the efficacy of that plan, was directing the whole business of the war. With Pfuel was Wolzogen, who expressed Pfuel's thought in a more comprehensible way than Pfuel himself – who was a harsh, bookish theorist, self-confident to the point of despising everyone else – was able to do.

Besides these Russians and foreigners who propounded new and unexpected ideas every day – especially the foreigners, who did so with a boldness characteristic of people employed in a country not their own – there were many secondary personages accompanying the army because their principals were there.

Among the opinions and voices in this immense, restless, brilliant, and proud sphere, Prince Andrew noticed the following sharply defined sub-divisions of tendencies and parties.

The first party consisted of Pfuel and his adherents – military theorists who believed in a science of war with immutable laws – laws of oblique movements, outflankings, and so forth. Pfuel and his adherents demanded a retirement into the depths of the country in accordance with precise laws defined by a pseudo-theory of war, and they saw only barbarism, ignorance, or evil intention in every deviation from that theory. To this party belonged the foreign nobles, Wolzgen, Wintzingerode, and others, chiefly Germans.

The second party was directly opposed to the first; one extreme, as always happens, was met by representatives of the other. The members of this party were those who had demanded an advance from Vilna into Poland, and freedom from all pre-arranged plans. Besides being advocates of bold action, this section also represented nationalism, which made them still more one-sided in the dispute. They were Russians: Bagration, Ermolov (who was beginning to come to the front), and others. At that time a famous joke of Ermolov's was being circulated, that as a great favour he had petitioned the Emperor to make him a German. The men of that party, remembering Suvorov, said that what one had to do was not to reason, or stick pins into maps, but to fight, beat the enemy, keep him out of Russia and not let the army get discouraged.

To the third party – in which the Emperor had most confidence – belonged the courtiers who tried to arrange compromises between the other two. The members of this party, chiefly civilians, and to whom Arakcheev belonged, thought and said what men who have no convictions but wish to seem to have some, generally say. They said that undoubtedly war, particularly against such a genius as Bonaparte (they called him Bonaparte again now), needs most deeply devised plans and profound scientific knowledge, and in that respect Pfuel was a genius, but at the same time it had to be acknowledged that theorists are often one-sided, and therefore one should not trust them absolutely, but should also listen to what Pfuel's opponents and practical men of experience in warfare had to say, and then choose a middle course. They insisted on the retention of the camp at Drissa according to Pfuel's plan, but on changing the movements of the other armies. Though by this course neither one aim nor the other could be attained, yet it seemed best to the adherents of this third party.

Of a fourth opinion the most conspicuous representative was the Tsarevich, who could not forget his disillusionment at Austerlitz, where he had ridden out at the head of the Guards, in his casque and cavalry uniform as to review, expecting to crush the French gallantly; but unexpectedly finding himself in the front line had narrowly escaped amid the general confusion. The men of this party had both the quality and the defect of frankness in their opinions. They feared Napoleon, recognized his strength and their own weakness, and frankly said so. They said: 'Nothing but sorrow, shame, and ruin will come of all this! We have abandoned Vilna and Vitebsk and shall abandon Drissa. The only reasonable thing left to do is to conclude peace as soon as possible, before we are turned out of Petersburg.'

This view was very general in the upper army circles, and found support also in Petersburg, and from the chancellor, Rumyantsev, who for other reasons of state was in favour of peace.

The fifth party consisted of those who were adherents of Barclay de Tolly, not so much as a man but as minister of war and commander-in-chief. 'Be he what he may' (they always began like that), 'he is an honest, practical man and we have nobody better. Give him real power, for war cannot be conducted successfully without unity of command, and he will show what he can do, as he did in Finland. If our army is well organized and strong and has withdrawn to Drissa without suffering any defeats, we owe this entirely to Barclay. If Barclay is now to be superseded by Bennigsen all will be lost, for Bennigsen showed his incapacity already in 1807.'

The sixth party, the Bennigsenites, said, on the contrary, that at any rate there was no one more active and experienced than Bennigsen: 'and twist about as you may you will have to come to

Bennigsen eventually. Let the others make mistakes now!' said they, arguing that our retirement to Drissa was a most shameful reverse and an unbroken series of blunders. 'The more mistakes that are made the better. It will at any rate be understood all the sooner that things cannot go on like this. What is wanted is not some Barclay or other, but a man like Bennigsen, who made his mark in 1807, and to whom Napoleon himself did justice – a man whose authority would be willingly recognized, and Bennigsen is the only such man.'

The seventh party consisted of the sort of people who are always to be found, especially around young sovereigns, and of whom there were particularly many round Alexander – generals and imperial aides-de-camp passionately devoted to the Emperor, not merely as a monarch but as a man, adoring him sincerely and disinterestedly, as Rostov had done in 1805, and who saw in him not only all the virtues but all human capabilities as well. These men, though enchanted with the sovereign for refusing the command of the army, yet blamed him for such excessive modesty, and only desired and insisted that their adored sovereign should abandon his diffidence and openly announce that he would place himself at the head of the army, gather round him a commander-in-chief's staff and, consulting experienced theoreticians and practical men where necessary, would himself lead the troops, whose spirits would thereby be raised to the highest pitch.

The eighth and largest group, which in its enormous numbers was to the others as ninety-nine to one, consisted of men who desired neither peace nor war, neither an advance nor a defensive camp at the Drissa or anywhere else, neither Barclay nor the Emperor, neither Pfuel nor Bennigsen, but only one most essential thing – as much advantage and pleasure for themselves as possible. In the troubled waters of conflicting and intersecting intrigues that eddied about the Emperor's head-quarters, it was possible to succeed in many ways unthinkable at other times. A man who simply wished to retain his lucrative post would to-day agree with Pfuel, to-morrow with his opponent, and the day after, merely to avoid responsibility or to please the Emperor, would declare that he had no opinion at all on the matter. Another who wished to gain some advantage would attract the Emperor's attention by loudly advocating the very thing the Emperor had hinted at the day before, and would dispute and shout at the council, beating his breast and challenging those who did not agree with him to duels, thereby proving that he was prepared to sacrifice himself for the common good. A third, in the absence of opponents and between two councils, would take the chance to solicit a special gratuity for his faithful services, well knowing that people would be too busy to refuse him. A fourth would continually come accidentally under the Emperor's eye while overwhelmed with work. A fifth, to achieve his long-cherished aim of dining with the Emperor, would stubbornly insist on the correctness or falsity of some newly emerging opinion, and for this object would produce arguments more or less forcible and correct.

All the men of this party were fishing for rubles, decorations, and promotions, and in this pursuit watched only the weather-cock of imperial favour, and directly they noticed it turning in any direction, this whole drone-population of the army began blowing hard that way, so that it was all the harder for the Emperor to turn it elsewhere. Amid the uncertainties of the position, with the menace of serious danger giving a peculiarly threatening character to everything, amid this vortex of intrigue, egotism, conflict of views and feelings, and the diversity of race among these people – this eighth and largest party of those preoccupied with personal interests imparted great confusion and obscurity to the common task. Whatever question arose, a swarm of these drones, without having finished their buzzing on a previous theme, flew over to the new one and by their hum drowned and obscured the voices of those who were disputing honestly.

From among all these parties, just at the time Prince Andrew reached the army, another, a ninth party, was being formed and was beginning to raise its voice. This was the party of the elders, reasonable men experienced and capable in state affairs, who without sharing any of those conflicting opinions were able to take a detached view of what was going on at the staff at head-quarters, and to consider means of escape from this muddle, indecision, intricacy, and weakness.

The men of this party said and thought that what was wrong resulted chiefly from the Emperor's presence in the army with his military court, and from the consequent presence there of an indefinite, conditional, and unsteady fluctuation of relations, which is in place at court but harmful in an army; that a sovereign should reign but not command the army, and that the only way out of the position would be for the Emperor and his court to leave the army; that the mere presence of the Emperor paralysed the action of fifty thousand men required to secure his personal safety, and that the worst commander-in-chief if independent would be better than the very best one trammelled by the presence and authority of the monarch.

Just at the time Prince Andrew was living unoccupied at Drissa, Shishkov, the Secretary of State and one of the chief representatives of this party, wrote a letter to the Emperor which Arakcheev and

Balashev agreed to sign. In this letter, availing himself of permission given him by the Emperor to discuss the general course of affairs, he respectfully suggested – on the plea that it was necessary for the sovereign to arouse a warlike spirit in the people of the capital – that the Emperor should leave the army.

That arousing of the people by their sovereign, and his call to them to defend their country – the very incitement which was the chief cause of Russia's triumph in so far as it was produced by the Tsar's personal presence in Moscow – was suggested to the Emperor, and accepted by him, as a pretext for quitting the army.

10

THIS letter had not yet been presented to the Emperor when Barclay one day at dinner informed Bolkonsky that the sovereign wished to see him personally, to question him about Turkey, and that Prince Andrew was to present himself at Bennigsen's quarters at six that evening.

News was received at the Emperor's quarters that very day of a fresh movement by Napoleon which might endanger the army – news subsequently found to be false. And that morning Colonel Michaud had ridden round the Drissa fortifications with the Emperor and had pointed out to him that this fortified camp constructed by Pfuel, and till then considered a *chef-d'œuvre* of tactical science which would ensure Napoleon's destruction, was an absurdity, threatening the destruction of the Russian army.

Prince Andrew arrived at Bennigsen's quarters – a country gentleman's house of moderate size situated on the very banks of the river. Neither Bennigsen nor the Emperor was there, but Chernyshev, the Emperor's aide-de-camp, received Bolkonsky and informed him that the Emperor, accompanied by General Bennigsen and Marquis Paulucci, had gone a second time that day to inspect the fortifications of the Drissa camp, of the suitability of which serious doubts were beginning to be felt.

Chernyshev was sitting at a window in the first room with a French novel in his hand. This room had probably been a music-room, there was still an organ in it on which some rugs were piled, and in one corner stood the folding bedstead of Bennigsen's adjutant. This adjutant was also there, and sat dozing on the rolled-up bedding, evidently exhausted by work or by feasting. Two doors led from the room, one straight on into what had been the drawing-room, and another on the right to the study. Through the first door came the sound of voices conversing in German and occasionally in French. In that drawing-room were gathered by the Emperor's wish, not a military council (the Emperor preferred indefiniteness) but certain persons whose opinions he wished to know in view of the impending difficulties. It was not a council of war, but, as it were, a council to elucidate certain questions for the Emperor personally. To this semi-council had been invited the Swedish General Armfelt, Adjutant-General Wolzogen, Wintzingerode (whom Napoleon had referred to as a renegade French subject), Michaud, Toll,* Count Stein who was not a military man at all, and Pfuel himself, who as Prince Andrew had heard was the mainspring of the whole affair. Prince Andrew had an opportunity of getting a good look at him, for Pfuel arrived soon after himself, and in passing through to the drawing-room stopped a minute to speak to Chernyshev.

At first sight Pfuel, in his ill-made uniform of a Russian general, which fitted him badly like a fancy costume, seemed familiar to Prince Andrew though he saw him now for the first time. There was about him something of Weyrother, Mack, and Schmidt, and many other German theorist-generals whom Prince Andrew had seen in 1805, but he was more typical than any of them. Prince Andrew had never yet seen a German theorist in whom all the characteristics of those others were united to such an extent.

Pfuel was short and very thin but broad-boned, of coarse, robust build, broad in the hips and with prominent shoulder-blades. His face was much wrinkled and his eyes deep set. His hair had evidently been hastily brushed smooth in front on the temples, but stuck up behind in quaint little tufts. He entered the room looking restlessly and angrily around, as if afraid of everything in that large apartment. Awkwardly holding up his sword he addressed Chernyshev, and asked in German where the Emperor was. One could see that he wished to pass through the rooms as quickly as possible, finish with the bows and greetings, and sit down to business in front of a map, where he would feel at home. He nodded hurriedly in reply to Chernyshev, and smiled ironically on hearing that the sovereign was inspecting the fortifications that he, Pfuel, had planned in accord with his theory. He muttered something to himself abruptly and in a bass voice, as self-assured Germans do – it might have been 'stupid fellow' ... or 'the whole affair will be ruined', or 'something absurd will come of it' ... Prince Andrew did not catch what he said and would have passed on, but Chernyshev introduced him to Pfuel, remarking that Prince Andrew was just back from Turkey where the war had terminated so fortunately. Pfuel barely glanced – not so much at Prince Andrew as past him – and said with a laugh: 'That must have been a fine tactical war'; and laughing contemptuously went on into the room from which the sound of voices was heard.

Pfuel, always inclined to be irritably sarcastic, was particularly disturbed that day, evidently by the fact that they had dared to inspect and criticize his camp in his absence. From this short interview with Pfuel, Prince Andrew, thanks to his Austerlitz experiences, was able to form a clear conception of the man. Pfuel was one of those hopelessly and immutably self-confident men, self-confident to the point of martyrdom as only Germans are, because only Germans are self-confident on the basis of an abstract notion – science, that is, the supposed knowledge of absolute truth. A Frenchman is self-assured because he regards himself personally both in mind and body as irresistibly attractive to men and women. An Englishman is self-assured as being a citizen of the best-organized state in the world and therefore, as an Englishman, always knows what he should do and knows that all he does as an Englishman is undoubtedly correct. An Italian is self-assured because he is excitable and easily forgets himself and other people. A Russian is self-assured just because he knows nothing and does not want to know anything, since he does not believe that anything can be known. The German's self-assurance is worst of all, stronger and more repulsive than any other, because he imagines that he knows the truth – science – which he himself has invented but which is for him the absolute truth.

Pfuel was evidently of that sort. He had a science – the theory of oblique movements deduced by him from the history of Frederick the Great's wars, and all he came across in the history of more recent warfare seemed to him absurd and barbarous – monstrous collisions in which so many blunders were committed by both sides that these wars could not be called wars, they did not accord with the theory, and therefore could not serve as material for science.

In 1806 Pfuel had been one of those responsible for the plan of campaign that ended in Jena and Auerstadt, but he did not see the least proof of the fallibility of his theory in the disasters of that war. On the contrary, the deviations made from his theory were, in his opinion, the sole cause of the whole disaster, and with characteristically gleeful sarcasm he would remark, 'There, I said the whole affair would go to the devil!' Pfuel was one of those theoreticians who so love their theory that they lose sight of the theory's object – its practical application. His love of theory made him hate everything practical, and he would not listen to it. He was even pleased by failure, for failures resulting from deviations in practice from the theory, only proved to him the accuracy of his theory.

He said a few words to Prince Andrew and Chernyshev about the present war, with the air of a man who knows beforehand that all will go wrong, and who is not displeased that it should be so. The unbrushed tufts of hair sticking up behind and the hastily brushed hair on his temples expressed this most eloquently.

He passed into the next room, and the deep, querulous sounds of his voice were at once heard from there.

11

PRINCE ANDREW'S eyes were still following Pfuel out of the room when Count Bennigsen entered hurriedly, and nodding to Bolkonsky, but not pausing, went into the study giving instructions to his adjutant as he went. The Emperor was following him, and Bennigsen had hastened on to make some preparations and to be ready to receive the sovereign. Chernyshev and Prince Andrew went out into the porch, where the Emperor, who looked fatigued, was dismounting. Marquis Paulucci was talking to him with particular warmth and the Emperor, with his head bent to the left, was listening with a dissatisfied air. The Emperor moved forward evidently wishing to end the conversation, but the flushed and excited Italian oblivious of decorum followed him and continued to speak.

'And as for the man who advised forming this camp – the Drissa camp,' said Paulucci as the Emperor mounted the steps and noticing Prince Andrew scanned his unfamiliar face, 'as to that person, Sire . . .' continued Paulucci desperately, apparently unable to restrain himself, 'the man who advised the Drissa camp – I see no alternative but the lunatic asylum or the gallows!'

Without heeding the end of the Italian's remarks, and as though not hearing them, the Emperor, recognizing Bolkonsky, addressed him graciously:

'I am very glad to see you! Go in there where they are meeting, and wait for me.'

The Emperor went into the study. He was followed by Prince Peter Mikhaylovich Volkonsky and Baron Stein, and the door closed behind them. Prince Andrew, taking advantage of the Emperor's permission, accompanied Paulucci, whom he had known in Turkey, into the drawing-room where the council was assembled.

Prince Peter Mikhaylovich Volkonsky occupied the position as it were of chief of the Emperor's staff. He came out of the study into the drawing-room with some maps which he spread on a table, and put questions on which he wished to hear the opinion of the gentlemen present. What had happened was that news (which

684

afterwards proved to be false) had been received during the night of a movement by the French to outflank the Drissa camp.

The first to speak was General Armfelt who, to meet the difficulty that presented itself, unexpectedly proposed a perfectly new position away from the Petersburg and Moscow roads. The reason for this was inexplicable (unless he wished to show that he, too, could have an opinion), but he urged that at this point the army should unite and there await the enemy. It was plain that Armfelt had thought out that plan long ago, and now expounded it not so much to answer the questions put – which in fact his plan did not answer – as to avail himself of the opportunity to air it. It was one of the millions of proposals, one as good as another, that could be made as long as it was quite unknown what character the war would take. Some disputed his arguments, others defended them. Young Count Toll objected to the Swedish general's views more warmly than anyone else, and in the course of the dispute drew from his side pocket a well-filled notebook which he asked permission to read to them. In these voluminous notes Toll suggested another scheme, totally different from Armfelt's or Pfuel's plan of campaign. In answer to Toll, Paulucci suggested an advance and an attack, which, he urged, could alone extricate us from the present uncertainty and from the trap (as he called the Drissa camp) in which we were situated. During all these discussions Pfuel and his interpreter Wolzogen (his 'bridge' in court relations) were silent. Pfuel only snorted contemptuously and turned away, to show that he would never demean himself by replying to such nonsense as he was now hearing. So when Prince Volkonsky, who was in the chair, called on him to give his opinion, he merely said:

'Why ask me? General Armfelt has proposed a splendid position with an exposed rear, or why not this Italian gentleman's attack – very fine, or a retreat, also good! Why ask me?' said he. 'Why, you yourselves know everything better than I do.'

But when Volkonsky said with a frown that it was in the Emperor's name that he asked his opinion, Pfuel rose and, suddenly growing animated, began to speak:

'Everything has been spoilt, everything muddled, everybody thought they knew better than I did, and now you come to me! How mend matters? There is nothing to mend! The principles laid down by me must be strictly adhered to,' said he, drumming on the table with his bony fingers. 'What is the difficulty? Nonsense, childishness!'

He went up to the map, and speaking rapidly began proving that no eventuality could alter the efficiency of the Drissa camp, that everything had been foreseen, and that if the enemy were really going to outflank it, the enemy would inevitably be destroyed.

Paulucci, who did not know German, began questioning him in French. Wolzogen came to the assistance of his chief, who spoke French badly, and began translating for him, hardly able to keep pace with Pfuel, who was rapidly demonstrating that not only all that had happened, but all that could happen, had been foreseen in his scheme, and that if there were now any difficulties the whole fault lay in the fact that his plan had not been precisely executed. He kept laughing sarcastically, he demonstrated, and at last contemptuously ceased to demonstrate, like a mathematician who ceases to prove in various ways the accuracy of a problem that has already been proven. Wolzogen took his place and continued to explain his views in French, every now and then turning to Pfuel and saying, 'Is it not so, your Excellency?' But Pfuel, like a man heated in a fight who strikes those on his own side, shouted angrily at his own supporter, Wolzogen:

'Well, of course, what more is there to explain?'

Paulucci and Michaud both attacked Wolzogen simultaneously in French. Armfelt addressed Pfuel in German. Toll explained to Volkonsky in Russian. Prince Andrew listened and observed in silence.

Of all these men Prince Andrew sympathized most with Pfuel, angry, determined, and absurdly self-confident as he was. Of all those present evidently he alone was not seeking anything for himself, nursed no hatred against any one, and only desired that the plan, formed on a theory arrived at by years of toil, should be carried out. He was ridiculous, and unpleasantly sarcastic, but yet he inspired involuntary respect by his boundless devotion to an idea. Besides this, the remarks of all except Pfuel had one common trait that had not been noticeable at the council of war in 1805: there was now a panic fear of Napoleon's genius, which though concealed was noticeable in every rejoinder. Everything was assumed to be possible for Napoleon, they expected him from every side, and invoked his terrible name to shatter each other's proposals. Pfuel alone seemed to consider Napoleon a barbarian like everyone else who opposed his theory. But besides this feeling of respect, Pfuel evoked pity in Prince Andrew. From the tone in which the courtiers addressed him, and the way Paulucci had allowed himself to speak of him to the Emperor, but above all from a certain desperation in Pfuel's own expressions, it was clear that the others knew, and Pfuel himself felt, that his fall was at hand. And despite his self-confidence and grumpy German sarcasm he was pitiable, with his hair smoothly brushed on the temples and sticking up in tufts behind. Though he concealed the fact under a show of irritation and contempt, he was evidently in despair that the sole remaining chance of verifying his theory by a huge experiment and proving its soundness to the whole world, was slipping away from him.

The discussions continued a long time, and the longer they lasted the more heated became the disputes, culminating in shouts and personalities, and the less was it possible to arrive at any general conclusion from all that had been said. Prince Andrew, listening to this polyglot talk and to these surmises, plans, refutations and shouts, felt nothing but amazement at what they were saying. A thought that had long since and often occurred to him during his military activities – the idea that there is not, and cannot be, any science of war, and that therefore there can be no such thing as a military genius – now appeared to him an obvious truth. 'What theory and science is possible about a matter the conditions and circumstances of which are unknown and cannot be defined, especially when the strength of the acting forces cannot be ascertained? No one was or is able to foresee in what condition our or the enemy's armies will be in a day's time, and no one can gauge the force of this or that detachment. Sometimes – when there is not a coward at the front to shout, "We are cut off" and start running, but a brave and jolly lad who shouts "Hurrah!" – a detachment of five thousand is worth thirty thousand, as at Schön Graben, while at times fifty thousand run from eight thousand as at Austerlitz. What science can there be in a matter in which, as in all practical matters, nothing can be defined, and everything depends on innumerable conditions the significance of which is determined at a particular moment which arrives no one knows when? Armfelt says our army is cut in half, and Paulucci says we have got the French army between two fires; Michaud says that the worthlessness of the Drissa camp lies in having the river behind it, and Pfuel says that is what constitutes its strength; Toll proposes one plan, Armfelt another, and they are all good and all bad, and the advantages of any suggestion can only be seen at the moment of trial. And why do they all speak of a "military genius"? Is a man a genius who can order bread to be brought up at the right time and say who is to go to the right and who to the left? It is only because military men are invested with pomp and power, and crowds of sycophants flatter power, attributing to it qualities of genius it does not possess. The best generals I have known were, on the contrary, stupid or absent-minded men. Bagration was the best, Napoleon himself admitted that. And Bonaparte himself! I remember his limited, self-satisfied face on the field of Austerlitz. Not only does a good army commander not need any special qualities, on the contrary he needs the absence of the highest and best human attributes – love, poetry, tenderness, and philosophic inquiring doubt. He should be limited, firmly convinced that what he is doing is very important (otherwise he will not have sufficient patience), and only then will he be a brave leader. God forbid that he should be humane, should love, or pity, or think of what is just and unjust. It is understandable that a theory of their "genius" was invented for them long ago because they have power! The success of a military action depends not on them, but on the man in the ranks who shouts "We are lost!" or who shouts "Hurrah!" And only in the ranks can one serve with assurance of being useful.'

So thought Prince Andrew as he listened to the talking, and he roused himself only when Paulucci called him and everyone was leaving.

At the review next day the Emperor asked Prince Andrew where he would like to serve, and Prince Andrew lost his standing in court circles for ever by not asking to remain attached to the sovereign's person, but for permission to serve in the army.

12

BEFORE the beginning of the campaign Rostov had received a letter from his parents in which they told him briefly of Natasha's illness and the breaking off of her engagement to Prince Andrew (which they explained by Natasha's having rejected him) and again asked Nicholas to retire from the army and return home. On receiving this letter Nicholas did not even make any attempt to get leave of absence or to retire from the army, but wrote to his parents that he was sorry Natasha was ill and her engagement broken off, and that he would do all he could to meet their wishes. To Sonya he wrote separately.

Adored friend of my soul! [he wrote] Nothing but honour could keep me from returning to the country. But now, at the commencement of the campaign, I should feel dishonoured not only in my comrades' eyes but in my own if I preferred my own happiness to my love and duty to the Fatherland. But this shall be our last separation. Believe me, directly the war is over, if I am still alive and still loved by you, I will throw up everything and fly to you, to press you for ever to my ardent breast.

It was, in fact, only the commencement of the campaign that prevented Rostov from returning home as he had promised, and marrying Sonya. The autumn in Otradnoe with the hunting, and the winter with the Christmas holidays and Sonya's love, had opened out to him a vista of tranquil rural joys and peace such as he had never known before, and which now allured him. 'A splendid wife, children, a good pack of hounds, a dozen leashes of smart borzois, agriculture, neighbours, service by election...' thought he. But now the campaign was beginning and he had to remain with his regiment. And since it had to be so, Nicholas Rostov, as was natural to him, felt contented with the life he led in the regiment, and was able to find pleasure in that life.

On his return from his furlough Nicholas, having been joyfully welcomed by his comrades, was sent to obtain remounts, and brought back from the Ukraine excellent horses which pleased him and earned him commendation from his commanders. During his absence he had been promoted Captain, and when the regiment was put on war-footing with an increase in numbers, he was again allotted his old squadron.

The campaign began, the regiment was moved into Poland on double pay, new officers arrived, new men and horses, and above all, everybody was infected with the merrily excited mood that goes with the commencement of a war, and Rostov, conscious of his advantageous position in the regiment, devoted himself entirely to the pleasures and interests of military service, though he knew that sooner or later he would have to relinquish them.

The troops retired from Vilna for various complicated reasons of state, political and strategic. Each step of the retreat was accompanied by a complicated interplay of interests, arguments, and passions, at head-quarters. For the Pavlograd Hussars, however, the whole of this retreat during the finest period of summer and with sufficient supplies, was a very simple and agreeable business.

It was only at head-quarters that there was depression, uneasiness, and intriguing; in the body of the army they did not ask themselves where they were going or why. If they regretted having to retreat, it was only because they had to leave billets they had grown accustomed to, or some pretty young Polish lady. If the thought that things looked bad chanced to enter anyone's head, he tried to be cheerful as befits a good soldier, and not to think of the general trend of affairs, but only of the task nearest to hand. First they camped gaily before Vilna, making acquaintance with the Polish landowners, preparing for reviews, and being reviewed by the Emperor and other high commanders. Then came an order to retreat to Sventsyani and destroy any provisions they could not carry away with them. Sventsyani was remembered by the hussars only as the *drunken camp*, a name the whole army gave to their encampment there, and because many complaints were made against the troops, who taking advantage of the order to collect provisions, took also horses, carriages, and carpets, from the Polish proprietors. Rostov remembered Sventsyani because on the first day of their arrival at that small town he changed his sergeant-major, and was unable to manage all the drunken men of the squadron who, unknown to him, had appropriated five barrels of old beer. From Sventsyani they retired farther and farther to Drissa, and thence again beyond Drissa, drawing near to the frontier of Russia proper.

On the 13th of July the Pavlograds took part in a serious action for the first time.

On the 12th of July, on the eve of that action, there was a heavy storm of rain and hail. In general the summer of 1812 was remarkable for its storms.

The two Pavlograd squadrons were bivouacking on a field of rye, which was already in ear but had been completely trodden down by cattle and horses. The rain was descending in torrents, and Rostov with a young officer named Ilyin, his protégé, was sitting in a hastily constructed shelter. An officer of their regiment, with long moustaches extending onto his cheeks, who after riding to the staff had been overtaken by the rain, entered Rostov's shelter.

'I have come from the staff, Count. Have you heard of Raevsky's exploit?'

And the officer gave them details of the Saltanov battle, which he had heard at the staff.

Rostov, smoking his pipe and turning his head about as the water trickled down his neck, listened inattentively, with an occasional glance at Ilyin who was pressing close to him. This officer, a lad of sixteen who had recently joined the regiment, was now in the same relation to Nicholas that Nicholas had been to Denisov seven years before. Ilyin tried to imitate Rostov in everything, and adored him as a girl might have done.

Zdrzhinsky, the officer with the long moustache, spoke grandiloquently of the Saltanov dam being 'a Russian Thermopylae,' and of how a deed worthy of antiquity had been performed by General Raevsky. He recounted how Raevsky had led his two sons onto the dam under terrific fire, and had charged with them beside him. Rostov heard the story and not only said nothing to encourage Zdrzhinsky's enthusiasm, but on the contrary looked like a man ashamed of what he was hearing, though with no intention of contradicting it. Since the campaigns of Austerlitz and of 1807 Rostov knew by experience that men always lie when describing military exploits, as he himself had done when recounting them; besides that, he had experience enough to know that nothing happens in war at all as we can imagine or relate it. And so he did not like Zdrzhinsky's tale, nor did he like Zdrzhinsky himself who, with his moustaches extending over his cheeks, bent low over the face of his hearer, as was his habit, and crowded Rostov in the narrow shanty. Rostov looked at him in silence. 'In the first place, there must have been such a confusion and crowding on the dam that was being attacked, that if Raevsky did lead his sons there it could have had no effect except perhaps on some dozen men nearest to him,' thought he, 'the rest could not have seen how or with whom Raevsky came onto the dam. And even those who did see it would not have been much stimulated by it, for what had they to do with Raevsky's tender paternal feelings when their own skins were in danger? And besides, the fate of the Fatherland did not depend on whether they took the Saltanov dam or not, as we are told was the case at Thermopylae. So why should he have made such a sacrifice? And why expose his own children in the battle? I would not have taken my brother Petya there, or even Ilyin, who's a stranger to me but a nice lad, but would have tried to put them somewhere under cover,' Nicholas continued to think, as he listened to Zdrzhinsky. But he did not express his thoughts for in such matters, too, he had gained experience. He knew that this tale redounded to the glory of our arms and so one had to pretend not to doubt it. And he acted accordingly.

'I can't stand this any more,' said Ilyin, noticing that Rostov did not relish Zdrzhinsky's conversation. 'My stockings and shirt . . . and the water is running on my seat! I'll go and look for shelter. The rain seems less heavy.'

Ilyin went out and Zdrzhinsky rode away.

Five minutes later Ilyin, splashing through the mud, came running back to the shanty.

'Hurrah! Rostov, come quick! I've found it! About two hundred yards away there's a tavern where *ours* have already gathered. We can at least get dry there, and Mary Hendrikhovna's there.'

Mary Hendrikhovna was the wife of the regimental doctor, a pretty young German woman he had married in Poland. The doctor, whether from lack of means or because he did not like to part from his young wife in the early days of their marriage, took her about with him wherever the hussar regiment went, and his jealousy had become a standing joke among the hussar officers.

Rostov threw his cloak over his shoulders, shouted to Lavrushka to follow with the things, and – now slipping in the mud, now splashing right through it – set off with Ilyin in the lessening rain, and the darkness that was occasionally rent by distant lightning.

'Rostov, where are you?'

'Here. What lightning!' they called to one another.

IN the tavern, before which stood the doctor's covered cart, there were already some five officers. Mary Hendrikhovna, a plump little blonde German, in a dressing-jacket and night-cap, was sitting on a broad bench in the front corner. Her husband, the doctor, lay asleep behind her. Rostov and Ilyin on entering the room were welcomed with merry shouts and laughter.

'Dear me, how jolly we are!' said Rostov laughing.

'And why do you stand there gaping?'

'What swells they are! Why, the water streams from them! Don't make our drawing-room so wet.'

'Don't mess Mary Hendrikhovna's dress!' cried other voices.

Rostov and Ilyin hastened to find a corner where they could change into dry clothes without offending Mary Hendrikhovna's modesty. They were going into a tiny recess behind a partition to change, but found it completely filled by three officers who sat playing cards by the light of a solitary candle on an empty box, and these officers would on no account yield their position. Mary Hendrikhovna obliged them with the loan of a petticoat, to be used as a curtain, and behind that screen Rostov and Ilyin, helped by Lavrushka who had brought their kits, changed their wet things for dry ones.

A fire was made up in the dilapidated brick stove. A board was found, fixed on two saddles and covered with a horse-cloth, a small samovar was produced and a cellaret and half a bottle of rum, and having asked Mary Hendrikhovna to preside they all crowded round her. One offered her a clean handkerchief to wipe her charming hands, another spread a jacket under her little feet to keep them from the damp, another hung his coat over the window to keep out the draught, and yet another waved the flies off her husband's face lest he should wake up.

'Leave him alone,' said Mary Hendrikhovna, smiling timidly and happily. 'He is sleeping well as it is, after a sleepless night.'

'Oh, no, Mary Hendrikhovna,' replied the officer, 'one must look after the doctor. Perhaps he'll take pity on me some day, when it comes to cutting off a leg or an arm for me.'

There were only three tumblers, the water was so muddy that one could not make out whether the tea was strong or weak, and the samovar held only six tumblers of water, but this made it all the pleasanter to take turns in order of seniority to receive one's tumbler from Mary Hendrikhovna's plump little hands with their short and not over-clean nails. All the officers appeared to be and really were in love with her that evening. Even those playing cards behind the partition soon left their game and came over to the samovar, yielding to the general mood of courting Mary Hendrikhovna. She, seeing herself surrounded by such brilliant and polite young men, beamed with satisfaction, try as she might to hide it, and perturbed as she evidently was each time her husband moved in his sleep behind her.

There was only one spoon, sugar was more plentiful than anything else but it took too long to dissolve, so it was decided that Mary Hendrikhovna should stir the sugar for everyone in turn. Rostov received his tumbler, and adding some rum to it asked Mary Hendrikhovna to stir it.

'But you take it without sugar?' she said, smiling all the time as if everything she said and everything the others said was very amusing and had a double meaning.

'It is not the sugar I want, but only that your little hand should stir my tea.'

Mary Hendrikhovna assented and began looking for the spoon which someone meanwhile had pounced on.

'Use your finger, Mary Hendrikhovna, it will be still nicer,' said Rostov.

'Too hot!' she replied, blushing with pleasure.

Ilyin put a few drops of rum into the bucket of water and brought it to Mary Hendrikhovna asking her to stir it with her finger.

'This is my cup,' said he. 'Only dip your finger in it and I'll drink it all up.'

When they had emptied the samovar Rostov took a pack of cards and proposed that they should play 'Kings' with Mary Hendrikhovna. They drew lots to settle who should make up her set. At Rostov's suggestion it was agreed that whoever became 'King' should have the right to kiss Mary Hendrikhovna's hand, and that the 'Booby' should go to refill and reheat the samovar for the doctor when the latter awoke.

'Well, but supposing Mary Hendrikhovna is "King"?' asked Ilyin.

'As it is, she is Queen, and her word is law!'

They had hardly begun to play before the doctor's dishevelled head suddenly appeared from behind Mary Hendrikhovna. He had been awake some time, listening to what was being said, and evidently found nothing entertaining or amusing in what was going on. His face was sad and depressed. Without greeting the officers, he scratched himself and asked to be allowed to pass as they were blocking the way. As soon as he had left the room all the officers burst into loud laughter, and Mary Hendrikhovna blushed till her eyes filled with tears and thereby became still more attractive to them. Returning from the yard the doctor told his wife (who had ceased to smile so happily, and looked at him in alarm awaiting her sentence) that the rain had ceased and they must go to sleep in their covered cart, or everything in it would be stolen.

'But I'll send an orderly ... Two of them!' said Rostov. 'What an idea, doctor!'

'I'll stand guard on it myself!' said Ilyin.

'No, gentlemen, you have had your sleep, but I have not slept for two nights,' replied the doctor, and he sat down morosely beside his wife waiting for the game to end.

Seeing his gloomy face as he frowned at his wife, the officers grew still merrier, and some of them could not refrain from laughter, for which they hurriedly sought plausible pretexts. When he had gone, taking his wife with him, and had settled down with her in their covered cart, the officers lay down in the tavern, covering themselves with their wet cloaks, but they did not sleep for a long time; now they exchanged remarks, recalling the doctor's uneasiness and his wife's delight, now they ran out into the porch and reported what was taking place in the covered trap. Several times Rostov, covering his head, tried to go to sleep, but some remark would arouse him and conversation would be resumed, to the accompaniment of unreasoning, merry, childlike laughter.

14

IT was nearly three o'clock but no one was yet asleep, when the quartermaster appeared with an order to move on to the little town of Ostrovna.

Still laughing and talking, the officers began hurriedly getting ready, and again boiled some muddy water in the samovar. But Rostov went off to his squadron without waiting for tea. Day was breaking, the rain had ceased and the clouds were dispersing. It felt damp and cold, especially in clothes that were still moist. As they left the tavern in the twilight of the dawn Rostov and Ilyin both glanced under the wet and glistening leather hood of the doctor's cart, from under the apron of which his feet were sticking out, and in the middle of which his wife's night-cap was visible and her sleepy breathing audible.

'She really is a dear little thing,' said Rostov to Ilyin who was following him.

'A charming woman!' said Ilyin with all the gravity of a boy of sixteen.

Half an hour later the squadron was lined up on the road. The command was heard to 'mount' and the soldiers crossed themselves and mounted. Rostov riding in front gave the order 'Forward!' and the hussars, with clanking sabres and subdued talk, their horses' hoofs splashing in the mud, defiled in fours and moved along the broad road planted with birch-trees on each side, following the infantry and a battery that had gone on in front.

Tattered, blue-purple clouds, reddening in the east, were scudding before the wind. It was growing lighter and lighter. That curly grass which always grows by country roadsides became clearly visible, still wet with the night's rain, the drooping branches of the birches, also wet, swayed in the wind and flung down bright drops of water to one side. The soldiers' faces were more and more clearly visible. Rostov, always closely followed by Ilyin, rode along the side of the road between two rows of birch-trees.

When campaigning, Rostov allowed himself the indulgence of riding not a regimental but a Cossack horse. A judge of horses and a sportsman, he had lately procured himself a large, fine, mettlesome, Donets horse, dun-coloured with light mane and tail, and when he rode it no one could out-gallop him. To ride this horse was a pleasure to him, and he thought of the horse, of the morning, of the doctor's wife, but not once of the impending danger.

Formerly, when going into action, Rostov had felt afraid, now he had not the least feeling of fear. He was fearless not because he had grown used to being under fire (one cannot grow used to danger), but because he had learned how to manage his thoughts when in danger. He had grown accustomed when going into action to think about anything but what would seem most likely to interest him – the impending danger. During the first period of his service, hard as he tried and much as he reproached himself with cowardice, he had not been able to do this, but with time it had come of itself. Now he rode beside Ilyin under the birch-trees, occasionally plucking leaves from a branch that met his hand, sometimes touching his horse's side with his foot, or without turning round handing a pipe he had finished to an hussar riding behind him, with as calm and careless an air as though he were merely out for a ride. He glanced with pity at the excited face of Ilyin, who talked much and in great agitation. He knew from experience the tormenting expectation of terror and death the cornet was suffering, and knew that only time could help him.

As soon as the sun appeared in a clear strip of sky beneath the clouds, the wind fell, as if it dared not spoil the beauty of the summer morning after the storm; drops continued to fall, but vertically now, and all was still. The whole sun appeared on the horizon and disappeared behind a long, narrow cloud that hung above it. A few minutes later it reappeared brighter still from behind the top of the cloud, tearing its edge. Everything grew bright and glittered. And with that light, and as if in reply to it, came the sound of guns ahead of them.

Before Rostov had had time to consider and determine the distance of that firing, Count Ostermann-Tolstoy's* adjutant came galloping from Vitebsk with orders to advance at a trot along the road.

The squadron overtook and passed the infantry and the battery – which had also quickened their pace – rode down a hill, and passing through an empty and deserted village again ascended. The horses began to lather and the men to flush.

'Halt! Dress your ranks!' the order of the regimental commander was heard ahead. 'Forward by the left. Walk, march!' came the order from in front.

And the hussars, passing along the line of troops on the left flank of our position, halted behind our uhlans who were in the front line. To the right stood our infantry in a dense column: they were the reserve. Higher up the hill, on the very horizon, our guns were visible through the wonderfully clear air, brightly illuminated by slanting morning sunbeams. In front, beyond a hollow dale, could be seen the enemy's columns and guns. Our advanced line, already in action, could be heard briskly exchanging shots with the enemy in the dale.

At these sounds, long unheard, Rostov's spirits rose as at the strains of the merriest music. *Trap-ta-ta-tap!* cracked the shots, now together, now several quickly one after another. Again all was silent, and then again it sounded as if someone were walking on detonators and exploding them.

The hussars remained in the same place for about an hour. A cannonade began. Count Ostermann with his suite rode up behind the squadron, halted, spoke to the commander of the regiment, and rode up the hill to the guns.

After Ostermann had gone a command rang out to the uhlans.

'Form column! Prepare to charge!'

The infantry in front of them parted into platoons to allow the cavalry to pass. The uhlans started, the streamers on their spears fluttering, and trotted downhill towards the French cavalry which was seen below to the left.

As soon as the uhlans descended the hill the hussars were ordered up the hill to support the battery. As they took the places vacated by the uhlans, bullets came from the front whining and whistling, but fell spent without taking effect.

These sounds, which he had not heard for so long, had an even more pleasurable and exhilarating effect on Rostov than the previous sounds of firing. Drawing himself up he viewed the field of battle opening out before him from the hill, and with his whole soul followed the movement of the uhlans. They swooped down close to the French dragoons, something confused happened there amid the smoke, and five minutes later our uhlans were galloping back, not to the place they had occupied but more to the left, and among the orange-coloured uhlans on chestnut horses and behind them in a large group, blue French dragoons on grey horses could be seen.

15

ROSTOV, with his keen sportsman's eye, was one of the first to catch sight of these blue French dragoons pursuing our uhlans. Nearer and nearer in disorderly crowds came the uhlans and the French dragoons pursuing them. He could already see how these men, who looked so small at the foot of the hill, jostled and overtook one another waving their arms and their sabres in the air.

Rostov gazed at what was happening before him as at a hunt. He felt instinctively that if the hussars struck at the French dragoons now, the latter could not withstand them, but if a charge was to be made it must be done now, that very moment, or it would be too late. He looked round. A captain, standing beside him, was gazing like himself with eyes fixed on the cavalry below them.

'Andrew Sevastyanych!' said Rostov. 'You know, we could crush them...'

'A fine thing, too!' replied the captain, 'and really...'

Rostov without waiting to hear him out touched his horse, galloped to the front of the squadron, and before he had time to finish giving the word of command, the whole squadron, sharing his feeling, was following him. Rostov himself did not know how or why he did it. He acted as he did when hunting, without reflecting or considering. He saw the dragoons near, and that they were galloping in disorder; he knew they could not withstand an attack – knew there was only that moment, and that if he let it slip it would not return. The bullets were whining and whistling so stimulatingly around him and his horse was so eager to go, that he could not restrain himself. He touched his horse, gave the word of command, and immediately, hearing behind him the tramp of the horses of his deployed squadron, rode at full trot downhill towards the dragoons. Hardly had they reached the bottom of the hill before their pace instinctively changed to a gallop, which grew faster and faster as they drew nearer to our uhlans and the French dragoons who galloped after them. The dragoons were now close at hand. On seeing our hussars the foremost began to turn while those behind began to halt. With the same feeling with which he had galloped across the path of a wolf, Rostov gave rein to his Donets horse and galloped to intersect the path of the dragoons' disordered lines. One uhlan stopped, another who was on foot flung himself to the ground to avoid being knocked over, and a riderless horse fell in among the hussars. Nearly all the French dragoons were galloping back. Rostov, picking out one on a grey horse, dashed after him. On the way he came upon a bush, his gallant horse cleared it, and almost before he had righted himself in his saddle he saw that he would immediately overtake the enemy he had selected. That Frenchman, by his uniform an officer, was going at a gallop crouching on his grey horse and urging it on with his sabre. In another moment Rostov's horse dashed its breast against the hind quarters of the officer's horse almost knocking it over, and at the same instant Rostov, without knowing why, raised his sabre and struck the Frenchman with it.

The instant he had done this, all Rostov's animation vanished. The officer fell, not so much from the blow – which had but slightly cut his arm above the elbow – as from the shock to his horse and from fright. Rostov reined in his horse, and his eyes sought his foe to see whom he had vanquished. The French dragoon officer was hopping with one foot on the ground, the other being caught in the stirrup. His eyes, screwed up with fear as if he every moment expected another blow, gazed up at Rostov with shrinking terror. His pale and mud-stained face – fair and young, with a dimple in the chin and light blue eyes – was not an enemy's face at all suited to a battlefield, but a most ordinary, homelike face. Before Rostov had decided what to do with him the officer cried, 'I surrender!' He hurriedly but vainly tried to get his foot out of the stirrup, and did not remove his frightened blue eyes from Rostov's face. Some hussars who galloped up disengaged his foot and helped him into the saddle. On all sides the hussars were busy with the dragoons; one was wounded, but though his face was bleeding he would not give up his horse; another was perched up behind an hussar with his arms round him; a third was being helped by an hussar to mount his horse. In front the French infantry were firing as they ran. The hussars galloped hastily back with their prisoners. Rostov galloped back with the rest, aware of an unpleasant feeling of depression in his heart. Something vague and confused, which he could not at all account for, had come over him with the capture of that officer and the blow he had dealt him.

Count Ostermann-Tolstoy met the returning hussars, sent for Rostov, thanked him, and said he would report his gallant deed to the Emperor and would recommend him for a St George's Cross. When sent for by Count Ostermann, Rostov, remembering that he had charged without orders, felt sure his commander was sending for him to punish him for breach of discipline. Ostermann's flattering words and promise of a reward should therefore have struck him all the more pleasantly, but he still felt that same vaguely disagreeable feeling of moral nausea. 'But what on earth is worrying me?' he asked himself as he rode back from the general. 'Ilyin? No, he's safe. Have I disgraced myself in any way? No, that's not it.' Something else, resembling remorse, tormented him. 'Yes, oh yes, that French officer with the dimple. And I remember how my arm paused when I raised it.'

Rostov saw the prisoners being led away, and galloped after them to have a look at his Frenchman with the dimple on his chin. He was sitting in his foreign uniform on an hussar pack-horse and looked anxiously about him. The sword-cut on his arm could scarcely be called a wound. He glanced at Rostov with a feigned smile, and waved his hand in greeting. Rostov still had the same indefinite feeling, as of shame.

All that day and the next his friends and comrades noticed that Rostov, without being dull or angry, was silent, thoughtful, and preoccupied. He drank reluctantly, tried to remain alone, and kept turning something over in his mind.

Rostov was always thinking about that brilliant exploit of his, which to his amazement had gained him the St George's Cross and even given him a reputation for bravery, and there was something he could not at all understand. 'So others are even more afraid than I am!' he thought. 'So that's all there is in what is called heroism! And did I do it for my country's sake? And how was he to blame, with his dimple and blue eyes? And how frightened he was! He thought I should kill him. Why should I kill him? My hand trembled. And they have given me a St George's Cross. I can't make it out at all.'

But while Nicholas was considering these questions and still could reach no clear solution of what puzzled him so, the wheel of fortune in the service, as often happens, turned in his favour. After the affair at Ostrovna he was brought into notice, received command of an hussar battalion, and when a brave officer was needed he was chosen.

On receiving news of Natasha's illness, the countess, though not quite well yet and still weak, went to Moscow with Petya and the rest of the household, and the whole family moved from Marya Dmitrievna's house to their own, and settled down in town.

Natasha's illness was so serious that, fortunately for her and for her parents, the consideration of all that had caused the illness, her conduct and the breaking off of her engagement, receded into the background. She was so ill that it was impossible for them to consider how far she was to blame for what had happened. She could not eat or sleep, grew visibly thinner, coughed and, as the doctors made them feel, was in danger. They could not think of anything but how to help her. Doctors came to see her singly and in consultation, talked much in French, German, and Latin, blamed one another, and prescribed a great variety of medicines for all the diseases known to them, but the simple idea never occurred to any of them that they could not know the disease Natasha was suffering from, as no disease suffered by a live man can be known, for every living person has his own peculiarities and always has his own peculiar, personal, novel, complicated disease, unknown to medicine – not a disease of the lungs, liver, skin, heart, nerves, and so on mentioned in medical books, but a disease consisting of one of the innumerable combinations of the maladies of those organs. This simple thought could not occur to the doctors (as it cannot occur to a wizard that he is unable to work charms) because the business of their lives was to cure, and they received money for it and had spent the best years of their lives on that business. But above all that thought was kept out of their minds by the fact that they saw they were really useful, as in fact they were to the whole Rostov family. Their usefulness did not depend on making the patient swallow substances for the most part harmful (the harm was scarcely perceptible as they were given in small doses) but they were useful, necessary, and indispensable because they satisfied a mental need of the invalid and of those who loved her – and that is why there are, and always will be, pseudo-healers, wise women, homoeopaths, and allopaths. They satisfied that eternal human need for hope of relief, for sympathy, and that something should be done, which is felt by those who are suffering. They satisfied the need seen in its most elementary form in a child, when it wants to have a place rubbed that has been hurt. A child knocks itself and runs at once to the arms of its mother or nurse to have the aching spot rubbed or kissed, and it feels better when this is done. The child cannot believe that the strongest and wisest of its people have no remedy for its pain, and the hope of relief and the expression of its mother's sympathy while she rubs the bump, comforts it. The doctors were of use to Natasha because they kissed and rubbed her bump, assuring her that it would soon pass if only the coachman went to the chemist's in the Arbat and got a powder and some pills in a pretty box for a ruble and seventy kopeks, and if she took those powders in boiled water at intervals of precisely two hours, neither more nor less.

What would Sonya and the count and countess have done, how would they have looked, if nothing had been done, if there had not been those pills to give by the clock, the warm drinks, the chicken cutlets, and all the other details of life ordered by the doctors, the carrying out of which supplied an occupation and consolation to the family circle? How would the count have borne his dearly loved daughter's illness had he not known that it was costing him a thousand rubles, and that he would not grudge thousands more to benefit her, or had he not known that if her illness continued he would not grudge yet other thousands and would take her abroad for consultations there, and had he not been able to explain the details of how Métivier and Feller had not understood the symptoms, but Frise had, and Mudrov had diagnosed them even better? What would the countess have done had she not been able sometimes to scold the invalid for not strictly obeying the doctor's orders?

'You'll never get well like that,' she would say, forgetting her grief in her vexation, 'if you won't obey the doctor and take your medicine at the right time! You mustn't trifle with it, you know, or it may turn to *pneumonia*,' she would go on, deriving much comfort from the utterance of that foreign word, incomprehensible to others as well as to herself.

What would Sonya have done without the glad consciousness that she had not undressed during the first three nights, in order to be ready to carry out all the doctor's injunctions with precision, and that she still kept awake at night so as not to miss the proper time when the slightly harmful pills in the little gilt box had to be administered? Even to Natasha herself it was pleasant to see that so many sacrifices were being made for her sake, and to know that she had to take medicine at certain hours, though she declared that no medicine would cure her and that it was all nonsense. And it was even pleasant to be able to show, by disregarding the orders, that she did not believe in medical treatment and did not value her life.

The doctor came every day, felt her pulse, looked at her tongue, and regardless of her grief-stricken face joked with her. But when he had gone into another room, to which the countess hurriedly followed him, he assumed a grave air and thoughtfully shaking his head said that though there was danger, he had hopes of the effect of this last medicine and one must wait and see, that the malady was chiefly mental, but...' And the countess, trying to conceal the action from herself and from him, slipped a gold coin into his hand, and always returned to the patient with a more tranquil mind.

The symptoms of Natasha's illness were that she ate little, slept little, coughed, and was always low-spirited. The doctors said that she could not get on without medical treatment, so they kept her in the stifling atmosphere of the town, and the Rostovs did not move to the country that summer of 1812.

In spite of the many pills she swallowed and the drops and powders out of the little bottles and boxes of which Madame Schoss, who was fond of such things, made a large collection, and in spite of being deprived of the country life to which she was accustomed, youth prevailed. Natasha's grief began to be overlaid by the impressions of daily life, it ceased to press so painfully on her heart, it gradually faded into the past, and she began to recover physically.

17

NATASHA was calmer but no happier. She not merely avoided all external forms of pleasure – balls, promenades, concerts, and theatres – but she never laughed without a sound of tears in her laughter. She could not sing. As soon as she began to laugh, or tried to sing by herself, tears choked her: tears of remorse, tears at the recollection of those pure times which could never return, tears of vexation that she should so uselessly have ruined her young life which might have been so happy. Laughter and singing in particular seemed to her like a blasphemy, in face of her sorrow. Without any need of self-restraint no wish to coquet ever entered her head. She said and felt at that time that no man was more to her than Nastasya Ivanovna, the buffoon. Something stood sentinel within her and forbade her every joy. Besides, she had lost all the old interests of her carefree girlish life that had been so full of hope. The previous autumn, the hunting, 'Uncle', and the Christmas holidays spent with Nicholas at Otradnoe, were what she recalled oftenest and most painfully. What would she not have given to bring back even a single day of that time! But it was gone for ever. Her presentiment at the time had not deceived her – that that state of freedom and readiness for any enjoyment would not return again. Yet it was necessary to live on.

It comforted her to reflect that she was not better, as she had formerly imagined, but worse, much worse, than anybody else in the world. But this was not enough. She knew that, and asked herself, 'What next?' But there was nothing to come. There was no joy in life, yet life was passing. Natasha apparently tried not to be a burden or a hindrance to anyone, but wanted nothing for herself. She kept away from everyone in the house, and only felt at ease with her brother Petya. She liked to be with him better than with the others, and when alone with him she sometimes laughed. She hardly ever left the house, and of those who came to see them was only glad to see one person, Pierre. It would have been impossible to treat her with more delicacy, greater care, and at the same time more seriously, than did Count Bezukhov. Natasha unconsciously felt this delicacy, and so found great pleasure in his society. But she was not even grateful to him for it, nothing good on Pierre's part seemed to her to be an effort, it seemed so natural for him to be kind to everyone that there was no merit in his kindness. Sometimes Natasha noticed embarrassment and awkwardness on his part in her presence, especially when he wanted to do something to please her, or feared that something they spoke of would awaken memories distressing to her. She noticed this and attributed it to his general kindness and shyness, which she imagined must be the same towards everyone as it was to her. After those involuntary words – that if he were free he would have asked on his knees for her hand and her love – uttered at a moment when she was so strongly agitated, Pierre never spoke to Natasha of his feelings; and it seemed plain to her that those words, which had then so comforted her, were spoken as all sorts of meaningless words are spoken to comfort a crying child. It was not because Pierre was a married man, but because Natasha very strongly felt with him that moral barrier the absence of which she had experienced with Kuragin, that it never entered her head that the relations between him and herself could lead to love on her part, still less on his, or even to the kind of tender, self-conscious, romantic friendship between a man and a woman of which she had known several instances.

Before the end of the fast of St Peter,* Agrafena Ivanovna Belova, a country neighbour of the Rostovs, came to Moscow to pay her devotions at the shrines of the Moscow saints. She suggested that Natasha should fast and prepare for Holy Communion, and Natasha gladly welcomed the idea. Despite the doctor's orders that she should not go out early in the morning, Natasha insisted on fasting and preparing for the sacrament, not as they generally prepared for it in the Rostov family by attending three services in their own house, but as Agrafena Ivanovna did, by going to church every day for a week and not once missing Vespers, Matins, or Mass.

The countess was pleased with Natasha's zeal; after the poor results of the medical treatment, in the depths of her heart she hoped that prayer might help her daughter more than medicines and, though not without fear, and concealing it from the doctor, she agreed to Natasha's wish and entrusted her to Belova. Agrafena Ivanovna used to come to wake Natasha at three in the morning, but generally found her already awake. She was afraid of being late for Matins. Hastily washing, and meekly putting on her shabbiest dress and an old mantilla, Natasha, shivering in the fresh air, went out into the deserted streets lit by the clear light of dawn. By Agrafena Ivanovna's advice Natasha prepared herself not in their own parish, but at a church where according to the devout Agrafena Ivanovna the priest was a man of very severe and lofty life. There were never many people in the church; Natasha always stood beside Belova in the customary place before an icon of the Blessed Virgin let into the screen before the choir on the left side, and a feeling, new to her, of humility before something great and incomprehensible, seized her when at that unusual morning hour, gazing at the dark face of the Virgin illuminated by the candles burning before it and by the morning light falling from the window, she listened to the words of the service which she tried to follow with understanding. When she understood them, her personal feeling became interwoven in the prayers with shades of its own. When she did not understand, it was sweeter still to think that the wish to understand everything is pride, that it is impossible to understand all, that it is only necessary to believe and to commit oneself to God, whom she felt guiding her soul at those moments. She crossed herself, bowed low, and when she did not understand, in horror at her own vileness, simply asked God to forgive her everything, everything, and to have mercy upon her. The prayers to which she surrendered herself most of all were those of repentance. On her way home at an early hour when she met no one but bricklayers going to work or men men sweeping the street, and everybody within the houses was still asleep, Natasha experienced a feeling new to her, a sense of the possibility of correcting her faults, the possibility of a new, clean life, and of happiness.

During the whole week she spent in this way, that feeling grew every day. And the happiness of taking communion, or 'communing' as Agrafena Ivanovna, joyously playing with the word, called it, seemed to Natasha so great that she felt she should never live till that blessed Sunday.

But the happy day came, and on that memorable Sunday, when dressed in white muslin she returned home after communion, for the first time for many months she felt calm and not oppressed by the thought of the life that lay before her.

The doctor who came to see her that day ordered her to continue the powders he had prescribed a fortnight previously.

'She must certainly go on taking them morning and evening,' said he, evidently sincerely satisfied with his success. 'Only, please be particular about it.

'Be quite easy,' he continued playfully, as he adroitly took the gold coin in his palm. 'She will soon be singing and frolicking about. Tht last medicine has done her a very great deal of good. She has freshened up very much.'

The countess, with a cheerful expression on her face, looked down at her nails and spat a little for luck as she returned to the drawing-room.

18

AT the beginning of July more and more disquieting reports about the war began to spread in Moscow; people spoke of an appeal by the Emperor to the people, and of his coming himself from the army to Moscow. And as up to the 11th of July no manifesto or appeal had been received exaggerated reports became current about them, and about the position of Russia. It was said that the Emperor was leaving the army because it was in danger, it was said that Smolensk had surrendered, that Napoleon had an army of a million and only a miracle could save Russia.

On the 11th of July, which was Saturday, the manifesto was received but was not yet in print, and Pierre, who was at the Rostovs', promised to come to dinner next day, Sunday, and bring a copy of the manifesto and appeal, which he would obtain from Count Rostopchin.

That Sunday the Rostovs went to Mass at the Razumovskys' private chapel as usual. It was a hot July day. Even at ten o'clock, when the Rostovs got out of their carriage at the chapel, the sultry air, the shouts of hawkers, the light and gay summer clothes of the crowd, the dusty leaves of the trees on the boulevard, the sounds of the band and the white trousers of a battalion marching to parade, the rattling of wheels on the cobble-stones, and the brilliant, hot sunshine, were all full of that summer languor, that content and discontent with the present, which is most strongly felt on a bright hot day in town. All the Moscow notabilities, all the Rostovs' acquaintances, were at the Razumovskys' chapel, for as if expecting something to happen, many wealthy families who usually left town for their country estates had not gone away that summer. As Natasha, at her mother's side, passed through the crowd behind a liveried footman who cleared the way for them, she heard a young man speaking about her in too loud a whisper.

'That's Rostova, the one who . . .'

'She's much thinner, but all the same she's pretty!'

She heard or thought she heard the names of Kuragin and Bolkonsky. But she was always imagining that. It always seemed to her that everyone who looked at her was thinking only of what had happened to her. With a sinking heart, wretched as she always was now when she found herself in a crowd, Natasha, in her lilac silk dress trimmed with black lace, walked – as women can walk – with the more repose and stateliness the greater the pain and shame in her soul. She knew for certain that she was pretty, but this no longer gave her satisfaction as it used to. On the contrary it had tormented her more than anything else of late, and particularly so on this bright, hot summer day in town. 'It's Sunday again – another week past,' she thought, recalling that she had been here the Sunday before, 'and always the same life that is no life, and the same surroundings in which it used to be so easy to live. I'm pretty, I'm young, and I know that now I am good. I used to be bad, but now I know I am good,' she thought, 'but yet my best years are slipping by and are no good to anyone.' She stood by her mother's side and exchanged nods with acquaintances near her. From habit she scrutinized the ladies' dresses, condemned the bearing of a lady standing close by who was not crossing herself properly but in a cramped manner, and again she thought with vexation that she was herself being judged and was judging others, and suddenly, at the sound of the service, she felt horrified at her own vileness, horrified that the former purity of her soul was again lost to her.

A comely fresh-looking old man was conducting the service with that mild solemnity which has so elevating and soothing an effect on the souls of the worshippers. The gates of the sanctuary-screen were closed, the curtain was slowly drawn, and from behind it a soft mysterious voice pronounced some words. Tears, the cause of which she herself did not understand, made Natasha's breast heave, and a joyous but oppressive feeling agitated her.

'Teach me what I should do, how to live my life, how I may grow good for ever, for ever!' she pleaded.

The deacon came out onto the raised space before the altar-screen, and holding his thumb extended, drew his long hair from under his dalmatic, and making the sign of the cross on his breast, began in a loud and solemn voice to recite the words of the prayer . . .

'In peace let us pray unto the Lord.'

'As one community,* without distinction of class, without enmity, united by brotherly love – let us pray!' thought Natasha.

'For the peace that is from above, and for the salvation of our souls.'

'For the world of angels and all the spirits who dwell above us,' prayed Natasha.

When they prayed for the warriors, she thought of her brother and Denisov. When they prayed for all travelling by land and sea she remembered Prince Andrew, prayed for him, and asked God to forgive her all the wrong she had done him. When they prayed for those who love us, she prayed for the members of her own family, her father and mother and Sonya, realizing for the first time how wrongly she had acted towards them, and feeling all the strength of her love for them. When they prayed for those who hate us, she tried to think of her enemies and people who hated her, in order to pray for them. She included among her enemies the creditors and all who had business dealings with her father, and always at the thought of enemies and those who hated her, she remembered Anatole who had done her so much harm – and though he did not hate her, she gladly prayed for him as for an enemy. Only at prayer did she feel able to think clearly and calmly of Prince Andrew and Anatole, as men for whom her feelings were as nothing compared with her awe and devotion to God. When they prayed for the Imperial family and the Synod, she bowed very low and made the sign of the cross, saying to herself that even if she did not understand, still she could not doubt, and at any rate loved the governing Synod and prayed for it.

When he had finished the Litany the deacon crossed the stole over his breast and said,

'Let us commit ourselves and our whole lives to Christ the Lord!'

'Commit ourselves to God,' Natasha inwardly repeated. 'Lord God, I submit myself to Thy will!' she thought. 'I want nothing, wish for nothing; teach me what to do and how to use my will! Take me, take me!' prayed Natasha with impatient emotion in her heart, not crossing herself but letting her slender arms hang down as if expecting some invisible power at any moment to take her and deliver her from herself, from her regrets, desires, remorse, hopes, and sins.

The countess looked round several times at her daughter's softened face and shining eyes, and prayed God to help her.

Unexpectedly, in the middle of the service, and not in the usual order Natasha knew so well, the deacon brought out a small stool, the one he knelt on when praying on Trinity Sunday, and placed it before the doors of the sanctuary-screen. The priest came out, with his purple velvet biretta* on his head, adjusted his hair, and knelt down with an effort. Everybody followed his example and looked at one another in surprise. Then came the prayer just received from the Synod – a prayer for the deliverance of Russia from hostile invasion.

'Lord God of might, God of our salvation!' began the priest in that voice, clear, not grandiloquent but mild, in which only the Slav clergy read and which acts so irresistibly on a Russian heart.

'Lord God of might, God of our salvation! Look this day in mercy and blessing on Thy humble people, and graciously hear us, spare us, and have mercy upon us! This foe confounding Thy land, desiring to lay waste the whole world, rises against us; these lawless men are gathered together to overthrow Thy kingdom, to destroy Thy dear Jerusalem, Thy beloved Russia: to defile Thy temples, to overthrow Thine altars and to desecrate our holy shrines. How long, O Lord, how long shall the wicked triumph? How long shall they wield unlawful power?

'Lord God! Hear us when we pray to Thee; strengthen with Thy might our most gracious sovereign lord the Emperor Alexander Pavlovich; be mindful of his uprightness and meekness, reward him according to his righteousness, and let it preserve us, Thy chosen Israel! Bless his counsels, his undertakings, and his work; strengthen his kingdom by Thine almighty hand, and give him victory over his enemy, even as Thou gavest Moses the victory over Amalek, Gideon over Midian, and David over Goliath. Preserve his army, put a bow of brass in the hands of those who have armed themselves in Thy Name, and gird their loins with strength for the fight. Take up the spear and shield and arise to help us; confound and put to shame those who have devised evil against us, may they be before the faces of Thy faithful warriors as dust before the wind, and may Thy mighty Angel confound them and put them to flight; may they be ensnared when they know it not, and may the plots they have laid in secret be turned against them; let them fall before Thy servants' feet and be laid low by our hosts! Lord, Thou art able to save both great and small; Thou art God, and man cannot prevail against Thee!

'God of our fathers! Remember Thy bounteous mercy and loving kindness which are from of old; turn not Thy face from us, but be gracious to our unworthiness, and in Thy great goodness and Thy many mercies regard not our transgressions and iniquities! Create in us a clean heart and renew a right spirit within us, strengthen us all in Thy faith, fortify our hope, inspire us with true love one for another, arm us with unity of spirit in the righteous defence of the heritage Thou gavest to us and to our fathers, and let not the sceptre of the wicked be exalted against the destiny of those Thou hast sanctified.

'O Lord our God, in whom we believe and in whom we put our trust, let us not be confounded in our hope of Thy mercy, and give us a token of Thy blessing, that those who hate us and our Orthodox faith may see it, and be put to shame and perish, and may all the nations know that Thou art the Lord and we are Thy people. Show Thy mercy upon us this day, O Lord, and grant us Thy salvation; make the hearts of Thy servants to rejoice in Thy mercy; smite down our enemies and destroy them swiftly beneath the feet of Thy faithful servants! For Thou art the defence, the succour, and the victory of them that put their trust in Thee, and to Thee be all glory, to Father, Son, and Holy Ghost, now and for ever, world without end. Amen.'

In Natasha's receptive condition of soul this prayer affected her strongly. She listened to every word about the victory of Moses over Amalek, of Gideon over Midian, and of David over Goliath, and about the destruction of 'Thy Jerusalem', and she prayed to God with the tenderness and emotion with which her heart was overflowing, but without fully understanding what she was asking of God in that prayer. She shared with all her heart in the prayer for the spirit of righteousness, for the strengthening of the heart by faith and hope, and its animation by love. But she could not pray that her enemies might be trampled under foot when but a few minutes before she had been wishing she had more of them that she might pray for them. But neither could she doubt the righteousness of the prayer that was being read on bended knees. She felt in her heart a devout and tremulous awe at the thought of the punishment that overtakes men for their sins, and especially of her own sins, and she prayed to God to forgive them all, and her too, and to give them all, and her too, peace and happiness. And it seemed to her that God heard her prayer.

FROM the day when Pierre, after leaving the Rostovs' with Natasha's grateful look fresh in his mind, had gazed at the comet that seemed to be fixed in the sky and felt that something new was appearing on his own horizon – from that day the problem of the vanity and uselessness of all earthly things, that had incessantly tormented him, no longer presented itself. That terrible question 'Why?' 'Wherefore?' which had come to him amid every occupation, was now replaced, not by another question or by a reply to the former question, but by *her* image. When he listened to, or himself took part in, trivial conversations, when he read or heard of human baseness or folly, he was not horrified as formerly, and did not ask himself why men struggled so about these things, when all is so transient and incomprehensible – but he remembered her as he had last seen her, and all his doubts vanished – not because she had answered the questions that had haunted him, but because his conception of her transferred him instantly to another, a brighter, realm of spiritual activity in which no one could be justified or guilty – a realm of beauty and love which it was worth living for. Whatever worldly baseness presented itself to him he said to himself.

'Well, supposing N. N. has swindled the country and the Tsar, and the country and the Tsar confer honours upon him, what does that matter? She smiled at me yesterday and asked me to come again, and I love her, and no one will ever know it.' And his soul felt calm and peaceful.

Pierre still went into society, drank as much, and led the same idle and dissipated life, because besides the hours he spent at the Rostovs' there were other hours he had to spend somehow, and the habits and acquaintances he had made in Moscow formed a current that bore him along irresistibly. But latterly, when more and more disquieting reports came from the seat of war and Natasha's health began to improve and she no longer aroused in him the former feeling of careful pity, an ever-increasing restlessness, which he could not explain, took possession of him. He felt that the condition he was in could not continue long, that a catastrophe was coming which would change his whole life, and he impatiently sought everywhere for signs of that approaching catastrophe. One of his brother Masons had revealed to Pierre the following prophecy concerning Napoleon, drawn from the Revelation of St John.

In chapter xiii, verse 18, of the Apocalypse, it is said:

Here is wisdom: Let him that hath understanding count the number of the beast: for it is the number of a man; and his number is Six hundred threescore and six.

And in the fifth verse of the same chapter:

And there was given unto him a mouth speaking great things and blasphemies; and power was given unto him to continue forty and two months.

The French alphabet, written out with the same numerical values as the Hebrew, in which the first nine letters denote units and the others tens, will have the following significance:

a	b	c	d	e	f	g	h	i	k	l	m	n	o	p
1	2	3	4	5	6	7	8	9	10	20	30	40	50	60

q	r	s	t	u	v	w	x	y	z
70	80	90	100	110	120	130	140	150	160.

Writing the words L'*Empereur Napoléon* in numbers, it appears that the sum of them is 666,* and that Napoleon was therefore the beast foretold in the Apocalypse. Moreover by applying the same system to the words *quarante-deux* (forty-two), which was the term allowed to the beast that 'spoke great things and blasphemies', the same number 666 was obtained; from which it followed that the limit fixed for Napoleon's power had come in the year 1812, when the French emperor was forty-two. This prophecy pleased Pierre very much, and he often asked himself what would put an end to the power of the beast, that is, of Napoleon, and tried by the same system of using letters as numbers and adding them up, to find an answer to the question that engrossed him. He wrote the words L'*Empereur Alexandre, La nation russe* and added up their numbers, but the sums were either more or less than 666. Once when making such calculations he wrote down his own name in French, Comte Pierre Besouhoff, but the sum of the numbers did not come right. Then he changed the spelling, substituting a *z* for the *s* and adding *de* and the article *le*, still without obtaining the desired result. Then it occurred to him that if the answer to the question were contained in his name, his nationality would also be given in the answer. So he wrote Le *russe Besuhof* and adding up the numbers got 671. This was only five too much, and five was represented by *e*, the very letter elided from the article *le* before the word *Empereur*. By omitting the *e*, though incorrectly, Pierre got the answer he sought. L'*russe Besuhof* made 666. This discovery excited him. How, or by what means, he was connected with the great event foretold in the Apocalypse he did not know, but he did not doubt that connexion for a moment. His love for Natasha,

Antichrist, Napoleon, the invasion, the comet, 666, *L'Empereur Napoléon*, and *L'russe Besuhof* – all this had to mature and culminate, to lift him out of that spellbound, petty sphere of Moscow habits in which he felt himself held captive, and lead him to a great achievement and great happiness.

On the eve of the Sunday when the special prayer was read, Pierre had promised the Rostovs to bring them, from Count Rostopchin whom he knew well, both the appeal to the people and the latest news from the army. In the morning, when he went to call at Rostopchin's he met there a courier fresh from the army, an acquaintance of his own, who often danced at Moscow balls.

'Do, please, for heaven's sake relieve me of something!' said the courier. 'I have a sackful of letters to parents.'

Among these letters was one from Nicholas Rostov to his father. Pierre took that letter, and Rostopchin also gave him the Emperor's appeal to Moscow which had just been printed, the last army orders, and his own most recent bulletin. Glancing through the army orders Pierre found in one of them, in the lists of killed, wounded, and rewarded, the name of Nicholas Rostov, awarded a St George's Cross of the Fourth Class for courage shown in the Ostrovna affair, and in the same order the name of Prince Andrew Bolkonsky, appointed to the command of a regiment of Chasseurs. Though he did not want to remind the Rostovs of Bolkonsky, Pierre could not refrain from making them happy by the news of their son's having received a decoration, so he sent that printed army order and Nicholas's letter to the Rostovs, keeping the appeal, the bulletin, and the other orders, to take with him when he went to dinner.

His conversation with Count Rostopchin and the latter's tone of anxious hurry, the meeting with the courier who talked casually of how badly things were going in the army, the rumours of the discovery of spies in Moscow and of a leaflet in circulation stating that Napoleon promised to be in both the Russian capitals by the autumn, and the talk of the Emperor's being expected to arrive next day – all aroused with fresh force that feeling of agitation and expectation in Pierre which he had been conscious of ever since the appearance of the comet, and especially since the beginning of the war.

He had long been thinking of entering the army and would have done so had he not been hindered, first, by his membership of the Society of Freemasons to which he was bound by oath and which preached perpetual peace and the abolition of war, and secondly, by the fact that when he saw the great mass of Moscovites who had donned uniform and were talking patriotism, he somehow felt ashamed to take the step. But the chief reason for not carrying out his intention to enter the army lay in the vague idea that he was *L'russe Besuhof* who had the number of the beast, 666; that his part in the great affair of setting a limit to the power of the beast that spoke great and blasphemous things had been predestined from eternity, and that therefore he ought not to undertake anything, but wait for what was bound to come to pass.

20

A FEW intimate friends were dining with the Rostovs that day, as usual on Sundays.

Pierre came early so as to find them alone.

He had grown so stout this year that he would have been abnormal had he not been so tall, so broad of limb, and so strong that he carried his bulk with evident ease.

He went up the stairs puffing and muttering something. His coachman did not even ask whether he was to wait. He knew that when his master was at the Rostovs he stayed till midnight. The Rostovs' footman rushed eagerly forward to help him off with his cloak and take his hat and stick. Pierre, from club habit, always left both hat and stick in the ante-room.

The first person he saw in the house was Natasha. Even before he saw her, while taking off his cloak, he heard her. She was practising sol-fa exercises in the music-room. He knew that she had not sung since her illness, and so the sound of her voice surprised and delighted him. He opened the door softly and saw her, in the lilac dress she had worn at church, walking about the room singing. She had her back to him when he opened the door, but when, turning quickly, she saw his broad, surprised face, she blushed and came rapidly up to him:

'I want to try to sing again,' she said, adding as if by way of excuse, 'it is at least something to do.'

'That's capital!'

'How glad I am you've come! I am so happy to-day,' she said, with the old animation Pierre had not seen in her for a long time. 'You know Nicholas has received a St George's Cross? I am so proud of him.'

'Oh yes, I sent that announcement. But I don't want to interrupt you,' he added, and was about to go to the drawing-room.

Natasha stopped him.

'Count, is it wrong of me to sing?' she said blushing, and fixing her eyes inquiringly on him.

'No ... Why should it be? On the contrary ... But why do you ask me?'

'I don't know myself,' Natasha answered quickly, 'but I should not like to do anything you disapproved of. I believe in you completely. You don't know how important you are to me, how much you've done for me ...' She spoke rapidly and did not notice how Pierre flushed at her words. 'I saw in that same army order that *he*, Bolkonsky' (she whispered the name hastily), 'is in Russia, and in the army again. What do you think?' – she was speaking hurriedly, evidently afraid her strength might fail her – 'Will he ever forgive me? Will he not always have a bitter feeling towards me? What do you think? What do you think?'

'I think ...' Pierre replied, 'that he has nothing to forgive ... If I were in his place ...'

By association of ideas Pierre was at once carried back to the day when, trying to comfort her, he had said that if he were not himself but the best man in the world and free, he would ask on his knees for her hand; and the same feeling of pity, tenderness, and love, took possession of him and the same words rose to his lips. But she did not give him time to say them.

'Yes, you ... you ...' she said, uttering the word *you* rapturously – 'that's a different thing. I know no one kinder, more generous, or better than you; nobody could be! Had you not been there then, and now too, I don't know what would have become of me, because ...'

Tears suddenly rose in her eyes, she turned away, lifted her music before her eyes, began singing again, and again began walking up and down the room.

Just then Petya came running in from the drawing-room.

Petya was now a handsome rosy lad of fifteen, with full red lips, and resembled Natasha. He was preparing to enter the university, but he and his friend Obolensky had lately, in secret, agreed to join the hussars.

Petya had come rushing out to talk to his namesake about this affair. He had asked Pierre to find out whether he would be accepted in the hussars.

Pierre walked up and down the drawing-room not listening to what Petya was saying.

Petya pulled him by the arm to attract his attention.

'Well, what about my plan? Peter Kirilych, for heaven's sake! You are my only hope!' said Petya.

'Oh yes, your plan. To join the hussars? I'll mention it, I'll bring it all up to-day.'

'Well, *mon cher*, have you got the manifesto?' asked the old count. 'The countess has been to Mass at the Razumovskys' and heard the new prayer. She says it's very fine.'

'Yes, I've got it,' said Pierre. 'The Emperor is to be here to-morrow ... there's to be an Extraordinary Meeting of the nobility, and they are talking of a levy of ten men per thousand. Oh yes, let me congratulate you!'

'Yes, yes, thank God! Well, and what news from the army?'

'We are again retreating. They say we're already near Smolensk,' replied Pierre.

'O Lord, O Lord!' exclaimed the count. 'Where is the manifesto?'

'The Emperor's appeal? Oh yes!'

Pierre began feeling in his pockets for the papers, but could not find them. Still slapping his pockets, he kissed the hand of the countess who entered the room, and glanced uneasily around evidently expecting Natasha, who had left off singing but had not yet come into the drawing-room.

'On my word, I don't know what I've done with it,' he said.

'There he is, always losing everything!' remarked the countess.

Natasha entered with a softened and agitated expression of face, and sat down looking silently at Pierre. As soon as she entered, Pierre's features, which had been gloomy, suddenly lighted up, and while still searching for the papers he glanced at her several times.

'No, really! I'll drive home, I must have left them there. I'll certainly ...'

'But you'll be late for dinner.'

'Oh! And my coachman has gone.'

But Sonya, who had gone to look for the papers in the ante-room, had found them in Pierre's hat, where he had carefully tucked them under the lining. Pierre was about to begin reading.

'No, after dinner,' said the old count, evidently expecting much enjoyment from that reading.

At dinner, at which champagne was drunk to the health of the new chevalier of St George, Shinshin told them the town news, of the illness of the old Georgian princess, of Métivier's disappearance from Moscow, and of how some German fellow had been brought to Rostopchin and accused of being a French 'spyer' (so Count Rostopchin had told the story), and how Rostopchin let him go and assured the people that he was 'not a spire at all, but only an old German ruin'.

'People are being arrested ...' said the count. 'I've told the countess she should not speak French so much. It's not the time for it now.'

'And have you heard?' Shinshin asked. 'Prince Golitsin has

engaged a master to teach him Russian. It is becoming dangerous to speak French in the streets.'*

'And how about you, Count Peter Kirilych? If they call up the militia, you too will have to mount a horse,' remarked the old count, addressing Pierre.

Pierre had been silent and preoccupied all through dinner, seeming not to grasp what was said. He looked at the count.

'Oh yes, the war,' he said. 'No! What sort of a warrior should I make? And yet everything is so strange, so strange! I can't make it out. I don't know, I am very far from having military tastes, but in these times no one can answer for himself.'

After dinner the count settled himself comfortably in an easy-chair and with a serious face asked Sonya, who was considered an excellent reader, to read the appeal.

'To Moscow, our ancient Capital!

'The enemy has entered the borders of Russia with immense forces. He comes to despoil our beloved country,' Sonya read painstakingly in her high-pitched voice. The count listened with closed eyes, heaving abrupt sighs at certain passages.

Natasha sat erect gazing with a searching look now at her father and now at Pierre.

Pierre felt her eyes on him and tried not to look round. The countess shook her head disapprovingly and angrily at every solemn expression in the manifesto. In all these words she saw only that the danger threatening her son would not soon be over. Shinshin, with a sarcastic smile on his lips, was evidently preparing to make fun of anything that gave him the opportunity: Sonya's reading, any remark of the count's, or even the manifesto itself should no better pretext present itself.

After reading about the dangers that threatened Russia, the hopes the Emperor placed on Moscow and especially on its illustrious nobility, Sonya, with a quiver in her voice due chiefly to the attention that was being paid to her, read the last words : 'We ourselves will not delay to appear among our people in that Capital and in other parts of our realm for consultation, and for the direction of all our levies, both those now barring the enemy's path and those freshly formed to defeat him wherever he may appear. May the ruin he hopes to bring upon us recoil on his own head, and may Europe delivered from bondage glorify the name of Russia!'

'Yes, that's it!' cried the count, opening his moist eyes and sniffing repeatedly as if a strong vinaigrette had been held to his nose; and he added, 'Let the Emperor but say the word and we'll sacrifice everything and begrudge nothing.'

Before Shinshin had time to utter the joke he was ready to

make on the count's patriotism, Natasha jumped up from her place and ran to her father.

'What a darling our papa is!' she cried kissing him, and she again looked at Pierre with the unconscious coquetry that had returned to her with her better spirits.

'There! Here's a patriot for you!' said Shinshin.

'Not a patriot at all, but simply . . .' Natasha replied in an injured tone. 'Everything seems funny to you, but this isn't at all a joke . . .'

'A joke indeed!' put in the count. 'Let him but say the word and we'll all go . . . We're not Germans!'

'But did you notice, it says, "for consultation"?' said Pierre.

'Never mind what it's for . . .'

At this moment Petya, to whom nobody was paying any attention, came up to his father with a very flushed face, and said in his breaking voice that was now deep and now shrill:

'Well papa, I tell you definitely, and mamma too, it's as you please, but I say definitely that you must let me enter the army, because I can't . . . that is all . . .'

The countess, in dismay, looked up to heaven, clasped her hands, and turned angrily to her husband.

'That comes of your talking!' said she.

But the count had already recovered from his excitement.

'Come, come!' said he. 'Here's a fine warrior! No! Nonsense! You must study.'

'It's not nonsense, papa! Fedya Obolensky is younger than I, and he's going too. Besides, all the same, I can't study now when . . .' Petya stopped short, flushed till he perspired, but still got out the words, 'when our Fatherland is in danger.'

'That'll do, that'll do – nonsense . . .'

'But you said yourself that we would sacrifice everything.'

'Petya! Be quiet, I tell you!' cried the count with a glance at his wife, who had turned pale and was staring fixedly at her son.

'And I tell you – Peter Kirilych here will also tell you . . .'

'Nonsense, I tell you. Your mother's milk has hardly dried on your lips and you want to go into the army! There, there, I tell you,' and the count moved to go out of the room, taking the papers, probably to re-read them in his study before having a nap.

'Well, Peter Kirilych, let's go and have a smoke,' he said.

Pierre was agitated and undecided. Natasha's unwontedly brilliant eyes, continually glancing at him with a more than cordial look, had reduced him to this condition.

'No, I think I'll go home.'

'Home? Why, you meant to spend the evening with us . . . You don't often come nowadays as it is, and this girl of mine,' said the count good-naturedly, pointing to Natasha, 'only brightens up when you're here.'

'Yes, I had forgotten ... I really must go home ... business ...' said Pierre hurriedly.

'Well then, *au revoir!*' said the count and went out of the room.

'Why are you going? Why are you upset?' asked Natasha, and she looked challengingly into Pierre's eyes.

'Because I love you!' was what he wanted to say, but he did not say it, and only blushed till the tears came, and lowered his eyes.

'Because it is better for me to come less often ... because ... No, simply I have business ...'

'Why? No, tell me!' Natasha began resolutely, and suddenly stopped.

They looked at each other with dismayed and embarrassed faces. He tried to smile but could not: his smile expressed suffering, and he silently kissed her hand and went out.

Pierre made up his mind not to go to the Rostovs' any more.

21

AFTER the definite refusal he had received, Petya went to his room and there locked himself in and wept bitterly. When he came in to tea, silent, morose, and with tear-stained face, everybody pretended not to notice anything.

Next day the Emperor arrived in Moscow, and several of the Rostovs' domestic serfs begged permission to go to have a look at him. That morning Petya was a long time dressing and arranging his hair and collar to look like a grown-up man. He frowned before his looking-glass, gesticulated, shrugged his shoulders, and finally without saying a word to anyone took his cap and left the house by the back door, trying to avoid notice. Petya had decided to go straight to where the Emperor was and to explain frankly to some gentleman-in-waiting (he imagined the Emperor to be always surrounded by gentlemen-in-waiting) that he, Count Rostov, in spite of his youth, wished to serve his country; that youth could be no hindrance to loyalty, and that he was ready to ... While dressing, Petya had prepared many fine things he meant to say to the gentleman-in-waiting.

It was on the very fact of being so young that Petya counted for success in reaching the Emperor – he even thought how surprised everyone would be at his youthfulness – and yet in the arrangement of his collar and hair and by his sedate deliberate walk he wished to appear a grown-up man. But the farther he went and the more his attention was diverted by the ever-increasing crowds moving towards the Kremlin, the less he remembered to walk with the sedateness and deliberation of a man. As he approached the Kremlin he began to be afraid of being crushed, and resolutely stuck out his elbows in a menacing way. But within the Trinity Gateway he was so pressed to the wall by people who probably were unaware of the patriotic intentions with which he had come, that in spite of all his determination he had to give in, and stop while carriages passed in, rumbling beneath the archway. Beside Petya stood a peasant woman, a footman, two tradesmen, and a discharged soldier. After standing some time in the gateway, Petya tried to move forward in front of the others without waiting for all the carriages to pass, and he began resolutely working his way with his elbows, but the woman just in front of him, who was the first against whom he directed his efforts, angrily shouted at him:

'What are you shoving for, young lordling? Don't you see we're all standing still? Then why push?'

'Anybody can shove,' said the footman, and also began working his elbows to such effect that he pushed Petya into a very filthy corner of the gateway.

Petya wiped his perspiring face with his hands, and pulled up the damp collar which he had arranged so well at home to seem like a man's.

He felt that he no longer looked presentable, and feared that if he presented himself to the gentlemen-in-waiting in that plight he would not be admitted to the Emperor. But it was impossible to smarten oneself up, or move to another place, because of the crowd. One of the generals who drove past was an acquaintance of the Rostovs' and Petya thought of asking his help, but came to the conclusion that that would not be a manly thing to do. When the carriages had all passed in, the crowd, carrying Petya with it, streamed forward into the Kremlin Square which was already full of people. There were people not only in the square, but everywhere – on the slopes and on the roofs. As soon as Petya found himself in the square he clearly heard the sound of the bells and the joyous voices of the crowd that filled the whole Kremlin.

For a while the crowd was less dense, but suddenly all heads were bared, and everyone rushed forward in one direction. Petya was being pressed so that he could scarcely breathe, and everybody shouted 'hurrah! hurrah! hurrah!' Petya stood on tiptoe, and pushed and pinched, but could see nothing except the people about him.

All the faces bore the same expression of excitement and enthusiasm. A tradesman's wife standing beside Petya sobbed, and the tears ran down her cheeks.

'Father! Angel! Dear one!' she kept repeating, wiping away her tears with her fingers.

'Hurrah!' was heard on all sides.

For a moment the crowd stood still, but then it made another rush forward.

Quite beside himself, Petya, clenching his teeth and rolling his eyes ferociously, pushed forward, elbowing his way and shouting 'hurrah!' as if he were prepared that instant to kill himself and everyone else, but on both sides of him other people with similarly ferocious faces pushed forward and everybody shouted 'hurrah!'

'So this is what the Emperor is!' thought Petya. 'No, I can't petition him myself – that would be too bold.' But in spite of this he continued to struggle desperately forward, and from between the backs of those in front he caught glimpses of an open space with a strip of red cloth spread out on it; but just then the crowd swayed back – the police in front were pushing back those who had pressed too close to the procession: the Emperor was passing from the palace to the Cathedral of the Assumption – and Petya unexpectedly received such a blow on his side and ribs, and was squeezed so hard, that suddenly everything grew dim before his eyes and he lost consciousness. When he came to himself a man of clerical appearance with a tuft of grey hair at the back of his head and wearing a shabby blue cassock – probably a church clerk and chanter – was holding him under the arm with one hand, while warding off the pressure of the crowd with the other.

'You've crushed the young gentleman!' said the clerk. 'What are you up to? Gently! . . . They've crushed him, crushed him!'

The Emperor entered the Cathedral of the Assumption. The crowd spread out again more evenly, and the clerk led Petya – pale and breathless – to the Tsar-cannon.* Several people were sorry for Petya, and suddenly a crowd turned towards him and crushed round him. Those who stood nearest attended to him, unbuttoned his coat, seated him on the raised platform of the cannon, and reproached those others (whoever they might be) who had crushed him.

'One might easily get killed that way! What do they mean by it! Killing people! Poor dear, he's as white as a sheet!' – various voices were heard saying.

Petya soon came to himself, the colour returned to his face, the pain had passed, and at the cost of that temporary unpleasantness he had obtained a place by the cannon, from where he hoped to see the Emperor who would be returning that way. Petya no longer thought of presenting his petition. If he could only see the Emperor he would be happy!

While the service was proceeding in the Cathedral of the Assumption – it was a combined service of prayer on the occasion of the Emperor's arrival and of thanksgiving for the conclusion of peace with the Turks – the crowd outside spread out and hawkers appeared, selling kvas, gingerbread, and poppy-seed sweets (of which Petya was particularly fond), and ordinary conversation could again be heard. A tradesman's wife was showing a rent in her shawl and telling how much the shawl had cost; another was saying that all silk goods had now got dear. The clerk who had rescued Petya was talking to a functionary about the priests who were officiating that day with the bishop. The clerk several times used the word 'plenary' (of the service), a word Petya did not understand. Two young citizens were joking with some serf-girls who were cracking nuts. All these conversations, especially the joking with the girls, were such as might have had a particular charm for Petya at his age, but they did not interest him now. He sat on his elevation – the pedestal of the cannon – still agitated as before by the thought of the Emperor and by his love for him. The feeling of pain and fear he had experienced when he was being crushed, together with that of rapture, still further intensified his sense of the importance of the occasion.

Suddenly the sound of a firing of cannon was heard from the embankment, to celebrate the signing of peace with the Turks, and the crowd rushed impetuously towards the embankment to watch the firing. Petya too would have run there, but the clerk who had taken the young gentleman under his protection stopped him. The firing was still proceeding when officers, generals, and gentlemen-in-waiting came running out of the cathedral, and after them others in a more leisurely manner: caps were again raised, and those who had run to look at the cannon ran back again. At last four men in uniforms and sashes emerged from the cathedral doors. 'Hurrah! hurrah!' shouted the crowd again.

'Which is he? Which?' asked Petya in a tearful voice of those around him, but no one answered him, everybody was too excited; and Petya, fixing on one of those four men, whom he could not clearly see for the tears of joy that filled his eyes, concentrated all his enthusiasm on him – though it happened not to be the Emperor – frantically shouted 'Hurrah!' and resolved that to-morrow, come what might, he would join the army.

The crowd ran after the Emperor, followed him to the palace, and began to disperse. It was already late, and Petya had not eaten anything and was drenched with perspiration, yet he did not go home but stood with that diminishing, but still considerable, crowd before the palace while the Emperor dined – looking in at the palace windows, expecting he knew not what, and envying alike the notables he saw arriving at the entrance to dine with the Emperor and the court footmen who served at table, glimpses of whom could be seen through the windows.

While the Emperor was dining, Valuev, looking out of the window, said:

'The people are still hoping to see your Majesty again.'

The dinner was nearly over, and the Emperor, munching a biscuit, rose and went out onto the balcony. The people, with Petya among them, rushed towards the balcony.

'Angel! Dear one! Hurrah! Father!' ... cried the crowd, and Petya with it, and again the women and men of weaker mould, Petya among them, wept with joy.

A largish piece of the biscuit the Emperor was holding in his hand broke off, fell on the balcony parapet, and then to the ground. A coachman in a jerkin, who stood nearest, sprang forward and snatched it up. Several people in the crowd rushed at the coachman. Seeing this the Emperor had a plateful of biscuits brought him,* and began throwing them down from the balcony. Petya's eyes grew bloodshot, and still more excited by the danger of being crushed, he rushed at the biscuits. He did not know why, but he had to have a biscuit from the Tsar's hand and he felt that he must not give way. He sprang forward and upset an old woman who was catching at a biscuit; – the old woman did not consider herself defeated though she was lying on the ground – she grabbed at some biscuits but her hand did not reach them. Petya pushed her hand away with his knee, seized a biscuit, and as if fearing to be too late, again shouted 'Hurrah!' with a voice already hoarse.

The Emperor went in, and after that the greater part of the crowd began to disperse.

'There! I said if only we waited – and so it was!' was being joyfully said by various people.

Happy as Petya was, he felt sad at having to go home knowing that all the enjoyment of that day was over. He did not go straight home from the Kremlin, but called on his friend Obolensky, who was fifteen and was also entering the regiment. On returning home Petya announced resolutely and firmly that if he was not allowed to enter the service he would run away. And next day Count Ilya Rostov – though he had not yet quite yielded – went to inquire how he could arrange for Petya to serve where there would be least danger.

Two days later, on the 15th of July, an immense number of carriages were standing outside the Sloboda Palace.*

The great halls were full. In the first were the nobility and gentry in their uniforms, in the second bearded merchants in full-skirted coats of blue cloth and wearing medals. In the noblemen's hall there was an incessant movement and buzz of voices. The chief magnates sat on high-backed chairs at a large table under the portrait of the Emperor, but most of the gentry were strolling about the room.

All these nobles, whom Pierre met every day at the club or in their own houses, were in uniform – some in that of Catherine's day, others in that of the Emperor Paul, others again in the new uniforms of Alexander's time, or the ordinary uniform of the nobility, and the general characteristic of being in uniform imparted something strange and fantastic to these diverse and familiar personalities, both old and young. The old men, dim-eyed, toothless, bald, sallow and bloated, or gaunt and wrinkled, were especially striking. For the most part they sat quietly in their places and were silent, or if they walked about and talked, attached themselves to someone younger. On all these faces, as on the faces of the crowd Petya had seen in the Square, there was a striking contradiction: the general expectation of a solemn event, and at the same time the everyday interests in a boston card-party, Peter the cook, Zinaida Dmitrievna's health, and so on.

Pierre was there too, buttoned up since early morning in a nobleman's uniform that had become too tight for him. He was agitated: this extraordinary gathering not only of nobles but also of the merchant-class – *les états généraux* (States-General) – evoked in him a whole series of ideas he had long laid aside but which were deeply graven in his soul: thoughts of the *Contrat Social* and the French Revolution. The words that had struck him in the Emperor's appeal – that the sovereign was coming to the capital for consultation with his people – strengthened this idea. And imagining that in this direction something important which he had long awaited was drawing near, he strolled about, watching and listening to conversations, but nowhere finding any confirmation of the ideas that occupied him.

The Emperor's manifesto was read, evoking enthusiasm, and then all moved about discussing it. Besides the ordinary topics of conversation, Pierre heard questions of where the marshals of the nobility were to stand when the Emperor entered, when a ball should be given in the Emperor's honour, whether they should group themselves by districts or by whole provinces ... and so on; but as soon as the war was touched on, or what the nobility had been convened for, the talk became undecided and indefinite. Then all preferred listening to speaking.

A middle-aged man, handsome and virile, in the uniform of a retired naval officer, was speaking in one of the rooms, and a small crowd was pressing round him. Pierre went up to the circle that had formed round the speaker, and listened. Count Ilya Rostov, in a military uniform of Catherine's time, was sauntering with a pleasant smile among the crowd, with all of whom he was acquainted. He too approached that group and listened with a kindly smile and nods of approval, as he always did, to what the speaker was saying. The retired naval man was speaking very boldly, as was evident from the expression on the faces of the listeners and from the fact that some people Pierre knew as the meekest and quietest of men walked away disapprovingly, or expressed disagreement with him. Pierre pushed his way into the middle of the group, listened, and convinced himself that the man was indeed a Liberal, but of views quite different from his own. The naval officer spoke in a particularly sonorous, musical, and aristocratic baritone voice, pleasantly swallowing his r's and generally slurring his consonants: the voice of a man calling out to his servant, 'Heah! Bwing me my pipe!' It was indicative of dissipation and the exercise of authority.

'What if the Smolensk people have offahd to waise militia for the Empewah? Ah we to take Smolensk as our patte'n? If the noble awistocwacy of the pwovince of Moscow thinks fit, it can show its loyalty to our sov'weign the Empewah in othah ways. Have we fo'gotten the waising of the militia in the yeah 'seven? All that did was to enwich the pwiests' sons, and thieves and wobbahs ...'

Count Ilya Rostov smiled blandly and nodded approval.

'And was our militia of any use to the Empia? Not at all! It only wuined our farming! Bettah have another conscwiption ... o' ou' men will wetu'n neithah soldiers no' peasants, and we'll get only depwavity fwom them. The nobility don't gwudge theah lives – evewy one of us will go and bwing in more wecwuits, and the sov'weign' (that was the way he referred to the Emperor) 'need only say the word and we'll all die fo' him!' added the orator with animation.

Count Rostov's mouth watered with pleasure and he nudged Pierre, but Pierre wanted to speak himself. He pushed forward, feeling stirred, but not yet sure what stirred him or what he would say. Scarcely had he opened his mouth when one of the senators, a man without a tooth in his head, with a shrewd though angry

724

expression, standing near the first speaker, interrupted him. Evidently accustomed to managing debates and to maintaining an argument, he began in low but distinct tones:

'I imagine, Sir,' said he, mumbling with his toothless mouth, that we have been summoned here not to discuss whether it's best for the empire at the present moment to adopt conscription or to call out the militia. We have been summoned to reply to the appeal with which our sovereign the Emperor has honoured us. But to judge what is best – conscription or the militia – we can leave to the supreme authority . . .'

Pierre suddenly saw an outlet for his excitement. He hardened his heart against the senator who was introducing this set and narrow attitude into the deliberations of the nobility. Pierre stepped forward and interrupted him. He himself did not yet know what he would say, but he began to speak eagerly, occasionally lapsing into French or expressing himself in bookish Russian.

'Excuse me, your Excellency,' he began. (He was well acquainted with the senator, but thought it necessary on this occasion to address him formally.) 'Though I don't agree with the gentleman . . .' (He hesitated: he wished to say *'Mon très honorable préopinant'* 'My very honourable opponent') 'with the gentleman . . . whom I have not the honour of knowing, I suppose that the nobility have been summoned not merely to express their sympathy and enthusiasm but also to consider the means by which we can assist our Fatherland! I imagine,' he went on, warming to his subject, 'that the Emperor himself would not be satisfied to find in us merely owners of serfs whom we are willing to devote to his service, and *chair à canon* we are ready to make of ourselves – and not obtain from us any co-co-counsel.'

Many persons withdrew from the circle, noticing the senator's sarcastic smile and the freedom of Pierre's remarks. Only Count Rostov was pleased with them as he had been pleased with those of the naval officer, the senator, and in general with whatever speech he had last heard.

'I think that before discussing these questions,' Pierre continued, 'we should ask the Emperor – most respectfully ask his Majesty – to let us know the number of our troops and the position in which our army and our forces now are, and then . . .'

But scarcely had Pierre uttered these words before he was attacked from three sides. The most vigorous attack came from an old acquaintance, a boston player who had always been well disposed towards him, Stepan Stepanovich Adraksin. Adraksin was in uniform, and whether as a result of the uniform or from some other cause Pierre saw before him quite a different man. With a sudden expression of malevolence on his aged face Adraksin shouted at Pierre:

'In the first place, I tell you we have no right to question the Emperor about that, and secondly, if the Russian nobility had that right, the Emperor could not answer such a question. The troops move according to the enemy's movements and the number of men increases and decreases . . .'

Another voice, that of a nobleman of medium height and about forty years of age, whom Pierre had formerly met at the gipsies' and knew as a bad card-player, and who, also transformed by his uniform, came up to Pierre, interrupted Adraskin.

'Yes, and this is not a time for discussing,' he continued, 'but for acting: there is war in Russia! The enemy is advancing to destroy Russia, to desecrate the tombs of our fathers, to carry off our wives and children.' The nobleman smote his breast. 'We will all arise, every one of us will go, for our father the Tsar!' he shouted, rolling his bloodshot eyes. Several approving voices were heard in the crowd. 'We are Russians and will not grudge our blood in defence of our faith, the throne, and the Fatherland! We must cease raving if we are sons of our Fatherland! We will show Europe how Russia rises to the defence of Russia!'

Pierre wished to reply, but could not get in a word. He felt that his words, apart from what meaning they conveyed, were less audible than the sound of his opponent's voice.

Count Rostov at the back of the crowd was expressing approval; several persons, briskly turning a shoulder to the orator at the end of a phrase, said:

'That's right, quite right! Just so!'

Pierre wished to say that he was ready to sacrifice his money, his serfs, or himself, only one ought to know the state of affairs in order to be able to improve it, but he was unable to speak. Many voices shouted and talked at the same time, so that Count Rostov had not time to signify his approval of them all, and the group increased, dispersed, re-formed, and then moved with a hum of talk into the largest hall and to the big table. Not only was Pierre's attempt to speak unsuccessful but he was rudely interrupted, pushed aside, and people turned away from him as from a common enemy. This happened not because they were displeased by the substance of his speech, which had even been forgotten after the many subsequent speeches, but to animate it the crowd needed a tangible object to love and a tangible object to hate. Pierre became the latter. Many other orators spoke after the excited nobleman, and all in the same tone. Many spoke eloquently and with originality.

Glinka, the editor of the *Russian Messenger*, who was recognized (cries of 'author! author!' were heard in the crowd), said that 'hell must be repulsed by hell,' and that he had seen a child smiling at lightning flashes and thunderclaps, but 'we will not be that child'.

'Yes, yes, at thunderclaps!' was repeated approvingly in the back rows of the crowd.

The crowd drew up to the large table, at which sat grey-haired or bald seventy-year-old magnates, uniformed and besashed, almost all of whom Pierre had seen in their own homes with their buffoons, or playing boston at the clubs. With an incessant hum of voices the crowd advanced to the table. Pressed by the throng against the high backs of the chairs, the orators spoke one after another and sometimes two together. Those standing behind noticed what a speaker omitted to say and hastened to supply it. Others in that heat and crush racked their brains to find some thought and hastened to utter it. The old magnates, whom Pierre knew, sat and turned to look first at one and then at another, and their faces for the most part only expressed the fact that they found it very hot. Pierre however felt excited, and the general desire to show that they were ready to go to all lengths – which found expression in the tones and looks more than in the substance of the speeches – infected him too. He did not renounce his opinions, but felt himself in some way to blame and wished to justify himself.

'I only said that it would be more to the purpose to make sacrifices when we know what is needed!' said he, trying to be heard above the other voices.

One of the old men nearest to him looked round, but his attention was immediately diverted by an exclamation at the other side of the table.

'Yes, Moscow will be surrendered! She will be our expiation!' shouted one man.

'He is the enemy of mankind!' cried another. 'Allow me to speak ...' 'Gentlemen, you are crushing me! ...'

23

AT that moment Count Rostopchin with his protruding chin and alert eyes, wearing the uniform of a general with sash over his shoulder, entered the room, stepping briskly to the front of the crowd of gentry.

'Our sovereign the Emperor will be here in a moment,' said Rostopchin. 'I am straight from the palace. Seeing the position we are in, I think there is little need for discussion. The Emperor has deigned to summon us and the merchants. Millions will pour forth from there' – he pointed to the merchants' hall – 'but our business is to supply men and not spare ourselves . . . That is the least we can do!'

A conference took place confined to the magnates sitting at the table. The whole consultation passed more than quietly. After all the preceding noise the sound of their old voices saying one after another, 'I agree' or for variety, 'I too am of that opinion' and so on, had even a mournful effect.

The secretary was told to write down the resolution of the Moscow nobility and gentry, that they would furnish ten men fully equipped out of every thousand serfs, as the Smolensk gentry had done. Their chairs made a scraping noise as the gentlemen who had conferred rose with apparent relief, and began walking up and down arm in arm to stretch their legs and converse in couples.

'The Emperor! The Emperor!' a sudden cry resounded through the halls, and the whole throng hurried to the entrance.

The Emperor entered the hall through a broad path between two lines of nobles. Every face expressed respectful, awe-struck curiosity. Pierre stood rather far off, and could not hear all that the Emperor said. From what he did hear he understood that the Emperor spoke of the danger threatening the empire and of the hopes he placed on the Moscow nobility. He was answered by a voice which informed him of the resolution just arrived at.

'Gentlemen!' said the Emperor with a quivering voice.

There was a rustling among the crowd and it again subsided, so that Pierre distinctly heard the pleasantly human voice of the Emperor saying with emotion:

'I never doubted the devotion of the Russian nobles, but to-day it has surpassed my expectations. I thank you in the name of the Fatherland! Gentlemen, let us act! Time is most precious . . .'

The Emperor ceased speaking, the crowd began pressing round him, and rapturous exclamations were heard from all sides.

'Yes, most precious . . . a royal word,' said Count Rostov with a sob. He stood at the back, and though he had heard hardly anything, understood everything in his own way.

From the hall of the nobility the Emperor went to that of the merchants. There he remained about ten minutes. Pierre was among those who saw him come out from the merchants' hall with tears of emotion in his eyes. As became known later, he had scarcely begun to address the merchants before tears gushed from his eyes and he concluded in a trembling voice. When Pierre saw the Emperor he was coming out accompanied by two merchants, one of whom Pierre knew, a fat *otkupshchik*.* The other was the mayor, a man with a thin sallow face and narrow beard. Both were weeping. Tears filled the thin man's eyes, and the fat *otkupshchik* sobbed outright like a child, and kept repeating:

'Our lives and property – take them, your Majesty!'

Pierre's one feeling at the moment was a desire to show that he was ready to go to all lengths and was prepared to sacrifice everything. He now felt ashamed of his speech with its constitutional tendency and sought an opportunity of effacing it. Having heard that Count Mamonov was furnishing a regiment, Bezukhov at once informed Rostopchin that he would give a thousand men and their maintenance.

Old Rostov could not tell his wife of what had passed without tears, and at once consented to Petya's request and went himself to enter his name.

Next day the Emperor left Moscow. The assembled nobles all took off their uniforms and settled down again in their homes and clubs, and not without some groans gave orders to their stewards about the enrolment, feeling amazed themselves at what they had done.

END OF PART ONE

PART TWO

1

NAPOLEON began the war with Russia because he could not resist going to Dresden, could not help having his head turned by the homage he received, could not help donning a Polish uniform and yielding to the stimulating influence of a June morning, and could not refrain from bursts of anger in the presence of Kurakin and then of Balashev.

Alexander refused negotiations because he felt himself to be personally insulted. Barclay de Tolly tried to command the army in the best way because he wished to fulfil his duty and earn fame as a great commander. Rostov charged the French because he could not restrain his wish for a gallop across a level field; and in the same way the innumerable people who took part in the war acted in accord with their personal characteristics, habits, circumstances, and aims. They were moved by fear or vanity, rejoiced or were indignant, reasoned, imagining that they knew what they were doing and did it of their own free will, but they all were involuntary tools of history, carrying on a work concealed from them but comprehensible to us. Such is the inevitable fate of men of action, and the higher they stand in the social hierarchy the less are they free.

The actors of 1812 have long since left the stage, their personal interests have vanished leaving no trace, and nothing remains of that time but its historic results.

Providence compelled all these men, striving to attain personal aims, to further the accomplishment of a stupendous result no one of them at all expected – neither Napoleon, nor Alexander, and still less any of those who did the actual fighting.

The cause of the destruction of the French army in 1812 is clear to us now. No one will deny that that cause was, on the one hand, its advance into the heart of Russia late in the season without any preparation for a winter campaign, and on the other, the character given to the war by the burning of Russian towns and the hatred of the foe this aroused among the Russian people. But no one at the time foresaw (what now seems so evident) that this was the only way an army of eight hundred thousand men – the best in the world and led by the best general – could be destroyed in conflict with a raw army of half its numerical strength, and led by inexperienced commanders as the Russian army was. *Not only did no one see this,* but *on the Russian side* every effort was made to hinder the only thing that could save Russia, while *on the French side,* despite Napoleon's experience and so-called military genius, every effort was directed to pushing on to Moscow at the end of the summer, that is, to doing the very thing that was bound to lead to destruction.

In historical works on the year 1812 French writers are very fond of saying that Napoleon felt the danger of extending his line, that he sought a battle, and that his marshals advised him to stop at Smolensk, and of making similar statements to show that the danger of the campaign was even then understood. Russian authors are still fonder of telling us that from the commencement of the campaign a Scythian war-plan was adopted to lure Napoleon into the depths of Russia, and this plan some of them attribute to Pfuel, others to a certain Frenchman, others to Toll, and others again to Alexander himself – pointing to notes, projects, and letters, which contain hints of such a line of action. But all these hints at what happened, both from the French side and the Russian, are advanced only because they fit in with the event. Had that event not occurred these hints would have been forgotten, as we have forgotten the thousands and millions of hints and expectations to the contrary which were current then but have now been forgotten because the event falsified them. There are always so many conjectures as to the issue of any event, that however it may end there will always be people to say: 'I said then that it would be so,' quite forgetting that amid their innumerable conjectures many were to quite the contrary effect.

Conjectures as to Napoleon's awareness of the danger of extending his line, and as to the Russians' deliberately luring the enemy into the depths of Russia, are evidently of that kind, and only by much straining can historians attribute such conceptions to Napoleon and his marshals, or such plans to the Russian commanders. All the facts are in flat contradiction of such conjectures. During the whole period of the war not only was there no wish on the Russian side to draw the French into the heart of the country, but from their first entry into Russia, everything was done to stop them. And not only was Napoleon not afraid to extend his line, but he welcomed every step forward as a triumph, and did not seek battle as eagerly as in former campaigns, but very lazily.

At the very beginning of the war our armies were divided, and our sole aim was to unite them, though uniting the armies was no advantage if we meant to retire and lure the enemy into the depths of the country. Our Emperor joined the army to encourage it to defend every inch of Russian soil and not to retreat. The enormous Drissa camp was formed on Pfuel's plan, and there was no intention of retiring farther. The Emperor reproached the commanders-in-chief for every step they retired. He could not bear the idea of letting the enemy even reach Smolensk, still less could he contemplate the burning of Moscow, and when our armies did unite he was displeased that Smolensk was abandoned and burnt without a general engagement having been fought under its walls.

So thought the Emperor, and the Russian commanders and people were still more provoked at the thought that our forces were retreating into the depths of the country.

Napoleon having cut our armies apart advanced far into the country and missed several chances of forcing an engagement. In August he was at Smolensk, and thought only of how to advance farther, though as we now see that advance was evidently ruinous to him.

The facts clearly show that Napoleon did not foresee the danger of the advance on Moscow, nor did Alexander and the Russian commanders then think of luring Napoleon on, but quite the contrary. The luring of Napoleon into the depths of the country was not the result of any plan, for no one believed it to be possible; it resulted from a most complex interplay of intrigues, aims, and wishes, among those who took part in the war and had no perception whatever of the inevitable, or of the one way of saving Russia. Everything came about fortuitously. The armies were divided at the commencement of the campaign. We tried to unite them, with the evident intention of giving battle and checking the enemy's advance, and by this effort to unite them while avoiding battle with a much stronger enemy, and necessarily withdrawing the armies at an actute angle – we led the French on to Smolensk. But we withdrew at an acute angle not only because the French advanced between our two armies; the angle became still more acute and we withdrew still farther, because Barclay de Tolly was an unpopular foreigner disliked by Bagration (who would come under his command), and Bagration – being in command of the second army – tried to postpone joining up and coming under Barclay's command as long as he could. Bagration was slow in effecting the junction – though that was the chief aim of all at head-quarters – because, as he alleged, he exposed his army to danger on this march, and it was best for him to retire more to the left and more to the south, worrying the enemy from flank and rear and securing from the Ukraine recruits for his army; and it looks as if he planned this in order not to come under the command of the detested foreigner Barclay, whose rank was inferior to his own.

The Emperor was with the army to encourage it, but his presence and ignorance of what steps to take, and the enormous number of advisers and plans, destroyed the first army's energy and it retired.

The intention was to make a stand at the Drissa camp, but Paulucci, aiming at becoming commander-in-chief, unexpectedly employed his energy to influence Alexander, and Pfuel's whole plan was abandoned and the command entrusted to Barclay. But as Barclay did not inspire confidence his power was limited. The armies were divided, there was no unity of command, and Barclay was unpopular; but from this confusion, division, and the unpopularity of the foreign commander-in-chief, there resulted on the one hand indecision and the avoidance of a battle (which we could not have refrained from had the armies been united and had someone else, instead of Barclay, been in command) and on the other an ever-increasing indignation against the foreigners and an increase of patriotic zeal.

At last the Emperor left the army, and as the most convenient and indeed the only pretext for his departure it was decided that it was necessary for him to inspire the people in the capitals and arouse the nation in general to a patriotic war. And by this visit of the Emperor to Moscow the strength of the Russian army was trebled.

He left in order not to obstruct the commander-in-chief's undivided control of the army, and hoping that more decisive action would then be taken, but the command of the armies became still more confused and enfeebled. Bennigsen, the Tsarevich, and a swarm of adjutants-general, remained with the army to keep the commander-in-chief under observation and arouse his energy, and Barclay, feeling less free than ever under the observation of all these 'eyes of the Emperor', became still more cautious of undertaking any decisive action, and avoided giving battle.

Barclay stood for caution. The Tsarevich hinted at treachery and demanded a general engagement. Lubomirski, Bronnitski, Wlocki, and the others of that group, stirred up so much trouble that Barclay, under pretext of sending papers to the Emperor, dispatched these Polish adjutants-general to Petersburg, and plunged into an open struggle with Bennigsen and the Tsarevich.

At Smolensk the armies at last reunited, much as Bagration disliked it.

Bagration drove up in a carriage to the house occupied by

Barclay. Barclay donned his sash and came out to meet and report to his senior officer Bagration.

Despite his seniority in rank, Bagration, in this contest of magnanimity, took his orders from Barclay, but having submitted, agreed with him less than ever. By the Emperor's orders Bagration reported direct to him. He wrote to Arakcheev, the Emperor's confidant: 'It must be as my Sovereign pleases, but I cannot work with the *Minister* (meaning Barclay). For God's sake send me somewhere else, if only in command of a regiment. I cannot stand it here. Head-quarters are so full of Germans that a Russian cannot exist and there is no sense in anything. I thought I was really serving my Sovereign and the Fatherland, but it turns out that I am serving Barclay. I confess I do not want to.'

The swarm of Bronnitskis and Wintzingerodes and their like still further embittered the relations between the commanders-in-chief, and even less unity resulted. Preparations were made to fight the French before Smolensk. A general was sent to survey the position. This general, hating Barclay, rode to visit a friend of his own, a corps commander, and having spent the day with him, returned to Barclay and condemned, as unsuitable from every point of view, the battleground he had not seen.

While disputes and intrigues were going on about the future field of battle, and while we were looking for the French – having lost touch with them – the French stumbled upon Neverovsky's division and reached the walls of Smolensk.

It was necessary to fight an unexpected battle at Smolensk to save our lines of communication. The battle was fought, and thousands were killed on both sides.

Smolensk was abandoned contrary to the wishes of the Emperor and of the whole people. But Smolensk was burnt by its own inhabitants who had been misled by their governor. And these ruined inhabitants, setting an example to other Russians, went to Moscow thinking only of their own losses but kindling hatred of the foe. Napoleon advanced farther and we retired, thus arriving at the very result which caused his destruction.

2

THE day after his son had left, Prince Nicholas sent for Princess Mary to come to his study.

'Well? Are you satisfied now?' said he. 'You've made me quarrel with my son! Satisfied, are you? That's all you wanted! Satisfied? ... It hurts me, it hurts. I'm old and weak and this is what you wanted. Well then, gloat over it! Gloat over it!'

After that Princess Mary did not see her father for a whole week. He was ill and did not leave his study.

Princess Mary noticed to her surprise that during this illness the old prince not only excluded her from his room, but did not admit Mademoiselle Bourienne either. Tikhon alone attended him.

At the end of the week the prince reappeared and resumed his former way of life, devoting himself with special activity to building operations and the arrangement of the gardens, and completely breaking off his relations with Mademoiselle Bourienne. His looks and his cold tone to his daughter seemed to say: 'There, you see? You plotted against me, you lied to Prince Andrew about my relations with the Frenchwoman and made me quarrel with him, but you see I need neither her nor you!'

Princess Mary spent half of every day with little Nicholas, watching his lessons, teaching him Russian and music herself, and talking to Dessalles; the rest of the day she spent over her books, with her old nurse, or with 'God's folk' who sometimes came by the back door to see her.

Of the war Princess Mary thought as women do think about wars. She feared for her brother who was in it, was horrified by and amazed at the strange cruelty that impels men to kill one another, but she did not understand the significance of this war, which seemed to her like all previous wars. She did not realize the significance of this war, though Dessalles with whom she constantly conversed was passionately interested in its progress and tried to explain his own conception of it to her, and though the 'God's folk' who came to see her reported, in their own way, the rumours current among the people of an invasion by Antichrist, and though Julie (now Princess Drubetskaya), who had resumed correspondence with her, wrote patriotic letters from Moscow.

I write you in Russian, my good friend, [wrote Julie in her Frenchified Russian*] because I have a detestation for all the French, and the same for their language which I cannot support to hear spoken ... We in Moscow are elated by enthusiasm for our adored Emperor.

My poor husband is enduring pains and hunger in Jewish taverns, but the news which I have inspires me yet more.

You heard probably of the heroic exploit of Raevsky, embracing his two sons and saying: 'I will perish with them but we will not shake!' And truly though the enemy was twice stronger than we, we were unshakeable. We pass the time as we can, but in war as in war! The princesses Aline and Sophie sit whole days with me, and we, unhappy widows of live men, make beautiful conversations over our *charpie*, only you my friend are missing ...

and so on.

The chief reason Princess Mary did not realize the full significance of this war was because the old prince never spoke of it, did not recognize it, and laughed at Dessalles when he mentioned it at dinner. The prince's tone was so calm and confident that Princess Mary unhesitatingly believed him.

All that July the old prince was exceedingly active and even animated. He planned another garden and began a new building for the domestic serfs. The only thing that made Princess Mary anxious about him was that he slept very little and, instead of sleeping in his study as usual, changed his sleeping place every day. One day he would order his camp-bed to be set up in the glass-gallery, another day he remained on the couch or on the lounge-chair in the drawing-room and dozed there without undressing, while – instead of Mademoiselle Bourienne – a serf-boy read to him. Then again he would spend a night in the dining-room.

On August 1st a second letter was received from Prince Andrew. In his first letter which came soon after he had left home Prince Andrew had dutifully asked his father's forgiveness for what he had allowed himself to say, and begged to be restored to his favour. To this letter the old prince had replied affectionately, and from that time had kept the Frenchwoman at a distance. Prince Andrew's second letter, written near Vitebsk after the French had occupied that town, gave a brief account of the whole campaign with a plan he had drawn in the letter and forecasts as to the further progress of the war. In this letter Prince Andrew pointed out to his father the danger of staying at Bald Hills, so near the theatre of war and on the army's direct line of march, and advised him to move to Moscow.

At dinner that day, on Dessalles's mentioning that the French were said to have already entered Vitebsk, the old prince remembered his son's letter.

'There was a letter from Prince Andrew to-day,' he said to Princess Mary – 'Haven't you read it?'

'No, father,' she replied in a frightened voice.

She could not have read the letter as she did not even know it had arrived.

'He writes about this war,' said the prince, with the ironic smile that had become habitual to him in speaking of the present war.

'That must be very interesting,' said Dessalles. 'Prince Andrew is in a position to know . . .'

'Oh, very interesting!' said Mademoiselle Bourienne.

'Go and get it for me,' said the old prince to Mademoiselle Bourienne. 'You know – under the paper-weight on the little table.'

Mademoiselle Bourienne jumped up eagerly.

'No, don't!' he exclaimed with a frown. 'You go, Michael Ivanovich.'

Michael Ivanovich rose and went to the study. But as soon as he had left the room the old prince, looking uneasily round, threw down his napkin and went himself.

'They can't do anything...always make some muddle,' he muttered.

While he was away Princess Mary, Dessalles, Mademoiselle Bourienne, and even little Nicholas, exchanged looks in silence. The old prince returned with quick steps, accompanied by Michael Ivanovich, bringing the letter and a plan. These he put down beside him – not letting anyone read them at dinner.

On moving to the drawing-room he handed the letter to Princess Mary and, spreading out before him the plan of the new building and fixing his eyes upon it, told her to read the letter aloud. When she had done so Princess Mary looked inquiringly at her father. He was examining the plan, evidently engrossed in his own ideas.

'What do you think of it, Prince?' Dessalles ventured to ask.

'I? I?...' said the prince as if unpleasantly awakened, and not taking his eyes from the plan of the building.

'Very possibly the theatre of war will move so near to us that...'

'Ha ha ha! The theatre of war!' said the prince. 'I have said and still say, that the theatre of war is Poland and the enemy will never get beyond the Niemen.'

Dessalles looked in amazement at the prince, who was talking of the Niemen when the enemy was already at the Dnieper, but Princess Mary, forgetting the geographical position of the Niemen, thought that what her father was saying was correct.

'When the snow melts they'll sink in the Polish swamps. Only they could fail to see it,' the prince continued, evidently thinking of the campaign of 1807 which seemed to him so recent. 'Bennigsen should have advanced into Prussia sooner, then things would have taken a different turn...'

'But, Prince,' Dessalles began timidly, 'the letter mentions Vitebsk...'

'Ah, the letter? Yes...' replied the prince, peevishly. 'Yes... yes...' His face suddenly took on a morose expression. He paused. 'Yes, he writes that the French were beaten at...at...what river is it?'

Dessalles dropped his eyes.

'The prince says nothing about that,' he remarked gently.

'Doesn't he? But I didn't invent it myself.'

No one spoke for a long time.

'Yes...yes...Well, Michael Ivanovich,' he suddenly went on, raising his head and pointing to the plan of the building, 'tell me how you mean to alter it...'

Michael Ivanovich went up to the plan, and the prince after speaking to him about the new building looked angrily at Princess Mary and Dessalles and went to his own room.

Princess Mary saw Dessalles's embarrassed and astonished look fixed on her father, noticed his silence, and was struck by the fact that her father had forgotten his son's letter on the drawing-room table, but she was not only afraid to speak of it and ask Dessalles the reason for his confusion and silence, but was afraid even to think about it.

In the evening Michael Ivanovich, sent by the prince, came to Princess Mary for Prince Andrew's letter which had been forgotten in the drawing-room. She gave it to him and, unpleasant as it was to her to do so, ventured to ask him what her father was doing.

'Always busy,' replied Michael Ivanovich with a respectfully ironic smile which caused Princess Mary to turn pale. 'He's worrying very much about the new building. He has been reading a little, but now' – Michael Ivanovich went on, lowering his voice – 'now he's at his desk, busy with his will I expect.' (One of the prince's favourite occupations of late had been the preparation of some papers he meant to leave at his death and which he called his 'will'.)

'And Alpatych is being sent to Smolensk?' asked Princess Mary.

'Oh, yes, he has been waiting to start for some time.'

3

WHEN Michael Ivanovich returned to the study with the letter, the old prince, with spectacles on and a shade over his eyes, was sitting at his open bureau with screened candles, holding a paper in his outstretched hand, and in a somewhat dramatic attitude was reading his manuscript – his 'Remarks' as he termed it – which was to be transmitted to the Emperor after his death.

When Michael Ivanovich went in there were tears in the prince's eyes evoked by the memory of the time when the paper he was now reading had been written. He took the letter from Michael Ivanovich's hand, put it in his pocket, folded up his papers, and called in Alpatych who had long been waiting.

The prince had a list of things to be bought in Smolensk, and walking up and down the room past Alpatych who stood by the door, he gave his instructions.

'First, notepaper – do you hear? Eight quires, like this sample, gilt-edged . . . it must be exactly like the sample. Varnish, sealing-wax, as in Michael Ivanovich's list.'

He paced up and down for a while and glanced at his notes. 'Then hand to the governor in person a letter about the deed.'

Next bolts for the doors of the new buildings were wanted and had to be of a special shape the prince had himself designed, and a bound case had to be ordered to keep the 'will' in.

The instructions to Alpatych took over two hours and still the prince did not let him go. He sat down, sank into thought, closed his eyes, and dozed off. Alpatych made a slight movement.

'Well, go, go! If anything more is wanted I'll send after you.'

Alpatych went out. The prince again went to his bureau, glanced into it, fingered his papers, closed the bureau again, and sat down at the table to write to the governor.

It was already late when he rose after sealing the letter. He wished to sleep, but he knew he would not be able to, and that most depressing thoughts came to him in bed. So he called Tikhon and went through the rooms with him to show him where to set up the bed for that night.

He went about looking at every corner. Every place seemed unsatisfactory, but worst of all was his customary couch in the study. That couch was dreadful to him, probably because of the oppressive thoughts he had had when lying there. It was unsatisfactory everywhere, but the corner behind the piano in the sitting-room was better than other places: he had never slept there yet.

With the help of a footman Tikhon brought in the bedstead and began putting it up.

'That's not right! That's not right!' cried the prince, and himself pushed it a few inches from the corner and then closer in again.

'Well, at last I've finished, now I'll rest,' thought the prince, and let Tikhon undress him.

Frowning with vexation at the effort necessary to divest himself of his coat and trousers, the prince undressed, sat down heavily on the bed, and appeared to be meditating as he looked contemptuously at his withered yellow legs. He was not meditating, but only deferring the moment of making the effort to lift those legs up and turn over on the bed. 'Ugh, how hard it is! Oh, that this toil might end and *you* would release me!' thought he. Pressing his lips together he made that effort for the twenty-thousandth time and lay down. But hardly had he done so before he felt the bed rocking backwards and forwards beneath him as if it were breathing heavily and jolting. This happened to him almost every night. He opened his eyes as they were closing.

'No peace, damn them!' he muttered, angry he knew not with whom. 'Ah yes, there was something else important, very important, that I was keeping till I should be in bed. The bolts? No, I told him about them. No, it was something, something in the drawing-room. Princess Mary talked some nonsense. Dessalles, that fool, said something. Something in my pocket – can't remember.'

'Tikhon, what did we talk about at dinner?'

'About Prince Michael . . .'

'Be quiet, quiet!' The prince slapped his hand on the table. 'Yes, I know, Prince Andrew's letter! Princess Mary read it. Dessalles said something about Vitebsk. Now I'll read it.'

He had the letter taken from his pocket, and the table – on which stood a glass of lemonade and a spiral wax candle – moved close to the bed, and putting on his spectacles he began reading. Only now in the stillness of the night, reading it by the faint light under the green shade, did he grasp its meaning for a moment.

'The French at Vitebsk, in four days' march they may be at Smolensk; perhaps are already there! Tikhon!' Tikhon jumped up. 'No, no, I don't want anything!' he shouted.

He put the letter under the candlestick and closed his eyes. And there rose before him the Danube at bright noonday: reeds, the Russian camp, and himself a young general without a wrinkle on his ruddy face, vigorous and alert, entering Potëmkin's gaily-coloured tent, and a burning sense of jealousy of 'the favourite' agitated him now as strongly as it had done then. He recalled all the words spoken at that first meeting with Potëmkin. And he saw before him a plump, rather sallow-faced, short, stout woman, the Empress-Mother, with her smile and her words at her first gracious reception of him, and then that same face on the catafalque, and the encounter he had with Zubov over her coffin about his right to kiss her hand.

'Oh, quicker, quicker! To get back to that time and have done with all the present! Quicker, quicker – and that they should leave me in peace!'

4

BALD HILLS, Prince Nicholas Bolkonsky's estate, lay forty miles east from Smolensk and two miles from the main road to Moscow.

The same evening that the prince gave his instructions to Alpatych, Dessalles having asked to see Princess Mary told her that, as the prince was not very well and was taking no steps to secure his safety, though from Prince Andrew's letter it was evident that to remain at Bald Hills might be dangerous, he respect-fully advised her to send a letter by Alpatych to the Provincial Governor at Smolensk, asking him to let her know the state of affairs and the extent of the danger to which Bald Hills was exposed. Dessalles wrote this letter to the governor for Princess Mary, she signed it, and it was given to Alpatych with instructions to hand it to the governor and to come back as quickly as possible if there was danger.

Having received all his orders Alpatych, wearing a white beaver hat – a present from the prince – and carrying a stick as the prince did, went out accompanied by his family. Three well-fed roans stood ready harnessed to a small conveyance with a leather hood.

The larger bell was muffled and the little bells on the harness stuffed with paper. The prince allowed no one at Bald Hills to drive with ringing bells, but on a long journey Alpatych liked to have them. His satellites – the senior clerk, a counting-house clerk, a scullery maid, a cook, two old women, a little page boy, the coachman, and various domestic serfs – were seeing him off.

His daughter placed chintz-covered down cushions for him to sit on and behind his back. His old sister-in-law popped in a small bundle, and one of the coachmen helped him into the vehicle.

'There! There! Women's fuss! Women, women!' said Alpatych, puffing and speaking rapidly just as the prince did, and he climbed into the trap.

After giving the clerk orders about the work to be done, Alpatych, not trying to imitate the prince now, lifted the hat from his bald head and crossed himself three times.

'If there is anything ... come back, Yakov Alpatych. For Christ's sake think of us!' cried his wife, referring to the rumours of war and the enemy.

'Women, women! Women's fuss!' muttered Alpatych to himself and started on his journey, looking round at the fields of yellow rye and the still green, thickly growing oats, and at other quite black fields just being ploughed a second time.

As he went along he looked with pleasure at the year's splendid crop of corn, scrutinized the strips of rye-field which here and there were already being reaped, made his calculations as to the sowing and the harvest, and asked himself whether he had not forgotten any of the prince's orders.

Having baited the horses twice on the way, he arrived at the town towards evening on the 4th of August.

Alpatych kept meeting and overtaking baggage-trains and troops on the road. As he approached Smolensk he heard the sounds of distant firing, but these did not impress him. What struck him most was the sight of a splendid field of oats in which a camp had been pitched, and which was being mown down by the soldiers evidently for fodder. This fact impressed Alpatych, but in thinking about his own business he soon forgot it.

All the interests of his life for more than thirty years had been bounded by the will of the prince, and he never went beyond that limit. Everything not connected with the execution of the prince's orders did not interest and did not even exist for Alpatych.

On reaching Smolensk on the evening of the 4th of August he put up in the Gachina suburb, across the Dnieper, at the inn kept by Ferapontov, where he had been in the habit of putting up for the last thirty years. Some thirty years ago, Ferapontov, by Alpatych's advice, had bought a wood from the prince, had begun to trade, and now had a house, an inn, and a corn-dealer's shop in that province. He was a stout, dark, red-faced peasant in the forties, with thick lips, a broad knob of a nose, similar knobs over his black frowning brows, and a round belly.

Wearing a waistcoat over his cotton shirt, Ferapontov was standing before his shop which opened onto the street. On seeing Alpatych he went up to him.

'You're welcome, Yakov Alpatych. Folks are leaving the town, but you have come to it,' said he.

'Why are they leaving the town?' asked Alpatych.

'That's what I say. Folks are foolish! Always afraid of the French.'

'Women's fuss, women's fuss!' said Alpatych.

'Just what I think, Yakov Alpatych. What I say is: orders have been given not to let them in, so that must be right. And the peasants are asking three rubles for carting – it isn't Christian!'

Yakov Alpatych heard without heeding. He asked for a samovar, and hay for his horses, and when he had had his tea he went to bed.

All night long troops were moving past the inn. Next morning Alpatych donned a jacket he only wore in town, and went out on business. It was a sunny morning and by eight o'clock it was already hot. 'A good day for harvesting,' thought Alpatych.

From beyond the town firing had been heard since early morning. At eight o'clock the booming of cannon was added to the sound of musketry. Many people were hurrying through the streets and there were many soldiers, but cabs were still driving about, tradesmen stood at their shops, and service was being held in the churches as usual. Alpatych went to the shops, to government offices, to the post office, and to the governor's. In the offices and shops and at the post office everyone was talking about the army and about the enemy who was already attacking the town, everybody was asking what should be done, and all were trying to calm one another.

In front of the governor's house Alpatych found a large number of people, Cossacks, and a travelling carriage belonging to the governor. At the porch he met two of the landed gentry, one of whom he knew. This man, an ex-captain of police, was saying angrily:

'It's no joke, you know! It's all very well if you're single. "One man though undone is but one," as the proverb says, but with thirteen in family and all the property.... They've brought us to utter ruin! What sort of governors are they to do that? They ought to be hanged – the brigands!...'

'Oh come, that's enough!' said the other.

'What do I care? Let him hear! We're not dogs,' said the ex-captain of police, and looking round he noticed Alpatych.

'Oh, Yakov Alpatych! What have you come for?'

'To see the governor, by his Excellency's order,' answered Alpatych, lifting his head and proudly thrusting his hand into the bosom of his coat as he always did when he mentioned the prince... 'He has ordered me to inquire into the position of affairs,' he added.

'Yes, go and find out!' shouted the angry gentleman. 'They've brought things to such a pass that there are no carts or anything! ... There it is again, do you hear?' said he, pointing in the direction whence came the sounds of firing.

'They've brought us all to ruin... the brigands!' he repeated, and descended the porch steps.

Alpatych swayed his head* and went upstairs. In the waiting-room were tradesmen, women, and officials, looking silently at one another. The door of the governor's room opened and they all rose and moved forward. An official ran out, said some words to a merchant, called a stout official with a cross hanging on his neck to follow him, and vanished again, evidently wishing to avoid the inquiring looks and questions addressed to him. Alpatych moved forward and next time the official came out addressed him, one hand placed in the breast of his buttoned coat, and handed him two letters.

'To his Honour Baron Asch, from General-in-Chief Prince Bolkonsky,' he announced with such solemnity and significance that the official turned to him and took the letters.

A few minutes later the governor received Alpatych and hurriedly said to him:

'Inform the prince and princess that I knew nothing: I acted on the highest instructions – here...' and he handed a paper to Alpatych. 'Still, as the prince is unwell, my advice is that they should go to Moscow. I am just starting myself. Inform them...'

But the governor did not finish: a dusty perspiring officer ran into the room and began to say something in French. The governor's face expressed terror.

'Go,' he said, nodding his head to Alpatych, and began questioning the officer.

Eager, frightened, helpless glances were turned on Alpatych when he came out of the governor's room. Involuntarily listening now to the firing, which had drawn nearer and was increasing in strength, Alpatych hurried to his inn. The paper handed to him by the governor was this:

I assure you that the town of Smolensk is not in the slightest danger as yet and it is unlikely that it will be threatened with any. I from the one side and Prince Bagration from the other are marching to unite our forces before Smolensk, which junction will be effected on the 22nd instant, and both armies with their united forces will defend our compatriots of the province entrusted to your care till our efforts shall have beaten back the enemies of our Fatherland, or till the last warrior in our valiant ranks has perished. From this you will see that you have a perfect right to reassure the inhabitants of Smolensk, for those defended by two such brave armies may feel assured of victory. (Instructions from Barclay de Tolly to the civil governor of Smolensk, Baron Asch, 1812.)

People were anxiously roaming about the streets.

Carts piled high with household utensils, chairs, and cupboards, kept emerging from the gates of the yards and moving along the streets. Loaded carts stood at the house next to Ferapontov's and women were wailing and lamenting as they said good-bye. A small watch-dog ran round barking in front of the harnessed horses.

Alpatych entered the inn yard at a quicker pace than usual and went straight to the shed where his horses and trap were. The coachman was asleep. He woke him up, told him to harness, and went into the passage. From the host's room came the sound of a child crying, the despairing sobs of a woman, and the hoarse angry shouting of Ferapontov. The cook began running hither and thither in the passage like a frightened hen, just as Alpatych entered.

'He's done her to death. Killed the mistress!...Beat her... dragged her about so!...'

'What for?' asked Alpatych.

'She kept begging to go away. She's a woman! "Take me away," says she, "don't let me perish with my little children; folks," she says, "are all gone, so why", she says, "don't we go?" And he began beating and pulling her about so!'

At these words Alpatych nodded as if in approval and not wishing to hear more went to the door of the room opposite the innkeeper's, where he had left his purchases.

'You brute, you murderer!' screamed a thin, pale woman who, with a baby in her arms and her kerchief torn from her head, burst through the door at that moment and down the steps into the yard.

745

Ferapontov came out after her, but on seeing Alpatych, adjusted his waistcoat, smoothed his hair, yawned, and followed Alpatych into the opposite room.

'Going already?' said he.

Alpatych, without answering or looking at his host, sorted his packages and asked how much he owed.

'We'll reckon up! Well, have you been to the governor's?' asked Ferapontov. 'What has been decided?'

Alpatych replied that the governor had not told him anything definite.

'With our business, how can we get away?' said Ferapontov. 'We'd have to pay seven rubles a cartload to Dorogobuzh and I tell them they're not Christians to ask it! Selivanov, now, did a good stroke last Thursday – sold flour to the army at nine rubles a sack. Will you have some tea?' he added.

While the horses were being harnessed Alpatych and Ferapontov over their tea talked of the price of corn, the crops, and the good weather for harvesting.

'Well, it seems to be getting quieter,' remarked Ferapontov, finishing his third cup of tea and getting up. 'Ours must have got the best of it. The orders were not to let them in. So we're in force, it seems ... They say the other day Matthew Ivanych Platov drove them into the river Marina and drowned some eighteen thousand in one day.'

Alpatych collected his parcels, handed them to the coachman who had come in, and settled up with the innkeeper. The noise of wheels, hoofs, and bells was heard from the gateway as a little trap passed out.

It was by now late in the afternoon. Half the street was in shadow, the other half brightly lit by the sun. Alpatych looked out of the window and went to the door. Suddenly the strange sound of a far-off whistling and thud was heard, followed by a boom of cannon blending into a dull roar that set the windows rattling.

He went out into the street: two men were running past towards the bridge. From different sides came whistling sounds and the thud of cannon-balls and bursting shells falling on the town. But these sounds were hardly heard in comparison with the noise of the firing outside the town, and attracted little attention from the inhabitants. The town was being bombarded by a hundred and thirty guns which Napoleon had ordered up after four o'clock. At first the people did not realize the meaning of this bombardment.

At first the noise of the falling bombs and shells only aroused curiosity. Ferapontov's wife who till then had not ceased wailing under the shed, became quiet, and with the baby in her arms went to the gate listening to the sounds and looking in silence at the people.

The cook and a shop-assistant came to the gate. With lively curiosity everyone tried to get a glimpse of the projectiles as they flew over their heads. Several people came round the corner talking eagerly.

'What force!' remarked one. 'Knocked the roof and ceiling all to splinters!'

'Routed up the earth like a pig,' said another.

'That's grand, it bucks one up!' laughed the first. 'Lucky you jumped aside, or it would have wiped you out!'

Others joined those men, and stopped and told how cannon-balls had fallen on a house close to them. Meanwhile still more projectiles, now with the swift sinister whistle of a cannon-ball, now with the agreeable intermittent whistle of a shell, flew over the people's heads incessantly, but not one fell close by, they all flew over. Alpatych was getting into his trap. The innkeeper stood at the gate.

'What are you staring at?' he shouted to the cook, who in her red skirt, with sleeves rolled up, swinging her bare elbows, had stepped to the corner to listen to what was being said.

'What marvels!' she exclaimed, but hearing her master's voice she turned back, pulling down her tucked-up skirt.

Once more something whistled, but this time quite close, swooping downwards like a little bird; a flame flashed in the middle of the street, something exploded, and the street was shrouded in smoke.

'Scoundrel, what are you doing?' shouted the innkeeper, rushing to the cook.

At that moment the pitiful wailing of women was heard from different sides, the frightened baby began to cry, and people crowded silently with pale faces round the cook. The loudest sound in that crowd was her wailing.

'Oh-h-h! Dear souls, dear kind souls! Don't let me die! My good souls! . . .'

Five minutes later no one remained in the street. The cook, with her thigh broken by a shell-splinter, had been carried into the kitchen. Alpatych, his coachman, Ferapontov's wife and children, and the house-porter, were all sitting in the cellar listening. The roar of guns, the whistling of projectiles, and the piteous moaning of the cook, which rose above the other sounds, did not cease for a moment. The mistress rocked and hushed her baby and when anyone came into the cellar asked in a pathetic whisper what had become of her husband who had remained in the street. A shopman who entered told her that her husband had gone with others to the cathedral, whence they were fetching the wonder-working icon of Smolensk.

Towards dusk the cannonade began to subside. Alpatych left the cellar and stopped in the doorway. The evening sky that had been so clear was clouded with smoke, through which, high up, the sickle of the new moon shone strangely. Now that the terrible din of the guns had ceased a hush seemed to reign over the town, broken only by the rustle of footsteps, the moaning, the distant cries, and the crackle of fires which seemed widespread everywhere. The cook's moans had now subsided. On two sides black curling clouds of smoke rose and spread from the fires. Through the streets soldiers in various uniforms walked or ran confusedly in different directions like ants from a ruined ant-hill. Several of them ran into Ferapontov's yard before Alpatych's eyes. Alpatych went out to the gate. A retreating regiment, thronging and hurrying, blocked the street.

Noticing him, an officer said: 'The town is being abandoned. Get away, get away!' and then turning to the soldiers, shouted:

'I'll teach you to run into the yards!'

Alpatych went back to the house, called the coachman, and told him to set off. Ferapontov's whole household came out too, following Alpatych and the coachman. The women, who had been silent till then, suddenly began to wail as they looked at the fires – the smoke and even the flames of which could be seen in the failing twilight – and as if in reply the same kind of lamentation was heard from other parts of the street. Inside the shed Alpatych and the coachman arranged the tangled reins and traces of their horses with trembling hands.

As Alpatych was driving out of the gate he saw some ten soldiers in Ferapontov's open shop, talking loudly and filling their bags and knapsacks with flour and sunflower seeds. Just then Ferapontov returned and entered his shop. On seeing the soldiers he was about to shout at them, but suddenly stopped, and clutching at his hair burst into sobs and laughter:

'Loot everything, lads! Don't let those devils get it!' he cried, taking some bags of flour himself and throwing them into the street.

Some of the soldiers were frightened and ran away, others went on filling their bags. On seeing Alpatych, Ferapontov turned to him:

'Russia is done for!' he cried. 'Alpatych, I'll set the place on fire myself. We're done for! . . .' and Ferapontov ran into the yard.

Soldiers were passing in a constant stream along the street blocking it completely, so that Alpatych could not pass out and had to wait. Ferapontov's wife and children were also sitting in a cart waiting till it was possible to drive out.

Night had come. There were stars in the sky and the new moon shone out amid the smoke that screened it. On the sloping descent to the Dnieper Alpatych's cart and that of the innkeeper's wife, which were slowly moving amid the rows of soldiers and of other vehicles, had to stop. In a side street near the cross-roads where the vehicles had stopped a house and some shops were on fire. This fire was already burning itself out. The flames now died down and were lost in the black smoke, now suddenly flared up again brightly, lighting up with strange distinctness the faces of the people crowding at the cross-roads. Black figures flitted about before the fire and through the incessant crackling of the flames talking and shouting could be heard. Seeing that his trap would not be able to move on for some time, Alpatych got down and turned into the side street to look at the fire. Soldiers were continually rushing backwards and forwards near it, and he saw two of them and a man in a frieze coat dragging burning beams into another yard across the street, while others carried bundles of hay.

Alpatych went up to a large crowd standing before a high barn which was blazing briskly. The walls were all on fire and the back wall had fallen in, the wooden roof was collapsing and the rafters were alight. The crowd was evidently watching for the roof to fall in, and Alpatych watched for it too.

'Alpatych!' a familiar voice suddenly hailed the old man.

'Mercy on us! Your Excellency!' answered Alpatych, immediately recognizing the voice of his young prince.

Prince Andrew in his riding cloak, mounted on a black horse, was looking at Alpatych from the back of the crowd.

'Why are you here?' he asked.

'Your ... your Excellency,' stammered Alpatych and broke into sobs. 'Are we really lost? Master! ...'

'Why are you here?' Prince Andrew repeated.

At that moment the flames flared up and showed his young master's pale worn face. Alpatych told how he had been sent there and how difficult it was to get away.

'Are we really quite lost, your Excellency?' he asked again.

Prince Andrew without replying took out a notebook, and raising his knee began writing in pencil on a page he tore out. He wrote to his sister:

Smolensk is being abandoned. Bald Hills will be occupied by the enemy within a week. Set off immediately for Moscow. Let me know at once when you will start. Send by special messenger to Usvyazh.

Having written this and given the paper to Alpatych, he told him how to arrange for the departure of the prince, the princess, his son, and the boy's tutor, and how and where to let him know immediately. Before he had had time to finish these instructions, a chief of staff followed by a suite galloped up to him.

'You are a colonel?' shouted the chief of staff with a German accent, in a voice familiar to Prince Andrew. 'Houses are set on fire in your presence and you stand by! What does this mean? You will answer for it!' shouted Berg, who was now assistant to the chief of staff of the commander of the left flank of the infantry of the First Army, a place, as Berg said, 'very agreeable and well *en évidence*'.

Prince Andrew looked at him and without replying went on speaking to Alpatych.

'So tell them that I shall await a reply till the 10th and if by the 10th I don't receive news that they have all got away, I shall have to throw up everything and come myself to Bald Hills.'

'Prince,' said Berg, recognizing Prince Andrew, 'I only spoke because I have to obey orders, because I always do obey exactly... You must please excuse me,' he went on apologetically.

Something cracked in the flames. The fire died down for a moment and wreaths of black smoke rolled from under the roof. There was another terrible crash and something huge collapsed.

'Ou-rou-rou!' yelled the crowd, echoing the crash of the collapsing roof of the barn, the burning grain in which diffused a cake-like aroma all around. The flames flared up again, lighting the animated, delighted, exhausted faces of the spectators.

The man in the frieze coat raised his arms and shouted:

'It's fine, lads! Now it's raging. It's fine!'

'That's the owner himself,' cried several voices.

'Well then,' continued Prince Andrew to Alpatych, 'report to them as I have told you'; and not replying a word to Berg, who was now mute beside him, he touched his horse and rode down the side street.

5

FROM Smolensk the troops continued to retreat, followed by the enemy. On the 10th of August the regiment Prince Andrew commanded was marching along the high road past the avenue leading to Bald Hills. Heat and drought had continued for more than three weeks. Each day fleecy clouds floated across the sky and occasionally veiled the sun, but towards evening the sky cleared again and the sun set in reddish-brown mist. Heavy night-dews alone refreshed the earth. The unreaped corn was scorched and shed its grain. The marshes dried up. The cattle lowed from hunger, finding no food on the sun-parched meadows. Only at night and in the forests while the dew lasted was there any freshness. But on the road, the high road along which the troops marched, there was no such freshness even at night or when the road passed through the forest: the dew was imperceptible on the sandy dust churned up more than six inches deep. As soon as day dawned the march began. The artillery and baggage-wagons moved noiselessly through the deep dust that rose to the very hubs of the wheels, and the infantry sank ankle deep in that soft, choking, hot dust that never cooled even at night. Some of this dust was kneaded by the feet and wheels, while the rest rose and hung like a cloud over the troops, settling in eyes, ears, hair and nostrils, and worst of all in the lungs of the men and beasts as they moved along that road. The higher the sun rose the higher rose that cloud of dust, and through the screen of its hot fine particles one could look with naked eye at the sun, which showed like a huge crimson ball in the unclouded sky. There was no wind, and the men choked in that motionless atmosphere. They marched with handkerchiefs tied over their noses and mouths. When they passed through a village they all rushed to the wells and fought for the water, and drank it down to the mud.

Prince Andrew was in command of a regiment, and the management of that regiment, the welfare of the men and the necessity of receiving and giving orders, engrossed him. The burning of Smolensk and its abandonment made an epoch in his life. A novel feeling of anger against the foe made him forget his own sorrow. He was entirely devoted to the affairs of his regiment and was considerate and kind to his men and officers. In the regiment they called him 'our Prince', were proud of him and loved him. But he was kind and gentle only to those of his regiment, to Timokhin and the like – people quite new to him, belonging to a different world, and who could not know and understand his past. As soon as he came across a former acquaintance, or anyone from the staff, he bristled up immediately, and grew spiteful, ironical, and contemptuous. Everything that reminded him of his past was repugnant to him, and so in his relations with that former circle he confined himself to trying to do his duty and not to be unfair.

In truth everything presented itself in a dark and gloomy light to Prince Andrew, especially after the abandonment of Smolensk on the 6th of August (he considered that it could and should have been defended) and after his sick father had had to flee to Moscow, abandoning to pillage his dearly beloved Bald Hills which he had built and peopled. But despite this, thanks to his regiment, Prince Andrew had something to think about entirely apart from general questions. Two days previously he had received news that his father, son, and sister had left for Moscow; and though there was nothing for him to do at Bald Hills, Prince Andrew with a characteristic desire to foment his own grief decided that he must ride there.

He ordered his horse to be saddled and, leaving his regiment on the march, rode to his father's estate, where he had been born and spent his childhood. Riding past the pond where there used always to be dozens of women chattering as they rinsed their linen or beat it with wooden beetles, Prince Andrew noticed that there was not a soul about, and that the little washing-wharf, torn from its place and half submerged, was floating on its side in the middle of the pond. He rode to the keeper's lodge. No one was at the stone entrance-gates of the drive and the door stood open. Grass had already begun to grow on the garden paths, and horses and calves were straying in the English park. Prince Andrew rode up to the hot-house; some of the glass panes were broken, and of the trees in tubs some were overturned and others dried up. He called for Taras the gardener, but no one replied. Having gone round the corner of the hot-house to the ornamental garden, he saw that the carved garden fence was broken and branches of the plum trees had been torn off with the fruit. An old peasant whom Prince Andrew in his childhood had often seen at the gate, was sitting on a green garden-seat, plaiting a bast shoe.

He was deaf and did not hear Prince Andrew ride up. He was sitting on the seat the old prince used to like to sit on, and beside him strips of bast were hanging on the broken and withered branch of a magnolia.

Prince Andrew rode up to the house. Several limes in the old garden had been cut down and a piebald mare and her foal were wandering in front of the house among the rose bushes. The shutters were all closed, except at one window which was open. A little serf boy, seeing Prince Andrew, ran into the house. Alpatych, having sent his family away, was alone at Bald Hills and was sitting indoors reading the *Lives of the Saints*. On hearing that Prince Andrew had come, he went out with his spectacles on his nose, buttoning his coat, and hastily stepping up without a word began weeping and kissing Prince Andrew's knee.

Then, vexed at his own weakness, he turned away and began to report on the position of affairs. Everything precious and valuable had been removed to Bogucharovo. Seventy quarters of grain had also been carted away. The hay and the spring corn, of which Alpatych said there had been a remarkable crop that year, had been commandeered by the troops and mown down while still green. The peasants were ruined; some of them too had gone to Bogucharovo, only a few remained.

Without waiting to hear him out, Prince Andrew asked:

'When did my father and sister leave?' meaning when did they leave for Moscow.

Alpatych, understanding the question to refer to their departure for Bogucharovo, replied that they had left on the 7th, and again went into details concerning the estate management, asking for instructions.

'Am I to let the troops have the oats, and to take a receipt for them? We have still six hundred quarters left,' he inquired.

'What am I to say to him?' thought Prince Andrew, looking down on the old man's bald head shining in the sun and seeing by the expression on his face that the old man himself understood how untimely such questions were, and only asked them to allay his grief.

'Yes, let them have it,' replied Prince Andrew.

'If you noticed some disorder in the garden,' said Alpatych, 'it was impossible to prevent it. Three regiments have been here and spent the night, dragoons mostly. I took down the name and rank of their commanding officer, to hand in a complaint about it.'

'Well, and what are you going to do? Will you stay here if the enemy occupies the place?' asked Prince Andrew.

Alpatych turned his face to Prince Andrew, looked at him, and suddenly with a solemn gesture raised his arm.

'He is my refuge! His will be done!' he exclaimed.

A group of bareheaded peasants was approaching across the meadow towards the prince.

'Well, good-bye!' said Prince Andrew, bending over to Alpatych. 'You must go away too, take away what you can, and tell the serfs to go to the Ryazan estate or to the one near Moscow.'

Alpatych clung to Prince Andrew's leg and burst into sobs. Gently disengaging himself, the prince spurred his horse and rode down the avenue at a gallop.

The old man was still sitting in the ornamental garden, like a fly impassive on the face of a loved one who is dead, tapping the last on which he was making the bast shoe, and two little girls, running out from the hot-house carrying in their skirts plums they had plucked from the trees there, came upon Prince Andrew. On seeing the young master the elder one, with frightened look, clutched her younger companion by the hand and hid with her behind a birch tree, not stopping to pick up some green plums they had dropped.

Prince Andrew turned away with startled haste, unwilling to let them see that they had been observed. He was sorry for the pretty frightened little girl, was afraid of looking at her, and yet felt an irresistible desire to do so. A new sensation of comfort and relief came over him when, seeing these girls, he realized the existence of other human interests entirely aloof from his own and just as legitimate as those that occupied him. Evidently these girls passionately desired one thing – to carry away and eat those green plums without being caught – and Prince Andrew shared their wish for the success of their enterprise. He could not resist looking at them once more. Believing their danger past, they sprang from their ambush and chirruping something in their shrill little voices and holding up their skirts, their bare little sunburnt feet scampered merrily and quickly across the meadow grass.

Prince Andrew was somewhat refreshed by having ridden off the dusty high road along which the troops were moving. But not far from Bald Hills he again came out on the road and overtook his regiment at its halting-place by the dam of a small pond. It was past one o'clock. The sun, a red ball through the dust, burnt and scorched his back intolerably through his black coat. The dust always hung motionless above the buzz of talk that came from the resting troops. There was no wind. As he crossed the dam Prince Andrew smelt the ooze and freshness of the pond. He longed to get into that water however dirty it might be, and he glanced round at the pool from whence came sounds of shrieks and laughter. The small, muddy, green pond had risen visibly more than a foot, flooding the dam, because it was full of the naked white bodies of soldiers with brick-red hands, necks, and faces, who were splashing about in it. All this naked white human flesh, laughing and shrieking, floundered about in that dirty pool like carp stuffed into a watering can, and the suggestion of merriment in that floundering mass rendered it specially pathetic.

One fair-haired young soldier of the third company, whom Prince Andrew knew and who had a strap round the calf of one leg, crossed himself, stepped back to get a good run, and plunged into the water; another, a dark non-commissioned officer who was always shaggy, stood up to his waist in the water joyfully wriggling his muscular figure and snorted with satisfaction as he poured the water over his head with hands blackened to the wrists. There were sounds of men slapping one another, yelling, and puffing.

Everywhere on the bank, on the dam, and in the pond, there was healthy, white, muscular flesh. The officer, Timokhin, with his red little nose, standing on the dam wiping himself with a towel, felt confused at seeing the prince, but made up his mind to address him nevertheless.

'It's very nice, your Excellency! Wouldn't you like to?' said he.

'It's dirty,' replied Prince Andrew, making a grimace.

'We'll clear it out for you in a minute,' said Timokhin, and, still undressed, ran off to clear the men out of the pond.

'The prince wants to bathe.'

'What prince? Ours?' said many voices, and the men were in such haste to clear out that the prince could hardly stop them. He decided that he would rather souse himself with water in the barn.

'Flesh, bodies, cannon-fodder!' he thought, and he looked at his own naked body and shuddered, not from cold but from a sense of disgust and horror he did not himself understand, aroused by the sight of that immense number of bodies splashing about in the dirty pond.

On the 7th of August Prince Bagration wrote as follows from his quarters at Mikhaylovka on the Smolensk road:

Dear Count Alexis Andreevich [he was writing to Arakcheev but knew that his letter would be read by the Emperor, and therefore weighed every word in it to the best of his ability.]

I expect the Minister [Barclay de Tolly] has already reported the abandonment of Smolensk to the enemy. It is pitiable and sad, and the whole army is in despair that this most important place has been wantonly abandoned. I, for my part, begged him personally most urgently and finally wrote him, but nothing would induce him to consent. I swear to you on my honour that Napoleon was in such a fix as never before, and might have lost half his army but could not have taken Smolensk. Our troops fought, and are fighting, as never before. With fifteen thousand men I held the enemy at bay for thirty-five hours and beat him; but *he* would not hold out even for fourteen hours. It is disgraceful, a stain on our army, and as for him, he ought, it seems to me, not to live. If he reports that our losses were great, it is not true; perhaps about four thousand, not more, and not even that; but even were they ten thousand, that's war! But the enemy has lost masses ...

What would it have cost him to hold out for another two days? They would have had to retire of their own accord, for they had no water for men or horses. He gave his word he would not retreat, but suddenly sent instructions that he was retiring that night. We cannot fight in this way, or we may soon bring the enemy to Moscow ...

There is a rumour that you are thinking of peace. God forbid that you should make peace after all our sacrifices and such insane retreats! You would set all Russia against you and every one of us would feel ashamed to wear the uniform. If it has come to this – we must fight as long as Russia can and as long as there are men able to stand ...

One man ought to be in command, and not two. Your Minister may perhaps be good as a Minister, but as a General he is not merely bad but execrable, yet to him is entrusted the fate of our whole country ... I am really frantic with vexation; forgive my writing boldly. It is clear that the man who advocates the conclusion of a peace, and that the Minister should command the army, does not love our Sovereign and desires the ruin of us all. So I write you frankly: call out the militia. For the Minister is leading these visitors after him to Moscow in a most masterly way. The whole army feels great suspicion of the Imperial aide-de-camp Wolzogen. He is said to be more Napoleon's man than ours, and he is always advising the Minister. I am not merely civil to him but obey him like a corporal, though I am his senior. This is painful, but loving my benefactor and Sovereign I submit. Only I am sorry for the Emperor that he entrusts our fine army to such as he. Consider that on our retreat we have lost by fatigue and left in the hospital more than fifteen thousand men, and had we attacked this would not have happened. Tell me, for God's sake, what will Russia, our mother Russia, say to our being so frightened, and why are we abandoning our good and gallant Fatherland to such rabble, and implanting feelings of hatred and shame in all our subjects? What are we scared at and of whom are we afraid? I am not to blame that the Minister is vacillating, a coward, dense, dilatory, and has all bad qualities. The whole army bewails it and calls down curses upon him ...

6

AMONG the innumerable categories applicable to the phenomena of human life one may discriminate between those in which substance prevails and those in which form prevails. To the latter – as distinguished from village, country, provincial, or even Moscow life – we may allot Petersburg life, and especially the life of its salons. That life of the salons is unchanging. Since the year 1805 we had made peace and had again quarrelled with Bonaparte and had made constitutions and unmade them again, but the salons of Anna Pavlovna and Hélène remained just as they had been – the one seven and the other five years before. At Anna Pavlovna's they talked with perplexity of Bonaparte's successes just as before, and saw in them and in the subservience shown to him by the European sovereigns a malicious conspiracy the sole object of which was to cause unpleasantness and anxiety to the court circle of which Anna Pavlovna was the representative. And in Hélène's salon, which Rumyantsev himself honoured with his visits, regarding Hélène as a remarkably intelligent woman, they talked with the same ecstasy in 1812 as in 1808 of the 'great nation' and the 'great man', and regretted our rupture with France, a rupture which according to them ought to be promptly terminated by peace.

Of late, since the Emperor's return from the army, there had been some excitement in these conflicting salon-circles and some demonstrations of hostility to one another, but each camp retained its own tendency. In Anna Pavlovna's circle only those Frenchmen were admitted who were deep-rooted legitimists, and patriotic views were expressed to the effect that one ought not to go to the French theatre, and that to maintain the French troupe was costing the government as much as a whole army corps. The progress of the war was eagerly followed, and only the reports most flattering to our army were circulated. In the French circle of Hélène and Rumyantsev the reports of the cruelty of the enemy and of the war were contradicted and all Napoleon's attempts at conciliation were discussed. In that circle they discountenanced those who advised hurried preparations for a removal to Kazan of the Court and the girls' educational establishments under the patronage of the Dowager Empress. In Hélène's circle the war in general was regarded as a series of formal demonstrations which would very soon end in peace, and the view prevailed expressed by Bilibin – who now in Petersburg was quite at home in Hélène's house, which every clever man was obliged to visit – that not by gunpowder but by those who invented it would matters be settled. In that circle the Moscow enthusiasm – news of which had reached Petersburg simultaneously with the Emperor's return – was ridiculed sarcastically and very cleverly, though with much caution.

Anna Pavlovna's circle on the contrary was enraptured by this enthusiasm, and spoke of it as Plutarch speaks of the deeds of the ancients. Prince Vasíli, who still occupied his former important posts, formed a connecting link between these two circles. He visited his 'good friend, Anna Pavlovna' as well as his daughter's 'diplomatic salon', and often in his constant comings and goings between the two camps became confused, and said at Hélène's what he should have said at Anna Pavlovna's and vice versa.

Soon after the Emperor's return Prince Vasíli in a conversation about the war at Anna Pavlovna's severely condemned Barclay de Tolly, but was undecided as to who ought to be appointed commander-in-chief. One of the visitors, usually spoken of as 'a man of great merit',* having described how he had that day seen Kutúzov, the newly chosen chief of the Petersburg militia, presiding over the enrolment of recruits at the Treasury, cautiously ventured to suggest that Kutúzov would be the man to satisfy all requirements.

Anna Pavlovna remarked with a melancholy smile that Kutúzov had done nothing but cause the Emperor annoyance.

'I have talked and talked at the Assembly of the Nobility,' Prince Vasíli interrupted, 'but they did not listen to me. I told

757

them his election as chief of the militia would not please the Emperor. They did not listen to me.'

'It's all this mania for opposition,' he went on. 'And who for? It is all because we want to ape the foolish enthusiasm of those Moscovites,' Prince Vasili continued, forgetting for a moment that though at Hélène's one had to ridicule the Moscow enthusiasm, at Anna Pavlovna's one had to be ecstatic about it. But he retrieved his mistake at once. 'Now, is it suitable that Count Kutuzov, the oldest general in Russia, should preside at that tribunal? He will get nothing for his pains! How could they make a man commander-in-chief who cannot mount a horse, who drops asleep at a council, and has the very worst morals! A good reputation he made for himself at Bucharest! I don't speak of his capacity as a general, but at a time like this how can they appoint a decrepit, blind old man, positively blind? A fine idea to have a blind general! He can't see anything. To play blindman's buff? He can't see at all!'

No one replied to his remarks.

This was quite correct on the 24th of July. But on the 29th of July Kutuzov received the title of Prince. This might indicate a wish to get rid of him, and therefore Prince Vasili's opinion continued to be correct though he was not now in any hurry to express it. But on the 8th of August a committee, consisting of Field-Marshal Saltykov, Arakcheev, Vyazmitinov, Lopukhin, and Kochubey met to consider the progress of the war. This committee came to the conclusion that our failures were due to a want of unity in the command, and though the members of the committee were aware of the Emperor's dislike of Kutuzov, after a short deliberation they agreed to advise his appointment as Commander-in-Chief. That same day Kutuzov was appointed Commander-in-Chief with full powers over the armies and over the whole region occupied by them.

On the 9th of August Prince Vasili at Anna Pavlovna's again met the 'man of great merit'. The latter was very attentive to Anna Pavlovna because he wanted to be appointed director of one of the educational establishments for young ladies. Prince Vasili entered the room with the air of a happy conqueror who has attained the object of his desires.

'Well, have you heard the great news? Prince Kutuzov is field-marshal! All dissensions are at an end! I am so glad, so delighted! At last we have a man!' said he, glancing sternly and significantly round at everyone in the drawing-room.

The 'man of great merit', despite his desire to obtain the post of director, could not refrain from reminding Prince Vasili of his former opinion. Though this was impolite to Prince Vasili in Anna

Pavlovna's drawing-room, and also to Anna Pavlovna herself who had received the news with delight, he could not resist the temptation.

'But, Prince, they say he is blind!' said he, reminding Prince Vasili of his own words.

'Eh? Nonsense! He sees well enough,' said Prince Vasili rapidly, in a deep voice and with a slight cough – the voice and cough with which he was wont to dispose of all difficulties.

'He sees well enough,' he added. 'And what I am so pleased about,' he went on, 'is that our Sovereign has given him full powers over all the armies and the whole region – powers no commander-in-chief ever had before. He is a second autocrat,' he concluded with a victorious smile.

'God grant it! God grant it!' said Anna Pavlovna.

The 'man of great merit', who was still a novice in court circles, wishing to flatter Anna Pavlovna by defending her former position on this question observed:

'It is said that the Emperor was reluctant to give Kutuzov those powers. They say he blushed like a girl to whom *Joconde** is read, when he said to Kutuzov: "Your Emperor and the Fatherland award you this honour."'

'Perhaps the heart took no part in that speech,' said Anna Pavlovna.

'Oh, no, no!' warmly rejoined Prince Vasili, who would not now yield Kutuzov to anyone: in his opinion Kutuzov was not only admirable himself, but was adored by everybody. 'No, that's impossible,' said he, 'for our Sovereign appreciated him so highly before.'

'God grant only that Prince Kutuzov assumes real power and does not allow *anyone* to put a spoke in his wheel,' observed Anna Pavlovna.

Understanding at once to whom she alluded, Prince Vasili said in a whisper:

'I know for a fact that Kutuzov made it an absolute condition that the Tsarevich should not be with the army. Do you know what he said to the Emperor?'

And Prince Vasili repeated the words supposed to have been spoken by Kutuzov to the Emperor. 'I can neither punish him if he does wrong nor reward him if he does right.'

'Oh, a very wise man is Prince Kutuzov! I have known him a long time!'

'They even say,' remarked the 'man of great merit' who did not yet possess courtly tact, 'that his Excellency made it an express condition that the Sovereign himself should not be with the army.'

As soon as he said this both Prince Vasili and Anna Pavlovna turned away from him and glanced sadly at one another with a sigh at his naïveté.

7

WHILE this was taking place in Petersburg the French had already passed Smolensk and were drawing nearer and nearer to Moscow. Napoleon's historian, Thiers, like other of his historians, trying to justify his hero says that he was drawn to the walls of Moscow against his will. He is as right as other historians who look for the explanation of historic events in the will of one man; he is as right as the Russian historians who maintain that Napoleon was drawn to Moscow by the skill of the Russian commanders. Here besides the law of retrospection, which regards all the past as a preparation for events that subsequently occur, the law of reciprocity comes in, confusing the whole matter. A good chess-player having lost a game is sincerely convinced that his loss resulted from a mistake he made, and looks for that mistake in the opening, but forgets that at each stage of the game there were similar mistakes and that none of his moves were perfect. He only notices the mistake to which he pays attention, because his opponent took advantage of it. How much more complex than this is the game of war, which occurs under certain limits of time, and where it is not one will that manipulates lifeless objects, but everything results from innumerable conflicts of various wills!

After Smolensk Napoleon sought a battle beyond Dorogobuzh at Vyazma, and then at Tzarevo-Zaymishche, but it happened that owing to a conjunction of innumerable circumstances the Russians could not give battle till they reached Borodino, seventy miles from Moscow. From Vyazma Napoleon ordered a direct advance on Moscow.

Moscou, la capitale asiatique de ce grand empire, la ville sacrée des peuples d'Alexandre, Moscou avec ses innombrables églises en forme de pagodes chinoises, this Moscow gave Napoleon's imagination no rest. On the march from Vyazma to Tsarevo-Zaymishche he rode his light bay bob-tailed ambler accompanied by his Guards, his bodyguard, his pages, and aides-de-camp. Berthier, his chief of staff, dropped behind to question a Russian prisoner captured by the cavalry. Followed by Lelorgne d'Ideville, an interpreter, he overtook Napoleon at a gallop and reined in his horse with an amused expression.

'Well?' asked Napoleon.

'One of Platov's Cossacks says that Platov's corps is joining up with the main army and that Kutuzov has been appointed commander-in-chief. He is a very shrewd and garrulous fellow.'

Napoleon smiled and told them to give the Cossack a horse and bring the man to him. He wished to talk to him himself. Several adjutants galloped off, and an hour later, Lavrushka, the serf Denisov had handed over to Rostov, rode up to Napoleon in an orderly's jacket and on a French cavalry saddle, with a roguish, merry, and tipsy face. Napoleon told him to ride by his side, and began questioning him.

'You are a Cossack?'

'Yes, a Cossack, your Honour.'

'The Cossack, not knowing in what company he was, for Napoleon's plain appearance had nothing about it that would reveal the presence of a monarch to an oriental mind, talked with extreme familiarity of the incidents of the war,' says Thiers, narrating this episode. In reality Lavrushka having got drunk the day before and left his master dinnerless, had been whipped and sent to the village in quest of chickens, where he engaged in looting till the French took him prisoner. Lavrushka was one of those coarse, bare-faced lackeys who have seen all sorts of things, consider it necessary to do everything in a mean and cunning way, are ready to render any sort of service to their master, and are keen at guessing their master's baser impulses, especially those prompted by vanity and pettiness.

Finding himself in the company of Napoleon, whose identity he had easily and surely recognized, Lavrushka was not in the least abashed but merely did his utmost to gain his new master's favour.

He knew very well that this was Napoleon, but Napoleon's presence could no more intimidate him than Rostov's, or a sergeant-major's with the rods, would have done, for he had nothing that either the sergeant-major or Napoleon could deprive him of.

So he rattled on, telling all the gossip he had heard among the orderlies. Much of it was true. But when Napoleon asked him whether the Russians thought they would beat Bonaparte or not, Lavrushka screwed up his eyes and considered.

In this question he saw subtle cunning, as men of his type see cunning in everything, so he frowned and did not answer immediately.

'It's like this,' he said thoughtfully, 'if there's a battle soon, yours will win. That's right. But if three days pass, then after that, well then that same battle will not soon be over.'

Lelorgne d'Ideville smilingly interpreted this speech to Napoleon thus: 'If a battle takes place within the next three days the French will win, but if later, God knows what will happen.' Napoleon did not smile, though he was evidently in high good humour, and he ordered these words to be repeated.

Lavrushka noticed this and to entertain him further, pretending not to know who Napoleon was, added:

'We know that you have Bonaparte and that he has beaten everybody in the world, but we are a different matter ...' – without knowing why or how this bit of boastful patriotism slipped out at the end.

The interpreter translated these words without the last phrase, and Bonaparte smiled. 'The young Cossack made his mighty interlocutor smile,' says Thiers. After riding a few paces in silence, Napoleon turned to Berthier and said he wished to see how the news that he was talking to the Emperor himself, to that very Emperor who had written his immortally victorious name on the Pyramids, would affect this *enfant du Don*.

The fact was accordingly conveyed to Lavrushka.

Lavrushka, understanding that this was done to perplex him and that Napoleon expected him to be frightened, to gratify his new masters promptly pretended to be astonished and awestruck, opened his eyes wide, and assumed the expression he usually put on when taken to be whipped. 'As soon as Napoleon's interpreter had spoken,' says Thiers, 'the Cossack, seized by amazement, did not utter another word, but rode on, his eyes fixed on the conqueror whose fame had reached him across the steppes of the East. All his loquacity was suddenly arrested and replaced by a naïve and silent feeling of admiration. Napoleon, after making the Cossack a present, had him set free like a bird restored to its native fields.'

Napoleon rode on, dreaming of the Moscow that so appealed to his imagination, and 'the bird restored to its native fields' galloped to our outposts, inventing on the way all that had not taken place but that he meant to relate to his comrades. What had really taken place he did not wish to relate because it seemed to him not worth telling. He found the Cossacks, inquired for the regiment operating with Platov's detachment, and by evening found his master, Nicholas Rostov, quartered at Yankovo. Rostov was just mounting to go for a ride round the neighbouring villages with Ilyin; he let Lavrushka have another horse and took him along with him.

8

PRINCESS MARY was not in Moscow and out of danger as Prince Andrew supposed.

After the return of Alpatych from Smolensk the old prince suddenly seemed to awake as from a dream. He ordered the militiamen to be called up from the villages and armed, and wrote a letter to the commander-in-chief informing him that he had resolved to remain at Bald Hills to the last extremity and to defend it, leaving to the commander-in-chief's discretion to take measures or not for the defence of Bald Hills, where one of Russia's oldest generals would be captured or killed, and he announced to his household that he would remain at Bald Hills.

But while himself remaining, he gave instructions for the departure of the princess and Dessalles with the little prince to Bogucharovo and thence to Moscow. Princess Mary, alarmed by her father's feverish and sleepless activity after his previous apathy, could not bring herself to leave him alone, and for the first time in her life ventured to disobey him. She refused to go away and her father's fury broke over her in a terrible storm. He repeated every injustice he had ever inflicted on her. Trying to convict her, he told her she had worn him out, had caused his quarrel with his son, had harboured nasty suspicions of him making it the object of her life to poison his existence, and he drove her from his study telling her that if she did not go away it was all the same to him. He declared that he did not wish to remember her existence and warned her not to dare to let him see her. The fact that he did not, as she had feared, order her to be carried away by force but only told her not to let him see her, cheered Princess Mary. She knew it was a proof that in the depth of his soul he was glad she was remaining at home and had not gone away.

The morning after little Nicholas had left, the old prince donned his full uniform and prepared to visit the commander-in-chief. His calèche was already at the door. Princess Mary saw him walk out of the house in his uniform, wearing all his Orders, and go down the garden to review his armed peasants and domestic serfs. She sat by the window listening to his voice which reached her from the garden. Suddenly several men came running up the avenue with frightened faces.

Princess Mary ran out to the porch, down the flower-bordered path and into the avenue. A large crowd of militiamen and domestics was moving towards her, and in their midst several men were supporting by the armpits and dragging along a little old man in a uniform and decorations. She ran up to him and, in the play of the sunlight that fell in small round spots through the shade of the lime-tree avenue, could not be sure what change there was in his face. All she could see was that his former stern and determined expression had altered to one of timidity and submission. On seeing his daughter he moved his helpless lips and made a hoarse sound. It was impossible to make out what he wanted. He was lifted up, carried to his study, and laid on the very couch he had so feared of late.

The doctor, who was fetched that same night, bled him, and said that the prince had had a seizure paralysing his right side.

It was becoming more and more dangerous to remain at Bald Hills, and next day they moved the prince to Bogucharovo, the doctor accompanying him.

By the time they reached Bogucharovo, Dessalles and the little prince had already left for Moscow.

For three weeks the old prince lay stricken by paralysis* in the new house Prince Andrew had built at Bogucharovo, ever in the same state, getting neither better nor worse. He was unconscious and lay like a distorted corpse. He muttered unceasingly, his eyebrows and lips twitching, and it was impossible to tell whether he understood what was going on around him or not. One thing was certain – that he was suffering and wished to say something. But what it was, no one could tell: it might be some caprice of a sick and half-crazy man, or it might relate to public affairs, or possibly to family concerns.

The doctor said this restlessness did not mean anything and was due to physical causes; but Princess Mary thought he wished to tell her something, and the fact that her presence always increased his restlessness confirmed her opinion.

He was evidently suffering both physically and mentally. There was no hope of recovery. It was impossible for him to travel, it would not do to let him die on the road. 'Would it not be better if the end did come, the very end?' Princess Mary sometimes thought. Night and day, hardly sleeping at all, she watched him, and terrible to say, often watched him not with hope of finding signs of improvement but wishing to find symptoms of the approach of the end.

Strange as it was to her to acknowledge this feeling in herself, yet there it was. And what seemed still more terrible to her was that since her father's illness began (perhaps even sooner, when she stayed with him expecting something to happen), all the personal desires and hopes that had been forgotten or sleeping with her had re-awakened. Thoughts that had not entered her mind for years – thoughts of a life free from the fear of her father, and even the possibility of love and family happiness – floated continually in her imagination like temptations of the devil. Thrust them aside as she would, questions continually recurred to her as to how she would order her life now, after *that*. These were temptations of the devil and Princess Mary knew it. She knew that the sole weapon against *him* was prayer, and she tried to pray.

She assumed an attitude of prayer, looked at the icons, repeated the words of a prayer, but she could not pray. She felt that a different world had now taken possession of her – the life of a world of strenuous and free activity, quite opposed to the spiritual world in which till now she had been confined and in which her greatest comfort had been prayer. She could not pray, could not weep, and worldly cares took possession of her.

It was becoming dangerous to remain in Bogucharovo. News of the approach of the French came from all sides; and in one village, ten miles from Bogucharovo, a homestead had been looted by French marauders.

The doctor insisted on the necessity of moving the prince; the provincial Marshal of the Nobility sent an official to Princess Mary to persuade her to get away as quickly as possible, and the head of the rural police having come to Bogucharovo urged the same thing, saying that the French were only some twenty-five miles away, that French proclamations were circulating in the villages, and that if the princess did not take her father away before the 15th, he could not answer for the consequences.

The princess decided to leave on the 15th. The cares of preparation and giving orders, for which everyone came to her, occupied her all day. She spent the night of the 14th as usual, without undressing, in the room next to the one where the prince lay. Several times, waking up, she heard his groans and muttering, the creak of his bed, and the steps of Tikhon and the doctor when they turned him over. Several times she listened at the door, and it seemed to her that his mutterings were louder than usual and that they turned him over oftener. She could not sleep, and several times went to the door and listened, wishing to enter but not deciding to do so. Though he did not speak, Princess Mary saw and knew how unpleasant every sign of anxiety on his account was to him. She had noticed with what dissatisfaction he turned from the look she sometimes involuntarily fixed on him. She knew that her going in during the night at an unusual hour would irritate him.

But never had she felt so grieved for him or so much afraid of losing him. She recalled all her life with him, and in every word and act of his found an expression of his love of her. Occasionally amid these memories temptations of the devil would surge into her imagination: thoughts of how things would be after his death, and how her new, liberated life would be ordered. But she drove these thoughts away with disgust. Towards morning he became quiet and she fell asleep.

She woke late. That sincerity which often comes with waking

showed her clearly what chiefly concerned her about her father's illness. On waking she listened to what was going on behind the door and, hearing him groan, said to herself with a sigh that things were still the same.

'But what could have happened? What did I want? I want his death!' she cried with a feeling of loathing for herself.

She washed, dressed, said her prayers, and went out to the porch. In front of it stood carriages without horses, and things were being packed in the vehicles.

It was a warm, grey morning. Princess Mary stopped at the porch, still horrified by her spiritual baseness and trying to arrange her thoughts before going to her father.

The doctor came downstairs and went out to her.

'He is a little better to-day,' said he. 'I was looking for you. One can make out something of what he is saying. His head is clearer. Come in, he is asking for you . . .'

Princess Mary's heart beat so violently at this news that she grew pale and leant against the wall to keep from falling. To see him, talk to him, feel his eyes on her now that her whole soul was overflowing with those dreadful, wicked temptations – was a torment of joy and terror.

'Come,' said the doctor.

Princess Mary entered her father's room and went up to his bed. He was lying on his back propped up high, and his small bony hands with their knotted purple veins were lying on the quilt; his left eye gazed straight before him, his right eye was awry and his brows and lips motionless. He seemed altogether so thin, small, and pathetic. His face seemed to have shrivelled or melted, his features had grown smaller. Princess Mary went up and kissed his hand. His left hand pressed hers so that she understood that he had long been waiting for her to come. He twitched her hand, and his brows and lips quivered angrily.

She looked at him in dismay trying to guess what he wanted of her. When she changed her position so that his left eye could see her face he calmed down, not taking his eyes off her for some seconds. Then his lips and tongue moved, sounds came, and he began to speak, gazing timidly and imploringly at her, evidently afraid that she might not understand.

Straining all her faculties Princess Mary looked at him. The comic efforts with which he moved his tongue made her drop her eyes and with difficulty repress the sobs that rose to her throat. He said something, repeating the same words several times. She could not understand them, but tried to guess what he was saying, and inquiringly repeated the words he uttered.

766

'Mmm ... ar ... ate ... ate ...' he repeated several times.

It was quite impossible to understand these sounds. The doctor thought he had guessed them, and inquiringly repeated: '*Mary, are you afraid?*' The prince shook his head, and again repeated the same sounds.

'*My mind, my mind aches?*' questioned Princess Mary.

He made a mumbling sound in confirmation of this, took her hand and began pressing it to different parts of his breast as if trying to find the right place for it.

'Always thoughts ... about you ... thoughts ...' he then uttered much more clearly than he had done before, now that he was sure of being understood.

Princess Mary pressed her head against his hand trying to hide her sobs and tears.

He moved his hand over her hair.

'I have been calling you all night ...' he brought out.

'If only I had known ...' she said through her tears. 'I was afraid to come in.'

He pressed her hand.

'Weren't you asleep?'

'No, I didn't sleep,' said Princess Mary, shaking her head.

Unconsciously imitating her father, she now tried to express herself as he did, as much as possible by signs, and her tongue too seemed to move with difficulty.

'Dear one ... Dearest ...' Princess Mary could not quite make out what he said, but from his look it was clear that he had uttered a tender caressing word such as he had never used to her before. 'Why didn't you come in?'

'And I, I was wishing for his death!' thought Princess Mary.

He was silent awhile.

'Thank you ... daughter dear! ... for all, for all ... forgive! ... thank you! ... forgive! ... thank you! ...' and tears began to flow from his eyes. 'Call Andrew!' he said suddenly, and a childish, timid expression of doubt showed itself on his face as he spoke.

He himself seemed aware that his demand was meaningless. So at least it seemed to Princess Mary.

'I have a letter from him,' she replied.

He glanced at her with timid surprise.

'Where is he?'

'He's with the army, father, at Smolensk.'

He closed his eyes and remained silent a long time. Then as if in answer to his doubts and to confirm the fact that now he under-stood and remembered everything, he nodded his head and reopened his eyes.

'Yes,' he said, softly and distinctly. 'Russia has perished. They've destroyed her.'

And he began to sob, and again tears flowed from his eyes. Princess Mary could no longer restrain herself and wept while she gazed at his face.

Again he closed his eyes. His sobs ceased, he pointed to his eyes, and Tikhon, understanding him, wiped away the tears.

Then he again opened his eyes and said something none of them could understand for a long time, till at last Tikhon understood and repeated it. Princess Mary had sought the meaning of his words in the mood in which he had just been speaking. She thought he was speaking of Russia, or Prince Andrew, of herself, of his grandson, or of his own death, and so she could not guess his words.

'Put on your white dress. I like it,' was what he said.

Having understood this, Princess Mary sobbed still louder, and the doctor taking her arm led her out to the veranda, soothing her and trying to persuade her to prepare for her journey. When she had left the room, the prince again began speaking about his son, about the war, and about the Emperor, angrily twitching his brows and raising his hoarse voice, and then he had a second and final stroke.

Princess Mary stayed on the veranda. The day had cleared, it was hot and sunny. She could understand nothing, think of nothing, and feel nothing, except passionate love for her father, love such as she thought she had never felt till that moment. She ran out sobbing into the garden and as far as the pond, along the avenues of young lime trees Prince Andrew had planted.

'Yes...I...I...I wished for his death! Yes, I wanted it to end quicker...I wished to be at peace...And what will become of me? What use will peace be when he is no longer here?' Princess Mary murmured, pacing the garden with hurried steps and pressing her hands to her bosom which heaved with convulsive sobs.

When she had completed the tour of the garden, which brought her again to the house, she saw Mademoiselle Bourienne – who had remained at Bogucharovo and did not wish to leave it – coming towards her with a stranger. This was the Marshal of the Nobility of the district, who had come personally to point out to the princess the necessity for her prompt departure. Princess Mary listened without understanding him; she led him to the house, offered him lunch, and sat down with him. Then, excusing herself, she went to the door of the old prince's room. The doctor came out with an agitated face and said she could not enter.

'Go away, Princess! Go away...go away!'

She returned to the garden and sat down on the grass at the foot of the slope by the pond, where no one could see her. She did not know how long she had been there when she was aroused by the sound of a woman's footsteps running along the path. She rose and saw Dunyasha, her maid, who was evidently looking for her, and who stopped suddenly as if in alarm on seeing her mistress.

'Please come, Princess...The prince...' said Dunyasha in a breaking voice.

'Immediately, I'm coming, I'm coming!' replied the princess hurriedly, not giving Dunyasha time to finish what she was saying, and trying to avoid seeing the girl she ran towards the house.

'Princess, it's God's will! You must be prepared for everything,' said the Marshal, meeting her at the house door.

'Let me alone; it's not true!' she cried angrily to him.

The doctor tried to stop her. She pushed him aside and ran to her father's door. 'Why are these people with frightened faces stopping me? I don't want any of them! And what are they doing here?' she thought. She opened the door and the bright daylight in that previously darkened room startled her. In the room were her nurse and other women. They all drew back from the bed, making way for her. He was still lying on the bed as before, but the stern expression of his quiet face made Princess Mary stop short on the threshold.

'No, he's not dead – it's impossible!' she told herself and approached him, and repressing the terror that seized her, she pressed her lips to his cheek. But she stepped back immediately. All the force of the tenderness she had been feeling for him vanished instantly and was replaced by a feeling of horror at what lay there before her. 'No, he is no more! He is not, but here, where he was, is something unfamiliar and hostile, some dreadful terrifying repellent mystery!' And hiding her face in her hands, Princess Mary sank into the arms of the doctor, who held her up.

In the presence of Tikhon and the doctor the women washed what had been the prince, tied his head up with a handkerchief that the mouth should not stiffen while open, and with another handkerchief tied together the legs that were already spreading apart. Then they dressed him in uniform with his decorations, and placed his shrivelled little body on a table. Heaven only knows who arranged all this and when, but it all got done as if of its own accord. Towards night candles were burning round his coffin, a pall was spread over it, the floor was strewn with sprays of juniper, a printed band was tucked in under his shrivelled head, and in a corner of the room sat a chanter reading the psalms.

Just as horses shy and snort and gather about a dead horse, so the inmates of the house and strangers crowded into the drawing-room round the coffin – the Marshal, the village Elder, peasant women – and all with fixed and frightened eyes, crossing themselves, bowed, and kissed the old prince's cold and stiffened hand.

9

UNTIL Prince Andrew settled in Bogucharovo its owners had always been absentees, and its peasants were of quite a different character from those of Bald Hills. They differed from them in speech, dress, and disposition. They were called steppe-peasants. The old prince used to approve of them for their endurance at work when they came to Bald Hills to help with the harvest or to dig ponds and ditches, but he disliked them for their boorishness.

Prince Andrew's last stay at Bogucharovo, when he introduced hospitals and schools and reduced the quit-rent the peasants had to pay, had not softened their disposition but had on the contrary strengthened in them the traits of character the old prince called boorishness. Various obscure rumours were always current among them: at one time a rumour that they would all be enrolled as Cossacks; at another of a new religion to which they were all to be converted; then of some proclamation of the Tsar's and of an oath to the Tsar Paul in 1797 (in connexion with which it was rumoured that freedom had been granted them but the landowners had stopped it), then of Peter Fëdorovich's return to the throne* in seven years' time, when everything would be made free and so 'simple' that there would be no restrictions. Rumours of the war with Bonaparte and his invasion were connected in their minds with the same sort of vague notions of Antichrist, the end of the world, and 'pure freedom'.

In the vicinity of Bogucharovo were large villages belonging to the crown or to owners whose serfs paid quit-rent and could work where they pleased. There were very few resident landlords in the neighbourhood and also very few domestic or literate serfs, and in the lives of the peasantry of those parts the mysterious undercurrents in the life of the Russian people, the causes and meaning of which are so baffling to contemporaries, were more clearly and strongly noticeable than among others. One instance, which had occurred some twenty years before, was a movement among the peasants to emigrate to some unknown 'warm rivers'. Hundreds of peasants, among them the Bogucharovo folk, suddenly began selling their cattle and moving in whole families towards the south-east. As birds migrate to somewhere beyond the sea, so these men with their wives and children streamed to the south-east, to parts where none of them had ever been. They set off in caravans, bought their freedom one by one or ran away, and drove or walked towards the 'warm rivers'. Many of them were punished, some sent to Siberia, many died of cold and hunger on the road, many returned of their own accord, and the movement died down of itself just as it had sprung up, without apparent reason. But such undercurrents still existed among the people and gathered new forces ready to manifest themselves just as strangely, unexpectedly, and at the same time simply, naturally, and forcibly. Now, in 1812, to any-one living in close touch with these people it was apparent that these undercurrents were acting strongly and nearing an eruption.

Alpatych, who had reached Bogucharovo shortly before the old prince's death, noticed an agitation among the peasants, and that contrary to what was happening in the Bald Hills district, where over a radius of sixty versts all the peasants were moving away and leaving their villages to be devastated by the Cossacks, the peasants in the steppe region round Bogucharovo were, it was rumoured, in touch with the French, received leaflets from them that passed from hand to hand, and did not migrate. He learnt from domestic serfs loyal to him that the peasant Karp, who possessed great influence in the village commune and had recently been away driving a government transport, had returned with news that the Cossacks were destroying deserted villages, but that the French did not harm them. Alpatych also knew that on the previous day another peasant had even brought from the village of Visloukhovo, which was occupied by the French, a proclamation by a French general that no harm would be done to the inhabitants, and if they remained they would be paid for anything taken from them. As proof of this the peasant had brought from Visloukhovo a hundred rubles in notes (he did not know that they were false) paid to him in advance for hay.

More important still, Alpatych learnt that on the morning of the very day he gave the village Elder orders to collect carts to move the princess's luggage from Bogucharovo, there had been a village meeting at which it had been decided not to move but to wait. Yet there was no time to waste. On the 15th, the day of the old prince's death, the Marshal had insisted on Princess Mary's leaving at once, as it was becoming dangerous. He had told her that after the 16th he could not be responsible for what might happen. On the evening of the day the old prince died the Marshal went away, promising to return next day for the funeral.

But this he was unable to do, for he received tidings that the French had unexpectedly advanced, and had barely time to remove his own family and valuables from his estate.

For some thirty years Bogucharovo had been managed by the village Elder, Dron, whom the old prince called by the diminutive 'Dronushka'.

Dron was one of those physically and mentally vigorous peasants who grow big beards as soon as they are of age, and go on unchanged till they are sixty or seventy, without a grey hair or the loss of a tooth, as straight and strong at sixty as at thirty.

Soon after the migration to the 'warm rivers', in which he had taken part like the rest, Dron was made village Elder and overseer of Bogucharovo, and had since filled the post irreproachably for twenty-three years. The peasants feared him more than they did their master. The masters, both the old prince and the young, and the steward, respected him, and jestingly called him 'the Minister'. During the whole time of his service Dron had never been drunk or ill, never after sleepless nights or the hardest tasks had he shown the least fatigue, and though he could not read, he had never forgotten a single money account, or the number of quarters of flour in any of the endless cartloads he sold for the prince, nor a single shock of the whole corn crop on any single acre of the Bogucharovo fields.

Alpatych, arriving from the devastated Bald Hills estate, sent for this Dron on the day of the prince's funeral, and told him to have twelve horses got ready for the princess's carriages and eighteen carts for the things to be removed from Bogucharovo. Though the peasants paid quit-rent, Alpatych thought no difficulty would be made about complying with this order, for there were two hundred and thirty households at work in Bogucharovo and the peasants were well-to-do. But on hearing the order Dron lowered his eyes and remained silent. Alpatych named certain peasants he knew, from whom he told him to take the carts.

Dron replied that the horses of these peasants were away carting. Alpatych named others, but they too, according to Dron, had no horses available: some horses were carting for the government, others were too weak, and others had died for want of fodder. It seemed that no horse could be had even for the carriages, much less for the carting.

Alpatych looked intently at Dron and frowned. Just as Dron was a model village Elder, so Alpatych had not managed the prince's estates in vain for twenty years. He was a model steward, possessing in the highest degree the faculty of divining the needs and instincts of those he dealt with. Having glanced at Dron he at once understood that his answers did not express his personal views, but the general mood of the Bogucharovo commune, by which the Elder had already been carried away. But he also knew that Dron, who had acquired property and was hated by the commune, must be hesitating between the two camps: the masters' and the serfs'. He noticed this hesitation in Dron's look, and therefore frowned and moved closer up to him.

'Now just listen, Dronushka,' said he. 'Don't talk nonsense to me. His Excellency Prince Andrew himself gave me orders to move all the people away and not leave them with the enemy, and there is an order from the Tsar about it too. Anyone who stays is a traitor to the Tsar. Do you hear?'

'I hear,' Dron answered without lifting his eyes.

Alpatych was not satisfied with this reply.

'Eh, Dron, it will turn out badly!' he said, shaking his head.

'The power is in your hands,' Dron rejoined sadly.

'Eh, Dron, drop it!' Alpatych repeated, withdrawing his hand from his bosom and solemnly pointing to the floor at Dron's feet. 'I can see through you and three yards into the ground under you,' he continued, gazing at the floor in front of Dron.

Dron was disconcerted, glanced furtively at Alpatych, and again lowered his eyes.

'You drop this nonsense and tell the people to get ready to leave their homes and go to Moscow, and to get carts ready for to-morrow morning for the princess's things, And don't go to any meeting yourself, do you hear?'

Dron suddenly fell on his knees.

'Yakov Alpatych, discharge me! Take the keys from me and discharge me, for Christ's sake!'

'Stop that!' cried Alpatych sternly. 'I see through you and three yards under you,' he repeated, knowing that his skill in bee-keeping, his knowledge of the right time to sow the oats, and the fact that he had been able to retain the old prince's favour for twenty years, had long since gained him the reputation of being a wizard, and that the power of seeing three yards under a man is considered an attribute of wizards.

Dron got up and was about to say something, but Alpatych interrupted him.

'What is it you have got into your heads, eh? . . . What are you thinking of, eh?'

'What am I to do with the people?' said Dron. 'They're quite beside themselves; I have already told them . . .'

'"Told them", I daresay!' said Alpatych. 'Are they drinking?' he asked abruptly.

'Quite beside themselves, Yakov Alpatych; they've fetched another barrel.'

'Well, then, listen! I'll go to the police officer, and you tell them so, and that they must stop this and the carts must be got ready.'

'I understand.'

Alpatych did not insist further. He had managed people for a long time, and knew that the chief way to make them obey is to show no suspicion that they can possibly disobey. Having wrung a submissive 'I understand' from Dron, Alpatych contented himself with that, though he not only doubted but felt almost certain that without the help of troops the carts would not be forthcoming.

And so it was, for when evening came no carts had been provided. In the village, outside the drink-shop, another meeting was being held, which decided that the horses should be driven out into the woods and the carts should not be provided. Without saying anything of this to the princess, Alpatych had his own belongings taken out of the carts which had arrived from Bald Hills, and had those horses got ready for the princess's carriages. Meanwhile he went himself to the police authorities.

10

AFTER her father's funeral Princess Mary shut herself up in her room and did not admit anyone. A maid came to the door to say that Alpatych was asking for orders about their departure. (This was before his talk with Dron.) Princess Mary raised herself on the sofa on which she had been lying and replied through the closed door that she did not mean to go away and begged to be left in peace.

The windows of the room in which she was lying looked westward. She lay on the sofa with her face to the wall, fingering the buttons of the leather cushion and seeing nothing but that cushion, and her confused thoughts were centred on one subject – the irrevocability of death and her own spiritual baseness, which she had not suspected, but which had shown itself during her father's illness. She wished to pray but did not dare to, dared not in her present state of mind address herself to God. She lay for a long time in that position.

The sun had reached the other side of the house, and its slanting rays shone into the open window, lighting up the room and part of the morocco cushion at which Princess Mary was looking. The flow of her thoughts suddenly stopped. Unconsciously she sat up, smoothed her hair, got up, and went to the window, involuntarily inhaling the freshness of the clear but windy evening.

'Yes, you can well enjoy the evening now! He is gone and no one will hinder you,' she said to herself, and sinking into a chair she let her head fall on the window-sill.

Someone spoke her name in a soft and tender voice from the garden, and kissed her head. She looked up. It was Mademoiselle Bourienne in a black dress and weepers. She softly approached Princess Mary, sighed, kissed her, and immediately began to cry. The princess looked up at her. All their former disharmony and her own jealousy recurred to her mind. But she remembered too how *he* had changed of late towards Mademoiselle Bourienne and could not bear to see her, thereby showing how unjust were the reproaches Princess Mary had mentally addressed to her. 'Besides, is it for me, for me who desired his death, to condemn anyone?' she thought.

Princess Mary vividly pictured to herself the position of Mademoiselle Bourienne, whom she had of late kept at a distance, but who yet was dependent on her and living in her house. She felt sorry for her, and held out her hand with a glance of gentle inquiry. Mademoiselle Bourienne at once began crying again and kissed that hand, speaking of the princess's sorrow and making herself a partner in it. She said her only consolation was the fact that the princess allowed her to share her sorrow, that all the old misunderstandings should sink into nothing before this great grief; that she felt herself blameless in regard to everyone, and that *he*, from above, saw her affection and gratitude. The princess heard her, not heeding her words but occasionally looking up at her and listening to the sound of her voice.

'Your position is doubly terrible, dear Princess,' said Mademoiselle Bourienne after a pause. 'I understand that you could not, and cannot, think of yourself, but with my love for you I must do so . . . Has Alpatych been to you? Has he spoken to you of going away?' she asked.

Princess Mary did not answer. She did not understand who was to go or where to. 'Is it possible to plan or think of anything now? Is it not all the same?' she thought, and did not reply.

'You know, *chère Marie*,' said Mademoiselle Bourienne, 'that we are in danger – are surrounded by the French. It would be dangerous to move now. If we go we are almost sure to be taken prisoners, and God knows . . .'

Princess Mary looked at her companion without understanding what she was talking about.

'Oh, if anyone knew how little anything matters to me now,'

she said. 'Of course I would on no account wish to go away from him ... Alpatych did say something about going ... Speak to him; I can do nothing, nothing, and don't want to ...'

'I've spoken to him. He hopes we should be in time to get away to-morrow, but I think it would now be better to stay here,' said Mademoiselle Bourienne. 'Because, you will agree, *chère Marie*, to fall into the hands of the soldiers or of riotous peasants would be terrible.'

Mademoiselle Bourienne took from her reticule a proclamation (not printed on ordinary Russian paper) of General Rameau's, telling people not to leave their homes and that the French authorities would afford them proper protection. She handed this to the princess.

'I think it would be best to appeal to that general,' she continued, 'and I am sure that all due respect would be shown you.'

Princess Mary read the paper, and her face began to quiver with stifled sobs.

'From whom did you get this?' she asked.

'They probably recognized that I am French, by my name,' replied Mademoiselle Bourienne, blushing.

Princess Mary, with the paper in her hand, rose from the window, and with a pale face went out of the room and into what had been Prince Andrew's study.

'Dunyasha, send Alpatych, or Dronushka, or somebody to me!' she said, 'and tell Mademoiselle Bourienne not to come to me,' she added, hearing Mademoiselle Bourienne's voice. 'We must go at once, at once!' she said, appalled at the thought of being left in the hands of the French.

'If Prince Andrew heard that I was in the power of the French! That I, the daughter of Prince Nicholas Bolkonsky, asked General Rameau for protection and accepted his favour!' This idea horrified her, made her shudder, blush, and feel such a rush of anger and pride as she had never experienced before. All that was distressing, and especially all that was humiliating, in her position rose vividly to her mind. 'They, the French, would settle in this house: M. le Général Rameau would occupy Prince Andrew's study and amuse himself by looking through and reading his letters and papers. Mademoiselle Bourienne would do the honours of Bogucharovo for him. I should be given a small room as a favour, the soldiers would violate my father's newly dug grave to steal his crosses and stars, they would tell me of their victories over the Russians, and would pretend to sympathize with my sorrow ...' thought Princess Mary, not thinking her own thoughts, but feeling bound to think like her father and her brother. For herself she did not care where she remained or what happened to her, but she felt herself the representative of her dead father and of Prince Andrew. Involuntarily she thought their thoughts and felt their feelings. What they would have said and what they would have done she felt bound to say and do. She went into Prince Andrew's study trying to enter completely into his ideas, and considered her position.

The demands of life, which had seemed to her annihilated by her father's death, all at once rose before her with a new, previously unknown force, and took possession of her.

Agitated and flushed she paced the room, sending now for Michael Ivanovich and now for Tikhon or Dron. Dunyasha, the nurse, and the other maids could not say in how far Mademoiselle Bourienne's statement was correct. Alpatych was not at home, he had gone to the police. Neither could the architect, Michael Ivanovich, who came in with sleepy eyes on being sent for, tell Princess Mary anything. With just the same smile of agreement with which for fifteen years he had been accustomed to answer the old prince without expressing views of his own, he now replied to Princess Mary, so that nothing definite could be got from his answers. The old valet, Tikhon, with sunken, emaciated face that bore the stamp of inconsolable grief, replied: 'Yes, Princess' to all Princess Mary's questions, and hardly refrained from sobbing as he looked at her.

At length the village Elder, Dron, entered the room, and with a deep bow to Princess Mary came to a halt by the doorpost.

Princess Mary walked up and down the room and stopped in front of him.

'Dronushka,' she said, regarding as a sure friend this Dronushka who always used to bring a special kind of ginger-bread from his visit to the fair at Vyazma every year and smilingly offer it to her. 'Dronushka, now since our misfortune . . .' she began, but could not go on.

'We are all in God's hands,' said he, with a sigh.

They were silent for a while.

'Dronushka, Alpatych has gone off somewhere and I have no one to turn to. Is it true, as they tell me, that I can't even go away?'

'Why shouldn't you go away, your Excellency? You can go,' said Dron.

'I was told it would be dangerous because of the enemy. Dear friend, I can do nothing. I understand nothing. I have nobody. I want to go away to-night or early to-morrow morning.'

Dron paused. He looked askance at Princess Mary and said:

'There are no horses; I told Yakov Alpatych so.'

'Why are there none?' asked the princess.

'It's all God's scourge,' said Dron. 'What horses we had have been taken for the army or have died – this is such a year! It's not a case of feeding horses – we may die of hunger ourselves! As it is, some go three days without eating. We've nothing, we've been ruined.'

Princess Mary listened attentively to what he told her.

'The peasants are ruined? They have no bread?' she asked.

'They're dying of hunger,' said Dron. 'It's not a case of carting.'

'But why didn't you tell me, Dronushka? Isn't it possible to help them? I'll do all I can . . .'

To Princess Mary it was strange that now, at a moment when such sorrow was filling her soul, there could be rich people and poor, and the rich could refrain from helping the poor. She had heard vaguely that there was such a thing as 'landlord's corn' which was sometimes given to the peasants. She also knew that neither her father nor her brother would refuse to help the peasants in need, she only feared to make some mistake in speaking about the distribution of the grain she wished to give. She was glad such cares presented themselves, enabling her without scruple to forget her own grief. She began asking Dron about the peasants' needs, and what there was in Bogucharovo that belonged to the landlord.

'But we have grain belonging to my brother?' she said.

'The landlord's grain is all safe,' replied Dron proudly. 'Our prince did not order it to be sold.'

'Give it to the peasants, let them have all they need; I give you leave in my brother's name,' said she.

Dron made no answer but sighed deeply.

'Give them that corn if there is enough of it. Distribute it all. I give this order in my brother's name; and tell them that what is ours is theirs. We do not grudge them anything. Tell them so.'

Dron looked intently at the princess while she was speaking.

'Discharge me, little Mother, for God's sake! Order the keys to be taken from me,' said he. 'I have served twenty-three years and have done no wrong. Discharge me, for God's sake!'

Princess Mary did not understand what he wanted of her, or why he was asking to be discharged. She replied that she had never doubted his devotion and that she was ready to do anything for him and for the peasants.

AN hour later Dunyasha came to tell the princess that Dron had come, and all the peasants had assembled at the barn by the princess's order and wished to have word with their mistress.

'But I never told them to come,' said Princess Mary. 'I only told Dron to let them have the grain.'

'Only, for God's sake, Princess dear, have them sent away and don't go out to them. It's all a trick,' said Dunyasha, 'and when Yakov Alpatych returns let us get away ... and please dont ...'

'What is a trick?' asked Princess Mary in surprise.

'I know it is, only listen to me, for God's sake! Ask nurse too. They say they don't agree to leave Bogucharovo as you ordered.'

'You're making some mistake. I never ordered them to go away,' said Princess Mary. 'Call Dronushka.'

Dron came and confirmed Dunyasha's words; the peasants had come by the princess's order.

'But I never sent for them,' declared the princess. 'You must have given my message wrong. I only said that you were to give them the grain.'

Dron only sighed in reply.

'If you order it, they will go away,' said he.

'No, no. I'll go out to them,' said Princess Mary, and in spite of the nurse's and Dunyasha's protests she went out into the porch; Dron, Dunyasha, the nurse, and Michael Ivanovich following her.

'They probably think I am offering them the grain to bribe them to remain here, while I myself go away leaving them to the mercy of the French,' thought Princess Mary. 'I will offer them monthly rations and housing at our Moscow estate. I am sure Andrew would do even more in my place,' she thought as she went out in the twilight towards the crowd standing on the pasture by the barn.

The men crowded closer together, stirred, and rapidly took off their hats. Princess Mary lowered her eyes and, tripping over her skirt, came close up to them. So many different eyes, old and young, were fixed on her, and there were so many different faces, that she could not distinguish any of them, and feeling that she must speak to them all at once, did not know how to do it. But again the sense that she represented her father and her brother gave her courage, and she boldly began her speech.

'I am very glad you have come,' she said without raising her eyes, and feeling her heart beating quickly and violently. 'Dron-ushka tells me that the war has ruined you. That is our common misfortune, and I shall grudge nothing to help you. I am myself going away because it is dangerous here ... the enemy is near ... because ... I am giving you everything, my friends, and I beg you to take everything, all our grain, so that you may not suffer want! And if you have been told that I am giving you the grain to keep you here – that is not true. On the contrary, I ask you to go with all your belongings to our estate near Moscow, and I promise you I will see to it that there you shall want for nothing. You shall be given food and lodging.'

The princess stopped. Sighs were the only sound heard in the crowd.

'I am not doing this on my own account,' she continued, 'I do it in the name of my dead father, who was a good master to you, and of my brother and his son.'

Again she paused. No one broke the silence.

'Ours is a common misfortune and we will share it together. All that is mine is yours,' she concluded, scanning the faces before her.

All eyes were gazing at her with one and the same expression. She could not fathom whether it was curiosity, devotion, gratitude, or apprehension and distrust – but the expression on all the faces was identical.

'We are very thankful for your bounty, but it won't do for us to take the landlord's grain,' said a voice at the back of the crowd.

'But why not?' asked the princess.

No one replied, and Princess Mary, looking round at the crowd, found that every eye she met now was immediately dropped.

'But why don't you want to take it?' she asked again.

No one answered.

The silence began to oppress the princess, and she tried to catch someone's eye.

'Why don't you speak?' she inquired of a very old man who stood just in front of her leaning on his stick. 'If you think something more is wanted, tell me! I will do anything,' said she, catching his eye.

But as if this angered him, he bent his head quite low and muttered:

'Why should we agree? We don't want the grain.'

'Why should we give up everything? We don't agree. Don't agree ... We are sorry for you, but we're not willing. Go away yourself, alone ...' came from various sides of the crowd.

And again all the faces in that crowd bore an identical expression, though now it was certainly not an expression of curiosity or gratitude, but of angry resolve.

780

'But you can't have understood me,' said Princess Mary with a sad smile. 'Why don't you want to go? I promise to house and feed you, while here the enemy would ruin you . . .'

But her voice was drowned by the voices of the crowd.

'We're not willing. Let them ruin us! We won't take your grain. We don't agree!'

Again Princess Mary tried to catch someone's eye, but not a single eye in the crowd was turned to her; evidently they were all trying to avoid her look. She felt strange and awkward.

'Oh yes, an artful tale! Follow her into slavery! Pull down your houses and go into bondage! I daresay! "I'll give you grain, indeed!" she says', voices in the crowd were heard saying.

With drooping head Princess Mary left the crowd and went back to the house. Having repeated her order to Dron to have horses ready for her departure next morning, she went to her room and remained alone with her own thoughts.

12

FOR a long time that night Princess Mary sat by the open window of her room hearing the sound of the peasants' voices that reached her from the village, but it was not of them she was thinking. She felt that she could not understand them however much she might think about them. She thought only of one thing, her sorrow, which after the break caused by cares for the present, seemed already to belong to the past. Now she could remember it and weep or pray.

After sunset the wind had dropped. The night was calm and fresh. Towards midnight the voices began to subside, a cock crowed, the full moon began to show from behind the lime trees, a fresh white dewy mist began to rise, and stillness reigned over the village and the house.

Pictures of the near past – her father's illness and last moments – rose one after another to her memory. With mournful pleasure she now lingered over these images, repelling with horror only the last one, the picture of his death, which she felt she could not contemplate even in imagination at this still and mystic hour of night. And these pictures presented themselves to her so clearly and in such detail that they seemed now present, now past, and now future.

She vividly recalled the moment when he had his first stroke and was being dragged along by his armpits through the garden at Bald Hills, muttering something with his helpless tongue, twitching his grey eyebrows, and looking uneasily and timidly at her.

'Even then he wanted to tell me what he told me the day he died,' she thought. 'He had always thought what he said then.' And she recalled in all its detail the night at Bald Hills before he had the last stroke, when with a foreboding of disaster she had remained at home against his will. She had not slept, and had stolen downstairs on tiptoe, and going to the door of the conservatory where he slept that night had listened at the door. In a suffering and weary voice he was saying something to Tikhon, speaking of the Crimea and its warm nights and of the Empress. Evidently he had wanted to talk. 'And why didn't he call me? Why didn't he let me be there instead of Tikhon?' Princess Mary had thought and thought again now. 'Now he will never tell anyone what he had in his soul. Never will that moment return for him or for me when he might have said all he longed to say, and not Tikhon but I might have heard and understood him. Why didn't I enter the room?' she thought. 'Perhaps he would then have said to me what he said the day he died. While talking to Tikhon he asked about me twice. He wanted to see me, and I was standing close by, outside the door. It was sad and painful for him to talk to Tikhon who did not understand him. I remember how he began speaking to him about Lise as if she were alive – he had forgotten she was dead – and Tikhon reminded him that she was no more, and he shouted "Fool!" He was greatly depressed. From behind the door I heard how he lay down on his bed groaning and loudly exclaimed "My God!" Why didn't I go in then? What could he have done to me? What could I have lost? And perhaps he would then have been comforted and would have said that word to me.' And Princess Mary uttered aloud the caressing word he had said to her on the day of his death. 'Dear-est!' she repeated, and began sobbing, with tears that relieved her soul. She now saw his face before her. And not the face she had known ever since she could remember and had always seen at a distance, but the timid feeble face she had seen for the first time quite closely, with all its wrinkles and details, when she stooped near to his mouth to catch what he said.

'Dear-est!' she repeated again.

'What was he thinking when he uttered that word? What is he thinking now?' This question suddenly presented itself to her, and in answer she saw him before her with the expression that was on his face as he lay in his coffin with his chin bound up with a white handkerchief. And the horror that had seized her when she touched him and convinced herself that *that* was not *he*, but something mysterious and horrible, seized her again. She tried to think of something else and to pray, but could do neither. With wide-open eyes she gazed at the moonlight and the shadows, expecting every moment to see his dead face, and she felt that the silence brooding over the house and within it held her fast.

'Dunyasha,' she whispered. 'Dunyasha!' she screamed wildly, and tearing herself out of this silence she ran to the servants' quarters to meet her old nurse and the maid-servants who came running towards her.

13

On the 17th of August Rostov and Ilyin, accompanied by Lavrushka who had just returned from captivity and by an hussar orderly, left their quarters at Yankovo, ten miles from Bogucharovo, and went for a ride – to try a new horse Ilyin had bought and to find out whether there was any hay to be had in the villages.

For the last three days Bogucharovo had lain between the two hostile armies, so that it was as easy for the Russian rearguard to get to it as for the French vanguard, so Rostov, as a careful squadron-commander, wished to take such provisions as remained at Bogucharovo before the French could get them.

Rostov and Ilyin were in the merriest of moods. On the way to Bogucharovo, a princely estate with a dwelling house and farm where they hoped to find many domestic serfs and pretty girls, they questioned Lavrushka about Napoleon and laughed at his stories, and raced one another to try Ilyin's horse.

Rostov had no idea that the village he was entering was the property of that very Bolkonsky who had been engaged to his sister.

Rostov and Ilyin gave rein to their horses for a last race along the incline before reaching Bogucharovo, and Rostov, outstripping Ilyin, was the first to gallop into the village street.

'You're first!' cried Ilyin, flushed.

'Yes, always first both on the grass-land and here,' answered Rostov, stroking his heated Donets horse.

'And I'd have won on my Frenchy, your Excellency,' said Lavrushka from behind, alluding to his shabby cart-horse, 'only I didn't wish to mortify you.'

They rode at a foot-pace to the barn, where a large crowd of peasants was standing.

Some of the men bared their heads, others stared at the new arrivals without doffing their caps. Two tall old peasants with wrinkled faces and scanty beards emerged from the tavern, smiling, staggering, and singing some incoherent song, and approached the officers.

'Fine fellows!' said Rostov, laughing. 'Is there any hay here?'

'And how like one another,' said Ilyin.

'A mo-o-st me-r-r-y co-o-m-pa . . . !' sang one of the peasants with a blissful smile.

One of the men came out of the crowd and went up to Rostov.

'Who do you belong to?' he asked.

'The French,' replied Ilyin jestingly, 'and here is Napoleon himself' – and he pointed to Lavrushka.

'Then you are Russians?' the peasant asked again.

'And is there a large force of you here?' said another, a short man, coming up.

'Very large,' answered Rostov. 'But why have you collected here?' he added. 'Is it a holiday?'

'The old men have met to talk over the business of the commune,' replied the peasant moving away.

At that moment, on the road leading from the big house, two women and a man in a white hat were seen coming towards the officers.

'The one in pink is mine, so keep off!' said Ilyin on seeing Dunyasha running resolutely towards him.

'She'll be ours!' said Lavrushka to Ilyin, winking.

'What do you want, my pretty?' said Ilyin with a smile.

'The princess ordered me to ask your regiment and your name.'

'This is Count Rostov, squadron-commander, and I am your humble servant.'

'Co-o-om-pa-ny!' roared the tipsy peasant with a beatific smile as he looked at Ilyin talking to the girl. Following Dunyasha, Alpatych advanced to Rostov, having bared his head while still at a distance.

'May I make bold to trouble your Honour?' said he respectfully, but with a shade of contempt for the youthfulness of this officer and with a hand thrust into his bosom. 'My mistress, daughter of General-in-Chief Prince Nicholas Bolkonsky who died on the 15th of this month, finding herself in difficulties owing to the boorishness of these people' – he pointed to the peasants – 'asks you to come up to the house . . . Won't you, please; ride on a little farther,' said Alpatych with a melancholy smile, 'as it is not convenient in the presence of . . . ?' He pointed to the two peasants who kept as close to him as horseflies to a horse.

'Ah! . . . Alpatych . . . Ah, Yakov Alpatych . . . Grand! Forgive us for Christ's sake, eh?' said the peasants, smiling joyfully at him.

Rostov looked at the tipsy peasants and smiled.

'Or perhaps they amuse your Honour?' remarked Alpatych with a staid air, as he pointed at the old men with his free hand.

'No, there's not much to be amused at here,' said Rostov, and rode on a little way. 'What's the matter?' he asked.

'I make bold to inform your Honour that these rough peasants here don't wish to let the mistress leave the estate, and threaten to unharness her horses, so that though everything has been packed since morning, her Excellency cannot get away.'

'Impossible!' exclaimed Rostov.

'I have the honour to report to you the actual truth,' said Alpatych.

Rostov dismounted, gave his horse to the orderly, and followed Alpatych to the house, questioning him as to the state of affairs. It appeared that the princess's offer of corn to the peasants the previous day, and her talk with Dron and at the meeting, had actually had so bad an effect that Dron had finally given up the keys and joined the peasants, and had not appeared when Alpatych sent for him, and that in the morning when the princess gave orders to harness for her journey, the peasants had come in a large crowd to the barn and sent word that they would not let her leave the village: that there was an order not to move, and that they would unharness the horses. Alpatych had gone out to admonish them, but was told (it was chiefly Karp who did the talking, Dron not showing himself in the crowd) that they could not let the princess go, that there was an order to the contrary, but that if she stayed they would serve her as before and obey her in everything.

At the moment when Rostov and Ilyin were galloping along the road, Princess Mary, despite the dissuasions of Alpatych, her nurse, and the maids, had given orders to harness and intended to start, but when the cavalrymen were espied they were taken for Frenchmen, the coachman ran away, and the women in the house began to wail.

'Father! Benefactor! God has sent you!' exclaimed deeply moved voices as Rostov passed through the ante-room.

Princess Mary was sitting, helpless and bewildered, in the large sitting-room when Rostov was shown in. She could not grasp who he was and why he had come, or what was happening to her. When she saw his Russian face, and by his walk and the first words he uttered recognized him as a man of her own class, she glanced at him with her deep radiant look and began speaking in a voice that faltered and trembled with emotion. This meeting immediately struck Rostov as a romantic event. 'A helpless girl overwhelmed with grief, left to the mercy of coarse rioting peasants! And what a strange fate sent me here! What gentleness and nobility there is in her features and expression!' thought he as he looked at her and listened to her timid story.

When she began to tell him that all this had happened the day after her father's funeral, her voice trembled. She turned away, and then, as if fearing he might take her words as meant to move him to pity, looked at him with an apprehensive glance of inquiry. There were tears in Rostov's eyes. Princess Mary noticed this, and glanced gratefully at him with that radiant look which caused the plainness of her face to be forgotten.

'I cannot express, Princess, how glad I am that I happened to ride here and am able to show my readiness to serve you,' said Rostov, rising. 'Go when you please, and I give you my word of honour that no one shall dare to cause you annoyance if only you will allow me to act as your escort.' And bowing respectfully, as if to a lady of royal blood, he moved towards the door.

Rostov's deferential tone seemed to indicate that though he would consider himself happy to be acquainted with her, he did not wish to take advantage of her misfortunes to intrude upon her.

Princess Mary understood this and appreciated his delicacy.

'I am very, very grateful to you,' she said in French, 'but I hope it was all a misunderstanding and that no one is to blame for it.' She suddenly began to cry.

'Excuse me!' she said.

Rostov, knitting his brows, left the room with another low bow.

14

'Well, is she pretty? Ah, friend – my pink one is delicious; her name is Dunyasha . . .'

But on glancing at Rostov's face Ilyin stopped short. He saw that his hero and commander was following quite a different train of thought.

Rostov glanced angrily at Ilyin and without replying strode off with rapid steps to the village.

'I'll show them; I'll give it them, the brigands!' said he to himself.

Alpatych at a gliding trot, only just managing not to run, kept up with him with difficulty.

'What decision have you been pleased to come to?' said he.

Rostov stopped and, clenching his fists, suddenly and sternly turned on Alpatych.

'Decision? What decision? Old dotard! . . .' cried he. 'What have you been about? Eh? The peasants are rioting, and you can't manage them? You're a traitor yourself! I know you. I'll flay you all alive!'...And as if afraid of wasting his store of anger, he left Alpatych and went rapidly forward. Alpatych, mastering his offended feelings, kept pace with Rostov at a gliding gait and continued to impart his views. He said the peasants were obdurate and that at the present moment it would be imprudent to 'over-resist' them without an armed force, and would it not be better first to send for the military?

'I'll give them armed force...I'll "over-resist" them!' uttered Rostov meaninglessly, breathless with irrational animal fury and the need to vent it.

Without considering what he would do he moved unconsciously with quick resolute steps towards the crowd. And the nearer he drew to it the more Alpatych felt that this unreasonable action might produce good results. The peasants in the crowd were similarly impressed when they saw Rostov's rapid firm steps and resolute frowning face.

After the hussars had come to the village and Rostov had gone to see the princess, a certain confusion and dissension had arisen among the crowd. Some of the peasants said that these new arrivals were Russians and might take it amiss that the mistress was being detained. Dron was of this opinion, but as soon as he expressed it Karp and others attacked their ex-Elder.

'How many years have you been fattening on the commune?' Karp shouted at him. 'It's all one to you! You'll dig up your pot of money and take it away with you...What does it matter to you whether our homes are ruined or not?'

'We've been told to keep order, and that no one is to leave their homes or take away a single grain, and that's all about it!' cried another.

'It was your son's turn to be conscripted, but no fear! You begrudged your lump of a son,' a little old man suddenly began attacking Dron – 'and so they took my Vanka to be shaved for a soldier! But we all have to die.'

'To be sure, we all have to die. I'm not against the commune,' said Dron.

'That's it – not against it! You've filled your belly...'

The two tall peasants had their say. As soon as Rostov, followed by Ilyin, Lavrushka, and Alpatych, came up to the crowd, Karp, thrusting his fingers into his belt and smiling a little, walked to the front. Dron on the contrary retired to the rear, and the crowd drew closer together.

'Who is your Elder here? Hey?' shouted Rostov, coming up to the crowd with quick steps.

'The Elder? What do you want with him? . . .' asked Karp.

But before the words were well out of his mouth, his cap flew off and a fierce blow jerked his head to one side.

'Caps off, traitors!' shouted Rostov in a wrathful voice. 'Where's the Elder?' he cried furiously.

'The Elder . . . He wants the Elder! . . . Dron Zakharych, you!' meek and flustered voices here and there were heard calling, and the caps began to come off their heads.

'We don't riot, we're following the orders,' declared Karp, and at that moment several voices began speaking together.

'It's as the old men have decided – there's too many of you giving orders.'

'Arguing? Mutiny! . . . Brigands! Traitors!' cried Rostov unmeaningly in a voice not his own, gripping Karp by the collar. 'Bind him, bind him!' he shouted, though there was no one to bind him but Lavrushka and Alpatych.

Lavrushka however ran up to Karp and seized him by the arms from behind.

'Shall I call up our men from beyond the hill?' he called out.

Alpatych turned to the peasants and ordered two of them by name to come and bind Karp. The men obediently came out of the crowd, and began taking off their belts.

'Where's the Elder?' demanded Rostov in a loud voice.

With a pale and frowning face Dron stepped out of the crowd.

'Are you the Elder? Bind him, Lavrushka!' shouted Rostov, as if that order, too, could not possibly meet with any opposition.

And in fact two more peasants began binding Dron, who took off his own belt and handed it to them, as if to aid them.

'And you all listen to me!' said Rostov to the peasants. 'Be off to your houses at once, and don't let one of your voices be heard!'

'Why, we've not done any harm. We did it just out of foolishness. It's all nonsense . . . I said then that it was not in order,' voices were heard bickering with one another.

'There! What did I say?' said Alpatych, coming into his own again. 'It's wrong, lads!'

'All our stupidity, Yakov Alpatych,' came the answers, and the crowd began at once to disperse through the village.

The two bound men were led off to the master's house. The two drunken peasants followed them.

'Aye, when I look at you!' said one of them to Karp.

'How can one talk to the masters like that? What were you thinking of, you fool?' added the other – 'A real fool!'

Two hours later the carts were standing in the courtyard of the Bogucharovo house. The peasants were briskly carrying out the proprietor's goods and packing them on the carts, and Dron, liberated at Princess Mary's wish from the cupboard where he had been confined, was standing in the yard directing the men.

'Don't put it in so carelessly,' said one of the peasants, a man with a round smiling face, taking a casket from a housemaid. 'You know it has cost money! How can you chuck it in like that or shove it under the cord where it'll get rubbed? I don't like that way of doing things. Let it all be done properly, according to rule. Look here, put it under the bast-matting and cover it with hay — that's the way!'

'Eh, books books!' said another peasant bringing out Prince Andrew's library cupboards. 'Don't catch up against it! It's heavy, lads – solid books.'

'Yes, they worked all day and didn't play!' remarked the tall, round-faced peasant gravely, pointing with a significant wink at the dictionaries that were on the top.

Unwilling to obtrude himself on the princess, Rostov did not go back to the house but remained in the village awaiting her departure. When her carriage drove out of the house, he mounted, and accompanied her eight miles from Bogucharovo to where the road was occupied by our troops. At the inn at Yankovo he respectfully took leave of her, for the first time permitting himself to kiss her hand.

'How can you speak so!' he blushingly replied to Princess Mary's expressions of gratitude for her deliverance, as she termed what had occurred. 'Any police officer would have done as much! If we had had only peasants to fight, we should not have let the enemy come so far,' said he with a sense of shame and wishing to change the subject. 'I am only happy to have had the opportunity of making your acquaintance. Good-bye, Princess. I wish you happiness and consolation, and hope to meet you again in happier circumstances. If you don't want to make me blush, please don't thank me!'

But the princess, if she did not again thank him in words, thanked him with the whole expression of her face, radiant with gratitude and tenderness. She could not believe that there was nothing to thank him for. On the contrary it seemed to her certain that had he not been there she would have perished at the hands of the mutineers and of the French, and that he had exposed himself to terrible and obvious danger to save her, and even more certain was it that he was a man of lofty and noble soul, able to understand her position and her sorrow. His kind, honest eyes, with the tears rising in them when she herself had begun to cry as she spoke of her loss, did not leave her memory.

When she had taken leave of him and remained alone she suddenly felt her eyes filling with tears, and then not for the first time the strange question presented itself to her: did she love him?

On the rest of the way to Moscow, though the princess's position was not a cheerful one, Dunyasha, who went with her in the carriage, more than once noticed that her mistress leaned out of the window and smiled at something with an expression of mingled joy and sorrow.

'Well, supposing I do love him?' thought Princess Mary.

Ashamed as she was of acknowledging to herself that she had fallen in love with a man who would perhaps never love her, she comforted herself with the thought that no one would ever know it, and that she would not be to blame if, without ever speaking of it to anyone, she continued to the end of her life to love the man with whom she had fallen in love for the first and last time in her life.

Sometimes when she recalled his looks, his sympathy, and his words, happiness did not appear impossible to her. It was at those moments that Dunyasha noticed her smiling as she looked out of the carriage window.

'Was it not fate that brought him to Bogucharovo, and at that very moment?' thought Princess Mary, 'and that caused his sister to refuse my brother?'* And in all this Princess Mary saw the hand of Providence.

The impression the princess made on Rostov was a very agreeable one. To remember her gave him pleasure, and when his comrades, hearing of his adventure at Bogucharovo, rallied him on having gone to look for hay and having picked up one of the wealthiest heiresses in Russia, he grew angry. It made him angry just because the idea of marrying the gentle Princess Mary, who was attractive to him and had an enormous fortune, had against his will more than once entered his head. For himself personally Nicholas could not wish for a better wife: by marrying her he would make the countess his mother happy, would be able to put his father's affairs in order, and would even – he felt it – ensure Princess Mary's happiness.

But Sonya? And his plighted word? That was why Rostov grew angry when he was rallied about Princess Bolkonskaya.

ON receiving command of the armies Kutuzov remembered Prince Andrew and sent an order for him to report at head-quarters.

Prince Andrew arrived at Tsarevo-Zaymishche on the very day and at the very hour that Kutuzov was reviewing the troops for the first time. He stopped in the village at the priest's house in front of which stood the commander-in-chief's carriage, and he sat down on the bench at the gate awaiting his Serene Highness, as everyone now called Kutuzov. From the field beyond the village came, now sounds of regimental music and now the roar of many voices shouting 'Hurrah!' to the new commander-in-chief. Two orderlies, a courier, and a major-domo stood near by, some ten paces from Prince Andrew, availing themselves of Kutuzov's absence and of the fine weather. A short, swarthy lieutenant-colonel of hussars with thick moustaches and whiskers rode up to the gate and, glancing at Prince Andrew, inquired whether his Serene Highness was putting up there and whether he would soon be back.

Prince Andrew replied that he was not on his Serene Highness's staff but was himself a new arrival. The lieutenant-colonel turned to a smart orderly, who with the peculiar contempt with which a commander-in-chief's orderly speaks to officers, replied:

'What? His Serene Highness? I expect he'll be here soon. What do you want?'

The lieutenant-colonel of hussars smiled beneath his moustache at the orderly's tone, dismounted, gave his horse to a dispatch-runner, and approached Bolkonsky with a slight bow. Bolkonsky made room for him on the bench and the lieutenant-colonel sat down beside him.

'You're also waiting for the commander-in-chief?' said he. 'They say he weceives evewyone, thank God! ... It's awful with those sausage-eaters! Ermolov had weason to ask to be pwomoted to be a German! Now p'waps Wussians will get a look in. As it was, devil only knows what was happening. We kept wetweating and wetweating. Did you take part in the campaign?' he asked.

'I had the pleasure,' replied Prince Andrew, 'not only of taking part in the retreat but of losing in that retreat all I held dear — not to mention the estate and home of my birth — my father, who died of grief. I belong to the province of Smolensk.'

'Ah? You're Pwince Bolkonsky? Vewy glad to make your acquaintance! I'm Lieutenant-Colonel Denisov, better known as "Vaska",' said Denisov, pressing Prince Andrew's hand and looking into his face with a particularly kind attention. 'Yes, I heard,' said he sympathetically, and after a short pause added: 'Yes, it's Scythian warfare. It's all vewy well – only not for those who get it in the neck. So you are Pwince Andwew Bolkonsky?' He swayed his head. 'Vewy pleased, Pwince, to make your acquaintance!' he repeated again, smiling sadly, and he again pressed Prince Andrew's hand.

Prince Andrew knew Denisov from what Natasha had told him of her first suitor. The memory carried him sadly and sweetly back to those painful feelings of which he had not thought lately, but which still found place in his soul. Of late he had received so many new and very serious impressions – such as the retreat from Smolensk, his visit to Bald Hills, and the recent news of his father's death – and had experienced so many emotions, that for a long time past those memories had not entered his mind, and now that they did, they did not act on him with nearly their former strength. For Denisov, too, the memories awakened by the name of Bolkonsky belonged to a distant, romantic past, when after supper and after Natasha's singing he had proposed to a little girl of fifteen without realizing what he was doing. He smiled at the recollection of that time and of his love for Natasha, and passed at once to what now interested him passionately and exclusively. This was a plan of campaign he had devised while serving at the outposts during the retreat. He had proposed that plan to Barclay de Tolly and now wished to propose it to Kutuzov. The plan was based on the fact that the French line of operation was too extended, and it proposed that instead of, or concurrently with, action on the front to bar the advance of the French, we should attack their line of communication. He began explaining his plan to Prince Andrew.

'They can't hold all that line. It's impossible. I will undertake to bweak thwough. Give me five hundwed men and I will bweak the line, that's certain! There's only one way – guewilla warfare!'

Denisov rose and began gesticulating as he explained his plan to Bolkonsky. In the midst of his explanation shouts were heard from the army, growing more incoherent and more diffused, mingling with music and songs, and coming from the field where the review was held. Sounds of hoofs and shouts were nearing the village.

'He's coming! He's coming!' shouted a Cossack standing at the gate.

Bolkonsky and Denisov moved to the gate, at which a knot of soldiers (a guard of honour) was standing, and they saw Kutuzov coming down the street mounted on a rather small sorrel horse. A huge suite of generals rode behind him. Barclay was riding almost beside him, and a crowd of officers ran after and around them shouting 'Hurrah!'

His adjutants galloped into the yard before him. Kutuzov was impatiently urging on his horse, which ambled smoothly under his weight, and he raised his hand to his white horseguard's cap with a red band and no peak, nodding his head continually. When he came up to the guard of honour, a fine set of Grenadiers mostly wearing decorations, who were giving him the salute, he looked at them silently and attentively for nearly a minute with the steady gaze of a commander and then turned to the crowd of generals and officers surrounding him. Suddenly his face assumed a subtle expression, he shrugged his shoulders with an air of perplexity.

'And with such fine fellows to retreat and retreat! Well, good-bye, General,' he added, and rode into the yard past Prince Andrew and Denisov.

'Hurrah! hurrah! hurrah!' shouted those behind him.

Since Prince Andrew had last seen him Kutuzov had grown still more corpulent, flaccid, and fat. But the bleached eyeball, the scar, and the familiar weariness of his expression were still the same. He was wearing the white horseguard's cap and a military over-coat with a whip hanging over his shoulder by a thin strap. He sat heavily and swayed limply on his brisk little horse.

'Whew ... whew ... whew!' he whistled just audibly as he rode into the yard. His face expressed the relief of relaxed strain felt by a man who means to rest after a ceremony. He drew his left foot out of the stirrup and, lurching with his whole body and puckering his face with the effort, raised it with difficulty onto the saddle, leaned on his knee, groaned, and slipped down into the arms of the Cossacks and adjutants who stood ready to assist him.

He pulled himself together, looked round screwing up his eyes, glanced at Prince Andrew and, evidently not recognizing him, moved with his waddling gait to the porch. 'Whew ... whew ... whew!' he whistled, and again glanced at Prince Andrew. As often occurs with old men, it was only after some seconds that the impression produced by Prince Andrew's face linked itself up with Kutuzov's remembrance of his personality.

'Ah, how do you do, my dear Prince? How do you do, my dear boy? Come along...' said he glancing wearily round, and he stepped onto the porch which creaked under his weight.

He unbuttoned his coat and sat down on a bench in the porch.

'And how's your father?'

'I received news of his death yesterday,' replied Prince Andrew abruptly.

Kutuzov looked at him with eyes wide open with dismay, and then took off his cap and crossed himself:

'May the kingdom of Heaven be his! God's will be done to us all!' He sighed deeply, his whole chest heaving, and was silent for awhile. 'I loved him and respected him, and sympathize with you with all my heart.'

He embraced Prince Andrew, pressing him to his fat breast, and for some time did not let him go. When he released him Prince Andrew saw that Kutuzov's flabby lips were trembling and that tears were in his eyes. He sighed and pressed on the bench with both hands to raise himself.

'Come! Come with me, we'll have a talk,' said he.

But at that moment Denisov, no more intimidated by his superiors than by the enemy, came with jingling spurs up the steps of the porch, despite the angry whispers of the adjutants who tried to stop him. Kutuzov, his hands still pressed on the seat, glanced at him glumly. Denisov, having given his name, announced that he had to communicate to his Serene Highness a matter of great importance for their country's welfare. Kutuzov looked wearily at him, and lifting his hands with a gesture of annoyance folded them across his stomach repeating the words: 'For our country's welfare? Well, what is it? Speak!' Denisov blushed like a girl (it was strange to see the colour rise in that shaggy, bibulous, time-worn face) and boldly began to expound his plan of cutting the enemy's lines of communication between Smolensk and Vyazma. Denisov came from those parts and knew the country well. His plan seemed decidedly a good one, especially from the strength of conviction with which he spoke. Kutuzov looked down at his own legs, occasionally glancing at the door of the adjoining hut as if expecting something unpleasant to emerge from it. And from that hut, while Denisov was speaking, a general with a portfolio under his arm really did appear.

'What?' said Kutuzov, in the midst of Denisov's explanations, 'are you ready so soon?'

'Ready, your Serene Highness,' replied the general.

Kutuzov swayed his head, as much as to say: 'How is one man to deal with it all?' and again listened to Denisov.

'I give my word of honour as a Wussian officer,' said Denisov, 'that I can bweak Napoleon's line of communication!'

'What relation are you to Intendant-General Kiril Andreevich Denisov?' asked Kutuzov, interrupting him.

'He is my uncle, your Serene Highness.'

'Ah, we were friends,' said Kutuzov cheerfully. 'All right, all right, friend, stay here at the staff and to-morrow we'll have a talk.'

With a nod to Denisov he turned away and put out his hand for the papers Konovnitsyn had brought him.

'Would not your Serene Highness like to come inside?' said the general on duty in a discontented voice, 'the plans must be examined and several papers have to be signed.'

An adjutant came out and announced that everything was in readiness within. But Kutuzov evidently did not wish to enter that room till he was disengaged. He made a grimace ...

'No, tell them to bring a small table out here, my dear boy. I'll look at them here,' said he. 'Don't go away,' he added turning to Prince Andrew, who remained in the porch and listened to the general's report.

While this was being given, Prince Andrew heard the whisper of a woman's voice and the rustle of a silk dress behind the door. Several times on glancing that way he noticed behind that door a plump, rosy, handsome woman in a pink dress with a lilac silk kerchief on her head, holding a dish and evidently awaiting the entrance of the commander-in-chief. Kutuzov's adjutant whispered to Prince Andrew that this was the wife of the priest whose home it was, and that she intended to offer his Serene Highness bread and salt.* 'Her husband has welcomed his Serene Highness with the cross at the church, and she intends to welcome him in the house ... She's very pretty,' added the adjutant with a smile. At those words Kutuzov looked round. He was listening to the general's report – which consisted chiefly of a criticism of the position at Tsarevo-Zaymishche – as he had listened to Denisov, and seven years previously had listened to the discussion at the Austerlitz council of war. He evidently listened only because he had ears which, though there was a piece of tow in one of them, could not help hearing; but it was evident that nothing the general could say would surprise or even interest him, that he knew all that would be said beforehand, and heard it all only because he had to, as one has to listen to the chanting of a service of prayer. All that Denisov had said was clever and to the point. What the general was saying was even more clever and to the point, but it was evident that Kutuzov despised knowledge and cleverness, and knew of something else that would decide the matter – something independent of cleverness and knowledge. Prince Andrew watched the commander-in-chief's face attentively, and the only expression he could see there was one of boredom, curiosity as to the meaning of the feminine whispering behind the door, and a desire to observe propriety. It was evident that Kutuzov despised cleverness and learning and even the patriotic feeling shown by Denisov, but despised them not because of his own intellect, feelings, or knowledge – he did not try to display any of these – but because of something else. He despised them because of his old age and experience of life. The only instruction Kutuzov gave of his own accord during that report referred to looting by the Russian troops. At the end of the report the general put before him for signature a paper relating to the recovery of payment from army commanders for green oats mown down by the soldiers, when landowners lodged petitions for compensation.

After hearing the matter, Kutuzov smacked his lips together and shook his head.

'Into the stove . . . into the fire with it! I tell you once for all, my dear fellow,' said he, 'into the fire with all such things! Let them cut the crops and burn wood to their hearts' content. I don't order it or allow it, but I don't exact compensation either. One can't get on without it. "When wood is chopped, the chips will fly."' He looked at the paper again. 'Oh, this German precision!' he muttered, shaking his head.

16

'WELL, that's all!' said Kutuzov as he signed the last of the documents, and rising heavily and smoothing out the folds in his fat white neck he moved towards the door with a more cheerful expression.

The priest's wife, flushing rosy red, caught up the dish she had not managed to present at the right moment after all, though she had so long been preparing for it, and with a low bow offered it to Kutuzov.

He screwed up his eyes, smiled, lifted her chin with his hand and said:

'Ah, what a beauty! Thank you, sweetheart!'

He took some gold pieces from his trouser pocket and put them on the dish for her. 'Well, my dear, and how are we getting on?' he asked, moving to the door of the room assigned to him. The priest's wife smiled, and with dimples in her rosy cheeks followed him into the room. The adjutant came out to the porch and asked Prince Andrew to lunch with him. Half an hour later Prince Andrew was again called to Kutuzov. He found him reclining in an arm-chair, still in the same unbuttoned overcoat. He had in his hand a French book which he closed as Prince Andrew entered, marking the place with a knife. Prince Andrew saw by the cover that it was *Les Chevaliers du Cygne* by Madame de Genlis.

'Well, sit down, sit down here. Let's have a talk,' said Kutuzov.

'It's sad, very sad. But remember, my dear fellow, that I am a father to you, a second father . . .'

Prince Andrew told Kutuzov all he knew of his father's death, and what he had seen at Bald Hills when he passed through it.

'What . . . what they have brought us to!' Kutuzov suddenly cried in an agitated voice, evidently picturing vividly to himself from Prince Andrew's story the condition Russia was in. 'But give me time, give me time!' he said with a grim look evidently not wishing to continue this agitating conversation, and added: 'I sent for you to keep you with me.'

'I thank your Serene Highness, but fear I am no longer fit for the staff,' replied Prince Andrew with a smile which Kutuzov noticed.

Kutuzov glanced inquiringly at him.

'But above all,' added Prince Andrew, 'I have grown used to my regiment, am fond of the officers, and I fancy the men also like me. I should be sorry to leave the regiment. If I decline the honour of being with you, believe me . . .'

A shrewd, kindly, yet subtly derisive expression lit up Kutuzov's podgy face. He cut Bolkonsky short.

'I am sorry, for I need you. But you're right, you're right! It's not here that men are needed. Advisers are always plentiful, but men are not. The regiments would not be what they are if the would-be advisers served there as yóu do. I remember you at Austerlitz . . . I remember, yes, I remember you with the standard!' said Kutuzov, and a flush of pleasure suffused Prince Andrew's face at this recollection.

Taking his hand and drawing him downwards, Kutuzov offered his cheek to be kissed, and again Prince Andrew noticed tears in the old man's eyes. Though Prince Andrew knew that Kutuzov's tears came easily and that he was particularly tender to and considerate of him from a wish to show sympathy with his loss, yet this reminder of Austerlitz was both pleasant and flattering to him.

'Go your way and God be with you. I know your path is the path of honour!' He paused. 'I missed you at Bucharest, but I needed someone to send.' And changing the subject, Kutuzov began to speak of the Turkish war and the peace that had been concluded. 'Yes, I have been much blamed,' he said, 'both for that war and the peace . . . but everything came at the right time. *Tout vient à point à celui qui sait attendre.* And there were as many advisers there as here . . .' he went on, returning to the subject of 'advisers' which evidently occupied him. 'Ah, those advisers,' said he. 'If we had listened to them all we should not have made peace with Turkey and should not have been through with that war. Everything in haste, but more haste less speed. Kamensky would have been lost if he had not died. He stormed fortresses with thirty thousand men. It is not difficult to capture a fortress but it is difficult to win a campaign. For that, not storming and attacking but *patience and time* are wanted. Kamensky sent soldiers to Rustchuk, but I only employed these two things and took more fortresses than Kamensky and made the Turks eat horse-flesh!' He swayed his head. 'And the French shall too, believe me,' he went on, growing warmer and beating his chest, 'I'll make them eat horse-flesh!' And tears again dimmed his eyes.

'But shan't we have to accept battle?' remarked Prince Andrew.

'We shall if everybody wants it, it can't be helped . . . But believe me, my dear boy, there is nothing stronger than those two, *patience and time*, they will do it all. But the advisers *n'entendent pas de cette oreille, voilà le mal.* Some want a thing – others don't. What's one to do?' he asked, evidently expecting an answer. 'Well, what do you want us to do?' he repeated and his eye shone with a deep, shrewd look. 'I'll tell you what to do,' he continued, as Prince Andrew still did not reply: 'I will tell you what to do, and what I do. *Dans le doute, mon cher,*' he paused, '*abstiens-toi;*' he articulated the French proverb deliberately.

'Well, good-bye, my dear fellow; remember that with all my heart I share your sorrow, and that for you I am not a Serene Highness, nor a prince, nor a commander-in-chief, but a father! If you want anything, come straight to me. Good-bye, my dear boy.'

Again he embraced and kissed Prince Andrew, but before the latter had left the room Kutuzov gave a sigh of relief and went on with his unfinished novel, *Les Chevaliers du Cygne,* by Madame de Genlis.

Prince Andrew could not have explained how or why it was, but after that interview with Kutuzov he went back to his regiment reassured as to the general course of affairs and as to the man to whom it had been entrusted. The more he realized the absence of all personal motive in that old man – in whom there seemed to remain only the habit of passions, and in place of an intellect (grouping events and drawing conclusions) only the capacity calmly to contemplate the course of events – the more reassured he was that everything would be as it should. 'He will not bring in any plan of his own. He will not devise or undertake anything,' thought Prince Andrew, 'but he will hear everything, remember everything, and put everything in its place. He will not hinder anything useful nor allow anything harmful. He understands that there is something stronger and more important than

798

his own will – the inevitable course of events, and he can see them and grasp their significance, and seeing that significance can refrain from meddling and renounce his personal wish directed to something else. And above all,' thought Prince Andrew, 'one believes in him because he's Russian, despite the novel by Genlis and the French proverbs, and because his voice shook when he said: "What they have brought us to!" and had a sob in it when he said he would "make them eat horse-flesh!"'

On such feelings, more or less dimly shared by all, the unanimity and general approval were founded with which, despite court influences, the popular choice of Kutuzov as commander-in-chief was received.

17

AFTER the Emperor had left Moscow, life flowed on there in its usual course, and its course was so very usual that it was difficult to remember the recent days of patriotic elation and ardour, hard to believe that Russia was really in danger and that the members of the English Club were also sons of the Fatherland ready to sacrifice everything for it. The one thing that recalled the patriotic fervour everyone had displayed during the Emperor's stay was the call for contributions of men and money, a necessity that, as soon as the promises had been made, assumed a legal, official form and became unavoidable.

With the enemy's approach to Moscow the Moscovites' view of their situation did not grow more serious but on the contrary became even more frivolous, as always happens with people who see a great danger approaching. At the approach of danger there are always two voices that speak with equal power in the human soul: one very reasonably tells a man to consider the nature of the danger and the means of escaping it; the other, still more reasonably, says that it is too depressing and painful to think of the danger since it is not in man's power to foresee everything and avert the general course of events, and it is therefore better to disregard what is painful till it comes, and to think about what is pleasant. In solitude a man generally listens to the first voice, but in society to the second. So it was now with the inhabitants of Moscow. It was long since people had been as gay in Moscow as that year.

Rostopchin's broadsheets, headed by woodcuts of a drink-shop, a potman, and a Moscow burgher called Karpushka Chigirin, 'who – having been a militiaman and having had rather too much at *the pub – heard that Napoleon wished to come to Moscow, grew angry, abused the French in very bad language, came out of the drink-shop and, under the sign of the eagle, began to address the assembled people',* were read and discussed, together with the latest of Vasili Lvovich Pushkin's *bouts-rimés.**

In the corner room at the club, members gathered to read these broadsheets and some liked the way Karpushka jeered at the French,* saying: *'They will swell up with Russian cabbage, burst with our buck-wheat porridge, and choke themselves with cabbage-soup. They are all dwarfs, and one peasant woman will toss three of them with a hay-fork.'* Others did not like that tone and said it was stupid and vulgar. It was said that Rostopchin had expelled all Frenchmen and even all foreigners from Moscow, and that there had been some spies and agents of Napoleon among them, but this was told chiefly to introduce Rostopchin's witty remark on that occasion. The foreigners were deported to Nizhny by boat, and Rostopchin had said to them in French: *'Rentrez en vous-même, entrez dans la barque et n'en faites pas une barque de Charon.'* There was talk of all the government offices having been already removed from Moscow, and to this Shinshin's witticism was added – that for that alone Moscow ought to be grateful to Napoleon. It was said that Mamonov's regiment would cost him eight hundred thousand rubles, and that Bezukhov had spent even more on his, but the best thing about Bezukhov's action was that he himself was going to don a uniform and ride at the head of his regiment without charging anything for the show.

'You don't spare anyone,' said Julie Drubetskaya as she collected and pressed together a bunch of ravelled lint with her thin, beringed fingers.

Julie was preparing to leave Moscow next day and was giving a farewell soirée.

'Bezukhov est ridicule, but he is so kind and good-natured. What pleasure is there to be so *caustique?'*

'A forfeit!' cried a young man in militia uniform, whom Julie called *'mon chevalier',* and who was going with her to Nizhny.

In Julie's set, as in many other circles in Moscow, it had been agreed that they would speak nothing but Russian, and that those who made a slip and spoke French should pay fines to the Committee of Voluntary Contributions.

'Another forfeit for a Gallicism,' said a Russian writer who was present. ' "What pleasure is there to be" is not Russian!'

'You spare no one,' continued Julie to the young man without heeding the author's remark.

'For *caustique* – I am guilty and will pay, and I am prepared to pay again for the pleasure of telling you the truth. For Gallicisms I won't be responsible,' she remarked, turning to the author: 'I have neither the money nor the time, like Prince Galitsin, to engage a master to teach me Russian!'

'Ah, here he is!' she added. '*Quand on* ... No, no,' she said to the militia officer, 'you won't catch me. Speak of the sun and you see its rays!' and she smiled amiably at Pierre. 'We were just talking of you,' she said with the facility in lying natural to a society woman. 'We were saying that your regiment would be sure to be better than Mamonov's.'

'Oh, don't talk to me of my regiment,' replied Pierre, kissing his hostess's hand and taking a seat beside her. 'I am so sick of it.'

'You will, of course, command it yourself?' said Julie, directing a sly, sarcastic glance towards the militia officer.

The latter in Pierre's presence had ceased to be caustic, and his face expressed perplexity as to what Julie's smile might mean. In spite of his absent-mindedness and good nature, Pierre's personality immediately checked any attempt to ridicule him to his face.

'No,' said Pierre, with a laughing glance at his big, stout body. 'I should make too good a target for the French, besides I am afraid I should hardly be able to climb onto a horse.'

Among those whom Julie's guests happened to choose to gossip about were the Rostovs.

'I hear that their affairs are in a very bad way,' said Julie. 'And he is so unreasonable, the count himself I mean. The Razumovskys wanted to buy his house and his estate near Moscow, but it drags on and on. He asks too much.'

'No, I think the sale will come off in a few days,' said someone. 'Though it is madness to buy anything in Moscow now.'

'Why?' asked Julie. 'You don't think Moscow is in danger?'

'Then why are you leaving?'

'I? What a question! I am going because ... well, because everyone is going; and besides – I am not Joan of Arc, or an Amazon.'

'Well, of course, of course! Let me have some more strips of linen.'

'If he manages the business properly he will be able to pay off all his debts,' said the militia officer, speaking of Rostov.

'A kindly old man but not up to much. And why do they stay on so long in Moscow? They meant to leave for the country long ago. Natalie is quite well again now, isn't she?' Julie asked Pierre with a knowing smile.

'They are waiting for their younger son,' Pierre replied. 'He joined Obolensky's Cossacks and went to Belaya Tserkov where the regiment is being formed. But now they have had him transferred to my regiment and are expecting him every day. The count wanted to leave long ago, but the countess won't on any account leave Moscow till her son returns.'

'I met them the day before yesterday at the Arkharovs'. Natalie has recovered her looks and is brighter. She sang a song. How easily some people get over everything!'

'Get over what?' inquired Pierre looking displeased.

Julie smiled.

'You know, Count, such knights as you are only found in Madame de Souza's novels.'

'What knights? What do you mean?' demanded Pierre blushing.

'Oh, come, my dear Count! *C'est la fable de tout Moscou. Je vous admire, ma parole d'honneur.'*

'Forfeit, forfeit!' cried the militia officer.

'All right, one can't talk – how tiresome!'

'What is "the talk of all Moscow"?' Pierre asked angrily, rising to his feet.

'Come now, Count, you know!'

'I don't know anything about it,' said Pierre.

'I know you were friendly with Natalie, and so . . . but I was always more friendly with Vera – that dear Vera.'

'No, madame!' Pierre continued in a tone of displeasure, 'I have not taken on myself the role of Natalie Rostova's knight at all, and have not been to their house for nearly a month. But I cannot understand the cruelty . . .'

'*Qui s'excuse, s'accuse,*' said Julie, smiling and waving the lint triumphantly, and to have the last word she promptly changed the subject. 'Do you know what I heard to-day? Poor Mary Bolkonskaya arrived in Moscow yesterday. Do you know that she has lost her father?'

'Really? Where is she? I should very much like to see her,' said Pierre.

'I spent the evening with her yesterday. She is going to their estate near Moscow either to-day or to-morrow morning, with her nephew.'

'Well, and how is she?' asked Pierre.

'She is well, but sad. But do you know who rescued her? It is quite a romance. Nicholas Rostov. She was surrounded, and they wanted to kill her, and had wounded some of her people. He rushed in and saved her . . .'

'Another romance,' said the militia officer. 'Really this general flight has been arranged to get all the old maids married off. Catiche is one and Princess Bolkonskaya another.'

'Do you know, I really believe she is *un petit peu amoureuse du jeune homme?*'

'Forfeit, forfeit, forfeit!'

'But how could one say that in Russian?'

18

WHEN Pierre returned home he was handed two of Rostopchin's broadsheets that had been brought that day.

The first declared that the report that Count Rostopchin had forbidden people to leave Moscow was false; on the contrary he was glad that ladies and tradesmen's wives were leaving the city. 'There will be less panic and less gossip,' ran the broadsheet, 'but I will stake my life on it that that scoundrel will not enter Moscow.' These words showed Pierre clearly for the first time that the French would enter Moscow. The second broadsheet stated that our headquarters were at Vyazma, that Count Wittgenstein had defeated the French,* but that as many of the inhabitants of Moscow wished to be armed, weapons were ready for them at the arsenal: sabres, pistols, and muskets, which could be had at a low price. The tone of this proclamation was not as jocose as in the former Chigirin talks. Pierre pondered over these broadsheets. Evidently the terrible storm-cloud he had desired with the whole strength of his soul, but which yet aroused involuntary horror in him, was drawing near.

'Shall I join the army and enter the service or wait?' he asked himself for the hundredth time. He took a pack of cards that lay on the table and began to lay them out for a game of patience.

'If this patience comes out,' he said to himself after shuffling the cards, holding them in his hand and lifting his head, 'if it comes out, it means ... what does it mean?'

He had not decided what it should mean when he heard the voice of the eldest princess at the door asking whether she might come in.

'Then it will mean that I must go to the army,' said Pierre to himself. 'Come in, come in!' he added to the princess.

Only the eldest princess, the one with the stony face and long waist, was still living in Pierre's house. The two younger ones had both married.

'Excuse my coming to you, cousin,' she said in a reproachful and agitated voice. 'You know some decision must be come to. What is going to happen? Everyone has left Moscow and the people are rioting. How is it that we are staying on?'

'On the contrary things seem satisfactory, *ma cousine*,' said Pierre in the bantering tone he habitually adopted towards her, always feeling uncomfortable in the role of her benefactor.

'Satisfactory, indeed! Very satisfactory! Barbara Ivanovna told me to-day how our troops are distinguishing themselves. It certainly does them credit! And the people, too, are quite mutinous – they no longer obey, even my maid has taken to being rude. At this rate they will soon begin beating us. One can't walk in the streets. But, above all, the French will be here any day now, so what are we waiting for? I ask just one thing of you, cousin,' she went on, 'arrange for me to be taken to Petersburg. Whatever I may be, I can't live under Bonaparte's rule.'

'Oh, come, *ma cousine*! Where do you get your information from? On the contrary . . .'

'I won't submit to your Napoleon! Others may if they please . . . If you don't want to do this . . .'

'But I will, I'll give the order at once.'

The princess was apparently vexed at not having any one to be angry with. Muttering to herself, she sat down on a chair.

'But you have been misinformed,' said Pierre. 'Everything is quiet in the city and there is not the slightest danger. See! I've just been reading . . .' He showed her the broadsheet. 'Count Rostopchin writes that he will stake his life on it that the enemy will not enter Moscow.'

'Oh, that count of yours!' said the princess malevolently. 'He is a hypocrite, a rascal who has himself roused the people to riot. Didn't he write in those idiotic broadsheets that anyone "whoever it might be, should be dragged to the lock-up by his hair?" (How silly!) "And honour and glory to whoever captures him," he says. This is what his cajolery has brought us to! Barbara Ivanovna told me the mob nearly killed her because she said something in French.'

'Oh, but it's so . . . You take everything so to heart,' said Pierre, and began laying out his cards for patience.

Although that patience did come out, Pierre did not join the army, but remained in deserted Moscow ever in the same state of agitation, irresolution, and alarm, yet at the same time joyfully expecting something terrible.

Next day towards evening the princess set off, and Pierre's head steward came to inform him that the money needed for the equipment of his regiment could not be found without selling one of the estates. In general the head steward made out to Pierre that his project of raising a regiment would ruin him. Pierre listened to him, scarcely able to repress a smile.

'Well then, sell it,' said he. 'What's to be done? I can't draw back now!'

The worse everything became, especially his own affairs, the better was Pierre pleased and the more evident was it that the catastrophe he expected was approaching. Hardly anyone he knew was left in town. Julie had gone, and so had Princess Mary. Of his intimate friends only the Rostovs remained, but he did not go to see them.

To distract his thoughts he drove that day to the village of Vorontsovo to see the great balloon Leppich was constructing* to destroy the foe, and a trial balloon that was to go up next day. The balloon was not yet ready, but Pierre learnt that it was being constructed by the Emperor's desire. The Emperor had written to Count Rostopchin as follows:

'As soon as Leppich is ready, get together a crew of reliable and intelligent men for his car and send a courier to General Kutuzov to let him know. I have informed him of the matter.

'Please impress upon Leppich to be very careful where he descends for the first time, that he may not make a mistake and fall into the enemy's hands. It is essential for him to combine his movements with those of the commander-in-chief.'

On his way home from Vorontsovo, as he was passing the Bolotnoe Place, Pierre, seeing a large crowd round the Lobnoe Place,* stopped and got out of his trap. A French cook accused of being a spy was being flogged. The flogging was only just over, and the executioner was releasing from the flogging-bench a stout man with red whiskers, in blue stockings and a green jacket, who was moaning piteously. Another criminal, thin and pale, stood near. Judging by their faces they were both Frenchmen. With a frightened and suffering look resembling that on the thin French-man's face, Pierre pushed his way in through the crowd.

'What is it? Who is it? What is it for?' he kept asking.

But the attention of the crowd – officials, burghers, shopkeepers, peasants, and women in cloaks and in pelisses – was so eagerly centred on what was passing in Lobnoe Place that no one answered him. The stout man rose, frowned, shrugged his shoulders, and evidently trying to appear firm began to pull on his jacket without looking about him, but suddenly his lips trembled and he began to cry, in the way full-blooded grown-up men cry, though angry with himself for doing so. In the crowd people began talking loudly, to stifle their feelings of pity as it seemed to Pierre.

'He's cook to some prince.'

'Eh, mounseer, Russian sauce seems to be sour to a Frenchman ...

sets his teeth on edge!' said a wrinkled clerk who was standing behind Pierre, when the Frenchman began to cry.

The clerk glanced round, evidently hoping that his joke would be appreciated. Some people began to laugh, others continued to watch in dismay the executioner who was undressing the other man.

Pierre choked, his face puckered, and he turned hastily away, went back to his trap muttering something to himself as he went, and took his seat. As they drove along he shuddered, and exclaimed several times so audibly that the coachman asked him:

'What is your pleasure?'

'Where are you going?' shouted Pierre to the man, who was driving to Lubyanka Street.

'To the Governor's, as you ordered,' answered the coachman.

'Fool! Idiot!' shouted Pierre, abusing his coachman – a thing he rarely did. 'Home, I told you! And drive faster, blockhead!' 'I must get away this very day,' he murmured to himself.

At the sight of the tortured Frenchman and the crowd surrounding the Lobnoe Place, Pierre had so definitely made up his mind that he could no longer remain in Moscow, and would leave for the army that very day, that it seemed to him that either he had told the coachman this or that the man ought to have known it of himself.

On reaching home Pierre gave orders to Evstafey – his head coachman who knew everything, could do anything, and was known to all Moscow – that he would leave that night for the army at Mozhaysk, and that his saddle-horses should be sent there. This could not all be arranged that day, so on Evstafey's representation Pierre had to put off his departure till next day to allow time for the relay horses to be sent on in advance.

On the 24th the weather cleared up after a spell of rain, and after dinner Pierre left Moscow. When changing horses that night, in Perkhushkovo, he learnt that there had been a great battle that evening. (This was the battle of Shevardino.) He was told that there in Perkhushkovo the earth had trembled from the firing, but nobody could answer his questions as to who had won. At dawn next day Pierre was approaching Mozhaysk.

Every house in Mozhaysk had soldiers quartered in it, and at the hostel where Pierre was met by his groom and coachman there was no room to be had. It was full of officers.

Everywhere in Mozhaysk and beyond it troops were stationed or on the march. Cossacks, foot and horse soldiers, wagons, caissons and cannon, were everywhere. Pierre pushed forward as fast as he could, and the farther he left Moscow behind and the deeper he plunged into that sea of troops the more was he overcome by restless agitation and a new and joyful feeling he had not experienced before. It was a feeling akin to what he had felt at the Sloboda Palace during the Emperor's visit – a sense of the necessity of undertaking something and sacrificing something. He now experienced a glad consciousness that everything that constitutes men's happiness – the comforts of life, wealth, even life itself – is rubbish it is pleasant to throw away, compared with something ... With what? Pierre could not say, and he did not try to determine for whom and for what he felt such particular delight in sacrificing everything. He was not occupied with the question of what to sacrifice for, the fact of sacrificing in itself afforded him a new and joyous sensation.

19

On the 24th of August the battle of the Shevardino Redoubt was fought, on the 25th not a shot was fired by either side, and on the 26th the battle of Borodino itself took place.

Why and how were the battles at Shevardino and Borodino given and accepted? Why was the battle of Borodino fought? There was not the least sense in it for either the French or the Russians. Its immediate result for the Russians was, and was bound to be, that we were brought nearer to the destruction of Moscow – which we feared more than anything in the world; and for the French its immediate result was that they were brought nearer to the destruction of their whole army – which they feared more than anything in the world. What the result must be was quite obvious, and yet Napoleon offered and Kutuzov accepted that battle.

If the commanders had been guided by reason it would seem that it must have been obvious to Napoleon that by advancing thirteen hundred miles and giving battle with a probability of losing a quarter of his army, he was advancing to certain destruction, and it must have been equally clear to Kutuzov that by accepting battle and risking the loss of a quarter of his army he would certainly lose Moscow. For Kutuzov this was mathematically clear, as it is that if when playing draughts I have one man less and go on exchanging, I shall certainly lose, and therefore should not exchange. When my opponent has sixteen men and I have fourteen, I am only one-eighth weaker than he, but when I have exchanged thirteen more men he will be three times as strong as I.

Before the battle of Borodino our strength in proportion to the French was approximately as five to six, but after that battle as one to two: that is to say, before the battle we had a hundred thousand against a hundred and twenty thousand, and after the battle fifty thousand against a hundred thousand. Yet the shrewd and experienced Kutuzov accepted the battle, while Napoleon, who was said to be a commander of genius, gave it, losing a quarter of his army and lengthening his lines of communication still more. If it is said that he expected to end the campaign by occupying Moscow, as he had ended a previous campaign by occupying Vienna, there is much evidence to the contrary. Napoleon's historians themselves tell us that from Smolensk onwards he wished to stop, knew the danger of his extended position, and knew that the occupation of Moscow would not be the end of the campaign, for he had seen at Smolensk the state in which Russian towns were left to him, and had not received a single reply to his repeated announcements of his wish to negotiate.

In giving and accepting battle at Borodino Kutuzov acted involuntarily and irrationally. But later on, to fit what had occurred, the historians provided cunningly devised evidence of the foresight and genius of the generals who of all the blind tools of history were the most enslaved and involuntary.

The ancients have left us model heroic poems in which the heroes furnish the whole interest of the story, and we are still unable to accustom ourselves to the fact that for our epoch histories of that kind are meaningless.

On the other question, how the battle of Borodino and the preceding battle of Shevardino were fought, there also exists a definite and well-known, but quite false, conception. All the historians describe the affair as follows:

The Russian army, they say, in its retreat from Smolensk sought out for itself the best position for a general engagement and found such a position at Borodino.

The Russians, they say, fortified this position in advance on the left of the high road (from Moscow to Smolensk) and almost at a right angle to it, from Borodino to Utitsa, at the very place where the battle was fought.

In front of this position, they say, a fortified outpost was set up on the Shevardino mound to observe the enemy. On the 24th, we are told, Napoleon attacked this advanced post and took it, and on the 26th attacked the whole Russian army, which was in position on the field of Borodino.

So the histories say, and it is all quite wrong, as anyone who cares to look into the matter can easily convince himself.

The Russians did not seek out the best position but on the contrary during the retreat passed many positions better than

Borodino. They did not stop at any one of these positions because Kutuzov did not wish to occupy a position he had not himself chosen, because the popular demand for a battle had not yet expressed itself strongly enough, and because Miloradovich had not yet arrived with the militia, and for many other reasons. The fact is that other positions they had passed were stronger, and that the position at Borodino (the one where the battle was fought), far from being strong, was no more a *position* than any other spot one might find in the Russian Empire by sticking a pin into the map at hazard.

Not only did the Russians not fortify the position on the field of Borodino to the left of, and at a right angle to, the high road (that is, the position on which the battle took place) but never till the 25th of August 1812 did they think that a battle might be fought there. This is shown first by the fact that there were no entrenchments there by the 25th, and that those begun on the 25th and 26th were not completed, and secondly, by the position of the Shevardino Redoubt. That redoubt was quite senseless in front of the position where the battle was accepted. Why was it more strongly fortified than any other post? And why were all efforts exhausted and six thousand men sacrificed to defend it till late at night on the 24th? A Cossack patrol would have sufficed to observe the enemy. Thirdly, as proof that the position on which the battle was fought had not been foreseen and that the Shevardino Redoubt was not an advanced post of that position, we have the fact that up to the 25th Barclay de Tolly and Bagration were convinced that the Shevardino Redoubt was the *left flank* of the position, and that Kutuzov himself in his report written in hot haste after the battle, speaks of the Shevardino Redoubt as the *left flank* of the position. It was much later, when reports on the battle of Borodino were written at leisure, that the incorrect and extraordinary statement was invented (probably to justify the mistakes of a commander-in-chief who had to be represented as infallible) that the Shevardino Redoubt was an *advanced* post – whereas in reality it was simply a fortified point on the left flank – and that the battle of Borodino was fought by us on an entrenched position previously selected, whereas it was fought on a quite unexpected spot which was almost unentrenched.

The case was evidently this: a position was selected along the river Kolocha – which crosses the high road not at a right angle but at an acute angle – so that the left flank was at Shevardino, the right flank near the village of Novoe, and the centre at Borodino at the confluence of the rivers Kolocha and Voyna.

To any one who looks at the field of Borodino without thinking of how the battle was actually fought, this position, protected by the river Kolocha, presents itself as obvious for an army whose object was to prevent an enemy from advancing along the Smolensk road to Moscow.

Napoleon, riding to Valuevo on the 24th, did not see (as the history books say he did) the position of the Russians from Utitsa to Borodino (he could not have seen that position because it did not exist) nor did he see an advanced post of the Russian army, but while pursuing the Russian rearguard he came upon the left flank of the Russian position – at the Shevardino Redoubt – and unexpectedly for the Russians moved his army across the Kolocha. And the Russians, not having time to begin a general engagement, withdrew their left wing from the position they had intended to occupy and took up a new position which had not been foreseen and was not fortified. By crossing to the other side of the Kolocha to the left of the high road, Napoleon shifted the whole forthcoming battle from right to left (looking from the Russian side) and transferred it to the plain between Utitsa, Semënovsk, and Borodino – a plain no more advantageous as a position than any other plain in Russia – and there the whole battle of the 26th of August took place. A rough outline of the plan of the intended battle and of the battle that actually took place is given (see Map 5).

Had Napoleon not ridden out on the evening of the 24th to the Kolocha, and had he not then ordered an immediate attack on the redoubt but had begun the attack next morning, no one would have doubted that the Shevardino Redoubt was the left flank of our position, and the battle would have taken place where we expected it. In that case we should probably have defended the Shevardino Redoubt – our left flank – still more obstinately. We should have attacked Napoleon in the centre or on the right, and the general engagement would have taken place on the 25th, on the position we intended and had fortified. But as the attack on our left flank took place in the evening after the retreat of our rearguard (that is, immediately after the fight at Gridnëva), and as the Russian commanders did not wish, or were not in time, to begin a general engagement then on the evening of the 24th, the first and chief action of the battle of Borodino was already lost on the 24th, and obviously led to the loss of the one fought on the 26th.

After the loss of the Shevardino Redoubt we found ourselves on the morning of the 25th without a position for our left flank, and were forced to bend it back and hastily entrench it where it chanced to be.

But not only was the Russian army on the 26th defended by

weak, unfinished entrenchments, the disadvantage of that position was increased by the fact that the Russian commanders – not having fully realized what had happened, namely, the loss of our position on the left flank and the shifting of the whole field of the forthcoming battle from right to left – maintained their extended position from the village of Novoe to Utitsa, and consequently had to move their forces from right to left during the battle. So it happened that throughout the whole battle the Russians opposed the entire French army launched against our left flank with but half as many men. (Poniatowski's action against Utitsa, and Uvarov's on the right flank against the French, were actions distinct from the main course of the battle.) So the battle of Borodino did not take place at all as (in an effort to conceal our commanders' mistakes even at the cost of diminishing the glory due to the Russian army and people) it has been described. The battle of Borodino was not fought on a chosen and entrenched position with forces only slightly weaker than those of the enemy, but, as a result of the loss of the Shevardino Redoubt, the Russians fought the battle of Borodino on an open and almost unentrenched position, with forces only half as numerous as the French; that is to say, under conditions in which it was not merely unthinkable to fight for ten hours and secure an indecisive result, but unthinkable to keep an army even for three hours from complete disintegration and flight.

20

On the morning of the 25th Pierre was leaving Mozhaysk. At the descent of the high steep hill, down which a winding road led out of the town past the cathedral on the right, where a service was being held and the bells were ringing, Pierre got out of his vehicle and proceeded on foot. Behind him a cavalry regiment was coming down the hill preceded by its singers. Coming up towards him was a train of carts carrying men who had been wounded in the engagement the day before. The peasant drivers, shouting and lashing their horses, kept crossing from side to side. The carts, in each of which three or four wounded soldiers were lying or sitting, jolted over the stones that had been thrown on the steep incline to make it something like a road. The wounded, bandaged with rags, with pale cheeks, compressed lips, and knitted brows, held on to the sides of the carts as they were jostled and jolted against one another. Almost all of them stared with naïve, childlike curiosity at Pierre's white hat and green swallow-tail coat.

Pierre's coachman shouted angrily at the convoy of wounded to keep to one side of the road. The cavalry regiment, as it descended the hill with its singers, surrounded Pierre's carriage and blocked the road. Pierre stopped, being pressed against the side of the cutting in which the road ran. The sunshine from behind the hill did not penetrate into the cutting, and there it was cold and damp, but above Pierre's head was the bright August sunshine and the bells sounded merrily. One of the carts with wounded stopped by the side of the road close to Pierre. The driver in his bast shoes ran panting up to it, placed a stone under one of its tyreless hind wheels, and began arranging the breeching on his little horse, which had stopped.

One of the wounded, an old soldier with a bandaged arm, who was following the cart on foot, caught hold of it with his sound hand and turned to look at Pierre.

'I say, fellow-countryman, will they set us down here or take us on to Moscow?' he asked.

Pierre was so deep in thought that he did not hear the question. He was looking, now at the cavalry regiment that had met the convoy of wounded, now at the cart by which he was standing, in which two wounded men were sitting and one was lying. One of those sitting up in the cart had probably been wounded in the cheek. His whole head was wrapped in rags and one cheek was swollen to the size of a baby's head. His nose and mouth were twisted to one side. This soldier was looking at the cathedral and crossing himself. Another, a young lad, a fair-haired recruit as white as though there was no blood in his thin face, looked at Pierre kindly, with a fixed smile. The third lay prone so that his face was not visible. The cavalry singers were passing close by:

> Ah lost, quite lost . . . is my head so keen,
> Living in a foreign land . . .

they sang their soldiers' dance-song.

As if responding to them, but with a different sort of merriment, the metallic sound of the bells reverberated high above, and the hot rays of the sun bathed the top of the opposite slope with yet another sort of merriment. But beneath the slope, by the cart with the wounded near the panting little nag where Pierre stood, it was damp, sombre, and sad.

The soldier with the swollen cheek looked angrily at the cavalry singers.

'Oh, the coxcombs!' he muttered reproachfully.

'It's not the soldiers only, but I've seen peasants to-day, too . . . The peasants – even they have to go,' said the soldier behind the cart, addressing Pierre with a sad smile. 'No distinctions made nowadays ... They want the whole nation to fall on them – in a word, it's Moscow! They want to make an end of it.'

In spite of the obscurity of the soldier's words Pierre understood what he wanted to say, and nodded approval.

The road was clear again; Pierre descended the hill and drove on.

He kept looking to either side of the road for familiar faces, but only saw everywhere the unfamiliar faces of various military men of different branches of the service, who all looked with astonishment at his white hat and green tail-coat.

Having gone nearly three miles he at last met an acquaintance and eagerly addressed him. This was one of the head army-doctors. He was driving towards Pierre in a covered gig, sitting beside a young surgeon, and on recognizing Pierre he told the Cossack who occupied the driver's seat to pull up.

'Count! Your Excellency, how come you to be here?' asked the doctor.

'Well, you know, I wanted to see ...'

'Yes, yes, there will be something to see ...'

Pierre got out and talked to the doctor, explaining his intention of taking part in the battle.

The doctor advised him to apply direct to Kutuzov.

'Why should you be God knows where, out of sight, during the battle?' he said, exchanging glances with his young companion. 'Anyhow, his Serene Highness knows you and will receive you graciously. That's what you must do.'

The doctor seemed tired and in a hurry.

'You think so? ... Ah, I also wanted to ask you where our position is exactly?' said Pierre.

'The position?' repeated the doctor. 'Well, that's not my line. Drive past Tatarinova, a lot of digging is going on there. Go up the hillock and you'll see.'

'Can one see from there? ... If you would ...'

But the doctor interrupted him and moved towards his gig.

'I would go with you but on my honour I'm up to here' – and he pointed to his throat. 'I'm galloping to the commander of the corps. How do matters stand? ... You know, Count, there'll be a battle to-morrow. Out of an army of a hundred thousand we must expect at least twenty thousand wounded, and we haven't stretchers, or bunks, or dressers, or doctors enough for six thousand. We have ten thousand carts, but we need others things as well – we must manage as best we can!'

The strange thought, that of the thousands of men, young and old, who had stared with merry surprise at his hat (perhaps the very men he had noticed) twenty thousand were inevitably doomed to wounds and death, amazed Pierre.

'They may die to-morrow; why are they thinking of anything but death?' And by some latent sequence of thought the descent of the Mozhaysk hill, the carts with the wounded, the ringing bells, the slanting rays of the sun, and the songs of the cavalry-men, vividly recurred to his mind.

'The cavalry ride to battle and meet the wounded and do not for a moment think of what awaits them, but pass by, winking at the wounded. Yet from among these men twenty thousand are doomed to die, and they wonder at my hat! Strange!' thought Pierre, continuing his way to Tatarinova.

In front of a landowner's house to the left of the road stood carriages, wagons, and crowds of orderlies and sentinels. The com-mander-in-chief was putting up there, but just when Pierre arrived he was not in, and hardly any of the staff were there – they had gone to the church service. Pierre drove on towards Gorky.

When he had ascended the hill and reached the little village street, he saw for the first time peasant militiamen in their white shirts and with crosses on their caps, who, talking and laughing loudly, animated and perspiring, were at work on a huge knoll overgrown with grass to the right of the road.

Some of them were digging, others were wheeling barrow-loads of earth along planks, while others stood about doing nothing.

Two officers were standing on the knoll, directing the men. On seeing these peasants, who were evidently still amused by the novelty of their position as soldiers, Pierre once more thought of the wounded men at Mozhaysk, and understood what the soldier had meant when he said: 'They want the whole nation to fall on them.' The sight of these bearded peasants at work on the battle-field, with their queer, clumsy boots and perspiring necks, and their shirts, opening from the left towards the middle, unfastened, exposing their sunburnt collar-bones, impressed Pierre more strongly with the solemnity and importance of the moment than anything he had yet seen or heard.

21

PIERRE stepped out of his carriage and, passing the toiling militia-men, ascended the knoll from which according to the doctor the battlefield could be seen.

It was about eleven o'clock. The sun shone somewhat to the left and behind him, and brightly lit up the enormous panorama which, rising like an amphitheatre, extended before him in the clear rarefied atmosphere.

From above on the left, bisecting that amphitheatre, wound the Smolensk high road, passing through a village with a white church some five hundred paces in front of the knoll and below it. This was Borodino. Below the village the road crossed the river by a bridge, and winding down and up, rose higher and higher to the village of Valuevo visible about four miles away, where Napoleon was then stationed. Beyond Valuevo the road disappeared into a yellowing forest on the horizon. Far in the distance in that birch and fir forest to the right of the road, the cross and belfry of the Kolochà Monastery gleamed in the sun. Here and there over the whole of that blue expanse, to right and left of the forest and the road, smoking camp-fires could be seen and indefinite masses of troops – ours and the enemy's. The ground to the right – along the course of the Kolocha and Moskva rivers – was broken and hilly. Between the hollows the villages of Bezzubova and Zakharino showed in the distance. On the left the ground was more level; there were fields of grain, and the smoking village of Semënovsk, which had been burnt down, could be seen.

All that Pierre saw was so indefinite that neither the left nor the right side of the field fully satisfied his expectations. Nowhere could he see the battlefield he had expected to find, but only fields, meadows, troops, woods, the smoke of camp-fires, villages, mounds, and streams; and try as he would he could descry no military 'position' in this place which teemed with life, nor could he even distinguish our troops from the enemy's.

'I must ask someone who knows,' he thought, and addressed an officer who was looking with curiosity at his huge unmilitary figure.

'May I ask you,' said Pierre, 'what village that is in front?'

'Burdino, isn't it?' said the officer, turning to a companion.

'Borodino,' the other corrected him.

The officer, evidently glad of an opportunity for a talk, moved up to Pierre.

'Are those our men there?' Pierre inquired.

'Yes, and there further on are the French,' said the officer. 'There they are, there, you can see them.'

'Where? Where?' asked Pierre.

'One can see them with the naked eye . . . Why, there!'

The officer pointed with his hand to the smoke visible on the left beyond the river, and the same stern and serious expression that Pierre had noticed on many of the faces he had met came into his face.

'Ah, so those are the French! And over there?'... Pierre pointed to a knoll on the left, near which some troops could be seen.

'Those are ours.'

'Ah, ours! And there?'... Pierre pointed to another knoll in the distance with a big tree on it, near a village that lay in a hollow where some camp-fires were smoking too, and something black was visible.

'That's *his* again,' said the officer. (It was the Shevardino Redoubt.) 'It was ours yesterday, but now it is *his*.'

'Then how about our position?'

'Our position?' replied the officer with a smile of satisfaction. 'I can tell you quite clearly, because I constructed nearly all our entrenchments. There, you see? There's our centre, at Borodino, just there,' and he pointed to the village in front of them with the white church. 'That's where one crosses the Kolocha. You see down there where the rows of hay are lying in the hollow, there's the bridge. That's our centre. Our right flank is over there' – he pointed sharply to the right, far away in the broken ground – 'That's where the Moskva river is, and we have thrown up three redoubts there, very strong ones. The left flank...' here the officer paused. 'Well, you see, that's difficult to explain... Yesterday our left flank was there at Shevardino, you see, where the oak is, but now we have withdrawn our left wing – now, it is over there, do you see that village and the smoke? That's Semënovsk, yes, there,' he pointed to Raevsky's knoll. 'But the battle will hardly be there. *His* having moved his troops there is only a ruse; *he* will probably pass round to the right of the Moskva. But wherever it may be, many a man will be missing tomorrow!' he remarked.

An elderly sergeant who had approached the officer while he was giving these explanations had waited in silence for him to finish speaking, but at this point evidently not liking the officer's remark, interrupted him.

'Gabions must be sent for,' said he sternly.

The officer appeared abashed, as though he understood that one might think of how many men would be missing to-morrow but ought not to speak of it.

'Well, send number three company again,' the officer replied hurriedly.

'And you, are you one of the doctors?'

'No, I've come on my own,' answered Pierre, and he went down the hill again passing the militiamen.

'Oh, those damned fellows!' muttered the officer, who followed him holding his nose as he ran past the men at work.

'There they are... bringing her, coming... There they are...

They'll be here in a minute . . .' voices were suddenly heard saying; and officers, soldiers, and militiamen began running forward along the road.

A church procession was coming up the hill from Borodino. First along the dusty road came the infantry in ranks, bareheaded and with arms reversed. From behind them came the sound of church singing.

Soldiers and militiamen ran bareheaded past Pierre towards the procession.

'They are bringing her, our Protectress! . . . The Iberian Mother of God!'* someone cried.

'The Smolensk Mother of God,' another corrected him.

The militiamen, both those who had been in the village and those who had been at work on the battery, threw down their spades and ran to meet the church procession. Following the battalion that marched along the dusty road, came priests in their vestments – one little old man in a hood with attendants and singers. Behind them soldiers and officers bore a large, dark-faced icon with an embossed metal cover. This was the icon that had been brought from Smolensk and had since accompanied the army. Behind, before, and on both sides, crowds of militiamen with bared heads walked, ran, and bowed to the ground.

At the summit of the hill they stopped with the icon; the men who had been holding it up by the linen bands attached to it were relieved by others, the chanters relit their censers and service began. The hot rays of the sun beat down vertically, and a fresh soft wind played with the hair of the bared heads and with the ribbons decorating the icon. The singing did not sound loud under the open sky. An immense crowd of bareheaded officers, soldiers, and militiamen surrounded the icon. Behind the priest and a chanter stood the notabilities, on a spot reserved for them. A bald general with a St George's Cross on his neck stood just behind the priest's back, and without crossing himself (he was evidently a German) patiently awaited the end of the service, which he considered it necessary to hear to the end, probably to arouse the patriotism of the Russian people. Another general stood in a martial pose, crossing himself by shaking his hand in front of his chest while looking about him. Standing among the crowd of peasants, Pierre recognized several acquaintances among these notables, but did not look at them – his whole attention was absorbed in watching the serious expression on the faces of the crowd of soldiers and militiamen who were all gazing eagerly at the icon. As soon as the tired chanters, who were singing the service for the twentieth time that day, began lazily and mechanically to sing: 'Save from calamity Thy servants, O Mother of God,' and the priest and deacon chimed in: 'For to Thee under God we all flee as to an inviolable bulwark and protection,' there again kindled in all those faces the same expression of consciousness of the solemnity of the impending moment that Pierre had seen on the faces at the foot of the hill at Mozhaysk, and momentarily on many and many faces he had met that morning; and heads were bowed more frequently and hair tossed back, and sighs and the sound men made as they crossed themselves were heard.

The crowd round the icon suddenly parted, and pressed against Pierre. Someone, a very important personage judging by the haste with which way was made for him, was approaching the icon.

It was Kutuzov, who had been riding round the position and on his way back to Tatarinova had stopped where the service was being held. Pierre recognized him at once by his peculiar figure, which distinguished him from everybody else.

With a long overcoat on his exceedingly stout, round-shouldered body, with uncovered white head and puffy face showing the white ball of the eye he had lost, Kutuzov walked with plunging, swaying gait into the crowd and stopped behind the priest. He crossed himself with an accustomed movement, bent till he touched the ground with his hand, and bowed his white head with a deep sigh. Behind Kutuzov was Bennigsen and the suite. Despite the presence of the commander-in-chief who attracted the attention of all the superior officers, the militiamen and soldiers continued their prayers without looking at him.

When the service was over Kutuzov stepped up to the icon, sank heavily to his knees, bowed to the ground, and for a long time tried vainly to rise, but could not do so on account of his weakness and weight. His white head twitched with the effort. At last he rose, kissed the icon as a child does with naïvely pouting lips, and again bowed till he touched the ground with his hand. The other generals followed his example, then the officers, and after them with excited faces, pressing on one another, crowding, panting, and pushing, scrambled the soldiers and militiamen.

22

STAGGERING amid the crush Pierre looked about him.

'Count Peter Kirilovich! How did you get here?' said a voice.

Pierre looked round. Boris Drubetskoy, brushing his knees with his hand (he had probably soiled them when he, too had knelt before the icon) came up to him smiling. Boris was elegantly dressed, with a slightly martial touch appropriate to a campaign. He wore a long coat, and like Kutuzov had a whip slung across his shoulder.

Meanwhile Kutuzov had reached the village and seated himself in the shade of the nearest house, on a bench which one Cossack had run to fetch and another had hastily covered with a rug. An immense and brilliant suite surrounded him.

The icon was carried further, accompanied by the throng. Pierre stopped some thirty paces from Kutuzov, talking to Boris.

He explained his wish to be present at the battle and to see the position.

'This is what you must do,' said Boris. 'I will do the honours of the camp for you. You will see everything best from where Count Bennigsen will be. I am in attendance on him, you know; I'll mention it to him. But if you want to ride round the position, come along with us. We are just going to the left flank. Then when we get back, do spend the night with me and we'll arrange a game of cards. Of course you know Dmitri Sergeevich? Those are his quarters,' and he pointed to the third house in the village of Gorky.

'But I should like to see the right flank. They say it's very strong,' said Pierre. 'I should like to start from the Moskva river and ride round the whole position.'

'Well, you can do that later, but the chief thing is the left flank.'

'Yes, yes. But where is Prince Bolkonsky's regiment? Can you point it out to me?'

'Prince Andrew's? We shall pass it and I'll take you to him.'

'What about the left flank?' asked Pierre.

'To tell you the truth, between ourselves, God only knows what state our left flank is in,' said Boris, confidentially lowering his voice. 'It is not at all what Count Bennigsen intended. He meant to fortify that knoll quite differently, but . . .' Boris shrugged his shoulders, 'his Serene Highness would not have it, or some one persuaded him. You see . . .' but Boris did not finish, for at that moment Kaysarov, Kutuzov's adjutant, came up to Pierre. 'Ah, Kaysarov!' said Boris, addressing him with an unembarrassed smile, 'I was just trying to explain our position to the Count. It is amazing how his Serene Highness could so foresee the intentions of the French!'

'You mean the left flank?' asked Kaysarov.

'Yes, exactly; the left flank is now extremely strong.'

Though Kutuzov had dismissed all unnecessary men from the staff, Boris had contrived to remain at head-quarters after the changes. He had established himself with Count Bennigsen, who, like all on whom Boris had been in attendance, considered young Prince Drubetskoy an invaluable man.

In the higher command there were two sharply defined parties: Kutuzov's party and that of Bennigsen, the chief of staff. Boris belonged to the latter, and no one else, while showing servile respect to Kutuzov, could so create an impression that the old fellow was not much good, and that Bennigsen managed everything. Now the decisive moment of battle had come when Kutuzov would be destroyed and the power pass to Bennigsen, or even if Kutuzov won the battle it would be felt that everything was done by Bennigsen. In any case many great rewards would have to be given for to-morrow's action, and new men would come to the front. So Boris was full of nervous vivacity all that day.

After Kaysarov, others whom Pierre knew came up to him, and he had not time to reply to all the questions about Moscow that were showered upon him, or to listen to all that was told him. The faces all expressed animation and apprehension, but it seemed to Pierre that the cause of the excitement shown in some of these faces lay chiefly in questions of personal success; his mind, however, was occupied by the different expression he saw on other faces – an expression that spoke not of personal matters but of the universal questions of life and death. Kutuzov noticed Pierre's figure and the group gathered round him.

'Call him to me,' said Kutuzov.

An adjutant told Pierre of his Serene Highness's wish, and Pierre went towards Kutuzov's bench. But a militiaman got there before him. It was Dolokhov.

'How did that fellow get here?' asked Pierre.

'He's a creature that wriggles in anywhere!' was the answer. 'He has been degraded, you know. Now he wants to bob up again. He's been proposing some scheme or other and has crawled into the enemy's piquet line at night . . . He's a brave fellow.'

Pierre took off his hat and bowed respectfully to Kutuzov.

'I concluded that if I reported to your Serene Highness, you might send me away or say that you knew what I was reporting, but then I shouldn't lose anything . . .' Dolokhov was saying.

'Yes, yes.'

'But if I were right, I should be rendering a service to my Fatherland for which I am ready to die.'

'Yes, yes.'

'And should your Serene Highness require a man who will not spare his skin, please think of me . . . Perhaps I may prove useful to your Serene Highness.'

'Yes ... Yes ...' Kutuzov repeated, his laughing eye narrowing more and more as he looked at Pierre.

Just then Boris, with his courtier-like adroitness, stepped up to Pierre's side near Kutuzov, and in a most natural manner, without raising his voice, said to Pierre as though continuing an interrupted conversation:

'The militia have put on clean white shirts to be ready to die. What heroism, Count!'

Boris evidently said this to Pierre in order to be overheard by his Serene Highness. He knew Kutuzov's attention would be caught by those words, and so it was.

'What are you saying about the militia?' he asked Boris.

'Preparing for to-morrow, your Serene Highness – for death – they have put on clean shirts.'

'Ah ... a wonderful, a matchless people!' said Kutuzov; and he closed his eyes and swayed his head. 'A matchless people!' he repeated with a sigh.

'So you want to smell gunpowder?' he said to Pierre. 'Yes, it's a pleasant smell. I have the honour to be one of your wife's adorers. Is she well? My quarters are at your service.'

And as often happens with old people, Kutuzov began looking about absent-mindedly as if forgetting all he wanted to say or do.

Then, evidently remembering what he wanted, he beckoned to Andrew Kaysarov, his adjutant's brother.

'Those verses ... those verses of Marin's ... how do they go, eh? Those he wrote about Gerakov.* "Lectures for the corps inditing".... Recite them, recite them!' said he, evidently preparing to laugh.

Kaysarov recited ... Kutuzov smilingly nodded his head to the rhythm of the verses.

When Pierre had left Kutuzov, Dolokhov came up to him and took his hand.

'I am very glad to meet you here, Count,' he said aloud, regardless of the presence of strangers and in a particularly resolute and solemn tone. 'On the eve of a day when God alone knows who of us is fated to survive, I am glad of this opportunity to tell you that I regret the misunderstandings that occurred between us, and should wish you not to have any ill feeling for me. I beg you to forgive me.'

Pierre looked at Dolokhov with a smile, not knowing what to say to him. With tears in his eyes Dolokhov embraced Pierre and kissed him.

Boris said a few words to his general, and Count Bennigsen

turned to Pierre and proposed that he should ride with him along the line.

'It will interest you,' said he.

'Yes, very much,' replied Pierre.

Half an hour later Kutuzov left for Tatarinova, and Bennigsen and his suite, with Pierre among them, set out on their ride along the line.

23

From Gorky Bennigsen descended the high road to the bridge which, when they had looked at it from the hill, the officer had pointed out as being the centre of our position and where rows of fragrant new-mown hay lay by the riverside. They rode across that bridge into the village of Borodino and thence turned to the left, passing an enormous number of troops and guns, and came to a high knoll where militiamen were digging. This was the redoubt, as yet unnamed, which afterwards became known as the Raevsky Redoubt, or the Knoll-Battery, but Pierre paid no special attention to it. He did not know that it would become more memorable to him than any other spot on the plain of Borodino.

They then crossed the hollow to Semënovsk, where the soldiers were dragging away the last logs from the huts and barns. Then they rode downhill and uphill, across a rye-field trodden and beaten down as if by hail, following a track freshly made by the artillery over the furrows of the ploughed land, and reached some flèches* which were still being dug.

At the flèches Bennigsen stopped, and began looking at the Shevardino Redoubt opposite, which had been ours the day before and where several horsemen could be descried. The officers said that either Napoleon or Murat was there, and they all gazed eagerly at this little group of horsemen. Pierre also looked at them, trying to guess which of the scarcely discernible figures was Napoleon. At last those mounted men rode away from the mound and disappeared.

Bennigsen spoke to a general who approached him, and began explaining the whole position of our troops. Pierre listened to him, straining each faculty to understand the essential points of the impending battle, but was mortified to feel that his mental capacity was inadequate for the task. He could make nothing of it. Bennigsen stopped speaking, and noticing that Pierre was listening, suddenly said to him:

'I don't think this interests you?'

'On the contrary it's very interesting!' replied Pierre not quite truthfully.

From the flèches they rode still farther to the left, along a road winding through a thick, low-growing birch wood. In the middle of the wood a brown hare with white feet sprang out and, scared by the tramp of the many horses, grew so confused that it leapt along the road in front of them for some time, arousing general attention and laughter, and only when several voices shouted at it did it dart to one side and disappear in the thicket. After going through the wood for about a mile and a half they came out on a glade where troops of Tuchkov's corps were stationed to defend the left flank.

Here, at the extreme left flank, Bennigsen talked a great deal and with much heat, and, as it seemed to Pierre, gave orders of great military importance. In front of Tuchkov's troops was some high ground not occupied by troops. Bennigsen loudly criticized this mistake, saying that it was madness to leave a height which commanded the country around unoccupied and to place troops below it. Some of the generals expressed the same opinion. One in particular declared with martial heat that they were put there to be slaughtered. Bennigsen on his own authority ordered the troops to occupy the high ground.

This disposition on the left flank increased Pierre's doubt of his own capacity to understand military matters. Listening to Bennigsen and the generals criticizing the position of the troops behind the hill, he quite understood them and shared their opinion, but for that very reason he could not understand how the man who put them there behind the hill could have made so gross and palpable a blunder.

Pierre did not know that these troops were not, as Bennigsen supposed, put there to defend the position, but were in a concealed position, as an ambush, that they should not be seen and might be able to strike an approaching enemy unexpectedly. Bennigsen did not know this, and moved the troops forward according to his own ideas without mentioning the matter to the commander-in-chief.

24

On that bright evening of August the 25th, Prince Andrew lay leaning on his elbow in a broken-down shed in the village of Knyazkovo at the further end of his regiment's encampment. Through a gap in the broken wall he could see, beside the wooden fence, a row of thirty-year-old birches with their lower branches lopped off, a field on which shocks of oats were standing, and some bushes near which rose the smoke of camp-fires – the soldiers' kitchens.

Narrow and burdensome and useless to anyone as his life now seemed to him, Prince Andrew on the eve of battle felt agitated and irritable, as he had done seven years before at Austerlitz.

He had received and given the orders for next day's battle, and had nothing more to do. But his thoughts – the simplest, clearest, and therefore most terrible thoughts – would give him no peace. He knew that to-morrow's battle would be the most terrible of all he had taken part in, and for the first time in his life the possibility of death presented itself to him – not in relation to any worldly matter or with reference to its effect on others, but simply in relation to himself, to his own soul – vividly, plainly, terribly, and almost as a certainty. And from the height of this perception all that had previously tormented and preoccupied him suddenly became illumined by a cold white light without shadows, without perspective, and without distinction of outline. All life appeared to him like magic-lantern pictures at which he had long been gazing by artificial light through a glass. Now he suddenly saw those badly daubed pictures in clear daylight and without a glass. 'Yes, yes! There they are, those false images that agitated, enraptured, and tormented me,' said he to himself, passing in review the principal pictures of the magic lantern of life and regarding them now in the cold white daylight of his clear perception of death. 'There they are, those rudely painted figures that once seemed splendid and mysterious. Glory, the good of society, love of a woman, the Fatherland itself – how important these pictures appeared to me, with what profound meaning they seemed to be filled! And it is all so simple, pale, and crude in the cold white light of this morning which I feel is dawning for me.' The three great sorrows of his life held his attention in particular: his love for a woman, his father's death, and the French invasion which had overrun half Russia. 'Love! . . . that little girl who seemed to me brimming over with mystic forces! Yes, indeed I loved her. I made romantic plans of love and happiness with her! Oh, what a boy I was!' he said aloud bitterly. 'Ah me! I believed in some ideal love which was to keep her faithful to me for the whole year of my absence! Like the gentle dove in the fable she was to pine apart from me . . . But it was much simpler really . . . It was all very simple and horrible.

'When my father built Bald Hills he thought the place was his, his land, his air, his peasants. But Napoleon came and swept him aside, unconscious of his existence, as he might brush a chip from his path, and his Bald Hills and his whole life fell to pieces. Princess Mary says it is a trial sent from above. What is the trial for, when he is not here and will never return? He is not here! For whom then is the trial intended? The Fatherland, the destruction of Moscow! And to-morrow I shall be killed, perhaps not even by a Frenchman but by one of our own men, by a soldier discharging a musket close to my ear, as one of them did yesterday, and the French will come and take me by head and heels and fling me into a hole that I may not stink under their noses, and new conditions of life will arise, which will seem quite ordinary to others and about which I shall know nothing. I shall not exist.'

He looked at the row of birches shining in the sunshine with their motionless green and yellow foliage and white bark. 'To die ... to be killed to-morrow ... That I should not exist ... That all this should still be, but no me ...'

And the birches with their light and shade, the curly clouds, the smoke of the camp-fires, and all that was around him, changed and seemed terrible and menacing. A cold shiver ran down his spine. He rose quickly, went out of the shed, and began to walk about.

After he had returned, voices were heard outside the shed. 'Who's that?' he cried.

The red-nosed Captain Timokhin, formerly Dolokhov's squadron commander, but now from lack of officers a battalion commander, shyly entered the shed, followed by an adjutant and the regimental paymaster.

Prince Andrew rose hastily, listened to the business they had come about, gave them some further instructions and was about to dismiss them when he heard a familiar, lisping voice behind the shed.

'Devil take it!' said the voice of a man stumbling over something.

Prince Andrew looked out of the shed and saw Pierre, who had tripped over a pole on the ground and had nearly fallen, coming his way. It was unpleasant to Prince Andrew to meet people of his own set in general, and Pierre especially, for he reminded him of all the painful moments of his last visit to Moscow.

'You? What a surprise!' said he. 'What brings you here? This is unexpected!'

As he said this his eyes and face expressed more than coldness – they expressed hostility, which Pierre noticed at once. He had approached the shed full of animation, but on seeing Prince Andrew's face he felt constrained and ill at ease.

'I have come ... simply ... you know ... come ... it interests me,' said Pierre, who had so often that day senselessly repeated that word 'interesting'. 'I wish to see the battle.'

'Oh yes, and what do the masonic brothers say about war? How would they stop it?' said Prince Andrew sarcastically. 'Well, and how's Moscow? And my people? Have they reached Moscow at last?' he asked seriously.

'Yes, they have. Julie Drubetskaya told me so. I went to see them, but missed them. They have gone to your estate near Moscow.'

25

THE officers were about to take leave, but Prince Andrew, apparently reluctant to be left alone with his friend, asked them to stay and have tea. Seats were brought in and so was the tea. The officers gazed with surprise at Pierre's huge stout figure, and listened to his talk of Moscow and the position of our army, round which he had ridden. Prince Andrew remained silent, and his expression was so forbidding that Pierre addressed his remarks chiefly to Timokhin, the good-natured battalion commander.

'So you understand the whole position of our troops?' Prince Andrew interrupted him.

'Yes — that is, how do you mean?' said Pierre. 'Not being a military man I can't say I have understood it fully, but I understand the general position.'

'Well, then, you know more than anyone else, be it who it may,' said Prince Andrew.

'Oh!' said Pierre, looking over his spectacles in perplexity at Prince Andrew. 'Well, and what do you think of Kutuzov's appointment?' he asked.

'I was very glad of his appointment, that's all I know,' replied Prince Andrew.

'And tell me your opinion of Barclay de Tolly. In Moscow they are saying heaven knows what about him ... What do you think of him?'

'Ask them,' replied Prince Andrew, indicating the officers.

Pierre looked at Timokhin with the condescendingly interrogative smile with which everybody involuntarily addressed that officer.

'We see light again, since his Serenity has been appointed,* your Excellency,' said Timokhin, timidly and continually turning to glance at his colonel.

'Why so?' asked Pierre.

'Well, to mention only fire-wood and fodder, let me inform you. Why, when we were retreating from Sventsyani we dare not touch a stick, or a wisp of hay or anything. You see, we were going away, so *he* would get it all;* wasn't it so, your Excellency?' and again Timokhin turned to the prince. 'But we daren't. In our regiment two officers were court-martialled for that kind of thing. But when his Serenity took command everything became straight-forward. Now we see light . . .'

'Then why was it forbidden?'

Timokhin looked about in confusion, not knowing what or how to reply to such a question. Pierre put the same question to Prince Andrew.

'Why, so as not to lay waste the country we were abandoning to the enemy,' said Prince Andrew with venomous irony. 'It is very sound: one can't permit the land to be pillaged and accustom the troops to marauding. At Smolensk too he judged correctly that the French might outflank us, as they had larger forces. But he could not understand this,' cried Prince Andrew in a shrill voice that seemed to escape him involuntarily: 'He could not understand that there, for the first time, we were fighting for Russian soil, and that there was a spirit in the men such as I had never seen before, that we had held the French for two days, and that that success had increased our strength tenfold. He ordered us to retreat, and all our efforts and losses went for nothing. He had no thought of betraying us, he tried to do the best he could, he thought out everything, and that is why he is unsuitable. He is unsuitable now, just because he plans out everything very thoroughly and accurately as every German has to. How can I explain? . . . Well, say your father has a German valet, and he is a splendid valet and satisfies your father's requirements better than you could, then it's all right to let him serve. But if your father is mortally sick you'll send the valet away and attend to your father with your own unpractised, awkward hands, and will soothe him better than a skilled man who is a stranger could. So it has been with Barclay. While Russia was well, a foreigner could serve her and be a splendid Minister; but as soon as she is in danger she needs one of her own kin. But in your club they have been making him out a traitor! They slander him as a traitor, and the only result will be that afterwards, ashamed of their false accusations, they will make him out a hero or a genius instead of a traitor, and that will be still more unjust. He is an honest and very punctilious German.'

'And they say he's a skilful commander,' rejoined Pierre.

'I don't understand what is meant by "a skilful commander",' replied Prince Andrew ironically.

'A skilful commander?' replied Pierre. 'Why, one who foresees all contingencies . . . and foresees the adversary's intentions.'

'But that's impossible,' said Prince Andrew as if it were a matter settled long ago.

Pierre looked at him in surprise.

'And yet they say that war is like a game of chess?' he remarked.

'Yes,' replied Prince Andrew, 'but with this little difference, that in chess you may think over each move as long as you please and are not limited for time, and with this difference too, that a knight is always stronger than a pawn, and two pawns are always stronger than one, while in war a battalion is sometimes stronger than a division and sometimes weaker than a company. The relative strength of bodies of troops can never be known to anyone. Believe me,' he went on, 'if things depended on arrangements made by the staff, I should be there making arrangements, but instead of that I have the honour to serve here in the regiment with these gentlemen, and I consider that on us to-morrow's battle will depend and not on those others . . . Success never depends, and never will depend, on position, or equipment, or even on numbers, and least of all on position.'

'But on what then?'

'On the feeling that is in me and in him,' he pointed to Timokhin, 'and in each soldier.'

Prince Andrew glanced at Timokhin, who looked at his commander in alarm and bewilderment. In contrast to his former reticent taciturnity Prince Andrew now seemed excited. He could apparently not refrain from expressing the thoughts that had suddenly occurred to him.

'A battle is won by those who firmly resolve to win it! Why did we lose the battle at Austerlitz? The French losses were almost equal to ours, but very early we said to ourselves that we were losing the battle, and we did lose it. And we said so because we had nothing to fight for there, we wanted to get away from the battlefield as soon as we could. "We've lost, so let us run," and we ran. If we had not said that till the evening, heaven knows what might not have happened. But to-morrow we shan't say it. You talk about our position, the left flank weak and the right flank too extended,' he went on. 'That's all nonsense, there's nothing of the kind. But what awaits us to-morrow? A hundred million most diverse chances which will be decided on the instant by the fact that our men or theirs run or do not run, and that this man or that man is killed; but all that is being done at present is only play. The fact is that those men with whom you have ridden round the position not only do not help matters, but hinder. They are only concerned with their own petty interests.'

'At such a moment?' said Pierre reproachfully.

'At *such a moment!*' Prince Andrew repeated. 'To them it is only a moment affording opportunities to undermine a rival and obtain an extra cross or ribbon. For me to-morrow means this: a Russian army of a hundred thousand and a French army of a hundred thousand have met to fight, and the thing is that these two hundred thousand men *will* fight and the side that fights more fiercely and spares itself least will win. And if you like I will tell you that whatever happens, and whatever muddles those at the top may make, we shall win to-morrow's battle. To-morrow, happen what may, we shall win!'

'There now, your Excellency! That's the truth, the real truth,' said Timokhin. 'Who would spare himself now? The soldiers in my battalion, believe me, wouldn't drink their vodka! "It's not the day for that!" they say.'

All were silent. The officers rose. Prince Andrew went out of the shed with them, giving final orders to the adjutant. After they had gone, Pierre approached Prince Andrew and was about to start a conversation when they heard the clatter of three horses' hoofs on the road not far from the shed, and looking in that direction Prince Andrew recognized Wolzogen and Clausewitz* accompanied by a Cossack. They rode close by, continuing to converse and Prince Andrew involuntarily heard these words:

'*Der Krieg muss in Raum verlegt werden. Der Ansicht kann ich nicht genug Preis geben,*' said one of them.

'*Oh, ja,*' said the other, '*der Zweck ist nur den Feind zu schwächen, so kann man gewiss nicht den Verlust der Privat-Personen in Achtung nehmen.*'*

'Oh, no,' agreed the other.

'Extend widely!' said Prince Andrew with an angry snort, when they had ridden past. 'In that "extent" were my father, son, and sister, at Bald Hills. That's all the same to him! That's what I was saying to you – those German gentlemen won't win the battle to-morrow but will only make all the mess they can, because they have nothing in their German heads but theories not worth an empty egg-shell, and haven't in their hearts the one thing needed to-morrow – that which Timokhin has. They have yielded up all Europe to *him*, and have now come to teach us. Fine teachers!' and again his voice grew shrill.

'So you think we shall win to-morrow's battle?' asked Pierre.

'Yes, yes,' answered Prince Andrew absently. 'One thing I would do if I had the power,' he began again, 'I would not take prisoners. Why take prisoners? It's chivalry! The French have destroyed my home and are on their way to destroy Moscow, they have outraged and are outraging me every moment. They are my enemies. In my opinion they are all criminals. And so thinks Timokhin and the whole army. They should be executed! Since they are my foes they cannot be my friends, whatever may have been said at Tilsit.'

'Yes, yes,' muttered Pierre, looking with shining eyes at Prince Andrew. 'I quite agree with you!'

The question that had perturbed Pierre on the Mozhaysk hill and all that day now seemed to him quite clear and completely solved. He now understood the whole meaning and importance of this war and of the impending battle. All he had seen that day, all the significant and stern expressions on the faces he had seen in passing, were lit up for him by a new light. He understood that latent heat (as they say in physics) of patriotism which was present in all these men he had seen, and this explained to him why they all prepared for death calmly, and as it were light-heartedly.

'Not take prisoners,' Prince Andrew continued. 'That by itself would quite change the whole war and make it less cruel. As it is we have played at war – that's what's vile! We play at magnanimity and all that stuff. Such magnanimity and sensibility are like the magnanimity and sensibility of a lady who faints when she sees a calf being killed: she is so kind-hearted that she can't look at blood, but enjoys eating the calf served up with sauce. They talk to us of the rules of war, of chivalry, of flags of truce, of mercy to the unfortunate, and so on. It's all rubbish. I saw chivalry and flags of truce in 1805; they humbugged us and we humbugged them. They plunder other people's houses, issue false paper money, and worst of all they kill my children and my father, and then talk of rules of war and magnanimity to foes! Take no prisoners, but kill and be killed! He who has come to this as I have through the same sufferings . . .'

Prince Andrew, who had thought it was all the same to him whether or not Moscow was taken as Smolensk had been, was suddenly checked in his speech by an unexpected cramp in his throat. He paced up and down a few times in silence, but his eyes glittered feverishly and his lips quivered as he began to speak again.

'If there was none of this magnanimity in war, we should go to war only when it was worth while going to certain death, as now. Then there would not be war because Paul Ivanovich had offended Michael Ivanovich. And when there was a war, like this one, it would be war! And then the determination of the troops would be quite different. Then all these Westphalians and Hessians whom Napoleon is leading would not follow him into Russia, and we should not go to fight in Austria and Prussia without knowing why. War is not courtesy but the most horrible thing in life; and we ought to understand that, and not play at war. We ought to accept this terrible necessity sternly and seriously. It all lies in that: get rid of falsehood and let war be war and not a game. As it is now, war is the favourite pastime of the idle and frivolous. The military calling is the most highly honoured.

'But what is war? What is needed for success in warfare? What are the habits of the military? The aim of war is murder,* the methods of war are spying, treachery, and their encouragement, the ruin of a country's inhabitants, robbing them or stealing to provision the army, and fraud and falsehood termed military craft. The military life is characterized by absence of freedom, that is, discipline, idleness, ignorance, cruelty, debauchery and drunkenness. And in spite of all this it is the highest class, respected by everyone. All the kings, except the Chinese, wear military uniforms, and he who kills most people receives the highest rewards.

'They meet, as we shall meet to-morrow, to murder one another; they kill and maim tens of thousands, and then have thanksgiving services for having killed so many people (they even exaggerate the number), and they announce a victory, supposing that the more people they have killed the greater their achievement. How does God above look at them and hear them?' exclaimed Prince Andrew in a shrill, piercing voice. 'Ah, my friend, it has of late become hard for me to live. I see that I have begun to understand too much. And it doesn't do for man to taste of the tree of knowledge of good and evil ... Ah, well, it's not for long!' he added.

'However, you're sleepy, and it's time for me to sleep. Go back to Gorky!' said Prince Andrew suddenly.

'Oh, no!' Pierre replied, looking at Prince Andrew with frightened, compassionate eyes.

'Go, go! Before a battle one must have one's sleep out,' repeated Prince Andrew.

He came quickly up to Pierre and embraced and kissed him.

'Good-bye, be off!' he shouted. 'Whether we meet again or not ...' and turning away hurriedly he entered the shed.

It was already dark, and Pierre could not make out whether the expression of Prince Andrew's face was angry or tender.

For some time he stood in silence considering whether he should follow him or go away. 'No, he does not want it!' Pierre concluded, 'and I know that this is our last meeting!' He sighed deeply and rode back to Gorky.

On re-entering the shed Prince Andrew lay down on a rug, but he could not sleep.

He closed his eyes. One picture succeeded another in his imagination. On one of them he dwelt long and joyfully. He vividly recalled an evening in Petersburg. Natasha with animated and excited face was telling him how she had gone to look for mushrooms the previous summer and had lost her way in the big forest. She incoherently described the depths of the forest, her feelings, and a talk with a bee-keeper she met, and constantly interrupted her story to say: 'No, I can't, I'm not telling it right; no, you don't understand,' though he encouraged her by saying that he did understand, and he really had understood all she wanted to say. But Natasha was not satisfied with her own words: she felt that they did not convey the passionately poetic feeling she had experienced that day and wished to convey. 'He was such a delightful old man, and it was so dark in the forest . . . and he had such kind . . . No, I can't describe it,' she had said, flushed and excited. Prince Andrew smiled now the same happy smile as then when he had looked into her eyes. 'I understood her,' he thought. 'I not only understood her, but it was just that inner, spiritual force, that sincerity, that frankness of soul – that very soul of hers which seemed to be fettered by her body – it was that soul I loved in her . . . loved so strongly and happily . . .' and suddenly he remembered how his love had ended. '*He* did not need anything of that kind. *He* neither saw nor understood anything of the sort. He only saw in her a pretty and *fresh* young girl, with whom he did not deign to unite his fate. And I? . . . and he is still alive and gay!'

Prince Andrew jumped up as if someone had burnt him, and again began pacing up and down in front of the shed.

26

ON August 25th, the eve of the battle of Borodino, M. de Beausset, prefect of the French Emperor's palace, arrived at Napoleon's quarters at Valuevo with Colonel Fabvier, the former from Paris and the latter from Madrid.

Donning his court uniform, M. de Beausset ordered a box he had brought for the Emperor to be carried before him, and entered the first compartment of Napoleon's tent, where he began opening the box while conversing with Napoleon's aides-de-camp who surrounded him.

Fabvier, not entering the tent, remained at the entrance talking to some generals of his acquaintance.

The Emperor Napoleon had not yet left his bedroom and was finishing his toilette. Slightly snorting and grunting, he presented now his back and now his plump hairy chest to the brush with which his valet was rubbing him down. Another valet, with his finger over the mouth of a bottle, was sprinkling eau-de-Cologne on the Emperor's pampered body with an expression which seemed to say that he alone knew where and how much eau-de-Cologne should be sprinkled. Napoleon's short hair was wet and matted on the forehead, but his face, though puffy and yellow, expressed physical satisfaction. 'Go on, harder, go on!' he muttered to the valet who was rubbing him, slightly twitching and grunting. An aide-de-camp, who had entered the bedroom to report to the Emperor the number of prisoners taken in yesterday's action, was standing by the door after delivering his message, awaiting permission to withdraw. Napoleon, frowning, looked at him under his brows.

'No prisoners!' said he, repeating the aide-de-camp's words. 'They are forcing us to exterminate them. So much the worse for the Russian army . . . Go on . . . harder, harder!' he muttered, hunching his back and presenting his fat shoulders.

'All right. Let Monsieur de Beausset enter, and Fabvier too,' he said, nodding to the aide-de-camp.

'Yes, Sire,' and the aide-de-camp disappeared through the door of the tent.

Two valets rapidly dressed his Majesty, and wearing the blue uniform of the Guards he went with firm quick steps to the reception room.

De Beausset's hands meanwhile were busily engaged arranging the present he had brought from the Empress, on two chairs directly in front of the entrance. But Napoleon had dressed and come out with such unexpected rapidity that he had not time to finish arranging the surprise.

Napoleon noticed at once what they were about and guessed that they were not ready. He did not wish to deprive them of the pleasure of giving him a surprise, so he pretended not to see de Beausset and called Fabvier to him, listening silently and with a stern frown to what Fabvier told him of the heroism and devotion of his troops fighting at Salamanca, at the other end of Europe, with but one thought – to be worthy of their Emperor, and but one fear – to fail to please him. The result of that battle had been deplorable.* Napoleon made ironic remarks during Fabvier's account, as if he had not expected that matters could go otherwise in his absence.

'I must make up for that in Moscow,' said Napoleon. 'I'll see you later,' he added, and summoned de Beausset, who by that time had prepared the surprise, having placed something on the chairs and covered it with a cloth.

De Beausset bowed low, with that courtly French bow which only the old retainers of the Bourbons knew how to make, and approached him, presenting an envelope.

Napoleon turned to him gaily and pulled his ear.

'You have hurried here. I am very glad. Well, what is Paris saying?' he asked, suddenly changing his former stern expression for a most cordial tone.

'Sire, all Paris regrets your absence,' replied de Beausset as was proper.

But though Napoleon knew that de Beausset had to say something of this kind, and though in his lucid moments he knew it was untrue, he was pleased to hear it from him. Again he honoured him by touching his ear.

'I am very sorry to have made you travel so far,' said he.

'Sire, I expected nothing less than to find you at the gates of Moscow,' replied de Beausset.

Napoleon smiled, and lifting his head absent-mindedly looked to the right. An aide-de-camp approached with gliding steps and offered him a gold snuff-box, which he took.

'Yes, it has happened luckily for you,' he said, raising the open snuff-box to his nose. 'You are fond of travel, and in three days you will see Moscow. You surely did not expect to see that Asiatic capital. You will have a pleasant journey.'

De Beausset bowed gratefully at this regard for his taste for travel (of which he had not till then been aware).

'Ha, what's this?' asked Napoleon, noticing that all the courtiers were looking at something concealed under a cloth.

With courtly adroitness de Beausset half turned, and without turning his back to the Emperor retired two steps, twitching off the cloth at the same time, and said:

'A present to your Majesty from the Empress.'*

It was a portrait, painted in bright colours by Gérard, of the son born to Napoleon by the daughter of the Emperor of Austria, the boy whom for some reason everyone called 'The King of Rome'.

A very pretty curly-headed boy, with a look of the Christ in the Sistine Madonna, was depicted playing at stick and ball. The ball represented the terrestrial globe and the stick in his other hand a sceptre.

Though it was not clear what the artist meant to express by depicting the so-called King of Rome spiking the earth with a stick, the allegory apparently seemed to Napoleon, as it had done to all who had seen it in Paris, quite clear and very pleasing.

'The King of Rome!' he said, pointing to the portrait with a graceful gesture. 'Admirable!'

With the natural capacity of an Italian for changing the expression of his face at will, he drew nearer to the portrait and assumed a look of pensive tenderness. He felt that what he said now and did would be historical, and it seemed to him that it would now be best for him – whose grandeur enabled his son to play stick and ball with the terrestrial globe – to show, in contrast to that grandeur, the simplest paternal tenderness. His eyes grew dim, he moved forward, glanced round at a chair (which seemed to place itself under him), and sat down on it before the portrait. At a single gesture from him everyone went out on tiptoe, leaving the great man to himself and his emotion.

Having sat still for a while he touched – himself not knowing why – the thick spot of paint representing the highest light in the portrait, rose, and recalled de Beausset and the officer on duty. He ordered the portrait to be carried outside his tent, that the Old Guard, stationed round it, might not be deprived of the pleasure of seeing the King of Rome, the son and heir of their adored monarch.

And while he was doing M. de Beausset the honour of breakfasting with him, they heard, as Napoleon had anticipated, the rapturous cries of the officers and men of the Old Guard who had run up to see the portrait.

'Vive l'Empereur! Vive le roi de Rome! Vive l'Empereur!' came those ecstatic cries.

After breakfast Napoleon in de Beausset's presence dictated his order of the day to the army.

'Short and energetic!' he remarked when he had read over the proclamation which he had dictated straight off without corrections. It ran:

Soldiers! This is the battle you have so longed for. Victory depends on you. It is essential for us; it will give us all we need, comfortable quarters and a speedy return to our country. Behave as you did at Austerlitz, Friedland, Vitebsk, and Smolensk. Let our remotest posterity recall your achievements this day with pride. Let it be said of each of you: 'He was in the great battle before Moscow!'

'Before Moscow!' repeated Napoleon, and inviting M. de Beausset, who was so fond of travel, to accompany him on his ride, he went out of the tent to where the horses stood saddled.

'Your Majesty is too kind!' replied de Beausset to the invitation to accompany the Emperor: he wanted to sleep, did not know how to ride, and was afraid of doing so.

But Napoleon nodded to the traveller, and de Beausset had to mount. When Napoleon came out of the tent the shouting of the Guards before his son's portrait grew still louder. Napoleon frowned.

'Take him away!' he said, pointing with a gracefully majestic gesture to the portrait. 'It is too soon for him to see a field of battle.'

De Beausset closed his eyes, bowed his head, and sighed deeply, to indicate how profoundly he valued and comprehended the Emperor's words.

<h1 style="text-align:center">27</h1>

ON the 25th of August, so his historians tell us, Napoleon spent the whole day on horseback inspecting the locality, considering plans submitted to him by his marshals, and personally giving commands to his generals.

The original line of the Russian forces along the river Kolocha had been dislocated by the capture of the Shevardino Redoubt on the 24th, and part of the line – the left flank – had been drawn back. That part of the line was not entrenched and in front of it the ground was more open and level than elsewhere. It was evident to anyone, military or not, that it was here the French should attack. It would seem that not much consideration was needed to reach this conclusion, nor any particular care or trouble on the part of the Emperor and his marshals, nor was there any need of that special and supreme quality called genius that people are so apt to ascribe to Napoleon; yet the historians who described the event later and the men who then surrounded Napoleon, and he himself, thought otherwise.

Napoleon rode over the plain and surveyed the locality with a profound air and in silence, nodded with approval or shook his head dubiously, and without communicating to the generals around him the profound course of ideas which guided his decisions merely gave them his final conclusions in the form of commands. Having listened to a suggestion from Davout, who was now called Prince d'Eckmühl, to turn the Russian left wing, Napoleon said it should not be done, without explaining why not. To a proposal made by General Campan (who was to attack the flèches) to lead his division through the woods, Napoleon agreed, though the so-called Duke of Elchingen (Ney) ventured to remark that a movement through the woods was dangerous and might disorder the division.

Having inspected the country opposite the Shevardino Redoubt, Napoleon pondered a little in silence and then indicated the spots where two batteries should be set up by the morrow to act against the Russian entrenchments, and the places where, in line with them, the field artillery should be placed.

After giving these and other commands he returned to his tent, and the dispositions for the battle were written down from his dictation.

These dispositions, of which the French historians write with enthusiasm and other historians with profound respect, were as follows:

At dawn the two new batteries established during the night on the plain occupied by the Prince d'Eckmühl will open fire on the two opposing batteries of the enemy.

At the same time the commander of the artillery of the 1st Corps, General Pernetti, with thirty cannon of Campan's division and all the howitzers of Dessaix's and Friant's divisions, will move forward, open fire, and overwhelm with shell-fire the enemy's battery, against which will operate:

24 guns of the artillery of the Guards

30 guns of Campan's division

and   8 guns of Friant's and Dessaix's divisions

in all   62 guns

The commander of the artillery of the 3rd Corps, General Fouché, will place the howitzers of the 3rd and 8th Corps, sixteen in all, on the flanks of the battery that is to bombard the entrenchment on the left, which will have forty guns in all directed against it.

General Sorbier must be ready at the first order to advance with all the howitzers of the Guards' artillery against either one or other of the entrenchments.

During the cannonade Prince Poniatowski is to advance through the wood on the village and turn the enemy's position.

General Campan will move through the wood to seize the first fortification.

After the advance has begun in this manner, orders will be given in accordance with the enemy's movements.

The cannonade on the left flank will begin as soon as the guns of the right wing are heard. The sharpshooters of Morand's division and of the viceroy's* division will open a heavy fire on seeing the attack commence on the right wing.

The viceroy will occupy the village* and cross by its three bridges, advancing to the same heights as Morand's and Gérard's divisions, which under his leadership will be directed against the redoubt and come into line with the rest of the forces.

'All this must be done in good order (le tout se fera avec ordre et méthode) as far as possible retaining troops in reserve.

The Imperial Camp near Mozhaysk,
  6th September 1812.

These dispositions, which are very obscure and confused if one allows oneself to regard the arrangements without religious awe of his genius, related to Napoleon's orders to deal with four points – four different orders. Not one of these was, or could be, carried out.

In the disposition it is said first, *that the batteries placed on the spot chosen by Napoleon, with the guns of Pernetti and Fouché which were to come in line with them, 102 guns in all, were to open fire and shower shells on the Russian flèches and redoubts.* This could not be done, as from the spots selected by Napoleon the projectiles did not carry to the Russian works, and those 102 guns shot into the air until the nearest commander, contrary to Napoleon's instructions, moved them forward.

The second order was that *Poniatowski, moving to the village through the wood, should turn the Russian left flank.* This could not be done and was not done, because Poniatowski, advancing on the village through the wood, met Tuchkov there barring his way, and could not and did not turn the Russian position.

The third order was: *General Campan will move through the wood to seize the first fortification.* General Campan's division did not seize the first fortification, but was driven back, for on emerging from the wood it had to re-form under grape-shot, of which Napoleon was unaware.

The fourth order was: *The viceroy will occupy the village (Borodino) and cross by its three bridges, advancing to the same heights as Morand's and Gérard's divisions* (for whose movements no directions are given), *which under his leadership will be directed against the redoubt and come into line with the rest of the forces.*

As far as one can make out, not so much from this unintelligible sentence as from the attempts the viceroy made to execute the orders given him, he was to advance from the left through Borodino to the redoubt, while the divisions of Morand and Gérard were to advance simultaneously from the front.

All this, like the other parts of the disposition, was not and could not be executed. After passing through Borodino the viceroy was driven back to the Kolocha and could get no farther; while the divisions of Morand and Gérard did not take the redoubt but were driven back, and the redoubt was only taken at the end of the battle by the cavalry (a thing probably unforeseen and not heard of by Napoleon). So not one of the orders in the disposition was, or could be, executed. But in the disposition it is said that, *after the advance has begun in this manner, orders will be given in accordance with the enemy's movements,* and so it might be supposed that all necessary arrangements would be made by Napoleon during the battle. But this was not and could not be done, for during the whole battle Napoleon was so far away that, as appeared later, he could not know the course of the battle, and not one of his orders during the fight could be executed.

28

MANY historians say that the French did not win the battle of Borodino because Napoleon had a cold, and that if he had not had a cold the orders he gave before and during the battle would have been still more full of genius and Russia would have been lost and the face of the world have been changed. To historians who believe that Russia was shaped by the will of one man – Peter the Great – and that France from a republic became an empire and French armies went to Russia at the will of one man – Napoleon – to say that Russia remained a power because Napoleon had a bad cold on the 24th of August may seem logical and convincing.

If it had depended on Napoleon's will to fight or not to fight the battle of Borodino, and if this or that other arrangement depended on his will, then evidently a cold affecting the manifestation of his will might have saved Russia, and consequently the valet who omitted to bring Napoleon his waterproof-boots on the 24th would have been the saviour of Russia. Along that line of thought such a deduction is indubitable, as indubitable as the deduction Voltaire made in jest (without knowing what he was jesting at) when he said that the Massacre of St Bartholomew was due to Charles IX's stomach being deranged. But to men who do not admit that Russia was formed by the will of one man, Peter I, or that the French Empire was formed and the war with Russia begun by the will of one man, Napoleon, that argument seems not merely untrue and irrational, but contrary to all human reality. To the question of what causes historic events, another answer presents itself, namely, that the course of human events is predetermined from on high – depends on the coincidence of the wills of all who take part in the events, and that a Napoleon's influence on the course of these events is purely external and fictitious.

Strange as at first glance it may seem to suppose that the Massacre of St Bartholomew was not due to Charles IX's will, though he gave the order for it and thought it was done as a result of that order; and strange as it may seem to suppose that the slaughter of eighty thousand men at Borodino was not due to Napoleon's will, though he ordered the commencement and conduct of the battle and thought it was done because he ordered it; strange as these suppositions appear, yet human dignity – which

839

tells me that each of us is, if not more, at least not less a man than the great Napoleon – demands the acceptance of that solution of the question, and historic investigation abundantly confirms it.

At the battle of Borodino Napoleon shot at no one and killed no one. That was all done by the soldiers. Therefore it was not he who killed people.

The French soldiers went to kill and be killed at the battle of Borodino not because of Napoleon's orders, but by their own volition. The whole army – French, Italian, German, Polish, and Dutch – hungry, ragged, and weary of the campaign, felt at the sight of an army blocking their road to Moscow, that the wine was drawn and must be drunk. Had Napoleon then forbidden them to fight the Russians, they would have killed him and have proceeded to fight the Russians because it was inevitable.

When they heard Napoleon's proclamation offering them, as compensation for mutilation and death, the words of posterity about their having been in the battle before Moscow, they cried 'Vive l'Empereur!' just as they had cried 'Vive l'Empereur!' at the sight of the portrait of the boy piercing the terrestrial globe with a toy stick, and just as they would have cried 'Vive l'Empereur!' at any nonsense that might be told them. There was nothing left for them to do but cry 'Vive l'Empereur!' and go to fight in order to get food and rest as conquerors in Moscow. So it was not because of Napoleon's commands that they killed their fellow men.

And it was not Napoleon who directed the course of the battle, for none of his orders were executed and during the battle he did not know what was going on before him. So the way in which these people killed one another was not decided by Napoleon's will but occurred independently of him, in accord with the will of hundreds of thousands of people who took part in the common action. It *only seemed* to Napoleon that it all took place by his will. And so the question whether he had or had not a cold has no more historic interest than the cold of the least of the transport soldiers.

Moreover the assertion made by various writers that his cold was the cause of his dispositions not being as well planned as on former occasions, and of his orders during the battle not being as good as previously, is quite baseless which again shows that Napoleon's cold on the 26th of August was unimportant.

The dispositions cited above are not at all worse, but are even better, than previous dispositions by which he had won victories. His pseudo-orders during the battle were also no worse than formerly, but much the same as usual. These dispositions and orders only seem worse than previous ones because the battle of

Borodino was the first Napoleon did not win. The profoundest and most excellent dispositions and orders seem very bad, and every learned militarist criticizes them with looks of importance, when they relate to a battle that has been lost, and the very worst dispositions and orders seem very good, and serious people fill whole volumes to demonstrate their merits, when they relate to a battle that has been won.

The dispositions drawn up by Weyrother for the battle of Austerlitz were a model of perfection for that kind of composition, but still they were criticized – criticized for their very perfection, for their excessive minuteness.

Napoleon at the battle of Borodino fulfilled his office as representative of authority as well as, and even better than, at other battles. He did nothing harmful to the progress of the battle; he inclined to the most reasonable opinions, he made no confusion, did not contradict himself, did not get frightened or run away from the field of battle, but with his great tact and military experience carried out his role of appearing to command, calmly and with dignity.

29

On returning from a second careful inspection of the lines, Napoleon remarked:

'The chessmen are set up, the game will begin to-morrow!'

Having ordered punch and summoned de Beausset, he began to talk to him about Paris and about some changes he meant to make in the Empress's household, surprising the prefect by his memory of minute details relating to the Court.

He showed an interest in trifles, joked about de Beausset's love of travel, and chatted carelessly, as a famous, self-confident surgeon who knows his job does when turning up his sleeves and putting on his apron while a patient is being strapped to the operating-table. 'The matter is in my hands and is clear and definite in my head. When the time comes to set to work I shall do it as no one else could, but now I can jest, and the more I jest and the calmer I am the more tranquil and confident you ought to be, and the more amazed at my genius.'

Having finished his second glass of punch, Napoleon went to rest before the serious business which, he considered, awaited him next day. He was so much interested in that task that he was unable to sleep, and in spite of his cold which had grown worse from the dampness of the evening, he went into the large division of the tent at three o'clock in the morning, loudly blowing his nose. He asked whether the Russians had not withdrawn, and was told that the enemy's fires were still in the same places. He nodded approval.

The adjutant in attendance came into the tent.

'Well, Rapp, do you think we shall do good business to-day?' Napoleon asked him.

'Without doubt, Sire,' replied Rapp.

Napoleon looked at him.

'Do you remember, Sire, what you did me the honour to say at Smolensk?' continued Rapp. 'The wine is drawn and must be drunk.'

Napoleon frowned, and sat silent for a long time leaning his head on his hand.

'This poor army!' he suddenly remarked. 'It has diminished greatly since Smolensk. Fortune is frankly a courtesan, Rapp. I have always said so and I am beginning to experience it. But the Guards, Rapp, the Guards are intact?' he remarked interrogatively.

'Yes, Sire,' replied Rapp.

Napoleon took a lozenge, put it in his mouth, and glanced at his watch. He was not sleepy and it was still not nearly morning. It was impossible to give further orders for the sake of killing time, for the orders had all been given and were now being executed.

'Have the biscuits and rice been served out to the regiments of the Guards?' asked Napoleon sternly.

'Yes, Sire.'

'The rice too?'

Rapp replied that he had given the Emperor's order about the rice, but Napoleon shook his head in dissatisfaction as if not believing that his order had been executed. An attendant came in with punch. Napoleon ordered another glass to be brought for Rapp, and silently sipped his own.

'I have neither taste nor smell,' he remarked, sniffing at his glass. 'This cold is tiresome. They talk about medicine – what is the good of medicine when it can't cure a cold! Corvisart gave me these lozenges but they don't help at all. What can doctors cure? One can't cure anything. Our body is a machine for living. It is organized for that, it is its nature. Let life go on in it unhindered and let it defend itself, it will do more than if you paralyse it by encumbering it with remedies. Our body is like a perfect watch that should go for a certain time; the watchmaker cannot open it, he can only adjust it by fumbling, and that blindfold . . . Yes, our body is a machine for living, that is all.'

And having entered on the path of definition, of which he

was fond, Napoleon suddenly and unexpectedly gave a new one.

'Do you know, Rapp, what military art is?' asked he. 'It is the art of being stronger than the enemy at a given moment. That's all.'

Rapp made no reply.

'To-morrow we shall have to deal with Kutuzov!' said Napoleon. 'We shall see! Do you remember at Braunau he commanded an army for three weeks and did not once mount a horse to inspect his entrenchments ... We shall see!'

He looked at his watch. It was still only four o'clock. He did not feel sleepy. The punch was finished and there was still nothing to do. He rose, walked to and fro, put on a warm overcoat and a hat, and went out of the tent. The night was dark and damp, a scarcely perceptible moisture was descending from above. Near by, the camp-fires were dimly burning among the French Guards, and in the distance those of the Russian line shone through the smoke. The weather was calm, and the rustle and tramp of the French troops already beginning to move to take up their positions was clearly audible.

Napoleon walked about in front of his tent, looked at the fires, and listened to these sounds, and as he was passing a tall guardsman in a shaggy cap, who was standing sentinel before his tent and had drawn himself up like a black pillar at sight of the Emperor, Napoleon stopped in front of him.

'What year did you enter the service?' he asked with that affectation of military bluntness and geniality with which he always addressed the soldiers.

The man answered the question.

'Ah! One of the old ones! Has your regiment had its rice?'

'It has, your Majesty.'

Napoleon nodded and walked away.

At half-past five Napoleon rode to the village of Shevardino.

It was growing light, the sky was clearing, only a single cloud lay in the east. The abandoned camp-fires were burning themselves out in the faint morning light.

On the right a single deep report of a cannon resounded and died away in the prevailing silence. Some minutes passed. A second and a third report shook the air, then a fourth and a fifth boomed solemnly near by on the right.

The first shots had not yet ceased to reverberate before others rang out and yet more were heard mingling with and overtaking one another.

Napoleon with his suite rode up to the Shevardino Redoubt where he dismounted. The game had begun.

843

ON returning to Gorky after having seen Prince Andrew, Pierre ordered his groom to get the horses ready and to call him early in the morning, and then immediately fell asleep behind a partition in a corner Boris had given up to him.

Before he was thoroughly awake next morning, everybody had already left the hut. The panes were rattling in the little windows and his groom was shaking him.

'Your Excellency! Your Excellency! Your Excellency!' he kept repeating pertinaciously while he shook Pierre by the shoulder without looking at him, having apparently lost hope of getting him to wake up.

'What? Has it begun? Is it time?' Pierre asked, waking up.

'Hear the firing,' said the groom, a discharged soldier. 'All the gentlemen have all gone out, and his Serene Highness himself rode past long ago.'

Pierre dressed hastily and ran out to the porch. Outside all was bright, fresh, dewy, and cheerful. The sun, just bursting forth from behind a cloud that had concealed it, was shining, with rays still half broken by the clouds, over the roofs of the street opposite, on the dew-besprinkled dust of the road, on the walls of the houses, on the windows, the fence, and on Pierre's horses standing before the hut. The roar of guns sounded more distinct outside. An adjutant accompanied by a Cossack passed by at a sharp trot.

'It's time, Count; it's time!' cried the adjutant.

Telling the groom to follow him with the horses, Pierre went down the street to the knoll from which he had looked at the field of battle the day before. A crowd of military men was assembled there, members of the staff could be heard conversing in French, and Kutuzov's grey head in a white cap with a red band was visible, his grey nape sunk between his shoulders. He was looking through a field-glass down the high road before him.

Mounting the steps to the knoll, Pierre looked at the scene before him, spellbound by its beauty. It was the same panorama he had admired from that spot the day before, but now the whole place was full of troops and covered by smoke-clouds from the guns, and the slanting rays of the bright sun, rising slightly to the left behind Pierre, cast upon it through the clear morning air penetrating streaks of rosy, golden-tinted light and long dark shadows. The forest at the farthest extremity of the panorama seemed carved in some precious stone of a yellowish-green colour, its undulating outline was silhouetted against the horizon and was pierced beyond

Valuevo by the Smolensk high road, crowded with troops. Nearer at hand glittered golden cornfields interspersed with copses. There were troops to be seen everywhere, in front and to the right and left. All this was vivid, majestic, and unexpected; but what impressed Pierre most of all was the view of the battlefield itself, of Borodino and the hollows on both sides of the Kolocha.

Above the Kolocha, in Borodino and on both sides of it, especially to the left where the Voyna flowing between its marshy banks falls into the Kolocha, a mist had spread which seemed to melt, to dissolve and to become translucent when the brilliant sun appeared and magically coloured and outlined everything. The smoke of the guns mingled with this mist, and over the whole expanse and through that mist the rays of the morning sun were reflected, flashing back like lightning from the water, from the dew, and from the bayonets of the troops crowded together by the river banks and in Borodino. A white church could be seen through the mist, and here and there the roofs of huts in Borodino, as well as dense masses of soldiers, or green ammunition-chests and ordnance. And all this moved, or seemed to move, as the smoke and mist spread out over the whole space. Just as in the mist-enveloped hollow near Borodino, so along the entire line outside and above it and especially in the woods and fields to the left, in the valleys and on the summits of the high ground, clouds of powder-smoke seemed continually to spring up out of nothing, now singly now several at a time, some translucent others dense, which, swelling, growing, rolling, and blending, extended over the whole expanse.

These puffs of smoke and (strange to say) the sound of the firing, produced the chief beauty of the spectacle.

'*Puff!*' – suddenly a round compact cloud of smoke was seen merging from violet into grey and milky-white, and '*boom!*' came the report a second later.

'*Puff! puff!*' – and two clouds arose pushing one another and blending together; and '*boom, boom!*' came the sounds confirming what the eye had seen.

Pierre glanced round at the first cloud, which he had seen as a round compact ball, and in its place already were balloons of smoke floating to one side, and – '*puff*' (with a pause) – '*puff, puff!*' three and then four more appeared and then from each, with the same interval – '*boom – boom, boom!*' came the fine, firm, precise sounds in reply. It seemed as if those smoke-clouds sometimes ran, and sometimes stood still while woods, fields, and glittering bayonets ran past them. From the left, over fields and bushes, those large balls of smoke were continually appearing followed by their solemn reports, while nearer still, in the hollows and woods, there burst from the muskets small cloudlets that had no time to become balls, but had their little echoes in just the same way. '*Trakh-ta-ta-takh!*' came the frequent crackle of musketry, but it was irregular and feeble in comparison with the reports of the cannon.

Pierre wished to be there with that smoke, those shining bayonets, that movement, and those sounds. He turned to look at Kutuzov and his suite, to compare his impressions with those of others. They were all looking at the field of battle as he was, and, as it seemed to him, with the same feelings. All their faces were now shining with that latent warmth of feeling Pierre had noticed the day before, and had fully understood after his talk with Prince Andrew.

'Go, my dear fellow, go ... and Christ be with you!' Kutuzov was saying to a general who stood beside him, not taking his eye from the battlefield.

Having received this order the general passed by Pierre on his way down the knoll.

'To the crossing!' said the general coldly and sternly in reply to one of the staff who asked where he was going.

'I'll go there too, I too!' thought Pierre, and followed the general.

The general mounted a horse a Cossack had brought him. Pierre went to his groom who was holding his horses, and asking which was the quietest, clambered onto it, seized it by the mane, and turning out his toes, pressed his heels against its sides and, feeling that his spectacles were slipping off but unable to let go of the mane and reins, he galloped after the general, causing the staff officers to smile as they watched him from the knoll.

31

HAVING descended the hill the general after whom Pierre was galloping turned sharply to the left, and Pierre, losing sight of him, galloped in among some ranks of infantry marching ahead of him. He tried to pass either in front of them or to the right or left, but there were soldiers everywhere, all with the same preoccupied expression and busy with some unseen but evidently important task. They all gazed with the same dissatisfied and inquiring expression at this stout man in a white hat, who for some unknown reason threatened to trample them under his horse's hoofs.

'Why ride into the middle of the battalion?' one of them shouted at him.

Another prodded his horse with the butt-end of a musket, and Pierre, bending over his saddle-bow and hardly able to control his shying horse, galloped ahead of the soldiers where there was a free space.

There was a bridge ahead of him, where other soldiers stood firing. Pierre rode up to them. Without being aware of it he had come to the bridge across the Kolocha between Gorky and Borodino, which the French (having occupied Borodino) were attacking in the first phase of the battle. Pierre saw that there was a bridge in front of him and that soldiers were doing something on both sides of it and in the meadow, among the rows of new-mown hay which he had taken no notice of amid the smoke of the camp-fires the day before; but despite the incessant firing going on there, he had no idea that this was the field of battle. He did not notice the sound of the bullets whistling from every side, or the projectiles that flew over him, did not see the enemy on the other side of the river, and for a long time did not notice the killed and wounded, though many fell near him. He looked about him with a smile which did not leave his face.

'Why's that fellow in front of the line?' shouted somebody at him again.

'To the left! . . . Keep to the right!' the men shouted to him.

Pierre went to the right, and unexpectedly encountered one of Raevsky's adjutants whom he knew. The adjutant looked angrily at him, evidently also intending to shout at him, but on recognizing him he nodded.

'How have you got here?' he said, and galloped on.

Pierre, feeling out of place there, having nothing to do, and afraid of getting in someone's way again, galloped after the adjutant.

'What's happening here? May I come with you?' he asked.

'One moment, one moment!' replied the adjutant, and riding up to a stout colonel who was standing in the meadow, he gave him some message and then addressed Pierre.

'Why have you come here, Count?' he asked with a smile. 'Still inquisitive?'

'Yes, yes,' assented Pierre.

But the adjutant turned his horse about and rode on.

'Here it's tolerable,' said he, 'but with Bagration on the left flank they're getting it frightfully hot.'

'Really?' said Pierre. 'Where is that?'

'Come along with me to our knoll. We can get a view from there and in our battery it is still bearable,' said the adjutant. 'Will you come?'

'Yes, I'll come with you,' replied Pierre, looking round for his groom.

It was only now that he noticed wounded men, staggering along or being carried on stretchers. On that very meadow he had ridden over the day before, a soldier was lying athwart the rows of scented hay, with his head thrown awkwardly back and his shako off.

'Why haven't they carried him away?' Pierre was about to ask, but seeing the stern expression of the adjutant who was also looking that way, he checked himself.

Pierre did not find his groom, and rode along the hollow with the adjutant to Raevsky's Redoubt. His horse lagged behind the adjutant's and jolted him at every step.

'You don't seem to be used to riding, Count?' remarked the adjutant.

'No, it's not that, but her action seems so jerky,' said Pierre in a puzzled tone.

'Why ... she's wounded!' said the adjutant. 'In the off foreleg above the knee. A bullet, no doubt. I congratulate you, Count, on your baptism of fire!'

Having ridden in the smoke past the Sixth Corps, behind the artillery which had been moved forward and was in action, deafening them with the noise of firing, they came to a small wood. There it was cool and quiet, with a scent of autumn. Pierre and the adjutant dismounted and walked up the hill on foot.

'Is the general here?' asked the adjutant on reaching the knoll.

'He was here a minute ago but has just gone that way,' someone told him, pointing to the right.

The adjutant looked at Pierre as if puzzled what to do with him now.

'Don't trouble about me,' said Pierre. 'I'll go up onto the knoll if I may?'

'Yes, do. You'll see everything from there and it's less dangerous, and I'll come for you.'

Pierre went to the battery and the adjutant rode on. They did not meet again, and only much later did Pierre learn that he lost an arm that day.

The knoll to which Pierre ascended was that famous one afterwards known to the Russians as the Knoll Battery or Raevsky's Redoubt, and to the French as *la grande redoute, la fatale redoute, la redoute du centre*, around which tens of thousands fell, and which the French regarded as the key to the whole position.

This redoubt consisted of a knoll, on three sides of which trenches had been dug. Within the entrenchment stood ten guns, that were being fired through openings in the earthwork.

In line with the knoll on both sides stood other guns which also fired incessantly. A little behind the guns stood infantry. When ascending that knoll Pierre had no notion that this spot, on which small trenches had been dug and from which a few guns were firing, was the most important point of the battle.

On the contrary, just because he happened to be there he thought it one of the least significant parts of the field.

Having reached the knoll, Pierre sat down at one end of a trench surrounding the battery, and gazed at what was going on around him with an unconsciously happy smile. Occasionally he rose and walked about the battery, still with that same smile, trying not to obstruct the soldiers who were loading, hauling the guns, and continually running past him with bags and charges. The guns of that battery were being fired continually one after another with a deafening roar, enveloping the whole neighbourhood in powder-smoke.

In contrast with the dread felt by the infantrymen placed in support, here, in the battery where a small number of men busy at their work were separated from the rest by a trench, everyone experienced a common and as it were family feeling of animation.

The intrusion of Pierre's non-military figure in a white hat made an unpleasant impression at first. The soldiers looked askance at him with surprise and even alarm as they went past him. The senior artillery officer, a tall, long-legged, pock-marked man, moved over to Pierre as if to see the action of the farthest gun, and looked at him with curiosity.

A young round-faced officer, quite a boy still and evidently only just out of the Cadet College, who was zealously commanding the two guns entrusted to him, addressed Pierre sternly.

'Sir,' he said, 'permit me to ask you to stand aside. You must not be here.'

The soldiers shook their heads disapprovingly as they looked at Pierre. But when they had convinced themselves that this man in the white hat was doing no harm, but either sat quietly on the slope of the trench with a shy smile, or, politely making way for the soldiers, paced up and down the battery under fire as calmly as if he were on a boulevard, their feeling of hostile distrust gradually began to change into a kindly and bantering sympathy, such as soldiers feel for their dogs, cocks, goats, and in general for the animals that live with the regiment. The men soon accepted Pierre into their family, adopted him, gave him a nickname ('our gentleman'), and made kindly fun of him among themselves.

A shell tore up the earth two paces from Pierre and he looked around with a smile as he brushed from his clothes some earth it had thrown up.

'And how's it you're not afraid, sir, really now?' a red-faced, broad-shouldered soldier asked Pierre, with a grin that disclosed a set of sound, white teeth.

'Are you afraid, then?' said Pierre.

'What else do you expect?' answered the soldier. 'She has no mercy, you know! When she comes spluttering down, out go your innards. One can't help being afraid,' he said laughing.

Several of the men, with bright kindly faces, stopped beside Pierre. They seemed not to have expected him to talk like anybody else, and the discovery that he did so delighted them.

'It's the business of us soldiers. But in a gentleman it's wonderful! There's a gentleman for you!'

'To your places!' cried the young officer to the men gathered round Pierre.

The young officer was evidently exercising his duties for the first or second time, and therefore treated both his superiors and the men with great precision and formality.

The booming cannonade and the fusillade of musketry was growing more intense over the whole field, especially to the left where Bagration's flèches were, but where Pierre was the smoke of the firing made it almost impossible to distinguish anything. Moreover his whole attention was engrossed by watching the family circle – separated from all else – formed by the men in the battery. His first unconscious feeling of joyful animation produced by the sights and sounds of the battlefield was now replaced by another, especially since he had seen that soldier lying alone in the hayfield. Now, seated on the slope of the trench, he observed the faces of those around him.

By ten o'clock some twenty men had already been carried away from the battery; two guns were smashed and cannon-balls fell more and more frequently on the battery; and spent bullets buzzed and whistled around. But the men in the battery seemed not to notice this, and merry voices and jokes were heard on all sides.

'A live one!' shouted a man as a whistling shell approached.

'Not this way! To the infantry!' added another with loud laughter, seeing the shell fly past and fall into the ranks of the supports.

'Are you bowing to a friend, eh?' remarked another, chaffing a peasant who ducked low as a cannon-ball flew over.

Several soldiers gathered by the wall of the trench, looking out to see what was happening in front.

'They've withdrawn the front line, it has retired,' said they, pointing over the earthwork.

'Mind your own business,' an old sergeant shouted at them. 'If they've retired it's because there's work for them to do farther back.'

And the sergeant, taking one of the men by the shoulders, gave him a shove with his knee. This was followed by a burst of laughter.

'To the fifth gun, wheel it up!' came shouts from one side.

'Now then, all together, like bargees!' rose the merry voices of those who were moving the gun.

'Oh, she nearly knocked our gentleman's hat off!' cried the red-faced humorist, showing his teeth and chaffing Pierre. 'Awkward baggage!' he added reproachfully to a cannon-ball that struck a cannon-wheel and a man's leg.

'Now then, you foxes!' another said, laughing at some militiamen who, stooping low, entered the battery to carry away the wounded man.

'So this gruel isn't to your taste? Oh, you crows! You're scared!' they shouted at the militiamen who stood hesitating before the man whose leg had been torn off.

'There lads...oh, oh!' they mimicked the peasants, 'they don't like it at all!'

Pierre noticed that after every ball that hit the redoubt, and after every loss, the liveliness increased more and more.

As the flames of the fire hidden within come more and more vividly and rapidly from an approaching thunder-cloud, so, as if in opposition to what was taking place, the lightning of hidden fire growing more and more intense glowed in the faces of these men.

Pierre did not look out at the battlefield and was not concerned to know what was happening there, he was entirely absorbed in watching this fire which burnt ever more brightly and which he felt was flaming up in the same way in his own soul.

At ten o'clock the infantry that had been among the bushes in front of the battery and along the Kamenka streamlet retreated. From the battery they could be seen running back past it carrying their wounded on their muskets. A general with his suite came to the battery, and after speaking to the colonel gave Pierre an angry look and went away again having ordered the infantry supports behind the battery to lie down, so as to be less exposed to fire. After this from amid the ranks of infantry to the right of the battery came the sound of a drum and shouts of command, and from the battery one saw how those ranks of infantry moved forward.

Pierre looked over the wall of the trench, and was particularly struck by a pale young officer who, letting his sword hang down, was walking backwards and kept glancing uneasily round.

The ranks of the infantry disappeared amid the smoke but their long-drawn shout and rapid musketry firing could still be heard. A few minutes later crowds of wounded men and stretcher-bearers came back from that direction. Projectiles began to fall still more frequently in the battery. Several men were lying about who had not been removed. Around the cannon the men moved still more briskly and busily. No one any longer took notice of Pierre. Once or twice he was shouted at for being in the way. The senior officer moved with big, rapid strides from one gun to another with a frowning face. The young officer, with his face still more flushed, commanded the men more scrupulously than ever. The soldiers handed up the charges, turned, loaded, and did their business with strained smartness. They gave little jumps as they walked, as though they were on springs.

The storm-cloud had come upon them, and in every face the fire which Pierre had watched kindle burnt up brightly. Pierre was standing beside the commanding officer. The young officer, his hand to his shako, ran up to his superior.

'I have the honour to report, sir, that only eight rounds are left. Are we to continue firing?' he asked.

'Grape-shot!' the senior shouted, without answering the question, looking over the wall of the trench.

Suddenly something happened; the young officer gave a gasp, and bending double sat down on the ground like a bird shot on the wing. Everything became strange, confused, and misty in Pierre's eyes.

One cannon-ball after another whistled by and struck the earth-work, a soldier, or a gun. Pierre, who had not noticed these sounds before, now heard nothing else. On the right of the battery soldiers shouting 'Hurrah!' were running not forwards but backwards it seemed to Pierre.

A cannon-ball struck the very end of the earthwork by which he was standing, crumbling down the earth; a black ball flashed before his eyes and at the same instant plumped into something. Some militiamen who were entering the battery ran back.

'All with grape-shot!' shouted the officer.

The sergeant ran up to the officer and in a frightened whisper informed him (as a butler at dinner informs his master that there is no more of some wine asked for) that there were no more charges.

'The scoundrels! What are they doing?' shouted the officer, turning to Pierre.

The officer's face was red and perspiring and his eyes glittered under his frowning brow.

'Run to the reserves and bring up the ammunition-boxes!' he yelled, angrily avoiding Pierre with his eyes and speaking to his men.

'I'll go,' said Pierre.

The officer, without answering him, strode across to the opposite side.

'Don't fire . . . Wait!' he shouted.

The man who had been ordered to go for ammunition stumbled against Pierre.

'Eh, sir, this is no place for you,' said he, and ran down the slope.

Pierre ran after him, avoiding the spot where the young officer was sitting.

One cannon-ball, another, and a third, flew over him, falling in front, beside, and behind him. Pierre ran down the slope. 'Where am I going?' he suddenly asked himself when he was already near the green ammunition-wagons. He halted irresolutely, not knowing whether to return or go on. Suddenly a terrible concussion threw him backwards to the ground. At the same instant he was dazzled by a great flash of flame, and immediately a deafening roar, crackling and whistling, made his ears tingle.

When he came to himself he was sitting on the ground leaning on his hands; the ammunition-wagons he had been approaching no longer existed, only charred green boards and rags littered the scorched grass, and a horse, dangling fragments of its shafts behind it, galloped past, while another horse lay, like Pierre, on the ground, uttering prolonged and piercing cries.

32

BESIDE himself with terror Pierre jumped up and ran back to the battery, as to the only refuge from the horrors that surrounded him.

On entering the earthwork he noticed that there were men doing something there but that no shots were being fired from the battery. He had no time to realize who these men were. He saw the senior officer lying on the earth wall with his back turned as if he were examining something down below, and that one of the soldiers he had noticed before was struggling forward shouting 'Brothers!' and trying to free himself from some men who were holding him by the arm. He also saw something else that was strange.

But he had not time to realize that the colonel had been killed, that the soldier shouting 'Brothers!' was a prisoner, and that another man had been bayoneted in the back before his eyes, for hardly had he run into the redoubt before a thin, sallow-faced, perspiring man in a blue uniform rushed on him sword in hand, shouting something. Instinctively guarding against the shock – for they had been running together at full speed before they saw one another – Pierre put out his hands and seized the man (a French officer) by the shoulder with one hand and by the throat with the other. The officer, dropping his sword, seized Pierre by his collar.

For some seconds they gazed with frightened eyes at one another's unfamiliar faces, and both were perplexed at what they had done and what they were to do next. 'Am I taken prisoner or have I taken him prisoner?' each was thinking. But the French officer was evidently more inclined to think he had been taken prisoner, because Pierre's strong hand, impelled by instinctive fear, squeezed his throat ever tighter and tighter. The Frenchman was about to say something, when just above their heads, terrible and low, a cannon-ball whistled, and it seemed to Pierre that the French officer's head had been torn off, so swiftly had he ducked it.

Pierre too bent his head and let his hands fall. Without further thought as to who had taken whom prisoner, the Frenchman ran back to the battery and Pierre ran down the slope stumbling over the dead and wounded who, it seemed to him, caught at his feet. But before he reached the foot of the knoll he was met by a dense crowd of Russian soldiers who, stumbling, tripping up, and shouting, ran merrily and wildly towards the battery. (This was the attack for which Ermolov claimed the credit, declaring that only his courage and good luck made such a feat possible: it was the attack in which he was said to have thrown some St George's Crosses he had in his pocket into the battery, for the first soldiers to take who got there.)

The French who had occupied the battery fled, and our troops, shouting 'Hurrah!' pursued them so far beyond the battery that it was difficult to call them back.

The prisoners were brought down from the battery and among them was a wounded French general, whom the officers surrounded. Crowds of wounded – some known to Pierre and some unknown – Russians and French, with faces distorted by suffering, walked, crawled, and were carried on stretchers, from the battery. Pierre again went up onto the knoll where he had spent over an hour, and of that family circle which had received him as a member he did not find a single one. There were many dead whom he did not know, but some he recognized. The young officer still sat in the same way bent double, in a pool of blood at the edge of the earth wall. The red-faced man was still twitching, but they did not carry him away.

Pierre ran down the slope once more.

'Now they will stop it, now they will be horrified at what they have done!' he thought, aimlessly going towards a crowd of stretcher-bearers moving from the battlefield.

But behind the veil of smoke the sun was still high, and in front and especially to the left, near Semënovsk, something seemed to be seething in the smoke, and the roar of cannon and musketry did not diminish, but even increased to desperation like a man who, straining himself, shrieks with all his remaining strength.

33

THE chief action of the battle of Borodino was fought within the seven thousand feet between Borodino and Bagration's flèches. Beyond that space there were, on the one side, a demonstration made by the Russians with Uvarov's cavalry at midday, and on the other side, beyond Utitsa, Poniatowski's collision with Tuchkov; but these two were detached and feeble actions in comparison with what took place in the centre of the battlefield. On the field between Borodino and the flèches, beside the wood, the chief action of the day took place on an open space visible from both sides, and was fought in the simplest and most artless way.

The battle began on both sides with a cannonade from several hundred guns.

Then when the whole field was covered with smoke, two divisions, Campan's and Dessaix's, advanced from the French right, while Murat's troops advanced on Borodino from their left.

From the Shevardino Redoubt where Napoleon was standing the flèches were a verst away, and it was more than two versts as the crow flies to Borodino, so that Napoleon could not see what was happening there, especially as the smoke mingling with the mist hid the whole locality. The soldiers of Dessaix's division advancing against the flèches could only be seen till they had entered the hollow that lay between them and the flèches. As soon as they had descended into that hollow the smoke of the guns and musketry on the flèches grew so dense that it covered the whole approach on that side of it. Through the smoke glimpses could be caught of something black – probably men – and at times the glint of bayonets. But whether they were moving or stationary, whether they were French or Russian, could not be discovered from the Shevardino Redoubt.

The sun had risen brightly, and its slanting rays struck straight into Napoleon's face as, shading his eyes with his hand, he looked at the flèches. The smoke spread out before them, and at times it looked as if the smoke were moving, at times as if the troops moved. Sometimes shouts were heard through the firing, but it was impossible to tell what was being done there.

Napoleon, standing on the knoll, looked through a field-glass, and in its small circlet saw smoke and men, sometimes his own and sometimes Russians, but when he looked again with the naked eye, he could not tell where what he had seen was.

He descended the knoll and began walking up and down before it. Occasionally he stopped, listened to the firing, and gazed intently at the battlefield.

But not only was it impossible to make out what was happening from where he was standing down below, or from the knoll above on which some of his generals had taken their stand, but even from the flèches themselves – in which by this time there were now Russian and now French soldiers, alternately or together, dead, wounded, alive, frightened, or maddened – even at those flèches themselves it was impossible to make out what was taking place. There for several hours amid incessant cannon and musketry fire, now Russians were seen alone, now Frenchmen alone, now infantry and now cavalry; they appeared, fired, fell, collided not knowing what to do with one another, screamed and ran back again.

From the battlefield adjutants he had sent out and orderlies from his marshals kept galloping up to Napoleon with reports of the progress of the action, but all these reports were false, both because it was impossible in the heat of battle to say what was happening at any given moment, and because many of the adjutants did not go to the actual place of conflict, but reported what they had heard from others; and also because while an adjutant was riding the couple of versts to Napoleon circumstances changed and the news he brought was already becoming false. Thus an adjutant galloped up from Murat with tidings that Borodino had been occupied and the bridge over the Kolocha was in the hands of the French. The adjutant asked whether Napoleon wished the troops to cross it? Napoleon gave orders that the troops should form up on the farther side and wait. But before that order was given – almost as soon in fact as the adjutant had left Borodino – the bridge had been retaken by the Russians and burnt, in the very skirmish at which Pierre had been present at the beginning of the battle.

An adjutant galloped up from the flèches with a pale and frightened face and reported to Napoleon that their attack had been repulsed, Campan wounded, and Davout killed; yet at the very time the adjutant had been told that the French had been repulsed, the flèches had in fact been recaptured by other French troops, and Davout was alive and only slightly bruised. On the basis of these necessarily untrustworthy reports Napoleon gave his orders, which had either been executed before he gave them or could not be and were not executed.

The marshals and generals, who were nearer to the field of battle but, like Napoleon, did not take part in the actual fighting and only occasionally went within musket range, made their own arrangements without asking Napoleon and issued orders where and in what direction to fire, and where cavalry should gallop and infantry should run. But even their orders, like Napoleon's, were seldom carried out, and then but partially. For the most part things happened contrary to their orders. Soldiers ordered to advance ran back on meeting grape-shot; soldiers ordered to remain where they were, suddenly seeing Russians unexpectedly before them, sometimes rushed back and sometimes forward, and the cavalry dashed without orders in pursuit of the flying Russians. In this way two cavalry regiments galloped through the Semënovsk hollow and as soon as they reached the top of the incline turned round and galloped full speed back again. The infantry moved in the same way, sometimes running to quite other places than those they were ordered to go to. All orders as to where and when to move the guns, when to send infantry to shoot or horsemen to ride down the Russian infantry – all such orders were given by the officers on the spot nearest to the units concerned, without asking either Ney, Davout, or Murat, much less Napoleon. They did not fear getting into trouble for not fulfilling orders or for acting on their own initiative, for in battle what is at stake is what is dearest to man – his own life, and it sometimes seems that safety lies in running back, sometimes in running forward; and these men who were right in the heat of the battle, acted according to the mood of the moment. In reality however all these movements forward and backward did not improve or alter the position of the troops. All their rushing and galloping at one another did little harm, the harm of disablement and death was caused by the balls and bullets that flew over the fields on which these men were floundering about. As soon as they left the place where the balls and bullets were flying about, their superiors, located in the background, re-formed them and brought them under discipline, and under the influence of that discipline led them back to the zone of fire, where under the influence of fear of death they lost their discipline and rushed about according to the chance promptings of the throng.

34

NAPOLEON'S generals – Davout, Ney, and Murat, who were near the region of fire and sometimes even entered it – repeatedly led into it huge masses of well-ordered troops. But contrary to what had always happened in their former battles, instead of the news they expected of the enemy's flight, these orderly masses returned thence as disorganized and terrified mobs. The generals re-formed them, but their numbers constantly decreased. In the middle of the day Murat sent his adjutant to Napoleon to demand reinforcements.

Napoleon sat at the foot of the knoll, drinking punch, when Murat's adjutant galloped up with an assurance that the Russians would be routed if his Majesty would let him have another division.

'Reinforcements?' said Napoleon in a tone of stern surprise, looking at the adjutant – a handsome lad with long black curls arranged like Murat's own – as though he did not understand his words.

'Reinforcements!' thought Napoleon to himself. 'How can they need reinforcements when they already have half the army directed against a weak, unentrenched Russian wing?'

'Tell the King of Naples,' said he sternly, 'that it is not noon yet, and I don't yet see my chess-board clearly. Go! . . .'

The handsome boy-adjutant with the long hair sighed deeply without removing his hand from his hat, and galloped back to where men were being slaughtered.

Napoleon rose, and having summoned Caulaincourt and Berthier began talking to them about matters unconnected with the battle.

In the midst of this conversation, which was beginning to interest Napoleon, Berthier's eyes turned to look at a general with a suite who was galloping towards the knoll on a lathering horse. It was Belliard. Having dismounted he went up to the Emperor with rapid strides, and in a loud voice began boldly demonstrating the necessity of sending reinforcements. He swore on his honour that the Russians were lost if the Emperor would give another division.

Napoleon shrugged his shoulders and continued to pace up and down without replying. Belliard began talking loudly and eagerly to the generals of the suite around him.

'You are very fiery, Belliard,' said Napoleon when he again came up to the general. 'In the heat of a battle it is easy to make a mistake. Go and have another look and then come back to me.'

Before Belliard was out of sight a messenger from another part of the battlefield galloped up.

'Now then, what do you want?' asked Napoleon in the tone of a man irritated at being continually disturbed.

'Sire, the prince . . .' began the adjutant.

'Asks for reinforcements?' said Napoleon with an angry gesture.

The adjutant bent his head affirmatively and began to report, but the Emperor turned from him, took a couple of steps, stopped, came back, and called Berthier.

'We must give reserves,' he said, moving his arms slightly apart. 'Who do you think should be sent there?' he asked of Berthier (whom he subsequently termed 'that gosling I have made an eagle').

'Send Claparède's division, Sire,' replied Berthier who knew all the divisions, regiments, and battalions by heart.

Napoleon nodded assent.

The adjutant galloped to Claparède's division and a few minutes later the Young Guards stationed behind the knoll moved forward. Napoleon gazed silently in that direction.

'No!' he suddenly said to Berthier. 'I can't send Claparède. Send Friant's division.'

Though there was no advantage in sending Friant's division instead of Claparède's, and even an obvious inconvenience and delay in stopping Claparède and sending Friant now, the order was carried out exactly. Napoleon did not notice that in regard to his army he was playing the part of a doctor who hinders by his medicines – a role he so justly understood and condemned.

Friant's division disappeared, as the others had done, into the smoke of the battlefield. From all sides adjutants continued to arrive at a gallop, and as if by agreement all said 'the same thing. They all asked for reinforcements, and all said that the Russians were holding their positions and maintaining a hellish fire under which the French army was melting away.

Napoleon sat on a camp-stool wrapped in thought.

M. de Beausset, the man so fond of travel, having fasted since morning came up to the Emperor and ventured respectfully to suggest lunch to his Majesty.

'I hope I may now congratulate your Majesty on a victory?' said he.

Napoleon silently shook his head in negation. Assuming the negation to refer only to the victory and not to the lunch, M. de

Beausset ventured with respectful jocularity to remark that there is no reason for not having lunch when one can get it.

'Go away . . .' exclaimed Napoleon suddenly and morosely, and turned aside.

A beatific smile of regret, repentance, and ecstasy beamed on M. de Beausset's face and he glided away to the other generals.

Napoleon was experiencing a feeling of depression like that of an ever-lucky gambler who after recklessly flinging money about and always winning, suddenly, just when he has calculated all the chances of the game, finds that the more he considers his play the more surely he loses.

His troops were the same, his generals the same, the same preparations had been made, the same dispositions, and the same proclamation *courte et énergique*, he himself was still the same, he knew that and knew that he was now even more experienced and skilful than before. Even the enemy was the same as at Austerlitz and Friedland – yet the terrible stroke of his arm had supernaturally become impotent.

All the old methods that had been unfailingly crowned with success: the concentration of batteries on one point, an attack by reserves to break the enemy's line and a cavalry attack by 'the men of iron', all these methods had already been employed, yet not only was there no victory, but from all sides came news of generals killed and wounded, of reinforcements needed, of the impossibility of driving back the Russians, and of disorganization among his own troops.

Formerly, after he had given two or three orders and uttered a few phrases, marshals and adjutants had come galloping up with congratulations and happy faces, announcing the trophies taken, the corps of prisoners, bundles of enemy eagles and standards, cannon and stores, and Murat had only begged leave to loose the cavalry to gather in the baggage-wagons. So it had been at Lodi, Marengo, Arcola, Jena, Austerlitz, Wagram,* and so on. But now something strange was happening to his troops.

Despite news of the capture of the flèches, Napoleon saw that this was not the same, not at all the same, as what had happened in his former battles. He saw that what he was feeling was felt by all the men about him experienced in the art of war. All their faces looked dejected, and they all shunned one another's eyes – only a de Beausset could fail to grasp the meaning of what was happening.

But Napoleon with his long experience of war well knew the meaning of a battle not gained by the attacking side in eight hours, after all efforts had been expended. He knew that it was a lost battle and that the least accident might now – with the fight balanced on such a strained centre – destroy him and his army.

When he ran his mind over the whole of this strange Russian campaign, in which not one battle had been won, and in which not a flag, or cannon, or army corps, had been captured in two months, when he looked at the concealed depression on the faces around him and heard reports of the Russians still holding their ground – a terrible feeling like a nightmare took possession of him, and all the unlucky accidents that might destroy him occurred to his mind. The Russians might fall on his left wing, might break through his centre, he himself might be killed by a stray cannon-ball. All this was possible. In former battles he had only considered the possibilities of success, but now innumerable unlucky chances presented themselves, and he expected them all. Yes, it was like a dream in which a man fancies that a ruffian is coming to attack him, and raises his arm to strike that ruffian a terrible blow which he knows should annihilate him, but then feels that his arm drops powerless and limp like a rag, and the horror of unavoidable destruction seizes him in his helplessness.

The news that the Russians were attacking the left flank of the French army aroused that horror in Napoleon. He sat silently on a camp-stool below the knoll, with head bowed and elbows on his knees. Berthier approached and suggested that they should ride along the line to ascertain the position of affairs.

'What? What do you say?' asked Napoleon. 'Yes, tell them to bring me my horse.'

He mounted and rode towards Semënovsk.

Amid the powder-smoke slowly dispersing over the whole space through which Napoleon rode, horses and men were lying in pools of blood, singly or in heaps. Neither Napoleon nor any of his generals had ever before seen such horrors or so many slain in such a small area. The roar of guns, that had not ceased for ten hours, wearied the ear and gave a peculiar significance to the spectacle, as music does to *tableaux vivants*. Napoleon rode up the high ground at Semënovsk, and through the smoke saw ranks of men in uniforms of a colour unfamiliar to him. They were Russians.

The Russians stood in serried ranks behind Semënovsk village and its knoll, and their guns boomed incessantly along their line and sent forth clouds of smoke. It was no longer a battle: it was a continuous slaughter which could be of no avail either to the French or the Russians. Napoleon stopped his horse and again fell into the reverie from which Berthier had roused him. He could not stop what was going on before him and around him and was supposed to be directed by him and to depend on him, and from its lack of success this affair, for the first time, seemed to him unnecessary and horrible.

One of the generals rode up to Napoleon and ventured to offer to lead the Old Guard into action. Ney and Berthier, standing near Napoleon, exchanged looks and smiled contemptuously at this general's senseless offer.

Napoleon bowed his head and remained silent a long time.

'At eight hundred leagues from France I will not have my Guard destroyed!' he said, and turning his horse rode back to Shevardino.

35

ON the rug-covered bench where Pierre had seen him in the morning sat Kutuzov, his grey head hanging, his heavy body relaxed. He gave no orders, but only assented to or dissented from what others suggested.

'Yes, yes, do that,' he replied to various proposals. 'Yes, yes: go, dear boy, and have a look,' he would say to one or another of those about him; or, 'No, don't, we'd better wait!' He listened to the reports that were brought him, and gave directions when his subordinates demanded that of him; but when listening to the reports it seemed as if he were not interested in the import of the words spoken, but rather in something else – in the expression of face and the tone of voice of those who were reporting. By long years of military experience he knew, and with the wisdom of age understood, that it is impossible for one man to direct hundreds of thousands of others struggling with death, and he knew that the result of a battle is decided not by the orders of a commander-in-chief, nor the place where the troops are stationed, not by the number of cannon or of slaughtered men, but by that intangible force called the spirit of the army, and he watched this force and guided it in as far as that was in his power.

Kutuzov's general expression was one of concentrated quiet attention, and his face wore a strained look as if he found it difficult to master the fatigue of his old and feeble body.

At eleven o'clock they brought him news that the flèches captured by the French had been retaken, but that Prince Bagration was wounded. Kutuzov groaned and swayed his head.

'Ride over to Prince Peter Ivanovich* and find out about it exactly,' he said to one of his adjutants, and then turned to the Duke of Würtemburg* who was standing behind him.

'Will your Highness, please, take command of the First Army?'

Soon after the Duke's departure – before he could possibly have reached Semënovsk – his adjutant came back from him and told Kutuzov that the Duke asked for more troops.

Kutuzov made a grimace and sent an order to Dokhturov to take over the command of the First Army, and a request to the Duke – whom he said he could not spare at such an important moment – to return to him. When they brought him news that Murat had been taken prisoner,* and the staff-officers congratulated him, Kutuzov smiled.

'Wait a little, gentlemen,' said he. 'The battle is won, and there is nothing extraordinary in the capture of Murat. Still, it is better to wait before we rejoice.'

But he sent an adjutant to take the news round the army.

When Scherbinin came galloping from the left flank with news that the French had captured the flèches and the village of Semënovsk, Kutuzov, guessing by the sounds of the battle and by Scherbinin's looks that the news was bad, rose as if to stretch his legs, and taking Scherbinin's arm led him aside.

'Go, my dear fellow,' he said to Ermolov, 'and see whether something can't be done.'

Kutuzov was in Gorky, near the centre of the Russian position. The attack directed by Napoleon against our left flank had been several times repulsed. In the centre the French had not got beyond Borodino, and on their left flank Uvarov's cavalry had put the French to flight.

Towards three o'clock the French attacks ceased. On the faces of all who came from the field of battle, and of those who stood around him, Kutuzov noticed an expression of extreme tension. He was satisfied with the day's success – a success exceeding his expectation, but the old man's strength was failing him. Several times his head dropped low as if it were falling, and he dozed off. Dinner was brought him.

Adjutant-General Wolzogen, the man who when riding past Prince Andrew had said, 'the war should be extended widely,' and whom Bagration so detested, rode up while Kutuzov was at dinner. Wolzogen had come from Barclay de Tolly to report on the progress of affairs on the left flank. The sagacious Barclay de Tolly, seeing crowds of wounded men running back and the disordered rear of the army, weighed all the circumstances, concluded that the battle was lost, and sent his favourite officer to the commander-in-chief with that news.

Kutuzov was chewing a piece of roast chicken with difficulty, and glanced at Wolzogen with eyes that brightened under their puckering lids.

Wolzogen, nonchalantly stretching his legs, approached Kutuzov with a half-contemptuous smile on his lips, scarcely touching the peak of his cap.

He treated his Serene Highness with a somewhat affected nonchalance intended to show that, as a highly trained military man, he left it to Russians to make an idol of this useless old man, but that he knew whom he was dealing with. 'Der alte Herr' (as in their own set the Germans called Kutuzov) 'is making himself very comfortable,' thought Wolzogen, and looking severely at the dishes in front of Kutuzov he began to report to 'the old gentleman' the position of affairs on the left flank as Barclay had ordered him to and as he had himself seen and understood it.

'All the points of our position are in the enemy's hands and we cannot dislodge them for lack of troops, the men are running away and it is impossible to stop them,' he reported.

Kutuzov ceased chewing and fixed an astonished gaze on Wolzogen, as if not understanding what was said to him. Wolzogen, noticing 'the old gentleman's' agitation, said with a smile:

'I have not considered it right to conceal from your Serene Highness what I have seen. The troops are in complete disorder . . .'

'You have seen? You have seen? . . .' Kutuzov shouted frowning, and rising quickly he went up to Wolzogen.

'How . . . how dare you! . . .' he shouted, choking and making a threatening gesture with his trembling arms: 'How dare you, sir, say that to me? You know nothing about it. Tell General Barclay from me that his information is incorrect and that the real course of the battle is better known to me, the commander-in-chief, than to him.'

Wolzogen was about to make a rejoinder, but Kutuzov interrupted him.

'The enemy has been repulsed on the left and defeated on the right flank. If you have seen amiss, sir, do not allow yourself to say what you don't know! Be so good as to ride to General Barclay and inform him of my firm intention to attack the enemy tomorrow,' said Kutuzov sternly.

All were silent, and the only sound audible was the heavy breathing of the panting old general.

'They are repulsed everywhere, for which I thank God and our brave army! The enemy is beaten, and to-morrow we shall drive him from the sacred soil of Russia,' said Kutuzov crossing himself, and he suddenly sobbed as his eyes filled with tears.

Wolzogen, shrugging his shoulders and curling his lips, stepped silently aside, marvelling at 'the old gentleman's' conceited stupidity.

'Ah, here he is, my hero!' said Kutuzov to a portly, handsome, dark-haired general, who was just ascending the knoll.

This was Raevsky, who had spent the whole day at the most important part of the field of Borodino.

Raevsky reported that the troops were firmly holding their ground and that the French no longer ventured to attack.

After hearing him, Kutuzov said in French:

'Then you do not think *like some others* that we must retreat?'

'On the contrary, your Highness, in indecisive actions it is always the most stubborn who remain victors,' replied Raevsky, 'and in my opinion . . .'

'Kaysarov!' Kutuzov called to his adjutant. 'Sit down and write out the order of the day for to-morrow. And you,' he continued, addressing another, 'ride along the line and announce that to-morrow we attack.'

While Kutuzov was talking to Raevsky and dictating the order of the day, Wolzogen returned from Barclay, and said that General Barclay de Tolly wished to have written confirmation of the order the field-marshal had given.

Kutuzov, without looking at Wolzogen, gave directions for the order to be written out which the former commander-in-chief, to avoid personal responsibility, very judiciously wished to receive.

And by means of that mysterious indefinable bond which maintains throughout an army one and the same temper, known as 'the spirit of the army', and which constitutes the chief sinew of war, Kutuzov's words, his order for a battle next day, immediately became known from one end of the army to the other.

It was far from being the same words or the same order that reached the farthest links of that chain. The tales passing from mouth to mouth at different ends of the army did not even resemble what Kutuzov had said, but the sense of his words spread everywhere because what he said was not the outcome of cunning calculations, but of a feeling that lay in the commander-in-chief's soul as in that of every Russian.

And on learning that to-morrow they were to attack the enemy, and hearing from the highest quarters a confirmation of what they wanted to believe, the exhausted wavering men felt comforted and inspired.

36

PRINCE ANDREW'S regiment was among the reserves which till after one o'clock were stationed inactive behind Semënovsk under heavy artillery fire. Towards two o'clock the regiment, having already lost more than two hundred men, was moved forward into a trampled oatfield in the gap between Semënovsk and the Knoll Battery where thousands of men perished that day and on which an intense, concentrated fire from several hundred enemy guns was directed between one and two o'clock.

Without moving from that spot or firing a single shot the regiment here lost another third of its men. From in front and especially from the right, in the unlifting smoke the guns boomed, and out of the mysterious domain of smoke that overlay the whole space in front, quick hissing cannon-balls and slow whistling shells flew unceasingly. At times, as if to allow them a respite, a quarter of an hour passed during which the cannon-balls and shells all flew overhead, but sometimes several men were torn from the regiment in a minute, and the slain were continually being dragged away and the wounded carried off.

With each fresh blow less and less chance of life remained for those not yet killed. The regiment stood in columns of battalion three hundred paces apart, but nevertheless the men were always in one and the same mood. All alike were taciturn and morose. Talk was rarely heard in the ranks, and it ceased altogether every time the thud of a successful shot and the cry of 'stretchers!' was heard. Most of the time, by their officers' order, the men sat on the ground. One, having taken off his shako carefully loosened the gathers of its lining and drew them tight again; another, rubbing some dry clay between his palms, polished his bayonet; another fingered the strap and pulled the buckle of his bandolier, while another smoothed and refolded his leg-bands and put his boots on again. Some built little houses of the tufts in the ploughed ground, or plaited baskets from the straw in the cornfield. All seemed fully absorbed in these pursuits. When men were killed or wounded, when rows of stretchers went past, when some troops retreated, and when great masses of the enemy came into view through the smoke, no one paid any attention to these things. But when our artillery or cavalry advanced or some of our infantry were seen to move forward, words of approval were heard on all sides. But the liveliest attention was attracted by occurrences quite apart from, and unconnected with, the battle. It was as if the minds of these morally exhausted men found relief in everyday, commonplace occurrences. A battery of artillery was passing in front of the regiment. The horse of an ammunition cart put its leg over a trace. 'Hey, look at the trace horse!... Get her leg out! She'll fall... Ah, they don't see it!' came identical shouts from the ranks all along the regiment. Another time general attention was attracted by a small brown dog, coming heaven knows whence, which trotted in a preoccupied manner in front of the ranks with tail stiffly erect till suddenly a shell fell close by, when it yelped, tucked its tail between its legs, and darted aside. Yells and shrieks of laughter rose from the whole regiment. But such distractions lasted only a moment, and for eight hours the men had been inactive, without food, in constant fear of death, and their pale and gloomy faces grew ever paler and gloomier.

Prince Andrew, pale and gloomy like everyone in the regiment, paced up and down from the border of one patch to another, at the edge of a meadow beside an oat-field, with head bowed and arms behind his back. There was nothing for him to do and no orders to be given. Everything went on of itself. The killed were dragged from the front, the wounded carried away, and the ranks closed up. If any soldiers ran to the rear they returned immediately and hastily. At first Prince Andrew, considering it his duty to rouse the courage of the men and to set them an example, walked about among the ranks, but he soon became convinced that this was unnecessary and that there was nothing he could teach them. All the powers of his soul, as of every soldier there, were unconsciously bent on avoiding the contemplation of the horrors of their situation. He walked along the meadow, dragging his feet, rustling the grass, and gazing at the dust that covered his boots; now he took big strides trying to keep to the footprints left on the meadow by mowers, then he counted his steps, calculating how often he must walk from one strip to another to walk a mile, then he stripped the flowers from the wormwood that grew along a boundary rut, rubbed them in his palms, and smelt their pungent sweetly bitter scent. Nothing remained of the previous day's thoughts. He thought of nothing. He listened with weary ears to the ever-recurring sounds, distinguishing the whistle of flying projectiles from the booming of the reports, glanced at the tiresomely familiar faces of the men of the first battalion, and waited. 'Here it comes . . . this one is coming our way again!' he thought, listening to the approaching whistle in the hidden region of smoke. 'One, another! Again! It has hit . . .' He stopped and looked at the ranks. 'No, it has gone over. But this one has hit!' And again he started trying to reach the boundary strip in sixteen paces. A whizz and a thud! Five paces from him a cannon-ball tore up the dry earth and disappeared. A chill ran down his back. Again he glanced at the ranks. Probably many had been hit – a large crowd had gathered near the second battalion.

'Adjutant!' he shouted. 'Order them not to crowd together.'

The adjutant, having obeyed this instruction, approached Prince Andrew. From the other side a battalion commander rode up.

867

'Look out!' came a frightened cry from a soldier and, like a bird whirring in rapid flight and alighting on the ground, a shell dropped with little noise within two steps of Prince Andrew and close to the battalion commander's horse. The horse first, regardless of whether it was right or wrong to show fear, snorted, reared almost throwing the major, and galloped aside. The horse's terror infected the men.

'Lie down!' cried the adjutant, throwing himself flat on the ground.

Prince Andrew hesitated. The smoking shell spun like a top between him and the prostrate adjutant near a wormwood plant between the field and the meadow.

'Can this be death?' thought Prince Andrew, looking with a quite new, envious glance at the grass, the wormwood, and the streamlet of smoke that curled up from the rotating black ball. 'I cannot, I do not wish to die. I love life – I love this grass, this earth, this air...' He thought this, and at the same time remembered that people were looking at him.

'It's shameful, sir!' he said to the adjutant. 'What...'

He did not finish speaking. At one and the same moment came the sound of an explosion, a whistle of splinters as from a breaking window frame, a suffocating smell of powder, and Prince Andrew started to one side, raising his arm, and fell on his chest. Several officers ran up to him. From the right side of his abdomen blood was welling out making a large stain on the grass.

The militiamen with stretchers, who were called up, stood behind the officers. Prince Andrew lay on his chest with his face in the grass, breathing heavily and noisily.

'What are you waiting for? Come along!'

The peasants went up and took him by his shoulders and legs, but he moaned piteously and, exchanging looks, they set him down again.

'Pick him up, lift him, it's all the same!' cried someone.

They again took him by the shoulders and laid him on the stretcher.

'Ah God! My God! What is it? The stomach? That means death! My God!' – voices among the officers were heard saying.

'It flew a hair's breadth past my ear,' said the adjutant.

The peasants, adjusting the stretcher to their shoulders, started hurriedly along the path they had trodden down, to the dressing-station.

'Keep in step! Ah... those peasants!' shouted an officer, seizing by their shoulders and checking the peasants, who were walking unevenly and jolting the stretcher.

'Get into step, Fëdor . . . I say, Fëdor!' said the foremost peasant.

'Now that's right!' said the one behind joyfully, when he had got into step.

'Your Excellency! Eh. Prince!' said the trembling voice of Timokhin, who had run up and was looking down on the stretcher.

Prince Andrew opened his eyes and looked up at the speaker from the stretcher into which his head had sunk deep, and again his eyelids drooped.

The militiamen carried Prince Andrew to the dressing-station by the wood, where wagons were stationed. The dressing-station consisted of three tents with flaps turned back, pitched at the edge of a birch wood. In the wood, wagons and horses were standing. The horses were eating oats from their movable troughs and sparrows flew down and pecked the grains that fell. Some crows, scenting blood, flew among the birch trees cawing impatiently. Around the tents, over more than five acres, bloodstained men in various garbs stood, sat, or lay. Around the wounded stood crowds of soldier stretcher-bearers with dismal and attentive faces, whom the officers keeping order tried in vain to drive from the spot. Disregarding the officers' orders the soldiers stood leaning against their stretchers and gazing intently, as if trying to comprehend the difficult problem of what was taking place before them. From the tents came now loud angry cries, and now plaintive groans. Occasionally dressers ran out to fetch water, or to point out those who were to be brought in next. The wounded men awaiting their turn outside the tents groaned, sighed, wept, screamed, swore, or asked for vodka. Some were delirious. Prince Andrew's bearers stepping over the wounded who had not yet been bandaged, took him, as a regimental commander, close up to one of the tents and there stopped, awaiting instructions. Prince Andrew opened his eyes and for a long time could not make out what was going on around him. He remembered the meadow, the wormwood, the field, the whirling black ball, and his sudden rush of passionate love of life. Two steps from him, leaning against a branch and talking loudly and attracting general attention, stood a tall, handsome, black-haired non-commissioned officer with a bandaged head. He had been wounded in the head and leg by bullets. Around him, eagerly listening to his talk, a crowd of wounded and stretcher-bearers was gathered.

'We kicked *him* out from there so that he chucked everything, we grabbed the King himself!' cried he, looking around him with eyes that glittered with fever. 'If only reserves had come up just then, lads, there wouldn't have been nothing left of him! I tell you surely . . .'

Like all the others near the speaker, Prince Andrew looked at him with shining eyes and experienced a sense of comfort. 'But isn't it all the same now?' thought he. 'And what will be there, and what has there been here? Why was I so reluctant to part with life? There was something in this life I did not and do not understand . . .'

37

ONE of the doctors came out of the tent in a bloodstained apron, holding a cigar between the thumb and little finger of one of his small bloodstained hands, so as not to smear it. He raised his head and looked about him, but above the level of the wounded men. He evidently wanted a little respite. After turning his head from right to left for some time he sighed and looked down.

'All right, immediately,' he replied to a dresser who pointed Prince Andrew out to him, and he told them to carry him into the tent.

Murmurs arose among the wounded who were waiting.

'It seems that even in the next world only the gentry are to have a chance!' remarked one.

Prince Andrew was carried in and laid on a table that had only just been cleared, and which a dresser was washing down. Prince Andrew could not make out distinctly what was in that tent. The pitiful groans from all sides, and the torturing pain in his thigh, stomach, and back, distracted him. All he saw about him merged into a general impression of naked bleeding human bodies that seemed to fill the whole of the low tent, as a few weeks previously, on that hot August day, such bodies had filled the dirty pond beside the Smolensk road. Yes, it was the same flesh, the same *chair à canon*, the sight of which had even then filled him with horror, as by a presentiment.

There were three operating tables in the tent. Two were occupied, and on the third they placed Prince Andrew. For a little while he was left alone and involuntarily witnessed what was taking place on the other two tables. On the nearest one sat a Tartar, probably a Cossack judging by the uniform thrown down beside him. Four soldiers were holding him, and a spectacled doctor was cutting into his muscular brown back.

'Ooh, ooh, ooh!' grunted the Tartar, and suddenly lifting up his swarthy snub-nosed face with its high cheekbones, and baring his white teeth, he began to wriggle and twitch his body and utter piercing, ringing, and prolonged yells. On the other table, round which many people were crowding, a tall well-fed man lay on his back with his head thrown back. His curly hair, its colour and the shape of his head, seemed strangely familiar to Prince Andrew. Several dressers were pressing on his chest to hold him down. One large white plump leg twitched rapidly all the time with a feverish tremor. The man was sobbing and choking convulsively. Two doctors – one of whom was pale and trembling – were silently doing something to this man's other, gory leg. When he had finished with the Tartar, whom they covered with an overcoat, the spectacled doctor came up to Prince Andrew wiping his hands.

He glanced at Prince Andrew's face and quickly turned away.

'Undress him! What are you waiting for?' he cried angrily to the dressers.

His very first remotest recollections of childhood came back to Prince Andrew's mind when the dresser with sleeves rolled up began hastily to undo the buttons of his clothes and undressed him. The doctor bent down over the wound, felt it, and sighed deeply. Then he made a sign to someone, and the torturing pain in his abdomen caused Prince Andrew to lose consciousness. When he came to himself the splintered portions of his thigh-bone had been extracted, the torn flesh cut away, and the wound bandaged. Water was being sprinkled on his face. As soon as Prince Andrew opened his eyes, the doctor bent over, kissed him silently on the lips, and hurried away.

After the sufferings he had been enduring Prince Andrew enjoyed a blissful feeling such as he had not experienced for a long time. All the best and happiest moments of his life – especially his earliest childhood, when he used to be undressed and put to bed, and when leaning over him his nurse sang him to sleep and he, burying his head in the pillow, felt happy in the mere consciousness of life – returned to his memory, not merely as something past but as something present.

The doctors were busily engaged with the wounded man the shape of whose head seemed familiar to Prince Andrew: they were lifting him up and trying to quiet him.

'Show it me ... Oh, ooh ... oh! Oh, ooh!' his frightened moans could be heard, subdued by suffering and broken by sobs.

Hearing those moans Prince Andrew wanted to weep. Whether because he was dying without glory, or because he was sorry to part with life, or because of those memories of a childhood that could not return, or because he was suffering and others were suffering and that man near him was groaning so piteously – he felt like weeping childlike, kindly, and almost happy, tears.

The wounded man was shown his amputated leg stained with clotted blood and with the boot still on.

'Oh! Oh, ooh!' he sobbed, like a woman.

The doctor who had been standing beside him, preventing Prince Andrew from seeing his face, moved away.

'My God! What is this? Why is he here?' said Prince Andrew to himself.

In the miserable, sobbing, enfeebled man whose leg had just been amputated he recognized Anatole Kuragin. Men were supporting him in their arms and offering him a glass of water, but his trembling, swollen lips could not grasp its rim. Anatole was sobbing painfully. 'Yes, it is he! Yes, that man is somehow closely and painfully connected with me,' thought Prince Andrew, not yet clearly grasping what he saw before him. 'What is the connexion of that man with my childhood and my life?' he asked himself, without finding an answer. And suddenly a new unexpected memory from that realm of pure and loving childhood presented itself to him. He remembered Natasha as he had seen her for the first time at the ball in 1810, with her slender neck and arms, and with a frightened happy face ready for rapture, and love and tenderness for her, stronger and more vivid than ever, awoke in his soul. He now remembered the connexion that existed between himself and this man who was dimly gazing at him through tears that filled his swollen eyes. He remembered everything, and ecstatic pity and love for that man overflowed his happy heart.

Prince Andrew could no longer restrain himself, and wept tender loving tears for his fellow men, for himself, and for his own and their errors.

'Compassion, love of our brothers, for those who love us and for those who hate us, love of our enemies; yes, that love which God preached on earth and which Princess Mary taught me and I did not understand – that is what made me sorry to part with life, that is what remained for me had I lived. But now it is too late. I know it!'

38

THE terrible spectacle of the battlefield covered with dead and wounded, together with the heaviness of his head and the news that some twenty generals he knew personally had been killed or wounded, and the consciousness of the impotence of his once mighty arm, produced an unexpected impression on Napoleon, who usually liked to look at the killed and wounded, thereby, he considered, testing his strength of mind. This day the horrible appearance of the battlefield overcame that strength of mind which he thought constituted his merit and his greatness. He rode hurriedly from the battlefield and returned to the Shevardino knoll, where he sat on his camp stool, his sallow face swollen and heavy, his eyes dim, his nose red, and his voice hoarse, involuntarily listening with downcast eyes to the sounds of firing. With painful dejection he awaited the end of this action, in which he regarded himself as a participant and which he was unable to arrest. A personal, human feeling for a brief moment got the better of the artificial phantasm of life he had served so long. He felt in his own person the sufferings and death he had witnessed on the battlefield. The heaviness of his head and chest reminded him of the possibility of suffering and death for himself. At that moment he did not desire Moscow, or victory, or glory (what need had he of more glory?). The one thing he wished for was rest, tranquillity, and freedom. But when he had been on the Semënovsk heights the artillery commander had proposed to him to bring several batteries of artillery up to those heights to strengthen the fire on the Russian troops crowded in front of Knyazkovo. Napoleon had assented and had given orders that news should be brought him of the effect those batteries produced.

An adjutant came now to inform him that the fire of two hundred guns had been concentrated on the Russians, as he had ordered, but that they still held their ground.

'Our fire is mowing them down by rows, but still they hold on,' said the adjutant.

'They want more! . . .' said Napoleon in a hoarse voice.

'Sire?' asked the adjutant, who had not heard the remark.

'They want more!' croaked Napoleon frowning. 'Let them have it!'

Even before he gave that order the thing he did not desire, and for which he only gave the order because he thought it was expected of him, was being done. And he fell back into that artificial realm of imaginary greatness, and again – as a horse walking a treadmill thinks it is doing something for itself – he submissively fulfilled the cruel, sad, gloomy, and inhuman role predestined for him.

And not for that day and hour alone were the mind and conscience of this man darkened on whom the responsibility for what was happening lay more than on all the others who took part in it. Never to the end of his life could he understand goodness, beauty, or truth, or the significance of his actions, which were too contrary to goodness and truth, too remote from everything

873

human, for him ever to be able to grasp their meaning. He could not disavow his actions, belauded as they were by half the world, and so he had to repudiate truth, goodness, and all humanity.

Not only on that day, as he rode over the battlefield strewn with men killed and maimed (by his will as he believed) did he reckon as he looked at them how many Russians there were for each Frenchman and, deceiving himself, find reason for rejoicing in the calculation that there were five Russians for every Frenchman. Not on that day alone did he write in a letter to Paris, that 'the battlefield was superb', because fifty thousand corpses lay there, but even on the island of St Helena, in the peaceful solitude where he said he intended to devote his leisure to an account of the great deeds he had done, he wrote:

The Russian war should have been the most popular war of modern times: it was a war of good sense, for real interests, for the tranquillity and security of all; it was purely pacific and conservative.

It was a war for a great cause, the end of uncertainties and the beginning of security. A new horizon and new labours were opening out, full of well-being and prosperity for all. The European system was already founded; all that remained was to organize it.

Satisfied on these great points, and with tranquillity everywhere, I too should have had my *Congress* and my *Holy Alliance*. Those ideas were stolen from me. In that reunion of great sovereigns we should have discussed our interests like one family, and have rendered account to the peoples as clerk to master.

Europe would in this way soon have been, in fact, but one people, and anyone who travelled anywhere would have found himself always in the common fatherland. I should have demanded the freedom of all the navigable rivers for everybody, that the seas should be common to all, and that the great standing armies should be reduced henceforth to mere guards for the Sovereigns.

On returning to France, to the bosom of the great, strong, magnificent, peaceful, and glorious fatherland, I should have proclaimed her frontiers immutable; all future wars purely *defensive*, all aggrandizement *anti-national*. I should have associated my son in the Empire; my *dictatorship* would have been finished, and his constitutional reign would have begun.

Paris would have been the capital of the world, and the French the envy of the nations!

My leisure then, and my old age, would have been devoted, in company with the Empress and during the royal apprenticeship of my son, to leisurely visiting, with our own horses and like a true country couple, every corner of the Empire, receiving complaints, redressing wrongs, and scattering public buildings and benefactions on all sides and everywhere.

Napoleon, predestined by Providence for the gloomy role of executioner of the peoples, assured himself that the aim of his actions had been the peoples' welfare, and that he could control the fate of millions and by the employment of power confer bene-factions.

Of four hundred thousand men who crossed the Vistula [he wrote further of the Russian war] half were Austrians, Prussians, Saxons, Poles, Bavarians, Würtembergers, Mecklenbergers, Spaniards, Italians, and Neapolitans. The Imperial army, strictly speaking, was one-third composed of Dutch, Belgians, men from the borders of the Rhine, Piedmontese, Swiss, Genevese, Tuscans, Romans, inhabitants of the Thirty-Second Military Division, of Bremen, of Hamburg, and so on: it included scarcely a hundred and forty thousand who spoke French. The Russian expedition actually cost France less than fifty thousand men; the Russian army in the retreat from Vilna to Moscow lost in the various battles four times more men than the French army; the burning of Moscow cost the lives of a hundred thousand Russians who died of cold and want in the woods; finally, in its march from Moscow to the Oder the Russian army also suffered from the severity of the season; so that by the time it reached Vilna it numbered only fifty thousand and at Kalisch less than eighteen thousand.

He imagined that the war with Russia came about by his will, and the horrors that occurred did not stagger his soul. He boldly took the whole responsibility for what happened, and his darkened mind found justification in the belief that among the hundreds of thousands who perished there were fewer Frenchmen than Hessians and Bavarians.

39

SEVERAL tens of thousands of the slain lay in diverse postures and various uniforms on the fields and meadows belonging to the Davydov family and to the Crown serfs – those fields and meadows where for hundreds of years the peasants of Borodino, Gorky, Shevardino, and Semënovsk had reaped their harvests and pastured their cattle. At the dressing-stations the grass and earth were soaked with blood for a space of some three acres around. Crowds of men of various arms, wounded and unwounded, with frightened faces, dragged themselves back to Mozhaysk from the one army, and back to Valuevo from the other. Other crowds, exhausted and hungry, went forward led by their officers. Others held their ground and continued to fire.

Over the whole field, previously so gaily beautiful with the glitter of bayonets and cloudlets of smoke in the morning sun, there now spread a mist of damp and smoke and a strange acid smell of saltpetre and blood. Clouds gathered, and drops of rain began to fall on the dead and wounded, on the frightened, exhausted, and hesitating men, as if to say: 'Enough, men! Enough! Cease . . . bethink yourselves! What are you doing?'

To the men of both sides alike, worn out by want of food and rest, it began equally to appear doubtful whether they should continue to slaughter one another; all the faces expressed hesitation, and the question arose in every soul: 'For what, for whom, must I kill and be killed? . . . You may go and kill whom you please, but I don't want to do so any more!' By evening this thought had ripened in every soul. At any moment these men might have been seized with horror at what they were doing, and might have thrown up everything and run away anywhere.

But though towards the end of the battle the men felt all the horror of what they were doing, though they would have been glad to leave off, some incomprehensible, mysterious power continued to control them, and they still brought up the charges, loaded, aimed, and applied the match, though only one artilleryman survived out of every three, and though they stumbled and panted with fatigue, perspiring and stained with blood and powder. The cannon-balls flew just as swiftly and cruelly from both sides, crushing human bodies, and that terrible work, which was not done by the will of a man, but at the will of Him who governs men and worlds, continued.

Anyone looking at the disorganized rear of the Russian army would have said that, if only the French made one more slight effort, it would disappear; and anyone looking at the rear of the French army would have said that the Russians need only make one more slight effort and the French would be destroyed. But neither the French nor the Russians made that effort, and the flame of battle burnt slowly out.

The Russians did not make that effort because they were not attacking the French. At the beginning of the battle they stood blocking the way to Moscow and they still did so at the end of the battle as at the beginning. But even had the aim of the Russians been to drive the French from their positions, they could not have made this last effort, for all the Russian troops had been broken up, there was no part of the Russian army that had not suffered in the battle, and though still holding their positions they had lost one-half of their army.

The French with the memory of all their former victories during fifteen years, with the assurance of Napoleon's invincibility, with the consciousness that they had captured part of the battlefield and had lost only a quarter of their men and still had their Guards intact, twenty thousand strong, might easily have made that effort. The French who had attacked the Russian army in order to drive it from its position ought to have made that effort, for as long as the Russians continued to block the road to Moscow as before, the aim of the French had not been attained and all their efforts and losses were in vain. But the French did not make that effort. Some historians say that Napoleon need only have used his Old Guards, who were intact, and the battle would have been won. To speak of what would have happened had Napoleon sent his Guards is like talking of what would happen if autumn became spring. It could not be. Napoleon did not give his Guards, not because he did not want to, but because it could not be done. All the generals, officers, and soldiers of the French army knew it could not be done, because the flagging spirit of the troops would not permit it.

It was not Napoleon alone who had experienced that nightmare feeling of the mighty arm being stricken powerless, but all the generals and soldiers of his army, whether they had taken part in the battle or not, after all their experience of previous battles – when after one-tenth of such efforts the enemy had fled – experienced a similar feeling of terror before an enemy who, after losing HALF his men, stood as threateningly at the end as at the beginning of the battle. The moral force of the attacking French army was exhausted. Not that sort of victory which is defined by the capture of pieces of material fastened to sticks, called standards, and of the ground on which the troops had stood and were standing, but a moral victory that convinces the enemy of the moral superiority of his opponent and of his own impotence, was gained by the Russians at Borodino. The French invaders, like an infuriated animal that has in its onslaught received a mortal wound, felt that they were perishing, but could not stop, any more than the Russian army, weaker by one-half, could help swerving. By the impetus gained, the French army was still able to roll forward to Moscow, but there, without further effort on the part of the Russians, it had to perish, bleeding from the mortal wound it had received at Borodino. The direct consequence of the battle of Borodino was Napoleon's senseless flight from Moscow, his retreat along the old Smolensk road, the destruction of the invading army of five hundred thousand men, and the downfall of Napoleonic France, on which at Borodino for the first time the hand of an opponent of stronger spirit had been laid.

END OF PART TWO

PART THREE

1

ABSOLUTE continuity of motion is not comprehensible to the human mind. Laws of motion of any kind only become comprehensible to man when he examines arbitrarily selected elements of that motion; but at the same time, a large proportion of human error comes from the arbitrary division of continuous motion into discontinuous elements. There is a well-known so-called sophism of the ancients consisting in this, that Achilles could never catch up with a tortoise he was following, in spite of the fact that he travelled ten times as fast as the tortoise. By the time Achilles has covered the distance that separated him from the tortoise, the tortoise has covered one-tenth of that distance ahead of him: when Achilles has covered that tenth, the tortoise has covered another one-hundredth, and so on for ever. This problem seemed to the ancients insoluble. The absurd answer (that Achilles could never overtake the tortoise) resulted from this: that motion was arbitrarily divided into discontinuous elements, whereas the motion both of Achilles and of the tortoise was continuous.

By adopting smaller and smaller elements of motion we only approach a solution of the problem, but never reach it. Only when we have admitted the conception of the infinitely small, and the resulting geometrical progression with a common ratio of one-tenth, and have found the sum of this progression to infinity, do we reach a solution of the problem.

A modern branch of mathematics, having achieved the art of dealing with the infinitely small, can now yield solutions in other more complex problems of motion, which used to appear insoluble.

This modern branch of mathematics, unknown to the ancients, when dealing with problems of motion, admits the conception of the infinitely small, and so conforms to the chief condition of motion (absolute continuity) and thereby corrects the inevitable error which the human mind cannot avoid when dealing with separate elements of motion instead of examining continuous motion.

In seeking the laws of historical movement just the same thing happens. The movement of humanity, arising as it does from innumerable arbitrary human wills, is continuous.

To understand the laws of this continuous movement is the aim of history. But to arrive at these laws, resulting from the sum of all those human wills, man's mind postulates arbitrary and disconnected units. The first method of history is to take an arbitrarily selected series of continuous events and examine it apart from others, though there is and can be no *beginning* to any event, for one event always flows uninterruptedly from another.

The second method is to consider the actions of some one man – a king or a commander – as equivalent to the sum of many individual wills; whereas the sum of individual wills is never expressed by the activity of a single historic personage.

Historical science in its endeavour to draw nearer to truth continually takes smaller and smaller units for examination. But however small the units it takes, we feel that to take any unit disconnected from others, or to assume a *beginning* of any phenomenon, or to say that the will of many men is expressed by the actions of any one historic personage, is in itself false.

It needs no critical exertion to reduce utterly to dust any deductions drawn from history. It is merely necessary to select some larger or smaller unit as the subject of observation – as criticism has every right to do, seeing that whatever unit history observes must always be arbitrarily selected.

Only by taking an infinitesimally small unit for observation (the differential of history, that is, the individual tendencies of men) and attaining to the art of integrating them (that is, finding the sum of these infinitesimals) can we hope to arrive at the laws of history.

The first fifteen years of the nineteenth century in Europe present an extraordinary movement of millions of people. Men leave their customary pursuits, hasten from one side of Europe to the other, plunder and slaughter one another, triumph and are plunged in despair, and for some years the whole course of life is altered and presents an intensive movement which first increases and then slackens. What was the cause of this movement, by what laws was it governed? asks the mind of man.

The historians, replying to this question, lay before us the sayings and doings of a few dozen men in a building in the city of Paris, calling these sayings and doings 'the Revolution'; then they give a detailed biography of Napoleon, and of certain people favourable or hostile to him; tell of the influence some of these people had on others, and say: That is why this movement took place and those are its laws.

But the mind of man not only refuses to believe this explanation, but plainly says that this method of explanation is fallacious, because in it a weaker phenomenon is taken as the cause of a stronger. The sum of human wills produced the Revolution and Napoleon, and only the sum of those wills first tolerated and then destroyed them.

'But every time there have been conquests there have been conquerors; every time there has been a revolution in any state there have been great men,' says history. And indeed, every time conquerors appear there have been wars, human reason replies, but this does not prove that the conquerors caused the wars and that it is possible to find the laws of a war in the personal activity of a single man. Whenever I look at my watch and its hands point to ten, I hear the bells of the neighbouring church; but I have no right to assume that because the bells begin to ring when the hands of the watch reach ten, the movement of the bells is caused by the position of the hands of the watch.

Whenever I see the movement of a locomotive I hear the whistle and see the valves opening and wheels turning; but I have no right to conclude that the whistling and the turning of wheels are the cause of the movement of the engine.

The peasants say that a cold wind blows in late spring because the oaks are budding, and really every spring cold winds do blow when the oak is budding. But though I do not know what causes the cold winds to blow when the oak-buds unfold, I cannot agree with the peasants that the unfolding of the oak-buds is the cause of the cold wind, for the force of the wind is beyond the influence of the buds. I see only a coincidence of occurrences such as happens with all the phenomena of life, and I see that however much and however carefully I observe the hands of the watch, and the valves and wheels of the engine, and the oak, I shall not discover the cause of the bells ringing, the engine moving, or of the winds of spring. To do that I must entirely change my point of view and study the laws of the movement of steam, of the bells, and of the wind. History must do the same. And attempts in this direction have already been made.

To study the laws of history we must completely change the subject of our observation, must leave aside kings, ministers, and generals, and study the common, infinitesimally small elements by which the masses are moved. No one can say in how far it is possible for man to advance in this way towards an understanding of the laws of history; but it is evident that only along that path does the possibility of discovering the laws of history lie; and that as yet not a millionth part as much mental effort has been applied in this direction by historians as has been devoted to describing the actions of various kings, commanders, and ministers and propounding reflections of their own concerning these actions.

2

THE forces of a dozen European nations burst into Russia. The Russian army and people avoided a collision till Smolensk was reached, and again from Smolensk to Borodino. The French army pushed on to Moscow, its goal, its impetus ever increasing as it neared its aim, just as the velocity of a falling body increases as it approaches the earth. Behind it were a thousand versts of hunger-stricken, hostile country, ahead were a few dozen versts separating it from its goal. Every soldier in Napoleon's army felt this and the invasion moved on by its own momentum.

The more the Russian army retreated the more fiercely a spirit of hatred of the enemy flared up: and while it retreated the army increased and consolidated. At Borodino a collision took place. Neither army was broken up, but the Russian army retreated immediately after the collision, as inevitably as a ball recoils after colliding with another having a greater momentum, and with equal inevitability the ball of invasion that had advanced with such momentum rolled on for some distance, though the collision had deprived it of all its force.

The Russians retreated eighty miles – to beyond Moscow – and the French reached Moscow and there came to a standstill. For five weeks after that there was not a single battle. The French did not move. As a bleeding, mortally wounded animal licks its wounds, they remained inert in Moscow for five weeks, and then suddenly, with no fresh reason, fled back; they made a dash for the Kaluga road, and (after a victory – for at Malo-Yaroslavets the field of conflict again remained theirs) without undertaking a single serious battle, they fled still more rapidly back to Smolensk, beyond Smolensk, beyond the Berëzina, beyond Vilna, and farther still.

On the evening of the 26th of August, Kutuzov and the whole Russian army were convinced that the battle of Borodino was a victory. Kutuzov reported so to the Emperor. He gave orders to prepare for a fresh conflict to finish the enemy, and did this not to deceive anyone, but because he knew that the enemy was beaten, as everyone who had taken part in the battle knew it.

But all that evening and next day reports came in one after another of unheard-of losses, of the loss of half the army, and a fresh battle proved physically impossible.

It was impossible to give battle before information had been collected, the wounded gathered in, the supplies of ammunition replenished, the slain reckoned up, new officers appointed to replace those who had been killed, and before the men had had food and sleep. And meanwhile, the very next morning after the battle, the French army advanced of itself upon the Russians, carried forward by the force of its own movement now seemingly increased in inverse proportion to the square of the distance from its aim. Kutuzov's wish was to attack next day, and the whole army desired to do so. But to make an attack the wish to do so is not sufficient, there must also be a possibility of doing it, and that possibility did not exist. It was impossible not to retreat a day's march, and then in the same way it was impossible not to retreat another and a third day's march, and at last, on the 1st of September when the army drew near Moscow – despite the strength of the feeling that had arisen in all ranks, the force of circumstances compelled it to retire beyond Moscow. And the troops retired one more, last, day's march, and abandoned Moscow to the enemy.

For people accustomed to think that plans of campaign and battles are made by generals – as any one of us sitting over a map in his study may imagine how he would have arranged things in this or that battle – the questions present themselves: Why did Kutuzov during the retreat not do this or that? Why did he not take up a position before reaching Fili? Why did he not retire at once by the Kaluga road, abandoning Moscow? and so on. People accustomed to think in that way forget, or do not know, the inevitable conditions which always limit the activities of any commander-in-chief. The activity of a commander-in-chief does not at all resemble the activity we imagine to ourselves when we sit at ease in our studies examining some campaign on the map, with a certain number of troops on this and that side in a certain known locality, and begin our plans from some given moment. A commander-in-chief is never dealing with the *beginning* of any event – the position from which we always contemplate it. The commander-in-chief is always in the midst of a series of shifting events and so he never can at any moment consider the whole import of an event that is occurring. Moment by moment the event is imperceptibly shaping itself, and at every moment of this continuous, uninterrupted shaping of events the commander-in-chief is in the midst of a most complex play of intrigues, worries, contingencies, authorities, projects, counsels, threats, and deceptions, and is continually obliged to reply to innumerable questions addressed to him, which constantly conflict with one another.

Learned military authorities quite seriously tell us that Kutuzov should have moved his army to the Kaluga road long before reaching Fili, and that somebody actually submitted such a proposal to him. But a commander-in-chief, especially at a difficult moment, has always before him not one proposal but dozens simultaneously. And all these proposals, based on strategies and tactics, contradict each other.

A commander-in-chief's business, it would seem, is simply to choose one of these projects. But even that he cannot do. Events and time do not wait. For instance, on the 28th it is suggested to him to cross to the Kaluga road, but just then an adjutant gallops up from Miloradovich asking whether he is to engage the French or retire. An order must be given him at once, that instant. And the order to retreat carries us past the turn to the Kaluga road. And after the adjutant comes the commissary-general asking where the stores are to be taken, and the chief of the hospitals asks where the wounded are to go, and a courier from Petersburg brings a letter from the sovereign which does not admit of the possibility of abandoning Moscow, and the commander-in-chief's rival, the man who is undermining him (and there are always not merely one but several such), presents a new project diametrically opposed to that of turning to the Kaluga road, and the commander-in-chief himself needs sleep and refreshment to maintain his energy, and a-respectable general who has been overlooked in the distribution of rewards comes to complain, and the inhabitants of the district pray to be defended, and an officer sent to inspect the locality comes in and gives a report quite contrary to what was said by the officer previously sent, and a spy, a prisoner, and a general who has been on reconnaissance, all describe the position of the enemy's army differently. People accustomed to misunderstand or to forget these inevitable conditions of a commander-in-chief's actions describe to us, for instance, the position of the army at Fili and assume that the commander-in-chief could, on the 1st of September, quite freely decide whether to abandon Moscow or defend it; whereas, with the Russian army less than four miles from Moscow, no such question existed. When had that question been settled? At Drissa, and at Smolensk, and most palpably of all on the 24th of August at Shevardino and on the 26th at Borodino, and each day and hour and minute of the retreat from Borodino to Fili.

WHEN Ermolov, having been sent by Kutuzov to inspect the position, told the field-marshal that it was impossible to fight there before Moscow and that they must retreat, Kutuzov looked at him in silence.

'Give me your hand,' said he, and turning it over so as to feel the pulse, added: 'You are not well, my dear fellow. Think what you are saying.'

Kutuzov could not yet admit the possibility of retreating beyond Moscow without a battle.

On the Poklonny Hill, four miles from the Dorgomilov gate of Moscow, Kutuzov got out of his carriage and sat down on a bench by the roadside. A great crowd of generals gathered round him, and Count Rostopchin, who had come out from Moscow, joined them. This brilliant company separated into several groups who all discussed the advantages and disadvantages of the position, the state of the army, the plans suggested, the situation of Moscow, and military questions generally. Though they had not been summoned for the purpose, and though it was not so called, they all felt that this was really a council of war. The conversations all dealt with public questions. If anyone gave or asked for personal news, it was done in a whisper and they immediately reverted to general matters. No jokes, or laughter, or smiles even, were seen among all these men. They evidently all made an effort to hold themselves at the height the situation demanded. And all these groups, while talking among themselves, tried to keep near the commander-in-chief (whose bench formed the centre of the gathering) and to speak so that he might overhear them. The commander-in-chief listened to what was being said and sometimes asked them to repeat their remarks, but did not himself take part in the conversations or express any opinion. After hearing what was being said by one or other of these groups he generally turned away with an air of disappointment, as though they were not speaking of anything he wished to hear. Some discussed the position that had been chosen, criticizing not the position itself so much as the mental capacity of those who had chosen it. Others argued that a mistake had been made earlier and that a battle should have been fought two days before. Others again spoke of the battle of Salamanca, which was described by Crosart, a newly arrived Frenchman in a Spanish uniform. (This Frenchman and one of the German princes serving with the Russian army were discussing the siege of Saragossa* and considering the possibility of defending

Moscow in a similar manner.) Count Rostopchin was telling a fourth group that he was prepared to die with the city train-bands under the walls of the capital, but that he still could not help regretting having been left in ignorance of what was happening, and that had he known it sooner things would have been different. ...A fifth group, displaying the profundity of their strategic perceptions, discussed the direction the troops would now have to take. A sixth group was talking absolute nonsense. Kutuzov's expression grew more and more preoccupied and gloomy. From all this talk he saw only one thing: that to defend Moscow was a *physical impossibility* in the full meaning of those words, that is to say, so utterly impossible that if any senseless commander were to give orders to fight, confusion would result but the battle would still not take place. It would not take place because the commanders not merely all recognized the position to be impossible, but in their conversations were only discussing what would happen after its inevitable abandonment. How could the commanders lead their troops to a field of battle they considered it impossible to hold? The lower-grade officers and even the soldiers (who also reason) also considered the position impossible, and therefore could not go to fight fully convinced as they were of defeat. If Bennigsen insisted on the position being defended and others still discussed it, the question was no longer important in itself but only as a pretext for disputes and intrigue. This Kutuzov knew well.

Bennigsen, who had chosen the position, warmly displayed his Russian patriotism (Kutuzov could not listen to this without wincing) by insisting that Moscow must be defended. His aim was as clear as daylight to Kutuzov: if the defence failed, to throw the blame on Kutuzov who had brought the army as far as the Sparrow Hills without giving battle; if it succeeded, to claim the success as his own; or if battle were not given, to clear himself of the crime of abandoning Moscow. But this intrigue did not now occupy the old man's mind. One terrible question absorbed him and to that question he heard no reply from anyone. The question for him now was: 'Have I really allowed Napoleon to reach Moscow, and when did I do so? When was it decided? Can it have been yesterday when I ordered Platov to retreat, or was it the evening before when I had a nap and told Bennigsen to issue orders? Or was it earlier still? ... When, when was this terrible affair decided? Moscow must be abandoned. The army must retreat and the order to do so must be given.' To give that terrible order seemed to him equivalent to resigning the command of the army. And not only did he love power, to which he was accustomed (the honours awarded to Prince Prozorovsky, under whom he had served in Turkey, galled him), but he was convinced that he was destined to save Russia and that that was why, against the Emperor's wish and by the will of the people, he had been chosen commander-in-chief. He was convinced that he alone could maintain command of the army in these difficult circumstances, and that in all the world he alone could encounter the invincible Napoleon without fear, and he was horrified at the thought of the order he had to issue. But something had to be decided, and these conversations around him which were assuming too free a character must be stopped.

He called the most important generals to him.

'My head, be it good or bad, must depend on itself,' said he, rising from the bench, and he rode to Fili where his carriages were waiting.

4

THE Council of War began to assemble at two in the afternoon in the better and roomier part of Andrew Savostyanov's hut. The men, women, and children of the large peasant family crowded into the back room across the passage. Only Malasha, Andrew's six-year-old grand-daughter, whom his Serene Highness had petted and to whom he had given a lump of sugar while drinking his tea, remained on the top of the brick oven in the larger room. Malasha looked down from the oven with shy delight at the faces, uniforms, and decorations of the generals, who one after another came into the room and sat down on the broad benches in the corner under the icons. 'Grandad' himself, as Malasha in her own mind called Kutuzov, sat apart in a dark corner behind the oven. He sat sunk deep in a folding arm-chair and continually cleared his throat and pulled at the collar of his coat which, though it was unbuttoned, still seemed to pinch his neck. Those who entered went up one by one to the field-marshal; he pressed the hands of some and nodded to others. His adjutant, Kaysarov, was about to draw back the curtain of the window facing Kutuzov, but the latter moved his hand angrily and Kaysarov understood that his Serene Highness did not wish his face to be seen.

Round the peasant's deal table on which lay maps, plans, pencils, and papers, so many people gathered that the orderlies brought in another bench and put it beside the table. Ermolov, Kaysarov, and Toll, who had just arrived, sat down on this bench. In the foremost place, immediately under the icons, sat Barclay de Tolly, his high forehead merging into his bald crown. He had a St George's Cross round his neck and looked pale and ill. He had been feverish for two days and was now shivering and in pain. Beside him sat

Uvarov, who with rapid gesticulations was giving him some information, speaking in low tones as they all did. Chubby little Dokhturov was listening attentively with eyebrows raised and arms folded on his stomach. On the other side sat Count Ostermann-Tolstoy, seemingly absorbed in his own thoughts. His broad head with its bold features and glittering eyes was resting on his hand. Raevsky, twitching forward the black hair on his temples as was his habit, glanced now at Kutuzov and now at the door, with a look of impatience. Konovnitsyn's firm, handsome and kindly face was lit up by a tender, sly smile. His glance met Malasha's, and the expression of his eyes caused the little girl to smile.

They were all waiting for Bennigsen, who on the pretext of inspecting the position was finishing his savoury dinner. They waited for him from four till six o'clock and did not begin their deliberations all that time but talked in low tones of other matters.

Only when Bennigsen had entered the hut did Kutuzov leave his corner and draw towards the table, but not near enough for the candles that had been placed there to light up his face.

Bennigsen opened the council with the question: 'Are we to abandon Russia's ancient and sacred capital without a struggle, or are we to defend it?' A prolonged and general silence followed. There was a frown on every face and only Kutuzov's angry grunts and occasional cough broke the silence. All eyes were gazing at him. Malasha too looked at 'Grandad'. She was nearest to him and saw how his face puckered; he seemed about to cry, but this did not last long.

'Russia's ancient and sacred capital!' he suddenly said, repeating Bennigsen's words in an angry voice and thereby drawing attention to the false note in them. 'Allow me to tell you, your Excellency, that that question has no meaning for a Russian.' (He lurched his heavy body forward.) 'Such a question cannot be put, it is senseless. The question I have asked these gentlemen to meet to discuss is a military one. The question is that of saving Russia. Is it better to give up Moscow without a battle, or by accepting battle to risk losing the army as well as Moscow? That is the question on which I want your opinion,' and he sank back in his chair.

The discussion began. Bennigsen did not yet consider his game lost. Admitting the view of Barclay and others that a defensive battle at Fili was impossible, but imbued with Russian patriotism and the love of Moscow, he proposed to move troops from the right to the left flank during the night, and attack the French right flank the following day. Opinions were divided, and arguments were advanced for and against that project. Ermolov,

Dokhturov, and Raevsky agreed with Bennigsen. Whether feeling it necessary to make a sacrifice before abandoning the capital, or guided by other, personal, considerations, these generals seemed not to understand that this council could not alter the inevitable course of events, and that Moscow was in effect already abandoned. The other generals however understood it and, leaving aside the question of Moscow, spoke of the direction the army should take in its retreat. Malasha, who kept her eyes fixed on what was going on before her, understood the meaning of the council differently. It seemed to her that it was only a personal struggle between 'Grandad' and 'Long-coat' as she termed Bennigsen. She saw that they grew spiteful when they spoke to one another, and in her heart she sided with 'Grandad'. In the midst of the conversation she noticed 'Grandad' give Bennigsen a quick, subtle glance, and then to her joy she saw that 'Grandad' said something to 'Long-coat' which settled him. Bennigsen suddenly reddened, and paced angrily up and down the room. What so affected him was Kutuzov's calm and quiet comment on the advantage or disadvantage of Bennigsen's proposal to move troops by night from the right to the left flank to attack the French right wing.

'Gentlemen,' said Kutuzov, 'I cannot approve of the Count's plan. Moving troops in close proximity to an enemy is always dangerous, and military history supports that view. For instance...' Kutuzov seemed to reflect, searching for an example, then with a clear naïve look at Bennigsen, he added: 'Oh yes; take the battle of Friedland,* which I think the Count well remembers, and which was...not fully successful, only because our troops were re-arranged too near the enemy...'

There followed a momentary pause, which seemed very long to them all.

The discussion recommenced, but pauses frequently occurred and they all felt that there was no more to be said.

During one of those pauses Kutuzov heaved a deep sigh as if preparing to speak. They all looked at him.

'Well, gentlemen, I see that it is I who will have to pay for the broken crockery,' said he, and rising slowly he moved to the table. 'Gentlemen, I have heard your views. Some of you will not agree with me. But I,' he paused, 'by the authority entrusted to me by my Sovereign and country, order a retreat.'

After that the generals began to disperse with the solemnity and circumspect silence of people who are leaving after a funeral.

Some of the generals, in low tones and in a strain very different from the way they had spoken during the council, communicated something to their commander-in-chief.

Malasha, who had long been expected for supper, climbed carefully backwards down from the oven, her bare little feet catching at its projections, and slipping between the legs of the generals she darted out of the room.

When he had dismissed the generals Kutuzov sat a long time with his elbows on the table, thinking always of the same terrible question: 'When, when did the abandonment of Moscow become inevitable? When was that done which settled the matter? And who was to blame for it?'

'I did not expect this,' said he to his adjutant Schneider, when the latter came in late that night. 'I did not expect this! I did not think this would happen.'

'You should take some rest, your Serene Highness,' replied Schneider.

'But no! They shall eat horse-flesh yet, like the Turks!' exclaimed Kutuzov without replying, striking the table with his podgy fist. 'They shall too, if only ...'

5

AT that very time, in circumstances even more important than retreating without a battle, namely, the evacuation and burning of Moscow, Rostopchin, who is usually represented as being the instigator of that event, acted in an altogether different manner from Kutuzov.

After the battle of Borodino the abandonment and burning of Moscow was as inevitable as the retreat of the army beyond Moscow without fighting.

Every Russian might have predicted it, not by reasoning, but by the feeling implanted in each of us and in our fathers.

The same thing that took place in Moscow had happened in all the towns and villages on Russian soil beginning with Smolensk, without the participation of Count Rostopchin and his broadsheets. The people awaited the enemy unconcernedly, did not riot or become excited or tear anyone to pieces, but faced its fate, feeling within it the strength to find what it should do at that most difficult moment. And as soon as the enemy drew near, the wealthy classes went away abandoning their property, while the poorer remained and burnt and destroyed what was left.

The consciousness that this would be so and would always be so, was and is present in the heart of every Russian. And a consciousness of this, and a foreboding that Moscow would be taken, was present in Russian Moscow society in 1812. Those who had quitted Moscow already in July and at the beginning of August showed that they expected this. Those who went away, taking what they could and abandoning their houses and half their belongings, did so from that latent patriotism which expresses itself not by phrases or by giving one's children to save the fatherland, and by similar unnatural exploits, but unobtrusively, simply, organically, and therefore in the way that always produces the most powerful results.

'It is disgraceful to run away from danger, only cowards are running away from Moscow,' they were told. In his broadsheets Rostopchin impressed on them that to leave Moscow was shameful. They were ashamed to be called cowards, ashamed to leave, but still they left, knowing it had to be done. Why did they go? It is impossible to suppose that Rostopchin had scared them by his accounts of horrors Napoleon had commited in conquered countries. The first people to go away were the rich educated people who knew quite well that Vienna and Berlin had remained intact, and that during Napoleon's occupation the inhabitants had spent their time pleasantly in the company of the charming Frenchmen whom the Russians, and especially the Russian ladies, then liked so much.

They went away because for Russians there could be no question as to whether things would go well or ill under French rule in Moscow. It was out of the question to be under French rule, it would be the worst thing that could happen. They went away even before the battle of Borodino and still more rapidly after it, despite Rostopchin's calls to defend Moscow, or the announcement of his intention to take the wonder-working icon of the Iberian Mother of God and go to fight, or of the balloons that were to destroy the French, and despite all the nonsense Rostopchin wrote in his broadsheets. They knew that it was for the army to fight, and that if it could not succeed it would not do to take young ladies and house-serfs to the Three Hills quarter of Moscow to fight Napoleon, and that they must go away, sorry as they were to abandon their property to destruction. They went away without thinking of the tremendous significance of that immense and wealthy city being given over to destruction, for a great city with wooden buildings was certain, when abandoned by its inhabitants, to be burnt. They went away each on his own account, and yet it was only in consequence of their going away that the momentous event was accomplished that will always remain the greatest glory of the Russian people. The lady who, afraid of being stopped by Count Rostopchin's orders, had already in June moved with her negroes and her women-jesters from Moscow to her Saratov estate with a vague consciousness that she was not Bonaparte's servant, was really, simply, and truly carrying out the great work which saved

Russia. But Count Rostopchin, who now taunted those who left Moscow and now had the Government offices removed; now distributed quite useless weapons to the drunken rabble; now had processions displaying the icons, and now forbade Father Augustin to remove icons or the relics of saints; now seized all the private carts in Moscow and on one hundred and thirty-six of them removed the balloon that was being constructed by Leppich; now hinted that he would burn Moscow and related how he had set fire to his own house; now wrote a proclamation to the French solemnly upbraiding them for having destroyed his Orphanage; now claimed the glory of having hinted that he would burn Moscow and now repudiated the deed; now ordered the people to catch all spies and bring them to him, and now reproached them for doing so; now expelled all the French residents from Moscow, and now allowed Madame Aubert-Chalmé* (the centre of the whole French colony in Moscow) to remain, but ordered the venerable old postmaster Klyucharëv to be arrested and exiled for no particular offence; now assembled the people at the Three Hills to fight the French and now, to get rid of them, handed over to them a man to be killed, and himself drove away by a back gate; now declared that he would not survive the fall of Moscow, and now wrote French verses in albums* concerning his share in the affair – this man did not understand the meaning of what was happening but merely wanted to do something himself that would astonish people, to perform some patriotically heroic feat; and like a child he made sport of the momentous and unavoidable event – the abandonment and burning of Moscow – and tried with his puny hand now to speed and now to stay the enormous, popular tide that bore him along with it.

6

Hélène, having returned with the court from Vilna to Petersburg, found herself in a difficult position.

In Petersburg she had enjoyed the special protection of a grandee who occupied one of the highest posts in the Empire. In Vilna she had formed an intimacy with a young foreign prince. When she returned to Petersburg both the magnate and the prince were there, and both claimed their rights. Hélène was faced by a new problem – how to preserve her intimacy with both without offending either.

What would have seemed difficult or even impossible to another woman did not cause the least embarrassment to Countess Bezukhova, who evidently deserved her reputation of being a very clever woman. Had she attempted concealment, or tried to extricate herself from her awkward position by cunning, she would have spoilt her case by acknowledging herself guilty. But Hélène, like a really great man who can do whatever he pleases, at once assumed her own position to be correct, as she sincerely believed it to be, and that everyone else was to blame.

The first time the young foreigner allowed himself to reproach her, she lifted her beautiful head and, half turning to him, said firmly:

'That's just like a man – selfish and cruel! I expected nothing else. A woman sacrifices herself for you, she suffers, and this is her reward! What right have you, Monseigneur, to demand an account of my attachments and friendships? He is a man who has been more than a father to me!'

The prince was about to say something, but Hélène interrupted him.

'Well, yes,' said she, 'it may be that he has other sentiments for me than those of a father, but that is not a reason for me to shut my door on him. I am not a man, that I should repay kindness with ingratitude! Know, Monseigneur, that in all that relates to my intimate feelings I render account only to God and to my conscience,' she concluded, laying her hand on her beautiful, fully expanded bosom and looking up to heaven.

'But for heaven's sake listen to me!'

'Marry me, and I will be your slave!'

'But that's impossible.'

'You won't deign to demean yourself by marrying me, you...' said Hélène, beginning to cry.

The prince tried to comfort her, but Hélène, as if quite distraught, said through her tears that there was nothing to prevent her marrying, that there were precedents (there were up to that time very few, but she mentioned Napoleon and some other exalted personages), that she had never been her husband's wife, and that she had been sacrificed.

'But the law, religion...' said the prince, already yielding.

'The law, religion... What have they been invented for, if they can't arrange that?' said Hélène.

The prince was surprised that so simple an idea had not occurred to him, and he applied for advice to the holy brethren of the Society of Jesus, with whom he was on intimate terms.

A few days later at one of those enchanting fêtes which Hélène gave at her country house on the Stone Island, the charming Monsieur de Jobert, a man no longer young, with snow-white hair and brilliant black eyes, a Jesuit *à robe courte*,* was presented to

893

her, and in the garden by the light of the illuminations and to the sound of music talked to her for a long time of the love of God, of Christ, of the Sacred Heart, and of the consolations the one true Catholic religion affords in this world and the next. Hélène was touched, and more than once tears rose to her eyes and to those of Monsieur de Jobert and their voices trembled. A dance, for which her partner came to seek her, put an end to her discourse with her future *directeur de conscience,* but the next evening Monsieur de Jobert came to see Hélène when she was alone, and after that often came again.

One day he took the countess to a Roman Catholic church, where she knelt down before the altar to which she was led. The enchanting, middle-aged Frenchman laid his hands on her head and, as she herself afterwards described it, she felt something like a fresh breeze wafted into her soul. It was explained to her that this was *la grâce.*

After that a long-frocked abbé was brought to her. She confessed to him, and he absolved her from her sins. Next day she received a box containing the Sacred Host, which was left at her house for her to partake of. A few days later Hélène learnt with pleasure that she had now been admitted to the true Catholic Church, and that in a few days the Pope himself would hear of her and would send her a certain document.

All that was done around her and to her at this time, all the attention devoted to her by so many clever men and expressed in such pleasant, refined ways, and the state of dove-like purity she was now in (she wore only white dresses and white ribbons all that time) gave her pleasure, but her pleasure did not cause her for a moment to forget her aim. And as it always happens in contests of cunning that a stupid person gets the better of cleverer ones, Hélène – having realized that the main object of all these words and all this trouble was, after converting her to Catholicism, to obtain money from her for Jesuit institutions (as to which she received indications) – before parting with her money insisted that the various operations necessary to free her from her husband should be performed. In her view the aim of every religion was merely to preserve certain proprieties while affording satisfaction to human desires. And with this aim, in one of her talks with her Father Confessor she insisted on an answer to the question, how far was she bound by her marriage?

They were sitting in the twilight by a window in the drawing-room. The scent of flowers came in at the window. Hélène was wearing a white dress, transparent over her shoulders and bosom. The abbé, a well-fed man with a plump, clean-shaven chin, a pleasant firm mouth, and white hands meekly folded on his knees, sat close to Hélène and with a subtle smile on his lips and a peaceful look of delight at her beauty, occasionally glanced at her face as he explained his opinion on the subject. Hélène, with an uneasy smile, looked at his curly hair and his plump clean-shaven blackish cheeks, and every moment expected the conversation to take a fresh turn. But the abbé, though he evidently enjoyed the beauty of his companion, was absorbed in his mastery of the matter.

The course of the Father Confessor's arguments ran as follows: 'Ignorant of the import of what you were undertaking, you made a vow of conjugal fidelity to a man who on his part, by entering the married state without faith in the religious significance of marriage, committed an act of sacrilege. That marriage lacked the dual significance it should have had. Yet in spite of this your vow was binding. You swerved from it. What did you commit by so acting? A venial, or a mortal, sin? A venial sin, for you acted without evil intention. If now you married again with the object of bearing children, your sin might be forgiven. But the question is again a twofold one: firstly . . .'

But suddenly Hélène, who was getting bored, said with one of her bewitching smiles: 'But I think that having espoused the true religion, I cannot be bound by what a false religion laid upon me.'

The director of her conscience was astounded at having the case presented to him thus with the simplicity of Columbus's egg. He was delighted at the unexpected rapidity of his pupil's progress, but could not abandon the edifice of argument he had laboriously constructed.

'Let us understand one another, Countess,' said he with a smile, and began refuting his spiritual daughter's arguments.

7

HÉLÈNE understood that the question was very simple and easy from the ecclesiastical point of view, and that her directors were making difficulties only because they were apprehensive as to how the matter would be regarded by the secular authorities.

So she decided that it was necessary to prepare the opinion of society. She provoked the jealousy of the elderly magnate and told him what she had told her other suitor, that is, she put the matter so that the only way for him to obtain a right over her was to marry her. The elderly magnate was at first as much taken aback by this suggestion of marriage with a woman whose husband was alive, as the younger man had been, but Hélène's imperturbable conviction that it was as simple and natural as marrying a maiden had its effect on him too. Had Hélène herself shown the least sign of hesitation, shame, or secrecy, her cause would certainly have been lost; but not only did she show no signs of secrecy or shame, on the contrary, with good-natured naïveté she told her intimate friends (and these were all Petersburg) that both the prince and the magnate had proposed to her, and that she loved both and was afraid of grieving either.

A rumour immediately spread in Petersburg, not that Hélène wanted to be divorced from her husband (had such a report spread many would have opposed so illegal an intention) but simply that the unfortunate and interesting Hélène was in doubt which of the two men she should marry. The question was no longer whether this was possible, but only which was the better match and how the matter would be regarded at court. There were, it is true, some rigid individuals unable to rise to the height of such a question, who saw in the project a desecration of the sacrament of marriage, but there were not many such and they remained silent, while the majority were interested in Hélène's good fortune and in the question which match would be the more advantageous. Whether it was right or wrong to re-marry while one had a husband living they did not discuss, for that question had evidently been settled by people 'wiser than you or me', as they said, and to doubt the correctness of that decision would be to risk exposing one's stupidity and incapacity to live in society.

Only Marya Dmitrievna Akhrosimova, who had come to Petersburg that summer to see one of her sons, allowed herself plainly to express an opinion contrary to the general one. Meeting Hélène at a ball, she stopped her in the middle of the room and, amid general silence, said in her gruff voice: 'So wives of living men have started marrying again! Perhaps you think you have invented a novelty? You have been forestalled, my dear! It was thought of long ago. It is done in all the brothels,' and with these words Marya Dmitrievna, turning up her wide sleeves with her usual threatening gesture and glancing sternly round, moved across the room.

Though people were afraid of Marya Dmitrievna, she was regarded in Petersburg as a buffoon, and so of what she had said they only noticed, and repeated in a whisper, the one coarse word she had used, supposing the whole sting of her remark to lie in that word.

Prince Vasili, who of late very often forgot what he had said and repeated one and the same thing a hundred times, remarked to his daughter whenever he chanced to see her:

Hélène, I have a word to say to you,' and he would lead her aside, drawing her hand downwards. 'I have heard of certain projects concerning... you know. Well, my dear child, you know how your father's heart rejoices to know that you... You have suffered so much... But my dear child, consult only your own heart. That is all I have to say,' and concealing his unvarying emotion he would press his cheek against his daughter's and move away.

Bilibin, who had not lost his reputation of an exceedingly clever man, and who was one of the disinterested friends so brilliant a woman as Hélène always has – men-friends who can never change into lovers – once gave her his view of the matter at a small and intimate gathering.

'Listen, Bilibin,' said Hélène (she always called friends of that sort by their surnames), and she touched his coat-sleeve with her white, beringed fingers. 'Tell me, as you would a sister, what I ought to do. Which of the two?'

Bilibin wrinkled up the skin over his eyebrows and pondered, with a smile on his lips.

'You are not taking me unawares, you know,' said he. 'As a true friend, I have thought and thought again about your affair. You see, if you marry the prince' – he meant the younger man – and he crooked one finger, 'you forever lose the chance of marrying the other, and you will displease the court besides. (You know there is some kind of connexion.) But if you marry the old count you will make his last days happy, and as widow of the Grand..., the prince would no longer be making a mésalliance by marrying you,' and Bilibin smoothed out his forehead.

'That's a true friend!' said Hélène beaming, and again touching Bilibin's sleeve. 'But I love both, you know, and don't want to distress either of them. I would give my life for the happiness of them both.'

Bilibin shrugged his shoulders, as much as to say that not even he could help in that difficulty.

'*Une maîtresse-femme!* That's what is called putting things squarely. She would like to be married to all three at the same time,' thought he.

'But tell me, how will your husband look at the matter?' Bilibin asked, his reputation being so well-established that he did not fear to ask so naïve a question. 'Will he agree?'

'Oh, he loves me so!' said Hélène, who for some reason imagined that Pierre, too, loved her. 'He will do anything for me.'

Bilibin puckered his skin in preparation for something witty.

'Even divorce you?' said he.

Hélène laughed.

Among those who ventured to doubt the justifiability of the

897

proposed marriage was Hélène's mother, Princess Kuragina. She was continually tormented by jealousy of her daughter, and now that her jealousy concerned a subject near to her own heart, she could not reconcile herself to the idea. She consulted a Russian priest as to the possibility of divorce and re-marriage during a husband's lifetime, and the priest told her that it was impossible, and to her delight showed her a text in the Gospel which (as it seemed to him) plainly forbids remarriage while the husband is alive.

Armed with these arguments, which appeared to her unanswerable, she drove to her daughter's early one morning so as to find her alone.

Having listened to her mother's objections, Hélène smiled blandly and ironically.

'But it says plainly: "Whosoever shall marry her that is divorced..."' said the old princess.

'Ah, maman, ne dites pas de bêtises. Vous ne comprenez rien. Dans ma position j'ai des devoirs,' said Hélène changing from Russian, in which language she always felt that her case did not sound quite clear, into French which suited it better.

'But, my dear...'

'Oh, mamma, how is it you don't understand that the Holy Father, who has the right to grant dispensations...'

Just then the lady companion who lived with Hélène came in to announce that his Highness was in the ballroom and wished to see her.

'Non, dites lui que je ne veux pas le voir, que je suis furieuse contre lui, parce qu'il m'a manqué parole.'

'Comtesse, à tout péché miséricorde,' said a fair-haired young man, with a long face and nose, as he entered the room.

The old princess rose respectfully and curtsied. The young man who had entered took no notice of her. The princess nodded to her daughter and sidled out of the room.

'Yes, she is right,' thought the old princess, all her convictions dissipated by the appearance of his Highness. 'She is right, but how is it that we in our irrecoverable youth did not know it? Yet it is so simple,' she thought as she got into her carriage.

By the beginning of August Hélène's affairs were clearly defined and she wrote a letter to her husband – who as she imagined loved her very much – informing him of her intention to marry N.N. and of her having embraced the one true faith, and asking him to carry out all the formalities necessary for a divorce, which would be explained to him by the bearer of the letter.

'And so I pray God to have you, my friend, in His holy and powerful keeping – Your friend Hélène.'

This letter was brought to Pierre's house when he was on the field of Borodino.

8

TOWARDS the end of the battle of Borodino, Pierre, having run down from Raevsky's battery a second time, made his way through a gully to Knyazkovo with a crowd of soldiers, reached the dressing station, and, seeing blood and hearing cries and groans, hurried on, still entangled in the crowds of soldiers.

The one thing he now desired with his whole soul was to get away quickly from the terrible sensations amid which he had lived that day, and return to ordinary conditions of life and sleep quietly in a room in his own bed. He felt that only in the ordinary conditions of life would he be able to understand himself and all he had seen and felt. But such ordinary conditions of life were nowhere to be found.

Though shells and bullets did not whistle over the road along which he was going, still on all sides there was what there had been on the field of battle. There were still the same suffering, exhausted, and sometimes strangely indifferent faces, the same blood, the same soldiers' overcoats, the same sounds of firing, which though distant now still aroused terror, and besides this there was the foul air and the dust.

Having gone a couple of miles along the Mozhaysk road, Pierre sat down by the roadside.

Dusk had fallen, and the roar of guns died away. Pierre lay leaning on his elbow for a long time, gazing at the shadows that moved past him in the darkness. He was continually imagining that a cannon-ball was flying towards him with a terrific whizz, and then he shuddered and sat up. He had no idea how long he had been there. In the middle of the night three soldiers, having brought some fire-wood, settled down near him and began lighting a fire.

The soldiers, who threw sidelong glances at Pierre, got the fire to burn and placed an iron pot on it into which they broke some dried bread and put a little dripping. The pleasant odour of greasy viands mingled with the smell of smoke. Pierre sat up and sighed. The three soldiers were eating and talking among themselves, taking no notice of him.

'And who may you be?' one of them suddenly asked Pierre,

evidently meaning what Pierre himself had in mind, namely: 'If you want to eat we'll give you some food, only let us know whether you are an honest man.'

'I, I . . .' said Pierre, feeling it necessary to minimize his social position as much as possible so as to be nearer to the soldiers and better understood by them. 'By rights I am a militia officer, but my men are not here. I came to the battle and have lost them.'

'There now!' said one of the soldiers.

Another shook his head.

'Would you like a little mash?' the first soldier asked, and handed Pierre a wooden spoon after licking it clean.

Pierre sat down by the fire and began eating the mash, as they called the food in the cauldron, and he thought it more delicious than any food he had ever tasted. As he sat bending greedily over it, helping himself to large spoonfuls and chewing one after another, his face was lit up by the fire and the soldiers looked at him in silence.

'Where have you to go to? Tell us!' said one of them.

'To Mozhaysk.'

'You're a gentleman, aren't you?'

'Yes.'

'And what's your name?'

'Peter Kirilych.'

'Well then, Peter Kirilych, come along with us, we'll take you there.'

In total darkness the soldiers walked with Pierre to Mozhaysk.

By the time they got near Mozhaysk and began ascending the steep hill into the town, the cocks were already crowing. Pierre went on with the soldiers, quite forgetting that his inn was at the bottom of the hill and that he had already passed it. He would not soon have remembered this, such was his state of forgetfulness, had he not, half-way up the hill, stumbled upon his groom, who had been to look for him in the town and was returning to the inn. The groom recognized Pierre in the darkness by his white hat.

'Your Excellency!' he said. 'Why, we were beginning to despair! How is it you are on foot? And where are you going, please?'

'Oh, yes!' said Pierre.

The soldiers stopped.

'So you've found your folk?' said one of them. 'Well, good-bye, Peter Kirilych! – isn't it?'

'Good-bye, Peter Kirilych!' Pierre heard the other voices repeat.

'Good-bye!' he said and turned with his groom towards the inn.

'I ought to give them something!' he thought, and felt in his pocket. 'No, better not!' said another inner voice.

There was not a room to be had at the inn, they were all occupied. Pierre went out into the yard and, covering himself up head and all, lay down in his carriage.

9

SCARCELY had Pierre laid his head on the pillow before he felt himself falling asleep, but suddenly, almost with the distinctness of reality, he heard the *boom, boom, boom* of firing, the thud of projectiles, groans and cries, and smelt blood and powder, and a feeling of horror and dread of death seized him. Filled with fright he opened his eyes and lifted his head from under his cloak. All was tranquil in the yard. Only someone's orderly passed through the gateway, splashing through the mud, and talked to the inn-keeper. Above Pierre's head some pigeons, disturbed by the move-ment he had made in sitting up, fluttered under the dark roof of the penthouse. The whole courtyard was permeated by a strong peaceful smell of stable-yards, delightful to Pierre at that moment. He could see the clear starry sky between the dark roofs of two penthouses.

'Thank God, there is no more of that!' he thought, covering up his head again. 'Oh, what a terrible thing is fear, and how shame-fully I yielded to it! But they ... *they* were steady and calm all the time, to the end ...' thought he.

They, in Pierre's mind, were the soldiers, those who had been at the battery, those who had given him food, and those who had prayed before the icon. *They*, those strange men he had not pre-viously known, stood out clearly and sharply from everyone else.

'To be a soldier, just a soldier!' thought Pierre as he fell asleep, 'to enter communal life completely, to be imbued by what makes them what they are. But how cast off all the superfluous, devilish burden of my outer man? There was a time when I could have done it. I could have run away from my father, as I wanted to. Or I might have been sent to serve as a soldier after the duel with Dolokhov.' And the memory of the dinner at the English Club when he had challenged Dolokhov flashed through Pierre's mind, and then he remembered his benefactor at Torzhok. And now a picture of a solemn meeting of the Lodge presented itself to his mind. It was taking place at the English Club and someone near and dear to him sat at the end of the table. 'Yes, that is he! It is my benefactor. But he died!' thought Pierre. 'Yes, he died, and I did not know he was alive. How sorry I am that he died, and how glad I am that he is alive again!' On one side of the table sat

Anatole, Dolokhov, Nesvitsky, Denisov, and others like them (in his dream the category to which these men belonged was as clearly defined in his mind as the category of those he termed *they*), and he heard those people, Anatole and Dolokhov, shouting and singing loudly; yet through their shouting the voice of his benefactor was heard speaking all the time and the sound of his words was as weighty and uninterrupted as the booming on the battlefield, but pleasant and comforting. Pierre did not understand what his benefactor was saying, but he knew (the categories of thoughts were also quite distinct in his dream) that he was talking of goodness and the possibility of being what *they* were. And *they* with their simple, kind, firm faces surrounded his benefactor on all sides. But though they were kindly they did not look at Pierre and did not know him. Wishing to speak and to attract their attention, he got up, but at that moment his legs grew cold and bare.

He felt ashamed, and with one arm covered his legs, from which the cloak had in fact slipped. For a moment as he was rearranging his cloak Pierre opened his eyes and saw the same penthouse roofs, posts, and yard, but now they were all bluish, lit up, and glittering with frost or dew.

'It is dawn,' thought Pierre. 'But that's not what I want. I want to hear and understand my benefactor's words.' Again he covered himself up with the cloak, but now neither the Lodge nor his benefactor was there. There were only thoughts clearly expressed in words, thoughts that someone was uttering, or that he himself was formulating.

Afterwards when he recalled those thoughts Pierre was convinced that someone outside himself had spoken them, though the impressions of that day had evoked them. He had never it seemed to him been able to think and express his thoughts like that when awake.

'To endure war is the most difficult subordination of man's freedom to the law of God,' the voice had said. 'Simplicity is submission to the will of God, you cannot escape from Him. And *they* are simple. *They* do not talk but act. The spoken word is silver but the unspoken is golden. Man can be master of nothing while he fears death, but he who does not fear it possesses all. If there were no suffering man would not know his limitations, would not know himself. The hardest thing (Pierre went on thinking, or hearing, in his dream) is to be able in your soul to unite the meaning of all. To unite all?' he asked himself. 'No, not to unite. Thoughts cannot be united, but to *harness* all these thoughts together is what we need! Yes, one *must harness* them, *must harness* them!'

he repeated to himself with inward rapture, feeling that these words and they alone expressed what he wanted to say and solved the question that tormented him.

'Yes, one must harness, it is time to harness.'

'Time to harness, time to harness, your Excellency! Your Excellency!' some voice was repeating. 'We must harness, it is time to harness...'

It was the voice of the groom trying to wake him. The sun shone straight into Pierre's face. He glanced at the dirty inn-yard in the middle of which soldiers were watering their lean horses at the pump while carts were passing out of the gate. Pierre turned away with repugnance, and closing his eyes quickly fell back on the carriage seat. 'No, I don't want that, I don't want to see and understand that. I want to understand what was revealing itself to me in my dream. One second more and I should have understood it all! But what am I to do? Harness, but how can I harness everything?' and Pierre felt with horror that the meaning of all he had seen and thought in the dream had been destroyed.

The groom, the coachman, and the innkeeper told Pierre that an officer had come with news that the French were already near Mozhaysk and that our men were leaving it.

Pierre got up, and having told them to harness and overtake him, went on foot through the town.

The troops were moving on, leaving about ten thousand wounded behind them. There were wounded in the yards, at the windows of the houses, and the streets were crowded with them. In the streets, around carts that were to take some of the wounded away, shouts, curses and blows could be heard. Pierre offered the use of his carriage, which had overtaken him, to a wounded general he knew, and drove with him to Moscow. On the way Pierre heard of the death of his brother-in-law, Anatole, and of Prince Andrew.

10

ON the 30th of August Pierre reached Moscow. Close to the gates of the city he was met by Count Rostopchin's adjutant.

'We have been looking for you everywhere,' said the adjutant. 'The count wants to see you particularly. He asks you to come to him at once on a very important matter.'

Without going home Pierre took a cab and drove to see the Moscow commander-in-chief.

Count Rostopchin had only that morning returned to town from his summer villa at Sokolniki. The ante-room and reception-room of his house were full of officials who had been summoned or had come for orders. Vasilchikov and Platov had already seen the count and explained to him that it was impossible to defend Moscow and that it would have to be surrendered. Though this news was being concealed from the inhabitants, the officials – the heads of the various Government departments – knew that Moscow would soon be in the enemy's hands, just as Count Rostopchin himself knew it, and to escape personal responsibility they had all come to the governor to ask how they were to deal with their various departments.

As Pierre was entering the reception-room a courier from the army came out of Rostopchin's private room.

In answer to questions with which he was greeted, the courier made a despairing gesture with his hand and passed through the room.

While waiting in the reception-room Pierre, with weary eyes, watched the various officials, old and young, military and civilian, who were there. They all seemed dissatisfied and uneasy. Pierre went up to a group of men, one of whom he knew. After greeting Pierre they continued their conversation.

'If they're sent out and brought back again later on it will do no harm, but as things are now one can't answer for anything.'

'But you see what he writes...' said another, pointing to a printed sheet he held in his hand.

'That's another matter. That's necessary for the people,' said the first.

'What is it?' asked Pierre.

'Oh, it's a fresh broadsheet.'

Pierre took it and began reading.

'His Serene Highness has passed through Mozhaysk in order to join up with the troops moving towards him, and has taken up a strong position where the enemy will not soon attack him. Forty-eight guns with ammunition have been sent him from here, and his Serene Highness says he will defend Moscow to the last drop of blood and is even ready to fight in the streets. Do not be upset, brothers, that the Law Courts are closed; things have to be put in order, and we will deal with villains in our own way! When the time comes I shall want both town and peasant lads and will raise the cry a day or two beforehand, but they are not wanted yet so I hold my peace. An axe will be useful, a hunting-spear not bad, but a three-pronged fork will be best of all: a Frenchman is no heavier than a sheaf of rye. To-morrow after dinner I shall take the Iberian icon of the Mother of God to the wounded in the Catherine Hospital where we will have some water blessed. That

904

will help them to get well quicker. I, too, am well now: one of my eyes was sore but now I am on the look-out with both.'

'But military men have told me that it is impossible to fight in the town,' said Pierre, 'and that the position . . .'

'Well, of course! That's what we were saying,' replied the first speaker.

'And what does he mean by "One of my eyes was sore but now I am on the look-out with both"?' asked Pierre.

'The count had a sty,' replied the adjutant smiling, 'and was very much upset when I told him people had come to ask what was the matter with him. By the by, Count,' he added suddenly, addressing Pierre with a smile, 'we heard that you have family troubles and that the countess your wife . . .'

'I have heard nothing,' Pierre replied unconcernedly. 'But what have you heard?'

'Oh, well, you know people often invent things. I only say what I heard.'

'But what did you hear?'

'Well, they say,' continued the adjutant with the same smile, 'that the countess, your wife, is preparing to go abroad. I expect it's nonsense . . .'

'Possibly,' remarked Pierre, looking about him absent-mindedly. 'And who is that?' he asked, indicating a short old man in a clean blue peasant overcoat, with a big snow-white beard and eyebrows and a ruddy face.

'He? That's a tradesman, that is to say, he's the restaurant-keeper, Vereshchagin. Perhaps you have heard of that affair with the proclamation.'

'Oh, so that is Vereshchagin!' said Pierre, looking at the firm calm face of the old man and seeking any indication of his being a traitor.

'That's not he himself, that's the father of the fellow who wrote the proclamation,' said the adjutant. 'The young man is in prison and I expect it will go hard with him.'

An old gentleman wearing a star, and another official, a German wearing a cross round his neck, approached the speaker.

'It's a complicated story, you know,' said the adjutant. 'That proclamation appeared about two months ago. The count was informed of it. He gave orders to investigate the matter. Gabriel Ivanovich here made the inquiries. The proclamation had passed through exactly sixty-three hands. He asked one, "From whom did you get it?" "From so-and-so." He went to the next one. "From whom did you get it?" and so on till he reached Vereshchagin, a half-educated tradesman, you know, "a pet of a trader",' said the adjutant smiling. 'They asked him, "Who gave it you?" And the point is that we knew whom he had it from. He could only have had it from the Postmaster. But evidently they had come to some understanding. He replied: "From no one; I made it up myself." They threatened and questioned him, but he stuck to that: "I made it up myself." And so it was reported to the count, who sent for the man. "From whom did you get the proclamation?" "I wrote it myself." Well, you know the count,' said the adjutant cheerfully with a smile of pride, 'he flared up dreadfully – and just think of the fellow's audacity, lying, and obstinacy.'

'And the count wanted him to say it was from Klyucharëv? I understand!' said Pierre.

'Not at all,' rejoined the adjutant in dismay. 'Klyucharëv had his own sins to answer for without that and that is why he has been banished. But the point is that the count was much annoyed. "How could you have written it yourself?" said he, and he took up the Hamburg Gazette that was lying on the table. "Here it is! You did not write it yourself but translated it, and translated it abominably, because you don't even know French, you fool." And what do you think? "No," said he, "I have not read any papers, I made it up myself." "If that's so you're a traitor and I'll have you tried, and you'll be hanged! Say from whom you had it." "I have seen no papers, I made it up myself." And that was the end of it. The count had the father fetched, but the fellow stuck to it. He was sent for trial and condemned to hard labour, I believe. Now the father has come to intercede for him. But he's a good-for-nothing lad! You know that sort of tradesman's son, a dandy and lady-killer. He attended some lectures somewhere and imagines that the devil is no match for him. That's the sort of fellow he is. His father keeps a cookshop here by the Stone Bridge, and you know there was a large icon of God Almighty painted with a sceptre in the one hand and an orb in the other. Well, he took that icon home with him for a few days and what did he do? He found some scoundrel of a painter ...'

11

IN the middle of this fresh tale Pierre was summoned to the commander-in-chief.

When he entered the private room Count Rostopchin, puckering his face, was rubbing his forehead and eyes with his hand. A short man was saying something, but when Pierre entered he stopped speaking and went out.

'Ah, how do you do, great warrior?' said Rostopchin as soon as the short man had left the room. 'We have heard of your prowess. But that's not the point. Between ourselves, *mon cher*, do you belong to the Masons?' he went on severely, as though there were something wrong about it which he nevertheless intended to pardon. Pierre remained silent. 'I am well-informed, my friend, but I am aware that there are Masons who on pretence of saving mankind wish to ruin Russia.'

'Yes, I am a Mason,' Pierre replied.

'There you see, *mon cher!* I expect you know that Messrs. Speransky and Magnitsky have been deported to their proper place. Mr Klyucharëv has been treated in the same way, and so have others who on the plea of building up the temple of Solomon have tried to destroy the temple of their fatherland. You can understand that there are reasons for this and that I could not have exiled the Postmaster had he not been a harmful person. It has now come to my knowledge that you lent him your carriage for his removal from town, and that you have even accepted papers from him for safe custody. I like you and don't wish you any harm and – as you are only half my age – I advise you as a father would to cease all communication with men of that stamp and to leave here as soon as possible.'

But what did Klyucharëv do wrong, Count?' asked Pierre.

'That is for me to know, but not for you to ask,' shouted Rostopchin.

'If he is accused of circulating Napoleon's proclamation it is not proved that he did so,' said Pierre without looking at Rostopchin, 'and Vereshchagin . . .'

'There we are!' Rostopchin shouted at Pierre louder than before, frowning suddenly. 'Vereshchagin is a renegade and a traitor who will be punished as he deserves,' said he with the vindictive heat with which people speak when recalling an insult. 'But I did not summon you to discuss my actions, but to give you advice – or an order if you prefer it. I beg you to leave the town and break off all communication with such men as Klyucharëv. And I will knock the nonsense out of anybody' – but, probably realizing that he was shouting at Bezukhov who so far was not guilty of anything, he added, taking Pierre's hand in a friendly manner, 'We are on the eve of a public disaster and I haven't time to be polite to everybody who has business with me. My head is sometimes in a whirl. Well, *mon cher*, what are you doing personally?'

'Why, nothing,' answered Pierre without raising his eyes or changing the thoughtful expression of his face.

The count frowned.

'A word of friendly advice, *mon cher*. Be off as soon as you can, that's all I have to tell you. Happy he who has ears to hear. Good-bye, my dear fellow. Oh, by the by!' he shouted through the doorway after Pierre, 'is it true that the countess has fallen into the clutches of the holy fathers of the Society of Jesus?'

Pierre did not answer, and left Rostopchin's room more sullen and angry than he had ever before shown himself.

When he reached home it was already getting dark. Some eight people came to see him that evening: the secretary of a committee, the colonel of his battalion, his steward, his major-domo, and various petitioners. They all had business with Pierre and wanted decisions from him. Pierre did not understand and was not interested in any of these questions, and only answered them in order to get rid of these people. When left alone at last he opened and read his wife's letter.

'*They*, the soldiers at the battery, Prince Andrew killed ... that old man ... Simplicity is submission to God. Suffering is necessary ... the meaning of all ... one must harness ... my wife is getting married ... One must forget and understand ...' And going to his bed he threw himself on it without undressing and immediately fell asleep.

When he awoke next morning the major-domo came to inform him that a special messenger, a police officer, had come from Count Rostopchin to know whether Count Bezukhov had left or was leaving the town.

A dozen persons who had business with Pierre were awaiting him in the drawing-room. Pierre dressed hurriedly, and instead of going to see them went to the back porch and out through the gate.

From that time till the end of the destruction of Moscow no one of Bezukhov's household, despite all the search they made, saw Pierre again or knew where he was.

12

THE Rostovs remained in Moscow till the 1st of September, that is, till the eve of the enemy's entry into the city.

After Petya had joined Obolensky's regiment of Cossacks and left for Belaya Tserkov where that regiment was forming, the countess was seized with terror. The thought that both her sons were at the war, had both gone from under her wing, that to-day or to-morrow either or both of them might be killed like the three sons of one of her acquaintances, struck her that summer for the first time with cruel clearness. She tried to get Nicholas back, and wished to go herself to join Petya, or to get him an appointment somewhere in Petersburg, but neither of these proved possible. Petya could not return unless his regiment did so or unless he was transferred to another regiment on active service. Nicholas was somewhere with the army and had not sent a word since his last letter, in which he had given a detailed account of his meeting with Princess Mary. The countess did not sleep at night, or when she did fall asleep dreamed that she saw her sons lying dead. After many consultations and conversations the count at last devised means to tranquillize her. He got Petya transferred from Obolensky's regiment to Bezukhov's, which was in training near Moscow. Though Petya would remain in the service, this transfer would give the countess the consolation of seeing at least one of her sons under her wing, and she hoped to arrange matters for her Petya so as not to let him go again, but always get him appointed to places where he could not possibly take part in a battle. As long as Nicholas alone was in danger the countess imagined that she loved her first-born more than all her other children and even reproached herself for it; but when her youngest, the scapegrace who had been bad at lessons, was always breaking things in the house and making himself a nuisance to everybody, that snub-nosed Petya with his merry black eyes and fresh rosy cheeks where soft down was just beginning to show – when he was thrown amid those big, dreadful, cruel men who were fighting somewhere about something and apparently finding pleasure in it – then his mother thought she loved him more, much more, than all her other children. The nearer the time came for Petya to return, the more uneasy grew the countess. She began to think she would never live to see such happiness. The presence of Sonya, of her beloved Natasha, or even of her husband, irritated her. 'What do I want with them? I want no one but Petya,' she thought.

At the end of August the Rostovs received another letter from Nicholas. He wrote from the province of Voronezh where he had been sent to procure remounts, but that letter did not set the countess at ease. Knowing that one son was out of danger she became the more anxious about Petya.

Though by the 20th of August nearly all the Rostovs' acquaintances had left Moscow, and though everybody tried to persuade the countess to get away as quickly as possible, she would not hear of leaving before her treasure, her adored Petya, returned. On the 28th of August he arrived. The passionate tenderness with which his mother received him did not please the sixteen-year-old officer. Though she concealed from him her intention of keeping him under her wing, Petya guessed her designs, and instinctively fearing that he might give way to emotion when with her – might 'become womanish' as he termed it to himself – he treated her coldly, avoided her, and during his stay in Moscow attached himself exclusively to Natasha for whom he had always had a particular brotherly tenderness, almost lover-like.

Owing to the count's customary carelessness nothing was ready for their departure by the 28th of August and the carts that were to come from their Ryazan and Moscow estates to remove their household belongings did not arrive till the 30th.

From the 28th to the 31st all Moscow was in a bustle and commotion. Every day thousands of men wounded at Borodino were brought in by the Dorogomilov gate and taken to various parts of Moscow, and thousands of carts conveyed the inhabitants and their possessions out by the other gates. In spite of Rostopchin's broadsheets, or because of them or independently of them, the strangest and most contradictory rumours were current in the town. Some said that no one was to be allowed to leave the city, others on the contrary said that all the icons had been taken out of the churches and everybody was to be ordered to leave. Some said there had been another battle after Borodino at which the French had been routed, while others on the contrary reported that the Russian army had been destroyed. Some talked about the Moscow militia which, preceded by the clergy, would go to the Three Hills, others whispered that Augustin had been forbidden to leave,* that traitors had been seized, that the peasants were rioting and robbing people on their way from Moscow, and so on. But all this was only talk; in reality (though the Council of Fili at which it was decided to abandon Moscow had not yet been held), both those who went away and those who remained behind felt, though they did not show it, that Moscow would certainly be abandoned, and that they ought to get away as quickly as possible and save their belongings. It was felt that everything would suddenly break up and change, but up to the 1st of September nothing had done so. As a criminal who is being led to execution knows that he must die immediately, but yet looks about him and straightens the cap that is awry on his head, so Moscow involuntarily continued its wonted life, though it knew that the time of its destruction was near when the conditions of life to which its people were accustomed to submit would be completely upset.

During the three days preceding the occupation of Moscow the whole Rostov family was absorbed in various activities. The head of the family, Count Ilya Rostov, continually drove about the city collecting the current rumours from all sides, and gave superficial and hasty orders at home about the preparations for their departure.

The countess watched the things being packed, was dissatisfied with everything, was constantly in pursuit of Petya who was always running away from her, and was jealous of Natasha with whom he spent all his time. Sonya alone directed the practical side of matters by getting things packed. But of late Sonya had been particularly sad and silent. Nicholas's letter in which he mentioned Princess Mary had elicited, in her presence, joyous comments from the countess, who saw an intervention of Providence in this meeting of the princess and Nicholas.

'I was never pleased at Bolkonsky's engagement to Natasha,' said the countess, 'but I always wanted Nicholas to marry the princess, and had a presentiment that it would happen. What a good thing it would be!'

Sonya felt that this was true: that the only possibility of retrieving the Rostovs' affairs was by Nicholas marrying a rich woman, and that the princess was a good match. It was very bitter for her. But despite her grief, or perhaps just because of it, she took on herself all the difficult work of directing the storing and packing of their things and was busy for whole days. The count and countess turned to her when they had any orders to give. Petya and Natasha on the contrary, far from helping their parents, were generally a nuisance and a hindrance to everyone. Almost all day long the house resounded with their running feet, their cries, and their spontaneous laughter. They laughed and were gay not because there was any reason to laugh, but because gaiety and mirth were in their hearts and so everything that happened was a cause for gaiety and laughter to them. Petya was in high spirits because having left home a boy he had returned (as everybody told him) a fine young man, because he was at home, because he had left Belaya Tserkov where there was no hope of soon taking part in a battle, and had come to Moscow where there was to be fighting in a few days, and chiefly because Natasha, whose lead he always followed, was in high spirits. Natasha was gay because she had been sad too long and now nothing reminded her of the cause of her sadness, and because she was feeling well. She was also happy because she had someone to adore her: the adoration of others was a lubricant the wheels of her machine needed to make them run freely – and Petya adored her. Above all, they were gay because there was a war near Moscow, there would be fighting at the town gates, arms were being given out, everybody was escaping – going away somewhere, and in general something extraordinary was happening, and that is always exciting, especially to the young.

ON Saturday the 31st of August everything in the Rostovs' house seemed topsy-turvy. All the doors were open, all the furniture was being carried out or moved about, and the mirrors and pictures had been taken down. There were trunks in the rooms, and hay, wrapping-paper and cords were scattered about. The peasants and house-serfs carrying out the things were treading heavily on the parquet floors. The yard was crowded with peasant carts, some loaded high and already corded up, others still empty.

The voices and footsteps of the many servants and of the peasants who had come with their carts, resounded as they shouted to one another in the yard and in the house. The count had been out since morning. The countess had a headache brought on by all the noise and turmoil, and was lying down in the new sitting-room with a vinegar compress on her head. Petya was not at home, he had gone to visit a friend with whom he meant to obtain a transfer from the militia to the active army. Sonya was in the ball-room looking after the packing of the glass and china. Natasha was sitting on the floor of her dismantled room with dresses, ribbons and scarves strewn all about her, gazing fixedly at the floor and holding in her hands the old ball-dress (already out of fashion) which she had worn at her first Petersburg ball.

Natasha was ashamed of doing nothing when everyone else was so busy, and several times that morning had tried to set to work, but her heart was not in it, and she could not and did not know how to do anything except with all her heart and all her might. For a while she had stood beside Sonya while the china was being packed, and tried to help, but soon gave it up and went to her room to pack her own things. At first she found it amusing to give away dresses and ribbons to the maids, but when that was done and what was left had still to be packed, she found it dull.

'Dunyasha, you pack! You will, won't you, dear?' And when Dunyasha willingly promised to do it all for her, Natasha sat down on the floor, took her old ball-dress, and fell into a reverie quite unrelated to what ought to have occupied her thoughts now. She was roused from her reverie by the talk of the maids in the next room (which was theirs) and by the sound of their hurried foot-steps going to the back porch. Natasha got up and looked out of the window. An enormously long row of carts full of wounded men had stopped in the street.

The housekeeper, the old nurse, the cooks, coachmen, maids,

footmen, postilions and scullions, stood at the gate staring at the wounded.

Natasha, throwing a clean pocket-handkerchief over her hair and holding an end of it in each hand, went out into the street.

The former housekeeper, old Mavra Kuzminishna, had stepped out of the crowd by the gate, gone up to a cart with a hood constructed of bast mats, and was speaking to a pale young officer who lay inside. Natasha moved a few steps forward and stopped shyly, still holding her handkerchief, and listened to what the housekeeper was saying.

'Then you have nobody in Moscow?' she was saying. 'You would be more comfortable somewhere in a house...in ours for instance...the family are leaving.'

'I don't know if it would be allowed,' replied the officer in a weak voice. 'Here is our commanding officer...ask him,' and he pointed to a stout major, who was walking back along the street past the row of carts.

Natasha glanced with frightened eyes at the face of the wounded officer and at once went to meet the major.

'May the wounded men stay in our house?' she asked.

The major raised his hand to his cap with a smile.

'Which one do you want, Ma'moiselle?' said he, screwing up his eyes and smiling.

Natasha quietly repeated her question, and her face and whole manner were so serious, though she was still holding the ends of her handkerchief, that the major ceased smiling and after some reflection – as if considering how far the thing was possible – replied in the affirmative.

'Oh yes, why not? They may,' he said.

With a slight inclination of her head, Natasha stepped back quickly to Mavra Kuzminishna who stood talking compassionately to the officer.

'They may. He says they may!' whispered Natasha.

The cart in which the officer lay was turned into the Rostovs' yard, and dozens of carts with wounded men began at the invitation of the townsfolk to turn into the yards and to draw up at the entrances of the houses in Povarskaya Street. Natasha was evidently pleased to be dealing with new people outside the ordinary routine of her life. She and Mavra Kuzminishna tried to get as many of the wounded as possible into their yard.

'Your papa must be told, though,' said Mavra Kuzminishna.

'Never mind, never mind, what does it matter? For one day we can move into the drawing-room. They can have all our half of the house.'

'There now, young lady, you do take things into your head! Even if we put them into the wing, the men's room, or the nurse's room, we must ask permission.'

'Well, I'll ask.'

Natasha ran into the house, and went on tiptoe through the half-open door into the sitting-room where there was a smell of vinegar and Hoffman's drops.*

'Are you asleep, mamma?'

'Oh, what sleep—?' said the countess, waking up just as she was dropping into a doze.

'Mamma darling!' said Natasha, kneeling by her mother and bringing her face close to her mother's, 'I am sorry, forgive me, I'll never do it again; I woke you up! Mavra Kuzminishna has sent me: they have brought some wounded here – officers. Will you let them come? They have nowhere to go. I knew you'd let them come . . .' she said quickly all in one breath.

'What officers? Whom have they brought? I don't understand anything about it,' said the countess.

Natasha laughed, and the countess too smiled slightly.

'I knew you'd give permission . . . so I'll tell them,' and having kissed her mother, Natasha got up and went to the door.

In the hall she met her father, who had returned with bad news.

'We've stayed too long!' said the count with involuntary vexation. 'The club is closed and the police are leaving.'

'Papa, is it all right – I've invited some of the wounded into the house?' said Natasha.

'Of course it is,' he answered absently. 'That's not the point. I beg you not to indulge in trifles now, but to help to pack, and to-morrow we must go, go, go! . . .'

And the count gave a similar order to the major-domo and the servants.

At dinner Petya having returned home told them the news he had heard. He said the people had been getting arms in the Kremlin, and that though Rostopchin's broadsheet had said that he would sound a call two or three days in advance, the order had certainly already been given for everyone to go armed to the Three Hills to-morrow, and that there would be a big battle there.

The countess looked with timid horror at her son's eager excited face as he said this. She realized that if she said a word about his not going to this battle (she knew he enjoyed the thought of the impending engagement) he would say something about men, honour, and the fatherland – something senseless, masculine, and obstinate which there would be no contradicting, and her plans would be spoilt; and so, hoping to arrange to leave before then and take Petya with her as their protector and defender, she did not answer him, but after dinner called the count aside and implored him with tears to take her away quickly, that very night if possible. With a woman's involuntary loving cunning she, who till then had not shown any alarm, said that she would die of fright if they did not leave that very night. Without any pretence she was now afraid of everything.

14

MADAME SCHOSS, who had been out to visit her daughter, increased the countess's fears still more by telling what she had seen at a spirit-dealer's in Myasnitsky Street. When returning by that street she had been unable to pass because of a drunken crowd rioting in front of the shop. She had taken a cab and driven home by a side street and the cabman had told her that the people were breaking open the barrels at the drink store, having received orders to do so.

After dinner the whole Rostov household set to work with enthusiastic haste packing their belongings and preparing for their departure. The old count, suddenly setting to work, kept passing from the yard to the house and back again, shouting confused instructions to the hurrying people, and flurrying them still more. Petya directed things in the yard. Sonya owing to the count's contradictory orders lost her head and did not know what to do. The servants ran noisily about the house and yard, shouting and disputing. Natasha with the ardour characteristic of all she did suddenly set to work too. At first her intervention in the business of packing was received sceptically. Everybody expected some prank from her, and did not wish to obey her; but she resolutely and passionately demanded obedience, grew angry and nearly cried because they did not heed her, and at last succeeded in making them believe in her. Her first exploit, which cost her immense effort and established her authority, was the packing of the carpets. The count had valuable Gobelin tapestries and Persian carpets in the house. When Natasha set to work two cases were standing open in the ball-room, one almost full up with crockery, the other with carpets. There was also much china standing on the tables, and still more was being brought in from the store-room. A third case was needed and servants had gone to fetch it.

'Sonya, wait a bit – we'll pack everything into these,' said Natasha.

'You can't, Miss, we have tried to,' said the butler's assistant.

'No, wait a minute, please.'

And Natasha began rapidly taking out of the case dishes and plates wrapped in paper.

'The dishes must go in here among the carpets,' said she.

'Why, it's a mercy if we can get the carpets alone into three cases,' said the butler's assistant.

'Oh, wait please!' And Natasha began rapidly and deftly sorting out the things. 'These aren't needed,' said she, putting aside some plates of Kiev ware. 'These – yes, these must go among the carpets,' she said, referring to the Saxony china dishes.

'Don't, Natasha! Leave it alone! We'll get it all packed,' urged Sonya reproachfully.

'What a young lady she is!' remarked the major-domo.

But Natasha would not give in. She turned everything out and began quickly repacking, deciding that the inferior Russian carpets and unnecessary crockery should not be taken at all. When everything had been taken out of the cases, they recommenced packing, and it turned out that when the cheaper things not worth taking had nearly all been rejected, the valuable ones really did all go into the two cases. Only the lid of the case containing the carpets would not shut down. A few more things might have been taken out, but Natasha insisted on having her own way. She packed, repacked, pressed, made the butler's assistant and Petya – whom she had drawn into the business of packing – press on the lid, and made desperate efforts herself.

'That's enough, Natasha,' said Sonya. 'I see you were right, but just take out the top one.'

'I won't!' cried Natasha, with one hand holding back the hair that hung over her perspiring face, while with the other she pressed down the carpets. 'Now press, Petya! Press, Vasilich, press hard!' she cried.

The carpets yielded and the lid closed. Natasha, clapping her hands, screamed with delight, and tears fell from her eyes. But this only lasted a moment. She at once set to work afresh and they now trusted her completely. The count was not angry even when they told him that Natasha had countermanded an order of his, and the servants now came to her to ask whether a cart was sufficiently loaded, and whether it might be corded up. Thanks to Natasha's directions the work now went on expeditiously, unnecessary things were left and the most valuable packed as compactly as possible.

But hard as they all worked till quite late that night, they could not get everything packed. The countess had fallen asleep and the count, having put off their departure till next morning, went to bed.

Sonya and Natasha slept in the sitting-room without undressing.

That night another wounded man was driven down the Povar-skaya, and Mavra Kuzminishna, who was standing at the gate, had him brought into the Rostovs' yard. Mavra Kuzminishna concluded that he was a very important man. He was being conveyed in a calèche with a raised hood, and was quite covered by an apron. On the box beside the driver sat a venerable old attendant. A doctor and two soldiers followed the carriage in a cart.

'Please come in here. The masters are going away and the whole house will be empty,' said the old woman to the old attendant.

'Well, perhaps,' said he with a sigh. 'We don't expect to get him home alive! We have a house of our own in Moscow but it's a long way from here, and there's nobody living in it.'

'Do us the honour to come in, there's plenty of everything in the master's house. Come in,' said Mavra Kuzminishna. 'Is he very ill?' she asked.

The attendant made a hopeless gesture.

'We don't expect to get him home! We must ask the doctor.'

And the old servant got down from the box and went up to the cart.

'All right!' said the doctor.

The old servant returned to the calèche, looked into it, shook his head disconsolately, told the driver to turn into the yard, and stopped beside Mavra Kuzminishna.

'O, Lord Jesus Christ!' she murmured.

She invited them to take the wounded man into the house.

'The masters won't object . . .' she said.

But they had to avoid carrying the man upstairs, and so they took him into the wing and put him in the room that had been Madame Schoss's.

This wounded man was Prince Andrew Bolkonsky.

15

MOSCOW'S last day had come. It was a clear bright autumn day, a Sunday. The church bells everywhere were ringing for service, just as usual on Sundays. Nobody seemed yet to realize what awaited the city.

Only two things indicated the social condition of Moscow – the rabble, that is the poor people, and the price of commodities. An enormous crowd of factory hands, house-serfs and peasants, with whom some officials, seminarists, and gentry were mingled, had gone early that morning to the Three Hills. Having waited there for Rostopchin who did not turn up, they became convinced that Moscow would be surrendered, and then dispersed all about the town to the public houses and cookshops. Prices too that day indicated the state of affairs. The price of weapons, of gold, of carts and horses, kept rising, but the value of paper money and city articles kept falling, so that by mid-day there were instances of carters removing valuable goods, such as cloth, and receiving in payment a half of what they carted, while peasant horses were fetching five hundred rubles each, and furniture, mirrors and bronzes were being given away for nothing.

In the Rostovs' staid old-fashioned house the dissolution of former conditions of life was but little noticeable. As to the serfs the only indication was that three out of their huge retinue disappeared during the night, but nothing was stolen; and as to the value of their possessions, the thirty peasant carts that had come in from their estates and which many people envied, proved to be extremely valuable and they were offered enormous sums of money for them. Not only were huge sums offered for the horses and carts, but on the previous evening and early in the morning of the 1st of September, orderlies and servants sent by wounded officers came to the Rostovs' yard, and wounded men dragged themselves in from the Rostovs' and from neighbouring houses where they were accommodated, entreating the servants to try to get them a lift out of Moscow. The major-domo to whom these entreaties were addressed, though he was sorry for the wounded, resolutely refused, saying that he dare not even mention the matter to the count. Pity these wounded men as one might, it was evident that if they were given one cart there would be no reason to refuse another, or all the carts and one's own carriages as well. Thirty carts could not save all the wounded and in the general catastrophe one could not disregard oneself and one's own family. So thought the major-domo on his master's behalf.

On waking up that morning Count Ilya Rostov left his bedroom softly, so as not to wake the countess who had fallen asleep only towards morning, and came out to the porch in his lilac silk dressing-gown. In the yard stood the carts ready corded. The carriages were at the front porch. The major-domo stood at the porch talking to an elderly orderly and to a pale young officer with a bandaged arm. On seeing the count the major-domo made a significant and stern gesture to them both to go away.

'Well, Vasilich, is everything ready?' asked the count, and stroking his bald head he looked good-naturedly at the officer and the orderly and nodded to them. (He liked to see new faces.)

'We can harness at once, your Excellency.'

'Well, that's right. As soon as the countess wakes we'll be off, God willing! What is it, gentlemen?' he added, turning to the officer, 'Are you staying in my house?'

The officer came nearer and suddenly his face flushed crimson.

'Count, be so good as to allow me ... for God's sake, to get into some corner of one of your carts! I have nothing here with me ... I should be all right on a loaded cart ...'

Before the officer had finished speaking the orderly made the same request on behalf of his master.

'Oh yes, yes!' said the count hastily. 'I shall be very pleased, very pleased. Vasilich, you'll see to it. Just unload one or two carts. Well, what of it ... do what's necessary ...' said the count muttering some indefinite order.

But at the same moment an expression of warm gratitude on the officer's face had already sealed the order. The count looked round him. In the yard, at the gates, at the window of the wing, wounded officers and their orderlies were to be seen. They were all looking at the count and moving towards the porch.

'Please step into the gallery, your Excellency,' said the major-domo. 'What are your orders about the pictures?'

The count went into the house with him, repeating his order not to refuse the wounded who asked for a lift.

'Well, never mind, some of the things can be unloaded,' he added in a soft, confidential voice, as though afraid of being over-heard.

At nine o'clock the countess woke up, and Matrëna Timofeevna who had been her lady's maid before her marriage and now performed a sort of chief gendarme's duty for her, came to say that Madame Schoss was much offended and the young ladies' summer dresses could not be left behind. On inquiry, the countess learnt that Madame Schoss was offended because her trunk had been taken down from its cart, and all the loads were being uncorded and the luggage taken out of the carts to make room for wounded men, whom the count in the simplicity of his heart had ordered that they should take with them. The countess sent for her husband.

'What is this, my dear? I hear that the luggage is being unloaded.'

'You know, love, I wanted to tell you ... Countess dear ... an officer came to me to ask for a few carts for the wounded. After all, ours are things that can be bought but think what being left behind means to them! ... Really now, in our own yard – we asked them in ourselves and there are officers among them ... You know, I think, my dear ... let them be taken ... where's the hurry?'

The count spoke timidly as he always did when talking of

919

money matters. The countess was accustomed to this tone as a precursor of news of something detrimental to the children's interests, such as the building of a new gallery or conservatory, the inauguration of a private theatre or an orchestra. She was accustomed always to oppose anything announced in that timid tone, and considered it her duty to do so.

She assumed her dolefully submissive manner and said to her husband:

'Listen to me, Count, you have managed matters so that we are getting nothing for the house, and now you wish to throw away all our – all *the children's* property! You said yourself that we have a hundred thousand rubles' worth of things in the house. I don't consent, my dear, I don't! Do as you please! It's the government's business to look after the wounded; they know that. Look at the Lopukhins opposite, they cleared out everything two days ago. That's what other people do. It's only we who are such fools. If you have no pity on me, have some for the children.'

Flourishing his arms in despair the count left the room without replying.

'Papa, what are you doing that for?' asked Natasha, who had followed him into her mother's room.

'Nothing! What business is it of yours?' muttered the count angrily.

'But I heard,' said Natasha. 'Why does mamma object?'

'What business is it of yours?' cried the count.

Natasha stepped up to the window and pondered.

'Papa! Here's Berg coming to see us,' said she, looking out of the window.

16

BERG, the Rostovs' son-in-law, was already a colonel wearing the orders of Vladimir and Anna, and he still filled the quiet and agreeable post of assistant to the head of the staff of the assistant-commander of the first division of the Second Army.

On the 1st of September he had come to Moscow from the army.

He had nothing to do in Moscow, but he had noticed that everyone in the army was asking for leave to visit Moscow and had something to do there. So he considered it necessary to ask for leave of absence for family and domestic reasons.

Berg drove up to his father-in-law's house in his spruce little trap with a pair of sleek roans, exactly like those of a certain prince. He looked attentively at the carts in the yard and while going up to the porch took out a clean pocket handkerchief and tied a knot in it.

From the ante-room Berg ran with smooth though impatient steps into the drawing-room, where he embraced the count, kissed the hands of Natasha and Sonya, and hastened to inquire after 'mamma's' health.

'Health, at a time like this?' said the count. 'Come, tell us the news! Is the army retreating or will there be another battle?'

'God Almighty alone can decide the fate of our Fatherland, papa,' said Berg. 'The army is burning with a spirit of heroism and the leaders, so to say, have now assembled in council. No one knows what is coming. But in general I can tell you, papa, that such an heroic spirit, the truly antique valour of the Russian army, which they – which it' (he corrected himself) 'has shown or displayed in the battle of the 26th – there are no words worthy to do it justice. I tell you, papa' (he smote himself on the breast as a general he had heard speaking had done, but Berg did it a trifle late for he should have struck his breast at the words 'Russian army'), 'I tell you frankly that we, the commanders, far from having to urge the men on or anything of that kind, could hardly restrain those . . . those . . . yes, those exploits of antique valour,' he went on rapidly. 'General Barclay de Tolly risked his life everywhere at the head of the troops, I can assure you. Our corps was stationed on a hill-side. You can imagine!'

And Berg related all that he remembered of the various tales he had heard those days. Natasha watched him with an intent gaze that confused him, as if she were trying to find in his face the answer to some question.

'Altogether such heroism as was displayed by the Russian warriors cannot be imagined or adequately praised!' said Berg, glancing round at Natasha, and as if anxious to conciliate her, replying to her intent look with a smile. '"Russia is not in Moscow, she lives in the hearts of her sons!" Isn't it so, papa?' said he.

Just then the countess came in from the sitting-room with a weary and dissatisfied expression. Berg hurriedly jumped up, kissed her hand, inquired about her health, and, swaying his head from side to side to express sympathy, remained standing beside her.

'Yes, mamma, I tell you sincerely that these are hard and sad times for every Russian. But why are you so anxious? You have still time to get away . . .'

'I can't think what the servants are about,' said the countess, turning to her husband. 'I have just been told that nothing is ready yet. Somebody after all must see to things. One misses Mitenka at such times. There won't be any end to it.'

The count was about to say something, but evidently restrained himself. He got up from his chair and went to the door.

At that moment Berg drew out his handkerchief as if to blow his nose, and seeing the knot in it pondered, shaking his head sadly and significantly.

'And I have a great favour to ask of you, papa,' said he.

'Hm . . .' said the count and stopped.

'I was driving past Yusupov's house just now,' said Berg with a laugh, 'when the steward, a man I know, ran out and asked me whether I wouldn't buy something. I went in out of curiosity, you know, and there is a small chiffonier and a dressing-table. You know how dear Vera wanted a chiffonier like that and how we had a dispute about it.' (At the mention of the chiffonier and dressing-table, Berg involuntarily changed his tone to one of pleasure at his admirable domestic arrangements.) 'And it's such a beauty! It pulls out and has a secret English drawer, you know! And dear Vera has long wanted one. I wish to give her a surprise you see. I saw so many of those peasant carts in your yard. Please let me have one, I will pay the man well, and . . .'

The count frowned and coughed.

'Ask the countess, I don't give orders.'

'If it's inconvenient, please don't,' said Berg. 'Only I so wanted it, for dear Vera's sake.'

'Oh, go to the devil, all of you! To the devil, the devil, the devil . . . !' cried the old count. 'My head's in a whirl!'

And he left the room. The countess began to cry.

'Yes mamma! Yes, these are very hard times!' said Berg.

Natasha left the room with her father and, as if finding it difficult to reach some decision, first followed him and then ran downstairs.

Petya was in the porch, engaged in giving out weapons to the servants who were to leave Moscow. The loaded carts were still standing in the yard. Two of them had been uncorded, and a wounded officer was climbing into one of them helped by an orderly.

'Do you know what it's about?' Petya asked Natasha.

She understood that he meant what were their parents quarrelling about. She did not answer.

'It's because papa wanted to give up all the carts to the wounded,' said Petya. 'Vasilich told me. I consider . . .'

'I consider,' Natasha suddenly almost shouted, turning her angry face to Petya, 'I consider it so horrid, so abominable, so . . . I don't know what. Are we despicable Germans?'

Her throat quivered with convulsive sobs and, afraid of weakening and letting the force of her anger run to waste, she turned and rushed headlong up the stairs.

Berg was sitting beside the countess consoling her with the respectful attention of a relative. The count, pipe in hand, was pacing up and down the room, when Natasha, her face distorted by anger, burst in like a tempest and approached her mother with rapid steps.

'It's horrid! It's abominable!' she screamed. 'You can't possibly have ordered it!'

Berg and the countess looked at her, perplexed and frightened. The count stood still at the window and listened.

'Mamma, it's impossible: see what is going on in the yard!' she cried. 'They will be left!...'

'What's the matter with you? Who are "they"? What do you want?'

'Why, the wounded! It's impossible, mamma. It's monstrous... No, mamma darling, it's not the thing. Please forgive me, darling ... Mamma, what does it matter what we take away? Only look what is going on in the yard... Mamma!... It's impossible!'

The count stood by the window and listened without turning round. Suddenly he sniffed and put his face closer to the window.

The countess glanced at her daughter, saw her face full of shame for her mother, saw her agitation, and understood why her husband did not turn to look at her now, and she glanced round quite disconcerted.

'Oh, do as you like! Am I hindering anyone?' she said, not surrendering at once.

'Mamma, darling, forgive me.'

But the countess pushed her daughter away and went up to her husband.

'My dear, you order what is right... You know I don't understand about it,' said she dropping her eyes shamefacedly.

'The eggs... the eggs are teaching the hen...' muttered the count through tears of joy, and he embraced his wife, who was glad to hide her look of shame on his breast.

'Papa! Mamma! May I see to it? May I?...' asked Natasha. 'We will still take all the most necessary things.'

The count nodded affirmatively, and Natasha, at the rapid pace at which she used to run when playing at tag, ran through the ball-room to the ante-room and downstairs into the yard.

The servants gathered round Natasha, but could not believe the strange order she brought them, until the count himself in his wife's name confirmed the order to give up all the carts to the wounded and take the trunks to the store-rooms. When they

923

understood that order the servants set to work at this new task with pleasure and zeal. It no longer seemed strange to them but on the contrary it seemed the only thing that could be done, just as a quarter of an hour before it had not seemed strange to anyone that the wounded should be left behind and the goods carted away but had seemed the only thing to do.

The whole household, as if to atone for not having done it sooner, set eagerly to work at the new task of placing the wounded in the carts. The wounded dragged themselves out of their rooms and stood with pale but happy faces round the carts. The news that carts were to be had spread to the neighbouring houses, from which wounded men began to come into the Rostovs' yard. Many of the wounded asked them not to unload the carts but only to let them sit on the top of the things. But the work of unloading, once started, could not be arrested. It seemed not to matter whether all or only half the things were left behind. Cases full of china, bronzes, pictures and mirrors, that had been so carefully packed the night before, now lay about the yard, and still they went on searching for and finding possibilities of unloading this or that and letting the wounded have another and yet another cart.

'We can take four more men,' said the steward. 'They can have my trap, or else what is to become of them?'

'Let them have my wardrobe cart,' said the countess. 'Dunyasha can go with me in the carriage.'

They unloaded the wardrobe cart and sent it to take wounded men from a house two doors off. The whole household, servants included, was bright and animated. Natasha was in a state of rapturous excitement such as she had not known for a long time.

'What could we fasten this onto?' asked the servants, trying to fix a trunk on the narrow footboard behind a carriage. 'We must keep at least one cart.'

'What's in it?' asked Natasha.

'The count's books.'

'Leave it, Vasilich will put it away. It's not wanted.'

The phaeton was full of people and there was a doubt as to where Count Peter could sit.

'On the box. You'll sit on the box, won't you, Petya?' cried Natasha.

Sonya too was busy all this time, but the aim of her efforts was quite different from Natasha's. She was putting away the things that had to be left behind and making a list of them as the countess wished, and she tried to get as much taken away with them as possible.

BEFORE two o'clock in the afternoon the Rostovs' four carriages, packed full and with the horses harnessed, stood at the front door. One by one the carts with the wounded had moved out of the yard.

The calèche in which Prince Andrew was being taken attracted Sonya's attention as it passed the front porch. With the help of a maid she was arranging a seat for the countess in the huge high coach that stood at the entrance.

'Whose calèche is that?' she inquired, reaching out of the carriage window.

'Why, didn't you know, Miss?' replied the maid. 'The wounded prince: he spent the night in our house and is going with us.'

'But who is it? What's his name?'

'It's our intended that was – Prince Bolkonsky himself! They say he is dying,' replied the maid with a sigh.

Sonya jumped out of the coach and ran to the countess. The countess, tired out and already dressed in shawl and bonnet for her journey, was pacing up and down the drawing-room waiting for the household to assemble for the usual silent prayer with closed doors before starting. Natasha was not in the room

'Mamma,' said Sonya, 'Prince Andrew is here, mortally wounded. He is going with us.'

The countess opened her eyes in dismay, and seizing Sonya's arm glanced around.

'Natasha?' she murmured.

At that moment this news had only one significance for both of them. They knew their Natasha, and alarm as to what would happen if she heard this news stifled all sympathy for the man they both liked.

'Natasha does not know yet, but he is going with us,' said Sonya.

'You say he is dying?'

Sonya nodded.

The countess put her arms round Sonya and began to cry.

'The ways of God are past finding out!'* she thought, feeling that the Almighty Hand, hitherto unseen, was becoming manifest in all that was now taking place.

'Well, mamma? Everything is ready. What's the matter?' asked Natasha, as with animated face she ran into the room.

'Nothing,' answered the countess. 'If everything is ready let us start.'

And the countess bent over her reticule to hide her agitated face. Sonya embraced Natasha and kissed her.

Natasha looked at her inquiringly.

'What is it? What has happened?'

'Nothing ... No ...'

'Is it something very bad for me? What is it?' persisted Natasha with her quick intuition.

Sonya sighed and made no reply. The count, Petya, Madame Schoss, Mavra Kuzminishna and Vasilich came into the drawing-room, and having closed the doors they all sat down and remained for some moments silently seated without looking at one another.

The count was the first to rise, and with a loud sigh crossed himself before the icon. All the others did the same. Then the count embraced Mavra Kuzminishna and Vasilich, who were to remain in Moscow, and while they caught at his hand and kissed his shoulder he patted their backs lightly with some vaguely affectionate and comforting words. The countess went into the oratory and there Sonya found her on her knees before the icons that had been left here and there hanging on the wall. (The most precious ones, with which some family tradition was connected, were being taken with them.)

In the porch and in the yard the men whom Petya had armed with swords and daggers, with trousers tucked inside their high boots and with belts and girdles tightened, were taking leave of those remaining behind.

As is always the case at a departure, much had been forgotten or put in the wrong place, and for a long time two men-servants stood one each side of the open door and the carriage steps waiting to help the countess in, while maids rushed with cushions and bundles from the house to the carriages, the calèche, the phaeton, and back again.

'They always will forget everything!' said the countess. 'Don't you know I can't sit like that?'

And Dunyasha, with clenched teeth, without replying but with an aggrieved look on her face, hastily got into the coach to rearrange the seat.

'Oh, those servants!' said the count, swaying his head.

Efim, the old coachman, who was the only one the countess trusted to drive her, sat perched up high on the box and did not so much as glance round at what was going on behind him. From thirty years' experience he knew it would be some time yet before the order 'Be off, in God's name!' would be given him: and he knew that even when it was said he would be stopped once or twice more while they sent back to fetch something that had been forgotten, and even after that he would again be stopped and the countess herself would lean out of the window and beg him for the love of Heaven to drive carefully down the hill. He knew all this and therefore waited calmly for what would happen, with more patience than the horses, especially the near one, the chestnut Falcon, who was pawing the ground and champing his bit. At last all were seated, the carriage steps were folded and pulled up, the door was shut, somebody was sent for a travelling-case, and the countess leaned out and said what she had to say. Then Efim deliberately doffed his hat and began crossing himself. The postilion and all the other servants did the same. 'Off, in God's name!' said Efim, putting on his hat. 'Start!' The postilion started the horses, the off pole-horse tugged at his collar, the high springs creaked and the body of the coach swayed. The footman sprang onto the box of the moving coach which jolted as it passed out of the yard onto the uneven roadway; the other vehicles jolted in their turn, and the procession of carriages moved up the street. In the carriages, the calèche and the phaeton, all crossed themselves as they passed the church opposite the house. Those who were to remain in Moscow walked on either side of the vehicles seeing the travellers off.

Rarely had Natasha experienced so joyful a feeling as now, sitting in the carriage beside the countess and gazing at the slowly receding walls of forsaken agitated Moscow. Occasionally she leaned out of the carriage window and looked back and then forward at the long train of wounded in front of them. Almost at the head of the line she could see the raised hood of Prince Andrew's calèche. She did not know who was in it, but each time she looked at the procession her eyes sought that calèche. She knew it was right in front.

In Kudrino, from the Nikitsky, Presnya, and Podnovinsk Streets came several other trains of vehicles similar to the Rostovs', and as they passed along the Sadovaya Street the carriages and carts formed two rows abreast.

As they were going round the Sukharev water-tower Natasha, who was inquisitively and alertly scrutinizing the people driving or walking past, suddenly cried out in joyful surprise:

'Dear me! Mamma, Sonya, look, it's he!'

'Who? Who?'

'Look! Yes, on my word, it's Bezukhov!' said Natasha, putting her head out of the carriage and staring at a tall, stout man in a coachman's long coat, who from his manner of walking and moving was evidently a gentleman in disguise, and who was passing under the arch of the Sukharev tower accompanied by a small sallow-faced, beardless old man in a frieze coat.

'Yes, it really is Bezukhov in a coachman's coat, with a queer-looking old boy. Really,' said Natasha, 'Look, look!'

'No, it's not he. How can you talk such nonsense?'

'Mamma,' screamed Natasha, 'I'll stake my head it's he! I assure you! Stop, stop!' she cried to the coachman.

But the coachman could not stop, for from the Meshchansky Street came more carts and carriages, and the Rostovs were being shouted at to move on and not block the way.

In fact however, though now much farther off than before, the Rostovs all saw Pierre – or someone extraordinarily like him – in a coachman's coat, going down the street with head bent and a serious face beside a small, beardless old man who looked like a footman. That old man noticed a face thrust out of the carriage window gazing at them, and respectfully touching Pierre's elbow said something to him and pointed to the carriage. Pierre, evidently engrossed in thought, could not at first understand him. At length when he had understood and looked in the direction the old man indicated, he recognized Natasha, and following his first impulse stepped instantly and rapidly towards the coach. But having taken a dozen steps he seemed to remember something and stopped.

Natasha's face leaning out of the window beamed with quizzical kindliness.

'Peter Kirilovich, come here! We have recognized you! This is wonderful!' she cried holding out her hand to him. 'What are you doing? Why are you like this?'

Pierre took her outstretched hand and kissed it awkwardly as he walked beside her while the coach still moved on.

'What is the matter, Count?' asked the countess in a surprised and commiserating tone.

'What? What? Why? Don't ask me,' said Pierre, and looked round at Natasha whose radiant happy expression – of which he was conscious without looking at her – filled him with enchantment.

'Are you remaining in Moscow, then?'

Pierre hesitated.

'In Moscow?' he said in a questioning tone. 'Yes, in Moscow. Good-bye!'

'Ah, if only I were a man! I'd certainly stay with you. How splendid!' said Natasha. 'Mamma, if you'll let me, I'll stay.'

Pierre glanced absently at Natasha and was about to say something, but the countess interrupted him.

'You were at the battle, we heard?'

'Yes, I was,' Pierre answered. 'There will be another battle to-morrow . . .' he began, but Natasha interrupted him.

'But what is the matter with you, Count? You are not like yourself...'

'Oh, don't ask me, don't ask me! I don't know myself. To-morrow...But no! Good-bye, good-bye!' he muttered. 'It's an awful time!' and dropping behind the carriage he stepped onto the pavement.

Natasha continued to lean out of the window for a long time, beaming at him with her kindly, slightly quizzical, happy smile.

18

FOR the last two days, ever since leaving home, Pierre had been living in the empty house of his deceased benefactor, Bazdeev. This is how it happened.

When he woke up on the morning after his return to Moscow and his interview with Count Rostopchin, he could not for some time make out where he was and what was expected of him. When he was informed that among others awaiting him in his reception-room there was a Frenchman who had brought a letter from his wife, the Countess Hélène, he felt suddenly overcome by that sense of confusion and hopelessness to which he was apt to succumb. He felt that everything was now at an end, all was in confusion and crumbling to pieces, that nobody was right or wrong, the future held nothing, and there was no escape from this position. Smiling unnaturally and muttering to himself, he first sat down on the sofa in an attitude of despair, then rose, went to the door of the reception-room and peeped through the crack, returned flourishing his arms, and took up a book. His major-domo came in a second time to say that the Frenchman who had brought the letter from the countess was very anxious to see him if only for a minute, and that someone from Bazdeev's widow had called to ask Pierre to take charge of her husband's books, as she herself was leaving for the country.

'Oh, yes, in a minute; wait...or no! No of course...go and say I will come directly,' Pierre replied to the major-domo.

But as soon as the man had left the room Pierre took up his hat which was lying on the table and went out of his study by the other door. There was no one in the passage. He went along the whole length of this passage to the stairs and, frowning and rubbing his forehead with both hands, went down as far as the first landing. The hall-porter was standing at the front door. From the landing where Pierre stood there was a second staircase leading to the back entrance. He went down that staircase and out into the yard. No one had seen him. But there were some carriages waiting, and as soon as Pierre stepped out of the gate the coachmen and the yard-porter noticed him and raised their caps to him. When he felt he was being looked at he behaved like an ostrich which hides its head in a bush in order not to be seen: he hung his head and quickening his pace went down the street.

Of all the affairs awaiting Pierre that day the sorting of Joseph Bazdeev's books and papers appeared to him the most necessary.

He hired the first cab he met and told the driver to go to the Patriarch's Ponds, where the widow Bazdeev's house was.

Continually turning round to look at the rows of loaded carts that were making their way from all sides out of Moscow, and balancing his bulky body so as not to slip out of the ramshackle old vehicle, Pierre, experiencing the joyful feeling of a boy escaping from school, began to talk to his driver.

The man told him that arms were being distributed to-day at the Kremlin, and that to-morrow everyone would be sent out beyond the Three Hills gates, and a great battle would be fought there.

Having reached the Patriarch's Ponds Pierre found the Bazdeevs' house, where he had not been for a long time past. He went up to the gate. Gerasim, that sallow beardless old man Pierre had seen at Torzhok five years before with Joseph Bazdeev, came out in answer to his knock.

'At home?' asked Pierre.

'Owing to the present state of things Sophia Danilovna has gone to the Torzhok estate with the children, your Excellency.'

'I will come in all the same, I have to look through the books,' said Pierre.

'Be as good as to step in. Makar Alexeevich, the brother of my late master – may the kingdom of heaven be his – has remained here, but he is in a weak state, as you know,' said the old servant.

Pierre knew that Makar Alexeevich was Joseph Bazdeev's half-insane brother, and a hard drinker.

'Yes, yes, I know. Let us go in ...' said Pierre, and entered the house.

A tall, bald-headed old man with a red nose, wearing a dressing-gown and with goloshes on his bare feet, stood in the ante-room. On seeing Pierre he muttered something angrily and went away along the passage.

'He was a very clever man but has now grown quite feeble, as your Honour sees,' said Gerasim. 'Will you step into the study?' Pierre nodded. 'As it was sealed up, so it has remained, but Sophia Danilovna gave orders that if anyone should come from you they were to have the books.'

Pierre went into that gloomy study which he had entered with such trepidation in his benefactor's life-time. The room, dusty and untouched since the death of Joseph Bazdeev, was now even gloomier.

Gerasim opened one of the shutters and left the room on tiptoe. Pierre went round the study, approached the cupboard in which the manuscripts were kept, and took out what had once been one of the most important, the holy of holies of the Order. This was the authentic Scotch Acts with Bazdeev's notes and explanations. He sat down at the dusty writing-table, and having laid the manuscripts before him, opened them out, closed them, finally pushed them away, and resting his head on his hand sank into meditation.

Gerasim looked cautiously into the study several times and saw Pierre always sitting in the same attitude.

More than two hours passed and Gerasim took the liberty of making a slight noise at the door to attract his attention, but Pierre did not hear him.

'Is the cabman to be discharged, your Honour?'

'Oh yes!' said Pierre, rousing himself and rising hurriedly. 'Look here,' he added, taking Gerasim by a button of his coat and looking down at the old man with moist, shining, and ecstatic eyes, 'I say, do you know that there is going to be a battle to-morrow?'

'We heard so,' replied the man.

'I beg you not to tell anyone who I am, and to do what I ask you.'

'Yes, your Excellency,' replied Gerasim. 'Will you have something to eat?'

'No, but I want something else. I want peasant clothes and a pistol,' said Pierre, unexpectedly blushing.

'Yes, your Excellency,' said Gerasim after thinking for a moment.

All the rest of that day Pierre spent alone in his benefactor's study, and Gerasim heard him pacing restlessly from one corner to another and talking to himself. And he spent the night on a bed made up for him there.

Gerasim, being a servant who in his time had seen many strange things, accepted Pierre's taking up his residence in the house without surprise, and seemed pleased to have someone to wait on. That same evening – without even asking himself what they were wanted for – he procured a coachman's coat and cap for Pierre, and promised to get him the pistol next day. Makar Alexeevich came twice that evening shuffling along in his goloshes as far as the door, and stopped and looked ingratiatingly at Pierre. But as soon as Pierre turned towards him he wrapped his dressing-gown round him with a shamefaced and angry look and hurried away. It was when Pierre, wearing the coachman's coat which Gerasim had procured for him and had disinfected by steam, was on his way with the old man to buy the pistol at the Sukharev market, that he met the Rostovs.

19

KUTUZOV'S order to retreat through Moscow to the Ryazan Road was issued at night on the 1st of September.

The first troops started at once, and during the night they marched slowly and steadily without hurry. At daybreak however those nearing the town at the Dorogomilov bridge saw ahead of them masses of soldiers crowding and hurrying across the bridge, ascending on the opposite side and blocking the streets and alleys, while endless masses of troops were bearing down on them from behind, and an unreasoning hurry and alarm overcame them. They all rushed forward to the bridge, onto it, and to the fords and to the boats. Kutuzov himself had driven round by side streets to the other side of Moscow.

By ten o'clock in the morning of the 2nd of September only the rearguard remained in the Dorogomilov suburb, where they had ample room. The main army was on the other side of Moscow or beyond it.

At that very time, at ten in the morning of the 2nd of September, Napoleon was standing among his troops on the Poklonny Hill looking at the panorama spread out before him. From the 26th of August to the 2nd of September, that is from the battle of Borodino to the entry of the French into Moscow, during the whole of that agitating, memorable week, there had been the extraordinary autumn weather that always comes as a surprise, when the sun hangs low and gives more heat than in spring, when everything shines so brightly in the rare clear atmosphere that the eyes smart, when the lungs are strengthened and refreshed by inhaling the aromatic autumn air, when even the nights are warm, and when, in those dark warm nights, golden stars startle and delight us continually by falling from the sky.

At ten in the morning of the 2nd of September this weather still held.

The brightness of the morning was magical. Moscow, seen from the Poklonny Hill, lay spaciously spread out with her river, her gardens and her churches, and she seemed to be living her usual life, her cupolas glittering like stars in the sunlight.

The view of the strange city with its peculiar architecture such as he had never seen before, filled Napoleon with the rather envious and uneasy curiosity men feel when they see an alien form of life that has no knowledge of them. The city was evidently living with the full force of its own life. By the indefinite signs which, even at a distance, distinguish a living body from a dead one, Napoleon from the Poklonny Hill perceived the throb of life in the town and felt, as it were, the breathing of that great and beautiful body.

Every Russian looking at Moscow feels her to be a mother; every foreigner who sees her, even if ignorant of her significance as the mother city, must feel her feminine character, and Napoleon felt it.

'*Cette ville asiatique aux innombrables églises, Moscou la sainte. La voilà donc enfin, cette fameuse ville! Il était temps,*' said he, and dismounting he ordered a plan of Moscow to be spread out before him, and summoned Lelorgne d'Ideville, the interpreter.

'A town captured by the enemy is like a maid who has lost her honour,' thought he (he had said so to Tuchkov at Smolensk). From that point of view he gazed at the oriental beauty he had not seen before. It seemed strange to him that his long-felt wish, which had seemed unattainable, had at last been realized. In the clear morning light he gazed now at the city and now at the plan, considering its details, and the assurance of possessing it agitated and awed him.

'But could it be otherwise?' he thought. 'Here is this capital at my feet. Where is Alexander now, and of what is he thinking? A strange, beautiful and majestic city; and a strange and majestic moment! In what light must I appear to them!' he thought, thinking of his troops. 'Here she is, the reward for all those faint-hearted men,' he reflected, glancing at those near him and at the troops who were approaching and forming up. 'One word from me, one movement of my hand, and that ancient capital of the Tsars would perish. But my clemency is always ready to descend upon the vanquished. I must be magnanimous and truly great. But no, it can't be true that I am in Moscow,' he suddenly thought. 'Yet here she is lying at my feet, with her golden domes and crosses scintillating and twinkling in the sunshine. But I shall spare her. On the ancient monuments of barbarism and despotism I will inscribe great words of justice and mercy ... It is just this which Alexander will feel most painfully, I know him.' (It seemed to Napoleon that the chief import of what was taking place lay in the personal struggle between himself and Alexander.) 'From the height of the Kremlin – yes, there is the Kremlin, yes – I will give them just laws; I will teach them the meaning of true civilization, I will make generations of boyars remember their conqueror with love. I will tell the deputation that I did not, and do not, desire war, that I have waged war only against the false policy of their court; that I love and respect Alexander and that in Moscow I will accept terms of peace worthy of myself and of my people. I do not wish to utilize the fortunes of war to humiliate an honoured monarch. 'Boyars,' I will say to them,* 'I do not desire war, I desire the peace and welfare of all my subjects.' However, I know their presence will inspire me, and I shall speak to them as I always do: clearly, impressively, and majestically. But can it be true that I am in Moscow? Yes, there she lies.'

'*Qu'on m'amène les boyars,*' said he to his suite.

A general with a brilliant suite galloped off at once to fetch the boyars.

Two hours passed. Napoleon had lunched and was again standing in the same place on the Poklonny Hill awaiting the deputation. His speech to the boyars had already taken definite shape in his imagination. That speech was full of dignity and greatness as Napoleon understood it.

He was himself carried away by the tone of magnanimity he intended to adopt towards Moscow. In imagination he appointed days for assemblies at the palace of the Tsars, at which Russian notables and his own would mingle. He mentally appointed a governor, one who would win the hearts of the people. Having learnt that there were many charitable institutions in Moscow he mentally decided that he would shower favours on them all. He thought that, as in Africa he had had to put on a burnous and sit in a mosque, so in Moscow he must be beneficent like the Tsars. And in order finally to touch the hearts of the Russians – and being like all Frenchmen unable to imagine anything sentimental without a reference to *ma chère, ma tendre, ma pauvre mère* – he decided that he would place an inscription on all these establishments in large letters: 'This establishment is dedicated to my dear mother'. Or no, it should be simply: *Maison de ma Mère*, he concluded. 'But am I really in Moscow? Yes, here it lies before me, but why is the deputation from the city so long in appearing?' he wondered.

Meanwhile an agitated consultation was being carried on in whispers among his generals and marshals at the rear of his suite. Those sent to fetch the deputation had returned with the news that Moscow was empty, that everyone had left it. The faces of those who were conferring together were pale and perturbed. They were not alarmed by the fact that Moscow had been abandoned by its inhabitants (grave as that fact seemed), but by the question how to tell the Emperor – without putting him in the terrible position of appearing ridiculous – that he had been awaiting the boyars so long in vain: that there were drunken mobs left in Moscow but no one else. Some said that a deputation of some sort must be scraped together, others disputed that opinion and maintained that the Emperor should first be carefully and skilfully prepared, and then told the truth.

'He will have to be told, all the same,' said some gentlemen of the suite. 'But, gentlemen...'

The position was the more awkward because the Emperor, meditating upon his magnanimous plans, was pacing patiently up and down before the outspread map, occasionally glancing along the road to Moscow from under his lifted hand with a bright and proud smile.

'But it's impossible...' declared the gentlemen of the suite, shrugging their shoulders but not venturing to utter the implied word – *le ridicule*...

At last the Emperor, tired of futile expectation, his actor's instinct suggesting to him that the sublime moment having been too long drawn out was beginning to lose its sublimity, gave a sign with his hand. A single report of a signalling-gun followed, and the troops, who were already spread out on different sides of Moscow, moved into the city through the Tver, Kaluga, and Dorogomilov gates. Faster and faster, vying with one another, they moved at the double or at a trot, vanishing amid the clouds of dust they raised and making the air ring with a deafening roar of mingling shouts.

Drawn on by the movement of his troops Napoleon rode with them as far as the Dorogomilov gate, but there again stopped and, dismounting from his horse, paced for a long time by the Kammer-Kollezhsky rampart awaiting the deputation.

20

MEANWHILE Moscow was empty. There were still people in it, perhaps a fiftieth part of its former inhabitants had remained, but it was empty. It was empty in the sense that a dying queenless hive is empty.

In a queenless hive no life is left though to a superficial glance it seems as much alive as other hives.

The bees circle round a queenless hive in the hot beams of the midday sun as gaily as around the living hives; from a distance it smells of honey like the others, and bees fly in and out in the same way. But one has only to observe that hive to realize that there is no longer any life in it. The bees do not fly in the same way, the smell and the sound that meet the bee-keeper are not the same. To the bee-keeper's tap on the wall of the sick hive, instead of the former instant unanimous humming of tens of thousands of bees with their abdomens threateningly compressed, and producing by the rapid vibration of their wings an aerial living sound, the only reply is a disconnected buzzing from different parts of the deserted hive. From the alighting-board, instead of the former spirituous fragrant smell of honey and venom, and the warm whiffs of crowded life, comes an odour of emptiness and decay mingling with the smell of honey. There are no longer sentinels there sounding the alarm with their abdomens raised, and ready to die in defence of the hive. There is no longer the measured quiet sound of throbbing activity, like the sound of boiling water, but diverse discordant sounds of disorder. In and out of the hive long black robber-bees smeared with honey fly timidly and shiftily. They do not sting, but crawl away from danger. Formerly only bees laden with honey flew into the hive, and they flew out empty; now they fly out laden. The bee-keeper opens the lower part of the hive and peers in. Instead of black, glossy bees – tamed by toil, clinging to one another's legs and drawing out the wax, with a ceaseless hum of labour – that used to hang in long clusters down to the floor of the hive, drowsy shrivelled bees crawl about separately in various directions on the floor and walls of the hive. Instead of a neatly glued floor, swept by the bees with the fanning of their wings, there is a floor littered with bits of wax, excrement, dying bees scarcely moving their legs, and dead ones that have not been cleared away.

The bee-keeper opens the upper part of the hive and examines the super. Instead of serried rows of bees sealing up every gap in the combs and keeping the brood warm, he sees the skilful complex structures of the combs, but no longer in their former state of purity. All is neglected and foul. Black robber-bees are swiftly and stealthily prowling about the combs, and the short home-bees, shrivelled and listless as if they were old, creep slowly about without trying to hinder the robbers, having lost all desire and all sense of life. Drones, bumble-bees, wasps, and butterflies, knock awkwardly against the wall of the hive in their flight. Here and there among the cells containing dead brood and honey an angry buzzing can sometimes be heard. Here and there a couple of bees, by force of habit and custom cleaning out the brood-cells, with efforts beyond their strength laboriously drag away a dead bee or bumble-bee without knowing why they do it. In another corner two old bees are languidly fighting, or cleaning themselves, or feeding one another, without themselves knowing whether they do it with friendly or hostile intent. In a third place a crowd of bees, crushing one another, attack some victim and fight and smother it, and the victim, enfeebled or killed, drops from above slowly and lightly as a feather, among the heap of corpses. The keeper opens the two centre partitions to examine the brood-cells. In place of the former close dark circles formed by thousands of bees sitting back to back and guarding the high mystery of generation, he sees hundreds of dull, listless, and sleepy shells of bees. They have almost all died unawares, sitting in the sanctuary they had guarded and which is now no more. They reek of decay and death. Only a few of them still move, rise, and feebly fly to settle on the enemy's hand, lacking the spirit to die stinging him: the rest are dead and fall as lightly as fish-scales. The bee-keeper closes the hive, chalks a mark on it, and when he has time tears out its contents and burns it clean.*

So in the same way Moscow was empty when Napoleon, weary, uneasy, and morose, paced up and down in front of the Kammer-Kollezsky rampart, awaiting what to his mind was a necessary, if but formal, observance of the proprieties – a deputation.

In various corners of Moscow there still remained a few people aimlessly moving about, following their old habits and hardly aware of what they were doing.

When with due circumspection Napoleon was informed that Moscow was empty, he looked angrily at his informant, turned away, and silently continued to walk to and fro.

'My carriage!' he said.

He took his seat beside the aide-de-camp on duty and drove into the suburb. 'Moscow deserted!' he said to himself. 'What an incredible event!'

He did not drive into the town, but put up at an inn in the Dorogomilov suburb.

The *coup de théâtre* had not come off.

21

THE Russian troops were passing through Moscow from two o'clock at night till two in the afternoon, and bore away with them the wounded and the last of the inhabitants who were leaving.

The greatest crush during the movement of the troops took place at the Stone, Moskva, and Yauza bridges.

While the troops, dividing into two parts when passing around the Kremlin, were thronging the Moskva and the Stone bridges, a great many soldiers, taking advantage of the stoppage and congestion, turned back from the bridges and slipped stealthily and silently past the church of Vasili the Beatified and under the Borovitsky gate, back up the hill to the Red Square where some instinct told them they could easily take things not belonging to them. Crowds of the kind seen at cheap sales filled all the passages and alleys of the Bazaar. But there were no dealers with voices of ingratiating affability inviting customers to enter; there were no hawkers, nor the usual motley crowd of female purchasers – but only soldiers, in uniform and overcoats though without muskets, entering the Bazaar empty-handed and silently making their way out through its passages with bundles. Tradesmen and their assistants (of whom there were but few) moved about among the soldiers quite bewildered. They unlocked their shops and locked them up again, and themselves carried goods away with the help of their assistants. On the square in front of the Bazaar were drummers beating the muster-call. But the roll of the drums did not make the looting soldiers run in the direction of the drum as formerly, but made them, on the contrary, run farther away. Among the soldiers in the shops and passages some men were to be seen in grey coats, with closely-shaven heads.* Two officers, one with a scarf over his uniform and mounted on a lean dark-grey horse, the other in an overcoat and on foot, stood at the corner of the Ilyinka Street, talking. A third officer galloped up to them.

'The general orders them all to be driven out at once, without fail. This is outrageous! Half the men have dispersed.'

'Where are you off to? ... Where? ...' he shouted to three infantrymen without muskets who, holding up the skirts of their overcoats, were slipping past him into the Bazaar passage. 'Stop, you rascals!'

'But how are you going to stop them?' replied another officer. 'There is no getting them together. The army should push on before the rest bolt, that's all!'

'How can one push on? They are stuck there, wedged on the bridge, and don't move. Shouldn't we put a cordon round to prevent the rest from running away?'

'Come, go in there and drive them out!' shouted the senior officer.

The officer in the scarf dismounted, called up a drummer, and went with him into the arcade. Some soldiers started running away in a group. A shopkeeper with red pimples on his cheeks near the nose, and a calm, persistent, calculating expression on his plump face, hurriedly and ostentatiously approached the officer, swinging his arms.

'Your Honour!' said he. 'Be so good as to protect us! We won't grudge trifles, you are welcome to anything – we shall be delighted! Pray!... I'll fetch a piece of cloth at once for such an honourable gentleman, or even two pieces with pleasure. For we feel how it is; but what's all this – sheer robbery! If you please, could not guards be placed if only to let use close the shop...'

Several shopkeepers crowded round the officer.

'Eh, what twaddle!' said one of them, a thin stern-looking man. 'When one's head is gone one doesn't weep for one's hair! Take what any of you like!' And flourishing his arm energetically he turned sideways to the officer.

'It's all very well for you, Ivan Sidorych, to talk,' said the first tradesman angrily. 'Please step inside, your Honour!'

'Talk indeed!' cried the thin one. 'In my three shops here I have a hundred thousand rubles' worth of goods. Can they be saved when the army has gone? Eh, what people! "Against God's might our hands can't fight."'

'Come inside, your Honour!' repeated the first tradesman, bowing.

The officer stood perplexed and his face showed indecision.

'It's not my business!' he exclaimed, and strode on quickly down one of the passages.

From one open shop came the sound of blows and vituperation, and just as the officer came up to it a man in a grey coat with a shaven head was flung out violently.

This man, bent double, rushed past the tradesman and the officer. The officer pounced on the soldiers who were in the shops, but at that moment fearful screams reached them from the huge crowd on the Moskva bridge and the officer ran out into the square.

'What is it? What is it?' he asked, but his comrade was already galloping off past Vasili the Beatified in the direction from which the screams came.

The officer mounted his horse and rode after him. When he reached the bridge he saw two unlimbered guns, the infantry crossing the bridge, several overturned carts, and frightened and laughing faces among the troops. Beside the cannon a cart was standing to which two horses were harnessed. Four borzois with collars were pressing close to the wheels. The cart was loaded high, and at the very top, beside a child's chair with its legs in the air, sat a peasant woman uttering piercing and desperate shrieks. He was told by his fellow-officers that the screams of the crowd and the shrieks of the woman were due to the fact that General Ermolov, coming up to the crowd and learning that soldiers were dispersing among the shops while crowds of civilians blocked the bridge, had ordered two guns to be unlimbered and made a show of firing at the bridge. The crowd, crushing one another, upsetting carts, and shouting and squeezing desperately, had cleared off the bridge and the troops were now moving forward.

22

MEANWHILE the city itself was deserted. There was hardly anyone in the streets. The gates and shops were all closed, only here and there round the taverns solitary shouts or drunken songs could be heard. Nobody drove through the streets and footsteps were rarely heard. The Povarskaya was quite still and deserted. The huge courtyard of the Rostovs' house was littered with wisps of hay and with dung from the horses, and not a soul was to be seen there. In the great drawing-room of the house, which had been left with all it contained, were two people. They were the yard-porter Ignat and the page-boy Mishka, Vasilich's grandson who had stayed in Moscow with his grandfather. Mishka had opened the clavichord and was strumming on it with one finger. The yard-porter, his arms akimbo, stood smiling with satisfaction before the large mirror.

'Isn't it fine, eh, Uncle Ignat?' said the boy, suddenly beginning to strike the keyboard with both hands.

'Only fancy!' answered Ignat, surprised at the broadening grin on his face in the mirror.

'Impudence! Impudence!' They heard behind them the voice of Mavra Kuzminishna who had entered silently. 'How he's grinning, the fat mug! Is that what you're here for? Nothing's cleared away down there and Vasilich is worn out. Just you wait a bit!'

Ignat left off smiling, adjusted his belt, and went out of the room with meekly downcast eyes.

'Aunt, I did it gently,' said the boy.

'I'll give you something gently, you monkey you!' cried Mavra Kuzminishna, raising her arm threateningly. 'Go and get the samovar to boil for your grandfather.'

Mavra Kuzminishna flicked the dust off the clavichord and closed it, and with a deep sigh left the drawing-room and locked its main door.

Going out into the yard she paused to consider where she should go next – to drink tea in the servants' wing with Vasilich, or into the store-room to put away what still lay about.

She heard the sound of quick footsteps in the quiet street. Someone stopped at the gate, and the latch rattled as someone tried to open it.

Mavra Kuzminishna went to the gate.

'Who do you want?'

'The Count – Count Ilya Andreevich Rostov.'

'And who are you?'

'An officer, I have to see him,' came the reply in a pleasant, well-bred Russian voice.

Mavra Kuzminishna opened the gate and an officer of eighteen, with the round face of a Rostov, entered the yard.

'They have gone away, sir. Went away yesterday at vesper-time,' said Mavra Kuzminishna cordially.

The young officer standing in the gateway, as if hesitating whether to enter or not, clicked his tongue.

'Ah, how annoying!' he muttered. 'I should have come yesterday ... Ah, what a pity.'

Meanwhile Mavra Kuzminishna was attentively and sympathetically examining the familiar Rostov features of the young man's face, his tattered coat and downtrodden boots.

'What did you want to see the count for?' she asked.

'Oh well ... it can't be helped!' said he in a tone of vexation and placed his hand on the gate as if to leave.

He again paused in indecision.

'You see,' he suddenly said, 'I am a kinsman of the count's and he has been very kind to me. As you see' (he glanced with an amused and good-natured smile at his coat and boots) 'my things are worn out and I have no money, so I was going to ask the count ...'

Mavra Kuzminishna did not let him finish.

'Just wait a minute, sir. One little moment,' said she.

And as soon as the officer let go of the gate-handle she turned, and hurrying away on her old legs went through the back-yard to the servants' quarters.

While Mavra Kuzminishna was running to her room the officer walked about the yard gazing at his worn-out boots with lowered head and a faint smile on his lips. 'What a pity I've missed uncle! What a nice old woman! Where has she run off to? And how am I to find the nearest way to overtake my regiment, which must by now be getting near the Rogozhsky gate?' thought he. Just then Mavra Kuzminishna appeared from behind the corner of the house with a frightened yet resolute look, carrying a rolled-up check kerchief in her hand. While still a few steps from the officer she unfolded the kerchief and took out of it a white twenty-five ruble assignat* and hastily handed it to him.

'If his Excellency had been at home, as a kinsman he would of course ... but as it is ...'

Mavra Kuzminishna grew abashed and confused. The officer did not decline, but took the note quietly and thanked her.

'If the count had been at home...' Mavra Kuzminishna went on apologetically. 'Christ be with you, sir! May God preserve you!' said she, bowing as she saw him out.

Swaying his head and smiling as if amused at himself the officer ran almost at a trot through the deserted streets towards the Yauza bridge to overtake his regiment.

But Mavra Kuzminishna stood at the closed gate for some time with moist eyes, pensively swaying her head and feeling an unexpected flow of motherly tenderness and pity for the unknown young officer.

23

FROM an unfinished house on the Varvarka, the ground floor of which was a dram-shop, came drunken shouts and songs. On benches round the tables in a dirty little room sat some ten factory hands. Tipsy and perspiring, with dim eyes and wide-open mouths, they were all laboriously singing some song or other. They were singing discordantly, arduously, and with great effort, evidently not because they wished to sing, but because they wanted to show they were drunk and on the spree. One, a tall fair-haired lad in a clean blue coat, was standing over the others. His face with its fine straight nose would have been handsome had it not been for his thin, compressed, twitching lips and dull, gloomy, fixed eyes. Evidently possessed by some idea, he stood over those who were singing and solemnly and jerkily flourished above their heads his white arm with the sleeve turned up to the elbow, trying unnaturally to spread out his dirty fingers. The sleeve of his coat kept slipping down and he always carefully rolled it up again with his left hand, as if it were most important that the sinewy white arm he was flourishing should be bare. In the midst of the song cries were heard, and fighting and blows in the passage and the porch. The tall lad waved his arm.

'Stop it!' he exclaimed peremptorily. 'There's a fight, lads!' And, still rolling up his sleeve, he went out to the porch.

The factory hands followed him. These men, who under the leadership of the tall lad were drinking in the dram-shop that morning, had brought the publican some skins from the factory and for this had had drink served them. The blacksmiths from a neighbouring smithy, hearing the sounds of revelry in the tavern and supposing it to have been broken into, wished to force their way in too and a fight in the porch had resulted.

The publican was fighting one of the smiths at the door, and when the workmen came out the smith, wrenching himself free from the tavern-keeper, fell face downward on the pavement.

Another smith tried to enter the doorway, pressing against the publican with his chest.

The lad with the turned-up sleeve gave the smith a blow in the face and cried wildly:

'They're fighting us, lads!'

At that moment the first smith got up and, scratching his bruised face to make it bleed, shouted in a tearful voice:

'Police! Murder! . . . They've killed a man, lads!'

'Oh, gracious me, a man beaten to death – killed! . . .' screamed a woman coming out of a gate close by.

A crowd gathered round the bloodstained smith.

'Haven't you robbed people enough – taking their last shirts?' said a voice addressing the publican. 'What have you killed a man for, you thief?'

The tall lad, standing in the porch, turned his bleared eyes from the publican to the smith and back again as if considering whom he ought to fight now.

'Murder!' he shouted suddenly to the publican. 'Bind him, lads!'

'I daresay you would like to bind me!' shouted the publican, pushing away the men advancing on him, and snatching his cap from his head he flung it on the ground.

As if this action had some mysterious and menacing significance, the workmen surrounding the publican paused in indecision.

'I know the law very well, mates! I'll take the matter to the captain of police. You think I won't get to him? Robbery is permitted to anybody nowadays!' shouted the publican, picking up his cap.

'Come along then! Come along then!' the publican and the tall young fellow repeated one after the other, and they moved up the street together.

The bloodstained smith went beside them. The factory hands and others followed behind talking and shouting.

At the corner of the Moroseyka, opposite a large house with closed shutters and bearing a bootmaker's sign-board, stood a score of thin, worn-out, gloomy-faced bootmakers, wearing overalls and long tattered coats.

'He should pay folks off properly,' a thin working man, with frowning brows and a straggly beard, was saying.

'But he's sucked our blood and now he thinks he's quit of us! He's been misleading us all the week and now that he's brought us to this pass he's made off.'

On seeing the crowd and the bloodstained man the workman

ceased speaking, and with eager curiosity all the bootmakers joined the moving crowd.

'Where are all the folks going?'

'Why, to the police, of course!'

'I say, is it true that we have been beaten?'

'And what did you think? Look what folks are saying.'

Questions and answers were heard. The publican, taking advantage of the increased crowd, dropped behind and returned to his tavern.

The tall youth, not noticing the disappearance of his foe, waved his bare arm and went on talking incessantly, attracting general attention to himself. It was around him that the people chiefly crowded, expecting answers from him to the questions that occupied all their minds.

'He must keep order, keep the law, that's what the government is there for. Am I not right, good Christians?' said the tall youth, with a scarcely perceptible smile. 'He thinks there's no government! How can one do without government? Or else there would be plenty who'd rob us.'

'Why talk nonsense?' rejoined voices in the crowd. 'Will they give us Moscow like this? They told you that for fun, and you believed it! Aren't there plenty of troops on the march? Let *him* in, indeed! That's what the government is for. You'd better listen to what people are saying,' said some of the mob pointing to the tall youth.

By the wall of China-Town* a smaller group of people were gathered round a man in a frieze coat who held a paper in his hand.

'An ukase, they are reading an ukase! Reading an ukase!' cried voices in the crowd, and the people rushed towards the reader.

The man in the frieze coat was reading the broadsheet of August 31st. When the crowd collected round him he seemed confused, but at the demand of the tall lad who had pushed his way up to him, he began in a rather tremulous voice to read the sheet from the beginning.

'Early to-morrow I shall go to his Serene Highness,' he read ('*Sirin Highness*' said the tall fellow with a triumphant smile on his lips and a frown on his brow) 'to consult with him, to act, and to aid the army to exterminate these scoundrels. We too will take part ...' the reader went on and then paused ('Do you see,' shouted the youth victoriously, 'he's going to clear up the whole affair for you ...') 'in destroying them, and will send these visitors to the devil. I will come back to dinner, and we'll set to work. We will do, completely do, and undo these scoundrels.'

The last words were read out in the midst of complete silence.

The tall lad hung his head gloomily. It was evident that no one had understood the last part. In particular, the words 'I will come back to dinner', evidently displeased both reader and audience. The people's minds were tuned to a high pitch and this was too simple and needlessly comprehensible – it was what any one of them might have said, and therefore was what an ukase emanating from the highest authority should not say.

They all stood despondent and silent. The tall youth moved his lips and swayed from side to side.

'We should ask him . . . that's he himself!' . . . 'Yes, ask him indeed!' . . . 'Why not? He'll explain' . . . voices in the rear of the crowd were suddenly heard saying, and the general attention turned to the police-superintendent's trap which drove into the square attended by two mounted dragoons.

The superintendent of police who had gone that morning by Count Rostopchin's orders to burn the barges, and had in connexion with that matter acquired a large sum of money which was at that moment in his pocket, on seeing a crowd bearing down upon him told his coachman to stop.

'What people are these?' he shouted to the men, who were moving singly and timidly in the direction of his trap.

'What people are these?' he shouted again, receiving no answer.

'Your Honour . . .' replied the shopman in the frieze coat, 'your Honour, in accord with the proclamation of his Highest Excellency, the count, they desire to serve, not sparing their lives, and it is not any kind of riot, but as his Highest Excellency said . . .'

'The count has not left, he is here, and an order will be issued concerning you,' said the superintendent of police. 'Go on!' he ordered his coachman.

The crowd halted, pressing around those who had heard what the superintendent had said, and looking at the departing trap.

The superintendent of police turned round at that moment with a scared look, said something to his coachman, and his horses increased their speed.

'It's a fraud, lads! Lead the way to him, himself!' shouted the tall youth. 'Don't let him go, lads! Let him answer us! Keep him!' shouted different voices, and the people dashed in pursuit of the trap.

Following the superintendent of police and talking loudly the crowd went in the direction of the Lubyanka Street.

'There now, the gentry and merchants have gone away and left us to perish. Do they think we're dogs?' voices in the crowd were heard saying more and more frequently.

On the evening of the 1st of September, after his interview with Kutuzov, Count Rostopchin had returned to Moscow mortified and offended because he had not been invited to attend the council of war, and because Kutuzov had paid no attention to his offer to take part in the defence of the city, amazed also at the novel outlook revealed to him at the camp, which treated the tranquillity of the capital and its patriotic fervour as not merely secondary but quite irrelevant and unimportant matters. Distressed, offended, and surprised by all this, Rostopchin had returned to Moscow. After supper he lay down on a sofa without undressing, and was awakened soon after midnight by a courier bringing him a letter from Kutuzov. This letter requested the count to send police officers to guide the troops through the town, as the army was retreating to the Ryazan road beyond Moscow. This was not news to Rostopchin. He had known that Moscow would be abandoned not merely since his interview the previous day with Kutuzov on the Poklonny Hill but ever since the battle of Borodino, for all the generals who came to Moscow after that battle had said unanimously that it was impossible to fight another battle, and since then government property had been removed every night, and half the inhabitants had left the city with Rostopchin's own permission. Yet all the same this information astonished and irritated the count, coming as it did in the form of a simple note with an order from Kutuzov, and received at night, breaking in on his beauty sleep.

When later on in his memoirs Count Rostopchin explained his actions at this time, he repeatedly says that he was then actuated by two important considerations: to maintain tranquillity in Moscow and expedite the departure of the inhabitants. If one accepts this twofold aim all Rostopchin's actions appear irreproachable. 'Why were the holy relics, the arms, ammunition, gunpowder, and stores of corn not removed? Why were thousands of the inhabitants deceived into believing that Moscow would not be given up – and thereby ruined?' 'To preserve the tranquillity of the city,' explains Count Rostopchin. 'Why were bundles of useless papers from the government offices, and Leppich's balloon and other articles removed?' 'To leave the town empty,' explains Count Rostopchin. One need only admit that public tranquillity is in danger and any action finds a justification.

All the horrors of the reign of terror were based only on solicitude for public tranquillity.

On what, then, was Count Rostopchin's fear for the tranquillity of Moscow based in 1812? What reason was there for assuming any probability of an uprising in the city? The inhabitants were leaving it and the retreating troops were filling it. Why should that cause the masses to riot?

Neither in Moscow nor anywhere in Russia did anything resembling an insurrection ever occur when the enemy entered a town. More than ten thousand people were still in Moscow on the 1st and 2nd of September, and except for a mob in the governor's courtyard, assembled there at his bidding, nothing happened. It is obvious that there would have been even less reason to expect a disturbance among the people if after the battle of Borodino, when the surrender of Moscow became certain or at least probable, Rostopchin instead of exciting the people by distributing arms and broadsheets had taken steps to remove all the holy relics, the gunpowder, munitions, and money, and had told the population plainly that the town would be abandoned.

Rostopchin, though he had patriotic sentiments, was a sanguine and impulsive man who had always moved in the highest administrative circles and had no understanding at all of the people he supposed himself to be guiding. Ever since the enemy's entry into Smolensk he had in imagination been playing the role of director of the popular feeling of 'the heart of Russia'. Not only did it seem to him (as to all administrators) that he controlled the external actions of Moscow's inhabitants, but he also thought he controlled their mental attitude by means of his broadsheets and posters, written in a coarse tone which the people despise in their own class and do not understand from those in authority. Rostopchin was so pleased with the fine role of leader of popular feeling, and had grown so used to it, that the necessity of relinquishing that role and abandoning Moscow without any heroic display took him unawares and he suddenly felt the ground slip away from under his feet, so that he positively did not know what to do. Though he knew it was coming, he did not till the last moment wholeheartedly believe that Moscow would be abandoned, and did not prepare for it. The inhabitants left against his wishes. If the government offices were removed, this was only done on the demand of officials to whom the count yielded reluctantly. He was absorbed in the role he had created for himself. As is often the case with those gifted with an ardent imagination, though he had long known that Moscow would be abandoned, he knew it only with his intellect, he did not believe it in his heart and did not adapt himself mentally to this new position of affairs.

All his painstaking and energetic activity (how far it was useful and had any effect on the people is another question) had been simply directed towards arousing in the masses his own feeling of patriotic hatred of the French.

But when events assumed their true historical character, when expressing hatred for the French in words proved insufficient, when it was not even possible to express that hatred by fighting a battle, when self-confidence was of no avail in relation to the one question before Moscow, when the whole population streamed out of Moscow as one man, abandoning their belongings and proving by that negative action all the depth of their national feeling, then the role chosen by Rostopchin suddenly appeared senseless. He unexpectedly felt himself ridiculous, weak, and alone, with no ground to stand on.

When, awakened from his sleep, he received that cold, peremptory note from Kutuzov, he felt the more irritated the more he felt himself to blame. All that he had been specially put in charge of, the state property which he should have removed, was still in Moscow and it was no longer possible to take the whole of it away.

'Who is to blame for it? Who has let things come to such a pass?' he ruminated. 'Not I, of course. I had everything ready. I had Moscow firmly in hand. And this is what they have let it come to! Villains! Traitors!' he thought, without clearly defining who the villains and traitors were, but feeling it necessary to hate those traitors whoever they might be, who were to blame for the false and ridiculous position in which he found himself.

All that night Count Rostopchin issued orders, for which people came to him from all parts of Moscow. Those about him had never seen the count so morose and irritable.

'Your Excellency, the Director of the Registrar's Department has sent for instructions... From the Consistory, from the Senate, from the University, from the Foundling Hospital, the Suffragan has sent... asking for information... What are your orders about the Fire Brigade? From the governor of the prison... from the superintendent of the lunatic asylum...' All night long such announcements were continually being received by the count.

To all these inquiries he gave brief and angry replies indicating that orders from him were not now needed, that the whole affair, carefully prepared by him, had now been ruined by somebody, and that that somebody would have to bear the whole responsibility for all that might happen.

'Oh, tell that blockhead,' he said in reply to the question from the Registrar's Department, 'that he should remain to guard his documents. Now why are you asking silly questions about the Fire Brigade? They have horses, let them be off to Vladimir, and not leave them to the French.'

'Your Excellency, the superintendent of the lunatic asylum has come: what are your commands?'

'My commands? Let them go away, that's all ... And let the lunatics out into the town. When lunatics command our armies God evidently means these other madmen to be free.'

In reply to an inquiry about the convicts in the prison, Count Rostopchin shouted angrily at the governor:

'Do you expect me to give you two battalions – which we have not got – for a convoy? Release them, that's all about it!'

'Your Excellency, there are some political prisoners, Meshkov, Vereshchagin ...'

'Vereshchagin! Hasn't he been hanged yet?' shouted Rostopchin. 'Bring him to me!'

25

TOWARDS nine o'clock in the morning, when the troops were already moving through Moscow, nobody came to the count any more for instructions. Those who were able to get away were going of their own accord, those who remained behind decided for themselves what they must do.

The count ordered his carriage that he might drive to Sokolniki, and sat in his study with folded hands, morose, sallow, and taciturn.

In quiet and troubled times it seems to every administrator that it is only by his efforts that the whole population under his rule is kept going, and in this consciousness of being indispensable every administrator finds the chief reward of his labour and efforts. While the sea of history remains calm the ruler-administrator in his frail bark, holding on with a boat-hook to the ship of the people, and himself moving, naturally imagines that his efforts move the ship he is holding on to. But as soon as a storm arises and the sea begins to heave and the ship to move, such a delusion is no longer possible. The ship moves independently with its own enormous motion, the boat-hook no longer reaches the moving vessel, and suddenly the administrator, instead of appearing a ruler and a source of power, becomes an insignificant, useless, feeble man.

Rostopchin felt this, and it was this which exasperated him.

The superintendent of police, whom the crowd had stopped, went in to see him at the same time as an adjutant who informed the count that the horses were harnessed. They were both pale, and the superintendent of police, after reporting that he had executed the instructions he had received, informed the count that an immense crowd had collected in the courtyard and wished to see him.

Without saying a word Rostopchin rose and walked hastily to his light luxurious drawing-room, went to the balcony door, took hold of the handle, let it go again, and went to the window from which he had a better view of the whole crowd. The tall lad was standing in front, flourishing his arm and saying something with a stern look. The bloodstained smith stood beside him with a gloomy face. A drone of voices was audible through the closed window.

'Is my carriage ready?' asked Rostopchin, stepping back from the window.

'It is, your Excellency,' replied the adjutant.

Rostopchin went again to the balcony door.

'But what do they want?' he asked the superintendent of police.

'Your Excellency, they say they have got ready, according to your orders, to go against the French, and they shouted something about treachery. But it is a turbulent crowd, your Excellency – I hardly managed to get away from it. Your Excellency, I venture to suggest . . .'

'You may go. I don't need you to tell me what to do!' exclaimed Rostopchin angrily.

He stood by the balcony door looking at the crowd.

'This is what they have done with Russia! This is what they have done with me!' thought he, full of an irrepressible fury that welled up within him against the someone to whom what was happening might be attributed. As often happens with passionate people, he was mastered by anger but was still seeking an object on which to vent it. 'Here is that mob, the dregs of the people,' he thought as he gazed at the crowd: 'this rabble they have roused by their folly! They want a victim,' he thought as he looked at the tall lad flourishing his arm. And this thought occurred to him just because he himself desired a victim, something on which to vent his rage.

'Is the carriage ready?' he asked again.

'Yes, your Excellency. What are your orders about Vereshchagin? He is waiting at the porch,' said the adjutant.

'Ah!' exclaimed Rostopchin, as if struck by an unexpected recollection.

And rapidly opening the door he went resolutely out onto the balcony. The talking instantly ceased, hats and caps were doffed and all eyes were raised to the count.

'Good morning, lads!' said the count briskly and loudly. 'Thank you for coming. I'll come out to you in a moment, but we must first settle with the villain. We must punish the villain who has caused the ruin of Moscow. Wait for me!'

And the count stepped as briskly back into the room and slammed the door behind him.

A murmur of approbation and satisfaction ran through the crowd. 'He'll settle with all the villains, you'll see! And you said the French . . . He'll show you what law is!' the mob were saying as if reproving one another for their lack of confidence.

A few minutes later an officer came hurriedly out of the front door, gave an order, and the dragoons formed up in line. The crowd moved eagerly from the balcony towards the porch. Rostopchin, coming out there with quick angry steps, looked hastily around as if seeking someone.

'Where is he?' he inquired. And as he spoke he saw a young man coming round the corner of the house between two dragoons. He had a long thin neck, and his head, that had been half shaved, was again covered by short hair. This young man was dressed in a threadbare blue cloth coat lined with fox fur, that had once been smart, and dirty hempen convict trousers, over which were pulled his thin, dirty, down-trodden boots. On his thin weak legs were heavy chains which hampered his irresolute movements.

'Ah!' said Rostopchin, hurriedly turning away his eyes from the young man in the fur-lined coat and pointing to the bottom step of the porch. 'Put him there.'

The young man in his clattering chains stepped clumsily to the spot indicated, holding away with one finger the coat-collar which chafed his neck, turned his long neck twice this way and that, sighed, and submissively folded before him his thin hands, unused to work.

For several seconds while the young man was taking his place on the step the silence continued. Only among the back rows of the people, who were all pressing towards the one spot, could sighs, groans, and the shuffling of feet be heard.

While waiting for the young man to take his place on the step Rostopchin stood frowning and rubbing his face with his hand.

'Lads!' said he, with a metallic ring in his voice. 'This man, Vereshchagin, is the scoundrel by whose doing Moscow is perishing.'

The young man in the fur-lined coat, stooping a little, stood in a submissive attitude, his fingers clasped before him. His emaciated young face, disfigured by the half-shaven head, hung down hopelessly. At the count's first words he raised it slowly and looked up at him as if wishing to say something or at least to meet his eye. But Rostopchin did not look at him. A vein in the young man's long thin neck swelled like a cord and went blue behind the ear, and suddenly his face flushed.

All eyes were fixed on him. He looked at the crowd, and rendered more hopeful by the expression he read on the faces there, he smiled sadly and timidly, and lowering his head shifted his feet on the step.

'He has betrayed his Tsar and his country, he has gone over to Bonaparte. He alone of all the Russians has disgraced the Russian name, he has caused Moscow to perish,' said Rostopchin in a sharp, even voice, but suddenly he glanced down at Vereshchagin who continued to stand in the same submissive attitude. As if inflamed by the sight, he raised his arm and addressed the people, almost shouting:

'Deal with him as you think fit! I hand him over to you.'

The crowd remained silent and only pressed closer and closer to one another. To keep one another back, to breathe in that stifling atmosphere, to be unable to stir, and to await something unknown, uncomprehended, and terrible, was becoming unbearable. Those standing in front, who had seen and heard what had taken place before them, all stood with wide open eyes and mouths, straining with all their strength, and held back the crowd that was pushing behind them.

'Beat him! . . . Let the traitor perish and not disgrace the Russian name!' shouted Rostopchin. 'Cut him down. I command it.'

Hearing not so much the words as the angry tone of Rostopchin's voice, the crowd moaned and heaved forward, but again paused.

'Count!' exclaimed the timid yet theatrical voice of Vereshchagin in the midst of the momentary silence that ensued, 'Count! One God is above us both . . .' He lifted his head and again the thick vein in his thin neck filled with blood and the colour rapidly came and went in his face.

He did not finish what he wished to say.

'Cut him down! I command it . . .' shouted Rostopchin, suddenly growing pale like Vereshchagin.

'Draw sabres!' cried the dragoon officer, drawing his own.

Another still stronger wave flowed through the crowd and reaching the front ranks carried it swaying to the very steps of the porch. The tall youth, with a stony look on his face, and rigid and uplifted arm, stood beside Vereshchagin.

'Sabre him!' the dragoon officer almost whispered.

And one of the soldiers, his face all at once distorted with fury, struck Vereshchagin on the head with the blunt side of his sabre.

'Ah!' cried Vereshchagin in meek surprise, looking round with a frightened glance as if not understanding why this was done to him. A similar moan of surprise and horror ran through the crowd. 'O Lord!' exclaimed a sorrowful voice.

But after the exclamation of surprise that had escaped from

Vereshchagin he uttered a plaintive cry of pain, and that cry was fatal. The barrier of human feeling, strained to the utmost, that had held the crowd in check, suddenly broke. The crime had begun and must now be completed. The plaintive moan of reproach was drowned by the threatening and angry roar of the crowd. Like the seventh and last wave that shatters a ship, that last irresistible wave burst from the rear and reached the front ranks, carrying them off their feet and engulfing them all. The dragoon was about to repeat his blow. Vereshchagin with a cry of horror, covering his head with his hands, rushed towards the crowd. The tall youth, against whom he stumbled, seized his thin neck with his hands and, yelling wildly, fell with him under the feet of the pressing struggling crowd.

Some beat and tore at Vereshchagin, others at the tall youth. And the screams of those that were being trampled on and of those who tried to rescue the tall lad, only increased the fury of the crowd. It was a long time before the dragoons could extricate the bleeding youth, beaten almost to death. And for a long time, despite the feverish haste with which the mob tried to end the work that had been begun, those who were hitting, throttling, and tearing at Vereshchagin were unable to kill him, for the crowd pressed from all sides, swaying as one mass with them in the centre and rendering it impossible for them either to kill him or let him go.

'Hit him with an axe, eh! . . . Crushed? . . . Traitor, he sold Christ . . . Still alive . . . tenacious. . . serve him right! Torture serves a thief right. Use the hatchet! . . . What – still alive?'

Only when the victim ceased to struggle and his cries changed to a long-drawn, measured death-rattle, did the crowd around his prostrate, bleeding corpse begin rapidly to change places. Each one came up, glanced at what had been done, and with horror, reproach, and astonishment, pushed back again.

'O Lord! The people are like wild beasts! How could he be alive?' voices in the crowd could be heard saying. 'Quite a young fellow too . . . must have been a merchant's son. What men! . . . and they say he's not the right one . . . How not the right one? . . . O Lord! And there's another has been beaten too – they say he's nearly done for . . . Oh, the people . . . Aren't they afraid of sinning? . . .' said the same mob now, looking with pained distress at the dead body with its long thin half-severed neck and its livid face stained with blood and dust.

A painstaking police officer, considering the presence of a corpse in his Excellency's courtyard unseemly, told the dragoons to take it away. Two dragoons took it by its distorted legs and dragged it along the ground. The gory, dust-stained, half-shaven head with its long neck, trailed twisting along on the ground. The crowd shrank back from it.

At the moment when Vereshchagin fell and the crowd closed in with savage yells and swayed about him, Rostopchin suddenly turned pale and, instead of going to the back entrance where his carriage awaited him, went with hurried steps and bent head, not knowing where and why, along the passage leading to the rooms on the ground floor. The count's face was white and he could not control the feverish twitching of his lower jaw.

'This way, your Excellency . . . Where are you going? . . . This way, please . . .' said a trembling, frightened voice behind him.

Count Rostopchin was unable to reply and, turning obediently, went in the direction indicated. At the back entrance stood his calèche. The distant roar of the yelling crowd was audible even there. He hastily took his seat and told the coachman to drive him to his country house in Sokolniki.

When they reached the Myasnitsky Street and could no longer hear the shouts of the mob, the count began to repent. He remembered with dissatisfaction the agitation and fear he had betrayed before his subordinates. 'The mob is terrible – disgusting,' he said to himself in French. 'They are like wolves whom nothing but flesh can appease.' 'Count! One God is above us both!' – Vereshchagin's words suddenly recurred to him, and a disagreeable shiver ran down his back. But this was only a momentary feeling and Count Rostopchin smiled disdainfully at himself. 'I had other duties,' thought he. 'The people had to be appeased. Many other victims have perished and are perishing for the public good' – and he began thinking of his social duties to his family and to the city entrusted to him, and of himself – not himself as Theodore Vasilyevich Rostopchin (he fancied that Theodore Vasilyevich Rostopchin was sacrificing himself for the public good) but himself as Governor, the representative of authority and of the Tsar. 'Had I been simply Theodore Vasilyevich my course of action would have been quite different, but it was my duty to safeguard my life and dignity as Commander-in-Chief.'

Lightly swaying on the flexible springs of his carriage and no longer hearing the terrible sounds of the crowd, Rostopchin grew physically calm and, as always happens, as soon as he became physically tranquil his mind devised reasons why he should be mentally tranquil too. The thought which tranquillized Rostopchin was not a new one. Since the world began and men have killed one another no one has ever committed such a crime against his fellow-man without comforting himself with this same idea. This idea is *le bien public*, the hypothetical welfare of other people.

To a man not swayed by passion, that welfare is never certain, but he who commits such a crime always knows just where that welfare lies. And Rostopchin now knew it.

Not only did his reason not reproach him for what he had done but he even found cause for self-satisfaction in having so successfully contrived to avail himself of a convenient opportunity to punish a criminal and at the same time pacify the mob.

'Vereshchagin was tried and condemned to death,' thought Rostopchin (though the Senate had only condemned Vereshchagin to hard labour), 'he was a traitor and a spy. I could not let him go unpunished and so I have killed two birds with one stone: to appease the mob I gave them a victim, and at the same time punished a miscreant.'

Having reached his country house and begun to give orders about domestic arrangements, the count grew quite tranquil.

Half an hour later he was driving with his fast horses across the Sokolniki field, no longer thinking of what had occurred but considering what was to come. He was driving to the Yauza bridge where he had heard that Kutuzov was. Count Rostopchin was mentally preparing the angry and stinging reproaches he meant to address to Kutuzov for his deception. He would make that foxy old courtier feel that the responsibility for all the calamities that would follow the abandonment of the city and the ruin of Russia (as Rostopchin regarded it) would fall upon his doting old head. Planning beforehand what he would say to Kutuzov, Rostopchin turned angrily in his calèche and gazed sternly from side to side.

The Sokolniki field was deserted. Only at the end of it, in front of the almshouse and the lunatic asylum, could be seen some people in white, and others like them walking singly across the field shouting and gesticulating.

One of these was running to cross the path of Count Rostopchin's carriage, and the count himself, his coachman, and his dragoons, looked with vague horror and curiosity at these released lunatics and especially at the one running towards them.

Swaying from side to side on his long thin legs in his fluttering dressing-gown, this lunatic was running impetuously, his gaze fixed on Rostopchin, shouting something in a hoarse voice and making signs to him to stop. The lunatic's solemn, gloomy face was thin and yellow, with its beard growing in uneven tufts. His black, agate pupils with saffron-yellow whites, moved restlessly near the lower eyelids.

'Stop! Pull up, I tell you!' he cried in a piercing voice, and again shouted something breathlessly with emphatic intonations and gestures.

Coming abreast of the calèche he ran beside it.

'Thrice have they slain me, thrice have I risen from the dead. They stoned me, crucified me . . . I shall rise . . . shall rise . . . shall rise. They have torn my body. The kingdom of God will be overthrown . . . Thrice will I overthrow it and thrice re-establish it!' he cried, raising his voice higher and higher.

Count Rostopchin suddenly grew pale as he had done when the crowd closed in on Vereshchagin. He turned away. 'Go fas . . . faster!' he cried in a trembling voice to his coachman. The calèche flew over the ground as fast as the horses could draw it, but for a long time Count Rostopchin still heard the insane despairing screams growing fainter in the distance, while his eyes saw nothing but the astonished, frightened, bloodstained face of 'the traitor' in the fur-lined coat.

Recent as that mental picture was, Rostopchin already felt that it had cut deep into his heart and drawn blood. Even now he felt clearly that the gory trace of that recollection would not pass with time, but that the terrible memory would, on the contrary, dwell in his heart ever more cruelly and painfully to the end of his life. He seemed still to hear the sound of his own words: 'Cut him down! I command it . . .'

'Why did I utter those words? It was by some accident I said them . . . I need not have said them,' he thought. 'And then nothing would have happened.' He saw the frightened and then infuriated face of the dragoon who dealt the blow, and the look of silent, timid reproach that boy in the fur-lined coat had turned upon him. 'But I did not do it for my own sake. I was bound to act that way . . . The mob, the traitor . . . the public welfare,' he thought.

Troops were still crowding at the Yauza bridge. It was hot. Kutuzov, dejected and frowning, sat on a bench by the bridge toying with his whip in the sand when a calèche dashed up noisily. A man in a general's uniform with plumes in his hat went up to Kutuzov and said something in French. It was Count Rostopchin. He told Kutuzov that he had come because Moscow, the capital, was no more and only the army remained.

'Things would have been different if your Serene Highness had not told me that you would not abandon Moscow without another battle; all this would not have happened,' he said.

Kutuzov looked at Rostopchin as if, not grasping what was said to him, he was trying to read something peculiar, written at that moment on the face of the man addressing him. Rostopchin grew confused and became silent. Kutuzov slightly shook his head and not taking his penetrating gaze from Rostopchin's face muttered softly:

'No! I shall not give up Moscow without a battle!'

Whether Kutuzov was thinking of something entirely different when he spoke those words, or uttered them purposely, knowing them to be meaningless, at any rate Rostopchin made no reply and hastily left him. And, strange to say, the Governor of Moscow, the proud Count Rostopchin, took up a Cossack whip and went to the bridge, where he began with shouts to drive on the carts that blocked the way.

26

TOWARDS four o'clock in the afternoon Murat's troops were entering Moscow. In front rode a detachment of Würtemberg hussars, and behind them rode the King of Naples himself, accompanied by a numerous suite.

About the middle of the Arbat street, near the Church of the Miraculous Icon of St Nicholas, Murat halted to await news from the advanced detachment as to the condition in which they had found the citadel, *le Kremlin*.*

Around Murat gathered a group of those who had remained in Moscow. They all stared in timid bewilderment at the strange, long-haired commander dressed up in feathers and gold.

'Is that their Tsar himself? He's not bad!' low voices could be heard saying.

An interpreter rode up to the group.

'Take off your cap ... your caps!' These words went from one to another in the crowd. The interpreter addressed an old porter and asked if it was far to the Kremlin. The porter, listening in perplexity to the unfamiliar Polish accent and not realizing that the interpreter was speaking Russian, did not understand what was being said to him and slipped behind the others.

Murat approached the interpreter and told him to ask where the Russian army was. One of the Russians understood what was asked and several voices at once began answering the interpreter. A French officer, returning from the advanced detachment, rode up to Murat and reported that the gates of the citadel had been barricaded and that there was probably an ambuscade there.

'Good!' said Murat and, turning to one of the gentlemen in his suite, ordered four light guns to be moved forward to fire at the gates.

The guns emerged at a trot from the column following Murat,

and advanced up the Arbat. When they reached the end of the Vozdvizhenka Street they halted and drew up in the Square. Several French officers superintended the placing of the guns and looked at the Kremlin through field-glasses.

The bells in the Kremlin were ringing for vespers, and this sound troubled the French. They imagined it to be a call to arms. A few infantrymen ran to the Kutafyev Gate. Beams and wooden screens had been put there, and two musket shots rang out from under the gate as soon as an officer and men began to run towards it. A general who stood by the guns shouted some words of command to the officer, and the latter ran back again with his men.

The sound of three more shots came from the gate.

One shot struck a French soldier's foot, and from behind the screens came the strange sound of a few voices shouting. Instantly as at a word of command the expression of cheerful serenity on the faces of the French general, officers, and men, changed to one of determined concentrated readiness for strife and suffering. To all of them from the marshal to the least soldier, that place was not the Vozdvizhenka, Mokhavaya or Kutafyev Street, nor the Troitsa Gate but a new battlefield which would probably prove sanguinary. And all made ready for that battle. The cries from the gates ceased. The guns were advanced, the artillerymen blew the ash off their linstocks, and an officer gave the word: 'Fire!' This was followed by two whistling sounds of canister-shot one after another. The shot rattled against the stone of the gate and upon the wooden beams and screens, and two wavering clouds of smoke rose over the Square.

A few instants after the echo of the reports resounding over the stone-built Kremlin had died away, the French heard a strange sound above their heads. Thousands of crows rose above the walls and circled in the air, cawing and noisily flapping their wings. Together with that sound came a solitary human cry from the gateway, and amid smoke appeared the figure of a bare-headed man in a peasant's coat. He grasped a musket and took aim at the French. 'Fire!' repeated the officer once more, and the reports of a musket and of two cannon-shots were heard simultaneously. The gate was again hidden by smoke.

Nothing more stirred behind the screens and the French infantry soldiers and officers advanced to the gate. In the gateway lay three wounded and four dead. Two men in peasant coats ran away at the foot of the wall, towards the Znamenka.

'Clear that away!' said the officer, pointing to the beams and the corpses, and the French soldiers, after dispatching the wounded, threw the corpses over the parapet.

Who those men were nobody knew. 'Clear that away!' was all that was said of them, and they were thrown over the parapet, and removed later on that they might not stink. Thiers alone dedicates a few eloquent lines to their memory: 'These wretches had occupied the sacred citadel, having supplied themselves with guns from the arsenal, and fired' (the wretches) 'at the French. Some of them were sabred and the Kremlin was purged of their presence.'

Murat was informed that the way had been cleared. The French entered the gates, and began pitching their camp in the Senate Square. Out of the windows of the Senate House the soldiers threw chairs into the Square for fuel, and kindled fires there.

Other detachments passed through the Kremlin and encamped along the Moroseyka, the Lubyanka, and Pokrovka streets. Others quartered themselves along the Vozdvizhenka, the Nikolsky, and the Tverskoy streets. No masters of the houses being found anywhere the French were not billeted on the inhabitants as is usual in towns, but lived in it as in a camp.

Though tattered, hungry, worn out, and reduced to a third of their original number, the French entered Moscow in good marching order. It was a weary and famished, but still a fighting and menacing army. But it only remained an army until its soldiers had dispersed into their different lodgings. As soon as the men of the various regiments began to disperse among the wealthy and deserted houses, the army was lost for ever and there came into being something nondescript, neither citizens nor soldiers but what are known as marauders. When five weeks later these same men left Moscow, they no longer formed an army. They were a mob of marauders, each carrying a quantity of articles which seemed to him valuable or useful. The aim of each man when he left Moscow was no longer, as it had been, to conquer, but merely to keep what he had acquired. Like a monkey which puts its paw into the narrow neck of a jug, and having seized a handful of nuts will not open its fist for fear of losing what it holds, and therefore perishes, the French when they left Moscow had inevitably to perish because they carried their loot with them, yet to abandon what they had stolen was as impossible for them as it is for the monkey to open its paw and let go of its nuts. Ten minutes after each regiment had entered a Moscow district, not a soldier or officer was left. Men in military uniforms and Hessian boots could be seen through the windows laughing and walking through the rooms. In cellars and store-rooms similar men were busy among the provisions, and in the yards unlocking or breaking open coach-house and stable doors; lighting fires in kitchens and kneading and baking bread with rolled-up sleeves, and cooking; or frightening, amusing, or caressing women and children. There were many such men both in the shops and houses – but there was no army.

Order after order was issued by the French commanders that day forbidding the men to disperse about the town, sternly forbidding any violence to the inhabitants, or any looting, and announcing a roll-call for that very evening. But despite all these measures the men, who had till then constituted an army, flowed all over the wealthy, deserted city with its comforts and plentiful supplies. As a hungry herd of cattle keeps well together when crossing a barren field, but gets out of hand and at once disperses uncontrollably as soon as it reaches rich pastures, so did the army disperse all over the wealthy city.

No residents were left in Moscow, and the soldiers – like water percolating through sand – spread irresistibly through the city in all directions from the Kremlin into which they had first marched. The cavalry, on entering a merchant's house that had been abandoned and finding there stabling more than sufficient for their horses, went on, all the same, to the next house which seemed to them better. Many of them appropriated several houses, chalked their names on them. and quarrelled and even fought with other companies for them. Before they had had time to secure quarters the soldiers ran out into the streets to see the city, and hearing that everything had been abandoned, rushed to places where valuables were to be had for the taking. The officers followed to check the soldiers, and were involuntarily drawn into doing the same. In Carriage Row, carriages had been left in the shops, and generals flocked there to select calèches and coaches for themselves. The few inhabitants who had remained invited commanding officers to their houses, hoping thereby to secure themselves from being plundered. There were masses of wealth and there seemed no end to it. All around the quarters occupied by the French were other regions still unexplored and unoccupied where, they thought, yet greater riches might be found. And Moscow engulfed the army ever deeper and deeper. When water is spilt on dry ground both the dry ground and the water disappear and mud results; and in the same way the entry of the faminished army into the rich and deserted city resulted in fires and looting and the destruction of both the army and the wealthy city.

The French attributed the Fire of Moscow *au patriotisme féroce de Rostopchine*, the Russians to the barbarity of the French. In reality however it was not, and could not be, possible to explain the burning of Moscow by making any individual, or any group of people, responsible for it. Moscow was burnt because it found itself in a position in which any town built of wood was bound to burn, quite apart from whether it had, or had not, a hundred and thirty inferior fire-engines. Deserted Moscow had to burn as inevitably as a heap of shavings has to burn on which sparks continually fall for several days. A town built of wood where scarcely a day passes without conflagrations when the house-owners are in residence and a police force is present, cannot help burning when its inhabitants have left it and it is occupied by soldiers who smoke pipes, make camp-fires of the Senate chairs in the Senate Square, and cook themselves meals twice a day. In peace time it is only necessary to billet troops in the villages of any district, and the number of fires in that district immediately increases. How much then must the probability of fire be increased in an abandoned, wooden town where foreign troops are quartered. 'Le patriotisme féroce de Rostopchine' and the barbarity of the French were not to blame in the matter. Moscow was set on fire by the soldiers' pipes, kitchens, and camp-fires, and by the careless-ness of enemy soldiers occupying houses they did not own. Even if there was any arson (which is very doubtful, for no one had any reason to burn the houses – in any case a troublesome and dangerous thing to do), arson cannot be regarded as the cause, for the same thing would have happened without any incendiar-ism.

However tempting it might be for the French to blame Rostop-chin's ferocity and for Russians to blame the scoundrel Bonaparte, or later on to place an heroic torch in the hands of their own people, it is impossible not to see that there could be no such direct cause of the fire, for Moscow had to burn as every village, factory, or house must burn which is left by its owners and in which strangers are allowed to live and cook their porridge. Moscow was burnt by its inhabitants it is true, but by those who had abandoned it and not by those who remained in it. Moscow when occupied by the enemy did not remain intact like Berlin, Vienna, and other towns, simply because its inhabitants abandoned it and did not welcome the French with bread and salt, nor bring them the keys of the city.

27

THE absorption of the French by Moscow, radiating star-wise as it did, only reached the quarter where Pierre was staying by the evening of the 2nd of September.

After the last two days spent in solitude and unusual circum-stances, Pierre was in a state bordering on insanity. He was completely obsessed by one persistent thought. He did not know how or when this thought had taken such possession of him, but he remembered nothing of the past, understood nothing of the present, and all he saw and heard appeared to him like a dream.

He had left home only to escape the intricate tangle of life's demands that enmeshed him, and which in his present condition he was unable to unravel. He had gone to Joseph Alexeevich's house, on the plea of sorting the deceased's books and papers, only in search of rest from life's turmoil, for in his mind the memory of Joseph Alexeevich was connected with a world of eternal, solemn, and calm thoughts, quite contrary to the restless confusion into which he felt himself being drawn. He sought a quiet refuge, and in Joseph Alexeevich's study he really found it. When he sat with his elbows on the dusty writing table in the deathlike stillness of the study, calm and significant memories of the last few days rose one after another in his imagination, particularly of the battle of Borodino, and of that vague sense of his own insignificance and insincerity compared with the truth, simplicity, and strength of the class of men he mentally classed as *they*. When Gerasim roused him from his reverie the idea occurred to him of taking part in the popular defence of Moscow which he knew was projected. And with that object he had asked Gerasim to get him a peasant's coat and a pistol, confiding to him his intention of remaining in Joseph Alexeevich's house and keeping his name secret. Then during the first day spent in inaction and solitude (he tried several times to fix his attention on the masonic manuscripts, but was unable to do so) the idea that had previously occurred to him of the cabalistic significance of his name in connexion with Bonaparte's more than once vaguely presented itself. But the idea that he, *L'russe Besuhof*, was destined to set a limit to the power of *the Beast*, was as yet only one of the fancies that often passed through his mind and left no trace behind.

When, having bought the coat merely with the object of taking part among the people in the defence of Moscow, Pierre had met the Rostovs and Natasha had said to him: 'Are you remaining in Moscow? ... How splendid!' the thought flashed into his mind that it really would be a good thing, even if Moscow were taken, for him to remain there and do what he was predestined to do.

Next day, with the sole idea of not sparing himself and not lagging in any way behind *them*, Pierre went to the Three Hills gate. But when he returned to the house convinced that Moscow would not be defended, he suddenly felt that what before had seemed to him merely a possibility had now become absolutely necessary and inevitable. He must remain in Moscow, concealing his name, and must meet Napoleon and kill him, and either perish or put an end to the misery of all Europe – which it seemed to him was solely due to Napoleon.

Pierre knew all the details of the attempt on Bonaparte's life in 1809 by a German student in Vienna, and knew that the student had been shot. And the risk to which he would expose his life by carrying out his design excited him still more.

Two equally strong feelings drew Pierre irresistibly to this purpose. The first was a feeling of the necessity of sacrifice and suffering in view of the common calamity, the same feeling that had caused him to go to Mozhaysk on the 25th and to make his way to the very thick of the battle, and had now caused him to run away from his home and, in place of the luxury and comfort to which he was accustomed, to sleep on a hard sofa without undressing and eat the same food as Gerasim. The other was that vague and quite Russian feeling of contempt for everything conventional, artificial, and human – for everything the majority of men regard as the greatest good in the world. Pierre had first experienced this strange and fascinating feeling at the Sloboda Palace, when he had suddenly felt that wealth, power, and life – all that men so painstakingly acquire and guard – if it has any worth has so only by reason of the joy with which it can all be renounced.

It was the feeling that induces a volunteer-recruit to spend his last penny on drink, and a drunken man to smash mirrors or glasses for no apparent reason and knowing that it will cost him all the money he possesses; the feeling which causes a man to perform actions which from an ordinary point of view are insane, to test, as it were, his personal power and strength, affirming the existence of a higher, non-human, criterion of life.

From the very day Pierre had experienced this feeling for the first time at the Sloboda Palace he had been continuously under its influence, but only now found full satisfaction for it. Moreover at this moment Pierre was supported in his design and prevented from renouncing it by what he had already done in that direction. If he were now to leave Moscow like everyone else, his flight from home, the peasant coat, the pistol, and his announcement to the Rostovs that he would remain in Moscow, would all become not merely meaningless, but contemptible and ridiculous, and to this Pierre was very sensitive.

Pierre's physical condition, as is always the case, corresponded to his mental state. The unaccustomed coarse food, the vodka he drank during those days, the absence of wine and cigars, his dirty unchanged linen, two almost sleepless nights passed on a short sofa without bedding – all this kept him in a state of excitement bordering on insanity.

It was two o'clock in the afternoon. The French had already entered Moscow. Pierre knew this, but instead of acting, he only thought about his undertaking, going over its minutest details in his mind. In his fancy he did not clearly picture to himself either the striking of the blow or the death of Napoleon, but with extraordinary vividness and melancholy enjoyment imagined his own destruction and heroic endurance.

'Yes, alone, for the sake of all, I must do it or perish!' he thought. 'Yes, I will approach ... and then suddenly ... with pistol or dagger? But that is all the same! "It is not I but the hand of Providence that punishes thee," I shall say,' he thought, imagining what he would say when killing Napoleon. 'Well then, take me and execute me!' he went on, speaking to himself and bowing his head with a sad but firm expression.

While Pierre, standing in the middle of the room, was talking to himself in this way, the study door opened and on the threshold appeared the figure of Makar Alexeevich, always so timid before but now quite transformed.

His dressing-gown was unfastened, his face red and distorted. He was obviously drunk. On seeing Pierre he grew confused at first, but noticing embarrassment on Pierre's face, immediately grew bold and, staggering on his thin legs, advanced into the middle of the room.

'They're frightened,' he said confidentially in a hoarse voice. 'I say, I won't surrender, I say ... Am I not right, sir?'

He paused and then suddenly seeing the pistol on the table seized it with unexpected rapidity, and ran out into the corridor.

Gerasim and the porter, who had followed Makar Alexeevich, stopped him in the vestibule and tried to take the pistol from him. Pierre, coming out into the corridor, looked with pity and repulsion at the half-crazy old man. Makar Alexeevich, frowning with exertion, held on to the pistol and screamed hoarsely, evidently with some heroic fancy in his head.

'To arms! Board them! No, you shan't get it,' he yelled.

'That will do, please, that will do. Have the goodness – please sir, to let go! Please sir ...' pleaded Gerasim, trying carefully to steer Makar Alexeevich by the elbows back to the door.

'Who are you? Bonaparte! ...' shouted Makar Alexeevich.

'That's not right, sir. Come to your room, please, and rest. Allow me to have the pistol.'

'Be off, thou base slave! Touch me not! See this?' shouted Makar Alexeevich, brandishing the pistol. 'Board them!'

'Catch hold!' whispered Gerasim to the porter.

They seized Makar Alexeevich by the arms and dragged him to the door.

The vestibule was filled with the discordant sounds of a struggle and of a tipsy, hoarse voice.

Suddenly a fresh sound, a piercing feminine scream, reverberated from the porch, and the cook came running into the vestibule.

'It's them! Gracious heavens! O Lord, four of them, horsemen!' she cried.

Gerasim and the porter let Makar Alexeevich go, and in the now silent corridor the sound of several hands knocking at the front door could be heard.

28

PIERRE, having decided that until he had carried out his design he would disclose neither his identity nor his knowledge of French, stood at the half-open door of the corridor, intending to conceal himself as soon as the French entered. But the French entered and still Pierre did not retire – an irresistible curiosity kept him there.

There were two of them. One was an officer – a tall, soldierly, handsome man – the other evidently a private or an orderly, sunburnt, short, and thin, with sunken cheeks and a dull expression. The officer walked in front, leaning on a stick and slightly limping. When he had advanced a few steps he stopped, having apparently decided that these were good quarters, turned round to the soldiers standing at the entrance and in a loud voice of command ordered them to put up the horses. Having done that, the officer lifting his elbow with a smart gesture stroked his moustache and lightly touched his hat.

'*Bonjour, la compagnie!*' said he gaily, smiling and looking about him.

No one gave any reply.

'*Vous êtes le bourgeois?*' the officer asked Gerasim.

Gerasim gazed at the officer with an alarmed and inquiring look.

'*Quartier, quartier, logement!*' said the officer, looking down at the little man with a condescending and good-natured smile. '*Les Français sont de bons enfants. Que diable! Voyons! Ne nous fâchons pas, mon vieux!*' added he, clapping the scared and silent Gerasim on the shoulder. 'Well, does no one speak French in this establishment?' he asked again in French, looking around and meeting Pierre's eyes. Pierre moved away from the door.

Again the officer turned to Gerasim and asked him to show him the rooms in the house.

'Master, not here – don't understand . . . me, you . . .' said Gerasim, trying to render his words more comprehensible by contorting them.

Still smiling, the French officer spread his hands out before Gerasim's nose, intimating that he did not understand him either, and moved, limping, to the door at which Pierre was standing. Pierre wished to go away and conceal himself, but at that moment he saw Makar Alexeevich appearing at the open kitchen door with the pistol in his hand. With a madman's cunning Makar Alexeevich eyed the Frenchman, raised his pistol, and took aim.

'Board them!' yelled the tipsy man trying to press the trigger. Hearing the yell the officer turned round, and at the same moment Pierre threw himself on the drunkard. Just when Pierre snatched at and struck up the pistol, Makar Alexeevich at last got his fingers on the trigger, there was a deafening report and all were enveloped in a cloud of smoke. The Frenchman turned pale and rushed to the door.

Forgetting his intention of concealing his knowledge of French, Pierre, snatching away the pistol and throwing it down, ran up to the officer and addressed him in French.

'You are not wounded?' he asked.

'I think not,' answered the Frenchman, feeling himself over. 'But I have had a lucky escape this time,' he added pointing to the damaged plaster of the wall. 'Who is that man?' said he, looking sternly at Pierre.

'Oh, I am really in despair at what has occurred,' said Pierre rapidly, quite forgetting the part he had intended to play. 'He is an unfortunate madman who did not know what he was doing.'

The officer went up to Makar Alexeevich and took him by the collar.

Makar Alexeevich was standing with parted lips, swaying, as if about to fall asleep, as he leant against the wall.

'Brigand! You shall pay for this,' said the Frenchman, letting go of him. 'We French are merciful after victory, but we do not pardon traitors,' he added with a look of gloomy dignity and a fine energetic gesture.

Pierre continued, in French, to persuade the officer not to hold that drunken imbecile to account. The Frenchman listened in silence with the same gloomy expression, but suddenly turned to Pierre with a smile. For a few seconds he looked at him in silence. His handsome face assumed a melodramatically gentle expression and he held out his hand.

'You have saved my life. You are French,' said he.

For a Frenchman that deduction was indubitable. Only a Frenchman could perform a great deed, and to save his life – the life of M. Ramballe, captain of the 13th Light Regiment – was undoubtedly a very great deed.

But however indubitable that conclusion and the officer's conviction based upon it, Pierre felt it necessary to disillusion him.

'I am Russian,' he said quickly.

'Tut, tut, tut! Tell that to others,' said the officer, waving his finger before his nose and smiling. 'You shall tell me all about that presently. I am delighted to meet a compatriot. Well and what are we to do with this man?' he added, addressing himself to Pierre as to a brother.

Even if Pierre were not a Frenchman, having once received that loftiest of human appellations he could not renounce it, said the officer's look and tone. In reply to his last question Pierre again explained who Makar Alexeevich was, and how just before their arrival that drunken imbecile had seized the loaded pistol which they had not had time to recover from him, and begged the officer to let the deed go unpunished.

The Frenchman expanded his chest and made a majestic gesture with his arm.

'You have saved my life! You are French. You ask his pardon? I grant it you. Lead that man away!' said he quickly and energetically, and taking the arm of Pierre, whom he had promoted to be a Frenchman for saving his life, he went with him into the room.

The soldiers in the yard, hearing the shot, came into the passage asking what had happened, and expressed their readiness to punish the culprits, but the officer sternly checked them.

'You will be called in when you are wanted,' he said.

The soldiers went out again, and the orderly, who had meanwhile had time to visit the kitchen, came up to his officer.

'Captain, there is soup and a leg of mutton in the kitchen,' said he. 'Shall I serve them up?'

'Yes, and some wine,' answered the captain.

29

WHEN the French officer went into the room with Pierre the latter again thought it his duty to assure him that he was not French, and wished to go away, but the officer would not hear of it. He was so very polite, amiable, good-natured, and genuinely grateful to Pierre for saving his life, that Pierre had not the heart to refuse, and sat down with him in the parlour – the first room they entered. To Pierre's assurances that he was not a Frenchman, the captain, evidently not understanding how anyone could decline so flattering an appellation, shrugged his shoulders and said that if Pierre absolutely insisted on passing for a Russian let it be so, but for all that he would be for ever bound to Pierre by gratitude for saving his life.

Had this man been endowed with the slightest capacity for perceiving the feelings of others, and had he at all understood what Pierre's feelings were, the latter would probably have left him, but the man's animated obtuseness to everything other than himself disarmed Pierre.

'A Frenchman or a Russian prince incognito,' said the officer, looking at Pierre's fine though dirty linen and at the ring on his finger. 'I owe my life to you and offer you my friendship. A Frenchman never forgets either an insult or a service. I offer you my friendship. That is all I can say.'

There was so much good-nature and nobility (in the French sense of the word) in the officer's voice, in the expression of his face, and in his gestures, that Pierre, unconsciously smiling in response to the Frenchman's smile, pressed the hand held out to him.

'Captain Ramballe, of the 13th Light Regiment, Chevalier of the Legion of Honour for the affair on the 7th of September,' he introduced himself, a self-satisfied irrepressible smile puckering his lips under his moustache. 'Will you now be so good as to tell me with whom I have the honour of conversing so pleasantly, instead of being in the ambulance with that maniac's bullet in my body?'

Pierre replied that he could not tell him his name and, blushing, began to try to invent a name and to say something about his reason for concealing it, but the Frenchman hastily interrupted him.

'Oh. please!' said he. 'I understand your reasons. You are an officer . . . a superior officer perhaps. You have borne arms against us. That's not my business. I owe you my life. That is enough for me. I am quite at your service. You belong to the gentry?' he concluded with a shade of inquiry in his tone. Pierre bent his head. 'Your baptismal name, if you please. That is all I ask. Monsieur Pierre, you say . . . Excellent! That's all I want to know.'

When the mutton and an omelette had been served and a samovar and vodka brought, with some wine which the French had taken from a Russian cellar and brought with them, Ramballe invited Pierre to share his dinner, and himself began to eat greedily and quickly like a healthy and hungry man, munching his food rapidly with his strong teeth, continually smacking his lips, and repeating – 'Excellent! Delicious!' His face grew red and was covered with perspiration. Pierre was hungry and shared the dinner with pleasure. Morel, the orderly, brought some hot water in a saucepan and placed a bottle of claret in it. He also brought a bottle of kvas, taken from the kitchen for them to try. That beverage was already known to the French and had been given a special name. They called it *limonade de cochon* (pig's lemonade), and Morel spoke well of the *limonade de cochon* he had found in the kitchen. But as the captain had the wine they had taken while passing through Moscow, he left the kvas to Morel and applied himself to the bottle of Bordeaux. He wrapped the bottle up to its neck in a table-napkin and poured out wine for himself and for Pierre. The satisfaction of his hunger and the wine rendered the captain still more lively and he chatted incessantly all through dinner.

'Yes, my dear Monsieur Pierre, I owe you a fine votive candle for saving me from that maniac... You see, I have bullets enough in my body already. Here is one I got at Wagram,' (he touched his side) 'and a second at Smolensk,' – he showed a scar on his cheek – 'and this leg which as you see does not want to march, I got that on the 7th at the great battle of la Moskowa.* *Sacré Dieu!* It was splendid! That deluge of fire was worth seeing. It was a tough job you set us there, my word! You may be proud of it! And on my honour, in spite of the cough I caught there, I should be ready to begin again. I pity those who did not see it.'

'I was there,' said Pierre.

'Bah, really? So much the better! You are certainly brave foes. The great redoubt held out well, by my pipe!' continued the Frenchman, 'And you made us pay dear for it. I was at it three times – sure as I sit here. Three times we reached the guns and three times we were thrown back like cardboard figures. Oh, it was beautiful, Monsieur Pierre! Your grenadiers were splendid, by heaven! I saw them close up their ranks six times in succession and march as if on parade. Fine fellows! Our King of Naples, who knows what's what, cried "Bravo!" Ha, ha! So you are one of us soldiers!' he added smiling, after a momentary pause. 'So much the better, so much the better, Monsieur Pierre! Terrible in battle... gallant... with the fair' (he winked and smiled), 'that's what the French are, Monsieur Pierre, aren't they?'

The captain was so naïvely and good-humouredly gay, so real, and so pleased with himself, that Pierre almost winked back as he looked merrily at him. Probably the word 'gallant' turned the captain's thoughts to the state of Moscow.

'Apropos, tell me please, is it true that the women have all left Moscow? What a queer idea! What had they to be afraid of?'

'Would not the French ladies leave Paris if the Russians entered it?' asked Pierre.

'Ha, ha, ha!' The Frenchman emitted a merry, sanguine chuckle, patting Pierre on the shoulder. 'What a thing to say!' he exclaimed. 'Paris? ... But Paris, Paris ...'

'Paris – the capital of the world,' Pierre finished his remark for him.

The captain looked at Pierre. He had a habit of stopping short in the middle of his talk and gazing intently with his laughing, kindly eyes.

'Well, if you hadn't told me you were Russian, I should have wagered that you were Parisian! You have that ... I don't know what, that ...' and having uttered this compliment, he again gazed at him in silence.

'I have been in Paris. I spent years there,' said Pierre.

'Oh yes, one sees that plainly. Paris! ... A man who doesn't know Paris is a savage. You can tell a Parisian two leagues off. Paris is Talma, la Duchénois, Potier, the Sorbonne,* the boulevards,' and noticing that his conclusion was weaker than what had gone before, he added quickly: 'There is only one Paris in the world. You have been to Paris and have remained Russian. Well, I don't esteem you the less for it.'

Under the influence of the wine he had drunk, and after the days he had spent alone with his depressing thoughts, Pierre involuntarily enjoyed talking with this cheerful and good-natured man.

'To return to your ladies – I hear they are lovely. What a wretched idea to go and bury themselves in the steppes when the French army is in Moscow. What a chance those girls have missed! Your peasants, now – that's another thing, but you civilized people, you ought to know us better than that. We took Vienna, Berlin, Madrid, Naples, Rome, Warsaw, all the world's capitals ... We are feared, but we are loved. We are nice to know. And then the Emperor ...' he began, but Pierre interrupted him.

'The Emperor,' Pierre repeated, and his face suddenly became sad and embarrassed, 'Is the Emperor ...?'

'The Emperor? He is generosity, mercy, justice, order, genius – that's what the Emperor is! It is I, Ramballe, who tell you so ... I assure you I was his enemy eight years ago. My father was an emigrant count ... But that man has vanquished me. He has taken hold of me. I could not resist the sight of the grandeur and glory with which he has covered France. When I understood what he wanted – when I saw that he was preparing a bed of laurels for us, you know, I said to myself: "That is a monarch", and I devoted myself to him! So there! Oh yes, *mon cher*, he is the greatest man of the ages past or future.'

'Is he in Moscow?' Pierre stammered with a guilty look.

The Frenchman looked at his guilty face, and smiled.

'No, he will make his entry to-morrow,' he replied, and continued his talk.

Their conversation was interrupted by the cries of several voices at the gate and by Morel, who came to say that some Würtemberg hussars had come and wanted to put up their horses in the yard where the captain's horses were. This difficulty had arisen chiefly because the hussars did not understand what was said to them in French.

The captain had their senior sergeant called in, and in a stern voice asked him to what regiment he belonged, who was his commanding officer, and by what right he allowed himself to claim quarters that were already occupied. The German who knew little French, answered the two first questions by giving the names of his regiment and of his commanding officer, but in reply to the third question which he did not understand, said, introducing broken French into his own German, that he was the quartermaster of the regiment and his commander had ordered him to occupy all the houses one after another. Pierre, who knew German, translated what the German said to the captain and gave the captain's reply to the Würtemberg hussar in German. When he had understood what was said to him, the German submitted and took his men elsewhere. The captain went out into the porch and gave some orders in a loud voice.

When he returned to the room Pierre was sitting in the same place as before, with his head in his hands. His face expressed suffering. He really was suffering at that moment. When the captain went out and he was left alone, he suddenly came to himself and realized the position he was in. It was not that Moscow had been taken nor that the happy conquerors were masters in it and were patronizing him. Painful as that was it was not that which tormented Pierre at the moment. He was tormented by the consciousness of his own weakness. The few glasses of wine he had drunk and the conversation with this good-natured man had destroyed the mood of concentrated gloom in which he had spent the last few days and which was essential for the execution of his design. The pistol, dagger, and peasant coat were ready. Napoleon was to enter the town next day. Pierre still considered that it would be a useful and worthy action to slay the evil-doer, but he now felt that he would not do it. He did not know why, but he felt a foreboding that he would not carry out his intention. He struggled against the confession of his weakness but dimly felt that he could not overcome it and that his former gloomy frame of mind, concerning vengeance, killing, and self-sacrifice, had been dispersed like dust by contact with the first man he met.

The captain returned to the room, limping slightly and whistling a tune.

The Frenchman's chatter which had previously amused Pierre, now repelled him. The tune he was whistling, his gait, and the gesture with which he twirled his moustache, all now seemed offensive. 'I will go away immediately. I won't say another word to him,' thought Pierre. He thought this but still sat in the same place. A strange feeling of weakness tied him to the spot, he wished to get up and go away but could not do so.

The captain, on the other hand, seemed very cheerful. He paced up and down the room twice. His eyes shone and his moustache twitched as if he were smiling to himself at some amusing thought.

'The colonel of those Würtembergers is delightful,' he suddenly said. 'He is a German, but a nice fellow all the same ... But he's a German.' He sat down facing Pierre. 'By the way, you know German, then?'

Pierre looked at him in silence.

'What is the German for "shelter"?'

'Shelter?' Pierre repeated. 'The German for shelter is *Unterkunft.*'

'How do you say it?' the captain asked quickly and doubtfully.

'*Unterkunft,*' Pierre repeated.

'Onterkoff,' said the captain and looked at Pierre for some seconds with laughing eyes. 'These Germans are first-rate fools, don't you think so, Monsieur Pierre?' he concluded.

'Well, let's have another bottle of this Moscow Bordeaux, shall we? Morel will warm us up another little bottle. Morel!' he called out gaily.

Morel brought candles and a bottle of wine. The captain looked at Pierre by the candle-light and was evidently struck by the troubled expression on his companion's face. Ramballe, with genuine distress and sympathy in his face, went up to Pierre and bent over him.

'There now, we're sad,' said he, touching Pierre's hand. 'Have I upset you? No, really, have you anything against me?' he asked Pierre. 'Perhaps it's the state of affairs?'

Pierre did not answer, but looked cordially into the Frenchman's eyes whose expression of sympathy was pleasing to him.

'Honestly, without speaking of what I owe you, I feel friendship for you. Can I do anything for you? Dispose of me. It is for life and death. I say it with my hand on my heart!' said he, striking his chest.

'Thank you,' said Pierre.

The captain gazed intently at him as he had done when he learnt that 'shelter' was *Unterkunft* in German, and his face suddenly brightened.

'Well, in that case, I drink to our friendship!' he cried gaily, filling two glasses with wine.

Pierre took one of the glasses and emptied it. Ramballe emptied his too, again pressed Pierre's hand, and leaned his elbows on the table in a pensive attitude.

'Yes, my dear friend,' he began, 'such is fortune's caprice. Who would have said that I should be a soldier and a captain of dragoons in the service of Bonaparte, as we used to call him? Yet here I am in Moscow with him. I must tell you, *mon cher*,' he continued in the sad and measured tones of a man who intends to tell a long story, 'that our name is one of the most ancient in France.'

And with a Frenchman's easy and naïve frankness the captain told Pierre the story of his ancestors, his childhood, youth, and manhood, and all about his relations and his financial and family affairs, '*ma pauvre mère*' playing of course an important part in the story.

'But all that is only life's setting, the real thing is love – love! Am I not right, Monsieur Pierre?' said he, growing animated. 'Another glass?'

Pierre again emptied his glass and poured himself out a third.

'Oh, women, women!' and the captain, looking with glistening eyes at Pierre, began talking of love and of his love affairs.

There were very many of these, as one could easily believe, looking at the officer's handsome self-satisfied face, and noting the eager enthusiasm with which he spoke of women. Though all Ramballe's love stories had the sensual character which Frenchmen regard as the special charm and poetry of love, yet he told his story with such sincere conviction that he alone had experienced and known all the charm of love, and he described women so alluringly, that Pierre listened to him with curiosity.

It was plain that *l'amour* which the Frenchman was so fond of was not that low and simple kind that Pierre had once felt for his wife, nor was it the romantic love that he felt for Natasha. (Ramballe despised both these kinds of love equally: the one he considered the 'love of clod-hoppers' and the other the 'love of simpletons'.) *L'amour* which the Frenchman worshipped consisted principally in the unnaturalness of his relations to the woman and in a combination of incongruities giving the chief charm to the feeling.

Thus the captain touchingly recounted the story of his love for a fascinating Marquise of thirty-five and at the same time for a charming, innocent child of seventeen, daughter of the bewitching Marquise. The conflict of magnanimity between the mother and the daughter, ending in the mother's sacrificing herself and offering her daughter in marriage to her lover, even now agitated the captain, though it was the memory of a distant past. Then he recounted an episode in which the husband played the part of the lover, and he – the lover – assumed the rôle of the husband, as well as several droll incidents from his recollections of Germany, where 'shelter' is called *Unterkunft*, and where the husbands eat sauerkraut and the young girls are 'too blonde'.

Finally, the latest episode in Poland still fresh in the captain's memory and which he narrated with rapid gestures and glowing face, was of how he had saved the life of a Pole (in general the saving of life continually occurred in the captain's stories) and the Pole had entrusted to him his enchanting wife (*parisienne de cœur*) while himself entering the French service. The captain was happy, the enchanting Polish lady wished to elope with him, but prompted by magnanimity the captain restored the wife to the husband, saying as he did so: 'I have saved your life and I save your honour!' Having repeated these words the captain wiped his eyes and gave himself a shake, as if driving away the weakness which assailed him at this touching recollection.

Listening to the captain's tales, Pierre – as often happens late in the evening and under the influence of wine – followed all that was told him, understood it all, and at the same time followed a train of personal memories which, he knew not why, suddenly arose in his mind. While listening to these love stories his own love for Natasha unexpectedly rose to his mind, and going over the pictures of that love in his imagination he mentally compared them with Ramballe's tales. Listening to the story of the struggle between love and duty, Pierre saw before his eyes every minutest detail of his last meeting with the object of his love at the Sukharev Water-Tower. At the time of that meeting it had not produced an effect upon him – he had not even once recalled it. But now it seemed to him that that meeting had had in it something very important and poetic.

'Peter Kirilovich, come here! We have recognized you,' he now seemed to hear the words she had uttered and to see before him her eyes, her smile, her travelling hood, and a stray lock of her hair . . . and there seemed to him something pathetic and touching in all this.

Having finished his tale about the enchanting Polish lady, the captain asked Pierre if he had ever experienced a similar impulse to sacrifice himself for love and a feeling of envy of the legitimate husband.

Challenged by this question Pierre raised his head and felt a need to express the thoughts that filled his mind. He began to explain that he understood love for a woman somewhat differently. He said that in all his life he had loved and still loved only one woman, and that she could never be his.

'*Tiens!*' said the captain.

Pierre then explained that he had loved this woman from his earliest years, but that he had not dared to think of her because she was too young, and because he had been an illegitimate son without a name. Afterwards when he had received a name and wealth he dared not think of her because he loved her too well, placing her far above everything in the world, and especially therefore above himself.

When he had reached this point, Pierre asked the captain whether he understood that.

The captain made a gesture signifying that even if he did not understand it he begged Pierre to continue.

'Platonic love, clouds . . .' he muttered.

Whether it was the wine he had drunk, or an impulse of frankness, or the thought that this man did not, and never would, know any of those who played a part in his story, or whether it was all these things together, something loosened Pierre's tongue. Speaking thickly, and with a far-away look in his shining eyes, he told the whole story of his life: his marriage, Natasha's love for his best friend, her betrayal of him, and all his own simple relations with her. Urged on by Ramballe's questions he also told what he had at first concealed – his own position and even his name.

More than anything else in Pierre's story the captain was impressed by the fact that Pierre was very rich, had two mansions in Moscow, and that he had abandoned everything and not left the city, but remained there concealing his name and station.

When it was late at night they went out together into the street. The night was warm and light. To the left of the house on the Pokrovka, a fire glowed – the first of those that were beginning in Moscow. To the right, and high up in the sky, was the sickle of the waning moon and opposite to it hung that bright comet which was connected in Pierre's heart with his love. At the gate stood

975

Gerasim, the cook, and two Frenchmen. Their laughter and their mutually incomprehensible remarks in two languages could be heard. They were looking at the glow seen in the town.

There was nothing terrible in the one small, distant fire in the immense city.

Gazing at the high starry sky, at the moon, at the comet, and at the glow from the fire, Pierre experienced a joyful emotion. 'There now, how good it is, what more does one need?' thought he. And suddenly remembering his intention he grew dizzy, and felt so faint that he leaned against the fence to save himself from falling.

Without taking leave of his new friend Pierre left the gate with unsteady steps, and returning to his room lay down on the sofa and immediately fell asleep.

30

THE glow of the first fire that began on the 2nd of September was watched from the various roads by the fugitive Moscovites, and by the retreating troops, with many different feelings.

The Rostov party spent that night at Mytishchy, fourteen miles from Moscow. They had started so late on the 1st of September, the road had been so blocked by vehicles and troops, so many things had been forgotten for which servants were sent back, that they had decided to spend that night at a place three miles out of Moscow. The next morning they woke late and were again delayed so often that they only got as far as Great Mytischy. At ten o'clock that evening the Rostov family, and the wounded travelling with them, were all distributed in the yards and huts of that large village. The Rostovs' servants and coachmen and the orderlies of the wounded officers, after attending to their masters, had supper, fed the horses, and came out into the porches.

In a neighbouring hut lay Raevsky's adjutant with a fractured wrist. The awful pain he suffered made him moan incessantly and piteously, and his moaning sounded terrible in the darkness of the autumn night. He had spent the first night in the same yard as the Rostovs. The countess said she had been unable to close her eyes on account of his moaning, and at Mytishchy she moved into a worse hut simply to be farther away from the wounded man.

In the darkness of the night one of the servants noticed, above the high body of a coach standing before the porch, the small glow of another fire. One glow had long been visible and everybody knew that it was Little Mytishchy burning – set on fire by Mamonov's Cossacks.

'But look here, brothers, there's another fire!' remarked an orderly.

All turned their attention to the glow.

'But they told us Little Mytishchy had been set on fire by Mamonov's Cossacks.'

'But that's not Mytishchy, it's farther away.'

'Look, it must be in Moscow!'

Two of the gazers went round to the other side of the coach and sat down on its steps.

'It's more to the left, why, Little Mytishchy is over there, and this is right on the other side.'

Several men joined the first two.

'See how it's flaring,' said one. 'That's a fire in Moscow: either in the Sushchevsky or the Rogozhsky quarter.'

No one replied to this remark and for some time they all gazed silently at the spreading flames of the second fire in the distance.

Old Daniel Terentich, the count's valet (as he was called), came up to the group and shouted at Mishka.

'What are you staring at, you good-for-nothing...? The count will be calling, and there's nobody there; go and gather the clothes together.'

'I only ran out to get some water,' said Mishka.

'But what do you think, Daniel Terentich? Doesn't it look as if that glow were in Moscow?' remarked one of the footmen.

Daniel Terentich made no reply, and again for a long time they were all silent. The glow spread, rising and falling, farther and farther still.

'God have mercy... It's windy and dry...' said another voice.

'Just look! See what it's doing now. O Lord! You can even see the crows flying. Lord have mercy on us sinners!'

'They'll put it out, no fear!'

'Who's to put it out?' Daniel Terenitch, who had hitherto been silent, was heard to say. His voice was calm and deliberate. 'Moscow it is, brothers,' said he. 'Mother Moscow, the white...' his voice faltered, and he gave way to an old man's sob.

And it was as if they had all only waited for this to realize the significance for them of the glow they were watching. Sighs were heard, words of prayer, and the sobbing of the count's old valet.

THE valet, returning to the cottage, informed the count that Moscow was burning. The count donned his dressing-gown and went out to look. Sonya and Madame Schoss, who had not yet undressed, went out with him. Only Natasha and the countess remained in the room. Petya was no longer with the family, he had gone on with his regiment which was making for Troitsa.*

The countess, on hearing that Moscow was on fire, began to cry. Natasha, pale, with a fixed look, was sitting on the bench under the icons just where she had sat down on arriving, and paid no attention to her father's words. She was listening to the ceaseless moaning of the adjutant, three houses off.

'Oh, how terrible,' said Sonya, returning from the yard chilled and frightened. 'I believe the whole of Moscow will burn, there's an awful glow! Natasha, do look! You can see it now from the window,' she said to her cousin, evidently wishing to distract her mind.

But Natasha looked at her as if not understanding what was said to her, and again fixed her eyes on the corner of the stove. She had been in this condition of stupor since the morning, when Sonya, to the surprise and annoyance of the countess, had for some unaccountable reason found it necessary to tell Natasha of Prince Andrew's wound and of his being with their party. The countess had seldom been so angry with anyone as she was with Sonya. Sonya had cried and begged to be forgiven, and now, as if trying to atone for her fault, paid unceasing attention to her cousin.

'Look, Natasha, how dreadfully it is burning!' said she.

'What's burning?' asked Natasha. 'Oh, yes, Moscow.'

And as if in order not to offend Sonya and to get rid of her, she turned her face to the window, looked out in such a way that it was evident that she could not see anything, and again settled down in her former attitude.

'But you didn't see it!'

'Yes, really I did,' Natasha replied in a voice that pleaded to be left in peace.

Both the countess and Sonya understood that, naturally, neither Moscow, nor the burning of Moscow, nor anything else, could seem of importance to Natasha.

The count returned and lay down behind the partition. The countess went up to her daughter and touched her head with the back of her hand as she was wont to do when Natasha was ill, then touched her forehead with her lips as if to feel whether she was feverish, and finally kissed her.

'You are cold. You are trembling all over. You'd better lie down,' said the countess.

'Lie down? All right, I will. I'll lie down at once,' said Natasha.

When Natasha had been told that morning that Prince Andrew was seriously wounded and was travelling with their party, she had at first asked many questions: Where was he going? How was he wounded? Was it serious? And could she see him? But after she had been told that she could not see him, that he was seriously wounded, but that his life was not in danger, she ceased to ask questions or to speak at all, evidently disbelieving what they told her, and convinced that say what she might she would still be told the same. All the way she had sat motionless in a corner of the coach with wide-open eyes, and the expression in them which the countess knew so well and feared so much, and now she sat in the same way on the bench where she had seated herself on arriving. She was planning something, and either deciding or had already decided something in her mind. The countess knew this, but what it might be she did not know, and this alarmed and tormented her.

'Natasha, undress, darling; lie down on my bed.'

A bed had been made on a bedstead for the countess only. Madame Schoss and the two girls were to sleep on some hay on the floor.

'No, mamma, I will lie down here on the floor,' Natasha replied irritably and she went to the window and opened it. Through the open window the moans of the adjutant could be heard more distinctly. She put her head out into the damp night air, and the countess saw her slim neck shaking with sobs and throbbing against the window-frame. Natasha knew it was not Prince Andrew who was moaning. She knew Prince Andrew was in the same yard as themselves and in a part of the hut across the passage; but this dreadful incessant moaning made her sob. The countess exchanged a look with Sonya.

'Lie down, darling; lie down, my pet,' said the countess, softly touching Natasha's shoulders. 'Come, lie down.'

'Oh, yes . . . I'll lie down at once,' said Natasha, and began hurriedly undressing, tugging at the tapes of her petticoat.

When she had thrown off her dress and put on a dressing-jacket she sat down with her feet under her, on the bed that had been made up on the floor, jerked her thin and rather short plait of hair to the front, and began re-plaiting it. Her long, thin, practised fingers rapidly unplaited, re-plaited, and tied up the plait. Her head moved from side to side from habit, but her eyes, feverishly wide, looked fixedly before her. When her toilette for the night was finished she sank gently onto the sheet spread over the hay on the side nearest the door.

'Natasha, you'd better lie in the middle,' said Sonya.

'I'll stay here,' muttered Natasha. 'Do lie down,' she added crossly, and buried her face in the pillow.

The countess, Madame Schoss, and Sonya undressed hastily and lay down. The small lamp in front of the icons was the only light left in the room. But in the yard there was light from the fire at Little Mytishchy a mile and a half away, and through the night came the noise of people shouting at a tavern Mamonov's Cossacks had set up across the street, and the adjutant's unceasing moans could still be heard.

For a long time Natasha listened attentively to the sounds that reached her from inside and outside the room and did not move. First she heard her mother praying and sighing and the creaking of her bed under her, then Madame Schoss's familiar whistling snore and Sonya's gentle breathing. Then the countess called to Natasha. Natasha did not answer.

'I think she's asleep, mamma,' said Sonya softly.

After a short silence the countess spoke again, but this time no one replied.

Soon after that Natasha heard her mother's even breathing. Natasha did not move, though her little bare foot, thrust out from under the quilt, was growing cold on the bare floor.

As if to celebrate a victory over everybody, a cricket chirped in a crack in the wall. A cock crowed far off and another replied near by. The shouting in the tavern had died down, only the moaning of the adjutant was heard. Natasha sat up.

'Sonya, are you asleep? Mamma?' she whispered.

No one replied. Natasha rose slowly and carefully, crossed herself, and stepped cautiously on the cold and dirty floor with her slim supple bare feet. The boards of the floor creaked. Stepping cautiously from one foot to the other she ran like a kitten the few steps to the door and grasped the cold door-handle.

It seemed to her that something heavy was beating rhythmically against all the walls of the room: it was her own heart, sinking with alarm and terror and overflowing with love.

She opened the door and stepped across the threshold and onto the cold damp earthen floor of the passage. The cold she felt refreshed her. With her bare feet she touched a sleeping man, stepped over him, and opened the door into the part of the hut where

Prince Andrew lay. It was dark in there. In the farthest corner, on a bench beside the bed on which something was lying, stood a tallow candle with a long thick and smouldering wick.

From the moment she had been told that morning of Prince Andrew's wound and his presence there, Natasha had resolved to see him. She did not know why she had to, she knew the meeting would be painful, but felt the more convinced that it was necessary.

All day she had lived only in the hope of seeing him that night. But now that the moment had come she was filled with dread of what she might see. How was he maimed? What was left of him? Was he like that incessant moaning of the adjutant's? Yes, he was altogether like that. In her imagination he was that terrible moaning personified. When she saw an indistinct shape in the corner, and mistook his knees raised under the quilt for his shoulders, she imagined a horrible body there, and stood still in terror. But an irresistible impulse drew her forward. She cautiously took one step and then another, and found herself in the middle of a small room containing baggage. Another man – Timokhin – was lying in a corner on the benches beneath the icons, and two others – the doctor and a valet – lay on the floor.

The valet sat up and whispered something. Timokhin, kept awake by the pain in his wounded leg, gazed with wide-open eyes at this strange apparition of a girl in a white chemise, dressing-jacket, and night-cap. The valet's sleepy, frightened exclamation, 'What do you want? What's the matter?' made Natasha approach more swiftly to what was lying in the corner. Horribly unlike a man as that body looked, she must see him. She passed the valet, the snuff fell from the candle wick, and she saw Prince Andrew clearly with his arms outside the quilt, and such as she had always seen him.

He was the same as ever, but the feverish colour of his face, his glittering eyes rapturously turned towards her, and especially his neck, delicate as a child's, revealed by the turn-down collar of his shirt, gave him a peculiarly innocent, childlike look, such as she had never seen on him before. She went up to him, and with a swift, flexible, youthful movement dropped on her knees.

He smiled and held out his hand to her.

32

SEVEN days had passed since Prince Andrew found himself in the ambulance station on the field of Borodino. His feverish state and the inflammation of his bowels, which were injured, were in the doctor's opinion sure to carry him off. But on the seventh day he ate with pleasure a piece of bread with some tea, and the doctor noticed that his temperature was lower. He had regained consciousness that morning. The first night after they left Moscow had been fairly warm, and he had remained in the calèche, but at Mytishchy the wounded man himself asked to be taken out and given some tea. The pain caused by his removal into the hut had made him groan aloud and again lose consciousness. When he had been placed on his camp-bed he lay for a long time motionless with closed eyes. Then he opened them and whispered softly: 'And the tea?' His remembering such a small detail of everyday life astonished the doctor. He felt Prince Andrew's pulse, and to his surprise and dissatisfaction found it had improved. He was dissatisfied because he knew by experience that if his patient did not die now, he would do so a little later with greater suffering. Timokhin, the red-nosed major of Prince Andrew's regiment, had joined him in Moscow and was being taken along with him, having been wounded in the leg at the battle of Borodino. They were accompanied by a doctor, Prince Andrew's valet, his coachman, and two orderlies.

They gave Prince Andrew some tea. He drank it eagerly, looking with feverish eyes at the door in front of him as if trying to understand and remember something.

'I don't want any more. Is Timokhin here?' he asked.

Timokhin crept along the bench to him.

'I am here, your Excellency.'

'How's your wound?'

'Mine, sir? All right. But how about you?'

Prince Andrew again pondered as if trying to remember something.

'Couldn't one get a book?' he asked.

'What book?'

'The Gospels. I haven't one.'

The doctor promised to procure it for him, and began to ask how he was feeling. Prince Andrew answered all his questions reluctantly but reasonably, and then said he wanted a bolster placed under him as he was uncomfortable and in great pain. The doctor and valet lifted the cloak with which he was covered, and making wry faces at the noisome smell of mortifying flesh that came from the wound began examining that dreadful place. The doctor was very much displeased about something, and made a change in the dressings, turning the wounded man over so that he groaned again and grew unconscious and delirious from the agony. He kept asking them to get him the book and put it under him.

'What trouble would it be to you?' he said. 'I have not got one. Please get it for me and put it under me for a moment,' he pleaded in a piteous voice.

The doctor went into the passage to wash his hands.

'You fellows have no conscience,' said he to the valet who was pouring water over his hands. 'For just one moment I didn't look after you...It's such pain, you know, that I wonder how he can bear it.'

'I thought we had put something under him, by the Lord Jesus Christ!' said the valet.

The first time Prince Andrew understood where he was and what was the matter with him, and remembered being wounded and how, was when he asked to be carried into the hut after his calèche had stopped at Mytishchy. After growing confused from pain while being carried into the hut he again regained consciousness, and while drinking tea once more recalled all that had happened to him, and above all vividly remembered the moment at the ambulance station when, at sight of the sufferings of a man he disliked, those new thoughts had come to him which promised him happiness. And those thoughts, though now vague and indefinite, again possessed his soul. He remembered that he had now a new source of happiness and that this happiness had something to do with the Gospels. That was why he asked for a copy of them. The uncomfortable position in which they had put him and turned him over, again confused his thoughts, and when he came to himself a third time it was in the complete stillness of the night. Everybody near him was sleeping. A cricket chirped from across the passage; someone was shouting and singing in the street; cockroaches rustled on the table, on the icons, and on the walls, and a big fly flopped at the head of his bed and around the candle beside him, the wick of which was charred and had shaped itself like a mushroom.

His mind was not in a normal state. A healthy man usually thinks of, feels, and remembers, innumerable things simultaneously, but has the power and will to select one sequence of thoughts or events on which to fix his whole attention. A healthy man can tear himself away from the deepest reflections to say a civil word to someone who comes in, and can then return again to his own thoughts. But Prince Andrew's mind was not in a normal state in that respect. All the powers of his mind were more active and clearer than ever, but they acted apart from his will. Most diverse thoughts and images occupied him simultantously. At times his brain suddenly began to work with a vigour, clearness, and depth it had never reached when he was in health, but suddenly in the midst of its work it would turn to some unexpected idea and he had not the strength to turn it back again.

'Yes, a new happiness was revealed to me of which man cannot be deprived,' he thought as he lay in the semi-darkness of the quiet hut gazing fixedly before him with feverish, wide-open eyes. 'A happiness lying beyond material forces, outside the material influences that act on man – a happiness of the soul alone, the happiness of loving. Every man can understand it, but to conceive it and enjoin it was possible only for God. But how did God enjoin that law? And why was the Son . . . ?'

And suddenly the sequence of these thoughts broke off, and Prince Andrew heard (without knowing whether it was delusion or reality) a soft, whispering voice incessantly and rhythmically repeating 'piti-piti-piti', and then 'ti-ti', and then again 'piti-piti-piti', and 'ti-ti' once more. At the same time he felt that above his face, above the very middle of it, some strange airy structure was being erected out of slender needles or splinters, to the sound of this whispered music. He felt that he had to balance carefully (though it was difficult), so that this airy structure should not collapse; but nevertheless it kept collapsing and again slowly rising to the sound of whispered rhythmic music – 'it stretches, stretches, spreading out and stretching,' said Prince Andrew to himself. While listening to this whispering, and feeling the sensation of this drawing out and the construction of this edifice of needles, he also saw by glimpses a red halo round the candle, and heard the rustle of the cockroaches and the buzzing of the fly that flopped against his pillow and his face. Each time the fly touched his face it gave him a burning sensation and yet to his surprise it did not destroy the structure, though it knocked against the very region of his face where it was rising. But besides this there was something else of importance. It was something white by the door – the statue of a sphinx, which also oppressed him.

'But perhaps that's my shirt on the table,' he thought, 'and that's my legs, and that is the door, but why is it always stretching and drawing itself out, and "piti-piti-piti" and "ti-ti" and "piti-piti-piti" . . . ? That's enough, please leave off!' Prince Andrew painfully entreated someone. And suddenly thoughts and feelings again swam to the surface of his mind with peculiar clearness and force.

'Yes – love,' he thought again quite clearly. 'But not love which loves for something, for some quality, for some purpose, or for some reason, but the love which I – while dying – first experienced when I saw my enemy and yet loved him. I experienced that feeling of love which is the very essence of the soul and does not require an object. Now again I feel that bliss. To love one's neighbours, to love one's enemies, to love everything, to love God in all His manifestations. It is possible to love someone dear to you with human love, but an enemy can only be loved by divine love. That is why I experienced such joy when I felt that I loved that man. What has become of him? Is he alive . . .?

'When loving with human love one may pass from love to hatred, but divine love cannot change. No, neither death nor anything else can destroy it. It is the very essence of the soul. Yet how many people have I hated in my life? And of them all, I loved and hated none as I did her.' And he vividly pictured to himself Natasha, not as he had done in the past with nothing but her charms which gave him delight, but for the first time picturing to himself her soul. And he understood her feelings, her sufferings, shame, and remorse. He now understood for the first time all the cruelty of his rejection of her, the cruelty of his rupture with her. 'If only it were possible for me to see her once more. Just once, looking into those eyes to say . . .'

'Piti-piti-piti and ti-ti and piti-piti-piti boom!' flopped the fly . . . And his attention was suddenly carried into another world, a world of reality and delirium in which something particular was happening. In that world some structure was still being erected and did not fall, something was still stretching out, and the candle with its red halo was still burning, and the same shirt-like sphinx lay near the door: but besides all this, something creaked, there was a whiff of fresh air, and a new white sphinx appeared, standing at the door. And that sphinx had the pale face and shining eyes of the very Natasha of whom he had just been thinking.

'Oh, how oppressive this continual delirium is,' thought Prince Andrew, trying to drive that face from his imagination. But the face remained before him with the force of reality and drew nearer. Prince Andrew wished to return to that former world of pure thought, but he could not, and delirium drew him back into its domain. The soft whispering voice continued its rhythmic murmur, something oppressed him and stretched out, and the strange face was before him. Prince Andrew collected all his strength in an effort to recover his senses, he moved a little, and suddenly there was a ringing in his ears, a dimness in his eyes, and like a man plunged into water he lost consciousness. When he came to himself, Natasha, that same living Natasha whom of all people he most longed to love with this new pure divine love that had been revealed to him, was kneeling before him. He realized that it was the real living Natasha, and he was not surprised, but quietly happy. Natasha, on her knees motionless (she was unable to stir), with frightened eyes riveted on him, was restraining her sobs. Her face was pale and rigid. Only in the lower part of it something quivered.

Prince Andrew sighed with relief, smiled, and held out his hand.

'You?' he said. 'How fortunate!'

With a rapid but careful movement Natasha drew nearer to him on her knees, and taking his hand carefully, bent her face over it and began kissing it, just touching it lightly with her lips.

'Forgive me!' she whispered, raising her head and glancing at him. 'Forgive me!'

'I love you,' said Prince Andrew.

'Forgive . . . !'

'Forgive what?' he asked.

'Forgive me for what I ha-ve do-ne!' faltered Natasha in a scarcely audible, broken whisper, and began kissing his hand more rapidly, just touching it with her lips.

'I love you more, better than before,' said Prince Andrew, lifting her face with his hand so as to look into her eyes.

Those eyes, filled with happy tears, gazed at him timidly, compassionately and with joyous love. Natasha's thin pale face, with its swollen lips, was more than plain – it was dreadful. But Prince Andrew did not see that, he saw her shining eyes which were beautiful. They heard the sound of voices behind them.

Peter, the valet, who was now wide awake, had roused the doctor. Timokhin, who had not slept at all because of the pain in his leg, had long been watching all that was going on, carefully covering his bare body with the sheet as he huddled up on his bench.

'What's this?' said the doctor, rising from his bed. 'Please go away, madam!'

At that moment a maid, sent by the countess who had noticed her daughter's absence, knocked at the door.

Like a somnambulist aroused from her sleep, Natasha went out of the room and returning to her hut fell sobbing on her bed.

From that time, during all the rest of the Rostovs' journey, at every halting place and wherever they spent a night, Natasha never left the wounded Bolkonsky, and the doctor had to admit that he had not expected from a young girl either such firmness, or such skill in nursing a wounded man.

Dreadful as the countess imagined it would be should Prince Andrew die in her daughter's arms during the journey – as, judging by what the doctor said, seemed might easily happen – she could not oppose Natasha. Though with the intimacy now established between the wounded man and Natasha, the thought occurred that should he recover their former engagement would be renewed, no one – least of all Natasha and Prince Andrew – spoke of this: the unsettled question of life and death, which hung not only over Bolkonsky but over all Russia, shut out all other considerations.

On the 3rd of September Pierre awoke late. His head was aching, the clothes in which he had slept without undressing felt uncomfortable on his body, and his mind had a dim consciousness of something shameful he had done the day before. That something shameful was his yesterday's conversation with Captain Ramballe.

It was eleven by the clock, but it seemed peculiarly dark out of doors. Pierre rose, rubbed his eyes, and seeing the pistol with an engraved stock which Gerasim had replaced on the writing-table, he remembered where he was and what lay before him that very day.

'Am I not too late?' he thought. 'No, probably *he* won't make his entry into Moscow before noon.'

Pierre did not allow himself to reflect on what lay before him, but hastened to act.

After arranging his clothes, he took the pistol and was about to go out. But it then occurred to him for the first time that he certainly could not carry the weapon in his hand through the streets. It was difficult to hide such a big pistol even under his wide coat. He could not carry it unnoticed in his belt, nor under his arm. Besides it had been discharged, and he had not had time to reload it. 'No matter, the dagger will do,' he said to himself, though when planning his design he had more than once come to the conclusion that the chief mistake made by the student in 1809 had been to try to kill Napoleon with a dagger. But as if his chief aim consisted not in carrying out his design, but in proving to himself that he would not abandon his intention and was doing all he could to achieve it, Pierre hastily took the blunt jagged dagger in a green sheath which he had bought at the Sukharev market with the pistol, and hid it under his waistcoat.

Having tied a girdle over his coat and pulled his cap low on his head, Pierre went down the corridor trying to avoid making a noise or meeting the captain, and passed out into the street.

The conflagration, at which he had looked with so much indifference the evening before, had greatly increased during the night. Moscow was on fire in several places. The buildings in Carriage Row, across the river, in the Bazaar and the Povarskoy, as well as the barges on the Moskva River and the timber yards by the Dorogomilov bridge, were all ablaze.

Pierre's way led through side streets to the Povarskoy and from there to the church of St Nicholas on the Arbat, where he had long before decided that the deed should be done. The gates of most of the houses were locked and the shutters up. The streets and lanes were deserted. The air was full of smoke and the smell of burning. Now and then he met Russians with anxious and timid faces, and Frenchmen with an air not of the city but of the camp, walking in the middle of the streets. Both the Russians and the French looked at Pierre with surprise. Besides his height and stoutness, and the strange morose look of suffering in his face and whole figure, the Russians stared at him because they could not make out to what class he could belong. The French followed him with astonishment in their eyes chiefly because Pierre, unlike all the other Russians who gazed at the French with fear or curiosity, paid no attention to them. At the gate of one house three French-men, who were explaining something to some Russians who did not understand them, stopped Pierre asking if he did not know French.

Pierre shook his head and went on. In another side street a sentinel standing beside a green caisson shouted at him, but only when the shout was threateningly repeated and he heard the click of the man's musket as he raised it did Pierre understand that he had to pass on the other side of the street. He heard nothing and saw nothing of what went on around him. He carried his resolu-tion within himself in terror and haste, like something dreadful and alien to him, for after the previous night's experience he was afraid of losing it. But he was not destined to bring his mood safely to his destination. Moreover, had he not been hindered by anything on the way, his intention could not now have been carried out, for Napoleon had passed the Arbat more than four hours previously on his way from the Dorogomilov suburb to the Kremlin, and was now sitting in a very gloomy frame of mind in a royal study in the Kremlin, giving detailed and exact orders as to measures to be taken immediately to extinguish the fire, to prevent looting, and to reassure the inhabitants. But Pierre did not know this: he was entirely absorbed in what lay before him, and was tortured – as those are who obstinately undertake a task that is impossible for them not because of its difficulty but because of its incompatibility with their natures – by the fear of weakening at the decisive moment and so losing his self-esteem.

Though he heard and saw nothing around him he found his way by instinct, and did not go wrong in the side streets that led to the Povarskoy.

As Pierre approached that street the smoke became denser and denser – he even felt the heat of the fire. Occasionally curly tongues of flame rose from under the roofs of the houses. He met more people in the streets and they were more excited. But Pierre, though he felt that something unusual was happening around him, did not realize that he was approaching the fire. As he was going along a foot-path across a wide open space adjoining the Povarskoy on one side and the gardens of Prince Gruzinsky's house on the other, Pierre suddenly heard the desperate weeping of a woman close to him. He stopped as if awakening from a dream, and lifted his head.

By the side of the path, on the dusty dry grass, all sorts of household goods lay in a heap: feather-beds, a samovar, icons, and trunks. On the ground, beside the trunks, sat a thin woman no longer young, with long prominent upper teeth, and wearing a black cloak and cap. This woman, swaying to and fro and muttering something, was choking with sobs. Two girls of about ten and twelve, dressed in dirty short frocks and cloaks, were staring at their mother with a look of stupefaction on their pale frightened faces. The youngest child, a boy of about seven, who wore an overcoat and an immense cap evidently not his own, was crying in his old nurse's arms. A dirty, bare-footed maid was sitting on a trunk, and having undone her pale-coloured plait was pulling it straight and sniffing at her singed hair. The woman's husband, a short, round-shouldered man in the undress uniform of a civilian official, with sausage-shaped whiskers, and showing under his square-set cap the hair smoothly brushed forward over his temples, with expressionless face was moving the trunks which were placed one on another, and was dragging some garments from under them.

As soon as she saw Pierre the woman almost threw herself at his feet.

'Dear people, good Christians, save me, help me, dear friends... help us, somebody,' she muttered between her sobs. 'My girl... My daughter! My youngest daughter is left behind. She's burnt! Ooh! Was it for this I nursed you... Ooh!'

'Don't, Mary Nikolaevna!' said her husband to her in a low voice, evidently only to justify himself before the stranger. 'Sister must have taken her, or else where can she be?' he added.

'Monster! Villain!' shouted the woman angrily, suddenly ceasing to weep. 'You have no heart, you don't feel for your own child! Another man would have rescued her from the fire. But this is a monster and neither a man nor a father! You, honoured sir, are a noble man,' she went on, addressing Pierre rapidly between her sobs. 'The fire broke out alongside, and blew our way, the maid called out "Fire!" and we rushed to collect our things. We ran out just as we were... This is what we have brought away... The icons, and my dowry bed, all the rest is lost. We seized the

989

children. But not Katie! Ooh! O Lord...!' and again she began to sob. 'My child, my dear one! Burnt, burnt!'

'But where was she left?' asked Pierre.

From the expression of his animated face the woman saw that this man might help her.

'Oh, dear sir!' she cried, seizing him by the legs. 'My benefactor, set my heart at ease... Aniska, go, you horrid girl, show him the way!' she cried to the maid, angrily opening her mouth and still farther exposing her long teeth

'Show me the way, show me, I...I'll do it,' gasped Pierre rapidly.

The dirty maid-servant stepped from behind the trunk, put up her plait, sighed, and went on her short, bare feet along the path. Pierre felt as if he had come back to life after a heavy swoon. He held his head higher, his eyes shone with the light of life, and with swift steps he followed the maid, overtook her and came out on the Povarskoy. The whole street was full of clouds of black smoke. Tongues of flame here and there broke through that cloud. A great number of people crowded in front of the conflagration. In the middle of the street stood a French general saying something to those around him. Pierre, accompanied by the maid, was advancing to the spot where the general stood, but the French soldiers stopped him.

'*On ne passe pas!*' cried a voice.

'This way, uncle,' cried the girl. 'We'll pass through the side street, by the Nikulins'!'

Pierre turned back, giving a spring now and then to keep up with her. She ran across the street, turned down a side street on the left and, passing three houses, turned into a yard on the right.

'It's here, close by,' said she, and running across the yard opened a gate in a wooden fence and, stopping, pointed out to him a small wooden wing of the house, which was burning brightly and fiercely. One of its sides had fallen in, another was on fire, and bright flames issued from the openings of the windows and from under the roof.

As Pierre passed through the fence gate he was enveloped by hot air, and involuntarily stopped.

'Which is it? Which is your house?' he asked.

'Ooh!' wailed the girl, pointing to the wing. 'That's it, that was our lodging. You've burnt to death, our treasure. Katie, my precious little missy! Ooh!' lamented Aniska, who at sight of the fire felt that she too must give expression to her feelings.

Pierre rushed to the wing, but the heat was so great that he involuntarily passed round in a curve and came upon the large house that was as yet burning only at one end, just below the roof, and around which swarmed a crowd of Frenchmen. At first Pierre did not realize what these men, who were dragging something out, were about; but seeing before him a Frenchman hitting a peasant with a blunt sabre and trying to take from him a fox-fur coat, he vaguely understood that looting was going on there, but he had no time to dwell on that idea.

The sounds of crackling and the din of falling walls and ceilings, the whistle and hiss of the flames, the excited shouts of the people and the sight of the swaying smoke, now gathering into thick black clouds and now soaring up with glittering sparks, with here and there dense sheaves of flame (now red and now like golden fish-scales creeping along the walls) and the heat and smoke and rapidity of motion, produced on Pierre the usual animating effects of a conflagration. It had a peculiarly strong effect on him because at sight of the fire he felt himself suddenly freed from the ideas that had weighed him down. He felt young, bright, adroit, and resolute. He ran around to the other side of the lodge and was about to dash into that part of it which was still standing, when just above his head he heard several voices shouting, and then a cracking sound and the ring of something heavy falling close beside him.

Pierre looked up and saw at a window of the large house some Frenchmen who had just thrown out the drawer of a chest, filled with metal articles. Other French soldiers standing below went up to the drawer.

'What does this fellow want?' shouted one of them, referring to Pierre.

'There's a child in that house. Haven't you seen a child?' cried Pierre.

'What's he talking about? Get along!' said several voices, and one of the soldiers, evidently afraid that Pierre might want to take from them some of the plate and bronzes that were in the drawer, moved threateningly towards him.

'A child?' shouted a Frenchman from above. 'I did hear something squealing in the garden. Perhaps it's his brat that the fellow is looking for. After all one must be human, you know . . .'

'Where is it? Where?' said Pierre.

'There! There! shouted the Frenchman at the window, pointing to the garden at the back of the house. 'Wait a bit – I'm coming down.'

And a minute or two later the Frenchman, a black-eyed fellow with a spot on his cheek, in shirt-sleeves, really did jump out of a window on the ground floor, and clapping Pierre on the shoulder ran with him into the garden.

'Hurry up, you others!' he called out to his comrades. 'It's getting hot.'

When they reached a gravel path behind the house the Frenchman pulled Pierre by the arm and pointed to a round, gravelled space where a three-year-old girl in a pink dress was lying under a seat.

'There is your child! Oh, a girl, so much the better!' said the Frenchman. 'Good-bye, Fatty. We must be human, we are all mortal you know!' and the Frenchman with the spot on his cheek ran back to his comrades.

Breathless with joy, Pierre ran to the little girl and was going to take her in his arms. But seeing a stranger the sickly, scrofulous-looking child, unattractively like her mother, began to yell and run away. Pierre however seized her and lifted her in his arms. She screamed desperately and angrily and tried with her little hands to pull Pierre's hands away, and to bite them with her slobbering mouth. Pierre was seized by a sense of horror and repulsion such as he had experienced when touching some nasty little animal. But he made an effort not to throw the child down, and ran with her to the large house. It was now however impossible to get back the way he had come; the maid, Aniska, was no longer there, and Pierre with a feeling of pity and disgust pressed the wet, painfully-sobbing child to himself as tenderly as he could and ran with her through the garden seeking another way out.

34

HAVING run through different yards and side streets, Pierre got back with his little burden to the Gruzinsky garden at the corner of the Povarskoy. He did not at first recognize the place from which he had set out to look for the child, so crowded was it now with people and goods that had been dragged out of the houses. Besides Russian families who had taken refuge here from the fire with their belongings, there were several French soldiers in a variety of clothing. Pierre took no notice of them. He hurried to find the family of that civil servant, in order to restore the daughter to her mother and go to save someone else. Pierre felt that he had still much to do and to do quickly. Glowing with the heat and from running, he felt at that moment more strongly than ever the sense of youth, animation, and determination that had come on him when he ran to save the child. She had now become quiet and, clinging with her little hands to Pierre's coat, sat on his arm gazing about her like some little wild animal. He glanced at her occasionally with a slight smile. He fancied he saw something pathetically innocent in that frightened sickly little face.

He did not find the civil servant or his wife where he had left them. He walked among the crowd with rapid steps scanning the various faces he met. Involuntarily he noticed a Georgian or Armenian family consisting of a very handsome old man of oriental type, wearing a new, cloth-covered, sheepskin coat and new boots, an old woman of similar type and a young woman. That very young woman seemed to Pierre the perfection of oriental beauty, with her sharply outlined, arched black eyebrows and the extraordinarily soft bright colour of her long, beautiful, expressionless face. Amid the scattered property and the crowd on the open space, she in her rich satin cloak with a bright lilac shawl on her head suggested a delicate exotic plant thrown out onto the snow. She was sitting on some bundles a little behind the old woman, and looked from under her long lashes with motionless, large, almond-shaped eyes at the ground before her. Evidently she was aware of her beauty and fearful because of it. Her face struck Pierre, and hurrying along by the fence he turned several times to look at her. When he had reached the fence, still without finding those he sought, he stopped and looked about him.

With the child in his arms his figure was now more conspicuous than before, and a group of Russians, both men and women, gathered about him.

'Have you lost anyone, my dear fellow? You're of the gentry yourself, aren't you? Whose child is it?' they asked him.

Pierre replied that the child belonged to a woman in a black cloak who had been sitting there with her other children, and he asked whether anyone knew where she had gone.

'Why, that must be the Anferovs,' said an old deacon, addressing a pock-marked peasant woman. 'Lord have mercy, Lord have mercy!' he added in his customary bass.

'The Anferovs? No,' said the woman. 'They left in the morning. That must be either Mary Nikolaevna's or the Ivanovs'!'

'He says "a woman", and Mary Nikolaevna is a lady,' remarked a house-serf.

'Do you know her? She's thin, with long teeth.' said Pierre.

'That's Mary Nikolaevna! They went inside the garden when these wolves swooped down,' said the woman pointing to the French soldiers.

'O Lord, have mercy!' added the deacon.

'Go over that way, they're there. It's she. She kept on lamenting and crying,' continued the woman. 'It's she. Here, this way!'

But Pierre was not listening to the woman. He had for some seconds been intently watching what was going on a few steps away. He was looking at the Armenian family and at two French soldiers who had gone up to them. One of these, a nimble little man, was wearing a blue coat tied round the waist with a rope. He had a nightcap on his head and his feet were bare. The other, whose appearance particularly struck Pierre, was a long, lank, round-shouldered, fair-haired man, slow in his movements and with an idiotic expression of face. He wore a woman's loose gown of frieze, blue trousers, and large torn Hessian boots. The little bare-footed Frenchman in the blue coat went up to the Armenians, and saying something, immediately seized the old man by his legs and the old man at once began pulling off his boots. The other, in the frieze gown, stopped in front of the beautiful Armenian girl and with his hands in his pockets stood staring at her, motionless and silent.

'Here, take the child!' said Pierre peremptorily and hurriedly to the woman, handing the little girl to her. 'Give her back to them, give her back!' he almost shouted, putting the child, who began screaming, on the ground, and again looking at the Frenchman and the Armenian family.

The old man was already sitting barefoot. The little Frenchman had secured his second boot and was slapping one boot against the other. The old man was saying something in a voice broken by sobs, but Pierre caught but a glimpse of this, his whole attention was directed to the Frenchman in the frieze gown who meanwhile, swaying slowly from side to side, had drawn nearer to the young woman and taking his hands from his pockets had seized her by the neck.

The beautiful Armenian still sat motionless and in the same attitude, with her long lashes drooping as if she did not see or feel what the soldier was doing to her.

While Pierre was running the few steps that separated him from the Frenchman, the tall marauder in the frieze gown was already tearing from her neck the necklace the young Armenian was wearing, and the young woman, clutching at her neck, screamed piercingly.

'Let that woman alone!' exclaimed Pierre hoarsely in a furious voice, seizing the soldier by his round shoulders and throwing him aside.

The soldier fell, got up, and ran away. But his comrade, throwing down the boots and drawing his sword, moved threateningly towards Pierre.

'Voyons, pas de bêtises!' he cried.

Pierre was in such a transport of rage that he remembered nothing and his strength increased tenfold. He rushed at the barefooted Frenchman and, before the latter had time to draw his sword, knocked him off his feet and hammered him with his fists. Shouts of approval were heard from the crowd around, and at the same moment a mounted patrol of French Uhlans appeared from round the corner. The Uhlans came up at a trot to Pierre and the Frenchman and surrounded them. Pierre remembered nothing of what happened after that. He only remembered beating someone and being beaten, and finally feeling that his hands were bound and that a crowd of French soldiers stood around him and were searching him.

'Lieutenant, he has a dagger,' were the first words Pierre understood.

'Ah, a weapon?' said the officer and turned to the bare-footed soldier who had been arrested with Pierre. 'All right, you can tell all about it at the court martial.' Then he turned to Pierre. 'Do you speak French?'

Pierre looked around him with bloodshot eyes and did not reply. His face probably looked very terrible, for the officer said something in a whisper and four more Uhlans left the ranks and placed themselves on both sides of Pierre.

'Do you speak French?' the officer asked again, keeping at a distance from Pierre. 'Call the interpreter.'

A little man in Russian civilian clothes rode out from the ranks, and by his clothes and manner of speaking Pierre at once knew him to be a French salesman from one of the Moscow shops.

'He does not look like a common man,' said the interpreter, after a searching look at Pierre.

'Ah, he looks very much like an incendiary,' remarked the officer. 'And ask him who he is,' he added.

'Who are you?' asked the interpreter in poor Russian. 'You must answer the chief.'

'I will not tell you who I am. I am your prisoner – take me!' Pierre suddenly replied in French.

'Ah, ah!' muttered the officer with a frown. 'Well then, march!'

A crowd had collected round the Uhlans. Nearest to Pierre stood the pock-marked peasant woman with the little girl, and when the patrol started she moved forward.

'Where are they talking you to, you poor dear?' said she. 'And the little girl, the little girl, what am I to do with her if she's not theirs?' said the woman.

'What does that woman want?' asked the officer.

Pierre was as if intoxicated. His elation increased at the sight of the little girl he had saved.

'What does she want?' he murmured. 'She is bringing me my daughter, whom I have just saved from the flames,' said he. 'Goodbye!' And without knowing how this aimless lie had escaped him, he went along with resolute and triumphant steps between the French soldiers.

The French patrol was one of those sent out through the various streets of Moscow by Durosnel's order to put a stop to the pillage, and especially to catch the incendiaries who, according to the general opinion which had that day originated among the higher French officers, were the cause of the conflagrations. After marching through a number of streets the patrol arrested five more Russian suspects: a small shopkeeper, two seminary students, a peasant, and a house-serf, besides several looters. But of all these various suspected characters, Pierre was considered to be the most suspicious of all. When they had all been brought for the night to a large house on the Zubov Rampart that was being used as a guardhouse, Pierre was placed apart under strict guard.

END OF BOOK THREE

WAR AND PEACE

*

BOOK FOUR

PART ONE

1

IN Petersburg at that time a complicated struggle was being carried on with greater heat than ever in the highest circles, between the parties of Rumyantsev, the French, Maria Fëdorovna, the Tsarevich, and others, drowned as usual by the buzzing of the Court drones. But the calm luxurious life of Petersburg, concerned only about phantoms and reflections of real life, went on in its old way, and made it hard, except by a great effort, to realize the danger and the difficult position of the Russian people. There were the same receptions and balls, the same French theatre, the same Court interests and service interests and intrigues as usual. Only in the very highest circles were attempts made to keep in mind the difficulties of the actual position. Stories were whispered of how differently the two Empresses* behaved in these difficult circumstances. The Empress Maria, concerned for the welfare of the charitable and educational institutions under her patronage, had given directions that they should all be removed to Kazan, and the things belonging to these institutions had already been packed up. The Empress Elisabeth, however, when asked what instructions she would be pleased to give – with her characteristic Russian patriotism had replied that she could give no directions about State institutions, for that was the affair of the Sovereign, but as far as she personally was concerned she would be the last to quit Petersburg.

At Anna Pavlovna's on the 26th of August, the very day of the battle of Borodino, there was a soirée, the chief feature of which was to be the reading of a letter from his Lordship the Bishop when sending the Emperor an icon of the Venerable Sergius. It was regarded as a model of ecclesiastical, patriotic eloquence. Prince Vasili himself, famed for his elocution, was to read it. (He used to read at the Empress's.) The art of his reading was supposed to lie in rolling out the words, quite independently of their meaning, in a loud and sing-song voice alternating between a despairing wail and a tender murmur, so that the wail fell quite at random on one word and the murmur on another. This reading, as was always the case at Anna Pavlovna's soirées, had a political significance. That evening she expected several important personages who had to be made ashamed of their visits to the French theatre and aroused to a patriotic temper. A good many people had already arrived, but Anna Pavlovna, not yet seeing all those whom she wanted in her drawing-room, did not let the reading begin but wound up the springs of a general conversation.

The news of the day in Petersburg was the illness of Countess Bezukhova. She had fallen ill unexpectedly a few days previously, had missed several gatherings of which she was usually the ornament, and was said to be receiving no one, and, instead of the celebrated Petersburg doctors who usually attended her, had entrusted herself to some Italian doctor who was treating her in some new and unusual way.

They all knew very well that the enchanting countess's illness arose from an inconvenience resulting from marrying two husbands at the same time, and that the Italian's cure consisted in removing such inconvenience; but in Anna Pavlovna's presence no one dared to think of this or even appear to know it.

'They say the poor countess is very ill. The doctor says it is angina pectoris.'

'Angina? Oh, that's a terrible illness!'

'They say that the rivals are reconciled, thanks to the angina . . .' and the word *angina* was repeated with great satisfaction.

'The old count is pathetic, they say. He cried like a child when the doctor told him the case was dangerous.'

'Oh, it would be a terrible loss, she is an enchanting woman.'

'You are speaking of the poor countess?' said Anna Pavlovna, coming up just then. 'I sent to ask for news, and hear that she is a little better. Oh, she is certainly the most charming woman in the world,' she went on, with a smile at her own enthusiasm. 'We belong to different camps, but that does not prevent my esteeming her as she deserves. She is very unfortunate!' added Anna Pavlovna.

Supposing that by these words Anna Pavlovna was somewhat lifting the veil from the secret of the countess's malady, an unwary young man ventured to express surprise that well-known doctors had not been called in and that the countess was being attended by a charlatan who might employ dangerous remedies.

'Your information may be better than mine,' Anna Pavlovna suddenly and venomously retorted on the inexperienced young man, 'but I know on good authority that this doctor is a very learned and able man. He is private physician to the Queen of Spain.'

And having thus demolished the young man, Anna Pavlovna

turned to another group where Bilibin was talking about the Austrians: having wrinkled up his face he was evidently preparing to smooth it out again and utter one of his *mots*.

'I think it is delightful,' he said, referring to a diplomatic note that had been sent to Vienna with some Austrian banners captured from the French by Wittgenstein,* 'the hero of Petropol' as he was then called in Petersburg.

'What? What's that?' asked Anna Pavlovna, securing silence for the *mot*, which she had heard before.

And Bilibin repeated the actual words of the diplomatic dispatch, which he had himself composed.

'The Emperor returns these Austrian banners,' said Bilibin, 'friendly banners gone astray and found on a wrong path,' and his brow became smooth again.

'Charming, charming!' observed Prince Vasili.

'The path to Warsaw, perhaps,' Prince Hippolyte remarked loudly and unexpectedly. Everybody looked at him, not understanding what he meant. Prince Hippolyte himself glanced around with amused surprise. He knew no more than the others what his words meant. During his diplomatic career he had more than once noticed that such sudden utterances were received as very witty, and at every opportunity he uttered in that way the first words that entered his head. 'It may turn out very well,' he thought, 'but if not, they'll know how to arrange matters.' And really, during the awkward silence that ensued, that insufficiently patriotic person entered whom Anna Pavlovna had been waiting for and wished to convert, and she, smiling and shaking a finger at Hippolyte, invited Prince Vasili to the table and bringing him two candles and the manuscript begged him to begin. Everyone became silent.

'Most Gracious Sovereign and Emperor!' Prince Vasili sternly declaimed, looking round at his audience as if to inquire whether anyone had anything to say to the contrary. But no one said anything. 'Moscow, our ancient Capital, the New Jerusalem, receives *her* Christ' – he placed a sudden emphasis on the word *her* – 'as a mother receives her zealous sons into her arms, and through the gathering mists, foreseeing the brilliant glory of thy rule, sings in exultation, "Hosanna, blessed is he that cometh!"'

Prince Vasili pronounced these last words in a tearful voice.

Bilibin attentively examined his nails, and many of those present appeared intimidated, as if asking in what they were to blame. Anna Pavlovna whispered the next words in advance, like an old woman muttering the prayer at Communion: 'Let the bold and insolent Goliath . . .' she whispered.

Prince Vasili continued.

'Let the bold and insolent Goliath from the borders of France encompass the realms of Russia with death-bearing terrors; humble Faith, the sling of the Russian David, shall suddenly smite his head in his bloodthirsty pride. This icon of the Venerable Sergius, the servant of God and zealous champion of old of our country's weal, is offered to your Imperial Majesty. I grieve that my waning strength prevents my rejoicing in the sight of your most gracious presence. I raise fervent prayers to Heaven that the Almighty may exalt the race of the just, and mercifully fulfil the desires of your Majesty.'

'What force! What a style!' was uttered in approval both of reader and of author.

Animated by that address Anna Pavlovna's guests talked for a long time of the state of the Fatherland, and offered various conjectures as to the result of the battle to be fought in a few days.

'You will see,' said Anna Pavlovna, 'that to-morrow, on the Emperor's birthday, we shall receive news. I have a favourable presentiment!'

2

ANNA PAVLOVNA'S presentiment was in fact fulfilled. Next day during the service at the Palace church in honour of the Emperor's birthday, Prince Volkonsky was called out of the church and received a dispatch from Prince Kutuzov. It was Kutuzov's report, written from Tatarinova* on the day of the battle. Kutuzov wrote that the Russians had not retreated a step, that the French losses were much heavier than ours, and that he was writing in haste from the field of battle before collecting full information. It followed that there must have been a victory. And at once, without leaving the church, thanks were rendered to the Creator for His help, and for the victory.

Anna Pavlovna's presentiment was justified, and all that morning a joyously festive mood reigned in the city. Everyone believed the victory to have been complete, and some even spoke of Napoleon's having been captured, of his deposition, and of the choice of a new ruler for France.

It is very difficult for events to be reflected in their real strength and completeness amid the conditions of Court life and far from the scene of action. General events involuntarily group themselves around some particular incident. So now the courtiers' pleasure was based as much on the fact that the news had arrived on the Emperor's birthday, as on the fact of the victory itself. It was like a successfully arranged surprise. Mention was made in Kutuzov's report of the Russian losses, among which figured the names of Tuchkov, Bagration, and Kutaysov. In the Petersburg world this sad side of the affair again involuntarily centred round a single incident: Kutaysov's death. Everybody knew him, the Emperor liked him, and he was young and interesting. That day everyone met with the words:

'What a wonderful coincidence! Just during the service. But what a loss Kutaysov is! How sorry I am!'

'What did I tell you about Kutuzov?' Prince Vasili now said with a prophet's pride. 'I always said he was the only man capable of defeating Napoleon.'

But next day no news arrived from the army and the public mood grew anxious. The courtiers suffered because of the suffering the suspense occasioned the Emperor.

'Fancy the Emperor's position!' said they, and instead of extolling Kutuzov as they had done the day before, they condemned him as the cause of the Emperor's anxiety. That day Prince Vasili no longer boasted of his protégé Kutuzov, but remained silent when the commander-in-chief was mentioned. Moreover towards the evening, as if everything conspired to make Petersburg society anxious and uneasy, a terrible piece of news was added. Countess Hélène Bezukhova had suddenly died of that terrible malady it had been so agreeable to mention. Officially, at large gatherings, everyone said that Countess Bezukhova had died of a terrible attack of angina pectoris, but in intimate circles details were mentioned of how the private physician of the Queen of Spain had prescribed small doses of a certain drug to produce a certain effect; but Hélène, tortured by the fact that the old count suspected her and that her husband to whom she had written (that wretched, profligate Pierre) had not replied, had suddenly taken a very large dose of the drug, and had died in agony before assistance could be rendered her. It was said that Prince Vasili and the old count had turned upon the Italian, but the latter had produced such letters from the unfortunate deceased that they had immediately let the matter drop.

Talk in general centred round three melancholy facts: the Emperor's lack of news, the loss of Kutaysov, and the death of Hélène.

On the third day after Kutuzov's report a country gentleman arrived from Moscow, and news of the surrender of Moscow to the French spread through the whole town. This was terrible! What a position for the Emperor to be in! Kutuzov was a traitor, and Prince Vasili, during the visits of condolence paid to him on the occasion of his daughter's death, said of Kutuzov whom he had formerly praised (it was excusable for him in his grief to forget what he had said) that it was impossible to expect anything else from a blind and depraved old man.

'I only wonder that the fate of Russia could have been entrusted to such a man.'

As long as this news remained unofficial it was possible to doubt it, but the next day the following communication was received from Count Rostopchin:

'Prince Kutuzov's adjutant has brought me a letter in which he demands police-officers to guide the army to the Ryazan road. He writes that he is regretfully abandoning Moscow. Sire! Kutuzov's action decides the fate of the capital and of your empire! Russia will shudder to learn of the abandonment of the city in which her greatness is centred, and in which lie the ashes of your ancestors! I shall follow the army. I have had everything removed, and it only remains for me to weep over the fate of my fatherland.'

On receiving this dispatch the Emperor sent Prince Volkonsky to Kutuzov with the following rescript:

'Prince Michael Ilarionovich! Since the 29th of August I have received no communication from you, yet on the 1st of September I received from the commander-in-chief of Moscow, via Yaroslavl, the sad news that you, with the army, have decided to abandon Moscow. You can yourself imagine the effect this news has had on me, and your silence increases my astonishment. I am sending this by Adjutant-General Prince Volkonsky, to hear from you the situation of the army and the reasons that have induced you to take this melancholy decision.'

3

NINE days after the abandonment of Moscow, a messenger from Kutuzov reached Petersburg with the official announcement of that event. This messenger was Michaud, a Frenchman who did not know Russian, but who was *quoique étranger, russe de cœur et d'âme*, as he said of himself.

The Emperor at once received this messenger in his study at the palace on Stone Island. Michaud, who had never seen Moscow before the campaign and who did not know Russian, yet felt deeply moved (as he wrote) when he appeared before *notre très gracieux souverain* with the news of the burning of Moscow, *dont les flammes éclairaient sa route.*

Though the source of M. Michaud's chagrin must have been different from that which caused Russians to grieve, he had such a sad face when shown into the Emperor's study that the latter at once asked:

'Have you brought me sad news, Colonel?'

'Very sad, Sire,' replied Michaud, lowering his eyes with a sigh. 'The abandonment of Moscow.'

'Have they surrendered my ancient capital without a battle?' asked the Emperor quickly, his face suddenly flushing.

Michaud respectfully delivered the message Kutuzov had entrusted to him, which was that it had been impossible to fight before Moscow, and that as the only remaining choice was between losing the army as well as Moscow, or losing Moscow alone, the field-marshal had to choose the latter.

The Emperor listened in silence not looking at Michaud.

'Has the enemy entered the city?' he asked.

'Yes, Sire, and Moscow is now in ashes. I left it all in flames,' replied Michaud in a decided tone, but glancing at the Emperor he was frightened by what he had done.

The Emperor began to breathe heavily and rapidly, his lower lip trembled and tears instantly appeared in his fine blue eyes.

But this lasted only a moment. He suddenly frowned, as if blaming himself for his weakness, and raising his head addressed Michaud in a firm voice:

'I see, Colonel, from all that is happening, that Providence requires great sacrifices of us ... I am ready to submit myself in all things to His will; but tell me, Michaud, how did you leave the army when it saw my ancient capital abandoned without a battle? Did you not notice discouragement? ...'

Seeing that his most gracious ruler was calm once more, Michaud also grew calm, but was not immediately ready to reply to the Emperor's direct and relevant question which required a direct answer.

'Sire, will you allow me to speak frankly as befits a loyal soldier?' he asked to gain time.

'Colonel, I always require it,' replied the Emperor. 'Conceal nothing from me, I wish to know absolutely how things are.'

'Sire!' said Michaud with a subtle, scarcely perceptible smile on his lips, having now prepared a well-phrased reply, 'Sire I left the whole army, from its chiefs to the lowest soldier, without exception in desperate and agonized terror ...'

'How is that?' the Emperor interrupted him, frowning sternly. 'Would misfortune make my Russians lose heart? ... Never.'

Michaud had only waited for this to bring out the phrase he had prepared.

'Sire,' he said with respectful playfulness, 'they are only afraid lest your Majesty, in the goodness of your heart, should allow yourself to be persuaded to make peace. They are burning for the combat,' declared this representative of the Russian nation, 'and to prove to your Majesty by the sacrifice of their lives how devoted they are . . .'

'Ah!' said the Emperor reassured, and with a kindly gleam in his eyes he patted Michaud on the shoulder. 'You set me at ease, Colonel.'

He bent his head and was silent for some time.

'Well then, go back to the army,' he said drawing himself up to his full height and addressing Michaud with a gracious and majestic gesture, 'and tell our brave men and all my good subjects wherever you go, that when I have not a soldier left, I shall put myself at the head of my beloved nobility and my good peasants and so use the last resources of my empire. It still offers me more than my enemies suppose,' said the Emperor growing more and more animated; 'but should it ever be ordained by Divine Providence,' he continued, raising to heaven his fine eyes shining with emotion, 'that my dynasty should cease to reign on the throne of my ancestors, then after exhausting all the means at my command, I shall let my beard grow to here' (he pointed half-way down his chest) 'and go and eat potatoes with the meanest of my peasants, rather than sign the disgrace of my country and of my beloved people whose sacrifices I know how to appreciate.'

Having uttered these words in an agitated voice the Emperor suddenly turned away, as if to hide from Michaud the tears that rose to his eyes, and went to the further end of his study. Having stood there a few moments, he strode back to Michaud and pressed his arm below the elbow with a vigorous movement. The Emperor's mild and handsome face was flushed and his eyes gleamed with resolution and anger.

'Colonel Michaud, do not forget what I say to you here, perhaps we may recall it with pleasure some day . . . Napoleon or I,' said the Emperor, touching his breast. 'We can no longer both reign together. I have learnt to know him, and he will not deceive me any more . . .'

And the Emperor paused, with a frown.

When he heard these words and saw the expression of firm resolution in the Emperor's eyes, Michaud – *quoique étranger, russe de cœur et d'âme* – at that solemn moment felt himself enraptured by all that he had heard (as he used afterwards to say), and gave expression to his own feelings and those of the Russian people whose representative he considered himself to be, in the following words:

'Sire!' said he, 'your Majesty is at this moment signing the glory of the nation and the salvation of Europe!'

With an inclination of the head the Emperor dismissed him.

4

IT is natural for us who were not living in those days to imagine that when half Russia had been conquered and the inhabitants were fleeing to distant provinces, and one levy after another was being raised for the defence of the fatherland, all Russians from the greatest to the least were solely engaged in sacrificing themselves, saving their fatherland, or weeping over its downfall. The tales and descriptions of that time without exception speak only of the self-sacrifice, patriotic devotion, despair, grief, and the heroism of the Russians. But it was not really so. It appears so to us because we see only the general historic interest of that time and do not see all the personal human interests that people had. Yet in reality those personal interests of the moment so much transcend the general interests, that they always prevent the public interest from being felt or even noticed. Most of the people at that time paid no attention to the general progress of events but were guided only by their private interests, and they were the very people whose activities at that period were most useful.

Those who tried to understand the general course of events, and to take part in it by self-sacrifice and heroism, were the most useless members of society, they saw everything upside down, and all they did for the common good turned out to be useless and foolish – like Pierre's and Mamonov's regiments which looted Russian villages, and the lint the young ladies prepared and that never reached the wounded, and so on. Even those, fond of intellectual talk and of expressing their feelings, who discussed Russia's position at the time, involuntarily introduced into their conversation either a shade of pretence and falsehood, or useless condemnation and anger directed against people accused of actions no one could possibly be guilty of. In historic events the rule forbidding us to eat of the fruit of the Tree of Knowledge is specially applicable. Only unconscious action bears fruit, and he who plays a part in an historic event never understands its significance. If he tries to realize it his efforts are fruitless.

The more closely a man was engaged in the events then taking place in Russia the less did he realize their significance. In Petersburg and in the provinces at a distance from Moscow, ladies, and gentlemen in militia uniforms, wept for Russia and its ancient capital and talked of self-sacrifice and so on; but in the army which retired beyond Moscow there was little talk or thought of Moscow, and when they caught sight of its burnt ruins no one swore to be avenged on the French, but they thought about the term's pay, their next quarters, of Matrëshka the vivandière, and like matters.

As the war had caught him in the service, Nicholas Rostov took a close and prolonged part in the defence of his country, but did so casually, without any aim at self-sacrifice, and he therefore looked at what was going on in Russia without despair and without dismally racking his brains over it. Had he been asked what he thought of the state of Russia, he would have said that it was not his business to think about it, that Kutuzov and others were there for that purpose, but that he had heard that the regiments were to be made up to their full strength, that fighting would probably go on for a long time yet, and that things being so, it was quite likely he might be in command of a regiment in a couple of years' time.

As he looked at the matter in this way he learnt that he was being sent to Voronezh to buy remounts for his division, not only without regret at being prevented from taking part in the coming battle, but with the greatest pleasure – which he did not conceal and which his comrades fully understood.

A few days before the battle of Borodino Nicholas received the necessary money and warrants, and having sent some hussars on in advance, he set out with post-horses for Voronezh.

Only a man who has experienced it – that is, has passed some months continuously in an atmosphere of campaigning and war – can understand the delight Nicholas felt when he escaped from the region covered by the army's foraging operations, provision-trains, and hospitals. When – free from soldiers, wagons, and the filthy traces of a camp – he saw villages with peasants and peasant-women, gentlemen's country houses, fields where cattle were grazing, post-houses with station-masters asleep in them, he rejoiced as though seeing all this for the first time. What for a long while specially surprised and delighted him were the women, young and healthy, without a dozen officers making up to each of them; women, too, who were pleased and flattered that a passing officer should joke with them.

In the highest spirits Nicholas arrived at night at an hotel in Voronezh, ordered things he had long been deprived of in camp, and next day, very clean-shaven and in a full-dress uniform he had not worn for a long time, went to present himself to the authorities.

The commander of the militia was a civilian general, an old

man who was evidently pleased with his military designation and rank. He received Nicholas brusquely (imagining this to be characteristically military) and questioned him with an important air, as if considering the general progress of affairs and approving and disapproving with full right to do so. Nicholas was in such good spirits that this merely amused him.

From the commander of the militia he drove to the governor. The governor was a brisk little man, very simple and affable. He indicated the stud-farms at which Nicholas might procure horses, recommended to him a horse-dealer in the town and a landowner fourteen miles out of town who had the best horses, and promised to assist him in every way.

'You are Count Ilya Rostov's son? My wife was a great friend of your mother's. We are at home on Thursdays – to-day is Thursday, so please come and see us quite informally,' said the governor, taking leave of him.

Immediately on leaving the governor's Nicholas hired post-horses, and taking his squadron quartermaster with him, drove at a gallop to the landowner fourteen miles away who had the stud. Everything seemed to him pleasant and easy during the first part of his stay in Voronezh, and as usually happens when a man is in a pleasant state of mind, everything went well and easily.

The landowner to whom Nicholas went was a bachelor, an old cavalry man, a horse-fancier, a sportsman, the possessor of some century-old brandy and some old Hungarian wine, who had a snuggery where he smoked, and who owned some splendid horses.

In very few words Nicholas bought seventeen picked stallions for six thousand roubles – to serve as he said as samples of his remounts. After dining and taking rather too much of the Hungarian wine, Nicholas – having exchanged kisses with the landowner, with whom he was already on the friendliest terms – galloped back over abominable roads, in the brightest frame of mind, continually urging on the driver so as to be in time for the governor's party.

When he had changed, poured water over his head, and scented himself, Nicholas arrived at the governor's rather late, but with the phrase 'better late than never' on his lips.

It was not a ball, nor had dancing been announced, but everyone knew that Catherine Petrovna would play valses and the écossaise on the clavichord and that there would be dancing, and so everyone had come as to a ball.

Provincial life in 1812 went on very much as usual, but with this difference, that it was livelier in the towns in consequence of the arrival of many wealthy families from Moscow, and as in everything that went on in Russia at that time, a special recklessness was noticeable, an 'in for a penny, in for a pound – who cares?' spirit, and the inevitable small talk, instead of turning on the weather and mutual acquaintances, now turned on Moscow, the army, and Napoleon.

The society gathered together at the governor's was the best in Voronezh.

There were a great many ladies and some of Nicholas's Moscow acquaintances, but there were no men who could at all vie with the cavalier of St George, the hussar remount-officer, the good-natured and well-bred Count Rostov. Among the men was an Italian prisoner, an officer of the French army; and Nicholas felt that the presence of that prisoner enhanced his own importance as a Russian hero. The Italian was, as it were, a war trophy. Nicholas felt this, it seemed to him that everyone regarded the Italian in the same light, and he treated him cordially though with dignity and restraint.

As soon as Nicholas entered in his hussar uniform, diffusing around him a fragrance of perfume and wine, and had uttered the words 'better late than never' and heard them repeated several times by others, people clustered around him; all eyes turned on him, and he felt at once that he had entered into his proper position in the province – that of a universal favourite: a very pleasant position, and intoxicatingly so after his long privations. At posting-stations, at inns, and in the landowner's snuggery, maid-servants had been flattered by his notice, and here too at the governor's party there were (as it seemed to Nicholas) an inexhaustible number of pretty young women, married and unmarried, impatiently awaiting his notice. The women and girls flirted with him and, from the first day, the old people concerned themselves to get this fine young dare-devil of an hussar married and settled down. Among these was the governor's wife herself, who welcomed Rostov as a near relative and called him 'Nicholas'.

Catherine Petrovna did actually play valses and the écossaise, and dancing began in which Nicholas still further captivated the provincial society by his agility. His particularly free manner of dancing even surprised them all. Nicholas was himself rather surprised at the way he danced that evening. He had never danced like that in Moscow and would even have considered such a very free and easy manner improper and in bad form, but here he felt it incumbent on him to astonish them all by something unusual, something they would have to accept as the regular thing in the capital though new to them in the provinces.

All the evening Nicholas paid attention to a blue-eyed, plump, and pleasing little blonde, the wife of one of the provincial officials.

With the naïve conviction of young men in a merry mood that other men's wives were created for them, Rostov did not leave the lady's side and treated her husband in a friendly and conspiratorial style, as if, without speaking of it, they knew how capitally Nicholas and the lady would get on together. The husband however did not seem to share that conviction and tried to behave morosely with Rostov. But the latter's good-natured naïveté was so boundless that sometimes even he involuntarily yielded to Nicholas's good-humour. Towards the end of the evening, however, as the wife's face grew more flushed and animated the husband's became more and more melancholy and solemn, as though there were but a given amount of animation between them and as the wife's share increased the husband's diminished.

5

NICHOLAS sat leaning slightly forward in an arm-chair, bending closely over the blonde lady and paying her mythological compliments with a smile that never left his face.

Jauntily shifting the position of his legs in their tight riding-breeches, diffusing an odour of perfume, and admiring his partner, himself, and the fine outlines of his legs in their well-fitting Hessian boots, Nicholas told the blonde lady that he wished to run away with a certain lady here in Voronezh.

'Which lady?'

'A charming lady, a divine one. Her eyes' (Nicholas looked at his partner) 'are blue, her mouth coral and ivory; her figure' (he glanced at her shoulders) 'like Diana's . . .'

The husband came up and sullenly asked his wife what she was talking about.

'Ah, Nikita Ivanych!' cried Nicholas, rising politely, and as if wishing Nikita Ivanych to share his joke he began to tell him of his intention to elope with a blonde lady.

The husband smiled gloomily, the wife gaily. The governor's good-natured wife came up with a look of disapproval.

'Anna Ignatyevna wants to see you, Nicholas,' said she, pronouncing the name so that Nicholas at once understood that Anna Ignatyevna was a very important person. 'Come, Nicholas! You know you let me call you so?'

'Oh, yes, aunt. Who is she?'

'Anna Ignatyevna Malvintseva. She has heard from her niece how you rescued her . . . Can you guess?'

'I rescued such a lot of them!' said Nicholas.

'Her niece, Princess Bolkonskaya. She is here in Voronezh with her aunt. Oho! How you blush. Why, are ... ?'

'Not a bit! Please don't, aunt!'

'Very well, very well! ... Oh, what a fellow you are!'

The governor's wife led him up to a tall and very stout old lady with a blue head-dress, who had just finished her game of cards with the most important personages of the town. This was Malvintseva, Princess Mary's aunt on her mother's side, a rich childless widow who always lived in Voronezh. When Rostov approached her she was standing settling up for the game. She looked at him, and screwing her eyes up sternly, continued to upbraid the general who had won from her.

'Very pleased, *mon cher*,' she then said, holding out her hand to Nicholas. 'Pray come and see me.'

After a few words about Princess Mary and her late father, whom Malvintseva had evidently not liked, and having asked what Nicholas knew of Prince Andrew, who also was evidently no favourite of hers, the important old lady dismissed Nicholas after repeating her invitation to come to see her.

Nicholas promised to come and blushed again as he bowed. At the mention of Princess Mary he experienced a feeling of shyness and even of fear, which he himself did not understand.

When he had parted from Malvintseva Nicholas wished to return to the dancing, but the governor's little wife placed her plump hand on his sleeve and, saying that she wanted to have a talk with him, led him to her sitting-room, from which those who were there immediately withdrew so as not to be in her way.

'Do you know, dear boy,' began the governor's wife with a serious expression on her kind little face, 'that really would be the match for you: would you like me to arrange it?'

'Whom do you mean, aunt?' asked Nicholas.

'I will make a match for you with the princess. Catherine Petrovna speaks of Lily, but I say, no – the princess! Do you want me to do it? I am sure your mother will be grateful to me. What a charming girl she is, really! And she is not at all so plain, either.'

'Not at all,' replied Nicholas as if offended at the idea. 'As befits a soldier, aunt, I don't force myself on anyone nor refuse anything,' he said before he had time to consider what he was saying.

'Well then, remember, this is not a joke!'

'Of course not!'

'Yes, yes,' the governor's wife said as if talking to herself. 'But, my dear boy, among other things you are too attentive to the other, the blonde. One is sorry for the husband, really ...'

'Oh no, we are good friends with him,' said Nicholas in the

simplicity of his heart: it did not enter his head that a pastime so pleasant to himself might not be pleasant to anyone else.

'But what nonsense I have been saying to the governor's wife!' thought Nicholas suddenly at supper. 'She will really begin to arrange a match...and Sonya...?' And on taking leave of the governor's wife, when she again smilingly said to him, 'Well then, remember!' he drew her aside.

'But see here, to tell you the truth, aunt...'

'What is it, my dear? Come, let's sit down here,' said she.

Nicholas suddenly felt a desire and need to tell his most intimate thoughts (which he would not have told to his mother, his sister, or his friend) to this woman who was almost a stranger. When he afterwards recalled that impulse to unsolicited and inexplicable frankness, which had very important results for him, it seemed to him – as it seems to everyone in such cases – that it was merely some silly whim that seized him: yet that burst of frankness, together with other trifling events, had immense consequences for him and for all his family.

'You see, aunt, mamma has long wanted me to marry an heiress, but the very idea of marrying for money is repugnant to me.'

'Oh yes, I understand,' said the governor's wife.

'But Princess Bolkonskaya – that's another matter. I will tell you the truth. In the first place, I like her very much, I feel drawn to her; and then, after I met her under such circumstances – so strangely, the idea often occurred to me: "This is fate". Especially if you remember that mamma had long been thinking of it; but I had never happened to meet her before, somehow it had always happened that we did not meet. And as long as my sister Natasha was engaged to her brother it was of course out of the question for me to think of marrying her. And it must needs happen that I should meet her just when Natasha's engagement had been broken off...and then everything...So you see...I never told this to anyone and never will, only to you.'

The governor's wife pressed his elbow gratefully.

'You know Sonya, my cousin? I love her, and promised to marry her, and will do so...So you see there can be no question about—' said Nicholas incoherently and blushing.

'My dear boy, what a way to look at it! You know Sonya has nothing, and you yourself say your papa's affairs are in a very bad way. And what about your mother? It would kill her, that's one thing. And what sort of a life would it be for Sonya – if she's a girl with a heart? Your mother in despair, and you all ruined... No, my dear, you and Sonya ought to understand that.'

Nicholas remained silent. It comforted him to hear these arguments.

'All the same, aunt, it is impossible,' he rejoined with a sigh, after a short pause. 'Besides, would the princess have me? And besides, she is now in mourning. How can one think of it!'

'But you don't suppose I'm going to get you married at once? There is always a right way of doing things,' replied the governor's wife.

'What a matchmaker you are, aunt...' said Nicholas, kissing her plump little hand.

6

ON reaching Moscow after her meeting with Rostov Princess Mary had found her nephew there with his tutor, and a letter from Prince Andrew giving her instructions how to get to her Aunt Malvintseva at Voronezh. That feeling akin to temptation which had tormented her during her father's illness, since his death, and especially since her meeting with Rostov, was smothered by arrangements for the journey, anxiety about her brother, settling in a new house, meeting new people, and attending to her nephew's education. She was sad. Now, after a month passed in quiet surroundings, she felt more and more deeply the loss of her father which was associated in her mind with the ruin of Russia. She was agitated and incessantly tortured by the thought of the dangers to which her brother, the only intimate person now remaining to her, was exposed. She was worried too about her nephew's education for which she had always felt herself incompetent, but in the depths of her soul she felt at peace – a peace arising from consciousness of having stifled those personal dreams and hopes that had been on the point of awakening within her and were related to her meeting with Rostov.

The day after her party the governor's wife came to see Malvintseva and, after discussing her plan with the aunt, remarked that though under present circumstances a formal betrothal was, of course, not to be thought of, all the same the young people might be brought together and could get to know one another. Malvintseva expressed approval, and the governor's wife began to speak of Rostov in Mary's presence, praising him and telling how he had blushed when Princess Mary's name was mentioned. But Princess Mary experienced a painful rather than a joyful feeling – her mental tranquillity was destroyed, and desires, doubts, self-reproach and hopes re-awoke.

During the two days that elapsed before Rostov called, Princess Mary continually thought of how she ought to behave to him. First she decided not to come to the drawing-room when he called to see her aunt – that it would not be proper for her, in her deep mourning, to receive visitors; then she thought this would be rude, after what he had done for her; then it occurred to her that her aunt and the governor's wife had intentions concerning herself and Rostov — their looks and words at times seemed to confirm this supposition – then she told herself that only she, with her sinful nature, could think this of them: they could not forget that situated as she was, while still wearing deep mourning, such match-making would be an insult to her and to her father's memory. Assuming that she did go down to see him, Princess Mary imagined the words he would say to her and what she would say to him, and these words sometimes seemed undeservedly cold, and then to mean too much. More than anything she feared lest the confusion she felt might overwhelm her and betray her as soon as she saw him.

But when on Sunday after church the footman announced in the drawing-room that Count Rostov had called, the princess showed no confusion, only a slight blush suffused her cheeks and her eyes lit up with a new and radiant light.

'You have met him, aunt?' said she in a calm voice, unable herself to understand that she could be outwardly so calm and natural.

When Rostov entered the room the princess dropped her eyes for an instant, as if to give the visitor time to greet her aunt, and then just as Nicholas turned to her she raised her head and met his look with shining eyes. With a movement full of dignity and grace she half rose with a smile of pleasure, held out her slender delicate hand to him, and began to speak in a voice in which for the first time new deep womanly notes vibrated. Mademoiselle Bourienne, who was in the drawing-room, looked at Princess Mary in bewildered surprise. Herself a consummate coquette, she could not have manœuvred better on meeting a man she wished to attract.

'Either black is particularly becoming to her or she really has greatly improved without my having noticed it. And above all, what tact and grace!' thought Mademoiselle Bourienne.

Had Princess Mary been capable of reflexion at that moment, she would have been more surprised than Mademoiselle Bourienne at the change that had taken place in herself. From the moment she recognized that dear, loved face, a new life-force took possession of her and compelled her to speak and act apart from her own will.

From the time Rostov entered, her face became suddenly transformed. It was as if a light had been kindled in a carved and painted lantern and the intricate, skilful, artistic work on its sides, that previously seemed dark, coarse, and meaningless, was suddenly shown up in unexpected and striking beauty. For the first time all that pure, spiritual, inward travail through which she had lived appeared on the surface. All her inward labour, her dissatisfaction with herself, her sufferings, her strivings after goodness, her meekness, love, and self-sacrifice – all this now shone in those radiant eyes, in her delicate smile, and in every trait of her gentle face.

Rostov saw all this as clearly as if he had known her whole life. He felt that the being before him was quite different from, and better than, anyone he had met before, and above all better than himself.

Their conversation was very simple and unimportant. They spoke of the war, and like everyone else unconsciously exaggerated their sorrow about it; they spoke of their last meeting – Nicholas trying to change the subject – they talked of the governor's kind wife, of Nicholas's relations, and of Princess Mary's.

She did not talk about her brother, diverting the conversation as soon as her aunt mentioned Andrew. Evidently she could speak of Russia's misfortunes with a certain artificiality, but her brother was too near her heart and she neither could nor would speak lightly of him. Nicholas noticed this, as he noticed every shade of Princess Mary's character with an observation unusual to him, and everything confirmed his conviction that she was a quite unusual and extraordinary being. Nicholas blushed and was confused when people spoke to him about the princess (as she did when he was mentioned) and even when he thought of her, but in her presence he felt quite at ease, and said not at all what he had prepared, but what, quite appropriately, occurred to him at the moment.

When a pause occurred during his short visit, Nicholas, as is usual when there are children, turned to Prince Andrew's little son, caressing him and asking whether he would like to be an hussar. He took the boy on his knee, played with him, and looked round at Princess Mary. With a softened, happy, and timid look she watched the boy she loved in the arms of the man she loved. Nicholas also noticed that look and, as if understanding it, flushed with pleasure and began to kiss the boy with good-natured playfulness.

As she was in mourning, Princess Mary did not go out into society, and Nicholas did not think it the proper thing to visit her again; but all the same the governor's wife went on with her matchmaking, passing on to Nicholas the flattering things Princess Mary said of him and vice versa, and insisting on his declaring himself to Princess Mary. For this purpose she arranged a meeting between the young people at the bishop's house before Mass.

Though Rostov told the governor's wife that he would not make any declaration to Princess Mary, he promised to go.

As at Tilsit Rostov had not allowed himself to doubt that what everybody considered right was right, so now, after a short but sincere struggle between his efforts to arrange his life by his own sense of justice, and in obedient submission to circumstances, he chose the latter and yielded to the power he felt irresistibly carrying him he knew not where. He knew that after his promise to Sonya, it would be what he deemed base to declare his feelings to Princess Mary. And he knew that he would never act basely. But he also knew (or rather felt at the bottom of his heart) that by resigning himself now to the force of circumstances and to those who were guiding him, he was not only doing nothing wrong, but was doing something very very important – more important than anything he had ever done in his life.

After meeting Princess Mary, though the course of his life went on externally as before, all his former amusements lost their charm for him and he often thought about her. But he never thought about her as he had thought of all the young ladies without exception whom he had met in society, nor as he had for a long time, and at one time rapturously, thought about Sonya. He had pictured each of those young ladies as almost all honest-hearted young men do, that is, as a possible wife, adapting her in his imagination to all the conditions of married life: a white dressing-gown, his wife at the tea-table, his wife's carriage, little ones, mamma and papa, their relations to her and so on – and these pictures of the future had given him pleasure. But with Princess Mary, to whom they were trying to get him engaged, he could never picture anything of future married life. If he tried, his pictures seemed incongruous and false. It made him afraid.

7

THE dreadful news of the battle of Borodino, of our losses in killed and wounded, and the still more terrible news of the loss of Moscow, reached Voronezh in the middle of September.* Princess Mary having learnt of her brother's wound only from the Gazette and having no definite news of him, prepared (so Nicholas heard, he had not seen her again himself) to set off in search of Prince Andrew.

When he received the news of the battle of Borodino and the abandonment of Moscow, Rostov was not seized with despair, anger, the desire for vengeance, or any feeling of that kind, but everything in Voronezh suddenly seemed to him dull and tiresome, and he experienced an indefinite feeling of shame and awkwardness. The conversations he heard seemed to him insincere; he did not know how to judge all these affairs and felt that only in the regiment would everything again become clear to him. He made haste to finish buying the horses, and often became unreasonably angry with his servant and squadron quartermaster.

A few days before his departure a special thanksgiving, at which Nicholas was present, was held in the cathedral for the Russian victory. He stood a little behind the governor, and held himself with military decorum through the service, meditating on a great variety of subjects. When the service was over the governor's wife beckoned him to her.

'Have you seen the princess?' she asked, indicating with a movement of her head a lady standing on the opposite side, beyond the choir.

Nicholas immediately recognized Princess Mary not so much by the profile he saw under her bonnet as by the feeling of solicitude, timidity, and pity, that immediately overcame him. Princess Mary, evidently engrossed by her thoughts, was crossing herself for the last time before leaving the church.

Nicholas looked at her face with surprise. It was the same face he had seen before, there was the same general expression of refined, inner, spiritual labour, but now it was quite differently lit up. There was a pathetic expression of sorrow, prayer, and hope in it. As had occurred before when she was present, Nicholas went up to her without waiting to be prompted by the governor's wife and not asking himself whether or not it was right and proper to address her here in church, and told her he had heard of her trouble and sympathized with his whole soul. As soon as she heard his voice a vivid glow kindled in her face, lighting up both her sorrow and her joy.

'There is one thing I wanted to tell you, Princess,' said Rostov. 'It is that if your brother, Prince Andrew Nikolaevich, were not living, it would have been at once announced in the Gazette, as he is a colonel.'

The princess looked at him, not grasping what he was saying, but cheered by the expression of regretful sympathy on his face.

'And I have known so many cases of a splinter-wound' (the

Gazette said it was a shell) 'either proving fatal at once, or being very slight,' continued Nicholas. 'We must hope for the best, and I am sure...'

Princess Mary interrupted him.

'Oh, that would be so dread...' she began and, prevented by agitation from finishing, she bent her head with a movement as graceful as everything she did in his presence and looking up at him gratefully, went out, following her aunt.

That evening Nicholas did not go out, but stayed at home to settle some accounts with the horsedealers. When he had finished that business it was already too late to go anywhere but still too early to go to bed, and for a long time he paced up and down the room reflecting on his life, a thing he rarely did.

Princess Mary had made an agreeable impression on him when he had met her in Smolensk Province. His having encountered her in such exceptional circumstances, and his mother's having at one time mentioned her to him as a good match, had drawn his particular attention to her. When he met her again in Voronezh the impression she made on him was not merely pleasing but powerful. Nicholas had been struck by the peculiar moral beauty he observed in her at this time. He was however preparing to go away and it had not entered his head to regret that he was thus depriving himself of chances of meeting her. But that day's encounter in church had, he felt, sunk deeper than was desirable for his peace of mind. That pale, sad, refined face, that radiant look, those gentle graceful gestures, and especially the deep and tender sorrow expressed in all her features, agitated him and evoked his sympathy. In men Rostov could not bear to see the expression of a higher spiritual life (that was why he did not like Prince Andrew) and he referred to it contemptuously as philosophy and dreaminess, but in Princess Mary that very sorrow which revealed the depth of a whole spiritual world foreign to him, was an irresistible attraction.

'She must be a wonderful woman. A real angel!' he said to himself. 'Why am I not free? Why was I in such a hurry with Sonya?' And he involuntarily compared the two: the lack of spirituality in the one and the abundance of it in the other – a spirituality he himself lacked and therefore valued most highly. He tried to picture what would happen were he free. How he would propose to her and how she would become his wife. But no, he could not imagine that. He felt awed, and no clear picture presented itself to his mind. He had long ago pictured to himself a future with Sonya, and that was all clear and simple just because it had all been thought out and he knew all there was in Sonya, but it was impossible to picture a future with Princess Mary, because he did not understand her but simply loved her.

Reveries about Sonya had had something merry and playful in them, but to dream of Princess Mary was always difficult and a little frightening.

'How she prayed!' he thought. 'It was plain that her whole soul was in her prayer. Yes, that was the prayer that moves mountains, and I am sure her prayer will be answered. Why don't I pray for what I want?' he suddenly thought. 'What do I want? To be free, released from Sonya ... She was right', he thought, remembering what the governor's wife had said: 'Nothing but misfortune can come of marrying Sonya. Muddles, grief for mamma ... business difficulties ... muddles, terrible muddles! Besides, I don't love her – not as I should. O God! release me from this dreadful, inextricable position!' he suddenly began to pray. 'Yes, prayer can move mountains, but one must have faith and not pray as Natasha and I used to as children, that the snow might turn into sugar – and then run out into the yard to see whether it had done so. No, but I am not praying for trifles now,' he thought as he put his pipe down in a corner, and, folding his hands, placed himself before the icon. Softened by memories of Princess Mary he began to pray as he had not done for a long time. Tears were in his eyes and in his throat when the door opened and Lavrushka came in with some papers.

'Blockhead! Why do you come in without being called?' cried Nicholas, quickly changing his attitude.

'From the governor,' said Lavrushka in a sleepy voice. 'A courier has arrived and there's a letter for you.'

'Well, all right, thanks. You can go!'

Nicholas took the two letters, one of which was from his mother and the other from Sonya. He recognized them by the handwriting and opened Sonya's first. He had only read a few lines when he turned pale and his eyes opened wide with fear and joy.

'No, it's not possible!' he cried aloud.

Unable to sit still he paced up and down the room holding the letter and reading it. He glanced through it, then read it again, and then again, and standing still in the middle of the room he raised his shoulders, stretching out his hands with his mouth wide open and his eyes fixed. What he had just been praying for with confidence that God would hear him had come to pass;* but Nicholas was as much astonished as if it were something extraordinary and unexpected, and as if the very fact that it had happened so quickly proved that it had not come from God to whom he had prayed, but by some ordinary coincidence.

This unexpected and as it seemed to Nicholas quite voluntary letter from Sonya, freed him from the knot that fettered him and from which there had seemed no escape. She wrote that the last unfortunate events – the loss of almost the whole of the Rostovs' Moscow property – and the countess's repeatedly expressed wish that Nicholas should marry Princess Bolkonskaya, together with his silence and coldness of late, had all combined to make her decide to release him from his promise and set him completely free.

'It would be too painful to me to think that I might be a cause of sorrow or discord in the family that has been so good to me,' she wrote, 'and my love has no aim but the happiness of those I love; so, Nicholas, I beg you to consider yourself free, and to be assured that, in spite of everything, no one can love you more than does

Your Sonya.'

Both letters were written from Troitsa. The other, from the countess, described their last days in Moscow, their departure, the fire, and the destruction of all their property. In this letter the countess also mentioned that Prince Andrew was among the wounded travelling with them; his state was very critical, but the doctor said there was now more hope. Sonya and Natasha were nursing him.

Next day Nicholas took his mother's letter and went to see Princess Mary. Neither he nor she said a word about what 'Natasha nursing him' might mean, but thanks to this letter Nicholas suddenly became almost as intimate with the princess as if they were relations.

The following day he saw Princess Mary off on her journey to Yaroslavl,* and a few days later left to rejoin his regiment.

8

SONYA'S letter written from Troitsa, which had come as an answer to Nicholas's prayer, was prompted by this: the thought of getting Nicholas married to an heiress occupied the old countess's mind more and more. She knew that Sonya was the chief obstacle to this happening, and Sonya's life in the countess's house had grown harder and harder, especially after they had received a letter from Nicholas telling of his meeting with Princess Mary in Bogucharovo. The countess let no occasion slip of making humiliating or cruel allusions to Sonya.

But a few days before they left Moscow, moved and excited by all that was going on, she called Sonya to her and, instead of reproaching and making demands on her, tearfully implored her to sacrifice herself and repay all that the family had done for her by breaking off her engagement with Nicholas.

'I shall not be at peace till you promise me this.'

Sonya burst into hysterical tears and replied through her sobs that she would do anything and was prepared for anything, but gave no actual promise, and could not bring herself to decide to do what was demanded of her. She must sacrifice herself for the family that had reared and brought her up. To sacrifice herself for others was Sonya's habit. Her position in the house was such that only by sacrifice could she show her worth, and she was accustomed to this and loved doing it. But in all her former acts of self-sacrifice she had been happily conscious that they raised her in her own esteem and in that of others, and so made her more worthy of Nicholas whom she loved more than anything in the world. But now they wanted her to sacrifice the very thing that constituted the whole reward for her self-sacrifice and the whole meaning of her life. And for the first time she felt bitterness against those who had been her benefactors only to torture her the more painfully: she felt jealous of Natasha who had never experienced anything of this sort, had never needed to sacrifice herself, but made others sacrifice themselves for her and yet was beloved by everybody. And for the first time Sonya felt that out of her pure, quiet love for Nicholas a passionate feeling was beginning to grow up which was stronger than principle, virtue, or religion. Under the influence of this feeling Sonya, whose life of dependence had taught her involuntarily to be secretive, having answered the countess in vague general terms, avoided talking with her, and resolved to wait till she should see Nicholas, not in order to set him free but on the contrary at that meeting to bind him to her for ever.

The bustle and terror of the Rostovs' last days in Moscow stifled the gloomy thoughts that oppressed Sonya. She was glad to find escape from them in practical activity. But when she heard of Prince Andrew's presence in their house, despite her sincere pity for him and for Natasha, she was seized by a joyful and superstitious feeling that God did not intend her to be separated from Nicholas. She knew that Natasha loved no one but Prince Andrew and had never ceased to love him. She knew that being thrown together again under such terrible circumstances they would again fall in love with one another, and that Nicholas would then not be able to marry Princess Mary as they would be within the prohibited degrees of affinity. Despite all the terror of what had happened during those last days and during the first days of their journey, this feeling that Providence was intervening in her personal affairs cheered Sonya.

At the Troitsa monastery the Rostovs first broke their journey for a whole day.

Three large rooms were assigned to them in the monastery hostelry, one of which was occupied by Prince Andrew. The wounded man was much better that day and Natasha was sitting with him. In the next room sat the count and countess respectfully conversing with the prior, who was calling on them as old acquaintances and benefactors of the monastery. Sonya was there too, tormented by curiosity as to what Prince Andrew and Natasha were talking about. She heard the sound of their voices through the door. That door opened and Natasha came out, looking excited. Not noticing the monk who had risen to greet her and was drawing back the wide sleeve on his right arm, she went up to Sonya and took her hand.

'Natasha, what are you about? Come here!' said the countess.

Natasha went up to the monk for his blessing, and he advised her to turn for aid to God and His Saint.*

As soon as the prior withdrew, Natasha took her friend by the hand and went with her into the unoccupied room.

'Sonya, will he live?' she asked. 'Sonya, how happy I am, and how unhappy!...Sonya, lovey, everything is as it used to be. If only he lives! He cannot...because...because...of...' and Natasha burst into tears.

'Yes! I knew it! Thank God!' murmured Sonya. 'He will live.'

Sonya was not less agitated than her friend by the latter's fear and grief and by her own personal feelings which she shared with no one. Sobbing, she kissed and comforted Natasha. 'If only he lives!' she thought. Having wept, talked, and wiped away their tears, the two friends went together to Prince Andrew's door. Natasha opened it cautiously and glanced into the room, Sonya standing beside her at the half-open door.

Prince Andrew was lying raised high on three pillows. His pale face was calm, his eyes closed, and they could see his regular breathing.

'O Natasha!' Sonya suddenly almost screamed, catching her companion's arm and stepping back from the door.

'What? What is it?' asked Natasha.

'It's that, that...' said Sonya, with a white face and trembling lips.

Natasha softly closed the door and went with Sonya to the window, not yet understanding what the latter was telling her.

'You remember,' said Sonya with a solemn and frightened

expression. 'You remember when I looked in the mirror for you ... at Otradnoe at Christmas? Do you remember what I saw?'

'Yes, yes!' cried Natasha opening her eyes wide, and vaguely recalling that Sonya had told her something about Prince Andrew whom she had seen lying down.

'You remember?' Sonya went on. 'I saw it then and told everybody, you and Dunyasha. I saw him lying on a bed,' said she, making a gesture with her hand and a lifted finger at each detail, 'and that he had his eyes closed and was covered just with a pink quilt, and that his hands were folded,' she concluded, convincing herself that the details she had just seen were exactly what she had seen in the mirror.

She had in fact seen nothing then but had mentioned the first thing that came into her head, but what she had invented then seemed to her now as real as any other recollection. She not only remembered what she had then said – that he turned to look at her and smiled and was covered with something red – but was firmly convinced that she had then seen and said that he was covered with a pink quilt and that his eyes were closed.

'Yes, yes, it really was pink!' cried Natasha, who now thought she too remembered the word pink being used, and saw in this the most extraordinary and mysterious part of the prediction.

'But what does it mean?' she added meditatively.

'Oh, I don't know, it is all so strange,' replied Sonya, clutching at her head.

A few minutes later Prince Andrew rang and Natasha went to him, but Sonya, feeling unusually excited and touched, remained at the window thinking about the strangeness of what had occurred.

They had an opportunity that day to send letters to the army, and the countess was writing to her son.

'Sonya!' said the countess, raising her eyes from her letter as her niece passed, 'Sonya, won't you write to Nicholas?' She spoke in a soft tremulous voice, and in the weary eyes that looked over her spectacles Sonya read all that the countess meant to convey by these words. Those eyes expressed entreaty, shame at having to ask, fear of a refusal, and readiness for relentless hatred in case of such refusal.

Sonya went up to the countess and, kneeling down, kissed her hand.

'Yes, mamma, I will write,' said she.

Sonya was softened, excited, and touched by all that had occurred that day, especially by the mysterious fulfilment she had just seen of her vision. Now that she knew that the renewal of

Natasha's relations with Prince Andrew would prevent Nicholas from marrying Princess Mary, she was joyfully conscious of a return of that self-sacrificing spirit in which she was accustomed to live and loved to live. So with a joyful consciousness of performing a magnanimous deed – interrupted several times by the tears that dimmed her velvety black eyes – she wrote that touching letter the arrival of which had so amazed Nicholas.

9

THE officer and soldiers who had arrested Pierre treated him with hostility but yet with respect, in the guard-house to which he was taken. In their attitude towards him could still be felt both uncertainty as to who he might be – perhaps a very important person – and hostility as a result of their recent personal conflict with him.

But when the guard was relieved next morning, Pierre felt that for the new guard – both officers and men – he was not as interesting as he had been to his captors; and in fact the guard of the second day did not recognize in this big, stout man in a peasant coat the vigorous person who had fought so desperately with the marauder and the convoy and had uttered those solemn words about saving a child; they saw in him only No. 17 of the captured Russians, arrested and detained for some reason by order of the Higher Command. If they noticed anything remarkable about Pierre, it was only his unabashed meditative concentration and thoughtfulness, and the way he spoke French, which struck them as surprisingly good. In spite of this he was placed that day with the other arrested suspects, as the separate room he had occupied was required by an officer.

All the Russians confined with Pierre were men of the lowest class and, recognizing him as a gentleman, they all avoided him, more especially as he spoke French. Pierre felt sad at hearing them making fun of him.

That evening he learnt that all these prisoners (he, probably, among them) were to be tried for incendiarism. On the third day he was taken with the others to a house where a French general with a white moustache sat with two colonels and other Frenchmen with scarves on their arms. With the precision and definiteness customary in addressing prisoners, and which is supposed to preclude human frailty, Pierre like the others was questioned as to who he was, where he had been, with what object, and so on.

These questions, like questions put at trials generally, left the essence of the matter aside, shut out the possibility of that essence being revealed, and were designed only to form a channel through which the judges wished the answers of the accused to flow so as to lead to the desired result, namely a conviction. As soon as Pierre began to say anything that did not fit in with that aim, the channel was removed and the water could flow to waste. Pierre felt, moreover, what the accused always feel at their trial, perplexity as to why these questions were put to him. He had a feeling that it was only out of condescension or a kind of civility that this device of placing a channel was employed. He knew he was in these men's power, that only by force had they brought him there, that force alone gave them a right to demand answers to their questions, and that the sole object of that assembly was to inculpate him. And so, as they had the power and wish to inculpate him, this expedient of an inquiry and trial seemed unnecessary. It was evident that any answer would lead to conviction. When asked what he was doing when he was arrested, Pierre replied in a rather tragic manner that he was restoring to its parents a child he had saved from the flames. Why had he fought the marauder? Pierre answered that he 'was protecting a woman', and that 'to protect a woman who was being insulted, was the duty of every man; that' ... They interrupted him, for this was not to the point. Why was he in the yard of a burning house where witnesses had seen him? He replied that he had gone out to see what was happening in Moscow. Again they interrupted him: they had not asked where he was going, but why he was found near the fire? Who was he? they asked, repeating their first question, which he had declined to answer. Again he replied that he could not answer it.

'Put that down, that's bad ... very bad,' sternly remarked the general with the white moustache and red flushed face.

On the fourth day fires broke out on the Zubovsky Rampart.

Pierre and thirteen others were moved to the coach-house of a merchant's house near the Crimean bridge. On his way through the streets Pierre felt stifled by the smoke which seemed to hang over the whole city. Fires were visible on all sides. He did not then realize the significance of the burning of Moscow, and looked at the fires with horror.

He passed four days in the coach-house near the Crimean bridge and during that time learnt, from the talk of the French soldiers, that all those confined there were awaiting a decision which might come any day from the marshal. What marshal this was, Pierre could not learn from the soldiers. Evidently for them 'the marshal' represented a very high and rather mysterious power.

These first days, before the 8th of September when the prisoners were had up for a second examination, were the hardest of all for Pierre.

10

On the 8th of September an officer – a very important one judging by the respect the guards showed him – entered the coach-house where the prisoners were. This officer, probably someone on the staff, was holding a paper in his hand, and called over all the Russians there, naming Pierre as 'the man who does not give his name'. Glancing indolently and indifferently at all the prisoners, he ordered the officer in charge to have them decently dressed and tidied up before taking them to the marshal. An hour later a squad of soldiers arrived and Pierre with thirteen others was led to the Virgin's Field. It was a fine day, sunny after rain, and the air was unusually pure. The smoke did not hang low as on the day when Pierre had been taken from the guard-house on the Zubovsky Rampart, but rose through the pure air in columns. No flames were seen, but columns of smoke rose on all sides, and all Moscow as far as Pierre could see was one vast charred ruin. On all sides there were waste spaces with only stoves and chimney stacks still standing, and here and there the blackened walls of the brick houses. Pierre gazed at the ruins and did not recognize districts he had known well. Here and there he could see churches that had not been burnt. The Kremlin, which was not destroyed, gleamed white in the distance with its towers and the belfry of Ivan the Great. The domes of the New Convent of the Virgin glittered brightly and its bells were ringing particularly clearly. These bells reminded Pierre that it was Sunday, and the feast of the Nativity of the Virgin. But there seemed to be no one to celebrate this holiday: everywhere were blackened ruins, and the few Russians to be seen were tattered and frightened people, who tried to hide when they saw the French.

It was plain that the Russian nest was ruined and destroyed, but in place of the Russian order of life that had been destroyed, Pierre unconsciously felt that a quite different, firm French order had been established over this ruined nest. He felt this in the looks of the soldiers who, marching in regular ranks briskly and gaily, were escorting him and the other criminals; he felt it in the looks of an important French official in a carriage and pair driven by a soldier, whom they met on the way. He felt it in the merry sounds of regimental music he heard from the left side of the field, and felt and realized it especially from that list of prisoners the

1027

French officer had read out when he came that morning. Pierre had been taken by one set of soldiers and led first to one and then to another place with dozens of other men, and it seemed that they might have forgotten him, or confused him with the others. But no: the answers he had given when questioned had come back to him in his designation as 'the man who does not give his name', and under that appellation, which to Pierre seemed terrible, they were now leading him somewhere with unhesitating assurance on their faces that he and all the other prisoners were exactly the ones they wanted and that they were being taken to the proper place. Pierre felt himself to be an insignificant chip fallen among the wheels of a machine whose action he did not understand but which was working well.

He and the other prisoners were taken to the right side of the Virgin's Field, to a large white house with an immense garden not far from the convent. This was Prince Shcherbatov's house, where Pierre had often been in other days, and which, as he learnt from the talk of the soldiers, was now occupied by the marshal, the Duke of Eckmühl (Davout).*

They were taken to the entrance, and led into the house one by one. Pierre was the sixth to enter. He was conducted through a glass gallery, an ante-room, and a hall, which were familiar to him, into a long low study at the door of which stood an adjutant.

Davout, spectacles on nose, sat bent over a table at the further end of the room. Pierre went close up to him, but Davout, evidently consulting a paper that lay before him, did not look up. Without raising his eyes he said in a low voice:

'Who are you?'

Pierre was silent because he was incapable of uttering a word. To him, Davout was not merely a French general, but a man notorious for his cruelty. Looking at his cold face, as he sat like a stern schoolmaster who was prepared to wait a while for an answer, Pierre felt that every instant of delay might cost him his life; but he did not know what to say. He did not venture to repeat what he had said at his first examination, yet to disclose his rank and position was dangerous and embarrassing. So he was silent. But before he had decided what to do, Davout raised his head, pushed his spectacles back on his forehead, screwed up his eyes, and looked intently at him.

'I know that man,' he said in a cold, measured tone, evidently calculated to frighten Pierre.

The chill that had been running down Pierre's back now seized his head as in a vice.

'You cannot know me, General, I have never seen you ...'

'He is a Russian spy,' Davout interrupted, addressing another general who was present, but whom Pierre had not noticed.

Davout turned away. With an unexpected reverberation in his voice Pierre rapidly began:

'No, Monseigneur,' he said, suddenly remembering that Davout was a duke. 'No, Monseigneur, you cannot have known me. I am a militia officer and have not quitted Moscow.'

'Your name?' asked Davout.

'Bezukhov.'

'What proof have I that you are not lying?'

'Monseigneur!' exclaimed Pierre not in an offended but in a pleading voice.

Davout looked up and gazed intently at him. For some seconds they looked at one another, and that look saved Pierre. Apart from conditions of war and law, that look established human relations between the two men. At that moment an immense number of things passed dimly through both their minds, and they realized that they were both children of humanity and were brothers.

At the first glance, when Davout had only raised his head from the paper where human affairs and lives were indicated by numbers, Pierre was merely a circumstance and Davout could have shot him without burdening his conscience with an evil deed, but now he saw in him a human being. He reflected for a moment.

'How can you show me that you are telling the truth?' said Davout coldly.

Pierre remembered Ramballe, and named him and his regiment and the street where the house was.

'You are not what you say,' returned Davout.

In a trembling, faltering voice Pierre began adducing proofs of the truth of his statements.

But at that moment an adjutant entered and reported something to Davout.

Davout brightened up at the news the adjutant brought and began buttoning up his uniform. It seemed that he had quite forgotten Pierre.

When the adjutant reminded him of the prisoner, he jerked his head in Pierre's direction with a frown and ordered him to be led away. But where they were to take him Pierre did not know: back to the coach-house or to the place of execution his companions had pointed out to him as they crossed the Virgin's Field.

He turned his head and saw that the adjutant was putting another question to Davout.

'Yes, of course!' replied Davout, but what this 'yes' meant, Pierre did not know.

Pierre could not afterwards remember how he went, whether it was far, or in which direction. His faculties were quite numbed, he was stupefied, and noticing nothing around him went on moving his legs as the others did till they all stopped and he stopped too. The only thought in his mind at that time was: Who was it that had really sentenced him to death? Not the men on the Commission that had first examined him – not one of them had wished to or, evidently, could have done it. It was not Davout, who had looked at him in so human a way. In another moment Davout would have realized that he was doing wrong, but just then the adjutant had come in and interrupted him. The adjutant, also, had evidently had no evil intent though he might have refrained from coming in. Then who was executing him, killing him, depriving him of life – him, Pierre, with all his memories, aspirations, hopes, and thoughts? Who was doing this? And Pierre felt that it was no one.

It was a system – a concurrence of circumstances.

A system of some sort was killing him – Pierre – depriving him of life, of everything, annihilating him.

11

FROM Prince Shcherbatov's house the prisoners were led straight down the Virgin's Field, to the left of the nunnery, as far as a kitchen-garden in which a post had been set up. Beyond that post a fresh pit had been dug in the ground, and near the post and the pit a large crowd stood in a semi-circle. The crowd consisted of a few Russians and many of Napoleon's soldiers who were not on duty – Germans, Italians, and Frenchmen in a variety of uniforms. To the right and left of the post stood rows of French troops in blue uniforms with red epaulettes and high boots and shakos.

The prisoners were placed in a certain order, according to the list (Pierre was sixth), and were led to the post. Several drums suddenly began to beat on both sides of them, and at that sound Pierre felt as if part of his soul had been torn away. He lost the power of thinking or understanding. He could only hear and see. And he had only one wish – that the frightful thing that had to happen should happen quickly. Pierre looked round at his fellow-prisoners and scrutinized them.

The first two were convicts with shaven heads. One was tall and thin, the other dark, shaggy, and sinewy, with a flat nose. The third was a domestic serf, about forty-five years old, with grizzled hair and a plump well-nourished body. The fourth was a peasant, a very handsome man with a broad light-brown beard and black eyes. The fifth was a factory hand, a thin, sallow-faced lad of eighteen in a loose cloak.

Pierre heard the French consulting whether to shoot them separately or two at a time. 'In couples,' replied the officer in command in a calm cold voice. There was a stir in the ranks of the soldiers and it was evident that they were all hurrying – not as men hurry to do something they understand, but as people hurry to finish a necessary but unpleasant and incomprehensible task.

A French official wearing a scarf came up to the right of the row of prisoners, and read out the sentence in Russian and French.

Then two pairs of Frenchmen approached the criminals, and at the officer's command took the two convicts who stood first in the row. The convicts stopped when they reached the post and, while sacks were being brought, looked dumbly around as a wounded beast looks at an approaching huntsman. One crossed himself continually, the other scratched his back and made a movement of the lips resembling a smile. With hurried hands the soldiers blind-folded them, drawing the sacks over their heads, and bound them to the post.

Twelve sharpshooters with muskets stepped out of the ranks with a firm regular tread, and halted eight paces from the post. Pierre turned away to avoid seeing what was about to happen. Suddenly a cracking rolling noise was heard which seemed to him louder than the most terrific thunder, and he looked round. There was some smoke, and the Frenchmen were doing something near the pit with pale faces and trembling hands. Two more prisoners were led up. In the same way, and with similar looks, these two glanced vainly at the onlookers with only a silent appeal for protection in their eyes, evidently unable to understand or believe what was going to happen to them. They could not believe it because they alone knew what their life meant to them, and so they neither understood nor believed that it could be taken from them.

Again Pierre did not wish to look, and again turned away; but again the sound as of a frightful explosion struck his ear, and at the same moment he saw smoke, blood, and the pale scared faces of the Frenchmen who were again doing something by the post, their trembling hands impeding one another. Pierre, breathing heavily, looked round as if asking what it meant. The same question was expressed in all the looks that met his.

On the faces of all the Russians, and of the French soldiers and officers without exception, he read the same dismay, horror, and conflict that were in his own heart. 'But who, after all, is doing

this? They are all suffering as I am. Who then is it? Who?'
flashed for an instant through his mind.

'Sharpshooters of the 86th, forward!' shouted someone. The fifth
prisoner, the one next to Pierre, was led away – alone. Pierre did
not understand that he was saved, that he and the rest had been
brought there only to witness the execution. With ever-growing
horror, and no sense of joy or relief, he gazed at what was taking
place. The fifth man was the factory lad in the loose cloak. The
moment they laid hands on him, he sprang aside in terror and
clutched at Pierre. (Pierre shuddered and shook himself free.) The
lad was unable to walk. They dragged him along holding him up
under the arms, and he screamed. When they got him to the post
he grew quiet, as if he had suddenly understood something.
Whether he understood that screaming was useless, or whether he
thought it incredible that men should kill him, at any rate he took
his stand at the post, waiting to be blindfolded like the others,
and like a wounded animal looked around him with glittering eyes.
Pierre was no longer able to turn away and close his eyes. His
curiosity and agitation, like that of the whole crowd, reached the
highest pitch at this fifth murder. Like the others this fifth man
seemed calm; he wrapped his loose cloak closer and rubbed one
bare foot with the other.

When they began to blindfold him he himself adjusted the knot
which hurt the back of his head; then when they propped him
against the bloodstained post, he leaned back and, not being comfortable in that position, straightened himself, adjusted his feet,
and leaned back again more comfortably. Pierre did not take his
eyes from him and did not miss his slightest movement.

Probably a word of command was given and was followed by the
reports of eight muskets; but try as he would Pierre could not afterwards remember having heard the slightest sound of the shots. He
only saw how the workman suddenly sank down on the cords that
held him, how blood showed itself in two places, how the ropes
slackened under the weight of the hanging body, and how the
workman sat down, his head hanging unnaturally and one leg
bent under him. Pierre ran up to the post. No one hindered him.
Pale frightened people were doing something around the workman.
The lower jaw of an old Frenchman with a thick moustache
trembled as he untied the ropes. The body collapsed. The soldiers
dragged it awkwardly from the post and began pushing it into
the pit.

They all plainly and certainly knew that they were criminals
who must hide the traces of their guilt as quickly as possible.

Pierre glanced into the pit, and saw that the factory lad was lying with his knees close up to his head and one shoulder higher than the other. That shoulder rose and fell rhythmically and convulsively, but spadesful of earth were already being thrown over the whole body. One of the soldiers, evidently suffering, shouted gruffly and angrily at Pierre to go back. But Pierre did not understand him, and remained near the post, and no one drove him away.

When the pit had been filled up a command was given. Pierre was taken back to his place, and the rows of troops on both sides of the post made a half turn and went past it at a measured pace. The twenty-four sharpshooters with discharged muskets, standing in the centre of the circle, ran back to their places as the companies passed by.

Pierre gazed now with dazed eyes at these sharpshooters who ran in couples out of the circle. All but one rejoined their companies. This one, a young soldier, his face deadly pale, his shako pushed back, and his musket resting on the ground, still stood near the pit at the spot from which he had fired. He swayed like a drunken man, taking some steps forwards and back to save himself from falling. An old, non-commissioned officer ran out of the ranks and taking him by the elbow dragged him to his company. The crowd of Russians and Frenchmen began to disperse. They all went away silently and with drooping heads.

'That will teach them to start fires,' said one of the Frenchmen.

Pierre glanced round at the speaker and saw that it was a soldier who was trying to find some relief after what had been done, but was not able to do so. Without finishing what he had begun to say he made a hopeless movement with his arm and went away.

12

AFTER the execution Pierre was separated from the rest of the prisoners and placed alone in a small, ruined, and befouled church.

Towards evening a non-commissioned officer entered with two soldiers and told him that he had been pardoned and would now go to the barracks for the prisoners-of-war. Without understanding what was said to him, Pierre got up and went with the soldiers. They took him to the upper end of the field, where there were some sheds built of charred planks, beams, and battens, and led him into one of them. In the darkness some twenty different men surrounded Pierre. He looked at them without understanding who they were, why they were there, or what they wanted of him. He heard what they said, but did not understand the meaning of the words and made no kind of deduction from or application of them. He replied to questions they put to him, but did not consider who was listening to his replies, nor how they would understand them. He looked at their faces and figures, but they all seemed to him equally meaningless.

From the moment Pierre had witnessed those terrible murders committed by men who did not wish to commit them, it was as if the mainspring of his life, on which everything depended and which made everything appear alive, had suddenly been wrenched out and everything had collapsed into a heap of meaningless rubbish. Though he did not acknowledge it to himself, his faith in the right ordering of the universe, in humanity, in his own soul and in God, had been destroyed. He had experienced this before, but never so strongly as now. When similar doubts had assailed him before, they had been the result of his own wrongdoing, and at the bottom of his heart he had felt that relief from his despair and from those doubts was to be found within himself. But now he felt that the universe had crumbled before his eyes and only meaningless ruins remained, and this not by any fault of his own. He felt that it was not in his power to regain faith in the meaning of life.

Around him in the darkness men were standing, and evidently something about him interested them greatly. They were telling him something and asking him something. Then they led him away somewhere, and at last he found himself in a corner of the shed among men who were laughing and talking on all sides.

'Well, then, mates . . . that very prince *who* . . .' some voice at the other side of the shed was saying, with a strong emphasis on the word *who*.

Sitting silent and motionless on a heap of straw against the wall, Pierre sometimes opened and sometimes closed his eyes. But as soon as he closed them he saw before him the dreadful face of the factory lad – especially dreadful because of its simplicity – and the faces of the murderers, even more dreadful because of their disquiet. And he opened his eyes again and stared vacantly into the darkness around him.

Beside him in a stooping position sat a small man, of whose presence he was first made aware by a strong smell of perspiration which came from him every time he moved. This man was doing something to his legs in the darkness, and though Pierre could not see his face he felt that the man continually glanced at him. On growing used to the darkness Pierre saw that the man was taking off his legbands, and the way he did it aroused Pierre's interest.

Having unwound the string that tied the band on one leg, he

carefully coiled it up and immediately set to work on the other leg, glancing up at Pierre. While one hand hung up the first string, the other was already unwinding the band on the second leg. In this way, having carefully removed the legbands by deft circular motions of his arm following one another uninterruptedly, the man hung the legbands up on some pegs fixed above his head. Then he took out a knife, cut something, closed the knife, placed it under the head of his bed, and seating himself more comfortably, clasped his arms round his lifted knees and fixed his eyes on Pierre. The latter was conscious of something pleasant, comforting, and well rounded in these deft movements, in the man's well-ordered arrangements in his corner, and even in his very smell, and he looked at the man without taking his eyes from him.

'You've sees a lot of trouble, sir, eh?' the little man suddenly said.

And there was so much kindliness and simplicity in his sing-song voice, that Pierre tried to reply, but his jaw trembled and he felt tears rising to his eyes. The little fellow, giving Pierre no time to betray his confusion, instantly continued in the same pleasant tones:

'Eh, lad, don't fret!' said he, in the tender sing-song caressing voice old Russian peasant women employ. 'Don't fret, friend – "suffer an hour, live for an age!" that's how it is, my dear fellow. And here we live, thank Heaven, without offence. Among these folk, too, there are good men as well as bad,' said he, and, still speaking, he turned on his knees with a supple movement, got up, coughed, and went off to another part of the shed.

'Eh, you rascal!' Pierre heard the same kind voice saying at the other end of the shed. 'So you've come, you rascal? She remembers ... Now, now, that'll do!'

And the soldier, pushing away a little dog that was jumping up at him, returned to his place and sat down. In his hands he had something wrapped in a rag.

'Here, eat a bit, sir,' said he, resuming his former respectful tone as he unwrapped and offered Pierre some baked potatoes. 'We had soup for dinner and the potatoes are grand!'

Pierre had not eaten all day, and the smell of the potatoes seemed extremely pleasant to him. He thanked the soldier and began to eat.

'Well, are they all right?' said the soldier with a smile. 'You should do like this.'

He took a potato, drew out his clasp knife, cut the potato into two equal halves on the palm of his hand, sprinkled some salt on it from the rag, and handed it to Pierre.

'The potatoes are grand!' he said once more. 'Eat some like that!'

Pierre thought he had never eaten anything that tasted better.

'Oh, I'm all right,' said he, 'but why did they shoot those poor fellows? The last one was hardly twenty.'

'Tss, tt...!' said the little man. 'Ah, what a sin...what a sin!' he added quickly, and as if his words were always waiting ready in his mouth and flew out involuntarily he went on: 'How was it, sir, that you stayed in Moscow?'

'I didn't think they would come so soon. I stayed accidentally,' replied Pierre.

'And how did they arrest you, dear lad? At your house?'

'No, I went to look at the fire, and they arrested me there, and tried me as an incendiary.'

'Where there's law there's injustice,' put in the little man.

'And have you been here long?' Pierre asked as he munched the last of the potato.

'I? It was last Sunday they took me, out of a hospital in Moscow.'

'Why, are you a soldier then?'

'Yes, we are soldiers of the Apsheron regiment. I was dying of fever. We weren't told anything. There were some twenty of us lying there. We had no idea, never guessed at all.'

'And do you feel sad here?' Pierre inquired.

'How can one help it, lad? My name is Platon, and the surname is Karataev,' he added, evidently wishing to make it easier for Pierre to address him. 'They call me "little falcon" in the regiment. How is one to help feeling sad? Moscow – she's the mother of cities. How can one see all this and not feel sad? But "the maggot gnaws the cabbage, yet dies first"; that's what the old folk used to tell us,' he added rapidly.

'What? What did you say?' asked Pierre.

'Who? I?' said Karataev. 'I say things happen not as we plan but as God judges,' he replied, thinking that he was repeating what he had said before, and immediately continued:

'Well, and you, have you a family estate, sir? And a house? So you have abundance, then? And a housewife? And your old parents, are they still living?' he asked.

And though it was too dark for Pierre to see, he felt that a suppressed smile of kindliness puckered the soldier's lips as he put these questions. He seemed grieved that Pierre had no parents, especially that he had no mother.

'A wife for counsel, a mother-in-law for welcome, but there's none as dear as one's own mother!' said he. 'Well, and have you little ones?' he went on asking.

Again Pierre's negative answer seemed to distress him, and he hastened to add:

'Never mind! You're young folks yet, and please God may still have some. The great thing is to live in harmony . . .'

'But it's all the same now,' Pierre could not help saying.

'Ah, my dear fellow!' rejoined Karataev, 'never decline a prison or a beggar's sack!'

He seated himself more comfortably, and coughed, evidently preparing to tell a long story.

'Well, my dear fellow, I was still living at home,' he began. 'We had a well-to-do homestead, plenty of land, we peasants lived well and our house was one to thank God for. When father and we went out mowing there were seven of us. We lived well. We were real peasants. It so happened . . .'

And Platon Karataev told a long story of how he had gone into someone's copse to take wood, how he had been caught by the keeper, had been tried, flogged, and sent to serve as a soldier.

'Well, lad,' and a smile changed the tone of his voice, 'we thought it was a misfortune but it turned out a blessing! If it had not been for my sin, my brother would have had to go as a soldier. But he, my younger brother, had five little ones, while I, you see, only left a wife behind. We had a little girl, but God took her before I went as a soldier. I come home on leave and I'll tell you how it was, I look and see that they are living better than before. The yard full of cattle, the women at home, two brothers away earning wages, and only Michael, the youngest, at home. Father, he says, "All my children are the same to me: it hurts the same whichever finger gets bitten. But if Platon hadn't been shaved for a soldier, Michael would have had to go." He called us all to him and, will you believe it, placed us in front of the icons. "Michael," he says, "come here and bow down to his feet; and you, young woman, you bow down too; and you, grandchildren, also bow down before him! Do you understand?" he says. That's how it is, dear fellow. Fate looks for a head. But we are always judging, "that's not well – that's not right!" Our luck is like water in a drag-net: you pull at it and it bulges, but when you've drawn it out it's empty! That's how it is.'

And Platon shifted his seat on the straw.

After a short silence he rose.

'Well, I think you must be sleepy,' said he, and began rapidly crossing himself and repeating:

'Lord Jesus Christ, holy Saint Nicholas, Frola and Lavra! Lord Jesus Christ, holy Saint Nicholas, Frola and Lavra!* Lord Jesus Christ, have mercy on us and save us!' he concluded, then bowed to the ground, got up, sighed, and sat down again on his heap of straw. 'That's the way. Lay me down like a stone, O God, and raise me up like a loaf,' he muttered as he lay down, pulling his coat over him.

'What prayer was that you were saying?' asked Pierre.

'Eh?' murmured Platon, who had almost fallen asleep. 'What was I saying? I was praying. Don't you pray?'

'Yes, I do,' said Pierre. 'But what was that you said: Frola and Lavra?'

'Well, of course,' replied Platon quickly, 'the horses' saints. One must pity the animals too. Eh, the rascal! Now you've curled up and got warm, you daughter of a bitch!' said Karataev, touching the dog that lay at his feet, and again turning over he fell asleep immediately.

Sounds of crying and screaming came from somewhere in the distance outside, and flames were visible through the cracks of the shed, but inside it was quiet and dark. For a long time Pierre did not sleep, but lay with eyes open in the darkness listening to the regular snoring of Platon, who lay beside him, and he felt that the world that had been shattered was once more stirring in his soul with a new beauty and on new and unshakable foundations.

13

TWENTY-THREE soldiers, three officers, and two officials were confined in the shed in which Pierre had been placed and where he remained for four weeks.

When Pierre remembered them afterwards they all seemed misty figures to him except Platon Karataev, who always remained in his mind a most vivid and precious memory and the personification of everything Russian, kindly, and round. When Pierre saw his neighbour next morning at dawn, the first impression of him, as of something round, was fully confirmed: Platon's whole figure – in a French overcoat girdled with a cord, a soldier's cap, and bast shoes – was round. His head was quite round, his back, chest, shoulders, and even his arms, which he held as if ever ready to embrace something, were rounded, his pleasant smile and his large gentle brown eyes were also round.

Platon Karataev must have been fifty judging by his stories of campaigns he had been in, told as by an old soldier. He did not himself know his age and was quite unable to determine it. But his brilliantly white, strong teeth, which showed in two unbroken semicircles when he laughed – as he often did – were all sound and good, there was not a grey hair in his beard or on his head, and his whole body gave an impression of suppleness and especially of firmness and endurance.

His face, despite its fine, rounded wrinkles, had an expression of innocence and youth, his voice was pleasant and musical. But the chief peculiarity of his speech was its directness and appositeness. It was evident that he never considered what he had said or was going to say, and consequently the rapidity and justice of his intonation had an irresistible persuasiveness.

His physical strength and agility during the first days of his imprisonment were such that he seemed not to know what fatigue and sickness meant. Every night, before lying down, he said: 'Lord, lay me down as a stone and raise me up as a loaf!' and every morning on getting up he said: 'I lay down and curled up, I get up and shake myself.' And indeed he only had to lie down, to fall asleep like a stone, and he only had to shake himself, to be ready without a moment's delay for some work, just as children are ready for play directly they awake. He could do everything, not very well but not badly. He baked, cooked, sewed, planed, and mended boots. He was always busy, and only at night allowed himself conversation – of which he was fond – and songs. He did not sing like a trained singer who knows he is listened to, but like the birds, evidently giving vent to the sounds in the same way that one stretches oneself, or walks about to get rid of stiffness, and the sounds were always high-pitched, mournful, delicate, and almost feminine, and his face at such times was very serious.

Having been taken prisoner and allowed his beard to grow, he seemed to have thrown off all that had been forced upon him – everything military and alien to himself – and had returned to his former peasant habits.

'A soldier on leave – a shirt outside the breeches,'* he would say.

He did not like talking about his life as a soldier, though he did not complain, and often mentioned that he had not been flogged once during the whole of his army service. When he related anything it was generally some old and evidently precious memory of his 'Christian' life,* as he called his peasant existence. The proverbs of which his talk was full were for the most part not the coarse and indecent saws soldiers employ, but those folk-sayings which taken without a context seem so insignificant, but when used appositely suddenly acquire a significance of profound wisdom.

He would often say the exact opposite of what he had said on a previous occasion, yet both would be right. He liked to talk and he talked well, adorning his speech with terms of endearment and with folk-sayings which Pierre thought he invented himself, but the chief charm of his talk lay in the fact that the commonest events – sometimes just such as Pierre had witnessed without taking notice of them – assumed in Karataev's speech a character of solemn fitness. He liked to hear the folk-tales one of the soldiers used to tell of an evening (they were always the same), but most of all he liked to hear stories of real life. He would smile joyfully when listening to such stories, now and then putting in a word or asking a question to make the moral beauty of what was told clear to himself. Karataev had no attachments, friendships, or love, as Pierre understood them, but loved and lived affectionately with everything life brought him in contact with, particularly with man – not any particular man, but those with whom he happened to be. He loved his dog, his comrades, the French, and Pierre who was his neighbour, but Pierre felt that in spite of Karataev's affectionate tenderness for him (by which he unconsciously gave Pierre's spiritual life its due) he would not have grieved for a moment at parting from him. And Pierre began to feel in the same way towards Karataev.

To all the other prisoners Platon Karataev seemed a most ordinary soldier. They called him 'little falcon' or 'Platosha', chaffed him good-naturedly, and sent him on errands. But to Pierre he always remained what he had seemed that first night: an unfathomable, rounded, eternal personification of the spirit of simplicity and truth.

Platon Karataev knew nothing by heart, except his prayers. When he began to speak he seemed not to know how he would conclude.

Sometimes Pierre, struck by the meaning of his words, would ask him to repeat them, but Platon could never recall what he had said a moment before, just as he never could repeat to Pierre the words of his favourite song: *native* and *birch-tree* and *my heart is sick* occurred in it, but when spoken and not sung no meaning could be got out of it. He did not, and could not, understand the meaning of words apart from their context. Every word and action of his was the manifestation of an activity unknown to him, which was his life. But his life, as he regarded it, had no meaning as a separate thing. It had meaning only as part of a whole of which he was always conscious. His words and actions flowed from him as evenly, inevitably, and spontaneously as fragrance exhales from a flower. He could not understand the value or significance of any word or deed taken separately.

14

WHEN Princess Mary heard from Nicholas that her brother was with the Rostovs at Yaroslavl she at once prepared to go there, in spite of her aunt's efforts to dissuade her – and not merely to go herself but to take her nephew with her. Whether it were difficult or easy, possible or impossible, she did not ask and did not want to know: it was her duty not only herself to be near her brother who was perhaps dying, but to do everything possible to take his son to him, and so she prepared to set off. That she had not heard from Prince Andrew himself Princess Mary attributed to his being too weak to write or to his considering the long journey too hard and too dangerous for her and his son.

In a few days Princess Mary was ready to start. Her equipages were the huge family coach in which she had travelled to Voronezh, a semi-open trap, and a baggage-cart. With her travelled Mademoiselle Bourienne, little Nicholas and his tutor, her old nurse, three maids, Tikhon, and a young footman and courier her aunt had sent to accompany her.

The usual route through Moscow could not be thought of and the roundabout way Princess Mary was obliged to take through Lipetsk, Ryazan, Vladimir, and Shuya was very long. As post-horses were not everywhere obtainable, it was difficult, and, near Ryazan where the French were said to have shown themselves, even dangerous.

During this difficult journey Mademoiselle Bourienne, Dessalles, and Princess Mary's servants were astonished at her energy and firmness of spirit. She went to bed later and rose earlier than any of them, and no difficulties daunted her. Thanks to her activity and energy, which infected her fellow-travellers, they approached Yaroslavl by the end of the second week.

The last days of her stay in Voronezh had been the happiest of her life. Her love for Rostov no longer tormented or agitated her. It filled her whole soul, had become an integral part of herself, and she no longer struggled against it. Latterly she had become convinced that she loved and was beloved, though she never said this definitely to herself in words. She had become convinced of it at her last interview with Nicholas, when he had come to tell her that her brother was with the Rostovs. Not by a single word had Nicholas alluded to the fact that Prince Andrew's relations with Natasha might, if he recovered, be renewed, but Princess Mary saw by his face that he knew and thought of this.

Yet in spite of that his relation to her – considerate, delicate, and loving – not only remained unchanged, but it sometimes seemed to Princess Mary that he was even glad that the family connexion between them allowed him to express his friendship more freely. She knew that she loved for the first and only time in her life, and felt that she was beloved, and was happy in regard to it.

But this happiness on one side of her spiritual nature did not prevent her feeling grief for her brother with full force; on the contrary that spiritual tranquillity on the one side made it the more possible for her to give full play to her feeling for her brother. That feeling was so strong at the moment of leaving Voronezh that those who saw her off, as they looked at her careworn despairing face, felt sure she would fall ill on the journey. But the very difficulties and preoccupations of the journey, which she took so actively in hand, saved her for a while from her grief and gave her strength.

As always happens when travelling, Princess Mary thought only of the journey itself, forgetting its object. But as she approached Yaroslavl the thought of what might await her there – not after many days, but that very evening – again presented itself to her and her agitation increased to its utmost limit.

The courier who had been sent on in advance to find out where the Rostovs were staying in Yaroslavl and in what condition Prince Andrew was, when he met the big coach just entering the town gates was appalled by the terrible pallor of the princess's face that looked out at him from the window.

'I have found out everything, your Excellency: the Rostovs are staying at the merchant Bronnikov's house, in the Square, not far from here, right above the Volga,' said the courier.

Princess Mary looked at him with frightened inquiry, not understanding why he did not reply to what she chiefly wanted to know: how was her brother? Mademoiselle Bourienne put that question for her.

'How is the prince?' she asked.

'His Excellency is staying in the same house with them.'

'Then he is alive,' thought Princess Mary, and asked in a low voice: 'How is he?'

'The servants say, he is still the same.'

What 'still the same' might mean Princess Mary did not ask, but with an unnoticed glance at little seven-year-old Nicholas, who was sitting in front of her looking with pleasure at the town, she bowed her head and did not raise it again till the heavy coach, rumbling, shaking, and swaying, came to a stop. The carriage steps clattered as they were let down.

The carriage door was opened. On the left there was water – a great river – and on the right a porch. There were people at the entrance: servants, and a rosy girl with a large plait of black hair, smiling as it seemed to Princess Mary in an unpleasantly affected way. (This was Sonya.) Princess Mary ran up the steps. 'This way, this way!' said the girl, with the same artificial smile, and the princess found herself in the hall facing an elderly woman of oriental type, who came rapidly to meet her with a look of emotion. This was the countess. She embraced Princess Mary and kissed her.

'*Mon enfant!*' she muttered, '*je vous aime et vous connais depuis longtemps.*'

Despite her excitement, Princess Mary realized that this was the countess and that it was necessary to say something to her. Hardly knowing how she did it she contrived to utter a few polite phrases in French in the same tone as those that had been addressed to her, and asked: 'How is he?'

'The doctor says that he is not in danger,' said the countess, but as she spoke she raised her eyes with a sigh, and her gesture conveyed a contradiction of her words.

'Where is he? Can I see him – can I?' asked the princess.

'One moment, Princess, one moment, my dear. Is this his son?' said the countess, turning to little Nicholas who was coming in with Dessalles. 'There will be room for everybody, this is a big house. Oh, what a lovely boy!'

The countess took Princess Mary into the drawing-room, where Sonya was talking to Mademoiselle Bourienne. The countess caressed the boy, and the old count came in and welcomed the princess. He had changed very much since Princess Mary had last seen him. Then he had been a brisk, cheerful, self-assured old man, now he seemed a pitiful bewildered person. While talking to Princess Mary he continually looked round as if asking everyone whether he was doing the right thing. After the destruction of Moscow and of his property, thrown out of his accustomed groove, he seemed to have lost the sense of his own significance and to feel that there was no longer a place for him in life.

In spite of her one desire to see her brother as soon as possible, and her vexation that at the moment when all she wanted was to see him they should be trying to entertain her and pretending to admire her nephew, the princess noticed all that was going on around her and felt the necessity of submitting, for a time, to this new order of things which she had entered. She knew it to be necessary, and though it was hard for her she was not vexed with these people.

'This is my niece,' said the count, introducing Sonya – 'You don't know her, Princess?'

Princess Mary turned to Sonya, and trying to stifle the hostile feeling that arose in her towards the girl, she kissed her. But she felt oppressed by the fact that the mood of everyone around her was so far from what was in her own heart.

'Where is he?' she asked again, addressing them all.

'He is downstairs. Natasha is with him,' answered Sonya flushing. 'We have sent to ask. I think you must be tired, Princess.'

Tears of vexation showed themselves in Princess Mary's eyes. She turned away, and was about to ask the countess again how to go to him, when light, impetuous and seemingly buoyant steps were heard at the door. The princess looked round and saw Natasha coming in, almost running – that Natasha whom she had liked so little at their meeting in Moscow long since.

But hardly had the princess looked at Natasha's face before she realized that here was a real comrade in her grief, and consequently a friend. She ran to meet her, embraced her, and began to cry on her shoulder.

As soon as Natasha, sitting at the head of Prince Andrew's bed, heard of Princess Mary's arrival, she softly left his room, and hastened to her with those swift steps that had sounded buoyant to Princess Mary.

There was only one expression on her agitated face when she ran into the drawing-room – that of love – boundless love for him, for her, and for all that was near to the man she loved; and of pity, suffering for others, and passionate desire to give herself entirely to helping them. It was plain that at that moment there was in Natasha's heart no thought of herself or of her own relations with Prince Andrew.

Princess Mary, with her acute sensibility, understood all this at the first glance at Natasha's face, and wept on her shoulder with sorrowful pleasure.

'Come, come to him, Mary,' said Natasha, leading her into the other room.

Princess Mary raised her head, dried her eyes, and turned to Natasha. She felt that from her she would be able to understand and learn everything.

'How . . .' she began her question but stopped short.

She felt that it was impossible to ask, or to answer, in words. Natasha's face and eyes would have to tell her all more clearly and profoundly.

Natasha was gazing at her, but seemed afraid and in doubt whether to say all she knew or not; she seemed to feel that before those luminous eyes which penetrated into the very depths of her heart, it was impossible not to tell the whole truth which she saw. And suddenly Natasha's lips twitched, ugly wrinkles gathered round her mouth, and covering her face with her hands, she burst into sobs.

Princess Mary understood.

But she still hoped, and asked, in words she herself did not trust:

'But how is his wound? What is his general condition?'

'You, you ... will see,' was all Natasha could say.

They sat a little while downstairs near his room till they had left off crying and were able to go to him with calm faces.

'How has his whole illness gone? Is it long since he grew worse? When did *this* happen?' Princess Mary inquired.

Natasha told her that at first there had been danger from his feverish condition and the pain he suffered, but at Troitsa that had passed and the doctor had only been afraid of gangrene. That danger had also passed. When they reached Yaroslavl the wound had begun to fester (Natasha knew all about such things as festering) and the doctor had said that the festering might take a normal course. Then fever set in, but the doctor had said the fever was not very serious.

'But two days ago *this* suddenly happened,' said Natasha, struggling with her sobs. 'I don't know why, but you will see what he is like.'

'Is he weaker? Thinner?' asked the princess.

'No, it's not that, but worse. You will see. Oh, Mary, he is too good, he cannot, cannot live, because ...'

15

WHEN Natasha opened Prince Andrew's door with a familiar movement and let Princess Mary pass into the room before her, the princess felt the sobs rising in her throat. Hard as she had tried to prepare herself and now tried to remain tranquil, she knew that she would be unable to look at him without tears.

The princess understood what Natasha had meant by the words: 'two days ago *this* suddenly happened'. She understood those words to mean that he had suddenly softened, and that this softening and gentleness were signs of approaching death. As she stepped to the door she already saw in imagination Andrew's face as she remembered it in childhood, a gentle, mild, sympathetic face which he had rarely shown, and which therefore affected her very strongly. She was sure he would speak soft, tender words to her such as her father had uttered before his death, and that she would not be able to bear it and would burst into sobs in his presence. Yet sooner or later it had to be, and she went in. The sobs rose higher and higher in her throat as she more and more clearly distinguished his form and her short-sighted eyes tried to make out his features, and then she saw his face and met his gaze.

He was lying in a squirrel-fur dressing-gown on a divan,

surrounded by pillows. He was thin and pale. In one thin, trans-lucently white hand he held a handkerchief, while with the other he stroked the delicate moustache he had grown, moving his fingers slowly. His eyes gazed at them as they entered.

On seeing his face and meeting his eyes Princess Mary's pace suddenly slackened, she felt her tears dry up and her sobs ceased. She suddenly felt guilty and grew timid on catching the expression of his face and eyes.

'But in what am I to blame?' she asked herself. 'Because you are alive and thinking of the living, while I . . .' his cold stern look replied.

In the deep gaze that seemed to look not outwards but inwards there was an almost hostile expression as he slowly regarded his sister and Natasha.

He kissed his sister, holding her hand in his as was their wont.

'How are you, Mary? How did you manage to get here?' said he in a voice as calm and aloof as his look.

Had he screamed in agony, that scream would not have struck such horror into Princess Mary's heart as the tone of his voice.

'And have you brought little Nicholas?' he asked in the same slow, quiet manner and with an obvious effort to remember.

'How are you now?' said Princess Mary, herself surprised at what she was saying.

'That, my dear, you must ask the doctor,' he replied, and again making an evident effort to be affectionate, he said with his lips only (his words clearly did not correspond to his thoughts):

'Merci, chère amie, d'être venue.'

Princess Mary pressed his hand. The pressure made him wince just perceptibly. He was silent, and she did not know what to say. She now understood what had happened to him two days before. In his words, his tone, and especially in that calm almost antagon-istic look, could be felt an estrangement from everything belonging to this world, terrible in one who is alive. Evidently only with an effort did he understand anything living; but it was obvious that he failed to understand, not because he lacked the power to do so but because he understood something else – something the living did not and could not understand – and which wholly occupied his mind.

'There, you see how strangely fate has brought us together,' said he, breaking the silence and pointing to Natasha. 'She looks after me all the time.'

Princess Mary heard him and did not understand how he could say such a thing. He, the sensitive, tender Prince Andrew, how could he say that, before her whom he loved and who loved him?

Had he expected to live he could not have said those words in that offensively cold tone. If he had not known that he was dying, how could he have failed to pity her and how could he speak like that in her presence? The only explanation was that he was indifferent, because something else, much more important, had been revealed to him.

The conversation was cold and disconnected, and continually broke off.

'Mary came by way of Ryazan,' said Natasha.

Prince Andrew did not notice that she called his sister Mary, and only after calling her so in his presence did Natasha notice it herself.

'Really?' he asked.

'They told her that all Moscow has been burnt down, and that...'

Natasha stopped. It was impossible to talk. It was plain he was making an effort to listen, but could not do so.

'Yes, they say it's burnt,' he said. 'It's a great pity,' and he gazed straight before him absently stroking his moustache with his fingers.

'And so you have met Count Nicholas, Mary?' Prince Andrew suddenly said, evidently wishing to speak pleasantly to them. 'He wrote here that he took a great liking to you,' he went on simply and calmly, evidently unable to understand all the complex significance his words had for living people. 'If you liked him too, it would be a good thing for you to get married,' he added rather more quickly, as if pleased at having found words he had long been seeking.

Princess Mary heard his words but they had no meaning for her, except as a proof of how far away he now was from everything living.

'Why talk of me?' she said quietly and glanced at Natasha.

Natasha, who felt her glance, did not look at her. All three were again silent.

'Andrew, would you like...' Princess Mary suddenly said in a trembling voice. 'Would you like to see little Nicholas? He is always talking about you!'

Prince Andrew smiled just perceptibly and for the first time, but Princess Mary, who knew his face so well, saw with horror that he did not smile with pleasure or affection for his son, but with quite gentle irony because he thought she was trying what she believed to be the last means of arousing him.

'Yes, I shall be very glad to see him. Is he quite well?'

When little Nicholas was brought into Prince Andrew's room he looked at his father with frightened eyes, but did not cry, because no one else was crying. Prince Andrew kissed him and evidently did not know what to say to him.

When Nicholas had been led away, Princess Mary again went up to her brother, kissed him, and unable to restrain her tears any longer, began to cry.

He looked at her attentively.

'Is it about Nicholas?' he asked.

Princess Mary nodded her head, weeping.

'Mary, you know the Gosp . . .' but he broke off.

'What did you say?'

'Nothing. You mustn't cry here,' he said, looking at her with the same cold expression.

When Princess Mary began to cry he understood that she was crying at the thought that little Nicholas would be left without a father. With a great effort he tried to return to life and to see things from their point of view.

'Yes, to them it must seem sad!' he thought. 'But how simple it is.

'The fowls of the air sow not, neither do they reap, yet your Father feedeth them,' he said to himself and wished to say to Princess Mary; 'but no, they will take it their own way, they won't understand! They can't understand that all those feelings they prize so – all our feelings, all those ideas that seem so important to us, are *unnecessary*. We cannot understand one another,' and he remained silent.

Prince Andrew's little son was seven. He could scarcely read, and knew nothing. After that day he lived through many things, gaining knowledge, observation, and experience, but had he possessed all the faculties he afterwards acquired, he could not have had a better or more profound understanding of the meaning of the scene he had witnessed between his father, Mary, and Natasha, than he had then. He understood it completely, and leaving the room without crying, went silently up to Natasha who had come out with him and looked shyly at her with his beautiful, thoughtful eyes, then his uplifted, rosy upper lip trembled and leaning his head against her he began to cry.

After that he avoided Dessalles and the countess who caressed him, and either sat alone, or came timidly to Princess Mary, or to Natasha of whom he seemed even fonder than of his aunt, and clung to them quietly and shyly.

When Princess Mary had left Prince Andrew she fully understood what Natasha's face had told her. She did not speak any more to Natasha of hopes of saving his life. She took turns with her beside his sofa, and did not cry any more, but prayed continually, turning in soul to that Eternal and Unfathomable, whose presence above the dying man was now so evident.

16

NOT only did Prince Andrew know he would die, but he felt that he was dying and was already half dead. He was conscious of an aloofness from everything earthly and a strange and joyous lightness of existence. Without haste or agitation he awaited what was coming. That inexorable, eternal, distant, and unknown – the presence of which he had felt continually all his life – was now near to him, and, by the strange lightness he experienced, almost comprehensible and palpable . . .

Formerly he had feared the end. He had twice experienced that terribly tormenting fear of death – the end – but now he no longer understood that fear.

He had felt it for the first time when the shell spun like a top before him, and he looked at the fallow field, the bushes and the sky, and knew that he was face to face with death. When he came to himself after being wounded and the flower of eternal, unfettered love had instantly unfolded itself in his soul as if freed from the bondage of life that had restrained it, he no longer feared death, and ceased to think about it.

During the hours of solitude, suffering, and partial delirium he spent after he was wounded, the more deeply he penetrated into the new principle of eternal love revealed to him, the more he unconsciously detached himself from earthly life. To love everything and everybody and always to sacrifice oneself for love, meant not to love anyone, not to live this earthly life. And the more imbued he became with that principle of love, the more he renounced life and the more completely he destroyed that dreadful barrier which – in the absence of such love – stands between life and death. When during those first days he remembered that he would have to die, he said to himself: 'Well, what of it? So much the better!'

But after the night in Mytishchy when, half delirious, he had seen her for whom he longed appear before him, and having pressed her hand to his lips, had shed gentle happy tears, love for a particular woman again crept unobserved into his heart and once more bound him to life. And joyful and agitating thoughts began to occupy his mind. Recalling the moment at the ambulance station when he had seen Kuragin, he could not now regain the feeling he then had, but was tormented by the question whether Kuragin was alive. And he dared not inquire.

His illness pursued its normal physical course, but what Natasha referred to when she said: 'This suddenly happened' had occurred two days before Princess Mary arrived. It was the last spiritual struggle between life and death, in which death gained the victory. It was the unexpected realization of the fact that he still valued life as presented to him in the form of his love for Natasha, and a last, though ultimately vanquished, attack of terror before the unknown.

It was evening. As usual after dinner he was slightly feverish, and his thoughts were preternaturally clear. Sonya was sitting by the table. He began to doze. Suddenly a feeling of happiness seized him.

'Ah, she has come!' thought he.

And so it was: in Sonya's place sat Natasha who had just come in noiselessly.

Since she had begun looking after him he had always experienced this physical consciousness of her nearness. She was sitting in an arm-chair placed sideways, screening the light of the candle from him, and was knitting a stocking. She had learned to knit stockings since Prince Andrew had casually mentioned that no one nursed the sick so well as old nurses who knit stockings, and that there is something soothing in the knitting of stockings. The needles clicked lightly in her slender, rapidly moving hands, and he could clearly see the thoughtful profile of her drooping face. She moved, and the ball rolled off her knees. She started, glanced round at him, and screening the candle with her hand stooped carefully with a supple and exact movement, picked up the ball, and regained her former position.

He looked at her without moving and saw that she wanted to draw a deep breath after stooping, but refrained from doing so and breathed cautiously.

At the Troitsa monastery they had spoken of the past, and he had told her that if he lived he would always thank God for his wound, which had brought them together again, but after that they never spoke of the future.

'Can it or can it not be?' he now thought as he looked at her and listened to the light click of the steel needles. 'Can fate have brought me to her so strangely only for me to die? ... Is it possible that the truth of life has been revealed to me only to show me that I have spent my life in falsity? I love her more than anything in the world! But what am I to do if I love her?' he thought, and he involuntarily groaned, from a habit acquired during his sufferings.

On hearing that sound Natasha put down the stocking, leaned nearer to him, and suddenly, noticing his shining eyes, stepped lightly up to him and bent over him.

'You are not asleep?'

'No, I have been looking at you a long time. I felt you come in. No one else gives me that sense of soft tranquillity that you do ... that light. I want to weep for joy.'

Natasha drew closer to him. Her face shone with rapturous joy.

'Natasha, I love you too much! More than anything in the world.'

'And I!' – She turned away for an instant. 'Why too much?' she asked.

'Why too much? ... Well, what do you think, what do you feel in your soul, your whole soul – shall I live? What do you think?'

'I am sure of it, sure!' Natasha almost shouted, taking hold of both his hands with a passionate movement.

He remained silent awhile.

'How good it would be!' and taking her hand he kissed it.

Natasha felt happy and agitated, but at once remembered that this would not do and that he had to be quiet.

'But you have not slept,' she said, repressing her joy. 'Try to sleep ... please!'

He pressed her hand and released it, and she went back to the candle and sat down again in her former position. Twice she turned and looked at him, and her eyes met his beaming at her. She set herself a task on her stocking and resolved not to turn round till it was finished.

Soon he really shut his eyes and fell asleep. He did not sleep long, and suddenly awoke with a start and in a cold perspiration.

As he fell asleep he had still been thinking of the subject that now always occupied his mind – about life and death, and chiefly about death. He felt himself nearer to it.

'Love? What is love?' he thought.

'Love hinders death. Love is life. All, everything that I understand, I understand only because I love. Everything is, everything exists, only because I love. Everything is united by it alone. Love is God, and to die means that I, a particle of love, shall return to the general and eternal source.' These thoughts seemed to him comforting. But they were only thoughts. Something was lacking in them, they were not clear, they were too one-sidedly personal and brain-spun. And there was the former agitation and obscurity. He fell asleep.

He dreamt that he was lying in the room he really was in, but that he was quite well and unwounded. Many various indifferent and insignificant people appeared before him. He talked to them, and discussed something trivial. They were preparing to go away somewhere. Prince Andrew dimly realized that all this was trivial and that he had more important cares, but he continued to speak, surprising them by empty witticisms. Gradually, unnoticed, all these persons began to disappear and a single question, that of the closed door, superseded all else. He rose and went to the door to bolt and lock it. Everything depended on whether he was, or was not, in time to lock it. He went, and tried to hurry, but his legs refused to move and he knew he would not be in time to lock the door though he painfully strained all his powers. He was seized by an agonizing fear. And that fear was the fear of death. It stood behind the door. But just when he was clumsily creeping towards the door, that dreadful something on the other side was already pressing against it and forcing its way in. Something not human – death – was breaking in through that door and had to be kept out. He seized the door, making a final effort to hold it back – to lock it was no longer possible – but his efforts were weak and clumsy and the door, pushed from behind by that terror, opened and closed again.

Once again it pushed from outside. His last superhuman efforts were vain and both halves of the door noiselessly opened. It entered, and it was *death*, and Prince Andrew died.

But at the instant he died, Prince Andrew remembered that he was asleep, and at the very instant he died, having made an effort, he awoke.

'Yes, it was death! I died – and woke up. Yes, death is an awakening!' And all at once it grew light in his soul and the veil that had till then concealed the unknown was lifted from his spiritual vision. He felt as if powers till then confined within him had been liberated, and that strange lightness did not again leave him.

When, waking in a cold perspiration, he moved on the divan, Natasha went up and asked him what was the matter. He did not answer and looked at her strangely, not understanding.

That was what had happened to him two days before Princess Mary's arrival. From that day, as the doctor expressed it, the wasting fever assumed a malignant character, but what the doctor said did not interest Natasha, she saw the terrible moral symptoms which to her were more convincing.

From that day an awakening from life came to Prince Andrew together with his awakening from sleep. And compared to the duration of life it did not seem to him slower than an awakening from sleep compared to the duration of a dream.

There was nothing terrible or violent in this comparatively slow awakening.

His last days and hours passed in an ordinary and simple way. Both Princess Mary and Natasha, who did not leave him, felt this. They did not weep or shudder and during these last days they themselves felt that they were not attending on him (he was no longer there, he had left them) but on what reminded them most closely of him – his body. Both felt this so strongly that the outward and terrible side of death did not affect them and they did not feel it necessary to foment their grief. Neither in his presence nor out of it did they weep, nor did they ever talk to one another about him. They felt that they could not express in words what they understood.

They both saw that he was sinking slowly and quietly, deeper and deeper, away from them, and they both knew that this had to be so and that it was right.

He confessed, and received communion: everyone came to take leave of him. When they brought his son to him, he pressed his lips to the boy's and turned away, not because he felt it hard and sad (Princess Mary and Natasha understood that) but simply because he thought it was all that was required of him, but when they told him to bless the boy, he did what was demanded and looked round as if asking whether there was anything else he should do.

When the last convulsions of the body, which the spirit was leaving, occurred, Princess Mary and Natasha were present.

'Is it over?' said Princess Mary when his body had for a few minutes lain motionless, growing cold before them. Natasha went up, looked at the dead eyes, and hastened to close them. She closed them and did not kiss them, but clung to that which reminded her most nearly of him – his body.

'Where has he gone? Where is he now? . . .'

When the body, washed and dressed, lay in the coffin on a table, everyone came to take leave of him, and they all wept.

Little Nicholas cried because his heart was rent by painful perplexity. The countess and Sonya cried from pity for Natasha and because he was no more. The old count cried because he felt that before long he, too, must take the same terrible step.

Natasha and Princess Mary also wept now, but not because of their own personal grief; they wept with a reverent and softening

emotion, which had taken possession of their souls at the consciousness of the simple and solemn mystery of death that had been
accomplished in their presence.

END OF PART ONE

PART TWO

1

MAN'S mind cannot grasp the causes of events in their completeness, but the desire to find those causes is implanted in man's soul. And without considering the multiplicity and complexity of the conditions any one of which taken separately may seem to be the cause, he snatches at the first approximation to a cause that seems to him intelligible, and says: 'This is the cause!' In historical events (where the actions of men are the subject of observation) the first and most primitive approximation to present itself was the will of the gods, and after that, the will of those who stood in the most prominent position – the heroes of history. But we need only penetrate to the essence of any historic event – which lies in the activity of the general mass of men who take part in it – to be convinced that the will of the historic hero does not control the actions of the mass but is itself continually controlled. It may seem to be a matter of indifference whether we understand the meaning of historical events this way or that; yet there is the same difference between a man who says that the people of the West moved on the East because Napoleon wished it, and a man who says that this happened because it had to happen, as there is between those who declared that the earth was stationary and that the planets moved round it, and those who admitted that they did not know what upheld the earth, but knew there were laws directing its movement and that of the other planets. There is, and can be, no cause of an historical event except the one cause of all causes. But there are laws directing events, and some of these laws are known to us while we are conscious of others we cannot comprehend. The discovery of these laws is only possible when we have quite abandoned the attempt to find the cause in the will of some one man, just as the discovery of the laws of the motion of the planets was possible only when men abandoned the conception of the fixity of the earth.

The historians consider that, next to the battle of Borodino and the occupation of Moscow by the enemy and its destruction by fire, the most important episode of the war of 1812 was the movement of the Russian army from the Ryazan to the Kaluga road and to the Tarutino camp – the so-called flank march across the Krasnaya Pakhra river.* They ascribe the glory of that achievement of genius to different men, and dispute to whom the honour is due. Even foreign historians, including the French, acknowledge the genius of the Russian commanders when they speak of that flank march. But it is hard to understand why military writers, and following them others, consider this flank march to be the profound conception of some one man who saved Russia and destroyed Napoleon. In the first place it is hard to understand where the profundity and genius of this movement lay, for not much mental effort was needed to see that the best position for an army, when it is not being attacked, is where there are most provisions; and even a dull boy of thirteen could have guessed that the best position for the army after its retreat from Moscow in 1812 was on the Kaluga road. So it is impossible to understand by what reasoning the historians reach the conclusion that this manœuvre was a profound one. And it is even more difficult to understand just why they think that this manœuvre was calculated to save Russia and destroy the French; for this flank march, had it been preceded, accompanied, or followed by other circumstances, might have proved ruinous to the Russians and salutary for the French. If the position of the Russian army really began to improve from the time of that march, it does not at all follow that the march was the cause of it.

That flank march might not only have failed to give any advantage to the Russian army, but might in other circumstances have led to its destruction. What would have happened had Moscow not burnt down? If Murat had not lost sight of the Russians? If Napoleon had not remained inactive? If the Russian army at Krasnaya Pakhra had given battle as Bennigsen and Barclay advised? What would have happened had the French attacked the Russians while they were marching beyond the Pakhra? What would have happened if on approaching Tarutino Napoleon had attacked the Russians with but a tenth of the energy he had shown when he attacked them at Smolensk? What would have happened had the French moved on Petersburg? ... In any of these eventualities the flank march that brought salvation might have proved disastrous.

The third and most incomprehensible thing is that people studying history deliberately avoid seeing that this flank march cannot be attributed to any one man, that no one ever foresaw it, and that in reality, like the retreat from Fili, it did not suggest itself to anyone in its entirety, but resulted – moment by moment, step by step, event by event – from an endless number of most diverse circumstances, and was only seen in its entirety when it had been accomplished and belonged to the past.

At the council at Fili* the prevailing thought in the minds of the Russian commanders was the one naturally suggesting itself, namely, a direct retreat by the Nizhny road. In proof of this there is the fact that the majority of the council voted for such a retreat, and above all there is the well-known conversation, after the council, between the commander-in-chief and Lanskoy who was in charge of the commissariat department. Lanskoy informed the commander-in-chief that the army supplies were for the most part stored along the Oka in the Tula and Ryazan provinces, and that if they retreated on Nizhny the army would be separated from its supplies by the broad river Oka, which cannot be crossed early in winter.* This was the first indication of the necessity of deviating from what had previously seemed the most natural course – a direct retreat on Nizhny-Novgorod. The army turned more to the south, along the Ryazan road and nearer to its supplies. Subsequently the inactivity of the French (who even lost sight of the Russian army), concern for the safety of the arsenal at Tula, and especially the advantages of drawing nearer to its supplies, caused the army to turn still farther south, to the Tula road. Having crossed over, by a forced march, to the Tula road beyond the Pakhra, the Russian commanders intended to remain at Podolsk and had no thought of the Tarutino position; but innumerable circumstances and the reappearance of French troops who had for a time lost touch with the Russians, and projects of giving battle, and above all the abundance of provisions in Kaluga province, obliged our army to turn still more to the south and to cross from the Tula to the Kaluga road and go to Tarutino, which was between the roads along which those supplies lay. Just as it is impossible to say when it was decided to abandon Moscow, so it is impossible to say precisely when, or by whom, it was decided to move to Tarutino. Only when the army had got there as the result of innumerable and varying forces, did people begin to assure themselves that they had desired this movement and long ago foreseen its result.

2

THE famous flank movement merely consisted in this: after the advance of the French had ceased, the Russian army, which had been continually retreating straight back from the invaders, deviated from that direct course and, not finding itself pursued, was naturally drawn towards the district where supplies were abundant.

If instead of imagining to ourselves commanders of genius leading the Russian army, we picture that army without any leaders, it could not have done anything but make a return movement towards Moscow, describing an arc in the direction where most provisions were to be found and where the country was richest.

That movement from the Nizhny to the Ryazan, Tula, and Kaluga roads was so natural that even the Russian marauders moved in that direction, and demands were sent from Petersburg for Kutuzov to take his army that way. At Tarutino Kutuzov received what was almost a reprimand from the Emperor for having moved the army along the Ryazan road, and the Emperor's letter indicated to him the very position he had already occupied near Kaluga.

Having rolled like a ball in the direction of the impetus given by the whole campaign and by the battle of Borodino, the Russian army – when the strength of that impetus was exhausted and no fresh push was received – assumed the position natural to it.

Kutuzov's merit lay, not in any strategic manœuvre of genius, as it is called, but in the fact that he alone understood the significance of what had happened. He alone then understood the meaning of the French army's inactivity, he alone continued to assert that the battle of Borodino had been a victory, he alone – who as commander-in-chief might have been expected to be eager to attack – employed his whole strength to restrain the Russian army from useless engagements.

The beast wounded at Borodino was lying where the fleeing hunter had left him; but whether he was still alive, whether he was strong and merely lying low, the hunter did not know. Suddenly the beast was heard to moan.

The moan of that wounded beast (the French army) which betrayed its calamitous condition, was the sending of Lauriston to Kutuzov's camp with overtures for peace.*

Napoleon, with his usual assurance that whatever entered his head was right, wrote to Kutuzov the first words that occurred to him, though they were meaningless.

Monsieur le prince Koutouzov [he wrote],
I am sending one of my adjutants-general to discuss several interesting questions with you. I beg your Highness to credit what he says to you, *especially when he expresses the sentiment of esteem and special regard I have long entertained for your person. This letter having no other object, I pray God, monsieur le prince Koutouzov, to keep you in His holy and gracious protection!*

Napoleon.

Moscow, 30th October 1812.

1058

Kutuzov replied:

I should be cursed by posterity were I looked on as the initiator of a settlement of any sort. *Such is the present spirit of my nation.*

But he continued to exert all his powers to restrain his troops from attacking.

During the month that the French troops were pillaging in Moscow and the Russian troops were quietly encamped at Tarutino, a change had taken place in the relative strength of the two armies – both in spirit and in number – as a result of which the superiority had passed to the Russian side. Though the condition and numbers of the French army were unknown to the Russians, as soon as that change occurred the need of attacking at once showed itself by countless signs. These signs were: Lauriston's mission; the abundance of provisions at Tarutino; the reports coming in from all sides of the inactivity and disorder of the French; the flow of recruits to our regiments; the fine weather; the long rest the Russian soldiers had enjoyed, and the impatience to do what they had been assembled for, which usually shows itself in an army that has been resting; curiosity as to what the French army, so long lost sight of, was doing; the boldness with which our outposts now scouted close up to the French stationed at Tarutino; the news of easy successes gained by peasants and guerrilla troops over the French, the envy aroused by this; the desire for revenge that lay in the heart of every Russian as long as the French were in Moscow, and (above all) a dim consciousness in every soldier's mind that the relative strength of the armies had changed and that the advantage was now on our side. There was a substantial change in the relative strength, and an advance had become inevitable. And at once, as a clock begins to strike and chime as soon as the minute hand has completed a full circle, this change was shown by an increased activity, whizzing, and chiming, in the higher spheres.

3

THE Russian army was commanded by Kutuzov and his staff, and also by the Emperor from Petersburg. Before the news of the abandonment of Moscow had been received in Petersburg, a detailed plan for the whole campaign had been drawn up and sent to Kutuzov for his guidance. Though this plan had been drawn up on the supposition that Moscow was still in our hands, it was approved by the staff and accepted as a basis for action. Kutuzov only replied that movements arranged from a distance were always difficult to execute. So fresh instructions were sent for the solution of difficulties that might be encountered, as well as fresh people who were to watch Kutuzov's actions and report upon them.

Besides this, the whole staff of the Russian army was now reorganized. The posts left vacant by Bagration who had been killed and by Barclay who had gone away in dudgeon, had to be filled. Very serious consideration was given to the question whether it would be better to put A in B's place and B in D's, or on the contrary to put D in A's place, and so on – as if anything more than A's or B's satisfaction depended on this.

As a result of the hostility between Kutuzov and his Chief of Staff, Bennigsen; the presence of confidential representatives of the Emperor; and these transfers, a more than usually complicated play of parties was going on among the staff of the army. A was undermining B, D was undermining C, and so on in all possible combinations and permutations. In all these plottings the subject of intrigue was generally the conduct of the war, which all these men believed they were directing; but this affair of the war went on independently of them as it had to go: that is, never in the way people devised, but flowing always from the essential attitude of the masses. Only in the highest spheres did all these schemes, crossings, and interminglings, appear to be a true reflection of what had to happen.

Prince Michael Ilarionovich! [wrote the Emperor on the 2nd of October in a letter that reached Kutuzov after the battle at Tarutino] Since September 2nd Moscow has been in the hands of the enemy. Your last reports were written on the 20th, and during all this time not only has no action been taken against the enemy or for the relief of the ancient capital, but according to your last report you have even retreated farther. Serpukhov is already occupied by an enemy detachment and Tula with its famous arsenal so indispensable to the army, is in danger. From General Wintzingerode's reports I see that an enemy corps of ten thousand men is moving on the Petersburg road. Another corps of several thousand men is moving on Dmitrov. A third has advanced along the Vladimir road, and a fourth, rather considerable detachment, is stationed between Ruza and Mozhaysk. Napoleon himself was in Moscow as late as the 25th. In view of all this information, when the enemy has scattered his forces in large detachments, and with Napoleon and his Guards in Moscow, is it possible that the enemy's forces confronting you are so considerable as not to allow of your taking the offensive? On the contrary, he is probably pursuing you with detachments, or at most with an army corps, much weaker than the army entrusted to you. It would seem that, availing yourself of these circumstances, you might advantageously attack a weaker enemy and annihilate him, or at least oblige him to retreat, retaining in our hands an important part of the provinces now occupied by the enemy, and thereby averting danger from Tula and other towns in the interior. You will be responsible if the enemy is able to direct a force of any size against Petersburg to threaten this capital in which it has not been possible to retain many troops; for with the army entrusted to you, and acting with resolution and energy, you have ample means to avert this fresh calamity. Remember that you have still to answer to our offended country for the loss of Moscow. You have experienced my readiness to reward you. That readiness will not weaken in me, but I and Russia have a right to expect from you all the zeal, firmness, and success, which your intellect, military talent, and the courage of the troops you command, justify us in expecting.

But by the time this letter, which proved that the real relation of the forces had already made itself felt in Petersburg, was dispatched, Kutuzov had found himself unable any longer to restrain the army he commanded from attacking and a battle had taken place.

On the 2nd of October a Cossack, Shapovalov, who was out scouting, killed one hare and wounded another. Following the wounded hare, he made his way far into the forest and came upon the left flank of Murat's army encamped there without any precautions. The Cossack laughingly told his comrades how he had almost fallen into the hands of the French. A cornet, hearing the story, informed his commander.

The Cossack was sent for and questioned. The Cossack officers wished to take advantage of this chance to capture some horses, but one of the superior officers, who was acquainted with the higher authorities, reported the incident to a general on the staff. The state of things on the staff had of late been exceedingly strained. Ermolov had been to see Bennigsen a few days previously and had entreated him to use his influence with the commander-in-chief to induce him to take the offensive.

'If I did not know you I should think you did not want what you are asking for. I need only advise anything and his Highness is sure to do the opposite,' replied Bennigsen.

The Cossack's report, confirmed by horse patrols who were sent out, was the final proof that events had matured. The tightly coiled spring was released, the clock began to whirr and the chimes to play. Despite all his supposed power, his intellect, his experience, and his knowledge of men, Kutuzov – having taken into consideration the Cossack's report; a note from Bennigsen, who sent personal reports to the Emperor; the wishes he supposed the Emperor to hold; and the fact that all the generals expressed the same wish, could no longer check the inevitable movement, and gave the order to do what he regarded as useless and harmful — gave his approval, that is, to the accomplished fact.

4

BENNIGSEN'S note and the Cossack's information that the left flank of the French was unguarded were merely final indications that it was necessary to order an attack, and it was fixed for the 5th of October.

In the morning of the 4th of October Kutuzov signed the dispositions. Toll read them to Ermolov, asking him to attend to the further arrangements.

'All right — all right. I haven't time just now,' replied Ermolov, and left the hut.

The dispositions drawn up by Toll were very good. As in the Austerlitz dispositions, it was written — though not in German this time:

'The First Column will march here and here', 'the Second Column will march there and there', and so on; and on paper all these columns arrived at their places at the appointed time and destroyed the enemy. Everything had been admirably thought out as is usual in dispositions, and as is always the case not a single column reached its place at the appointed time.

When the necessary number of copies of the dispositions had been prepared, an officer was summoned and sent to deliver them to Ermolov to deal with. A young officer of the Horse Guards, Kutuzov's orderly, pleased at the importance of the mission entrusted to him, went to Ermolov's quarters.

'Gone away,' said Ermolov's orderly.

The officer of the Horse Guards went to a general with whom Ermolov was often to be found.

'No, and the general's out too.'

The officer, mounting his horse, rode off to someone else.

'No, he's gone out.'

'If only they don't make me responsible for this delay! What a nuisance it is!' thought the officer, and he rode round the whole camp. One man said he had seen Ermolov ride past with some other generals, others said he must have returned home. The officer searched till six o'clock in the evening without even stopping to eat. Ermolov was nowhere to be found and no one knew where he was. The officer snatched a little food at a comrade's, and rode again to the vanguard to find Miloradovich. Miloradovich too was away, but here he was told that he had gone to a ball at General Kikin's and that Ermolov was probably there too.

1062

'But where is it?'

'Why, there, over at Echkino,' said a Cossack officer, pointing to a country house in the far distance.

'What, outside our lines?'

'They've put two regiments as outposts, and they're having such a spree there, it's awful! Two bands and three sets of singers!'

The officer rode out beyond our lines to Echkino. While still at a distance he heard as he rode the merry sounds of a soldiers' dance-song proceeding from the house.

'In the meadows . . . in the meadows!' he heard, accompanied by whistling and the sound of a *torban*,* drowned every now and then by shouts. These sounds made his spirits rise, but at the same time he was afraid that he would be blamed for not having executed sooner the important order entrusted to him. It was already past eight o'clock. He dismounted, and went up into the porch of a large country house which had remained intact between the Russian and French forces. In the refreshment room and the hall footmen were bustling about with wine and viands. Groups of singers stood outside the windows. The officer was admitted and immediately saw all the chief generals of the army together, and among them Ermolov's big imposing figure. They all had their coats unbuttoned and were standing in a semi-circle with flushed and animated faces, laughing loudly. In the middle of the room a short handsome general with a red face was dancing the *trepak* with much spirit and agility.

'Ha, ha, ha! Bravo, Nicholas Ivanych! Ha, ha, ha!'

The officer felt that by arriving with important orders at such a moment he was doubly to blame, and he would have preferred to wait; but one of the generals espied him and, hearing what he had come about, informed Ermolov.

Ermolov came forward with a frown on his face and, hearing what the officer had to say, took the papers from him without a word.

'You think he went off just by chance?' said a comrade who was on the staff that evening to the officer of the Horse Guards, referring to Ermolov. 'It was a trick. It was done on purpose to get Konovnitsyn into trouble. You'll see what a mess there'll be to-morrow.'

5

NEXT day the decrepit Kutuzov, having given orders to be called early, said his prayers, dressed, and with an unpleasant consciousness of having to direct a battle he did not approve of, got into his calèche and drove from Letashovka (a village three and a half miles from Tarutino) to the place where the attacking columns were to meet. He sat in the calèche dozing and waking up by turns, and listening for any sound of firing on the right as an indication that the action had begun. But all was still quiet. A damp dull autumn morning was just dawning. On approaching Tarutino, Kutuzov noticed cavalrymen leading their horses to water across the road along which he was driving. Kutuzov looked at them searchingly, stopped his carriage, and inquired what regiment they belonged to. They belonged to a column that should have been far in front and in ambush long before then. 'It may be a mistake,' thought the old commander-in-chief. But a little farther on he saw infantry regiments with their arms piled and the soldiers, only partly dressed, eating their rye-porridge and carrying fuel. He sent for an officer. The officer reported that no order to advance had been received.

'How! Not rec . . .' Kutuzov began, but checked himself immediately and sent for a senior officer. Getting out of his calèche, with drooping head and breathing heavily, he waited, pacing silently up and down. When Eykhen, the officer of the general staff whom he had summoned, appeared, Kutuzov went purple in the face not because that officer was to blame for the mistake, but because he was an object of sufficient importance for him to vent his wrath on. Trembling and panting the old man fell into that state of fury in which he sometimes used to roll on the ground, and he fell upon Eykhen, threatening him with his hands, shouting, and loading him with gross abuse. Another man, Captain Brozin, who happened to turn up and who was not at all to blame, suffered the same fate.

'What sort of another blackguard are you? You should be shot! Scoundrels!' yelled Kutuzov in a hoarse voice, waving his arms and reeling.

He was suffering physically. He, the commander-in-chief, a Serene Highness who everybody said possessed powers such as no man had ever had in Russia, to be placed in this position – made the laughing-stock of the whole army! 'I needn't have been in such a hurry to pray about to-day, or have kept awake thinking everything over all night,' thought he to himself. 'When I was a chit of an officer no one would have dared to mock me so . . . and now!' He was in a state of physical suffering as if from corporal punishment, and could not avoid expressing it by cries of anger and distress. But his strength soon began to fail him, and looking about him, conscious of having said much that was amiss, he again got into his calèche and drove back in silence.

His wrath, once expended, did not return, and blinking feebly he listened to excuses and self-justifications (Ermolov did not come to see him till the next day) and to the insistence of Bennigsen, Konovnitsyn, and Toll, that the movement that had miscarried should be executed next day. And once more Kutuzov had to consent.

6

NEXT day the troops assembled at their appointed places in the evening and advanced during the night. It was an autumn night with dark purple clouds, but no rain. The ground was damp but not muddy, and the troops advanced noiselessly, only occasionally a jingling of the artillery could be faintly heard. The men were forbidden to talk aloud, to smoke their pipes, or to strike a light, and they tried to prevent their horses neighing. The secrecy of the undertaking heightened its charm and they marched gaily. Some columns, supposing they had reached their destination, halted, piled arms, and settled down on the cold ground, but the majority marched all night and arrived at places where they evidently should not have been.

Only Count Orlov-Denisov with his Cossacks (the least important detachment of all) got to his appointed place at the right time. This detachment halted at the outskirts of a forest, on the path leading from the village of Stromilova to Dmitrovsk.

Towards dawn Count Orlov-Denisov, who had dozed off, was awakened by a deserter from the French army being brought to him. This was a Polish sergeant of Poniatowski's corps, who explained in Polish that he had come over because he had been slighted in the service: that he ought long ago to have been made an officer, that he was braver than any of them, and so he had left them and wished to pay them out. He said that Murat was spending the night only a verst from where they were, and that if they would let him have a convoy of a hundred men he would capture him alive. Count Orlov-Denisov consulted his fellow-officers. The offer was too tempting to be refused. Everyone volunteered to go and everybody advised making the attempt. After much disputing and arguing, Major-General Grekov with two Cossack regiments decided to go with the Polish sergeant.

'Now remember,' said Count Orlov-Denisov to the sergeant at parting, 'if you have been lying I'll have you hanged like a dog; but if it's true you shall have a hundred gold pieces!'

Without replying the sergeant, with a resolute air, mounted and rode away with Grekov whose men had quickly assembled. They disappeared into the forest, and Count Orlov-Denisov, having seen Grekov off, returned, shivering from the freshness of the early dawn and excited by what he had undertaken on his own responsibility, and began looking at the enemy camp, now just visible in the deceptive light of dawn and the dying camp-fires. Our columns ought to have begun to appear on an open declivity to his right. He looked in that direction, but though the columns would have been visible quite far off, they were not to be seen. It seemed to the count that things were beginning to stir in the French camp, and his keen-sighted adjutant confirmed this.

'Oh, it is really too late,' said Count Orlov, looking at the camp.

As often happens when someone we have trusted is no longer before our eyes, it suddenly seemed quite clear and obvious to him that the sergeant was an impostor, that he had lied, and that the whole Russian attack would be ruined by the absence of those two regiments, which he would lead away heaven only knew where. How could one capture a commander-in-chief from among such a mass of troops!

'I am sure that rascal was lying,' said the count.

'They can still be called back,' said one of his suite, who like Count Orlov felt distrustful of the adventure when he looked at the enemy's camp.

'Eh? Really . . . what do you think? Should we let them go on or not?'

'Will you have them fetched back?'

'Fetch them back, fetch them back!' said Count Orlov with sudden determination, looking at his watch. 'It will be too late. It is quite light.'

And the adjutant galloped through the forest after Grekov. When Grekov returned, Count Orlov-Denisov, excited both by the abandoned attempt and by vainly awaiting the infantry columns that still did not appear, as well as by the proximity of the enemy, resolved to advance. All his men felt the same excitement.

'Mount!' he commanded in a whisper. The men took their places and crossed themselves . . . 'Forward, with God's aid!'

'Hurrah-ah-ah!' reverberated in the forest, and the Cossack companies, trailing their lances and advancing one after another as if poured out of a sack, dashed gaily across the brook towards the camp.

One desperate frightened yell from the first French soldier who saw the Cossacks – and all who were in the camp, undressed and only just waking up, ran off in all directions, abandoning cannons, muskets and horses.

Had the Cossacks pursued the French without heeding what

was behind and around them they would have captured Murat and everything there. That was what the officers desired. But it was impossible to make the Cossacks budge when once they had got booty and prisoners. None of them listened to orders. Fifteen hundred prisoners and thirty-eight guns were taken on the spot, besides standards and (what seemed most important to the Cossacks) horses, saddles, horse-cloths, and the like. All this had to be dealt with, the prisoners and guns secured, the booty divided – not without some shouting and even a little fighting among themselves – and it was on this that the Cossacks all busied themselves.

The French, not being farther pursued, began to recover themselves: they formed into detachments and began firing. Orlov-Denisov, still waiting for the other columns to arrive, advanced no further.

Meantime according to the dispositions which said that 'the First Column will march' and so on, the infantry of the belated columns, commanded by Bennigsen and directed by Toll, had started in due order and, as always happens, had got somewhere, but not to their appointed places. As always happens the men, starting cheerfully, began to halt; murmurs were heard, there was a sense of confusion, and finally a backward movement. Adjutants and generals galloped about, shouted, grew angry, quarrelled, said they had come quite wrong and were late, gave vent to a little abuse, and at last gave it all up and went forward, simply to get somewhere. 'We shall get somewhere or other!' And they did indeed get somewhere, though not to their right places; a few eventually even got to their right place, but too late to be of any use, and only in time to be fired at. Toll, who in this battle played the part of Weyrother at Austerlitz, galloped assiduously from place to place finding everything upside down everywhere. Thus he stumbled on Bagovut's corps in a wood when it was already broad daylight, though the corps should long before have joined Orlov-Denisov. Excited and vexed by the failure, and supposing that someone must be responsible for it, Toll galloped up to the commander of the corps and began upbraiding him severely, saying that he ought to be shot. General Bagovut, a fighting old soldier of placid temperament, being also upset by all the delay, confusion, and cross-purposes, fell into a rage, to everybody's surprise and quite contrary to his usual character, and said disagreeable things to Toll.

'I prefer not to take lessons from anyone, but I can die with my men as well as anybody,' he said, and advanced with a single division.

Coming out onto a field under the enemy's fire, this brave

general went straight ahead leading his men under fire, without considering in his agitation whether going into action now, with a single division, would be of any use or no. Danger, cannon-balls, and bullets, were just what he needed in his angry mood. One of the first bullets killed him, and other bullets killed many of his men. And his division remained under fire for some time quite uselessly.

7

MEANWHILE another column was to have attacked the French from the front, but Kutuzov accompanied that column. He well knew that nothing but confusion would come of this battle undertaken against his will, and as far as was in his power held the troops back. He did not advance.

He rode silently on his small grey horse, indolently answering suggestions that they should attack.

'The word *attack* is always on your tongue, but you don't see that we are unable to execute complicated manœuvres,' said he to Miloradovich who asked permission to advance.

'We couldn't take Murat prisoner this morning or get to the place in time, and nothing can be done now!' he replied to someone else.

When Kutuzov was informed that at the French rear – where according to the reports of the Cossacks there had previously been nobody – there were now two battalions of Poles, he gave a sidelong glance at Ermolov who was behind him and to whom he had not spoken since the previous day.

'You see! They are asking to attack and making plans of all kinds, but as soon as one gets to business nothing is ready, and the enemy, forewarned, takes measures accordingly.'

Ermolov screwed up his eyes and smiled faintly on hearing these words. He understood that for him the storm had blown over, and that Kutuzov would content himself with that hint.

'He's having a little fun at my expense,' said Ermolov softly, nudging with his knee Raevsky who was at his side.

Soon after this, Ermolov moved up to Kutuzov and respectfully remarked:

'It is not too late yet, your Highness – the enemy has not gone away – if you were to order an attack! If not, the Guards will not so much as see smoke.'

Kutuzov did not reply, but when they reported to him that Murat's troops were in retreat he ordered an advance, though at every hundred paces he halted for three-quarters of an hour.

The whole battle consisted in what Orlov-Denisov's Cossacks had done: the rest of the army merely lost some hundreds of men uselessly.

In consequence of this battle Kutuzov received a diamond decoration, and Bennigsen some diamonds and a hundred thousand rubles; others also received pleasant recognitions corresponding to their various grades, and following the battle fresh changes were made in the staff.

'That's how everything is done with us, all topsy-turvy!' said the Russian officers and generals after the Tarutino battle, letting it be understood that some fool there is doing things all wrong but that we ourselves should not have done so, just as people speak to-day. But people who talk like that either do not know what they are talking about, or deliberately deceive themselves. No battle – Tarutino, Borodino, or Austerlitz – takes place as those who planned it anticipated. That is an essential condition.

A countless number of free forces (for nowhere is man freer than during a battle, where it is a question of life and death) influence the course taken by the fight, and that course never can be known in advance and never coincides with the direction of any one force.

If many simultaneously and variously directed forces act on a given body, the direction of its motion cannot coincide with any one of those forces, but will always be a mean – what in mechanics is represented by the diagonal of a parallelogram of forces.

If in the descriptions given by historians, especially French ones, we find their wars and battles carried out in accordance with previously formed plans, the only conclusion to be drawn is that those descriptions are false.

The battle of Tarutino obviously did not attain the aim Toll had in view – to lead the troops into action in the order prescribed by the dispositions; nor that which Count Orlov-Denisov may have had in view – to take Murat prisoner; nor the result of immediately destroying the whole corps, which Bennigsen and others may have had in view; nor the aim of the officer who wished to go into action to distinguish himself; nor that of the Cossack who wanted more booty than he got, and so on. But if the aim of the battle was what actually resulted and what all the Russians of that day desired – to drive the French out of Russia and destroy their army – it is quite clear that the battle of Tarutino, just because of its incongruities, was exactly what was wanted at that stage of the campaign. It would be difficult and even impossible to imagine any result more opportune than the actual outcome of this battle. With a minimum of effort and insignificant losses, despite the greatest confusion, the most important results of the whole campaign were attained: the transition from retreat to advance, an exposure of the weakness of the French, and the administration of that shock which Napoleon's army had only awaited to begin its flight.

8

NAPOLEON enters Moscow after the brilliant victory *de la Moskowa*; there can be no doubt about the victory, for the battlefield remains in the hands of the French. The Russians retreat and abandon their ancient capital. Moscow, abounding in provisions, arms, munitions, and incalculable wealth, is in Napoleon's hands. The Russian army, only half the strength of the French, does not make a single attempt to attack for a whole month. Napoleon's position is most brilliant. He can either fall on the Russian army with double its strength and destroy it; negotiate an advantageous peace, or in case of refusal make a menacing move on Petersburg; or even, in case of a reverse, return to Smolensk or Vilna, or remain in Moscow: in short, no special genius would seem to be required to retain the brilliant position the French held at that time. For that, only very simple and easy steps were necessary: not to allow the troops to loot; to prepare winter clothing – of which there was sufficient in Moscow for the whole army; and methodically to collect the provisions, of which (according to the French historians) there were enough in Moscow to supply the whole army for six months. Yet Napoleon, that greatest of all geniuses, who the historians declare had control of the army, took none of these steps.

He not merely did nothing of the kind, but on the contrary, he used his power to select the most foolish and ruinous of all the courses open to him. Of all that Napoleon might have done: wintering in Moscow, advancing on Petersburg or on Nizhny-Novgorod, or retiring by a more northerly or more southerly route (say by the road Kutuzov afterwards took), nothing more stupid or disastrous can be imagined than what he actually did. He remained in Moscow till October, letting the troops plunder the city, then – hesitating whether to leave a garrison behind him – he quitted Moscow, approached Kutuzov without joining battle, turned to the right and reached Malo-Yaroslavets, again without attempting to break through and take the road Kutuzov took, but retiring instead to Mozhaysk along the devastated Smolensk road. Nothing more stupid than that could have been devised, or more disastrous for the army, as the sequel showed. Had Napoleon's aim been to destroy his army, the most skilful strategist could hardly have devised any series of actions that would so completely have accomplished that purpose, independently of anything the Russian army might do.

Napoleon, the man of genius, did this! But to say that he destroyed his army because he wished to or because he was very stupid, would be as unjust as to say that he had brought his troops to Moscow because he wished to and because he was very clever and a genius.

In both cases his personal activity, having no more force than the personal activity of any soldier, merely coincided with the laws that guided the event.

The historians quite falsely represent Napoleon's faculties as having weakened in Moscow, and do so only because the results did not justify his actions. He employed all his ability and strength to do the best he could for himself and his army as he had done previously, and as he did subsequently in 1813. His activity at that time was no less astounding than it was in Egypt, in Italy, in Austria, and in Prussia. We do not know for certain how far his genius was genuine in Egypt – where forty centuries looked down upon his grandeur – for his great exploits there are all told us by Frenchmen. We cannot estimate his genius in Austria or Prussia accurately, for we have to draw our information from French or German sources, and the incomprehensible surrender of whole corps without fighting, and of fortresses without a siege, must incline Germans to recognize his genius as the only explanation of the war carried on in Germany. But we, thank God, have no need to recognize his genius in order to hide our shame. We have paid for the right to look at the matter plainly and simply, and we will not abandon that right.

His activity in Moscow was as amazing and as full of genius as elsewhere. Order after order and plan after plan was issued by him from the time he entered Moscow till the time he left it. The absence of citizens and of a deputation, and even the burning of Moscow, did not disconcert him. He did not lose sight either of the welfare of his army or of the doings of the enemy, or of the welfare of the people of Russia, or of the direction of affairs in Paris, or of diplomatic considerations concerning the terms of the anticipated peace.

WITH regard to military matters, Napoleon immediately on his entry into Moscow gave General Sébastiani strict orders to observe the movements of the Russian army, sent army corps out along the different roads, and charged Murat to find Kutuzov. Then he gave careful directions about the fortification of the Kremlin, and drew up a brilliant plan for a future campaign over the whole map of Russia.

With regard to diplomatic questions, Napoleon summoned Captain Yakovlev, who had been robbed and was in rags* and did not know how to get out of Moscow, minutely explained to him his whole policy and his magnanimity, and having written a letter to the Emperor Alexander in which he considered it his duty to inform his Friend and Brother that Rostopchin had managed affairs badly in Moscow, he dispatched Yakovlev to Petersburg.

Having similarly explained his views and his magnanimity to Tutolmin, he dispatched that old man also to Petersburg to negotiate.

With regard to legal matters, immediately after the fires he gave orders to find and execute the incendiaries. And the scoundrel Rostopchin was punished by an order to burn down his houses.

With regard to administrative matters, Moscow was granted a constitution. A municipality was established and the following announcement issued:

INHABITANTS OF MOSCOW!

Your misfortunes are cruel, but his Majesty the Emperor and King desires to arrest their course. Terrible examples have taught you how he punishes disobedience and crime. Strict measures have been taken to put an end to disorder and to re-establish public security. A paternal administration, chosen from among yourselves, will form your municipality or city government. It will take care of you, of your needs, and of your welfare. Its members will be distinguished by a red ribbon worn across the shoulder, and the mayor of the city will wear a white belt as well. But when not on duty they will only wear a red ribbon round the left arm.

The city police is established on its former footing, and better order already prevails in consequence of its activity. The government has appointed two commissaries-general, or chiefs of police, and twenty commissaries or captains of wards have been appointed to the different wards of the city. You will recognize them by the white ribbon they will wear on the left arm. Several churches of different denominations are open, and divine service is performed in them unhindered. Your fellow-citizens are returning every day to their homes and orders have been given that they should find in them the help and protection due in this misfortune. These are the measures the government has adopted to re-establish order and relieve your condition. But to achieve this aim it is necessary that you should add your efforts and should, if possible, forget the misfortunes you have suffered, should entertain the hope of a less cruel fate, should be certain that inevitable and ignominious death awaits those who make any attempt on your persons or on what remains of your property, and finally that you should not doubt that these will be safeguarded, since such is the will of the greatest and most just of monarchs. Soldiers and citizens, of whatever nation you may be, re-establish public confidence, the source of the welfare of a state, live like brothers, render mutual aid and protection one to another, unite to defeat the intentions of the evil-minded, obey the military and civil authorities, and your tears will soon cease to flow!

With regard to supplies for the army, Napoleon decreed that all the troops in turn should enter Moscow *à la maraude* to obtain provisions for themselves, so that the army might have its future provided for.

With regard to religion, Napoleon ordered the priests to be brought back and services to be again performed in the churches.

With regard to commerce and to provisioning the army, the following was placarded everywhere:

PROCLAMATION

You, peaceful inhabitants of Moscow, artisans and workmen whom misfortune has driven from the city, and you scattered tillers of the soil, still kept out in the fields by groundless fear, listen! Tranquillity is returning to this capital and order is being restored in it. Your fellow-countrymen are emerging boldly from their hiding-places on finding that they are respected. Any violence to them or to their property is promptly punished. His Majesty the Emperor and King protects them, and considers no one among you his enemy except those who disobey his orders. He desires to end your misfortunes and restore you to your homes and families. Respond therefore to his benevolent intentions and come to us without fear. Inhabitants, return with confidence to your abodes! You will soon find means of satisfying your needs. Craftsmen and industrious artisans, return to your work, your houses, your shops, where the protection of guards awaits you! You shall receive proper pay for your work. And lastly you too, peasants, come from the forests where you are hiding in terror, return to your huts without fear, in full assurance that you will find protection! Markets are established in the city where peasants can bring their surplus supplies and the products of the soil. The government has taken the following steps to ensure freedom of sale for them: (1) From to-day, peasants, husbandmen, and those living in the neighbourhood of Moscow, may without any danger bring their supplies of all kinds to two appointed markets, of which one is on the Mokhovaya Street and the other at the Provision Market.

(2) Such supplies will be bought from them at such prices as seller and buyer may agree on, and if a seller is unable to obtain a fair price he will be free to take his goods back to his village and no one may hinder him under any pretext. (3) Sunday and Wednesday of each week are appointed as the chief market-days, and to that end a sufficient number of troops will be stationed along the high roads on Tuesdays and Saturdays at such distances from the town as to protect the carts. (4) Similar measures will be taken that peasants with their carts and horses may meet with no hindrance on their return journey. (5) Steps will immediately be taken to re-establish ordinary trading.

Inhabitants of the city and villages, and you, working men and artisans, to whatever nation you belong, you are called on to carry out the paternal intentions of his Majesty the Emperor and King and to co-operate with him for the public welfare! Lay your respect and confidence at his feet and do not delay to unite with us!

With the object of raising the spirits of the troops and of the people, reviews were constantly held and rewards distributed. The Emperor rode through the streets to comfort the inhabitants, and despite his preoccupation with state affairs himself visited the theatres that were established by his order.

In regard to philanthropy, the greatest virtue of crowned heads, Napoleon also did all in his power. He caused the words *Maison de ma Mère* to be inscribed on the charitable institutions,* thereby combining tender filial affection with the majestic benevolence of a monarch. He visited the Foundling Hospital and, allowing the orphans saved by him to kiss his white hands, graciously conversed with Tutolmin. Then, as Thiers eloquently recounts, he ordered his soldiers to be paid in forged Russian money which he had prepared: 'Dignifying these measures by an act worthy of himself and of the French army, he let relief be distributed to those who had been burnt out. But as food was too precious to be given to foreigners, who were for the most part enemies, Napoleon preferred to supply them with money with which to purchase food from outside, and had paper rubles distributed to them.'

With reference to army discipline, orders were continually being issued to inflict severe punishment for the non-performance of military duties and to suppress robbery.

10

BUT strange to say all these measures, efforts, and plans – which were not at all worse than others issued in similar circumstances – did not affect the essence of the matter but, like the hands of a clock detached from the mechanism, swung about in an arbitrary and aimless way without engaging the cogwheels.

With reference to the military side – the plan of campaign – that work of genius of which Thiers remarks that 'His genius never devised anything more profound, more skilful, or more admirable', and enters into a polemic with M. Fain* to prove that this work of genius must be referred not to the 4th but to the 15th of October – that plan never was or could be executed, for it was quite out of touch with the facts of the case. The fortifying of the Kremlin, for which *la Mosquée* (as Napoleon termed the church of Basil the Beatified) was to have been razed to the ground, proved quite useless. The mining of the Kremlin only helped towards fulfilling Napoleon's wish that it should be blown up when he left Moscow – as a child wants the floor on which he has hurt himself to be beaten. The pursuit of the Russian army, about which Napoleon was so concerned, produced an unheard-of result. The French generals lost touch with the Russian army of sixty thousand men, and according to Thiers it was only eventually found, like a lost pin, by the skill and – apparently – the genius of Murat.

With reference to diplomacy, all Napoleon's arguments as to his magnanimity and justice, both to Tutolmin and to Yakovlev (whose chief concern was to obtain a greatcoat and a conveyance), proved useless: Alexander did not receive these envoys and did not reply to their embassage.

With regard to legal matters, after the execution of the supposed incendiaries, the rest of Moscow burnt down.

With regard to administrative matters, the establishment of a municipality did not stop the robberies and was only of use to certain people who formed part of that municipality and – under pretext of preserving order – looted Moscow or saved their own property from being looted.

With regard to religion, as to which in Egypt matters had so easily been settled by Napoleon's visit to a mosque, no results were achieved. Two or three priests who were found in Moscow did try to carry out Napoleon's wish, but one of them was slapped in the face by a French soldier while conducting service, and a French official reported of another that: 'The priest whom I found and invited to say Mass, cleaned and locked up the church. That night the doors were again broken open, the padlocks smashed, the books mutilated, and other disorders perpetrated.'

With reference to commerce, the proclamation to industrious workmen and to peasants evoked no response. There were no industrious workmen, and the peasants caught the commissaries who ventured too far out of town with the proclamation, and killed them.

As to the theatres for the entertainment of the people and the troops, these did not meet with success either. The theatres set up in the Kremlin and in Posnyakov's house were closed again at once, because the actors and actresses were robbed.

Even philanthropy did not have the desired effect. The genuine as well as the false paper-money which flooded Moscow lost its value. The French, collecting booty, cared only for gold. Not only was the paper-money which Napoleon so graciously distributed to the unfortunate valueless, but even silver lost its value in relation to gold.

But the most amazing example of the ineffectiveness of the orders given by the authorities at that time was Napoleon's attempt to stop the looting and re-establish discipline.

This is what the army authorities were reporting:

Looting continues in the city despite the decrees against it. Order is not yet restored and not a single merchant is carrying on trade in a lawful manner. The sutlers alone venture to trade, and they sell stolen goods.

The neighbourhood of my ward continues to be pillaged by soldiers of the 3rd Corps, who not satisfied with taking from the unfortunate inhabitants hiding in the cellars the little they have left, even have the ferocity to wound them with their sabres, as I have repeatedly witnessed.

Nothing new, except that the soldiers are robbing and pillaging – 9th October.

Robbery and pillaging continue. There is a band of thieves in our district who ought to be arrested by a strong force – 11th October.

The Emperor is extremely displeased that, despite the strict orders to stop pillage, parties of marauding Guards are continually seen returning to the Kremlin. Among the Old Guard disorder and pillage were renewed more violently than ever yesterday evening, last night, and to-day. The Emperor sees with regret that the picked soldiers appointed to guard his person, who should set an example of discipline, carry disobedience to such a point that they break into the cellars and stores containing army supplies. Others have disgraced themselves to the extent of disobeying sentinels and officers, and have abused and beaten them.

The Grand Marshal of the palace [wrote the governor] complains bitterly that in spite of repeated orders the soldiers continue to commit nuisances in all the courtyards, and even under the very windows of the Emperor.

That army, like a herd of cattle run wild and trampling underfoot the provender which might have saved it from starvation, disintegrated and perished with each additional day it remained in Moscow. But it did not go away.

It began to run away only when suddenly seized by a panic caused by the capture of transport trains on the Smolensk road, and by the battle of Tarutino. The news of that battle of Tarutino, unexpectedly received by Napoleon at a review, evoked in him a desire to punish the Russians (Thiers says), and he issued the order for departure which the whole army was demanding.

Fleeing from Moscow the soldiers took with them everything they had stolen. Napoleon, too, carried away his own personal *trésor*, but on seeing the baggage-trains that impeded the army he was (Thiers says) horror-struck. And yet with his experience of war he did not order all the superfluous vehicles to be burnt, as he had done with those of a certain marshal when approaching Moscow. He gazed at the calèches and carriages in which soldiers were riding and remarked that it was a very good thing, as those vehicles could be used to carry provisions, the sick, and the wounded.

The plight of the whole army resembled that of a wounded animal which feels it is perishing and does not know what it is doing. To study the skilful tactics and aims of Napoleon and his army from the time it entered Moscow till it was destroyed, is like studying the dying leaps and shudders of a mortally wounded animal. Very often a wounded animal, hearing a rustle, rushes straight at the hunter's gun, runs forward and back again, and hastens its own end. Napoleon, under pressure from his whole army, did the same thing. The rustle of the battle of Tarutino frightened the beast, and it rushed forward onto the hunter's gun, reached him, turned back, and finally – like any wild beast – ran back along the most disadvantageous and dangerous path, where the old scent was familiar.

During the whole of that period Napoleon, who seems to us to have been the leader of all those movements – as the figure-head of a ship may seem to a savage to guide the vessel – acted like a child who, holding a couple of strings inside a carriage, thinks he is driving it.

11

EARLY in the morning of the 6th of October Pierre went out of the shed, and on returning stopped by the door to play with a little blue-grey dog with a long body and short bandy legs, that jumped about him. This little dog lived in their shed, sleeping beside Karataev at night; it sometimes made excursions into the town but always returned again. Probably it had never had an owner, and it still belonged to nobody and had no name. The French called it Azor; the soldier who told stories called it Femgalka; Karataev and others called it Grey, or sometimes Flabby. Its lack of a master, a name, and even of a breed or any definite colour, did not seem to trouble the blue-grey dog in the least. Its furry tail stood up firm and round as a plume, its bandy legs served it so well that it would often gracefully lift a hind leg and run very easily and quickly on three legs, as if disdaining to use all four. Everything pleased it. Now it would roll on its back yelping with delight, now bask in the sun with a thoughtful air of importance, and now frolic about playing with a chip of wood or a straw.

Pierre's attire by now consisted of a dirty torn shirt (the only remnant of his former clothing), a pair of soldier's trousers which by Karataev's advice he tied with string round the ankles for warmth, and a peasant coat and cap. Physically he had changed much during this time. He no longer seemed stout, though he still had the appearance of solidity and strength hereditary in his family. A beard and moustache covered the lower part of his face, and a tangle of hair, infested with lice, curled round his head like a cap. The look of his eyes was resolute, calm, and animatedly alert, as never before. The former slackness which had shown itself even in his eyes was now replaced by an energetic readiness for action and resistance. His feet were bare.

Pierre first looked down the field across which vehicles and horsemen were passing that morning, then into the distance across the river, then at the dog who was pretending to be in earnest about biting him, and then at his bare feet which he placed with pleasure in various positions, moving his dirty thick big toes. Every time he looked at his bare feet a smile of animated self-satisfaction flitted across his face. The sight of them reminded him of all he had experienced and learned during these weeks, and this recollection was pleasant to him.

For some days the weather had been calm and clear with slight frosts in the mornings – what is called an 'old wives' summer'.

In the sunshine the air was warm, and that warmth was particularly pleasant with the invigorating freshness of the morning frost still in the air.

On everything – far and near – lay the magic crystal glitter seen only at that time of autumn. The Sparrow Hills were visible in the distance, with the village, the church, and the large white house. The bare trees, the sand, the bricks and roofs of the houses, the green church spire and the corners of the white house in the distance, all stood out in the transparent air in most delicate outline and with unnatural clearness. Near by could be seen the familiar ruins of a half-burnt mansion occupied by the French, with lilac bushes still showing dark green beside the fence. And even that ruined and befouled house – which in dull weather was repulsively ugly – seemed quietly beautiful now, in the clear motionless brilliance.

A French corporal with coat unbuttoned in a homely way, a skull-cap on his head and a short pipe in his mouth, came from behind a corner of the shed and approached Pierre with a friendly wink.

'What sunshine, Monsieur Kiril!' (their name for Pierre). 'Eh? Just like spring.'

And the corporal leant against the door and offered Pierre his pipe, though whenever he offered it Pierre always declined it.

'To be on the march in such weather . . .' he began.

Pierre inquired what was being said about leaving, and the corporal told him that nearly all the troops were starting and there ought to be an order about the prisoners that day. Sokolov, one of the soldiers in the shed with Pierre, was dying, and Pierre told the corporal that something should be done about him. The corporal replied that Pierre need not worry about that as they had an ambulance and a permanent hospital, and arrangements would be made for the sick, and that in general everything that could happen had been foreseen by the authorities.

'Besides, Monsieur Kiril, you have only to say a word to the captain, you know. He is a man who never forgets anything. Speak to the captain when he makes his round, he will do anything for you.'

(The captain of whom the corporal spoke often had long chats with Pierre and showed him all sorts of favours.)

'"You see, St Thomas," he said to me the other day, "Monsieur Kiril is a man of education, who speaks French. He is a Russian seigneur who has had misfortunes, but he is a man. He knows what's what . . . If he wants anything and asks me, he won't get a refusal. When one has studied, you see, one likes education and well-bred people." It is for your sake I mention it, Monsieur Kiril. The other day if it had not been for you that affair would have ended ill.'

And after chatting a while longer the corporal went away. (The affair he had alluded to had happened a few days before – a fight between the prisoners and the French soldiers, in which Pierre had succeeded in pacifying his comrades.) Some of the prisoners, who had heard Pierre talking to the corporal, immediately asked what the Frenchman had said. While Pierre was repeating what he had been told about the army leaving Moscow, a thin, sallow, tattered French soldier came up to the door of the shed. Rapidly and timidly raising his fingers to his forehead by way of greeting, he asked Pierre whether the soldier Platoche, to whom he had given a shirt to sew, was in that shed.

The French had had boot-leather and linen issued to them a week before, which they had given out to the prisoners to make up into boots and shirts for them.

'Ready, ready, dear fellow!' said Karataev, coming out with a neatly folded shirt.

Karataev, on account of the warm weather and for convenience at work, was wearing only trousers and a tattered shirt as black as soot. His hair was bound round, workman-fashion, with a wisp of lime-tree bast, and his round face seemed rounder and pleasanter than ever.

'A promise is own brother to performance. I said Friday and here it is, ready,' said Platon, smiling and unfolding the shirt he had sewn.

The Frenchman glanced round uneasily and then, as if overcoming his hesitation, rapidly threw off his uniform and put on the shirt. He had a long greasy flowered silk waistcoat next to his sallow thin bare body, but no shirt. He was evidently afraid the prisoners looking on would laugh at him, and thrust his head into the shirt hurriedly. None of the prisoners said a word.

'See, it fits well!' Platon kept repeating, pulling the shirt straight.

The Frenchman having pushed his head and hands through without raising his eyes, looked down at the shirt and examined the seams.

'You see, dear man, this is not a sewing shop, and I had no proper tools; and as they say, one needs a tool even to kill a louse,' said Platon with one of his round smiles, obviously pleased with his work.

'It's good, quite good, thank you,' said the Frenchman in French, 'but there must be some linen left over.'

'It will fit better still when it sets to your body,' said Karataev, still admiring his handiwork. 'You'll be nice and comfortable...'

'Thanks, thanks, old fellow... But the bits left over?' said the Frenchman again, and smiled. He took out an assignation ruble note and gave it to Karataev. 'But give me the pieces that are over.'

Pierre saw that Platon did not want to understand what the Frenchman was saying, and he looked on without interfering. Karataev thanked the Frenchman for the money and went on admiring his own work. The Frenchman insisted on having the pieces returned that were left over and asked Pierre to translate what he said.

'What does he want the bits for?' said Karataev. 'They'd make fine foot-wrappings for us. Well, never mind.' And Karataev with a suddenly changed and saddened expression took a small bundle of scraps from inside his shirt and gave it to the Frenchman without looking at him. 'Oh dear!' muttered Karataev and went away. The Frenchman looked at the linen, considered for a moment, then looked inquiringly at Pierre and, as if Pierre's look had told him something, suddenly blushed and shouted in a squeaky voice:

'Platoche! Eh, Platoche! Keep them yourself!' And handing back the odd bits he turned and went out.

'There, look at that,' said Karataev, swaying his head. 'People said they were not Christians, but they too have souls. It's what the old folk used to say: "A sweating hand's an open hand, a dry hand's close". He's naked, but yet he's given it back.'

Karataev smiled thoughtfully, and was silent awhile looking at the pieces.

'But they'll make grand foot-wrappings, dear friend,' he said, and went back into the shed.

12

FOUR weeks had passed since Pierre had been taken prisoner and, though the French had offered to move him from the men's to the officers' shed, he had stayed in the shed where he was first put.

In burnt and devastated Moscow Pierre experienced almost the extreme limits of privation a man can endure; but thanks to his physical strength and health, of which he had till then been unconscious, and thanks especially to the fact that the privations came so gradually that it was impossible to say when they began, he endured his position not only lightly but joyfully. And just at this time he obtained the tranquillity and ease of mind he had formerly striven in vain to reach. He had long sought in different ways that tranquillity of mind, that inner harmony, which had so impressed him in the soldiers at the battle of Borodino. He had sought it in philanthropy, in Freemasonry, in the dissipations of town life, in wine, in heroic feats of self-sacrifice, and in romantic love for Natasha; he had sought it by reasoning – and all these quests and experiments had failed him. And now without thinking about it, he had found that peace and inner harmony only through the horror of death, through privation, and through what he recognized in Karataev.

Those dreadful moments he had lived through at the executions had as it were for ever washed away from his imagination and memory the agitating thoughts and feelings that had formerly seemed so important. It did not now occur to him to think of Russia, or the war, or politics, or Napoleon. It was plain to him that all these things were no business of his, and that he was not called on to judge concerning them and therefore could not do so. 'Russia and summer weather are not bound together', he thought, repeating words of Karataev's which he found strangely consoling. His intention of killing Napoleon and his calculations of the cabalistic number of the beast of the Apocalypse, now seemed to him meaningless and even ridiculous. His anger with his wife and anxiety that his name should not be smirched, now seemed not merely trivial but even amusing. What concern was it of his that somewhere or other that woman was leading the life she preferred? What did it matter to anybody, and especially to him, whether or not they found out that their prisoner's name was Count Bezukhov?

He now often remembered his conversation with Prince Andrew and quite agreed with him, though he understood Prince Andrew's thoughts somewhat differently. Prince Andrew had thought and said that happiness could only be negative, but had said it with a shade of bitterness and irony as though he was really saying that all desire for positive happiness is implanted in us merely to torment us and never to be satisfied. But Pierre believed it without any mental reservation. The absence of suffering, the satisfaction of one's needs, and consequent freedom in the choice of one's occupation, that is, of one's way of life, now seemed to Pierre to be indubitably man's highest happiness. Here and now for the first time he fully appreciated the enjoyment of eating when he wanted to eat, drinking when he wanted to drink, sleeping when he wanted to sleep, of warmth when he was cold, of talking to a fellow-man when he wished to talk and to hear a human voice. The satisfaction of one's needs – good food, cleanliness, and freedom – now that he was deprived of all this, seemed to Pierre to constitute perfect happiness; and the choice of occupation, that is, of his way of life – now that that choice was so restricted – seemed to him such an easy matter that he forgot that a superfluity of the comforts of life destroys all joy in satisfying one's needs, while great freedom in the choice of occupation – such freedom as his wealth, his education, and his social position had given him in his own life – is just what makes the choice of occupation insolubly difficult, and destroys the desire and possibility of having an occupation.

All Pierre's day-dreams now turned on the time when he would be free. Yet subsequently, and for the rest of his life, he thought and spoke with enthusiasm of that month of captivity, of those irrecoverable, strong, joyful sensations, and chiefly of the complete peace of mind and inner freedom which he only experienced during those weeks.

When on the first day he got up early, went out of the shed at dawn, and saw the cupolas and crosses of the New Convent of the Virgin still dark at first, the hoar frost on the dusty grass, the Sparrow Hills, and the wooded banks above the winding river vanishing in the purple distance, when he felt the contact of the fresh air, and heard the noise of the crows flying from Moscow across the field, and when afterwards light gleamed from the east and the sun's rim appeared solemnly from behind a cloud, and the cupolas and crosses, the hoar frost, the distance and the river, all began to sparkle in the glad light – Pierre felt a new joy and strength in life such as he had never before known. And this not only stayed with him during the whole of his imprisonment, but even grew in strength as the hardships of his position increased.

That feeling of alertness and of readiness for anything was still further strengthened in him by the high opinion his fellow-prisoners formed of him soon after his arrival at the shed. With his knowledge of languages, the respect shown him by the French, his simplicity, his readiness to give anything asked of him (he received the allowance of three rubles a week made to officers); with his strength, which he showed to the soldiers by pressing nails into the walls of the hut; his gentleness to his companions, and his capacity for sitting still and thinking without doing anything (which seemed to them incomprehensible), he appeared to them a rather mysterious and superior being. The very qualities that had been a hindrance if not actually harmful to him in the world he had lived in – his strength, his disdain for the comforts of life, his absent-mindedness and simplicity – here among these people gave him almost the status of a hero. And Pierre felt that their opinion placed responsibilities upon him.

13

THE French evacuation began on the night between the 6th and 7th of October: kitchens and sheds were dismantled, carts loaded, and troops and baggage-trains started.

At seven in the morning a French convoy in marching trim, wearing shakos and carrying muskets, knapsacks and enormous sacks, stood in front of the sheds, and animated French talk mingled with curses sounded all along the lines.

In the shed everyone was ready, dressed, belted, shod, and only awaited the order to start. The sick soldier Sokolov, pale and thin with dark shadows round his eyes, alone sat in his place barefoot and not dressed. His eyes, prominent from the emaciation of his face, gazed inquiringly at his comrades who were paying no attention to him, and he moaned regularly and quietly. It was evidently not so much his sufferings that caused him to moan (he had dysentery) as his fear and grief at being left alone.

Pierre, girt with a rope round his waist and wearing shoes Karataev had made for him from some leather a French soldier had torn off a tea-chest and brought to have his boots mended with, went up to the sick man and squatted down beside him.

'You know, Sokolov, they are not all going away! They have a hospital here. You may be better off than we others,' said Pierre.

'O Lord! Oh, it will be the death of me! O Lord!' moaned the man in a louder voice.

'I'll go and ask them again directly,' said Pierre, rising and going to the door of the shed.

Just as Pierre reached the door, the corporal who had offered him a pipe the day before came up to it with two soldiers. The corporal and soldiers were in marching kit with knapsacks and shakos that had metal straps, and these changed their familiar faces.

The corporal came, according to orders, to shut the door. The prisoners had to be counted before being let out.

'Corporal, what will they do with the sick man?...' Pierre began.

But even as he spoke he began to doubt whether this was the corporal he knew or a stranger, so unlike himself did the corporal seem at that moment. Moreover, just as Pierre was speaking a sharp rattle of drums was suddenly heard from both sides. The corporal frowned at Pierre's words, and uttering some meaningless oaths slammed the door. The shed became semi-dark, and the sharp rattle of the drums on two sides drowned the sick man's groans.

'There it is!... It again!...' said Pierre to himself, and an involuntary shudder ran down his spine. In the corporal's changed face, in the sound of his voice, in the stirring and deafening noise of the drums, he recognized that mysterious, callous force which compelled people against their will to kill their fellow-men – that force the effect of which he had witnessed during the executions. To fear or to try to escape that force, to address entreaties or exhortations to those who served as its tools, was useless. Pierre knew this now. One had to wait and endure. He did not again go to the sick man, nor turn to look at him, but stood frowning by the door of the hut.

When that door was opened and the prisoners, crowding against one another like a flock of sheep, squeezed into the exit, Pierre pushed his way forward and approached that very captain who as the corporal had assured him was ready to do anything for him. The captain was also in marching dress, and on his cold face appeared that same *it* which Pierre had recognized in the corporal's words and the roll of the drums.

'Pass on, pass on!' the captain reiterated, frowning sternly, and looking at the prisoners who thronged past him.

Pierre went up to him, though he knew his attempt would be vain.

'What now?' the officer asked with a cold look as if not recognizing Pierre.

Pierre told him about the sick man.

'He'll manage to walk, devil take him!' said the captain. 'Pass on, pass on!' he continued without looking at Pierre.

'But he is dying,' Pierre again began.

'Be so good ...' shouted the captain, frowning angrily.

'*Dram-da-da-dam, dam-dam* ...' rattled the drums, and Pierre understood that this mysterious force completely controlled these men and that it was now useless to say any more.

The officer-prisoners were separated from the soldiers and told to march in front. There were about thirty officers, with Pierre among them, and about three hundred men.

The officers, who had come from the other sheds, were all strangers to Pierre and much better dressed than he. They looked at him and at his shoes mistrustfully, as at an alien. Not far from him walked a fat major with a sallow, bloated, angry face, who was wearing a Kazan dressing-gown tied round with a towel, and who evidently enjoyed the respect of his fellow-prisoners. He kept one hand, in which he clasped a tobacco-pouch, inside the bosom of his dressing-gown and held the stem of his pipe firmly with the other. Panting and puffing the major grumbled and growled at everybody because he thought he was being pushed, and that they were all hurrying when they had nowhere to hurry to, and were all surprised at something when there was nothing to be surprised at. Another, a thin little officer, was speaking to everyone, conjecturing where they were now being taken and how far they would get that day. An official in felt boots and wearing a commissariat uniform, ran round from side to side and gazed at the ruins of Moscow, loudly announcing his observations as to what had been burnt down, and what this or that part of the city was that they could see. A third officer, who by his accent was a Pole, disputed with the commissariat officer, arguing that he was mistaken in his identification of the different wards of Moscow.

'What are you disputing about?' said the major angrily. 'What does it matter whether it is St Nicholas or St Blasius? You see it's burnt down, and there's an end of it ... What are you pushing for? Isn't the road wide enough?' said he, turning to a man behind him who was not pushing him at all.

'Oh, oh, oh! What have they done?' the prisoners on one side and another were heard saying as they gazed on the charred ruins. 'All beyond the river, and Zubova, and in the Kremlin ... Just look! There's not half of it left. Yes, I told you – the whole quarter beyond the river, and so it is.'

'Well, you know it's burnt, so what's the use of talking?' said the major.

As they passed near a church in the Khamovniky (one of the few unburnt quarters of Moscow) the whole mass of prisoners suddenly started to one side and exclamations of horror and disgust were heard.

'Ah, the villains! What heathens! Yes; dead, dead, so he is ... And smeared with something!'

Pierre too drew near the church where the thing was that evoked these exclamations, and dimly made out something leaning against the palings surrounding the church. From the words of his comrades who saw better than he did, he found that this was the body of a man, set upright against the palings, with its face smeared with soot.

'Go on! What the devil ... Go on! Thirty thousand devils! ...' the convoy guards began cursing and the French soldiers, with fresh virulence, drove away with their swords the crowd of prisoners who were gazing at the dead man.

14

THROUGH the cross-streets of the Khamovniky quarter the prisoners marched followed only by their escort and the vehicles and wagons belonging to that escort, but when they reached the supply-stores they came among a huge and closely packed train of artillery mingled with private vehicles.

At the bridge they all halted, waiting for those in front to get across. From the bridge they had a view of endless lines of moving baggage-trains before and behind them. To the right, where the Kaluga road turns near Neskuchny, endless rows of troops and carts stretched away into the distance. These were troops of Beauharnais's corps which had started before any of the others. Behind, along the riverside and across the Stone bridge, were Ney's troops and transport.

Davout's troops, in whose charge were the prisoners, were crossing the Crimean bridge and some were already debouching into the Kaluga road. But the baggage-trains stretched out so that the last of Beauharnais's train had not yet got out of Moscow and reached the Kaluga road when the vanguard of Ney's army was already emerging from the Great Ordynka street.

When they had crossed the Crimean bridge the prisoners moved a few steps forward, halted, and again moved on, and from all sides vehicles and men crowded closer and closer together. They advanced the few hundred paces that separated the bridge from the Kaluga road, taking more than an hour to do so, and came out upon the square where the streets of the Transmoskva ward and the Kaluga road converge, and the prisoners jammed close together had to stand for some hours at that cross-way. From all sides, like the roar of the sea, was heard the rattle of wheels, the tramp of feet, and incessant shouts of anger and abuse. Pierre stood pressed against the wall of a charred house, listening to that noise, which mingled in his imagination with the roll of the drums.

To get a better view several officer-prisoners climbed onto the wall of the half-burnt house against which Pierre was leaning.

'What crowds! Just look at the crowds!... They've loaded goods even on the cannon! Look there, those are furs!' they exclaimed. 'Just see what the blackguards have looted... There! See what that one has behind in the cart... Why, those are settings taken from some icons, by heaven!... Oh, the rascals!... See how that fellow has loaded himself up, he can hardly walk! Good lord, they've even grabbed those chaises!... See that fellow there sitting on the trunks... Heavens! They're fighting.'

'That's right, hit him on the snout – on his snout! Like this we shan't get away before evening. Look, look there... Why, that must be Napoleon's own. See what horses! And the monograms with a crown! It's like a portable house... That fellow's dropped his sack and doesn't see it. Fighting again... A woman with a baby, and not bad-looking either! Yes, I dare say, that's the way they'll let you pass... Just look, there's no end to it. Russian wenches, by heaven, so they are! In carriages – see how comfortably they've settled themselves!'

Again, as at the church in Khamovniky, a wave of general curiosity bore all the prisoners forward onto the road, and Pierre thanks to his stature saw over the heads of the others what so attracted their curiosity. In three carriages involved among the munition carts, closely squeezed together, sat women with rouged faces, dressed in glaring colours, who were shouting something in shrill voices.

From the moment Pierre had recognized the appearance of the mysterious force nothing had seemed to him strange or dreadful: neither the corpse smeared with soot for fun, nor these women hurrying away, nor the burnt ruins of Moscow. All that he now witnessed hardly made any impression on him – as if his soul, making ready for a hard struggle, refused to receive impressions that might weaken it.

The women's vehicles drove by. Behind them came more carts, soldiers, wagons, soldiers, gun-carriages, carriages, soldiers, ammunition carts, more soldiers, and now and then women.

Pierre did not see the people as individuals but saw their movement.

All these people and horses seemed driven forward by some invisible power. During the hour Pierre watched them they all came flowing from the different streets with one and the same desire to get on quickly: they all jostled one another, began to grow angry and to fight, white teeth gleamed, brows frowned, ever the same words of abuse flew from side to side, and all the faces bore the same swaggeringly resolute and coldly cruel expression that had struck Pierre that morning on the corporal's face when the drums were beating.

It was not till nearly evening that the officer commanding the escort collected his men and with shouts and quarrels forced his way in among the baggage-trains, and the prisoners hemmed in on all sides emerged onto the Kaluga road.

They marched very quickly, without resting, and halted only when the sun began to set. The baggage-carts drew up close together and the men began to prepare for their night's rest. They all appeared angry and dissatisfied. For a long time oaths, angry shouts, and fighting, could be heard from all sides. A carriage that followed the escort ran into one of the carts and knocked a hole in it with its pole. Several soldiers ran towards the cart from different sides: some beat the carriage horses on their heads, turning them aside, others fought among themselves, and Pierre saw that one German was badly wounded on the head by a sword.

It seemed that all these men now that they had stopped amid fields in the chill dusk of the autumn evening, experienced one and the same feeling of unpleasant awakening from the hurry and eagerness to push on that had seized them at the start. Once at a standstill they all seemed to understand that they did not yet know where they were going, and that much that was painful and difficult awaited them on this journey.

During this halt the escort treated the prisoners even worse than they had done at the start. It was here that the prisoners for the first time received horse-flesh for their meat-ration.

From the officers down to the lowest soldier they all showed what seemed like personal spite against each of the prisoners, in unexpected contrast to their former friendly relations.

This spite increased still more when, on calling over the roll of prisoners, it was found that in the bustle of leaving Moscow one Russian soldier, who had pretended to suffer from colic, had escaped. Pierre saw a Frenchman beat a Russian soldier cruelly for straying too far from the road, and heard his friend the captain reprimand and threaten to courtmartial a non-commissioned officer on account of the escape of the Russian. To the non-commissioned officer's excuse that the prisoner was ill and could not walk, the officer replied that the order was to shoot those who lagged behind. Pierre felt that that fatal force which had crushed him during the executions, but which he had not felt during his imprisonment, now again controlled his existence. It was terrible, but he felt that in proportion to the efforts of that fatal force to crush him, there grew and strengthened in his soul a power of life independent of it.

He ate his supper of rye-flour soup with horse-flesh, and chatted with his comrades.

Neither Pierre nor any of the others spoke of what they had seen in Moscow, or of the roughness of their treatment by the French, or of the order to shoot them which had been announced to them. As if in reaction against the worsening of their position they were all particularly animated and gay. They spoke of personal reminiscences, of amusing scenes they had witnessed during the campaign, and avoided all talk of their present situation.

The sun had set long since. Bright stars shone out here and there in the sky. A red glow as of a conflagration spread above the horizon from the rising full moon, and that vast red ball swayed strangely in the grey haze. It grew light. The evening was ending but the night had not yet come. Pierre got up and left his new companions, crossing between the camp-fires to the other side of the road where he had been told the common soldier-prisoners were stationed. He wanted to talk to them. On the road he was stopped by a French sentinel who ordered him back.

Pierre turned back, not to his companions by the camp-fire but to an unharnessed cart where there was nobody. Tucking his legs under him and dropping his head he sat down on the cold ground by a wheel of the cart and remained motionless a long while sunk in thought. Suddenly he burst out into a fit of his broad, good-natured laughter, so loud that men from various sides turned with surprise to see what this strange and evidently solitary laughter could mean.

'Ha-ha-ha!' laughed Pierre. And he said aloud to himself: 'The soldier did not let me pass. They took me and shut me up. They hold me captive. What, me? Me? My immortal soul? Ha-ha-ha! Ha-ha-ha!...' and he laughed till tears started to his eyes.

A man got up and came to see what this queer big fellow was laughing at all by himself. Pierre stopped laughing, got up, went farther away from the inquisitive man, and looked around him.

The huge endless bivouac that had previously resounded with the crackling of camp-fires and the voices of many men had grown quiet, the red camp-fires were growing paler and dying down. High up in the light sky hung the full moon. Forests and fields beyond the camp, unseen before, were now visible in the distance. And farther still, beyond those forests and fields, the bright, oscillating, limitless distance lured one to itself. Pierre glanced up at the sky and the twinkling stars in its far-away depths. 'And all that is me, all that is within me, and it is all I!' thought Pierre. 'And they caught all that and put it into a shed boarded up with planks!' He smiled, and went and lay down to sleep beside his companions.

15

IN the early days of October another envoy came to Kutuzov with a letter from Napoleon proposing peace, and falsely dated from Moscow, though Napoleon was already not far from Kutuzov on the old Kaluga road. Kutuzov replied to this letter as he had done to the one formerly brought by Lauriston, saying that there could be no question of peace.

Soon after that a report was received from Dorokhov's guerrilla detachment operating to the left of Tarutino, that troops of Broussier's division had been seen at Forminsk, and that being separated from the rest of the French army they might easily be destroyed. The soldiers and officers again demanded action. Generals on the staff, excited by the memory of the easy victory at Tarutino, urged Kutuzov to carry out Dorokhov's suggestion. Kutuzov did not consider any offensive necessary. The result was a compromise, which was inevitable: a small detachment was sent to Forminsk to attack Broussier.

By a strange coincidence this task, which turned out to be a most difficult and important one, was entrusted to Dokhturov – that same modest little Dokhturov whom no one has described to us as drawing up plans of battles, dashing about in front of regiments, showering crosses on batteries, and so on, and who was thought to be and was spoken of as undecided and undiscerning – but whom we find commanding wherever the position was most difficult all through the Russo–French wars from Austerlitz to the year 1813. At Austerlitz he remained last at the Augezd dam, rallying the regiments, saving what was possible when all were flying and perishing and not a single general was left in the rear-guard. Ill with fever he went to Smolensk with twenty thousand men to defend the town against Napoleon's whole army. In Smolensk, at the Malakhov gate, he had hardly dozed off in a paroxysm of fever before he was awakened by the bombardment of the town – and Smolensk held out all day long. At the battle of Borodino when Bagration was killed and nine-tenths of the men of our left flank had fallen and the full force of the French artillery fire was directed against it, the man sent there was this same irresolute and undiscerning Dokhturov – Kutuzov hastening to rectify a mistake he had made by sending someone else there first. And the quiet little Dokhturov rode thither, and Borodino became the greatest glory of the Russian army. Many heroes have been described to us in verse and prose, but of Dokhturov scarcely a word has been said.

It was Dokhturov again whom they sent to Forminsk and from there to Malo-Yaroslavets, the place where the last battle with the French was fought and where the obvious disintegration of the French army began; and we are told of many geniuses and heroes of that period of the campaign, but of Dokhturov nothing or very little is said and that dubiously. And this silence about Dokhturov is the clearest testimony to his merit.

It is natural for a man who does not understand the working of a machine to imagine that a shaving that has fallen into it by chance and is interfering with its action and tossing about in it, is its important part. The man who does not understand the construction of the machine cannot conceive that the small connecting cog-wheel which revolves quietly is one of the most essential parts of the machine, and not the shaving which merely harms and hinders the working.

On the 10th of October, when Dokhturov had gone half-way to Forminsk and stopped at the village of Aristovo, preparing faith-fully to execute the orders he had received – the whole French army, having, in its convulsive movement, reached Murat's position apparently in order to give battle, suddenly without any reason turned off to the left on to the new Kaluga road and began to enter Forminsk, where only Broussier had been till then. At that time Dokhturov had under his command, besides Dorokhov's detachment, the two small guerrilla detachments of Figner and Seslavin.

On the evening of October the 11th, Seslavin came to the Aristovo head-quarters with a French guardsman he had captured. The prisoner said that the troops that had entered Forminsk that day were the vanguard of the whole army, that Napoleon was there and the whole army had left Moscow four days previously. That same evening a house-serf, who had come from Borovsk, said he had seen an immense army entering the town. Some Cossacks of Dokhturov's detachment reported having sighted the French Guards marching along the road to Borovsk. From all these reports it was evident that where they had expected to meet a single division there was now the whole French army marching from Moscow in an unexpected direction – along the Kaluga road. Dokhturov was unwilling to undertake any action, as it was not clear to him now what he ought to do. He had been ordered to attack Forminsk. But only Broussier had been there at that time and now the whole French army was there. Ermolov wished to act on his own judgement, but Dokhturov insisted that he must have Kutuzov's instructions. So it was decided to send a dispatch to the staff.

For this purpose a capable officer, Bolkhovitinov, was chosen, who was to explain the whole affair by word of mouth besides delivering a written report. Towards midnight Bolkhovitinov, having received the dispatch and verbal instructions, galloped off to the General Staff, accompanied by a Cossack with spare horses.

16

IT was a warm dark autumn night. It had been raining for four days. Having changed horses twice and galloped twenty miles in an hour and a half over a sticky muddy road, Bolkhovitinov reached Litashëvka after one o'clock at night. Dismounting at a cottage, on whose wattle fence hung a signboard 'General Staff', and throwing down his reins, he entered a dark passage.

'The General on duty, quick! It's very important!' said he to someone who had risen and was sniffing in the dark passage.

'He has been very unwell since the evening and this is the third night he has not slept,' said the orderly pleadingly in a whisper. 'You should wake the captain first.'

'But this is very important, from General Dokhturov,' said Bolkhovitinov, entering the open door which he had found by feeling in the dark.

The orderly had gone in before him and began waking somebody.

'Your Honour, your Honour! A courier.'

'What? What's that? From whom?' came a sleepy voice.

'From Dokhturov and from Alexey Petrovich. Napoleon is at Forminsk,' said Bolkhovitinov, unable to see in the dark who was speaking but guessing by the voice that it was not Konovnitsyn.

The man who had been awakened yawned and stretched himself.

'I don't like waking him,' he said, fumbling for something. 'He is very ill. Perhaps this is only a rumour.'

'Here is the dispatch,' said Bolkhovitinov. 'My orders are to give it at once to the general on duty.'

'Wait a moment, I'll light a candle. You damned rascal, where do you always hide it?' said the voice of the man who was stretching himself, to the orderly. (This was Shcherbinin, Konovnitsyn's adjutant.) 'I've found it, I've found it!' he added.

The orderly was striking a light, and Shcherbinin was fumbling for something on the candlestick.

'Oh, the nasty beasts!' said he with disgust.

By the light of the sparks Bolkhovitinov saw Shcherbinin's youthful face as he held the candle, and the face of another man who was still asleep. This was Konovnitsyn.

When the flame of the sulphur-splinters kindled by the tinder burnt up, first blue and then red, Shcherbinin lit the tallow candle, from the candlestick of which the cockroaches that had been gnawing it were running away, and looked at the messenger. Bolkhovitinov was bespattered all over with mud, and had smeared his face by wiping it with his sleeve.

'Who gave the report?' inquired Shcherbinin, taking the envelope.

'The news is reliable,' said Bolkhovitinov. 'Prisoners, Cossacks, and the scouts, all say the same thing.'

'There's nothing to be done, we'll have to wake him,' said Shcherbinin, rising and going up to the man in the nightcap who lay covered by a great-coat. 'Peter Petrovich!' said he (Konovnitsyn did not stir). 'To the General Staff!' he said with a smile, knowing that those words would be sure to arouse him.

And in fact the head in the nightcap was lifted at once. On Konovnitsyn's handsome resolute face, with cheeks flushed by fever, there still remained for an instant a far-away dreamy expression remote from present affairs, but then he suddenly started and his face assumed its habitual calm and firm appearance.

'Well, what is it? From whom?' he asked immediately but without hurry, blinking at the light.

While listening to the officer's report Konovnitsyn broke the seal and read the dispatch. Hardly had he done so before he lowered his legs in their woollen stockings to the earthen floor and began putting on his boots. Then he took off his nightcap, combed his hair over his temples, and donned his cap.

'Did you get here quickly? Let us go to his Highness.'

Konovnitsyn had understood at once that the news brought was of great importance and that no time must be lost. He did not consider or ask himself whether the news was good or bad. That did not interest him. He regarded the whole business of the war not with his intelligence or his reason but by something else. There was within him a deep unexpressed conviction that all would be well, but that one must not trust to this and still less speak about it, but must only attend to one's own work. And he did his work, giving his whole strength to the task.

Peter Petrovich Konovnitsyn, like Dokhturov, seems to have been included merely for propriety's sake in the list of the so-called heroes of 1812 – the Barclays, Raevskys, Ermolovs, Platovs, and Miloradoviches. Like Dokhturov he had the reputation of being a man of very limited capacity and information, and like Dokhturov he never made plans of battle but was always found where the situation was most difficult. Since his appointment as general on duty he had always slept with his door open, giving orders that every messenger should be allowed to wake him up. In battle he was always under fire, so that Kutuzov reproved him for it and feared to send him to the front, and like Dokhturov he was one of those unnoticed cog-wheels that, without clatter or noise, constitute the most essential part of the machine.

Coming out of the hut into the damp dark night Konovnitsyn frowned – partly from an increased pain in his head and partly at the unpleasant thought that occurred to him, of how all that nest of influential men on the staff would be stirred up by this news, especially Bennigsen, who ever since Tarutino had been at daggers drawn with Kutuzov; and how they would make suggestions, quarrel, issue orders, and rescind them. And this premonition was disagreeable to him, though he knew it could not be helped.

And in fact, Toll, to whom he went to communicate the news, immediately began to expound his plans to a general sharing his quarters, until Konovnitsyn, who listened in weary silence, reminded him that they must go to see his Highness.

17

KUTUZOV like all old people did not sleep much at night. He often fell asleep unexpectedly in the day-time, but at night, lying on his bed without undressing, he generally remained awake thinking.

So he lay now on his bed, supporting his large, heavy, scarred head on his plump hand, with his one eye open, meditating and peering into the darkness.

Since Bennigsen, who corresponded with the Emperor and had more influence than anyone else on the staff, had begun to avoid him, Kutuzov was more at ease as to the possibility of himself and his troops being obliged to take part in useless aggressive movements. The lesson of the Tarutino battle and of the day before it, which Kutuzov remembered with pain, must he thought have some effect on others too.

'They must understand that we can only lose by taking the offensive. Patience and time are my warriors, my champions,' thought Kutuzov. He knew that an apple should not be plucked while it is green. It will fall of itself when ripe, but if picked unripe the apple is spoilt, the tree is harmed, and your teeth are set on edge. Like an experienced sportsman, he knew that the beast was wounded and wounded as only the whole strength of Russia could have wounded it, but whether it was mortally wounded or not was still an undecided question. Now by the fact of Lauriston and Barthelemy having been sent, and by the reports of the guerrillas, Kutuzov was almost sure that the wound was mortal. But he needed further proofs and it was necessary to wait.

'They want to run to see how they have wounded it. Wait and we shall see! Continual manœuvres, continual advances!' thought he. 'What for? Only to distinguish themselves! As if fighting were fun. They are like children from whom one can't get any sensible account of what has happened because they all want to show how well they can fight. But that's not what is needed now.'

'And what ingenious manœuvres they all propose to me! It seems to them that when they have thought of two or three contingencies' (he remembered the general plan sent him from Petersburg), 'they have foreseen everything. But the contingencies are endless.'

The undecided question as to whether the wound inflicted at Borodino was mortal or not had hung over Kutuzov's head for a whole month. On the one hand the French had occupied Moscow. On the other Kutuzov felt assured with all his being that the terrible blow into which he and all the Russians had put their whole strength must have been mortal. But in any case proofs were needed; he had waited a whole month for them and grew more impatient the longer he waited. Lying on his bed during those sleepless nights he did just what he reproached those younger generals for doing. He imagined all sorts of possible contingencies, just like the younger men, but with this difference, that he saw thousands of contingencies instead of two or three and based nothing on them. The longer he thought the more contingencies presented themselves. He imagined all sorts of movements of the Napoleonic army as a whole or in sections – against Petersburg, or against him, or to outflank him. He thought too of the possibility (which he feared most of all) that Napoleon might fight him with his own weapon and remain in Moscow awaiting him. Kutuzov even imagined that Napoleon's army might turn back through Medyn and Yukhnov,* but the one thing he could not foresee was what happened – the insane, convulsive stampede of Napoleon's army during its first eleven days after leaving Moscow: a stampede which made possible what Kutuzov had not yet even dared to think of – the complete extermination of the French. Dorokhov's report about Broussier's division, the guerrillas' reports of distress in Napoleon's army, rumours of preparations for leaving Moscow – all confirmed the supposition that the French army was beaten and preparing for flight. But these were only suppositions, which seemed important to the younger men but not to Kutuzov. With his sixty years' experience he knew what value to attach to rumours, knew how apt people who desire anything are to group all news so that it appears to confirm what they desire, and he knew how readily in such cases they omit all that makes for the contrary. And the more he desired it the less he allowed himself to believe it. This question absorbed all his mental powers. All else was to him only life's customary routine. To such customary routine belonged his conversations with the staff, the letters he wrote from Tarutino to Madame de Staël,* the reading of novels, the distribution of awards, his correspondence with Petersburg, and so on. But the destruction of the French, which he alone foresaw, was his heart's one desire.

On the night of the 11th of October he lay leaning on his arm and thinking of that.

There was a stir in the next room and he heard the steps of Toll, Konovnitsyn, and Bolkhovitinov.

'Eh, who's there? Come in, come in! What news?' the field marshal called out to them.

While a footman was lighting a candle Toll communicated the substance of the news.

'Who brought it?' asked Kutuzov with a look which, when the candle was lit, struck Toll by its cold severity.

'There can be no doubt about it, your Highness.'

'Call him in, call him here.'

Kutuzov sat up with one leg hanging down from the bed and his big paunch resting against the other which was doubled under him. He screwed up his seeing eye to scrutinize the messenger more carefully, as if wishing to read in his face what preoccupied his own mind.

'Tell me, tell me, friend,' said he to Bolkhovitinov in his low, aged voice, as he pulled together the shirt which gaped open on his chest, 'come nearer – nearer. What news have you brought me? Eh? That Napoleon has left Moscow? Are you sure? Eh?'

Bolkhovitinov gave a detailed account from the beginning of all he had been told to report.

'Speak quicker, quicker! Don't torture me!' Kutuzov interrupted him.

Bolkhovitinov told him everything and was then silent, awaiting instructions. Toll was beginning to say something but Kutuzov checked him. He tried to say something, but his face suddenly puckered and wrinkled; he waved his arm at Toll and turned to the opposite side of the room, to the corner darkened by the icons that hung there.

'O Lord, my Creator, Thou has heard our prayer . . .' said he in a tremulous voice with folded hands. 'Russia is saved. I thank Thee, O Lord!' and he wept.

18

FROM the time he received this news to the end of the campaign all Kutuzov's activity was directed towards restraining his troops, by authority, by guile and by entreaty, from useless attacks, manœuvres, or encounters with the perishing enemy. Dokhturov went to Malo-Yaroslavets, but Kutuzov lingered with the main army and gave orders for the evacuation of Kaluga – a retreat beyond which town seemed to him quite possible.

Everywhere Kutuzov retreated, but the enemy without waiting for his retreat fled in the opposite direction.

Napoleon's historians describe to us his skilled manœuvres at Tarutino and Malo-Yaroslavets, and make conjectures as to what would have happened had Napoleon been in time to penetrate into the rich southern provinces.

But not to speak of the fact that nothing prevented him from advancing into those southern provinces (for the Russian army did not bar his way), the historians forget that nothing could have saved his army, for then already it bore within itself the germs of inevitable ruin. How could that army – which had found abundant supplies in Moscow and had trampled them underfoot instead of keeping them, and on arriving at Smolensk had looted provisions instead of storing them – how could that army recuperate in Kaluga province, which was inhabited by Russians such as those who lived in Moscow, and where fire had the same property of consuming what was set ablaze?

That army could not recover anywhere. Since the battle of Borodino and the pillage of Moscow it had borne within itself, as it were, the chemical elements of dissolution.

The members of what had once been an army – Napoleon himself and all his soldiers – fled without knowing whither, each concerned only to make his escape as quickly as possible from this position, of the hopelessness of which they were all more or less vaguely conscious.

So it came about that at the council at Malo-Yaroslavets, when the generals pretending to confer together expressed various opinions, all mouths were closed by the opinion uttered by the simple-minded soldier Mouton* who, speaking last, said what they all felt, that the one thing needful was to get away as quickly as possible; and no one, not even Napoleon, could say anything against that truth which they all recognized.

But though they all realized that it was necessary to get away, there still remained a feeling of shame at admitting that they must fly. An external shock was needed to overcome that shame, and this shock came in due time. It was what the French called 'le hourra de l'Empereur'.*

The day after the council at Malo-Yaroslavets Napoleon rode out early in the morning amid the lines of his army, with his suite of marshals and an escort, on the pretext of inspecting the army and the scene of the previous and of the impending battle. Some Cossacks on the prowl for booty fell in with the Emperor and very nearly captured him. If the Cossacks did not capture Napoleon then, what saved him was the very thing that was destroying the French army, the booty on which the Cossacks fell. Here as at Tarutino they went after plunder, leaving the men. Disregarding Napoleon they rushed after the plunder, and Napoleon managed to escape.

When *les enfants du Don* might so easily have taken the Emperor himself in the midst of his army, it was clear that there was nothing for it but to fly as fast as possible along the nearest, familiar road. Napoleon, with his forty-year-old stomach, understood that hint, not feeling his former agility and boldness, and under the influence of the fright the Cossacks had given him he at once agreed with Mouton and issued orders – as the historians tell us – to retreat by the Smolensk road.

That Napoleon agreed with Mouton, and that the army retreated, does not prove that Napoleon caused it to retreat, but that the forces which influenced the whole army and directed it along the Mozhaysk (that is, the Smolensk) road, acted simultaneously on him also.

19

A MAN in motion always devises an aim for that motion. To be able to go a thousand versts he must imagine that something good awaits him at the end of those thousand versts. One must have the prospect of a promised land to have the strength to move.

The promised land for the French during their advance had been Moscow, during their retreat it was their native land. But that native land was too far off, and for a man going a thousand versts it is absolutely necessary to set aside his final goal and to say to himself: 'To-day I shall get to a place forty versts off where I shall rest and spend the night', and during the first day's journey that resting-place eclipses his ultimate goal and attracts all his hopes and desires. And the impulses felt by a single person are always magnified in a crowd.

For the French retreating along the old Smolensk road, the final goal – their native land – was too remote, and their immediate goal was Smolensk, towards which all their desires and hopes, enormously intensified in the mass, urged them on. It was not that they knew that much food and fresh troops awaited them in Smolensk, nor that they were told so (on the contrary their superior officers, and Napoleon himself, knew that provisions were scarce there), but because this alone could give them strength to move on and endure their present privations. So both those who knew, and those who did not know, deceived themselves, and pushed on to Smolensk as to a promised land.

Coming out onto the high road the French flew with surprising energy and unheard-of rapidity towards the goal they had fixed on. Besides the common impulse which bound the whole crowd of French into one mass and supplied them with a certain energy, there was another cause binding them together – their great numbers. As with the physical law of gravity, their enormous mass drew the individual human atoms to itself. In their hundreds of thousands they moved like a whole nation.

Each of them desired nothing more than to give himself up as a prisoner to escape from all this horror and misery; but on the one hand the force of this common attraction to Smolensk, their goal, drew each of them in the same direction; on the other hand an army corps could not surrender to a company, and though the

French availed themselves of every convenient opportunity to detach themselves and to surrender on the slightest decent pretext, such pretexts did not always occur. Their very numbers and their crowded and swift movement deprived them of that possibility and rendered it not only difficult but impossible for the Russians to stop this movement to which the French were directing all their energies. Beyond a certain limit no mechanical disruption of the body could hasten the process of decomposition.

A lump of snow cannot be melted instantaneously. There is a certain limit of time in less than which no amount of heat can melt the snow. On the contrary the greater the heat the more solidified the remaining snow becomes.

Of the Russian commanders Kutuzov alone understood this. When the flight of the French army along the Smolensk road became well defined, what Konovnitsyn had foreseen on the night of the 11th of October began to occur. The superior officers all wanted to distinguish themselves, to cut off, to seize, to capture, and to overthrow the French, and all clamoured for action.

Kutuzov alone used all his power (and such power is very limited in the case of any commander-in-chief) to prevent an attack.

He could not tell them what we say now: 'Why fight, why block the road, losing our own men and inhumanly slaughtering unfortunate wretches? What is the use of that, when a third of their army has melted away on the road from Moscow to Vyazma without any battle?' But drawing from his aged wisdom what they could understand, he told them of the golden bridge, and they laughed at and slandered him, flinging themselves on, rending and exulting over the dying beast.

Ermolov, Miloradovich, Platov, and others in proximity to the French near Vyazma, could not resist their desire to cut off and break up two French corps, and by way of reporting their intention to Kutuzov they sent him a blank sheet of paper in an envelope.

And try as Kutuzov might to restrain the troops, our men attacked, trying to bar the road. Infantry regiments, we are told, advanced to the attack with music and with drums beating, and killed and lost thousands of men.

But they did not cut off or overthrow anybody, and the French army, closing up more firmly at the danger, continued, while steadily melting away, to pursue its fatal path to Smolensk.

END OF PART TWO

PART THREE

1

THE battle of Borodino, with the occupation of Moscow that followed it and the flight of the French without further conflicts, is one of the most instructive phenomena in history.

All historians agree that the external activity of states and nations in their conflicts with one another is expressed in wars and that as a direct result of greater or less success in war the political strength of states and nations increases or decreases.

Strange as may be the historical account of how some king or emperor, having quarrelled with another, collects an army, fights his enemy's army, gains a victory by killing three, five, or ten thousand men, and subjugates a kingdom and an entire nation of several millions, all the facts of history (as far as we know it) confirm the truth of the statement that the greater or lesser success of one army against another is the cause, or at least an essential indication, of an increase or decrease in the strength of the nation, even though it is unintelligible why the defeat of an army – a hundredth part of a nation – should oblige that whole nation to submit. An army gains a victory, and at once the rights of the conquering nation have increased to the detriment of the defeated. An army has suffered defeat, and at once a people loses its rights in proportion to the severity of the reverse, and if its army suffers a complete defeat the nation is quite subjugated.

So according to history it has been from the most ancient times, and so it is to our own day. All Napoleon's wars serve to confirm this rule. In proportion to the defeat of the Austrian army Austria loses its rights, and the rights and the strength of France increase. The victories of the French at Jena and Auerstädt destroy the independent existence of Prussia.

But then, in 1812, the French gain a victory near Moscow. Moscow is taken and after that, with no further battles, it is not Russia that ceases to exist, but the French army of six hundred thousand, and then Napoleonic France itself. To strain the facts to fit the rules of history: to say that the field of battle at Borodino remained in the hands of the Russians, or that after Moscow there were other battles that destroyed Napoleon's army, is impossible.

After the French victory at Borodino there was no general engagement nor any that were at all serious, yet the French army ceased to exist. What does this mean? If it were an example taken from the history of China, we might say that it was not an historic phenomenon (which is the historians' usual expedient when anything does not fit their standards); if the matter concerned some brief conflict, in which only a small number of troops took part, we might treat it as an exception; but this event occurred before our fathers' eyes and for them it was a question of the life or death of their fatherland, and it happened in the greatest of all known wars.

The period of the campaign of 1812 from the battle of Borodino to the expulsion of the French proved that the winning of a battle does not produce a conquest and is not even an invariable indication of conquest; it proved that the force which decides the fate of people lies not in the conquerors, nor even in armies and battles, but in something else.

The French historians, describing the condition of the French army before it left Moscow, affirm that all was in order in the Grand Army, except the cavalry, the artillery, and the transport – there was no forage for the horses or the cattle. That was a misfortune no one could remedy, for the peasants of the district burnt their hay rather than let the French have it.

The victory gained did not bring the usual results because the peasants, Karp and Vlas (who after the French had evacuated Moscow drove in their carts to pillage the town and in general personally failed to manifest any heroic feelings) and the whole innumerable multitude of such peasants, did not bring their hay to Moscow for the high price offered them, but burnt it instead.

Let us imagine two men who have come out to fight a duel with rapiers according to all the rules of the art of fencing. The fencing has gone on for some time: suddenly one of the combatants, feeling himself wounded and understanding that the matter is no joke but concerns his life, throws down his rapier, and seizing the first cudgel that comes to hand begins to brandish it. Then let us imagine that the combatant who so sensibly employed the best and simplest means to attain his end, was at the same time influenced by traditions of chivalry and, desiring to conceal the facts of the case, insisted that he had gained his victory with the rapier according to all the rules of art. One can imagine what confusion and obscurity would result from such an account of the duel.

The fencer who demanded a contest according to the rules of fencing was the French army; his opponent who threw away the rapier and snatched up the cudgel was the Russian people; those who try to explain the matter according to the rules of fencing are the historians who have described the event.

After the burning of Smolensk a war began which did not follow any previous traditions of war. The burning of towns and villages, the retreats after battles, the blow dealt at Borodino and the renewed retreat, the burning of Moscow, the capture of marauders, the seizure of transport, and the guerrilla war – were all departures from the rules.

Napoleon felt this, and from the time he took up the correct fencing attitude in Moscow and instead of his opponent's rapier saw a cudgel raised above his head, he did not cease to complain to Kutuzov and to the Emperor Alexander that the war was being carried on contrary to all the rules – as if there were any rules for killing people. In spite of the complaints of the French as to the non-observance of the rules, in spite of the fact that to some highly placed Russians it seemed rather disgraceful to fight with a cudgel and they wanted to assume a pose *en quarte* or *en tierce* according to all the rules and to make an adroit thrust *en prime*, and so on – the cudgel of the people's war was lifted with all its menacing and majestic strength, and without consulting anyone's tastes or rules, and regardless of anything else, it rose and fell with stupid simplicity, but consistently, and belaboured the French till the whole invasion had perished.

And it is well for a people who do not – as the French did in 1813 – salute according to all the rules of art, and presenting the hilt of their rapier gracefully and politely hand it to their magnanimous conqueror, but at the moment of trial, without asking what rules others have adopted in similar cases, simply and easily pick up the first cudgel that comes to hand, and strike with it till the feeling of resentment and revenge in their soul yields to a feeling of contempt and compassion.

2

ONE of the most obvious and advantageous departures from the so-called laws of war is the action of scattered groups against men pressed together in a mass. Such action always occurs in wars that take on a national character. In such actions, instead of two crowds opposing each other, the men disperse, attack singly, run away when attacked by stronger forces, but again attack when opportunity offers. This was done by the guerrillas in Spain, by the mountain tribes in the Caucasus,* and by the Russians in 1812.

People have called this kind of war 'guerrilla warfare' and assume that by so calling it they have explained its meaning. But such a war does not fit in under any rule and is directly opposed to a well-known rule of tactics which is accepted as infallible. That rule says that an attacker should concentrate his forces in order to be stronger than his opponent at the moment of conflict.

Guerrilla war (always successful, as history shows) directly infringes that rule.

This contradiction arises from the fact that military science assumes the strength of an army to be identical with its numbers. Military science says that the more troops the greater the strength. *Les gros bataillons ont toujours raison.*

For military science to say this is like defining momentum in mechanics by reference to the mass only: stating that momenta are equal or unequal to each other simply because the masses involved are equal or unequal.

Momentum (quantity of motion) is the product of mass and velocity.

In military affairs the strength of an army is the product of its mass and some unknown x.

Military science, seeing in history innumerable instances of the fact that the size of any army does not coincide with its strength and that small detachments defeat larger ones, obscurely admits the existence of this unknown factor and tries to discover it – now in a geometric formation, now in the equipment employed, now, and most usually, in the genius of the commanders. But the assignment of these various meanings to the factor does not yield results which accord with the historic facts.

Yet it is only necessary to abandon the false view (adopted to gratify the 'heroes') of the efficacy of the directions issued in wartime by commanders, in order to find this unknown quantity.

That unknown quantity is the spirit of the army, that is to say, the greater or lesser readiness to fight and face danger felt by all the men composing an army, quite independently of whether they are, or are not, fighting under the command of a genius: in two or three line formation: with cudgels or with rifles that repeat thirty times a minute. Men who want to fight will always put themselves in the most advantageous conditions for fighting.

The spirit of an army is the factor which multiplied by the mass gives the resulting force. To define and express the significance of this unknown factor – the spirit of an army – is a problem for science.

This problem is only solvable if we cease arbitrarily to substitute for the unknown x itself, the conditions under which that force becomes apparent – such as the commands of the general, the equipment employed, and so on – mistaking these for the real significance of the factor, and if we recognize this unknown quantity in its entirety as being the greater or lesser desire to fight and to face danger. Only then, expressing known historic facts by equations and comparing the relative significance of this factor, can we hope to define the unknown.

Ten men, battalions, or divisions, fighting fifteen men, battalions, or divisions, conquer – that is, kill or take captive – all the others, while themselves losing four, so that on the one side four and on the other fifteen were lost. Consequently the four were equal to the fifteen, and therefore $4x=15y$. Consequently $x/y=15/4$. This equation does not give us the value of the unknown factor but gives us a ratio between two unknowns. And by bringing variously selected historic units (battles, campaigns, periods of war) into such equations, a series of numbers could be obtained in which certain laws should exist and might be discovered.

The tactical rule that an army should act in masses when attacking and in smaller groups in retreat unconsciously confirms the truth that the strength of an army depends on its spirit. To lead men forward under fire more discipline (obtainable only by movement in masses) is needed than is needed to resist attacks. But this rule which leaves out of account the spirit of the army continually proves incorrect, and is in particularly striking contrast to the facts when some strong rise or fall in the spirit of the troops occurs, as in all national wars.

The French, retreating in 1812 – though according to tactics they should have separated into detachments to defend themselves – congregated into a mass because the spirit of the army had so fallen that only the mass held the army together. The Russians on the contrary ought according to tactics to have attacked in mass, but in fact they split up into small units, because their spirit had so risen that separate individuals, without orders, dealt blows at the French without needing any compulsion to induce them to expose themselves to hardships and dangers.

3

THE so-called partisan war began with the entry of the French into Smolensk.

Before partisan warfare had been officially recognized by the government, thousands of enemy stragglers, marauders, and foragers had been destroyed by the Cossacks and the peasants, who killed them off as instinctively as dogs worry a stray mad dog to death. Denis Davydov, with his Russian instinct, was the first to recognize the value of this terrible cudgel which regardless of the rules of military science destroyed the French, and to him belongs the credit of taking the first step towards regularizing this method of warfare.

On August 24th Davydov's first partisan detachment was formed, and then others were recognized. The further the campaign progressed the more numerous these detachments became.

The irregulars destroyed the great army piecemeal. They gathered the fallen leaves that dropped of themselves from that withered tree – the French army – and sometimes shook that tree itself. By October, when the French were fleeing towards Smolensk, there were hundreds of such companies, of various sizes and characters. There were some that adopted all the army methods and had infantry, artillery, staffs, and the comforts of life. Others consisted solely of Cossack cavalry. There were also small scratch groups of foot and horse, and groups of peasants and landowners that remained unknown. A sacristan commanded one party which captured several hundred prisoners in the course of a month; and there was Vasilisa, the wife of a village elder, who slew hundreds of the French.

The partisan warfare flamed up most fiercely in the latter days of October. Its first period had passed, when the partisans themselves, amazed at their own boldness, feared every minute to be surrounded and captured by the French, and hid in the forests without unsaddling, hardly daring to dismount and always expecting to be pursued. By the end of October this kind of warfare had taken definite shape: it had become clear to all what could be ventured against the French and what could not. Now only the commanders of detachments with staffs, and moving according to rules at a distance from the French, still regarded many things as impossible. The small bands that had started their activities long before and had already observed the French closely, considered things possible which the commanders of the big detachments did not dare to contemplate. The Cossacks and peasants who crept in among the French now considered everything possible.

On October 22nd, Denisov (who was one of the irregulars) was with his group at the height of the guerrilla enthusiasm. Since early morning he and his party had been on the move. All day long he had been watching, from the forest that skirted the high road, a large French convoy of cavalry baggage and Russian prisoners separated from the rest of the army, which – as was learnt from spies and prisoners – was moving under a strong escort to

Smolensk. Besides Denisov and Dolokhov (who also led a small party and moved in Denisov's vicinity), the commanders of some large divisions with staffs also knew of this convoy and, as Denisov expressed it, were sharpening their teeth for it. Two of the commanders of large parties – one a Pole and the other a German – sent invitations to Denisov, almost simultaneously, requesting him to join up with their divisions to attack the convoy.

'No, bwother, I have gwown moustaches myself,' said Denisov on reading these documents, and he wrote to the German that, despite his heartfelt desire to serve under so valiant and renowned a general, he had to forgo that pleasure because he was already under the command of the Polish general.* To the Polish general he replied to the same effect, informing him that he was already under the command of the German.

Having arranged matters thus, Denisov and Dolokhov intended, without reporting matters to the higher command, to attack and seize that convoy with their own small forces. On October 22nd it was moving from the village of Mikulino to that of Shamshevo. To the left of the road between Mikulino and Shamshevo there were large forests extending in some places up to the road itself, though in others a verst or more back from it. Through these forests Denisov and his party rode all day, sometimes keeping well back in them and sometimes coming to the very edge, but never losing sight of the moving French. That morning, Cossacks of Denisov's party had seized and carried off into the forest two wagons loaded with cavalry saddles, which had stuck in the mud not far from Mikulino where the forest ran close to the road. Since then, and until evening, the party had watched the movements of the French without attacking. It was necessary to let the French reach Shamshevo quietly without alarming them and then, after joining Dolokhov who was to come that evening to a consultation at a watchman's hut in the forest a verst from Shamshevo, to surprise the French at dawn, falling like an avalanche on their heads from two sides, and rout and capture them all at one blow.

In their rear, two versts from Mikulino where the forest came right up to the road, six Cossacks were posted to report at once if any fresh columns of French should show themselves.

Beyond Shamshevo Dolokhov was to observe the road in the same way, to find out at what distance there were other French troops. They reckoned that the convoy had fifteen hundred men. Denisov had two hundred, and Dolokhov might have as many more. But the disparity of numbers did not deter Denisov. All that he now wanted to know was what troops these were, and to learn that he had to capture a 'tongue' – that is, a man from the enemy column.

That morning's attack on the wagons had been made so hastily that the Frenchmen with the wagons had all been killed; only a little drummer-boy had been taken alive, and as he was a straggler he could tell them nothing definite about the troops in that column.

Denisov considered it dangerous to make a second attack for fear of putting the whole column on the alert, so he sent Tikhon Shcherbaty, a peasant of his party, to Shamshevo to try and seize at least one of the French quartermasters who had been sent on in advance.

4

It was a warm rainy autumn day. The sky and the horizon were both the colour of muddy water. At times a sort of mist descended, and then suddenly heavy slanting rain came down.

Denisov in a felt cloak and a sheepskin cap, from which the rain ran down, was riding a thin thoroughbred horse with sunken sides. Like his horse, which turned its head and laid its ears back, he shrank from the driving rain and gazed anxiously before him. His thin face with its short thick black beard looked angry.

Beside Denisov rode an esaul, Denisov's fellow-worker, also in felt cloak and sheepskin cap, and riding a large sleek Don horse.

Esaul Lovaysky* the Third was a tall man as straight as an arrow, pale-faced, fair-haired, with narrow light eyes and with calm self-satisfaction in his face and bearing. Though it was impossible to say in what the peculiarity of the horse and rider lay, yet at first glance at the esaul and Denisov one saw that the latter was wet and uncomfortable and was a man mounted on a horse, while looking at the esaul one saw that he was as comfortable and as much at ease as always, and that he was not a man who had mounted a horse, but a man who was one with his horse, a being consequently possessed of twofold strength.

A little ahead of them walked a peasant guide, wet to the skin and wearing a grey peasant coat and a white knitted cap.

A little behind, on a poor small lean Kirghiz mount with an enormous tail and mane and a bleeding mouth, rode a young officer in a blue French overcoat.

Beside him rode an hussar, with a boy in tattered French uniform and blue cap behind him on the crupper of his horse. The boy held on to the hussar with cold red hands, and raising his eyebrows gazed about him with surprise. This was the French drummer-boy captured that morning.

Behind them along the narrow, sodden, cut-up forest road came hussars in threes and fours, and then Cossacks, some in felt cloaks, some in French greatcoats, and some with horse-cloths over their heads. The horses, being drenched by the rain, all looked black whether chestnut or bay. Their necks, with their wet close-clinging manes, looked strangely thin. Steam rose from them. Clothes, saddles, reins, were all wet, slippery, and sodden, like the ground and the fallen leaves that strewed the road. The men sat huddled up trying not to stir, so as to warm the water that had trickled to their bodies, and not admit the fresh cold water that was leaking under their seats, their knees, and at the back of their necks. In the midst of the outspread line of Cossacks, two wagons, drawn by French horses and by saddled Cossack horses that had been hitched on in front, rumbled over the tree-stumps and branches and splashed through the water that lay in the ruts.

Denisov's horse swerved aside to avoid a pool in the track and bumped his rider's knee against a tree.

'Oh, the devil!' exclaimed Denisov angrily, and showing his teeth he struck the horse three times with his whip, splashing himself and his comrades with mud.

Denisov was out of sorts both because of the rain and also from hunger (none of them had eaten anything since morning), and yet more because he had still no news from Dolokhov, and the man sent to capture a 'tongue' had not returned.

'There'll hardly be another such chance to fall on a transport as to-day. It's too risky to attack them by oneself, and if we put it off till another day one of the big guerrilla detachments will snatch the prey from under our noses,' thought Denisov, continually peering forward, hoping to see a messenger from Dolokhov.

On coming to a path in the forest along which he could see far to the right, Denisov stopped.

'There's someone coming,' said he.

The esaul looked in the direction Denisov indicated.

'There are two, an officer and a Cossack. But it is not *presupposable* that it is the lieutenant-colonel himself,' said the esaul, who was fond of using words the Cossacks did not know.

The approaching riders having descended a decline were no longer visible, but they reappeared a few minutes later. In front, at a weary gallop and using his leather whip, rode an officer, dishevelled and drenched, whose trousers had worked up to above his knees. Behind him, standing in the stirrups, trotted a Cossack. The officer, a very young lad with a broad rosy face and keen merry eyes, galloped up to Denisov and handed him a sodden envelope.

'From the general,' said the officer. 'Please excuse its not being quite dry.'

Denisov, frowning, took the envelope and opened it.

'There, they kept telling us: "It's dangerous, it's dangerous,"' said the officer, addressing the esaul while Denisov was reading the dispatch. 'But Komarov and I' – he pointed to the Cossack – 'were prepared. We have each of us two pistols . . . But what's this?' he asked, noticing the French drummer-boy. 'A prisoner? You've already been in action? May I speak to him?'

'Wostov! Petya!' exclaimed Denisov, having run through the dispatch. 'Why didn't you say who you were?' and turning with a smile he held out his hand to the lad.

The officer was Petya Rostov.

All the way Petya had been preparing himself to behave with Denisov as befitted a grown-up man and an officer – without hinting at their previous cquaintance. But as soon as Denisov smiled at him Petya brightened up, blushed with pleasure, forgot the official manner he had been rehearsing, and began telling him how he had already been in a battle near Vyazma, and how a certain hussar had distinguished himself there.

'Well, I am glad to see you,' Denisov interrupted him, and his face again assumed its anxious expression.

'Michael Feoklitych,' said he to the esaul, 'this is again fwom that German, you know. He' – he indicated Petya – 'is serving under him.'

And Denisov told the esaul that the dispatch just delivered was a repetition of the German general's demand that he should join forces with him for an attack on the transport.

'If we don't take it to-mowwwow he'll snatch it from under our noses,' he added.

While Denisov was talking to the esaul, Petya – abashed by Denisov's cold tone and supposing that it was due to the condition of his trousers – furtively tried to pull them down under his greatcoat so that no one should notice it, while maintaining as martial an air as possible.

'Will there be any orders, your Honour?' he asked Denisov, holding his hand at the salute and resuming the game of adjutant and general for which he had prepared himself, 'or shall I remain with your Honour?'

'Orders?' Denisov repeated thoughtfully. 'But can you stay till to-mowwwow?'

'Oh, please . . . May I stay with you?' cried Petya.

'But, just what did the genewal tell you? To weturn at once?' asked Denisov.

Petya blushed.

'He gave me no instructions. I think I could?' he returned inquiringly.

'Well, all wight,' said Denisov.

And turning to his men he directed a party to go on to the halting-place arranged, near the watchman's hut in the forest, and told the officer on the Kirghiz horse (who performed the duties of an adjutant) to go and find out where Dolokhov was and whether he would come that evening. Denisov himself intended going with the esaul and Petya to the edge of the forest where it reached out to Shamshevo, to have a look at the part of the French bivouac they were to attack next day.

'Well, old fellow,' said he to the peasant guide, 'lead us to Shamshevo.'

Denisov, Petya, and the esaul, accompanied by some Cossacks and the hussar who had the prisoner, rode to the left across a ravine to the edge of the forest.

5

THE rain had stopped, and only the mist was falling and drops from the trees. Denisov, the esaul, and Petya rode silently, following the peasant in the knitted cap who, stepping lightly with out-turned toes and moving noiselessly in his bast shoes over the roots and wet leaves, silently led them to the edge of the forest.

He ascended an incline, stopped, looked about him, and advanced to where the screen of trees was less dense. On reaching a large oak tree that had not yet shed its leaves, he stopped and beckoned mysteriously to them with his hand.

Denisov and Petya rode up to him. From the spot where the peasant was standing they could see the French. Immediately beyond the forest, on a downward slope, lay a field of spring rye. To the right, beyond a steep ravine, was a small village and a landowner's house with a broken roof. In the village, in the house, in the garden, by the well, by the pond, over all the rising ground, and all along the road uphill from the bridge leading to the village not more than five hundred yards away, crowds of men could be seen through the shimmering mist. Their un-Russian shouting at their horses which were straining uphill with the carts, and their calls to one another, could be clearly heard.

'Bwing the pwisoner here,' said Denisov in a low voice, not taking his eyes off the French.

A Cossack dismounted, lifted the boy down, and took him to Denisov. Pointing to the French troops, Denisov asked him what these and those of them were. The boy, thrusting his cold hands into his pockets and lifting his eyebrows, looked at Denisov in affright, but in spite of an evident desire to say all he knew, gave confused answers, merely assenting to everything Denisov asked him. Denisov turned away from him frowning, and addressed the esaul, conveying his own conjectures to him.

Petya, rapidly turning his head, looked now at the drummer-boy, now at Denisov, now at the esaul, and now at the French in the village and along the road, trying not to miss anything of importance.

'Whether Dolokhov comes or not, we must seize it, eh?' said Denisov with a merry sparkle in his eyes.

'It is a very suitable spot,' said the esaul.

'We'll send the infantwy down by the swamps,' Denisov continued. 'They'll cweep up to the garden; you'll wide up from there with the Cossacks' – he pointed to a spot in the forest beyond the village – 'and I with my hussars from here. And at the signal shot . . .'

'The hollow is impassable – there's a swamp there,' said the esaul. 'The horses would sink. We must ride round more to the left . . .'

While they were talking in undertones, the crack of a shot sounded from the low ground by the pond, a puff of white smoke appeared, and another, and the sound of hundreds of seemingly merry French voices shouting together came up from the slope. For a moment Denisov and the esaul drew back. They were so near that they thought they were the cause of the firing and shouting. But the firing and shouting did not relate to them. Down below, a man wearing something red was running through the marsh. The French were evidently firing and shouting at him.

'Why, that's our Tikhon,' said the esaul.

'So it is! It is!'

'The wascal!' said Denisov.

'He'll get away!' said the esaul, screwing up his eyes.

The man whom they called Tikhon, having run to the stream plunged in so that the water splashed in the air, and having disappeared for an instant, scrambled out on all fours, all black with the wet, and ran on. The French who had been pursuing him stopped.

'Smart, that!' said the esaul.

'What a beast!' said Denisov with his former look of vexation. 'What has he been doing all this time?'

'Who is he?' asked Petya.

'He's our *plastun*.* I sent him to capture a "tongue".'

'Oh, yes,' said Petya, nodding at the first words Denisov uttered, as if he understood it all, though he really did not understand anything of it.

Tikhon Shcherbaty was one of the most indispensable men in their band. He was a peasant from Pokrovsk, near the river Gzhat. When Denisov had come to Pokrovsk at the beginning of his operations and had as usual summoned the village Elder and asked him what he knew about the French, the Elder, as though shielding himself, had replied as all village Elders did, that he had neither seen nor heard anything of them. But when Denisov explained that his purpose was to kill the French, and asked if no French had strayed that way, the Elder replied that some 'moreorderers' had really been at their village, but that Tikhon Shcherbaty was the only man who dealt with such matters. Denisov had Tikhon called, and having praised him for his activity, said a few words in the Elder's presence about loyalty to the Tsar and the country and the hatred of the French all sons of the fatherland should cherish.

'We don't do the French any harm,' said Tikhon, evidently frightened by Denisov's words. 'We only fooled about with the lads for fun, you know. We killed a score or so of "moreorderers", but we did no harm else . . .'

Next day when Denisov had left Pokrovsk, having quite forgotten about this peasant, it was reported to him that Tikhon had attached himself to their party and asked to be allowed to remain with it. Denisov gave orders to let him do so.

Tikhon, who at first did rough work, laying camp-fires, fetching water, flaying dead horses, and so on, soon showed a great liking and aptitude for partisan warfare. At night he would go out for booty and always brought back French clothing and weapons, and when told to would bring in French captives also. Denisov then relieved him from drudgery and began taking him with him when he went out on expeditions, and had him enrolled among the Cossacks.

Tikhon did not like riding, and always went on foot, never lagging behind the cavalry. He was armed with a musketoon (which he carried rather as a joke), a pike and an axe, which latter he used as a wolf uses its teeth, with equal ease picking fleas out of its fur or crunching thick bones. Tikhon with equal accuracy would split logs with blows at arm's length, or holding the head of the axe would cut thin little pegs or carve spoons. In Denisov's party he held a peculiar and exceptional position. When anything particularly difficult or nasty had to be done – to push a cart out of the mud with one's shoulder, pull a horse out of a swamp by its tail, skin it, slink in among the French, or walk more than thirty miles in a day – everybody pointed laughingly at Tikhon.

'It won't hurt that devil – he's as strong as a horse!' they said of him.

Once a Frenchman Tikhon was trying to capture fired a pistol at him and shot him in the fleshy part of the back. That wound (which Tikhon only treated with internal and external applications of vodka) was the subject of the liveliest jokes by the whole detachment – jokes in which Tikhon readily joined.

'Hallo, mate! Never again? Gave you a twist?' the Cossacks would banter him. And Tikhon, purposely writhing and making faces, pretended to be angry and swore at the French with the funniest curses. The only effect of this incident on Tikhon was that after being wounded he seldom brought in prisoners.

He was the bravest and most useful man in the party. No one found more opportunities for attacking, no one captured or killed more Frenchmen, and consequently he was made the buffoon of all the Cossacks and hussars and willingly accepted that role. Now he had been sent by Denisov over night to Shamshevo to capture a 'tongue'. But whether because he had not been content to take only one Frenchman, or because he had slept through the night, he had crept by day into some bushes right among the French, and, as Denisov had witnessed from above, had been detected by them.

6

AFTER talking for some time with the esaul about next day's attack, which now, seeing how near they were to the French, he seemed to have definitely decided on, Denisov turned his horse and rode back.

'Now, my lad, we'll go and get dwy,' he said to Petya.

As they approached the watch-house Denisov stopped, peering into the forest. Among the trees a man with long legs and long swinging arms, wearing a short jacket, bast shoes, and a Kazan hat, was approaching with long light steps. He had a musketoon over his shoulder and an axe stuck in his girdle. When he espied Denisov he hastily threw something into the bushes, removed his sodden hat by its floppy brim, and approached his commander. It was Tikhon. His wrinkled and pock-marked face and narrow little eyes beamed with self-satisfied merriment. He lifted his head high and gazed at Denisov as if repressing a laugh.

'Well, where did you disappear to?' inquired Denisov.

'Where did I disappear to? I went to get Frenchmen,' answered Tikhon boldly and hurriedly, in a husky but melodious bass voice.

'Why did you push yourself in there by daylight? You ass! Well, why haven't you taken one?'

'Oh, I took one all right,' said Tikhon.

'Where is he?'

'You see, I took him first thing at dawn,' Tikhon continued, spreading out his flat feet with out-turned toes in their bast shoes. 'I took him into the forest. Then I see he's no good and think I'll go and fetch a likelier one.'

'You see? ... What a wogue – it's just as I thought,' said Denisov to the esaul. 'Why didn't you bwing that one?'

'What was the good of bringing him?' Tikhon interrupted hastily and angrily – 'that one wouldn't have done for you. As if I don't know what sort you want!'

'What a bwute you are! ... Well?'

'I went for another one,' Tikhon continued, 'and I crept like this through the wood and lay down.' (He suddenly lay down on his stomach with a supple movement to show how he had done it.) 'One turned up and I grabbed him, like this.' (He jumped up quickly and lightly.) '"Come along to the colonel," I said. He starts yelling, and suddenly there were four of them. They rushed at me with their little swords. So I went for them with my axe, this way: "What are you up to?" says I. "Christ be with you!"' shouted Tikhon, waving his arms with an angry scowl and throwing out his chest.

'Yes, we saw from the hill how you took to your heels through the puddles!' said the esaul screwing up his glittering eyes.

Petya badly wanted to laugh, but noticed that they all refrained from laughing. He turned his eyes rapidly from Tikhon's face to the esaul's and Denisov's, unable to make out what it all meant.

'Don't play the fool!' said Denisov, coughing angrily. 'Why didn't you bwing the first one?'

Tikhon scratched his back with one hand and his head with the other, then suddenly his whole face expanded into a beaming foolish grin, disclosing a gap where he had lost a tooth (that was why he was called Shcherbaty – the gap-toothed). Denisov smiled, and Petya burst into a peal of merry laughter in which Tikhon himself joined.

'Oh, but he was a regular good-for-nothing,' said Tikhon. 'The clothes on him – poor stuff! How could I bring him? And so rude, your Honour! Why, he says: "I'm a general's son myself, I won't go!" he says.'

'You are a bwute!' said Denisov. 'I wanted to question ...'

'But I questioned him,' said Tikhon. 'He said he didn't know much. "There are a lot of us," he says, "but all poor stuff – only soldiers in name," he says. "Shout loud at them," he says "and you'll take them all,"' Tikhon concluded, looking cheerfully and resolutely into Denisov's eyes.

'I'll give you a hundwed sharp lashes – that'll teach you to play the fool!' said Denisov severely.

'But why are you angry?' remonstrated Tikhon, 'just as if I'd never seen your Frenchmen! Only wait till it gets dark and I'll fetch any of them you want – three if you like.'

'Well, let's go,' said Denisov, and rode all the way to the watch-house in silence and frowning angrily.

Tikhon followed behind and Petya heard the Cossacks laughing with him and at him, about some pair of boots he had thrown into the bushes.

When the fit of laughter that had seized him at Tikhon's words and smile had passed and Petya realized for a moment that this Tikhon had killed a man, he felt uneasy. He looked round at the captive drummer-boy and felt a pang in his heart. But this uneasiness lasted only a moment. He felt it necessary to hold his head higher, to brace himself, and to question the esaul with an air of importance about to-morrow's undertaking, that he might not be unworthy of the company in which he found himself.

The officer who had been sent to inquire, met Denisov on the way with news that Dolokhov was soon coming and that all was well with him.

Denisov at once cheered up and calling Petya to him, said: 'Well, tell me about yourself.'

7

PETYA, having left his people after their departure from Moscow, joined his regiment and was soon taken as orderly by a general commanding a large guerrilla detachment. From the time he received his commission, and especially since he had joined the active army and taken part in the battle of Vyazma,* Petya had been in a constant state of blissful excitement at being grown up, and in a perpetual ecstatic hurry not to miss any chance to do something really heroic. He was highly delighted with what he saw and experienced in the army, but at the same time it always seemed to him that the really heroic exploits were being performed just where he did not happen to be. And he was always in a hurry to get where he was not.

When on the 21st of October his general expressed a wish to send somebody to Denisov's detachment, Petya begged so piteously to be sent that the general could not refuse. But when dispatching him he recalled Petya's mad action at the battle of Vyazma, where instead of riding by the road to the place to which he had been sent, he had galloped to the advanced line under the fire of the

French and had there twice fired his pistol. So now the general explicitly forbade his taking part in any action whatever of Denisov's. That was why Petya had blushed and grown confused when Denisov asked him whether he could stay. Before they had ridden to the outskirts of the forest Petya had considered that he must carry out his instructions strictly and return at once. But when he saw the French and saw Tikhon, and learnt that there would certainly be an attack that night, he decided, with the rapidity with which young people change their views, that the general, whom he had greatly respected till then, was a rubbishy German, that Denisov was a hero, the esaul a hero, and Tikhon a hero too, and that it would be shameful for him to leave them at a moment of difficulty.

It was already growing dusk when Denisov, Petya, and the esaul rode up to the watch-house. In the twilight saddled horses could be seen, and Cossacks and hussars who had rigged up rough shelters in the glade and were kindling glowing fires in a hollow of the forest where the French could not see the smoke. In the passage of the small watch-house a Cossack with sleeves rolled up was chopping some mutton. In the room three officers of Denisov's band were converting a door into a tabletop. Petya took off his wet clothes, gave them to be dried, and at once began helping the officers to fix up the dinner-table.

In ten minutes the table was ready and a napkin spread on it. On the table were vodka, a flask of rum, white bread, roast mutton and salt.

Sitting at table with the officers and tearing the fat savoury mutton with his hands, down which the grease trickled, Petya was in an ecstatic childish state of love for all men, and consequently of confidence that others loved him in the same way.

'So then, what do you think, Vasili Dmitrich?' said he to Denisov, 'it's all right my staying a day with you?' And not waiting for a reply he answered his own question: 'You see I was told to find out – well, I am finding out ... Only do let me into the very ... into the chief ... I don't want a reward ... But I want ...'

Petya clenched his teeth and looked around, throwing back his head and flourishing his arms.

'Into the very chief ...' Denisov repeated with a smile.

'Only, please let me command something, so that I may really command ...' Petya went on. 'What would it be to you? ... Oh, you want a knife?' he said, turning to an officer who wished to cut himself a piece of mutton.

And he handed him his clasp-knife. The officer admired it.

'Please keep it. I have several like it,' said Petya, blushing. 'Heavens! I was quite forgetting,' he suddenly cried. 'I have some raisins, fine ones; you know, seedless ones. We have a new sutler and he has such capital things. I bought ten pounds. I am used to something sweet. Would you like some? . . .' and Petya ran out into the passage to his Cossack and brought back some bags which contained about five pounds of raisins. 'Have some, gentlemen, have some!'

'You want a coffee-pot, don't you?' he asked the esaul. 'I bought a capital one from our sutler! He has splendid things. And he's very honest, that's the chief thing. I'll be sure to send it you. Or perhaps your flints are giving out, or are worn out — that happens sometimes, you know. I have brought some with me, here they are,' — and he showed a bag — 'a hundred flints. I bought them very cheap. Please take as many as you want, or all if you like . . .'

Then suddenly, dismayed lest he had said too much, Petya stopped and blushed.

He tried to remember whether he had not done anything else that was foolish. And running over the events of the day he remembered the French drummer-boy. 'It's capital for us here, but what of him? Where have they put him? Have they fed him? Haven't they hurt his feelings?' he thought. But having caught himself saying too much about the flints, he was now afraid to speak out.

'I might ask,' he thought, 'but they'll say: "He's a boy himself and so he pities the boy."' I'll show them to-morrow whether I'm a boy. Will it seem odd if I ask?' Petya thought. 'Well, never mind!' and immediately, blushing and looking anxiously at the officers to see if they appeared ironical, he said:

'May I call in that boy who was taken prisoner and give him something to eat? . . . Perhaps . . .'

'Yes, he's a poor little fellow,' said Denisov, who evidently saw nothing shameful in this reminder. 'Call him in. His name is Vincent Bosse. Have him fetched.'

'I'll call him,' said Petya.

'Yes, yes, call him. A poor little fellow,' Denisov repeated.

Petya was standing at the door when Denisov said this. He slipped in between the officers, came close to Denisov, and said:

'Let me kiss you, dear old fellow! Oh, how fine, how splendid!' And having kissed Denisov he ran out of the hut.

'Bosse! Vincent!' Petya cried, stopping outside the door.

'Who do you want, sir?' asked a voice in the darkness.

Petya replied that he wanted the French lad who had been captured that day.

'Ah, Vesenny?' said a Cossack.

Vincent, the boy's name, had already been changed by the Cossacks into *Vesénny* (vernal) and into *Vesénya* by the peasants and soldiers. In both these adaptations the reference to spring (*vesná*) matched the impression made by the young lad.

'He is warming himself there by the bonfire. Ho, Vesenya! Vesenya! – Vesenny!' laughing voices were heard calling to one another in the darkness.

'He's a smart lad,' said an hussar standing near Petya. 'We gave him something to eat a while ago. He was awfully hungry!'

The sound of bare feet splashing through the mud was heard in the darkness, and the drummer-boy came to the door.

'Ah, *c'est vous!*' said Petya. '*Voulez-vous manger? N'ayez pas peur, on ne vous fera pas de mal,*' he added shyly and affectionately, touching the boy's hand. '*Entrez, entrez.*'

'*Merci, monsieur,*' said the drummer-boy in a trembling almost childish voice, and he began scraping his dirty feet on the threshold.

There were many things Petya wanted to say to the drummer-boy, but did not dare to. He stood irresolutely beside him in the passage. Then in the darkness he took the boy's hand and pressed it.

'Come in, come in!' he repeated in a gentle whisper. 'Oh, what can I do for him?' he thought, and opening the door he let the boy pass in first.

When the boy had entered the hut, Petya sat down at a distance from him, considering it beneath his dignity to pay attention to him. But he fingered the money in his pocket, and wondered whether it would seem ridiculous to give some to the drummer-boy.

8

THE arrival of Dolokhov diverted Petya's attention from the drummer-boy, to whom Denisov had had some mutton and vodka given, and whom he had had dressed in a Russian coat so that he might be kept with their band and not sent away with the other prisoners. Petya had heard in the army many stories of Dolokhov's extraordinary bravery and of his cruelty to the French, so from the moment he entered the hut Petya did not take his eyes from him, but braced himself up more and more and held his head high, that he might not be unworthy even of such company.

Dolokhov's appearance amazed Petya by its simplicity.

Denisov wore a Cossack coat, had a beard, had an icon of Nicholas the Wonder-Worker on his breast, and his way of speaking, and everything he did, indicated his unusual position. But

Dolokhov, who in Moscow had worn a Persian costume, had now the appearance of a most correct officer of the Guards. He was clean-shaven and wore a Guardsman's padded coat with an Order of St George at his buttonhole and a plain forage cap set straight on his head. He took off his wet felt cloak in a corner of the room, and without greeting anyone went up to Denisov and began questioning him about the matter in hand. Denisov told him of the designs the large detachments had on the transport, of the message Petya had brought, and his own replies to both generals. Then he told him all he knew of the French detachment.

'That's so. But we must know what troops they are and their numbers,' said Dolokhov. 'It will be necessary to go there. We can't start the affair without knowing for certain how many of them there are. I like to work accurately. Here now – wouldn't one of these gentlemen like to ride over to the French camp with me? I have brought a spare uniform.'

'I, I . . . I'll go with you!' cried Petya.

'There's no need for you to go at all,' said Denisov, addressing Dolokhov, 'and as for him, I won't let him go on any account.'

'I like that!' exclaimed Petya. 'Why shouldn't I go?'

'Because it's useless.'

'Well, you must excuse me, because . . . because . . . I shall go, and that's all. You'll take me, won't you?' he said, turning to Dolokhov.

'Why not?' Dolokhov answered absently, scrutinizing the face of the French drummer-boy. 'Have you had that youngster with you long?' he asked Denisov.

'He was taken to-day but he knows nothing. I'm keeping him with me.'

'Yes, and where do you put the others?' inquired Dolokhov.

'Where? I send them away and take a weceipt for them,' shouted Denisov, suddenly flushing. 'And I say boldly that I have not a single man's life on my conscience. Would it be difficult for you to send thirty or thwee-hundwed men to town under escort, instead of staining – I speak bluntly – staining the honour of a soldier?'

'That kind of amiable talk would be suitable from this young count of sixteen,' said Dolokhov with cold irony, 'but it's time for you to drop it.'

'Why, I've not said anything! I only say that I'll certainly go with you,' said Petya shyly.

'But for you and me, old fellow, it's time to drop these amenities,' continued Dolokhov, as if he found particular pleasure in speaking of this subject which irritated Denisov. 'Now why have you kept this lad?' he went on, swaying his head. 'Because you are sorry for him! Don't we know those "receipts" of yours? You send a hundred men away, and thirty get there. The rest either starve or get killed. So isn't it all the same not to send them?'

The esaul, screwing up his light-coloured eyes, nodded approvingly.

'That's not the point. I'm not going to discuss the matter. I do not wish to take it on my conscience. You say they'll die. All wight. Only not by my doing!'

Dolokhov began laughing.

'Who has told them not to capture me these twenty times over? But if they did catch me they'd string me up to an aspen tree, and you with all your chivalry just the same.' He paused. 'However, we must get to work. Tell the Cossack to fetch my kit. I have two French uniforms in it. Well, are you coming with me?' he asked Petya.

'I? Yes, yes, certainly!' cried Petya, blushing almost to tears and glancing at Denisov.

While Dolokhov had been disputing with Denisov what should be done with prisoners, Petya had once more felt awkward and restless; but again he had no time to grasp fully what they were talking about. 'If grown-up, distinguished men think so, it must be necessary and right,' thought he. 'But above all Denisov must not dare to imagine that I'll obey him and that he can order me about. I will certainly go to the French camp with Dolokhov. If he can, so can I!'

And to all Denisov's persuasions, Petya replied that he too was accustomed to do everything accurately and not just anyhow, and that he never considered personal danger.

'For you'll admit that if we don't know for sure how many of them there are . . . hundreds of lives may depend on it, while there are only two of us. Besides, I want to go very much, and certainly will go, so don't hinder me,' said he. 'It will only make things worse . . .'

9

HAVING put on French greatcoats and shakos, Petya and Dolokhov rode to the clearing from which Denisov had reconnoitred the French camp, and emerging from the forest in pitch darkness they descended into the hollow. On reaching the bottom, Dolokhov told the Cossacks accompanying him to await him there and rode on at a quick trot along the road to the bridge. Petya, his heart in his mouth with excitement, rode by his side.

'If we're caught I won't be taken alive! I have a pistol,' whispered he.

'Don't talk Russian,' said Dolokhov in a hurried whisper, and at that very moment they heard through the darkness the challenge: '*Qui vive?*' and the click of a musket.

The blood rushed to Petya's face and he grasped his pistol.

'*Lanciers du 6-me,*' replied Dolokhov neither hastening nor slackening his horse's pace.

The black figure of a sentinel stood on the bridge.

'*Mot d'ordre.*'

Dolokhov reined in his horse and advanced at a walk.

'*Dites donc, le colonel Gérard est ici?*' he asked.

'*Mot d'ordre,*' repeated the sentinel, barring the way and not replying.

'*Quand un officier fait sa ronde, les sentinelles ne demandent pas le mot d'ordre...*' cried Dolokhov suddenly flaring up and riding straight at the sentinel. '*Je vous demande si le colonel est ici?*'

And without waiting for an answer from the sentinel, who had stepped aside, Dolokhov rode up the incline at a walk.

Noticing the black outline of a man crossing the road, Dolokhov stopped him and inquired where the commander and officers were. The man, a soldier with a sack over his shoulder, stopped, came close up to Dolokhov's horse, touched it with his hand, and explained simply and in a friendly way that the commander and the officers were higher up the hill to the right in the courtyard of the farm, as he called the landowner's house.

Having ridden up the road, on both sides of which French talk could be heard around the camp-fires, Dolokhov turned into the courtyard of the landowner's house. Having ridden in, he dismounted and approached a big blazing camp-fire, around which sat several men talking noisily. Something was boiling in a small cauldron at the edge of the fire and a soldier in a peaked cap and blue overcoat, lit up by the fire, was kneeling beside it stirring its contents with a ramrod.

'Oh, he's a hard nut to crack,' said one of the officers who was sitting in the shadow at the other side of the fire.

'He'll make them get a move on, those fellows!' said another, laughing.

Both fell silent, peering out through the darkness at the sound of Dolokhov and Petya's steps as they advanced to the fire leading their horses.

'*Bonjour, messieurs!*' said Dolokhov loudly and clearly.

There was a stir among the officers in the shadow beyond the fire, and one tall long-necked officer, walking round the fire, came up to Dolokhov.

'Is that you, Clément?' he asked. 'Where the devil ... ?' But noticing his mistake he broke off short and, with a frown, greeted Dolokhov as a stranger, asking what he could do for him.

Dolokhov said that he and his companion were trying to over-take their regiment, and addressing the company in general asked whether they knew anything of the 6th Regiment. None of them knew anything, and Petya thought the officers were beginning to look at him and Dolokhov with hostility and suspicion. For some seconds all were silent.

'If you were counting on the evening soup, you have come too late,' said a voice from behind the fire with a repressed laugh.

Dolokhov replied that they were not hungry and must push on farther that night.

He handed the horses over to the soldier who was stirring the pot, and squatted down on his heels by the fire beside the officer with the long neck. That officer did not take his eyes from Dolo-khov and again asked to what regiment he belonged. Dolokhov, as if he had not heard the question, did not reply, but lighting a short French pipe which he took from his pocket, began asking the officers how far the road before them was safe from Cossacks.

'Those brigands are everywhere,' replied an officer from behind the fire.

Dolokhov remarked that the Cossacks were a danger only to stragglers such as his companion and himself, 'but probably they would not dare attack large detachments?' he added inquiringly. No one replied.

'Well, now he'll come away,' Petya thought every moment as he stood by the camp-fire listening to the talk.

But Dolokhov restarted the conversation which had dropped, and began putting direct questions as to how many men there were in the battalion, how many battalions, and how many prisoners. Asking about the Russian prisoners with that detachment, Dolo-khov said:

'A horrid business dragging these corpses about with one! It would be better to shoot such rabble,' and burst into loud laughter, so strange that Petya thought the French would immediately detect their disguise, and involuntarily took a step back from the camp-fire.

No one replied a word to Dolokhov's laughter, and a French officer whom they could not see (he lay wrapped in a greatcoat) rose and whispered something to a companion. Dolokhov got up and called to the soldier who was holding their horses.

'Will they bring our horses or not?' thought Petya, instinctively drawing nearer to Dolokhov.

The horses were brought.

'Good evening, gentlemen,' said Dolokhov.

Petya wished to say 'Good night' but could not utter a word. The officers were whispering together. Dolokhov was a long time mounting his horse which would not stand still, then he rode out of the yard at a foot-pace. Petya rode beside him, longing to look round to see whether or no the French were running after them, but not daring to.

Coming out on to the road, Dolokhov did not ride back across the open country, but through the village. At one spot he stopped and listened. 'Do you hear?' he asked. Petya recognized the sound of Russian voices and saw the dark figures of Russian prisoners round their camp-fires. When they had descended to the bridge Petya and Dolokhov rode past the sentinel, who without saying a word paced morosely up and down it, then they descended into the hollow where the Cossacks awaited them.

'Well now, good-bye. Tell Denisov, "at the first shot at day-break",' said Dolokhov and was about to ride away, but Petya seized hold of him.

'Really!' he cried, 'you are such a hero! Oh, how fine, how splendid! How I love you!'

'All right, all right!' said Dolokhov. But Petya did not let go of him and Dolokhov saw through the gloom that Petya was bending towards him and wanted to kiss him. Dolokhov kissed him, laughed, turned his horse, and vanished into the darkness.

10

HAVING returned to the watchman's hut, Petya found Denisov in the passage. He was awaiting Petya's return in a state of agitation, anxiety, and self-reproach for having let him go.

'Thank God!' he exclaimed. 'Yes, thank God!' he repeated, listening to Petya's rapturous account. 'But, devil take you, I haven't slept because of you! Well, thank God. Now lie down. We can still get a nap before morning.'

'But . . . no,' said Petya, 'I don't want to sleep yet. Besides I know myself, if I fall asleep it's finished. And then I am used to not sleeping before a battle.'

He sat awhile in the hut joyfully recalling the details of his expedition and vividly picturing to himself what would happen next day. Then noticing that Denisov was asleep, he rose and went out of doors.

It was still quite dark outside. The rain was over, but drops were still falling from the trees. Near the watchman's hut the black shapes of the Cossacks' shanties and of horses tethered together could be seen. Behind the hut the dark shapes of the two wagons, with their horses beside them, were discernible, and in the hollow the dying camp-fire gleamed red. Not all the Cossacks and hussars were asleep: here and there, amid the sounds of falling drops and the munching of the horses near by, could be heard low voices which seemed to be whispering.

Petya came out, peered into the darkness, and went up to the wagons. Someone was snoring under them, and around them stood saddled horses munching their oats. In the dark Petya recognized his own horse, which he called 'Karabakh'* though it was of Ukrainian breed, and went up to it.

'Well, Karabakh! We'll do some service to-morrow,' said he, sniffing its nostrils and kissing it.

'Why aren't you asleep, sir?' said a Cossack who was sitting under a wagon.

'No, ah . . . Likhachëv – isn't that your name? Do you know I have only just come back. We've been into the French camp.'

And Petya gave the Cossack a detailed account not only of his ride but also of his object, and why he considered it better to risk his life than to act 'just anyhow'.

'Well you should get some sleep now,' said the Cossack.

'No, I am used to this,' said Petya. 'I say, aren't the flints in your pistols worn out? I brought some with me. Don't you want any? You can have some.'

The Cossack bent forward from under the wagon to get a closer look at Petya.

'Because I am accustomed to doing everything accurately,' said Petya. 'Some fellows do things just anyhow, without preparation, and then they're sorry for it afterwards. I don't like that.'

'Just so,' said the Cossack.

'Oh yes, another thing! Please, my dear fellow, will you sharpen my sabre for me? It's got blun . . .' (Petya feared to tell a lie) '– it has never been sharpened. Can you do it?'

'Of course I can.'

Likhachëv got up, rummaged in his pack, and soon Petya heard the warlike sound of steel on whetstone. He climbed onto the wagon and sat on its edge. The Cossack was sharpening the sabre under the wagon.

'I say! Are the lads asleep?' asked Petya.

'Some are, and some aren't – like us.'

'Well, and that boy?'

'Vesenny? Oh, he's thrown himself down there in the passage. Fast asleep after his fright. He was that glad!'

After that Petya remained silent for a long time, listening to the sounds. He heard footsteps in the darkness and a black figure appeared.

'What are you sharpening?' asked a man coming up to the wagon.

'Why, this gentleman's sabre.'

'That's right,' said the man, whom Petya took to be an hussar. 'Was the cup left here?'

'There, by the wheel!'

The hussar took the cup.

'It must be daylight soon,' said he yawning, and went away.

Petya ought to have known that he was in a forest with Denisov's guerrilla band, a verst from the road, sitting on a wagon captured from the French beside which horses were tethered, that under it Likhachëv was sitting sharpening a sabre for him, that the big dark blotch to the right was the watchman's hut, and the red blotch below to the left was the dying embers of a camp-fire, that the man who had come for the cup was an hussar who wanted a drink; but he neither knew nor wanted to know anything of all this. He was in a fairy kingdom where nothing resembled reality. The big dark blotch might really be the watchman's hut or it might be a cavern leading to the very depths of the earth. Perhaps the red spot was a fire, or it might be the eye of an enormous monster. Perhaps he was really sitting on a wagon but it might very well be that he was not sitting on a wagon but on a terribly high tower from which, if he fell, he would have to fall for a whole day or a whole month, or go on falling and never reach the bottom. Perhaps it was just the Cossack, Likhachëv, who was sitting under the wagon, but it might be the kindest, bravest, most wonderful, most splendid man in the world, whom no one knew of. It might really have been that an hussar came for water and went back into the hollow, but perhaps he had simply vanished – disappeared altogether and dissolved into nothingness.

Nothing Petya could have seen now would have surprised him. He was in a fairy kingdom where everything was possible.

He looked up at the sky. And the sky was a fairy realm like the earth. It was clearing, and over the tops of the trees clouds were swiftly sailing as if unveiling the stars. Sometimes it looked as if the clouds were passing, and a clear black sky appeared. Sometimes it seemed as if the black spaces were clouds. Sometimes the sky seemed to be rising high, high overhead, and then it seemed to sink so low that one could touch it with one's hand.

Petya's eyes began to close and he swayed a little.

The trees were dripping. Quiet talking was heard. The horses neighed and jostled one another. Someone snored.

'Ozheg-zheg, Ozheg-zheg...' hissed the sabre against the whetstone, and suddenly Petya heard an harmonious orchestra playing some unknown, sweetly solemn hymn. Petya was as musical as Natasha and more so than Nicholas, but had never learnt music or thought about it, and so the melody that unexpectedly came to his mind seemed to him particularly fresh and attractive. The music became more and more audible. The melody grew and passed from one instrument to another. And what was played was a fugue – though Petya had not the least conception of what a fugue is. Each instrument – now resembling a violin and now a horn, but better and clearer than violin or horn – played its own part, and before it had finished the melody merged with another instrument that began almost the same air, and then with a third and a fourth; and they all blended into one, and again became separate and again blended, now into solemn church music, now into something dazzlingly brilliant and triumphant.

'Oh – why, that was in a dream!' Petya said to himself as he lurched forward. 'It's in my ears. But perhaps it's music of my own. Well, go on, my music! Now!...'

He closed his eyes, and from all sides, as if from a distance, sounds fluttered, grew into harmonies, separated, blended, and again all mingled into the same sweet and solemn hymn. 'Oh, this is delightful! As much as I like, and as I like it!' said Petya to himself. He tried to conduct that enormous orchestra.

'Now softly, softly die away!' and the sounds obeyed him. 'Now fuller, more joyful. Still more and more joyful!' And from an unknown depth rose increasingly triumphant sounds. 'Now voices join in!' ordered Petya. And at first from afar he heard men's voices and then women's. The voices grew in harmonious triumphant strength, and Petya listened to their surpassing beauty in awe and joy.

With a solemn triumphal march there mingled a song, the drip from the trees, and the hissing of the sabre, 'Ozheg-zheg-zheg...' and again the horses jostled one another and neighed, not disturbing the choir but joining in it.

Petya did not know how long this lasted: he enjoyed himself all the time, wondered at his enjoyment and regretted that there was no one to share it. He was awakened by Likhachëv's kindly voice.

'It's ready, your Honour; you can split a Frenchman in half with it!'

Petya woke up.

'It's getting light, it's really getting light!' he exclaimed.

The horses that had previously been invisible could now be seen to their very tails, and a watery light showed itself through the bare branches. Petya shook himself, jumped up, took a ruble from his pocket and gave it to Likhachëv; then he flourished the sabre, tested it, and sheathed it. The Cossacks were untying their horses and tightening their saddle-girths.

'And here's the commander,' said Likhachëv.

Denisov came out of the watchman's hut and, having called Petya, gave orders to get ready.

11

THE men rapidly picked out their horses in the semi-darkness, tightened their saddle girths, and formed companies. Denisov stood by the watchman's hut giving final orders. The infantry of the detachment passed along the road and quickly disappeared amid the trees in the mist of early dawn, hundreds of feet splashing through the mud. The esaul gave some orders to his men. Petya held his horse by the bridle, impatiently awaiting the order to mount. His face, having been bathed in cold water, was all aglow, and his eyes were particularly brilliant. Cold shivers ran down his spine and his whole body pulsed rhythmically.

'Well, is ev'wything weady?' asked Denisov. 'Bwing the horses.'

The horses were brought. Denisov was angry with the Cossack because the saddle-girths were too slack, reproved him, and mounted. Petya put his foot in the stirrup. His horse by habit made as if to nip his leg, but Petya leapt quickly into the saddle unconscious of his own weight, and turning to look at the hussars starting in the darkness behind him, rode up to Denisov.

'Vasili Dmitrich, entrust me with some commission! Please . . . For God's sake . . . !' said he.

Denisov seemed to have forgotten Petya's very existence. He turned to glance at him.

'I ask one thing of you,' he returned sternly, 'To obey me and not shove you'self fo'ward anywhere.'

He did not say another word to Petya but rode in silence all the way. When they had come to the edge of the forest it was noticeably growing light over the field. Denisov talked in whispers with the esaul, and the Cossacks rode past Petya and Denisov.

When they had all ridden by, Denisov touched his horse and rode down the hill. Slipping onto their haunches and sliding, the horses descended with their riders into the ravine. Petya rode beside Denisov, the pulsation of his body constantly increasing. It was getting lighter and lighter but the mist still hid distant objects. Having reached the valley Denisov looked back and nodded to a Cossack beside him.

'The signal!' said he.

The Cossack raised his arm and a shot rang out. In an instant the tramp of horses galloping forward was heard, shouts came from various sides, and then more shots.

At the first sound of trampling hoofs and shouting, Petya lashed his horse and loosening his rein galloped forward, not heeding Denisov who shouted at him. It seemed to Petya that at the moment the shot was fired it suddenly became as bright as noon. He galloped to the bridge. Cossacks were galloping along the road in front of him. On the bridge he collided with a Cossack who had fallen behind, but he galloped on. In front of him soldiers, probably Frenchmen, were running from right to left across the road. One of them fell in the mud under his horse's feet.

Cossacks were crowding about a hut, busy with something. From the midst of that crowd terrible screams arose. Petya galloped up, and the first thing he saw was the pale face and trembling jaw of a Frenchman clutching the handle of a lance that had been aimed at him.

'Hurrah!...Lads!...ours!' shouted Petya, and giving rein to his excited horse he galloped forward along the village street.

He could hear shooting ahead of him. Cossacks, hussars, and ragged Russian prisoners, who had come running from both sides of the road, were shouting something loudly and incoherently. A gallant-looking Frenchman in a blue overcoat, capless, and with a frowning red face, had been defending himself with his bayonet against the hussars. When Petya galloped up the Frenchman had already fallen. 'Too late again!' flashed through Petya's mind and he galloped on to the place from which the rapid firing could be heard. The shots came from the yard of the landowner's house he had visited the night before with Dolokhov. The French were making a stand there behind a wattle fence in a garden thickly overgrown with bushes, and were firing at the Cossacks who crowded at the gateway. Through the smoke, as he approached the gate, Petya saw Dolokhov, whose face was of a pale greenish tint, shouting to his men. 'Go round! Wait for the infantry!' he exclaimed, as Petya rode up to him.

'Wait?...Hurrah-ah-ah!' shouted Petya, and without pausing a moment, galloped to the place whence came the sounds of firing and where the smoke was thickest.

A volley was heard, and some bullets whistled past, while others plashed against something. The Cossacks and Dolokhov galloped after Petya into the gateway of the courtyard. In the dense wavering smoke some of the French threw down their arms and ran out of the bushes to meet the Cossacks, while others ran down the hill towards the pond. Petya was galloping along the courtyard, but instead of holding the reins he waved both his arms about rapidly and strangely, slipping farther and farther to one side in his saddle. His horse, having galloped up to a camp-fire that was smouldering in the morning light, stopped suddenly, and Petya fell heavily on to the wet ground. The Cossacks saw that his arms and legs jerked rapidly though his head was quite motionless. A bullet had pierced his skull.

After speaking to the senior French officer, who came out of the house with a white handkerchief tied to his sword and announced that they surrendered, Dolokhov dismounted and went up to Petya, who lay motionless with outstretched arms.

'Done for!' he said with a frown, and went to the gate to meet Denisov who was riding towards him.

'Killed?' cried Denisov, recognizing from a distance the unmistakably lifeless attitude – very familiar to him – in which Petya's body was lying.

'Done for!' repeated Dolokhov, as if the utterance of these words afforded him pleasure, and he quickly went up to the prisoners, who were surrounded by Cossacks who had hurried up. 'We won't take them!' he called out to Denisov.

Denisov did not reply; he rode up to Petya, dismounted, and with trembling hands turned towards himself the bloodstained, mud-bespattered face, which had already gone white.

'I am used to something sweet. Raisins, fine ones ... take them all!' he recalled Petya's words. And the Cossacks looked round in surprise at the sound, like the yelp of a dog, with which Denisov turned away, walked to the wattle fence, and seized hold of it.

Among the Russian prisoners rescued by Denisov and Dolokhov was Pierre Bezukhov.

12

DURING the whole of their march from Moscow no fresh orders had been issued by the French authorities concerning the party of prisoners among whom was Pierre. On the 22nd of October that party was no longer with the same troops and baggage trains as when it had left Moscow. Half the wagons laden with hard-tack that had travelled the first stages with them had been captured by Cossacks, the other half had gone on ahead. Not one of those dismounted cavalrymen who had marched in front of the prisoners was left; they had all disappeared. The artillery the prisoners had seen in front of them during the first days was now replaced by Marshal Junot's enormous baggage-train, convoyed by Westphalians. Behind the prisoners came a cavalry baggage-train.

From Vyazma onwards the French army, which had till then moved in three columns, went on as a single group. The symptoms of disorder that Pierre had noticed at their first halting-place after leaving Moscow had now reached the utmost limit.

The road along which they moved was bordered on both sides by dead horses; ragged men who had fallen behind from various regiments continually changed about, now joining the moving column, now again lagging behind it.

Several times during the march false alarms had been given, and the soldiers of the escort had raised their muskets, fired, and run headlong, crushing one another, but had afterwards reassembled and abused each other for their causeless panic.

These three groups travelling together - the cavalry stores, the convoy of prisoners, and Junot's baggage-train - still constituted a separate and united whole, though each of the groups was rapidly melting away.

Of the artillery baggage-train, which had consisted of a hundred and twenty wagons, not more than sixty now remained, the rest had been captured or left behind. Some of Junot's wagons had also been captured or abandoned. Three wagons had been raided and robbed by stragglers from Davout's corps. From the talk of the Germans, Pierre learned that a larger guard had been allotted to that baggage-train than to the prisoners, and that one of their comrades, a German soldier, had been shot by the marshal's own order, because a silver spoon belonging to the marshal had been found in his possession.

The group of prisoners had thawed away most of all. Of the three hundred and thirty men who had set out from Moscow less than a hundred now remained. The prisoners were more burdensome to the escort than even the cavalry-saddles or Junot's baggage. They understood that the saddles and Junot's spoons might be of some use, but that cold and hungry soldiers should have to stand and guard equally cold and hungry Russians who froze and lagged behind on the road (in which case the order was to shoot them) was not merely incomprehensible but revolting. And the escort, as if afraid, in the grievous condition they themselves were in, of giving way to the pity they felt for the prisoners, and so rendering their own plight still worse, treated them with particular moroseness and severity.

At Dorogobuzh while the soldiers of the convoy, having locked the prisoners in a stable, had gone off to pillage their own stores, several of the soldier-prisoners tunnelled under the wall and ran away, but were re-captured by the French and shot.

The arrangement adopted when they started, that the officer-prisoners should be kept separate from the rest, had long since been abandoned. All who could walk went together, and after the third stage Pierre had rejoined Karataev and the grey-blue bandy-legged dog that had chosen Karataev for its master.

On the third day after leaving Moscow Karataev again fell ill with the fever he had suffered from in hospital in Moscow, and as he grew gradually weaker Pierre kept away from him. Pierre did not know why, but since Karataev had begun to grow weaker it had cost him an effort to go near him. When he did so and heard the subdued moaning with which Karataev generally lay down at the halting places, and when he smelt the odour emanating from him which was now stronger than before, Pierre moved further away and did not think about him.

While imprisoned in the shed Pierre had learned, not with his intellect but with his whole being, by life itself, that man is created for happiness, that happiness is within him, in the satisfaction of simple human needs, and that all unhappiness arises not from privation but from superfluity. And now during these last three weeks of the march he had learned still another new, consolatory truth – that there is nothing in the world that is terrible. He had learned that, as there is no condition in which man can be happy and entirely free, so there is no condition in which he need be unhappy and not free. He learned that suffering and freedom have their limits and that those limits are very near together; that the person in a bed of roses with one crumpled petal suffered as keenly as he now, sleeping on the bare damp earth with one side growing chilled while the other was warming; and that when he had put on tight dancing shoes he had suffered just as he did now when he walked with bare feet that were covered with sores – his foot-gear having long since fallen to pieces. He discovered that when he had married his wife – of his own free will as it had seemed to him – he had been no more free than now when they locked him up at night in a stable. Of all that he himself subsequently termed his sufferings, but which at the time he scarcely felt, the worst was the state of his bare, rubbed, and scab-covered feet. (The horseflesh was appetising and nourishing, the saltpetre flavour of the gunpowder they used instead of salt was even pleasant; there was no great cold, it was always warm walking in the daytime, and at night there were the camp-fires; the lice that devoured him warmed his body.) The one thing that was at first hard to bear was his feet.

After the second day's march Pierre, having examined his feet by the camp-fire, thought it would be impossible to walk on them; but when everybody got up, he went along, limping, and when he had warmed up, walked without feeling the pain, though at night his feet were more terrible to look at than before. But he did not look at them and thought of other things.

Only now did Pierre realize the full strength of life in man, and the saving power he has of transferring his attention from one thing to another, which is like the safety valve of a boiler that allows superfluous steam to blow off when the pressure exceeds a certain limit.

He did not see and did not hear how they shot the prisoners who lagged behind, though more than a hundred had perished in that way. He did not think of Karataev, who grew weaker every day and evidently would soon have to share that fate. Still less did Pierre think about himself. The harder his position became and the more terrible the future, the more independent of that position in which he found himself were the joyful and comforting thoughts, memories, and imaginings, that came to him.

13

AT mid-day on the 22nd of October Pierre was going uphill along the muddy, slippery road, looking at his feet and at the roughness of the way. Occasionally he glanced at the familiar crowd around him, and then again at his feet. The former and the latter were alike familiar and his own. The blue-grey bandy-legged dog ran merrily along the side of the road, sometimes in proof of its agility and self-satisfaction lifting one hind leg and hopping along on three, and then again going on all four and rushing to bark at the crows that sat on the carrion. The dog was merrier and sleeker than it had been in Moscow. All around lay the flesh of different animals – from men to horses – in various stages of decomposition; and as the wolves were kept off by the passing men the dog could eat all it wanted.

It had been raining since morning and had seemed as if at any moment it might cease and the sky clear, but after a short break it began raining again harder than before. The saturated road no longer absorbed the water, which ran along the ruts in streams.

Pierre walked along, looking from side to side, counting his steps in threes, and reckoning them off on his fingers. Mentally addressing the rain, he repeated: 'Now then, now then, go on! Pelt harder!'

It seemed to him that he was thinking of nothing, but far down and deep within him his soul was occupied with something important and comforting. This something was a most subtle spiritual deduction from a conversation with Karataev the day before.

At their yesterday's halting-place, feeling chilly by a dying camp-fire, Pierre had got up and gone to the next one, which was burning better. There Platon Karataev was sitting, covered up – head and all – with his greatcoat as if it were a vestment, telling the soldiers in his effective and pleasant though now feeble voice a story Pierre knew. It was already past midnight, the hour when Karataev was usually free of his fever and particularly lively. When Pierre reached the fire and heard Platon's voice enfeebled by illness, and saw his pathetic face brightly lit up by the blaze, he felt a painful prick at his heart. His feeling of pity for this man frightened him and he wished to go away, but there was no other fire, and Pierre sat down, trying not to look at Platon.

'Well, how are you?' he asked.

'How am I? If we grumble at sickness, God won't grant us death,' replied Platon, and at once resumed the story he had begun.

'And so, brother,' he continued, with a smile on his pale, emaciated face and a particularly happy light in his eyes, 'you see, brother . . .'

Pierre had long been familiar with that story.* Karataev had told it to him alone some half dozen times and always with a specially joyful emotion. But well as he knew it Pierre now listened to that tale as to something new, and the quiet rapture Karataev evidently felt as he told it communicated itself also to Pierre. The story was of an old merchant who lived a good and God-fearing life with his family, and who went once to the Nizhny fair with a companion – a rich merchant.

Having put up at an inn, they both went to sleep and next morning his companion was found robbed and with his throat cut. A bloodstained knife was found under the old merchant's pillow. He was tried, knouted, and his nostrils having been torn off, 'all in due order' as Karataev put it, he was sent to hard labour in Siberia.

'And so, brother' (it was at this point that Pierre came up), 'ten years or more passed by. The old man was living as a convict, submitting as he should, and doing no wrong. Only he prayed to God for death. Well one night the convicts were gathered, just as we are, with the old man among them. And they began telling what each was suffering for, and how they had sinned against God. One told how he had taken a life, another had taken two, a third had set a house on fire, while another had simply been a vagrant and had done nothing. So they asked the old man: "What are you being punished for, Daddy?" – "I, my dear brothers," he said, "am being punished for my own and other men's sins. But I have not killed anyone, or taken anything that was not mine, but have only helped my poorer brothers. I was a merchant, my dear brothers, and had much property." And he went on to tell them all about it in due order. "I don't grieve for myself," he says. "God it seems has chastened me. Only I am sorry for my old wife and the children," and the old man began to weep. Now it happened that among the group was the very man who had killed the other merchant. "Where did it happen, Daddy?" he said. "When, and in what month?" He asked all about it and his heart began to ache. So he comes up to the old man like this, and falls down at his feet! "You are perishing because of me, Daddy," he says. "It is quite true, lads, that this man," he says, "is being tortured innocently and for nothing! I," he says, "did that deed, and I put the knife under your head while you were asleep. Forgive me, Daddy," he says, "for Christ's sake!"'

Karataev paused, smiling joyously as he gazed into the fire, and he drew the logs together.

'And the old man said, "God will forgive you, we are all sinners in His sight. I suffer for my own sins," and he wept bitter tears. Well and what do you think, dear friends?' Karataev continued, his face brightening more and more with a rapturous smile, as if what he now had to tell contained the chief charm and the whole meaning of his story: 'What do you think, dear fellow? That murderer confessed to the authorities. "I have taken six lives," he says (he was a great sinner) "but what I am most sorry for is this old man. Don't let him suffer because of me." So he confessed, and it was all written down and the papers sent off in due order. The place was a long way off, and while they were judging, with one thing and another, filling in the papers all in due order – the authorities I mean – time passed. The affair reached the Tsar. After a while the Tsar's decree came: to set the merchant free and give him a compensation that had been awarded. The paper arrived and they began to look for the old man. "Where is the old man who has been suffering innocently and in vain? A paper has come from the Tsar!" So they began looking for him,' here Karataev's lower jaw trembled, 'but God had already forgiven him – he was dead! That's how it was, dear fellow!' Karataev concluded, and sat for a long time silent gazing before him with a smile.

And Pierre's soul was dimly but joyfully filled not by the story itself but by its mysterious significance: by the rapturous joy that lit up Karataev's face as he told it, and the mystic significance of that joy.

14

'À vos places!' suddenly cried a voice.

A pleasant feeling of excitement and an expectation of something joyful and solemn was aroused among the soldiers of the convoy and the prisoners. From all sides came shouts of command, and from the left came smartly-dressed cavalrymen on good horses, passing the prisoners at a trot. The expression on all faces showed the tension people feel at the approach of those in authority. The prisoners thronged together and were pushed off the road. The convoy formed up.

'The Emperor! The Emperor! The Marshal! The Duke!' and hardly had the sleek cavalry passed, before a carriage drawn by six grey horses rattled by. Pierre caught a glimpse of a man in a three-cornered hat with a tranquil look on his handsome, plump, white face. It was one of the marshals. His eye fell on Pierre's large and striking figure, and in the expression with which he frowned and looked away Pierre thought he detected sympathy and a desire to conceal that sympathy.

The general in charge of the stores galloped after the carriage with a red and frightened face, whipping up his skinny horse. Several officers formed a group, and some soldiers crowded round them. Their faces all looked excited and worried.

'What did he say? What did he say?' Pierre heard them ask.

While the marshal was passing, the prisoners had huddled together in a crowd and Pierre saw Karataev, whom he had not yet seen that morning. He sat in his small overcoat leaning against a birch tree. On his face, besides the look of joyful emotion it had worn yesterday while telling the tale of the merchant who suffered innocently, there was now an expression of quiet solemnity.

Karataev looked at Pierre with his kindly round eyes now filled with tears, evidently wishing him to come near that he might say something to him. But Pierre was not sufficiently sure of himself. He made as if he did not notice that look, and moved hastily away.

When the prisoners again went forward Pierre looked round.

Karataev was still sitting at the side of the road under the birch tree and two Frenchmen were talking over his head. Pierre did not look round again but went limping up the hill.

From behind, where Karataev had been sitting, came the sound of a shot. Pierre heard it plainly, but at that moment he remembered that he had not yet finished reckoning up how many stages there still remained to Smolensk – a calculation he had begun before the marshal went by. And he again started reckoning. Two French soldiers ran past Pierre, one of whom carried a lowered and smoking gun. They both looked pale, and in the expression on their faces – one of them glanced timidly at Pierre – there was something resembling what he had seen on the face of the young soldier at the execution. Pierre looked at this soldier and remembered that, two days before, that man had burnt his shirt while drying it at the fire, and how they had laughed at him.

Behind him, where Karataev had been sitting, the dog began to howl. 'What a stupid beast! Why is it howling?' thought Pierre.

His comrades, the prisoner-soldiers walking beside him, avoided looking back at the place where the shot had been fired and the dog was howling, just as Pierre did, but there was a set look on all their faces.

15

THE stories, the prisoners, and the marshal's baggage-train, stopped at the village of Shamshevo. The men crowded together round the camp-fires. Pierre went up to the fire, ate some roast horseflesh, lay down with his back to the fire and immediately fell asleep. He again slept as he had done at Mozhaysk after the battle of Borodino.

Again real events mingled with dreams and again someone, he or another, gave expression to his thoughts, and even to the same thoughts that had been expressed in his dream at Mozhaysk.

'Life is everything. Life is God. Everything changes and moves and that movement is God. And while there is life there is joy in consciousness of the divine. To love life is to love God. Harder and more blessed than all else is to love this life in one's sufferings, in innocent sufferings.'

'Karataev!' came to Pierre's mind.

And suddenly he saw vividly before him a long-forgotten, kindly old man who had given him geography lessons in Switzerland. 'Wait a bit,' said the old man, and showed Pierre a globe. This globe was alive – a vibrating ball without fixed dimensions. Its whole surface consisted of drops closely pressed together, and all these drops moved and changed places, sometimes several of them merging into one, sometimes one dividing into many. Each drop tried to spread out and occupy as much space as possible, but others, striving to do the same, compressed it, sometimes destroyed it, and sometimes merged with it.

'That is life,' said the old teacher.

'How simple and clear it is,' thought Pierre. 'How is it I did not know it before?'

'God is in the midst, and each drop tries to expand so as to reflect Him to the greatest extent. And it grows, merges, disappears from the surface, sinks to the depths and again emerges. There now, Karataev has spread out and disappeared. Do you understand, my child?' said the teacher.

'Do you understand,* damn you?' shouted a voice and Pierre woke up.

He lifted himself and sat up. A Frenchman who had just pushed a Russian soldier away was squatting by the fire engaged in roasting a piece of meat stuck on a ramrod. His sleeves were rolled up and his sinewy, hairy, red hands with their short fingers deftly turned the ramrod. His brown morose face with frowning brows was clearly visible by the glow of the charcoal.

'It's all the same to him,' he muttered, turning quickly to a soldier who stood behind him. 'Brigand! Get away!'

And twisting the ramrod he looked gloomily at Pierre, who turned away and gazed into the darkness. A prisoner, the Russian soldier the Frenchman had pushed away, was sitting near the fire patting something with his hand. Looking more closely, Pierre recognized the blue-grey dog, sitting beside the soldier wagging his tail.

'Ah, he's come?' said Pierre. 'And Plat—', he began, but did not finish.

Suddenly and simultaneously a crowd of memories awoke in his fancy – of the look Platon had given him as he sat under the tree, of the shot heard from that spot, of the dog's howl, of the guilty faces of the two Frenchmen as they ran past him, of the lowered and smoking gun, and of Karataev's absence at this halt – and he was on the point of realizing that Karataev had been killed, but just at that instant, he knew not why, the recollection came to his mind of a summer evening he had spent with a beautiful Polish lady on the verandah of his house in Kiev. And without linking up the events of the day or drawing a conclusion from them, Pierre closed his eyes, seeing a vision of the country in summer-time mingled with memories of bathing and of the liquid, vibrating globe, and he sank into water so that it closed over his head.

Before sunrise he was awakened by shouts and loud and rapid firing. French soldiers were running past him.

'The Cossacks!' one of them shouted, and a moment later a crowd of Russians surrounded Pierre.

For a long time he could not understand what was happening to him. All around he heard his comrades sobbing with joy.

'Brothers! Dear fellows! Darlings!' old soldiers exclaimed weeping, as they embraced Cossacks and hussars.

The hussars and Cossacks crowded round the prisoners, one offered them clothes, another boots, and a third bread. Pierre sobbed as he sat among them, and could not utter a word. He hugged the first soldier who approached him, and kissed him, weeping.

Dolokhov stood at the gate of the ruined house letting a crowd of disarmed Frenchmen pass by. The French, excited by all that had happened, were talking loudly among themselves, but as they passed Dolokhov, who gently switched his boots with his whip and watched them with cold glassy eyes that boded no good, they became silent. On the opposite side stood Dolokhov's Cossacks, counting the prisoners and marking off each hundred with a chalk line on the gate.

'How many?' Dolokhov asked the Cossack.

'The second hundred,' replied the Cossack.

'*Filez, filez!*' Dolokhov kept saying, having adopted this expression from the French, and when his eyes met those of the prisoners they flashed with a cruel light.

Denisov, bare-headed and with a gloomy face, walked behind some Cossacks who were carrying the body of Petya Rostov to a hole that had been dug in the garden.

16

AFTER the 28th of October, when the frosts began, the flight of the French assumed a still more tragic character, with men freezing, or roasting themselves to death at the camp-fires, while carriages with people dressed in furs continued to drive past carrying away the property that had been stolen by the Emperor, the kings, and the dukes; but the process of the flight and disintegration of the French army went on essentially as before.

From Moscow to Vyazma the French army of seventy-three

thousand men, not reckoning the Guards (who did nothing during the whole war but pillage), was reduced to thirty-six thousand, though not more than five thousand had fallen in battle. From this beginning the succeeding terms of the progression could be determined mathematically. The French army melted away and perished at the same rate from Moscow to Vyazma, from Vyazma to Smolensk, from Smolensk to the Berëzina, and from the Berëzina to Vilna – independently of the greater or lesser intensity of the cold, the pursuit, the barring of the way, or any other particular conditions. Beyond Vyazma the French army instead of moving in three columns huddled together into one mass, and so went on to the end. Berthier wrote to his Emperor (we know how far commanding officers allow themselves to diverge from the truth in describing the condition of an army) and this is what he said:

I deem it my duty to report to your Majesty the condition of the various corps I have had occasion to observe during different stages of the last two or three days' march. They are almost disbanded. Scarcely a quarter of the soldiers remain with the standards of their regiments, the others go off by themselves in different directions, hoping to find food and escape discipline. In general they regard Smolensk as the place where they hope to recover. During the last few days many of the men have been seen to throw away their cartridges and their arms. In such a state of affairs, whatever your ultimate plans may be, the interest of your Majesty's service demands that the army should be rallied at Smolensk, and should first of all be freed from ineffectives, such as dismounted cavalry, unnecessary baggage, and artillery material that is no longer in proportion to the present forces. The soldiers, who are worn out with hunger and fatigue, need supplies as well as a few days' rest. Many have died these last days on the road or at the bivouacs. This state of things is continually becoming worse, and makes one fear that unless a prompt remedy is applied the troops will no longer be under control in case of an engagement.

9th of November: thirty versts from Smolensk.

After staggering into Smolensk which seemed to them a promised land, the French, searching for food, killed one another, sacked their own stores, and when everything had been plundered, fled farther.

They all went without knowing whither, or why they were going. Still less did that genius, Napoleon, know it, for no one issued any orders to him. But still he and those about him retained their old habits: wrote commands, letters, reports, and orders of the day; called one another *sire, mon cousin, prince d'Eckmühl, roi de Naples*, and so on. But these orders and reports were only on paper, nothing in them was acted upon, for they could not be carried out, and though they entitled one another Majesties, High-nesses, or Cousins, they all felt that they were miserable wretches who had done much evil, for which they had now to pay. And though they pretended to be concerned about the army, each was thinking only of himself and of how to get away quickly and save himself.

17

THE movements of the Russian and French armies during the campaign from Moscow back to the Niemen were like those in a game of Russian blindman's buff, in which two players are blind-folded and one of them occasionally rings a little bell to inform the catcher of his whereabouts. First he rings his bell fearlessly, but when he gets into a tight place he runs away as quietly as he can, and often, thinking to escape, runs straight into his opponent's arms.

At first, while they were still moving along the Kaluga road, Napoleon's armies made their presence known, but later when they reached the Smolensk road they ran holding the clapper of their bell tight – and often, thinking that they were escaping, ran right into the Russians.

Owing to the rapidity of the French flight and the Russian pursuit, and the consequent exhaustion of the horses, the chief means of approximately ascertaining the enemy's position – by cavalry scouting – was not available. Besides, as a result of the frequent and rapid change of position by each army, even what information was obtained could not be delivered in time. If news was received one day that the enemy had been in a certain posi-tion the day before, by the third day, when something could have been done, that army was already two days' march further on and in quite another position.

One army fled and the other pursued. Beyond Smolensk there were several different roads available for the French, and one would have thought that during their stay of four days they might have learnt where the enemy was, might have arranged some more advantageous plan and undertaken something new. But after a four days' halt the mob, with no manœuvres or plans, again began running along the beaten track, neither to the right nor to the left but along the old – the worst – road, through Krasnoe and Orsha.

Expecting the enemy from behind and not in front, the French separated in their flight and spread out over a distance of twenty-four hours. In front of them all fled the Emperor, then the kings, then the dukes. The Russian army, expecting Napoleon to take the road to the right beyond the Dnieper – which was the only reasonable thing for him to do – themselves turned to the right and came out onto the high road at Krasnoe. And here, as in a game of blindman's buff, the French ran into our vanguard. Seeing their enemy unexpectedly, the French fell into confusion and stopped short from the sudden fright, but then they resumed their flight, abandoning their comrades who were further behind. Then for three days separate portions of the French army – first Murat's (the viceroy's), then Davout's, and then Ney's – ran, as it were, the gauntlet of the Russian army. They abandoned one another, abandoned all their heavy baggage, their artillery, and half their men, and fled, getting past the Russians by night by making semicircles to the right.

Ney, who came last, had been busying himself blowing up the walls of Smolensk which were in nobody's way, because despite the unfortunate plight of the French, or because of it, they wished to punish the floor against which they had hurt themselves. Ney, who had had a corps of ten thousand men, reached Napoleon at Orsha with only one thousand men left, having abandoned all the rest and all his cannon, and having crossed the Dnieper at night by stealth at a wooded spot.

From Orsha they fled farther along the road to Vilna, still playing at blindman's buff with the pursuing army. At the Berëzina they again became disorganized, many were drowned and many surrendered, but those who got across the river fled farther. Their supreme chief donned a fur coat and, having seated himself in a sledge, galloped on alone, abandoning his companions. Those others who could do so drove away too, leaving those who could not to surrender or die.

18

THIS campaign consisted in a flight of the French during which they did all they could to destroy themselves. From the time they turned onto the Kaluga road to the day their leader fled from the army, none of the movements of the crowd had any sense. So one might have thought that of this period of the campaign the historians, who attribute the actions of the mass to the will of one man, would have found it impossible to make the story of the retreat fit their theory. But no! Mountains of books have been written by the historians about this campaign, and everywhere Napoleon's arrangements are described, the manœuvres, and his profound plans which guided the army, as well as the military genius shown by his marshals.

The retreat from Malo-Yaroslavets when he had a free road into a well-supplied district and the parallel road was open to him along which Kutuzov afterwards pursued him – this unnecessary retreat along a devastated road – is explained to us as being due to profound considerations. Similarly profound considerations are given for his retreat from Smolensk to Orsha. Then his heroism at Krasnoe is described, where he is reported to have been prepared to accept battle and take personal command and to have walked about with a birch stick and said:

'*J'ai assez fait l'empereur; il est temps de faire le général,*' but nevertheless immediately ran away again, abandoning to its fate the scattered fragments of the army he left behind.

Then we are told of the greatness of soul of the marshals, especially of Ney – a greatness of soul consisting in this: that he made his way by night round through the forest and across the Dnieper, and escaped to Orsha abandoning standards, artillery, and nine-tenths of his men.

And lastly, the final departure of the great Emperor from his heroic army is presented to us by the historians as something great and characteristic of genius. Even that final running away, described in ordinary language as the lowest depth of baseness which every child is taught to be ashamed of – even that act finds justification in the historians' language.

When it is impossible to stretch the very elastic threads of historical ratiocination any farther, when actions are clearly contrary to all that humanity calls right or even just, the historians produce a saving conception of 'greatness'. 'Greatness,' it seems, excludes the standards of right and wrong. For the 'great' man nothing is wrong; there is no atrocity for which a 'great' man can be blamed.

'*C'est grand!*' say the historians, and there no longer exists either good or evil, but only '*grand*' and '*not grand*'. *Grand* is good, not *grand* is bad. *Grand* is the characteristic, in their conception, of some special animals called 'heroes'. And Napoleon escaping home in a warm fur coat and leaving to perish those who were not merely his comrades but were (in his opinion) men he had brought there, feels *que c'est grand*, and his soul is tranquil.

'*Du sublime*' (he saw something sublime in himself) '*au ridicule il n'y a qu'un pas,*'* said he. And the whole world for fifty years has been repeating: '*Sublime! Grand! Napoléon le Grand!*' *Du sublime au ridicule il n'y a qu'un pas.*

And it occurs to no one that to admit a greatness not

commensurable with the standard of right and wrong is merely to admit one's own nothingness and immeasurable meanness.

For us, with the standard of good and evil given us by Christ, no human actions are incommensurable. And there is no greatness there where simplicity, goodness, and truth are absent.

·19·

WHAT Russian, reading the account of the last part of the campaign of 1812, has not experienced an uncomfortable feeling of regret, dissatisfaction, and perplexity? Who has not asked himself how it is that the French were not all captured or destroyed when our three armies surrounded them in superior numbers, when the disordered French, hungry and freezing, surrendered in crowds, and when (as the historians relate) the aim of the Russians was to stop the French, to cut them off, and to capture them all?

How was it that the Russian army, which when numerically weaker than the French had given battle at Borodino, did not achieve its purpose when it had surrounded the French on three sides and when its aim was to capture them? Can the French be so enormously superior to us that when we had surrounded them with superior forces we could not beat them? How could that happen?

History (or what is called by that name), replying to these questions, says that this occurred because Kutuzov and Tormasov and Chichagov, and this man and that man, did not execute such and such manœuvres...

But why did they not execute those manœuvres? And why, if they were guilty of not carrying out a prearranged aim, were they not tried and punished? But even if we admitted that Kutuzov, Chichagov, and others were the cause of the Russian failures, it is still incomprehensible why, the position of the Russian army being what it was at Krasnoe and at the Berëzina (in both cases we had superior forces), the French army with its marshals, kings, and Emperor was not captured if that was what the Russians aimed at.

The explanation of this strange fact given by Russian military historians (to the effect that Kutuzov hindered an attack) is unfounded, for we know that he could not restrain the troops from attacking at Vyazma and Tarutino.

Why was the Russian army – which with inferior forces had withstood the enemy in full strength at Borodino – defeated at Krasnoe and the Berëzina* by the disorganized crowds of the French when it was numerically superior?

If the aim of the Russians consisted in cutting off and capturing Napoleon and his marshals – and that aim was not merely frustrated but all attempts to attain it were most shamefully baffled – then this last period of the campaign is quite rightly considered by the French to be a series of victories, and quite wrongly considered victorious by Russian historians.

The Russian military historians in so far as they submit to claims of logic must admit that conclusion, and in spite of their lyrical rhapsodies about valour, devotion, and so forth, must reluctantly admit that the French retreat from Moscow was a series of victories for Napoleon and defeats for Kutuzov.

But putting national vanity entirely aside, one feels that such a conclusion involves a contradiction, since the series of French victories brought them to complete destruction, while the series of Russian defeats led to the total destruction of their enemy and the liberation of their country.

The source of this contradiction lies in the fact that the historians, studying the events from the letters of the sovereigns and the generals, from memoirs, reports, projects, and so forth, have attributed to this last period of the war of 1812 an aim that never existed, namely, that of cutting off and capturing Napoleon with his marshals and his army.

There never was or could have been such an aim, for it would have been senseless and its attainment quite impossible.

It would have been senseless, first because Napoleon's disorganized army was flying from Russia with all possible speed, that is to say was doing just what every Russian desired. So what was the use of performing various operations on the French who were running away as fast as they possibly could?

Secondly, it would have been senseless to block the passage of men whose whole energy was directed to flight.

Thirdly, it would have been senseless to sacrifice one's own troops in order to destroy the French army which, without external interference, was destroying itself at such a rate that though its path was not blocked it could not carry across the frontier more than it actually took in December, namely, a one-hundredth part of the original army.

Fourthly, it would have been senseless to wish to take captive the Emperor, kings, and dukes – whose capture would have been in the highest degree embarrassing for the Russians, as the most adroit diplomatists of the time (Joseph de Maistre and others) recognized. Still more senseless would have been the wish to capture army-corps of the French, when our own army had melted away to half before reaching Krasnoe, and a whole division would have been needed to convoy a corps of prisoners, and when our men were not always getting full rations and the prisoners already taken were perishing of hunger.

All the profound plans about cutting off and capturing Napoleon and his army were like the plan of a market-gardener who, when driving out of his garden a cow that had trampled down the beds he had planted, should run to the gate and hit the cow on the head. The only thing to be said in excuse of that gardener would be that he was very angry. But not even that could be said for those who drew up this project, for it was not they who had suffered from the trampled beds.

But besides the fact that cutting off Napoleon with his army would have been senseless, it was impossible.

It was impossible, first because, as experience shows that a three-mile movement of columns on a battlefield never coincides with the plans, the probability of Chichagov, Kutuzov, and Wittgenstein effecting a junction on time at an appointed place was so remote as to be tantamount to impossibility, as in fact Kutuzov thought, who when he received the plan remarked that diversions planned over great distances do not yield the desired results.

Secondly, it was impossible because to paralyse the momentum with which Napoleon's army was retiring, incomparably greater forces than the Russians possessed would have been required.

Thirdly, it was impossible because the military term 'to cut off' has no meaning. One can cut off a slice of bread, but not an army. To cut off an army – to bar its road – is quite impossible, for there is always plenty of room to avoid capture, and there is the night when nothing can be seen, as the military scientists might convince themselves by the example of Krasnoe and of the Berëzina. It is only possible to capture prisoners if they agree to be captured, just as it is only possible to catch a swallow if it settles on one's hand. Men can be taken prisoner only if they surrender according to the rules of strategy and tactics as the Germans did. But the French troops quite rightly did not consider that this suited them, since death by hunger and cold awaited them in flight or captivity alike.

Fourthly and chiefly, it was impossible because never since the world began has a war been fought under such terrible conditions as those that obtained in 1812, and the Russian army in its pursuit of the French strained its strength to the utmost, and could not have done more without destroying itself.

During the movement of the Russian army from Tarutino to Krasnoe it lost fifty thousand sick or stragglers, that is, a number equal to the population of a large provincial town. Half the men fell out of the army without a battle.

And it is of this period of the campaign – when the army lacked boots and sheepskin coats, was short of provisions and without vodka, and was camping out at night for months in the snow with fifteen degrees of frost,* when there were only seven or eight hours of daylight and the rest was night in which the influence of discipline cannot be maintained, when men were taken into that region of death where discipline fails, not for a few hours only as in a battle, but for months, when they were every moment fighting death from hunger and cold, when half the army perished in a single month – it is of this period of the campaign that the historians tell us how Miloradovich should have made a flank march to such and such a place, Tormasov to another place, and Chichagov should have crossed (more than knee-deep in snow) to somewhere else, and how so and so 'routed' and 'cut off' the French, and so on and so on.

The Russians, half of whom died, did all that could and should have been done to attain an end worthy of the nation, and they are not to blame because other Russians, sitting in warm rooms, proposed that they should do what was impossible.

All that strange contradiction, now difficult to understand, between the facts and the historical accounts, only arises because the historians dealing with the matter have written the history of the beautiful words and sentiments of various generals, and not the history of the events.

To them the words of Miloradovich seem very interesting, and so do their surmises, and the rewards this or that general received; but the question of those fifty thousand men who were left in hospitals and in graves does not even interest them, for it does not come within the range of their investigation.

Yet one need only discard the study of the reports and general plans and consider the movement of those hundreds of thousands of men who took a direct part in the events, and all the questions that seemed insoluble easily and simply receive an immediate and certain solution.

The aim of cutting off Napoleon and his army never existed except in the imaginations of a dozen people. It could not exist, because it was senseless and unattainable.

The people had a single aim: to free their land from invasion. That aim was attained in the first place of itself as the French ran away, and so it was only necessary not to stop their flight. Secondly, it was attained by the guerrilla warfare which was destroying the French, and thirdly by the fact that a large Russian army was

1147

following the French, ready to use its strength in case their movement stopped.

The Russian army had to act like a whip to a running animal. And the experienced driver knew it was better to hold the whip raised as a menace than to strike the running animal on the head.

END OF PART THREE

PART FOUR

1

WHEN seeing a dying animal a man feels a sense of horror: substance similar to his own is perishing before his eyes. But when it is a beloved and intimate human being that is dying, besides this horror at the extinction of life there is a severance, a spiritual wound, which like a physical wound is sometimes fatal and sometimes heals, but always aches and shrinks at any external irritating touch.

After Prince Andrew's death Natasha and Princess Mary alike felt this. Drooping in spirit and closing their eyes before the menacing cloud of death that overhung them, they dared not look life in the face. They carefully guarded their open wounds from any rough and painful contact. Everything: a carriage passing rapidly in the street, a summons to dinner, the maid's inquiry what dress to get out, or worse still, any word of insincere or feeble sympathy, seemed an insult, painfully irritated the wound, infringed that necessary quiet in which they both tried to listen to the stern and dreadful choir that still resounded in their imagination, and hindered their gazing into those mysterious limitless vistas that for an instant had opened out before them.

Only when alone together were they free from such outrage and pain. They spoke little even to one another and when they did it was of very unimportant matters.

Both avoided any allusion to the future. To admit the possibility of a future seemed to them to insult his memory. Still more carefully did they avoid anything relating to him who was dead. It seemed to them that what they had lived through and experienced could not be expressed in words, and that any reference to the details of his life infringed the majesty and sacredness of the mystery that had been accomplished before their eyes.

Continued abstention from speech, and constant avoidance of everything that might lead up to the subject – this halting on all sides at the boundary of what they might not mention – brought before their minds with still greater purity and clearness what they were both feeling.

But pure and complete sorrow is as impossible as pure and complete joy. Princess Mary in her position as absolute and independent arbiter of her own fate and guardian and instructor of her nephew was the first to be called back to life from that realm of sorrow in which she had dwelt for the first fortnight. She received letters from her relations to which she had to reply; the room in which little Nicholas had been put was damp, and he began to cough; Alpatych came to Yaroslavl with reports on the state of their affairs and with advice and suggestions that they should return to Moscow to the house on Vozdvizhenka street, which had remained uninjured and needed only slight repairs. Life did not stand still and it was necessary to live. Hard as it was for Princess Mary to emerge from the realm of secluded contemplation in which she had lived till then, and sorry and almost ashamed as she felt to leave Natasha alone, yet the cares of life demanded her attention and she involuntarily yielded to them. She went through the accounts with Alpatych, conferred with Dessalles about her nephew, and gave orders and made preparations for the journey to Moscow.

Natasha remained alone, and from the time Princess Mary began making preparations for departure held aloof from her too.

Princess Mary asked the countess to let Natasha go with her to Moscow, and both parents gladly accepted this offer, for they saw their daughter losing strength every day and thought that a change of scene and the advice of Moscow doctors would be good for her.

'I am not going anywhere,' Natasha replied when this was proposed to her. 'Do, please, just leave me alone!' And she ran out of the room, with difficulty refraining from tears of vexation and irritation rather than of sorrow.

After she felt herself deserted by Princess Mary and alone in her grief, Natasha spent most of the time in her room by herself, sitting huddled up feet and all in the corner of the sofa, tearing and twisting something with her slender nervous fingers and gazing intently and fixedly at whatever her eyes chanced to fall on. This solitude exhausted and tormented her, but she was in absolute need of it. As soon as anyone entered she got up quickly, changed her position and expression, and picked up a book or some sewing, evidently waiting impatiently for the intruder to go.

She felt all the time as if she might at any moment penetrate that on which – with a terrible questioning too great for her strength – her spiritual gaze was fixed.

One day towards the end of December Natasha, pale and thin, dressed in a black woollen gown, her plaited hair negligently twisted into a knot, was crouched feet and all in the corner of her sofa, crumpling and smoothing out the end of her sash while she looked at a corner of the door.

She was gazing in the direction in which he had gone – to the other side of life. And that other side of life, of which she had never before thought and which had formerly seemed to her so far away and improbable, was now nearer and more akin and more comprehensible than this side of life where everything was either emptiness and desolation, or suffering and indignity.

She was gazing where she knew him to be; but she could not imagine him otherwise than as he had been here. She now saw him again as he had been at Mytishchi, at Troitsa, and Yaroslavl.

She saw his face, heard his voice, repeated his words and her own, and sometimes devised other words they might have spoken.

There he is lying back in an armchair in his velvet cloak, leaning his head on his thin pale hand. His chest is dreadfully hollow and his shoulders raised. His lips are firmly closed, his eyes glitter, and a wrinkle comes and goes on his pale forehead. One of his legs twitches just perceptibly, but rapidly. Natasha knows that he is struggling with terrible pain. 'What is that pain like? Why does he have that pain? What does he feel? How does it hurt him?' thought Natasha. He noticed her watching him, raised his eyes, and began to speak seriously:

'One thing would be terrible,' said he, 'to bind oneself for ever to a suffering man. It would be continual torture.' And he looked searchingly at her. Natasha, as usual, answered before she had time to think what she would say. She said: 'This can't go on – it won't. You will get well – quite well.'

She now saw him from the commencement of that scene and re-lived what she had then felt. She recalled his long sad and severe look at those words, and understood the meaning of the rebuke and despair in that protracted gaze.

'I agreed,' Natasha now said to herself, 'that it would be dreadful if he always continued to suffer. I said it then only because it would have been dreadful for him, but he understood it differently. He thought it would be dreadful for me. He then still wished to live and feared death. And I said it so awkwardly and stupidly! I did not say what I meant. I thought quite differently. Had I said what I thought, I should have said: even if he had to go on dying, to die continually before my eyes, I should have been happy compared with what I am now. Now there is nothing ... nobody. Did he know that? No, he did not and never will know it. And now it will never, never, be possible to put it right.' And now he again seemed to be saying the same words to her, only in her imagination Natasha now gave him a different answer. She stopped him, and said: 'Terrible for you, but not for me. You know that for me there is nothing in life but you, and to suffer with you is the greatest happiness for me,' and he took her hand and pressed it as he had pressed it that terrible evening four days before his death. And in her imagination she said other tender and loving words which she might have said then, but only spoke now: 'I love thee!... thee! I love, love...' she said, convulsively pressing her hands and setting her teeth with a desperate effort...

She was overcome by sweet sorrow, and tears were already rising to her eyes: then she suddenly asked herself to whom she was saying this? Again everything was shrouded in hard, dry perplexity, and again with a strained frown she peered towards the world where he was. And now, now, it seemed to her she was penetrating the mystery... But at the instant when it seemed that the incomprehensible was revealing itself to her a loud rattle of the door-handle struck painfully on her ears. Dunyasha, her maid, entered the room quickly and abruptly, with a frightened look on her face and showing no concern for her mistress.

'Come to your papa at once, please!' said she with a strange, excited look. 'A misfortune... about Peter Ilyich... a letter,' she finished with a sob.

2

BESIDES a feeling of aloofness from everybody Natasha was feeling a special estrangement from the members of her own family. All of them – her father, mother, and Sonya – were so near to her, so familiar, so commonplace, that all their words and feelings seemed an insult to the world in which she had been living of late, and she felt not merely indifferent to them but regarded them with hostility. She heard Dunyasha's words about Peter Ilyich and a misfortune, but did not grasp them.

'What misfortune? What misfortune can happen to them? They just live their own old quiet and commonplace life,' thought Natasha.

As she entered the ball-room her father was hurriedly coming out of her mother's room. His face was puckered up and wet with tears. He had evidently run out of that room to give vent to the sobs that were choking him. When he saw Natasha he waved his arms despairingly and burst into convulsively painful sobs that distorted his soft round face.

'Pe ... Petya ... Go, go, she ... is calling ...' and weeping like a child and quickly shuffling on his feeble legs to a chair, he almost fell into it, covering his face with his hands.

Suddenly an electric shock seemed to run through Natasha's whole being. Terrible anguish struck her heart, she felt a dreadful ache as if something were being torn inside her and she were dying. But the pain was immediately followed by a feeling of release from the oppressive restraint that had prevented her taking part in life. The sight of her father, the terrible wild cries of her mother that she heard through the door, made her immediately forget herself and her own grief.

She ran to her father, but he feebly waved his arm pointing to her mother's door. Princess Mary, pale and with quivering chin, came out from that room and taking Natasha by the arm said something to her. Natasha neither saw nor heard her. She went in with rapid steps, pausing at the door for an instant as if struggling with herself, and then ran to her mother.

The countess was lying in an arm-chair in a strange and awkward position, stretching out and beating her head against the wall. Sonya and the maids were holding her arms.

'Natasha! Natasha! ...' cried the countess. 'It's not true ... it's not true ... He's lying ... Natasha!' she shrieked, pushing those around her away. 'Go away all of you; it's not true! Killed! ... ha, ha, ha! ... It's not true!'

Natasha put one knee on the arm-chair, stooped over her mother, embraced her, and with unexpected strength raised her, turned her face towards herself, and clung to her.

'Mummy! ... darling ...! I am here, my dearest mummy,' she kept on whispering, not pausing an instant.

She did not let go of her mother but struggled tenderly with her, demanded a pillow and hot water, and unfastened and tore open her mother's dress.

'My dearest darling.... Mummy, my precious! ...' she whispered incessantly, kissing her head, her hands, her face, and feeling her own irrepressible and streaming tears tickling her nose and cheeks.

The countess pressed her daughter's hand, closed her eyes, and became quiet for a moment. Suddenly she sat up with unaccustomed swiftness, glanced vacantly around her, and seeing Natasha, began to press her head with all her strength. Then she turned towards her daughter's face which was wincing with pain, and gazed long at it.

'Natasha, you love me?' she said in a soft trustful whisper. 'Natasha, you would not deceive me? You'll tell me the whole truth?'

Natasha looked at her with eyes full of tears, and in her look there was nothing but love and an entreaty for forgiveness.

'My darling mummy!' she repeated, straining all the power of her love to find some way of taking on herself the excess of grief that crushed her mother.

And again, in a futile struggle with reality, her mother, refusing to believe that she could live when her beloved boy was killed in the bloom of life, escaped from reality into a world of delirium.

Natasha did not remember how that day passed nor that night, nor the next day and night. She did not sleep and did not leave her mother. Her persevering and patient love seemed completely to surround the countess every moment, not explaining or consoling but recalling her to life.

During the third night the countess kept very quiet for a few minutes, and Natasha rested her head on the arm of her chair and closed her eyes, but opened them again on hearing the bedstead creak. The countess was sitting up in bed speaking softly.

'How glad I am you have come. You are tired. Won't you have some tea?' Natasha went up to her. 'You have improved in looks and grown more manly,' continued the countess, taking her daughter's hand.

'Mamma! What are you saying? ...'

'Natasha, he is no more, no more!'

And embracing her daughter, the countess began to weep for the first time.

3

PRINCESS MARY postponed her departure. Sonya and the count tried to replace Natasha but could not. They saw that she alone was able to restrain her mother from unreasoning despair. For three weeks Natasha remained constantly at her mother's side, sleeping on a lounge chair in her room, making her eat and drink, and talking to her incessantly because the mere sound of her tender caressing tones soothed her mother.

The mother's wounded spirit could not heal. Petya's death had torn from her half her life. She had been a fresh and vigorous woman of fifty when the news of Petya's death had come, but a month later she left her room a listless old woman taking no interest in life. But the same blow that almost killed the countess, this second blow, restored Natasha to life.

A spiritual wound produced by a rending of the spiritual body is like a physical wound and, strange as it may seem, just as a deep wound may heal and its edges join, yet physical and spiritual wounds alike can heal completely only as the result of a vital force from within.

Natasha's wound healed in that way. She thought her life was ended, but her love for her mother unexpectedly showed her that the essence of life – love – was still active within her. Love awoke, and so did life.

Prince Andrew's last days had bound Princess Mary and Natasha together; this new sorrow brought them still closer to one another. Princess Mary put off her departure and for three weeks looked after Natasha as if she had been a sick child. The last weeks, passed in her mother's bedroom, had strained Natasha's physical strength.

One afternoon, noticing Natasha shivering with fever, Princess Mary took her to her own room and made her lie down on the bed. Natasha lay down, but when Princess Mary had drawn the blinds and was going away she called her back.

'I don't want to sleep, Mary, sit by me a little.'

'You are tired – try to sleep.'

'No, no. Why did you bring me away? She will be asking for me.'

'She is much better. She spoke so well to-day,' said Princess Mary.

Natasha lay on the bed and in the semi-darkness of the room scanned Princess Mary's face.

'Is she like him?' thought Natasha. 'Yes, like and yet not like. But she is quite original, strange, new, and unknown. And she loves me. What is in her heart? All this is good. But how? What is her mind like? What does she think about me? Yes, she is splendid!'

'Mary,' she said timidly, drawing Princess Mary's hand to herself. 'Mary, you mustn't think me wicked. No? Mary darling, how I love you! Let us be quite, quite friends.'

And Natasha, embracing her, began kissing her face and hands, making Princess Mary feel shy but happy by this demonstration of her feelings.

From that day a tender and passionate friendship, such as exists only between women, was established between Princess Mary and Natasha. They were continually kissing and saying tender things to one another and spent most of their time together. When one went out the other became restless and hastened to rejoin her. Together they felt more in harmony with one another than either of them felt with herself when alone. A feeling stronger than friendship sprang up between them; an exclusive feeling of life being possible only in each other's presence.

Sometimes they were silent for hours; sometimes after they were already in bed they would begin talking and go on till morning. They spoke most of what was long past. Princess Mary spoke of her childhood, of her mother, her father, and her day-dreams; and Natasha, who with a passive lack of understanding had formerly turned away from that life of devotion, submission, and the poetry of Christian self-sacrifice, now, feeling herself bound to Princess Mary by affection, learnt to love her past too and to understand a side of life previously incomprehensible to her. She did not think of applying submission and self-abnegation to her own life, for she was accustomed to seek other joys, but she understood and loved in another those previously incomprehensible virtues. For Princess Mary, listening to Natasha's tales of childhood and early youth, there also opened out a new and hitherto uncomprehended side of life: belief in life and its enjoyment.

Just as before, they never mentioned *him* so as not to lower (as they thought) their exalted feelings by words: but this silence about him had the effect of their gradually beginning to forget him, without being conscious of it.

Natasha had grown thin and pale, and physically so weak that they all talked about her health, and this pleased her. But sometimes she was suddenly overcome by fear not only of death but of sickness, weakness, and loss of good looks, and involuntarily she examined her bare arm carefully, surprised at its thinness, and in the morning noticed her drawn and, as it seemed to her, piteous face in her glass. It seemed to her that things must be so, and yet it was dreadfully sad.

One day she went quickly upstairs and found herself out of breath. Unconsciously she immediately invented a reason for going down, and then, testing her strength, ran upstairs again, observing the result.

Another time when she called Dunyasha her voice trembled, so she called again – though she could hear Dunyasha coming – called her in the deep chest tones in which she had been wont to sing, and listened attentively to herself.

She did not know and would not have believed it, but beneath the layer of slime that covered her soul and seemed to her impenetrable, delicate young shoots of grass were already sprouting, which, taking root, would so cover with their living verdure the grief that weighed her down that it would soon no longer be seen or noticed. The wound had begun to heal from within.

At the end of January Princess Mary left for Moscow, and the count insisted on Natasha's going with her to consult the doctors.

AFTER the encounter at Vyazma, where Kutuzov had been unable to hold back his troops from their anxiety to overwhelm and cut off the enemy and so on, the farther movement of the fleeing French, and of the Russians who pursued them, continued as far as Krasnoe without a battle. The flight was so rapid that the Russian army pursuing the French could not keep up with them; cavalry and artillery horses broke down, and the information received of the movements of the French was never reliable.

The men in the Russian army were so worn out by this continuous marching at the rate of twenty-seven miles a day, that they could not go any faster.

To realize the degree of exhaustion of the Russian army it is only necessary to grasp clearly the meaning of the fact that, while not losing more than five thousand killed and wounded after Tarutino and less than a hundred prisoners, the Russian army, which left that place a hundred thousand strong, reached Krasnoe with only fifty thousand.

The rapidity of the Russian pursuit was just as destructive to our army as the flight of the French was to theirs. The only difference was that the Russian army moved voluntarily, with no such threat of destruction as hung over the French, and that the sick Frenchmen were left behind in enemy hands while the sick Russians left behind were among their own people. The chief cause of the wastage of Napoleon's army was the rapidity of its movement, and a convincing proof of this is the corresponding decrease of the Russian army.

Kutuzov, as far as was in his power, instead of trying to check the movement of the French as was desired in Petersburg and by the Russian army generals, directed his whole activity here, as he had done at Tarutino and Vyazma, to hastening it on, while easing the movement of our army.

But besides this, since the exhaustion and enormous diminution of the army caused by the rapidity of the advance had become evident, another reason for slackening the pace and delaying presented itself to Kutuzov. The aim of the Russian army was to pursue the French. The road the French would take was unknown, and so the closer our troops trod on their heels the greater distance they had to cover. Only by following at some distance could one cut across the zigzag path of the French. All the artful manœuvres suggested by our generals meant fresh movements of the army and a lengthening of its marches, whereas the only reasonable aim was to shorten those marches. To that end Kutuzov's activity was directed during the whole campaign from Moscow to Vilna – not casually or intermittently, but so consistently that he never once deviated from it.

Kutuzov felt and knew – not by reasoning or science but with the whole of his Russian being – what every Russian soldier felt, that the French were beaten, that the enemy was flying and must be driven out; but at the same time he, like the soldiers, realized all the hardship of this march, the rapidity of which was unparalleled for such a time of the year.

But to the generals, especially the foreign ones in the Russian army, who wished to distinguish themselves, to astonish somebody, and for some reason to capture a king or a duke, it seemed that now – when any battle must be horrible and senseless – was the very time to fight and conquer somebody. Kutuzov merely shrugged his shoulders when one after another they presented projects of manœuvres to be made with those soldiers – ill-shod, insufficiently clad, and half starved – who within a month, and without fighting a battle, had dwindled to half their number, and who at best if the flight continued would have to go a greater distance than that they had already traversed before they reached the frontier.

This longing to distinguish themselves, to manœuvre, to overthrow, and to cut off, showed itself particularly whenever the Russians stumbled on the French army.

So it was at Krasnoe, where they expected to find one of the three French columns and stumbled instead on Napoleon himself with sixteen thousand men. Despite all Kutuzov's efforts to avoid that ruinous encounter and to preserve his troops, the massacre of the broken mob of French soldiers by worn-out Russians continued at Krasnoe for three days.

Toll wrote a disposition: 'The first column will march to so and so,' &c. And as usual, nothing happened in accord with the disposition. Prince Eugène of Würtemberg fired from a hill over the French crowds that were running past, and demanded reinforcements which did not arrive. The French, avoiding the Russians, dispersed and hid themselves in the forest by night making their way round as best they could, and continued their flight.

Miloradovich, who said he did not want to know anything about the commissariat affairs of his detachment and could never be found when he was wanted – that *chevalier sans peur et sans reproche* as he styled himself, who was fond of parleys with the French – sent envoys demanding their surrender, wasted time, and did not do what he was ordered to do.

'I give you that column, lads,' he said, riding up to the troops and pointing out the French to the cavalry.

And the cavalry, with spurs and sabres urging on horses that could scarcely move, trotted with much effort to the column presented to them – that is to say, to a crowd of Frenchmen stark with cold, frost-bitten and starving – and the column that had been presented to them threw down its arms and surrendered, as it had long been anxious to do.

At Krasnoe they took twenty-six thousand prisoners, several hundred cannon, and a stick called a 'marshal's staff', and disputed as to who had distinguished himself, and were pleased with their achievement, though they much regretted not having taken Napoleon, or at least a marshal or a hero of some sort, and reproached one another and especially Kutuzov for having failed to do so.

These men, carried away by their passions, were but blind tools of the most melancholy law of necessity, but considered themselves heroes and imagined that they were accomplishing a most noble and honourable achievement. They blamed Kutuzov and said that from the very beginning of the campaign he had prevented their vanquishing Napoleon, that he thought of nothing but satisfying his passions, and would not advance from the Linen Factories because he was comfortable there, that at Krasnoe he checked the advance because on learning that Napoleon was there he had quite lost his head, and that it was probable that he had an understanding with Napoleon and had been bribed by him,* and so on, and so on.

Not only did his contemporaries, carried away by their passions, talk in this way, but posterity and history have acclaimed Napoleon as *grand*, while Kutuzov is described by foreigners as a crafty, dissolute, weak old courtier, and by Russians as something indefinite – a sort of puppet, useful only because he had a Russian name.

5

In 1812 and 1813 Kutuzov was openly accused of blundering. The Emperor was dissatisfied with him. And in a history recently written by order of the Highest Authorities it is said that Kutuzov was a cunning court liar, frightened of the name of Napoleon, and that by his blunders at Krasnoe and the Berëzina he deprived the Russian army of the glory of complete victory over the French.*

Such is the fate, not of great men (*grands hommes*) whom the Russian mind does not acknowledge, but of those rare and always solitary individuals who discerning the will of Providence submit their personal will to it. The hatred and contempt of the crowd punishes such men for discerning the higher laws.

For Russian historians, strange and terrible to say, Napoleon – that most insignificant tool of history who never anywhere, even in exile, showed human dignity – Napoleon is the object of adulation and enthusiasm; he is *grand*. But Kutuzov – the man who, from the beginning to the end of his activity in 1812, never once swerving by word or deed from Borodino to Vilna, presented an example, exceptional in history, of self-sacrifice and a present consciousness of the future importance of what was happening – Kutuzov seems to them something indefinite and pitiful, and when speaking of him and of the year 1812 they always seem a little ashamed.

And yet it is difficult to imagine an historical character whose activity was so unswervingly directed to a single aim; and it would be difficult to imagine any aim more worthy or more consonant with the will of the whole people. Still more difficult would it be to find an instance in history of the aim of an historical personage being so completely accomplished as that to which all Kutuzov's efforts were directed in 1812.

Kutuzov never talked of 'forty centuries looking down from the Pyramids', of the sacrifices he offered for the fatherland, or of what he intended to accomplish or had accomplished: in general he said nothing about himself, adopted no pose, always appeared to be the simplest and most ordinary of men, and said the simplest and most ordinary things. He wrote letters to his daughters and to Madame de Staël, read novels, liked the society of pretty women, jested with generals, officers, and soldiers, and never contradicted those who tried to prove anything to him. When Count Rostopchin at the Yauza bridge galloped up to Kutuzov with personal reproaches for having caused the destruction of Moscow, and said: 'How was it you promised not to abandon Moscow without a battle?' Kutuzov replied: 'And I shall not abandon Moscow without a battle', though Moscow was then already abandoned. When Arakcheev, coming to him from the Emperor, said that Ermolov ought to be appointed chief of the artillery, Kutuzov replied: 'Yes, I was just saying so myself', though a moment before he had said quite the contrary. What did it matter to him – who then alone amid a senseless crowd understood the whole tremendous significance of what was happening – what did it matter to him whether Rostopchin attributed the calamities of Moscow to him or to himself? Still less could it matter to him who was appointed chief of the artillery.

Not merely in these cases, but continually, did that old man –

who by experience of life had reached the conviction that thoughts, and the words serving as their expression, are not what move people – use quite meaningless words that happened to enter his head.

But that man, so heedless of his words, did not once during the whole time of his activity utter one word inconsistent with the single aim towards which he moved throughout the whole war. Obviously in spite of himself, in very diverse circumstances, he repeatedly expressed his real thoughts with the bitter conviction that he would not be understood. Beginning with the battle of Borodino, from which time his disagreement with those about him began, he alone said that *the battle of Borodino was a victory* and repeated this both verbally and in his dispatches and reports up to the time of his death. He alone said that *the loss of Moscow is not the loss of Russia.* In reply to Lauriston's proposal of peace, he said: *There can be no peace, for such is the people's will.* He alone during the retreat of the French said that *all our manœuvres are useless, everything is being accomplished of itself better than we could desire,* that *the enemy must be offered 'a golden bridge',* that *neither the Tarutino, the Vyazma, nor the Krasnoe battles were necessary,* that *we must keep some force to reach the frontier with,* and that *he would not sacrifice a single Russian for ten Frenchmen.*

And this courtier, as he is described to us, who lies to Arakcheev to please the Emperor, he alone – incurring thereby the Emperor's displeasure – said in Vilna that *to carry the war beyond the frontier is useless and harmful.*

Nor do words alone prove that only he understood the meaning of the events. His actions – without the smallest deviation – were all directed to one and the same threefold aim: (1) to brace all his strength for conflict with the French, (2) to defeat them, and (3) to drive them out of Russia, minimizing as far as possible the sufferings of our people and of our army.

This procrastinator Kutuzov, whose motto was 'Patience and Time', this enemy of decisive action, gave battle at Borodino, investing the preparations for it with unparalleled solemnity. This Kutuzov who before the battle of Austerlitz began said that it would be lost, he alone, in contradiction to everyone else, declared till his death that Borodino was a victory, despite the assurance of generals that the battle was lost and despite the fact that for an army to have to retire after winning a battle was unprecedented. He alone during the whole retreat insisted that battles, which were useless then, should not be fought, and that a new war should not be begun nor the frontiers of Russia crossed.

It is easy now to understand the significance of those events –

if only we abstain from attributing to the activity of the mass aims that existed only in the heads of a dozen individuals – for the events and their results now lie before us.

But how did that old man, alone, in opposition to the general opinion, so truly discern the importance of the people's view of the events that in all his activity he was never once untrue to it?

The source of that extraordinary power of penetrating the meaning of the events then occurring, lay in the national feeling he possessed in full purity and strength.

Only the recognition of the fact that he possessed this feeling caused the people in so strange a manner, contrary to the Tsar's wish, to select him – an old man in disfavour – to be their representative in the national war. And only that feeling placed him on that highest human pedestal from which he, the commander-in-chief, devoted all his powers not to slaying and destroying men but to saving and showing pity on them.

That simple, modest, and therefore truly great, figure could not be cast in the false mould of a European hero – the supposed ruler of men – that history has invented.

To a lackey no man can be great, for a lackey has his own conception of greatness.

6

THE 5th of November was the first day of what is called the battle of Krasnoe. Towards evening – after much disputing and many mistakes made by generals who did not go to their proper places, and after adjutants had been sent about with counter orders – when it had become plain that the enemy was everywhere in flight and that there could and would be no battle, Kutuzov left Krasnoe and went to Dobroe, to which place his head-quarters had that day been transferred.

The day was clear and frosty. Kutuzov rode to Dobroe on his plump little white horse, followed by an enormous suite of discontented generals who whispered among themselves behind his back. All along the road groups of French prisoners captured that day (there were seven thousand of them) were crowding to warm themselves at camp-fires. Near Dobroe an immense crowd of tattered prisoners buzzing with talk, and wrapped and bandaged in anything they had been able to get hold of, were standing in the road beside a long row of unharnessed French guns. At the approach of the commander-in-chief the buzz of talk ceased and all eyes were fixed on Kutuzov who, wearing a white cap with a red band

and a padded overcoat that bulged on his round shoulders, moved slowly along the road on his white horse. One of the generals was reporting to him where the guns and prisoners had been captured.

Kutuzov seemed preoccupied and did not listen to what the general was saying. He screwed up his eyes with a dissatisfied look as he gazed attentively and fixedly at these prisoners who presented a specially wretched appearance. Most of them were disfigured by frost-bitten noses and cheeks, and nearly all had red, swollen, and festering eyes.

One group of the French stood close to the road, and two of them, one of whom had his face covered with sores, were tearing a piece of raw flesh with their hands. There was something horrible and bestial in the fleeting glance they threw at the riders, and in the malevolent expression with which after a glance at Kutuzov the soldier with the sores immediately turned away and went on with what he was doing.

Kutuzov looked long and intently at these two soldiers. He puckered his face, screwed up his eyes, and pensively swayed his head. At another spot he noticed a Russian soldier laughingly patting a Frenchman on the shoulder saying something to him in a friendly manner, and Kutuzov with the same expression on his face again swayed his head.

'What were you saying?' he asked the general, who continuing his report directed the commander-in-chief's attention to some standards captured from the French and standing in front of the Preobrazhensk regiment.

'Ah, the standards!' said Kutuzov, evidently detaching himself with difficulty from the thoughts that preoccupied him.

He looked about him absently. Thousands of eyes were looking at him from all sides, awaiting a word from him.

He stopped in front of the Preobrazhensk regiment, sighed deeply and closed his eyes. One of his suite beckoned to the soldiers carrying the standards to advance and surround the commander-in-chief with them. Kutuzov was silent for a few seconds and then, submitting with evident reluctance to the duty imposed by his position, raised his head and began to speak. A throng of officers surrounded him. He looked around attentively at the circle of officers, recognizing several of them.

'I thank you all!' he said, addressing the soldiers and then again the officers. In the stillness around him his slowly uttered words were distinctly heard. 'I thank you all for your hard and faithful service. The victory is complete and Russia will not forget you! Honour to you for ever.'

He paused and looked round.

'Lower its head, lower it!' he said to a soldier who had accident-ally lowered the French eagle he was holding before the Pre-obrazhensk standards. 'Lower, lower, that's it. Hurrah, lads!' he added addressing the men with a rapid movement of his chin.

'Hur-r-rah!' roared thousands of voices.

While the soldiers were shouting Kutuzov leaned forward in his saddle and bowed his head and his eye lit up with a mild and apparently ironic gleam.

'You see, brothers...' said he when the shouts had ceased... and all at once his voice and the expression of his face changed. It was no longer the commander-in-chief speaking, but an ordinary old man who wanted to tell his comrades something very important.

There was a stir among the throng of officers and in the ranks of the soldiers, who moved that they might hear better what he was going to say.

'You see, brothers, I know it's hard for you, but it can't be helped! Bear up; it won't be for long now. We'll see our visitors off and then we'll rest. The Tsar won't forget your service. It is hard for you, but still you are at home while they – you see what they have come to,' he said, pointing to the prisoners. 'Worse off than our poorest beggars. While they were strong we didn't spare ourselves, but now we may even pity them. They are human beings too. Isn't it so, lads?'

He looked around, and in the direct, respectful, wondering gaze fixed upon him he read sympathy with what he had said. His face grew brighter and brighter with an old man's mild smile which drew the corners of his lips and eyes into a cluster of wrinkles. He ceased speaking and bowed his head as if in perplexity.

'But after all, who asked them here? Serves them right, the b...b...!...' he cried, suddenly lifting his head.

And flourishing his whip he rode off at a gallop for the first time during the whole campaign, and left the broken ranks of the soldiers laughing joyfully and shouting 'hurrah!'

Kutuzov's words were hardly understood by the troops. No one could have repeated the field-marshal's address, begun solemnly and then changing into an old man's simple-hearted talk; but the hearty sincerity of that speech, the feeling of majestic triumph combined with pity for the foe and consciousness of the justice of our cause, exactly expressed by that old man's good-natured ex-pletives, was not merely understood but lay in the soul of every soldier and found expression in their joyous and long-sustained shouts. Afterwards, when one of the generals addressed Kutuzov asking whether he wished his calèche to be sent for, Kutuzov in answering unexpectedly gave a sob, being evidently greatly moved.

WHEN the troops reached their night's halting-place on the 8th of November, the last day of the Krasnoe battles, it was already growing dusk. All day it had been calm and frosty with occasional lightly falling snow, and towards evening it began to clear. Through the falling snow a purple-black and starry sky showed itself, and the frost grew keener.

An infantry regiment, which had left Tarutino three thousand strong but now numbered only nine hundred, was one of the first to arrive at its halting-place that night – a village on the high road. The quartermasters who met the regiment announced that all the huts were full of sick and dead Frenchmen, cavalrymen, and members of the staff. There was only one hut available for the regimental commander.

The commander rode up to his hut. The regiment passed through the village and stacked its arms in front of the last huts.

Like some huge, many-limbed animal, the regiment began to prepare its lair and its food. One part of it dispersed and waded knee-deep through the snow into a birch forest to the right of the village, and immediately the sound of axes and swords, the crashing of branches, and merry voices, could be heard from there. Another section, amid the regimental wagons and horses which were standing in a group, was busy getting out cauldrons and rye biscuit, and feeding the horses. A third section scattered through the village arranging quarters for the staff officers, carrying out the French corpses that were in the huts, and dragging away boards, dry wood, and thatch, from the roofs for the camp-fires, or wattle fences to serve for shelter.

Some fifteen men, with merry shouts, were shaking down the high wattle wall of a shed the roof of which had already been removed.

'Now then, all together, shove!' cried the voices, and the huge surface of the wall, sprinkled with snow and creaking with frost, was seen swaying in the gloom of the night. The lower stakes cracked more and more and at last the wall fell, and with it the men who had been pushing it. Loud and coarse laughter and joyous shouts ensued.

'Now then, catch hold in twos! Hand up the lever! That's it. Where are you shoving to?'

'Now, all together! But wait a moment, boys.... With a song!'

All stood silent, and a soft, pleasant, velvety voice began to sing. At the end of the third verse, as the last note died away, twenty voices roared out at once: 'Oo-oo-oo-oo! That's it. All together! Heave away, boys!...', but despite their united efforts the wattle hardly moved, and in the silence that followed the heavy breathing of the men was audible.

'Here, you of the Sixth Company! Devils that you are! Lend a hand...will you? You may want us one of these days.'

Some twenty men of the Sixth Company, who were on their way into the village, joined the haulers, and the wattle wall, which was about thirty-five feet long and seven feet high, moved forward along the village street, swaying, pressing upon and cutting the shoulders of the gasping men.

'Get along...Falling? What are you stopping for? There now...'

Merry, senseless words of abuse flowed freely.

'What are you up to?' suddenly came the authoritative voice of a sergeant-major who came upon the men who were hauling their burden. 'There are gentry here; the general himself is in that hut, and you foul-mouthed devils, you brutes! I'll give it you!' shouted he, hitting the first man who came in his way a swinging blow on the back. 'Can't you make less noise?'

The men became silent. The soldier who had been struck groaned and wiped his face, which had been scratched till it bled by his falling against the wattle.

'There, how that devil hits out! He's made my face all bloody,' said he in a frightened whisper when the sergeant-major had passed on.

'Don't you like it?' said a laughing voice, and moderating their tones the men moved forward.

When they were out of the village they began talking again as loud as before, interlarding their talk with the same aimless expletives.

In the hut which the men had passed, the chief officers had gathered and were in animated talk over their tea about the events of the day and the manœuvres suggested for to-morrow. It was proposed to make a flank march to the left, cut off the Viceroy (Murat) and capture him.

By the time the soldiers had dragged the wattle fence to its place the camp-fires were blazing on all sides ready for cooking, the wood crackled, the snow was melting, and black shadows of soldiers flitted to and fro all over the occupied space where the snow had been trodden down.

Axes and choppers were plied all around. Everything was done without any orders being given. Stores of wood were brought for the night, shelters were rigged up for the officers, cauldrons were being boiled, and muskets and accoutrements put in order.

The wattle wall the men had brought was set up in a semicircle by the Eighth Company as a shelter from the north, propped up by musket-rests, and a camp-fire was built up before it. They beat the tattoo, called the roll, had supper, and settled down round the fires for the night – some repairing their footgear, some smoking pipes, and some stripping themselves naked to steam the lice out of their shirts.

8

ONE would have thought that under the almost incredibly wretched conditions the Russian soldiers were in at that time – lacking warm boots and sheepskin coats, without a roof over their heads, in the snow with eighteen degrees of frost,* and without even full rations (the commissariat did not always keep up with the troops) – they would have presented a very sad and depressing spectacle.

On the contrary the army had never under the best material conditions presented a more cheerful and animated aspect. This was because all who began to grow depressed or lost strength were sifted out of the army day by day. All the physically or morally weak had long since been left behind and only the flower of the army – physically and mentally – remained.

More men collected behind the wattle fence of the Eighth Company than anywhere else. Two sergeant-majors were sitting with them and their camp-fire blazed brighter than the others. For leave to sit by their wattle they demanded contributions of fuel.

'Eh, Makeev! What has become of you, you son of a bitch? Are you lost or have the wolves eaten you? Fetch some more wood!' shouted a red-haired and red-faced man, screwing up his eyes and blinking because of the smoke but not moving back from the fire. 'And you, Jackdaw, go and fetch some wood!' said he to another soldier.

This red-haired man was neither a sergeant nor a corporal, but being robust he ordered about those weaker than himself. The soldier they called 'Jackdaw', a thin little fellow with a sharp nose, rose obediently and was about to go, but at that instant there came into the light of the fire the slender, handsome figure of a young soldier carrying a load of wood.

'Bring it here – that's fine!'

They split up the wood, pressed it down on the fire, blew at it with their mouths, and fanned it with the skirts of their greatcoats, making the flames hiss and crackle. The men drew nearer and lit their pipes. The handsome young soldier who had brought the wood, setting his arms akimbo began stamping his cold feet rapidly and deftly on the spot where he stood.

'Mother! The dew is cold but clear. It's well that I'm a musketeer . . .' he sang, pretending to hiccough after each syllable.

'Look out, your soles will fly off!' shouted the red-haired man, noticing that the sole of the dancer's boot was hanging loose. 'What a fellow you are for dancing!'

The dancer stopped, pulled off the loose piece of leather, and threw it on the fire.

'Right enough, friend,' said he, and having sat down, took out of his knapsack a scrap of blue French cloth and wrapped it round his foot. 'It's the steam that spoils them,' he added, stretching out his feet towards the fire.

'They'll soon be issuing us new ones. They say that when we've finished hammering *them*, we're to receive double kits!'

'And that son of a bitch Petrov has lagged behind after all, it seems,' said one sergeant-major.

'I've had an eye on him this long while,' said the other.

'Well, he's a poor sort of soldier . . .'

'But in the Third Company they say nine men were missing yesterday.'

'Yes, it's all very well, but when a man's feet are frozen how can he walk?'

'Eh? Don't talk nonsense!' said a sergeant-major.

'Do you want to be doing the same?' said an old soldier, turning reproachfully to the man who had spoken of frozen feet.

'Well, you know,' said the sharp-nosed man they called Jackdaw in a squeaky and unsteady voice, raising himself at the other side of the fire, 'a plump man gets thin, but for a thin one it's death. Take me, now! I've got no strength left,' he added with sudden resolution, turning to the sergeant-major. 'Tell them to send me to hospital; I'm aching all over; anyway I shan't be able to keep up.'

'That'll do, that'll do,' replied the sergeant-major quietly.

The soldier said no more and the talk went on.

'What a lot of those Frenchies were taken to-day, and the fact is that not one of them had what you might call real boots on,' said a soldier, starting a new theme. 'They were no more than make-believes.'

'The Cossacks have taken their boots. They were clearing the hut for the colonel and carried them out. It was pitiful to see them, boys,' put in the dancer. 'As they turned them over, one seemed still alive and, would you believe it, he jabbered something in their lingo.'

'But they're a clean folk, lads,' the first man went on; 'he was white – as white as birch-bark – and some of them are such fine fellows, you might think they were nobles.'

'Well, what do you suppose? They make soldiers of all classes there.'

'But they don't understand our talk at all,' said the dancer with a puzzled smile. 'I asked him whose subject he was, and he jabbered his own way. A queer lot!'

'But it's strange, friends,' continued the man who had wondered at their whiteness, 'the peasants at Mozhaysk were saying that when they began burying the dead – where the battle was you know – well, those dead had been lying there for nearly a month, and, says the peasant, "they lie as white as paper, clean, and not as much smell as a puff of powder smoke."'

'Was it from the cold?' asked someone.

'You're a clever fellow! From the cold indeed! Why, it was hot. If it had been from the cold, ours would not have rotted either. "But," he says, "go up to ours and they are all rotten and maggoty. So," he says, "we tie our faces up with kerchiefs and turn our heads away as we drag them off: we can hardly do it. But theirs," he says, "are white as paper and not so much smell as a whiff of gunpowder."'

All were silent.

'It must be from their food,' said the sergeant-major. 'They used to gobble the same food as the gentry.'

No one contradicted him.

'That peasant near Mozhaysk, where the battle was, said the men were all called up from ten villages around and carted for twenty days, and still didn't finish carting the dead away. And as for the wolves, he says . . .'

'That was a real battle,' said an old soldier. 'It's the only one worth remembering; but since that . . . it's only been tormenting folk.'

'And do you know, daddy, the day before yesterday we ran at them and, my word, they didn't let us get near before they just threw down their muskets and went on their knees. "Pardon!" they say. That's only one case. They say Platov took 'Poleon himself twice. But he didn't know the right charm. He catches him and catches him – no good! He turns into a bird in his hands and flies away. And there's no way of killing him either.'

'You're a first-class liar, Kiselëv, when I come to look at you!'

'Liar, indeed! It's the real truth.'

'If he fell into my hands, when I'd caught him I'd bury him

1169

in the ground with an aspen-stake to fix him down. What a lot of men he's ruined!'

'Well, anyhow we're going to end it. He won't come here again,' remarked the old soldier, yawning.

The conversation flagged and the soldiers began settling down to sleep.

'Look at the stars. It's wonderful how they shine! You would think the women had spread out their linen,' said one of the men, gazing with admiration at the Milky Way.

'That's a sign of a good harvest next year.'

'We shall want some more wood.'

'You warm your back and your belly gets frozen. That's queer.'

'O Lord!'

'What are you pushing for? Is the fire only for you? Look how he's sprawling!'

In the silence that ensued, the snoring of those who had fallen asleep could be heard. Others turned over and warmed themselves, now and again exchanging a few words. From a camp-fire a hundred paces off came a sound of general, merry laughter.

'Hark at them roaring there in the Fifth Company!' said one of the soldiers, 'and what a lot of them there are!'

One of the men got up and went over to the Fifth Company.

'They're having such fun,' said he coming back. 'Two Frenchies have turned up. One's quite frozen and the other's an awful swaggerer. He's singing songs . . .'

'Oh, I'll go across and have a look . . .'

And several of the men went over to the Fifth Company.

9

THE Fifth Company was bivouacking at the very edge of the forest. A huge camp-fire was blazing brightly in the midst of the snow, lighting up the branches of trees heavy with hoar-frost.

About midnight they heard the sound of steps in the snow of the forest and the crackling of dry branches.

'A bear, lads,' said one of the men.

They all raised their heads to listen, and out of the forest into the bright firelight stepped two strangely clad human figures cling-ing to one another.

These were two Frenchmen who had been hiding in the forest. They came up to the fire hoarsely uttering something in a language our soldiers did not understand. One was taller than the other;

he wore an officer's hat and seemed quite exhausted. On approaching the fire he had been going to sit down, but fell. The other, a short sturdy soldier with a shawl tied round his head, was stronger. He raised his companion and said something, pointing to his mouth. The soldiers surrounded the Frenchmen, spread a greatcoat on the ground for the sick man, and brought some buckwheat porridge and vodka for both of them.

The exhausted French officer was Ramballe and the man with his head wrapped in the shawl was Morel, his orderly.

When Morel had drunk some vodka and finished his bowl of porridge he suddenly became unnaturally merry and chattered incessantly to the soldiers, who could not understand him. Ramballe refused food and resting his head on his elbow lay silent beside the camp-fire, looking at the Russian soldiers with red and vacant eyes. Occasionally he emitted a long-drawn groan and then again became silent. Morel, pointing to his shoulders, tried to impress on the soldiers the fact that Ramballe was an officer and ought to be warmed. A Russian officer who had come up to the fire sent to ask his colonel whether he would not take a French officer into his hut to warm him, and when the messenger returned and said that the colonel wished the officer to be brought to him, Ramballe was told to go. He rose and tried to walk, but staggered and would have fallen had not a soldier standing by held him up.

'You won't do it again, eh?' said one of the soldiers, winking and turning mockingly to Ramballe.

'Oh, you fool! Why talk rubbish, lout that you are – a real peasant!' came rebukes from all sides addressed to the jesting soldier.

They surrounded Ramballe, lifted him on the crossed arms of two soldiers, and carried him to the hut. Ramballe put his arms around their necks while they carried him and began wailing plaintively:

'Oh, you fine fellows, my kind, kind friends! These are men! Oh, my brave, kind friends,' and he leaned his head against the shoulder of one of the men like a child.

Meanwhile Morel was sitting in the best place by the fire, surrounded by the soldiers.

Morel, a short sturdy Frenchman with inflamed and streaming eyes, was wearing a woman's cloak and had a shawl tied woman-fashion round his head over his cap. He was evidently tipsy, and was singing a French song in a hoarse broken voice, with an arm thrown round the nearest soldier. The soldiers simply held their sides as they watched him.

'Now then, now then, teach us how it goes! I'll soon pick it up.

How is it?' said the man – a singer and a wag – whom Morel was embracing.

'Vive Henri Quatre! Vive ce roi vaillant!' sang Morel, winking. 'Ce diable à quatre...'

'Vivarika! Vif-seruvaru! Sedyablyaka!' repeated the soldier, flourishing his arm and really catching the tune.

'Bravo! Ha, ha, ha!' rose their rough joyous laughter from all sides.

Morel, wrinkling up his face, laughed too.

'Well, go on, go on!'

> 'Qui eut le triple talent,
> De boire, de battre,
> Et d'être un vert galant...'

'It goes smoothly, too. Well, now, Zaletaev!'

'Ke...' Zaletaev brought out with effort: 'ke-e-e-e,' he drawled, laboriously pursing his lips, 'le-trip-ta-la-de-bu-de-ba, e de-tra-va-ga-la!' he sang.

'Fine! Just like the Frenchie! Oh, ho, ho! Do you want some more to eat?'

'Give him some porridge: it takes a long time to get filled up after starving.'

They gave him some more porridge, and Morel with a laugh set to work on his third bowl. All the young soldiers smiled gaily as they watched him. The older men, who thought it undignified to amuse themselves with such nonsense, continued to lie at the opposite side of the fire, but one would occasionally raise himself on an elbow and glance at Morel with a smile.

'They are men, too,' said one of them as he wrapped himself up in his coat. 'Even wormwood grows on its own root.'

'O Lord, O Lord! How starry it is! Tremendous! That means a hard frost...'

They all grew silent. The stars, as if knowing that no one was looking at them, began to disport themselves in the dark sky: now flaring up, now vanishing, now trembling, they were busy whispering something gladsome and mysterious to one another.

10

THE French army melted away at the uniform rate of a mathematical progression; and that crossing of the Berëzina, about which so much has been written, was only one intermediate stage in its destruction, and not at all the decisive episode of the campaign. If so much has been and still is written about the Berëzina, on the French side this is only because at the broken bridge across that river the calamities their army had been regularly enduring were suddenly concentrated at one moment into a tragic spectacle that remained in every memory, and on the Russian side merely because in Petersburg – far from the seat of war – a plan (again one of Pfuel's) had been devised to catch Napoleon in a strategic trap at the Berëzina river. Everyone assured himself that all would happen according to plan and therefore insisted that it was just the crossing of the Berëzina that destroyed the French army. In reality the results of the crossing were much less disastrous to the French – in guns and men lost – than Krasnoe had been, as the figures show.

The sole importance of the crossing of the Berëzina lies in the fact that it plainly and indubitably proved the fallacy of all the plans for cutting off the enemy's retreat, and the soundness of the only possible line of action – the one Kutuzov and the general mass of the army demanded – namely, simply to follow the enemy up. The crowd of French fled at a continually increasing speed and all its energy was directed to reaching its goal. It fled like a wounded animal and it was impossible to stand in its path. This was shown not so much by the arrangements it made for crossing as by what took place at the bridges. When the bridges broke down, unarmed soldiers, people from Moscow, and women with children who were with the French transport, all – carried on by *vis inertiæ* – pressed forward into boats and into the ice-covered water, and did not surrender.

That impulse was reasonable. The condition of fugitives and of pursuers was equally bad. As long as they remained with their own people each might hope for help from his fellows and the definite place he held among them. But those who surrendered, while remaining in the same pitiful plight, would be on a lower level to claim a share in the necessities of life. The French did not need to be informed of the fact that half the prisoners – with whom the Russians did not know what to do – perished of cold and hunger despite their captors' desire to save them; they felt that it could not be otherwise. The most compassionate Russian commanders, those favourable to the French – and even the Frenchmen in the Russian service – could do nothing for the prisoners. The French perished from the conditions to which the Russian army was exposed. It was impossible to take bread and clothes from our hungry and indispensable soldiers to give to the French who, though not harmful, or hated, or guilty, were simply unnecessary. Some Russians even did that, but they were exceptions.

Certain destruction lay behind the French, but in front there was hope. Their boats had been burnt, there was no salvation save in collective flight and on that the whole strength of the French was concentrated.

The farther they fled the more wretched became the plight of the remnant, especially after the Berëzina, on which (in consequence of the Petersburg plan) special hopes had been placed by the Russians, and the keener grew the passions of the Russian commanders who blamed one another and Kutuzov most of all. Anticipation that the failure of the Petersburg Berëzina plan would be attributed to Kutuzov led to dissatisfaction, contempt, and ridicule, more and more strongly expressed. The ridicule and contempt were of course expressed in a respectful form, making it impossible for him to ask wherein he was to blame. They did not talk seriously to him; when reporting to him or asking for his sanction they appeared to be fulfilling a regrettable formality, but they winked behind his back and tried to mislead him at every turn.

Because they could not understand him, all these people assumed that it was useless to talk to the old man; that he would never grasp the profundity of their plans, that he would answer with his phrases (which they thought were mere phrases) about a 'golden bridge', about the impossibility of crossing the frontier with a crowd of tatterdemalions, and so forth. They had heard all that before. And all he said – that it was necessary to await provisions, or that the men had no boots – was so simple, while what they proposed was so complicated and clever, that it was evident that he was old and stupid and that they, though not in power, were commanders of genius.

After the junction with the army of the brilliant admiral and Petersburg hero Wittgenstein, this mood and the gossip of the staff reached their maximum. Kutuzov saw this and merely sighed and shrugged his shoulders. Only once, after the affair of the Berëzina, did he get angry and write to Bennigsen (who reported separately to the Emperor) the following letter:

'On account of your fits of ill health, will your Excellency please be so good as to set off for Kaluga on receipt of this, and there await further commands and appointments from his Imperial Majesty.'

But after Bennigsen's departure the Grand Duke Tsarevich Constantine Pavlovich joined the army. He had taken part in the beginning of the campaign but had subsequently been removed from the army by Kutuzov. Now having come to the army he informed Kutuzov of the Emperor's displeasure at the poor success of our forces and the slowness of their advance. The Emperor intended to join the army personally in a few days' time.

The old man, experienced in court as well as in military affairs, – this same Kutuzov who in August had been chosen commander-in-chief against the Sovereign's wishes and who had removed the Grand Duke and heir-apparent* from the army – who on his own authority and contrary to the Emperor's will had decided on the abandonment of Moscow, now realized at once that his day was over, that his part was played, and that the power he was supposed to hold was no longer his. And he understood this not merely from the attitude of the court. He saw on the one hand that the military business in which he had played his part was ended and felt that his mission was accomplished. And at the same time he began to be conscious of the physical weariness of his aged body and of the necessity of physical rest.

On the 29th of November Kutuzov entered Vilna – his 'dear Vilna' as he called it. Twice during his career Kutuzov had been Governor of Vilna. In that wealthy town which had not been injured, he found old friends and associations, besides the comforts of life of which he had so long been deprived. And he suddenly turned from the cares of army and state and, as far as the passions that seethed around him allowed, immersed himself in the quiet life to which he had formerly been accustomed, as if all that was taking place and all that had still to be done in the realm of history did not concern him at all.

Chichagov, one of the most zealous 'cutters-off' and 'breakers-up', who had first wanted to effect a diversion in Greece and then in Warsaw but never wished to go where he was sent: Chichagov, noted for the boldness with which he spoke to the Emperor, and who considered Kutuzov to be under an obligation to him because when he was sent to make peace with Turkey in 1811 independently of Kutuzov, and found that peace had already been concluded, had admitted to the Emperor that the merit of securing that peace was really Kutuzov's; this Chichagov was the first to meet Kutuzov at the castle where the latter was to stay. In undress naval uniform, with a dirk, and holding his cap under his arm, he handed Kutuzov a garrison-report and the keys of the town. The contemptuously respectful attitude of the younger men to the old man in his dotage was expressed in the highest degree by the behaviour of Chichagov, who knew of the accusations that were being directed against Kutuzov.

When speaking to him, Kutuzov incidentally mentioned that the vehicles packed with china that had been captured from him at Borisov had been recovered and would be restored to him.

'You mean to imply that I have nothing to eat out of ... On the contrary, I can supply you with everything even if you want to give dinner-parties,' warmly replied Chichagov, who tried by every word he spoke to prove his own rectitude and therefore imagined Kutuzov to be animated by the same desire.

Kutuzov, shrugging his shoulders, replied with his subtle, penetrating smile: 'I meant merely to say what I said.'

Contrary to the Emperor's wish Kutuzov detained the greater part of the army in Vilna. Those about him said that he became extraordinarily slack and physically feeble during his stay in that town. He attended to army affairs reluctantly, left everything to his generals, and while awaiting the Emperor's arrival led a dissipated life.

Having left Petersburg on the 7th of December with his suite – Count Tolstoy, Prince Volkonsky, Arakcheev, and others – the Emperor reached Vilna on the 11th, and drove straight to the castle in his travelling sledge. In spite of the severe frost, some hundred generals and staff-officers in full parade uniform stood in front of the castle, as well as a guard of honour of the Semënov regiment.

A courier who galloped to the castle in advance in a troyka with three foam-flecked horses, shouted, 'Coming!', and Konovnitsyn rushed into the vestibule to inform Kutuzov, who was waiting in the hall-porter's little lodge.

A minute later the old man's large stout figure in full dress uniform, his chest covered with Orders and a scarf drawn round his stomach, waddled out into the porch. He put on his hat with its peaks to the sides,* and holding his gloves in his hand and walking sideways down the steps to the level of the street with an effort, took in his hand the report he had prepared for the Emperor.

There was running to and fro, whispering, another troyka flew furiously up, and then all eyes were turned on an approaching sledge in which the figures of the Emperor and Volkonsky could already be descried.

From the habit of fifty years all this had a physically agitating effect on the old general. He carefully and hastily felt himself all over, re-adjusted his hat, and pulling himself together drew himself up, and at the very moment when the Emperor, having alighted from the sledge, lifted his eyes to him, handed him the report and began speaking in his smooth, ingratiating voice.

The Emperor scanned Kutuzov with a rapid glance from head to foot, frowned for an instant, but immediately mastering himself went up to the old man, extended his arms, and embraced him.

And this embrace too, owing to a long-standing impression related to his innermost feelings, had its usual effect on Kutuzov and he gave a sob.

The Emperor greeted the officers and the Seménov guard, and again pressing the old man's hand went with him into the castle.

When alone with the field-marshal the Emperor expressed his dissatisfaction at the slowness of the pursuit and at the mistakes made at Krasnoe and the Berëzina, and informed him of his intentions for a future campaign abroad. Kutuzov made no rejoinder or remark. The same submissive, expressionless look with which he had listened to the Emperor's commands on the field of Austerlitz, seven years before, settled on his face now.

When Kutuzov came out of the study and with downcast head was crossing the ball-room with his heavy waddling gait, he was arrested by someone's voice saying:

'Your Serene Highness!'

Kutuzov raised his head and looked for a long while into the eyes of Count Tolstoy, who stood before him holding a silver salver on which lay a small object. Kutuzov seemed not to understand what was expected of him.

Suddenly he seemed to remember; a scarcely perceptible smile flashed across his puffy face, and bowing low and respectfully he took the object that lay on the salver. It was the Order of St George of the First Class.*

11

NEXT day the field-marshal gave a dinner and ball which the Emperor honoured by his presence. Kutuzov had received the Order of St George of the First Class and the Emperor showed him the highest honours, but everyone knew of the Imperial dissatisfaction with him. The proprieties were observed, and the Emperor was the first to set that example, but everybody understood that the old man was blameworthy and good-for-nothing. When Kutuzov, conforming to a custom of Catherine's day, ordered the standards that had been captured to be lowered at the Emperor's feet on his entering the ball-room, the Emperor made a wry face and muttered something in which some people caught the words, 'the old comedian'.

The Emperor's displeasure with Kutuzov was specially increased at Vilna by the fact that Kutuzov evidently could not, or would not, understand the importance of the coming campaign.

When on the following morning the Emperor said to the officers assembled about him: 'You have not only saved Russia, you have saved Europe!' they all understood that the war was not ended.

Kutuzov alone would not see this, and openly expressed his opinion that no fresh war could improve the position or add to the glory of Russia, but could only spoil and lower the glorious position that Russia had gained. He tried to prove to the Emperor the impossibility of levying fresh troops, spoke of the hardships already endured by the people, of the possibility of failure, and so forth.

This being the field-marshal's frame of mind, he was naturally regarded as merely a hindrance and obstacle to the impending war.

To avoid unpleasant encounters with the old man, the natural method was to do what had been done with him at Austerlitz and with Barclay at the beginning of the Russian campaign – to transfer the authority to the Emperor himself, thus cutting the ground from under the commander-in-chief's feet without upsetting the old man by informing him of the change.

With this object his staff was gradually reconstructed and its real strength removed and transferred to the Emperor. Toll, Konovnitsyn, and Ermolov received fresh appointments. Everyone spoke loudly of the field-marshal's great weakness and failing health.

His health had to be bad for his place to be taken away and given to another. And in fact his health was poor.

So naturally, simply, and gradually – just as he had come from Turkey to the Treasury in Petersburg to recruit the militia, and then to the army when he was needed there – now, when his part was played out, Kutuzov's place was taken by a new and necessary performer.

The war of 1812, besides its national significance dear to every Russian heart, was to assume another, a European, significance.

The movement of peoples from west to east was to be succeeded by a movement of peoples from east to west, and for this fresh war another leader was necessary, having qualities and views differing from those of Kutuzov and moved by different motives.

Alexander I was as necessary for the movement of the peoples from east to west and for the refixing of national frontiers as Kutuzov had been for the salvation and glory of Russia.

Kutuzov did not understand what Europe, the balance of power, or Napoleon, meant. He could not understand it. For the representative of the Russian people, after the enemy had been destroyed and Russia had been liberated and raised to the summit of her glory, there was nothing left to do as a Russian. Nothing remained for the representative of the national war but to die, and Kutuzov died.

As generally happens, Pierre only felt the full effects of the physical privation and strain he had suffered as prisoner after they were over. After his liberation he reached Orël, and on the third day there, when preparing to go to Kiev, he fell ill and was laid up for three months. He had what the doctors termed 'bilious fever'. But despite the fact that the doctors treated him, bled him, and gave him medicines to drink – he recovered.

Scarcely any impression was left on Pierre's mind by all that happened to him from the time of his rescue till his illness. He only remembered the dull grey weather, now rainy and now snowy, internal physical distress, and pains in his feet and side. He remembered a general impression of the misfortunes and sufferings of people, and of being worried by the curiosity of officers and generals who questioned him; he also remembered his difficulty in procuring a conveyance and horses, and above all he remembered his incapacity to think and feel all that time. On the day of his rescue he had seen the body of Petya Rostov. That same day he had learned that Prince Andrew, after surviving for more than a month after the battle of Borodino, had recently died in the Rostovs' house at Yaroslavl, and Denisov, who told him this news, also mentioned Hélène's death, supposing that Pierre had heard of it long before. All this at the time seemed merely strange to Pierre: he felt he could not grasp its significance. Just then he was only anxious to get away as quickly as possible from places where people were killing one another, to some peaceful refuge where he could recover himself, rest, and think over all the strange new facts he had learnt; but on reaching Orël he immediately fell ill. When he came to himself after his illness, he saw in attendance on him two of his servants, Terenty and Vaska, who had come from Moscow, and also his cousin, the eldest princess, who had been living on his estate at Elets and hearing of his rescue and illness had come to look after him.

It was only gradually during his convalescence that Pierre lost the impressions he had become accustomed to during the last few months, and got used to the idea that no one would oblige him to go anywhere to-morrow, that no one would deprive him of his warm bed, and that he would be sure to get his dinner, tea, and supper. But for a long time in his dreams he still saw himself in the conditions of captivity. In the same way, little by little, he came to understand the news he had been told after his rescue, about the death of Prince Andrew, the death of his wife, and the destruction of the French.

A joyous feeling of freedom – that complete inalienable freedom natural to man which he had first experienced at the first halt outside Moscow – filled Pierre's soul during his convalescence. He was surprised to find that this inner freedom which was independent of external conditions, now had, as it were, an additional setting of external liberty. He was alone in a strange town, without acquaintances. No one demanded anything of him or sent him anywhere. He had all he wanted: the thought of his wife which had been a continual torment to him was no longer there, since she was no more.

'Oh, how good! How splendid!' said he to himself when a cleanly-laid table was moved up to him with savoury beef-tea, or when he lay down for the night on a soft clean bed, or when he remembered that the French had gone and that his wife was no more. 'Oh, how good, how splendid!'

And by old habit he asked himself the question: 'Well, and what then? What am I going to do?' And he immediately gave himself the answer: 'Well, I shall live. Ah, how splendid!'

The very question that had formerly tormented him, the thing he had continually sought to find – the aim of life – no longer existed for him now. That search for the aim of life had not merely disappeared temporarily; he felt that it no longer existed for him and could not present itself again. And this very absence of an aim gave him the complete, joyous sense of freedom which constituted his happiness at this time.

He could not see an aim, for he now had faith – not faith in any kind of rule, or words, or ideas, but faith in an ever-living ever-manifest God. Formerly he had sought Him in aims he set himself. That search for an aim had been simply a search for God, and suddenly in his captivity he had learnt, not by words or reasoning but by direct feeling, what his nurse had told him long ago: that God is here and everywhere. In his captivity he had learnt that in Karataev God was greater, more infinite and unfathomable, than in the Architect of the Universe the Freemasons acknowledged. He felt like a man who, after straining his eyes to see into the far distance, finds what he sought at his very feet. All his life he had looked over the heads of the men around him, when he should have merely looked in front of him without straining his eyes.

In the past he had never been able to find that great inscrutable infinite *something*. He had only felt that it must exist somewhere and had looked for it. In everything near and comprehensible he had seen only what was limited, petty, commonplace, and senseless. He had equipped himself with a mental telescope and looked into remote space, where that petty worldliness, hiding itself in misty distance, had seemed to him great and infinite merely because it was not clearly seen. And such had European life, politics, Freemasonry, philosophy, and philanthropy, seemed to him. But even then, at moments of weakness as he had accounted them, his mind had penetrated to those distances and he had there seen the same pettiness, worldliness, and senselessness. Now, however, he had learnt to see the great, eternal, and infinite in everything, and therefore – to see it and enjoy its contemplation – he naturally threw away the telescope through which he had till now gazed over men's heads, and gladly regarded the ever-changing, eternally great, unfathomable and infinite life around him. And the closer he looked the more tranquil and happy he became. That dreadful question, What for? which had formerly destroyed all his mental edifices, no longer existed for him. To that question, What for? a simple answer was now always ready in his soul: 'Because there is a God, that God without whose will not one hair falls from a man's head.'

13

IN external ways Pierre had hardly changed at all. In appearance he was just what he used to be. As before he was absent-minded and seemed occupied not with what was before his eyes but with something special of his own. The difference between his former and present self was that formerly, when he did not grasp what lay before him or what was said to him, he had puckered his forehead painfully as if vainly seeking to distinguish something at a distance. Now he still forgot what was said to him and still did not see what was before his eyes, but he now looked with a scarcely perceptible and seemingly ironic smile at what was before him and listened to what was said, though he evidently saw and heard something quite different. Formerly he had appeared to be a kind-hearted but unhappy man and so people had been inclined to avoid him. Now a smile of the joy of life always played round his lips, and sympathy for others shone in his eyes and a questioning look as to whether they were as contented as he was, and people felt pleased by his presence.

Previously he had talked a great deal, grew excited when he talked, and seldom listened; now he was seldom carried away in conversation and knew how to listen so that people readily told him their most intimate secrets.

The princess, who had never liked Pierre and had been particularly hostile to him since she had felt herself under obligations to him after the old count's death, now, after staying a short time in Orël – where she had come intending to show Pierre that in spite of his ingratitude she considered it her duty to nurse him – felt to her surprise and vexation that she had become fond of him. Pierre did not in any way seek her approval, he merely studied her with interest. Formerly she had felt that he regarded her with indifference and irony, and so had shrunk into herself as she did with others, and had shown him only the combative side of her nature: but now she felt that he seemed to be trying to understand the most sacred places of her heart, and mistrustfully at first but afterwards gratefully, she let him see the hidden, kindly sides of her character.

The most cunning man could not have crept into her confidence more successfully, evoking memories of the best times of her youth and showing sympathy with them. Yet Pierre's cunning consisted simply in finding pleasure in drawing out the human qualities of the embittered, hard, and (in her own way) proud princess.

'Yes, he is a very, very kind man when he is not under the influence of bad people, but of people such as myself,' thought the princess.

His servants too – Terenty and Vaska – in their own way noticed the change that had taken place in Pierre. They considered that he had become much 'simpler'.* Terenty, when he had helped him to undress and wished him good-night, often lingered with his master's boots in his hand and clothes over his arm, to see whether he would not start a talk. And Pierre, noticing that Terenty wanted a chat, generally kept him there.

'Well, tell me ... now, how did you get food?' he would ask.

And Terenty would begin talking of the destruction of Moscow, and of the old count, and would stand for a long time holding the clothes and talking, or sometimes listening to Pierre's stories, and then with a pleasant sense of intimacy with his master and affection for him would go out into the hall.

The doctor who attended Pierre and visited him every day, though he considered it his duty as a doctor to pose as a man whose every moment was of value to suffering humanity, would sit for hours with Pierre telling him his favourite anecdotes and his observations of the characters of his patients in general, and especially of the ladies.

'It's a pleasure to talk to a man like that; he is not like our provincials,' he would say.

There were several prisoners from the French army in Orël,

and the doctor brought one of them, a young Italian,* to see Pierre.

This officer began visiting Pierre, and the princess used to make fun of the tenderness the Italian expressed for him.

The Italian seemed happy only when he could come to see Pierre, talk with him, tell him about his past, his life at home, and his love, and pour out to him his indignation against the French and especially against Napoleon.

'If all Russians are in the least like you, it is sacrilege to fight such a nation,' he said to Pierre. 'You, who have suffered so from the French, do not even feel animosity towards them.'

Pierre had earned the passionate affection of the Italian merely by evoking the best side of his nature and taking a pleasure in so doing.

During the last days of Pierre's stay in Orël his old masonic acquaintance Count Willarski, who had introduced him to the Lodge in 1807, came to see him. Willarski was married to a Russian heiress who had a large estate in Orël province, and he occupied a temporary post in the commissariat department in that town.

Hearing that Bezukhov was in Orël, Willarski, though they had never been intimate, came to him with the professions of friendship and intimacy that people who meet in a desert generally express for one another. Willarski felt dull in Orël and was pleased to meet a man of his own circle and, as he supposed, of similar interests.

But to his surprise Willarski soon noticed that Pierre had lagged much behind the times, and had sunk, as he expressed it to himself, into apathy and egotism.

'You are letting yourself go, my dear fellow,' he said.

But for all that, Willarski found it pleasanter to be with Pierre now than it had been formerly, and came to see him every day. To Pierre, as he looked at and listened to Willarski, it seemed strange to think that he had been like that himself but a short time before.

Willarski was a married man with a family, busy with his family affairs, his wife's affairs, and his official duties. He regarded all these occupations as hindrances to life, and considered that they were all contemptible because their aim was the welfare of himself and his family. Military, administrative, political, and masonic interests continually absorbed his attention. And Pierre, without trying to change the other's views and without condemning him, but with the quiet joyful and amused smile now habitual to him, was interested in this strange, though very familiar, phenomenon.

There was a new feature in Pierre's relations with Willarski, with the princess, with the doctor, and with all the people he now met, which gained for him the general goodwill. This was his acknowledgement of the impossibility of changing a man's convictions by words, and his recognition of the possibility of everyone thinking, feeling, and seeing things each from his own point of view. This legitimate peculiarity of each individual, which used to excite and irritate Pierre, now became a basis of the sympathy he felt for, and the interest he took in, other people. The difference, and sometimes complete contradiction, between men's opinions and their lives, and between one man and another, pleased him and evoked from him and amused and gentle smile.

In practical matters Pierre unexpectedly felt within himself a centre of gravity he had previously lacked. Formerly all money questions, especially requests for money to which, as a very wealthy man, he was very frequently exposed, produced in him a state of hopeless agitation and perplexity. 'To give or not to give?' he had asked himself. 'I have it and he needs it. But someone else needs it still more. Who needs it most? And perhaps they are both impostors?' In the old days he had been unable to find a way out of all these surmises and had given to all who asked as long as he had anything to give. Formerly he had been in a similar state of perplexity with regard to every question concerning his property, when one person advised one thing and another something else.

Now to his surprise he found that he no longer felt either doubt or perplexity about these questions. There was now within him a judge who by some rule unknown to him decided what should or should not be done.

He was as indifferent as heretofore to money matters, but now he felt certain of what ought and what ought not to be done. The first time he had recourse to this new judge was when a French prisoner, a colonel, came to him, and after talking a great deal about his exploits, concluded by making what amounted to a demand that Pierre should give him four thousand francs to send to his wife and children. Pierre refused without the least difficulty or effort, and was afterwards surprised how simple and easy had been what used to appear so insurmountably difficult. At the same time that he refused the colonel's demand he made up his mind that he must have recourse to artifice when leaving Orël to induce the Italian officer to accept some money of which he was evidently in need. A further proof to Pierre of his own more settled outlook on practical matters was furnished by his decision with regard to his wife's debts and to the rebuilding of his houses in and near Moscow.

His head steward came to him at Orël and Pierre reckoned up with him his diminished income. The burning of Moscow had cost him, according to the head steward's calculation, about two million rubles.

To console Pierre for these losses the head steward gave him an estimate showing that, despite these losses, his income would not be diminished but would even be increased if he refused to pay his wife's debts, which he was under no obligation to meet, and did not rebuild his Moscow house and the country house on his Moscow estate, which had cost him eighty thousand rubles a year and brought in nothing.

'Yes, of course that's true,' said Pierre with a cheerful smile. 'I don't need all that at all. By being ruined I have become much richer.'

But in January Savelich came from Moscow and gave him an account of the state of things there, and spoke of the estimate an architect had made of the cost of rebuilding the town and country houses, speaking of this as of a settled matter. About the same time he received letters from Prince Vasili and other Petersburg acquaintances speaking of his wife's debts. And Pierre decided that the steward's proposals which had so pleased him were wrong, and that he must go to Petersburg and settle his wife's affairs and must rebuild in Moscow. Why this was necessary he did not know, but he knew for certain that it was necessary. His income would be reduced by three-fourths, but he felt it must be done.

Willarski was going to Moscow and they agreed to travel together.

During the whole time of his convalescence in Orël Pierre had experienced a feeling of joy, freedom, and life; but when during his journey he found himself in the open world and saw hundreds of new faces, that feeling was intensified. Throughout his journey he felt like a schoolboy on holiday. Everyone – the stage-coach driver, the post-house overseers, the peasants on the roads and in the villages – had a new significance for him. The presence and remarks of Willarski, who continually deplored the ignorance and poverty of Russia and its backwardness compared with Europe, only heightened Pierre's pleasure. Where Willarski saw deadness Pierre saw an extraordinary strength of vitality – the strength which in that vast space amid the snows maintained the life of this original, peculiar and unique people. He did not contradict Willarski and even seemed to agree with him – an apparent agreement being the simplest way to avoid discussions that could lead to nothing – and he smiled joyfully as he listened to him.

IT would be difficult to explain why, and where to, ants whose heap has been destroyed are hurrying: some from the heap, dragging bits of rubbish, eggs and corpses, others back to the heap; why they jostle, overtake one another, and fight, and it would be equally difficult to explain what caused the Russians, after the departure of the French, to throng to the place that had formerly been Moscow. But when we watch the ants round their ruined heap, the tenacity, energy, and the immense number of the delving insects prove that, despite the destruction of the heap, something indestructible, which though intangible is the real strength of the colony, still exists; and similarly though in Moscow in the month of October there was no government, and no churches, shrines, riches, or houses – it was still the Moscow it had been in August. All was destroyed, except something intangible yet powerful and indestructible.

The motives of those who thronged from all sides to Moscow after it had been cleared of the enemy were most diverse and personal, and at first, for the most part, savage and brutal. One motive only they all had in common: a desire to get to the place that had been called Moscow, to apply their activities there.

Within a week Moscow already had fifteen thousand inhabitants, in a fortnight twenty-five thousand, and so on. By the autumn of 1813 the number, ever increasing and increasing, exceeded what it had been in 1812.

The first Russians to enter Moscow were the Cossacks of Wintzingerode's detachment, peasants from the adjacent villages, and residents who had fled from Moscow and had been hiding in its vicinity. The Russians who entered Moscow, finding it plundered, plundered it in their turn. They continued what the French had begun. Trains of peasant carts came to Moscow to carry off to the villages what had been abandoned in the ruined houses and the streets. The Cossacks carried off what they could to their camps, and the householders seized all they could find in other houses, and moved it to their own, pretending that it was their property.

But the first plunderers were followed by a second and a third contingent, and with increasing numbers plundering became more and more difficult and assumed more definite forms.

The French found Moscow abandoned but with all the organizations of regular life, with diverse branches of commerce and craftsmanship, with luxury, and governmental and religious institutions. These forms were lifeless, but still existed. There were bazaars, shops, warehouses, market-stalls, granaries – for the most part still stocked with goods – and there were factories and workshops, palaces and wealthy houses filled with luxuries, hospitals, prisons, Government offices, churches and cathedrals. The longer the French remained the more these forms of town life perished, until finally all was merged into one confused, lifeless scene of plunder.

The more the plundering by the French continued, the more both the wealth of Moscow and the strength of its plunderers was destroyed. But plundering by the Russians, with which the reoccupation of the city began, had an opposite effect: the longer it continued and the greater the number of people taking part in it, the more rapidly was the wealth of the city and its regular life restored.

Besides the plunderers, very various people, some drawn by curiosity, some by official duties, some by self-interest: house-owners, clergy, officials of all kinds, tradesmen, artisans, and peasants, streamed into Moscow as blood flows to the heart.

Within a week the peasants who came with empty carts to carry off plunder were stopped by the authorities and made to cart the corpses out of the town. Other peasants, having heard of their comrades' discomfiture, came to town bringing rye, oats, and hay, and beat down one another's prices to below what they had been in former days. Gangs of carpenters hoping for high pay arrived in Moscow every day, and on all sides logs were being hewn, new houses built, and old charred ones repaired. Tradesmen began trading in booths. Cookshops and taverns were opened in partially-burned houses. The clergy resumed the services in many of the churches that had not been burnt. Donors contributed Church property that had been stolen. Government clerks set up their baize-covered tables and their pigeon-holes of documents in small rooms. The higher authorities and the police organized the distribution of goods left behind by the French. The owners of houses in which had been left much property brought there from other houses, complained of the injustice of taking everything to the Faceted Palace in the Kremlin, others insisted that as the French had gathered things from different houses into this or that house, it would be unfair to allow its owner to keep all that was found there. They abused the police and bribed them, made out estimates at ten times their value for Government stores that had perished in the fire, and demanded relief. And Count Rostopchin wrote proclamations.

AT the end of January Pierre went to Moscow and stayed in an annexe of his house, which had not been burnt. He called on Count Rostopchin and on some acquaintances who were back in Moscow, and he intended to leave for Petersburg two days later. Everybody was celebrating the victory, everything was bubbling with life in the ruined but reviving city. Everyone was pleased to see Pierre, everyone wished to meet him, and everyone questioned him about what he had seen. Pierre felt particularly well disposed towards them all, but was now instinctively on his guard for fear of binding himself in any way. To all questions put to him – whether important or quite trifling – such as, Where would he live? Was he going to rebuild? When was he going to Petersburg and would he mind taking a parcel for someone? – he replied: 'Yes, perhaps', or, 'I think so', and so on.

He had heard that the Rostovs were at Kostroma but the thought of Natasha seldom occurred to him. If it did, it was only as a pleasant memory of the distant past. He felt himself not only free from social obligations but also from that feeling which it seemed to him he had aroused in himself.

On the third day after his arrival he heard from the Drubetskoys that Princess Mary was in Moscow. The death, sufferings, and last days of Prince Andrew had often occupied Pierre's thoughts and now recurred to him with fresh vividness. Having heard at dinner that Princess Mary was in Moscow and living in her house – which had not been burnt – in Vozdvizhenka street, he drove that same evening to see her.

On his way to the house Pierre kept thinking of Prince Andrew, of their friendship, of his various meetings with him, and especially of the last one at Borodino.

'Is it possible that he died in the bitter frame of mind he was then in? Is it possible that the meaning of life was not disclosed to him before he died?' thought Pierre. He recalled Karataev and his death, and involuntarily began to compare those two men, so different and yet so similar in that they had both lived and both died and in the love he felt for both of them.

Pierre drove up to the house of the old prince in a most serious mood. The house had escaped; it showed signs of damage but its general aspect was unchanged. The old footman, who met Pierre with a stern face as if wishing to make the visitor feel that the absence of the old prince had not disturbed the order of things in the house, informed him that the princess had gone to her own apartments, and that she received on Sundays.

'Announce me. Perhaps she will see me,' said Pierre.

'Yes, sir,' said the man. 'Please step into the portrait-gallery.'

A few minutes later the footman returned with Dessalles, who brought word from the princess that she would be very glad to see Pierre if he would excuse her want of ceremony and come upstairs to her apartment.

In a rather low room lit by one candle sat the princess, and with her another person dressed in black. Pierre remembered that the princess always had lady companions, but who they were and what they were like he never knew or remembered. 'This must be one of her companions,' he thought, glancing at the lady in the black dress.

The princess rose quickly to meet him and held out her hand.

'Yes,' she said, looking at his altered face after he had kissed her hand, 'so this is how we meet again. He often spoke of you even at the very last,' she went on, turning her eyes from Pierre to her companion with a shyness that surprised him for an instant.

'I was so glad to hear of your safety. It was the first piece of good news we had received for a long time.'

Again the princess glanced round at her companion with even more uneasiness in her manner, and was about to add something but Pierre interrupted her.

'Just imagine – I knew nothing about him!' said he. 'I thought he had been killed. All I know I heard at second-hand from others. I only know that he fell in with the Rostovs ... What a strange coincidence!'

Pierre spoke rapidly and with animation. He glanced once at the companion's face, saw her attentive and kindly gaze fixed on him and, as often happens when one is talking, felt somehow that this companion in the black dress was a good, kind, excellent creature, who would not hinder his conversing freely with Princess Mary.

But when he mentioned the Rostovs, Princess Mary's face expressed still greater embarrassment. She again glanced rapidly from Pierre's face to that of the lady in the black dress, and said:

'Do you really not recognize her?'

Pierre looked again at the companion's pale delicate face, with its black eyes and peculiar mouth, and something near to him, long forgotten and more than sweet, looked at him from those attentive eyes.

'But no, it can't be!' he thought. 'This stern, thin, pale face that looks so much older! It cannot be she. It merely reminds me of her.' But at that moment Princess Mary said 'Natasha!' And with difficulty, effort, and stress, like the opening of a door grown rusty on its hinges, a smile appeared on the face with the attentive eyes, and from that opening door came a breath of fragrance which suffused Pierre with a happiness he had long forgotten and of which he had not even been thinking – especially at that moment. It suffused him, seized him, and enveloped him completely. When she smiled, doubt was no longer possible, it was Natasha and he loved her.

At that moment Pierre involuntarily betrayed to her, to Princess Mary, and above all to himself, a secret of which he himself had been unaware. He flushed joyfully yet with painful distress. He tried to hide his agitation. But the more he tried to hide it the more clearly – clearer than any words could have done – did he betray to himself, to her, and to Princess Mary, that he loved her.

'No, it's only the unexpectedness of it,' thought Pierre. But as soon as he tried to continue the conversation he had begun with Princess Mary he again glanced at Natasha, and a still deeper flush suffused his face and a still stronger agitation of mingled joy and fear seized his soul. He became confused in his speech and stopped in the middle of what he was saying.

Pierre had failed to notice Natasha because he did not at all expect to see her there, but he had failed to recognize her because the change in her since he last saw her was immense. She had grown thin and pale, but that was not what made her unrecognizable: she was unrecognizable at the moment he entered because on that face whose eyes had always shone with a suppressed smile of the joy of life, now when he first entered and glanced at her there was not the least shadow of a smile: only her eyes were kindly attentive and sadly interrogative.

Pierre's confusion was not reflected by any confusion on Natasha's part, but only by the pleasure that just perceptibly lit up her whole face.

16

'SHE has come to stay with me,' said Princess Mary. 'The count and countess will be here in a few days. The countess is in a dreadful state. But it was necessary for Natasha herself to see a doctor. They insisted on her coming with me.'

'Yes, is there a family free from sorrow now?' said Pierre, addressing Natasha. 'You know it happened the very day we were rescued. I saw him. What a delightful boy he was!'

Natasha looked at him, and by way of answer to his words her eyes widened and lit up.

'What can one say or think of as a consolation?' said Pierre. 'Nothing! Why had such a splendid boy, so full of life, to die?'

'Yes, in these days it would be hard to live·without faith...' remarked Princess Mary.

'Yes, yes, that is really true,' Pierre hastily interrupted her.

'Why is it true?' Natasha asked, looking attentively into Pierre's eyes.

'How can you ask why?' said Princess Mary. 'The thought alone of what awaits...'

Natasha, without waiting for Princess Mary to finish, again looked inquiringly at Pierre.

'And because', Pierre continued, 'only one who believes that there is a God ruling us can bear a loss such as hers and...yours.'

Natasha had already opened her mouth to speak but suddenly stopped. Pierre hurriedly turned away from her and again addressed Princess Mary, asking her about his friend's last days.

Pierre's confusion had now almost vanished, but at the same time he felt that his freedom had also completely gone. He felt that there was now a judge of his every word and action whose judgement mattered more to him than that of all the rest of the world. As he spoke now he was considering what impression his words would make on Natasha. He did not purposely say things to please her, but whatever he was saying he regarded from her standpoint.

Princess Mary – reluctantly, as usual in such cases – began telling of the condition in which she had found Prince Andrew. But Pierre's face quivering with emotion, his questions, and his eager restless expression, gradually compelled her to go into details which she feared to recall for her own sake.

'Yes, yes, and so...?' Pierre kept saying as he leant towards her with his whole body and eagerly listened to her story. 'Yes, yes, so he grew tranquil, and softened? He had always sought one thing with his whole soul – to be perfectly good – so he could not be afraid of death. The faults he had – if he had any – were not of his making. So he did soften?...What a happy thing that he saw you again,' he added, suddenly turning to Natasha and looking at her with his eyes full of tears.

Natasha's face twitched. She frowned and lowered her eyes for a moment. She hesitated for an instant whether to speak or not.

'Yes, that was a happiness,' she then said in her quiet voice with its deep chest notes. 'For me it certainly was a happiness.' She paused. 'And he...he...he said he was wishing for it at the very moment I entered the room...'

Natasha's voice broke. She blushed, pressed her clasped hands on her knees, and then, controlling herself with an evident effort, lifted her head and began to speak rapidly.

'We knew nothing of it when we started from Moscow. I did not dare to ask about him. Then suddenly Sonya told me he was travelling with us. I had no idea and could not imagine what state he was in, all I wanted was to see him and be with him,' she said, trembling and breathing quickly.

And not letting them interrupt her, she went on to tell what she had never yet mentioned to anyone – all she had lived through during those three weeks of their journey and life at Yaroslavl.

Pierre listened to her with lips parted and eyes fixed upon her full of tears. As he listened he did not think of Prince Andrew, nor of death, nor of what she was telling. He listened to her, and felt only pity for her, for what she was suffering now while she was speaking.

Princess Mary, frowning in her effort to hold back her tears, sat beside Natasha, and heard for the first time the story of those last days of her brother's and Natasha's love.

Evidently Natasha needed to tell that painful yet joyful tale.

She spoke, mingling most trifling details with the intimate secrets of her soul, and it seemed as if she could never finish. Several times over she repeated the same thing twice.

Dessalles's voice was heard outside the door asking whether little Nicholas might come in to say good-night.

'Well, that's all – everything,' said Natasha.

She got up quickly just as Nicholas entered, almost ran to the door which was hidden by curtains, struck her head against it, and rushed from the room with a moan either of pain or sorrow.

Pierre gazed at the door through which she had disappeared, and did not understand why he suddenly felt all alone in the world.

Princess Mary roused him from his abstraction by drawing his attention to her nephew, who had entered the room.

At that moment of emotional tenderness, little Nicholas's face, which resembled his father's, affected Pierre so much that when he had kissed the boy he got up quickly, took out his handkerchief, and went to the window. He wished to take leave of Princess Mary, but she would not let him go.

'No, Natasha and I sometimes don't go to sleep till after two, so please don't go. I will order supper. Go downstairs, we will come immediately.'

Before Pierre left the room Princess Mary told him: 'This is the first time she has talked of him like that.'

PIERRE was shown into the large brightly-lit dining-room; a few minutes later he heard footsteps and Princess Mary entered with Natasha. Natasha was calm, though a severe and grave expression had again settled on her face. They all three of them now experienced that feeling of awkwardness which usually follows after a serious and heartfelt talk. It is impossible to go back to the same conversation, to talk of trifles is awkward, and yet the desire to speak is there and silence seems like affectation. They went silently to table. The footmen drew back the chairs and pushed them up again. Pierre unfolded his cold table-napkin and, resolving to break the silence, looked at Natasha and at Princess Mary. They had evidently both formed the same resolution, the eyes of both shone with satisfaction and a confession that besides its sorrow life also has joy.

'Do you take vodka, Count?' asked Princess Mary, and those words suddenly banished the shadows of the past. 'Now tell us about yourself,' said she. 'One hears such improbable wonders about you.'

'Yes,' replied Pierre with the smile of mild irony now habitual to him. 'They even tell me of wonders I myself never dreamt of! Mary Abramovna invited me to her house and kept telling me what had happened, or ought to have happened, to me. Stepan Stepanych also instructed me how I ought to tell of my experiences. In general I have noticed that it is very easy to be an interesting man (I am an interesting man now); people invite me out and tell me all about myself.'

Natasha smiled and was on the point of speaking.

'We have been told,' Princess Mary interrupted her, 'that you lost two millions in Moscow. Is that true?'

'But I am three times as rich as before,' returned Pierre.

Though the position was now altered by his decision to pay his wife's debts and to rebuild his houses, Pierre still maintained that he had become three times as rich as before.

'What I have certainly gained is freedom,' he began seriously, but did not continue, noticing that this theme was too egotistic.

'And are you building?'

'Yes. Savelich says I must!'

'Tell me, you did not know of the countess's death when you decided to remain in Moscow?' asked Princess Mary, and immediately blushed, noticing that her question, following his mention of freedom, ascribed to his words a meaning he had perhaps not intended.

'No,' answered Pierre, evidently not considering the meaning Princess Mary had given to his words awkward. 'I heard of it in Orël and you cannot imagine how it shocked me. We were not an exemplary couple,' he added quickly, glancing at Natasha and noticing on her face curiosity as to how he would speak of his wife, 'but her death shocked me terribly. When two people quarrel they are always both at fault, and one's own guilt suddenly becomes terribly serious when the other is no longer alive. And then such a death...without friends and without consolation! I am very, very sorry for her,' he concluded, and was pleased to notice a look of glad approval on Natasha's face.

'Yes, and so you are once more an eligible bachelor,' said Princess Mary.

Pierre suddenly flushed crimson and for a long time tried not to look at Natasha. When he ventured to glance her way again her face was cold, stern, and he fancied even contemptuous.

'And did you really see and speak to Napoleon, as we have been told?' said Princess Mary.

Pierre laughed.

'No, never once! Everybody seems to imagine that being taken prisoner means being Napoleon's guest. Not only did I never see him, but I heard nothing about him – I was in much lower company!'

Supper was over, and Pierre, who at first declined to speak about his captivity, was gradually led on to do so.

'But it's true that you remained in Moscow to kill Napoleon?' Natasha asked with a slight smile. 'I guessed it then, when we met at the Sukharev Tower, do you remember?'

Pierre admitted that it was true, and from that was gradually led on by Princess Mary's questions and especially by Natasha's to giving a detailed account of his adventures.

At first he spoke with the amused and mild irony now customary with him towards everybody and especially towards himself, but when he came to describe the horrors and sufferings he had witnessed he was unconsciously carried away, and began speaking with the suppressed emotion of a man re-experiencing in recollection strong impressions he has lived through.

Princess Mary with a gentle smile looked now at Pierre and now at Natasha. In the whole narrative she saw only Pierre and his goodness. Natasha, leaning on her elbow, the expression of her face constantly changing with the narrative, watched Pierre with an attention that never wandered – evidently herself experiencing all that he described. Not only her look, but her exclamations and the brief questions she put, showed Pierre that she understood just what he wished to convey. It was clear that she understood not only what he said, but also what he wished to, but could not, express in words. The account Pierre gave of the incident with the child and the woman for protecting whom he was arrested, was this: 'It was an awful sight – children abandoned, some in the flames ... One was snatched out before my eyes ... and there were women who had their things snatched off and their ear-rings torn out ...' he flushed and grew confused. 'Then a patrol arrived and all the men – all those who were not looting that is – were arrested, and I among them.'

'I am sure you're not telling us everything; I am sure you did something ...' said Natasha, and pausing added 'something fine?'

Pierre continued. When he spoke of the execution he wanted to pass over the horrible details, but Natasha insisted that he should not omit anything.

Pierre began to tell about Karataev, but paused. By this time he had risen from table and was pacing the room, Natasha following him with her eyes. Then he added:

'No, you can't understand what I learned from that illiterate man – that simple fellow.'

'Yes, yes: go on!' said Natasha. 'Where is he?'

'They killed him almost before my eyes.'

And Pierre, his voice trembling continually, went on to tell of the last days of their retreat, of Karataev's illness, and of his death.

He told of his adventures as he had never yet recalled them. He now, as it were, saw a new meaning in all he had gone through. Now that he was telling it all to Natasha, he experienced that pleasure which a man has when women listen to him – not clever women who when listening either try to remember what they hear to enrich their minds, and when opportunity offers to re-tell it, or who wish to adapt it to some thought of their own and promptly contribute their own clever comments prepared in their own little mental workshop – but the pleasure real women give who are gifted with a capacity to select and absorb the very best a man shows of himself. Natasha, without knowing it, was all attention: she did not lose a word, no single quiver in Pierre's voice, no look, no twitch of a muscle in his face, or a single gesture. She caught the unfinished word in its flight and took it straight into her open heart, divining the secret meaning of all Pierre's mental travail.

Princess Mary understood his story and sympathized with him, but she now saw something else that absorbed all her attention.

She saw the possibility of love and happiness between Natasha and Pierre, and the first thought of this filled her heart with gladness.

It was three o'clock in the morning. The footmen came in with sad and stern faces to change the candles, but no one noticed them.

Pierre finished his story. Natasha continued to look at him intently and attentively with bright animated eyes, as if trying to understand something more, which he had perhaps left untold. Pierre in shamefaced and happy confusion glanced occasionally at her and tried to think what to say next to introduce a fresh subject. Princess Mary was silent. It occurred to none of them that it was three o'clock and time to go to bed.

'People speak of misfortunes and sufferings,' remarked Pierre, 'but if at this moment I were asked: "Would you rather be what you were before you were taken prisoner, or go through this all again?" then for heaven's sake let me again have captivity and horse flesh! We imagine that when we are thrown out of our usual ruts all is lost, but it is only then that what is new and good begins. While there is life there is happiness. There is much, much before us. I say this to you,' he added, turning to Natasha.

'Yes, yes,' she said, answering something quite different. 'I too should wish nothing but to re-live it all from the beginning.'

Pierre looked intently at her.

'Yes, and nothing more,' said Natasha.

'It's not true, not true!' cried Pierre. 'I am not to blame for being alive and wishing to live – nor you either.'

Suddenly Natasha bent her head, covered her face with her hands, and began to cry.

'What is it, Natasha?' said Princess Mary.

'Nothing, nothing.' She smiled at Pierre through her tears. 'Good-night. It's time for bed.'

Pierre rose and took his leave.

Princess Mary and Natasha met as usual in the bedroom. They talked of what Pierre had told them. Princess Mary did not express her opinion of Pierre nor did Natasha speak of him.

'Well, good-night, Mary!' said Natasha. 'Do you know, I am often afraid that by not speaking of him' (she meant Prince Andrew) 'for fear of not doing justice to our feelings, we forget him.'

Princess Mary sighed deeply, and thereby acknowledged the justice of Natasha's remark, but she did not express agreement in words.

'Is it possible to forget?' said she.

'It did me so much good to tell all about it to-day. It was hard and painful, but good. Very good!' said Natasha. 'I am sure he really loved him. That is why I told him ... Was it all right?' she added, suddenly blushing.

'To tell Pierre? Oh, yes. What a splendid man he is!' said Princess Mary.

'Do you know, Mary ...' Natasha suddenly said with a mischievous smile such as Princess Mary had not seen on her face for a long time, 'he has somehow grown so clean, smooth, and fresh – as if he had just come out of a Russian bath: do you understand? Out of a moral bath. Isn't it true?'

'Yes,' replied Princess Mary. 'He has greatly improved.'

'With a short coat and his hair cropped; just as if, well, just as if he had come straight from the bath ... papa used to ...'

'I understand why *he*' (Prince Andrew) 'liked no one as much as him,' said Princess Mary.

'Yes, and he is quite different. They say men are friends when they are quite different. That must be true. Really he is quite unlike him – in everything.'

'Yes, but he's wonderful.'

'Well, good-night,' said Natasha.

And the same mischievous smile lingered for a long time on her face as if it had been forgotten there.

18

It was a long time before Pierre could fall asleep that night. He paced up and down his room, now turning his thoughts on a difficult problem and frowning, now suddenly shrugging his shoulders and wincing, and now smiling happily.

He was thinking of Prince Andrew, of Natasha, and of their love, one moment jealous of her past, then reproaching himself for that feeling. It was already six in the morning and he still paced up and down the room.

'Well, what's to be done if it cannot be avoided? What's to be done? Evidently it has to be so,' said he to himself, and hastily undressing he got into bed, happy and agitated but free from hesitation or indecision.

'Strange and impossible as such happiness seems, I must do everything that she and I may be man and wife,' he told himself.

A few days previously Pierre had decided to go to Petersburg on the Friday. When he awoke on the Thursday, Savelich came to ask him about packing for the journey.

'What, to Petersburg? What is Petersburg? Who is there in Petersburg?' he asked involuntarily, though only to himself. 'Oh, yes, long ago, before this happened, I did for some reason mean to go to Petersburg,' he reflected. 'Why? But perhaps I shall go. What a good fellow he is and how attentive, and how he remembers everything,' he thought, looking at Savelich's old face, 'and what a pleasant smile he has!'

'Well, Savelich, do you still not wish to accept your freedom?' Pierre asked him.

'What's the good of freedom to me, your Excellency? We lived under the late count – the Kingdom of Heaven be his! – and we have lived under you too, without ever being wronged.'

'And your children?'

'The children will live just the same. With such masters one can live.'

'But what about my heirs?' said Pierre. 'Supposing I suddenly marry ... it might happen,' he added with an involuntary smile.

'If I may take the liberty, your Excellency, it would be a good thing.'

'How easy he thinks it,' thought Pierre. 'He doesn't know how terrible it is and how dangerous. Too soon or too late ... it is terrible!'

'So what are your orders? Are you starting to-morrow?' asked Savelich.

'No, I'll put it off for a bit. I'll tell you later. You must forgive the trouble I have put you to,' said Pierre, and seeing Savelich smile, he thought: 'But how strange it is that he should not know that now there is no Petersburg for me, and that *that* must be settled first of all! But probably he knows it well enough and is only pretending. Shall I have a talk with him and see what he thinks?' Pierre reflected. 'No, another time.'

At breakfast Pierre told the princess, his cousin, that he had been to see Princess Mary the day before and had there met – 'Whom do you think? Natasha Rostova!'

The princess seemed to see nothing more extraordinary in that than if he had seen Anna Semënovna.

'Do you know her?' asked Pierre.

'I have seen the princess,' she replied. 'I heard that they were arranging a match for her with young Rostov. It would be a very good thing for the Rostovs, they are said to be utterly ruined.'

'No; I mean do you know Natasha Rostova?'

'I heard about that affair of hers at the time. It was a great pity.'

'No, she either doesn't understand or is pretending,' thought Pierre. 'Better not say anything to her either.'

The princess too had prepared provisions for Pierre's journey.

'How kind they all are,' thought Pierre. 'What is surprising is that they should trouble about these things now, when it can no longer be of interest to them. And all for me!'

On the same day the Chief of Police came to Pierre inviting him to send a representative to the Faceted Palace to recover things that were to be returned to their owners that day.

'And this man too,' thought Pierre, looking into the face of the Chief of Police. 'What a fine, good-looking officer, and how kind! Fancy bothering about such trifles *now*! And they actually say he is not honest and takes bribes. What nonsense! Besides, why shouldn't he take bribes? That's the way he was brought up, and everybody does it. But what a kind, pleasant face and how he smiles as he looks at me.'

Pierre went to Princess Mary's to dinner.

As he drove through the streets past the houses that had been burnt down he was surprised by the beauty of those ruins. The picturesqueness of the chimney-stacks and tumble-down walls of the burnt-out quarters of the town, stretching out and concealing one another, reminded him of the Rhine and the Colosseum. The cabmen he met and their passengers, the carpenters cutting the timber for new houses with their axes, the women hawkers, and the shopkeepers, all looked at him with cheerful beaming eyes that seemed to say: 'Ah, there he is! Let's see what will come of it!'

At the entrance to Princess Mary's house Pierre felt doubtful whether he had really been there the night before and had really seen Natasha and talked to her. 'Perhaps I imagined it; perhaps I shall go in and find no one there.' But he had hardly entered the room before he felt her presence with his whole being, by the loss of his sense of freedom. She was in the same black dress with soft folds and her hair was done the same way as the day before, yet she was quite different. Had she been like this when he entered the day before he could not for a moment have failed to recognize her.

She was as he had known her almost as a child, and later on as Prince Andrew's fiancée. A bright questioning light shone in her eyes, and on her face was a friendly and strangely roguish expression.

Pierre dined with them and would have spent the whole evening there, but Princess Mary was going to Vespers and Pierre left the house with her.

Next day he came early, dined, and spent the whole evening there. Though Princess Mary and Natasha were evidently glad to see their visitor and though all Pierre's interest was now centred in that house, by the evening they had talked over everything and the conversation passed from one trivial topic to another and repeatedly broke off. He stayed so long that Princess Mary and Natasha exchanged glances, evidently wondering when he would go. Pierre noticed this, but could not go. He felt uneasy and embarrassed, but sat on because he simply could not get up and take his leave.

Princess Mary, foreseeing no end to this, rose first, and complaining of a headache began to say good-night.

'So you are going to Petersburg to-morrow?' she asked.

'No, I am not going,' Pierre replied hastily, in a surprised tone and as though offended. 'Yes . . . no . . . to Petersburg? To-morrow – but I won't say good-bye yet. I will call round in case you have any commissions for me,' said he, standing before Princess Mary and turning red, but not taking his departure.

Natasha gave him her hand and went out. Princess Mary on the other hand instead of going away sank into an arm-chair and looked sternly and intently at him with her deep, radiant eyes. The weariness she had plainly shown before had now quite passed off. With a deep and long-drawn sigh she seemed to be prepared for a lengthy talk.

When Natasha left the room Pierre's confusion and awkwardness immediately vanished and were replaced by eager excitement. He quickly moved an arm-chair up to Princess Mary.

'Yes, I wanted to tell you,' said he, answering her look as if she had spoken. 'Princess, help me! What am I to do? Can I hope? Princess, my dear friend, listen! I know it all. I know I am not worthy of her, I know it's impossible to speak of it now. But I want to be a brother to her. No, not that, I don't, I can't . . .'

He paused and rubbed his face and eyes with his hands.

'Well,' he went on, with an evident effort at self-control and coherence. 'I don't know when I began to love her, but I have loved her, and her alone, all my life, and I love her so that I cannot imagine life without her. I cannot propose to her at present but the thought that perhaps she might some day be my wife and that I may be missing that possibility . . . that possibility . . . is terrible. Tell me, can I hope? Tell me what I am to do, dear Princess!' he added after a pause, and touched her hand as she did not reply.

'I am thinking of what you have told me,' answered Princess Mary. 'This is what I will say. You are right that to speak to her of love at present . . .'

Princess Mary stopped. She was going to say that to speak of love was impossible, but she stopped because she had seen by

Natasha's sudden change two days before, that she would not only not be hurt if Pierre spoke of his love, but that it was the very thing she wished for.

'To speak to her now wouldn't do,' said the princess all the same.

'But what am I to do?'

'Leave it to me,' said Princess Mary. 'I know ...'

Pierre was looking into Princess Mary's eyes.

'Well? ... Well? ...' he said.

'I know that she loves ... will love you,' Princess Mary corrected herself.

Before her words were out, Pierre had sprung up and with a frightened expression seized Princess Mary's hand.

'What makes you think so? You think I may hope? You think ...?'

'Yes, I think so,' said Princess Mary with a smile. 'Write to her parents, and leave it to me. I will tell her when I can. I wish it to happen, and my heart tells me it will.'

'No, it cannot be! How happy I am! But it can't be ... How happy I am! No, it can't be!' Pierre kept saying as he kissed Princess Mary's hands.

'Go to Petersburg, that will be best. And I will write to you,' she said.

'To Petersburg? Go there? Very well, I'll go. But I may come again to-morrow?'

Next day Pierre came to say good-bye. Natasha was less animated than she had been the day before; but that day as he looked at her Pierre sometimes felt as if he was vanishing and that neither he nor she existed any longer, that nothing existed but happiness. 'Is it possible? No, it can't be,' he told himself at every look, gesture, and word that filled his soul with joy.

When on saying good-bye he took her thin slender hand he could not help holding it a little longer in his own.

'Is it possible that this hand, that face, those eyes, all this treasure of feminine charm so strange to me now, is it possible that it will one day be mine for ever, as familiar to me as I am myself? ... No, that's impossible ... !'

'Good-bye, Count,' she said aloud. 'I shall look forward very much to your return,' she added in a whisper.

And these simple words, her look, and the expression on her face which accompanied them, formed for two months the subject of inexhaustible memories, interpretations, and happy meditations for Pierre. '"I shall look forward very much to your return ..." Yes, yes, how did she say it? Yes, "I shall look forward very much

to your return." Oh, how happy I am! What is happening to me?
How happy I am!' said Pierre to himself.

THERE was nothing in Pierre's soul now at all like what had
troubled it during his courtship of Hélène.

He did not repeat to himself, with a sickening feeling of shame,
the words he had spoken, or say: 'Oh, why did I not say that?'
and, 'whatever made me say "Je vous aime"?' On the contrary, he
now repeated in imagination every word that he or Natasha had
spoken and pictured every detail of her face and smile, and did not
wish to diminish or add anything, but only to repeat it again
and again. There was now not a shadow of doubt in his mind as
to whether what he had undertaken was right or wrong. Only
one terrible doubt sometimes crossed his mind: 'Wasn't it all a
dream? Isn't Princess Mary mistaken? Am I not too conceited and
self-confident? I believe all this; and suddenly Princess Mary will
tell her, and she will be sure to smile and say: "How strange! He
must be deluding himself. Doesn't he know that he is a man, just
a man, while I...? I am something altogether different and
higher."'

That was the only doubt often troubling Pierre. He did not now
make any plans. The happiness before him appeared so inconceivable that if only he could attain it, it would be the end of all
things. Everything ended with it.

A joyful, unexpected frenzy, of which he had thought himself
incapable, possessed him. The whole meaning of life – not for
him alone but for the whole world – seemed to him centred in his
love and the possibility of being loved by her. At times everybody
seemed to him to be occupied with one thing only – his future
happiness. Sometimes it seemed to him that other people were all
as pleased as he was himself, and merely tried to hide that pleasure
by pretending to be busy with other interests. In every word and
gesture he saw allusions to his happiness. He often surprised those
he met by his significantly happy looks and smiles, which seemed
to express a secret understanding between him and them. And
when he realized that people might not be aware of his happiness,
he pitied them with all his heart and felt a desire somehow to
explain to them that all that occupied them was a mere frivolous
trifle unworthy of attention.

When it was suggested to him that he should enter the Civil
Service, or when the war or any general political affairs were dis-

cussed on the assumption that everybody's welfare depended on this or that issue of events, he would listen with a mild and pitying smile, and surprise people by his strange comments. But at this time he saw everybody – both those who as he imagined understood the real meaning of life (that is, what he was feeling) and those unfortunates who evidently did not understand it – in the bright light of the emotion that shone within himself, and at once without any effort saw in everyone he met everything that was good and worthy of being loved.

When dealing with the affairs and papers of his dead wife her memory aroused in him no feeling but pity that she had not known the bliss he now knew. Prince Vasili, who having obtained a new post and some fresh decorations was particularly proud at this time, seemed to him a pathetic, kindly old man, much to be pitied.

Often in after-life Pierre recalled this period of blissful insanity. All the views he formed of men and circumstances at this time remained true for him always. He not only did not renounce them subsequently, but when he was in doubt or inwardly at variance, he appealed to the views he had held at this time of his madness, and they always proved correct.

'I may have appeared strange and queer then,' he thought, 'but I was not so mad as I seemed. On the contrary, I was then wiser and had more insight than at any other time, and understood all that is worth understanding in life, because ... because I was happy.'

Pierre's insanity consisted in not waiting, as he used to do, to discover personal attributes, which he termed 'good qualities', in people before loving them; his heart was now overflowing with love, and by loving people without cause he discovered indubitable causes for loving them.

20

AFTER Pierre's departure that first evening, when Natasha had said to Princess Mary with a gaily mocking smile: 'He looks just, yes, just as if he had come out of a Russian bath – in a short coat and with his hair cropped', something hidden and unknown to herself, but irrepressible, awoke in Natasha's soul.

Everything: her face, walk, look, and voice, was suddenly altered. To her own surprise a power of life and hope of happiness rose to the surface and demanded satisfaction. From that evening she seemed to have forgotten all that had happened to her. She no longer complained of her position, did not say a word about the past, and no longer feared to make happy plans for the future. She spoke little of Pierre, but when Princess Mary mentioned him a long-extinguished light once more kindled in her eyes and her lips curved with a strange smile.

The change that took place in Natasha at first surprised Princess Mary; but when she understood its meaning it grieved her. 'Can she have loved my brother so little as to be able to forget him so soon?' she thought when she reflected on the change. But when she was with Natasha she was not vexed with her and did not reproach her. The reawakened power of life that had seized Natasha was so evidently irrepressible and unexpected by her, that in her presence Princess Mary felt that she had no right to reproach her even in her heart.

Natasha gave herself up so fully and frankly to this new feeling that she did not try to hide the fact that she was no longer sad, but bright and cheerful.

When Princess Mary returned to her room after her nocturnal talk with Pierre, Natasha met her on the threshold.

'He has spoken? Yes? He has spoken?' she repeated.

And a joyful yet pathetic expression, which seemed to beg forgiveness for her joy, settled on Natasha's face.

'I wanted to listen at the door, but I knew you would tell me.'

Understandable and touching as the look with which Natasha gazed at her seemed to Princess Mary, and sorry as she was to see her agitation, these words pained her for a moment. She remembered her brother and his love.

'But what's to be done? She can't help it,' thought the princess.

And with a sad and rather stern look she told Natasha all that Pierre had said. On hearing that he was going to Petersburg Natasha was astounded.

'To Petersburg!' she repeated as if unable to understand.

But noticing the grieved expression on Princess Mary's face, she guessed the reason of that sadness and suddenly began to cry.

'Mary,' said she, 'tell me what I should do! I am afraid of being bad. Whatever you tell me, I will do. Tell me . . .'

'You love him?'

'Yes,' whispered Natasha.

'Then why are you crying? I am happy for your sake,' said Princess Mary, who because of those tears quite forgave Natasha's joy.

'It won't be just yet – some day. Think what fun it will be when I am his wife and you marry Nicholas!'

'Natasha, I have asked you not to speak of that. Let us talk about you.'

They were silent awhile.

'But why go to Petersburg?' Natasha suddenly asked, and hastily replied to her own question. 'But no, no, he must ... Yes, Mary. He must ...'

END OF BOOK FOUR

WAR AND PEACE

*

FIRST EPILOGUE

FIRST EPILOGUE

1

SEVEN years had passed. The storm-tossed sea of European history had subsided within its shores and seemed to have become calm. But the mysterious forces that move humanity (mysterious because the laws of their motion are unknown to us) continued to operate.

Though the surface of the sea of history seemed motionless the movement of humanity went on as unceasingly as the flow of time. Various groups of people formed and dissolved, the coming formation and dissolution of kingdoms and displacement of peoples was in course of preparation.

The sea of history was not driven spasmodically from shore to shore as previously. It was seething in its depths. Historic figures were not borne by the waves from one shore to another as before. They now seemed to rotate on one spot. The historical figures at the head of armies, who formerly reflected the movement of the masses by ordering wars, campaigns, and battles, now reflected the restless movement by political and diplomatic combinations, laws and treaties.

The historians call this activity of the historical figures 'the reaction'.

In dealing with this period they sternly condemn the historical personages who, in their opinion, caused what they describe as *the reaction*. All the well-known people of that period, from Alexander and Napoleon to Madame de Staël, Photius, Schelling, Fichte, Chateaubriand,* and the rest, pass before their stern judgement seat and are acquitted or condemned according to whether they conduced to *progress* or to *reaction*.

According to their accounts, a reaction took place at that time in Russia also, and the chief culprit was Alexander I, the same man who, according to them, was the chief cause of the Liberal movement at the commencement of his reign, as well as of saving Russia.

There is no one in Russian literature now, from school-boy essayist to learned historian, who does not throw his little stone at Alexander for things he did wrong at this period of his reign.

'He ought to have acted in this way and in that way. In this case he did well and in that case badly. He behaved admirably at the beginning of his reign and during 1812, but acted badly by giving a constitution to Poland,* forming the Holy Alliance,* entrusting power to Arakcheev, favouring Golitsyn* and mysticism, and afterwards Shishkov and Photius. He also acted badly by concerning himself with the active army and disbanding the Semënov regiment.'*

It would take a dozen pages to enumerate all the reproaches the historians address to him, based on their knowledge of what is good for humanity.

What do these reproaches mean?

Do not the very actions for which the historians praise Alexander I (the liberal attempts at the beginning of his reign, his struggle with Napoleon, the firmness he displayed in 1812 and the campaign of 1813) flow from the same sources: the circumstances of his birth, education, and life, that made his personality what it was and from which the actions for which they blame him (the Holy Alliance, the restoration of Poland, and the reaction of 1820 and later) also flowed?

In what does the substance of those reproaches lie?

It lies in the fact that an historic character like Alexander I, standing on the highest possible pinnacle of human power with the blinding light of history focused upon him – a character exposed to those strongest of all influences, the intrigues, flattery and self-deception inseparable from power – a character who at every movement of his life felt a responsibility for all that was happening in Europe; and not a fictitious but a live character, who like every man had his personal habits, passions, and impulses towards goodness, beauty and truth; that this character – though not lacking in virtue (the historians do not accuse him of that) — had not the same conception of the welfare of humanity fifty years ago as a present-day professor who from his youth upwards has been occupied with learning – that is with books and lectures and with taking notes from them.

But even if we assume that fifty years ago Alexander I was mistaken in his view of what was good for the people, we must inevitably assume that the historian who judges Alexander will also, after the lapse of some time, turn out to be mistaken in his view of what is good for humanity. This assumption is all the more natural and inevitable because, watching the movement of history, we see that every year, and with each new writer, opinion as to what is good for mankind changes; so that what once seemed good, ten years later seems bad, and vice versa. And what is more, we find at one and the same time quite contradictory views as to what is bad and what is good in history: some people regard giving a constitution to Poland and forming the Holy Alliance as praiseworthy in Alexander, while others regard it as blameworthy.

The activity of Alexander or of Napoleon cannot be called useful or harmful, for it is impossible to say for what it was useful or harmful. If that activity displeases somebody, this is only because it does not agree with his limited understanding of what is good. Whether the preservation of my father's house in Moscow, or the glory of the Russian arms, or the prosperity of the Petersburg and other universities, or the freedom of Poland, or the greatness of Russia, or the balance of power in Europe, or a certain kind of European culture called 'progress', appear to me to be good or bad, I must admit that, besides these things, the action of every historic character has other more general purposes inaccessible to me.

But let us assume that what is called science can harmonize all contradictions and possesses an unchanging standard of good and bad by which to try historic characters and events: let us say that Alexander could have done everything differently, let us say that – by guidance from those who blame him and who profess to know the ultimate aim of the movement of humanity – he might have arranged matters according to the programme his present accusers would have given him – of nationality, freedom, equality, and progress (these I think cover the ground). Let us assume that this programme was possible and had then been formulated, and that Alexander had acted on it. What would then have become of the activity of all those who opposed the tendency that then prevailed in the Government – the activity that in the opinion of the historians was good and beneficent? Their activity would not have existed: there would have been no life, there would have been nothing.

If we admit that human life can be ruled by reason, the possibility of life is destroyed.

2

IF we assume, as the historians do, that great men lead humanity to the attainment of certain ends – the greatness of Russia or of France, the balance of power in Europe, the diffusion of the ideas of the Revolution, general progress, or anything else – then it is impossible to explain the facts of history without introducing the conceptions of *chance* and *genius*.

If the aim of the European wars at the beginning of the nineteenth century had been the aggrandizement of Russia, that aim might have been accomplished without all the preceding wars, and without the invasion. If the aim was the aggrandizement of France, that might have been attained without the Revolution and without the Empire. If the aim was the dissemination of ideas, the printing-press could have accomplished that much better than warfare. If the aim was the progress of civilization, it is easy to see that there are other ways of diffusing civilization more expedient than by the destruction of wealth and of human lives.

Why did it happen in this and not in some other way?

Because it happened so! 'Chance created the situation; genius utilized it,' says history.

But what is chance? What is genius?

The words chance and genius do not denote any really existing thing and therefore cannot be defined. Those words only denote a certain stage of understanding of phenomena. I do not know why a certain event occurs; I think that I cannot know it; so I do not try to know it and I talk about chance. I see a force producing effects beyond the scope of ordinary human agencies; I do not understand why this occurs and I talk of genius.

To a herd of rams, the ram the herdsman drives each evening into a special enclosure to feed, and that becomes twice as fat as the others, must seem to be a genius. And it must appear an astonishing conjunction of genius with a whole series of extraordinary chances that this ram, who instead of getting into the general fold every evening gets into a special enclosure where there are oats – this very ram, swelling with fat, is killed for meat.

But the rams need only cease to suppose that all that happens to them happens solely for the attainment of their sheepish aims, they need only admit that what happens to them may also have purposes beyond their ken, and they will at once perceive a unity and coherence in what happened to the ram that was fattened. Even if they do not know for what purpose they are fattened, they will at least know that all that happened to the ram did not happen accidentally, and will no longer need the conceptions of chance or genius.

Only by renouncing our claim to discern a purpose immediately intelligible to us, and admitting the ultimate purpose to be beyond our ken, may we discern the sequence of experiences in the lives of historic characters, and perceive the cause of the effect they produce (incommensurable with ordinary human capabilities) and then the words chance and genius become superfluous.

We need only confess that we do not know the purpose of the

European convulsions and that we know only the facts – that is the murders, first in France, then in Italy, in Africa, in Prussia, in Austria, in Spain, and in Russia – and that the movements from the west to the east and from the east to the west form the essence and purpose of these events, and not only shall we have no need to see exceptional ability and genius in Napoleon and Alexander, but we shall be unable to consider them to be anything but men like other men, and we shall not be obliged to have recourse to *chance* for an explanation of those small events which made these people what they were, but it will be clear that all those small events were inevitable.

By discarding a claim to knowledge of the ultimate purpose, we shall clearly perceive that just as one cannot imagine a blossom or seed for any single plant better suited to it than those it produces, so it is impossible to imagine any two people more completely adapted down to the smallest detail for the purpose they had to fulfil than Napoleon and Alexander with all their antecedents.

3

THE fundamental and essential significance of the European events of the beginning of the nineteenth century lies in the movement of the mass of the European peoples from west to east and afterwards from east to west. The commencement of that movement was the movement from west to east. For the peoples of the west to be able to make their warlike movement to Moscow it was necessary, (1) that they should form themselves into a military group of a size able to endure a collision with the warlike military group of the east, (2) that they should abandon all established traditions and customs, and (3) that during their military movement they should have at their head a man who could justify to himself and to them the deceptions, robberies, and murders which would have to be committed during that movement.

And beginning with the French Revolution the old inadequately large group was destroyed, as well as the old habits and traditions, and step by step a group was formed of larger dimensions with new customs and traditions, and a man was produced who would stand at the head of the coming movement and bear the responsibility for all that had to be done.

A man without convictions, without habits, without traditions, without a name, and not even a Frenchman, emerges – by what seem the strangest chances – from among all the seething French parties, and, without joining any one of them, is borne forward to a prominent position.

The ignorance of his colleagues, the weakness and insignificance of his opponents, the frankness of his falsehoods and the dazzling and self-confident limitations of this man, raise him to the head of the army. The brilliant qualities of the soldiers of the army sent to Italy, his opponents' reluctance to fight, and his own childish audacity and self-confidence, secure him military fame. Innumerable so-called *chances* accompany him everywhere. The disfavour into which he falls* with the rulers of France turns to his advantage. His attempts to avoid his predestined path are unsuccessful: he is not received into the Russian service, and the appointment he seeks in Turkey comes to nothing.* During the war in Italy he is several times on the verge of destruction and each time is saved in an unexpected manner. Owing to various diplomatic considerations the Russian armies – just those which might have destroyed his prestige – do not appear upon the scene till he is no longer there.*

On his return from Italy he finds the Government in Paris in a process of dissolution in which all those who are in it are inevitably wiped out and destroyed. And by chance an escape from this dangerous position presents itself in the form of an aimless and senseless expedition to Africa. Again so-called *chance* accompanies him. Impregnable Malta surrenders without a shot; his most reckless schemes are crowned with success. The enemy's fleet, which subsequently did not let a single boat pass, allows his entire army to elude it. In Africa a whole series of outrages are committed against the almost unarmed inhabitants. And the men who commit these crimes, especially their leader, assure themselves that this is admirable, this is glory – it resembles Caesar and Alexander the Great, and is therefore good.

This ideal of *glory* and *grandeur* – which consists not merely in considering nothing wrong that one does, but in priding oneself on every crime one commits, ascribing to it an incomprehensible supernatural significance – that ideal, destined to guide this man and his associates, had scope for its development in Africa. Whatever he does succeeds. The plague does not touch him. The cruelty of murdering prisoners is not imputed to him as a fault. His childishly rash, uncalled-for and ignoble departure from Africa, leaving his comrades in distress, is set down to his credit, and again the enemy's fleet twice lets him slip past. When, intoxicated by the crimes he has committed so successfully, he reaches Paris, the dissolution of the Republican government, which a year earlier might have ruined him, has reached its extreme limit, and his presence there now, as a newcomer free from party entanglements, can only serve to exalt him – and though he himself has no plan, he is quite ready for his new role.

He had no plan, he was afraid of everything, but the parties snatched at him and demanded his participation.

He alone – with his ideal of glory and grandeur developed in Italy and Egypt, his insane self-adulation, his boldness in crime and frankness in lying – he alone could justify what had to be done.

He is needed for the place that awaits him, and so, almost apart from his will, and despite his indecision, his lack of a plan, and all his mistakes, he is drawn into a conspiracy that aims at seizing power, and the conspiracy is crowned with success.

He is pushed into a meeting of the legislature. In alarm he wishes to flee, considering himself lost. He pretends to fall into a swoon, and says senseless things that should have ruined him. But the once proud and shrewd rulers of France, feeling that their part is played out, are now even more bewildered than he, and do not say the words they should have said to destroy him and retain their power.

Chance, millions of *chances*, give him power, and all men, as if by agreement, cooperate to confirm that power. *Chance* forms the characters of the rulers of France, who submit to him; *chance* forms the character of Paul I of Russia who recognizes his government; *chance* contrives a plot against him which not only fails to harm him but confirms his power.* *Chance* puts the Duc d'Enghien in his hands, and unexpectedly causes him to kill him – thereby convincing the mob more forcibly than in any other way that he had the right, since he had the might. *Chance* contrives that though he directs all his efforts to prepare an expedition against England (which would inevitably have ruined him) he never carries out that intention, but unexpectedly falls upon Mack and the Austrians, who surrender without a battle. *Chance* and *genius* give him the victory at Austerlitz; and by *chance* all men, not only the French but all Europe – except England, which does not take part in the events about to happen – despite their former horror and detestation of his crimes, now recognize his authority, the title he has given himself, and his ideal of grandeur and glory, which seems excellent and reasonable to them all.

As if measuring themselves and preparing for the coming movement, the western forces push towards the east several times in 1805, 1806, 1807, and 1809, gaining strength and growing. In 1811 the group of people that had formed in France unites into one great group with the peoples of Central Europe. The strength of the justification of the man who stands at the head of the movement grows with the increased size of the group. During the ten-year preparatory period this man had formed relations with all the crowned heads of Europe. The discredited rulers of the world can oppose no reasonable ideal to the insensate Napoleonic ideal of *glory* and *grandeur*. One after another they hasten to display their insignificance before him. The King of Prussia sends his wife to seek the great man's mercy; the Emperor of Austria considers it a favour that this man receives a daughter of the Caesars into his bed; the Pope, the guardian of all that the nations hold sacred, utilizes religion for the aggrandizement of the great man. It is not Napoleon who prepares himself for the accomplishment of his role, so much as all those round him who prepare him to take on himself the whole responsibility for what is happening and has to happen. There is no step, no crime or petty fraud he commits, which in the mouths of those around him is not at once represented as a great deed. The most suitable fête the Germans can devise for him is a celebration of Jena and Auerstädt. Not only is he great, but so are his ancestors, his brothers, his stepsons, and his brothers-in-law. Everything is done to deprive him of the remains of his reason and to prepare him for his terrible part. And when he is ready so are the forces.

The invasion pushes eastwards and reaches its final goal – Moscow. That city is taken; the Russian army suffers heavier losses than the opposing armies had suffered in the former wars from Austerlitz to Wagram. But suddenly instead of those *chances* and that *genius* which had so consistently led him hitherto by an uninterrupted series of successes to the predestined goal, an innumerable sequence of inverse *chances* occur – from the cold in his head at Borodino to the sparks which set Moscow on fire, and the frosts – and instead of *genius*, stupidity and immeasurable baseness becomes evident.

The invaders flee, turn back, flee again, and all the chances are now not for Napoleon but always against him.

A counter-movement is then accomplished from east to west with a remarkable resemblance to the preceding movement from west to east. Attempted drives from east to west – similar to the contrary movements of 1805, 1807, and 1809 – precede the great westward movement; there is the same coalescence into a group of enormous dimensions; the same adhesion of the people of Central Europe to the movement; the same hesitation midway, and the same increasing rapidity as the goal is approached.

Paris, the ultimate goal, is reached. The Napoleonic government and army are destroyed. Napoleon himself is no longer of any account; all his actions are evidently pitiful and mean, but again an inexplicable *chance* occurs. The allies detest Napoleon whom they regard as the cause of their sufferings. Deprived of power and authority, his crimes and his craft exposed, he should have appeared to them what he appeared ten years previously and one year later – an outlawed brigand. But by some strange chance no one perceives this. His part is not yet ended. The man who ten years before and a year later was considered an outlawed brigand is sent to an island two days' sail from France, which for some reason is presented to him as his dominion, and guards are given to him and millions are paid him.

4

THE flood of nations begins to subside into its normal channels. The waves of the great movement abate, and on the calm surface eddies are formed in which float the diplomatists who imagine that they have caused the floods to abate.

But the smooth sea again suddenly becomes disturbed. The diplomatists think that their disagreements are the cause of this fresh pressure of natural forces; they anticipate war between their sovereigns; the position seems to them insoluble. But the wave they feel to be rising does not come from the quarter they expect. It rises again from the same point as before – Paris. The last backwash of the movement from the west occurs: a backwash which serves to solve the apparently insuperable diplomatic difficulties and ends the military movement of that period of history.

The man who had devastated France returns to France alone, without any conspiracy and without soldiers. Any guard might arrest him; but by a strange chance no one does so, and all rapturously greet the man they cursed the day before and will curse again a month later.

This man is still needed to justify the final collective act.

That act is performed.

The last role is played. The actor is bidden to disrobe and wash off his powder and paint: he will not be wanted any more.

And some years pass during which he plays a pitiful comedy to himself in solitude on his island, justifying his actions by intrigues and lies when the justification is no longer needed, and displaying to the whole world what it was that people had mistaken for strength as long as an unseen hand directed his actions.

The manager, having brought the drama to a close and stripped the actor, shows him to us.

'See what you believed in! This is he! Do you now see that it was not he, but I, who moved you?'

But dazed by the force of the movement, it was long before people understood this.

Still greater coherence and inevitability is seen in the life of Alexander I, the man who stood at the head of the counter-movement from east to west.

What was needed for him, who overshadowing others stood at the head of that movement from east to west?

What was needed was a sense of justice and a sympathy with European affairs, but a remote sympathy not dulled by petty interests; a moral superiority over those sovereigns of the day who cooperated with him; a mild and attractive personality; and a personal grievance against Napoleon. And all this was found in Alexander I; all this had been prepared by innumerable so-called *chances* in his life: his education, his early liberalism, the advisers who surrounded him, and by Austerlitz, and Tilsit, and Erfurt.

During the national war he was inactive because he was not needed. But as soon as the necessity for a general European war presented itself, he appeared in his place at the given moment and, uniting the nations of Europe, led them to the goal.

The goal is reached. After the final war of 1815 Alexander possesses all possible power. How does he use it?

Alexander I – the pacifier of Europe, the man who from his early years had striven only for his people's welfare, the originator of the liberal innovations in his fatherland – now that he seemed to possess the utmost power and therefore to have the possibility of bringing about the welfare of his peoples – at the time when Napoleon in exile was drawing up childish and mendacious plans of how he would have made mankind happy had he retained power – Alexander I, having fulfilled his mission and feeling the hand of God upon him, suddenly recognizes the insignificance of that supposed power, turns away from it, and gives it into the hands of contemptible men whom he despises, saying only:

'Not unto us, not unto us, but unto Thy Name!* ... I too am a man like the rest of you. Let me live like a man, and think of my soul and of God.'*

As the sun and each atom of ether is a sphere complete in itself, and yet at the same time only a part of a whole too immense for man to comprehend, so each individual bears within himself his own aims and yet bears them to serve a general purpose incomprehensible to man.

A bee settling on a flower has stung a child. And the child is afraid of bees and declares that bees exist to sting people. A poet admires the bee sucking from the chalice of a flower, and says it exists to suck the fragrance of flowers. A beekeeper, seeing the bee collect pollen from flowers and carry it to the hive, says that it exists to gather honey. Another beekeeper who has studied the life of the hive more closely, says that the bee gathers pollen-dust to feed the young bees and rear a queen, and that it exists to perpetuate its race. A botanist notices that the bee flying with the pollen of a male flower to a pistil fertilizes the latter, and sees in this the purpose of the bee's existence. Another, observing the migration of plants, notices that the bee helps in this work, and may say that in this lies the purpose of the bee. But the ultimate purpose of the bee is not exhausted by the first, the second, or any of the processes the human mind can discern. The higher the human intellect rises in the discovery of these purposes, the more obvious it becomes that the ultimate purpose is beyond our comprehension.

All that is accessible to man is the relation of the life of the bee to other manifestations of life. And so it is with the purpose of historic characters and nations.

5

NATASHA'S wedding to Bezukhov, which took place in 1813, was the last happy event in the family of the old Rostovs. Count Ilya Rostov died that same year, and as always happens, after the father's death the family group broke up.

The events of the previous year: the burning of Moscow and the flight from it, the death of Prince Andrew, Natasha's despair, Petya's death, and the old countess's grief, fell blow after blow on the old count's head. He seemed to be unable to understand the meaning of all these events, and bowed his old head in a spiritual sense as if expecting and inviting further blows which would finish him. He seemed now frightened and distraught and now unnaturally animated and enterprising.

The arrangements for Natasha's marriage occupied him for a while. He ordered dinners and suppers and obviously tried to appear cheerful; but his cheerfulness was not infectious as it used to be, on the contrary it evoked the compassion of those who knew and liked him.

When Pierre and his wife had left he grew very quiet and began to complain of depression. A few days later he fell ill and took to his bed. He realized from the first that he would not get up again, despite the doctor's encouragement. The countess passed a fortnight in an arm-chair by his pillow, without undressing. Every time she gave him his medicine he sobbed, and silently kissed her hand. On his last day, sobbing, he asked her and his absent son to forgive him for having dissipated their property – that being the chief fault of which he was conscious. After receiving communion and unction he quietly died, and next day a throng of acquaintances, who had so often dined and danced at his house and had so often laughed at him, now said, with a common feeling of self-reproach and emotion, as if justifying themselves: 'Well, whatever he may have been he was a most worthy man. You don't meet such men nowadays...And which of us has not weaknesses of his own?'

It was just when the count's affairs had become so involved that it was impossible to say what would happen if he lived another year, that he unexpectedly died.

Nicholas was with the Russian army in Paris when the news of his father's death reached him. He at once resigned his commission, and without waiting for it to be accepted, took leave of absence and went to Moscow. The state of the count's affairs became quite obvious a month after his death, surprising everyone by the immense total of the small debts the existence of which no one had suspected. The debts amounted to double the value of the property.

Friends and relations advised Nicholas to decline the inheritance. But he regarded such a refusal as a slur on his father's memory, which he held sacred, and therefore would not hear of refusing, and accepted the inheritance together with the obligation to pay the debts.

The creditors who, restrained by a vague but powerful influence exerted on them while he lived by the count's careless good nature, had so long been silent, all proceeded to enforce their claims at once. As always happens in such cases rivalry sprang up as to which should get paid first, and those who, like Mitenka, held promissory notes given them as presents, now became the most exacting creditors. Nicholas was allowed no respite and no peace, and those who had seemed to pity the old man – the cause of their losses (if they were losses) – now remorselessly pursued the young heir who had voluntarily undertaken the debts and was obviously not guilty of contracting them.

Not one of the plans Nicholas tried succeeded; the estate was sold by auction for half its value, and half the debts still remained unpaid. Nicholas accepted thirty thousand rubles offered him by his brother-in-law Bezukhov to pay off debts he regarded as genuinely due for value received. And to avoid being imprisoned for the remainder, as the creditors threatened, he re-entered the government service.

He could not rejoin the army, where he would have been made colonel at the next vacancy, for his mother now clung to him as her one hold on life; and so, despite his reluctance to remain in Moscow among people who had known him before, and despite his abhorrence of the civil service, he accepted a post in Moscow in that service, doffed the uniform of which he was so fond, and moved with his mother and Sonya to a small house on the Sivtsev Vrazhëk.

Natasha and Pierre were living in Petersburg at the time and had no clear idea of Nicholas's circumstances. Having borrowed money from his brother-in-law, Nicholas tried to hide his wretched condition from him. His position was the more difficult because with his salary of twelve hundred rubles he had not only to keep himself, his mother, and Sonya, but had to shield his mother from knowledge of their poverty. The countess could not conceive of life without the luxurious conditions she had been used to from child-hood and, unable to realize how hard it was for her son, kept demanding now a carriage (which they did not keep) to send for a friend, now some expensive article of food for herself, or wine for her son, or money to buy a present as a surprise for Natasha, or Sonya, or for Nicholas himself.

Sonya kept house, attended on her aunt, read to her, put up with her whims and secret ill-will, and helped Nicholas to conceal their poverty from the old countess. Nicholas felt himself irredeem-ably indebted to Sonya for all she was doing for his mother, and greatly admired her patience and devotion, but tried to keep aloof from her.

He seemed in his heart to reproach her for being too perfect, and because there was nothing to reproach her with. She had all that people are valued for, but little that could have made him love her. He felt that the more he valued her the less he loved her. He had taken her at her word when she wrote giving him his freedom, and now behaved as if all that had passed between them had been long forgotten and could never in any case be renewed.

Nicholas's position became worse and worse. The idea of putting something aside out of his salary proved a dream. Not only did he not save anything, but to comply with his mother's demands he even incurred some small debts. He could see no way out of this situation. The idea of marrying some rich woman, which was suggested to him by his female relations, was repugnant to him. The other way out – his mother's death – never entered his head. He wished for nothing and hoped for nothing, and deep in his heart experienced a gloomy and stern satisfaction in an uncomplaining endurance of his position. He tried to avoid his old acquaintances, with their commiseration and offensive offers of assistance; he avoided all distraction and recreation, and even at home did nothing but play cards with his mother, pace silently up and down the room, and smoke one pipe after another. He seemed carefully to cherish within himself the gloomy mood which alone enabled him to endure his position.

6

AT the beginning of winter Princess Mary came to Moscow. From reports current in town she learnt how the Rostovs were situated, and how 'the son has sacrificed himself for his mother', as people were saying.

'I never expected anything else of him,' said Princess Mary to herself, feeling a joyous sense of her love for him. Remembering her friendly relations with all the Rostovs, which had made her almost a member of the family, see thought it her duty to go to see them. But remembering her relations with Nicholas in Voronezh she was timid about doing so. Making a great effort she did however go to call on them a few weeks after her arrival in Moscow.

Nicholas was the first to meet her, as the countess's room could only be reached through his. But instead of being greeted with pleasure as she had expected, at his first glance at her his face assumed a cold, stiff, and proud expression she had not seen on it before. He inquired about her health, led the way to his mother, and having sat there for five minutes left the room.

When the princess came out of the countess's room Nicholas met her again, and with marked solemnity and stiffness accompanied her to the ante-room. To her remarks about his mother's health he made no reply. 'What's that to you? Leave me in peace,' his looks seemed to say.

'Why does she come prowling here? What does she want? I can't bear these ladies and all these civilities!' said he aloud in Sonya's presence, evidently unable to repress his vexation, after the princess's carriage had disappeared.

'Oh Nicholas, how can you talk like that?' cried Sonya, hardly able to conceal her delight. 'She is so kind, and mamma is so fond of her!'

Nicholas did not reply, and tried to avoid speaking of the princess any more. But after her visit the old countess spoke of her several times a day.

She sang her praises, insisted that her son must call on her, expressed a wish to see her often, yet always became ill-humoured when she began to talk about her.

Nicholas tried to keep silence when his mother spoke of the princess, but his silence irritated her.

'She is a very admirable and excellent young woman,' said she, 'and you must go and call on her. You would at least be seeing somebody; and I think it must be dull for you only seeing us.'

'But I don't in the least want to, mamma.'

'You used to want to, and now you don't. Really I don't understand you, my dear. One day you are dull and the next you refuse to see anyone.'

'But I never said I was dull.'

'Why, you said yourself you don't want even to see her. She is a very admirable young woman and you always liked her, but now suddenly you have got some notion or other in your head. You hide everything from me.'

'Not at all, mamma.'

'If I were asking you to do something disagreeable now – but I only ask you to return a call. One would think mere politeness required it . . . Well, I have asked you, and now I won't interfere any more since you have secrets from your mother.'

'Well then, I'll go if you wish it.'

'It doesn't matter to me. I only wish it for your sake.'

Nicholas sighed, bit his moustache, and laid out the cards for patience, trying to divert his mother's attention to another topic.

The same conversation was repeated next day, and the day after, and the day after that.

After her visit to the Rostovs and her unexpectedly chilly reception by Nicholas, Princess Mary confessed to herself that she had been right in not wishing to be the first to call.

'I expected nothing else,' she told herself, calling up her pride to her aid. 'I have nothing to do with him and I only wanted to see the old lady, who was always kind to me and to whom I am under many obligations.'

But she could not pacify herself with these reflections: a feeling akin to remorse troubled her when she thought of her visit. Though she had firmly resolved not to call on the Rostovs again and to forget the whole matter, she felt herself all the time in an awkward position. And when she asked herself what distressed her, she had to admit that it was her relation to Rostov. His cold polite manner did not express his feeling for her (she knew that) but it concealed something, and until she could discover what that something was, she could not, she felt, be at ease.

One day in midwinter, when sitting in the schoolroom attending to her nephew's lessons, she was informed that Rostov had called. With a firm resolution not to betray herself and not show her agitation, she sent for Mademoiselle Bourienne and went with her to the drawing-room.

Her first glance at Nicholas's face told her that he had only come to fulfil the demands of politeness, and she firmly resolved to maintain the tone in which he addressed her.

They spoke of the countess's health, of their mutual friends, of the latest war news, and when the ten minutes required by propriety had elapsed, after which a visitor may rise, Nicholas got up to say good-bye.

With Mademoiselle Bourienne's help the princess had maintained the conversation very well, but at the very last moment, just when he rose, she was so tired of talking of what did not interest her and her mind was so full of the question why she alone was granted so little happiness in life, that in a fit of absent-mindedness she sat still, her luminous eyes gazing fixedly before her, not noticing that he had risen.

Nicholas glanced at her and, wishing to appear not to notice her abstraction, made some remark to Mademoiselle Bourienne and then again looked at the princess. She still sat motionless with a look of suffering on her gentle face. He suddenly felt sorry for her, and was vaguely conscious that he might be the cause of the sadness her face expressed. He wished to help her and say something pleasant to her, but could think of nothing to say.

'Good-bye, Princess!' he said.

She started, flushed, and sighed deeply.

'Oh, I beg your pardon,' she said, as if waking up. 'Are you going already, Count? Well then, good-bye! Oh, but the cushion for the countess!'

'Wait a moment, I'll fetch it,' said Mademoiselle Bourienne, and she left the room.

They both sat silent, with an occasional glance at one another.

'Yes, Princess,' said Nicholas at last, with a sad smile, 'it doesn't seem long ago since we first met at Bogucharovo, but how much water has flowed since then! In what distress we all seemed to be then, yet I would give much to bring back that time . . . but there's no bringing it back.'

Princess Mary gazed intently into his eyes with her own luminous ones as he said this. She seemed to be trying to fathom the hidden meaning of his words which would explain his feeling for her.

'Yes, yes,' said she, 'but you have no reason to regret the past, Count. As I understand your present life, I think you will always recall it with satisfaction, because the self-sacrifice that fills it now . . .'

'I cannot accept your praise,' he interrupted her hurriedly. 'On the contrary I continually reproach myself . . . But this is not at all an interesting or cheerful subject.'

His face again resumed its former stiff and cold expression. But the princess had caught a glimpse of the man she had known and loved, and it was to him that she now spoke.

'I thought you would allow me to tell you this,' she said. 'I had come so near to you . . . and to all your family, that I thought you would not consider my sympathy misplaced, but I was mistaken,' and suddenly her voice trembled. 'I don't know why,' she continued, recovering herself, 'but you used to be different, and . . .'

'There are a thousand reasons *why*,' – he laid special emphasis on the *why*. 'Thank you, Princess,' he added softly. 'Sometimes it is hard.'

'So that's why! That's why!' a voice whispered in Princess Mary's soul. 'No, it was not only that gay, kind, and frank look, not only that handsome exterior, that I loved in him. I divined his noble, resolute, self-sacrificing spirit too,' she said to herself. 'Yes, he is poor now and I am rich . . . Yes, that's the only reason . . . Yes, were it not for that . . .' And remembering his former tenderness, and looking now at his kind sorrowful face, she suddenly understood the cause of his coldness.

'But why, Count, why?' she almost cried, unconsciously moving closer to him. 'Why? Tell me. You must tell me!'

He was silent.

'I don't understand your *why*, Count,' she continued, 'but it's hard for me . . . I confess it. For some reason you wish to deprive me öf our former friendship. And that hurts me.' There were tears in her eyes and in her voice. 'I have had so little happiness in life that every loss is hard for me to bear . . . Excuse me, good-bye!' and suddenly she began to cry and was hurrying from the room.

'Princess, for God's sake!' he exclaimed, trying to stop her. 'Princess!'

She turned round. For a few seconds they gazed silently into one another's eyes – and what had seemed impossible and remote suddenly became possible, inevitable, and very near.

7

IN the winter of 1813 Nicholas married Princess Mary and moved to Bald Hills with his wife, his mother, and Sonya.

Within four years he had paid off all his remaining debts without selling any of his wife's property, and having received a small inheritance on the death of a cousin he paid his debt to Pierre as well.

In another three years, by 1820, he had so managed his affairs that he was able to buy a small estate adjoining Bald Hills, and was negotiating to buy back Otradnoe – that being his pet dream.

Having started farming from necessity, he soon grew so devoted to it that it became his favourite and almost his sole occupation. Nicholas was a plain farmer: he did not like innovations, especially the English ones then coming into vogue. He laughed at theoretical treatises on estate management, disliked factories, the raising of expensive products and the buying of expensive seed corn, and did not make a hobby of any particular part of the work on his estate. He always had before his mind's eye *the estate* as a whole, and not any particular part of it. The chief thing in his eyes was not the nitrogen in the soil, or the oxygen in the air, nor manures, or special ploughs, but that most important agent by which nitrogen, oxygen, manure, and plough were made effective – the peasant labourer. When Nicholas first began farming and began to understand its different branches, it was the serf who especially attracted his attention. The peasant seemed to him not merely a tool, but also a judge of farming and an end in himself. At first he watched the serfs, trying to understand their aims and what they considered good and bad, and only pretended to direct them and give orders while in reality learning from them their methods, their manner of speech, and their judgement of what was good and bad. Only when he had understood the peasants' tastes and aspirations, had learnt to talk their language, to grasp the hidden meaning of their words, and felt akin to them, did he begin boldly to manage his serfs, that is, to perform towards them the duties demanded of him. And Nicholas's management produced very brilliant results.

Guided by some gift of insight, on taking up the management of the estates he at once unerringly appointed as bailiff, village Elder, and delegate the very men the serfs would themselves have chosen had they had the right to choose, and these posts never changed hands. Before analysing the properties of manure, before entering into the *debit* and *credit* (as he ironically called it), he found out how many cattle the peasants had, and increased the number by all possible means. He kept the peasant families together in the largest groups possible, not allowing the family groups to divide into separate households. He was hard alike on the lazy, the depraved, and the weak, and tried to get them expelled from the Commune.

He was as careful of the sowing and reaping of the peasants' hay and corn as of his own, and few landowners had their crops sown and harvested so early and so well, or got so good a return, as Nicholas.

He disliked having anything to do with the domestic serfs – the 'drones' as he called them – and everyone said he spoilt them by his laxity. When a decision had to be taken regarding a domestic serf, especially if one had to be punished, he always felt undecided and consulted everybody in the house; but when it was possible to have a domestic serf conscripted instead of a land worker he did so without the least hesitation. He never felt any hesitation in dealing with the peasants. He knew that his every decision would be approved by all of them with very few exceptions.

He did not allow himself either to be hard on or punish a man, or to make things easy for or reward anyone, merely because he felt inclined to do so. He could not have said by what standard he judged what he should or should not do, but the standard was quite firm and definite in his own mind.

Often, speaking with vexation of some failure or irregularity, he would say: 'What can one do with our Russian peasants?' and imagined that he could not bear them.

Yet he loved 'our Russian peasants' and their way of life with his whole soul, and for that very reason had understood and assimilated the one way and manner of farming which produced good results.

Countess Mary was jealous of this passion of her husband's and regretted that she could not share it; but she could not understand the joys and vexations he derived from that world, to her so remote and alien. She could not understand why he was so particularly animated and happy when, after getting up at day-break and spending the whole morning in the fields or on the threshing-floor, he returned from the sowing, or mowing, or reaping to have tea with her. She did not understand why he spoke with such admiration and delight of the farming of the thrifty and well-to-do peasant Matthew Ermishin, who with his family had carted corn all night; or of the fact that his (Nicholas's) sheaves were already stacked before anyone else had his harvest in. She did not understand why he stepped out from the window to the verandah and smiled under his moustache and winked so joy-fully when warm steady rain began to fall on the dry and thirsty shoots of the young oats, or why, when the wind carried away a threatening cloud during the hay harvest, he would return from the barn, flushed, sunburnt and perspiring, with a smell of worm-wood and gentian in his hair and, gleefully rubbing his hands, would say: 'Well, one more day and my grain and the peasants' will all be under cover.'

Still less did she understand why he, kind-hearted and always ready to anticipate her wishes, should become almost desperate when she brought him a petition from some peasant men or women who had appealed to her to be excused some work; why he, that kind Nicholas, should obstinately refuse her, angrily asking her not to interfere in what was not her business. She felt he had a world apart, which he loved passionately and which had laws she had not fathomed.

Sometimes when, trying to understand him, she spoke of the good work he was doing for his serfs, he would be vexed and reply: 'Not in the least; it never entered my head; and I wouldn't do *that* for their good! That's all poetry and old wives' talk – all that doing good to one's neighbour. What I want is that our children should not have to go begging. I must put our affairs in order while I am alive, that's all. And to do that, order and strictness are essential . . . That's all about it!' said he, clenching his vigorous fist. 'And fairness, of course,' he added, 'for if the peasant is naked and hungry and has only one miserable horse, he can do no good either for himself or for me.'

And all Nicholas did was fruitful – probably just because he refused to allow himself to think that he was doing good to others for virtue's sake. His means increased rapidly: serfs from neighbour-ing estates came to beg him to buy them, and long after his death the memory of his administration was devoutly preserved among the serfs. 'He was a master . . . the peasants' affairs first and then his own. Of course he was not to be trifled with either – in a word, he was a real master!'

8

ONE matter connected with his management sometimes worried Nicholas, and that was his quick temper together with his old hussar habit of making free use of his fists. At first he saw nothing reprehensible in this, but in the second year of his marriage his view of that form of punishment suddenly changed.

Once in summer he had sent for the village Elder from Bogucharovo, a man who had succeeded to the post when Dron died and
who was accused of dishonesty and various irregularities. Nicholas
went out into the porch to question him, and immediately after
the Elder had given a few replies the sound of cries and blows
was heard. On returning to lunch Nicholas went up to his wife,
who sat with her head bent low over her embroidery frame, and
as usual began to tell her what he had been doing that morning.
Among other things he spoke of the Bogucharovo Elder. Countess Mary turned red and then pale, but continued to sit
with head bowed and lips compressed and gave her husband no
reply.

'Such an insolent scoundrel!' he cried, growing hot again at the
mere recollection of him. 'If he had told me he was drunk and did
not see . . . But what is the matter with you, Mary?' he suddenly
asked.

Countess Mary raised her head and tried to speak, but hastily
looked down again and her lips puckered.

'Why, whatever is the matter, my dearest?'

The looks of the plain Countess Mary always improved when she
was in tears. She never cried from pain or vexation, but always
from sorrow or pity, and when she wept her radiant eyes acquired
an irresistible charm.

The moment Nicholas took her hand she could no longer restrain
herself and began to cry.

'Nicholas, I saw it . . . he was to blame, but why do you . . .
Nicholas!' and she covered her face with her hands.

Nicholas said nothing. He flushed crimson, left her side, and
paced up and down the room. He understood what she was weeping about, but could not in his heart at once agree with her that
what he had regarded from childhood as quite an everyday event
was wrong. 'Is it just sentimentality, old wives' tales, or is she
right?' he asked himself. Before he had solved that point he
glanced again at her face filled with love and pain, and he suddenly realized that she was right and that he had long been
sinning against himself.

'Mary,' he said softly, going up to her, 'it will never happen
again; I give you my word. Never,' he repeated in a trembling
voice like a boy asking for forgiveness.

The tears flowed faster still from the countess's eyes. She took
his hand and kissed it.

'Nicholas, when did you break your camera?' she asked, to change
the subject, looking at his finger on which he wore a ring with a
cameo of Laocoön's head.

'To-day – it was the same affair. Oh Mary, don't remind me of it!' and again he flushed. 'I give you my word of honour it shan't occur again. And let this always be a reminder to me,' and he pointed to the broken ring.

After that, when in discussions with his village Elders or the stewards the blood rushed to his face and his fists began to clench, Nicholas would turn the broken ring on his finger and would drop his eyes before the man who was making him angry. But he did forget himself once or twice within a twelvemonth, and then he would go and confess to his wife, and would again promise that this should really be the very last time.

'Mary, you must despise me!' he would say. 'I deserve it.'

'You should go, go away at once, if you don't feel strong enough to control yourself,' she would reply sadly, trying to comfort her husband.

Among the gentry of the province Nicholas was respected, but not liked. He did not concern himself with the interests of his own class, and consequently some thought him proud and others thought him stupid. The whole summer, from spring sowing to harvest, he was busy with the work on his farm. In autumn he gave himself up to hunting with the same business-like seriousness – leaving home for a month, or even two, with his hunt. In winter he visited his other villages or spent his time reading. The books he read were chiefly historical, and on these he spent a certain sum every year. He was collecting, as he said, a serious library, and he made it a rule to read through all the books he bought. He would sit in his study with a grave air, reading – a task he first imposed upon himself as a duty, but which afterwards became a habit affording him a special kind of pleasure and a consciousness of being occupied with serious matters. In winter, except for business excursions, he spent most of his time at home making himself one with his family and entering into all the details of his children's relations with their mother. The harmony between him and his wife grew closer and closer, and he daily discovered fresh spiritual treasures in her.

From the time of his marriage Sonya had lived in his house. Before that, Nicholas had told his wife all that had passed between himself and Sonya, blaming himself and commending her. He had asked Princess Mary to be gentle and kind to his cousin. She thoroughly realized the wrong he had done Sonya, felt herself to blame towards her, and imagined that her wealth had influenced Nicholas's choice. She could not find fault with Sonya in any way, and tried to be fond of her, but often felt ill-will towards her which she could not overcome.

Once she had a talk with her friend Natasha about Sonya and about her own injustice towards her.

'You know,' said Natasha, 'you have read the Gospels a great deal – there is a passage in them that just fits Sonya.

'What?' asked Countess Mary, surprised.

'"To him that hath shall be given, and from him that hath not shall be taken away." You remember? She is one that hath not; why, I don't know. Perhaps she lacks egotism, I don't know, but from her is taken away, and everything has been taken away. Sometimes I am dreadfully sorry for her. Formerly I very much wanted Nicholas to marry her, but I always had a sort of presentiment that it would not come off. She is a *sterile flower*, you know – like some strawberry blossoms. Sometimes I am sorry for her, and sometimes I think she doesn't feel it as you or I would.'

Though Countess Mary told Natasha that those words in the Gospel must be understood differently, yet looking at Sonya she agreed with Natasha's explanation. It really seemed that Sonya did not feel her position trying, and had grown quite reconciled to her lot as a *sterile flower*. She seemed to be fond not so much of individuals as of the family as a whole. Like a cat, she had attached herself not to the people but to the home. She waited on the old countess, petted and spoiled the children, was always ready to render the small services for which she had a gift, and all this was unconsciously accepted from her with insufficient gratitude.

The country seat at Bald Hills had been rebuilt, though not on the same scale as under the old prince.

The buildings, begun under straitened circumstances, were more than simple. The immense house on the old stone foundations was of wood, plastered only inside. It had bare deal floors and was furnished with very simple hard sofas,* arm-chairs, tables, and chairs, made by their own serf-carpenters out of their own birch-wood. The house was spacious and had rooms for the house-serfs and apartments for visitors. Whole families of the Rostovs' and Bolkonskys' relations sometimes came to Bald Hills with sixteen horses and dozens of servants and stayed for months. Besides that, four times a year, on the name-days and birthdays of the hosts, as many as a hundred visitors would gather there for a day or two. The rest of the year life pursued its unbroken routine with its ordinary occupations, and its breakfasts, lunches, dinners, and suppers, provided out of the produce of the estate.

IT was the eve of St Nicholas, the fifth of December, 1820. Natasha had been staying at her brother's with her husband and children since early autumn. Pierre had gone to Petersburg on business of his own for three weeks as he said, but had remained there nearly seven weeks and was expected back every minute.

Besides the Bezukhov family, Nicholas's old friend the retired General Vasili Dmitrich Denisov was staying with the Rostovs this 5th of December.

On the 6th, which was his name-day when the house would be full of visitors, Nicholas knew he would have to exchange his Tartar tunic for a tail-coat, and put on narrow boots with pointed toes and drive to the new church he had built, and then receive visitors who would come to congratulate him, offer them refreshments, and talk about the elections of the nobility,* but he considered himself entitled to spend the eve of that day in his usual way. He examined the bailiff's accounts of the village in Ryazan which belonged to his wife's nephew, wrote two business letters, and walked over to the granaries, the cattle-yards, and the stables, before dinner. Having taken precautions against the general drunkenness to be expected on the morrow because it was a great saint's day, he returned to dinner, and without having time for a private talk with his wife sat down to the long table laid for twenty persons, at which the whole household had assembled. At that table were his mother, his mother's old lady-companion Belova, his wife, their three children with their governess and tutor, his wife's nephew with his tutor, Sonya, Denisov, Natasha, her three children, their governess, and old Michael Ivanovich the late prince's architect, who was living on in retirement at Bald Hills.

Countess Mary sat at the other end of the table. When her husband took his place she concluded, from the rapid manner in which after taking up his table-napkin he pushed back the tumbler and wine-glass standing before him, that he was out of humour, as was sometimes the case when he came in to dinner straight from the farm – especially before the soup. Countess Mary knew that mood of his well, and when she herself was in a good frame of mind quietly waited till he had had his soup and then began to talk to him and make him admit that there was no cause for his ill-humour. But to-day she quite forgot that, and was hurt that he should be angry with her without any reason, and she felt unhappy. She asked him where he had been. He replied. She again inquired whether everything was going well on the farm. Her unnatural tone made him wince unpleasantly and he replied hastily.

'Then I'm not mistaken,' thought Countess Mary. 'Why is he cross with me?' She concluded from his tone that he was vexed with her and wished to end the conversation. She knew her remarks sounded unnatural, but could not refrain from asking some more questions.

Thanks to Denisov the conversation at table soon became general and lively and she did not talk to her husband. When they left the table and went as usual to thank the old countess,* Countess Mary held out her hand and kissed her husband, and asked him why he was angry with her.

'You always have such strange fancies. I didn't even think of being angry,' he replied.

But the word *always* seemed to her to imply: 'Yes, I am angry but I won't tell you why.'

Nicholas and his wife lived together so happily that even Sonya and the old countess, who felt jealous and would have liked them to disagree, could find nothing to reproach them with; but even they had their moments of antagonism. Occasionally, and it was always just after they had been happiest together, they suddenly had a feeling of estrangement and hostility, which occurred most frequently during Countess Mary's pregnancies, and this was such a time.

'Well, *messieurs et mesdames*,' said Nicholas loudly and with apparent cheerfulness (it seemed to Countess Mary that he did it on purpose to vex her), 'I have been on my feet since six this morning. To-morrow I shall have to suffer, so to-day I'll go and rest.'

And without a word to his wife he went to the little sitting-room and lay down on the sofa.

'That's always the way,' thought Countess Mary. 'He talks to everyone except me. I see ... I see that I am repulsive to him, especially when I am in this condition.' She looked down at her expanded figure, and in the glass at her pale, sallow, emaciated face in which her eyes now looked larger than ever.

And everything annoyed her – Denisov's shouting and laughter, Natasha's talk, and especially a quick glance Sonya gave her.

Sonya was always the first excuse Countess Mary found for feeling irritated.

Having sat awhile with her visitors without understanding anything of what they were saying, she softly left the room and went to the nursery.

The children were playing at 'going to Moscow' in a carriage made of chairs, and invited her to go with them. She sat down and played with them a little, but the thought of her husband and his unreasonable crossness worried her. She got up and, walking on tiptoe with difficulty, went to the small sitting-room.

'Perhaps he is not asleep; I'll have an explanation with him,' she said to herself. Little Andrew, her eldest boy, imitating his mother, followed her on tiptoe. She did not notice him.

'Mary, dear, I think he is asleep – he was so tired,' said Sonya, meeting her in the large sitting-room (it seemed to Countess Mary that she crossed her path everywhere), 'Andrew may wake him.'

Countess Mary looked round, saw little Andrew following her, felt that Sonya was right and, for that very reason, flushed and with evident difficulty refrained from saying something harsh. She made no reply, but, to avoid obeying Sonya, beckoned to Andrew to follow her quietly and went to the door. Sonya went away by another door. From the room in which Nicholas was sleeping came the sound of his even breathing, every slightest tone of which was familiar to his wife. As she listened to it she saw before her his smooth handsome forehead, his moustache and his whole face as she had so often seen it in the stillness of the night when he slept. Nicholas suddenly moved and cleared his throat. And at that moment little Andrew shouted from outside the door: 'Papa! Mamma's standing here!' Countess Mary turned pale with fright and made signs to the boy. He grew silent, and quiet ensued for a moment, terrible to Countess Mary. She knew how Nicholas disliked being waked. Then through the door she heard Nicholas clearing his throat again and stirring, and his voice said crossly:

'I can't get a moment's peace. Mary, is that you? Why did you bring him here?'

'I only came in to look, and did not notice ... forgive me ...'

Nicholas coughed and said no more. Countess Mary moved away from the door and took the boy back to the nursery. Five minutes later little black-eyed three-year-old Natasha, her father's pet, having learnt from her brother that papa was asleep and mamma was in the sitting-room, ran to her father unobserved by her mother. The dark-eyed little girl boldly opened the creaking door, went up to the sofa with energetic steps of her sturdy little legs, and having examined the position of her father, who was asleep with his back to her, rose on tiptoe and kissed the hand which lay under his head. Nicholas turned with a tender smile on his face.

'Natasha, Natasha!' came Countess Mary's frightened whisper from the door. 'Papa wants to sleep.'

'No, mamma, he doesn't want to sleep,' said little Natasha with conviction. 'He's laughing.'

Nicholas lowered his legs, rose, and took his daughter in his arms.

'Come in, Mary,' he said to his wife.

She went in and sat down by her husband.

'I did not notice him following me,' she said timidly. 'I just looked in.'

Holding his little girl with one arm, Nicholas glanced at his wife and, seeing her guilty expression, put his other arm round her and kissed her hair.

'May I kiss mamma?' he asked Natasha.

Natasha smiled bashfully.

'Again!' she commanded, pointing with a peremptory gesture to the spot where Nicholas had placed the kiss.

'I don't know why you think I am cross,' said Nicholas, replying to the question he knew was in his wife's mind.

'You have no idea how unhappy, how lonely, I feel when you are like that. It always seems to me . . .'

'Mary, don't talk nonsense. You ought to be ashamed of yourself!' he said gaily.

'It seems to me that you can't love me, that I am so plain . . . always . . . and now . . . in this cond. . . .'

'Oh, how absurd you are! It is not beauty that endears, it's love that makes us see beauty. It is only Malvinas and women of that kind who are loved for their beauty. But do I love my wife? I don't love her, but . . . I don't know how to put it. Without you, or when something comes between us like this, I seem lost and can't do anything. Now do I love my finger? I don't love it, but just try to cut it off!'

'I'm not like that myself, but I understand. So you're not angry with me?'

'Awfully angry!' he said, smiling and getting up. And smoothing his hair he began to pace the room.

'Do you know, Mary, what I've been thinking?' he began, immediately thinking aloud in his wife's presence now that they had made it up.

He did not ask if she was ready to listen to him. He did not care. A thought had occurred to him, and so it belonged to her also. And he told her of his intention to persuade Pierre to stay with them till spring.

Countess Mary listened till he had finished, made some remark, and in her turn began thinking aloud. Her thoughts were about the children.

'You can see the woman in her already,' she said in French, pointing to little Natasha. 'You reproach us women with being illogical. Here is our logic. I say: "Papa wants to sleep!" but she says, "No, he's laughing." And she was right,' said Countess Mary with a happy smile.

'Yes, yes.' And Nicholas, taking his little daughter in his strong hand, lifted her high, placed her on his shoulder, held her by the legs and paced the room with her. There was an expression of carefree happiness on the faces of both father and daughter.

'But you know you may be unfair. You are too fond of this one,' his wife whispered in French.

'Yes, but what am I to do? ... I try not to show ...'

At that moment they heard the sound of the door-pulley and footsteps in the hall and ante-room, as if someone had arrived.

'Somebody has come.'

'I am sure it is Pierre. I will go and see,' said Countess Mary, and left the room.

In her absence Nicholas allowed himself to give his little daughter a gallop round the room. Out of breath, he took the laughing child quickly from his shoulder and pressed her to his heart. His capers reminded him of dancing, and looking at the child's round happy little face he thought of what she would be like when he was an old man, taking her into society and dancing the mazurka with her as his old father had danced *Daniel Cooper* with his daughter.

'It's he, it's he, Nicholas,' said Countess Mary re-entering the room a few minutes later. 'Now our Natasha has come to life. You should have seen her ecstasy, and how he caught it for having stayed away so long. Well, come along now, quick quick! It's time you two were parted,' she added, looking smilingly at the little girl who clung to her father.

Nicholas went out holding the child by the hand.

Countess Mary remained in the sitting-room.

'I should never, never have believed that one could be so happy,' she whispered to herself. A smile lit up her face, but at the same time she sighed, and her deep eyes expressed a quiet sadness, as though she felt, through her happiness, that there is another sort of happiness unattainable in this life, and of which she involuntarily thought at that instant.

10

NATASHA had married in the early spring of 1813, and in 1820 already had three daughters, besides a son for whom she had longed and whom she was now nursing. She had grown stouter and broader, so that it was difficult to recognize the slim lively Natasha of former days in this robust motherly woman. Her features were more defined and had a calm, soft and serene expression. In her face there was none of the ever-glowing animation that had formerly burned there and constituted its charm. Now her face and body were often all that one saw, and her soul was not visible at all. All that struck the eye was a strong, handsome and fertile woman. The old fire very rarely kindled in her face now. That happened only when, as was the case that day, her husband returned home, or a sick child was convalescent, or when she and Countess Mary spoke of Prince Andrew (she never mentioned him to her husband, who she imagined was jealous of Prince Andrew's memory), or on the rare occasions when something happened to induce her to sing, a practice she had quite abandoned since her marriage. At the rare moments when the old fire kindled in her handsome fully-developed body she was even more attractive than in former days.

Since their marriage Natasha and her husband had lived in Moscow, in Petersburg, on their estate near Moscow, or with her mother, that is to say, in Nicholas's house. The young Countess Bezukhova was not often seen in society, and those who met her there were not pleased with her and found her neither attractive nor amiable. Not that Natasha liked solitude – she did not know whether she liked it or not, she even thought that she did not – but with her pregnancies, her confinements, the nursing of her children, and sharing every moment of her husband's life, she had demands on her time which could only be satisfied by renouncing society. All who had known Natasha before her marriage wondered at the change in her as at something extraordinary. Only the old countess, with her maternal instinct, had realized that all Natasha's outbursts had been due to her need of children and a husband – as she herself had once exclaimed at Otradnoe not so much in fun as in earnest – and her mother was now surprised by the surprise expressed by those who had never understood Natasha, and kept saying that she had always known that Natasha would make an exemplary wife and mother.

'Only she lets her love of her husband and children overflow all bounds,' said the countess, 'so that it even becomes absurd.'

Natasha did not follow the golden rule advocated by clever folk, especially the French, which says that a girl should not let herself go when she marries, should not neglect her accomplishments, should be even more careful of her appearance than when she was unmarried, and should fascinate her husband as much as she did before he became her husband. Natasha, on the contrary, had at once abandoned all her witchery, of which her singing had been an unusually powerful part. She gave it up just because it was so powerfully seductive. She took no pains with her manners, or with delicacy of speech, or with her toilet, or to show herself to her husband in her most becoming attitudes, or to avoid inconveniencing him by being too exacting. She acted in contradiction to all those rules. She felt that the allurements instinct had formerly taught her to use would now be merely ridiculous in the eyes of her husband, to whom she had from the first moment given herself up entirely – that is, with her whole soul, leaving no corner of it hidden from him. She felt that her unity with her husband was not maintained by the poetic feelings that had attracted him to her, but by something else – indefinite but firm as the bond between her own body and soul.

To fluff out her curls, put on fashionable dresses, and sing romantic songs to fascinate her husband, would have seemed as strange as to adorn herself to attract herself. To adorn herself for others might perhaps have been agreeable – she did not know – but she had no time at all for it. The chief reason for devoting no time either to singing, to dress, or to choosing her words, was that she really had no time to spare for these things.

It is known that man has the faculty of becoming completely absorbed in a subject however trivial it may be. And it is known that there is no subject so trivial that it will not grow to infinite proportions if one's entire attention is devoted to it.

The subject which wholly engrossed Natasha's attention was her family, that is, her husband whom she had to keep so that he should belong entirely to her and to the home – and the children whom she had to bear, bring into the world, nurse, and bring up.

And the deeper she penetrated, not with her mind only but with her whole soul, her whole being, into the subject that absorbed her, the larger did that subject grow and the weaker and more inadequate her own powers appeared, so that she concentrated them all on that one thing and yet was unable to accomplish all that she considered necessary.

There were then, as there are now, conversations and discussions about women's rights, the relations of husband and wife, and their freedom and rights, though these themes were not yet termed *questions* as they are now; but these topics were not merely uninteresting to Natasha, she positively did not understand them.

Those questions, then as now, existed only for those who see nothing in marriage but the pleasure married people get from one another, that is, only the beginnings of marriage and not its whole significance, which lies in the family.

Discussions and questions of that kind, which are like the question of how to get the greatest gratification from one's dinner, did not then, and do not now, exist for those for whom the purpose of a dinner is the nourishment it affords, and the purpose of marriage is the family.

If the purpose of dinner is to nourish the body, a man who eats two dinners at once may perhaps get more enjoyment, but will not attain his purpose for his stomach will not digest the two dinners.

If the purpose of marriage is the family, the person who wishes to have many wives or husbands may perhaps obtain much pleasure, but in that case will not have a family.

If the purpose of food is nourishment, and the purpose of marriage is the family, the whole question resolves itself into not eating more than one can digest, and not having more wives or husbands than are needed for the family – that is, one wife or one husband. Natasha needed a husband. A husband was given her, and he gave her a family. And she not only saw no need of any other or better husband, but as all the powers of her soul were intent on serving that husband and family she could not imagine, and saw no interest in imagining, how it would be if things were different.

Natasha did not care for society in general, but prized the more the society of her relatives – Countess Mary and her brother, her mother, and Sonya. She valued the company of those to whom she could come striding dishevelled from the nursery in her dressing-gown, and with joyful face show a yellow instead of a green stain on baby's napkin, and from whom she could hear reassuring words to the effect that baby was much better.

To such an extent had Natasha let herself go, that the way she dressed and did her hair, her ill-chosen words, and her jealousy – she was jealous of Sonya, of the governess, and of every woman, pretty or plain – were habitual subjects of jest to those about her. The general opinion was that Pierre was under his wife's thumb, which was really true. From the very first days of their married life Natasha had announced her demands. Pierre was greatly surprised by his wife's view, to him a perfectly novel one, that every moment of his life belonged to her and to the family. His wife's demands astonished him, but they also flattered him, and he submitted to them.

Pierre's subjection consisted in the fact that he not only dared not flirt with, but dared not even speak smilingly to, any other woman; did not dare to dine at the club as a pastime, did not dare to spend money on a whim, and did not dare absent himself for any length of time, except on business – in which his wife included his intellectual pursuits, which she did not in the least understand but to which she attributed great importance. To make up for this, Pierre had the right of completely regulating his life at home as he chose, as well as that of the whole family. At home Natasha placed herself in the position of a slave to her husband, and the whole household went on tiptoe when he was occupied – that is, was reading or writing in his study. Pierre had but to show a partiality for anything, to get just what he liked done always. He had only to express a wish and Natasha would jump up and run to fulfil it.

The entire household was governed according to Pierre's supposed orders, that is, by his wishes which Natasha tried to guess. Their way of life and place of residence, their acquaintances and ties, Natasha's occupations, the children's upbringing, were all selected not merely with regard to Pierre's expressed wishes, but to what Natasha supposed his wishes to be from the thoughts he expressed in conversation. And she deduced the essentials of his wishes quite correctly, and having once arrived at them clung to them tenaciously. When Pierre himself wanted to change his mind she would fight him with his own weapons.

Thus in a time of trouble ever memorable to him, after the birth of their first child who was delicate, when they had to change the wet-nurse three times and Natasha fell ill from despair, Pierre one day told her of Rousseau's view, with which he quite agreed, that to have a wet-nurse is unnatural and harmful. When her next baby was born, despite the opposition of her mother, the doctors, and even of her husband himself – who were all vigorously opposed to her nursing her baby herself, a thing then unheard of and considered injurious – she insisted on having her own way, and after that nursed all her babies herself.

It very often happened that in a moment of irritation husband and wife would have a dispute, but long afterwards Pierre, to his surprise and delight, would find in his wife's ideas and actions the very thought against which she had argued, but divested of everything superfluous that in the excitement of the dispute he had added when expressing his opinion.

After seven years of marriage Pierre had the joyous and firm consciousness that he was not a bad man, and he felt this because he saw himself reflected in his wife. He felt the good and bad within himself inextricably mingled and overlapping. But only what was really good in him was reflected in his wife, all that was not quite good was rejected. And this was not the result of logical reasoning but was a direct and mysterious reflection.

Two months previously, when Pierre was already staying with the Rostovs, he had received a letter from Prince Theodore asking him to come to Petersburg to confer on some important questions that were being discussed there by a society of which Pierre was one of the principal founders.

On reading that letter (she always read her husband's letters) Natasha herself suggested that he should go to Petersburg, though she would feel his absence very acutely. She attributed immense importance to all her husband's intellectual and abstract interests though she did not understand them, and she always dreaded being a hindrance to him in such matters. To Pierre's timid look of inquiry after reading the letter, she replied by asking him to go, but to fix a definite date for his return. He was given four weeks' leave of absence.

Ever since that leave of absence had expired, more than a fortnight before, Natasha had been in a constant state of alarm, depression, and irritability.

Denisov, now a general on the retired list and much dissatisfied with the present state of affairs, had arrived during that fortnight. He looked at Natasha with sorrow and surprise, as at a bad likeness of someone once dear. A dull dejected look, random replies, and talk about the nursery, was all he saw and heard from his former enchantress.

Natasha was sad and irritable all that time, especially when her mother, her brother, Sonya, or Countess Mary, in their efforts to console her tried to excuse Pierre and suggested reasons for his delay in returning.

'It's all nonsense, all rubbish – those discussions which lead to nothing, and all those idiotic societies!' Natasha declared of the very affairs in the immense importance of which she firmly believed.

And she would go to the nursery to nurse Petya, her only boy. No one else could tell her anything so comforting or so reasonable as this little three-months-old creature when he lay at her breast and she was conscious of the movement of his lips and snuffling of his little nose. That creature said: 'You are angry, you are jealous, you would like to pay him out, you are afraid – but here am I! And he is in me'; and that was unanswerable. It was more than true.

During that fortnight of anxiety Natasha resorted to the infant for comfort so often, and fussed over him so much, that she overfed him and he fell ill. She was terrified by his illness, and yet that was just what she needed. While attending to him she bore the anxiety about her husband more easily.

She was nursing her baby when the sound of Pierre's sleigh was heard at the front door, and the old nurse – knowing how to please her mistress – entered the room inaudibly but hurriedly and with a beaming face.

'Has he come?' Natasha asked quickly in a whisper, afraid to move lest she should rouse the dozing baby.

'He's come, ma'am,' whispered the nurse.

The blood rushed to Natasha's face and her feet involuntarily moved, but she could not jump up and run out. The baby again opened his eyes and looked at her. 'You are here?' he seemed to be saying, and again lazily smacked his lips.

Cautiously withdrawing her breast, Natasha rocked him a little, handed him to the nurse and went with rapid steps towards the door. But at the door she stopped as if her conscience reproached her for having in her joy left the child too soon, and she glanced round. The nurse, with raised elbows, was lifting the infant over the rail of his cot.

'Go, ma'am! Don't worry, go!' she whispered smiling, with the kind of familiarity that grows up between a nurse and her mistress.

Natasha ran with light footsteps to the ante-room.

Denisov, who with his pipe had come out of the study into the dancing-room, now recognized the old Natasha for the first time. A flood of brilliant, joyful light poured from her transfigured face.

'He's come!' she exclaimed as she ran past, and Denisov felt that he was delighted that Pierre, whom he did not much care for, had returned.

On reaching the vestibule Natasha saw a tall figure in a fur coat unwinding his scarf. 'It's he! It's really he! He has come!' she said to herself, and rushing at him, embraced him, pressed his head to her breast, and then pushed him back and gazed at his ruddy, happy face covered with hoar-frost. 'Yes, it is he, happy and contented ...'

Then all at once she remembered the tortures of suspense she had experienced for the last fortnight: the joy that had lit up her face vanished, she frowned, and overwhelmed Pierre with a torrent of reproaches and angry words.

'Yes, it's all very well for you. You are pleased, you've had a good time ... But what about me? You might at least have shown consideration for the children. I am nursing, and my milk was spoilt ... Petya was at death's door. But you were enjoying yourself. Yes, enjoying ...'

Pierre knew he was not to blame, for he could not have come

sooner; he knew this outburst was unseemly and would blow over in a minute or two; above all, he knew that he himself was bright and happy. He wanted to smile but dared not even think of doing so. He made a piteous, frightened face and stooped down.

'I could not, on my honour. But how is Petya?'

'All right now. Come along! I wonder you're not ashamed! If only you could see what I was like without you, how I suffered!'

'You are well?'

'Come, come!' she said, not letting go of his arm. And they went to their rooms.

When Nicholas and his wife came to look for Pierre he was in the nursery holding his baby son, who was again awake, on his huge right palm and dandling him. A blissful bright smile was fixed on the baby's broad face, with its toothless open mouth. The storm was long since over and there was bright, joyous sunshine on Natasha's face as she gazed tenderly at her husband and child.

'And have you talked everything well over with Prince Theodore?' she asked.

'Yes, capitally.'

'You see, he holds it up.' (She meant the baby's head.) 'But how he did frighten me . . . You've seen the princess? Is it true she's in love with that . . .'

'Yes, just fancy . . .'

At that moment Nicholas and Countess Mary came in. Pierre, with the baby on his hand, stooped down, kissed them, and replied to their inquiries. But in spite of much that was interesting and had to be discussed, the baby with the little cap on its unsteady head evidently absorbed all his attention.

'How sweet!' said Countess Mary, looking at and playing with the baby. 'Now, Nicholas,' she added turning to her husband, 'I can't understand how it is you don't see the charm of these delicious marvels.'

'I don't and can't,' replied Nicholas, looking coldly at the baby. 'A lump of flesh. Come along, Pierre!'

'And yet he's such an affectionate father,' said Countess Mary, vindicating her husband, 'but only after they are a year old or so . . .'

'Now Pierre nurses them splendidly,' said Natasha. 'He says his hand is just made for a baby's seat. Just look!'

'Only not for this . . .' Pierre suddenly exclaimed with a laugh, and shifting the baby he gave him to the nurse.

As in every large household, there were at Bald Hills several perfectly distinct worlds which merged into one harmonious whole, though each retained its own peculiarities and made concessions to the others. Every event, joyful or sad, that took place in that house, was important to all these worlds, but each had its own special reasons to rejoice or grieve over that occurrence, independently of the others.

For instance, Pierre's return was a joyful and important event and they all felt it to be so.

The servants – the most reliable judges of their masters, because they judge not by their conversation or expressions of feeling but by their acts and way of life – were glad of Pierre's return because they knew that when he was there Count Nicholas would cease going every day to attend to the estate and would be in better spirits and temper, and also because they would all receive handsome presents for the holidays.

The children and their governesses were glad of Pierre's return because no one else drew them into the social life of the household as he did. He alone could play on the clavichord that écossaise (his only piece) to which, as he said, all possible dances could be danced, and they felt sure he had brought presents for them all.

Young Nicholas, now a slim lad of fifteen, delicate and intelligent, with curly light-brown hair and beautiful eyes, was delighted because Uncle Pierre, as he called him, was the object of his rapturous and passionate affection. No one had instilled into him this love for Pierre, whom he only saw occasionally. Countess Mary, who had brought him up, had done her utmost to make him love her husband as she loved him, and little Nicholas did love his uncle, but loved him with just a shade of contempt. Pierre however he adored. He did not want to be an hussar or a Knight of St George like his uncle Nicholas; he wanted to be learned, wise and kind like Pierre. In Pierre's presence his face always shone with pleasure, and he flushed and was breathless when Pierre spoke to him. He did not miss a single word he uttered, and would afterwards, with Dessalles or by himself, recall and reconsider the meaning of everything Pierre had said. Pierre's past life and his unhappiness prior to 1812 (of which young Nicholas had formed a vague poetic picture from some words he had overheard), his adventures in Moscow, his captivity, Platon Karataev (of whom he had heard from Pierre), his love for Natasha (of whom the lad was also particularly fond), and especially Pierre's friendship with the father whom Nicholas could not remember – all this made Pierre in his eyes a hero and a saint.

From broken remarks about Natasha and his father, from the emotion with which Pierre spoke of that dead father, and from the careful reverent tenderness with which Natasha spoke of him, the boy, who was only just beginning to guess what love is, derived the notion that his father had loved Natasha and when dying had left her to his friend. But the father whom the boy did not remember appeared to him a divinity who could not be pictured, and of whom he never thought without a swelling heart and tears of sadness and rapture. So the boy also was happy that Pierre had arrived.

The guests welcomed Pierre because he always helped to enliven and unite any company he was in.

The grown-up members of the family, not to mention his wife, were pleased to have back a friend whose presence made life run more smoothly and peacefully.

The old ladies were pleased with the presents he brought them, and especially that Natasha would now be herself again.

Pierre felt the different outlooks of these various worlds, and made haste to satisfy all their expectations.

Though the most absent-minded and forgetful of men, Pierre, with the aid of a list his wife drew up, had now bought everything, not forgetting his mother and brother-in-law's commissions, nor the dress material for a present to Belova, nor the toys for his wife's nephews. In the early days of his marriage it had seemed strange to him that his wife should expect him not to forget to procure all the things he undertook to buy, and he had been taken aback by her serious annoyance when on his first trip he forgot everything. But in time he grew used to this demand. Knowing that Natasha asked nothing for herself and only gave him commissions for others when he himself had offered to undertake them, he now found an unexpected and childlike pleasure in this purchase of presents for everyone in the house, and never forgot anything. If he now incurred Natasha's censure it was only for buying too many and too expensive things. To her other defects (as most people thought them, but which to Pierre were qualities) of untidiness and neglect of herself, she now added stinginess.

From the time that Pierre began life as a family man on a footing entailing heavy expenditure, he had noticed to his surprise that he spent only half as much as before and that his affairs – which had been in disorder of late, chiefly because of his first wife's debts – had begun to improve.

Life was cheaper because it was circumscribed: that most expensive luxury, the kind of life that can be changed at any moment, was no longer his, nor did he wish for it. He felt that his way of life had now been settled once for all till death and that to change it was not in his power, and so that way of life proved economical.

With a merry, smiling face Pierre was sorting his purchases.

'What do you think of this?' said he, unrolling a piece of stuff like a shopman.

Natasha, who was sitting opposite to him with her eldest daughter on her lap, turned her sparkling eyes swiftly from her husband to the things he showed her.

'That's for Belova? Excellent!' She felt the quality of the material. 'It was a ruble an arshin, I suppose?'

Pierre told her the price.

'Too dear!' Natasha remarked. 'How pleased the children will be, and mamma too! Only you need not have bought me this,' she added, unable to suppress a smile as she gazed admiringly at a gold comb set with pearls, of a kind then just coming into fashion.

'Adèle tempted me: she kept on telling me to buy it,' returned Pierre.

'When am I to wear it?' and Natasha stuck it in her coil of hair. 'When I take little Masha into society? Perhaps they will be fashionable again by then. Well, let's go now.'

And collecting the presents they went first to the nursery and then to the old countess's rooms.

The countess was sitting with her companion, Belova, playing grand-patience as usual, when Pierre and Natasha came into the drawing-room with parcels under their arms.

The countess was now over sixty, was quite grey and wore a cap with a frill that surrounded her face. Her face had shrivelled, her upper lip had sunk in, and her eyes were dim.

After the deaths of her son and husband in such rapid succession, she felt herself a being accidentally forgotten in this world and left without aim or object for her existence. She ate, drank, slept, or kept awake, but did not live. Life gave her no new impressions. She wanted nothing from life but tranquillity, and that tranquillity only death could give her. But until death came she had to go on living, that is, to use her vital forces. A peculiarity one sees in very young children and very old people was particularly evident in her. Her life had no external aims – only a need to exercise her various functions and inclinations was apparent. She had to eat, sleep, think, speak, weep, work, give vent to her anger, and so on, merely because she had a stomach, a brain, muscles, nerves, and a liver. She did these things not under any external impulse as people in the full vigour of life do, when behind the aim for which they strive the other aim of exercising their functions remains unnoticed. She talked only because she physically needed to exercise her tongue and lungs. She cried, as a child does, because her nose had to be cleared, and so on. What for people in their full vigour is an aim was for her evidently merely a pretext.

Thus in the morning – especially if she had eaten anything rich the day before – she felt a need of being angry, and would choose as the handiest pretext Belova's deafness.

She would begin to say something to her in a low tone from the other end of the room.

'It seems a little warmer to-day, my dear,' she would murmur.

And when Belova replied: 'Oh yes, they've come,' she would mutter angrily: 'O Lord! How stupid and deaf she is!'

Another pretext would be her snuff, which would seem too dry or too damp, or not rubbed fine enough. After these fits of irritability her face would grow yellow, and her maids knew by infallible symptoms when Belova would again be deaf, the snuff damp, and the countess's face yellow. Just as she needed to work off her spleen so she had sometimes to exercise her still existing faculty of thinking – and the pretext for that was a game of patience. When she needed to cry, the deceased count would be the pretext. When she wanted to be agitated, Nicholas and his health would be the pretext, and when she felt a need to speak spitefully, the pretext would be Countess Mary. When her vocal organs needed exercise, which was usually towards seven o'clock when she had had an after-dinner rest in a darkened room, the pretext would be the re-telling of the same stories over and over again to the same audience.

The old lady's condition was understood by the whole household, though no one ever spoke of it, and they all made every possible effort to satisfy her needs. Only by a rare glance exchanged with a sad smile between Nicholas, Pierre, Natasha, and Countess Mary, was the common understanding of her condition expressed.

But those glances expressed something more: they said that she had played her part in life, that what they now saw was not her whole self, that we must all become like her, and that they were glad to yield to her, to restrain themselves for this once precious being, formerly as full of life as themselves but now so much to be pitied. '*Memento mori*', said these glances.

Only the really heartless, the stupid ones of that household, and the little children, failed to understand this and avoided her.

WHEN Pierre and his wife entered the drawing-room the countess was in one of her habitual states in which she needed the mental exertion of playing patience, and so – though by force of habit she greeted him with the words she always used when Pierre or her son returned after an absence: 'High time, my dear, high time! We were all weary of waiting for you. Well, thank God!' and received her presents with another customary remark: 'It's not the gift that's precious, my dear, but that you give it to me, an old woman...' – it was evident that she was not pleased by Pierre's arrival at that moment, when it diverted her attention from the unfinished game.

She finished her game of patience and only then examined the presents. They consisted of a box for cards of splendid workmanship, a bright blue Sèvres tea-cup with shepherdesses depicted on it and with a lid, and a gold snuff-box with the count's portrait on the lid, which Pierre had had done by a miniaturist in Petersburg. The countess had long wished for such a box, but she did not want to cry just then, so she glanced indifferently at the portrait and gave her attention chiefly to the box for cards.

'Thank you, my dear, you have cheered me up,' said she, as she always did. 'But best of all you have brought yourself back – for I never saw anything like it, you ought to give your wife a scolding! What are we to do with her? She is like a mad woman when you are away. Doesn't see anything, doesn't remember anything,' she went on, repeating her usual phrases. 'Look, Anna Timofeevna,' she added to her companion, 'see what a box for cards my son has brought us!'

Belova admired the presents and was delighted with her dress material.

Though Pierre, Natasha, Nicholas, Countess Mary, and Denisov had much to talk about that they could not discuss before the old countess – not that anything was hidden from her, but she had dropped so far behindhand in many things that had they begun to converse in her presence they would have had to answer inopportune questions and to repeat what they had already told her many times: that so-and-so was dead and so-and-so was married, which she would again be unable to remember – yet they sat at tea round the samovar in the drawing-room from habit, and Pierre answered the countess's questions as to whether Prince Vasili had aged, and whether Countess Mary Alexeevna had sent greetings and still thought of them, and other matters that interested no one and to which she herself was indifferent.

Conversation of this kind, interesting to no one but unavoidable, continued all through tea-time. All the grown-up members of the family were assembled near the round tea-table at which Sonya presided beside the samovar. The children with their tutors and governesses had had tea and their voices were audible from the next room. At tea all sat in their accustomed places: Nicholas beside the stove at a small table where his tea was handed to him; Milka, the old grey borzoi bitch (daughter of the first Milka), with a quite grey face and large black eyes that seemed more prominent than ever, lay on the arm-chair beside him; Denisov, whose curly hair, moustache, and whiskers had turned half grey, sat beside Countess Mary with his general's tunic unbuttoned; Pierre sat between his wife and the old countess. He spoke of what he knew might interest the old lady and she could understand. He told of external social events and of the people who had formed the circle of her contemporaries and had once been a real, living and distinct group, but who were now for the most part scattered about the world and, like herself, were garnering the last ears of the harvests they had sown in earlier years. But to the old countess those contemporaries of hers seemed to be the only serious and real society. Natasha saw by Pierre's animation that his visit had been interesting and that he had much to tell them but dare not say it before the old countess. Denisov, not being a member of the family, did not understand Pierre's caution, and being, as a malcontent, much interested in what was occurring in Petersburg, kept urging Pierre to tell them about what had happened in the Semënovsk regiment, then about Arakcheev, and then about the Bible Society. Once or twice Pierre was carried away and began to speak of these things, but Nicholas and Natasha always brought him back to the health of Prince Ivan and Countess Mary Alexeevna.

'Well, and all this idiocy – Gossner and Tatawinova?'* Denisov asked. 'Is that weally still going on?'

'Going on?' Pierre exclaimed. 'Why, more than ever! The Bible Society is the whole government now!'

'What is that, *mon cher ami*?' asked the countess, who had finished her tea and evidently needed a pretext for being angry after her meal. 'What are you saying about the government? I don't understand.'

'Well, you know, *maman*,' Nicholas interposed, knowing how to translate things into his mother's language, 'Prince Alexander Golitsin has founded a society and in consequence has great influence, they say.'

'Arakcheev and Golitsin,' incautiously remarked Pierre, 'are now the whole government! And what a government! They see treason everywhere and are afraid of everything.'

'Well, and how is Prince Alexander to blame? He is a most estimable man. I used to meet him at Mary Antonovna's,' said the countess in an offended tone, and still more offended that they all remained silent, she went on: 'Nowadays everyone finds fault. A Gospel Society! Well, and what harm is there in that?' and she rose (everybody else got up too) and with a severe expression sailed back to her table in the sitting-room.

The melancholy silence that followed was broken by the sounds of the children's voices and laughter from the next room. Evidently some jolly excitement was going on there.

'Finished, finished!' little Natasha's gleeful yell rose above them all.

Pierre exchanged glances with Countess Mary and Nicholas (Natasha he never lost sight of) and smiled happily.

'That's delightful music!' said he.

'It means that Anna Makarovna has finished her stocking,' said Countess Mary.

'Oh, I'll go and see,' said Pierre, jumping up. 'You know,' he added, stopping at the door, 'why I'm especially fond of that music? It is always the first thing that tells me all is well. When I was driving here to-day, the nearer I got to the house the more anxious I grew. As I entered the ante-room I heard Andrusha's peals of laughter and that meant that all was well.'

'I know. I know that feeling,' said Nicholas. 'But I mustn't go there – those stockings are to be a surprise for me.'

Pierre went to the children, and the shouting and laughter grew still louder.

'Come, Anna Makarovna,' Pierre's voice was heard saying, 'come here into the middle of the room and at the word of command, "One, two," and when I say "three"... You stand here, and you in my arms – well now! "One, two...!"' said Pierre, and a silence followed: 'three!' – and a rapturously breathless cry of children's voices filled the room. 'Two, two!' they shouted.

This meant two stockings, which by a secret process known only to herself, Anna Makarovna used to knit at the same time on the same needles, and which, when they were ready, she always triumphantly drew one out of the other in the children's presence.

SOON after this the children came in to say good-night. They kissed everyone, the tutors and governesses made their bows, and they went out. Only little Nicholas and his tutor remained. Dessalles whispered to the boy to come downstairs.

'No, Monsieur Dessalles, I will ask my aunt to let me stay,' replied Nicholas Bolkonsky also in a whisper.

'*Ma tante*, please let me stay,' said he, going up to his aunt.

His face expressed entreaty, agitation and ecstasy. Countess Mary glanced at him and turned to Pierre.

'When you are here he can't tear himself away,' she said.

'I will bring him to you directly, Monsieur Dessalles. Good-night!' said Pierre giving his hand to the Swiss tutor, and he turned to young Nicholas with a smile. 'You and I haven't seen anything of one another yet . . . How like he is growing, Mary!' he added, addressing Countess Mary.

'Like my father?' asked the boy, flushing crimson and looking up at Pierre with bright ecstatic eyes.

Pierre nodded, and went on with what he had been saying when the children had interrupted. Countess Mary sat down doing wool-work; Natasha did not take her eyes off her husband. Nicholas and Denisov rose, asked for their pipes, smoked, went to fetch more tea from Sonya – who sat weary but resolute at the samovar – and questioned Pierre. The curly-headed, delicate boy sat with shining eyes unnoticed in a corner, starting every now and then and muttering something to himself, and evidently experiencing a new and powerful emotion as he turned his curly head, with his thin neck exposed by his turn-down collar, towards the place where Pierre sat.

The conversation turned on the contemporary gossip about those in power, in which most people see the chief interest of home politics. Denisov, dissatisfied with the government on account of his own disappointments in the service, heard with pleasure of the things done in Petersburg which seemed to him stupid, and made forcible and sharp comments on what Pierre told them.

'One used to have to be a German – now one must dance with Tatawinova and Madame Kwüdener,* and wead Ecka'tshausen and the bwethwen. Oh, they should let that fine fellow Bonaparte loose – he'd knock all this nonsense out of them! Fancy giving the command of the Semënov wegiment to a fellow like that Schwa'tz!' he cried.

Nicholas, though free from Denisov's readiness to find fault with everything, also thought that discussion of the government was a very serious and weighty matter, and the fact that A had been appointed Minister of This, and B Governor-General of That, and that the Emperor had said so-and-so, and this Minister so-and-so, seemed to him very important. And so he thought it necessary to take an interest in these things and to question Pierre. The questions put by these two kept the conversation from changing its ordinary character of gossip about the higher government circles.

But Natasha, knowing all her husband's ways and ideas, saw that he had long been wishing, but had been unable, to divert the conversation to another channel and express his own deeply-felt idea for the sake of which he had gone to Petersburg to consult with his new friend, Prince Theodore, and she helped him by asking how his affairs with Prince Theodore* had gone.

'What was it about?' asked Nicholas.

'Always the same thing,' said Pierre, looking round at his listeners. 'Everybody sees that things are going so badly that they cannot be allowed to go on so and that it is the duty of all decent men to counteract it as far as they can.'

'What can decent men do?' Nicholas inquired, frowning slightly. 'What can be done?'

'Why, this . . .'

'Come into my study,' said Nicholas.

Natasha, who had long expected to be fetched to nurse her baby, now heard the nurse calling her and went to the nursery. Countess Mary followed her. The men went into the study, and little Nicholas Bolkonsky followed them unnoticed by his uncle, and sat down at the writing-table in a dark corner by the window.

'Well, what would you do?' asked Denisov.

'Always some fantastic schemes,' said Nicholas.

'Why this,' began Pierre, not sitting down but pacing the room, sometimes stopping short, gesticulating and lisping: 'the position in Petersburg is this: the Emperor does not look into anything. He has abandoned himself altogether to this mysticism' (Pierre could not tolerate mysticism in anyone now). 'He seeks only for peace, and only these people *sans foi ni loi* can give it him – people who recklessly hack at and strangle everything – Magnitsky, Arakcheev, and *tutti quanti* . . . You will agree that if you did not look after your estates yourself but only wanted a quiet life, the harsher your steward was the more readily your object might be attained,' he said to Nicholas.

'Well, what does that lead up to?' said Nicholas.

'Well, everything is going to ruin! Robbery in the law-courts, in the army nothing but flogging, drilling, and Military Settlements;

the people are tortured, enlightenment is suppressed. All that is young and honest is crushed! Everyone sees that this cannot go on. Everything is strained to such a degree that it will certainly break,' said Pierre (as those who examine the actions of any government have always said* since governments began). 'I told them just one thing in Petersburg.'

'Told whom?'

'Well, you know whom,' said Pierre, with a meaning glance from under his brows. 'Prince Theodore and all those. To encourage culture and philanthropy is all very well of course. The aim is excellent, but in the present circumstances something else is needed.'

At that moment Nicholas noticed the presence of his nephew. His face darkened and he went up to the boy.

'Why are you here?'

'Why? Let him be,' said Pierre taking Nicholas by the arm and continuing. 'That is not enough, I told them. Something else is needed. When you stand expecting the overstrained string to snap at any moment, when everyone is expecting the inevitable catastrophe, as many as possible must join hands as closely as they can to withstand the general calamity. Everything that is young and strong is being enticed away and depraved. One is lured by women, another by honours, a third by ambition or money, and they go over to that camp. No independent men, such as you or I, are left. What I say is, widen the scope of our Society, let the *mot d'ordre* be not virtue alone, but independence and action as well!'

Nicholas, who had left his nephew, irritably pushed up an armchair, sat down in it, and listened to Pierre, coughing discontentedly and frowning more and more.

'But action with what aim?' he cried. 'And what position will you adopt towards the government?'

'Why, the position of assistants. The Society need not be secret if the government allows it. Not merely is it not hostile to government, but it is a society of true conservatives – a society of gentlemen in the full meaning of that word. It is only to prevent some Pugachëv* or other from killing my children and yours, and Arakcheev from sending me off to some Military Settlement. We join hands only for the public welfare and the general safety.'

'Yes, but it's a secret society and therefore a hostile and harmful one which can only cause harm.'

'Why? Did the Tugendbund which saved Europe* [they did not then venture to suggest that Russia had saved Europe] do any harm? The Tugendbund is an alliance of virtue: it is love, mutual help . . . it is what Christ preached on the Cross.'

Natasha, who had come in during the conversation, looked joyfully at her husband. It was not what he was saying that pleased her – that did not even interest her for it seemed to her that it was all extremely simple and that she had known it a long time (it seemed so to her because she knew that it sprang from Pierre's whole soul), but it was his animated and enthusiastic appearance that made her glad.

The boy with the thin neck stretching out from the turn-down collar – whom everyone had forgotten – gazed at Pierre with even greater and more rapturous joy. Every word of Pierre's burnt into his heart, and with a nervous movement of his fingers he unconsciously broke the sealing-wax and quill pens his hands came upon on his uncle's table.

'It is not at all what you suppose; but that is what the German Tugendbund was and what I am proposing.'

'No, my fwiend! The Tugendbund is all vewy well for the sausage-eaters, but I don't understand it and can't even pwonounce it,' interposed Denisov in a loud and resolute voice. 'I agwee that evewything here is wotten and howwible, but the *Tugendbund* I don't understand. If we're not satisfied, let us have a *bunt* of our own. That's all wight, *Je suis vot'e homme!*'

Pierre smiled, Natasha began to laugh, but Nicholas knitted his brows still more, and began proving to Pierre that there was no prospect of any great change and that all the danger he spoke of existed only in his imagination. Pierre maintained the contrary, and as his mental faculties were greater and more resourceful, Nicholas felt himself cornered. This made him still angrier, for he was fully convinced, not by reasoning but by something within him stronger than reason, of the justice of his opinion.

'I will tell you this,' he said, rising and trying with nervously twitching fingers to prop up his pipe in a corner, but finally abandoning the attempt. 'I can't prove it to you. You say that everything here is rotten and that an overthrow is coming: I don't see it. But you also say that our oath of allegiance is a conditional matter, and to that I reply: "You are my best friend, as you know, but if you formed a secret society and began working against the government – be it what it may – I know it is my duty to obey the government. And if Arakcheev ordered me to lead a squadron against you and cut you down, I should not hesitate an instant, but should do it." And you may argue about that as you like!'

An awkward silence followed these words. Natasha was the first to speak, defending her husband and attacking her brother. Her defence was weak and inept but she attained her object. The conversation was resumed, and no longer in the unpleasantly hostile tone of Nicholas's last remark.

When they all got up to go in to supper, little Nicholas Bolkonsky went up to Pierre, pale and with shining, radiant eyes.

'Uncle Pierre, you . . . no . . . If papa were alive . . . would he agree with you?' he asked.

And Pierre suddenly realized what a special, independent, complex and powerful process of thought and feeling must have been going on in this boy during that conversation, and remembering all he had said he regretted that the lad should have heard him. He had however to give him an answer.

'Yes, I think so,' he said reluctantly, and left the study.

The lad looked down and seemed now for the first time to notice what he had done to the things on the table. He flushed and went up to Nicholas.

'Uncle, forgive me, I did that . . . unintentionally,' he said, pointing to the broken sealing-wax and pens.

Nicholas started angrily.

'All right, all right,' he said, throwing the bits under the table.

And evidently suppressing his vexation with difficulty, he turned away from the boy.

'You ought not to have been here at all,' he said.

15

THE conversation at supper was not about politics or societies, but turned on the subject Nicholas liked best – recollections of 1812. Denisov started these, and Pierre was particularly agreeable and amusing about them. The family separated on the most friendly terms.

After supper Nicholas, having undressed in his study and given instructions to the steward who had been waiting for him, went to the bedroom in his dressing-gown, where he found his wife still at her table, writing.

'What are you writing, Mary?' Nicholas asked.

Countess Mary blushed. She was afraid that what she was writing would not be understood or approved of by her husband.

She had wanted to conceal what she was writing from him, but at the same time was glad he had surprised her at it and that she would now have to tell him.

'A diary,* Nicholas,' she replied, handing him a blue exercise-book filled with her firm, bold writing.

'A diary?' Nicholas repeated with a shade of irony, and he took up the book.

It was in French.

'4th December. To-day when Andrusha' (her eldest boy) 'woke up he did not wish to dress, and Mademoiselle Louise sent for me. He was naughty and obstinate. I tried threats, but he only grew angrier. Then I took the matter in hand: I left him alone and began with nurse's help to get the other children up, telling him that I did not love him. For a long time he was silent, as if astonished, then he jumped out of bed, ran to me in his shirt, and sobbed so that I could not calm him for a long time. It was plain that what troubled him most was that he had grieved me. Afterwards in the evening, when I gave him his ticket, he again began crying piteously and kissing me. One can do anything with him by tenderness.'

'What is a "ticket"?' Nicholas inquired.

'I have begun giving the elder ones marks every evening, showing how they have behaved.'

Nicholas looked into the radiant eyes that were gazing at him, and continued to turn over the pages and read. In the diary was set down everything in the children's lives that seemed noteworthy to their mother as showing their characters, or suggesting general reflections on educational methods. They were for the most part quite insignificant trifles, but did not seem so to the mother, or to the father either now that he read this diary about his children for the first time.

Under the date '5th' was entered:

'Mitya was naughty at table. Papa said he was to have no pudding. He had none, but looked so unhappily and greedily at the others while they were eating! I think that punishment by depriving children of sweets only develops their greediness. Must tell Nicholas this.'

Nicholas put down the book and looked at his wife. The radiant eyes gazed at him questioningly: would he approve or disapprove of her diary? There could be no doubt not only of his approval, but also of his admiration of his wife.

Perhaps it need not be done so pedantically, Nicholas thought, or even done at all, but this untiring continual spiritual effort, the sole aim of which was the children's moral welfare, delighted him. Had Nicholas been able to analyse his feelings he would have found that his steady, tender and proud love of his wife rested on his feeling of wonder at her spirituality and at the lofty moral world, almost beyond his reach, in which she had her being.

He was proud of her intelligence and goodness, recognized his own insignificance beside her in the spiritual world, and rejoiced all the more that she, with such a soul, not only belonged to him but was part of himself.

'I quite, quite approve, my dearest!' said he with a significant look, and after a short pause he added: 'And I behaved badly to-day. You weren't in the study. We began disputing – Pierre and I – and I lost my temper. But he is impossible: such a child! I don't know what would become of him if Natasha didn't keep him in hand ... Have you any idea why he went to Petersburg? They have formed ...'

'Yes, I know,' said Countess Mary. 'Natasha told me.'

'Well, then you know,' Nicholas went on, growing hot at the mere recollection of their discussion, 'he wanted to convince me that it is every honest man's duty to go against the government and that the oath of allegiance and duty ... I am sorry you weren't there. They all fell on me – Denisov and Natasha ... Natasha is absurd. How she rules over him! And yet there need only be a discussion, and she has no words of her own but only repeats his sayings ...' added Nicholas, yielding to that irresistible inclination which tempts us to judge those nearest and dearest to us. He forgot that what he was saying about Natasha could have been applied word for word to himself in relation to his wife.

'Yes, I have noticed that,' said Countess Mary.

'When I told him that duty and the oath were above everything, he started proving goodness knows what! A pity you were not there – what would you have said?'

'As I see it, you were quite right, and I told Natasha so. Pierre says everybody is suffering, is tortured, and is being corrupted, and that it is our duty to help our neighbour. Of course he is right there,' said Countess Mary, 'but he forgets that we have other duties nearer to us, duties indicated to us by God Himself, and that though we might expose ourselves to risks we must not risk our children.'

'Yes, that's it! That's just what I said to him,' put in Nicholas, who fancied he really had said it. 'But they insisted on their own view: love of one's neighbour and Christianity – and all this in the presence of little Nicholas, who had got into my study and broke all my things.'

'Ah, Nicholas, do you know I am often troubled about little Nicholas,' said Countess Mary. 'He is such an exceptional boy. I am afraid I neglect him for the sake of my own: we all have children and relations, while he has no one. He is constantly alone with his thoughts.'

'Well, I don't think you need reproach yourself on his account. All that the fondest mother could do for her son you have done, and are doing, for him, and of course I am glad of it. He is a fine lad, a fine lad! This evening he listened to Pierre in a sort of trance, and fancy – as we were going to supper I looked, and he had broken everything on my table to bits, and he told me of it himself at once! I never knew him tell an untruth. A fine lad, a fine lad!' repeated Nicholas, who at heart was not fond of Nicholas Bolkonsky but was always anxious to recognize that he was a fine lad.

'Still, I am not the same as his own mother,' said Countess Mary. 'I feel I am not the same and it troubles me. A wonderful boy, but I am dreadfully afraid for him. It would be good for him to have companions.'

'Well, it won't be for long. Next summer I'll take him to Petersburg,' said Nicholas. 'Yes, Pierre always was a dreamer and always will be,' he continued, returning to the talk in the study, which had evidently disturbed him. 'Well, what business is it of mine what goes on there – whether Arakcheev is bad, and all that? What business was it of mine when I married and was so deep in debt that I was threatened with prison, and had a mother who could not see or understand it? And then there are you and the children and our affairs. Is it for my own pleasure that I am at the farm or in the office from morning to night? No, but I know I must work to comfort my mother, to repay you, and not to leave the children such beggars as I was.'

Countess Mary wanted to tell him that man does not live by bread alone, and that he attached too much importance to those matters. But she knew she must not say this, and that it would be useless to do so. She only took his hand and kissed it. He took that as a sign of approval and a confirmation of his thoughts, and after a few minutes' reflection continued to think aloud.

'You know, Mary, to-day Elias Mitrofanych' (this was his overseer) 'came back from the Tambov estate and told me they are already offering eighty thousand rubles for the forest.'

And with an eager face Nicholas began to speak of the possibility of repurchasing Otradnoe before long, and added: 'Another ten years of life and I shall leave the children . . . in an excellent position.'

Countess Mary listened to her husband and understood all that he told her. She knew that when he thought aloud in this way he would sometimes ask her what he had been saying, and be vexed if he noticed that she had been thinking about something else. But she had to force herself to attend, for what he was saying did not interest her at all. She looked at him and did not think but felt about something different. She felt a submissive tender love for this man who would never understand all that she understood, and this seemed to make her love for him still stronger and added a touch of passionate tenderness. Besides this feeling which absorbed her altogether and hindered her from following the details of her husband's plans, thoughts that had no connexion with what he was saying flitted through her mind. She thought of her nephew. Her husband's account of the boy's agitation while Pierre was speaking struck her forcibly, and various traits of his gentle sensitive character recurred to her mind; and while thinking of her nephew she thought also of her own children. She did not compare them with him, but compared her feeling for them with her feeling for him, and felt with regret that there was something lacking in her feeling for little Nicholas.

Sometimes it seemed to her that this difference arose from the difference in their ages, but she felt herself to blame towards him, and promised in her heart to do better and to accomplish the impossible – in this life to love her husband, her children, little Nicholas, and all her neighbours, as Christ loved mankind. Countess Mary's soul always strove towards the infinite, the eternal, and the absolute, and could therefore never be at peace. A stern expression of the lofty, secret suffering of a soul burdened by the body appeared on her face. Nicholas gazed at her. 'O God! What will become of us if she dies, as I always fear when her face is like that?' thought he, and placing himself before the icon he began to say his evening prayers.

16

NATASHA and Pierre, left alone, also began to talk as only a husband and wife can talk, that is, with extraordinary clearness and rapidity, understanding and expressing each other's thoughts in ways contrary to all rules of logic, without premises, deductions, or conclusions, and in a quite peculiar way. Natasha was so used to this kind of talk with her husband that for her it was the surest sign of something being wrong between them if Pierre followed a line of logical reasoning. When he began proving anything or talking argumentatively and calmly and she, led on by his example, began to do the same, she knew that they were on the verge of a quarrel.

From the moment they were alone and Natasha came up to him with wide-open happy eyes and quickly seizing his head pressed it to her bosom, saying: 'Now you are all mine! You won't escape!' – from that moment this conversation began, contrary to all the laws of logic, and contrary to them because quite different subjects were talked about at one and the same time. This simultaneous discussion of many topics did not prevent a clear understanding, but on the contrary was the surest sign that they fully understood one another.

Just as in a dream when all is uncertain, unreasoning, and contradictory except the feeling that guides the dream, so in this intercourse, contrary to all laws of reason, the words themselves were not consecutive and clear, but only the feeling that prompted them.

Natasha spoke to Pierre about her brother's life and doings, of how she had suffered and lacked life during his absence, and of how she was fonder than ever of Mary, and how Mary was in every way better than herself. In saying this Natasha was sincere in acknowledging Mary's superiority, but at the same time by saying it she made a demand on Pierre that he should, all the same, prefer her to Mary and to all other women, and that now, especially after having seen many women in Petersburg, he should tell her so afresh.

Pierre, answering Natasha's words, told her how intolerable it had been for him to meet ladies at dinners and balls in Petersburg.

'I have quite lost the trick of talking to ladies,' he said. 'It was simply dull. Besides, I was very busy.'

Natasha looked intently at him and went on:

'Mary is so splendid,' she said. 'How she understands children! It is as if she saw straight into their souls. Yesterday, for instance, Mitya was naughty ...'

'How like his father he is,' Pierre interjected.

Natasha knew why he mentioned Mitya's likeness to Nicholas: the recollection of his dispute with his brother-in-law was unpleasant and he wanted to know what Natasha thought of it.

'Nicholas has the weakness of never agreeing with anything not generally accepted. But I understand that you value what opens up a fresh line,' said she, repeating words Pierre had once uttered.

'No, the chief point is that to Nicholas ideas and discussions are an amusement – almost a pastime,' said Pierre. 'For instance he is collecting a library and has made it a rule not to buy a new book till he has read what he had already bought – Sismondi, and Rousseau, and Montesquieu,' he added with a smile. 'You know how much I ...' he began, to soften down what he had said; but Natasha interrupted him to show that this was unnecessary.

'So you say ideas are an amusement to him ...'

'Yes, and for me nothing else is serious. All the time in Petersburg I saw everyone as in a dream. When I am taken up by a thought, all else is mere amusement.'

'Ah, I'm so sorry I wasn't there when you met the children,' said Natasha. 'Which was most delighted? Lisa I'm sure.'

'Yes,' Pierre replied, and went on with what was in his mind. 'Nicholas says we ought not to think. But I can't help it. Besides, when I was in Petersburg I felt (I can say this to you) that the whole affair would go to pieces without me – everyone was pulling his own way. But I succeeded in uniting them all; and then my idea is so clear and simple. You see, I don't say that we ought to oppose this and that. We may be mistaken. What I say is: "Join hands, you who love the right, and let there be but one banner – that of active virtue." Prince Sergey is a fine fellow, and clever.'

Natasha would have had no doubt as to the greatness of Pierre's idea, but one thing disconcerted her. 'Can a man so important and necessary to society be also my husband? How did this happen?' She wished to express this doubt to him. 'Now who could decide whether he is really cleverer than all the others?' she asked herself, and passed in review all those whom Pierre most respected. Judging by what he had said, there was no one he had respected so highly as Platon Karataev.

'Do you know what I am thinking about?' she asked. 'About Platon Karataev. Would he have approved of you now do you think?'

Pierre was not at all surprised at this question. He understood his wife's line of thought.

'Platon Karataev?' he repeated, and pondered, evidently sincerely trying to imagine Karataev's opinion on the subject. 'He would not have understood . . . yet perhaps he would.'

'I love you awfully!' Natasha suddenly said. 'Awfully, awfully!'

'No, he would not have approved,' said Pierre, after reflection. 'What he would have approved of is our family life. He was always so anxious to find seemliness, happiness, and peace, in everything, and I should have been proud to let him see us. There now – you talk of my absence, but you wouldn't believe what a special feeling I have for you after a separation . . .'

'Yes, I should think . . .' Natasha began.

'No, it's not that. I never leave off loving you. And one couldn't love more, but this is something special . . . Yes, of course—' he did not finish, because their eyes meeting said the rest.

'What nonsense it is,' Natasha suddenly exclaimed, 'about honeymoons, and that the greatest happiness is at first! On the contrary, now is the best of all. If only you did not go away! Do you remember how we quarrelled? And it was always my fault. Always mine. And what we quarrelled about – I don't even remember!'

'Always about the same thing,' said Pierre with a smile. 'Jealo . . .'

'Don't say it! I can't bear it!' Natasha cried, and her eyes glittered coldly and vindictively. 'Did you see her?'* she added, after a pause.

'No, and if I had I shouldn't have recognized her.'

They were silent for awhile.

'Oh, do you know? While you were talking in the study I was looking at you,' Natasha began, evidently anxious to disperse the cloud that had come over them. 'You are as like him as two peas – like the boy.' (She meant her little son.) 'Oh, it's time to go to him . . . The milk's come . . . But I'm sorry to leave you.'

They were silent for a few seconds. Then suddenly turning to one another at the same time, they both began to speak. Pierre began with self-satisfaction and enthusiasm, Natasha with a quiet happy smile. Having interrupted one another they both stopped to let the other continue.

'No. What did you say? Go on, I was talking nonsense,' said Natasha.

Pierre finished what he had begun. It was the sequel to his complacent reflections on his success in Petersburg. At that moment it seemed to him that he was chosen to give a new direction to the whole of Russian society and to the whole world.

'I only wished to say that ideas that have great results are always simple ones. The whole of my idea is that if vicious people are united and constitute a power, then honest folk must do the same. Now that's simple enough.'

'Yes.'

'And what were you going to say?'

'I? Only nonsense.'

'But all the same?'

'Oh, nothing, only a trifle,' said Natasha, smiling still more brightly. 'I only wanted to tell you about Petya: to-day nurse was coming to take him from me, and he laughed, shut his eyes, and clung to me. I'm sure he thought he was hiding. Awfully sweet! There, now he's crying. Well, good-bye!' and she left the room.

Meanwhile, downstairs in young Nicholas Bolkonsky's bedroom, a little lamp was burning as usual. (The boy was afraid of the dark and they could not cure him of it.) Dessalles slept propped up on four pillows, and his Roman nose emitted sounds of rhythmic snoring. Little Nicholas, who had just waked up in a cold perspiration, sat up in bed and gazed before him with wide-open eyes. He had awoken from a terrible dream. He had dreamt that he and Uncle Pierre, wearing helmets such as were depicted in his Plutarch, were leading a huge army. The army was made up of white slanting lines that filled the air like the cobwebs that float about in autumn, and which Dessalles called *le fil de la Vierge*. In front was Glory, which was similar to those threads but rather thicker. He and Pierre were borne along lightly and joyously, nearer and nearer to their goal. Suddenly the threads that moved them began to slacken and become entangled and it became difficult to move. And Uncle Nicholas stood before them in a stern and threatening attitude.

'Have you done this?' he said, pointing to some broken sealing-wax and pens. 'I loved you, but I have orders from Arakcheev and will kill the first of you who moves forward.' Little Nicholas turned to look at Pierre, but Pierre was no longer there. In his place was his father – Prince Andrew – and his father had neither shape nor form, but he existed, and when little Nicholas perceived him he grew faint with love: he felt himself powerless, limp, and formless. His father caressed and pitied him. But Uncle Nicholas came nearer and nearer to them. Terror seized young Nicholas, and he awoke.

'My father!' he thought. (Though there were two good portraits of Prince Andrew in the house, Nicholas never imagined him in human form.) 'My father has been with me and caressed me. He approved of me and of Uncle Pierre. Whatever he may tell me, I will do it. Mucius Scaevola burnt his hand. Why should not the same sort of thing happen to me? I know they want me to learn. And I will learn. But some day I shall have finished learning, and then I will do something. I only pray God that something may happen to me such as happened to Plutarch's men, and I will act as they did. I will do better. Everyone shall know me, love me, and be delighted with me.' And suddenly his bosom heaved with sobs and he began to cry.

'Are you ill?' he heard Dessalles's voice asking.

'No,' answered Nicholas, and lay back on his pillow.

'He is good and kind and I am fond of him!' he thought of Dessalles. 'But Uncle Pierre! Oh, what a wonderful man he is! And my father? Oh, father, father! Yes, I will do something with which even *he* would be satisfied . . .'

WAR AND PEACE

*

SECOND EPILOGUE

SECOND EPILOGUE

1

HISTORY is the life of nations and of humanity. To seize and put into words, to describe directly, the life of humanity or even of a single nation appears impossible.

The ancient historians all employed one and the same method to describe and seize the apparently elusive – the life of a people. They describe the activity of individuals who ruled the people, and regarded the activity of those men as representing the activity of the whole nation.

The question, how did individuals make nations act as they wished and by what was the will of these individuals themselves guided? the ancients met by recognizing a Divinity which subjected the nations to the will of a chosen man, and guided the will of that chosen man so as to accomplish ends that were predestined.

For the ancients these questions were solved by a belief in the direct participation of the Deity in human affairs.

Modern history, in theory, rejects both these principles.

It would seem that having rejected the belief of the ancients in man's subjection to the Deity and in a predetermined aim towards which nations are led, modern history should study not the manifestations of power but the causes that produce it. But modern history has not done this. Having in theory rejected the view held by the ancients, it still follows them in practice.

Instead of men endowed with divine authority and directly guided by the will of God, modern history has given us either heroes endowed with extraordinary, superhuman capacities, or simply men of very various kinds, from monarchs to journalists, who lead the masses. Instead of the former divinely appointed aims of the Jewish, Greek, or Roman nations, which ancient historians regarded as representing the progress of humanity, modern history has postulated its own aims – the welfare of the French, German, or English people, or, in its highest abstraction, the welfare and civilization of humanity in general, by which is usually meant that of the peoples occupying a small north-westerly portion of a large continent.

Modern history has rejected the beliefs of the ancients without replacing them by a new conception, and the logic of the situation has obliged the historians, after they had apparently rejected the divine authority of the kings and the 'fate' of the ancients, to reach the same conclusion by another road, that is, to recognize (1) nations guided by individual men, and (2) the existence of a known aim to which these nations and humanity at large are tending.

At the basis of the works of all the modern historians from Gibbon to Buckle, despite their seeming disagreements and the apparent novelty of their outlooks, lie those two old, unavoidable assumptions.

In the first place the historian describes the activity of individuals who in his opinion have directed humanity (one historian considers only monarchs, generals, and ministers as being such men, while another includes also orators, learned men, reformers, philosophers and poets). Secondly, it is assumed that the goal towards which humanity is being led is known to the historians: to one of them this goal is the greatness of the Roman, Spanish, or French realm, to another it is liberty, equality, and a certain kind of civilization of a small corner of the world called Europe.

In 1789 a ferment arises in Paris: it grows, spreads, and is expressed by a movement of peoples from west to east. Several times it moves eastwards and collides with a counter-movement from the east westwards; in 1812 it reaches its extreme limit, Moscow; and then, with remarkable symmetry, a counter-movement occurs from east to west, attracting to it, as the first movement had done, the nations of middle Europe. The counter-movement reaches the starting-point of the first movement in the west – Paris – and subsides.

During that twenty-year period an immense number of fields were left untilled, houses were burned, trade changed its direction, millions of men migrated, were impoverished or were enriched, and millions of Christian men professing the law of love of their fellows slew one another.

What does all this mean? Why did it happen? What made those people burn houses and slay their fellow-men? What were the causes of these events? What force made men act so? These are the instinctive, plain, and most legitimate questions humanity asks itself when it encounters the monuments and tradition of that period.

For a reply to these questions the common sense of mankind turns to the science of history, whose aim is to enable nations and humanity to know themselves.

If history had retained the conception of the ancients, it would have said that God, to reward or punish his people, gave Napoleon power and directed his will to the fulfilment of the divine ends; and that reply would have been clear and complete. One might believe or disbelieve in the divine significance of Napoleon, but for anyone believing in it there would have been nothing unintelligible in the history of that period, nor would there have been any contradictions.

But modern history cannot give that reply. Science does not admit the conception of the ancients as to the direct participation of the Deity in human affairs, and therefore history ought to give other answers.

Modern history replying to these questions says: You want to know what this movement means, what caused it, and what force produced these events? Listen:

'Louis XIV was a very proud and self-confident man: he had such and such mistresses and such and such ministers and he ruled France badly. His descendants were weak men and they too ruled France badly. And they had such and such favourites and such and such mistresses. Moreover certain men wrote some books at that time. At the end of the eighteenth century there were a couple of dozen men in Paris who began to talk about all men being free and equal. This caused people all over France to begin to slash at and drown one another. They killed the king and many other people. At that time there was in France a man of genius – Napoleon. He conquered everybody everywhere – that is, he killed many people because he was a great genius. And for some reason he went to kill Africans, and killed them so well and was so cunning and wise that when he returned to France he ordered everybody to obey him, and they all obeyed him. Having become an Emperor he again went out to kill people in Italy, Austria, and Prussia. And there too he killed a great many. In Russia there was an Emperor, Alexander, who decided to restore order in Europe and therefore fought against Napoleon. In 1807 he suddenly made friends with him, but in 1811 they again quarrelled and again began killing many people. Napoleon led six hundred thousand men into Russia and captured Moscow; then he suddenly ran away from Moscow, and the Emperor Alexander, helped by the advice of Stein and others, united Europe to arm against the disturber of its peace. All Napoleon's allies suddenly became his enemies and their forces advanced against the fresh forces he raised. The Allies defeated Napoleon, entered Paris, forced Napoleon to abdicate, and sent him to the island of Elba, not depriving him of the title of Emperor and showing him every respect, though five years before and one year later they all regarded him as an outlaw and a brigand. Then Louis XVIII, who till then had been the laughing-stock both of the French and the Allies, began to reign. And Napoleon, shedding tears before his Old Guards, renounced the throne and went into exile. Then the skilful statesmen and diplomatists (especially Talleyrand, who managed to sit down in a particular chair before anyone else, and thereby extended the frontiers of France) talked in Vienna, and by these conversations made the nations happy or unhappy. Suddenly the diplomatists and monarchs nearly quarrelled, and were on the point of again ordering their armies to kill one another, but just then Napoleon arrived in France with a battalion, and the French, who had been hating him, immediately submitted to him. But the Allied monarchs were angry at this and went to fight the French once more. And they defeated the genius Napoleon and, suddenly recognizing him as a brigand, sent him to the island of St Helena. And the exile, separated from the beloved France so dear to his heart, died a lingering death on that rock and bequeathed his great deeds to posterity. But in Europe a reaction occurred, and the sovereigns once again all began to oppress their subjects.'

It would be a mistake to think this ironic – a caricature of the historical accounts. On the contrary, it is a very mild expression of the contradictory replies, not meeting the questions, which *all* the historians give, from the compilers of memoirs and the histories of separate States to the writers of general histories and the new histories of the *culture* of that period.

The strangeness and absurdity of these replies arise from the fact that modern history, like a deaf man, answers questions no one asks.

If the purpose of history be to give a description of the movement of humanity and of the peoples, the first question – in the absence of a reply to which all the rest will be incomprehensible – is: What is the power that moves peoples? To this, modern history laboriously replies either that Napoleon was a great genius, or that Louis XIV was very proud, or that certain writers wrote certain books.

All that may be so, and mankind is ready to agree with it, but it is not what was asked. All that would be interesting if we recognized a divine power based on itself and always consistently directing its nations through Napoleons, Louis-es, and writers; but we do not acknowledge such a power, and therefore before speaking about Napoleons, Louis-es, and authors, we ought to be shown the connexion existing between these men and the movement of the nations.

If instead of a divine power some other force has appeared, it should be explained in what this new force consists, for the whole interest of history lies precisely in that force.

History seems to assume that this force is self-evident and known to everyone. But in spite of every desire to regard it as known, anyone reading many historical works cannot help doubting whether this new force, so variously understood by the historians themselves, is really quite well known to everybody.

2

WHAT force moves the nations?

Biographical historians and historians of separate nations understand this force as a power inherent in heroes and rulers. In their narration events occur solely by the will of a Napoleon, an Alexander, or in general the persons they describe. The answers given by this kind of historian to the question of what force causes events to happen are satisfactory only as long as there is but one historian to each event. As soon as historians of different nationalities and tendencies begin to describe the same event, the replies they give immediately lose all meaning, for this force is understood by them all not only differently but often in quite contradictory ways. One historian says that an event was produced by Napoleon's power, another that it was produced by Alexander's, a third that it was due to the power of some other person. Besides this, historians of that kind contradict each other even in their statement as to the force on which the authority of some particular person was based. Thiers, a Bonapartist, says that Napoleon's power was based on his virtue and genius. Lanfrey, a Republican,* says it was based on his trickery and deception of the people. So that the historians of this class, by mutually destroying one another's positions, destroy the understanding of the force which produces events, and furnish no reply to history's essential question.

Writers of universal history, who deal with all the nations, seem to recognize how erroneous is the specialist historians' view of the force which produces events. They do not recognize it as a power inherent in heroes and rulers but as the resultant of a multiplicity of variously directed forces. In describing a war, or the subjugation of a people, a general historian looks for the cause of the event not in the power of one man, but in the interaction of many persons connected with the event.

According to this view the power of historical personages, represented as the product of many forces, can no longer, it would seem, be regarded as a force that itself produces events. Yet in most cases universal historians still employ the conception of power as a force that itself produces events, and treat it as their cause. In their exposition, an historical character is first the product of his time and his power only the resultant of various forces, and then his power is itself a force producing events. Gervinus,* Schlosser and others, for instance, at one time prove Napoleon to be a product of the Revolution, of the ideas of 1789 and so forth, and at another plainly say that the campaign of 1812 and other things they do not like were simply the product of Napoleon's misdirected will, and that the very ideas of 1789 were arrested in their development by Napoleon's caprice. The ideas of the Revolution and the general temper of the age produced Napoleon's power. But Napoleon's power suppressed the ideas of the Revolution and the general temper of the age.

This curious contradiction is not accidental. Not only does it occur at every step, but the universal historians' accounts are all made up of a chain of such contradictions. This contradiction occurs because after entering the field of analysis the universal historians stop half-way.

To find component forces equal to the composite or resultant force, the sum of the components must equal the resultant. This condition is never observed by the universal historians, and so to explain the resultant forces they are obliged to admit, in addition to the insufficient components, another unexplained force affecting the resultant action.

Specialist historians describing the campaign of 1813, or the restoration of the Bourbons, plainly assert that these events were produced by the will of Alexander. But the universal historian Gervinus, refuting this opinion of the specialist historian, tries to prove that the campaign of 1813 and the restoration of the Bourbons were due to other things besides Alexander's will – such as the activity of Stein, Metternich, Madame de Staël, Talleyrand, Fichte, Chateaubriand, and others. The historian evidently decomposes Alexander's power into the components: Talleyrand, Chateaubriand, and the rest – but the sum of the components, that is, the interactions of Chateaubriand, Talleyrand, Madame de Staël and the others, evidently does not equal the resultant, namely the phenomenon of millions of Frenchmen submitting to the Bourbons. That Chateaubriand, Madame de Staël and others spoke certain words to one another only affected their mutual relations but does not account for the submission of millions. And therefore to explain how from these relations of theirs the submission of millions of people resulted – that is, how component forces equal to one A gave a resultant equal to a thousand times A – the historian is again obliged to fall back on the force he had denied – power – and to recognize it as the resultant of the forces, that is, he has to admit an unexplained force acting on the resultant. And that is just what the universal historians do, and consequently they not only contradict the specialist historians but contradict themselves.

Peasants having no clear idea of the cause of rain, say, according to whether they want rain or fine weather: 'The wind has blown the clouds away,' or, 'The wind has brought up the clouds.' And in the same way the universal historians sometimes, when it pleases them and fits in with their theory, say that power is the result of events, and sometimes, when they want to prove something else, say that power produces events.

A third class of historians – the so-called historians of culture – following the path laid down by the universal historians who sometimes accept writers and ladies as forces producing events – again take that force to be something quite different. They see it in what is called culture – in mental activity.

The historians of culture are quite consistent in regard to their progenitors, the writers of universal histories, for if historical events may be explained by the fact that certain persons treated one another in such and such ways, why not explain them by the fact that such and such people wrote such and such books? Of the immense number of indications accompanying every vital phenomenon these historians select the indication of intellectual activity, and say that this indication is the cause. But despite their endeavours to prove that the cause of events lies in intellectual activity, only by a great stretch can one admit that there is any connexion between intellectual activity and the movement of peoples, and in no case can one admit that intellectual activity controls people's actions, for that view is not confirmed by such facts as the very cruel murders of the French Revolution resulting from the doctrine of the equality of man, or the very cruel wars and executions resulting from the preaching of love.

But even admitting all the cunningly devised arguments with which these histories are filled to be correct: admitting that nations are governed by some indefined force called an *idea* – history's essential question still remains unanswered, and to the former power of monarchs and to the influence of advisers and other people introduced by the universal historians, another, newer force – the *idea* – is added, the connexion of which with the masses needs explanation. It is possible to understand that Napoleon had power and so events occurred; with some effort one may conceive that Napoleon together with other influences was the cause of an event; but how a book, *Le Contrat Social,* had the effect of making Frenchmen begin to drown one another, cannot be understood without an explanation of the causal nexus of this new force with the event.

Undoubtedly some connexion exists between all who live contemporaneously, and so it is possible to find some connexion between the intellectual activity of men and their historical movements, just as such a connexion may be found between the movements of humanity and commerce, handicraft, gardening, or anything else you please. But why intellectual activity is considered by the historians of culture to be the cause or expression of the whole historical movement is hard to understand. Only the following considerations can have led the historians to such a conclusion: (1) that history is written by learned men and so it is natural and agreeable for them to think that the activity of their class supplies the basis of the movement of all humanity, just as a similar belief is natural and agreeable to traders, agriculturists, and soldiers (if they do not express it, that is merely because traders and soldiers do not write history), and (2) that spiritual activity, enlightenment, civilization, culture, ideas, are all indistinct, indefinite conceptions under whose banner it is very easy to use words having a still less definite meaning and which can therefore be readily introduced into any theory.

But not to speak of the intrinsic quality of histories of this kind (which may possibly even be of use to someone for something), the histories of culture, to which all general histories tend more and more to approximate, are significant from the fact that after seriously and minutely examining various religious, philosophic, and political doctrines as causes of events, as soon as they have to describe an actual historical event, such as the campaign of 1812 for instance, they involuntarily describe it as resulting from an exercise of power – and say plainly that that campaign was the result of Napoleon's will. Speaking so, the historians of culture involuntarily contradict themselves, and show that the new force they have devised does not account for what happens in history, and that history can only be explained by introducing the power which they apparently do not recognize.

A LOCOMOTIVE is moving. Someone asks: What moves it? A peasant says the devil moves it. Another man says the locomotive moves because its wheels go round. A third asserts that the cause of its movement lies in the smoke which the wind carries away.

The peasant is irrefutable. He has devised a complete explanation. To refute him someone would have to prove to him that there is no devil, or another peasant would have to explain to him that it is not the devil, but a German, who moves the locomotive. Only then, as a result of the contradiction, will they see that they are both wrong. But the man who says that the movement of the wheels is the cause, refutes himself, for having once started on analysis he ought to go on and explain further why the wheels go round; and till he has reached the ultimate cause of the movement of the locomotive in the pressure of steam in the boiler, he has no right to stop in his search for the cause. The man who explains the movement of the locomotive by the smoke that is carried back, has noticed that the wheels do not supply an explanation, and has taken the first sign that occurs to him and in his turn has offered that as an explanation.

The only conception that can explain the movement of the locomotive is that of a force commensurate with the movement observed.

The only conception that can explain the movement of the peoples is that of some force commensurate with the whole movement of the peoples.

Yet to supply this conception various historians take forces of different kinds, all of which are incommensurate with the movement observed. Some see it as a force directly inherent in heroes, as the peasant sees the devil in the locomotive; others as a force resulting from several other forces, like the movement of the wheels; others again as an intellectual influence, like the smoke that is blown away.

So long as histories are written of separate individuals, whether Caesars, Alexanders, Luthers, or Voltaires, and not the histories of *all*, absolutely *all*, those who take part in an event, it is quite impossible to describe the movement of humanity without the conception of a force compelling men to direct their activity towards a certain end. And the only such conception known to historians is that of power.

This conception is the one handle by means of which the material of history, as at present expounded, can be dealt with, and anyone who breaks that handle off, as Buckle did, without finding some other method of treating historical material, merely deprives himself of the one possible way of dealing with it. The necessity for the conception of power as an explanation of historical events is best demonstrated by the universal historians and historians of culture themselves, for they professedly reject that conception but inevitably have recourse to it at every step.

In dealing with humanity's inquiry the science of history up to now is like money in circulation – paper money and coin. The biographies and special national histories are like paper money. They can be used and can circulate and fulfil their purpose without harm to anyone, and even advantageously, as long as no one asks what is the security behind them. You need only forget to ask how the will of heroes produces events, and such histories as Thiers's will be interesting and instructive, and may perhaps even possess a tinge of poetry. But just as doubts of the real value of paper money arise either because, being easy to make, too much of it gets made, or because people try to exchange it for gold, so also doubts concerning the real value of such histories arise either because too many of them are written, or because in his simplicity of heart someone inquires: By what force did Napoleon do this? – that is, wants to exchange the current paper money for the real gold of actual comprehension.

The writers of universal histories and of the history of culture are like people who, recognizing the defects of paper money, decide to substitute for it money made of metal that has not the specific gravity of gold. It may indeed make jingling coin, but will do no more than that. Paper money may deceive the ignorant, but nobody is deceived by tokens of base metal that have no value but merely jingle. As gold is gold only if it is serviceable not merely for exchange but also for use, so universal historians will only be valuable when they can reply to history's essential question: What is power? The universal historians give contradictory replies to that question, while the historians of culture evade it and answer something quite different. And as counters of imitation gold can only be used among a group of people who agree to accept them as gold or among those who do not know the nature of gold, so universal historians and historians of culture, not answering humanity's essential question, only serve as currency for some purposes of their own in universities and among the mass of readers who have a taste for what they call 'serious reading'.

HAVING abandoned the conception of the ancients as to the divine subjection of the will of a nation to some chosen man and the subjection of that man's will to the Deity, history cannot without contradictions take a single step till it has chosen one of two things: either a return to the former belief in the direct intervention of the Deity in human affairs, or a definite explanation of the meaning of the force producing historical events and termed 'power'.

A return to the first is impossible, the belief has been destroyed; and so it is essential to explain what is meant by power.

Napoleon ordered an army to be raised and go to war. We are so accustomed to that idea and have become so used to it, that the question why six hundred thousand men went to fight, when Napoleon uttered certain words seems to us senseless. He had the power and so what he ordered was done.

This reply is quite satisfactory if we believe that the power was given him by God. But as soon as we do not admit that, it becomes essential to determine what is this power one man had over others.

It cannot be the direct physical power of a strong man over a weak one – a domination based on the application or threat of physical force, like the power of Hercules; nor can it be based on the effect of moral force as in their simplicity some historians think, who say that the leading figures in history are heroes, that is, men gifted with a special strength of soul and mind called genius. This power cannot be based on the predominance of moral strength for, not to mention heroes such as Napoleon about whose moral qualities opinions differ widely, history shows us that neither a Louis XI nor a Metternich, who ruled over millions of people, had any particular moral qualities, but on the contrary were generally morally weaker than any of the millions they ruled over.

If the source of power lies neither in the physical nor the moral qualities of him who possesses it, it must evidently be looked for elsewhere – in the relations of the man who wields the power to the people.

And that is how power is understood by the science of jurisprudence, that exchange-bank of history, which offers to exchange history's understanding of power for true gold.

Power is the collective will of the people transferred, by expressed or tacit consent, to their chosen rulers.

In the domain of jurisprudence, which consists of discussions of how a State and power might be arranged were it possible for all that to be arranged, it is all very clear; but when applied to history that definition of power needs explanation.

The science of jurisprudence regards the State and power as the ancients regarded fire – namely, as something existing absolutely. But for history the State and power are merely phenomena, just as for modern physics fire is not an element but a phenomenon.

From this fundamental difference between the view held by history and that held by jurisprudence it follows that jurisprudence can tell minutely how, in its opinion, power should be constituted and what power – existing immutably, outside time – is, but to history's questions about the meaning of the mutations of power in time it can answer nothing.

If power be the collective will of the people transferred to their ruler, was Pugachëv a representative of the will of the people? If not, then why was Napoleon I? Why was Napoleon III a criminal when he was taken prisoner at Boulogne,* and why, later on, were those criminals whom he arrested?

Do palace revolutions – in which sometimes only two or three people take part – transfer the will of the people to a new ruler? In international relations, is the will of the people also transferred to their conqueror? Was the will of the Confederation of the Rhine transferred to Napoleon in 1808? Was the will of the Russian people transferred to Napoleon in 1809, when our army in alliance with the French went to fight the Austrians?

To these questions three answers are possible:

Either to assume (1) that the will of the people is always unconditionally transferred to the ruler or rulers they have chosen and that therefore every emergence of a new power, every struggle against the power once appointed, should be absolutely regarded as an infringement of the real power; or (2) that the will of the people is transferred to the rulers conditionally, under definite and known conditions, and to show that all limitations, conflicts, and even destructions of power, result from a non-observance by the rulers of the conditions under which their power was entrusted to them; or (3) that the will of the people is delegated to the rulers conditionally, but that the conditions are unknown and indefinite, and that the appearance of several authorities, their struggles, and their falls, result solely from the greater or lesser fulfilment by the rulers of these unknown conditions on which the will of the people is transferred from some people to others.

And these are the three ways in which the historians do explain the relation of the people to their rulers.

Some historians, failing in their simplicity to understand the question of the meaning of power – those biographical and special historians already referred to – seem to consider that the collective will of the people is unconditionally transferred to historical persons, and therefore when describing some single State they assume that particular power to be the one absolute and real power, and that any other force opposing this is not a power but a violation of power – mere violence.

Their theory, suitable for primitive and peaceful periods of history, has the inconvenience – in application to complex and stormy periods in the life of nations, during which various powers arise simultaneously and struggle with one another – that a Legitimist historian will prove that the National Convention, the Directory, and Bonaparte, were mere infringers of the true power, while a Republican and a Bonapartist will prove, the one that the Convention and the other that the Empire was the real power, and that all the others were violations of power. Evidently the explanations furnished by these historians, being mutually contradictory, can only satisfy young children.

Recognizing the falsity of this view of history, another set of historians say that power rests on a conditional delegation of the will of the people to their rulers, and that historical leaders have power only conditionally on carrying out the programme the will of the people has by tacit agreement prescribed to them. But what this programme consists in, these historians do not say, or if they do they continually contradict one another.

Each historian, according to his view of what constitutes a nation's progress, looks for these conditions in the greatness, wealth, freedom, or enlightenment, of the citizens of France or some other country. But not to mention the historians' contradictions as to the nature of this programme – or even admitting that some one general programme of these conditions exists – the facts of history almost always contradict that theory. If the conditions under which power is entrusted consist in the wealth, freedom, and enlightenment of the people, how is it that Louis XIV and Ivan the Terrible end their reigns tranquilly, while Louis XVI and Charles I are executed by their people? To this question the historians reply that Louis XIV's activity, contrary to the programme, reacted on Louis XVI. But why did it not react on Louis XIV or on Louis XV – why should it react just on Louis XVI? And what is the term for such reactions? To these questions there are, and can be, no answers. Equally little does this view explain why for several centuries the collective will is not withdrawn from certain rulers and their heirs, and then suddenly during a period of fifty years is transferred to the Convention, to the Directory, to Napoleon, to

Alexander, to Louis XVIII, to Napoleon again, to Charles X, to Louis Philippe, to a Republican government, and to Napoleon III. When explaining these rapid transfers of the people's will from one individual to another, especially in view of international relations, conquests, and alliances, the historians are obliged to admit that some of these transfers are not normal delegations of the people's will but are accidents, dependent on cunning, on mistakes, on craft, or on the weakness of a diplomatist, a ruler, or a party leader. So that the greater part of the events of history – civil wars, revolutions, and conquests – are presented by these historians not as the results of free transferences of the people's will, but as results of the ill-directed will of one or more individuals, that is, once again, as usurpations of power. And so these historians also see and admit historical events which are exceptions to the theory.

The historians resemble a botanist who, having noticed that some plants grow from seeds with two cotyledons, should insist that all that grows does so by sprouting into two leaves, and that the palm, the mushroom, and even the oak, which blossom in full growth and no longer resemble two leaves, are deviations from the theory.

Historians of the third class assume that the will of the people is transferred to historical personages conditionally, but that the conditions are unknown to us. They say that historical personages have power only because they fulfil the will of the people which has been delegated to them.

But in that case, if the force that moves nations lies not in the historical leaders but in the nations themselves, what significance have those leaders?

The leaders, these historians tell us, express the will of the people: the activity of the leaders represents the activity of the people.

But in that case the question arises whether all the activity of the leaders serves as an expression of the people's will or only some part of it? If the whole activity of the leaders serves as the expression of the people's will, as some historians suppose, then all the details of the court scandals contained in the biographies of a Napoleon or a Catherine serve to express the life of the nation, which is evident nonsense; but if it is only some particular side of the activity of an historical leader which serves to express the people's life, as other so-called 'philosophical' historians believe, then to determine which side of the activity of a leader expresses the nation's life we have first of all to know in what the nation's life consists.

Met by this difficulty historians of that class devise some most obscure, impalable, and general abstraction which can cover all conceivable occurrences, and declare this abstraction to be the aim of humanity's movement. The most usual generalizations, adopted by almost all the historians, are: freedom, equality, enlightenment, progress, civilization, and culture. Postulating some generalization as the goal of the movement of humanity, the historians study the men of whom the greatest number of monuments have remained: kings, ministers, generals, authors, reformers, popes, and journalists, to the extent to which in their opinion these persons have promoted or hindered that abstraction. But as it is in no way proven that the aim of humanity does consist in freedom, equality, enlightenment, or civilization, and as the connexion of the people with the rulers and enlighteners of humanity is only based on the arbitrary assumption that the collective will of the people is always transferred to the men whom we have noticed, it happens that the activity of the millions who migrate, burn houses, abandon agriculture, and destroy one another, never is expressed in the account of the activity of some dozen people who did not burn houses, practise agriculture, or slay their fellow-creatures.

History proves this at every turn. Is the ferment of the peoples of the west at the end of the eighteenth century and their drive eastwards explained by the activity of Louis XIV, XV, and XVI, their mistresses and ministers, and by the lives of Napoleon, Rousseau, Diderot, Beaumarchais and others?

Is the movement of the Russian people eastwards to Kazan and Siberia expressed by details of the morbid character of Ivan the Terrible and by his correspondence with Kurbsky?*

Is the movement of the peoples at the time of the Crusades explained by the life and activity of the Godfreys and the Louis-es and their ladies? For us that movement of the peoples from west to east, without leaders, with a crowd of vagrants, and with Peter the Hermit, remains incomprehensible. And yet more incomprehensible is the cessation of that movement when a rational and sacred aim for the Crusade – the deliverance of Jerusalem – had been clearly defined by historical leaders. Popes, kings, and knights incited the peoples to free the Holy Land; but the people did not go, for the unknown cause which had previously impelled them to go no longer existed. The history of the Godfreys and the Minnesingers can evidently not cover the life of the peoples. And the history of the Godfreys and the Minnesingers has remained the history of Godfreys and Minnesingers, but the history of the life of the peoples and their impulses has remained unknown.

Still less does the history of authors and reformers explain to us the life of the peoples.

The history of culture explains to us the impulses and conditions of life and thought of a writer or a reformer. We learn that Luther had a hot temper and said such and such things; we learn that Rousseau was suspicious and wrote such and such books; but we do not learn why after the Reformation the peoples massacred one another, nor why during the French Revolution they guillotined one another.

If we unite both these kinds of history, as is done by the newest historians, we shall have the history of monarchs and writers, but not the history of the life of the peoples.

5

THE life of the nations is not contained in the lives of a few men, for the connexion between those men and the nations has not been found. The theory that this connexion is based on the transference of the collective will of a people to certain historical personages is an hypothesis unconfirmed by the experience of history.

The theory of the transference of the collective will of the people to historical persons may perhaps explain much in the domain of jurisprudence and be essential for its purposes, but in its application to history, as soon as revolutions, conquests, or civil wars occur – that is, as soon as history begins – that theory explains nothing.

The theory seems irrefutable just because the act of transference of the people's will cannot be verified, for it never occurred.

Whatever happens and whoever may stand at the head of affairs, the theory can always say that such and such a person took the lead because the collective will was transferred to him.

The replies this theory gives to historical questions are like the replies of a man who, watching the movements of a herd of cattle and paying no attention to the varying quality of the pasturage in different parts of the field or to the driving of the herdsman, should attribute the direction the herd takes to what animal happens to be at its head.

'The herd goes in that direction because the animal in front leads it and the collective will of all the other animals is vested in that leader.' That is what historians of the first class say – those who assume the unconditional transference of the people's will.

'If the animals leading the herd change, this happens because the collective will of all the animals is transferred from one leader to another, according to whether the animal is or is not leading them in the direction selected by the whole herd.' Such is the reply of historians who assume that the collective will of the people is delegated to rulers under conditions which they regard as known. (With this method of observation it often happens that the observer, influenced by the direction he himself prefers, regards those as leaders who, owing to the people's change of direction, are no longer in front, but on one side, or even in the rear.)

'If the animals in front are continually changing and the direction of the whole herd is constantly altered, this is because, in order to follow a given direction, the animals transfer their will to the animals that have attracted our attention, and to study the movements of the herd we must watch the movements of all the prominent animals moving on all sides of the herd.' So say the third class of historians who regard all historical persons, from monarchs to journalists, as the expression of their age.

The theory of the transference of the will of the people to historical persons is merely a paraphrase – a restatement of the question in other words.

What causes historical events? Power. What is power? Power is the collective will of the people transferred to one person. Under what condition is the will of the people delegated to one person? On condition that that person expresses the will of the whole people. That is, power is power: in other words, power is a word the meaning of which we do not understand.

If the realm of human knowledge were confined to abstract reasoning, then having subjected to criticism the explanation of 'power' that juridical science gives us, humanity would conclude that power is merely a word and has no real existence. But for the knowledge of phenomena man has, besides abstract reasoning, experience by which he verifies his reflections. And experience tells us that power is not merely a word but an actually existing phenomenon.

Not to speak of the fact that no description of the collective activity of men can do without the conception of power, the existence of power is proved both by history and by observing contemporary events.

Whenever an event occurs a man appears, or men appear, by whose will the event seems to have taken place. Napoleon III issues a decree and the French go to Mexico.* The King of Prussia and Bismarck issue decrees and an army enters Bohemia.* Napoleon I issues a decree and an army enters Russia. Alexander I gives a command and the French submit to the Bourbons. Experience shows us that whatever event occurs it is always related to the will of one man or of several men who have decreed it.

The historians, in accord with the old habit of acknowledging divine intervention in human affairs, want to see the cause of events in the expression of the will of someone endowed with power, but that supposition is not confirmed either by reason or by experience.

On the one side reflection shows that the expression of a man's will – his words – are only part of the general activity expressed in an event, as for instance in a war or a revolution, and so without assuming an incomprehensible, supernatural force – a miracle – one cannot admit that words can be the immediate cause of the movements of millions of men. On the other hand, even if we admitted that words could be the cause of events, history shows that the expression of the will of historical personages does not in most cases produce any effect; that is to say, their commands are often not executed, and sometimes the very opposite of what they order occurs.

Without admitting divine intervention in the affairs of humanity we cannot regard 'power' as the cause of events.

Power, from the standpoint of experience, is merely the relation that exists between the expression of someone's will and the execution of that will by others.

To explain the conditions of that relationship we must first establish a conception of the expression of will, referring it to man and not to the Deity.

If the Deity issues a command, expresses His will as ancient history tells us, the expression of that will is independent of time and is not caused by anything, for the Divinity is not controlled by an event. But speaking of commands that are the expression of the will of men, acting in time and related to one another – to explain the connexion of commands with events we must restore: (1) the condition of all that takes place: the continuity of movement in time both of the events and of the person who commands, and (2) the inevitability of the connexion of the person commanding to those who execute his command.

6

ONLY the expression of the will of the Deity, not dependent on time, can relate to a whole series of events occurring over a period of years or centuries, and only the Deity, independent of everything, can by His sole will determine the direction of humanity's movement; but man acts in time and himself takes part in what occurs.

Reinstating the first condition omitted, that of time, we see that no command can be executed without some preceding command having been given, rendering the execution of the last command possible.

No command ever appears spontaneously, or itself covers a whole series of occurrences; but each command follows from another, and never refers to a whole series of events but always to one moment only of an event.

When, for instance, we say that Napoleon ordered armies to go to war, we combine in one simultaneous expression a whole series of consecutive commands dependent one on another. Napoleon could not have commanded an invasion of Russia and never did so. To-day he ordered such and such papers to be written to Vienna, to Berlin, and to Petersburg; to-morrow such and such decrees and orders to the army, the fleet, the commissariat, and so on and so on – millions of commands, which formed a whole series, corresponding to a series of events which brought the French armies into Russia.

If throughout his reign Napoleon gave commands concerning an invasion of England and expended on no other undertaking so much time and effort, and yet during his whole reign never once attempted to execute that design, but undertook an expedition into Russia, with which country he considered it desirable to be in alliance (a conviction he repeatedly expressed) – this came about because his commands did not correspond to the course of events in the first case, but did so in the latter.

For a command to be certainly executed it is necessary that a man should command what can be executed. But to know what can and what cannot be executed is impossible, not only in the case of Napoleon's invasion of Russia, in which millions participated, but even in the simplest event, for in either case millions of obstacles may arise to prevent its execution. Every command executed is always one of an immense number unexecuted. All the impossible commands inconsistent with the course of events remain unexecuted. Only the possible ones get linked up with a consecutive series of commands corresponding to a series of events, and are executed.

Our false conception that an event is caused by a command which precedes it is due to the fact that when the event has taken place, and out of thousands of others those few commands which were consistent with that event have been executed, we forget about the others that were not executed because they could not be. Apart from that, the chief source of our error in this matter is due to the fact that in the historical accounts a whole series of innumerable, diverse, and petty events, such as all those which led the French armies to Russia, for instance, is generalized into one event in accord with the result produced by that series of events, and corresponding with this generalization the whole series of commands is also generalized into a single expression of will.

We say that Napoleon wished to invade Russia and invaded it. In reality in all Napoleon's activity we never find anything resembling an expression of that wish, but find a series of commands, or expressions of his will, very variously and indefinitely directed. Of an innumerable series of unexecuted commands of Napoleon's, one series, for the campaign of 1812, was carried out – not because those orders differed in any way from the other unexecuted orders, but because they coincided with the course of events that led the French army into Russia; just as in stencil work this or that figure comes out, not because the colour was laid on from this side or in that way, but because it was laid on from all sides over the figure cut in the stencil.

So that examining the relation in time of the commands to the events, we find that a command can never be the cause of the event, but that a certain definite dependence exists between the two.

To understand in what this dependence consists it is necessary to reinstate another omitted condition of every command proceeding not from the Deity but from a man, which is, that the man who gives the command himself takes part in the event.

This relation of the commander to those he commands is just what is called power. This relation consists in the following:

For common action people always unite in certain combinations, in which, regardless of the difference of the aims set for the common action, the relation between those taking part in it is always the same.

Men uniting in these combinations always assume such relations towards one another that the larger number take a more direct share, and the smaller number a less direct share, in the collective action for which they have combined.

Of all the combinations in which men unite for collective action one of the most striking and definite examples is an army.

Every army is composed of lower ranks of the service – the rank and file – of whom there are always the greatest number; of the next higher military rank – corporals and non-commissioned officers – of whom there are fewer than of the former; and of still higher officers, of whom there are still fewer, and so on to the highest military command, which is concentrated in one person.

A military organization may be quite correctly compared to a cone, of which the base with the largest diameter consists of the rank and file; the next higher and smaller section of the cone consists of the next higher grades of the army, and so on to the apex, the point of which will represent the commander-in-chief.

The soldiers, of whom there are the most, form the lower section of the cone and its base. The soldier himself does the stabbing, hacking, burning, and pillaging, and always receives orders for these actions from men above him; he himself never gives an order. The non-commissioned officers (of whom there are fewer) perform the action itself less frequently than the soldiers, but they already give commands. An officer still less often acts directly himself, but commands still more frequently. A general does nothing but command the troops, indicates the objective, and hardly ever uses a weapon himself. The commander-in-chief never takes direct part in the action itself, but only gives general orders concerning the movement of the mass of the troops. A similar relation of people to one another is seen in every combination of men for common activity – in agriculture, trade, and every administration.

And so, without particularly analysing all the contiguous sections of a cone and of the ranks of an army, or the ranks and positions in any administrative or public business whatever, from the lowest to the highest, we see a law by which men, to take associated action, combine in such relations that the more directly they participate in performing the action the less they can command and the more numerous they are, while the less their direct participation in the action itself, the more they command and the fewer of them there are; rising in this way from the lowest ranks to the man at the top, who takes the least direct share in the action and directs his activity most of all to commanding.

This relation of the men who command to those they command is what constitutes the essence of the conception called power.

Having restored the condition of time, under which all events occur, we find that a command is executed only when it is related to a corresponding series of events. Restoring the essential condition of connexion between those who command and those who execute, we find that by the very nature of the case, those who command take the smallest part in the action itself, and that their activity is exclusively directed to commanding.

7

WHEN an event is taking place people express their opinions and wishes about it, and as the event results from the collective activity of many people, some one of the opinions or wishes expressed is sure to be fulfilled if but approximately. When one of the opinions expressed is fulfilled, that opinion gets connected with the event as a command preceding it.

Men are hauling a log. Each of them expresses his opinion as to how and where to haul it. They haul the log away, and it happens that this is done as one of them said. He ordered it. There we have command and power in their primary form. The man who worked most with his hands could not think so much about what he was doing, or reflect on or command what would result from the common activity; while the man who commanded more would evidently work less with his hands on account of his greater verbal activity.

When some larger concourse of men direct their activity to a common aim there is a yet sharper division of those who, because their activity is given to directing and commanding, take less part in the direct work.

When a man works alone he always has a certain set of reflections which, as it seems to him, directed his past activity, justify his present activity, and guide him in planning his future actions. Just the same is done by a concourse of people, allowing those who do not take a direct part in the activity to devise considerations, justifications, and surmises concerning their collective activity.

For reasons known or unknown to us the French began to drown and to kill one another. And corresponding to the event its justification appears in people's belief that this was necessary for the welfare of France, for liberty, and for equality. People ceased to kill one another, and this event was accompanied by its justification in the necessity for a centralization of power, resistance to Europe, and so on. Men went from the west to the east killing their fellow-men, and the event was accompanied by phrases about the glory of France, the baseness of England, and so on. History shows us that these justifications of the events have no common sense and are all contradictory, as in the instance of killing a man as the result of recognizing his rights, and the killing of millions in Russia for the humiliation of England. But these justifications have a very necessary significance in their own day.

These justifications release those who produce the events from moral responsibility. These temporary aims are like the broom fixed in front of a locomotive to clear the snow from the rails in front: they clear men's moral responsibilities from their path.

Without such justifications there would be no reply to the simplest question that presents itself when examining each historical event. How is it that millions of men commit collective crimes – make war, commit murder, and so on?

With the present complex forms of political and social life in

Europe, can any event that is not prescribed, decreed, or ordered by monarchs, ministers, parliaments, or newspapers, be imagined? Is there any collective action which cannot find its justification in political unity, in patriotism, in the balance-of-power, or in civilization? So that every event that occurs inevitably coincides with some expressed wish, and receiving a justification, presents itself as the result of the will of one man or of several men.

In whatever direction a ship moves the flow of the waves it cuts will always be noticeable ahead of it. To those on board the ship the movement of those waves will be the only perceptible motion.

Only by watching closely, moment by moment, the movement of that flow and comparing it with the movement of the ship, do we convince ourselves that every bit of it is occasioned by the forward movement of the ship and that we were led into error by the fact that we ourselves were imperceptibly moving.

We see the same if we watch, moment by moment, the movement of historical characters (that is, re-establish the inevitable condition of all that occurs – the continuity of movement in time) and do not lose sight of the essential connexion of historical persons with the masses.

When the ship moves in one direction there is one and the same wave ahead of it, when it turns frequently the wave ahead of it also turns frequently. But wherever it may turn there always will be the wave anticipating its movement.

Whatever happens it always appears that just that event was foreseen and decreed. Wherever the ship may go, the rush of water which neither directs nor increases its movement foams ahead of it, and at a distance seems to us not merely to move of itself but to govern the ship's movement also.

Examining only those expressions of the will of historical persons which were related to events as commands, historians have assumed that the events depended on those commands. But examining the events themselves and the connexion in which the historical persons stood to the people, we have found that they and their commands were dependent on events. The incontestable proof of this deduction is that however many commands were issued the event does not take place unless there are other causes for it, but as soon as an event occurs – be it what it may – then out of all the continually expressed wishes of different people some will always be found which by their meaning and their time of utterance are related to the events as commands.

Arriving at this conclusion we can reply directly and positively to those two essential questions of history:

(1) What is power?

(2) What force produces the movement of the nations?

(1) Power is the relation of a given person to other individuals, in which the more this person expresses opinions, predictions, and justifications of the collective action that is performed, the less is his participation in that action.

(2) The movement of nations is caused not by power, nor by intellectual activity, nor even by a combination of the two as historians have supposed, but by the activity of *all* the people who participate in the events, and who always combine in such a way that those taking the largest direct share in the event take on themselves the least responsibility and vice versa.

Morally the wielder of power appears to cause the event; physically it is those who submit to the power. But as the moral activity is inconceivable without the physical, the cause of the event is neither in the one nor in the other, but in the union of the two.

Or in other words, the conception of a cause is inapplicable to the phenomena we are examining.

In the last analysis we reach the circle of infinity – that final limit to which in every domain of thought man's reason arrives if it is not playing with its subject. Electricity produces heat, heat produces electricity. Atoms attract each other and atoms repel one another.

Speaking of the interaction of heat and electricity and of atoms we cannot say why this occurs, and we say that it is so because it is inconceivable otherwise, because it must be so, and that it is a law. The same applies to historical events. Why war and revolution occur we do not know. We only know that to produce the one or the other action people combine in a certain formation in which they all take part, and we say that this is so because it is unthinkable otherwise, or in other words that it is a law.

8

IF history dealt with external phenomena, the establishment of this simple and obvious law would suffice and we should have finished our argument. But the law of history relates to man. A particle of matter cannot tell us that it does not feel the law of attraction or repulsion and that that law is untrue, but man, who is the subject of history, says plainly: I am free, and am therefore not subject to the law.

The presence of the problem of man's freewill, though unexpressed, is felt at every step of history.

All seriously thinking historians have involuntarily encountered this question. All the contradictions and obscurities of history, and the false path historical science has followed, are due solely to the lack of a solution of that question.

If the will of every man were free, that is, if each man could act as he pleased, all history would be a series of disconnected accidents.

If in a thousand years even one man in a million could act freely, that is, as he chose, it is evident that one single free act of that man's in violation of the laws governing human action, would destroy the possibility of the existence of any laws for the whole of humanity.

If there be a single law governing the actions of men, freewill cannot exist, for man's will would be subject to that law.

In this contradiction lies the problem of freewill, which from most ancient times has occupied the best human minds and from most ancient times has been presented in its whole tremendous significance.

The problem is, that regarding man as a subject of observation from whatever point of view – theological, historical, ethical, or philosophic – we find a general law of necessity to which he (like all that exists) is subject. But regarding him from within ourselves, as what we are conscious of, we feel ourselves to be free.

This consciousness is a source of self-cognition quite apart from and independent of reason. Through his reason man observes himself, but only through consciousness does he know himself.

Apart from consciousness of self, no observation or application of reason is conceivable.

To understand, observe, and draw conclusions, man must first of all be conscious of himself as living. A man is only conscious of himself as a living being by the fact that he wills, that is, is conscious of his volition. But his will – which forms the essence of his life – man recognizes (and can only recognize) as being free.

If, observing himself, man sees that his will is always directed by one and the same law (whether he observes the necessity of taking food, using his brain, or anything else), he cannot recognize this never-varying direction of his will otherwise than as a limitation of it. Were it not free it could not be limited. A man's will seems to him to be limited just because he is not conscious of it except as free.

You say: I am not free. But I have lifted my hand and let it fall. Everyone understands that this illogical reply is an irrefutable demonstration of freedom.

That reply is the expression of a consciousness that is not subject to reason.

If the consciousness of freedom were not a separate and independent source of self-consciousness it would be subject to reasoning and to experience, but in fact such subjection does not exist and is inconceivable.

A series of experiments and arguments proves to every man that he, as an object of observation, is subject to certain laws, and man submits to them and never resists the laws of gravity or impermeability once he has become acquainted with them. But the same series of experiments and arguments proves to him that the complete freedom of which he is conscious in himself is impossible, and that his every action depends on his organization, his character, and the motives acting upon him; yet man never submits to the deductions of these experiments and arguments. Having learnt from experiment and argument that a stone falls downwards, a man indubitably believes this, and always expects the law he has learnt to be fulfilled.

But learning just as certainly that his will is subject to laws, he does not and cannot believe it.

However often experiment and reasoning may show a man that under the same conditions and with the same character he will do the same thing as before, yet when, under the same conditions and with the same character, he approaches for the thousandth time the action that always ends in the same way, he feels as certainly convinced as before the experiment that he can act as he pleases. Every man, savage or sage, however incontestably reason and experiment may prove to him that it is impossible to imagine two different courses of action in precisely the same conditions, feels that without this irrational conception (which constitutes the essence of freedom) he cannot imagine life. He feels that, however impossible it may be, it is so, for without this conception of freedom not only would he be unable to understand life, but he would be unable to live for a single moment.

He could not live, because all man's efforts, all his impulses to life, are only efforts to increase freedom. Wealth and poverty, fame and obscurity, power and subordination, strength and weakness, health and disease, culture and ignorance, work and leisure, repletion and hunger, virtue and vice, are only greater or lesser degrees of freedom.

A man having no freedom cannot be conceived of except as deprived of life.

If the conception of freedom appears to reason a senseless contradiction, like the possibility of performing two actions at one and the same instant of time, or of an effect without a cause, that only proves that consciousness is not subject to reason.

This unshakable, irrefutable, consciousness of freedom, un-controlled by experiment or argument, recognized by all thinkers and felt by everyone without exception, this consciousness without which no conception of man is possible, constitutes the other side of the question.

Man is the creation of an all-powerful, all-good, and all-seeing God. What is sin, the conception of which arises from the con-sciousness of man's freedom? That is the question for theology.

The actions of men are subject to general immutable laws ex-pressed in statistics. What is man's responsibility to society, the conception of which results from the conception of freedom? That is the question for jurisprudence.

Man's actions proceed from his innate character and the motives acting upon him. What is conscience, and the perception of right and wrong in actions, that follows from the consciousness of free-dom? That is the question for ethics.

Man in connexion with the general life of humanity appears subject to laws which determine that life. But the same man apart from that connexion appears to be free. How should the past life of nations and of humanity be regarded – as the result of the free, or as the result of the constrained, activity of man? That is the question for history.

Only in our self-confident day of the popularization of knowl-edge – thanks to that most powerful engine of ignorance, the diffusion of printed matter – has the question of the freedom of will been put on a level on which the question itself cannot exist. In our time the majority of so-called advanced people – that is, the crowd of ignoramuses – has taken the work of the naturalists who deal with one side of the question for a solution of the whole problem.

They say and write and print that the soul and freedom do not exist, for the life of man is expressed by muscular movements and muscular movements are conditioned by the activity of the nerves: the soul and freewill do not exist because at an unknown period of time we sprang from the apes. They say this not at all suspect-ing that thousands of years ago that same law of necessity which with such ardour they are now trying to prove by physiology and comparative zoology, was not merely acknowledged by all the religions and all the thinkers, but has never been denied. They do not see that the role of the natural sciences in this matter is merely to serve as an instrument for the illumination of one side of it. For the fact that, from the point of view of observation, reason and the will are merely secretions of the brain and that man, following the general law, may have developed from lower animals at some unknown period of time, only explains from a fresh side the truth admitted thousands of years ago by all the religious and philosophic theories – that from the point of view of reason man is subject to the law of necessity; but it does not advance by a hair's breadth the solution of the question, which has another, opposite, side based on the consciousness of freedom.

If men descended from the apes at an unknown period of time, that is as comprehensible as that they were made from a handful of earth at a certain period of time (in the first case the unknown quantity is the time, in the second case it is the origin); and the question of how man's consciousness of freedom is to be reconciled with the law of necessity to which he is subject, cannot be solved by comparative physiology and zoology, for in a frog, a rabbit, and an ape we can observe only the muscular nervous activity, but in man we observe consciousness as well as the muscular and nervous activity.

The naturalists and their followers, thinking they can solve the question, are like plasterers set to plaster one side of the walls of a church, who availing themselves of the absence of the chief superintendent of the work, should in an access of zeal plaster over the windows, icons, woodwork, and still unbuttressed walls, and should be delighted that, from their point of view as plasterers, everything is now so smooth and regular.

9

FOR the solution of the question of freewill or inevitability, history has this advantage over other branches of knowledge in which the question is dealt with, that for history this question does not refer to the essence of man's freewill, but to its manifestation in the past and under certain conditions.

In regard to this question history stands to the other sciences as experimental science stands to abstract science.

The subject for history is not man's will itself, but our presentation of it.

And so for history the insoluble mystery presented by the incompatibility of freewill and inevitability does not exist as it does for theology, ethics, and philosophy. History surveys a presentation of man's life in which the union of those two contradictions has already taken place.

In actual life each historical event, each human action, is very clearly and definitely understood without any sense of contradiction, although each event presents itself as partly free and partly compulsory.

To solve the question of how freedom and necessity are combined and what constitutes the essence of these two conceptions, the philosophy of history can and should follow a path contrary to that taken by other sciences. Instead of first defining the conceptions of freedom and inevitability in themselves, and then ranging the phenomena of life under those definitions, history should deduce a definition of the conception of freedom and inevitability themselves from the immense quantity of phenomena of which it is cognizant, and that always appear dependent on those two elements.

Whatever presentation of the activity of many men or of an individual we may consider, we always regard it as the result partly of man's freewill and partly of the law of inevitability.

Whether we speak of the migration of the peoples and the incursions of the barbarians, or of the decrees of Napoleon III, or of someone's action an hour ago in choosing one direction out of several for his walk, we are unconscious of any contradiction. The degree of freedom and inevitability governing the actions of these people is clearly defined for us.

Our conception of the degree of freedom often varies according to differences in the point of view from which we regard the event, but every human action appears to us as a certain combination of freedom and inevitability. In every action we examine, we see a certain measure of freedom and a certain measure of inevitability. And always, the more freedom we see in any action the less inevitability do we perceive, and the more inevitability the less freedom.

The proportion of freedom to inevitability decreases and increases according to the point of view from which the action is regarded, but their relation is always one of inverse proportion.

A sinking man who clutches at another and drowns him; or a hungry mother exhausted by feeding her baby, who steals some food; or a man trained to discipline who on duty, at the word of command, kills a defenceless man – seem less guilty, that is less free and more subject to the law of necessity, to one who knows the circumstances in which these people were placed, and more free to one who does not know that the man was himself drowning, that the mother was hungry, that the soldier was in the ranks, and so on. Similarly a man who committed a murder twenty years ago and has since lived peaceably and harmlessly in society, seems less guilty and his action more due to the law of inevitability, to someone who considers his action after twenty years have elapsed, than to one who examined it the day after it was committed. And in the same way every action of an insane, intoxicated, or highly excited man, appears less free and more inevitable to one who knows the mental condition of him who committed the action, and seems more free and less inevitable to one who does not know it. In all these cases the conception of freedom is increased or diminished, and the conception of compulsion is correspondingly deceased or increased, according to the point of view from which the action is regarded. So that the greater the conception of necessity the smaller the conception of freedom and vice versa.

Religion, the common sense of mankind, the science of jurisprudence, and history itself, understand alike this relation between necessity and freedom.

All cases without exception in which our conception of freedom and necessity is increased and diminished depend on three considerations:

(1) The relation to the external world of the man who commits the deeds.

(2) His relation to time.

(3) His relation to the causes leading to the action.

(1) The first consideration is the clearness of our perception of the man's relation to the external world, and the greater or lesser clearness of our understanding of the definite position occupied by the man in relation to everything co-existing with him. This is what makes it evident that a drowning man is less free and more subject to necessity than one standing on dry ground, and that makes the actions of a man closely connected with others in a thickly populated district, or of one bound by family, official, or business duties, seem certainly less free and more subject to necessity than those of a man living in solitude and seclusion.

If we consider a man alone, apart from his relation to everything around him, each action of his seems to us free. But if we see his relation to anything around him, if we see his connexion with anything whatever – with a man who speaks to him, a book he reads, the work on which he is engaged, even with the air he breathes or the light that falls on the things about him – we see that each of these circumstances has an influence on him and controls at least some side of his activity. And the more we perceive of these influences the more our conception of his freedom diminishes and the more our conception of the necessity that weighs on him increases.

(2) The second consideration is the more or less evident time relation of the man to the world and the clearness of our perception of the place the man's action occupies in time. That is the ground which makes the fall of the first man, resulting in the

production of the human race, appear evidently less free than a man's entry into marriage to-day. It is the reason why the life and activity of people who lived centuries ago and are connected with me in time, cannot seem to me as free as the life of a contemporary, the consequences of which are still unknown to me.

The degree of our conception of freedom or inevitability depends in this respect on the greater or lesser lapse of time between the performance of the action and our judgement of it.

If I examine an act I performed a moment ago in approximately the same circumstances as those I am in now, my action appears to me undoubtedly free. But if I examine an act performed a month ago, then, being in different circumstances, I cannot help recognizing that if that act had not been committed much that resulted from it – good, agreeable, and even essential – would not have taken place. If I reflect on an action still more remote, ten years ago or more, then the consequences of my action are still plainer to me, and I find it hard to imagine what would have happened had that action not been performed. The farther I go back in memory, or what is the same thing, the farther I go forward in my judgement, the more doubtful becomes my belief in the freedom of my action.

In history we find a very similar progress of conviction concerning the part played by freewill in the general affairs of humanity. A contemporary event seems to us to be indubitably the doing of all the known participants, but with a more remote event we already see its inevitable results which prevent our considering anything else possible. And the farther we go back in examining events the less arbitrary do they appear.

The Austro-Prussian war appears to us undoubtedly the result of the crafty conduct of Bismarck, and so on. The Napoleonic wars still seem to us, though already questionably, to be the outcome of their heroes' will. But in the Crusades we already see an event occupying its definite place in history, and without which we cannot imagine the modern history of Europe, though to the chroniclers of the Crusades that event appeared as merely due to the will of certain people. In regard to the migration of the peoples it does not enter anyone's head to-day to suppose that the renovation of the European world depended on Attila's caprice. The farther back in history the object of our observation lies, the more doubtful does the freewill of those concerned in the event become, and the more manifest the laws of inevitability.

(3) The third consideration is the degree to which we apprehend that endless chain of causation inevitably demanded by reason, in which each phenomenon comprehended, and therefore man's every

1297

action, must have its definite place as a result of what has gone before and a cause of what will follow.

The better we are acquainted with the physiological, psychological, and historical laws deduced by observation and by which man is controlled, and the more correctly we perceive the physiological, psychological, and historical causes of the action, and the simpler the action we are observing and the less complex the character and mind of the man in question, the more subject to inevitability and the less free do our actions and those of others appear.

When we do not at all understand the cause of an action, whether a crime, a good action, or even one that is simply non-moral, we ascribe a greater amount of freedom to it. In the case of a crime, we most urgently demand the punishment for such an act; in the case of a virtuous act we rate its merit most highly. In an indifferent case we recognize in it more individuality, originality, and independence. But if even one of the innumerable causes of the act is known to us we recognize a certain element of necessity and are less insistent on punishment for the crime, or the acknowledgement of the merit of the virtuous act, or the freedom of the apparently original action. That a criminal was reared among malefactors mitigates his fault in our eyes. The self-sacrifice of a father or a mother, or self-sacrifice with the possibility of a reward, is more comprehensible than gratuitous self-sacrifice, and therefore seems less deserving of sympathy and less the result of freewill. The founder of a sect or a party, or an inventor, impresses us less when we know how or by what the way was prepared for his activity. If we have a large range of examples, if our observation is constantly directed to seeking the correlation of cause and effect in people's actions, their actions appear to us more under compulsion and less free the more correctly we connect the effects with the causes. If we examined simple actions, and had a vast number of such actions under observation, our conception of their inevitability would be still greater. The dishonest conduct of the son of a dishonest father, the misconduct of a woman who had fallen into bad company, a drunkard's relapse into drunkenness, and so on, are actions that seem to us less free the better we understand their cause. If the man whose actions we are considering is on a very low stage of mental development, like a child, a madman, or a simpleton – then, knowing the causes of the act and the simplicity of the character and intelligence in question, we see so large an element of necessity and so little freewill that as soon as we know the cause prompting the action we can foretell the result.

On these three considerations alone is based the conception of irresponsibility for crimes, and the extenuating circumstances admitted by all legislative codes. The responsibility appears greater or less according to our greater or lesser knowledge of the circumstances in which the man was placed whose action is being judged, and according to the greater or lesser interval of time between the commission of the action and its investigation, and according to the greater or lesser understanding of the causes that led to the action.

10

THUS our conception of freewill and inevitability gradually diminishes or increases according to the greater or lesser connexion with the external world, the greater or lesser remoteness of time, and the greater or lesser dependence on the causes, under which we contemplate a man's life.

So that if we examine the case of a man whose connexion with the external world is well known, where the time between the action and its examination is great, and where the causes of the action are most accessible, we get the conception of a maximum of inevitability and a minimum of freewill. If we examine a man little dependent on external conditions, whose action was performed very recently, and the causes of whose action are beyond our ken, we get the conception of a minimum of inevitability and a maximum of freedom.

In neither case – however we may change our point of view, however plain we may make to ourselves the connexion between the man and the external world, however inaccessible it may be to us, however long or short the period of time, however intelligible or incomprehensible the causes of the action may be – can we ever conceive either complete freedom or complete necessity.

(1) To whatever degree we may imagine a man to be exempt from the influence of the external world, we never get a conception of freedom in space. Every human action is inevitably conditioned by what surrounds him and his own body. I lift my arm and let it fall. My action seems to me free; but asking myself whether I could raise my arm in every direction, I see that I raised it in the direction in which there was least obstruction to that action either from things around me or from the construction of my own body. I chose one out of all the possible directions because in it there were fewest obstacles. For my action to be free it was necessary that it should encounter no obstacles. To conceive of a man being free we must imagine him outside space, which is evidently impossible.

(2) However much we approximate the time of judgement to the time of the deed, we never get a conception of freedom in time. For if I examine an action committed a second ago I must still recognize it as not being free, for it is irrevocably linked to the moment at which it was committed. Can I lift my arm? I lift it, but ask myself: Could I have abstained from lifting my arm at the moment that has already passed? To convince myself of this I do not lift it the next moment. But I am not now abstaining from doing so at the first moment when I asked the question. Time has gone by which I could not detain, the arm I then lifted is no longer the same as the arm I now refrain from lifting, nor is the air in which I lifted it the same that now surrounds me. The moment in which the first movement was made is irrevocable, and at that moment I could only make one movement, and whatever movement I made would be the only one. That I did not lift my arm a moment later does not prove that I could have abstained from lifting it then. And since I could only make one movement at that single moment of time, it could not have been any other. To imagine it as free, it is necessary to imagine it in the present, on the boundary between the past and the future – that is, outside time, which is impossible.

(3) However much the difficulty of understanding the causes may be increased, we never reach a conception of complete freedom, that is, an absence of cause. However inaccessible to us may be the cause of the expression of will in any action, our own or another's, the first demand of reason is the assumption of and search for a cause, for without a cause no phenomenon is conceivable. I raise my arm to perform an action independently of any cause, but my wish to perform an action without a cause is the cause of my action.

But even if – imagining a man quite exempt from all influences, examining only his momentary action in the present unevoked by any cause – we were to admit so infinitely small a remainder of inevitability as equalled zero, we should even then not have arrived at the conception of complete freedom in man, for a being uninfluenced by the external world, standing outside of time, and independent of cause, is no longer a man.

In the same way we can never imagine the action of a man quite devoid of freedom and entirely subject to the law of inevitability.

(1) However we may increase our knowledge of the conditions of space in which man is situated, that knowledge can never be complete, for the number of those conditions is as infinite as the infinity of space. And therefore so long as not *all* the conditions

influencing man are defined, there is no complete inevitability but a certain measure of freedom remains.

(2) However we may prolong the period of time between the action we are examining and the judgement upon it, that period will be finite, while time is infinite, and so in this respect too there can never be absolute inevitability.

(3) However accessible may be the chain of causation of any action, we shall never know the whole chain since it is endless, and so again we never reach absolute inevitability.

But besides this, even if, admitting the remaining minimum of freedom to equal zero, we assumed in some given case – as for instance in that of a dying man, an unborn babe, or an idiot – complete absence of freedom, by doing so we should destroy the very conception of man in the case we are examining, for as soon as there is no freedom there is also no man. And so the conception of the action of a man subject solely to the law of inevitability, without any element of freedom, is just as impossible as the conception of a man's completely free action.

And so to imagine the action of a man entirely subject to the law of inevitability, without any freedom, we must assume the knowledge of an *infinite* number of space relations, an *infinitely* long period of time, and an *infinite* series of causes.

To imagine a man perfectly free and not subject to the law of inevitability, we must imagine him all alone, *beyond space, beyond time*, and *free from dependence on cause*.

In the first case, if inevitability were possible without freedom, we should have reached a definition of inevitability by the laws of inevitability itself, that is, a mere form without content.

In the second case, if freedom were possible without inevitability, we should have arrived at unconditioned freedom beyond space, time, and cause, which by the fact of its being unconditioned and unlimited would be nothing, or mere content without form.

We should in fact have reached those two fundamentals of which man's whole outlook on the universe is constructed – the incomprehensible essence of life, and the laws defining that essence.

Reason says: (1) Space with all the forms of matter that give it visibility is infinite and cannot be imagined otherwise. (2) Time is infinite motion without a moment of rest and is unthinkable otherwise. (3) The connexion between cause and effect has no beginning and can have no end.

Consciousness says: (1) I alone am, and all that exists is but me, consequently I include space. (2) I measure flowing time by the fixed moment of the present, in which alone I am conscious of myself as living, consequently I am outside time. (3) I am beyond cause, for I feel myself to be the cause of every manifestation of my life.

Reason gives expression to the laws of inevitability. Consciousness gives expression to the essence of freedom.

Freedom not limited by anything is the essence of life in man's consciousness. Inevitability without content is man's reason in its three forms.

Freedom is the thing examined. Inevitability is what examines. Freedom is the content. Inevitability is the form.

Only by separating the two sources of cognition, related to one another as form to content, do we get the mutually exclusive and separately incomprehensible conceptions of freedom and inevitability.

Only by uniting them do we get a clear conception of man's life.

Apart from these two concepts which in their union mutually define one another as form and content, no conception of life is possible.

All that we know of the life of man is merely a certain relation of freewill to inevitability, that is, of consciousness to the laws of reason.

All that we know of the external world of nature is only a certain relation of the forces of nature to inevitability, or of the essence of life to the laws of reason.

The great natural forces lie outside us and we are not conscious of them: we call those forces gravitation, inertia, electricity, animal force, and so on, but we are conscious of the force of life in man and we call it freedom.

But just as the force of gravitation, incomprehensible in itself but felt by every man, is only understood by us to the extent to which we know the laws of inevitability to which it is subject (from the first knowledge that all bodies have weight, up to Newton's law), so too the force of freewill, incomprehensible in itself but of which everyone is conscious, is only intelligible to us in as far as we know the laws of inevitability to which it is subject (from the fact that every man dies, up to the knowledge of the most complex economic and historical laws).

All knowledge is merely a bringing of this essence of life under the laws of reason.

Man's freewill differs from every other force in that man is directly conscious of it, but in the eyes of reason it in no way differs from any other force. The forces of gravitation, electricity, or chemical affinity, are only distinguished from one another in that they are differently defined by reason. Just so the force of man's freewill is distinguished by reason from the other forces of nature only by the definition reason gives it. Freedom apart from necessity, that is, apart from the laws of reason that define it, differs in no way from gravitation, or heat, or the force that makes things grow; for reason, it is only a momentary undefinable sensation of life.

And as the undefinable essence of the force moving the heavenly bodies, the undefinable essence of the forces of heat and electricity, or of chemical affinity, or of the vital force, forms the content of astronomy, physics, chemistry, botany, zoology and so on, just in the same way the force of freewill forms the content of history. But just as the subject of every science is the manifestation of this unknown essence of life, while that essence itself can only be the subject of metaphysics, even so the manifestation of the force of freewill in human beings in space, in time, and in dependence on cause, forms the subject of history, while freewill itself is the subject of metaphysics.

In the experimental sciences, what we know we call the laws of inevitability, what is unknown to us we call vital force. Vital force is only an expression for the unknown remainder over and above what we know of the essence of life.

So also in history what is known to us we call laws of inevitability, what is unknown we call freewill. Freewill is for history only an expression for the unknown remainder of what we know about the laws of human life.

11

HISTORY examines the manifestations of man's freewill in connexion with the external world in time and in dependence on cause, that is, it defines this freedom by the laws of reason, and so history is a science only in so far as this freewill is defined by those laws.

The recognition of man's freewill as something capable of influencing historical events, that is, as not subject to laws, is the same for history as the recognition of a free force moving the heavenly bodies would be for astronomy.

The assumption would destroy the possibility of the existence of laws, that is, of any science whatever. If there is even a single body moving freely, then the laws of Kepler and Newton are negatived and no conception of the movement of the heavenly bodies any longer exists. If any single action is due to freewill, then not a single historical law can exist, nor any conception of historical events.

For history, lines exist of the movement of human wills, one end of which is hidden in the unknown but at the other end of which a consciousness of man's will in the present moves in space, time, and dependence on cause.

The more this field of motion spreads out before our eyes, the more evident are the laws of that movement. To discover and define those laws is the problem of history.

From the standpoint from which the science of history now regards its subject on the path it now follows, seeking the causes of events in man's freewill, a scientific enunciation of those laws is impossible, for however man's freewill may be restricted, as soon as we recognize it as a force not subject to law, the existence of law becomes impossible.

Only by reducing this element of freewill to the infinitesimal, that is, by regarding it as an infinitely small quantity, can we convince ourselves of the absolute inaccessibility of the causes, and then instead of seeking causes, history will take the discovery of laws as its problem.

The search for these laws has long been begun and the new methods of thought which history must adopt are being worked out simultaneously with the self-destruction towards which – ever dissecting and dissecting the causes of phenomena – the old method of history is moving.

All human sciences have travelled along that path. Arriving at infinitesimals, mathematics, the most exact of sciences, abandons the process of analysis and enters on the new process of the integration of unknown, infinitely small, quantity. Abandoning the conception of cause, mathematics seeks law, that is, the property common to all unknown, infinitely small, elements.

In another form but along the same path of reflection the other sciences have proceeded. When Newton enunciated the law conception of cause, mathematics seeks law, that is, the property of attraction; he said that all bodies from the largest to the smallest have the property of attracting one another, that is, leaving aside the question of the cause of the movement of the bodies, he expressed the property common to all bodies from the infinitely large to the infinitely small. The same is done by the natural sciences: leaving aside the question of cause, they seek for laws. History stands on the same path. And if history has for its object the study of the movement of the nations and of humanity, and not the narration of episodes in the lives of individuals, it too, setting aside the conception of cause, should seek the laws common to all the inseparably interconnected infinitesimal elements of freewill.

FROM the time the law of Copernicus was discovered and proved, the mere recognition of the fact that it was not the sun but the earth that moves sufficed to destroy the whole cosmography of the ancients. By disproving that law it might have been possible to retain the old conception of the movements of the bodies, but without disproving it it would seem impossible to continue studying the Ptolemaic worlds. But even after the discovery of the law of Copernicus the Ptolemaic worlds were still studied for a long time.

From the time the first person said and proved that the number of births or of crimes is subject to mathematical laws, and that this or that mode of government is determined by certain geographical and economic conditions, and that certain relations of population to soil produce migrations of peoples, the foundations on which history had been built were destroyed in their essence.

By refuting these new laws the former view of history might have been retained; but without refuting them it would seem impossible to continue studying historic events as the results of man's freewill. For if a certain mode of government was established or certain migrations of peoples took place in consequence of such and such geographic, ethnographic, or economic conditions, then the freewill of those individuals who appear to us to have established that mode of government or evoked the migrations can no longer be regarded as the cause.

And yet the former history continues to be studied side by side with the laws of statistics, geography, political economy, comparative philology, and geology, which directly contradict its assumptions.

The struggle between the old views and the new was long and stubbornly fought out in physical philosophy. Theology stood on guard for the old views and accused the new of violating revelation. But when truth conquered, theology established itself just as firmly on the new foundation.

Just as prolonged and stubborn is the struggle now proceeding between the old and the new conception of history, and theology in the same way stands on guard for the old view and accuses the new view of subverting revelation.

In the one case as in the other, on both sides the struggle provokes passion and stifles truth. On the one hand there is fear and regret for the loss of the whole edifice constructed through the ages, on the other is the passion for destruction.

To the men who fought against the rising truths of physical

philosophy, it seemed that if they admitted that truth, it would destroy faith in God, in the creation of the firmament, and in the miracle of Joshua the son of Nun. To the defenders of the laws of Copernicus and Newton, to Voltaire for example, it seemed that the laws of astronomy destroyed religion, and he utilized the law of gravitation as a weapon against religion.

Just so it now seems as if we have only to admit the law of inevitability, to destroy the conception of the soul, of good and evil, and all the institutions of State and Church that have been built up on those conceptions.

So too, like Voltaire in his time, uninvited defenders of the law of inevitability to-day use that law as a weapon against religion, though the law of inevitability in history, like the law of Copernicus in astronomy, far from destroying, even strengthens the foundation on which the institutions of State and Church are erected.

As in the question of astronomy then, so in the question of history now, the whole difference of opinion is based on the recognition or non-recognition of something absolute serving as the measure of visible phenomena. In astronomy it was the immovability of the earth, in history it is the independence of personality – freewill.

As with astronomy the difficulty of recognizing the motion of the earth lay in abandoning the immediate sensation of the earth's fixity and of the motion of the planets, so in history the difficulty of recognizing the subjection of personality to the laws of space, time, and cause, lies in renouncing the direct feeling of the independence of one's own personality. But as in astronomy the new view said: 'It is true that we do not feel the movement of the earth, but by admitting its immobility we arrive at absurdity, while by admitting its motion (which we do not feel) we arrive at laws,' so also in history the new view says: 'It is true that we are not conscious of our dependence, but by admitting our freewill we arrive at absurdity, while by admitting our dependence on the external world, on time, and on cause, we arrive at laws.'

In the first case it was necessary to renounce the consciousness of an unreal immobility in space and to recognize a motion we did not feel; in the present case it is similarly necessary to renounce a freedom that does not exist, and to recognize a dependence of which we are not conscious.

THE END

APPENDIX

SOME WORDS ABOUT 'WAR AND PEACE'

(Published in *Russian Archive*, 1868)

ON publishing this work, on which I have spent five years of uninterrupted and exceptionally strenuous labour under the best conditions of life, I wish to express my own view of it and thus counteract misunderstandings which might arise in the reader's mind. I do not want readers of this book to see in it, or look for, what I did not wish, or was unable, to express, and I should like to direct their attention to what I wished to say but owing to the conditions of the work could not enlarge on. Neither my time nor capacity allowed me fully to accomplish what I intended, and I now avail myself of the hospitality of a specialist periodical to state, though but briefly and incompletely, the author's view of his work for those whom it may interest.

(1) What is *War and Peace*? It is not a novel, even less is it a poem, and still less an historical chronicle. *War and Peace* is what the author wished and was able to express in the form in which it is expressed. Such an announcement of disregard of conventional form in an artistic production might seem presumptuous were it premeditated, and were there no precedents for it. But the history of Russian literature since the time of Pushkin not merely affords many examples of such deviation from European forms, but does not offer a single example of the contrary. From Gogol's *Dead Souls* to Dostoevsky's *House of the Dead* in the recent period of Russian literature there is not a single artistic prose work, rising at all above mediocrity, which quite fits into the form of a novel, epic, or story.

(2) *The character of the period.* When the first part of this book appeared some readers told me that this is not sufficiently defined in my work. To that reproach I make the following reply: I know what 'the characteristics of the period' are that people do not find in my novel – the horrors of serfdom, the immuring of wives, the flogging of grown-up sons, Saltykova,* and so on; but I do not think that these characteristics of the period as they exist in our imagination are correct, and I did not wish to reproduce them. On studying letters, diaries, and traditions, I did not find the horrors of such savagery to a greater extent than I find them now, or at

1307

any other period. In those days also people loved, envied, sought truth and virtue, and were carried away by passion; and there was the same complex mental and moral life among the upper classes, who were in some instances even more refined than now. If we have come to believe in the perversity and coarse violence of that period, that is only because the traditions, memoirs, stories, and novels that have been handed to us, record for the most part exceptional cases of violence and brutality. To suppose that the predominant characteristic of that period was turbulence, is as unjust as it would be for a man, seeing nothing but the tops of trees beyond a hill, to conclude that there was nothing to be found in that locality but trees. That period had its own characteristics (as every epoch has), which resulted from the predominant alienation of the upper class from other classes, from the religious philosophy of the time, from peculiarities of education, from the habit of using the French language, and so forth. That is the character I tried to depict as well as I could.

(3) *The use of the French language in a Russian book.* Why in my book do Russians as well as Frenchmen sometimes speak Russian and sometimes French? The reproach that in a Russian book people speak and write French, is like the reproach of a man who, looking at a portrait, notices black spots (shadows) on it which do not exist in nature. The painter is not to blame if to some people the shadow he has put on the face of the portrait appears as a black spot non-existent in nature; he is only to blame if such shadows are put on wrongly or coarsely. Dealing with the beginning of the nineteenth century, and depicting the Russians of a certain class and Napoleon and other Frenchmen who had so direct a part in the life of that epoch, I was involuntarily carried away to an unnecessary extent by the form in which they expressed their French way of thought. And so, without denying that the shadows put on by me are probably incorrect and coarse, I would only ask those to whom it seems absurd that Napoleon should speak now Russian and now French, to realize that this seems so to them only because they, like the man looking at the portrait, notice a black spot under the nose instead of observing the face with its lights and shades.

(4) *The names of the people in the book.* Bolkonsky, Drubetskoy, Bilibin, Kuragin and others, suggest well-known Russian names. When confronting fictitious with historical characters I felt it awkward for the ear to make a Count Rostopchin speak to a Prince Pronsky, Strelsky, or other princes or counts bearing such invented (single or hyphenated) names. Bolkonsky or Drubetskoy, though they are neither Volkonsky nor Trubetskoy, sound familiar

and natural in a Russian aristocratic circle. I was unable to devise for all my characters names which did not sound false to my ear, such as Bezukhov and Rostov, and I could not find any other way to overcome this difficulty except by taking at random names quite familiar to a Russian ear and changing some of the letters in them. I should be very sorry if the similarity between the invented names and real ones should suggest to anyone that I wished to describe this or that actual person, more especially as the literary activity which consists of describing real people who exist or have existed has nothing in common with the activity I was engaged on.

M. D. Akhrosimova and Denisov are the only persons to whom I involuntarily and unreflectingly gave names closely resembling those of two particularly characteristic and charming people of the real society of that time. That was my mistake, arising from the specially typical character of those two persons, but my mistake in this matter is limited to their mere introduction, and readers will probably agree that nothing resembling the actual facts of their lives is ascribed to these characters in the novel. All the other people are entirely invented, and have for me no definite prototypes in tradition or in reality.

(5) *The divergence between my description of historical events and that given by the historians.* This was not accidental but inevitable. An historian and an artist describing an historic epoch have two quite different tasks before them. As an historian would be wrong if he tried to present an historical person in his entirety, in all the complexity of his relations with all sides of life, so the artist would fail to perform his task were he to represent the person always in his historic significance. Kutuzov did not always hold a telescope, point at the enemy, and ride a white horse. Rostopchin was not always setting fire with a torch to the Voronovsky House* (which in fact he never did) and the Empress Marya Fëdorovna did not always stand in an ermine cloak leaning her hand on the code of laws, but that is how the popular imagination pictures them.

For an historian considering the achievement of a certain aim, there are heroes; for the artist treating of man's relation to all sides of life there cannot and should not be heroes, but there should be men.

An historian is sometimes obliged by bending the truth to subordinate all the actions of an historical personage to the one idea he has ascribed to that person. The artist, on the contrary, finds the very singleness of that idea incompatible with his problem, and tries to understand and show not a certain actor but a man.

In the description of the events themselves the difference is still sharper and more essential.

The historian has to deal with the results of an event, the artist with the fact of the event. An historian in describing a battle says: 'The left flank of such and such an army was advanced to attack such and such a village and drove out the enemy, but was compelled to retire; then the cavalry, which was sent to attack, overthrew...' and so on. But these words have no meaning for an artist and do not actually touch the event itself. Either from his own experience, or from letters, memoirs, and accounts, the artist realizes a certain event to himself, and very often (to take the example of a battle) the deductions the historian permits himself to make as to the activity of such and such armies prove to be the very opposite of the artist's deductions. The difference of the results arrived at is also to be explained by the sources from which the two draw their information. For the historian (to keep to the case of a battle) the chief source is found in the reports of the commanding officers and of the commander-in-chief. The artist can draw nothing from such sources; they tell him nothing and explain nothing to him. More than that: the artist turns away from them as he finds inevitable falsehood in them. To say nothing of the fact that after any battle the two sides nearly always describe it in quite contradictory ways, in every description of a battle there is a necessary lie, resulting from the need of describing in a few words the actions of thousands of men spread over several miles, and subject to most violent moral excitement under the influence of fear, shame, and death.

In descriptions of battles it is generally said that such and such armies were sent to attack such and such points, and were then ordered to retire and so on, as if assuming that discipline, which subjects tens of thousand of men to the will of one man on a parade-ground, will have the same effect where it is a question of life and death. Anyone who has been in a war knows how untrue that is,* yet the reports are based on that assumption, and on them the military descriptions. Make a round of the troops immediately after a battle, or even next day or the day after before the reports have been drawn up, and ask any of the soldiers and senior and junior officers how the affair went: you will be told what all these men experienced and saw, and you will form a majestic, complex, infinitely varied, depressing and indistinct impression; and from no one – least of all from the commander-in-chief – will you learn what the whole affair was like. Two or three days later the reports begin to be handed in. Talkers begin to narrate how things happened which they did not see; finally a general report is drawn up, and on this report the general opinion of the army is formed. Everyone is glad to exchange his own doubts and questionings for this deceptive, but clear and always flattering, presentation. Question a month or two later a man who was in the battle, and you will no longer feel in this account the raw, vital material that was there before, but he will answer according to the report. Thus I was told of the battle of Borodino by many lively, clever participants in that affair. They all told me one and the same thing, and all in accord with the false accounts of Mikhaylovsky-Danilevsky, Glinka and others: even the details they mentioned were all identical, though the narrators had been several miles apart from one another.

After the fall of Sevastopol the Commander of the Artillery, Kryzhanovsky, sent me the reports of the officers of artillery from all the bastions, and asked me to draw up a report from these (more than twenty) separate accounts. I am sorry I did not take copies of them. It would have been the best example of the naïve, inevitable, military falsehoods from which reports are made. I imagine that many of my comrades who drew up those reports will laugh on reading these lines, at the recollection of how they, by order of their superior, wrote what they could not know. All who have had experience of war know how capable Russians are of doing their work in a war, and how little fit they are to describe it with the boastful falsity indispensable for that purpose. Everyone knows that in our armies that duty of drawing up reports and dispatches is generally carried out by men of foreign birth.

I say all this to show the inevitability of falsehood in military descriptions which serve as material for military historians, and thus to show how unavoidable are frequent disagreements between artists and historians in their understanding of historical events. But besides this necessary error in the narration of historical events, I noticed in the histories of the epoch on which I was engaged (probably as a result of the habit of grouping events to express them briefly, and of conforming to the tragic import of those events) a special kind of high-flown diction in which the falsehood and perversion extended not merely to the occurrences but also to the interpretation and significance of them. Often when studying the two chief historical works on that epoch, Thiers and Mikhaylovsky-Danilevsky, I felt perplexed that such books could have been printed and read. To say nothing of the fact that they present the same events in a most serious, significant tone, citing the sources they have drawn on, and are yet in diametrical opposition to one another, in these histories I came across such accounts that I did not know whether to laugh or to cry, remembering that these books are the chief memorials of that epoch and have had millions of readers. I will give a single example from the work of the famous historian Thiers. After telling how Napoleon brought with him forged paper rubles, he says: *Relevant l'emploi de ces moyens par un acte de bienfaisance* digne de lui et de l'armée française, *il fit distribuer des secours aux incendiés. Mais les vivres étant trop précieux pour être donnés longtemps à ces étrangers, la plupart ennemis, Napoléon aima mieux leur fournir de l'argent; et il leur fit distribuer des roubles papier.*

This passage when taken by itself amazes one, I will not say by its immorality but simply by its stupidity; but in the whole book it does not surprise one, for it is quite in accord with the general high-flown pompous style, devoid of any direct meaning.

So the tasks of artist and historian are quite different, and the reader should not be surprised when my book disagrees with an historian in the descriptions of events or persons.

But an artist must not forget that the popular conception of historical persons and events is not based on fancy, but on historical documents in so far as the historians have been able to group them, and therefore, though he understands and presents them differently, the artist like the historian should be guided by historical material. *Wherever in my novel historical persons speak or act, I have invented nothing, but have used historical material of which I have accumulated a whole library during my work. I do not think it necessary to cite the titles of those books here, but could cite them at any time in proof of what I say.*

(6) Finally, the sixth and for me most important consideration relates to the small significance that, in my conception, should be ascribed to so-called great men in historical events.

Studying so tragic an epoch, so rich in the importance of its events, so near to our own time, and regarding which so many varied traditions survive, I arrived at the evident fact that the causes of historical events when they take place cannot be grasped by our intelligence. To say (which seems to everyone very simple) that the causes of the events of 1812 lay in Napoleon's domineering disposition and the patriotic firmness of the Emperor Alexander I, is as meaningless as to say that the causes of the fall of the Roman Empire were that a certain barbarian led his people westwards and a certain Roman emperor ruled his State badly, or that an immense hill that was being levelled toppled over because the last labourer struck it with his spade.

The cause of such an event, in which millions of people fought one another and killed half a million men, cannot be the will of one man. Just as one man could not have levelled the hill, so no single man could cause five hundred thousand to die. But what were the causes? One historian says it was the aggressive spirit of the French and the patriotism of the Russians. Others speak of the democratic element Napoleon's hordes carried abroad, and of Russia's need to form relations with Europe, and so forth. But why did millions of people begin to kill one another? Who told them to do it? It would seem that it was clear to each of them that this could not benefit any of them but would be worse for them all. Why did they do it? Endless retrospective conjectures can be made, and are made, of the causes of this senseless event, but the immense number of these explanations, and their concurrence in one purpose, only proves that the causes were innumerable and that not one of them deserves to be called the cause.

Why did millions of people kill one another when it has been known since the world began that it is physically and morally bad to do so? Because it was such an inevitable necessity that in doing it men fulfilled the elemental zoological law which bees fulfil when they kill one another in autumn, and which causes male animals to destroy one another. One can give no other reply to that terrible question.

This truth is not only evident, but is so innate in every man's consciousness that it would not be worth while proving it were there not another sentiment in man which convinces him that he is free at each moment that he commits an action.

Taking a wide view of history we are indubitably convinced of a sempiternal law by which events occur. Looking at it from a personal point of view we are convinced of the opposite.

A man who kills another, Napoleon who orders the crossing of the Niemen, you or I handing in a petition to be admitted to the army, or lifting or lowering our arm, are all indubitably convinced that our every action is based on reasonable grounds and on our own freewill, and that it depends on us whether we do this or that. This conviction is so inherent in us and so precious to each of us, that in spite of the proofs of history and the statistics of crime (which convince us of absence of freedom in the actions of other people) we extend the consciousness of our freedom to all our actions.

The contradiction seems insoluble. When committing an act I am convinced that I do it by my own freewill, but considering that action in its connexion with the general life of mankind (in its historical significance), I am convinced that this action was predestined and inevitable. Where is the error?

Psychological observations of man's capacity for retrospectively supplying a whole series of supposedly free reasons for something that has been done (as I intend to expound in more detail in another place) confirm the assumption that man's consciousness of freedom in the commission of a certain kind of action is erroneous. But the same psychological observations prove that there is another series of actions in which the consciousness of freedom is not retrospective but instantaneous and indubitable. In spite of all that the materialists may say, I can undoubtedly commit an act or refrain from it if the act relates to me alone. I have undoubtedly by my own will just lifted and lowered my arm. I can at once stop writing. You can at once stop reading. I can certainly, by my own will and free from all obstacles, transfer my thoughts to America, or to any mathematical problem I choose. Testing my freedom I can lift and forcibly lower my hand in the air. I have done so. But near me stands a child and I raise my hand above him and want to lower it with the same force onto the child. I *cannot* do this. A dog rushes at that child, and I *cannot* refrain from lifting my hand at the dog. I am on parade, and cannot help following the movement of the regiment. In action I cannot refrain from attacking with my regiment or from running when all around me run – I *cannot*. When I appear in Court as the defender of an accused person, I cannot help speaking or knowing what I am going to say. I cannot help blinking when a blow is directed at my eye.

So there are two kinds of actions: some that do and others that do not depend on my will. And the mistake causing the contradiction is due only to the fact that I wrongly transfer the consciousness of freedom (which properly accompanies every act relating to my *ego*, to the highest abstractions of my existence) to actions performed in conjunction with others and dependent on the coincidence of other wills with my own. To define the limits of freedom and dependence is very difficult and the definition of those limits forms the sole and essential problem of psychology, but observing the conditions of the manifestation of our greatest freedom and greatest dependence, we cannot but see that the more abstract and therefore the less connected with the activity of others our activity is, the more free it is; and on the contrary, the more our activity is connected with other people the less free it is.

The strongest, most indissoluble, most burdensome, and constant bond with other men is what is called power over others, which in its real meaning is only the greatest dependence on them.

Having wrongly or rightly become fully convinced of this in the course of my work, I naturally was unable – when describing the historical events of 1805, 1807 and especially of 1812 in which this law of predetermination is most prominently displayed* – to attribute importance to the actions of those who thought they controlled the events, but who introduced less free human activity into them than did all the other participants. The activity of these people interested me only as an illustration of the law of predetermination which in my opinion guides history, and of that psychological law which compels a man who commits actions under the greatest compulsion to supply in his imagination a whole series of retrospective reflections to prove his freedom to himself.

NOTES

[M] indicates that the note is the translator's.

BOOK ONE

PART ONE

3 *Genoa and Lucca are now just family estates of the Buonapartes*: Napoleon seized them in June 1805. He had made himself Emperor of the French in December 1804, but Anna Scherer and her associates refer to him slightingly as 'Buonaparte' (the Corsican upstart).

4 *Novosiltsev's dispatch*: a new coalition which included England, Russia, Austria, and Prussia was being formed against France. Napoleon unexpectedly proposed peace to England. At the latter's request Tsar Alexander had sent N. N. Novosiltsev as intermediary, but on hearing at Berlin about the seizure of Genoa he turned back.

11 *the murder of the Duc d'Enghien*: the young duke, a member of the Bourbon family, was alleged to have taken part in a conspiracy of 1804 to assassinate Napoleon, then First Consul. He was kidnapped on neutral territory, tried by an irregular court martial, and shot.

13 *Mademoiselle George*: this celebrated French tragic actress (who failed to impress Pushkin) appeared in Petersburg and Moscow during the years 1808–12. Natasha hears her declaim in Hélène's drawing room (II v 13).

17 In 1805 M. I. Kutuzov (1745–1813) already enjoyed a great military reputation. He had taken part in the Turkish wars in Catherine's reign and together with Suvorov had captured the fortresses of Ochakov and Ismail, but had been seriously wounded and lost an eye. Having displeased Alexander in the post of Governor-General of Petersburg, he had been living for three years in disfavour in the country, but was now recalled to lead an army of 50,000 men to the aid of Austria [M].

Dieu me la donne, gare à qui la touche!: 'God has given it to me, let him beware who shall touch it'.

18 Maude dismisses Hippolyte's heraldry as 'untranslatable nonsense'.

20 *The prisoners he killed in Africa*: they were massacred in reprisal by Napoleon after the taking of Jaffa in 1799.

21 *the bridge of Arcole*: where, in 1796, Napoleon, fighting against the Austrians, seized the flag and led his troops across.

28 *and he waved his arm*: a forceful gesture employed by Russians to signify dismissal, 'giving it up as a bad job'.

31 *you part our hands*: the Russian custom was to shake hands on a bet, and for some third person, acting as a witness, to separate the hands [M].

35 Radzivilov was on the frontier between Russia and Galicia. Count Ilya Rostov bears a strong likeness to Count Ilya Tolstoy, the author's grandfather, and the Countess to his grandmother. Nicholas has some features of Tolstoy's father. Natasha is closer to his sister-in-law Tanya Behrs than to his wife. Vera resembles another sister-in-law. Sonya's relations with Nicholas are not unlike those between Tolstoy's father and his guardian Tatyana Ergolskaya. Maude remarks that 'the atmosphere of the Rostov family reproduces much that was characteristic of the Behrs' family circle.'

52 *performed his final duty*: i.e. to receive Unction.

59 Marya Dmitrievna Akhrosimova has much in common with N. D. Ofrosimova (1753–1826), a conspicuous figure of the time in Moscow society, though Tolstoy denies the derivation in 'Some Words about *War and Peace*' (p. 1309 below).

61 *summons to zakuska*: an *hors d'œuvre* eaten before the main meal, and consisting of caviare, salt fish etc., with vodka.

65 *Suvorov ... they beat him à plate couture* (hollow): A. S. Suvorov (1729–1800), owing to the failure of his Austrian allies in 1799 to supply him, was hard pressed in Switzerland. But although surrounded by 80,000 French, his army of not many more than 20,000 escaped from encirclement.

68 In the Russian Church cousins come within the prohibited degrees of affinity and a special permission has to be obtained for their marriage [M].

70 The *anglaise* was a contredanse with many figures to which arbitrary and fantastic names were given. Tolstoy obtained his knowledge of it from family tradition [M].

89 Prince Nicholas Andreevich Bolkonsky has many characteristics of Tolstoy's grandfather, Prince Nikolay Sergeevich Volkonsky (1753–1812), though it is suggested that he may derive more closely from Field Marshal M. F. Kamensky, another veteran of Catherine's wars. Princess Mary was modelled on Tolstoy's mother, Marya Nikolaevna Volkonskaya (who died when he was two

years old). Mlle Bourienne portrays a Frenchwoman who was her companion.

91 *From Heloise*: alluding to Rousseau's novel, *La Nouvelle Héloise* (1761). The correspondence between Princess Mary and Julie (the name of Rousseau's heroine) was suggested by that between M. A. Volkova and V. I. Lanskaya between 1812 and 1818. Tolstoy read it in manuscript.

92 *Some sort of Key to the Mysteries*: The book in question was a mystical one by Eckartshausen (1752–1803) – *A Key to the Mysteries of Nature*. In 1805 it had been recently translated into Russian and was being eagerly read, especially among the Freemasons [M].

96 *grasseyement*: burring the r's in the French manner.

100 *About Michelsen's army I understand*: The old prince is asking about Wintzingerode's plan for an attack on the French from three sides. Mikhelson with Russian and Austrian troops would advance from the east, to bring in Prussia; Tolstoy from the north; Kutuzov with the southern Russian army and Bavarians would fight in Galicia. There would be an Austrian army in northern Italy, and in central Italy a Russian corps with British and Neapolitans.

103 *Hofs-kriegs-wurst-schnapps-Rath*: 'Court-war-sausage-schnapps-councils'.

104 *The German, Pahlen ... to fetch the Frenchman Moreau*. P. A. Pahlen had been Governor-General of Petersburg under Paul, and took part in his assassination (1801). General Moreau had been exiled by Napoleon after the conspiracy of 1804.

105 *the siege of Ochakov*: a Turkish fort at the mouth of the Dnieper, stormed by Kutuzov in the war of 1787–91.

109 *Countess Zubova ... her mouth full of false teeth*: zub in Russian means 'tooth'.

111 *Michael Ilarionovich*: Kutuzov.

Lombard-bond: an interest-bearing bond from a state-run pawnshop, or Lombard.

PART TWO

114 *The Tsaritsin Meadow*: subsequently the 'Field of Mars', a parade ground in Petersburg.

121 *leg-bands*: strips of linen wound round in place of stockings.

Wasn't it fine when those Germans gave us lifts?: Kutuzov's army had moved very slowly from Radzivilov. Napoleon reached the Rhine early in September, and the Austrians supplied carts to speed up the arrival of the Russians.

130 *Schon fleissig? ... Hoch Oestreicher! Hoch Russen! Kaiser Alexander hoch!*: 'Busy already? Hurrah for the Austrians! Hurrah for the Russians! Hurrah for the Emperor Alexander!'

Und die ganze Welt hoch!: 'And hurrah for the whole world!'

139 After Mack's surrender, Kutuzov began to retreat towards Vienna, beating back as he went the attacks of the French advanced guard under Murat. On 23 October, O.S., he crossed the rapid river Enns. Murat was pressing all day on the troops under Bagration, trying to intercept him and cut him off from the crossing. Failing to do this, he reached the river almost simultaneously with Bagration and tried to seize the bridge. As described in the novel, the Pavlograd hussars managed to fire it after the Russian troops had crossed [M].

Murat had been with Napoleon in Egypt; he took part in the *coup d'état* of 18 Brumaire 1799 which established Napoleon as Consul; and married his sister in 1800. Napoleon made him King of Naples in 1808 – a title which failed to satisfy his ambition, and which Tolstoy constantly treats with sarcasm.

148 Colonel Schubert, as Maude points out, is one of many Russo-Germans serving the Tsar, and he speaks very poor Russian, which the translation indicates.

153 *actions at Lambach, Amstetten, and Melk*: all three were delaying actions under Bagration in late October, O.S., against the French advanced guard under Murat.

160 *Murat et tout le tremblement*: in the Tolstoy family *le tremblement* had long been ironically used to denote the bustle usually accompanying official celebrations and rejoicings ... [M].

161 The Berlin Conference in October 1805 was an attempt by Alexander I to bring Prussia into the war. A secret treaty was accorded by the sovereigns, with a solemn oath taken over the grave of Frederick the Great, but nothing followed.

il faut lui faire grâce de l'u: 'We must let him off the u' in Buonaparte (see note to p. 3 above).

His Sardinian Majesty: Prussia had wanted Napoleon to be made to compensate the king for his seizure in 1796 of Nice and Savoy.

167 *the Toulon that would lift him from the ranks*: like Napoleon, who was a young artillery captain at the siege of this Royalist stronghold in 1793. He gained his first military success and was promoted general.

176 Tolstoy quotes the letter to Murat from Thiers's *Histoire du Consulat et de l'Empire* (1845–62).

184 *my Toulon*: see note to p. 167 above.

uttering his words with an oriental accent: Prince Bagration was

1320

a Georgian, Bagrationi being the dynastic name of former Georgian kings.

191 'This was the attack of which Thiers says: "The Russians behaved courageously, and, what seldom happens in war, two bodies of infantry were seen marching resolutely against one another without either of them giving way before meeting." And Napoleon at St Helena said: "Some Russian battalions showed entire fearlessness." ' [Tolstoy's note.]

200 The 'unicorn', like all other guns of the period, was a smooth-bore muzzle-loader, but was peculiar in the way it narrowed towards the muzzle [M].

PART THREE

209 *Councillor of State*: in the fifth of the eleven classes in the civil service.

216 *Lëlya*: affectionate diminutive for Elena (Hélène).

247 *the Ismaylov regiment*: Tolstoy has made very few slips in this long novel, but here there seems to be one, for in Chapter 7 of Part One we were told that Boris had been transferred to the Semënov Guards [M].

251 Arnauts is a Turkish name of the Albanians, who supplied the Turks with irregular cavalry [M].

264 *sotnya*: company of a hundred men.

271 *Prishprish*: the Polish general Przebyszewski.

273 30 November, N.S. = 18 November, O.S.

276 Maude points out that the problem of death defeating 'man's greatest efforts and best hopes', here evaded by Prince Andrew, was to revolutionize Tolstoy's life sixteen years later, as described in Chapter 3 of A *Confession* (see also II ii 1, 12 and II ii 22).

281 *Hollabrünn*: Tolstoy refers to this battle as Schön Grabern, from the neighbouring village (I ii 16–21).

289 The conversation between Kutuzov and Alexander is recorded in Mikhaylovsky-Danilevsky's *War of 1805*. As R. F. Christian comments, Tolstoy reproduces the dialogue exactly, but 'fills in the reactions of the speakers' – the twitching of Kutuzov's upper lip, the shrugging of his 'rather round shoulders'.

BOOK TWO

PART ONE

318 The English Club in Moscow dated from the reign of Catherine in the previous century. Moscow, relegated to the standing of second capital by Petersburg, tended to what Maude styles 'informal opposition'. The club was the meeting place of its aristocracy.

321 *The men who set the tone in conversation*: Count F. V. Rostopchin (1763–1826), to become Governor-General and Commander-in-Chief of Moscow (III iii 11, 24–5); Prince Yu. V. Dolgorukov, Commander-in-Chief of Moscow under Paul; P. S. Valuev, an archaeologist; Count I. I. Markov, a general of Catherine's time; Prince A. N. Vyazemsky, high-ranking official and father of the writer Prince P. A. Vyazemsky.

325 The description of the banquet in honour of Bagration enlarges (with a few slips) the entry for 4 March 1806 in the diary of S. P. Zhikharev. The verses, in awkward Russian, were transcribed from there. Their author, Nikolov, was blind by 1806 and could not have read his verses to the company.

327 *Paul Ivanovich Kutuzov*: not to be confused with the general (Michael Ilarionovich).

334 *Anatole used to come to borrow money from her*: in the first drafts of the novel, Tolstoy made it plain that Hélène and her brother had been in guilty relations with one another, but afterwards he altered this so that only some hints remain [M].

335 *Mais que diable ... dans cette galère*: 'What the dickens did he get himself into that mess for?' or, more literally, 'What the devil was he going to do in that galley?' (*Les Fourberies de Scapin*).

340 *this morning's frushtique*: for *Frühstück*, breakfast.

346 In the Russian baptismal service the priest cuts off a little of the child's hair and sticks it together with wax from a taper. It is considered unlucky if this wax sinks in the font [M].

348 *In the autumn of 1806 everybody had again begun talking of the war with Napoleon*: all through 1806 Napoleon had been making preparations for a new campaign. Charles James Fox, the pacifically inclined British Foreign Secretary, died in September. At the end of the month Napoleon won victories at Jena and Auerstadt over the Prussians and occupied Berlin. Alexander had no time to give aid, with the French on the Vistula. He conscripted men for the army and militia to defend his borders. Maude notes that four-fifths of the militia would have had to carry pikes.

359 *some verses called 'Enchantress'*: Denisov has certain features of

the poet and partisan hero of 1812, Denis Davydov (1784–1839), but these verses cannot be traced to the latter.

368 *a half-cut novel ... by Madame de Souza: Émilie et Alphonse* (1799). Mme de Souza (1761–1836) was mentioned in an earlier draft along with Mrs Radcliffe, as a novelist much admired by women of the same generation as Tolstoy's mother.

369 Russian serfs and peasants often turn their tea-tumblers upside down as an indication that they do not want any more. From economy they do not dissolve the sugar, but nibble a little with their tea [M].

370 *The Brotherhood of the Freemasons:* Freemasonry came to Russia in the late seventeenth or early eighteenth century. By the 1760s many high officials were Masons. The Lodges were German or English by derivation. (The so-called 'Scottish' Lodges of II iii 8 were actually German.) Catherine closed down the order in 1790, by which time the Russian Freemasons had been formed into a province under a German Grandmaster, the Duke of Brunswick. There had been a revival of Freemasonry in Alexander's reign, with some revolutionary implications. (See note to p. 376.)

374 *in Novikov's time.* N. I. Novikov (1744–1818) was an active Mason, a prominent journalist who attacked serfdom, and publisher of Rosicrucian and other literature. One of the works he printed was L. C. de Saint Martin's *Des erreurs et de la vérité* (1785), the inspiration of the so-called Martinists. Novikov was imprisoned in 1792 for fifteen years in Schlüsselburg but released in 1796 following Catherine's death.

375 *Thomas à Kempis:* (1380–1471), the author of *De Imitatione Christi*, a celebrated devotional treatise.

376 Tolstoy took the ceremonies of the Freemasons from his study of books and manuscripts in the rich collection of the Rumyantsev Museum in Moscow. In a letter to his wife in the autumn of 1866 he wrote: 'After drinking my coffee I went to the Rumyantsev Museum and sat there till three o'clock reading very interesting Masonic manuscripts. I can't describe to you why the reading produced on me a depression I have not been able to get rid of all day. What is distressing is that all those Masons were fools.' Tolstoy sympathized with their aims but considered their methods futile [M].

387 *Tu l'as voulu, George Dandin:* a familiar quotation from Molière's comedy *George Dandin* (1668). (It should be 'Vous l'avez voulu'.)

388 *Vienna considers the bases of the proposed treaty so unattainable:* negotiations for the Bartenstein treaty between France and

Prussia, to which Austria was invited to adhere, were going on in April 1807. Napoleon had been discomfited by the battle of Preussisch Eylau (see note to p. 393 below). The treaty was still unconcluded when the battle of Friedland took place in June. After this the Emperors met at Tilsit (II ii 19–21).

388 *The man of profound intellect*: another of Tolstoy's apparent slips. It was the Danish *chargé d'affaires* who was referred to thus (p. 387). The speaker here is presumably Shitov, he who was described (also p. 387) as 'a man of great merit'.

389 *'For the King of Prussia'*, a phrase used in French to denote 'for a trifle of no value' [M].

393 *a complete victory over Buonaparte at Eylau*: the battle of Preussisch Eylau was fought on 27 January 1807, O. S. Bennigsen commanded the Russian army, losing a third of his men, but Napoleon too suffered heavy losses. Both sides claimed a victory.

395 *kibitka*: a covered wagon.

401 'The same day is kept by the Russian Church in honour of St Peter and St Paul, so that Pierre (Peter) had them both as patron saints [M].' Maude further points out that a chantry would bring people from outside to the fair, and the peasants resented having their children taken because they needed them to work on their own plots.

407 *to be their marshal*: *Maréchal de la Noblesse*, elected by them and the landed gentry as their representative.

409 *the serfs' backs and foreheads, which, beat and shave as you may*: a proprietor could send any of his serfs as exiles to Siberia, and when going there one side of the head was shaved, that the man might more easily be recaptured should he run away [M].

412 *God's folk*: Tolstoy tells of his aunt Alexandra that she harboured at Yasnaya Polyana, and loved to converse with, 'pilgrims, half-crazy devotees, monks and nuns'. These pilgrims wandered over Russia on their way to Holy Places.

413 *Il faut que vous sachiez . . . votre intimité avec ce jeune homme*: 'You realize that this is a woman.' . . . 'My dear, you ought on the contrary to be pleased I should explain to Pierre your intimacy with this young man.'

419 *Platov's division*: General M. I. Platov (1751–1818), Ataman (Chief) of the Cossack Host, was a former comrade-in-arms of Suvorov and Kutuzov.

neither provisions for the men nor fodder for the horses: Maude quotes from Mikhaylovsky-Danilevsky's *Description of the Wars of 1806–7*: 'The lack of grain in spring occasioned the slackness of the higher command and its inability to stop abuses which made their way into the management of the commissariat. In reply to a report of hunger in the army, Bennigsen once replied: "It is necessary to know how to endure. I only have three dishes for my own dinner." Money was issued to buy provisions, but money cannot buy provisions where there are none. Sometimes the generals seized one another's provision waggons almost by assault, and bread seldom reached Bennigsen's advanced guard, Soldiers swelled up and died of hunger. The hospitals were in a wretched condition.'

420 *quoits and skittles*: literally, *svayka* and *gorodki*. In the former a thick-headed nail has to be thrown into a ring. *Gorodki* is a game in which short, thick sticks are arranged in certain figures within squares. Each side has its own square, and each player in turn throws a stick to try to clear out the enemy's square. The side wins which first accomplishes this with the six figures in which the sticks are successively arranged [M].

431 *The French and Russian Emperors arrived in Tilsit*: this was to arrange a peace which lasted for five years. The King of Prussia was excluded from their two hours of discussion, and admitted only the next day when Napoleon treated him with contempt. Maude notes that their want of silver plate prevented the Preobrazhensk regiment from matching the style of hospitality shown by the French Guards.

PART THREE

447 *flying away! Like this*: Tolstoy at the age of seven or eight attempted to fly from a window eighteen yards up and was concussed by the fall.

450 *when the youthful Speransky was at the zenith of his fame*: M. M. Speransky (1772–1839), son of a village priest, whose abilities enabled him to rise rapidly in the civil service, was from 1808 the Tsar's adviser on home affairs. He worked to reform the finances and administration of Russia. His Plan of 1809, which proposed far-reaching reforms, was implemented only in part. Prince Andrew works on his commission for revising the laws (II iii 6). The civil code drafted by Speransky was indebted to the *Code Napoléon*. The Moscow opposition, led by the fanatically anti-French Rostopchin, who believed Speransky to be the evil genius of Russia and a leader of the Freemasons, campaigned for his overthrow. He was dismissed and exiled in 1812, shortly before Napoleon invaded Russia (II v 21).

450 *the grades of Collegiate Assessor and State Councillor*: the sixth and fifth, equivalent to lieutenant-colonel and full colonel.

450 Count Aleksey Arakcheev (1769–1834) was Alexander's military adviser. He is notorious for his military settlements of the 1820s in which state peasants had to combine army service and agriculture under the harshest discipline. Not only the young liberals of Pushkin's day but some of Alexander's leading generals intensely disliked the settlements.

451 *Sila Andreevich: sila* means 'force'.

453 Count V. P. Kochubey (1768–1834) was Minister of the Interior from 1802 until 1807.

456 *an admirer of Montesquieu*: Speransky himself approved the ideas of Montesquieu in *De l'esprit des lois* (1748), as he did those of the eighteenth-century English jurist Blackstone. The French here reads: 'That the principle of monarchies is honour seems to me incontestable. Certain rights and privileges for the aristocracy appear to me a means of maintaining that sentiment.'

461 *the three primordial elements – sulphur, mercury, and salt*: the Rosicrucian Masons, including Novikov, were interested in alchemy.

463 *dangerous designs of Illuminism*: the Illuminati were a Bavarian conspiratorial group with republican aims, founded in 1776 and suppressed by their government in 1785. They had followers in the Moscow Martinists.

For three days after the delivery of his speech at the Lodge: this incident recalls Tolstoy's own experience on the few occasions when he ventured to make a public speech ... [M].

466 *the circle of Count Rumyantsev and Caulaincourt*: Count N. P. Rumyantsev, Minister of Foreign Affairs in 1807, became Chancellor in 1809. The Marquis de Caulaincourt was French ambassador in Petersburg from 1807 until 1811.

Hélène had been at Erfurt: Alexander, Napoleon and the King of Prussia met there in the autumn of 1808. Napoleon proposed an alliance between France and Russia which Alexander rejected, knowing the strength of feeling at home. For promising not to intervene in Europe he was allowed to annex Finland and, if he could, Turkey's Danubian provinces.

The Prince de Ligne (1735–1814), famous as soldier, diplomat and author, spent some time in Russia. He accompanied Catherine on her tour to the Crimea in 1787.

473 *I have arranged that rent for them in the Baltic provinces*: throughout the nineteenth century the Russian government, as a reward for service, or simply by favouritism, used to make grants of 'rents' (*arenda*), that is to say, the usufruct of land [M].

478 *Natasha ... began kissing first one knuckle*: she is reckoning the knuckles of the closed fist as the months that have 31 days, the

spaces between as the shorter months, and Maude observes that she has to cheat in order to arrive at August.

484 *Marya Antonovna*: M. A. Naryshkina (1779–1854) was for a long time Alexander's mistress.

491 *Gervais, Magnitsky, and Stolypin*: A. A. Gervais, who served in the Ministry of Foreign Affairs, was a kinsman of Speransky's; M. L. Magnitsky (1778–1855), his friend and collaborator, also arrested and exiled in 1812; Senator A. A. Stolypin, a wealthy landowner. Tolstoy here handles ironically the reminiscences of Speransky's daughter in Baron M. A. Korf's *Life of Count Speransky* (1861).

493 *Napoleon's Spanish affairs*: Napoleon had invaded the Iberian peninsula in 1807. The following year he installed his brother Joseph (then King of Naples) in place of Ferdinand VII as King of Spain. By 1810 the combined pressure of Wellington's army and Spanish guerrillas was forcing the French out of Spain, a process completed in 1813.

498 *the table for boston*: boston was a card game invented by French officers at Boston, Massachusetts, during the Revolutionary war. It has a distant resemblance to auction bridge [M].

512 *her own brother, killed in Turkey*: following Tilsit the Russian army resumed hostilities against Turkey in the Caucasus and on the Danube. They had little success in the latter region until Kutuzov became Commander-in-Chief.

PART FOUR

525 *an unsurpassable morning for hunting*: Maude observes that 'the hounds in hunting of the kind here described were keen-scented but not very swift dogs. They had to find the game by scent and chase it in the desired direction, but the swift and strong borzois caught and killed the game. A borzoi has very poor scent and only chases the game when he sees it. It must be pointed out to him, and even when following it he sometimes loses sight of it. If the game shams dead, a borzoi is often balked and hesitates what to do, as in the case mentioned when the hare suddenly squatted and the borzoi did not seize it' (ch. 6).

529 *the buffoon…Nastasya Ivanovna*: the practice of keeping a buffoon in country houses lasted till after the abolition of serfdom. 'Alesha the Pot', from whom Tolstoy later made so tragic a story, was a sort of buffoon Tolstoy's wife found at Yasnaya Polyana when she arrived there after her marriage in 1862 [M].

546 *the pas de châle*: a French shawl dance.

548 *Dimmler the musician*: a real person who gave piano lessons at this time in Moscow.

551 Twenty degrees Réaumur is thirteen below zero Fahrenheit.

552 Feeding a fowl with grain arranged on the floor is a way of telling fortunes at Christmas time [M].

556 John Field (1782–1837), Irish-born pianist and composer, famous for his nocturnes, lived in Petersburg from 1804 until 1831. Pasternak in *An Essay in Autobiography* (1959) speaks of Chopin's originality in 'using the old idiom of Mozart and Field' for new purposes.

PART FIVE

571 *Sivtsev Vrazhok*: a Moscow slum.

573 *the Emperor Francis wants to offer him his daughter in an illegal marriage*: Napoleon had married Joséphine de Beauharnais in 1796. The marriage was childless. He divorced her in 1809, applied unsuccessfully for the hand of Alexander's sister Anna, and married the Archduchess Marie Louise of Austria in March 1810.

The Spanish victory over the French on 14 June appears to be Talavera (15–16 July 1809, O.S.)

Astræa Lodge against the Manna Seekers: they were both in Petersburg, and the intrigues could take the form of denunciations.

an authentic Scotch carpet: a carpet with symbolic signs on it was considered important for the equipment of each Lodge. The Lodges competed with one another in obtaining such carpets from the most ancient and highly esteemed masonic organizations, as well as copies of the ceremonies and 'acts' – that is, the rules of the Order [M].

580 *Napoleon's seizure of the Duke of Oldenburg's territory*: he annexed it in 1810, along with Hanseatic towns that had infringed the Continental System, his blockade against Britain. The Duke was Alexander's brother-in-law.

589 *to jails and prisons on affairs of which she never spoke to anyone*: Prisoners 'suffered much want, and to contribute to their needs was a recognized Christian duty [M]'.

590 *we'll drive to the Super-Rogue's*: There is a pun in the Russian. Akhrosimova refers to the dressmaker Mme Aubert-Chalmé as 'Ober-Shel'ma' ('arch-rogue').

625 *we have first to sit down*: according to Russian custom before a journey.

626 *Remember me to Stëshka*: she was a celebrated gypsy singer in Moscow at that time.

637 *Speransky – the news of whose sudden exile and alleged treachery had just reached Moscow*: for Speransky, see note to p. 450. He had neglected to find allies and supporters. In 1812 he was exiled, eventually to Perm on the Siberian border, but in 1814 the Tsar allowed him to settle on his small estate near Novgorod. In 1816 he became Governor of Penza, and three years later Governor-General of Siberia. In 1821 he returned to Petersburg. Under Nicholas I Speransky was responsible for the Digest of Russian Law, a great bureaucratic enterprise. A few months before his death he was made a Count.

BOOK THREE
PART ONE

645 This chapter is the first of Tolstoy's theoretical digressions on war and the philosophy of history. It has been calculated that in Books Three and Four they fill one chapter in six.

648 *honours he received in Dresden*: Napoleon spent a month there in May 1812, with his new allies – the Emperor of Austria, the King of Prussia (compelled to join in the impending war), the King of Saxony, and others. The date of his leaving Dresden is given N.S. in the following chapter. To be consistent with other dates here, it should be twelve days earlier.

651 *having summoned Berthier*: Marshal L.-A. Berthier, Prince of Neufchâtel (1753–1815), was chief of the general staff.

652 *Quos [Juppiter] vult perdere dementat [prius]*: 'Those whom God wishes to destroy he first drives mad.'

Each of the three armies had its own commander-in-chief: that of the western army was Prince M. Barclay de Tolly (1761–1818), born in Lithuania, of Scottish extraction. He was Minister of War in 1810–13, and was replaced in command of the army in 1812 by Kutuzov, after the fall of Smolensk. Pushkin was one who greatly admired Barclay de Tolly. Although recognizing that Kutuzov had performed a unique service to Russia, he believed that Barclay's crucial role had been underestimated.

Bagration commanded the southern army, and Tormasov a reserve army being formed near the Austrian frontier.

655 *Count Lauriston*: A. J. B. Law (1768–1828), a great-nephew of John Law of Lauriston, of Mississippi Scheme fame. He was a fellow pupil of Napoleon's at the Artillery School. He greatly distinguished himself at the battle of Wagram (1809), was Napoleon's ambassador in Petersburg (1811–12) and accompanied him through the greater part of the Russian campaign, but did not side with Napoleon after his return from Elba in 1815. He was subsequently made a marquis and a Marshal of France by Louis XVIII [M].

1329

Prince Kurakin: the Russian ambassador in Paris.

660 *his Mameluke, Rustan*: the Mamelukes were Egyptian cavalry under the Turks. After defeating them in 1798 at the battle of the Pyramids, Napoleon brought back Rustan as his personal bodyguard.

661 Napoleon's speeches to Balashev in this chapter, and at dinner in the following one, are taken from Thiers and Mikhaylovsky-Danilevsky. But Tolstoy manipulates the scene to bring out his vanity and inattentiveness to his interlocutor.

664 *peace with Turkey*: Kutuzov after a victorious campaign signed peace with the Turks at Bucharest in May 1812.

With Steins, Armfelts, Bennigsens, and Wintzingerodes: Baron H. F. K. von Stein (1757–1831) had been a Prussian minister until Napoleon secured his expulsion. He came to Russia in 1812, being invited there by Alexander, and was active in promoting the coalition against Napoleon.

Count G. M. Armfelt (1757–1814), a distinguished Swedish general, was now in the Russian service and responsible for the administration of Finland. He played an active part in the downfall of Speransky. In the campaign of 1812 he accompanied the Tsar.

Count L. A. von Bennigsen (1745–1826), 'a landowner in the Vilna province' (III i 3), was the Russian commander defeated at Friedland in 1807. He would 'awaken terrible memories in the Emperor Alexander's mind' since he had taken part in the conspiracy to assassinate Paul I.

Baron F. T. Wintzingerode (1770–1818) had been in Russian service since 1793. He was nominally a 'fugitive French subject' since Napoleon had annexed his native Hesse in 1806 to become part of the Confederation of the Rhine.

665 J. B. J. Bernadotte, one of Napoleon's Marshals, had been elected heir to the Swedish throne in 1810.

666 *re-erect against you that barrier*: namely, a reconstituted Poland.

667 J. B. Bessières (1768–1813), Marshal of France and Duke of Istria, had commanded the French cavalry at Austerlitz who routed 'the brilliant charge of the Horse Guards that amazed the French themselves' (I iii 17).

668 *the recent defeats of the French in Spain*: a number of successes in the last twelve months were leading up to Wellington's victory at Salamanca in July 1812 and his occupation of Madrid in August.

the road through Poltava: where Peter the Great won his notable victory over Charles XII of Sweden in 1709. The evidence that Napoleon put this question and Balashev made his pointed reply is doubtful.

670 *the army in Moldavia*: Kutuzov had become its commander-in-chief in March 1811.

671 At Drissa, where two rivers meet, a fortified camp had been constructed, chiefly to guard the road to Petersburg.

675 The second army was commanded by Bagration.

The 'Polish' provinces were those west of Smolensk which had been annexed several years earlier.

676 Marquis F. O. Paulucci, in 1812 for a time Chief of Staff to the First Army, had passed from the French to the Russian service in 1809.

Baron L. J. Wolzogen (1774–1845) was a Prussian general, from 1807 to 1815 on the Russian General Staff. He appears at the Council of War (III i 11), translating and speaking for Pfuel.

682 K. F. Toll (1778–1842), a Russian general of German origin, and in 1812 Quartermaster-General of the main army.

696 *Count Ostermann-Tolstoy*: he commanded a corps in the first western army.

703 *Before the end of the fast of St Peter*: that is, for two weeks before St Peter's Day (29 June, Old Style), and seventeen days after Napoleon had crossed the Russian frontier [M].

707 *As one community*: Maude points out that the Russian word *mir* (peace) has a homophone, meaning the world or the commune (village assembly), and this latter sense is the one taken by Natasha.

708 *biretta*: an approximation for the *skuf'ya*, worn by the 'white', or lower, married clergy.

711 Maude observes that to obtain the sum of 666 the *e* of *le*, elided before *Empereur*, had to be counted. Pierre juggles with *quarante-deux*, taking it to mean years, rather than months, and ignoring the fact that Napoleon would not be 42 until August. He chooses to transliterate his name Besuhof, though in IV i 10 it is spelt Besouhof.

716 *to speak French in the streets*: it was so customary for the Russian aristocracy of those days to speak French that many of them could neither write nor speak Russian correctly, though the mass of the people spoke nothing but Russian [M].

720 The Tsar-cannon (*Tsar'-pushka*), a very large cannon cast in 1488, which is preserved in the Moscow Kremlin as a curiosity [M].

722 *the Emperor had a plateful of biscuits brought him*: Tolstoy had declared in 'Some Words about *War and Peace*' that he could always produce supporting evidence for his statements. Prince Vyazemsky challenged Tolstoy about this episode, which he

considered uncharacteristic of the very self-conscious and formal Alexander. Tolstoy was unable to locate the reference. He probably had in mind another source that tells of the Tsar on this occasion sending out fruit to the crowd.

723 The scene at the Sloboda Palace is derived from the memoirs of an eyewitness, Sergey Glinka.

728 An *otkupshchik* leased the right to deal in spirits, a government monopoly.

PART TWO

736 *wrote Julie in her Frenchified Russian*: Tolstoy, as Maude has noted, wants to show the artificiality of her patriotism. But young ladies then did not write Russian easily. Even Pushkin's Tatyana, 'Russian at heart', uses French in her letter to Onegin.

744 *Alpatych swayed his head*: Russians have a habit of bending their heads from side to side to express surprise, dismay, or disapproval [M].

757 *a man of great merit*: usually taken to be Joseph de Maistre (1758–1821), Sardinian Ambassador in Petersburg from 1803 to 1817. Tolstoy draws freely on his *Correspondance diplomatique* and *Soirées de St. Pétersbourg* for anecdote and comment. Isaiah Berlin has discussed the influence of Maistre's ideas on Tolstoy's own thinking in *The Hedgehog and the Fox*, reprinted in *Russian Thinkers* (London, 1978).

759 *blushed like a girl to whom Joconde is read*: *Joconde* is one of the early and libertine *Contes* by Jean de la Fontaine (1621–95).

764 *For three weeks the old prince lay stricken by paralysis*: this is a rare instance of Tolstoy's making a mistake in the time-arrangement of his novel. On the 5th of August, the day Smolensk was bombarded, the old prince was still well. He died on the 15th, and could not therefore have lain stricken by paralysis for three weeks [M].

770 *Peter Fëdorovich's return to the throne*: Peter III, deposed in 1762 by his wife, Catherine the Great, was killed soon after in mysterious circumstances. The peasants refused to believe that he had died. There were many false Peters – the most famous being the Cossack Pugachev who led the great Urals and middle-Volga rebellion in 1773–5.

There were serious peasant disturbances in the Smolensk region in 1812.

790 *caused his sister to refuse my brother*: Princess Mary sees the hand of Providence in this because the Orthodox Church would not allow her to marry her brother's brother-in-law, which Nicholas would have been if Natasha married Prince Andrew.

795 to offer his *Serene Highness* bread and salt: it is a Russian custom to present 'bread and salt' to anyone who is taking up residence in a new place. In practice the 'bread and salt' is often represented by a cake and a silver dish of white powdered sugar [M].

800 *Vasili Lvovich Pushkin's bouts-rimés*: V. L. Pushkin (1767–1830), uncle of the poet, a skilled versifier and best known for his satirical poem *The Dangerous Neighbour* (1811) to which Pushkin refers in *Eugene Onegin*.

the way Karpushka jeered at the French: Rostopchin, Governor-General of Moscow, invented for his broadsheets a patriotic spokesman, one Chikhirin, 'a Moscow *meshchanin* (petty bourgeois) and former militiaman'.

803 *Count Wittgenstein had defeated the French*: he commanded a corps guarding the road to Petersburg. Marshal Oudinot opposing him suffered a reverse on 30 July. However, the real victor was not Wittgenstein but the general commanding the Russian rearguard.

805 *the great balloon Leppich was constructing*: Franz Leppich, a Dutchman, persuaded Rostopchin that he could construct a balloon to confound the French. (In 1811 he had tried to sell the invention to Napoleon, who banished him from the French Empire.) Much time and government money were spent on this project. At its trials in November 1812 the balloon leaked gas, and Leppich disappeared.

the Lobnoe Place: where executions in Moscow were carried out. It had formerly been in the Red Square. (Literally 'forehead place', named after *Golgotha*, or *calvary*, 'place of a skull'.)

810 The sketch map of Borodino is Tolstoy's own, made after a two-day visit in September 1867, when he surveyed the ground and talked to peasants who remembered the time. Tolstoy made a thorough study of the available resources. He promised his wife in a letter on returning from the scene, 'I'll write a battle of Borodino, the like of which there has never been before.'

817 *The Iberian Mother of God*: an icon.

821 *those verses of Marin's...about Gerakov*: S. N. Marin was an aide-de-camp of Alexander I, well known for his parodies and amusing verses. G. V. Gerakov was a captain in the army, a teacher in the military school, and the author of numerous patriotic works of very poor quality. He was the object of much ridicule. Marin's verse about him was in the form of a prophecy:

> You will always go on writing
> And to death your readers bore:
> Lectures for the corps inditing –
> Be a captain evermore [M].

822 *flèches*: salient outworks, known also as 'arrows'.

826 *We see light again, since his Serenity has been appointed*: a play on *svet* (light) and Kutuzov's title *Svetleyshiy* (Most Serene).

827 *going away, so he would get it all*: the enemy was always *he* to the Russians [M].

829 *Prince Andrew recognized Wolzogen and Clausewitz*: for Wolzogen, see note to p. 676. Karl von Clausewitz (1780–1831), the celebrated military theorist and historian (who wrote on the war of 1812), was a Prussian general now in the Russian service.

Der Krieg ... in Achtung nehmen: 'The war must be extended widely. I cannot sufficiently commend that view.' 'Oh yes, the only aim is to weaken the enemy, so one cannot, of course, take into account the losses of private persons.'

831 *The aim of war is murder*: Maude notes that in this chapter Prince Andrew comes near to expressing Tolstoy's own view then of the campaign, and in places anticipates his absolute condemnation of war in later years. He refers to 'The Raid' (1853) where Tolstoy writes: 'Can it be possible that in the midst of this entrancing Nature, feelings of hatred, vengeance, or the passion for exterminating their fellows, can endure in the souls of men?', and to the end of *Sevastopol in May* (1855). Eventually the seeds from such perceptions 'grew into great trees throwing their shade far around'.

833 *Salamanca ... The result of that battle had been deplorable*: Wellington with English, Portuguese, and Spanish troops defeated Marshal Marmont at Salamanca on 10 July 1812, N.S.

834 *A present to your Majesty from the Empress*: this episode is attested by the Memoirs of de Beausset himself, but Tolstoy's handling of it is ironical and somewhat unscrupulous. He stresses, as Maude has noted, the uneasiness Napoleon feels about the course of the war (calling for his snuff-box is a sign of this); and the whole scene is rendered to look slightly ridiculous – the 'courtly adroitness' of Beausset in 'twitching off the cloth' – and also insincere – Napoleon assuming 'a look oi pensive tenderness' because he has 'the natural capacity of an Italian for changing his face at will'. There is no evidence to show that he required all his officers to steal out on tiptoe, 'leaving the great man to himself and his emotion'.

837 The viceroy is Murat (King of Naples).

The village to be occupied is Borodino. The date of the proclamation, 6 September N.S., is 25 August O.S.

860 *Lodi, Marengo ... Jena, ... Wagram*. In Northern Italy Napoleon defeated the Austrians at Lodi in 1796, and at Marengo in 1800;

he destroyed the Prussians at Jena in 1806; and his final war
against Austria ended with victory at Wagram in 1809.

862 *Prince Peter Ivanovich*: Bagration.

The Duke of Würtemburg: brother-in-law of Paul I, he had been
in the Russian service since 1800.

863 *news that Murat had been taken prisoner*: this report turned
out to be false. It was General Bonnamy who had been captured.
Seeing a Russian grenadier's bayonet at his breast he cried out 'I
am the King', and was taken alive to Kutuzov. The false rumour
was spread by a major who spoke in a thick voice and rode
along the line indistinctly shouting news of the capture [M].

PART THREE

885 *the siege of Saragossa*: the Spanish garrison held out for more
than two months, and the city had to be taken house by house.

889 Bennigsen suffered a heavy defeat by Napoleon in 1807 at Friedland in East Prussia.

892 *Madame Aubert-Chalmé*: see n. to p. 590.

French verses in albums: quoted in Maude's note as follows:

> Je suis né Tartare.
> Je voulus être Romain.
> Les Français m'appelèrent barbare.
> Les Russes – Georges Dandin.

For Dandin see n. to p. 387.

893 *a Jesuit à robe courte*: 'in walking dress'. The Pope suppressed
the Society of Jesus in 1773, and for some years it was only
allowed to operate in Russia and Prussia. Catherine the Great
became its active protector, and Pius VII sanctioned the reconstruction of the Order in Russia in 1801. It was, however,
expelled from Petersburg and Moscow in 1813, and from Russia
altogether in 1820.

In France in the time of Louis XIV and XV *un Jésuite à robe
courte* was a term applied to lay sympathizers who helped the
Jesuits [M].

910 *Augustin had been forbidden to leave*: the monastic name of
A. V. Vinogradsky (1766–1818), a celebrated preacher.

914 *Hoffman's drops*: a medicine much used in Russia, composed of
two parts ether sulphuricus and three parts alcohol [M].

925 *The ways of God are past finding out*: the countess is thinking
of the Russian Church law of affinity: if Prince Andrew dies,
Nicholas can marry his sister. See n. to p. 709

934 *'Boyars,' I will say to them*: Napoleon did not know that the
boyars of medieval Russia – the Tsar's chief assistants from the

aristocracy – had lost their position under Peter the Great, and the term was now obsolete.

937 The Russian hives were usually made of hollowed-out tree-trunks, which were cleansed by charring [M].

938 *men ... with closely-shaven heads*: these were prisoners released from jail.

941 *a white twenty-five ruble assignat*: a bank note. One silver ruble was worth three and a half paper rubles.

944 China-Town (*Kitay-gorod*) was a part of Moscow.

957 *the citadel, le Kremlin*: Tolstoy likes to indicate the superficial and inaccurate knowledge the French had of Russia. Here, for instance, he mentions Murat as regarding the Kremlin, the brick walls of which were built in 1367, as a 'citadel'. It might really have served as a fortress in the Middle Ages, but was quite unsuited to resist artillery. Later [p. 1072] the mention of Napoleon giving 'careful directions about the fortification of the Kremlin' is again ironic. In 1812 the Kremlin walls served merely as an enclosure for the palaces, churches, law-courts, and state buildings, of which the Kremlin was constituted [M].

969 *great battle of la Moskowa*: i.e. Borodino, 7 September N.S.

970 *Paris is Talma, la Duchénois, Potier, the Sorbonne*: the famous tragedian Talma, the actress Duchénois, the comedian Potier, the University of Paris.

978 *his regiment which was making for Troitsa*: the Sergeyevo-Troitsky (or Trinity) Monastery founded by St Sergius is forty-four miles NE of Moscow. The town in which it stands is now called Zagorsk.

BOOK FOUR

PART ONE

999 *the two Empresses*: Maria Fëdorovna, widow of Paul I, and Elisabeth Alexeevna, wife of Alexander I – 'who had been a princess of Baden and developed her "Russian patriotism" after her marriage [M].'

1001 *Austrian banners captured from the French by Wittgenstein*: he took them on 18 and 19 June in a successful action against Oudinot. Austria had changed sides.

1002 *Kutuzov's report, written from Tatarinova*: Maude finds here 'one of the rare instances of Tolstoy going astray in his dates'. The report sent on 25 August anticipates the deaths on the next day of Bagration, Tuchkov, and Kutaysov, and Tolstoy has confused Alexander's birthday (12 December) with his name-day

(30 August). Rostopchin's letter, referring to the receipt of one from Kutuzov on the night of 1–2 September (p. 946), is unlikely to have reached Petersburg by 4 September.

1017 *news of the battle of Borodino...reached Voronezh in the middle of September*: Voronezh is about 175 miles south of Moscow: the news would have taken three weeks. Maude, writing fifty years ago, commented: 'The roads in Voronezh province...are exceptionally bad even today.'

1020 *What he had just been praying for...had come to pass*: Maude notes a similar experience of Tolstoy's own as a young man in the Caucasus. He was unable to meet a note-of-hand for gambling debts, prayed fervently, and the next day heard from his brother Nicholas that a Chechen who was attached to Tolstoy had won back the note of hand and wanted Nicholas to send it to him.

1021 *Nicholas saw Princess Mary off on her journey to Yaroslavl*: a distance of at least 500 miles from Voronezh since Moscow, in French hands, was impassable.

1023 *to turn for aid to God and His Saint*: St Sergius of Radonezh, who founded the Trinity Monastery in the fourteenth century.

1028 *the marshal, the Duke of Eckmühl (Davout)*: I. N. Davout (1770–1823), a Marshal of France who came from a noble family, was actually Duke of Auerstädt and Prince of Eckmühl. An exceedingly strict disciplinarian, he was respected but not loved by his men, and unpopular with the other marshals.

1037 *Frola and Lavra*: Florus and Laurus, brothers who were martyred under Diocletian, are numbered among the saints of the Russo-Greek church and are accounted the patron saints of horses by the peasants, who mispronounce their names [M].

1039 *A soldier on leave – a shirt outside the breeches*: the peasants wear their shirts fastened by a girdle at the waist and hanging loose outside their breeches, whereas a soldier's shirt is tucked inside [M].

his 'Christian' life: the Russian word for peasant is *krest'yanin* and originally meant 'one who has been christened'. A Christian is *khristianin*: in Karataev's pronunciation the distinction is lost.

PART TWO

1056 *the so-called flank march across the Krasnaya Pakhra river*: Kutuzov retreated from Moscow along the Ryazan road, but turned right to follow the Pakhra, a tributary of the Moskva river. This manœuvre was to defend the fertile southern provinces and the ordnance factories at Tula. Murat was deliberately misled by two Cossack regiments of the rearguard who kept on the Ryazan road, and he lost sight of Kutuzov's army. Napoleon in

Moscow did not know its whereabouts until 14 September O.S.

1057 *the council at Fili*: described on pp. 887–90. Fili was the last village reached by the Russian army in its retreat on Moscow.

The river Oka could not be crossed because at that time it was covered by thin ice.

1058 *overtures for peace*: Lauriston was sent with proposals to Kutuzov on 5 October (23 September O.S.).

1063 *torban*: a Ukrainian stringed instrument resembling the balalayka [M].

1072 *Captain Yakovlev, who had been robbed and was in rags*: Yakovlev's son, Alexander Herzen, himself an infant at this time, later described the episode in his memoirs, *My Life and Thoughts*. (The part containing this, published in 1856, was known to Tolstoy.) Yakovlev had delayed leaving Moscow. His house was burnt down and the family was destitute. His knowledge of Italian led an Italian officer to bring him to the notice of General Mortier, with whom he had been acquainted in Paris. He was presented, in grimy clothes and unwashed, to Napoleon, who gave him the safe conduct for which he asked on condition he carried a letter to the Tsar. On arriving in Petersburg Yakovlev was detained at Arakcheev's house and held under close arrest for a month. Then he was released, without blame, but he had to leave Petersburg at once, seeing only his brother. (See Herzen *Childhood, Youth and Exile*, The World's Classics, O.U.P. 1980, Part I.)

1074 *He caused the words Maison de ma Mère to be inscribed on the charitable institutions*: Tolstoy took this from a not altogether reliable source in the journal *Russian Archives*.

1075 *a polemic with M. Fain*: Napoleon's secretary, Baron Agathon Fain, who published in 1827 a work on the 1812 campaign.

1096 Medyn and Yukhnov lie to the north-west of Kaluga on a road running well to the south of the Mozhaysk–Smolensk road by which Napoleon eventually retreated westward [M].

the letters he wrote... to Madame de Staël: Mme de Staël (1766–1817), daughter of the Swiss financier Necker who tried to re-order the finances of the *ancien régime* in France, was the implacable enemy of Napoleon. He exiled her in 1807. In 1812 she spent six weeks in Russia, leaving it for Finland the day after Borodino. Pushkin praised her posthumous work, *Dix années d'exil* (1821), for speaking of Russia 'with respect and discretion'.

1098 *the simple-minded soldier Mouton*: General Mouton, Count of Lobau, who spoke last at the Council on 13 (25) October.

what the French called 'le hourra de l'Empereur': hourra was the cheer the Russian troops gave when charging the enemy [M].

1103 *the mountain tribes in the Caucasus*: against whom Tolstoy served in the army from 1851 to 1853.

1107 *because he was already under the command of the Polish general*: Tolstoy borrowed this expedient, by which Denisov preserved his independent command, from an incident recorded in Davydov's *Diary of Guerilla [sic] Operations* [M]. For Davydov, see II i 15.

1108 *Esaul Lovaysky*: What is here told is actual fact. After Davydov's (in the novel Denisov's) first successes, Kutuzov gave him two Cossack regiments to strengthen his force. Lovaysky is a familiar form of the well-known Cossack family name, Ilovaysky. An *esaul* is a captain of Cossacks [M].

  Unbegaun in *Russian Surnames* (O.U.P., 1972), cites Ilovaysky as a clergy name.

1112 *plastun*: an unmounted sharpshooter from the Kuban Cossack Host.

1116 *the battle of Vyazma*: the first battle of importance on Napoleon's retreat towards Smolensk was at Vyazma on 21 and 22 October (2 and 3 November). Miloradovich won a brilliant victory. Caulaincourt said in his memoirs, 'From this incident must be dated our disorganization and misfortune.'

1125 Karabakh is a district in the Southern Caucasus, famous for its breed of horses [M].

1134 *Pierre had long been familiar with that story*: in 1872 Tolstoy elaborated it as *God Sees the Truth but Waits* (translated by Maude in *Twenty-Three Tales*), and published it in his *Primer*. This is one of only two stories by himself which in *What Is Art?* (1898) he did not consign 'to the category of bad art'.

1138 *Do you understand*: as a young man Tolstoy was interested in the phenomena of dreams, and he adopted a theory that dreams, however complex and prolonged they may seem, occur at the instant of awakening and are suggested by external sounds, smells, or sensations [M].

1143 *Du sublime ... un pas*: 'From the sublime to the ridiculous there is but one step'.

1144 *defeated at Krasnoe and the Berëzina*: at Krasnoe on 3–6 (15–18) November 1812 Napoleon's troops, falling back from Smolensk to the Berëzina, had to break out of Russian encirclement. Napoleon was only able to cross the Berëzina a week later with enormous losses.

1147 *fifteen degrees of frost*: Réaumur – two degrees below zero Fahrenheit.

1159 *had an understanding with Napoleon and had been bribed by him*: Tolstoy adds the note 'Wilson's Diary'. Sir Robert Wilson (1777–1849) was the unofficial British military representative with the Russian army. He intrigued, with Bennigsen the Chief of Staff, to persuade Alexander that Kutuzov should be dismissed. Tolstoy would have been able to read in 1862 the relevant parts of Wilson's diary in the *Russian Messenger*.

deprived the Russian army of ... complete victory over the French: Tolstoy gives a general reference here to Bogdanovich's 'The character of Kutuzov and reflections on the unsatisfactory results of the battles at Krasnoe' (*History of the Year 1812*).

1167 *eighteen degrees of frost*: Réaumur – eight degrees below zero Fahrenheit.

1175 *the Grand Duke and heir-apparent*: Constantine Pavlovich (1779–1831) was Alexander I's brother.... He was to some extent responsible for the disaster at Austerlitz ... Constantine was personally courageous, but erratic and incompetent alike in war and politics. After marrying a Polish lady he renounced his right to the throne. The hesitation and confusion caused by the fact that this was not made public occasioned delay in proclaiming his younger brother Nicholas, as Emperor, and gave occasion for the 'Decembrist' revolt with which Nicholas I's reign inauspiciously began [M].

1176 *hat with its peaks to the sides*: a cocked hat with two peaks turned sideways.

1177 The Order of St George was founded by Catherine the Great in 1769 for distinguished exploits in war. The First Class – a very high honour indeed, seldom given – [was] a Star and Cross attached to a ribbon [M].

1182 *he had become much 'simpler'*: in the sense, common in Russia, of unpretentious, natural [M].

1183 *a young Italian*: Maude points out that only this mention remains of an Italian officer, Emilio Poncini, who in an early draft preceded Captain Ramballe (III iii 28).

FIRST EPILOGUE

1209 Photius was head of the Novgorod Monastery. 'In 1820...he instigated a persecution of "Masons and mystics", the Bible Society, and other movements tainted with Liberalism...Photius was an ascetic and frightened Alexander by dismal Apocalyptic predictions, but did not retain his influence long [M].'

F. W. G. Schelling (1775–1854) and J. G. Fichte (1762–1814) were German idealist philosophers and advocates of liberty who had much influence in Russia.

The Vicomte de Chateaubriand (1768–1848), minister under the Restoration, was a leading romantic writer celebrated for his eloquence.

1210 *a constitution to Poland*: the Kingdom of Poland re-established at the Congress of Vienna in 1815 was united to Russia, but had a constitution with certain democratic rights which remained in force until the Polish insurrection of 1830.

the Holy Alliance: founded in 1815 by Austria, Prussia, and Russia for the preservation of peace, it soon became an instrument of repression.

Prince Golitsyn, Minister of Education and Spiritual Affairs, was head of the Bible Society; Admiral Alexander Shishkov (1754–1841), a publicist, statesman, and President of the Academy of Sciences, is remembered for his stubborn defence of the Russian language against Gallicisms and neologisms.

disbanding the Semënov regiment: Alexander dealt severely with this regiment in 1820 when it mutinied in protest against the harsh discipline of its German commander.

1214 *The disfavour into which he falls*: when the government of Robespierre which had promoted him after Toulon fell in 1794 Napoleon was imprisoned for a month. He restored his position in 1795 and gained glory as 'saviour of the republic' for his part in putting down a Royalist rising in Paris.

the appointment he seeks in Turkey comes to nothing: in August 1795 Bonaparte applied to a Commission of the French Government to be sent to Constantinople to reform the Turkish artillery service [M].

the Russian armies ... do not appear upon the scene till he is no longer there: Suvorov's victories against the French took place in 1799, the year after Napoleon went to Egypt.

1215 *chance contrives a plot ... which ... confirms his power*: Napoleon used the failure of the conspiracy of 1804 (see n. to p. 11) to confirm his power by taking the title of Emperor.

1218 *Not unto us, not unto us, but unto Thy Name!*: the inscription on Alexander's medal to commemorate 1812.

Let me live like a man, and think of my soul and of God: Maude notes that Tolstoy seems here to 'refer to and adopt a belief widespread in Russia', that Alexander I had not died at Taganrog in 1825 but lived as a recluse in Siberia until 1866. (His sarco-

phagus when opened in 1927 was empty.) Tolstoy's posthumously
published *Fëdor Kuzmich* tells this story.

1231 *The immense house ... had bare deal floors and was furnished*
with very simple hard sofas: the simplicity of the house is similar
to that which always prevailed at Yasnaya Polyana – the prototype of Bald Hills. For purposes of literary effect much has been
written about the 'luxury' of Tolstoy's house and its contrast
with the simplicity he aimed at and preached in his later life. In
fact, however, he never liked, or indulged in, luxury. Compared
to most English country estates the frugal simplicity of Yasnaya
Polyana was conspicuous [M].

1232 *the elections of the nobility*: periodically held to fill offices in
the local administration.

1233 *to thank the old countess*: it was customary in Russia to thank
the hostess after dinner, and in this case the old countess,
though she was not the hostess, was thanked out of deference
[M].

1249 *Gossner and Tatawinova*: Johann Gossner, a clergyman and
mystic expelled from Bavaria in 1817, became Director of the
Bible Society in Petersburg (1820–4). E. F. Tatarinova in 1817
founded a mystical sect which induced ecstasy by dervish-like
dances. It lasted until 1837 when she was sent to a remote
nunnery.

1251 *Madame Kwüdener*: Baroness Barbara Juliana Krüdener (1764–
1825), born in Riga, sentimental novelist (*Valérie*, 1803) and
mystic, met Alexander I in 1815 and for a while influenced him
profoundly. She lived in Petersburg from 1821.

1252 *his affairs with Prince Theodore*: the aims Pierre mentions as
those of Prince Theodore's circle are very much those with
which many of the Decembrists began their conspiracy. Tolstoy
had planned a novel dealing with the Decembrist movement
before he began *War and Peace ... War and Peace* extends to the
time when the Decembrist conspiracy [of 1825] was taking shape,
and Tolstoy hints at it in this chapter. The careful description
of the Russian masonic movement in an earlier part of the novel
[II ii] was an outcome of his study of the Freemasons as an
organization intimately connected with the Decembrists [M].

1253 *as those who examine the actions of any government have*
always said: the anti-government trend of this passage ... indicates a fundamental connexion between Tolstoy's earlier and later
views [M].

to prevent some Pugachëv: leader of the great rising of the Ural
Cossacks in 1773, which spread through the Middle Volga region.
Pugachëv himself was captured and executed in 1775.

the *Tugendbund which saved Europe*: the Tugendbund or League of Virtue was a liberal and patriotic association, founded at Königsberg in 1808, which aimed at freeing Prussia from the interference of Napoleon. The Prussian government suppressed it in 1809, but it carried on the work illegally. Prussia rose against Napoleon in 1813. Its government after 1815, as a member of the Holy Alliance, continued to repress the Tugendbund. Denisov puns on the German *Bund* (union) and the Russian *bunt* (riot).

1255 A *diary*: these quotations from Countess Mary's diary very closely resemble similar notes written by Tolstoy's mother about her children and still preserved [M].

1262 *Did you see her?*: unreasonable jealousy of the kind here indicated was always a cause of distress between Tolstoy and his wife. His story *The Devil* suggests an exploration of the question: 'Did you see her?' [M].

SECOND EPILOGUE

1271 *Lanfrey, a Republican*: Pierre Lanfrey wrote a history of Napoleon I in four volumes (Paris, 1867–70).

1272 *Gervinus*: G. G. Gervinus (1805–71), 'a German historian and Shakespearian commentator with whom Tolstoy disagreed on both counts [M]'.

1278 *Why was Napoleon III a criminal when he was taken prisoner at Boulogne?* Louis Napoleon, nephew of Napoleon, was arrested at Boulogne in 1840 on his second attempt to seize the throne. He was imprisoned in a fortress but escaped in 1846 to England.

1281 *Ivan the Terrible and . . . his correspondence with Kurbsky*: Ivan the Terrible (1530–84), whom D. S. Mirsky describes as 'a pamphleteer of genius', carried on a polemical correspondence with his leading opponent, Prince Andrey Kurbsky (c.1528–83), who had deserted to the enemy in Lithuania.

1283 *Napoleon III issues a decree and the French go to Mexico*: the Archduke Maximilian (1832–67), brother of the Austrian Emperor Franz Josef, with aid from the French became Emperor of Mexico in 1864. When the Civil War ended, the Americans demanded the withdrawal of the French army. It left in 1867, and the Mexicans overthrew and executed Maximilian.

The King of Prussia and Bismarck issue decrees and an army enters Bohemia: Prussia defeated Austria in the war of 1866.

APPENDIX:
'SOME WORDS ABOUT WAR AND PEACE'

1307 Darya Nikolaevna Saltykova, popularly called 'Saltychikha' (1730–1801), was a landed proprietress who owned six hundred serfs, and in seven years tortured a hundred and thirty-nine of them to death. By bribery and family influence she escaped punishment for a while, but in 1776 a complaint reached Catherine II, and after a trial that lasted six years Saltykova was sentenced to death: this sentence, however, was commuted to exposure in the pillory and confinement for life in a nunnery [M].

1309 *Rostopchin ... setting fire with a torch to the Voronovsky House*: General Wilson, Bennigsen, and Ermolov accompanied Rostopchin, after the fall of Moscow, to his estate at Voronovo, thirty miles from the city. As a grand gesture of defiance, Rostopchin set fire to the mansion. 'All discussion was useless,' Wilson narrates, 'his resolve was inflexible.'

1310 *Anyone who has been in a war knows how untrue that is*: Tolstoy appends a footnote: 'After the description of the battle of Schön Graben had appeared in the first part of my novel, I was told of Nikolay Nikolaevich Muravëv Karsky's remark about that description – a remark which confirmed my conviction. He, a commander-in-chief, remarked that he had never read a truer account of a battle, and that his own experience had convinced him of the impossibility of a commander-in-chief's orders being carried out during a battle.'

N. N. Muravëv (1794–1866) took part in the 1812 campaign. In 1854–5, when Tolstoy met him, he was Governor-General of the Caucasus and Commander-in-Chief of the army there.

1314 *especially of 1812 in which this law of predetermination is most prominently displayed*: Tolstoy adds in a footnote: 'It is noteworthy that almost all those who have written of the campaign of 1812 have seen something special and fateful in that event.'

American Literature

British and Irish Literature

Children's Literature

Classics and Ancient Literature

Colonial Literature

Eastern Literature

European Literature

History

Medieval Literature

Oxford English Drama

Poetry

Philosophy

Politics

Religion

The Oxford Shakespeare

A complete list of Oxford Paperbacks, including Oxford World's Classics, Oxford Shakespeare, Oxford Drama, and Oxford Paperback Reference, is available in the UK from the Academic Division Publicity Department, Oxford University Press, Great Clarendon Street, Oxford OX2 6DP.

In the USA, complete lists are available from the Paperbacks Marketing Manager, Oxford University Press, 198 Madison Avenue, New York, NY 10016.

Oxford Paperbacks are available from all good bookshops. In case of difficulty, customers in the UK can order direct from Oxford University Press Bookshop, Freepost, 116 High Street, Oxford OX1 4BR, enclosing full payment. Please add 10 per cent of published price for postage and packing.